SHŌGUN

SHŌGUN

A NOVEL OF JAPAN

BY

JAMES CLAVELL

ATHENEUM   (1979)   NEW YORK

For two seafarers, Captains, Royal Navy,
who loved their ships more than their women
—as was expected of them.

AUTHOR'S NOTE

I would like to thank all those here, in Asia, and in Europe—the living and the dead—who helped to make this novel possible.

Lookout Mountain, California

SHŌGUN

PROLOGUE

THE gale tore at him and he felt its bite deep within and he knew that if they did not make landfall in three days they would all be dead. Too many deaths on this voyage, he thought, I'm Pilot-Major of a dead fleet. One ship left out of five—eight and twenty men from a crew of one hundred and seven and now only ten can walk and the rest near death and our Captain-General one of them. No food, almost no water and what there is, brackish and foul.

His name was John Blackthorne and he was alone on deck but for the bow-sprit lookout—Salamon the mute—who huddled in the lee, searching the sea ahead.

The ship heeled in a sudden squall and Blackthorne held on to the arm of the seachair that was lashed near the wheel on the quarterdeck until she righted, timbers squealing. She was the *Erasmus,* two hundred and sixty tons, a three-masted trader-warship out of Rotterdam, armed with twenty cannon and sole survivor of the first expeditionary force sent from the Netherlands to ravage the enemy in the New World. The first Dutch ships ever to breach the secrets of the Strait of Magellan. Four hundred and ninety-six men, all volunteers. All Dutch except for three Englishmen—two pilots, one officer. Their orders: to plunder Spanish and Portuguese possessions in the New World and put them to the torch; to open up permanent trading concessions; to discover new islands in the Pacific Ocean that could serve as permanent bases and to claim the territory for the Netherlands; and, within three years, to come home again.

Protestant Netherlands had been at war with Catholic Spain for more than four decades, struggling to throw off the yoke of their hated Spanish masters. The Netherlands, sometimes called Holland, Dutchland, or the Low Countries, were still legally part of the Spanish Empire. England, their only allies, the first country in Christendom to break with the Papal Court at Rome and become Protestant some seventy-odd years ago, had also been warring on Spain for the last twenty years, and openly allied with the Dutch for a decade.

The wind freshened even more and the ship lurched. She was riding under bare poles but for storm tops'ls. Even so the tide and the storm bore her strongly toward the darkening horizon.

There's more storm there, Blackthorne told himself, and more reefs and more shoals. And unknown sea. Good. I've set myself against the sea all my life and I've always won. I always will.

First English pilot ever to get through Magellan's Pass. Yes, the first—and first pilot ever to sail these Asian waters, apart from a few bastard Portuguese or motherless Spaniards who still think they own the world. First Englishman in these seas. . . .

So many firsts. Yes. And so many deaths to win them.

Again he tasted the wind and smelled it, but there was no hint of land. He searched the ocean but it was dull gray and angry. Not a fleck of seaweed or splash of color to give a hint of a sanding shelf. He saw the spire of another reef far on the starboard quarter but that told him nothing. For a month now outcrops had threatened them, but never a sight of land. This ocean's endless, he thought. Good. That's what you were trained for—to sail the unknown sea, to chart it

3

and come home again. How many days from home? One year and eleven months and two days. The last landfall Chile, one hundred and thirty-three days aft, across the ocean Magellan had first sailed eighty years ago called Pacific.

Blackthorne was famished and his mouth and body ached from the scurvy. He forced his eyes to check the compass course and his brain to calculate an approximate position. Once the plot was written down in his rutter—his sea manual—he would be safe in this speck of the ocean. And if he was safe, his ship was safe and then together they might find the Japans, or even the Christian King Prester John and his Golden Empire that legend said lay to the north of Cathay, wherever Cathay was.

And with my share of the riches I'll sail on again, westward for home, first English pilot ever to circumnavigate the globe, and I'll never leave home again. Never. By the head of my son!

The cut of the wind stopped his mind from wandering and kept him awake. To sleep now would be foolish. You'll never wake from that sleep, he thought, and stretched his arms to ease the cramped muscles in his back and pulled his cloak tighter around him. He saw that the sails were trimmed and the wheel lashed secure. The bow lookout was awake. So patiently he settled back and prayed for land.

"Go below, Pilot. I take this watch if it pleases you." The third mate, Hendrik Specz, was pulling himself up the gangway, his face gray with fatigue, eyes sunken, skin blotched and sallow. He leaned heavily against the binnacle to steady himself, retching a little. "Blessed Lord Jesus, piss on the day I left Holland."

"Where's the mate, Hendrik?"

"In his bunk. He can't get out of his *scheit voll* bunk. And he won't—not this side of Judgment Day."

"And the Captain-General?"

"Moaning for food and water." Hendrik spat. "I tell him I roast him a capon and bring it on a silver platter with a bottle of brandy to wash it down. *Scheit-huis! Coot!*"

"Hold your tongue!"

"I will, Pilot. But he's a maggot-eaten fool and we'll be dead because of him." The young man retched and brought up mottled phlegm. "Blessed Lord Jesus help me!"

"Go below. Come back at dawn."

Hendrik lowered himself painfully into the other seachair. "There's the reek of death below. I take the watch if it pleases you. What's the course?"

"Wherever the wind takes us."

"Where's the landfall you promised us? Where's the Japans—where is it, I ask?"

"Ahead."

"Always ahead! *Gottimhimmel,* it wasn't in our orders to sail into the unknown. We should be back home by now, safe, with our bellies full, not chasing St. Elmo's fire."

"Go below or hold your tongue."

Sullenly Hendrik looked away from the tall bearded man. Where are we now? he wanted to ask. Why can't I see the secret rutter? But he knew you don't ask those questions of a pilot, particularly this one. Even so, he thought, I wish I was as strong and healthy as when I left Holland. Then I wouldn't wait. I'd smash your gray-blue eyes now and stamp that maddening half-smile off your face and send you to the hell you deserve. Then I'd be Captain-Pilot and we'd have a Netherlander running the ship—not a foreigner—and the secrets would be safe for us. Because soon we'll be at war with you English. We want the same thing:

to command the sea, to control all trade routes, to dominate the New World, and to strangle Spain.

"Perhaps there is no Japans," Hendrik muttered suddenly. "It's *Gottbewonden* legend."

"It exists. Between latitudes thirty and forty north. Now hold your tongue or go below."

"There's death below, Pilot," Hendrik muttered and put his eyes ahead, letting himself drift.

Blackthorn shifted in his seachair, his body hurting worse today. You're luckier than most, he thought, luckier than Hendrik. No, not luckier. More careful. You conserved your fruit while the others consumed theirs carelessly. Against your warnings. So now your scurvy is still mild whereas the others are constantly hemorrhaging, their bowels diarrhetic, their eyes sore and rheumy, and their teeth lost or loose in their heads. Why is it men never learn?

He knew they were all afraid of him, even the Captain-General, and that most hated him. But that was normal, for it was the pilot who commanded at sea; it was he who set the course and ran the ship, he who brought them from port to port.

Any voyage today was dangerous because the few navigational charts that existed were so vague as to be useless. And there was absolutely no way to fix longitude.

"Find how to fix longitude and you're the richest man in the world," his old teacher, Alban Caradoc, had said. "The Queen, God bless her, 'll give you ten thousand pound and a dukedom for the answer to the riddle. The dung-eating Portuguese'll give you more—a golden galleon. And the motherless Spaniards'll give you twenty! Out of sight of land you're always lost, lad." Caradoc had paused and shaken his head sadly at him as always. "You're lost, lad. Unless . . ."

"Unless you have a rutter!" Blackthorne had shouted happily, knowing that he had learned his lessons well. He was thirteen then and had already been apprenticed a year to Alban Caradoc, pilot and shipwright, who had become the father he had lost, who had never beaten him but taught him and the other boys the secrets of shipbuilding and the intimate way of the sea.

A rutter was a small book containing the detailed observation of a pilot *who had been there before.* It recorded magnetic compass courses between ports and capes, headlands and channels. It noted the sounding and depths and color of the water and the nature of the seabed. It set down the *how we got there and how we got back:* how many days on a special tack, the pattern of the wind, when it blew and from where, what currents to expect and from where; the time of storms and the time of fair winds; where to careen the ship and where to water; where there were friends and where foes; shoals, reefs, tides, havens; at best, *everything* necessary for a safe voyage.

The English, Dutch, and French had rutters for their own waters, but the waters of the rest of the world had been sailed only by captains from Portugal and Spain, and these two countries considered all rutters secret. Rutters that revealed the seaways to the New World or unraveled the mysteries of the Pass of Magellan and the Cape of Good Hope—both Portuguese discoveries—and thence the seaways to Asia were guarded as national treasures by the Portuguese and Spanish, and sought after with equal ferocity by their Dutch and English enemies.

But a rutter was only as good as the pilot who wrote it, the scribe who hand-copied it, the very rare printer who printed it, or the scholar who translated it. A rutter could therefore contain errors. Even deliberate ones. A pilot never knew for certain *until he had been there himself.* At least once.

At sea the pilot was leader, sole guide, and final arbiter of the ship and her crew. Alone he commanded from the quarterdeck.

That's heady wine, Blackthorne told himself. And once sipped, never to be forgotten, always to be sought, and always necessary. That's one of the things that keep you alive when others die.

He got up and relieved himself in the scuppers. Later the sand ran out of the hourglass by the binnacle and he turned it and rang the ship's bell.

"Can you stay awake, Hendrik?"

"Yes. Yes, I believe so."

"I'll send someone to replace the bow lookout. See he stands in the wind and not in the lee. That'll keep him sharp and awake." For a moment he wondered if he should turn the ship into the wind and heave to for the night but he decided against it, went down the companionway, and opened the fo'c'sle door. The companionway led into the crew's quarters. The cabin ran the width of the ship and had bunks and hammock space for a hundred and twenty men. The warmth surrounded him and he was grateful for it and ignored the ever present stench from the bilges below. None of the twenty-odd men moved from his bunk.

"Get aloft, Maetsukker," he said in Dutch, the lingua franca of the Low Countries, which he spoke perfectly, along with Portuguese and Spanish and Latin.

"I'm near death," the small, sharp-featured man said, cringing deeper into the bunk. "I'm sick. Look, the scurvy's taken all my teeth. Lord Jesus help us, we'll all perish! If it wasn't for you we'd all be home by now, safe! I'm a merchant. I'm not a seaman. I'm not part of the crew. . . . Take someone else. Johann there's—" He screamed as Blackthorne jerked him out of the bunk and hurled him against the door. Blood flecked his mouth and he was stunned. A brutal kick in his side brought him out of his stupor.

"You get your face aloft and stay there till you're dead or we make landfall."

The man pulled the door open and fled in agony.

Blackthorne looked at the others. They stared back at him. "How are you feeling, Johann?"

"Good enough, Pilot. Perhaps I'll live."

Johann Vinck was forty-three, the chief gunner and bosun's mate, the oldest man aboard. He was hairless and toothless, the color of aged oak and just as strong. Six years ago he had sailed with Blackthorne on the ill-fated search for the Northeast Passage, and each man knew the measure of the other.

"At your age most men are already dead, so you're ahead of us all." Blackthorne was thirty-six.

Vinck smiled mirthlessly. "It's the brandy, Pilot, that an' fornication an' the saintly life I've led."

No one laughed. Then someone pointed at a bunk. "Pilot, the bosun's dead."

"Then get the body aloft! Wash it and close his eyes! You, you, and you!"

The men were quickly out of their bunks this time and together they half dragged, half carried the corpse from the cabin.

"Take the dawn watch, Vinck. And Ginsel, you're bow lookout."

"Yes sir."

Blackthorne went back on deck.

He saw that Hendrik was still awake, that the ship was in order. The relieved lookout, Salamon, stumbled past him, more dead than alive, his eyes puffed and red from the cut of the wind. Blackthorne crossed to the other door and went below. The passageway led to the great cabin aft, which was the Captain-General's quarters and magazine. His own cabin was starboard and the other, to port, was usually for the three mates. Now Baccus van Nekk, the chief merchant, Hendrik the third mate, and the boy, Croocq, shared it. They were all very sick.

He went into the great cabin. The Captain-General, Paulus Spillbergen, was lying half conscious in his bunk. He was a short, florid man, normally very fat, now very thin, the skin of his paunch hanging slackly in folds. Blackthorne took a water flagon out of a secret drawer and helped him drink a little.

"Thanks," Spillbergen said weakly. "Where's land—where's land?"

"Ahead," he replied, no longer believing it, then put the flagon away, closed his ears to the whines and left, hating him anew.

Almost exactly a year ago they had reached Tierra del Fuego, the winds favorable for the stab into the unknown of Magellan's Pass. But the Captain-General had ordered a landing to search for gold and treasure.

"Christ Jesus, look ashore, Captain-General! There's no treasure in those wastes."

"Legend says it's rich with gold and we can claim the land for the glorious Netherlands."

"The Spaniards have been here in strength for fifty years."

"Perhaps—but perhaps not this far south, Pilot-Major."

"This far south the seasons're reversed. May, June, July, August're dead winter here. The rutter says the timing's critical to get through the Straits—the winds turn in a few weeks, then we'll have to stay here, winter here for months."

"How many weeks, Pilot?"

"The rutter says eight. But seasons don't stay the same—"

"Then we'll explore for a couple of weeks. That gives us plenty of time and then, if necessary, we'll go north again and sack a few more towns, eh, gentlemen?"

"We've got to try now, Captain-General. The Spanish have very few warships in the Pacific. Here the seas are teeming with them and they're looking for us. I say we've got to go on now."

But the Captain-General had overridden him and put it to a vote of the other captains—not to the other pilots, one English and three Dutch—and had led the useless forays ashore.

The winds had changed early that year and they had had to winter there, the Captain-General afraid to go north because of Spanish fleets. It was four months before they could sail. By then one hundred and fifty-six men in the fleet had died of starvation, cold, and the flux and they were eating the calfskin that covered the ropes. The terrible storms within the Strait had scattered the fleet. *Erasmus* was the only ship that made the rendezvous off Chile. They had waited a month for the others and then, the Spaniards closing in, had set sail into the unknown. The secret rutter stopped at Chile.

Blackthorne walked back along the corridor and unlocked his own cabin door, relocking it behind him. The cabin was low-beamed, small, and orderly, and he had to stoop as he crossed to sit at his desk. He unlocked a drawer and carefully unwrapped the last of the apples he had hoarded so carefully all the way from Santa Maria Island, off Chile. It was bruised and tiny, with mold on the rotting section. He cut off a quarter. There were a few maggots inside. He ate them with the flesh, heeding the old sea legend that the apple maggots were just as effective against scurvy as the fruit and that, rubbed into the gums, they helped prevent your teeth from falling out. He chewed the fruit gently because his teeth were aching and his gums sore and tender, then sipped water from the wine skin. It tasted brackish. Then he wrapped the remainder of the apple and locked it away.

A rat scurried in the shadows cast by the hanging oil lantern over his head. Timbers creaked pleasantly. Cockroaches swarmed on the floor.

I'm tired. I'm so tired.

He glanced at his bunk. Long, narrow, the straw palliasse inviting.

I'm so tired.

Go to sleep for this hour, the devil half of him said. Even for ten minutes—and you'll be fresh for a week. You've had only a few hours for days now, and most of that aloft in the cold. You must sleep. Sleep. They rely on you. . . .

"I won't, I'll sleep tomorrow," he said aloud, and forced his hand to unlock his chest and take out his rutter. He saw that the other one, the Portuguese one, was safe and untouched and that pleased him. He took a clean quill and began to write: "April 21 1600. Fifth hour. Dusk. 133d day from Santa Maria Island, Chile, on the 32 degree North line of latitude. Sea still high and wind strong and the ship rigged as before. The color of the sea dull gray-green and bottomless. We are still running before the wind along a course of 270 degrees, veering to North North West, making way briskly, about two leagues, each of three miles this hour. Large reefs shaped like a triangle were sighted at half the hour bearing North East by North half a league distant.

"Three men died in the night of the scurvy—Joris sailmaker, Reiss gunner, 2d mate de Haan. After commending their souls to God, the Captain-General still being sick, I cast them into the sea without shrouds, for there was no one to make them. Today Bosun Rijckloff died.

"I could not take the declension of the sun at noon today, again due to overcast. But I estimate we are still on course and that landfall in the Japans should be soon. . . .

"But how soon?" he asked the sea lantern that hung above his head, swaying with the pitch of the ship. How to make a chart? There must be a way, he told himself for the millionth time. How to set longitude? There must be a way. How to keep vegetables fresh? What *is* scurvy. . . ?

"They say it's a flux from the sea, boy," Alban Caradoc had said. He was a huge-bellied, great-hearted man with a tangled gray beard.

"But could you boil the vegetables and keep the broth?"

"It sickens, lad. No one's ever discovered a way to store it."

"They say that Francis Drake sails soon."

"No. You can't go, boy."

"I'm almost fourteen. You let Tim and Watt sign on with him and he needs apprentice pilots."

"They're sixteen. You're just thirteen."

"They say he's going to try for Magellan's Pass, then up the coast to the unexplored region—to the Californias—to find the Straits of Anian that join Pacific with Atlantic. From the Californias all the way to Newfoundland, the Northwest Passage at long last . . ."

"The *supposed* Northwest Passage, lad. No one's proved that legend yet."

"He will. He's Admiral now and we'll be the first English ship through Magellan's Pass, the first in the Pacific, the first— I'll never get another chance like this."

"Oh, yes, you will, and he'll never breach Magellan's secret way 'less he can steal a rutter or capture a Portuguese pilot to guide him through. How many times must I tell you—a pilot must have patience. Learn patience, boy. You've plen—"

"Please!"

"No."

"Why?"

"Because he'll be gone two, three years, perhaps more. The weak and the young will get the worst of the food and the least of the water. And of the five ships that go, only his will come back. You'll never survive, boy."

"Then I'll sign for his ship only. I'm strong. He'll take me!"

"Listen, boy, I was with Drake in *Judith,* his fifty tonner, at San Juan de Ulua when we and Admiral Hawkins—he was in *Minion*—when we fought our way out of harbor through the dung-eating Spaniards. We'd been trading slaves from Guinea to the Spanish Main, but we had no Spanish license for the trade and they tricked Hawkins and trapped our fleet. They'd thirteen great ships, we six. We sank three of theirs, and they sank our *Swallow, Angel, Caravelle,* and the *Jesus of Lubeck.* Oh, yes, Drake fought us out of the trap and brought us home. With eleven men aboard to tell the tale. Hawkins had fifteen. Out of four hundred and eight jolly Jack Tars. Drake is merciless, boy. He wants glory and gold, but only for Drake, and too many men are dead proving it."

"But I won't die. I'll be one of—"

"No. You're apprenticed for twelve years. You've ten more to go and then you're free. But until that time, until 1588, you'll learn how to build ships and how to command them—you'll obey Alban Caradoc, Master Shipwright and Pilot and Member of Trinity House, or you'll never have a license. And if you don't have a license, you'll never pilot *any* ship in English waters, you'll never command the quarterdeck of *any* English ship in *any* waters because that was good King Harry's law, God rest his soul. It was the great whore Mary Tudor's law, may her soul burn in hell, it's the Queen's law, may she reign forever, it's England's law, and the best sea law that's ever been."

Blackthorne remembered how he had hated his master then, and hated Trinity House, the monopoly created by Henry VIII in 1514 for the training and licensing of all English pilots and masters, and hated his twelve years of semibondage, without which he knew he could never get the one thing in the world he wanted. And he had hated Alban Caradoc even more when, to everlasting glory, Drake and his hundred-ton sloop, the *Golden Hind* had miraculously come back to England after disappearing for three years, the first English ship to circumnavigate the globe, bringing with her the richest haul of plunder aboard ever brought back to those shores: an incredible million and a half sterling in gold, silver, spices, and plate.

That four of the five ships were lost and eight out of every ten men were lost and Tim and Watt were lost and a captured Portuguese pilot had led the expedition for Drake through the Magellan into the Pacific did not assuage his hatred; that Drake had hanged one officer, excommunicated the chaplain Fletcher, and failed to find the Northwest Passage did not detract from national admiration. The Queen took fifty percent of the treasure and knighted him. The gentry and merchants who had put up the money for the expedition received three hundred percent profit and pleaded to underwrite his next corsair voyage. And all seamen begged to sail with him, because he did get plunder, he did come home, and, with their share of the booty, the lucky few who survived were rich for life.

I would have survived, Blackthorne told himself. I would. And my share of the treasure then would have been enough to—

"*Rotz vooruiiiiiiit!*" Reef ahead!

He felt the cry at first more than he heard it. Then, mixed with the gale, he heard the wailing scream again.

He was out of the cabin and up the companionway onto the quarterdeck, his heart pounding, his throat parched. It was dark night now and pouring, and he was momentarily exulted for he knew that the canvas raintraps, made so many weeks ago, would soon be full to overflowing. He opened his mouth to the near horizontal rain and tasted its sweetness, then turned his back on the squall.

He saw that Hendrik was paralyzed with terror. The bow lookout, Maetsukker, cowered near the prow, shouting incoherently, pointing ahead. Then he too looked beyond the ship.

The reef was barely two hundred yards ahead, great black claws of rocks pounded by the hungry sea. The foaming line of surf stretched port and starboard, broken intermittently. The gale was lifting huge swathes of spume and hurling them at the night blackness. A forepeak halliard snapped and the highest top gallant spar was carried away. The mast shuddered in its bed but held, and the sea bore the ship inexorably to its death.

"All hands on deck!" Blackthorne shouted, and rang the bell violently.

The noise brought Hendrik out of his stupor. "We're lost!" he screamed in Dutch. "Oh, Lord Jesus help us!"

"Get the crew on deck, you bastard! You've been asleep! You've both been asleep!" Blackthorne shoved him toward the companionway, held onto the wheel, slipped the protecting lashing from the spokes, braced himself, and swung the wheel hard aport.

He exerted all his strength as the rudder bit into the torrent. The whole ship shuddered. Then the prow began to swing with increasing velocity as the wind bore down and soon they were broadside to the sea and the wind. The storm tops'ls bellied and gamely tried to carry the weight of the ship and all the ropes took the strain, howling. The following sea towered above them and they were making way, parallel to the reef, when he saw the great wave. He shouted a warning at the men who were coming from the fo'c'sle, and hung on for his life.

The sea fell on the ship and she heeled and he thought they'd floundered but she shook herself like a wet terrier and swung out of the trough. Water cascaded away through the scuppers and he gasped for air. He saw that the corpse of the bosun that had been put on deck for burial tomorrow was gone and that the following wave was coming in even stronger. It caught Hendrik and lifted him, gasping and struggling, over the side and out to sea. Another wave roared across the deck and Blackthorne locked one arm through the wheel and the water passed him by. Now Hendrik was fifty yards to port. The wash sucked him back alongside, then a giant comber threw him high above the ship, held him there for a moment shrieking, then took him away and pulped him against a rock spine and consumed him.

The ship nosed into the sea trying to make way. Another halliard gave and the block and tackle swung wildly until it tangled with the rigging.

Vinck and another man pulled themselves onto the quarterdeck and leaned on the wheel to help. Blackthorne could see the encroaching reef to starboard, nearer now. Ahead and to port were more outcrops, but he saw gaps here and there.

"Get aloft, Vinck. Fores'ls ho!" Foot by foot Vinck and two seamen hauled themselves into the shrouds of the foremast rigging as others, below, leaned on the ropes to give them a hand.

"Watch out for'ard," Blackthorne shouted.

The sea foamed along the deck and took another man with it and brought the corpse of the bosun aboard again. The bow soared out of the water and smashed down once more bringing more water aboard. Vinck and the other men cursed the sail out of its ropes. Abruptly it fell open, cracked like a cannonade as the wind filled it, and the ship lurched.

Vinck and his helpers hung there, swaying over the sea, then began their descent.

"Reef—reef ahead!" Vinck screamed.

Blackthorne and the other man swung the wheel to starboard. The ship hesitated then turned and cried out as the rocks, barely awash, found the side of the ship. But it was an oblique blow and the rock nose crumbled. The timbers held safe and the men aboard began to breathe once more.

Blackthorne saw a break in the reef ahead and committed the ship to it. The wind was harder now, the sea more furious. The ship swerved with a gust and the wheel spun out of their hands. Together they grabbed it and set her course again, but she bobbed and twisted drunkenly. Sea flooded aboard and burst into the fo'c'sle, smashing one man against the bulkhead, the whole deck awash like the one above.

"Man the pumps!" Blackthorne shouted. He saw two men go below.

The rain was slashing his face and he squinted against the pain. The binnacle light and aft riding light had long since been extinguished. Then as another gust shoved the ship further off course, the seaman slipped and again the wheel spun out of their grasp. The man shrieked as a spoke smashed the side of his head and he lay there at the mercy of the sea. Blackthorne pulled him up and held him until the frothing comber had passed. Then he saw that the man was dead so he let him slump into the seachair and the next sea cleaned the quarterdeck of him.

The gulch through the reef was three points to windward and, try as he could, Blackthorne could not gain way. He searched desperately for another channel but knew there was none, so he let her fall off from the wind momentarily to gain speed, then swung her hard to windward again. She gained way a fraction and held course.

There was a wailing, tormented shudder as the keel scraped the razor spines below and all aboard imagined they saw the oak timbers burst apart and the sea flood in. The ship reeled forward out of control now.

Blackthorne shouted for help but no one heard him so he fought the wheel alone against the sea. Once he was flung aside but he groped back and held on again, wondering in his thickening mind how the rudder had survived so long.

In the neck of the pass the sea became a maelstrom, driven by the tempest and hemmed in by the rocks. Huge waves smashed at the reef, then reeled back to fight the incomer until the waves fought among themselves and attacked on all quarters of the compass. The ship was sucked into the vortex, broadside and helpless.

"Piss on you, storm!" Blackthorne raged. "Get your dung-eating hands off my ship!"

The wheel spun again and threw him away and the deck heeled sickeningly. The bowsprit caught a rock and tore loose, part of the rigging with it, and she righted herself. The foremast was bending like a bow and it snapped. The men on deck fell on the rigging with axes to cut it adrift as the ship floundered down the raging channel. They hacked the mast free and it went over the side and one man went with it, caught in the tangled mess. The man cried out, trapped, but there was nothing they could do and they watched as he and the mast appeared and disappeared alongside, then came back no more.

Vinck and the others who were left looked back at the quarterdeck and saw Blackthorne defying the storm like a madman. They crossed themselves and doubled their prayers, some weeping with fear, and hung on for life.

The strait broadened for an instant and the ship slowed, but ahead it narrowed ominously again and the rocks seemed to grow, to tower over them. The current ricocheted off one side, taking the ship with it, turned her abeam again and flung her to her doom.

Blackthorne stopped cursing the storm and fought the wheel to port and hung there, his muscles knotted against the strain. But the ship knew not her rudder and neither did the sea.

"Turn, you whore from hell," he gasped, his strength ebbing fast. "Help me!"

The sea race quickened and he felt his heart near bursting but still he strained against the press of the sea. He tried to keep his eyes focused but his vision reeled, the colors wrong and fading. The ship was in the neck and dead but just then the keel scraped a mud shoal. The shock turned her head. The rudder bit into the sea. And then the wind and the sea joined to help and together they spun her before the wind and she sped through the pass to safety. Into the bay beyond.

BOOK ONE

CHAPTER 1

BLACKTHORNE was suddenly awake. For a moment he thought he was dreaming because he was ashore and the room unbelievable. It was small and very clean and covered with soft mats. He was lying on a thick quilt and another was thrown over him. The ceiling was polished cedar and the walls were lathes of cedar, in squares, covered with an opaque paper that muted the light pleasantly. Beside him was a scarlet tray bearing small bowls. One contained cold cooked vegetables and he wolfed them, hardly noticing the piquant taste. Another contained a fish soup and he drained that. Another was filled with a thick porridge of wheat or barley and he finished it quickly, eating with his fingers. The water in an odd-shaped gourd was warm and tasted curious—slightly bitter but savory.

Then he noticed the crucifix in its niche.

This house is Spanish or Portuguese, he thought aghast. Is this the Japans? or Cathay?

A panel of the wall slid open. A middle-aged, heavy-set, round-faced woman was on her knees beside the door and she bowed and smiled. Her skin was golden and her eyes black and narrow and her long black hair was piled neatly on her head. She wore a gray silk robe and short white socks with a thick sole and a wide purple band around her waist.

"Goshujinsama, gokibun wa ikaga desu ka?" she said. She waited as he stared at her blankly, then said it again.

"Is this the Japans?" he asked. "Japans? Or Cathay?"

She stared at him uncomprehendingly and said something else he could not understand. Then he realized that he was naked. His clothes were nowhere in sight. With sign language he showed her that he wanted to get dressed. Then he pointed at the food bowls and she knew that he was still hungry.

She smiled and bowed and slid the door shut.

He lay back exhausted, the untoward, nauseating nonmotion of the floor making his head spin. With an effort he tried to collect himself. I remember getting the anchor out, he thought. With Vinck. I think it was Vinck. We were in a bay and the ship had nosed a shoal and stopped. We could hear waves breaking on the beach but everything was safe. There were lights ashore and then I was in my cabin and blackness. I don't remember anything. Then there were lights through the blackness and strange voices. I was talking English, then Portuguese. One of the natives talked a little Portuguese. Or was he Portuguese? No, I think he was a native. Did I ask him where we were? I don't remember. Then we were back in the reef again and the big wave came once more and I was carried out to sea and drowning—it was freezing—no, the sea was warm and like a silk bed a fathom thick. They must have carried me ashore and put me here.

"It must have been this bed that felt so soft and warm," he said aloud. "I've never slept on silk before." His weakness overcame him and he slept dreamlessly.

When he awoke there was more food in earthenware bowls and his clothes were

15

beside him in a neat pile. They had been washed and pressed and mended with tiny, exquisite stitching.

But his knife was gone, and so were his keys.

I'd better get a knife and quickly, he thought. Or a pistol.

His eyes went to the crucifix. In spite of his dread, his excitement quickened. All his life he had heard legends told among pilots and sailormen about the incredible riches of Portugal's secret empire in the East, how they had by now converted the heathens to Catholicism and so held them in bondage, where gold was as cheap as pig iron, and emeralds, rubies, diamonds, and sapphires as plentiful as pebbles on a beach.

If the Catholic part's true, he told himself, perhaps the rest is too. About the riches. Yes. But the sooner I'm armed and back aboard *Erasmus* and behind her cannon, the better.

He consumed the food, dressed, and stood shakily, feeling out of his element as he always did ashore. His boots were missing. He went to the door, reeling slightly, and put out a hand to steady himself but the light, square lathes could not bear his weight and they shattered, the paper ripping apart. He righted himself. The shocked woman in the corridor was staring up at him.

"I'm sorry," he said, strangely ill at ease with his clumsiness. The purity of the room was somehow defiled.

"Where are my boots?"

The woman stared at him blankly. So, patiently, he asked her again with sign language and she hurried down a passage, knelt and opened another lathe door, and beckoned him. Voices were nearby, and the sound of running water. He went through the doorway and found himself in another room, also almost bare. This opened onto a veranda with steps leading to a small garden surrounded by a high wall. Beside this main entrance were two old women, three children dressed in scarlet robes, and an old man, obviously a gardener, with a rake in his hand. At once they all bowed gravely and kept their heads low.

To his astonishment Blackthorne saw that the old man was naked but for a brief, narrow loincloth, hardly covering his organs.

"Morning," he said to them, not knowing what to say.

They stayed motionless, still bowing.

Nonplussed, he stared at them, then, awkwardly he bowed back to them. They all straightened and smiled at him. The old man bowed once more and went back to work in the garden. The children stared at him, then, laughing, dashed away. The old women disappeared into the depths of the house. But he could feel their eyes on him.

He saw his boots at the bottom of the steps. Before he could pick them up, the middle-aged woman was there on her knees, to his embarrassment, and she helped him to put them on.

"Thank you," he said. He thought a moment and then pointed at himself. "Blackthorne," he said deliberately. "Blackthorne." Then he pointed at her. "What's your name?"

She stared at him uncomprehendingly.

"Black-thorne," he repeated carefully, pointing at himself, and again pointed at her. "What's your name?"

She frowned, then with a flood of understanding pointed at herself and said, *"Onna! Onna!"*

"Onna!" he repeated, very proud of himself as she was with herself. *"Onna."* She nodded happily. *"Onna!"*

The garden was unlike anything he had ever seen: a little waterfall and stream and small bridge and manicured pebbled paths and rocks and flowers and shrubs.

It's so clean, he thought. So neat.

"Incredible," he said.

" 'Nkerriberr?" she repeated helpfully.

"Nothing," he said. Then not knowing what else to do, he waved her away. Obediently she bowed politely and left.

Blackthorne sat in the warm sun, leaning against a post. Feeling very frail, he watched the old man weeding an already weedless garden. I wonder where the others are. Is the Captain-General still alive? How many days have I been asleep? I can remember waking and eating and sleeping again, the eating unsatisfactory like the dreams.

The children flurried past, chasing one another, and he was embarrassed for them at the gardener's nakedness, for when the man bent over or stooped you could see everything and he was astounded that the children appeared not to notice. He saw tiled and thatched roofs of other buildings over the wall and, far off, high mountains. A crisp wind broomed the sky and kept the cumulus advancing. Bees were foraging and it was a lovely spring day. His body begged for more sleep but he pushed himself erect and went to the garden door. The gardener smiled and bowed and ran to open the door and bowed and closed it after him.

The village was set around the crescent harbor that faced east, perhaps two hundred houses unlike any he'd ever seen nestling at the beginning of the mountain which spilled down to the shore. Above were terraced fields and dirt roads that led north and south. Below, the waterfront was cobbled and a stone launching ramp went from the shore into the sea. A good safe harbor and a stone jetty, and men and women cleaning fish and making nets, a uniquely designed boat being built at the northern side. There were islands far out to sea, to the east and to the south. The reefs would be there or beyond the horizon.

In the harbor were many other quaintly shaped boats, mostly fishing craft, some with one large sail, several being sculled—the oarsmen standing and pushing against the sea, not sitting and pulling as he would have done. A few of the boats were heading out to sea, others were nosing at the wooden dock, and *Erasmus* was anchored neatly, fifty yards from shore, in good water, with three bow cables. Who did that? he asked himself. There were boats alongside her and he could see native men aboard. But none of his. Where could they be?

He looked around the village and became conscious of the many people watching him. When they saw that he had noticed them they all bowed and, still uncomfortable, he bowed back. Once more there was happy activity and they passed to and fro, stopping, bargaining, bowing to each other, seemingly oblivious of him, like so many multicolored butterflies. But he felt eyes studying him from every window and doorway as he walked toward the shore.

What is it about them that's so weird? he asked himself. It's not just their clothes and behavior. It's—*they've no weapons,* he thought, astounded. No swords or guns! Why is that?

Open shops filled with odd goods and bales lined the small street. The floors of the shops were raised and the sellers and the buyers knelt or squatted on the clean wooden floors. He saw that most had clogs or rush sandals, some with the same white socks with the thick sole that were split between the big toe and the next to hold the thongs, but they left the clogs and sandals outside in the dirt. Those who were barefoot cleansed their feet and slipped on clean, indoor sandals that were waiting for them. That's very sensible if you think about it, he told himself, awed.

Then he saw the tonsured man approaching and fear swept sickeningly from his testicles into his stomach. The priest was obviously Portuguese or Spanish, and, though his flowing robe was orange, there was no mistaking the rosary and crucifix at his belt, or the cold hostility on his face. His robe was travel stained and his European-style boots besmirched with mud. He was looking out into the harbor at *Erasmus,* and Blackthorne knew that he must recognize her as Dutch or English, new to most seas, leaner, faster, a merchant fighting ship, patterned and improved on the English privateers that had wreaked so much havoc on the Spanish Main. With the priest were ten natives, black-haired and black-eyed, one dressed like him except that he had thong slippers. The others wore varicolored robes or loose trousers, or simply loincloths. But none was armed.

Blackthorne wanted to run while there was time but he knew he did not have the strength and there was nowhere to hide. His height and size and the color of his eyes made him alien in this world. He put his back against the wall.

"Who are you?" the priest said in Portuguese. He was a thick, dark, well-fed man in his middle twenties, with a long beard.

"Who are you?" Blackthorne stared back at him.

"That's a Netherlander privateer. You're a heretic Dutchman. You're pirates. God have mercy on you!"

"We're not pirates. We're peaceful merchants, except to our enemies. I'm pilot of that ship. Who are you?"

"Father Sebastio. How did you get here? How?"

"We were blown ashore. What is this place? Is it the Japans?"

"Yes. Japan. Nippon," the priest said impatiently. He turned to one of the men, older than the rest, small and lean with strong arms and calloused hands, his pate shaved and his hair drawn into a thin queue as gray as his eyebrows. The priest spoke haltingly to him in Japanese, pointing at Blackthorne. All of them were shocked and one made the sign of the cross protectively.

"Dutchmen are heretics, rebels, and pirates. What's your name?"

"Is this a Portuguese settlement?"

The priest's eyes were hard and bloodshot. "The village headman says he's told the authorities about you. Your sins have caught up with you. Where's the rest of your crew?"

"We were blown off course. We just need food and water and time to repair our ship. Then we'll be off. We can pay for every—"

"Where's the rest of your crew?"

"I don't know. Aboard. I suppose they're aboard."

Again the priest questioned the headman, who replied and motioned to the other end of the village, explaining at length. The priest turned back to Blackthorne. "They crucify criminals here, Pilot. You're going to die. The *daimyo's* coming with his samurai. God have mercy on you."

"What's a *daimyo?*"

"A feudal lord. He owns this whole province. How did you get here?"

"And *samurai?*"

"Warriors—soldiers—members of the warrior caste," the priest said with growing irritation. "Where did you come from and who are you?"

"I don't recognize your accent," Blackthorne said, to throw him off balance. "You're a Spaniard?"

"I'm Portuguese," the priest flared, taking the bait. "I told you, I'm Father Sebastio from Portugal. Where did you learn such good Portuguese. Eh?"

"But Portugal and Spain are the same country now," Blackthorne said, taunting. "You've the same king."

"We're a separate country. We're a different people. We have been forever. We fly our own flag. Our overseas possessions are separate, yes, separate. King Philip agreed when he stole my country." Father Sebastio controlled his temper with an effort, his fingers trembling. "He took my country by force of arms twenty years ago! His soldiers and that devil-spawned Spaniard tyrant, the Duke of Alva, they crushed our real king. *Que va!* Now Philip's son rules but he's not our real king either. Soon we'll have our own king back again." Then he added with venom, "You know it's the truth. What devil Alva did to your country he did to mine."

"That's a lie. Alva was a plague in the Netherlands, but he never conquered them. They're still free. Always will be. But in Portugal he smashed one small army and the whole country gave in. No courage. You could throw the Spaniard out if you wanted to, but you'll never do it. No honor. No *cojones.* Except to burn innocents in the name of God."

"May God burn you in hellfire for all eternity," the priest flared. "Satan walks abroad and will be stamped out. Heretics will be stamped out. You're cursed before God!"

In spite of himself Blackthorne felt the religious terror begin to rise within him. "Priests don't have the ear of God, or speak with His voice. We're free of your stinking yoke and we're going to stay free!"

It was only forty years ago that Bloody Mary Tudor was Queen of England and the Spaniard Philip II, Philip the Cruel, her husband. This deeply religious daughter of Henry VIII had brought back Catholic priests and inquisitors and heresy trials and the dominance of the foreign Pope again to England and had reversed her father's curbs and historic changes to the Church of Rome in England, against the will of the majority. She had ruled for five years and the realm was torn asunder with hatred and fear and bloodshed. But she had died and Elizabeth became queen at twenty-four.

Blackthorne was filled with wonder, and deep filial love, when he thought of Elizabeth. For forty years she's battled with the world. She's outfoxed and outfought Popes, the Holy Roman Empire, France and Spain combined. Excommunicated, spat on, reviled abroad, she's led us into harbor—safe, strong, separate.

"We're free," Blackthorne said to the priest. "You're broken. We've our own schools now, our own books, our own bible, our own Church. You Spaniards are all the same. Offal! You monks are all the same. Idol worshipers!"

The priest lifted his crucifix and held it between Blackthorne and himself as a shield. "Oh, God, protect us from this evil! I'm not Spanish, I tell you! I'm Portuguese. And I'm not a monk. I'm a brother of the Society of Jesus!"

"Ah, one of them. A Jesuit!"

"Yes. May God have mercy on your soul!" Father Sebastio snapped something in Japanese and the men surged toward Blackthorne. He backed against the wall and hit one man hard but the others swarmed over him and he felt himself choking.

"*Nanigoto da?*"

Abruptly the melee ceased.

The young man was ten paces away. He wore breeches and clogs and a light kimono and two scabbarded swords were stuck into his belt. One was daggerlike. The other, a two-handed killing sword, was long and slightly curved. His right hand was casually on the hilt.

"*Nanigoto da?*" he asked harshly and when no one answered instantly, "*NANIGOTO DA?*"

The Japanese fell to their knees, their heads bowed into the dirt. Only the priest stayed on his feet. He bowed and began to explain haltingly, but the man contemptuously cut him short and pointed at the headman. "Mura!"

Mura, the headman, kept his head bowed and began explaining rapidly. Several times he pointed at Blackthorne, once at the ship, and twice at the priest. Now there was no movement on the street. All who were visible were on their knees and bowing low. The headman finished. The armed man arrogantly questioned him for a moment and he was answered deferentially and quickly. Then the soldier said something to the headman and waved with open contempt at the priest, then at Blackthorne, and the gray-haired man put it more simply to the priest, who flushed.

The man, who was a head shorter and much younger than Blackthorne, his handsome face slightly pock-marked, stared at the stranger. *"Onushi ittai doko kara kitanoda? Doko no kuni no monoda?"*

The priest said nervously, "Kasigi Omi-san says, 'Where do you come from and what's your nationality?' "

"Is Mr. Omisan the *daimyo?"* Blackthorne asked, afraid of the swords in spite of himself.

"No. He's a samurai, the samurai in charge of the village. His surname's Kasigi, Omi's his given name. Here they always put their surnames first. 'San' means 'honorable,' and you add it to all names as a politeness. You'd better learn to be polite—and find some manners quickly. Here they don't tolerate lack of manners." His voice edged. "Hurry up and answer!"

"Amsterdam. I'm English."

Father Sebastio's shock was open. He said, "English. England," to the samurai and began an explanation but Omi impatiently cut him short and rapped out a flurry of words.

"Omi-san asks if you're the leader. The headman says there are only a few of you heretics alive and most are sick. Is there a Captain-General?"

"I'm the leader," Blackthorne answered even though, truly, now that they were ashore, the Captain-General was in command. "I'm in command," he added, knowing that Captain-General Spillbergen could command nothing, ashore or afloat, even when he was fit and well.

Another spate of words from the samurai. "Omi-san says, because you are the leader you are allowed to walk around the village freely, wherever you want, until his master comes. His master, the *daimyo,* will decide your fate. Until then, you are permitted to live as a guest in the headman's house and come and go as you please. But you are not to leave the village. Your crew are confined to their house and are not allowed to leave it. Do you understand?"

"Yes. Where are my crew?"

Father Sebastio pointed vaguely at a cluster of houses near a wharf, obviously distressed by Omi's decision and impatience. "There! Enjoy your freedom, pirate. Your evil's caught up with—"

"Wakarimasu ka?" Omi said directly to Blackthorne.

"He says, 'Do you understand?' "

"What's 'yes' in Japanese?"

Father Sebastio said to the samurai, *"Wakarimasu."*

Omi disdainfully waved them away. They all bowed low. Except one man who rose deliberately, without bowing.

With blinding speed the killing sword made a hissing silver arc and the man's head toppled off his shoulders and a fountain of blood sprayed the earth. The body rippled a few times and was still. Involuntarily, the priest had backed off a pace. No one else in the street had moved a muscle. Their heads remained low and motionless. Blackthorne was rigid, in shock.

Omi put his foot carelessly on the corpse.

"Ikinasai!" he said, motioning them away.

The men in front of him bowed again, to the earth. Then they got up and went away impassively. The street began to empty. And the shops.

Father Sebastio looked down at the body. Gravely he made the sign of the cross over him and said, *"In nomine Patris et Filii et Spiritus Sancti."* He stared back at the samurai without fear now.

"Ikinasai!" The tip of the gleaming sword rested on the body.

After a long moment the priest turned and walked away. With dignity. Omi watched him narrowly, then glanced at Blackthorne. Blackthorne backed away and then, when safely distant, he quickly turned a corner and vanished.

Omi began to laugh uproariously. The street was empty now. When his laughter was exhausted, he grasped his sword with both hands and began to hack the body methodically into small pieces.

Blackthorne was in a small boat, the boatman sculling happily toward *Erasmus.* He had had no trouble in getting the boat and he could see men on the main deck. All were samurai. Some had steel breastplates but most wore simple kimonos, as the robes were called, and the two swords. All wore their hair the same way: the top of the head shaved and the hair at the back and sides gathered into a queue, oiled, then doubled over the crown and tied neatly. Only samurai were allowed this style and, for them, it was obligatory. Only samurai could wear the two swords—always the long, two-handed killing sword and the short, daggerlike one—and, for them, the swords were obligatory.

The samurai lined the gunwales of his ship watching him.

Filled with disquiet, he climbed up the gangway and came on deck. One samurai, more elaborately dressed than the others, came over to him and bowed. Blackthorne had learned well and he bowed back equally and everyone on the deck beamed genially. He still felt the horror of the sudden killing in the street, and their smiles did not allay his foreboding. He went toward the companionway and stopped abruptly. Across the doorway was pasted a wide band of red silk and, beside it, a small sign with queer, squiggled writing. He hesitated, checked the other door, but that too was sealed up with a similar band, and a similar sign was nailed to the bulkhead.

He reached out to remove the silk.

"Hotté oké!" To make the point quite clear the samurai on guard shook his head. He was no longer smiling.

"But this is my ship and I want . . ." Blackthorne bottled his anxiety, eyes on the swords. I've got to get below, he thought. I've got to get the rutters, mine and the secret one. Christ Jesus, if they're found and given to the priests or to the Japaners we're finished. Any court in the world—outside of England and the Netherlands—would convict us as pirates with that evidence. My rutter gives dates, places, and amounts of plunder taken, the number of dead at our three landings in the Americas and the one in Spanish Africa, the number of churches sacked, and how we burned the towns and the shipping. And the Portuguese rutter? That's our death warrant, for of course it's stolen. At least it was bought from a Portuguese traitor, and by their law any foreigner caught in possession of any rutter of theirs, let alone one that unlocks the Magellan, is to be put to death at once. And if the rutter is found aboard an enemy ship, the ship is to be burned and all aboard executed without mercy.

"Nan no yoda?" one of the samurai said.

"Do you speak Portuguese?" Blackthorne asked in that language.

The man shrugged. *"Wakarimasen."*

Another came forward and deferentially spoke to the leader, who nodded in agreement.

"Portugeezu friend," this samurai said in heavily accented Portuguese. He opened the top of his kimono and showed the small wooden crucifix that hung from his neck.

"Christ'an!" He pointed at himself and smiled. "Christ'an." He pointed at Blackthorne. "Christ'an *ka?*"

Blackthorne hesitated, nodded. "Christian."

"Portugeezu?"

"English."

The man chattered with the leader, then both shrugged and looked back at him. "Portugeezu?"

Blackthorne shook his head, not liking to disagree with them on anything. "My friends? Where?"

The samurai pointed to the east end of the village. "Friends."

"This is my ship. I want to go below." Blackthorne said it in several ways and with signs and they understood.

"*Ah, so desu! Kinjiru,*" they said emphatically, indicating the notice, and beamed.

It was quite clear that he was not allowed to go below. *Kinjiru* must mean forbidden, Blackthorne thought irritably. Well, to hell with that! He snapped the handle of the door down and opened it a fraction.

"*KINJIRU!*"

He was jerked around to face the samurai. Their swords were half out of the scabbards. Motionlessly the two men waited for him to make up his mind. Others on deck watched impassively.

Blackthorne knew he had no option but to back down, so he shrugged and walked away and checked the hawsers and the ship as best he could. The tattered sails were down and tied in place. But the lashings were different from any he'd ever seen, so he presumed that the Japaners had made the vessel secure. He started down the gangway, and stopped. He felt the cold sweat as he saw them all staring at him malevolently and he thought, Christ Jesus, how could I be so stupid. He bowed politely and at once the hostility vanished and they all bowed and were smiling again. But he could still feel the sweat trickling down his spine and he hated everything about the Japans and wished himself and his crew back aboard, armed, and out to sea.

"By the Lord Jesus, I think you're wrong, Pilot," Vinck said. His toothless grin was wide and obscene. "If you can put up with the swill they call food, it's the best place I've been. Ever. I've had two women in three days and they're like rabbits. They'll do anything if you show 'em how."

"That's right. But you can't do nothing without meat or brandy. Nor for long. I'm tired out, and I could only do it once," Maetsukker said, his narrow face twitching. "The yellow bastards won't understand that we need meat and beer and bread. And brandy or wine."

"That's the worst! Lord Jesus, my kingdom for some grog!" Baccus van Nekk was filled with gloom. He walked over and stood close to Blackthorne and peered up at him. He was very nearsighted and had lost his last pair of spectacles in the storm. But even with them he would always stand as close as possible. He was chief merchant, treasurer, and representative of the Dutch East India Company that had put up the money for the voyage. "We're ashore and safe and I haven't had a drink yet. Not a beautiful drop! Terrible. Did you get any, Pilot?"

"No." Blackthorne disliked having anyone near him, but Baccus was a friend and almost blind so he did not move away. "Just hot water with herbs in it."

"They simply won't understand grog. Nothing to drink but hot water and

herbs—the good Lord help us! Suppose there's no liquor in the whole country!"
His eyebrows soared. "Do me a huge favor, Pilot. Ask for some liquor, will you?"

Blackthorne had found the house that they had been assigned on the eastern
edge of the village. The samurai guard had let him pass, but his men had confirmed that they themselves could not go out of the garden gate. The house was
many-roomed like his, but bigger and staffed with many servants of various ages,
both men and women.

There were eleven of his men alive. The dead had been taken away by the
Japanese. Lavish portions of fresh vegetables had begun to banish the scurvy and
all but two of the men were healing rapidly. These two had blood in their bowels
and their insides were fluxed. Vinck had bled them but this had not helped. By
nightfall he expected them to die. The Captain-General was in another room,
still very sick.

Sonk, the cook, a stocky little man, was saying with a laugh, "It's good here,
like Johann says, Pilot, excepting the food and no grog. And it's all right with
the natives so long as you don't wear your shoes in the house. It sends the little
yellow bastards mad if you don't take off your shoes."

"Listen," Blackstone said. "There's a priest here. A Jesuit."

"Christ Jesus!" All banter left them as he told them about the priest and about
the beheading.

"Why'd he chop the man's head off, Pilot?"

"I don't know."

"We better get back aboard. If Papists catch us ashore . . ."

There was great fear in the room now. Salamon, the mute, watched Blackthorne. His mouth worked, a bubble of phlegm appearing at the corners.

"No, Salamon, there's no mistake," Blackthorne said kindly, answering the
silent question. "He said he was Jesuit."

"Christ, Jesuit or Dominican or what-the-hell-ever makes no muck-eating
difference," Vinck said. "We'd better get back aboard. Pilot, you ask that samurai, eh?"

"We're in God's hands," Jan Roper said. He was one of the merchant adventur-
ers, a narrow-eyed young man with a high forehead and thin nose. "He will
protect us from the Satan worshipers."

Vinck looked back at Blackthorne. "What about Portuguese, Pilot? Did you
see any around?"

"No. There were no signs of them in the village."

"They'll swarm here soon as they know about us." Maetsukker said it for all
of them and the boy Croocq let out a moan.

"Yes, and if there's one priest, there's got to be others." Ginsel licked dry lips.
"And then their God-cursed conquistadores are never far away."

"That's right," Vinck added uneasily. "They're like lice."

"Christ Jesus! Papists!" someone muttered. "And conquistadores!"

"But we're in the Japans, Pilot?" van Nekk asked. "He told you that?"

"Yes. Why?"

Van Nekk moved closer and dropped his voice. "If priests are here, and some
of the natives are Catholic, perhaps the other part's true—about the riches, the
gold and silver and precious stones." A hush fell on them. "Did you see any,
Pilot? Any gold? Any gems on the natives, or gold?"

"No. None." Blackthorne thought a moment. "I don't remember seeing any.
No necklaces or beads or bracelets. Listen, there's something else to tell you. I
went aboard *Erasmus* but she's sealed up." He related what had happened and
their anxiety increased.

"Jesus, if we can't go back aboard and there are priests ashore and Papists. . . . We've got to get away from here." Maetsukker's voice began to tremble. "Pilot, what are we going to do? They'll burn us! Conquistadores—those bastards'll shove their swords . . ."

"We're in God's hands," Jan Roper called out confidently. "He will protect us from the anti-Christ. That's His promise. There's nothing to be afraid of."

Blackthorne said, "The way the samurai Omi-san snarled at the priest—I'm sure he hated him. That's good, eh? What I'd like to know is why the priest wasn't wearing their usual robes. Why the orange one? I've never seen that before."

"Yes, that's curious," van Nekk said.

Blackthorne looked up at him. "Maybe their hold here isn't strong. That could help us greatly."

"What should we do, Pilot?" Ginsel asked.

"Be patient and wait till their chief, this *daimyo,* comes. He'll let us go. Why shouldn't he? We've done them no harm. We've goods to trade. We're not pirates, we've nothing to fear."

"Very true, and don't forget the Pilot said the savages aren't all Papists," van Nekk said, more to encourage himself than the others. "Yes. It's good the samurai hated the priest. And it's only the samurai who are armed. That's not so bad, eh? Just watch out for the samurai and get our weapons back—that's the idea. We'll be aboard before you know it."

"What happens if this *daimyo's* Papist?" Jan Roper asked.

No one answered him. Then Ginsel said, "Pilot, the man with the sword? He cut the other wog into pieces, after chopping his head off?"

"Yes."

"Christ! They're barbarians! Lunatics!" Ginsel was tall, a good-looking youth with short arms and very bowed legs. The scurvy had taken all his teeth. "After he chopped his head off, the others just walked away? Without saying anything?"

"Yes."

"Christ Jesus, an unarmed man, murdered, just like that? Why'd he do it? Why'd he kill him?"

"I don't know, Ginsel. But you've never seen such speed. One moment the sword was sheathed, the next the man's head was rolling."

"God protect us!"

"Dear Lord Jesus," van Nekk murmered. "If we can't get back to the ship. . . . God damn that storm, I feel so helpless without my spectacles!"

"How many samurai were aboard, Pilot?" Ginsel asked.

"Twenty-two were on deck. But there were more ashore."

"The wrath of God will be upon the heathen and on sinners and they'll burn in hell for all eternity."

"I'd like to be sure of that, Jan Roper," Blackthorne said, an edge to his voice, as he felt the fear of God's vengeance sweep through the room. He was very tired and wanted to sleep.

"You can be sure, Pilot, oh yes, I am. I pray that your eyes are opened to God's truth. That you come to realize we're here only because of you—what's left of us."

"What?" Blackthorne said dangerously.

"Why did you really persuade the Captain-General to try for the Japans? It wasn't in our orders. We were to pillage the New World, to carry the war into the enemy's belly, then go home."

"There were Spanish ships south and north of us and nowhere else to run. Has your memory gone along with your wits? We had to sail west—it was our only chance."

"I never saw enemy ships, Pilot. None of us did."

"Come now, Jan," van Nekk said wearily. "The pilot did what he thought best. Of course the Spaniards were there."

"Aye, that's the truth, and we was a thousand leagues from friends and in enemy waters, by God!" Vinck spat. "That's the God's truth—and the God's truth was we put it to a vote. We all said yes."

"I didn't."

Sonk said, "No one asked me."

"Oh, Christ Jesus!"

"Calm down, Johann," van Nekk said, trying to ease the tension. "We're the first ones to reach Japans. Remember all the stories, eh? We're rich if we keep our wits. We have trade goods and there's gold here—there must be. Where else could we sell our cargo? Not there in the New World, hunted and harried! They were hunting us and the Spaniards knew we were off Santa Maria. We had to quit Chile and there was no escape back through the Strait—of course they'd be lying in wait for us, of course they would! No, here was our only chance and a good idea. Our cargo exchanged for spices and gold and silver, eh? Think of the profit—a thousandfold, that's usual. We're in the Spice Islands. You know the riches of the Japans and Cathay, you've heard about them forever. We all have. Why else did we all sign on? We'll be rich, you'll see!"

"We're dead men, like all the others. We're in the land of Satan."

Vinck said angrily, "Shut your mouth, Roper! The Pilot did right. Not his fault the others died—not his fault. Men always die on these voyages."

Jan Roper's eyes were flecked, the pupils tiny. "Yes, God rest their souls. My brother was one."

Blackthorne looked into the fanatic eyes, hating Jan Roper. Inside he was asking himself if he had really sailed west to elude the enemy ships. Or was it because he was the first English pilot through the Strait, first in position, ready and able to stab west and therefore first with the chance of circumnavigating?

Jan Roper hissed, "Didn't the others die through your ambition, Pilot? God will punish you!"

"Now hold your tongue." Blackthorne's words were soft and final.

Jan Roper stared back with the same frozen hatchet face, but he kept his mouth shut.

"Good." Blackthorne sat tiredly on the floor and rested against one of the uprights.

"What should we do, Pilot?"

"Wait and get fit. Their chief is coming soon—then we'll get everything settled."

Vinck was looking out into the garden at the samurai who sat motionless on his heels beside the gateway. "Look at that bastard. Been there for hours, never moves, never says anything, doesn't even pick his nose."

"He's been no trouble though, Johann. None at all," van Nekk said.

"Yes, but all we've been doing is sleeping and fornicating and eating the swill."

"Pilot, he's only one man. We're ten," Ginsel said quietly.

"I've thought of that. But we're not fit enough yet. It'll take a week for the scurvy to go," Blackthorne replied, disquieted. "There are too many of them aboard ship. I wouldn't like to take on even one without a spear or gun. Are you guarded at night?"

"Yes. They change guard three or four times. Has anyone seen a sentry asleep?" van Nekk asked.

They shook their heads.

"We could be aboard tonight," Jan Roper said. "With the help of God we'll overpower the heathen and take the ship."

"Clear the shit out of your ears! The pilot's just got through telling you! Don't you listen?" Vinck spat disgustedly.

"That's right," Pieterzoon, a gunner, agreed. "Stop hacking at old Vinck!"

Jan Roper's eyes narrowed even more. "Look to your soul, Johann Vinck. And yours, Hans Pieterzoon. The Day of Judgment approaches." He walked away and sat on the veranda.

Van Nekk broke the silence. "Everything is going to be all right. You'll see."

"Roper's right. It's greed that put us here," the boy Croocq said, his voice quavering. "It's God's punishment that—"

"Stop it!"

The boy jerked. "Yes, Pilot. Sorry, but—well . . ." Maximilian Croocq was the youngest of them, just sixteen, and he had signed on for the voyage because his father had been captain of one of the ships and they were going to make their fortune. But he had seen his father die badly when they had sacked the Spanish town of Santa Magdellana in the Argentine. The plunder had been good and he had seen what rape was and he had tried it, hating himself, glutted by the blood smell and the killing. Later he had seen more of his friends die and the five ships became one and now he felt he was the oldest among them. "Sorry. I'm sorry."

"How long have we been ashore, Baccus?" Blackthorne asked.

"This is the third day." Van Nekk moved close again, squatting on his haunches. "Don't remember the arrival too clearly, but when I woke up the savages were all over the ship. Very polite and kind though. Gave us food and hot water. They took the dead away and put the anchors out. Don't remember much but I think they towed us to a safe mooring. You were delirious when they carried you ashore. We wanted to keep you with us but they wouldn't let us. One of them spoke a few words of Portuguese. He seemed to be the headman, he had gray hair. He didn't understand 'Pilot-Major' but knew 'Captain.' It was quite clear he wanted our 'Captain' to have different quarters from us, but he said we shouldn't worry because you'd be well looked after. Us too. Then he guided us here, they carried us mostly, and said we were to stay inside until *his* captain came. We didn't want to let them take you but there was nothing we could do. Will you ask the headman about wine or brandy, Pilot?" Van Nekk licked his lips thirstily, then added, "Now that I think of it, he mentioned 'daimyo' too. What's going to happen when the *daimyo* arrives?"

"Has anyone got a knife or a pistol?"

"No," van Nekk said, scratching absently at the lice in his hair. "They took all our clothes away to clean them and kept the weapons. I didn't think anything about it at the time. They took my keys too, as well as my pistol. I had all my keys on a ring. The strong room, the strongbox, and the magazine."

"Everything's locked tight aboard. No need to worry about that."

"I don't like not having my keys. Makes me very nervous. Damn my eyes, I could use a brandy right now. Even a flagon of ale."

"Lord Jesus! The sameree cut him into pieces, did he?" Sonk said to no one in particular.

"For the love of God, shut your mouth. It's 'samurai.' You're enough to make a man shit himself," Ginsel said.

"I hope that bastard priest doesn't come here," Vinck said.

"We're safe in the good Lord's hands." Van Nekk was still trying to sound confident. "When the *daimyo* comes we'll be released. We'll get our ship back and our guns. You'll see. We'll sell all our goods and we'll get back to Holland rich and safe having gone round the world—the first Dutchmen ever. The Catholics'll go to hell and that's the end of it."

"No, it isn't," Vinck said. "Papists make my skin crawl. I can't help it. That and the thought of the conquistadores. You think they'll be here in strength, Pilot?"

"I don't know. I'd think yes! I wish we had all our squadron here."

"Poor bastards," Vinck said. "At least we're alive."

Maetsukker said, "Maybe they're back home. Maybe they turned back at the Magellan when the storms scattered us."

"I hope you're right," Blackthorne said. "But I think they're lost with all hands."

Ginsel shuddered. "At least we're alive."

"With Papists here, and these heathens with their stinking tempers, I wouldn't give an old whore's crack for our lives."

"Goddamn the day I left Holland," Pieterzoon said. "Goddamn all grog! If I hadn't been drunker than a fiddler's bitch I'd still be heads down in Amsterdam with my old woman."

"Damn what you like, Pieterzoon. But don't damn liquor. It's the stuff of life!"

"I'd say we're in the sewer, up to our chins, and the tide's coming in fast." Vinck rolled his eyes. "Yes, very fast."

"I never thought we'd reach land," Maetsukker said. He looked like a ferret, except he had no teeth. "Never. Least of all the Japans. Lousy stinking Papists! We'll never leave here alive! I wish we had some guns. What a rotten landfall! I didn't mean anything, Pilot," he said quickly as Blackthorne looked at him. "Just bad luck, that's all."

Later servants brought them food again. Always the same: vegetables—cooked and raw—with a little vinegar, fish soup, and the wheat or barley porridge. They all spurned the small pieces of raw fish and asked for meat and liquor. But they were not understood and then, near sunset, Blackthorne left. He had wearied of their fears and hates and obscenities. He told them that he would return after dawn.

The shops were busy on the narrow streets. He found his street and the gate of his house. The stains on the earth had been swept away and the body had vanished. It's almost as though I dreamed the whole thing, he thought. The garden gate opened before he could put a hand on it.

The old gardener, still loinclothed although there was a chill on the wind, beamed and bowed. *"Konbanwa."*

"Hello," Blackthorne said without thinking. He walked up the steps, stopped, remembering his boots. He took them off and went barefoot onto the veranda and into the room. He crossed it into a corridor but could not find his room.

"Onna!" he called out.

An old woman appeared. *"Hai?"*

"Where's Onna?"

The old woman frowned and pointed to herself. "Onna!"

"Oh, for the love of God," Blackthorne said irritably. "Where's my room? Where's Onna?" He slid open another latticed door. Four Japanese were seated on the floor around a low table, eating. He recognized one of them as the gray-haired man, the village headman, who had been with the priest. They all bowed. "Oh, sorry," he said, and pulled the door to.

"Onna!" he called out.

The old woman thought a moment, then beckoned. He followed her into another corridor. She slid a door aside. He recognized his room from the crucifix. The quilts were already laid out neatly.

"Thank you," he said, relieved. "Now fetch Onna!"

The old woman padded away. He sat down, his head and body aching, and wished there was a chair, wondering where they were kept. How to get aboard?

How to get some guns? There must be a way. Feet padded back and there were three women now, the old woman, a young round-faced girl, and the middle-aged lady.

The old woman pointed at the girl, who seemed a little frightened. "Onna."

"No." Blackthorne got up ill-temperedly and jerked a finger at the middle-aged woman. "This is Onna, for God's sake! Don't you know your name? Onna! I'm hungry. Could I have some food?" He rubbed his stomach parodying hunger. They looked at each other. Then the middle-aged woman shrugged, said something that made the others laugh, went over to the bed, and began to undress. The other two squatted, wide-eyed and expectant.

Blackthorne was appalled. "What are you doing?"

"*Ishimasho!*" she said, setting aside her wide waistband and opening her kimono. Her breasts were flat and dried up and her belly huge.

It was quite clear that she was going to get into the bed. He shook his head and told her to get dressed and took her arm and they all began chattering and gesticulating and the woman was becoming quite angry. She stepped out of her long underskirt and, naked, tried to get back into bed.

Their chattering stopped and they all bowed as the headman came quietly down the corridor. "*Nanda? Nanda?*" he asked.

The old woman explained what was the matter. "You want this woman?" he asked incredulously in heavily accented, barely understandable Portuguese, motioning at the naked woman.

"No. No, of course not. I just wanted Onna to get me some food." Blackthorne pointed impatiently at her. "Onna!"

"*Onna* mean 'woman.'" The Japanese motioned at all of them. "*Onna—onna—onna.* You want *onna?*"

Blackthorne wearily shook his head. "No. No, thank you. I made a mistake. Sorry. What's her name?"

"Please?"

"What's her name?"

"Ah! Namu is Haku. Haku," he said.

"Haku?"

"*Hai.* Haku!"

"I'm sorry, Haku-san. Thought *onna* your name."

The man explained to Haku and she was not at all pleased. But he said something and they all looked at Blackthorne and tittered behind their hands and left. Haku walked off naked, her kimono over her arm, with a vast amount of dignity.

"Thank you," Blackthorne said, enraged at his own stupidity.

"This my house. My namu Mura."

"Mura-san. Mine's Blackthorne."

"Please?"

"My namu. Blackthorne."

"Ah! Berr—rakk—fon." Mura tried to say it several times but could not. Eventually he gave up and continued to study the colossus in front of him. This was the first barbarian he had ever seen except for Father Sebastio, and the other priest, so many years ago. But anyway, he thought, the priests are dark-haired and dark-eyed and of normal height. But this man: tall and golden-haired and golden-bearded with blue eyes and a weird pallor to his skin where it is covered and redness where it is exposed. Astonishing! I thought *all* men had black hair and dark eyes. *We* all do. The Chinese do, and isn't China the whole world, except for the land of the southern Portugee barbarians? Astonishing! And why does Father Sebastio hate this man so much? Because he's a Satan worshiper? I wouldn't think so, because Father Sebastio could cast out the devil if he wanted. Eeee, I've never seen the good Father so angry. Never. Astonishing!

Are blue eyes and golden hair the mark of Satan?

Mura looked up at Blackthorne and remembered how he had tried to question him aboard the ship and then, when this Captain had become unconscious, he had decided to bring him to his own house because he was the leader and should have special consideration. They had laid him on the quilt and undressed him, more than just a little curious.

"His Peerless Parts are certainly impressive, *neh?*" Mura's mother, Saiko, had said. "I wonder how large he would be when erect?"

"Large," he had answered and they had all laughed, his mother and wife and friends and servants, and the doctor.

"I expect their women must be—must be as well endowed," his wife, Niji, said.

"Nonsense, girl," said his mother. "Any number of our courtesans could happily make the necessary accommodation." She shook her head in wonder. "I've never seen anything like him in my whole life. Very odd indeed, *neh?*"

They had washed him and he had not come out of his coma. The doctor had thought it unwise to immerse him in a proper bath until he was awake. "Perhaps we should remember, Mura-san, we don't know how the barbarian really is," he had said with careful wisdom. "So sorry, but we might kill him by mistake. Obviously he's at the limit of his strength. We should exercise patience."

"But what about the lice in his hair?" Mura had asked.

"They will have to stay for the time being. I understand all barbarians have them. So sorry, I'd advise patience."

"Don't you think we could at least shampoo his head?" his wife had said. "We'd be very careful. I'm sure the Mistress would supervise our poor efforts. That should help the barbarian and keep our house clean."

"I agree. You can shampoo him," his mother had said with finality. "But I'd certainly like to know how large he is when erect."

Now Mura glanced down at Blackthorne involuntarily. Then he remembered what the priest had told them about these Satanists and pirates. God the Father protect us from this evil, he thought. If I'd known that he was so terrible I would never have brought him into my house. No, he told himself. You are obliged to treat him as a special guest until Omi-san says otherwise. But you were wise to send word to the priest and send word to Omi-san instantly. Very wise. You're headman, you've protected the village and you, alone, are responsible.

Yes. And Omi-san will hold you responsible for the death this morning and the dead man's impertinence, and quite rightly.

"Don't be stupid, Tamazaki! You risk the good name of the village, *neh?*" he had warned his friend the fisherman a dozen times. "Stop your intolerance. Omi-san has no option but to sneer at Christians. Doesn't our *daimyo* detest Christians? What else can Omi-san do?"

"Nothing, I agree, Mura-san, please excuse me." Tamazaki had always replied as formally. "But Buddhists should have more tolerance, *neh?* Aren't they both Zen Buddhists?" Zen Buddhism was self-disciplining; it relied heavily on self-help and meditation to find Enlightenment. Most samurai belonged to the Zen Buddhist sect, since it suited, seemed almost to be designed for, a proud, death-seeking warrior.

"Yes, Buddhism teaches tolerance. But how many times must you be reminded they're samurai, and this is Izu and not Kyushu, and even if it were Kyushu, you're still the one that's wrong. Always. *Neh?*"

"Yes. Please excuse me, I know I'm wrong. But sometimes I feel I cannot live with my inner shame when Omi-san is so insulting about the True Faith."

And now, Tamazaki, you are dead of your own choosing because you insulted Omi-san by not bowing simply because he said, ". . . this smelly priest of the foreign religion." Even though the priest does smell and the True Faith is foreign. My poor friend. That truth will not feed your family now or remove the stain from my village.

Oh, Madonna, bless my old friend and give him the joy of thy Heaven.

Expect a lot of trouble from Omi-san, Mura told himself. And if that isn't bad enough, now our *daimyo* is coming.

A pervading anxiety always filled him whenever he thought of his feudal lord, Kasigi Yabu, *daimyo* of Izu, Omi's uncle—the man's cruelty and lack of honor, the way he cheated all the villages of their rightful share of their catch and their crops, and the grinding weight of his rule. When war comes, Mura asked himself, which side will Yabu declare for, Lord Ishido or Lord Toranaga? We're trapped between the giants and in pawn to both.

Northwards, Toranaga, the greatest general alive, Lord of the Kwanto, the Eight Provinces, the most important *daimyo* in the land, Chief General of the Armies of the East; to the west the domains of Ishido, Lord of Osaka Castle, conqueror of Korea, Protector of the Heir, Chief General of the Armies of the West. And to the north, the Tokaidō, the Great Coastal Road that links Yedo, Toranaga's capital city, to Osaka, Ishido's capital city—three hundred miles westward over which their legions must march.

Who will win the war?

Neither.

Because their war will envelop the empire again, alliances will fall apart, provinces will fight provinces until it is village against village as it ever was. Except for the last ten years. For the last ten years, incredibly, there had been a warlessness called peace throughout the empire, for the first time in history.

I was beginning to like peace, Mura thought.

But the man who made the peace is dead. The peasant soldier who became a samurai and then a general and then the greatest general and finally the Taikō, the absolute Lord Protector of Japan, is dead a year and his seven-year-old son is far too young to inherit supreme power. So the boy, like us, is in pawn. Between the giants. And war inevitable. Now not even the Taikō himself can protect his beloved son, his dynasty, his inheritance, or his empire.

Perhaps this is as it should be. The Taikō subdued the land, made the peace, forced all the *daimyos* in the land to grovel like peasants before him, rearranged fiefs to suit his whim—promoting some, deposing others—and then he died. He was a giant among pygmies. But perhaps it's right that all his work and greatness should die with him. Isn't man but a blossom taken by the wind, and only the mountains and the sea and the stars and this Land of the Gods real and everlasting?

We're all trapped and that is a fact; war will come soon and that is a fact; Yabu alone will decide which side we are on and that is a fact; the village will always be a village because the paddy fields are rich and the sea abundant and that is a last fact.

Mura brought his mind back firmly to the barbarian pirate in front of him. You're a devil sent to plague us, he thought, and you've caused us nothing but trouble since you arrived. Why couldn't you have picked another village?

"Captain-san want *onna?*" he asked helpfully. At his suggestion the village council made physical arrangements for the other barbarians, both as a politeness and as a simple means of keeping them occupied until the authorities came. That the village was entertained by the subsequent stories of the liaisons more than compensated for the money which had had to be invested.

"*Onna?*" he repeated, naturally presuming that as the pirate was on his feet, he would be equally content to be on his belly, his Heavenly Spear warmly encased before sleeping, and anyway, all the preparations had been made.

"No!" Blackthorne wanted only to sleep. But because he knew that he needed this man on his side he forced a smile, indicated the crucifix. "You're a Christian?"

Mura nodded. "Christian."

"I'm Christian."

"Father say not. Not Christian."

"I'm a Christian. Not a Catholic. But I'm still Christian."

But Mura could not understand. Neither was there any way Blackthorne could explain, however much he tried.

"Want *onna?*"

"The—the dimyo—when come?"

"Dimyo? No understand."

"Dimyo—ah, I mean *daimyo.*"

"Ah, *daimyo. Hai. Daimyo!*" Mura shrugged. "*Daimyo* come when come. Sleep. First clean. Please."

"What?"

"Clean. Bath, please."

"I don't understand."

Mura came closer and crinkled his nose distastefully.

"Stinku. Bad. Like all Portugeezu. Bath. This clean house."

"I'll bathe when I want and I don't stink!" Blackthorne fumed. "Everyone knows baths are dangerous. You want me to catch the flux? You think I'm God-cursed stupid? You get the hell out of here and let me sleep!"

"Bath!" Mura ordered, shocked at the barbarian's open anger—the height of bad manners. And it was not just that the barbarian stank, as indeed he did, but he had not bathed correctly for three days to his knowledge, and the courtesan quite rightly would refuse to pillow with him, however much the fee. These awful foreigners, he thought. Astonishing! How astoundingly filthy their habits are! Never mind. I'm responsible for you. You will be taught manners. You will bathe like a human being, and Mother will know that which she wants to know. "Bath!"

"Now get out before I snap you into pieces!" Blackthorne glowered at him, motioning him away.

There was a moment's pause and the other three Japanese appeared along with three of the women. Mura explained curtly what was the matter, then said with finality to Blackthorne, "Bath. Please."

"Out!"

Mura came forward alone into the room. Blackthorne shoved out his arm, not wanting to hurt the man, just to push him away. Suddenly Blackthorne let out a bellow of pain. Somehow Mura had chopped his elbow with the side of his hand and now Blackthorne's arm hung down, momentarily paralyzed. Enraged, he charged. But the room spun and he was flat on his face and there was another stabbing, paralyzing pain in his back and he could not move. "By God . . ."

He tried to get up but his legs buckled under him. Then Mura calmly put out his small but iron-hard finger and touched a nerve center in Blackthorne's neck. There was a blinding pain.

"Good sweet Jesus . . ."

"Bath? Please?"

"Yes—yes," Blackthorne gasped through his agony, astounded that he had been overcome so easily by such a tiny man and now lay helpless as any child, ready to have his throat cut.

Years ago Mura had learned the arts of judo and karate as well as how to fight with sword and spear. This was when he was a warrior and fought for Nakamura, the peasant general, the Taikō—long before the Taikō had become the Taikō —when peasants could be samurai and samurai could be peasants, or craftsmen or even lowly merchants, and warriors again. Strange, Mura thought absently, looking down at the fallen giant, that almost the first thing the Taikō did when he became all powerful was to order all peasants to cease being soldiers and at once give up all weapons. The Taikō had forbidden them weapons forever and set up the immutable caste system that now controlled all the lives in all the empire: samurai above all, below them the peasants, next craftsmen, then the merchants followed by actors, outcasts, and bandits, and finally at the bottom of the scale, the *eta,* the nonhumans, those who dealt with dead bodies, the curing of leather and handling of dead animals, who were also the public executioners, branders, and mutilators. Of course, any barbarian was beneath consideration in this scale.

"Please excuse me, Captain-san," Mura said, bowing low, ashamed for the barbarian's loss of face as he lay groaning like a baby still at suck. Yes, I'm very sorry, he thought, but it had to be done. You provoked me beyond all reasonableness, even for a barbarian. You shout like a lunatic, upset my mother, interrupt my house's tranquillity, disturb the servants, and my wife's already had to replace one shoji door. I could not possibly permit your obvious lack of manners to go unopposed. Or allow you to go against my wishes in my own house. It's really for your own good. Then, too, it's not so bad because you barbarians really have no face to lose. Except the priests—they're different. They still smell horrible, but they're the anointed of God the Father so they have great face. But you— you're a liar as well as a pirate. No honor. How astonishing! Claiming to be a Christian! Unfortunately that won't help you at all. Our *daimyo* hates the True Faith and barbarians and tolerates them only because he has to. But you're not a Portuguese or a Christian, therefore not protected by law, *neh?* So even though you are a dead man—or at least a mutilated one—it is my duty to see that you go to your fate clean. "Bath very good!"

He helped the other men carry the still dazed Blackthorne through the house, out into the garden, along a roofed-in walk of which he was very proud, and into the bath house. The women followed.

It became one of the great experiences of his life. He knew at the time that he would tell and retell the tale to his incredulous friends over barrels of hot saké, as the national wine of Japan was called; to his fellow elders, fishermen, villagers, to his children who also would not at first believe him. But they, in their turn, would regale their children and the name of Mura the fisherman would live forever in the village of Anjiro, which was in the province of Izu on the southeastern coast of the main island of Honshu. All because he, Mura the fisherman, had the good fortune to be headman in the first year after the death of the Taikō and therefore temporarily responsible for the leader of the strange barbarians who came out of the eastern sea.

CHAPTER 2

T HE *daimyo*, Kasigi Yabu, Lord of Izu, wants to know who you are, where you come from, how you got here, and what acts of piracy you have committed," Father Sebastio said.

"I keep telling you we're not pirates." The morning was clear and warm and Blackthorne was kneeling in front of the platform in the village square, his head still aching from the blow. Keep calm and get your brain working, he told himself. You're on trial for your lives. You're the spokesman and that's all there is to it. The Jesuit's hostile and the only interpreter available and you'll have no way of knowing what he's saying except you can be sure he'll not help you. . . . 'Get your wits about you boy,' he could almost hear old Alban Caradoc saying. 'When the storm's the worst and the sea the most dreadful, that's when you need your special wits. That's what keeps you alive and your ship alive—if you're the pilot. Get your wits about you and take the juice out of every day, however bad. . . .'

The juice of today is bile, Blackthorne thought grimly. Why do I hear Alban's voice so clearly?

"First tell the *daimyo* that we're at war, that we're enemies," he said. "Tell him England and the Netherlands are at war with Spain and Portugal."

"I caution you again to speak simply and not to twist the facts. The Netherlands—or Holland, Zeeland, the United Provinces, whatever you filthy Dutch rebels call it—is a small, rebellious province of the Spanish Empire. You're leader of traitors who are in a state of insurrection against their lawful king."

"England's at war and the Netherlands have been sepa—" Blackthorne did not continue because the priest was no longer listening but interpreting.

The *daimyo* was on the platform, short, squat, and dominating. He knelt comfortably, his heels tucked neatly under him, flanked by four lieutenants, one of whom was Kasigi Omi, his nephew and vassal. They all wore silk kimonos and, over them, ornate surcoats with wide belts nipping them in at the waist and huge, starched shoulders. And the inevitable swords.

Mura knelt in the dirt of the square. He was the only villager present and the only other onlookers were the fifty samurai who came with the *daimyo*. They sat in disciplined, silent rows. The rabble of the ship's crew were behind Blackthorne and, like him, were on their knees, guards nearby. They had had to carry the Captain-General with them when they were sent for, even though he was ailing badly. He had been allowed to lie down in the dirt, still in semicoma. Blackthorne had bowed with all of them when they had come in front of the *daimyo*, but this was not enough. Samurai had slammed all of them on their knees and pushed their heads into the dust in the manner of peasants. He had tried to resist and shouted to the priest to explain that it was not their custom, that he was the leader and an emissary of their country and should be treated as such. But the haft of a spear had sent him reeling. His men gathered themselves for an impulsive charge, but he shouted at them to stop and to kneel. Fortunately they obeyed. The *daimyo* had uttered something guttural and the priest interpreted this as a caution to him to tell the truth and tell it quickly. Blackthorne had asked for a chair but the priest said the Japanese did not use chairs and there were none in Japan.

33

Blackthorne was concentrating on the priest as he spoke to the *daimyo,* seeking a clue, a way through this reef.

There's arrogance and cruelty in the *daimyo's* face, he thought. I'll bet he's a real bastard. The priest's Japanese isn't fluent. Ah, see that? Irritation and impatience. Did the *daimyo* ask for another word, a clearer word? I think so. Why's the Jesuit wearing orange robes? Is the *daimyo* a Catholic? Look, the Jesuit's very deferential and sweating a lot. I'll bet the *daimyo's* not a Catholic. Be accurate! *Perhaps* he's not a Catholic. Either way you'll get no quarter from him. How can you use the evil bastard? How do you talk direct to him? How're you going to work the priest? How discredit him? What's the bait? Come on, think! You know enough about Jesuits—

"The *daimyo* says hurry up and answer his questions."

"Yes. Of course, I'm sorry. My name's John Blackthorne. I'm English, Pilot-Major of a Netherlands fleet. Our home port's Amsterdam."

"Fleet? What fleet? You're lying. There's no fleet. Why is an Englishman pilot of a Dutch ship?"

"All in good time. First please translate what I said."

"Why are you the pilot of a Dutch privateer? Hurry up!"

Blackthorne decided to gamble. His voice abruptly hardened and it cut through the morning warmth. *"Que va!* First translate what I said, *Spaniard!* Now!"

The priest flushed. "I'm Portuguese. I've told you before. Answer the question."

"I'm here to talk to the *daimyo,* not to you. Translate what I said, you motherless offal!" Blackthorne saw the priest redden even more and felt that this had not gone unnoticed by the *daimyo.* Be cautious, he warned himself. That yellow bastard will carve you into pieces quicker than a school of sharks if you overreach yourself. "Tell the lord *daimyo!"* Blackthorne deliberately bowed low to the platform and felt the chill sweat beginning to pearl as he committed himself irrevocably to his course of action.

Father Sebastio knew that his training should make him impervious to the pirate's insults and the obvious plan to discredit him in front of the *daimyo.* But, for the first time, it did not and he felt lost. When Mura's messenger had brought news of the ship to his mission in the neighboring province, he had been rocked by the implications. It can't be Dutch or English! he had thought. There had never been a heretic ship in the Pacific except those of the archdevil corsair Drake, and never one here in Asia. The routes were secret and guarded. At once he had prepared to leave and had sent an urgent carrier pigeon message to his superior in Osaka, wishing that he could first have consulted with him, knowing that he was young, almost untried and new to Japan, barely two years here, not yet ordained, and not competent to deal with this emergency. He had rushed to Anjiro, hoping and praying that the news was untrue. But the ship was Dutch and the pilot English, and all of his loathing for the satanic heresies of Luther, Calvin, Henry VIII, and the archfiend Elizabeth, his bastard daughter, had overwhelmed him. And still swamped his judgment.

"Priest, translate what the pirate said," he heard the *daimyo* say.

O Blessed Mother of God, help me to do thy will. Help me to be strong in front of the *daimyo* and give me the gift of tongues, and let me convert him to the True Faith.

Father Sebastio gathered his wits and began to speak more confidently.

Blackthorne listened carefully, trying to pick out the words and meanings. The Father used "England" and "Blackthorne" and pointed at the ship, which lay nicely at anchor in the harbor.

"How did you get here?" Father Sebastio said.

"By Magellan's Pass. This is the one hundred and thirty-sixth day from there. Tell the *daimyo*—"

"You're lying. Magellan's Pass is secret. You came via Africa and India. You'll have to tell the truth eventually. They use torture here."

"The Pass *was* secret. A Portuguese sold us a rutter. One of your own people sold you out for a little Judas gold. You're all manure! Now all English warships —and Dutch warships—know the way through to the Pacific. There's a fleet—twenty English ships-of-the-line, sixty-cannon warships—attacking Manila right now. Your empire's finished."

"You're lying!"

Yes, Blackthorne thought, knowing there was no way to prove the lie except to go to Manila. "That fleet will harry your sea lanes and stamp out your colonies. There's another Dutch fleet due here any week now. The Spanish-Portuguese pig is back in his pigsty and your Jesuit General's penis is in his anus—where it belongs!" He turned away and bowed low to the *daimyo*.

"God curse you and your filthy mouth!"

"*Ano mono wa nani o moshité oru?*" the *daimyo* snapped impatiently.

The priest spoke more quickly, harder, and said "Magellan" and "Manila" but Blackthorne thought that the *daimyo* and his lieutenants did not seem to understand too clearly.

Yabu was wearying of this trial. He looked out into the harbor, to the ship that had obsessed him ever since he had received Omi's secret message, and he wondered again if it was the gift from the gods that he hoped.

"Have you inspected the cargo yet, Omi-san?" he had asked this morning as soon as he had arrived, mud-spattered and very weary.

"No, Lord. I thought it best to seal up the ship until you came personally, but the holds are filled with crates and bales. I hope I did it correctly. Here are all their keys. I confiscated them."

"Good." Yabu had come from Yedo, Toranaga's capital city, more than a hundred miles away, post haste, furtively and at great personal risk, and it was vital that he return as quickly. The journey had taken almost two days over foul roads and spring-filled streams, partly on horseback and partly by palanquin. "I'll go to the ship at once."

"You should see the strangers, Lord," Omi had said with a laugh. "They're incredible. Most of them have blue eyes—like Siamese cats—and golden hair. But the best news of all is that they're pirates. . . ."

Omi had told him about the priest and what the priest had related about these corsairs and what the pirate had said and what had happened, and his excitement had tripled. Yabu had conquered his impatience to go aboard the ship and break the seals. Instead he had bathed and changed and ordered the barbarians brought in front of him.

"You, priest," he said, his voice sharp, hardly able to understand the priest's bad Japanese. "Why is he so angry with you?"

"He's evil. Pirate. He worship devil."

Yabu leaned over to Omi, the man on his left. "Can you understand what he's saying, nephew? Is he lying? What do you think?"

"I don't know, Lord. Who knows what barbarians really believe? I imagine the priest *thinks* the pirate is a devil worshiper. Of course, that's all nonsense."

Yabu turned back to the priest, detesting him. He wished that he could crucify him today and obliterate Christianity from his domain once and for all. But he could not. Though he and all other *daimyos* had total power in their own domains, they were still subject to the overriding authority of the Council of Regents, the military ruling junta to whom the Taikō had legally willed his power during his son's minority, and subject, too, to edicts the Taikō had issued in his lifetime, which were all still legally in force. One of these, promulgated years ago, dealt with the Portuguese barbarians and ordered that they were all protected persons and, within reason, their religion was to be tolerated and their priests allowed, within reason, to proselytize and convert. "You, priest! What else did the pirate say? What was he saying to you? Hurry up! Have you lost your tongue?"

"Pirate says bad things. Bad. About more pirate war boatings—many."

"What do you mean, 'war boatings'?"

"Sorry, Lord, I don't understand."

" 'War boatings' doesn't make sense, *neh?*"

"Ah! Pirate says other ships war are in Manila, in Philippines."

"Omi-san, do you understand what he's talking about?"

"No, Lord. His accent's appalling, it's almost gibberish. Is he saying that more pirate ships are east of Japan?"

"You, priest! Are these pirate ships off our coast? East? Eh?"

"Yes, Lord. But I think he's lying. He says at Manila."

"I don't understand you. Where's Manila?"

"East. Many days' journey."

"If any pirate ships come here, we'll give them a pleasant welcome, wherever Manila is."

"Please excuse me, I don't understand."

"Never mind," Yabu said, his patience at an end. He had already decided the strangers were to die and he relished the prospect. Obviously these men did not come within the Taikō's edict that specified "Portuguese barbarians," and anyway they were pirates. As long as he could remember he had hated barbarians, their stench and filthiness and disgusting meat-eating habits, their stupid religion and arrogance and detestable manners. More than that, he was shamed, as was every *daimyo,* by their stranglehold over this Land of the Gods. A state of war had existed between China and Japan for centuries. China would allow no trade. Chinese silk cloth was vital to make the long, hot, humid Japanese summer bearable. For generations only a minuscule amount of contraband cloth had slipped through the net and was available, at huge cost, in Japan. Then, sixty-odd years ago, the barbarians had first arrived. The Chinese Emperor in Peking gave them a tiny permanent base at Macao in southern China and agreed to trade silks for silver. Japan had silver in abundance. Soon trade was flourishing. Both countries prospered. The middlemen, the Portuguese, grew rich, and their priests—Jesuits mostly—soon became vital to the trade. Only the priests managed to learn to speak Chinese and Japanese and therefore could act as negotiators and interpreters. As trade blossomed, the priests became more essential. Now the yearly trade was huge and touched the life of every samurai. So the priests had to be tolerated and the spread of their religion tolerated or the barbarians would sail away and trade would cease.

By now there were a number of very important Christian *daimyos* and many hundreds of thousands of converts, most of whom were in Kyushu, the southern island that was nearest to China and contained the Portuguese port of Nagasaki. Yes, Yabu thought, we must tolerate the priests and the Portuguese, but not these barbarians, the new ones, the unbelievable golden-haired, blue-eyed ones. His excitement filled him. Now at last he could satisfy his curiosity as to how well a barbarian would die when put to torment. And he had eleven men, eleven different tests, to experiment with. He never questioned why the agony of others pleasured him. He only knew that it did and therefore it was something to be sought and enjoyed.

Yabu said, "This ship, alien, non-Portuguese, and pirate, is confiscated with all it contains. All pirates are sentenced to immediate—" His mouth dropped open as he saw the pirate leader suddenly leap at the priest and rip the wooden crucifix from his belt, snap it into pieces and hurl the pieces on the ground, then shout something very loudly. The pirate immediately knelt and bowed low to him as the guards jumped forward, swords raised.

"Stop! Don't kill him!" Yabu was astounded that anyone could have the impertinence to act with such lack of manners in front of him. "These barbarians are beyond belief!"

"Yes," Omi said, his mind flooding with the questions that such an action implied.

The priest was still kneeling, staring fixedly at the pieces of the cross. They watched as his hand reached out shakily and picked up the violated wood. He said something to the pirate, his voice low, almost gentle. His eyes closed, he steepled his fingers, and his lips began to move slowly. The pirate leader was looking up at them motionlessly, pale blue eyes unblinking, catlike, in front of his rabble crew.

Yabu said, "Omi-san. First I want to go on the ship. Then we'll begin." His voice thickened as he contemplated the pleasure he had promised himself. "I want to begin with that red-haired one on the end of the line, the small man."

Omi leaned closer and lowered his excited voice. "Please excuse me, but this has never happened before, Sire. Not since the Portuguese barbarians came here. Isn't the crucifix their sacred symbol? Aren't they *always* deferential to their priests? Don't they always kneel to them openly? Just like our Christians? Haven't the priests absolute control over them?"

"Come to your point."

"We all detest the Portuguese, Sire. Except the Christians among us, *neh?* Perhaps these barbarians are worth more to you alive than dead."

"How?"

"Because they're unique. They're anti-Christian! Perhaps a wise man could find a way to use their hatred—or irreligiousness—to our advantage. They're your property, to do with as you wish. *Neh?*"

Yes. And I want them in torment, Yabu thought. Yes, but you can enjoy that at any time. Listen to Omi. He's a good counselor. But is he to be trusted now? Does he have a secret reason for saying this? Think.

"Ikawa Jikkyu is Christian," he heard his nephew say, naming his hated enemy—one of Ishido's kinsmen and allies—who sat on his western borders. "Doesn't this filthy priest have his home there? Perhaps these barbarians could give you the key to unlock Ikawa's whole province. Perhaps Ishido's. Perhaps even Lord Toranaga's," Omi added delicately.

Yabu studied Omi's face, trying to reach what was behind it. Then his eyes went to the ship. He had no doubt now that it had been sent by the gods. Yes. But was it as a gift or a plague?

He put away his own pleasure for the security of his clan. "I agree. But first break these pirates. Teach them manners. Particularly *him.*"

"Good sweet Jesus' death!" Vinck muttered.

"We should say a prayer," van Nekk said.

"We've just said one."

"Perhaps we'd better say another. Lord God in Heaven, I could use a pint of brandy."

They were crammed into a deep cellar, one of the many that the fishermen used to store sun-dried fish. Samurai had herded them across the square, down a ladder, and now they were locked underground. The cellar was five paces long and five wide and four deep, with an earthen floor and walls. The ceiling was made of planks with a foot of earth above and a single trapdoor set into it.

"Get off my foot, you God-cursed ape!"

"Shut your face, shit picker!" Pieterzoon said genially. "Hey! Vinck, move up a little, you toothless old fart, you've got more room than anyone! By God, I could use a cold beer! Move up."

"I can't, Pieterzoon. We're tighter than a virgin's arse here."

"It's the Captain-General. He's got all the space. Give him a shove. Wake him up!" Maetsukker said.

"Eh? What's the matter? Leave me alone. What's going on? I'm sick. I've got to lie down. Where are we?"

"Leave him alone. He's sick. Come on, Maetsukker, get up, for the love of God." Vinck angrily pulled Maetsukker up and shoved him against the wall. There was not room enough for them all to lie down, or even to sit comfortably, at the same time. The Captain-General, Paulus Spillbergen, was lying full length under the trapdoor where there was the best air, his head propped on his bundled cloak. Blackthorne was leaning against a corner, staring up at the trapdoor. The crew had left him alone and stayed clear of him uneasily, as best they could, recognizing from long experience his mood, and the brooding, explosive violence that always lurked just below his quiet exterior.

Maetsukker lost his temper and smashed his fist into Vinck's groin. "Leave me alone or I'll kill you, you bastard."

Vinck flew at him, but Blackthorne grabbed both of them and rammed their heads against the wall.

"Shut up, all of you," he said softly. They did as they were ordered. "We'll split into watches. One watch sleeps, one sits, and one stands. Spillbergen lies down until he's fit. That corner's the latrine." He divided them up. When they had rearranged themselves it was more bearable.

We'll have to break out of here within a day or we'll be too weak, Blackthorne thought. When they bring the ladder back to give us food or water. It will have to be tonight or tomorrow night. Why did they put us here? We're no threat. We could help the *daimyo*. Will he understand? It was my only way to show him that the priest's our real enemy. Will he understand? The priest had.

"Perhaps God may forgive your sacrilege but I won't," Father Sebastio had said, very quietly. "I will never rest until you and your evil are obliterated."

The sweat was dribbling down his cheeks and chin. He wiped it away absently, ears tuned to the cellar as they would be when he was aboard and sleeping, or off watch and drifting; just enough to try to hear the danger before it happened.

We'll have to break out and take the ship. I wonder what Felicity's doing. And the children. Let's see, Tudor's seven years old now and Lisbeth is. . . . We're one year and eleven months and six days from Amsterdam, add thirty-seven days provisioning and coming from Chatham to there, add lastly, the eleven days that she was alive before the embarkation at Chatham. That's her age exactly—if all's well. All should be well. Felicity will be cooking and guarding and cleaning and chattering as the kids grow up, as strong and fearless as their mother. It will be fine to be home again, to walk together along the shore and in the forests and glades and beauty that is England.

Over the years he had trained himself to think about them as characters in a play, people that you loved and bled for, the play never ending. Otherwise the hurt of being away would be too much. He could almost count his days at home in the eleven years of marriage. They're few, he thought, too few. "It's a hard life for a woman, Felicity," he had said before. And she had said, "Any life is hard for a woman." She was seventeen then and tall and her hair was long and sensu—

His ears told him to beware.

The men were sitting or leaning or trying to sleep. Vinck and Pieterzoon, good friends, were talking quietly. Van Nekk was staring into space with the others. Spillbergen was half awake, and Blackthorne thought the man was stronger than he let everyone believe.

There was a sudden silence as they heard the footsteps overhead. The footsteps stopped. Muted voices in the harsh, strange-sounding language. Blackthorne thought he recognized the samurai's voice—Omi-san? Yes, that was his name— but he could not be certain. In a moment the voices stopped and the footsteps went away.

"You think they'll feed us, Pilot?" Sonk said.

"Yes."

"I could use a drink. Cold beer, by God," Pieterzoon said.

"Shut up," Vinck said. "You're enough to make a man sweat."

Blackthorne was conscious of his soaking shirt. And the stench. By the Lord God I could use a bath, he thought and abruptly he smiled, remembering.

Mura and the others had carried him into the warm room that day and laid him on a stone bench, his limbs still numb and slow moving. The three women, led by the old crone, had begun to undress him and he had tried to stop them but every time he moved, one of the men would stab a nerve and hold him powerless, and however much he raved and cursed they continued to undress him until he was naked. It was not that he was ashamed of being naked in front of a woman, it was just that undressing was always done in private and that was the custom. And he did not like being undressed by anyone, let alone these uncivilized natives. But to be undressed publicly like a helpless baby and to be washed everywhere like a baby with warm, soapy, scented water while they chattered and smiled as he lay on his back was too much. Then he had become erect and as much as he tried to stop it from happening, the worse it became—at least he thought so, but the women did not. Their eyes became bigger and he began to blush. Jesus Lord God the One and Only, I can't be blushing, but he was and this seemed to increase his size and the old woman clapped her hands in wonder and said something to which they all nodded and she shook her head awed and said something else to which they nodded even more.

Mura had said with enormous gravity, "Captain-san, Mother-san thank you, the best her life, now die happy!" and he and they had all bowed as one and then he, Blackthorne, had seen how funny it was and he had begun to laugh. They were startled, then they were laughing too, and his laughter took his strength away and the crone was a little sad and said so and this made him laugh more and them also. Then they had laid him gently into the vast heat of the deep water and soon he could bear it no longer, and they laid him gasping on the bench once more. The women had dried him and then an old blind man had come. Blackthorne had never known massage. As first he had tried to resist the probing fingers but then their magic seduced him and soon he was almost purring like a cat as the fingers found the knots and unlocked the blood or elixir that lurked beneath skin and muscle and sinew.

Then he had been helped to bed, strangely weak, half in dream, and the girl was there. She was patient with him, and after sleeping, when he had strength, he took her with care even though it had been so long.

He had not asked her name, and in the morning when Mura, tense and very frightened, had pulled him out of sleep, she was gone.

Blackthorne sighed. Life is marvelous, he thought.

In the cellar, Spillbergen was querulous again, Maetsukker was nursing his head and moaning, not from pain but from fear, the boy Croocq near breaking, and Jan Roper said, "What's there to smile about, Pilot?"

"Go to hell."

"With respect, Pilot," van Nekk said carefully, bringing into the open what was foremost in their minds, "you were most unwise to attack the priest in front of the rotten yellow bastard."

There was general though carefully expressed agreement.

"If you hadn't, I don't think we'd be in this filthy mess."

Van Nekk did not go near Blackthorne. "All you've got to do is put your head in the dust when the Lord Bastard's around and they're as meek as lambs."

He waited for a reply but Blackthorne made none, just turned back to the trapdoor. It was as though nothing had been said. Their unease increased.

Paulus Spillbergen lifted himself on one elbow with difficulty. "What are you talking about, Baccus?"

Van Nekk went over to him and explained about the priest and the cross and what had happened and why they were here, his eyes hurting today worse than ever.

"Yes, that was dangerous, Pilot-Major," Spillbergen said. "Yes, I'd say quite wrong—pass me some water. Now the Jesuits'll give us no peace at all."

"You should have broken his neck, Pilot. Jesuits'll give us no peace anyway," Jan Roper said. "They're filthy lice and we're here in this stink hole as God's punishment."

"That's nonsense, Roper," Spillbergen said. "We're here becau—"

"It is God's punishment! We should have burned all the churches in Santa Magdellana—not just two. We should have. Cesspits of Satan!"

Spillbergen slapped weakly at a fly. "The Spanish troops were regrouping and we were outnumbered fifteen to one. Give me some water! We'd sacked the town and got the plunder and rubbed their noses in the dust. If we'd stayed we would have been killed. For God's sake, give me some water, someone. We'd've all been killed if we hadn't retrea—"

"What does it matter if you're doing the work of God? We failed Him."

"Perhaps we're here to do God's work," van Nekk said, placatingly, for Roper was a good though zealous man, a clever merchant and his partner's son. "Perhaps we can show the natives here the error of their Papist ways. Perhaps we could convert them to the True Faith."

"Quite right," Spillbergen said. He still felt weak, but his strength was returning. "I think you should have consulted Baccus, Pilot-Major. After all, he's chief merchant. He's very good at parleying with savages. Pass the water, I said!"

"There isn't any, Paulus." Van Nekk's gloom increased. "They've given us no food or water. We haven't even got a pot to piss in."

"Well, ask for one! And some water! God in heaven, I'm thirsty. Ask for water! You!"

"Me?" Vinck asked.

"Yes. You!"

Vinck looked at Blackthorne but Blackthorne just watched the trapdoor obliviously, so Vinck stood under the opening and shouted, "Hey! You up there! Give us God-cursed water! We want food and water!"

There was no answer. He shouted again. No answer. The others gradually took up the shouts. All except Blackthorne. Soon their panic and the nausea of their close confinement crept into their voices and they were howling like wolves.

The trapdoor opened. Omi looked down at them. Beside him was Mura. And the priest.

"Water! And food, by God! Let us out of here!" Soon they were all screaming again.

Omi motioned to Mura, who nodded and left. A moment later Mura returned with another fisherman, carrying a large barrel between them. They emptied the contents, rotting fish offal and seawater, onto the heads of the prisoners.

The men in the cellar scattered and tried to escape, but all of them could not. Spillbergen was choking, almost drowned. Some of the men slipped and were trampled on. Blackthorne had not moved from the corner. He just stared up at Omi, hating him.

Then Omi began talking. There was a cowed silence now, broken only by coughing and Spillbergen's retching. When Omi had finished, the priest nervously came to the opening.

"These are Kasigi Omi's orders: You will begin to act like decent human beings. You will make no more noise. If you do, next time five barrels will be poured into the cellar. Then ten, then twenty. You will be given food and water twice a day. When you have learned to behave, you will be allowed up into the world of men. Lord Yabu has graciously spared all your lives, providing you serve him loyally. All except one. One of you is to die. At dusk. You are to choose who it will be. But you"—he pointed at Blackthorne—"you are not to be the one chosen." Ill at ease, the priest took a deep breath, half bowed to the samurai, and stepped back.

Omi peered down into the pit. He could see Blackthorne's eyes and he felt the hatred. It will take much to break that man's spirit, he thought. No matter. There's time enough.

The trapdoor slammed into place.

CHAPTER 3

YABU lay in the hot bath, more content, more confident than he had ever
been in his life. The ship had revealed its wealth and this wealth gave
him a power that he had never dreamed possible.

"I want everything taken ashore tomorrow," he had said. "Repack the muskets
in their crates. Camouflage everything with nets or sacking."

Five hundred muskets, he thought exultantly. With more gunpowder and shot
than Toranaga has in all the Eight Provinces. And twenty cannon, five thousand
cannon balls with an abundance of ammunition. Fire arrows by the crate. All
of the best European quality. "Mura, you will provide porters. Igurashi-san, I
want all this armament, including the cannon, in my castle at Mishima forthwith,
in secret. You will be responsible."

"Yes, Lord." They had been in the main hold of the ship and everyone had
gaped at him: Igurashi, a tall, lithe, one-eyed man, his chief retainer, Zukimoto
his quartermaster, together with ten sweat-stained villagers who had opened the
crates under Mura's supervision, and his personal bodyguard of four samurai.
He knew they did not understand his exhilaration or the need to be clandestine.
Good, he thought.

When the Portuguese had first discovered Japan in 1542, they had introduced
muskets and gunpowder. Within eighteen months the Japanese were manufactur-
ing them. The quality was not nearly as good as the European equivalent but
that did not matter because guns were considered merely a novelty and, for a
long time, used only for hunting—and even for that bows were far more accurate.
Also, more important, Japanese warfare was almost ritual; hand-to-hand individual combat, the sword being the most honorable weapon. The use of guns
was considered cowardly and dishonorable and completely against the samurai
code, *bushido,* the Way of the Warrior, which bound samurai to fight with honor,
to live with honor, and to die with honor; to have undying, unquestioning loyalty
to one's feudal lord; to be fearless of death—even to seek it in his service; and
to be proud of one's own name and keep it unsullied.

For years Yabu had had a secret theory. At long last, he thought exultantly,
you can expand it and put it into effect: Five hundred chosen samurai, armed
with muskets *but trained as a unit,* spearheading your twelve thousand conven-
tional troops, supported by twenty cannon used in a special way by special men,
also trained *as a unit.* A new strategy for a new era! In the coming war, guns
could be decisive!

What about *bushido?* the ghosts of his ancestors had always asked him.

What about *bushido?* he had always asked them back.

They had never answered.

Never in his wildest dreams had he thought he'd ever be able to afford five
hundred guns. But now he had them for nothing and he alone knew how to use
them. But whose side to use them for? Toranaga's or Ishido's? Or should he
wait—and perhaps be the eventual victor?

"Igurashi-san. You'll travel by night and maintain strict security."

"Yes, Lord."

"This is to remain secret, Mura, or the village will be obliterated."

"Nothing will be said, Lord. I can speak for my village. I cannot speak for the journey, or for other villages. Who knows where there are spies? But nothing will be said by us."

Next Yabu had gone to the strong room. It contained what he presumed to be pirate plunder: silver and gold plate, cups, candelabra and ornaments, some religious paintings in ornate frames. A chest contained women's clothes, elaborately embroidered with gold thread and colored stones.

"I'll have the silver and gold melted into ingots and put in the treasury," Zukimoto had said. He was a neat, pedantic man in his forties who was not a samurai. Years ago he had been a Buddhist warrior-priest, but the Taikō, the Lord Protector, had stamped out his monastery in a campaign to purge the land of certain Buddhist militant warrior monasteries and sects that would not acknowledge his absolute suzerainty. Zukimoto had bribed his way out of that early death and become a peddler, at length a minor merchant in rice. Ten years ago he had joined Yabu's commissariat and now he was indispensable. "As to the clothes, perhaps the gold thread and gems have value. With your permission, I'll have them packed and sent to Nagasaki with anything else I can salvage." The port of Nagasaki, on the southernmost coast of the south island of Kyushu, was the legal entrepôt and trading market of the Portuguese. "The barbarians might pay well for these odds and ends."

"Good. What about the bales in the other hold?"

"They all contain a heavy cloth. Quite useless to us, Sire, with no market value at all. But this should please you." Zukimoto had opened the strongbox.

The box contained twenty thousand minted silver pieces. Spanish doubloons. The best quality.

Yabu stirred in his bath. He wiped the sweat from his face and neck with the small white towel and sank deeper into the hot scented water. If, three days ago, he told himself, a soothsayer had forecast that all this would happen, you would have fed him his tongue for telling impossible lies.

Three days ago he had been in Yedo, Toranaga's capital. Omi's message had arrived at dusk. Obviously the ship had to be investigated at once but Toranaga was still away in Osaka for the final confrontation with General Lord Ishido and, in his absence, had invited Yabu and all friendly neighboring *daimyos* to wait until his return. Such an invitation could not be refused without dire results. Yabu knew that he and the other independent *daimyos* and their families were merely added protection for Toranaga's safety and, though of course the word would never be used, they were hostages against Toranaga's safe return from the impregnable enemy fortress at Osaka where the meeting was being held. Toranaga was President of the Council of Regents which the Taikō had appointed on his deathbed to rule the empire during the minority of his son Yaemon, now seven years old. There were five Regents, all eminent *daimyos*, but only Toranaga and Ishido had real power.

Yabu had carefully considered all the reasons for going to Anjiro, the risks involved, and the reasons for staying. Then he had sent for his wife and his favorite consort. A consort was a formal, legal mistress. A man could have as many consorts as he wished, but only one wife at one time.

"My nephew Omi has just sent secret word that a barbarian ship came ashore at Anjiro."

"One of the Black Ships?" his wife had asked excitedly. These were the huge, incredibly rich trading ships that plied annually with the monsoon winds between Nagasaki and the Portuguese colony of Macao that lay almost a thousand miles south on the China mainland.

"No. But it might be rich. I'm leaving immediately. You're to say that I've been taken sick and cannot be disturbed for any reason. I'll be back in five days."

"That's incredibly dangerous," his wife warned. "Lord Toranaga gave specific orders for us to stay. I'm sure he'll make another compromise with Ishido and he's too powerful to offend. Sire, we could never guarantee that someone won't suspect the truth—there are spies everywhere. If Toranaga returned and found you'd gone, your absence would be misinterpreted. Your enemies would poison his mind against you."

"Yes," his consort added. "Please excuse me, but you must listen to the Lady, your wife. She's right. Lord Toranaga would never believe that you'd disobeyed just to look at a barbarian ship. Please send someone else."

"But this isn't an ordinary barbarian ship. It's *not* Portuguese. Listen to me. Omi says it's from a different country. These men talk a different-sounding language among themselves and they have *blue eyes* and *golden hair.*"

"Omi-san's gone mad. Or he's drunk too much saké," his wife said.

"This is much too important to joke about, for him and for you."

His wife had bowed and apologized and said that he was quite right to correct her, but that the remark was not meant in jest. She was a small, thin woman, ten years older than he, who had given him a child a year for eight years until her womb had dried up, and of these, five had been sons. Three had become warriors and died bravely in the war against China. Another had become a Buddhist priest and the last, now nineteen, he despised.

His wife, the Lady Yuriko, was the only woman he had ever been afraid of, the only woman he had ever valued—except his mother, now dead—and she ruled his house with a silken lash.

"Again, please excuse me," she said. "Does Omi-san detail the cargo?"

"No. He didn't examine it, Yuriko-san. He says he sealed the ship at once because it was so unusual. There's never been a non-Portuguese ship before, *neh?* He says also it's a fighting ship. With twenty cannon on its decks."

"Ah! Then someone must go immediately."

"I'm going myself."

"Please reconsider. Send Mizuno. Your brother's clever and wise. I implore you not to go."

"Mizuno's weak and not to be trusted."

"Then order him to commit seppuku and have done with him," she said harshly. Seppuku, sometimes called hara-kiri, the ritual suicide by disembowelment, was the only way a samurai could expiate a shame, a sin, or a fault with honor, and was the sole prerogative of the samurai caste. All samurai—women as well as men—were prepared from infancy, either for the act itself or to take part in the ceremony as a second. Women committed seppuku only with a knife in the throat.

"Later, not now," Yabu told his wife.

"Then send Zukimoto. He's certainly to be trusted."

"If Toranaga hadn't ordered all wives and consorts to stay here too, I'd send you. But that would be too risky. I have to go. I have no option. Yuriko-san, you tell me my treasury's empty. You say I've no more credit with the filthy moneylenders. Zukimoto says we're getting the maximum tax out of my peasants. I have to have more horses, armaments, weapons, and more samurai. Perhaps the ship will supply the means."

"Lord Toranaga's orders were quite clear, Sire. If he comes back and finds—"

"Yes. *If* he comes back, Lady. I still think he's put himself into a trap. The Lord Ishido has eighty thousand samurai in and around Osaka Castle alone. For Toranaga to go there with a few hundred men was the act of a madman."

"He's much too shrewd to risk himself unnecessarily," she said confidently.

"If I were Ishido and I had him in my grasp I would kill him at once."

"Yes," Yuriko said. "But the mother of the Heir is still hostage in Yedo until Toranaga returns. General Lord Ishido dare not touch Toranaga until she's safely back at Osaka."

"I'd kill him. If the Lady Ochiba lives or dies, it doesn't matter. The Heir's safe in Osaka. With Toranaga dead, the succession is certain. Toranaga's the only real threat to the Heir, the only one with a chance at using the Council of Regents, usurping the Taikō's power, and killing the boy."

"Please excuse me, Sire, but perhaps General Lord Ishido can carry the other three Regents with him and impeach Toranaga, and that's the end of Toranaga, *neh?*" his consort said.

"Yes, Lady, if Ishido could he would, but I don't think he can—yet—nor can Toranaga. The Taikō picked the five Regents too cleverly. They despise each other so much it's almost impossible for them to agree on anything." Before taking power, the five great *daimyos* had publicly sworn eternal allegiance to the dying Taikō and to his son and his line forever. And they had taken public, sacred oaths agreeing to unanimous rule in the Council, and vowed to pass over the realm intact to Yaemon when he came of age on his fifteenth birthday. "Unanimous rule means nothing really can be changed until Yaemon inherits."

"But some day, Sire, four Regents will join against one—through jealousy, fear or ambition—*neh?* The four will bend the Taikō's orders just enough for war, *neh?*"

"Yes. But it will be a small war, Lady, and the *one* will always be smashed and his lands divided up by the victors, who will than have to appoint a fifth Regent and, in time, it will be four against one and again the one will be smashed and his lands forfeit—all as the Taikō planned. My only problem is to decide who will be the one this time—Ishido or Toranaga."

"Toranaga will be the one isolated."

"Why?"

"The others fear him too much because they all *know* he secretly wants to be Shōgun, however much he protests he doesn't."

Shōgun was the ultimate rank a mortal could achieve in Japan. Shōgun meant Supreme Military Dictator. Only one *daimyo* at a time could possess the title. And only His Imperial Highness, the reigning Emperor, the Divine Son of Heaven, who lived in seclusion with the Imperial Families at Kyoto, could grant the title.

With the appointment of Shōgun went absolute power: the Emperor's seal and mandate. The Shōgun ruled in the Emperor's name. All power was derived from the Emperor because he was directly descended from the gods. Therefore any *daimyo* who opposed the Shōgun was automatically in rebellion against the throne, and at once outcast and all his lands forfeit.

The reigning Emperor was worshiped as a divinity because he was descended in an unbroken line from the Sun Goddess, Amaterasu Omikami, one of the children of the gods Izanagi and Izanami, who had formed the islands of Japan from the firmament. By divine right the ruling Emperor owned all the land and ruled and was obeyed without question. But in practice, for more than six centuries real power had rested behind the throne.

Six centuries ago there had been a schism when two of the three great rival, semiregal samurai families, the Minowara, Fujimoto and Takashima, backed rival claimants to the throne and plunged the realm into civil war. After sixty years the Minowara prevailed over the Takashima, and the Fujimoto, the family that had stayed neutral, bided its time.

From then on, jealously guarding their rule, the Minowara Shōguns dominated the realm, decreed their Shōgunate hereditary and began to intermarry some of their daughters with the Imperial line. The Emperor and the entire Imperial Court were kept completely isolated in walled palaces and gardens in the small enclave at Kyoto, most times in penury, and their activities perpetually confined to observing the rituals of Shinto, the ancient animistic religion of Japan, and to intellectual pursuits such as calligraphy, painting, philosophy, and poetry.

The Court of the Son of Heaven was easy to dominate because, though it possessed all the land, it had no revenue. Only *daimyos,* samurai, possessed revenue and the right to tax. And so it was that although all members of the Imperial Court were above all samurai in rank, they still existed on a stipend granted the Court at the whim of the Shōgun, the Kwampaku—the civil Chief Adviser—or the ruling military junta of the day. Few were generous. Some Emperors had even had to barter their signatures for food. Many times there was not enough money for a coronation.

At length the Minowara Shōguns lost their power to others, to Takashima or Fujimoto descendants. And as the civil wars continued unabated over the centuries, the Emperor became more and more the creature of the *daimyo* who was strong enough to obtain physical possession of Kyoto. The moment the new conqueror of Kyoto had slaughtered the ruling Shōgun and his line, he would—providing he was Minowara, Takashima, or Fujimoto—with humility, swear allegiance to the throne and humbly invite the powerless Emperor to grant him the now vacant rank of Shōgun. Then, like his predecessors, he would try to extend his rule outward from Kyoto until he in his turn was swallowed by another. Emperors married, abdicated, or ascended the throne at the whim of the Shōgunate. But always the reigning Emperor's bloodline was inviolate and unbroken.

So the Shōgun was all powerful. Until he was overthrown.

Many were unseated over the centuries as the realm splintered into ever smaller factions. For the last hundred years no single *daimyo* had ever had enough power to become Shōgun. Twelve years ago the peasant General Nakamura had had the power and he had obtained the mandate from the present Emperor, Go-Nijo. But Nakamura could not be granted Shōgun rank however much he desired it, because he was born a peasant. He had to be content with the much lesser civilian title of Kwampaku, Chief Adviser, and later, when he resigned that title to his infant son, Yaemon—though keeping all power, as was quite customary—he had to be content with Taikō. By historic custom only the descendants of the sprawling, ancient, semidivine families of the Minowara, Takashima, and Fujimoto were entitled to the rank of Shōgun.

Toranaga was descended from the Minowara. Yabu could trace his lineage to a vague and minor branch of the Takashima, enough of a connection if ever he could become supreme.

"Eeeee, Lady," Yabu said, "of course Toranaga wants to be Shōgun, but he'll never achieve it. The other Regents despise and fear him. They neutralize him, as the Taikō planned." He leaned forward and studied his wife intently. "You say Toranaga's going to lose to Ishido?"

"He will be isolated, yes. But in the end I don't think he'll lose, Sire. I beg you not to disobey Lord Toranaga, and not to leave Yedo just to examine the barbarian ship, no matter how unusual Omi-san says it is. Please send Zukimoto to Anjiro."

"What if the ship contains bullion? Silver or gold? Would you trust Zukimoto or any of our officers with it?"

"No," his wife had said.

So that night he had slipped out of Yedo secretly, with only fifty men, and now he had wealth and power beyond his dreams and unique captives, one of whom was going to die tonight. He had arranged for a courtesan and a boy to be ready later. At dawn tomorrow he would return to Yedo. By sunset tomorrow the guns and the bullion would begin their secret journey.

Eeeee, the guns! he thought exultantly. The guns and the plan together will give me the power to make Ishido win, or Toranaga—whomever I chose. Then I'll become a Regent in the loser's place, *neh?* Then the most powerful Regent. Why not even Shōgun? Yes. It's all possible *now.*

He let himself drift pleasantly. How to use the twenty thousand pieces of silver? I can rebuild the castle keep. And buy special horses for the cannon. And expand our espionage web. What about Ikawa Jikkyu? Would a thousand pieces be enough to bribe Ikawa Jikkyu's cooks to poison him? More than enough! Five hundred, even one hundred in the right hands would be plenty. Whose?

The afternoon sun was slanting through the small window set into the stone walls. The bath water was very hot and heated by a wood fire built into the outside wall. This was Omi's house and it stood on a small hill overlooking the village and the harbor. The garden within its walls was neat and serene and worthy.

The bathroom door opened. The blind man bowed. "Kasigi Omi-san sent me, Sire. I am Suwo, his masseur." He was tall and very thin and old, his face wrinkled.

"Good." Yabu had always had a terror of being blinded. As long as he could remember he had had dreams of waking in blackness, knowing it was sunlight, feeling the warmth but not seeing, opening his mouth to scream, knowing that it was dishonorable to scream, but screaming even so. Then the real awakening and the sweat streaming.

But this horror of blindness seemed to increase his pleasure at being massaged by the sightless.

He could see the jagged scar on the man's right temple and the deep cleft in the skull below it. That's a sword cut, he told himself. Did that cause his blindness? Was he a samurai once? For whom? Is he a spy?

Yabu knew that the man would have been searched very carefully by his guards before being allowed to enter, so he had no fear of a concealed weapon. His own prized long sword was within reach, an ancient blade made by the master swordsmith Murasama. He watched the old man take off his cotton kimono and hang it up without seeking the peg. There were more sword scars on his chest. His loincloth was very clean. He knelt, waiting patiently.

Yabu got out of the bath when he was ready and lay on the stone bench. The old man dried Yabu carefully, put fragrant oil on his hands, and began to knead the muscles in the *daimyo's* neck and back.

Tension began to vanish as the very strong fingers moved over Yabu, probing deeply with surprising skill. "That's good. Very good," he said after a while.

"Thank you, Yabu-sama," Suwo said. *Sama,* meaning "Lord," was an obligatory politeness when addressing a superior.

"Have you served Omi-san long?"

"Three years, Sire. He is very kind to an old man."

"And before that?"

"I wandered from village to village. A few days here, half a year there, like a butterfly on the summer's breath." Suwo's voice was as soothing as his hands. He had decided that the *daimyo* wanted him to talk and he waited patiently for the next question and then he would begin. Part of his art was to know what was required and when. Sometimes his ears told him this, but mostly it was his fingers that seemed to unlock the secret of the man or woman's mind. His fingers were telling him to beware of this man, that he was dangerous and volatile, his age about forty, a good horseman and excellent sword fighter. Also that his liver was bad and that he would die within two years. Saké, and probably aphrodisiacs, would kill him. "You are strong for your age, Yabu-sama."

"So are you. How old are you, Suwo?"

The old man laughed but his fingers never ceased. "I'm the oldest man in the world—my world. Everyone I've ever known is dead long since. It must be more than eighty years—I'm not sure. I served Lord Yoshi Chikitada, Lord Toranaga's grandfather, when the clan's fief was no bigger than this village. I was even at the camp the day he was assassinated."

Yabu deliberately kept his body relaxed with an effort of will but his mind sharpened and he began to listen intently.

"That was a grim day, Yabu-sama. I don't know how old I was—but my voice hadn't broken yet. The assassin was Obata Hiro, a son of his most powerful ally. Perhaps you know the story, how the youth struck Lord Chikitada's head off with a single blow of his sword. It was a Murasama blade and that's what started the superstition that all Murasama blades are filled with unluck for the Yoshi clan."

Is he telling me that because of my own Murasama sword? Yabu asked himself. Many people know I possess one. Or is he just an old man who remembers a special day in a long life? "What was Toranaga's grandfather like?" he asked, feigning lack of interest, testing Suwo.

"Tall, Yabu-sama. Taller than you and much thinner when I knew him. He was twenty-five the day he died." Suwo's voice warmed. "Eeee, Yabu-sama, he was a warrior at twelve and our liege lord at fifteen when his own father was killed in a skirmish. At that time, Lord Chikitada was married and had already sired a son. It was a pity that he had to die. Obata Hiro was his friend as well as vassal, seventeen then, but someone had poisoned young Obata's mind, saying that Chikitada had planned to kill his father treacherously. Of course it was all lies but that didn't bring Chikitada back to lead us. Young Obata knelt in front of the body and bowed three times. He said that he had done the deed out of filial respect for his father and now wished to atone for his insult to us and our clan by committing seppuku. He was given permission. First he washed Chikitada's head with his own hands and set it in a place of reverence. Then he cut himself open and died manfully, with great ceremony, one of our men acting as his second and removing his head with a single stroke. Later his father came to collect his son's head and the Murasama sword. Things became bad for us. Lord Chikitada's only son was taken hostage somewhere and our part of the clan fell on evil times. That was—"

"You're lying, old man. You were never there." Yabu had turned around and he was staring up at the man, who had frozen instantly. "The sword was broken and destroyed after Obata's death."

"No, Yabu-sama. That is the legend. I saw the father come and collect the head and the sword. Who would want to destroy such a piece of art? That would have been sacrilege. His father collected it."

"What did he do with it?"

"No one knows. Some said he threw it into the sea because he liked and honored our Lord Chikitada as a brother. Others said that he buried it and that it lurks in wait for the grandson, Yoshi Toranaga."

"What do *you* think he did with it?"

"Threw it into the sea."

"Did you see him?"

"No."

Yabu lay back again and the fingers began their work. The thought that someone else knew that the sword had not been broken thrilled him strangely. You should kill Suwo, he told himself. Why? How could a blind man recognize the blade? It is like any Murasama blade and the handle and scabbard have been changed many times over the years. No one can know that your sword is *the* sword that has gone from hand to hand with increasing secrecy as the power of Toranaga increased. Why kill Suwo? The fact that he's alive has added a zest. You're stimulated. Leave him alive—you can kill him at any time. With the sword.

That thought pleased Yabu as he let himself drift once more, greatly at ease. One day soon, he promised himself, I will be powerful enough to wear my Murasama blade in Toranaga's presence. One day, perhaps, I will tell him the story of my sword.

"What happened next?" he asked, wishing to be lulled by the old man's voice.

"We just fell on evil times. That was the year of the great famine, and, now that my master was dead, I became *ronin.*" Ronin were landless or masterless peasant-soldiers or samurai who, through dishonor or the loss of their masters, were forced to wander the land until some other lord would accept their services. It was difficult for *ronin* to find new employment. Food was scarce, almost every man was a soldier, and strangers were rarely trusted. Most of the robber bands and corsairs who infested the land and the coast were *ronin.* "That year was very bad and the next. I fought for anyone—a battle here, a skirmish there. Food was my pay. Then I heard that there was food in plenty in Kyushu so I started to make my way west. That winter I found a sanctuary. I managed to become hired by a Buddhist monastery as a guard. I fought for them for half a year, protecting the monastery and their rice fields from bandits. The monastery was near Osaka and, at that time—long before the Taikō obliterated most of them—the bandits were as plentiful as swamp mosquitoes. One day, we were ambushed and I was left for dead. Some monks found me and healed my wound. But they could not give me back my sight."

His fingers probed deeper and ever deeper. "They put me with a blind monk who taught me how to massage and to see again with my fingers. Now my fingers tell me more than my eyes used to, I think.

"The last thing I can remember seeing with my eyes was the bandit's widespread mouth and rotting teeth, the sword a glittering arc and beyond, after the blow, the scent of flowers. I saw perfume in all its colors, Yabu-sama. That was all long ago, long before the barbarians came to our land—fifty, sixty years ago—but I saw the perfume's colors. I saw nirvana, I think, and for the merest moment, the face of Buddha. Blindness is a small price to pay for such a gift, *neh?*"

There was no answer. Suwo had expected none. Yabu was sleeping, as was planned. Did you like my story, Yabu-sama? Suwo asked silently, amused as an old man would be. It was all true but for one thing. The monastery was not near Osaka but across your western border. The name of the monk? Su, uncle of your enemy, Ikawa Jikkyu.

I could snap your neck so easily, he thought. It would be a favor to Omi-san. It would be a blessing to the village. And it would repay, in tiny measure, my patron's gift. Should I do it now? Or later?

Spillbergen held up the bundled stalks of rice straw, his face stretched. "Who wants to pick first?"

No one answered. Blackthorne seemed to be dozing, leaning against the corner from which he had not moved. It was near sunset.

"Someone's got to pick first," Spillbergen rasped. "Come on, there's not much time."

They had been given food and a barrel of water and another barrel as a latrine. But nothing with which to wash away the stinking offal or to clean themselves. And the flies had come. The air was fetid, the earth mud-mucous. Most of the men were stripped to the waist, sweating from the heat. And from fear.

Spillbergen looked from face to face. He came back to Blackthorne. "Why— why are you eliminated? Eh? Why?"

The eyes opened and they were icy. "For the last time: I—don't—know."

"It's not fair. Not fair."

Blackthorne returned to his reverie. There must be a way to break out of here. There must be a way to get the ship. That bastard will kill us all eventually, as certain as there's a north star. There's not much time, and I was eliminated because they've some particular rotten plan for me.

When the trapdoor had closed they had all looked at him, and someone had said, "What're we going to do?"

"I don't know," he had answered.

"Why aren't you to be picked?"

"I don't know."

"Lord Jesus help us," someone whimpered.

"Get the mess cleared up," he ordered. "Pile the filth over there!"

"We've no mops or—"

"Use *your hands!*"

They did as he ordered and he helped them and cleaned off the Captain-General as best he could. "You'll be all right now."

"How—how are we to choose someone?" Spillbergen asked.

"We don't. We fight them."

"With what?"

"You'll go like a sheep to the butcher? *You* will?"

"Don't be ridiculous—they don't want me—it wouldn't be right for me to be the one."

"Why?" Vinck asked.

"I'm the Captain-General."

"With respect, sir," Vinck said ironically, "maybe you should volunteer. It's your place to volunteer."

"A very good suggestion," Pieterzoon said. "I'll second the motion, by God."

There was general assent and everyone thought, Lord Jesus, anyone but me.

Spillbergen had begun to bluster and order but he saw the pitiless eyes. So he stopped and stared at the ground, filled with nausea. Then he said, "No. It—it wouldn't be right for someone to volunteer. It—we'll—we'll draw lots. Straws, one shorter than the rest. We'll put our hands—we'll put ourselves into the hands of God. Pilot, you'll hold the straws."

"I won't. I'll have nothing to do with it. I say we fight."

"They'll kill us all. You heard what the samurai said: Our lives are spared—except one." Spillbergen wiped the sweat off his face and a cloud of flies rose and then settled again. "Give me some water. It's better for one to die than all of us."

Van Nekk dunked the gourd in the barrel and gave it to Spillbergen. "We're ten. Including you, Paulus," he said. "The odds are good."

"Very good—unless you're the one." Vinck glanced at Blackthorne. "Can we fight those swords?"

"Can you go meekly to the torturer if you're the one picked?"

"I don't know."

Van Nekk said, "We'll draw lots. We'll let God decide."

"Poor God," Blackthorne said. "The stupidities He gets blamed for!"

"How else do we choose?" someone shouted.

"We don't!"

"We'll do as Paulus says. He's Captain-General," said van Nekk. "We'll draw straws. It's best for the majority. Let's vote. Are we all in favor?"

They had all said yes. Except Vinck. "I'm with the Pilot. To hell with sewer-sitting pissmaking witch-festering straws!"

Eventually Vinck had been persuaded. Jan Roper, the Calvinist, had led the prayers. Spillbergen broke the ten pieces of straw with exactitude. Then he halved one of them.

Van Nekk, Pieterzoon, Sonk, Maetsukker, Ginsel, Jan Roper, Salamon, Maximilian Croocq, and Vinck.

Again he said, "Who wants to pick first?"

"How do we know that—that the one who picks the wrong, the short straw'll go? How do we know that?" Maetsukker's voice was raw with terror.

"We don't. Not for certain. We should know for certain," Croocq, the boy, said.

"That's easy," Jan Roper said. "Let's swear we will do it in the name of God. In His name. To—to die for the others in His name. Then there's no worry. The anointed Lamb of God will go straight to Everlasting Glory."

They all agreed.

"Go on, Vinck. Do as Roper says."

"All right." Vinck's lips were parched. "If—if it's me—I swear by the Lord God that I'll go with them if—if I pick the wrong straw. In God's name."

They all followed. Maetsukker was so frightened he had to be prompted before he sank back into the quagmire of his living nightmare.

Sonk chose first. Pieterzoon was next. Then Jan Roper, and after him Salamon and Croocq. Spillbergen felt himself dying fast because they had agreed he would not choose but his would be the last straw and now the odds were becoming terrible.

Ginsel was safe. Four left.

Maetsukker was weeping openly, but he pushed Vinck aside and took a straw and could not believe that it was not the one.

Spillbergen's fist was shaking and Croocq helped him steady his arm. Feces ran unnoticed down his legs.

Which one do I take? van Nekk was asking himself desperately. Oh, God help me! He could barely see the straws through the fog of his myopia. If only I could see, perhaps I'd have a clue which to pick. Which one?

He picked and brought the straw close to his eyes to see his sentence clearly. But the straw was not short.

Vinck watched his fingers select the next to last straw and it fell to the ground but everyone saw that it was the shortest thus far. Spillbergen unclenched his knotted hand and everyone saw that the last straw was long. Spillbergen fainted.

They were all staring at Vinck. Helplessly he looked at them, not seeing them. He half shrugged and half smiled and waved absently at the flies. Then he slumped down. They made room for him, kept away from him as though he were a leper.

Blackthorne knelt in the ooze beside Spillbergen.

"Is he dead?" van Nekk asked, his voice almost inaudible.

Vinck shrieked with laughter, which unnerved them all, and ceased as violently as he had begun. "I'm the—the one that's dead," he said. "I'm dead!"

"Don't be afraid. You're the anointed of God. You're in God's hands," Jan

Roper said, his voice confident.

"Yes," van Nekk said. "Don't be afraid."

"That's easy now, isn't it?" Vinck's eyes went from face to face but none could hold his gaze. Only Blackthorne did not look away.

"Get me some water, Vinck," he said quietly. "Go over to the barrel and get some water. Go on."

Vinck stared at him. Then he got the gourd and filled it with water and gave it to him. "Lord Jesus God, Pilot," he muttered, "what am I going to do?"

"First help me with Paulus. Vinck! Do what I say! Is he going to be all right?"

Vinck pushed his agony away, helped by Blackthorne's calm. Spillbergen's pulse was weak. Vinck listened to his heart, pulled the eyelids away, and watched for a moment. "I don't know, Pilot. Lord Jesus, I can't think properly. His heart's all right, I think. He needs bleeding but—but I've no way—I—I can't concentrate. . . . Give me . . ." He stopped exhaustedly, sat back against the wall. Shudders began to rack him.

The trapdoor opened.

Omi stood etched against the sky, his kimono blooded by the dying sun.

CHAPTER 4

V INCK tried to make his legs move but he could not. He had faced death many times in his life but never like this, meekly. It had been decreed by the straws. Why me? his brain screamed. I'm no worse than the others and better than most. Dear God in Heaven, why me?

A ladder had been lowered. Omi motioned for the one man to come up, and quickly. *"Isogi!"* Hurry up!

Van Nekk and Jan Roper were praying silently, their eyes closed. Pieterzoon could not watch. Blackthorne was staring up at Omi and his men.

"Isogi!" Omi barked out again.

Once more Vinck tried to stand. "Help me, someone. Help me to get up!"

Pieterzoon, who was nearest, bent down and put his hand under Vinck's arm and helped him to his feet, then Blackthorne was at the foot of the ladder, both feet planted firmly in the slime.

"Kinjiru!" he shouted, using the word from the ship. A gasp rushed through the cellar. Omi's hand tightened on his sword and he moved to the ladder. Immediately Blackthorne twisted it, daring Omi to put a foot there.

"Kinjiru!" he said again.

Omi stopped.

"What's going on?" Spillbergen asked, frightened, as were all of them.

"I told him it's forbidden! None of my crew is walking to death without a fight."

"But—but we agreed!"

"I didn't."

"Have you gone mad!"

"It's all right, Pilot," Vinck whispered. "I—we did agree and it was fair. It's God's will. I'm going—it's . . . ." He groped to the foot of the ladder but Blackthorne stood implacably in the way, facing Omi.

"You're not going without a fight. No one is."

"Get away from the ladder, Pilot! You're ordered away!" Spillbergen shakily kept to his corner, as far from the opening as possible. His voice shrilled, "Pilot!"

But Blackthorne was not listening. "Get ready!"

Omi stepped back a pace and snarled orders to his men. At once a samurai, closely followed by two others, started down the steps, swords unsheathed. Blackthorne twisted the ladder and grappled with the lead man, swerving from his violent sword blow, trying to choke the man to death.

"Help me! Come on! For your *lives!*"

Blackthorne changed his grip to pull the man off the rungs, braced sickeningly as the second man stabbed downward. Vinck came out of his cataleptic state and threw himself at the samurai, berserk. He intercepted the blow that would have sliced Blackthorne's wrist off, held the shuddering sword arm at bay, and smashed his other fist into the man's groin. The samurai gasped and kicked viciously. Vinck hardly seemed to notice the blow. He climbed the rungs and tore at the man for possession of the sword, his nails ripping at the man's eyes. The other two samurai were hampered by the confined space and Blackthorne, but a kick from one of them caught Vinck in the face and he reeled away. The samurai on the ladder hacked at Blackthorne, missed, then the entire crew hurled themselves at the ladder.

Croocq hammered his fist onto the samurai's instep and felt a small bone give. The man managed to throw his sword out of the pit—not wishing the enemy armed—and tumbled heavily to the mud. Vinck and Pieterzoon fell on him. He fought back ferociously as others rushed for the encroaching samurai. Blackthorne picked up the cornered Japanese's dagger and started up the ladder, Croocq, Jan Roper, and Salamon following. Both samurai retreated and stood at the entrance, their killing swords viciously ready. Blackthorne knew his dagger was useless against the swords. Even so he charged, the others in close support. The moment his head was above ground one of the swords swung at him, missing him by a fraction of an inch. A violent kick from an unseen samurai drove him underground again.

He turned and jumped back, avoiding the writhing mass of fighting men who tried to subdue the samurai in the stinking ooze. Vinck kicked the man in the back of the neck and he went limp. Vinck pounded him again and again until Blackthorne pulled him off.

"Don't kill him—we can use him as a hostage!" he shouted and wrenched desperately at the ladder, trying to pull it down into the cellar. But it was too long. Above, Omi's other samurai waited impassively at the trapdoor's entrance.

"For God's sake, Pilot, stop it!" Spillbergen wheezed. "They'll kill us all—you'll kill us all! Stop him, someone!"

Omi was shouting more orders and strong hands aloft prevented Blackthorne from jamming the entrance with the ladder.

"Look out!" he shouted.

Three more samurai, carrying knives and wearing only loincloths, leapt nimbly into the cellar. The first two crashed deliberately onto Blackthorne, carrying him helpless to the floor, oblivious of their own danger, then attacked ferociously.

Blackthorne was crushed beneath the strength of the men. He could not use the knife and felt his will to fight subsiding and he wished he had Mura the headman's skill at unarmed combat. He knew, helplessly, that he could not survive much longer but he made a final effort and jerked one arm free. A cruel blow from a rock-hard hand rattled his head and another exploded colors in his brain but still he fought back.

Vinck was gouging at one of the samurai when the third dropped on him from the sky door, and Maetsukker screamed as a dagger slashed his arm. Van Nekk was blindly striking out and Pieterzoon was saying, "For Christ's sake, hit them not me," but the merchant did not hear for he was consumed with terror.

Blackthorne caught one of the samurai by the throat, his grip slipping from the sweat and slime, and he was almost on his feet like a mad bull, trying to shake them off when there was a last blow and he fell into blankness. The three samurai hacked their way up and the crew, now leaderless, retreated from the circling slash of their three daggers, the samurai dominating the cellar now with their whirling daggers, not trying to kill or to maim, but only to force the panting, frightened men to the walls, away from the ladder where Blackthorne and the first samurai lay inert.

Omi came down arrogantly into the pit and grabbed the nearest man, who was Pieterzoon. He jerked him toward the ladder.

Pieterzoon screamed and tried to struggle out of Omi's grasp, but a knife sliced his wrist and another opened his arm. Relentlessly the shrieking seaman was backed against the ladder.

"Christ help me, it's not me that's to go, it's not me it's not me—" Pieterzoon had both feet on the rung and he was retreating up and away from the agony of the knives and then, "Help me, for God's sake," he screamed a last time, turned and fled raving into the air.

Omi followed without hurrying.

A samurai retreated. Then another. The third picked up the knife that Blackthorne had used. He turned his back contemptuously, stepped over the prostrate body of his unconscious comrade, and climbed away.

The ladder was jerked aloft. Air and sky and light vanished. Bolts crashed into place. Now there was only gloom, and in it heaving chests and rending heartbeats and running sweat and the stench. The flies returned.

For a moment no one moved. Jan Roper had a small cut on his cheek, Maetsukker was bleeding badly, the others were mostly in shock. Except Salamon. He groped his way over to Blackthorne, pulled him off the unconscious samurai. He mouthed gutturally and pointed at the water. Croocq fetched some in a gourd, helped him to prop Blackthorne, still lifeless, against the wall. Together they began to clean the muck off his face.

"When those bastards—when they dropped on him I thought I heard his neck or shoulder go," the boy said, his chest heaving. "He looks like a corpse, Lord Jesus!"

Sonk forced himself to his feet and picked his way over to them. Carefully he moved Blackthorne's head from side to side, felt his shoulders. "Seems all right. Have to wait till he comes round to tell."

"Oh, Jesus God," Vinck began whimpering. "Poor Pieterzoon—I'm damned —I'm damned . . ."

"You were going. The Pilot stopped you. You were going like you promised, I saw you, by God." Sonk shook Vinck but he paid no attention. "I saw you, Vinck." He turned to Spillbergen, waving the flies away. "Wasn't that right?"

"Yes, he was going. Vinck, stop moaning! It was the Pilot's fault. Give me some water."

Jan Roper dipped some water with the gourd and drank and daubed the cut on his cheek. "Vinck should have gone. He was the lamb of God. He was ordained. And now his soul's forfeit. Oh, Lord God have mercy on him, he'll burn for all eternity."

"Give me some water," the Captain-General whimpered.

Van Nekk took the gourd from Jan Roper and passed it to Spillbergen. "It wasn't Vinck's fault," van Nekk said tiredly. "He couldn't get up, don't you remember? He asked someone to help him up. I was so frightened I couldn't move either, and I didn't have to go."

"It wasn't Vinck's fault," Spillbergen said. "No. It was him." They all looked at Blackthorne. "He's mad."

"All the English are mad," Sonk said. "Have you ever known one that wasn't? Scratch one of 'em and you find a maniac—and a pirate."

"Bastards, all of them!" Ginsel said.

"No, not all of them," van Nekk said. "The pilot was only doing what he felt was right. He's protected us and brought us ten thousand leagues."

"Protected us, piss! We were five hundred when we started and five ships. Now there's nine of us!"

"Wasn't his fault the fleet split up. Wasn't his fault that the storms blew us all—"

"Weren't for him we'd have stayed in the New World, by God. It was him who said we could get to the Japans. And for Jesus Christ's sweet sake, look where we are now."

"We agreed to try for the Japans. We all agreed," van Nekk said wearily. "We all voted."

"Yes. But it was him that persuaded us."

"Look out!" Ginsel pointed at the samurai, who was stirring and moaning. Sonk quickly slid over to him, crashed his fist into his jaw. The man went out again.

"Christ's death! What'd the bastards leave him here for? They could've carried him out with them, easy. Nothing we could've done."

"You think they thought he was dead?"

"Don't know! They must've seen him. By the Lord Jesus, I could use a cold beer," Sonk said.

"Don't hit him again, Sonk, don't kill him. He's a hostage." Croocq looked at Vinck, who sat huddled against a wall, locked into his whimpering self-hatred. "God help us all. What'll they do to Pieterzoon? What'll they do to us?"

"It's the pilot's fault," Jan Roper said. "Only him."

Van Nekk peered compassionately at Blackthorne. "It doesn't matter now. Does it? Whose fault it is or was."

Maetsukker reeled to his feet, the blood still flowing down his forearm. "I'm hurt, help me someone."

Salamon made a tourniquet from a piece of shirt and staunched the blood. The slice in Maetsukker's biceps was deep but no vein or artery had been cut. The flies began to worry the wound.

"God-cursed flies! And God curse the Pilot to hell," Maetsukker said. "It was agreed. But, oh no! He had to save Vinck! Now Pieterzoon's blood's on his hands and we'll all suffer because of him."

"Shut your face! He said none of his crew—"

There were footsteps above. The trapdoor opened. Villagers began pouring barrels of fish offal and seawater into the cellar. When the floor was six inches awash, they stopped.

The screams began when the moon was high.

Yabu was kneeling in the inner garden of Omi's house. Motionless. He watched the moonlight in the blossom tree, the branches jet against the lighter sky, the clustered blooms now barely tinted. A petal spiraled and he thought,

> *Beauty*
> *Is not less*
> *For falling*
> *In the breeze.*

Another petal settled. The wind sighed and took another. The tree was scarcely as tall as a man, kneaded between moss rocks that seemed to have grown from the earth, so cleverly had they been placed.

It took all of Yabu's will to concentrate on the tree and blossoms and sky and night, to feel the gentle touch of the wind, to smell its sea-sweetness, to think of poems, and yet to keep his ears reaching for the agony. His spine felt limp. Only his will made him graven as the rocks. This awareness gave him a level of sensuality beyond articulation. And tonight it was stronger and more violent than it had ever been.

"Omi-san, how long will our Master stay there?" Omi's mother asked in a frightened whisper from inside the house.

"I don't know."

"The screams are terrible. When will they stop?"

"I don't know," Omi said.

They were sitting behind a screen in the second best room. The best room, his mother's, had been given to Yabu, and both these rooms faced onto the garden that he had constructed with so much effort. They could see Yabu through the lattice, the tree casting stark patterns on his face, moonlight sparking on the handles of his swords. He wore a dark haori, or outer jacket, over his somber kimono.

"I want to go to sleep," the woman said, trembling. "But I can't sleep with all this noise. When will it stop?"

"I don't know. Be patient, Mother," Omi said softly. "The noise will stop soon. Tomorrow Lord Yabu will go back to Yedo. Please be patient." But Omi knew that the torture would continue to the dawn. It had been planned that way.

He tried to concentrate. Because his feudal lord meditated within the screams, he tried again to follow his example. But the next shriek brought him back and he thought, I can't. I can't, not yet. I don't have his control or power.

Or is it power? he asked himself.

He could see Yabu's face clearly. He tried to read the strange expression on his *daimyo's* face: the slight twisting of the slack full lips, a fleck of saliva at the corners, eyes set into dark slits that moved only with the petals. It's almost as though he's just climaxed—was almost climaxing—without touching himself. Is that possible?

This was the first time that Omi had been in close contact with his uncle, for he was a very minor link in the clan chain, and his fief of Anjiro and the surrounding area poor and unimportant. Omi was the youngest of three sons and his father, Mizuno, had six brothers. Yabu was the eldest brother and leader of the Kasigi clan, his father second eldest. Omi was twenty-one and had an infant son of his own.

"Where's your miserable wife," the old woman whimpered querulously. "I want her to rub my back and shoulders."

"She had to go to visit her father, don't you remember? He's very sick, Mother. Let me do it for you."

"No. You can send for a maid in a moment. Your wife's most inconsiderate. She could have waited a few days. I come all the way from Yedo to visit you. It took two weeks of terrible journeying and what happens? I've only been here a week and she leaves. She should have waited! Good for nothing, that's her. Your father made a very bad mistake arranging your marriage to her. You should tell her to stay away permanently—divorce the good-for-nothing once and for all. She can't even massage my back properly. At the very least you should give her a good beating. Those dreadful screams! Why won't they stop?"

"They will. Very soon."

"You should give her a good beating."

"Yes." Omi thought about his wife Midori and his heart leapt. She was so beautiful and fine and gentle and clever, her voice so clear, and her music as good as that of any courtesan in Izu.

"Midori-san, you must go at once," he had said to her privately.

"Omi-san, my father is not so sick and my place is here, serving your mother, *neh?*" she had responded. "If our lord *daimyo* arrives, this house has to be prepared. Oh, Omi-san, this is so important, the most important time of your whole service, *neh?* If the Lord Yabu is impressed, perhaps he'll give you a better fief, you deserve so much better! If anything happened while I was away, I'd never forgive myself and this is the first time you've had an opportunity to excel and it must succeed. He *must* come. Please, there's so much to do."

"Yes, but I would like you to go at once, Midori-san. Stay just two days, then hurry home again."

She had pleaded but he had insisted and she had gone. He had wanted her away from Anjiro before Yabu arrived and while the man was a guest in his house. Not that the *daimyo* would dare to touch her without permission—that was unthinkable because he, Omi, would then have the right, the honor, and the duty by law, to obliterate the *daimyo*. But he had noticed Yabu watching her just after they had been married in Yedo and he had wanted to remove a possible source of irritation, anything that could upset or embarrass his lord while he was here. It was so important that he impress Yabu-sama with his filial loyalty, his foresight, and with his counsel. And so far everything had succeeded beyond possibility. The ship had been a treasure trove, the crew another. Everything was perfect.

"I've asked our house *kami* to watch over you," Midori had said just before she left, referring to the particular Shinto spirit that had their house in his care, "and I've sent an offering to the Buddhist temple for prayers. I've told Suwo to be his most perfect, and sent a message to Kiku-san. Oh, Omi-san, please let me stay."

He had smiled and sent her on her way, the tears spoiling her makeup.

Omi was sad to be without her, but glad that she had gone. The screams would have pained her very much.

His mother winced under the torment on the wind, moved slightly to ease the ache in her shoulders, her joints bad tonight. It's the west sea breeze, she thought. Still, it's better here than in Yedo. Too marshy there and too many mosquitoes.

She could just see the soft outline of Yabu in the garden. Secretly she hated him and wanted him dead. Once Yabu was dead, Mizuno, her husband, would be *daimyo* of Izu and would lead the clan. That would be very nice, she thought. Then all the rest of the brothers and their wives and children would be subservient to her and, of course, Mizuno-san would make Omi heir when Yabu was dead and gone.

Another pain in her neck made her move slightly.

"I'll call Kiku-san," Omi said, referring to the courtesan who waited patiently for Yabu in the next room, with the boy. "She's very, very deft."

"I'm all right, just tired, *neh*? Oh, very well. She can massage me."

Omi went into the next room. The bed was ready. It consisted of over- and under-coverlets called futons that were placed on the floor matting. Kiku bowed and tried to smile and murmured she would be honored to try to use her modest skill on the most honorable mother of the household. She was even paler than usual and Omi could see the screams were taking their toll on her too. The boy was trying not to show his fear.

When the screams had begun Omi had had to use all his skill to persuade her to stay. "Oh, Omi-san, I cannot bear it—it's terrible. So sorry, please let me go—I want to close my ears but the sound comes through my hands. Poor man—it's terrible," she had said.

"Please, Kiku-san, please be patient. Yabu-sama has ordered this, *neh*? There is nothing to be done. It will stop soon."

"It's too much, Omi-san. I can't bear it."

By inviolate custom, money of itself could not buy a girl if she, or her employer, wished to refuse the client, whoever he was. Kiku was a courtesan of the First Class, the most famous in Izu, and though Omi was convinced she would not compare even to a courtesan of the Second Class of Yedo, Osaka, or Kyoto, here she was at the pinnacle and correctly prideful and exclusive. And even though he had agreed with her employer, the Mama-san Gyoko, to pay five times the usual price, he was still not sure that Kiku would stay.

Now he was watching her nimble fingers on his mother's neck. She was beautiful, tiny, her skin almost translucent and so soft. Usually she would bubble with zest for life. But how could such a plaything be happy under the weight of the screams, he asked himself. He enjoyed watching her, enjoyed the knowledge of her body and her warmth—

Abruptly the screams stopped.

Omi listened, his mouth half-open, straining to catch the slightest noise, waiting. He noticed Kiku's fingers had stopped, his mother uncomplaining, listening as intently. He looked through the lattice at Yabu. The *daimyo* remained statuelike.

"Omi-san!" Yabu called at last.

Omi got up and went onto the polished veranda and bowed. "Yes, Lord."

"Go and see what has happened."

Omi bowed again and went through the garden, out onto the tidily pebbled roadway that led down the hill to the village and onto the shore. Far below he could see the fire near one of the wharfs and the men beside it. And, in the square that fronted the sea, the trapdoor to the pit and the four guards.

As he walked toward the village he saw that the barbarian ship was safe at anchor, oil lamps on the decks and on the nestling boats. Villagers—men and women and children—were still unloading the cargo, and fishing boats and dinghies were going back and forth like so many fireflies. Neat mounds of bales and crates were piling up on the beach. Seven cannon were already there and another was being hauled by ropes from a boat onto a ramp, thence onto the sand.

He shuddered though there was no chill on the wind. Normally the villagers would be singing at their labors, as much from happiness as to help them pull in unison. But tonight the village was unusually quiet though every house was awake and every hand employed, even the sickest. People hurried back and forth, bowed and hurried on again. Silent. Even the dogs were hushed.

It's never been like this before, he thought, his hand unnecessarily tight on his sword. It's almost as though our village *kami* have deserted us.

Mura came up from the shore to intercept him, forewarned the moment Omi had opened the garden door. He bowed. "Good evening, Omi-sama. The ship will be unloaded by midday."

"Is the barbarian dead?"

"I don't know, Omi-sama. I'll go and find out at once."

"You can come with me."

Obediently Mura followed, half a pace behind. Omi was curiously glad of his company.

"By midday, you said?" Omi asked, not liking the quiet.

"Yes. Everything is going well."

"What about the camouflage?"

Mura pointed to groups of old women and children near one of the net houses who were platting rough mats, Suwo with them.

"We can dismantle the cannon from their carriages and wrap them up. We'll need at least ten men to carry one. Igurashi-san has sent for more porters from the next village."

"Good."

"I'm concerned that secrecy should be maintained, Sire."

"Igurashi-san will impress on them the need, *neh?*"

"Omi-sama, we'll have to expend all our rice sacks, all our twine, all our nets, all our matting straw."

"So?"

"How then can we catch fish or bale our harvest?"

"You will find a way." Omi's voice sharpened. "Your tax is increased by half again this season. Yabu-san has tonight ordered it."

"We have already paid this year's tax and next."

"That's a peasant's privilege, Mura. To fish and to till and to harvest and to pay tax. Isn't it?"

Mura said calmly, "Yes, Omi-sama."

"A headman who cannot control his village is a useless object, *neh?*"

"Yes, Omi-sama."

"That villager, he was a fool as well as insulting. Are there others like him?"

"None, Omi-sama."

"I hope so. Bad manners are unforgivable. His family is fined the value of one koku of rice—in fish, rice, grain, or whatever. To be paid within three moons."

"Yes, Omi-sama."

Both Mura and Omi the samurai knew that this sum was totally beyond the family's means. There was only the fishing boat and the single half-hectare rice paddy which the three Tamazaki brothers—now two—shared with their wives, four sons and three daughters, and Tamazaki's widow and three children. A koku of rice was a measure that approximated the amount of rice it took to keep one family alive for one year. About five bushels. Perhaps three hundred and fifty pounds of rice. All income in the realm was measured by koku. And all taxes.

"Where would this Land of the Gods be if we forgot manners?" Omi asked. "Both to those beneath us and to those above us?"

"Yes, Omi-sama." Mura was estimating where to gain that one koku of value, because the village would have to pay if the family could not. And where to obtain more rice sacks, twine, and nets. Some could be salvaged from the journey. Money would have to be borrowed. The headman of the next village owed him a favor. Ah! Isn't Tamazaki's eldest daughter a beauty at six, and isn't six the perfect age for a girl to be sold? And isn't the best child broker in all Izu my mother's sister's third cousin?—the money-hungry, hair-rending, detestable old hag. Mura sighed, knowing that he now had a series of furious bargaining sessions ahead. Never mind, he thought. Perhaps the child'll bring even two koku. She's certainly worth much more.

"I apologize for Tamazaki's misconduct and ask your pardon," he said.

"It was his misconduct—not yours," Omi replied as politely.

But both knew that it was Mura's responsibility and there had better be no more Tamazakis. Yet both were satisfied. An apology had been offered and it had been accepted but refused. Thus the honor of both men was satisfied.

They turned the corner of the wharf and stopped. Omi hesitated, then motioned Mura away. The headman bowed, left thankfully.

"Is he dead, Zukimoto?"

"No, Omi-san. He's just fainted again."

Omi went to the great iron cauldron that the village used for rendering blubber from the whales they sometimes caught far out to sea in the winter months, or for the rendering of glue from fish, a village industry.

The barbarian was immersed to his shoulders in the steaming water. His face was purple, his lips torn back from his mildewed teeth.

At sunset Omi watched Zukimoto, puffed with vanity, supervising while the barbarian was trussed like a chicken, his arms around his knees, his hands loosely to his feet, and put into cold water. All the time, the little red-headed barbarian that Yabu had wanted to begin with had babbled and laughed and wept, the Christian priest there at first droning his cursed prayers.

Then the stoking of the fire had begun. Yabu had not been at the shore, but his orders had been specific and had been followed diligently. The barbarian had begun shouting and raving, then tried to beat his head to pulp on the iron lip until he was restrained. Then came more praying, weeping, fainting, waking, shrieking in panic before the pain truly began. Omi had tried to watch as you would watch the immolation of a fly, trying not to see the man. But he could not and had gone away as soon as possible. He had discovered that he did not relish torture. There was no dignity in it, he had decided, glad for the opportunity to know the truth, never having seen it before. There was no dignity for either the sufferer or the torturer. It removed the dignity from death, and without that dignity, what was the ultimate point of life? he asked himself.

Zukimoto calmly poked the parboiled flesh of the man's legs with a stick as one would a simmered fish to see if it was ready. "He'll come to life again soon. Extraordinary how long he's lasted. I don't think they're made like us. Very interesting, eh?" Zukimoto said.

"No," Omi said, detesting him.

Zukimoto was instantly on his guard and his unctuousness returned. "I mean nothing, Omi-san," he said with a deep bow. "Nothing at all."

"Of course. Lord Yabu is pleased that you have done so well. It must require great skill not to give too much fire, yet to give enough."

"You're too kind, Omi-san."

"You've done it before?"

"Not like this. But Lord Yabu honors me with his favors. I just try to please him."

"He wants to know how long the man will live."

"Until dawn. With care."

Omi studied the cauldron thoughtfully. Then he walked up the beach into the square. All the samurai got up and bowed.

"Everything's quiet down there, Omi-san," one of them said with a laugh, jerking a thumb at the trapdoor. "At first there was some talk—it sounded angry—and some blows. Later, two of them, perhaps more, were whimpering like frightened children. But there's been quiet for a long time."

Omi listened. He could hear water sloshing and distant muttering. An occasional moan. "And Masijiro?" he asked, naming the samurai who, on his orders, had been left below.

"We don't know, Omi-san. Certainly he hasn't called out. He's probably dead."

How dare Masijiro be so useless, Omi thought. To be overpowered by defenseless men, most of whom are sick! Disgusting! Better he is dead. "No food or water tomorrow. At midday remove any bodies, *neh?* And I want the leader brought up then. Alone."

"Yes, Omi-san."

Omi went back to the fire and waited until the barbarian opened his eyes. Then he returned to the garden and reported what Zukimoto had said, the torment once more keening on the wind.

"You looked into the barbarian's eyes?"

"Yes, Yabu-sama."

Omi was kneeling now behind the *daimyo,* ten paces away. Yabu had remained immobile. Moonlight shadowed his kimono and made a phallus of his sword handle.

"What—what did you see?"

"Madness. The essence of madness. I've never seen eyes like that. And limitless terror."

Three petals fell gently.

"Make up a poem about him."

Omi tried to force his brain to work. Then, wishing he were more adequate, he said:

"His eyes
Were just the end
Of Hell—
All pain,
Articulate."

Shrieks came wafting up, fainter now, the distance seeming to make their cut more cruel.

Yabu said, after a moment:

"If you allow
Their chill to reach
Into the great, great deep,
You become one with them,
Inarticulate."

Omi thought about that a long time in the beauty of the night.

CHAPTER 5

JUST before first light, the cries had ceased.

Now Omi's mother slept. And Yabu.

The village was still restless in the dawn. Four cannon had yet to be brought ashore, fifty more kegs of powder, a thousand more cannon shot.

Kiku was lying under the coverlet watching the shadows on the shoji wall. She had not slept even though she was more exhausted than she had ever been. Wheezing snores from the old woman in the next room drowned the soft deep breathing of the *daimyo* beside her. The boy slept soundlessly on the other coverlets, one arm thrown over his eyes to shut out the light.

A slight tremor went through Yabu and Kiku held her breath. But he remained in sleep and this pleased her for she knew that very soon she would be able to leave without disturbing him. As she waited patiently, she forced herself to think of pleasant things. 'Always remember, child,' her first teacher had impressed on her, 'that to think bad thoughts is really the easiest thing in the world. If you leave your mind to itself it will spiral you down into ever-increasing unhappiness. To think good thoughts, however, requires effort. This is one of the things that discipline—training—is about. So train your mind to dwell on sweet perfumes, the touch of this silk, tender raindrops against the shoji, the curve of this flower arrangement, the tranquillity of dawn. Then, at length, you won't have to make such a great effort and you will be of value to yourself, a value to our profession —and bring honor to our world, the Willow World. . . .'

She thought about the sensuous glory of the bath she soon would have that would banish this night, and afterwards the soothing caress of Suwo's hands. She thought of the laughter she would have with the other girls and with Gyoko-san, the Mama-san, as they swapped gossip and rumors and stories, and of the clean, oh so clean, kimono that she would wear tonight, the golden one with yellow and green flowers and the hair ribbons that matched. After the bath she would have her hair dressed and from the money of last night there would be very much to pay off her debt to her employer, Gyoko-san, some to send to her father who was a peasant farmer, through the money exchanger, and still some for herself. Soon she would see her lover and it would be a perfect evening.

Life is very good, she thought.

Yes. But it's very difficult to put away the screams. Impossible. The other girls will be just as unhappy, and poor Gyoko-san! But never mind. Tomorrow we will all leave Anjiro and go home to our lovely Tea House in Mishima, the biggest city in Izu, which surrounds the *daimyo's* greatest castle in Izu, where life begins and is.

I'm sorry the Lady Midori sent for me.

Be serious, Kiku, she told herself sharply. You shouldn't be sorry. You are not sorry, *neh?* It was an honor to serve our Lord. Now that you have been honored, your value to Gyoko-san is greater than ever, *neh?* It was an experience, and now you will be known as the Lady of the Night of the Screams and, if you are lucky, someone will write a ballad about you and perhaps the ballad will even by sung in Yedo itself. Oh, that would be very good! Then certainly your lover will buy your contract and you will be safe and content and bear sons.

She smiled to herself. Ah, what stories the troubadours will make up about tonight that will be told in every Tea House throughout Izu. About the lord *daimyo,* who sat motionless in the screams, his sweat streaming. What did he do in the bed? they will all want to know. And why the boy? How was the pillowing? What did the Lady Kiku do and say and what did Lord Yabu do and say? Was his Peerless Pestle insignificant or full? Was it once or twice or never? Did nothing happen?

A thousand questions. But none ever directly asked or ever answered. That's wise, Kiku thought. The first and last rule of the Willow World was absolute secrecy, never to tell about a client or his habits or what was paid, and thus to be completely trustworthy. If someone else told, well, that was his affair, but with walls of paper and houses so small and people being what they are, stories always sped from the bed to the ballad—never the truth, always exaggerated, because people are people, *neh?* But nothing from *the* Lady. An arched eyebrow perhaps or hesitant shrug, a delicate smoothing of a perfect coiffure or fold of the kimono was all that was allowed. And always enough, if the girl had wit.

When the screams stopped, Yabu had remained statuelike in the moonlight for what had seemed a further eternity and then he had got up. At once she had hurried back into the other room, her silk kimono sighing like a midnight sea. The boy was frightened, trying not to show it, and wiped away the tears that the torment had brought. She had smiled at him reassuringly, forcing a calm that she did not feel.

Then Yabu was at the door. He was bathed in sweat, his face taut and his eyes half-closed. Kiku helped him take off his swords, then his soaking kimono and loin cloth. She dried him, helped him into a sun-fresh kimono and tied its silken belt. Once she had begun to greet him but he had put a gentle finger on her lips.

Then he had gone over to the window and looked up at the waning moon, trancelike, swaying slightly on his feet. She remained quiescent, without fear, for what was there now to fear? He was a man and she a woman, trained to be a woman, to give pleasure, in whatever way. But not to give or to receive pain. There were other courtesans who specialized in that form of sensuality. A bruise here or there, perhaps a bite, well, that was part of the pleasure-pain of giving and receiving, but always within reason, for honor was involved and she was a Lady of the Willow World of the First Class Rank, never to be treated lightly, always to be honored. But part of her training was to know how to keep a man tamed, within limits. Sometimes a man became untamed and then it became terrible. For the Lady was alone. With no rights.

Her coiffure was impeccable but for the tiny locks of hair so carefully loosed over her ears to suggest erotic disarray, yet, at the same time, to enhance the purity of the whole. The red- and black-checkered outer kimono, bordered with the purest green that increased the whiteness of her skin, was drawn tight to her tiny waist by a wide stiff sash, an obi, of iridescent green. She could hear the surf on the shore now and a light wind rustled the garden.

Finally Yabu had turned and looked at her, then at the boy.

The boy was fifteen, the son of a local fisherman, apprenticed at the nearby monastery to a Buddhist monk who was an artist, a painter and illustrator of books. The boy was one of those who was pleased to earn money from those who enjoyed sex with boys and not with women.

Yabu motioned to him. Obediently the boy, now also over his fear, loosed the sash of his kimono with a studied elegance. He wore no loincloth but a woman's wrapped underskirt that reached the ground. His body was smooth and curved and almost hairless.

Kiku remembered how still the room had been, the three of them locked together by the stillness and the vanished screams, she and the boy waiting for Yabu to indicate that which was required, Yabu standing there between them, swaying slightly, glancing from one to another.

At length he had signed to her. Gracefully she unknotted the ribbon of her obi, unwound it gently and let it rest. The folds of her three gossamer kimonos sighed open and revealed the misted underskirt that enhanced her loins. He lay on the bedding and at his bidding they lay on either side of him. He put their hands on him and held them equally. He warmed quickly, showing them how to use their nails in his flanks, hurrying, his face a mask, faster, faster and then his shuddering violent cry of utter pain. For a moment, he lay there panting, eyes tightly closed, chest heaving, then turned over and, almost instantly, was asleep.

In the quiet they caught their breaths, trying to hide their surprise. It had been over so quickly.

The boy had arched an eyebrow in wonder. "Were we inept, Kiku-san? I mean, everything was so fast," he whispered.

"We did everything he wanted," she said.

"He certainly reached the Clouds and the Rain," the boy said. "I thought the house was going to fall down."

She smiled. "Yes."

"I'm glad. At first I was very frightened. It's very good to please."

Together they dried Yabu gently and covered him with the quilt. Then the boy lay back languorously, half propped on one elbow and stifled a yawn.

"Why don't you sleep, too," she said.

The boy pulled his kimono closer and shifted his position to kneel opposite her. She was sitting beside Yabu, her right hand gently stroking the *daimyo's* arm, gentling his tremored sleep.

"I've never been together with a man and a lady at the same time before, Kiku-san," the boy whispered.

"Neither have I."

The boy frowned. "I've never been with a girl either. I mean I've never pillowed with one."

"Would you like me?" she had asked politely. "If you wait a little, I'm sure our Lord won't wake up."

The boy frowned. Then he said, "Yes please," and afterwards he said, "That was very strange, Lady Kiku."

She smiled within. "Which do you prefer?"

The boy thought a long time as they lay at peace, in each other's arms. "This way is rather hard work."

She buried her head in his shoulder and kissed the nape of his neck to hide her smile. "You are a marvelous lover," she whispered. "Now you must sleep after so much hard work." She caressed him to sleep, then left him and went to the other quilts.

The other bed had been cool. She did not want to move into Yabu's warmth lest she disturb him. Soon her side was warm.

The shadows from the shoji were sharpening. Men are such babies, she thought. So full of foolish pride. All the anguish of this night for something so transitory. For a passion that is in itself but an illusion, *neh?*

The boy stirred in his sleep. Why did you make the offer to him? she asked herself. For his pleasure—for him and not for me, though it amused me and passed the time and gave him the peace he needed. Why don't you sleep a little? Later. I'll sleep later, she told herself.

When it was time she slipped from the soft warmth and stood up. Her kimonos whispered apart and the air chilled her skin. Quickly she folded her robes perfectly and retied her obi. A deft but careful touch to her coiffure. And to her makeup.

She made no sound as she left.

The samurai sentry at the veranda entrance bowed and she bowed back and she was in the dawning sunshine. Her maid was waiting for her.

"Good morning, Kiku-san."

"Good morning."

The sun felt very good and washed away the night. It's very fine to be alive, she thought.

She slipped her feet into her sandals, opened her crimson parasol, and started through the garden, out onto the path that led down to the village, through the square, to the tea house that was her temporary home. Her maid followed.

"Good morning, Kiku-san," Mura called out, bowing. He was resting momentarily on the veranda of his house, drinking cha, the pale green tea of Japan. His mother was serving him. "Good morning, Kiku-san," she echoed.

"Good morning, Mura-san. Good morning, Saiko-san, how well you are looking," Kiku replied.

"How are you?" the mother asked, her old old eyes boring into the girl. "What a terrible night! Please join us for cha. You look pale, child."

"Thank you, but please excuse me, I must go home now. You do me too much honor. Perhaps later."

"Of course, Kiku-san. You honor our village by being here."

Kiku smiled and pretended not to notice their searching stares. To add spice to their day and to hers, she pretended a slight pain in her nether regions.

That will sail around the village, she thought happily as she bowed, winced again, and went off as though stoically covering an intensity of pain, the folds of her kimonos swaying to perfection, and her sunshade tilted to give her just that most marvelous light. She was very glad that she had worn this outer kimono and this parasol. On a dull day the effect would never have been so dramatic.

"Ah, poor, poor child! She's so beautiful, *neh?* What a shame! Terrible!" Mura's mother said with a heart-rending sigh.

"What's terrible, Saiko-san?" Mura's wife asked, coming onto the veranda.

"Didn't you see the poor girl's agony? Didn't you see how bravely she was trying to hide it? Poor child. Only seventeen and to have to go through all that!"

"She's eighteen," Mura said dryly.

"All of what, Mistress?" one of the maids said breathlessly, joining them.

The old woman looked around to ensure that everyone was listening and whispered loudly. "I heard"—she dropped her voice—"I heard that she'll . . . she'll be useless . . . for three months."

"Oh, no! Poor Kiku-san! Oh! But why?"

"He used his teeth. I have it on the best authority."

"Oh!"

"Oh!"

"But why does he have the boy as well, Mistress? Surely he doesn't—"

"Ah! Run along! Back to your work, good-for-nothings! This isn't for your ears! Go on, off with the lot of you. The Master and I have to talk."

She shooed them all off the veranda. Even Mura's wife. And sipped her cha, benign and very content.

Mura broke the silence. "Teeth?"

"Teeth. Rumor has it that the screams make him large because he was frightened by a dragon when he was small," she said in a rush. "He always has a boy there to remind him of himself when he was a boy and petrified, but actually the boy's there only to pillow with, to exhaust himself—otherwise he'd bite everything off, poor girl."

Mura sighed. He went into the small outhouse beside the front gate and farted involuntarily as he began to relieve himself into the bucket. I wonder what really happened, he asked himself, titillated. Why was Kiku-san in pain? Perhaps the *daimyo* really does use his teeth! How extraordinary!

He walked out, shaking himself to ensure that he did not stain his loincloth, and headed across the square deep in thought. Eeeee, how I would like to have one night with the Lady Kiku! What man wouldn't? How much did Omi-san have to pay her Mama-san—which we will have to pay eventually? Two koku? They say her Mama-san, Gyoko-san, demanded and got ten times the regular fee. Does she get five koku for one night? Kiku-san would certainly be worth it, *neh?* Rumor has it she's as practiced at eighteen as a woman twice her age. She's supposed to be able to prolong. . . . Eeeee, the joy of her! If it was me—how would *I* begin?

Absently he adjusted himself into his loincloth as his feet took him out of the square, up the well-worn path to the funeral ground.

The pyre had been prepared. The deputation of five men from the village was already there.

This was the most delightful place in the village, where the sea breezes were coolest in summer and the view the best. Nearby was the village Shinto shrine, a tiny thatched roof on a pedestal for the *kami,* the spirit, that lived there, or might wish to live there if it pleased him. A gnarled yew that had seeded before the village was born leaned against the wind.

Later Omi walked up the path. With him were Zukimoto and four guards. He stood apart. When he bowed formally to the pyre and to the shroud-covered, almost disjointed body that lay upon it, they all bowed with him, to honor the barbarian who had died that his comrades might live.

At his signal Zukimoto went forward and lit the pyre. Zukimoto had asked Omi for the privilege and the honor had been granted to him. He bowed a last time. And then, when the fire was well alight, they went away.

Blackthorne dipped into the dregs of the barrel and carefully measured a half cup of water and gave it to Sonk. Sonk tried to sip it to make it last, his hand trembling, but he could not. He gulped the tepid liquid, regretting that he had done so the moment it had passed his parched throat, groped exhaustedly to his place by the wall, stepping over those whose turn it was to lie down. The floor was now deep ooze, the stench and the flies hideous. Faint sunlight came into the pit through the slats of the trapdoor.

Vinck was next for water and he took his cup and stared at it, sitting near the barrel, Spillbergen on the other side. "Thanks," he muttered dully.

"Hurry up!" Jan Roper said, the cut on his cheek already festering. He was the last for water and, being so near, his throat was torturing him. "Hurry up, Vinck, for Christ's sweet sake."

"Sorry. Here, you take it," Vinck muttered, handing him the cup, oblivious of the flies that speckled him.

"Drink it, you fool! It's the last you'll get till sunset. Drink it!" Jan Roper shoved the cup back into the man's hands. Vinck did not look up at him but obeyed miserably, and slipped back once more into his private hell.

Jan Roper took his cup of water from Blackthorne. He closed his eyes and said a silent grace. He was one of those standing, his leg muscles aching. The cup gave barely two swallows.

And now that they had all been given their ration, Blackthorne dipped and sipped gratefully. His mouth and tongue were raw and burning and dusty. Flies and sweat and filth covered him. His chest and back were badly bruised.

He watched the samurai who had been left in the cellar. The man was huddled against the wall, between Sonk and Croocq, taking up as little space as possible, and he had not moved for hours. He was staring bleakly into space, naked but for his loincloth, violent bruises all over him, a thick weal around his neck.

When Blackthorne had first come to his senses, the cellar was in complete darkness. The screams were filling the pit and he thought that he was dead and in the choking depths of hell. He felt himself being sucked down into muck that was clammy and flesh-crawling beyond measure, and he had cried out and flailed in panic, unable to breathe, until, after an eternity, he had heard, "It's all right, Pilot, you're not dead, it's all right. Wake up, wake up, for the love of Christ, it's not hell but it might just as well be. Oh, Blessed Lord Jesus, help us all."

When he was fully conscious they had told him about Pieterzoon and the barrels of seawater.

"Oh, Lord Jesus, get us out of here!" someone whimpered.

"What're they doing to poor old Pieterzoon? What're they doing to him? Oh, God help us. I can't stand the screams!"

"Oh, Lord, let the poor man die. Let him die."

"Christ God, stop the screams! Please stop the screams!"

The pit and Pieterzoon's screams had measured them all, had forced them to look within themselves. And no man had liked what he had seen.

The darkness makes it worse, Blackthorne had thought.

It had been an endless night, in the pit.

With the gloaming the cries had vanished. When dawn trickled down to them they had seen the forgotten samurai.

"What're we going to do about him?" van Nekk had asked.

"I don't know. He looks as frightened as we are," Blackthorne said, his heart pumping.

"He'd better not start anything, by God."

"Oh, Lord Jesus, get me out of here—" Croocq's voice started to crescendo. *"Helllp!"*

Van Nekk, who was near him, shook him and gentled him. "It's all right, lad. We're in God's hands. He's watching over us."

"Look at my arm," Maetsukker moaned. The wound had festered already.

Blackthorne stood shakily. "We'll all be raving lunatics in a day or two if we don't get out of here," he said to no one in particular.

"There's almost no water," van Nekk said.

"We'll ration what there is. Some now—some at noon. With luck, there'll be enough for three turns. God curse all flies!"

So he had found the cup and had given them a ration, and now he was sipping his, trying to make it last.

"What about him—the Japaner?" Spillbergen said. The Captain-General had fared better than most during the night because he had shut his ears to the screams with a little mud, and, being next to the water barrel, had cautiously slaked his thirst. "What are we going to do about him?"

"He should have some water," van Nekk said.

"The pox on that," Sonk said. "I say he gets none."

They all voted on it and it was agreed he got none.

"I don't agree," Blackthorne said.

"You don't agree to anything we say," Jan Roper said. "He's the enemy. He's a heathen devil and he almost killed you."

"You've almost killed me. Half a dozen times. If your musket had fired at Santa Magdellana, you'd have blown my head off."

"I wasn't aiming at you. I was aiming at stinking Satanists."

"They were unarmed priests. And there was plenty of time."

"I wasn't aiming at you."

"You've almost killed me a dozen times, with your God-cursed anger, your God-cursed bigotry, and your God-cursed stupidity."

"Blasphemy's a mortal sin. Taking His name in vain is a sin. We're in His hands, not yours. You're not a king and this isn't a ship. You're not our keep—"

"But you will do what I say!"

Jan Roper looked round the cellar, seeking support in vain. "Do what you want," he said sullenly.

"I will."

The samurai was as parched as they, but he shook his head to the offered cup. Blackthorne hesitated, put the cup to the samurai's swollen lips, but the man smashed the cup away, spilling the water, and said something harshly. Blackthrone readied to parry the following blow. But it never came. The man made no further move, just looked away into space.

"He's mad. They're all mad," Spillbergen said.

"There's more water for us. Good," Jan Roper said. "Let him go to the hell he deserves."

"What's your name? *Namu?*" Blackthorne asked. He said it again in different ways but the samurai appeared not to hear.

They left him alone. But they watched him as if he were a scorpion. He did not watch them back. Blackthorne was certain the man was trying to decide on something, but he had no idea what it could be.

What's on his mind, Blackthorne asked himself. Why should he refuse water? Why was he left here? Was that a mistake by Omi? Unlikely. By plan? Unlikely. Could we use him to get out? Unlikely. The whole world's unlikely except it's likely we're going to stay here until they *let* us out . . . if they let us out. And if they let us out, what next? What happened to Pieterzoon?

The flies swarmed with the heat of the day.

Oh, God, I wish I could lie down—wish I could get into that bath—they wouldn't have to carry me there now. I never realized how important a bath is. That old blind man with the steel fingers! I could use him for an hour or two.

What a waste! All our ships and men and effort for this. A total failure. Well, almost. Some of us are still alive.

"Pilot!" Van Nekk was shaking him. "You were asleep. It's him—he's been bowing to you for a minute or more." He motioned to the samurai who knelt, head bowed in front of him.

Blackthorne rubbed the exhaustion out of his eyes. He made an effort and bowed back.

"*Hai?*" he asked curtly, remembering the Japanese word for "yes."

The samurai took hold of the sash of his shredded kimono and wrapped it around his neck. Still kneeling, he gave one end to Blackthorne and the other to Sonk, bowed his head, and motioned them to pull it tight.

"He's afraid we'll strangle him," Sonk said.

"Christ Jesus, I think that's what he wants us to do." Blackthorne let the sash fall and shook his head. "*Kinjiru,*" he said, thinking how useful that word was. How do you say to a man who doesn't speak your language that it's against your code to commit murder, to kill an unarmed man, that you're not executioners, that suicide is damned before God?

The samurai asked again, clearly begging him, but again Blackthorne shook his head. *"Kinjiru."* The man looked around wildly. Suddenly he was on his feet and he had shoved his head deep into the latrine bucket to try to drown himself. Jan Roper and Sonk immediately pulled him out, choking and struggling.

"Let him go," Blackthorne ordered. They obeyed. He pointed at the latrine. "Samurai, if that's what you want, go ahead!"

The man was retching, but he understood. He looked at the foul bucket and knew that he did not have the strength to hold his head there long enough. In abject misery the samurai went back to his place by the wall.

"Jesus," someone muttered.

Blackthorne dipped half a cup of water from the barrel, got to his feet, his joints stiff, went over to the Japanese and offered it. The samurai looked past the cup.

"I wonder how long he can hold out," Blackthorne said.

"Forever," Jan Roper said. "They're animals. They're not human."

"For Christ's sake, how much longer will they keep us here?" Ginsel asked.

"As long as they want."

"We'll have to do anything they want," van Nekk said. "We'll have to if we want to stay alive and get out of this hell hole. Won't we, Pilot?"

"Yes." Blackthorne thankfully measured the sun's shadows. "It's high noon, the watch changes."

Spillbergen, Maetsukker, and Sonk began to complain but he cursed them to their feet and when all were rearranged he lay down gratefully. The mud was foul and the flies worse than ever, but the joy of being able to stretch out full length was enormous.

What did they do to Pieterzoon? he asked himself, as he felt his fatigue engulfing him. Oh, God help us to get out of here. I'm so frightened.

There were footsteps above. The trapdoor opened. The priest stood there flanked by samurai.

"Pilot. You are to come up. You are to come up alone," he said.

CHAPTER 6

$\mathbf{A}$LL eyes in the pit went to Blackthorne.
"What do they want with me?"
"I don't know," Father Sebastio said gravely. "But you must come up at once."

Blackthorne knew that he had no option, but he did not leave the protective wall, trying to summon more strength.

"What happened to Pieterzoon?"

The priest told him. Blackthorne translated for those who did not speak Portuguese.

"The Lord have mercy on him," van Nekk whispered over the horrified silence. "Poor man. Poor man."

"I'm sorry. There was nothing I could do," the priest said with a great sadness. "I don't think he knew me or anyone the moment they put him into the water. His mind was gone. I gave him absolution and prayed for him. Perhaps, through God's mercy. . . . *In nomine Patris et Filii et Spiritus Sancti.* Amen." He made the sign of the cross over the cellar. "I beg you all to renounce your heresies and be accepted back into God's faith. Pilot, you must come up."

"Don't leave us, Pilot, for the love of God!" Croocq cried out.

Vinck stumbled to the ladder and started to climb. "They can take me—not the pilot. Me, not him. Tell him—" He stopped, helplessly, both feet on the rungs. A long spear was an inch away from his heart. He tried to grab the haft but the samurai was ready and if Vinck had not jumped back he would have been impaled.

This samurai pointed at Blackthorne and beckoned him up. Harshly. Still Blackthorne did not move. Another samurai shoved a long barbed staff into the cellar and tried to hook Blackthorne out.

No one moved to help Blackthorne except the samurai in the cellar. He caught the barb fast and said something sharply to the man above, who hesitated; then he looked across at Blackthorne, shrugged and spoke.

"What did he say?"

The priest replied, "It's a Japanese saying: 'A man's fate is a man's fate and life is but an illusion.' "

Blackthorne nodded to the samurai and went to the ladder without looking back and scaled it. When he came into full sunlight, he squinted against the painful brilliance, his knees gave way, and he toppled to the sandy earth.

Omi was to one side. The priest and Mura stood near the four samurai. Some distant villagers watched for a moment and then turned away.

No one helped him.

Oh, God, give me strength, Blackthorne prayed. I've got to get on my feet and pretend to be strong. That's the only thing they respect. Being strong. Showing no fear. Please help me.

He gritted his teeth and pushed against the earth and stood up, swaying slightly. "What the hell do you want with me, you poxy little bastard?" he said directly at Omi, then added to the priest, "Tell the bastard I'm a *daimyo* in my

71

own country and what sort of treatment is this? Tell him we've no quarrel with him. Tell him to let us out or it'll be the worse for him. Tell him I'm a *daimyo,* by God. I'm heir to Sir William of Micklehaven, may the bastard be dead long since. Tell him!"

The night had been terrible for Father Sebastio. But during his vigil he had come to feel God's presence and gained a serenity he had never experienced before. Now he knew that he could be an instrument of God against the heathen, that he was shielded against the heathen, and the pirate's cunning. He knew, somehow, that this night had been a preparation, a crossroads for him.

"Tell him."

The priest said in Japanese, "The pirate says he's a lord in his own country." He listened to Omi's reply. "Omi-san says he does not care if you are a king in your own country. Here you live at Lord Yabu's whim—you and all your men."

"Tell him he's a turd."

"You should beware of insulting him."

Omi began talking again.

"Omi-san says that you will be given a bath. And food and drink. If you behave, you will not be put back into the pit."

"What about my men?"

The priest asked Omi.

"They will stay below."

"Then tell him to go to hell." Blackthorne walked toward the ladder to go below again. Two of the samurai prevented him, and though he struggled against them, they held him easily.

Omi spoke to the priest, then to his men. They released him and Blackthorne almost fell.

"Omi-san says that unless you behave, another of your men will be taken up. There is plenty of firewood and plenty of water."

If I agree now, thought Blackthorne, they've found the means to control me and I'm in their power forever. But what does it matter, I'm in their power now and, in the end, I will have to do what they want. Van Nekk was right. I'll have to do anything.

"What does he want me to do? What does it mean to 'behave'?"

"Omi-san says, it means to obey. To do what you are told. To eat dung if need be."

"Tell him to go to hell. Tell him I piss on him and his whole country—and his *daimyo.*"

"I recommend you agree to wh—"

"Tell him what I said, exactly, by God!"

"Very well—but I did warn you, Pilot."

Omi listened to the priest. The knuckles on his sword hand whitened. All of his men shifted uneasily, their eyes knifing into Blackthorne.

Then Omi gave a quiet order.

Instantly two samurai went down into the pit and brought out Croocq, the boy. They dragged him over to the cauldron, trussed him while others brought firewood and water. They put the petrified boy into the brimming cauldron and ignited the wood.

Blackthorne watched the soundless mouthings of Croocq and the terror that was all of him. Life has no value to these people at all, he thought. God curse them to hell, they'll boil Croocq as certain as I'm standing on this God-forsaken earth.

Smoke billowed across the sand. Sea gulls were mewing around the fishing boats. A piece of wood fell out of the fire and was kicked back again by a samurai.

"Tell him to stop," Blackthorne said. "Ask him to stop."

"Omi-san says, you agree to behave?"

"Yes."

"He says, you will obey all orders?"

"As far as I can, yes."

Omi spoke again. Father Sebastio asked a question and Omi nodded.

"He wants you to answer directly to him. The Japanese for 'yes' is *'hai.'* He says, you will obey all orders?"

"As far as I can, *hai.*"

The fire was beginning to warm the water and a nauseating groan broke from the boy's mouth. Flames from the wooden fire that was set into the bricks below the iron licked the metal. More wood was piled on.

"Omi-san says, lie down. Immediately."

Blackthorne did as he was ordered.

"Omi-san says that he had not insulted you personally, neither was there any cause for you to insult him. Because you are a barbarian and know no better yet, you will not be killed. But you will be taught manners. Do you understand?"

"Yes."

"He wants you to answer direct to him."

There was a wailing cry from the boy. It went on and on and then the boy fainted. One of the samurai held his head out of the water.

Blackthorne looked up at Omi. Remember, he ordered himself, remember that the boy is in your hands alone, the lives of all your crew are in your hands. Yes, the devil half of him began, but there's no guarantee that the bastard'll honor a bargain.

"Do you understand?"

"*Hai.*"

He saw Omi hitch up his kimono and ease his penis out of his loincloth. He had expected the man to piss in his face. But Omi did not. He pissed on his back. By the Lord God, Blackthorne swore to himself, I will remember this day and somehow, somewhere, Omi will pay.

"Omi-san says, it is bad manners to say that you will piss on anyone. Very bad. It is bad manners and very stupid to say you will piss on anyone when you are unarmed. It is very bad manners and even more stupid to say you will piss on anyone when you are unarmed, powerless, and not prepared to allow your friends or family or whomever to perish first."

Blackthorne said nothing. He did not take his eyes off Omi.

"*Wakarimasu ka?*" Omi said.

"He says, do you understand?"

"*Hai.*"

"*Okiro.*"

"He says you will get up."

Blackthorne got up, pain hammering in his head. His eyes were on Omi and Omi stared back at him.

"You will go with Mura and obey his orders."

Blackthorne made no reply.

"*Wakarimasu ka?*" Omi said sharply.

"*Hai.*" Blackthorne was measuring the distance between himself and Omi. He could feel his fingers on the man's neck and face already, and he prayed he could be quick and strong enough to take Omi's eyes out before they tore him off the man. "What about the boy?" he said.

The priest spoke to Omi haltingly.

Omi glanced at the cauldron. The water was hardly tepid yet. The boy had fainted but was unharmed. "Take him out of there," he ordered. "Get a doctor if he needs one."

His men obeyed. He saw Blackthorne go over to the boy and listen to his heart.

Omi motioned to the priest. "Tell the leader that the youth can also stay out of the pit today. If the leader behaves and the youth behaves, another of the barbarians *may* come out of the pit tomorrow. Then another. Perhaps. Or more than one. Perhaps. It depends on how the ones above behave. But you—" he looked directly at Blackthorne—"you are responsible for the smallest infraction of any rule or order. Do you understand?"

After the priest had translated this, Omi heard the barbarian say, "Yes," and saw part of the blood-chilling anger go out of his eyes. But the hatred remained. How foolish, Omi thought, and how naïve to be so open. I wonder what he would have done if I had played with him further—pretended to go back on what I had promised, or implied that I had promised.

"Priest, what's his name again? Say it slowly."

He heard the priest say the name several times but it still sounded like gibberish.

"Can you say it?" he asked one of his men.

"No, Omi-san."

"Priest, tell him from now on his name is Anjin—Pilot—*neh?* When he merits it, he will be called Anjin-san. Explain to him that there are no sounds in our tongue for us to say his real name as it is." Omi added dryly, "Impress upon him that this is not meant to be insulting. Good-by, Anjin, for the moment."

They all bowed to him. He returned the salutation politely and walked away. When he was well clear of the square and certain that no one was watching, he allowed himself to smile broadly. To have tamed the chief of the barbarians so quickly! To have discerned at once how to dominate him, and them!

How extraordinary those barbarians are, he thought. Eeee, the sooner the Anjin speaks our language the better. Then we'll know how to smash the Christian barbarians once and for all!

"Why didn't you piss in his face?" Yabu asked.

"At first I'd intended to, Lord. But the Pilot's still an untamed animal, totally dangerous. To do it in his face—well, with us, to touch a man's face is the worst of insults, *neh?* So I reasoned that I might have insulted him so deeply he would lose control. So I pissed on his back—which I think will be sufficient."

They were seated on the veranda of his house, on silk cushions. Omi's mother was serving them cha—tea—with all the ceremony she could command, and she had been well trained in her youth. She offered the cup with a bow to Yabu. He bowed and politely offered it to Omi, who of course refused with a deeper bow; then he accepted it and sipped with enjoyment, feeling complete.

"I'm very impressed with you, Omi-san," he said. "Your reasoning is exceptional. Your planning and handling of this whole business has been splendid."

"You are too kind, Sire. My efforts could have been much better, much better."

"Where did you learn so much about the barbarian mind?"

"When I was fourteen, for a year I had a teacher who was the monk called Jiro. Once he'd been a Christian priest, at least he was an apprentice priest, but fortunately he learned the errors of his stupidity. I've always remembered one thing he told me. He said that the Christian religion was vulnerable because they taught that their chief deity, Jesu, said that all people should 'love' one another—he taught nothing about honor or duty, only love. And also that life was sacred—'Thou shalt not kill,' *neh?* And other stupidities. These new barbarians claim to be Christian also, even though the priest denies it, so I reasoned that perhaps they're just a different sect, and that's the cause of their enmity, just as some of the Buddhist sects hate each other. I thought if they 'love one another,' perhaps we could control the leader by taking the life or even threatening to take the life of one of his men." Omi knew that this conversation was dangerous because of the torture death, the befouled death. He felt his mother's unspoken warning crossing the space between them.

"Will you have more cha, Yabu-sama?" his mother asked.

"Thank you," Yabu said. "It's very, very good."

"Thank you, Sire. But Omi-san, is the barbarian broken for good?" his mother asked, twisting the conversation. "Perhaps you should tell our Lord if you think it's temporary or permanent."

Omi hesitated. "Temporary. But I think he should learn our language as fast as possible. That's very important to you, Sire. You will probably have to destroy one or two of them to keep him and the rest in control, but by that time he will have learned how to behave. Once you can talk directly to him, Yabu-sama, you can use his knowledge. If what the priest said is true—that he piloted the ship ten thousand *ri*—he must be more than just a little clever."

"You're more than just a little clever." Yabu laughed. "You're put in charge of the animals. Omi-san, trainer of men!"

Omi laughed with him. "I'll try, Lord."

"Your fief is increased from five hundred koku to three thousand. You will have control within twenty *ri*." A *ri* was a measure of distance that approximated one mile. "As a further token of my affection, when I return to Yedo I will send you two horses, twenty silk kimonos, one suit of armor, two swords, and enough arms to equip a further hundred samurai which you will recruit. When war comes you will immediately join my personal staff as a hatamoto." Yabu was feeling expansive: A hatamoto was a special personal retainer of a *daimyo* who had the right of access to his lord and could wear swords in the presence of his lord. He was delighted with Omi and felt rested, even reborn. He had slept exquisitely. When he had awoken he was alone, which was to be expected, because he had not asked either the girl or the boy to stay. He had drunk a little tea and eaten sparingly of rice gruel. Then a bath and Suwo's massage.

That was a marvelous experience, he thought. Never have I felt so close to nature, to the trees and mountains and earth, to the inestimable sadness of life and its transience. The screams had perfected everything.

"Omi-san, there's a rock in my garden at Mishima that I'd like you to accept, also to commemorate this happening, and that marvelous night and our good fortune. I'll send it with the other things," he said. "The stone comes from Kyushu. I called it 'The Waiting Stone' because we were waiting for the Lord Taikō to order an attack when I found it. That was, oh, fifteen years ago. I was part of his army which smashed the rebels and subdued the island."

"You do me much honor."

"Why not put it here, in your garden, and rename it? Why not call it 'The Stone of Barbarian Peace,' to commemorate the night and his endless waiting for peace."

"Perhaps I may be allowed to call it 'The Happiness Stone' to remind me and my descendants of the honors you do to me, Uncle?"

"No—better just simply name it 'The Waiting Barbarian.' Yes, I like that. That joins us further together—him and me. He was waiting as I was waiting. I lived, he died." Yabu looked at the garden, musing. "Good, 'The Waiting Barbarian'! I like that. There are curious flecks on one side of the rock that remind me of tears, and veins of blue mixed with a reddish quartz that remind me of flesh—the impermanence of it!" Yabu sighed, enjoying his melancholy. Then he added, "It's good for a man to plant a stone and name a stone. The barbarian took a long time to die, *neh?* Perhaps he will be reborn Japanese, to compensate for his suffering. Wouldn't that be marvelous? Then one day, perhaps, his descendants would see his stone and be content."

Omi poured out his heartfelt thanks, and protested that he did not deserve such bounty. Yabu knew that the bounty was not more than deserved. He could easily have given more, but he had remembered the old adage that you can always increase a fief, but to reduce one causes enmity. And treachery.

"Oku-san," he said to the woman, giving her the title of Honorable Mother, "my brother should have told me sooner about the great qualities of his youngest son. Then Omi-san would have been much further advanced today. My brother's too retiring, too thoughtless."

"My husband's too thoughtful for you, my Lord, to worry you," she replied, aware of the underlying criticism. "I'm glad that my son has had an opportunity of serving you, and that he's pleased you. My son has only done his duty, *neh?* It's our duty—Mizuno-san and all of us—to serve."

Horses clattered up the rise. Igurashi, Yabu's chief retainer, strode through the garden. "Everything's ready, Sire. If you want to get back to Yedo quickly we should leave now."

"Good. Omi-san, you and your men will go with the convoy and assist Igurashi-san to see it safely into the castle." Yabu saw a shadow cross Omi's face. "What?"

"I was just thinking about the barbarians."

"Leave a few guards for them. Compared to the convoy, they're unimportant. Do what you want with them—put them back into the pit, do what you like. When and if you obtain anything useful from them, send me word."

"Yes, Lord," Omi replied. "I'll leave ten samurai and specific instructions with Mura—they'll come to no harm in five or six days. What do you want done with the ship itself?"

"Keep it safe here. You're responsible for it, of course. Zukimoto has sent letters to a dealer at Nagasaki to offer it for sale to the Portuguese. The Portuguese can come and collect it."

Omi hesitated. "Perhaps you should keep the ship, Sire, and get the barbarians to train some of our sailors to handle it."

"What do I need with barbarian ships?" Yabu laughed derisively. "Should I become a filthy merchant?"

"Of course not, Sire," Omi said quickly. "I just thought Zukimoto might have found a use for such a vessel."

"What do I need with a trading ship?"

"The priest said this was a warship, Sire. He seemed afraid of it. When war starts, a warship could—"

"Our war will be fought on land. The sea's for merchants, all of whom are filthy usurers, pirates or fishermen." Yabu got up and began to walk down the steps toward the garden gate, where a samurai was holding the bridle of his horse. He stopped and stared out to sea. His knees went weak.

Omi followed his glance.

A ship was rounding the headland. She was a large galley with a multitude of oars, the swiftest of the Japanese coastal vessels because she depended neither upon the wind, nor upon the tide. The flag at the masthead carried the Toranaga crest.

CHAPTER 7

TODA Hiro-matsu, overlord of the provinces of Sagami and Kozuké, Toranaga's most trusted general and adviser, commander-in-chief of all his armies, strode down the gangplank onto the wharf alone. He was tall for a Japanese, just under six feet, a bull-like man with heavy jowls, who carried his sixty-seven years with strength. His military kimono was brown silk, stark but for the five small Toranaga crests—three interlocked bamboo sprays. He wore a burnished breastplate and steel arm protectors. Only the short sword was in his belt. The other, the killing sword, he carried loose in his hand. He was ready to unsheathe it instantly and to kill instantly to protect his liege lord. This had been his custom ever since he was fifteen.

No one, not even the Taikō, had been able to change him.

A year ago, when the Taikō died, Hiro-matsu had become Toranaga's vassal. Toranaga had given him Sagami and Kozuké, two of his eight provinces, to overlord, five hundred thousand koku yearly, and had also left him to his custom. Hiro-matsu was very good at killing.

Now the shore was lined with all the villagers—men, women, children—on their knees, their heads low. The samurai were in neat, formal rows in front of them. Yabu was at their head with his lieutenants.

If Yabu had been a woman or a weaker man, he knew that he would be beating his breast and wailing and tearing his hair out. This was too much of a coincidence. For the famous Toda Hiro-matsu to be here, on this day, meant that Yabu had been betrayed—either in Yedo by one of his household, or here in Anjiro by Omi, one of Omi's men, or one of the villagers. He had been trapped in disobedience. An enemy had taken advantage of his interest in the ship.

He knelt and bowed and all his samurai followed him, and he cursed the ship and all who sailed in it.

"Ah, Yabu-sama," he heard Hiro-matsu say, and saw him kneel on the matting that had been set out for him and return his bow. But the depth of the bow was less than correct and Hiro-matsu did not wait for him to bow again, so he knew, without being told, that he was in vast jeopardy. He saw the general sit back on his heels. "Iron Fist" he was called behind his back. Only Toranaga or one of three counselors would have the privilege of flying the Toranaga flag. Why send so important a general to catch me away from Yedo?

"You honor me by coming to one of my poor villages, Hiro-matsu-sama," he said.

"My Master ordered me here." Hiro-matsu was known for his bluntness. He had neither guile nor cunning, only an absolute trustworthiness to his liege lord.

"I'm honored and very glad," Yabu said. "I rushed here from Yedo because of that barbarian ship."

"Lord Toranaga invited all friendly *daimyos* to wait in Yedo until he returned from Osaka."

"How is our Lord? I hope everything goes well with him?"

"The sooner Lord Toranaga is safe in his own castle at Yedo the better. The sooner the clash with Ishido is open and we marshal our armies and cut a path

77

back to Osaka Castle and burn it to the bricks, the better." The old man's jowls reddened as his anxiety for Toranaga increased; he hated being away from him. The Taikō had built Osaka Castle to be invulnerable. It was the greatest in the Empire, with interlocking keeps and moats, lesser castles, towers, and bridges, and space for eighty thousand soldiers within its walls. And around the walls and the huge city were other armies, equally disciplined and equally well armed, all fanatic supporters of Yaemon, the Heir. "I've told him a dozen times that he was mad to put himself into Ishido's power. Lunatic!"

"Lord Toranaga had to go, *neh?* He had no choice." The Taikō had ordered that the Council of Regents, who ruled in Yaemon's name, were to meet for ten days at least twice a year and always within Osaka's castle keep, bringing with them a maximum of five hundred retainers within the walls. And all other *daimyos* were equally obliged to visit the castle with their families to pay their respects to the Heir, also twice a year. So all were controlled, all defenseless for part of the year, every year. "The meeting was fixed, *neh?* If he didn't go it would be treason, *neh?*"

"Treason against whom?" Hiro-matsu reddened even more. "Ishido's trying to isolate our Master. Listen, if I had Ishido in my power like he has Lord Toranaga, I wouldn't hesitate for a moment—whatever the risks. Ishido's head would have been off his shoulders long since, and his spirit awaiting rebirth." The general was involuntarily twisting the well-used sheath of the sword that he carried in his left hand. His right hand, gnarled and calloused, lay ready in his lap. He studied *Erasmus*. "Where are the cannon?"

"I had them brought ashore. For safety. Will Toranaga-sama make another compromise with Ishido?"

"When I left Osaka, all was quiet. The Council was to meet in three days."

"Will the clash become open?"

"I'd like it open. But my Lord? If he wants to compromise, he will compromise." Hiro-matsu looked back at Yabu. "He ordered all allied *daimyos* to wait for him at Yedo. Until he returned. This is not Yedo."

"Yes. I felt that the ship was important enough to our cause to investigate it immediately."

"There was no need, Yabu-san. You should have more confidence. Nothing happens without our Master's knowledge. He would have sent someone to investigate it. It happens he sent me. How long have you been here?"

"A day and a night."

"Then you were two days coming from Yedo?"

"Yes."

"You came very quickly. You are to be complimented."

To gain time Yabu began telling Hiro-matsu about his forced march. But his mind was on more vital matters. Who was the spy? How had Toranaga got the information about the ship as quickly as he himself? And who had told Toranaga about his departure? How could he maneuver now and deal with Hiro-matsu?

Hiro-matsu heard him out, then said pointedly, "Lord Toranaga has confiscated the ship and all its contents."

A shocked silence swamped the shore. This was Izu, Yabu's fief, and Toranaga had no rights here. Neither had Hiro-matsu any rights to order anything. Yabu's hand tightened on his sword.

Hiro-matsu waited with practiced calmness. He had done exactly as Toranaga had ordered and now he was committed. It was implacably kill or be killed.

Yabu knew also that now he must commit himself. There was no more waiting. If he refused to give up the ship he would have to kill Hiro-matsu Iron Fist, because Hiro-matsu Iron Fist would never leave without it. There were perhaps two hundred elite samurai on the galley that was moored to the dock. They would also have to die. He could invite them ashore and beguile them, and within a few hours he could easily have enough samurai in Anjiro to overwhelm them all, for he was a master at ambush. But that would force Toranaga to send armies against Izu. You will be swallowed up, he told himself, unless Ishido comes to your rescue. And why should Ishido rescue you when your enemy Ikawa Jikkyo is Ishido's kinsman and wants Izu for himself? Killing Hiro-matsu will open hostilities, because Toranaga will be honor bound to move against you, which would force Ishido's hand, and Izu would be the first battlefield.

What about my guns? My beautiful guns and my beautiful plan? I'll lose my immortal chance forever if I have to turn them over to Toranaga.

His hand was on the Murasama sword and he could feel the blood in his sword arm and the blinding urge to begin. He had discarded at once the possibility of not mentioning the muskets. If the news of the ship had been betrayed, certainly the identity of its cargo was equally betrayed. But how did Toranaga get the news so quickly? By carrier pigeon! That's the only answer. From Yedo or from here? Who possesses carrier pigeons here? Why haven't I such a service? That's Zukimoto's fault—he should have thought of it, *neh?*

Make up your mind. War or no war?

Yabu called down the ill will of Buddha, of all *kami,* of all gods that had ever been or were yet to be invented, upon the man or men who had betrayed him, upon their parents and upon their descendants for ten thousand generations. And he conceded.

"Lord Toranaga cannot confiscate the ship because it's already a gift to him. I've dictated a letter to that effect. Isn't that so, Zujimoto?"

"Yes, Sire."

"Of course, if Lord Toranaga wishes to consider it confiscated he may. But it was to be a gift." Yabu was pleased to hear that his voice sounded matter-of-fact. "He will be happy with the booty."

"Thank you on behalf of my Master." Hiro-matsu again marveled at Toranaga's foresight. Toranaga had predicted that this would happen and that there would be no fighting. 'I don't believe it,' Hiro-matsu had said. 'No *daimyo* would stand for such usurping of his rights. Yabu won't. I certainly wouldn't. Not even to you, Sire.'

'But you would have obeyed orders and you would have told me about the ship. Yabu must be manipulated, *neh?* I need his violence and cunning—he neutralizes Ikawa Jikkyu and guards my flank.'

Here on the beach under a good sun Hiro-matsu forced himself into a polite bow, hating his own duplicity. "Lord Toranaga will be delighted with your generosity."

Yabu was watching him closely. "It's not a Portuguese ship."

"Yes. So we heard."

"And it's pirate." He saw the general's eyes narrow.

"Eh?"

As he told him what the priest had said, Yabu thought, if that's news to you as it was to me, doesn't that mean that Toranaga had the same original information as I? But if you know the contents of the ship, then the spy is Omi, one of his samurai, or a villager. "There's an abundance of cloth. Some treasure. Muskets, powder, and shot."

Hiro-matsu hesitated. Then he said, "The cloth is Chinese silks?"

"No, Hiro-matsu-san," he said, using the "san." They were *daimyos* equally. But now that he was magnanimously "giving" the ship, he felt safe enough to use the less deferential term. He was pleased to see that the word had not gone unnoticed by the older man. I'm *daimyo* of Izu, by the sun, the moon, and the stars!

"It's very unusual, a thick heavy cloth, totally useless to us," he said. "I've had everything worth salvaging brought ashore."

"Good. Please put all of it aboard my ship."

"What?" Yabu's bowels almost burst.

"All of it. At once."

"Now?"

"Yes. So sorry, but you'll naturally understand that I want to return to Osaka as soon as possible."

"Yes but—but will there be space for everything?"

"Put the cannon back on the barbarian ship and seal it up. Boats will be arriving within three days to tow it to Yedo. As to the muskets, powder, and shot, there's—" Hiro-matsu stopped, avoiding the trap that he suddenly realized had been set for him.

'There's just enough space for the five hundred muskets,' Toranaga had told him. 'And all the powder and the twenty thousand silver doubloons aboard the galley. Leave the cannon on the deck of the ship and the cloth in the holds. Let Yabu do the talking and give him orders, don't let him have time to think. But don't get irritated or impatient with him. I need him, but I want those guns and that ship. Beware of his trying to trap you into revealing that you know the exactness of the cargo, because he must not uncover our spy.'

Hiro-matsu cursed his inability to play these necessary games. "As to the space needed," he said shortly, "perhaps you should tell me. And just exactly what is the cargo? How many muskets and shot and so forth? And is the bullion in bar or coins—is it silver or gold?"

"Zukimoto!"

"Yes, Yabu-sama."

"Get the list of the contents." I'll deal with you later, Yabu thought.

Zukimoto hurried away.

"You must be tired, Hiro-matsu-san. Perhaps some cha? Accommodations have been prepared for you, such as they are. The baths are totally inadequate, but perhaps one would refresh you a little."

"Thank you. You're very thoughtul. Some cha and a bath would be excellent. Later. First tell me everything that has happened since the ship arrived here."

Yabu told him the facts, omitting the part about the courtesan and the boy, which was unimportant. On Yabu's orders, Omi told his story, except for his private conversations with Yabu. And Mura told his, excluding the part about the Anjin's erection which, Mura reasoned, though interesting, might have offended Hiro-matsu, whose own, at his age, might be few and far between.

Hiro-matsu looked at the plume of smoke that still rose from the pyre. "How many of the pirates are left?"

"Ten, Sire, including the leader," Omi said.

"Where's the leader now?"

"In Mura's house."

"What did he do? What was the first thing he did there after getting out of the pit?"

"He went straight to the bath house, Sire," Mura said quickly. "Now he's asleep, Sire, like a dead man."

"You didn't have to carry him this time?"

"No, Sire."

"He seems to learn quickly." Hiro-matsu glanced back at Omi. "You think they can be taught to behave?"

"No. Not for certain, Hiro-matsu-sama."

"Could you clean away an enemy's urine from your back?"

"No, Lord."

"Nor could I. Never. Barbarians are very strange." Hiro-matsu turned his mind back to the ship. "Who will be supervising the loading?"

"My nephew, Omi-san."

"Good. Omi-san, I want to leave before dusk. My captain will help you be very quick. Within three sticks." The unit of time was the time it took for a standard stick of incense to smolder away, approximately one hour for one stick.

"Yes, Lord."

"Why not come with me to Osaka, Yabu-san?" Hiro-matsu said as though it was a sudden thought. "Lord Toranaga would be delighted to receive all these things from your hands. Personally. Please, there's room enough." When Yabu began to protest he allowed him to continue for a time, as Toranaga had ordered, and then he said, as Toranaga had ordered, "I insist. In Lord Toranaga's name, I insist. Your generosity needs to be rewarded."

With my head and my lands? Yabu asked himself bitterly, knowing that there was nothing he could do now but accept gratefully. "Thank you. I would be honored."

"Good. Well then, that's all done," Iron Fist said with obvious relief. "Now some cha. And a bath."

Yabu politely led the way up the hill to Omi's house. The old man was washed and scoured and then he lay gratefully in the steaming heat. Later Suwo's hands made him new again. A lttle rice and raw fish and pickled vegetables taken sparingly in private. Cha sipped from good porcelain. A short dreamless nap.

After three sticks the shoji slid open. The personal bodyguard knew better than to go into the room uninvited; Hiro-matsu was already awake and the sword half unsheathed and ready.

"Yabu-sama is waiting outside, Sire. He says the ship is loaded."

"Excellent."

Hiro-matsu went onto the veranda and relieved himself into the bucket. "Your men are very efficient, Yabu-san."

"Your men helped, Hiro-matsu-san. They are more than efficient."

Yes, and by the sun, they had better be, Hiro-matsu thought, then said genially, "Nothing like a good piss from a full bladder so long as there's plenty of power behind the stream. *Neh?* Makes you feel young again. At my age you need to feel young." He eased his loincloth comfortably, expecting Yabu to make some polite remark in agreement, but none was forthcoming. His irritation began to rise but he curbed it. "Have the pirate leader taken to my ship."

"What?"

"You were generous enough to make a gift of the ship and the contents. The crew are contents. So I'm taking the pirate leader to Osaka. Lord Toranaga wants to see him. Naturally you do what you like with the rest of them. But during your absence, please make certain that your retainers realize the barbarians are my Master's property and that there had better be nine in good health, alive, and here when he wants them."

Yabu hurried away to the jetty where Omi would be.

When, earlier, he had left Hiro-matsu to his bath, he had walked up the track that meandered past the funeral ground. There he had bowed briefly to the pyre and continued on, skirting the terraced fields of wheat and fruit to come out at length on a small plateau high above the village. A tidy *kami* shrine guarded this tender place. An ancient tree bequeathed shade and tranquillity. He had gone there to quell his rage and to think. He had not dared to go near the ship or Omi or his men for he knew that he would have ordered most, if not all of them, to commit seppuku, which would have been a waste, and he would have slaughtered the village, which would have been foolish—peasants alone caught the fish and grew the rice that provided the wealth of the samurai.

While he had sat and fumed alone and tried to sharpen his brain, the sun bent down and drove the sea mists away. The clouds that shrouded the distant mountains to the west had parted for an instant and he had seen the beauty of the snow-capped peaks soaring. The sight had settled him and he had begun to relax and think and plan.

Set your spies to find the spy, he told himself. Nothing that Hiro-matsu said indicated whether the betrayal was from here or from Yedo. In Osaka you've powerful friends, the Lord Ishido himself among them. Perhaps one of them can smell out the fiend. But send a private message at once to your wife in case the informer is there. What about Omi? Make him responsible for finding the informer here? Is he the informer? That's not likely, but not impossible. It's more than probable the betrayal began in Yedo. A matter of timing. If Toranaga in Osaka got the information about the ship when it arrived, then Hiro-matsu would have been here first. You've informers in Yedo. Let them prove their worth.

What about the barbarians? Now they're your only profit from the ship. How can you use them? Wait, didn't Omi give you the answer? You could use their knowledge of the sea and ships to barter with Toranaga for guns. *Neh?*

Another possibility: become Toranaga's *vassal* completely. Give him your plan. Ask him to allow you to lead the Regiment of the Guns—for *his* glory. But a *vassal should never expect his lord to reward his services or even acknowledge them: To serve is duty, duty is samurai, samurai is immortality.* That would be the best way, the very best, Yabu thought. Can I truly be his *vassal?* Or Ishido's?

No, that's unthinkable. Ally yes, vassal no.

Good, so the barbarians are an asset after all. Omi's right again.

He had felt more composed and then, when the time had come and a messenger had brought the information that the ship was loaded, he had gone to Hiro-matsu and discovered that now he had lost even the barbarians.

He was boiling when he reached the jetty.

"Omi-san!"

"Yes, Yabu-sama?"

"Bring the barbarian leader here. I'm taking him to Osaka. As to the others, see that they're well cared for while I'm away. I want them fit, and well behaved. Use the pit if you have to."

Ever since the galley had arrived, Omi's mind had been in a turmoil and he had been filled with anxiety for Yabu's safety. "Let me come with you, Lord. Perhaps I can help."

"No, now I want you to look after the barbarians."

"Please. Perhaps in some small way I can repay your kindness to me."

"There's no need," Yabu said, more kindly than he wanted to. He remembered that he had increased Omi's salary to three thousand koku and extended his fief because of the bullion and the guns. Which now had vanished. But he had seen the concern that filled the youth and had felt an involuntary warmth. With vassals like this, I will carve an empire, he promised himself. Omi will lead one of the units when I get back my guns. "When war comes—well, I'll have a very important job for you, Omi-san. Now go and get the barbarian."

Omi took four guards with him. And Mura to interpret.

*   *   *

Blackthorne was dragged out of sleep. It took him a minute to clear his head. When the fog lifted Omi was staring down at him.

One of the samurai had pulled the quilt off him, another had shaken him awake, the other two carried thin, vicious-looking bamboo canes. Mura had a short coil of rope.

Mura knelt and bowed. *"Konnichi wa"*—Good day.

"Konnichi wa." Blackthorne pulled himself onto his knees and, though he was naked, he bowed with equal politeness.

It's only a politeness, Blackthorne told himself. It's their custom and they bow for good manners so there's no shame to it. And nakedness is ignored and is also their custom, and there's no shame to nakedness either.

"Anjin. Please to dress," Mura said.

Anjin? Ah, I remember now. The priest said they can't pronounce my name so they've given me the name "Anjin" which means "pilot" and this is not meant as an insult. And I will be called "Anjin-san"—Mr. Pilot—when I merit it.

Don't look at Omi, he cautioned himself. Not yet. Don't remember the village square and Omi and Croocq and Pieterzoon. One thing at a time. That's what you're going to do. That's what you have sworn before God to do: One thing at a time. Vengeance will be mine, by the Lord God.

Blackthorne saw that his clothes had been cleaned again and he blessed whoever had done it. He had crawled out of his clothes in the bath house as though they had been plague-infested. Three times he had made them scour his back. With the roughest sponge and with pumice. But he could still feel the piss-burn.

He took his eyes off Mura and looked at Omi. He derived a twisted pleasure from the knowledge that his enemy was alive and nearby.

He bowed as he had seen equals bow and he held the bow. *"Konnichi wa, Omi-san,"* he said. There's no shame in speaking their language, no shame in saying "good day" or in bowing first as is their custom.

Omi bowed back.

Blackthorne noted that it was not quite equal, but it was enough for the moment.

"Konnichi wa, Anjin," Omi said.

The voice was polite, but not enough.

"Anjin-*san!*" Blackthorne looked directly at him.

Their wills locked and Omi was called as a man is called at cards or at dice. Do you have manners?

"Konnichi wa, Anjin-*san,"* Omi said at length, with a brief smile.

Blackthorne dressed quickly.

He wore loose trousers and a codpiece, socks and shirt and coat, his long hair tied into a neat queue and his beard trimmed with scissors the barber had loaned to him.

"Hai, Omi-san?" Blackthorne asked when he was dressed, feeling better but very guarded, wishing he had more words to use.

"Please, hand," Mura said.

Blackthorne did not understand and said so with signs. Mura held out his own hands and parodied tying them together.

"Hand, please."

"No." Blackthorne said it directly to Omi and shook his head. "That's not necessary," he said in English, "not necessary at all. I've given my word." He kept his voice gentle and reasonable, then added harshly, copying Omi, *"Wakarimasu ka,* Omi-san?" Do you understand?

Omi laughed. Then he said, *"Hai,* Anjin-san. *Wakarimasu."* He turned and left.

Mura and the others stared after him, astounded. Blackthorne followed Omi into the sun. His boots had been cleaned. Before he could slip them on, the maid "Onna" was there on her knees and she helped him.

"Thank you, Haku-san," he said, remembering her real name. What's the word for "thank you"? he wondered.

He walked through the gate, Omi ahead.

I'm after you, you God-cursed bas—Wait a minute! Remember what you promised yourself? And why swear at him, even to yourself? He hasn't sworn at you. Swearing's for the weak, or for fools. Isn't it?

One thing at a time. It is enough that you are after him. You know it clearly and he knows it clearly. Make no mistake, he knows it very clearly.

The four samurai flanked Blackthorne as he walked down the hill, the harbor still hidden from him, Mura discreetly ten paces back, Omi ahead.

Are they going to put me underground again? he wondered. Why did they want to bind my hands? Didn't Omi say yesterday—Christ Jesus, was that only yesterday?—'If you behave you can stay out of the pit. If you behave, tomorrow another man will be taken out of the pit. Perhaps. And more, perhaps.' Isn't that what he said? Have I behaved? I wonder how Croocq is. The lad was alive when they carried him off to the house where the crew first stayed.

Blackthorne felt better today. The bath and the sleep and the fresh food had begun to repair him. He knew that if he was careful and could rest and sleep and eat, within a month he would be able to run a mile and swim a mile and command a fighting ship and take her around the earth.

Don't think about that yet! Just guard your strength this day. A month's not much to hope for, eh?

The walk down the hill and through the village was tiring him. You're weaker than you thought. . . . No, you are stronger than you thought, he ordered himself.

The masts of *Erasmus* jutted over the tiled roofs and his heart quickened. Ahead the street curved with the contour of the hillside, slid down to the square and ended. A curtained palanquin stood in the sun. Four bearers in brief loincloths squatted beside it, absently picking their teeth. The moment they saw Omi they were on their knees, bowing mightily.

Omi barely nodded at them as he strode past, but then a girl came out of the neat gateway to go to the palanquin and he stopped.

Blackthorne caught his breath and stopped also.

A young maid ran out to hold a green parasol to shade the girl. Omi bowed and the girl bowed and they talked happily to each other, the strutting arrogance vanishing from Omi.

The girl wore a peach-colored kimono and a wide sash of gold and gold-thonged slippers. Blackthorne saw her glance at him. Clearly she and Omi were discussing him. He did not know how to react, or what to do, so he did nothing but wait patiently, glorying in the sight of her, the cleanliness and the warmth of her presence. He wondered if she and Omi were lovers, or if she was Omi's wife, and he thought, Is she truly real?

Omi asked her something and she answered and fluttered her green fan that shimmered and danced in the sunlight, her laugh musical, the delicacy of her exquisite. Omi was smiling too, then he turned on his heel and strode off, samurai once more.

Blackthorne followed. Her eyes were on him as he passed and he said, *"Konni-chi wa."*

"*Konnichi wa,* Anjin-san," she replied, her voice touching him. She was barely five feet tall and perfect. As she bowed slightly the breeze shook the outer silk and showed the beginnings of the scarlet under-kimono, which he found surprisingly erotic.

The girl's perfume still surrounded him as he turned the corner. He saw the trapdoor and *Erasmus.* And the galley. The girl vanished from his mind.

Why are our gun ports empty? Where are our cannon and what in the name of Christ is a slave galley doing here and what's happened in the pit?

One thing at a time.

First *Erasmus:* the stub of the foremast that the storm had carried away jutted nastily. That doesn't matter, he thought. We could get her out to sea easily. We could slip the moorings—the night airflow and the tide would take us out silently and we could careen tomorrow on the far side of that speck of island. Half a day to step the spare mast and then all sails ho and away into the far deep. Maybe it'd be better not to anchor but to flee to safer waters. But who'd crew? You can't take her out by yourself.

Where did that slaver come from? And why is it here?

He could see knots of samurai and sailors down at the wharf. The sixty-oared vessel—thirty oars a side—was neat and trim, the oars stacked with care, ready for instant departure, and he shivered involuntarily. The last time he'd seen a galley was off the Gold Coast two years ago when his fleet was outward bound, all five ships together. She had been a rich coastal trader, a Portuguese, and she was fleeing from him against the wind. *Erasmus* could not catch her, to capture her or sink her.

Blackthorne knew the North African coast well. He had been a pilot and ship's master for ten years for the London Company of Barbary Merchants, the joint stock company that fitted out fighting merchantmen to run the Spanish blockade and trade the Barbary Coast. He had piloted to West and North Africa, south as far as Lagos, north and eastward through the teacherous straits of Gibraltar —ever Spanish patrolled—as far as Salerno in the Kingdom of Naples. The Mediterranean was dangerous to English and Dutch shipping. Spanish and Portuguese enemy were there in strength and, worse, the Ottomans, the infidel Turks, swarmed the seas with slave galleys and with fighting ships.

These voyages had been very profitable for him and he had bought his own ship, a hundred-fifty-ton brig, to trade on his own behalf. But he had had her sunk under him and lost everything. They had been caught a-lee, windless off Sardinia, when the Turk galley had come out of the sun. The fight was cruel and then, toward sunset, the enemy ram caught their stern and they were boarded fast. He had never forgotten the screaming cry 'Allahhhhhhhh!' as the corsairs came over his gunwales. They were armed with swords and with muskets. He had rallied his men and the first attack had been beaten off, but the second overwhelmed them and he ordered the magazine fired. His ship was in flames and he decided that it was better to die than to be put to the oars. He had always had a mortal terror of being taken alive and made a galley slave—not an unusual fate for a captured seaman.

When the magazine blew, the explosion tore the bottom out of his ship and destroyed part of the corsair galley and, in the confusion, he managed to swim to the longboat and escape with four of the crew. Those who could not swim to him he had had to leave and he still remembered their cries for help in God's name. But God had turned His face from those men that day, so they had perished or gone to the oars. And God had kept His face on Blackthorne and the four men that time, and they had managed to reach Cagliari in Sardinia. And from there they had made it home, penniless.

That was eight years ago, the same year that plague had erupted again in London. Plague and famine and riots of the starving unemployed. His younger brother and family had been wiped out. His own first-born son had perished. But in the winter the plague vanished and he had easily got a new ship and gone to sea to repair his fortune. First for the London Company of Barbary Merchants. Then a voyage to the West Indies hunting Spaniards. After that, a little richer, he navigated for Kees Veerman, the Dutchman, on his second voyage to search for the legendary Northeast Passage to Cathay and the Spice Islands of Asia, that was supposed to exist in the Ice Seas, north of tsarist Russia. They searched for two years, then Kees Veerman died in the Arctic wastes with eighty percent of the crew and Blackthorne turned back and led the rest of the men home. Then, three years ago, he'd been approached by the newly formed Dutch East India Company and asked to pilot their first expedition to the New World. They whispered secretly that they had acquired, at huge cost, a contraband Portuguese rutter that supposedly gave away the secrets of Magellan's Strait, and they wanted to prove it. Of course the Dutch merchants would have preferred to use one of their own pilots, but there was none to compare in quality with Englishmen trained by the monopolistic Trinity House, and the awesome value of this rutter forced them to gamble on Blackthorne. But he was the perfect choice: He was the best Protestant pilot alive, his mother had been Dutch, and he spoke Dutch perfectly. Blackthorne had agreed enthusiastically and accepted the fifteen percent of all profit as his fee and, as was custom, had solemnly, before God, sworn allegiance to the Company and vowed to take their fleet out, and to bring it home again.

By God, I am going to bring *Erasmus* home, Blackthorne thought. And with as many of the men as He leaves alive.

They were crossing the square now and he took his eyes off the slaver and saw the three samurai guarding the trapdoor. They were eating deftly from bowls with the wooden sticks that Blackthorne had seen them use many times but could not manage himself.

"Omi-san!" With signs he explained that he wanted to go to the trapdoor, just to shout down to his friends. Only for a moment. But Omi shook his head and said something he did not understand and continued across the square, down the foreshore, past the cauldron, and on to the jetty. Blackthorne followed obediently. One thing at a time, he told himself. Be patient.

Once on the jetty, Omi turned and called back to the guards on the trapdoor. Blackthorne saw them open the trapdoor and peer down. One of them beckoned to villagers who fetched the ladder and a full fresh-water barrel and carried it below. The empty one they brought back aloft. And the latrine barrel.

There! If you're patient and play their game with their rules, you can help your crew, he thought with satisfaction.

Groups of samurai were collected near the galley. A tall old man was standing apart. From the deference that the *daimyo* Yabu showed him, and the way the others jumped at his slightest remark, Blackthorne immediately realized his importance. Is he their king? he wondered.

Omi knelt with humility. The old man half bowed, turned his eyes on him.

Mustering as much grace as he could, Blackthorne knelt and put his hands flat on the sand floor of the jetty, as Omi had done, and bowed as low as Omi.

"*Konnichi wa,* Sama," he said politely.

He saw the old man half bow again.

Now there was a discussion between Yabu and the old man and Omi. Yabu spoke to Mura.

Mura pointed at the galley. "Anjin-san. Please there."

"Why?"

"Go! Now. Go!"

Blackthorne felt his panic rising. "Why?"

"*Isogi!*" Omi commanded, waving him toward the galley.

"No, I'm not going to—"

There was an immediate order from Omi and four samurai fell on Blackthorne and pinioned his arms. Mura produced the rope and began to bind his hands behind him.

"You sons of bitches!" Blackthorne shouted. "I'm not going to go aboard that God-cursed slave ship!"

"Madonna! Leave him alone! Hey, you piss-eating monkeys, let that bastard alone! *Kinjiru, neh?* Is he the pilot? The Anjin, *ka?*"

Blackthorne could scarcely believe his ears. The boisterous abuse in Portuguese had come from the deck of the galley. Then he saw the man start down the gangway. As tall as he and about his age, but black-haired and dark-eyed and carelessly dressed in seaman's clothes, rapier by his side, pistols in his belt. A jeweled crucifix hung from his neck. He wore a jaunty cap and a smile split his face.

"Are you the pilot? The pilot of the Dutchman?"

"Yes," Blackthorne heard himself reply.

"Good. Good. I'm Vasco Rodrigues, pilot of this galley!" He turned to the old man and spoke a mixture of Japanese and Portuguese, and called him Monkey-sama and sometimes Toda-sama but the way it sounded it came out "Toady-sama." Twice he pulled out his pistol and pointed it emphatically at Blackthorne and stuck it back in his belt, his Japanese heavily laced with sweet vulgarities in gutter Portuguese that only seafarers would understand.

Hiro-matsu spoke briefly and the samurai released Blackthorne and Mura untied him.

"That's better. Listen, Pilot, this man's like a king. I told him I'd be responsible for you, that I'd blow your head off as soon as drink with you!" Rodrigues bowed to Hiro-matsu, then beamed at Blackthorne. "Bow to the Bastard-sama."

Dreamlike, Blackthorne did as he was told.

"You do that like a Japper," Rodrigues said with a grin. "You're really the pilot?"

"Yes."

"What's the latitude of The Lizard?"

"Forty-nine degrees fifty-six minutes North—and watch out for the reefs that bear sou' by sou'west."

"You're the pilot, by God!" Rodrigues shook Blackthorne's hand warmly. "Come aboard. There's food and brandy and wine and grog and all pilots should love all pilots, who're the sperm of the earth. Amen! Right?"

"Yes," Blackthorne said weakly.

"When I heard we were carrying a pilot back with us, good says I. It's years since I had the pleasure of talking to a real pilot. Come aboard. How did you sneak past Malacca? How did you avoid our Indian Ocean patrols, eh? Whose rutter did you steal?"

"Where are you taking me?"

"Osaka. The Great Lord High Executioner himself wants to see you."

Blackthorne felt his panic returning. "Who?"

"Toranaga! Lord of the Eight Provinces, wherever the hell they are! The chief *daimyo* of Japan—a *daimyo*'s like a king or feudal lord but better. They're all despots."

"What's he want with me?"

"I don't know but that's why we're here, and if Toranaga wants to see you, Pilot, he'll see you. They say he's got a million of these slant-eyed fanatics who'll die for the honor of wiping his arse if that's his pleasure! 'Toranaga wants you to bring back the pilot, Vasco,' his interpreter said. 'Bring back the pilot and the ship's cargo. Take old Toda Hiro-matsu there to examine the ship and—' Oh yes, Pilot, it's all confiscated, so I hear, your ship, and everything in it!"

"Confiscated?"

"It may be a rumor. Jappers sometimes confiscate things with one hand, give 'em back with the other—or pretend they've never given the order. It's hard to understand the poxy little bastards!"

Blackthorne felt the cold eyes of the Japanese boring into him and he tried to hide his fear. Rodrigues followed his glance. "Yes, they're getting restless. Time enough to talk. Come aboard." He turned but Blackthorne stopped him.

"What about my friends, my crew?"

"Eh?"

Blackthorne told him briefly about the pit. Rodrigues questioned Omi in pidgin Japanese. "He says they'll be all right. Listen, there's nothing you or me can do now. You'll have to wait—you can never tell with a Jappo. They're six-faced and three-hearted." Rodrigues bowed like a European courtier to Hiro-matsu. "This is the way we do it in Japan. Like we're at the court of Fornicating Philip II, God take that Spaniard to an early grave." He led the way on deck. To Blackthorne's astonishment there were no chains and no slaves.

"What's the matter? You sick?" Rodrigues asked.

"No. I thought this was a slaver."

"They don't have 'em in Japan. Not even in their mines. Lunatic, but there you are. You've never seen such lunatics and I've traveled the world three times. We've samurai rowers. They're soldiers, the old bugger's personal soldiers—and you've never seen slaves row better, or men fight better." Rodrigues laughed. "They put their arses into the oars and I push 'em just to watch the buggers bleed. They never quit. We came all the way from Osaka—three-hundred-odd sea miles in forty hours. Come below. We'll cast off shortly. You sure you're all right?"

"Yes. Yes, I think so." Blackthorne was looking at *Erasmus.* She was moored a hundred yards away. "Pilot, there's no chance of going aboard, is there? They haven't let me back aboard, I've no clothes and they sealed her up the moment we arrived. Please?"

Rodrigues scrutinized the ship.

"When did you lose the foremast?"

"Just before we made landfall here."

"There a spare still aboard?"

"Yes."

"Where's her home port?"

"Rotterdam."

"She was built there?"

"Yes."

"I've been there. Bad shoals but a pisscutter of a harbor. She's got good lines, your ship. New—haven't seen one of her class before. Madonna, she'd be fast, very fast. Very rough to deal with." Rodrigues looked at him. "Can you get your gear quickly?" He turned over the half-hour glass sand timer that was beside the hourglass, both attached to the binnacle.

"Yes." Blackthorne tried to keep his growing hope off his face.

"There'd be a condition, Pilot. No weapons, up your sleeve or anywhere. Your word as a pilot. I've told the monkeys I'd be responsible for you."

"I agree." Blackthorne watched the sand falling silently through the neck of the timer.

"I'll blow your head off, pilot or no, if there's the merest whiff of trickery, or cut your throat. *If* I agree."

"I give you my word, pilot to pilot, by God. And the pox on the Spanish!"

Rodrigues smiled and banged him warmly on the back. "I'm beginning to like you, Ingeles."

"How'd you know I'm English?" Blackthorne asked, knowing his Portuguese was perfect and that nothing he had said could have differentiated him from a Dutchman.

"I'm a soothsayer. Aren't all pilots?" Rodrigues laughed.

"You talked to the priest? Father Sebastio told you?"

"I don't talk to priests if I can help it. Once a week's more than enough for any man." Rodrigues spat deftly into the scuppers and went to the port gangway that overlooked the jetty. "Toady-sama! *Ikimasho ka?*"

"*Ikimasho,* Rodrigu-san. *Ima!*"

"*Ima* it is." Rodrigues looked at Blackthorne thoughtfully. " '*Ima*' means 'now,' 'at once.' We're to leave at once, Ingeles."

The sand had already made a small, neat mound in the bottom of the glass.

"Will you ask him, please? If I can go aboard my ship?"

"No, Ingeles. I won't ask him a poxy thing."

Blackthorne suddenly felt empty. And very old. He watched Rodrigues go to the railing of the quarterdeck and bellow to a small, distinguished seaman who stood on the raised fore-poop deck at the bow. "Hey, Captain-san. *Ikimasho?* Get samurai aboard-u, *ima! Ima, wakarimasu ka?*"

"*Hai,* Anjin-san."

Immediately Rodrigues rang the ship's bell loudly six times and the Captain-san began shouting orders to the seamen and samurai ashore and aboard. Seamen hurried up on deck from below to prepare for departure and, in the disciplined, controlled confusion, Rodrigues quietly took Blackthorne's arm and shoved him toward the starboard gangway, away from the shore.

"There's a dinghy below, Ingeles. Don't move fast, don't look around, and don't pay attention to anyone but me. If I tell you to come back, do it quickly."

Blackthorne walked across the deck, down the gangway, toward the small Japanese skiff. He heard angry voices behind him and he felt the hairs on his neck rising for there were many samurai all over the ship, some armed with bows and arrows, a few with muskets.

"You don't have to worry about him, Captain-san, I'm responsible. Me, Rodrigu-san, *ichi ban* Anjin-san, by the Virgin! *Wakarimasu ka?*" was dominating the other voices, but they were getting angrier every moment.

Blackthorne was almost in the dinghy now and he saw that there were no rowlocks. I can't scull like they do, he told himself. I can't use the boat! It's too far to swim. Or is it?

He hesitated, checking the distance. If he had had his full strength he would not have waited a moment. But now?

Feet clattered down the gangway behind him and he fought the impulse to turn.

"Sit in the stern," he heard Rodrigues say urgently. "Hurry up!"

He did as he was told and Rodrigues jumped in nimbly, grabbed the oars and, still standing, shoved off with great skill.

A samurai was at the head of the gangway, very perturbed, and two other samurai were beside him, bows ready. The captain samurai called out, unmistakably beckoning them to come back.

A few yards from the vessel Rodrigues turned. "Just go there," he shouted up at him, pointing at *Erasmus*. "Get samurai aboard!" He set his back firmly to his ship and continued sculling, pushing against the oars in Japanese fashion, standing amidships. "Tell me if they put arrows in their bows, Ingeles! Watch 'em carefully! What're they doing now?"

"The captain's very angry. You won't get into trouble, will you?"

"If we don't sail at the turn, Old Toady might have cause for complaint. What're those bowmen doing?"

"Nothing. They're listening to him. He seens undecided. No. Now one of them's drawing out an arrow."

Rodrigues prepared to stop. "Madonna, they're too God-cursed accurate to risk anything. Is it in the bow yet?"

"Yes—but wait a moment! The captain's—someone's come up to him, a seaman I think. Looks like he's asking him something about the ship. The captain's looking at us. He said something to the man with the arrow. Now the man's putting it away. The seaman's pointing at something on deck."

Rodrigues sneaked a quick look to make sure and breathed easier. "That's one of the mates. It'll take him all of the half hour to get his oarsmen settled."

Blackthorne waited, the distance increased. "The captain's looking at us again. No, we're all right. He's gone away. But one of the samurai's watching us."

"Let him." Rodrigues relaxed but he did not slacken the pace of his sculling or look back. "Don't like my back to samurai, not when they've weapons in their hands. Not that I've ever seen one of the bastards unarmed. They're all bastards!"

"Why?"

"They love to kill, Ingeles. It's their custom even to sleep with their swords. This is a great country, but samurai're dangerous as vipers and a sight more mean."

"Why?"

"I don't know why, Ingeles, but they are," Rodrigues replied, glad to talk to one of his own kind. "Of course, all Jappos are different from us—they don't feel pain or cold like us—but samurai are even worse. They fear nothing, least of all death. Why? Only God knows, but it's the truth. If their superiors say 'kill,' they kill, 'die' and they'll fall on their swords or slit their own bellies open. They kill and die as easily as we piss. Women're samurai too, Ingeles. They'll kill to protect their masters, that's what they call their husbands here, or they'll kill themselves if they're ordered to. They do it by slitting their throats. Here a samurai can order his wife to kill herself and that's what she's got to do, by law. Jesu Madonna, the women are something else though, a different species, Ingeles, nothing on earth like them, but the men. . . . Samurai're reptiles and the safest thing to do is treat them like poisonous snakes. You all right now?"

"Yes, thank you. A bit weak but all right."

"How was your voyage?"

"Rough. About them—the samurai—how do they get to be one? Do they just pick up the two swords and get that haircut?"

"You've got to be born one. Of course, there are all ranks of samurai from *daimyos* at the top of the muckheap to what we'd call a foot soldier at the bottom. It's hereditary mostly, like with us. In the olden days, so I was told, it was the same as in Europe today—peasants could be soldiers and soldiers peasants, with hereditary knights and nobles up to kings. Some peasant soldiers rose to the highest rank. The Taikō was one."

"Who's he?"

"The Great Despot, the ruler of all Japan, the Great Murderer of all times—I'll tell you about him one day. He died a year ago and now he's burning in hell."

Rodrigues spat overboard. "Nowadays you've got to be born samurai to be one. It's all hereditary, Ingeles. Madonna, you've no idea how much store they put on heritage, on family, rank, and the like—you saw how Omi bows to that devil Yabu and they both grovel to old Toady-sama. 'Samurai' comes from a Jappo word meaning 'to serve.' But while they'll all bow and scrape to the man above, they're all samurai equally, with a samurai's special privileges. What's happening aboard?"

"The captain's jabbering away at another samurai and pointing at us. What's special about them?"

"Here samurai rule everything, own everything. They've their own code of honor and sets of rules. Arrogant? Madonna, you've no idea! The lowest of them can legally kill any non-samurai, *any* man, woman, or child, for any reason or for no reason. They can kill, legally, just to test the edge of their piss-cutting swords—I've seen 'em do it—and they have the best swords in the world. Better'n Damascus steel. What's that fornicator doing now?"

"Just watching us. His bow's on his back now." Blackthorne shuddered. "I hate those bastards more than Spaniards."

Again Rodrigues laughed as he sculled. "If the truth's known, they curdle my piss too! But if you want to get rich quick you've got to work with them because they own everything. You sure you're all right?"

"Yes. Thanks. You were saying? Samurai own everything?"

"Yes. Whole country's split up into castes, like in India. Samurai at the top, peasants next important." Rodrigues spat overboard. "Only peasants can *own* land. Understand? But samurai own all the produce. They own all the rice and that's the only important crop, and they give back part to the peasants. Only samurai're allowed to carry arms. For anyone except a samurai to attack a samurai is rebellion, punishable by instant death. And anyone who sees such an attack and doesn't report it at once is equally liable, and so are their wives, and even their kids. The whole family's put to death if one doesn't report it. By the Madonna, they're Satan's whelps, samurai! I've seen kids chopped into mince-meat." Rodrigues hawked and spat. "Even so, if you know a thing or two this place is heaven on earth." He glanced back at the galley to reassure himself, then he grinned. "Well, Ingeles, nothing like a boat ride around the harbor, eh?"

Blackthorne laughed. The years dropped off him as he reveled in the familiar dip of the waves, the smell of the sea salt, gulls calling and playing overhead, the sense of freedom, the sense of arriving after so very long. "I thought you weren't going to help me get to *Erasmus!*"

"That's the trouble with all Ingeles. No patience. Listen, here you don't *ask* Japmen anything—samurai or others, they're all the same. If you do, they'll hesitate, than ask the man above for the decision. Here you have to *act*. Of course"—his hearty laugh ran across the waves—"sometimes you get killed if you act wrong."

"You scull very well. I was wondering how to use the oars when you came."

"You don't think I'd let you go alone, do you? What's your name?"

"Blackthorne. John Blackthorne."

"Have you ever been north, Ingeles? Into the far north?"

"I was with Kees Veerman in *Der Lifle*. Eight years ago. It was his second voyage to find the Northeast Passage. Why?"

"I'd like to hear about that—and all the places you've been. Do you think they'll ever find the way? The northern way to Asia, east or west?"

"Yes. You and the Spanish block both southern routes, so we'll have to. Yes, we will. Or the Dutch. Why?"

"And you've piloted the Barbary Coast, eh?"

"Yes. Why?"

"And you know Tripoli?"

"Most pilots have been there. Why?"

"I thought I'd seen you once. Yes, it was Tripoli. You were pointed out to me. The famous Ingeles pilot. Who went with the Dutch explorer, Kees Veerman, into the Ice Seas—and was once a captain with Drake, eh? At the Armada? How old were you then?"

"Twenty-four. What were you doing in Tripoli?"

"I was piloting an Ingeles privateer. My ship'd got taken in the Indies by this pirate, Morrow—Henry Morrow was his name. He burned my ship to the waterline after he'd sacked her and offered me the pilot's job—his man was useless, so he said—you know how it is. He wanted to go from there—we were watering off Hispaniola when he caught us—south along the Main, then back across the Atlantic to try to intercept the annual Spanish gold ship near the Canaries, then on through the Straits to Tripoli if we missed her to try for other prizes, then north again to England. He made the usual offer to free my comrades, give them food and boats in return if I joined them. I said, 'Sure, why not? Providing we don't take any Portuguese shipping and you put me ashore near Lisbon and don't steal my rutters.' We argued back and forth as usual—you know how it is. Then I swore by the Madonna and we both swore on the Cross and that was that. We had a good voyage and some fat Spanish merchantmen fell into our wake. When we were off Lisbon he asked me to stay aboard, gave me the usual message from Good Queen Bess, how she'd pay a princely bounty to any Portuguese pilot who'd join her and teach others the skill at Trinity House, and give five thousand guineas for the rutter of Magellan's Pass, or the Cape of Good Hope." His smile was broad, his teeth white and strong, and his dark mustache and beard well groomed. "I didn't have them. At least that's what I told him. Morrow kept his word, like all pirates should. He put me ashore with my rutters—of course he'd had them copied though he himself couldn't read or write, and he even gave me my share of the prize money. You ever sail with him, Ingeles?"

"No. The Queen knighted him a few years ago. I've never served on one of his ships. I'm glad he was fair with you."

They were nearing *Erasmus*. Samurai were peering down at them quizzically.

"That was the second time I'd piloted for heretics. The first time I wasn't so lucky."

"Oh?"

Rodrigues shipped his oars and the boat swerved neatly to the side and he hung onto the boarding ropes. "Go aloft but leave the talking to me."

Blackthorne began to climb while the other pilot tied the boat safely. Rodrigues was the first on deck. He bowed like a courtier. "*Konnichi wa* to all sod-eating samas!"

There were four samurai on deck. Blackthorne recognized one of them as a guard of the trapdoor. Nonplussed, they bowed stiffly to the Portuguese. Blackthorne aped him, feeling awkward, and would have preferred to bow correctly.

Rodrigues walked straight for the companionway. The seals were neatly in place. One of the samurai intercepted him.

"*Kinjiru, gomen nasai.*" It's forbidden, so sorry.

"*Kinjiru,* eh?" the Portuguese said, openly unimpressed. "I'm Rodrigu-san, anjin for Toda Hiro-matsu-sama. This seal," he said, pointing to the red stamp with the odd writing on it, "Toda Hiro-matsu-sama, *ka?*"

"*Iyé,*" the samurai said, shaking his head. "Kasigi Yabu-sama!"

"*IYÉ?*" Rodrigues said. "Kasigi Yabu-sama? I'm from Toda Hiro-matsu-sama, who's a bigger king than your bugger and Toady-sama's from Toranaga-sama, who's the biggest bugger-sama in this whole world. *Neh?*" He ripped the seal off the door, dropped a hand to one of his pistols. The swords were half out of their scabbards and he said quietly to Blackthorne, "Get ready to abandon ship," and to the samurai he said gruffly, "Toranaga-sama!" He pointed with his left hand at the flag which fluttered at his own masthead. *"Wakarimasu ka?"*

The samurai hesitated, their swords ready. Blackthorne prepared to dive over the side.

"Toranaga-sama!" Rodrigues crashed his foot against the door, the latch snapped and the door burst open. *"WAKARIMASU KA?"*

"Wakarimasu, Anjin-san." The samurai quickly put their swords away and bowed and apologized and bowed again and Rodrigues said hoarsely, "That's better," and led the way below.

"Christ Jesus, Rodrigues," Blackthorne said when they were on the lower deck. "Do you do this all the time and get away with it?"

"I do it very seldom," the Portuguese said, wiping the sweat from his brow, "and even then I wish I'd never started it."

Blackthorne leaned against the bulkhead. "I feel as if someone's kicked me in the stomach."

"It's the only way. You've got to act like a king. Even so, you can never tell with a samurai. They're as dangerous as a pissed priest with a candle in his arse sitting on a half-full powder keg."

"What did you say to them?"

"Toda Hiro-matsu is Toranaga's chief adviser—he's a bigger *daimyo* than this local one. That's why they gave in."

"What's he like, Toranaga?"

"Long story, Ingeles." Rodrigues sat on the step, pulled his boot off, and rubbed his ankle. "I nearly broke my foot on your lice-eaten door."

"It wasn't locked. You could have just opened it."

"I know. But that wouldn't have been as effective. By the Blessed Virgin, you've got a lot to learn!"

"Will you teach me?"

Rodrigues pulled his boot back on. "That depends," he said.

"On what?"

"We'll have to see, won't we? I've done all the talking so far, which is fair—I'm fit, you're not. Soon it'll be your turn. Which is your cabin?"

Blackthorne studied him for a moment. The smell below decks was stiff and weathered. "Thanks for helping me come aboard."

He led the way aft. His door was unlocked. The cabin had been ransacked and everything removable had been taken. There were no books or clothes or instruments or quills. His sea chest too was unlocked. And empty.

White with rage, he walked into the Great Cabin, Rodrigues watching intently. Even the secret compartment had been found and looted.

"They've taken everything. The sons of plague-infested lice!"

"What did you expect?"

"I don't know. I thought—with the seals—" Blackthorne went to the strong room. It was bare. So was the magazine. The holds contained only the bales of woolen cloth. "God curse all Jappers!" He went back to his cabin and slammed his sea chest closed.

"Where are they?" Rodrigues asked.

"What?"

"Your rutters. Where are your rutters?"

Blackthorne looked at him sharply.

"No pilot'd worry about clothes. You came for the rutters. Didn't you?"

"Yes."

"Why're you so surprised, Ingeles? Why do you think I came aboard? To help you get more rags? They're threadbare as it is and you'll need others. I've plenty for you. But where are the rutters?"

"They've gone. They were in my sea chest."

"I'm not going to steal them, Ingeles. I just want to read them. And copy them, if need be. I'll cherish them like my own, so you've no need to worry." His voice hardened. "Please get them, Ingeles, we've little time left."

"I can't. They've gone. They were in my sea chest."

"You wouldn't have left them there—not coming into a foreign port. You wouldn't forget a pilot's first rule—to hide them carefully, and leave only false ones unprotected. Hurry up!"

"They're stolen!"

"I don't believe you. But I'll admit you've hidden them very well. I searched for two hours and didn't get a fornicating whiff."

"What?"

"Why are you so surprised, Ingeles? Is your head up your arse? Naturally I came here from Osaka to investigate your rutters!"

"You've already been aboard?"

"Madonna!" Rodrigues said impatiently. "Yes, of course, two or three hours ago with Hiro-matsu, who wanted to look around. He broke the seals and then, when we left, this local *daimyo* sealed her up again. Hurry up, by God," he added. "The sand's running out."

"*They're stolen!*" Blackthorne told him how they had arrived and how he had awakened ashore. Then he kicked his sea chest across the room, infuriated at the men who had looted his ship. "They're stolen! All my charts! All my rutters! I've copies of some in England, but my rutter of this voyage's gone and the—" He stopped.

"And the Portuguese rutter? Come on, Ingeles, it had to be Portuguese."

"Yes, and the Portuguese one, it's gone too." Get hold of yourself, he thought. They're gone and that's the end. Who has them? The Japanese? Or did they give them to the priest? Without the rutters and the charts you can't pilot your way home. You'll never get home. . . . That's not true. You can pilot your way home, with care, and enormous luck. . . . Don't be ridiculous! You're half-way around the earth, in enemy land, in enemy hands, and you've neither rutter nor charts. "Oh, Lord Jesus, give me strength!"

Rodrigues was watching him intently. At length he said, "I'm sorry for you, Ingeles. I know how you feel—it happened to me once. He was an Ingeles too, the thief, may his ship drown and he burn in hell forever. Come on, let's go back aboard."

Omi and the others waited on the jetty until the galley rounded the headland and vanished. To the west layers of night already etched the crimson sky. To the east, night joined the sky and the sea together, horizonless.

"Mura, how long will it take to get all the cannon back on the ship?"

"If we work through the night, by midday tomorrow, Omi-san. If we begin at dawn, we'll be finished well before sunset. It would be safer to work during the day."

"Work through the night. Bring the priest to the pit at once."

Omi glanced at Igurashi, Yabu's chief lieutenant, who was still looking out toward the headland, his face stretched, the livid scar tissue over his empty eye socket eerily shadowed. "You'd be welcome to stay, Igurashi-san. My house is poor but perhaps we could make you comfortable."

"Thank you," the older man said, turning back to him, "but our Master said to return to Yedo at once, so I will return at once." More of his concern showed. "I wish I was on that galley."

"Yes."

"I hate the thought of Yabu-sama being aboard with only two men. I hate it."

"Yes."

He pointed at *Erasmus*. "A devil ship, that's what it is! So much wealth, then nothing."

"Surely everything? Won't Lord Toranaga be pleased, enormously pleased with Lord Yabu's gift?"

"That money-infected province grabber is so filled with his own importance, he won't even notice the amount of silver he'll have stolen from our Master. Where are your brains?"

"I presume only your anxiety over the possible danger to our Lord prompted you to make such a remark."

"You're right, Omi-san. No insult was intended. You've been very clever and helpful to our Master. Perhaps you're right about Toranaga too," Igurashi said, but he was thinking, Enjoy your newfound wealth, you poor fool. I know my Master better than you, and your increased fief will do you no good at all. Your advancement would have been a fair return for the ship, the bullion, and the arms. But now they've vanished. And because of you, my Master's in jeopardy. You sent the message and you said, 'See the barbarians first,' tempting him. We should have left yesterday. Yes, then my Master would have been safely away by now, with the money and arms. Are you a traitor? Are you acting for yourself, or your stupid father, or for an enemy? For Toranaga, perhaps? It doesn't matter. You can believe me, Omi, you dung-eating young fool, you and your branch of the Kasigi clan are not long for this earth. I'd tell you to your face but then I'd have to kill you and I would have spurned my Master's trust. He's the one to say when, not me.

"Thank you for your hospitality, Omi-san," he said. "I'll look forward to seeing you soon, but I'll be on my way now."

"Would you do something for me, please? Give my respects to my father. I'd appreciate it very much."

"I'd be happy to. He's a fine man. And I haven't congratulated you yet on your new fief."

"You're too kind."

"Thank you again, Omi-san." He raised his hand in friendly salutation, motioned to his men, and led the phalanx of horsemen out of the village.

Omi went to the pit. The priest was there. Omi could see the man was angry and he hoped that he would do something overt, publicly, so he could have him thrashed.

"Priest, tell the barbarians they are to come up, one by one. Tell them Lord Yabu has said they may live again in the world of men." Omi kept his language deliberately simple. "But the smallest breaking of a rule, and two will be put back into the pit. They are to behave and obey all orders. Is that clear?"

"Yes."

Omi made the priest repeat it to him as before. When he was sure the man had it all correctly, he made him speak it down into the pit.

The men came up, one by one. All were afraid. Some had to be helped. One man was in great pain and screamed every time someone touched his arm.

"There should be nine."

"One is dead. His body is down there, in the pit," the priest said.

Omi thought for a moment. "Mura, burn the corpse and keep the ashes with those of the other barbarian. Put these men in the same house as before. Give them plenty of vegetables and fish. And barley soup and fruit. Have them washed. They stink. Priest, tell them that if they behave and obey, the food will continue."

Omi watched and listened carefully. He saw them all react gratefully and he thought with contempt, how stupid! I deprive them for only two days, then give them back a pittance and now they'll eat dung, they really will. "Mura, make them bow properly and take them away."

Then he turned to the priest. "Well?"

"I go now. Go my home. Leave Anjiro."

"Better you leave and stay away forever, you and every priest like you. Perhaps the next time one of you comes into *my* fief it is because some of *my* Christian peasants or vassals are considering treason," he said, using the veiled threat and classic ploy that anti-Christian samurai used to control the indiscriminate spread of the foreign dogma in their fiefs, for though foreign priests were protected, their Japanese converts were not.

"Christians good Japanese. Always. Only good vassals. Never had bad thoughts. No."

"I'm glad to hear it. Don't forget my fief stretches twenty *ri* in every direction. Do you understand?"

"I understand. Yes. I understand very well."

He watched the man bow stiffly—even barbarian priests had to have manners—and walk away.

"Omi-san?" one of his samurai said. He was young and very handsome.

"Yes?"

"Please excuse me, I know you haven't forgotten but Masijiro-san is still in the pit." Omi went to the trapdoor and stared down at the samurai. Instantly the man was on his knees, bowing deferentially.

The two days had aged him. Omi weighed his past service and his future worth. Then he took the young samurai's dagger from his sash and dropped it into the pit.

At the bottom of the ladder Masijiro stared at the knife in disbelief. Tears began coursing his cheeks. "I don't deserve this honor, Omi-san," he said abjectly.

"Yes."

"Thank you."

The young samurai beside Omi said, "May I please ask that he be allowed to commit seppuku here, on the beach?"

"He failed in the pit. He stays in the pit. Order the villagers to fill it in. Obliterate all traces of it. The barbarians have defiled it."

Kiku laughed and shook her head. "No, Omi-san, so sorry, please no more saké for me or my hair will fall down, I'll fall down, and then where would we be?"

"I'd fall down with you and we'd pillow and be in nirvana, outside ourselves," Omi said happily, his head swimming from the wine.

"Ah, but I'd be snoring and you can't pillow a snoring, horrid drunken girl and get much pleasure. Certainly not, so sorry. Oh no, Omi-sama of the Huge New Fief, you deserve better than that!" She poured another thimble of the warm wine into the tiny porcelain cup and offered it with both hands, her left forefinger and thumb delicately holding the cup, the forefinger of her right hand touching the underside. "Here, because you are wonderful!"

He accepted it and sipped, enjoying its warmth and mellow tang. "I'm so glad

I was able to persuade you to stay an extra day, *neh?* You are so beautiful, Kiku-san."

"You are beautiful, and it is my pleasure." Her eyes were dancing in the light of a candle encased in a paper and bamboo flower that hung from the cedar rafter. This was the best suite of rooms in the Tea House near the Square. She leaned over to help him to some more rice from the simple wooden bowl that was on the low black lacquered table in front of him, but he shook his head.

"No, no, thank you."

"You should eat more, a strong man like you."

"I'm full, really."

He did not offer her any because she had barely touched her small salad— thinly sliced cucumbers and tiny sculptured radishes pickled in sweet vinegar— which was all she would accept of the whole meal. There had been slivers of raw fish on balls of tacky rice, soup, the salad, and some fresh vegetables served with a piquant sauce of soya and ginger. And rice.

She clapped her hands softly and the shoji was opened instantly by her personal maid.

"Yes, Mistress?"

"Suisen, take all these things away and bring more saké and a fresh pot of cha. And fruit. The saké should be warmer than last time. Hurry up, good-for-nothing!" She tried to sound imperious.

Suisen was fourteen, sweet, anxious to please, and an apprentice courtesan. She had been with Kiku for two years and Kiku was responsible for her training.

With an effort, Kiku took her eyes off the pure white rice that she would have loved to have eaten and dismissed her own hunger. You ate before you arrived and you will eat later, she reminded herself. Yes, but even then it was so little. 'Ah, but ladies have tiny appetites, very tiny appetites,' her teacher used to say. 'Guests eat and drink—the more the better. Ladies don't, and certainly never with guests. How can ladies talk or entertain or play the samisen or dance if they're stuffing their mouths? You will eat later, be patient. Concentrate on your guest.'

While she watched Suisen critically, gauging her skill, she told Omi stories to make him laugh and forget the world outside. The young girl knelt beside Omi, tidied the small bowls and chopsticks on the lacquer tray into a pleasing pattern as she had been taught. Then she picked up the empty saké flask, poured to make sure it was empty—it would have been very bad manners to have shaken the flask—then got up with the tray, noiselessly carried it to the shoji door, knelt, put the tray down, opened the shoji, got up, stepped through the door, knelt again, lifted the tray out, put it down again as noiselessly, and closed the door completely.

"I'll really have to get another maid," Kiku said, not displeased. That color suits her, she was thinking. I must send to Yedo for some more of that silk. What a shame it's so expensive! Never mind, with all the money Gyoko-san was given for last night and tonight, there will be more than enough from my share to buy little Suisen twenty kimonos. She's such a sweet child, and really very graceful. "She makes so much noise—it disturbs the whole room—so sorry."

"I didn't notice her. Only you," Omi said, finishing his wine.

Kiku fluttered her fan, her smile lighting her face. "You make me feel very good, Omi-san. Yes. And beloved."

Suisen brought the saké quickly. And the cha. Her mistress poured Omi some wine and gave it to him. The young girl unobtrusively filled the cups. She did not spill a drop and she thought the sound that the liquid made going into the cup had the right quiet kind of ring to it, so she sighed inwardly with vast relief, sat back on her heels, and waited.

Kiku was telling an amusing story that she had heard from one of her friends in Mishima and Omi was laughing. As she did so, she took one of the small oranges and, using her long fingernails, opened it as though it were a flower, the sections of the fruit the petals, the divisions of the skin its leaves. She removed a fleck of pith and offered it with both hands as if this were the usual way a lady would serve the fruit to her guest.

"Would you like an orange, Omi-san?"

Omi's first reaction was to say, I can't destroy such beauty. But that would be inept, he thought, dazzled by her artistry. How can I compliment her, and her unnamed teacher? How can I return the happiness that she has given me, letting me watch her fingers create something so precious yet so ephemeral?

He held the flower in his hands for a moment then nimbly removed four sections, equidistant from each other, and ate them with enjoyment. This left a new flower. He removed four more sections, creating a third floral design. Next he took one section, and moved a second so that the remaining three made still another blossom.

Then he took two sections and replaced the last in the orange cradle, in the center on its side, as though a crescent moon within a sun.

He ate one very slowly. When he had finished, he put the other in the center of his hand and offered it. "This you must have because it is the second to last. This is my gift to you."

Suisen could hardly breathe. What was the last one for?

Kiku took the fruit and ate it. It was the best she had ever tasted.

"This, the last one," Omi said, putting the whole flower gravely into the palm of his right hand, "this is my gift to the gods, whoever they are, wherever they are. I will never eat this fruit again, unless it is from your hands."

"That is too much, Omi-sama," Kiku said. "I release you from your vow! That was said under the influence of the *kami* who lives in all saké bottles!"

"I refuse to be released."

They were very happy together.

"Suisen," she said. "Now leave us. And please, child, please try to do it with grace."

"Yes, Mistress." The young girl went into the next room and checked that the futons were meticulous, the love instruments and pleasure beads near at hand, and the flowers perfect. An imperceptible crease was smoothed from the already smooth cover. Then, satisfied, Suisen sat down, sighed with relief, fanned the heat out of her face with her lilac fan, and contentedly waited.

In the next room, which was the finest of all the rooms in the tea house, the only one with a garden of its own, Kiku picked up the long-handled samisen. It was three-stringed, guitarlike, and Kiku's first soaring chord filled the room. Then she began to sing. At first soft, then trilling, soft again then louder, softer and sighing sweetly, ever sweetly, she sang of love and unrequited love and happiness and sadness.

"Mistress?" The whisper would not have awakened the lightest sleeper but Suisen knew that her mistress preferred not to sleep after the Clouds and the Rain, however strong. She preferred to rest, half awake, in tranquillity.

"Yes, Sui-chan?" Kiku whispered as quietly, using "chan" as one would to a favorite child.

"Omi-san's wife has returned. Her palanquin has just gone up the path to his house."

Kiku glanced at Omi. His neck rested comfortably on the padded wooden pillow, arms interlocked. His body was strong and unmarked, his skin firm and golden, a sheen there. She caressed him gently, enough to make the touch enter his dream but not enough to awaken him. Then she slid from under the quilt, gathering her kimonos around herself.

It took Kiku very little time to renew her makeup as Suisen combed and brushed her hair and retied it into the shimoda style. Then mistress and maid walked noiselessly along the corridor, out onto the veranda, through the garden to the square. Boats, like fireflies, plied from the barbarian ship to the jetty where seven of the cannon still remained to be loaded. It was still deep night, long before dawn.

The two women slipped along the narrow alley between a cluster of houses and began to climb the path.

Sweat-stained and exhausted bearers were collecting their strength around the palanquin on the hilltop outside Omi's house. Kiku did not knock on the garden door. Candles were lit in the house and servants were hurrying to and fro. She motioned to Suisen, who immediately went to the veranda near the front door, knocked, and waited. In a moment the door opened. The maid nodded and vanished. Another moment and the maid returned and beckoned Kiku and bowed low as she swept past. Another maid scurried ahead and opened the shoji of the best room.

Omi's mother's bed was unslept in. She was sitting, rigidly erect, near the small alcove that held the flower arrangement. A small window shoji was open to the garden. Midori, Omi's wife, was opposite her.

Kiku knelt. Is it only a night ago that I was here and terrified on the Night of the Screams? She bowed, first to Omi's mother, then to his wife, feeling the tension between the two women and she asked herself, Why is it there is always such violence between mother-in-law and daughter-in-law? Doesn't daughter-in-law, in time, become mother-in-law? Why does she then always treat her own daughter-in-law to a lashing tongue and make her life a misery, and why does that girl do the same in her turn? Doesn't anyone learn?

"I'm sorry to disturb you, Mistress-san."

"You're very welcome, Kiku-san," the old woman replied. "There's no trouble, I hope?"

"Oh, no, but I didn't know whether or not you'd want me to awaken your son," she said to her, already knowing the answer. "I thought I'd better ask you, as you, Midori-san"—she turned and smiled and bowed slightly to Midori, liking her greatly—"as you had returned."

The old woman said, "You're very kind, Kiku-san, and very thoughtful. No, leave him in peace."

"Very well. Please excuse me, disturbing you like this, but I thought it best to ask. Midori-san, I hope your journey was not too bad."

"So sorry, it was awful," Midori said. "I'm glad to be back and hated being away. Is my husband well?"

"Yes, very well. He laughed a lot this evening and seemed to be happy. He ate and drank sparingly and he's sleeping soundly."

"The Mistress-san was beginning to tell me some of the terrible things that happened while I was away and—"

"You shouldn't have gone. You were needed here," the old woman interrupted, venom in her voice. "Or perhaps not. Perhaps you should have stayed away permanently. Perhaps you brought a bad *kami* into our house along with your bed linen."

"I'd never do that, Mistress-san," Midori said patiently. "Please believe I would rather kill myself than bring the slightest stain to your good name. Please forgive my being away and my faults. I'm sorry."

"Since that devil ship came here we've had nothing but trouble. That's bad *kami*. Very bad. And where were you when you were needed? Gossiping in Mishima, stuffing yourself and drinking saké."

"My father died, Mistress-san. The day before I arrived."

"Huh, you haven't even got the courtesy or the foresight to be at your own father's deathbed. The sooner you permanently leave our house, the better for all of us. I want some cha. We have a guest here and you haven't even remembered your manners enough to offer her refreshment!"

"It was ordered, instantly, the moment she—"

"It hasn't arrived instantly!"

The shoji opened. A maid nervously brought cha and some sweet cakes. First Midori served the old woman, who cursed the maid roundly and chomped toothlessly on a cake, slurping her drink. "You must excuse the maid, Kiku-san," the old woman said. "The cha's tasteless. Tasteless! And scalding. I suppose that's only to be expected in this house."

"Here, please have mine." Midori blew gently on the tea to cool it.

The old woman took it grudgingly. "Why can't it be correct the first time?" She lapsed into sullen silence.

"What do you think about all this?" Midori asked Kiku. "The ship and Yabu-sama and Toda Hiro-matsu-sama?"

"I don't know what to think. As to the barbarians, who knows? They're certainly an extraordinary collection of men. And the great *daimyo,* Iron Fist? It's very curious that he arrived almost the same time as Lord Yabu, *neh?* Well, you must excuse me, no, please, I can see myself out."

"Oh, no, Kiku-san, I wouldn't hear of it."

"There, you see, Midori-san," the old woman interrupted impatiently. "Our guest's uncomfortable and the cha awful."

"Oh, the cha was sufficient for me, Mistress-san, really. No, if you'll excuse me, I am a little tired. Perhaps before I go tomorrow, I may be allowed to come to see you. It's always such a pleasure to talk with you."

The old woman allowed herself to be cajoled and Kiku followed Midori onto the veranda and into the garden.

"Kiku-san, you're so thoughtful," Midori said, holding her arm, warmed by her beauty. "It was very kind of you, thank you."

Kiku glanced back at the house momentarily, and shivered. "Is she always like that?"

"Tonight she was polite, compared to some times. If it wasn't for Omi and my son I swear I'd shake her dust off my feet, shave my head, and become a nun. But I have Omi and my son and that makes up for everything. I only thank all *kami* for that. Fortunately Mistress-san prefers Yedo and can't stay away from there for very long." Midori smiled sadly. "You train yourself not to listen, you know how it is." She sighed, so beautiful in the moonlight. "But that's unimportant. Tell me what's happened since I left."

This was why Kiku had come to the house so urgently, for obviously neither the mother nor the wife would wish Omi's sleep disturbed. She came to tell the lovely Lady Midori everything, so she could help to guard Kasigi Omi as she herself would try to guard him. She told her all that she knew except what had happened in the room with Yabu. She added the rumors she had heard and the stories the other girls had passed on to her or invented. And everything that Omi had told her—his hopes and fears and plans—everything about him, except what had happened in the room tonight. She knew that this was not important to his wife.

"I'm afraid, Kiku-san, afraid for my husband."

"Everything he advised was wise, Lady. I think everything he did was correct. Lord Yabu doesn't reward anyone lightly and three thousand koku is a worthy increase."

"But the ship's Lord Toranaga's now, and all that money."

"Yes, but for Yabu-sama to offer the ship as a gift was an idea of genius. Omi-san gave the idea to Yabu—surely this itself is payment enough, *neh?* Omi-san must be recognized as a preeminent vassal." Kiku twisted the truth just a trifle, knowing that Omi was in great danger, and all his house. What is to be will be, she reminded herself. But it does no harm to ease the brow of a nice woman.

"Yes, I can see that," Midori said. Let it be the truth, she prayed. Please let it be the truth. She embraced the girl, her eyes filling with tears. "Thank you. You're so kind, Kiku-san, so kind." She was seventeen.

CHAPTER 8

W HAT do you think, Ingeles?"
"I think there'll be a storm."
"When?"
"Before sunset."

It was near noon and they were standing on the quarterdeck of the galley under a gray overcast. This was the second day out to sea.

"If this was your ship, what would you do?"

"How far is it to our landfall?" Blackthorne asked.

"After sunset."

"How far to the nearest land?"

"Four or five hours, Ingeles. But to run for cover will cost us half a day and I can't afford that. What would you do?"

Blackthorne thought a moment. During the first night the galley had sped southward down the east coast of the Izu peninsula, helped by the large sail on the midships mast. When they had come abreast of the southmost cape, Cape Ito, Rodrigues had set the course West South West and had left the safety of the coast for the open sea, heading for a landfall at Cape Shinto two hundred miles away.

"Normally in one of these galleys we'd hug the coast—for safety," Rodrigues had said, "but that'd take too much time and time is important. Toranaga asked me to pilot Toady to Anjiro and back. Quickly. There's a bonus for me if we're very quick. One of their pilots'd be just as good on a short haul like this, but the poor son of a whore'd be frightened to death carrying so important a *daimyo* as Toady, particularly out of sight of land. They're not oceaners, Japmen. Great pirates and fighters and coastal sailors. But the deep frightens them. The old Taikō even made a law that the few ocean ships Japmen possess were always to have Portuguese pilots aboard. It's still the law of their land today."

"Why did he do that?"

Rodrigues shrugged. "Perhaps someone suggested it to him."

"Who?"

"Your stolen rutter, Ingeles, the Portuguese one. Whose was it?"

"I don't know. There was no name on it, no signature."

"Where'd you get it?"

"From the chief merchant of the Dutch East India Company."

"Where'd he get it from?"

Blackthorne shrugged.

Rodrigues' laugh had no humor in it. "Well, I never expected you to tell me—but whoever stole it and sold it, I hope he burns in hellfire forever!"

"You're employed by this Toranaga, Rodrigues?"

"No. I was just visiting Osaka, my Captain and I. This was just a favor to Toranaga. My Captain volunteered me. I'm pilot of the—" Rodrigues had stopped. "I keep forgetting you're the enemy, Ingeles."

"Portugal and England have been allies for centuries."

"But we're not now. Go below, Ingeles. You're tired and so am I and tired men make mistakes. Come on deck when you're rested."

So Blackthorne had gone below to the pilot's cabin and had lain on the bunk. Rodrigues' rutter of the voyage was on the sea desk which was pinned to the bulkhead like the pilot's chair on the quarterdeck. The book was leather-covered and used but Blackthorne did not open it.

"Why leave it there?" he had asked previously.

"If I didn't, you'd search for it. But you won't touch it there—or even look at it—uninvited. You're a pilot—not a pig-bellied whoring thieving merchant or soldier."

"I'll read it. You would."

"Not uninvited, Ingeles. No pilot'd do that. Even I wouldn't!"

Blackthorne had watched the book for a moment and then he closed his eyes. He slept deeply, all of that day and part of the night. It was just before dawn when he awoke as always. It took time to adjust to the untoward motion of the galley and the throb of the drum that kept the oars moving as one. He lay comfortably on his back in the dark, his arms under his head. He thought about his own ship and put away his worry of what would happen when they reached shore and Osaka. One thing at a time. Think about Felicity and Tudor and home. No, not now. Think that if other Portuguese are like Rodrigues, you've a good chance now. You'll get a ship home. Pilots are not enemies and the pox on other things! But you can't say that, lad. You're English, the hated heretic and anti-Christ. Catholics own this world. They *owned* it. Now we and the Dutch're going to smash them.

What nonsense it all is! Catholic and Protestant and Calvinist and Lutherist and every other shitist. You should have been born Catholic. It was only fate that took your father to Holland where he met a woman, Anneke van Droste, who became his wife and he saw Spanish Catholics and Spanish priests and the Inquisition for the first time. I'm glad he had his eyes opened, Blackthorne thought. I'm glad mine are open.

Then he had gone on deck. Rodrigues was in his chair, his eyes red-rimmed with sleeplessness, two Japanese sailors on the helm as before.

"Can I take this watch for you?"

"How do you feel, Ingeles?"

"Rested. Can I take the watch for you?" Blackthorne saw Rodrigues measuring him. "I'll wake you if the wind changes—anything."

"Thank you, Ingeles. Yes, I'll sleep a little. Maintain this course. At the turn, go four degrees more westerly and at the next, six more westerly. You'll have to point the new course on the compass for the helmsman. *Wakarimasu ka?*"

"*Hai!*" Blackthorne laughed. "Four points westerly it is. Go below, Pilot, your bunk's comfortable."

But Vasco Rodrigues did not go below. He merely pulled his sea cloak closer and settled deeper into the seachair. Just before the turn of the hourglass he awoke momentarily and checked the course change without moving and immediately went back to sleep again. Once when the wind veered he awoke and then, when he had seen there was no danger, again he slept.

Hiro-matsu and Yabu came on deck during the morning. Blackthorne noticed their surprise that he was conning the ship and Rodrigues sleeping. They did not talk to him, but returned to their conversation and, later, they went below again.

Near midday Rodrigues had risen from the seachair to stare northeast, sniffing the wind, all his senses concentrated. Both men studied the sea and the sky and the encroaching clouds.

"What would you do, Ingeles, if this was your ship?" Rodrigues said again.

"I'd run for the coast if I knew where it was—the nearest point. This craft won't take much water and there's a storm there all right. About four hours away."

"Can't be *tai-fun,*" Rodrigues muttered.

"What?"

"*Tai-fun.* They're huge winds—the worst storms you've ever seen. But we're not in *tai-fun* season."

"When's that?"

"It's not now, enemy." Rodrigues laughed. "No, not now. But it could be rotten enough so I'll take your piss-cutting advice. Steer North by West."

As Blackthorne pointed the new course and the helmsman turned the ship neatly, Rodrigues went to the rail and shouted at the captain, "*Isogi!* Captain-san. *Wakarimasu ka?*"

"*Isogi, hai!*"

"What's that? Hurry up?"

The corners of Rodrigues' eyes crinkled with amusement. "No harm in you knowing a little Japman talk, eh? Sure, Ingeles, *'isogi'* means to hurry. All you need here's about ten words and then you can make the buggers shit if you want to. If they're the right words, of course, and if they're in the mood. I'll go below now and get some food."

"You cook too?"

"In Japland, every civilized man has to cook, or personally has to train one of the monkeys to cook, or you starve to death. All they eat's raw fish, raw vegetables in sweet pickled vinegar. But life here can be a pisscutter if you know how."

"Is 'pisscutter' good or bad?"

"It's mostly very good but sometimes terribly bad. It all depends how you feel and you ask too many questions."

Rodrigues went below. He barred his cabin door and carefully checked the lock on his sea chest. The hair that he had placed so delicately was still there. And a similar hair, equally invisible to anyone but him, that he had put on the cover of his rutter was also untouched.

You can't be too careful in this world, Rodrigues thought. Is there any harm in his knowing that you're pilot of the *Nao del Trato,* this year's great Black Ship from Macao? Perhaps. Because then you'd have to explain that she's a leviathan, one of the richest, biggest ships in the world, more than sixteen hundred tons. You might be tempted to tell him about her cargo, about trade and about Macao and all sorts of illuminating things that are very, very private and very, very secret. But we are at war, us against the English and Dutch.

He opened the well-oiled lock and took out his private rutter to check some bearings for the nearest haven and his eyes saw the sealed packet the priest, Father Sebastio, had given him just before they had left Anjiro.

Does it contain the Englishman's rutters? he asked himself again.

He weighed the package and looked at the Jesuit seals, sorely tempted to break them and see for himself. Blackthorne had told him that the Dutch squadron had come by way of Magellan's Pass and little else. The Ingeles asks lots of questions and volunteers nothing, Rodrigues thought. He's shrewd, clever, and dangerous.

Are they his rutters or aren't they? If they are, what good are they to the Holy Fathers?

He shuddered, thinking of Jesuits and Franciscans and Dominicans and all monks and all priests and the Inquisition. There are good priests and bad priests and they're mostly bad, but they're still priests. The Church has to have priests and without them to intercede for us we're lost sheep in a Satanic world. Oh,

Madonna, protect me from all evil and bad priests!

Rodrigues had been in his cabin with Blackthorne in Anjiro harbor when the door had opened and Father Sebastio had come in uninvited. They had been eating and drinking and the remains of their food was in the wooden bowls.

"You break bread with heretics?" the priest had asked. "It's dangerous to eat with them. They're infectious. Did he tell you he's a pirate?"

"It's only Christian to be chivalrous to your enemies, Father. When I was in their hands they were fair to me. I only return their charity." He had knelt and kissed the priest's cross. Then he had got up and, offering wine, he said, "How can I help you?"

"I want to go to Osaka. With the ship."

"I'll ask them at once." He had gone and had asked the captain and the request had gradually gone up to Toda Hiro-matsu, who replied that Toranaga had said nothing about bringing a foreign priest from Anjiro so he regretted he could not bring the foreign priest from Anjiro.

Father Sebastio had wanted to talk privately so he had sent the Englishman on deck and then, in the privacy of the cabin, the priest had brought out the sealed package.

"I would like you to deliver this to the Father-Visitor."

"I don't know if his Eminence'll still be at Osaka when I get there." Rodrigues did not like being a carrier of Jesuit secrets. "I might have to go back to Nagasaki. My Captain-General may have left orders for me."

"Then give it to Father Alvito. Make absolutely sure you put it only in his hands."

"Very well," he had said.

"When were you last at Confession, my son?"

"On Sunday, Father."

"Would you like me to confess you now?"

"Yes, thank you." He was grateful that the priest had asked, for you never knew if your life depended on the sea, and, afterwards, he had felt much better as always.

Now in the cabin, Rodrigues put back the package, greatly tempted. Why Father Alvito? Father Martin Alvito was chief trade negotiator and had been personal interpreter for the Taikō for many years and therefore an intimate of most of the influential *daimyos*. Father Alvito plied between Nagasaki and Osaka and was one of the very few men, and the only European, who had had access to the Taikō at any time—an enormously clever man who spoke perfect Japanese and knew more about them and their way of life than any man in Asia. Now he was the Portuguese's most influential mediator to the Council of Regents, and to Ishido and Toranaga in particular.

Trust the Jesuits to get one of their men into such a vital position, Rodrigues thought with awe. Certainly if it hadn't been for the Society of Jesus the flood of heresy would never have been stopped, Portugal and Spain might have gone Protestant, and we'd have lost our immortal souls forever. Madonna!

"Why do you think about priests all the time?" Rodrigues asked himself aloud. "You know it makes you nervous!" Yes. Even so, why Father Alvito? If the package contains the rutters, is the package meant for one of the Christian *daimyos,* or Ishido or Toranaga, or just for his Eminence, the Father-Visitor himself? Or for my Captain-General? Or will the rutters be sent to Rome, for the Spaniards? Why Father Alvito? Father Sebastio could have easily said to give it to one of the other Jesuits.

And why does Toranaga want the Ingeles?

In my heart I know I should kill Blackthorne. He's the enemy, he's a heretic. But there's something else. I've a feeling this Ingeles is a danger to all of us. Why should I think that? He's a pilot—a great one. Strong. Intelligent. A good man. Nothing there to worry about. So why am I afraid? Is he evil? I like him very much but I feel I should kill him quickly and the sooner the better. Not in anger. Just to protect ourselves. Why?

I am afraid of him.

What to do? Leave it to the hand of God? The storm's coming and it'll be a bad one.

"God curse me and my lack of wits! Why don't I know what to do easily?"

The storm came before sunset and caught them out to sea. Land was ten miles away. The bay they raced for was haven enough and dead ahead when they had crested the horizon. There were no shoals or reefs to navigate between them and safety, but ten miles was ten miles and the sea was rising fast, driven by the rain-soaked wind.

The gale blew from the northeast, on the starboard quarter, and veered badly as gusts swirled easterly or northerly without pattern, the sea grim. Their course was northwest so they were mostly broadside to the swell, rolling badly, now in the trough, now sickeningly on the crest. The galley was shallow draft and built for speed and kind waters, and though the rowers were game and very disciplined, it was hard to keep their oars in the sea and their pull clean.

"You'll have to ship the oars and run before the wind," Blackthorne shouted.

"Maybe, but not yet! Where are your *cojones,* Ingeles?"

"Where they should be, by God, and where I want 'em to stay!"

Both men knew that if they turned into the wind they could never make way against the storm, so the tide and the wind would take them away from sanctuary and out to sea. And if they ran before the wind, the tide and the wind would take them away from sanctuary and out to sea as before, only faster. Southward was the Great Deep. There was no land southward for a thousand miles, or, if you were unlucky, for a thousand leagues.

They wore lifelines that were lashed to the binnacle and they were glad of them as the deck pitched and rolled. They hung on to the gunwales as well, riding her.

As yet, no water had come aboard. She was heavily ladened and rode lower in the water than either would have liked. Rodrigues had prepared properly in the hours of waiting. Everything had been battened down, the men forewarned. Hiro-matsu and Yabu had said that they would stay below for a time and then come on deck. Rodrigues had shrugged and told them clearly that it would be very dangerous. He was sure they did not understand.

"What'll they do?" Blackthorne had asked.

"Who knows, Ingeles? But they won't be weeping with fear, you can be sure."

In the well of the main deck the oarsmen were working hard. Normally there would be two men on each oar but Rodrigues had ordered three for strength and safety and speed. Others were waiting below decks to spell these rowers when he gave the order. On the foredeck the captain oar-master was experienced and his beat was slow, timed to the waves. The galley was still making way, though every moment the roll seemed more pronounced and the recovery slower. Then the squalls became erratic and threw the captain oar-master off stroke.

"Watch out for'ard!" Blackthorne and Rodrigues shouted almost in the same breath. The galley rolled sickeningly, twenty oars pulled at air instead of sea and there was chaos aboard. The first comber had struck and the port gunwale was awash. They were floundering.

"Go for'ard," Rodrigues ordered. "Get 'em to ship half the oars each side! Madonna, hurry, hurry!"

Blackthorne knew that without his lifeline he could easily be carried overboard. But the oars had to be shipped or they were lost.

He slipped the knot and fought along the heaving, greasy deck, down the short gangway to the main deck. Abruptly the galley swerved and he was carried to the down side, his legs taken away by some of the rowers who had also slipped their safety lines to try to fight order into their oars. The gunwale was under water and one man went overboard. Blackthorne felt himself going too. His hand caught the gunwale, his tendons stretched but his grip held, then his other hand reached the rail and, choking, he pulled himself back. His feet found the deck and he shook himself, thanking God, and thought, there's your seventh life gone. Alban Caradoc had always said a good pilot had to be like a cat, except that the pilot had to have at least ten lives whereas a cat is satisfied with nine.

A man was at his feet and he dragged him from the grip of the sea, held him until he was safe, then helped him to his place. He looked back at the quarterdeck to curse Rodrigues for letting the helm get away from him. Rodrigues waved and pointed and shouted, the shout swallowed by a squall. Blackthorne saw their course had changed. Now they were almost into the wind, and he knew the swerve had been planned. Wise, he thought. That'll give us a respite to get organized, but the bastard could have warned me. I don't like losing lives unnecessarily.

He waved back and hurled himself into the work of re-sorting the rowers. All rowing had stopped except for the two oars most for'ard, which kept them tidily into the wind. With signs and yelling, Blackthorne got the oars shipped, doubled up the men on the working ones, and went aft again. The men were stoic and though some were very sick they stayed and waited for the next order.

The bay was closer but it still seemed a million leagues away. To the northeast the sky was dark. Rain whipped them and the gusts strengthened. In *Erasmus* Blackthorne would not have been worried. They could have made harbor easily or could have turned back carelessly onto their real course, heading for their proper landfall. His ship was built and rigged for weather. This galley was not.

"What do you think, Ingeles?"

"You'll do what you want, whatever I think," he shouted against the wind. "But she won't take much water and we'll go down like a stone, and the next time I go for'ard, tell me you're putting her into wind. Better still, put her to windward while I've my line on and then we'll both reach port."

"That was the hand of God, Ingeles. A wave slammed her rump around."

"That nearly put me overboard."

"I saw."

Blackthorne was measuring their drift. "If we stay on this course we'll never make the bay. We'll be swept past the headland by a mile or more."

"I'm going to stay into the wind. Then, when the time's ripe, we'll stab for the shore. Can you swim?"

"Yes."

"Good. I never learned. Too dangerous. Better to drown quickly than slow, eh?" Rodrigues shuddered involuntarily. "Blessed Madonna, protect me from a water grave! This sow-bellied whore of a ship's going to get to harbor tonight. Has to. My nose says if we turn and run we'll flounder. We're too heavily laden."

"Lighten her. Throw the cargo overboard."

"King Toady'd never agree. He has to arrive with it or he might as well not arrive."

"Ask him."

"Madonna, are you deaf? I've told you! I know he won't agree!" Rodrigues went closer to the helmsman and made sure they understood they were to keep heading into the wind without fail.

"Watch them, Ingeles! You have the con." He untied his lifeline and went down the gangway, sure-footed. The rowers watched him intently as he walked to the captain-san on the forepoop deck to explain with signs and with words the plan he had in mind. Hiro-matsu and Yabu came on deck. The captain-san explained the plan to them. Both men were pale but they remained impassive and neither vomited. They looked shoreward through the rain, shrugged and went below again.

Blackthorne stared at the bay to port. He knew the plan was dangerous. They would have to wait until they were just past the near headland, then they would have to fall off from the wind, turn northwest again and pull for their lives. The sail wouldn't help them. It would have to be their strength alone. The southern side of the bay was rock-fanged and reefed. If they misjudged the timing they would be driven ashore there and wrecked.

"Ingeles, lay for'ard!"

The Portuguese was beckoning him.

He went forward.

"What about the sail?" Rodrigues shouted.

"No. That'll hurt more than help."

"You stay here then. If the captain fails with the beat, or we lose him, you take it up. All right?"

"I've never sailed one of these before—I've never mastered oars. But I'll try."

Rodrigues looked landward. The headland appeared and disappeared in the driving rain. Soon he would have to make the stab. The seas were growing and already whitecaps fled from the crests. The race between the headlands looked evil. This one's going to be filthy, he thought. Then he spat and decided.

"Go aft, Ingeles. Take the helm. When I signal, go West North West for that point. You see it?"

"Yes."

"Don't hesitate and hold that course. Watch me closely. This sign means hard aport, this hard astarboard, this steady as she goes."

"Very well."

"By the Virgin, you'll wait for my orders and you'll obey my orders?"

"You want me to take the helm or not?"

Rodrigues knew he was trapped. "I have to trust you, Ingeles, and I hate trusting you. Go aft," he said. He saw Blackthorne read what was behind his eyes and walk away. Then he changed his mind and called after him, "Hey, you arrogant pirate! Go with God!"

Blackthorne turned back gratefully. "And you, Spaniard!"

"Piss on all Spaniards and long live Portugal!"

"Steady as she goes!"

They made harbor but without Rodrigues. He was washed overboard when his lifeline snapped.

The ship had been on the brink of safety when the great wave came out of the north and, though they had taken much water previously and had already lost the Japanese captain, now they were awash and driven backward towards the rock-infested shore.

Blackthorne saw Rodrigues go and he watched him, gasping and struggling in the churning sea. The storm and the tide had taken them far to the south side of the bay and they were almost on the rocks, all aboard knowing that the ship was lost.

As Rodrigues was swept alongside, Blackthorne threw him a wooden life ring. The Portuguese flailed for the life ring but the sea swept it out of his reach. An oar crashed into him and he grabbed for it. The rain slashed down and the last Blackthorne saw of Rodrigues was an arm and the broken oar and, just ahead, the surf raging against the tormented shore. He could have dived overboard and swum to him and survived, perhaps, there was time, perhaps, but his first duty was to his ship and his last duty was to his ship and *his* ship was in danger.

So he turned his back on Rodrigues.

The wave had taken some rowers with it and others were struggling to fill the empty places. A mate had bravely slipped his safety line. He jumped onto the foredeck, secured himself, and restarted the beat. The chant leader also began again, the rowers tried to get order out of chaos.

"*Isogiiiiii!*" Blackthorne shouted, remembering the word. He bent his weight on the helm to help get the bow more into wind, then went to the rail and beat time, called out One-Two-One-Two, trying to encourage the crew.

"Come on, you bastards, *puuull!*"

The galley was on the rocks, at least the rocks were just astern and to port and to starboard. The oars dipped and pulled, but still the ship made no way, the wind and the tide winning, dragging her backward perceptibly.

"Come on, pull, you bastards!" Blackthorne shouted again, his hand beating time.

The rowers took strength from him.

First they held their own with the sea. Then they conquered her.

The ship moved away from the rocks. Blackthorne held the course for the lee shore. Soon they were in calmer waters. There was still gale but it was overhead. There was still tempest but it was out to sea.

"Let go the starboard anchor!"

No one understood the words but all seamen knew what was wanted. They rushed to do his bidding. The anchor splashed over the side. He let the ship fall off slightly to test the firmness of the seabed, the mate and rowers understanding his maneuver.

"Let go the port anchor!"

When his ship was safe, he looked aft.

The cruel shore line could hardly be seen through the rain. He gauged the sea and considered possibilities.

The Portuguese's rutter is below, he thought, drained. I can con the ship to Osaka. I could con it back to Anjiro. But were you right to disobey him? I didn't disobey Rodrigues. I was on the quarterdeck. Alone.

'Steer south,' Rodrigues had screamed when the wind and the tide carried them perilously near the rocks. 'Turn and run before the wind!'

'No!' he had shouted back, believing their only chance was to try for the harbor and that in the open sea they'd flounder. 'We can make it!'

'God curse you, you'll kill us all!'

But I didn't kill anyone, Blackthorne thought. Rodrigues, you knew and I knew that it was my responsibility to decide—if there was a time of decision. I was right. The ship's safe. Nothing else matters.

He beckoned to the mate, who hurried from the foredeck. Both helmsmen had collapsed, their arms and legs almost torn from their sockets. The rowers were like corpses, fallen helplessly over their oars. Others weakly came from below to help. Hiro-matsu and Yabu, both badly shaken, were assisted onto the deck, but once on deck both *daimyos* stood erect.

"*Hai,* Anjin-san?" the mate asked. He was a middle-aged man with strong white teeth and a broad, weatherbeaten face. A livid bruise marked his cheek where the sea had battered him against the gunwale.

"You did very well," Blackthorne said, not caring that his words would not be understood. He knew his tone would be clear and his smile. "Yes, very well. You're Captain-san now. *Wakarimasu?* You! Captain-san!"

The man stared at him open-mouthed, then he bowed to hide both his astonishment and his pleasure. "*Wakarimasu,* Anjin-san. *Hai. Arigato goziemashita.*"

"Listen, Captain-san," Blackthorne said. "Get the men food and drink. Hot food. We'll stay here tonight." With signs Blackthorne made him comprehend.

Immediately the new captain turned and shouted with new authority. Instantly seamen ran to obey him. Filled with pride, the new captain looked back at the quarterdeck. I wish I could speak your barbarian language, he thought happily. Then I could thank you, Anjin-san, for saving the ship and with the ship the life of our Lord Hiro-matsu. Your magic gave us all new strength. Without your magic we would have floundered. You may be a pirate but you are a great seaman, and while you are pilot I will obey you with my life. I'm not worthy to be captain, but I will try to deserve your trust. "What do you want me to do next?" he asked.

Blackthorne was looking over the side. The seabed was obscured. He took mental bearings and when he was sure that the anchors had not slipped and the sea was safe, he said, "Launch the skiff. And get a good sculler."

Again with signs and with words Blackthorne made himself understood.

The skiff was launched and manned instantly.

Blackthorne went to the gunwale and would have scaled down the side but a harsh voice stopped him. He looked around. Hiro-matsu was there, Yabu beside him.

The old man was badly bruised about the neck and shoulders but he still carried the long sword. Yabu was bleeding from his nose, his face bruised, his kimono blotched, and he tried to staunch the flow with a small piece of material. Both men were impassive, seemingly unaware of their hurts or the chill of the wind.

Blackthorne bowed politely. "*Hai,* Toda-sama?"

Again the harsh words and the old man pointed with his sword at the skiff and shook his head.

"Rodrigu-san there!" Blackthorne pointed to the south shore in answer. "I go look!"

"*Iyé!*" Hiro-matsu shook his head again, and spoke at length, clearly refusing him permission because of the danger.

"I'm Anjin-san of this whore-bitch ship and if I want to go ashore I'm going ashore." Blackthorne kept his voice very polite but strong and it was equally obvious what he meant. "I know that skiff won't live in that sea. *Hai!* But I'm going ashore there—by that point. You see that point, Toda Hiro-matsu-sama? By that small rock. I'm going to work my way around the headland, there. I'm in no hurry to die and I've nowhere to run. I want to get Rodrigu-san's body." He cocked a leg over the side. The scabbarded sword moved a fraction. So he froze. But his gaze was level, his face set.

Hiro-matsu was in a dilemma. He could understand the pirate wanting to find Rodrigu-san's body but it was dangerous to go there, even by foot, and Lord Toranaga had said to bring the barbarian back safely, so he was going to be brought safely. It was equally clear that the man intended to go.

He had seen him during the storm, standing on the pitching deck like an evil sea *kami,* unafraid, in his element and part of the storm, and he had thought grimly at the time, better to get this man and all barbarians like him on the land where we can deal with them. At sea we're in their power.

He could see the pirate was impatient. How insulting they are, he told himself. Even so I should thank you. Everyone says you alone are responsible for bringing the ship to harbor, that the Rodrigu anjin lost his nerve and waved us away from land, but you held our course. Yes. If we'd gone out to sea we'd have sunk certainly and then I would have failed my Master. Oh, Buddha, protect me from that!

All his joints were aching and his piles inflamed. He was exhausted by the effort it took to remain stoic in front of his men, Yabu, the crew, even this barbarian. Oh, Buddha, I'm so tired. I wish I could lie in a bath and soak and soak and have one day of rest from pain. Just one day. Stop your stupid womanish thoughts! You've been in pain for almost sixty years. What is pain to a man? A privilege! Masking pain is the measure of a man. Thank Buddha you are still alive to protect your Master when you should have been dead a hundred times. I do thank Buddha.

But I hate the sea. I hate the cold. And I hate pain.

"Stay where you are, Anjin-san," he said, pointing with his scabbard for clarity, bleakly amused by the ice-blue fire in the man's eyes. When he was sure the man understood he glanced at the mate. "Where are we? Whose fief is this?"

"I don't know, Sire. I think we're somewhere in Ise Province. We could send someone ashore to the nearest village."

"Can you pilot us to Osaka?"

"Providing we stay very close to shore, Sire, and go slowly, with great caution. I don't know these waters and I could never guarantee your safety. I don't have enough knowledge and there's no one aboard, Sire, who has. Except this pilot. If it was left to me I would advise you to go by land. We could get you horses or palanquins."

Hiro-matsu shook his head irascibly. To go overland was out of the question. It would take far too long—the way was mountainous and there were few roads —and they would have to go through many territories controlled by allies of Ishido, the enemy. Added to this danger were also the multitudinous bandit groups that infested the passes. This would mean he would have to take all his men. Certainly he could fight his way through the bandits, but he could never force a passage if Ishido or his allies decided to inhibit him. All this would delay him further, and his orders were to deliver the cargo, the barbarian, and Yabu, quickly and safely.

"If we follow the coast, how long would it take us?"

"I don't know, Sire. Four or five days, perhaps more. I would feel very unsure of myself—I'm not a captain, so sorry."

Which means, Hiro-matsu thought, that I have to have the cooperation of this barbarian. To prevent him going ashore I'll have to tie him up. And who knows if he'll be cooperative tied up?

"How long will we have to stay here?"

"The pilot said overnight."

"Will the storm be gone by then?"

"It should, Sire, but one never knows."

Hiro-matsu studied the mountain coast, then the pilot, hesitating.

"May I offer a suggestion, Hiro-matsu-san?" Yabu said.

"Yes, yes, of course," he said testily.

"As we seem to need the pirate's cooperation to get us to Osaka, why not let him go ashore but send men with him to protect him, and order them back before dark. As to going overland, I agree it would be too dangerous for you—I would never forgive myself if anything happened to you. Once the storm has blown itself out you'll be safer with the ship and you'll get to Osaka much quicker, *neh?* Surely by sunset tomorrow."

Reluctantly Hiro-matsu nodded. "Very well." He beckoned a samurai. "Takatashi-san! You will take six men and go with the Pilot. Bring the Portuguese's body back if you can find it. But if even one of this barbarian's eyelashes is damaged, you and your men will commit seppuku instantly."

"Yes, Lord."

"And send two men to the nearest village and find out exactly where we are and in whose fief we are."

"Yes, Lord."

"With your permission, Hiro-matsu-san, I will lead the party ashore," Yabu said. "If we arrived in Osaka without the pirate, I'd be so ashamed that I'd feel obliged to kill myself anyway. I'd like the honor of carrying out your orders."

Hiro-matsu nodded, inwardly surprised that Yabu would put himself in such jeopardy. He went below.

When Blackthorne realized that Yabu was going ashore with him, his pulse quickened. I haven't forgotten Pieterzoon or my crew or the pit—or the screams or Omi or any part of it. Look to your life, bastard.

CHAPTER 9

THEY were quickly on land. Blackthorne intended to lead but Yabu usurped that position and set a strong pace, which he was hard put to keep up with. The other six samurai were watching him carefully. I've nowhere to run, you fools, he thought, misunderstanding their concern, as his eyes automatically quartered the bay, looking for shoals or hidden reefs, measuring bearings, his mind docketing the important things for future transcription.

Their way led first along the pebbled shore, then a short climb over sea-smoothed rocks up onto a path that skirted the cliff and crept precariously around the headland southward. The rain had stopped but the gale had not. The closer they came to the exposed tongue of land, the higher the surf—hurled against the rocks below—sprayed into the air. Soon they were soaked.

Although Blackthorne felt chilled, Yabu and the others, who had their light kimonos carelessly tucked into their belts, did not seem to be affected by the wet or the cold. It must be as Rodrigues had said, he thought, his fear returning. Japmen just aren't built like us. They don't *feel* cold or hunger or privations or wounds as we do. They are more like animals, their nerves dulled, compared to us.

Above them the cliff soared two hundred feet. The shore was fifty feet below. Beyond and all around were mountains and not a house or hut in the whole bay area. This was not surprising for there was no room for fields, the shore pebbles quickly becoming foreshore rocks and then granite mountain with trees on the upper slopes.

The path dipped and rose along the cliff face, very unsafe, the surface loose. Blackthorne plodded along, leaning against the wind, and noticed that Yabu's legs were strong and muscular. Slip, you whore-bastard, he thought. Slip—splatter yourself on the rocks below. Would that make you scream? What would make you scream?

With an effort he took his eyes off Yabu and went back to searching the foreshore. Each crevice and cleft and gulley. The spume wind was gusting and tore the tears from him. Sea spilled back and forth, swirled and eddied. He knew there was a minimal hope of finding Rodrigues, there would be too many caves and hidden places that could never be investigated. But he had had to come ashore to try. He owed Rodrigues the try. All pilots prayed helplessly for death ashore and burial ashore. All had seen too many sea-bloated corpses and half-eaten corpses and crab-mutilated corpses.

They rounded the headland and stopped gratefully in the lee. There was no need to go further. If the body wasn't to windward then it was hidden or swallowed up or already carried out to sea, into the deep. Half a mile away a small fishing village nestled on the white-frothed shore. Yabu motioned to two of the samurai. Immediately they bowed and loped off toward it. A last look, then Yabu wiped the rain out of his face, glanced up at Blackthorne, motioning their return. Blackthorne nodded and they set off again, Yabu leading, the other samurai still watching him so carefully, and again he thought how stupid they were.

Then, when they were halfway back, they saw Rodrigues.

The body was caught in a cleft between two great rocks, above the surf but washed by part of it. One arm was sprawled in front. The other was still locked to the broken oar which moved slightly with the ebb and flow. It was this movement that had attracted Blackthorne's attention as he bent into the wind, trudging in Yabu's wake.

The only way down was over the short cliff. The climb would only be fifty or sixty feet but it was a sheer drop and there were almost no footholds.

What about the tide? Blackthorne asked himself. It's flowing, not ebbing. That'll take him out to sea again. Jesus, it looks foul down there. What's it to be?

He went closer to the edge and immediately Yabu moved in his way, shaking his head, and the other samurai surrounded him.

"I'm only trying to get a better look, for the love of Christ," he said. "I'm not trying to escape! Where the hell can I run to?"

He backed off a little and peered down. They followed his look and chatted among themselves, Yabu doing most of the talking.

There's no chance, he decided. It's too dangerous. We'll come back at dawn with ropes. If he's here, he's here, and I'll bury him ashore. Reluctantly he turned and, as he did, the edge of the cliff crumbled and he began to slip. Immediately Yabu and the others grabbed him and pulled him back, and all at once he realized that they were concerned only for his safety. They're only trying to protect me!

Why should they want me safe? Because of Tora— What was his name? Toranaga? Because of him? Yes, but also perhaps because there's no one else aboard to pilot us. Is that why they let me come ashore, gave me my way? Yes, it must be. So now I have power over the ship, over the old *daimyo*, and over this bastard. How can I use it?

He relaxed and thanked them and let his eyes roam below. "We've got to get him, Yabu-san. *Hai!* The only way's that way. Over the cliff. I'll bring him up, me, Anjin-san!" Again he moved forward as though he was going to climb down and again they restrained him and he said with feigned anxiety, "We've got to get Rodrigu-san. Look! There's not much time, light's going."

"*Iyé,* Anjin-san," Yabu said.

He stood towering over Yabu. "If you won't let me go, Yabu-san, then send one of your men. Or go yourself. You!"

The wind tore around them, whining off the cliff face. He saw Yabu look down, weighing the climb and the falling light, and he knew Yabu was hooked. You're trapped, bastard, your vanity's trapped you. If you start down there you'll get hurt. But don't kill yourself, please, just shatter your legs or ankles. Then drown.

A samurai began to climb down but Yabu ordered him back.

"Return to the ship. Fetch some ropes immediately," Yabu said. The man ran off.

Yabu kicked off his thong slippers. He took his swords out of his belt and put them safely under cover. "Watch them and watch the barbarian. If anything happens to either, I'll sit you on your own swords."

"Please let me go down there, Yabu-sama," Takatashi said. "If you're hurt or lost I'll—"

"You think that you can succeed where I will fail?"

"No, Sire, of course not."

"Good."

"Please wait for the ropes then. I'll never forgive myself if anything happens to you." Takatashi was short and stocky with a heavy beard.

Why not wait for the ropes? Yabu asked himself. It would be sensible, yes. But not clever. He glanced up at the barbarian and nodded briefly. He knew that he had been challenged. He had expected it. And hoped for it. That's why I volunteered for this mission, Anjin-san, he said to himself, silently amused. You're really very simple. Omi was right.

Yabu took off his soaking kimono and, clad only in his loincloth, went to the cliff edge and tested it through the soles of his cotton tabi—his sock-shoes. Better to keep them on, he thought, his will and his body, forged by a lifetime of training all samurai had to undergo, dominating the cold that cut into him. The tabi will give you a firmer grip—for a time. You'll need all your strength and skill to get down there alive. Is it worth it?

During the storm and the stab for the bay he had come on deck and, unnoticed by Blackthorne, had taken a place at the oars. Gladly he had used his strength with the rowers, detesting the miasma below and the sickness he had felt. He had decided that it was better to die in the air than suffocate below.

As he worked with the others in the driving cold, he began watching the pilots. He saw very clearly that, at sea, the ship and all aboard were in the power of these two men. The pilots were in their element, riding the pitching decks as carelessly as he himself rode a galloping horse. No Japanese aboard could match them. For skill or courage or knowledge. And gradually this awareness had spawned a majestic concept: modern barbarian ships filled with samurai, piloted by samurai, captained by samurai, sailed by samurai. *His* samurai.

If I had three barbarian ships initially, I could easily control the sea lanes between Yedo and Osaka. Based in Izu, I could strangle all shipping or let it pass. So nearly all the rice and all the silk. Wouldn't I then be arbiter between Toranaga and Ishido? At the very least, a balance between them?

No *daimyo* has ever yet taken to the sea.

No *daimyo* has ships or pilots.

Except me.

I have a ship—had a ship—and now I *might* have my ship back—if I'm clever. I have a pilot and therefore a trainer of pilots, if I can get him away from Toranaga. If I can dominate him.

Once he is my vassal of his own accord, he will train my men. And build ships. But how to make him a true vassal? The pit did not break his spirit.

First get him alone and keep him alone—isn't that what Omi said? Then this pilot could be persuaded to manners and taught to speak Japanese. Yes. Omi's very clever. Too clever perhaps—I'll think about Omi later. Concentrate on the pilot. How to dominate a barbarian—a Christian filth eater?

What was it Omi said? 'They value life. Their chief deity, Jesus the Christ, teaches them to love one another and to value life.' Could I give him back his life? Save it, yes, that would be very good. How to bend him?

Yabu had been so swept by his excitement he had hardly noticed the motion of the ship or the seas. A wave cascaded over him. He saw it envelop the pilot. But there was no fear in the man at all. Yabu was astounded. How could someone who had meekly allowed an enemy to piss on his back to save the life of an insignificant vassal, how could this man have the strength to forget such eternal dishonor and stand there on the quarterdeck calling the gods of the sea to battle like any legendary hero—to save the same enemies? And then, when the great wave had taken the Portuguese away and they were floundering, the Anjin-san had miraculously laughed at death and given them the strength to pull away from the rocks.

I'll never understand them, he thought.

On the cliff edge, Yabu looked back a last time. Ah, Anjin-san, I know you think I go to my death, that you've trapped me. I know you wouldn't go down there yourself. I was watching you closely. But I grew up in the mountains and here in Japan we climb for pride and for pleasure. So I pit myself now on *my* terms, not on yours. I will try, and if I die it is nothing. But if I succeed then you, as a man, you'll know I'm better than you, on *your* terms. You'll be in my debt, too, if I bring the body back.

You will be my vassal, Anjin-san!

He went down the side of the cliff with great skill. When he was halfway down he slipped. His left hand held onto an outcrop. This stopped his fall, and he swung between life and death. His fingers dug deeply as he felt his grip failing and he ground his toes into a crevice, fighting for another hold. As his left hand ripped away, his toes found a cleft and they held and he hugged the cliff desperately, still off-balance, pressing against it, seeking holds. Then his toehold gave way. Though he managed to catch another outcrop with both hands, ten feet below, and hang on momentarily, this outcrop gave way too. He fell the last twenty feet.

He had prepared as best he could and landed on his feet like a cat, tumbled the sloping rock face to break the shock, and came to rest in a wheezing ball. He clutched his lacerated arms around his head, protecting himself against the stone avalanche that could follow. But none did. He shook his head to clear it and got up. One ankle was twisted. A searing pain shot up his leg into his bowels and the sweat started. His toes and fingernails were bleeding but that was to be expected.

There's no pain. You will not feel pain. Stand upright. The barbarian is watching.

A column of spray doused him and the cold helped to ease the hurt. With care, he slid over the seaweeded boulders, and eased himself across the crevices and then he was at the body.

Abruptly Yabu realized that the man was still alive. He made sure, then sat back for a moment. Do I want him alive or dead? Which is better?

A crab scuttled from under a rock and plopped into the sea. Waves rushed in. He felt the salt rip his wounds. Which is better, alive or dead?

He got up precariously and shouted, "Takatashi-san! This pilot's still alive! Go to the ship, bring a stretcher and a doctor, if there's one on the ship!"

Takatashi's words came back faintly against the wind, "Yes, Lord," and to his men as he ran off, "Watch the barbarian, don't let anything happen to him!"

Yabu peered at the galley, riding her anchors gently. The other samurai he had sent back for ropes was already beside the skiffs. He watched while the man jumped into one and it was launched. He smiled to himself, glanced back. Blackthorne had come to the edge of the cliff and was shouting urgently at him.

What is he trying to say? Yabu asked himself. He saw the pilot pointing to the sea but that didn't mean anything to him. The sea was rough and strong but it was no different from before.

Eventually Yabu gave up trying to understand and turned his attention to Rodrigues. With difficulty he eased the man up onto the rocks, out of the surf. The Portuguese's breathing was halting, but his heart seemed strong. There were many bruises. A splintered bone jutted through the skin of the left calf. His right shoulder seemed dislocated. Yabu looked for blood seepage from any openings but there was none. If he's not hurt inside, then perhaps he will live, he thought.

The *daimyo* had been wounded too many times and had seen too many dying and wounded not to have gained some measure of diagnostic skill. If Rodrigu can be kept warm, he decided, given saké and strong herbs, plenty of warm baths, he'll live. He may not walk again but he'll live. Yes. I want this man to live. If he can't walk, no matter. Perhaps that would be better. I'll have a spare pilot— this man certainly owes me his life. If the pirate won't cooperate, perhaps I can use this man. Would it be worthwhile to pretend to become a Christian? Would that bring them both around to me?

What would Omi do?

That one's clever—Omi. Yes. Too clever? Omi sees too much too fast. If he can see that far, he must perceive that his father would lead the clan if I vanish—my son's too inexperienced yet to survive by himself—and after the father, Omi himself. *Neh?*

What to do about Omi?

Say I gave Omi to the barbarian? As a toy.

What about that?

There were anxious shouts from above. Then he realized what the barbarian had been pointing at. The tide! The tide was coming in fast. Already it was encroaching on this rock. He scrambled up and winced at a shaft of pain from his ankle. All other escape along the shore was blocked by the sea. He saw that the tide mark on the cliff was over a man's full height above the base.

He looked at the skiff. It was near the ship now. On the foreshore Takatashi was still running well. The ropes won't arrive in time, he told himself.

His eyes searched the area diligently. There was no way up the cliff. No rocks offered sanctuary. No caves. Out to sea there were outcrops but he could never reach them. He could not swim and there was nothing to use as a raft.

The men above were watching him. The barbarian pointed to the outcrops seaward and made motions of swimming, but he shook his head. He searched carefully again. Nothing.

There's no escape, he thought. Now you are committed to death. Prepare yourself.

Karma, he told himself, and turned away from them, settling himself more comfortably, enjoying the vast clarity that had come to him. Last day, last sea, last light, last joy, last everything. How beautiful the sea and the sky and the cold and salt. He began to think of the final poem-song that he should now, by custom, compose. He felt fortunate. He had time to think clearly.

Blackthorne was shouting, "Listen, you whore-bastard! Find a ledge—there's got to be a ledge somewhere!"

The samurai were standing in his way, gazing at him as though he were a madman. It was clear to them there was no escape and that Yabu was simply preparing for a sweet death, as they would be doing if they had been he. And they resented these ravings as they knew Yabu would.

"Look down there, all of you. Maybe there's a ledge!"

One of them went to the edge and peered down, shrugged, and talked to his comrades and they shrugged too. Each time Blackthorne tried to go closer to the edge to search for an escape they stopped him. He could have easily shoved one of them to his death and he was tempted to. But he understood them and their problems. Think of a way to help that bastard. You've got to save him to save Rodrigues.

"Hey, you rotten, no good, piss-cutting, shit-tailed Japman! Hey, *Kasigi Yabu!* Where are your *cojones?* Don't give up! Only cowards give up! Are you a man or a sheep!" But Yabu paid no attention. He was as still as the rock upon which he sat.

Blackthorne picked up a stone and hurled it at him. It fell unnoticed into the water and the samurai shouted at Blackthorne angrily. He knew that at any moment they were going to fall on him and bind him up. But how could they? They've no rope—

Rope! Get some rope! Can you make some?

His eyes fell on Yabu's kimono. He started tearing it into strips, testing them for strength. The silk was very strong. "Come on!" he ordered the samurai, taking off his own shirt. "Make a rope. *Hai?*"

They understood. Rapidly they untied their sashes, took off their kimonos, and copied him. He began knotting the ends, sashes as well.

While they completed the rope, Blackthorne carefully lay down and inched for the edge, making two of them hold onto his ankles for safety. He didn't need their help but he wanted to reassure them.

He stuck his head out as far as he dared, conscious of their anxiety. Then he began to search as you would search at sea. Quarter by quarter. Using every part of his vision but mostly the sides.

A complete sweep. Nothing.

Once more.

Nothing.

Again.

What's that? Just above the tide line? Is it a crack in the cliff? Or a shadow?

Blackthorne shifted position, keenly aware that the sea had almost covered the rock that Yabu sat on, and almost all of the rocks between him and the base of the cliff. Now he could see better and he pointed.

"There! What's that?"

One of the samurai was on his hands and knees and he followed Blackthorne's outstretched finger but saw nothing.

"There! Isn't that a ledge?"

With his hands he formed the ledge and with two fingers made a man and stood the man on the ledge and, with another finger, made a long bundle over the shoulder of the man, so now a man stood on a ledge—*that ledge*—with another over his shoulder.

"Quick! *Isogi!* Make him understand—Kasigi Yabu-sama! *Wakarimasu ka?*"

The man scrambled up and talked rapidly to the others and they looked too. Now they all saw the ledge. And they began to shout. Still no movement from Yabu. He seemed like a stone. They went on and Blackthorne added his shouts but it was as if they made no sound at all.

One of them spoke to the others briefly and they all nodded and bowed. He bowed back. Then, with a sudden screaming shout of *"Bansaiiiiiii!"* he cast himself off the cliff and fell to his death. Yabu came violently out of his trance, whirled around and scrambled up.

The other samurai shouted and pointed but Blackthorne heard nothing and saw nothing but the broken corpse that lay below, already being taken by the sea. What kind of men are these? he thought helplessly. Was that courage or just insanity? That man deliberately committed suicide on the off-chance he'd attract the attention of another man who had given up. It doesn't make sense! They don't make sense.

He saw Yabu stagger up. He expected him to scramble for safety, leaving Rodrigues. That's what I would have done. Is it? I don't know. But Yabu half crawled, half slid, dragging the unconscious man with him through the surf-disturbed shallows to the bottom of the cliff. He found the ledge. It was barely a foot wide. Painfully he shoved Rodrigues onto it, almost losing him once, then hauled himself up.

The rope was twenty feet short. Quickly the samurai added their loincloths. Now, if Yabu stood, he could just reach the end.

They shouted encouragement and began to wait.

In spite of Blackthorne's hatred he had to admire Yabu's courage. Half a dozen times waves almost engulfed him. Twice Rodrigues was lost but each time Yabu dragged him back, and held his head out of the grasping sea, long after Blackthorne knew that he himself would have given up. Where do you get the courage, Yabu? Are you just devil-born? All of you?

To climb down in the first place had taken courage. At first Blackthorne had thought that Yabu had acted out of bravado. But soon he had seen that the man was pitting his skill against the cliff and almost winning. Then he had broken his fall as deftly as any tumbler. And he had given up with dignity.

Christ Jesus, I admire that bastard, and detest him.

For almost an hour Yabu set himself against the sea and against his failing body, and then, in the dusk, Takatashi came back with the ropes. They made a cradle and shinned down the cliff with a skill that Blackthorne had never seen ashore.

Quickly Rodrigues was brought aloft. Blackthorne would have tried to succor him but a Japanese with close-cropped hair was already on his knees beside him. He watched as this man, obviously a doctor, examined the broken leg. Then a samurai held Rodrigues' shoulders as the doctor leaned his weight on the foot and the bone slid back under the flesh. His fingers probed and shoved and reset it and tied it to the splint. He began to wrap noxious-looking herbs around the angry wound and then Yabu was brought up.

The *daimyo* shook off any help, waved the doctor back to Rodrigues, sat down and began to wait.

Blackthorne looked at him. Yabu felt his eyes. The two men stared at each other.

"Thank you," Blackthorne said finally, pointing at Rodrigues. "Thank you for saving his life. Thank you, Yabu-san." Deliberately he bowed. That's for your courage, you black-eyed son of a shit-festered whore.

Yabu bowed back as stiffly. But inside, he smiled.

BOOK TWO

CHAPTER 10

THEIR journey from the bay to Osaka was uneventful. Rodrigues' rutters were explicit and very accurate. During the first night Rodrigues regained consciousness. In the beginning he thought he was dead but the pain soon reminded him differently.

"They've set your leg and dressed it," Blackthorne said. "And your shoulder's strapped up. It was dislocated. They wouldn't bleed you, much as I tried to make them."

"When I get to Osaka the Jesuits can do that." Rodrigues' tormented eyes bored into him. "How did I get here, Ingeles? I remember going overboard but nothing else."

Blackthorne told him.

"So now I owe you a life. God curse you."

"From the quarterdeck it looked as though we could make the bay. From the bow, your angle of sight would be a few degrees different. The wave was bad luck."

"That doesn't worry me, Ingeles. You had the quarterdeck, you had the helm. We both knew it. No, I curse you to hell because I owe you a life now— Madonna, my leg!" Tears welled because of the pain and Blackthorne gave him a mug of grog and watched him during the night, the storm abating. The Japanese doctor came several times and forced Rodrigues to drink hot medicine and put hot towels on his forehead and opened the portholes. And every time the doctor went away Blackthorne closed the portholes, for everyone knew that disease was airborne, that the tighter closed the cabin the safer and more healthy, when a man was as bad as Rodrigues.

At length the doctor shouted at him and posted a samurai on the portholes so they remained open.

At dawn Blackthorne went on deck. Hiro-matsu and Yabu were both there. He bowed like a courtier. "*Konnichi wa.* Osaka?"

They bowed in return. "Osaka. *Hai,* Anjin-san," Hiro-matsu said.

"*Hai! Isogi,* Hiro-matsu-sama. Captain-san! Weigh anchor!"

"*Hai,* Anjin-san!"

He smiled involuntarily at Yabu. Yabu smiled back, then limped away and thought, that's one hell of a man, although he's a devil and a murderer. Aren't *you* a murderer, too? Yes—but not that way, he told himself.

Blackthorne conned the ship to Osaka with ease. The journey took that day and the night and just after dawn the next day they were near the Osaka roads. A Japanese pilot came aboard to take the ship to her wharf so, relieved of his responsibility, he gladly went below to sleep.

Later the captain shook him awake, bowed, and pantomimed that Blackthorne should be ready to go with Hiro-matsu as soon as they docked.

"*Wakarimasu ka,* Anjin-san?"

"*Hai.*"

The seaman went away. Blackthorne stretched his back, aching, then saw Rodrigues watching him.

"How do you feel?"

123

"Good, Ingeles. Considering my leg's on fire, my head's bursting, I want to piss, and my tongue tastes like a barrel of pig shit looks."

Blackthorne gave him the chamber pot, then emptied it out the porthole. He refilled the tankard with grog.

"You make a foul nurse, Ingeles. It's your black heart." Rodrigues laughed and it was good to hear him laugh again. His eyes went to the rutter that was open on the desk, and to his sea chest. He saw that it had been unlocked. "Did I give you the key?"

"No. I searched you. I had to have the true rutter. I told you when you woke the first night."

"That's fair. I don't remember, but that's fair. Listen, Ingeles, ask any Jesuit where Vasco Rodrigues is in Osaka and they'll guide you to me. Come to see me—then you can make a copy of my rutter, if you wish."

"Thanks. I've already taken one. At least, I copied what I could, and I've read the rest very carefully."

"Thy mother!" Rodrigues said in Spanish.

"And thine."

Rodrigues turned to Portuguese again. "Speaking Spanish makes me want to retch, even though you can swear better in it than any language. There's a package in my sea chest. Give it to me, please."

"The one with the Jesuit seals?"

"Yes."

He gave it to him. Rodrigues studied it, fingering the unbroken seals, then seemed to change his mind and put the package on the rough blanket under which he lay, leaning his head back again. "Ah, Ingeles, life is so strange."

"Why?"

"If I live, it is because of God's grace, helped by a heretic and a Japman. Send the sod-eater below so I can thank him, eh?"

"Now?"

"Later."

"All right."

"This fleet of yours, the one you claim's attacking Manila, the one you told the Father about—what's the truth, Ingeles?"

"A fleet of our warships'll wreck your Empire in Asia, won't it?"

"Is there a fleet?"

"Of course."

"How many ships were in your fleet?"

"Five. The rest are out to sea, a week or so. I came ahead to probe Japan and got caught in the storm."

"More lies, Ingeles. But I don't mind—I've told my captors as many. There are no more ships or fleets."

"Wait and see."

"I will." Rodrigues drank heavily.

Blackthorne stretched and went to the porthole, wanting to stop this conversation, and looked out at the shore and the city. "I thought London was the biggest city on earth, but compared to Osaka it's a small town."

"They've dozens of cities like this one," Rodrigues said, also glad to stop the cat-and-mouse game that would never bear fruit without the rack. "Miyako, the capital, or Kyoto as it's sometimes called, is the biggest city in the Empire, more than twice the size of Osaka, so they say. Next comes Yedo, Toranaga's capital. I've never been there, nor any priest or Portuguese—Toranaga keeps his capital locked away—a forbidden city. Still," Rodrigues added, lying back in his bunk and closing his eyes, his face stretched with pain, "still, that's no different to everywhere. All Japan's officially forbidden to us, except the ports of Nagasaki and Hirado. Our priests rightly don't pay much attention to the orders and go where they please. But we seamen can't or traders, unless it's on a special pass from the Regents, or a great *daimyo,* like Toranaga. Any *daimyo* can seize one of our ships—like Toranaga's got yours—outside of Nagasaki or Hirado. That's their law."

"Do you want to rest now?"

"No, Ingeles. Talking's better. Talking helps to take the pain away. Madonna, my head hurts! I can't think clearly. Let's talk until you go ashore. Come back and see me—there's lots I want to ask you. Give me some more grog. Thank you, thank you, Ingeles."

"Why're you forbidden to go where you please?"

"What? Oh, here in Japan? It was the Taikō—he started all the trouble. Ever since we first came here in 1542 to begin God's work and to bring them civilization, we and our priests could move freely, but when the Taikō got all power he started the prohibitions. Many believe . . . could you shift my leg, take the blanket off my foot, it's burning . . . yes—oh, Madonna, be careful—there, thank you, Ingeles. Yes, where was I? Oh yes . . . many believe the Taikō was Satan's penis. Ten years ago he issued Edicts against the Holy Fathers, Ingeles, and all who wanted to spread the word of God. And he banished everyone, except traders, ten, twelve-odd years ago. It was before I came to these waters—I've been here seven years, off and on. The Holy Fathers say it was because of the heathen priests—the Buddhists—the stinking, jealous idol worshipers, these heathens, they turned the Taikō against our Holy Fathers, filled him with lies, when they'd almost converted him. Yes, the Great Murderer himself almost had his soul saved. But he missed his chance for salvation. Yes. Anyway, he ordered all of our priests to leave Japan. . . . Did I tell you this was ten-odd years ago?"

Blackthorne nodded, glad to let him ramble and glad to listen, desperate to learn.

"The Taikō had all the Fathers collected at Nagasaki, ready to ship them out to Macao with written orders never to return on pain of death. Then, as suddenly, he left them all alone and did no more. I told you Japmen are upside-downers. Yes, he left them alone and soon it was as before, except that most of the Fathers stayed in Kyushu where we're welcome. Did I tell you Japan's made up of three big islands, Kyushu, Shikoku, and Honshu? And thousands of little ones. There's another island far to the north—some say it's the mainland—called Hokkaido, but only hairy natives live there.

"Japan's an upside-down world, Ingeles. Father Alvito told me it became again as though nothing had ever happened. The Taikō was as friendly as before, though he never converted. He hardly shut down a church and only banished two or three of the Christian *daimyos*—but that was just to get their lands—and never enforced his Expulsion Edicts. Then, three years ago, he went mad again and martyred twenty-six Fathers. He crucified them at Nagasaki. For no reason. He was a maniac, Ingeles. But after murdering the twenty-six he did nothing more. He died soon after. It was the Hand of God, Ingeles. The curse of God was on him and is on his seed. I'm sure of it."

"Do you have many converts here?"

But Rodrigues did not seem to hear, lost in his own half-consciousness. "They're animals, the Japaners. Did I tell you about Father Alvito? He's the interpreter—Tsukku-san they call him, Mr. Interpreter. He was the Taikō's interpreter, Ingeles, now he's the official interpreter for the Council of Regents and he speaks Japanese better'n most Japanese and knows more about them than any man alive. He told me there's a mound of earth fifty feet high in Miyako—

that's the capital, Ingeles. The Taikō had the noses and ears of all the Koreans killed in the war collected and buried there—Korea's part of the mainland, west of Kyushu. It's the truth! By the Blessed Virgin, there was never a killer like him—and they're all as bad." Rodrigues' eyes were closed and his forehead flushed.

"Do you have many converts?" Blackthorne carefully asked again, wanting desperately to know how many enemies were here.

To his shock, Rodrigues said, "Hundreds of thousands, and more every year. Since the Taikō's death we have more than ever before, and those who were secretly Christian now go to the church openly. Most of the island of Kyushu's Catholic now. Most of the Kyushu *daimyos* are converts. Nagasaki's a Catholic city, Jesuits own it and run it and control all trade. All trade goes through Nagasaki. We have a cathedral, a dozen churches, and dozens more spread through Kyushu, but only a few yet here in the main island, Honshu, and . . ." Pain stopped him again. After a moment he continued, "There are three or four million people in Kyushu alone—they'll all be Catholic soon. There's another twenty-odd million Japmen in the islands and soon—"

"That's not possible!" Blackthorne immediately cursed himself for interrupting the flow of information.

"Why should I lie? There was a census ten years ago. Father Alvito said the Taikō ordered it and he should know, he was there. Why should he lie?" Rodrigues' eyes were feverish and now his mouth was running away with him. "That's more than the population of all Portugal, all Spain, all France, the Spanish Netherlands, and England added together and you could almost throw in the whole Holy Roman Empire as well to equal it!"

Lord Jesus, Blackthorne thought, the whole of England hasn't got more than three million people. And that includes Wales as well.

If there are that many Japanese, how can we deal with them? If there's twenty million, that'd mean they could easily press an army of more men than we've got in our entire population if they wanted. And if they're all as ferocious as the ones I've seen—and why shouldn't they be—by God's wounds, they'd be unbeatable. And if they're already partially Catholic, and if the Jesuits are here in strength, their numbers will increase, and there's no fanatic like a converted fanatic, so what chance have we and the Dutch got in Asia?

None at all.

"If you think that's a lot," Rodrigues was saying, "wait till you go to China. They're all yellow men there, all with black hair and eyes. Oh, Ingeles, I tell you you've so much new to learn. I was in Canton last year, at the silk sales. Canton's a walled city in south China, on the Pearl River, north of our City of the Name of God at Macao. There's a million of the heathen dog-eaters within those walls alone. China's got more people than all the rest of the world put together. Must have. Think of that!" A spasm of pain went through Rodrigues and his good hand held onto his stomach. "Was there any blood seeping out of me? Anywhere?"

"No. I made sure. It's just your leg and shoulder. You're not hurt inside, Rodrigues—at least, I don't think so."

"How bad is the leg?"

"It was washed by the sea and cleaned by the sea. The break was clean and the skin's clean, at the moment."

"Did you pour brandy over it and fire it?"

"No. They wouldn't let me—they ordered me off. But the doctor seemed to know what he's doing. Will your own people come aboard quickly?"

"Yes. Soon as we dock. That's more than likely."

"Good. You were saying? About China and Canton?"

"I was saying too much, perhaps. Time enough to talk about them."

Blackthorne watched the Portuguese's good hand toy with the sealed package and he wondered again what significance it had. "Your leg will be all right. You'll know within the week."

"Yes, Ingeles."

"I don't think it'll rot—there's no pus—you're thinking clearly so your brain's all right. You'll be fine, Rodrigues."

"I still owe you a life." A shiver ran through the Portuguese. "When I was drowning, all I could think of was the crabs climbing in through my eyes. I could feel them churning inside me, Ingeles. That's the third time I've been overboard and each time it's worse."

"I've been sunk at sea four times. Three times by Spaniards."

The cabin door opened and the captain bowed and beckoned Blackthorne aloft.

"*Hai!*" Blackthorne got up. "You owe me nothing, Rodrigues," he said kindly. "You gave me life and succor when I was desperate, and I thank you for that. We're even."

"Perhaps, but listen, Ingeles, here's some truth for you, in part payment: Never forget Japmen're six-faced and have three hearts. It's a saying they have, that a man has a false heart in his mouth for all the world to see, another in his breast to show his very special friends and his family, and the real one, the true one, the secret one, which is never known to anyone except himself alone, hidden only God knows where. They're treacherous beyond belief, vice-ridden beyond redemption."

"Why does Toranaga want to see me?"

"I don't know. By the Blessed Virgin! I don't know. Come back to see me, if you can."

"Yes. Good luck, Spaniard!"

"Thy sperm! Even so, go with God."

Blackthorne smiled back, unguarded, and then he was on deck and his mind whirled from the impact of Osaka, its immensity, the teaming anthills of people, and the enormous castle that dominated the city. From within the castle's vastness came the soaring beauty of the donjon—the central keep—seven or eight stories high, pointed gables with curved roofs at each level, the tiles all gilded and the walls blue.

That's where Toranaga will be, he thought, an ice barb suddenly in his bowels.

A closed palanquin took him to a large house. There he was bathed and he ate, inevitably, fish soup, raw and steamed fish, a few pickled vegetables, and the hot herbed water. Instead of wheat gruel, this house provided him with a bowl of rice. He had seen rice once in Naples. It was white and wholesome, but to him tasteless. His stomach cried for meat and bread, new-baked crusty bread heavy with butter, and a haunch of beef and pies and chickens and beer and eggs.

The next day a maid came for him. The clothes that Rodrigues had given him were laundered. She watched while he dressed, and helped him into new tabi sock-shoes. Outside was a new pair of thongs. His boots were missing. She shook her head and pointed at the thongs and then at the curtained palanquin. A phalanx of samurai surrounded it. The leader motioned him to hurry up and get in.

They moved off immediately. The curtains were tight closed. After an age, the palanquin stopped.

"You will not be afraid," he said aloud, and got out.

The gigantic stone gate of the castle was in front of him. It was set into a thirty-foot wall with interlocking battlements, bastions, and outworks. The door was huge and iron plated and open, the forged iron portcullis up. Beyond was a wooden bridge, twenty paces wide and two hundred long, that spanned the moat and ended at an enormous drawbridge, and another gate that was set into the second wall, equally vast.

Hundreds of samurai were everywhere. All wore the same somber gray uniform —belted kimonos, each with five small circular insignias, one on each arm, on each breast, and one in the center of the back. The insignia was blue, seemingly a flower or flowers.

"Anjin-san!"

Hiro-matsu was seated stiffly on an open palanquin carried by four liveried bearers. His kimono was brown and stark, his belt black, the same as the fifty samurai that surrounded him. Their kimonos, too, had five insignias, but these were scarlet, the same that had fluttered at the masthead, Toranaga's cipher. These samurai carried long gleaming spears with tiny flags at their heads.

Blackthorne bowed without thinking, taken by Hiro-matsu's majesty. The old man bowed back formally, his long sword loose in his lap, and signed for him to follow.

The officer at the gate came forward. There was a ceremonial reading of the paper that Hiro-matsu offered and many bows and looks toward Blackthorne and then they were passed on to the bridge, an escort of the Grays falling in beside them.

The surface of the deep moat was fifty feet below and stretched about three hundred paces on either side, then followed the walls as they turned north and Blackthorne thought, Lord God, I'd hate to have to try to mount an attack here. The defenders could let the outer-wall garrison perish and burn the bridge, then they're safe inside. Jesus God, the outer wall must be nearly a mile square and look, it must be twenty, thirty feet thick—the inner one, too. And it's made out of huge blocks of stone. Each one must be ten feet by ten feet! At least! And cut perfectly and set into place without mortar. They must weigh fifty tons at least. Better than any we could make. Siege guns? Certainly they could batter the outer walls, but the guns defending would give as good as they got. It'd be hard to get them up here, and there's no higher point from which to lob fireballs into the castle. If the outer wall was taken, the defenders could still blast the attackers off the battlements. But even if siege guns could be mounted there and they were turned on the next wall and battered it, they wouldn't hurt it. They could damage the far gate, but what would that accomplish? How could the moat be crossed? It's too vast for the normal methods. The castle must be impregnable—with enough soldiers. How many soldiers are here? How many townspeople would have sanctuary inside?

It makes the Tower of London like a pigsty. And the whole of Hampton Court would fit into one corner!

At the next gate there was another ceremonial checking of papers and the road turned left immediately, down a vast avenue lined with heavily fortified houses behind easily defended greater walls and lesser walls, then doubled on itself into a labyrinth of steps and roads. Then there was another gate and more checking, another portcullis and another vast moat and new twistings and turnings until Blackthorne, who was an acute observer with an extraordinary memory and sense of direction, was lost in the deliberate maze. And all the time numberless Grays stared down at them from escarpments and ramparts and battlements and parapets and bastions. And there were more on foot, guarding, marching, training or tending horses in open stables. Soldiers everywhere, by the thousand. All well armed and meticulously clothed.

He cursed himself for not being clever enough to get more out of Rodrigues. Apart from the information about the Taikō and the converts, which was staggering enough, Rodrigues had been as closemouthed as a man should be—as you were, avoiding his questions.

Concentrate. Look for clues. What's special about this castle? It's the biggest. No, something's different. What?

Are the Grays hostile to the Browns? I can't tell, they're all so serious.

Blackthorne watched them carefully and focused on details. To the left was a carefully tended, multicolored garden, with little bridges and a tiny stream. The walls were now spaced closer together, the roads narrower. They were nearing the donjon. There were no townspeople inside but hundreds of servants and— *There are no cannon!* That's what's different!

You haven't seen any cannon. Not one.

Lord God in Heaven, no cannon—therefore no siege guns!

If you had modern weapons and the defenders none, could you blow the walls down, the doors down, rain fireballs on the castle, set it afire and take it?

You couldn't get across the first moat.

With siege guns you could make it difficult for the defenders but they could hold out forever—if the garrison was determined, if there were enough of them, with enough food, water, and ammunition.

How to cross the moats? By boat? Rafts with towers?

His mind was trying to devise a plan when the palanquin stopped. Hiro-matsu got down. They were in a narrow cul-de-sac. A huge iron-fortified timber gate was let into the twenty-foot wall which melted into the outworks of the fortified strongpoint above, still distant from the donjon, which from here was mostly obscured. Unlike all other gateways this was guarded by Browns, the only ones Blackthorne had seen within the castle. It was clear that they were more than a little pleased to see Hiro-matsu.

The Grays turned and left. Blackthorne noted the hostile looks they had received from the Browns.

So they're enemies!

The gate swung open and he followed the old man inside. Alone. The other samurai stayed outside.

The inner courtyard was guarded by more Browns and so was the garden beyond. They crossed the garden and entered the fort. Hiro-matsu kicked off his thongs and Blackthorne did likewise.

The corridor inside was richly carpeted with tatamis, the same rush mats, clean and kind to the feet, that were set into the floors of all but the poorest houses. Blackthorne had noticed before that they were all the same size, about six feet by three feet. Come to think of it, he told himself, I've never seen any mats shaped or cut to size. And there's never been an odd-shaped room! Haven't all the rooms been exactly square or rectangular? Of course! That means that all houses—or rooms—must be constructed to fit an exact number of mats. So they're all standard! How very odd!

They climbed winding, defendable stairs, and went along additional corridors and more stairs. There were many guards, always Browns. Shafts of sunlight from the wall embrasures cast intricate patterns. Blackthorne could see that now they were high over the three encircling main walls. The city and the harbor were a patterned quilt below.

The corridor turned a sharp corner and ended fifty paces away.

Blackthorne tasted bile in his mouth. Don't worry, he told himself, you've decided what to do. You're committed.

Massed samurai, their young officer in front of them, protected the last door— each with right hand on the sword hilt, left on the scabbard, motionless and ready, staring toward the two men who approached.

Hiro-matsu was reassured by their readiness. He had personally selected these guards. He hated the castle and thought again how dangerous it had been for Toranaga to put himself into the enemy's power. Directly he had landed yesterday he had rushed to Toranaga, to tell him what had happened and to find out if anything untoward had occurred in his absence. But all was still quiet though their spies whispered about dangerous enemy buildups to the north and east, and that their main allies, the Regents, Onoshi and Kiyama, the greatest of the Christian *daimyos,* were going to defect to Ishido. He had changed the guard and the passwords and had again begged Toranaga to leave, to no avail.

Ten paces from the officer he stopped.

CHAPTER 11

YOSHI NAGA, officer of the watch, was a mean-tempered, dangerous youth of seventeen. "Good morning, Sire. Welcome back."

"Thank you. Lord Toranaga's expecting me."

"Yes." Even if Hiro-matsu had not been expected, Naga would still have admitted him. Toda Hiro-matsu was one of only three persons in the world who were to be allowed into Toranaga's presence by day or by night, without appointment.

"Search the barbarian," Naga said. He was Toranaga's fifth son by one of his consorts, and he worshiped his father.

Blackthorne submitted quietly, realizing what they were doing. The two samurai were very expert. Nothing would have escaped them.

Naga motioned to the rest of his men. They moved aside. He opened the thick door himself.

Hiro-matsu entered the immense audience room. Just beyond the doorway he knelt, put his swords on the floor in front of him, placed his hands flat on the floor beside them and bowed his head low, waiting in that abject position.

Naga, ever watchful, indicated to Blackthorne to do the same.

Blackthorne walked in. The room was forty paces square and ten high, the tatami mats the best quality, four fingers thick and impeccable. There were two doors in the far wall. Near the dais, in a niche, was a small earthenware vase with a single spray of cherry blossom and this filled the room with color and fragrance.

Both doors were guarded. Ten paces from the dais, circling it, were twenty more samurai, seated cross-legged and facing outward.

Toranaga sat on a single cushion on the dais. He was repairing a broken wing feather of a hooded falcon as delicately as any ivory carver.

Neither he nor anyone in the room had acknowledged Hiro-matsu or paid any attention to Blackthorne as he walked in and stopped beside the old man. But unlike Hiro-matsu, Blackthorne bowed as Rodrigues had shown him, then, taking a deep breath, he sat cross-legged and stared at Toranaga.

All eyes flashed to Blackthorne.

In the doorway Naga's hand was on his sword. Hiro-matsu had already grasped his, though his head was still bent.

Blackthorne felt naked but he had committed himself and now he could only wait. Rodrigues had said, 'With Japmen you've got to act like a king,' and though this wasn't acting like a king, it was more than enough.

Toranaga looked up slowly.

A bead of sweat started at Blackthorne's temple as everything Rodrigues had told him about samurai seemed to crystalize in this one man. He felt the sweat trickle down his cheek to his chin. He willed his blue eyes firm and unblinking, his face calm.

Toranaga's gaze was equally steady.

Blackthorne felt the almost overwhelming power of the man reach out to him. He forced himself to count slowly to six, and then he inclined his head and bowed slightly again and formed a small, calm smile.

131

Toranaga watched him briefly, his face impassive, then looked down and concentrated on his work again. Tension subsided in the room.

The falcon was a peregrine and she was in her prime. The handler, a gnarled old samurai, knelt in front of Toranaga and held her as though she were spun glass. Toranaga cut the broken quill, dipped the tiny bamboo imping needle into the glue and inserted it into the haft of the feather, then delicately slipped the new cut feather over the other end. He adjusted the angle until it was perfect and bound it with a silken thread. The tiny bells on her feet jingled, and he gentled the fear out of her.

Yoshi Toranaga, Lord of the Kwanto—the Eight Provinces—head of the clan Yoshi, Chief General of the Armies of the East, President of the Council of Regents, was a short man with a big belly and large nose. His eyebrows were thick and dark and his mustache and beard gray-flecked and sparse. Eyes dominated his face. He was fifty-eight and strong for his age. His kimono was simple, an ordinary Brown uniform, his sash belt cotton. But his swords were the best in the world.

"There, my beauty," he said with a lover's tenderness. "Now you are whole again." He caressed the bird with a feather as she sat hooded on the handler's gauntleted fist. She shivered and preened herself contentedly. "We'll fly her within the week."

The handler bowed and left.

Toranaga turned his eyes on the two men at the door. "Welcome, Iron Fist, I'm pleased to see you," he said. "So this is your famous barbarian?"

"Yes, Lord." Hiro-matsu came closer, leaving his swords at the doorway as was custom, but Toranaga insisted he bring them with him.

"I would feel uncomfortable if you didn't have them in your hands," he said.

Hiro-matsu thanked him. Even so, he sat five paces away. By custom, no one armed could safely come closer to Toranaga. In the front rank of the guards was Usagi, Hiro-matsu's favorite grandson-in-law, and he nodded to him briefly. The youth bowed deeply, honored and pleased to be noticed. Perhaps I should adopt him formally, Hiro-matsu told himself happily, warmed by the thought of his favorite granddaughter and his first great-grandson that they had presented him with last year.

"How is your back?" Toranaga asked solicitously.

"All right, thank you, Lord. But I must tell you I'm glad to be off that ship and on land again."

"I hear you've a new toy here to idle away the hours with, *neh?*"

The old man guffawed. "I can only tell you, Lord, the hours weren't idle. I haven't been so hard in years."

Toranaga laughed with him. "Then we should reward her. Your health is important to me. May I send her a token of my thanks?"

"Ah, Toranaga-sama, you're so kind." Hiro-matsu became serious. "You could reward all of us, Sire, by leaving this hornet's nest at once, and going back to your castle at Yedo where your vassals can protect you. Here we're naked. Any moment Ishido could—"

"I will. As soon as the Council of Regents meeting is concluded." Toranaga turned and beckoned the lean-faced Portuguese who was sitting patiently in his shadow. "Will you interpret for me now, my friend?"

"Certainly, Sire." The tonsured priest came forward, with practiced grace kneeled in Japanese style close to the dais, his body as spare as his face, his eyes dark and liquid, an air of serene concentration about him. He wore tabi socks and a flowing kimono that seemed, on him, to belong. A rosary and a carved golden cross hung at his belt. He greeted Hiro-matsu as an equal, then glanced pleasantly at Blackthorne.

"My name is Martin Alvito of the Society of Jesus, Captain-Pilot. Lord Toranaga has asked me to interpret for him."

"First tell him that we're enemies and that—"

"All in good time," Father Alvito interrupted smoothly. Then he added, "We can speak Portuguese, Spanish, or, of course, Latin—whichever you prefer."

Blackthorne had not seen the priest until the man came forward. The dais had hidden him, and the other samurai. But he had been expecting him, forewarned by Rodrigues, and loathed what he saw: the easy elegance, the aura of strength and natural power of the Jesuits. He had assumed the priest would be much older, considering his influential position and the way Rodrigues had talked about him. But they were practically of an age, he and the Jesuit. Perhaps the priest was a few years older.

"Portuguese," he said, grimly hoping that this might give him a slight advantage. "You're Portuguese?"

"I have that privilege."

"You're younger than I expected."

"Senhor Rodrigues is very kind. He gives me more credit than I deserve. He described you perfectly. Also your bravery."

Blackthorne saw him turn and talk fluently and affably to Toranaga for a while, and this further perturbed him. Hiro-matsu alone, of all the men in the room, listened and watched attentively. The rest stared stonily into space.

"Now, Captain-Pilot, we will begin. You will please listen to everything that Lord Toranaga says, without interruption," Father Alvito began. "Then you will answer. From now on I will be translating what you say almost simultaneously, so please answer with great care."

"What's the point? I don't trust you!"

Immediately Father Alvito was translating what he had said to Toranaga, who darkened perceptibly.

Be careful, thought Blackthorne, he's playing you like a fish! Three golden guineas to a chewed farthing he can land you whenever he wants. Whether or not he translates accurately, you've got to create the correct impression on Toranaga. This may be the only chance you'll ever have.

"You can trust me to translate exactly what you say as best I can." The priest's voice was gentle, in complete command. "This is the court of Lord Toranaga. I am the official interpreter to the Council of Regents, to General Lord Toranaga and to General Lord Ishido. Lord Toranaga has favored me with his confidence for many years. I suggest you answer truthfully because I can assure you he is a most discerning man. Also I should point out that I am not Father Sebastio, who is, perhaps, overzealous and does not, unfortunately, speak Japanese very well, or, unfortunately, have much experience in Japan. Your sudden presence took away God's grace from him and, regrettably, he allowed his personal past to overwhelm him—his parents and brothers and sisters were massacred in the most horrible way in the Netherlands by your—by forces of the Prince of Orange. I ask your indulgence for him and your compassion." He smiled benignly. "The Japanese word for 'enemy' is 'teki.' You may use it if you wish. If you point at me and use the word, Lord Toranaga will understand clearly what you mean. Yes, I am your enemy, Captain-Pilot John Blackthorne. Completely. But not your assassin. That you will do yourself."

Blackthorne saw him explain to Toranaga what he had said and heard the word "teki" used several times and he wondered if it truly meant "enemy." Of course it does, he told himself. This man's not like the other one.

"Please, for a moment, forget that I exist," Father Alvito said. "I'm merely an instrument for making your answers known to Lord Toranaga, exactly as I will put *his* questions to you." Father Alvito settled himself, turned to Toranaga, bowed politely.

Toranaga spoke curtly. The priest began translating simultaneously, a few words or so later, his voice an uncanny mirror of inflection and inner meaning.

"Why are you an enemy of Tsukku-san, my friend and interpreter, who's an enemy of no one?" Father Alvito added by way of explanation, "Tsukku-san's my nickname as Japanese cannot pronounce my name either. They have no 'l' or 'th' sounds in their language. Tsukku's a pun on the Japanese word '*tsuyaku*' —to interpret. Please answer the question."

"We're enemies because our countries are at war."

"Oh? What is your country?"

"England."

"Where's that?"

"It's an island kingdom, a thousand miles north of Portugal. Portugal's part of a peninsula in Europe."

"How long have you been at war with Portugal?"

"Ever since Portugal became a *vassal* state of Spain. That was in 1580, twenty years ago. Spain conquered Portugal. We're really at war with Spain. We've been at war with Spain for almost thirty years."

Blackthorne noticed Toranaga's surprise and his searching glance at Father Alvito, who stared serenely into the distance.

"You say Portugal's part of Spain?"

"Yes, Lord Toranaga. A vassal state. Spain conquered Portugal and now they're in effect the same country with the same king. But the Portuguese are subservient to Spain in most parts of the world and their leaders treated as unimportant in the Spanish Empire."

There was a long silence. Then Toranaga spoke directly to the Jesuit, who smiled and answered at length.

"What did he say?" Blackthorne asked sharply.

Father Alvito did not answer but translated as before, almost simultaneously, aping his inflection, continuing a virtuoso performance of interpreting.

Toranaga answered Blackthorne directly, his voice flinty and cruel. "What I said is no concern of yours. When I wish you to know something I will tell you."

"I'm sorry, Lord Toranaga, I did not mean to be rude. May I tell you that we come in peace—"

"You may not tell me anything at the moment. You will hold your tongue until I require an answer. Do you understand?"

"Yes."

Mistake number one. Watch yourself. You can't make mistakes, he told himself.

"Why are you at war with Spain? And Portugal?"

"Partially because Spain is bent on conquering the world and we English, and our allies the Netherlands, refuse to be conquered. And partially because of our religions."

"Ah! A religious war? What is your religion?"

"I'm a Christian. Our Church—"

"The Portuguese and Spanish are Christians! You said your religion was different. What is your religion?"

"It's Christian. It's difficult to explain simply and quickly, Lord Toranaga. They're both—"

"There's no need to be quick, Mr. Pilot, just accurate. I have plenty of time.

I'm very patient. You're a cultured man—obviously no peasant—so you can be simple or complicated as you wish, just so long as you're clear. If you stray from the point I will bring you back. You were saying?"

"My religion is Christian. There are two main Christian religions, Protestant and Catholic. Most English are Protestant."

"You worship the same God, the Madonna and Child?"

"No, Sire. Not the way the Catholics do." What does he want to know? Blackthorne was asking himself. Is he a Catholic? Should you answer what you think he wants to know, or what you think is the truth? Is he anti-Christian? Didn't he call the Jesuit "my friend"? Is Toranaga a Catholic sympathizer, or is he going to become a Catholic?

"Do you believe the Jesus is God?"

"I believe in God," he said carefully.

"Do not evade a direct question! Do you believe the Jesus is God? Yes or no?"

Blackthorne knew that in any Catholic court in the world he would have been damned long since for heresy. And in most, if not all, Protestant courts. Even to hesitate before answering such a question was an admission of doubt. Doubt was heresy. "You can't answer questions about God with a simple 'yes' or 'no.' There have to be shades of 'yes' or 'no.' You don't know for certain about God until you're dead. Yes, I believe Jesus was God, but no, I don't know for certain until I'm dead."

"Why did you smash the priest's cross when you first arrived in Japan?"

Blackthorne had not been expecting this question. Does Toranaga know everything that's happened since I arrived? "I—I wanted to show the *daimyo* Yabu that the Jesuit, Father Sebastio—the only interpreter there—that he was my enemy, that he wasn't to be trusted, at least, in my opinion. Because I was sure he wouldn't necessarily translate accurately, not as Father Alvito is doing now. He accused us of being pirates, for instance. We're not pirates, we come in peace."

"Ah yes! Pirates. I'll come back to piracy in a moment. You say both your sects are Christian, both venerate Jesus the Christ? Isn't the essence of his teaching 'to love one another'?"

"Yes."

"Then how can you be enemies?"

"Their faith—their version of Christianity is a false interpretation of the Scriptures."

"Ah! At last we're getting somewhere. So you're at war through a difference of opinion about what is God or not God?"

"Yes."

"That's a very stupid reason to go to war."

Blackthorne said, "I agree." He looked at the priest. "I agree with all my heart."

"How many ships are in your fleet?"

"Five."

"And you were the senior pilot?"

"Yes."

"Where are the others?"

"Out to sea," Blackthorne said carefully, continuing his lie, presuming that Toranaga had been primed to ask certain questions by Alvito. "We were split up in a storm and scattered. Where exactly I don't know, Sire."

"Your ships were English?"

"No, Sire. Dutch. From Holland."

"Why is an Englishman in charge of Dutch ships?"

"That's not unusual, Sire. We're allies—Portuguese pilots sometimes lead Spanish ships and fleets. I understand Portuguese pilots con some of your ocean-going ships by law."

"There are no Dutch pilots?"

"Many, Sire. But for such a long voyage English are more experienced."

"But why you? Why did they want *you* to lead their ships?"

"Probably because my mother was Dutch and I speak the language fluently and I'm experienced. I was glad of the opportunity."

"Why?"

"This was my first opportunity to sail into these waters. No English ships were planning to come so far. This was a chance to circumnavigate."

"You yourself, Pilot, you joined the fleet because of your religion and to war against your enemies Spain and Portugal?"

"I'm a pilot, Sire, first and foremost. No one English or Dutch has been in these seas before. We're primarily a trading fleet, though we've letters of marque to attack the enemy in the New World. We came to Japan to trade."

"What are letters of marque?"

"Legal licenses issued by the Crown—or government—giving authority to war on the enemy."

"Ah, and your enemies are here. Do you plan to war on them here?"

"We did not know what to expect when we got here, Sire. We came here only to trade. Your country's almost unknown—it's legend. The Portuguese and Spanish are very closemouthed about this area."

"Answer the question: Your enemies are here. Do you plan to war on them here?"

"If they war on me. Yes."

Toranaga shifted irritably. "What you do at sea or in your own countries is your own affair. But here there is one law for all and foreigners are in our land by permission only. *Any* public mischief or quarrel is dealt with immediately by death. Our laws are clear and will be obeyed. Do you understand?"

"Yes, Sire. But we come in peace. We came here to trade. Could we discuss trade, Sire? I need to careen my ship and make repairs—we can pay for everything. Then there's the ques—"

"When I wish to discuss trade or anything else I will tell you. Meanwhile please confine yourself to answering the questions. So you joined the expedition to trade, for profit, not because of duty or loyalty? For money?"

"Yes. It's our custom, Sire. To be paid and to have a share of all plun—of all trade and all enemy goods captured."

"So you're a mercenary?"

"I was hired as senior pilot to lead the expedition. Yes." Blackthorne could feel Toranaga's hostility but he did not understand why. What did I say that was wrong? Didn't the priest say I'd assassinate myself? "It's a normal custom with us, Toranaga-sama," he said again.

Toranaga started conversing with Hiro-matsu and they exchanged views in obvious agreement. Blackthorne thought he could see disgust in their faces. Why? Obviously it has something to do with "mercenary," he thought. What's wrong with that? Isn't everyone paid? How else do you make enough money to live on? Even if you've inherited land, you still—

"You said earlier you came here to trade peacefully," Toranaga was saying. "Why then do you carry so many guns and so much powder, muskets and shot?"

"Our Spanish and Portuguese enemies are very powerful and strong, Lord Toranaga. We have to protect ourselves and—"

"You're saying your arms are merely defensive?"

"No. We use them not only to protect ourselves but to attack our enemies. And we produce them in abundance for trade, the best quality arms in the world. Perhaps we could trade with you in these, or in the other goods we carried."

"What is a pirate?"

"An outlaw. A man who rapes, kills, or plunders for personal profit."

"Isn't that the same as mercenary? Isn't that what you are? A pirate and the leader of pirates?"

"No. The truth is my ships have letters of marque from the legal rulers of Holland authorizing us to carry the war into all seas and places dominated up to now by our enemies. And to find markets for our goods. To the Spanish—and most Portuguese—yes, we're pirates, and religious heretics, but I repeat, the truth is we're not."

Father Alvito finished translating, then began to talk quietly but firmly, direct to Toranaga.

I wish to God I could talk as directly, Blackthorne thought, cursing. Toranaga glanced at Hiro-matsu and the old man put some questions to the Jesuit, who answered lengthily. Then Toranaga returned to Blackthorne and his voice became even more severe.

"Tsukku-san says that these 'Dutchlands'—the Netherlands—were vassals of the Spanish king up to a few years ago. Is that true?"

"Yes."

"Therefore the Netherlands—your allies—are in a state of rebellion against their lawful king?"

"They're fighting against the Spaniard, yes. But—"

"Isn't that rebellion? Yes or no?"

"Yes. But there are mitigating circumstances. Serious miti—"

"There are no 'mitigating circumstances' when it comes to rebellion against a sovereign lord."

"Unless you win."

Toranaga looked intently at him. Then laughed uproariously. He said something to Hiro-matsu through his laughter and Hiro-matsu nodded.

"Yes, Mister Foreigner with the impossible name, yes. You named *the one* mitigating factor." Another chuckle, then the humor vanished as suddenly as it had begun. "Will you win?"

"*Hai.*"

Toranaga spoke again but the priest didn't translate at once. He was smiling peculiarly, his eyes fixed on Blackthorne. He sighed and said, "You're very sure?"

"Is that what he said or what you're saying?"

"Lord Toranaga said that. My—he said that."

"Yes. Tell him yes, I'm very sure. May I please explain why?"

Father Alvito talked to Toranaga, for much longer than it took to translate that simple question. Are you as calm as you make out? Blackthorne wanted to ask him. What's the key that'll unlock you? How do I destroy you?

Toranaga spoke and took a fan out of his sleeve.

Father Alvito began translating again with the same eerie unfriendliness, heavy with irony. "Yes, Pilot, you may tell me why you think you will win this war."

Blackthorne tried to remain confident, aware that the priest was dominating him. "We presently rule the seas in Europe—most of the seas in Europe," he said, correcting himself. Don't get carried away. Tell the truth. Twist it a little, just as the Jesuit's sure to be doing, but tell the truth. "We English smashed two huge Spanish and Portuguese war armadas—invasions—and they're unlikely to be able to mount any others. Our small island's a fortress and we're safe now. Our navy dominates the sea. Our ships are faster, more modern, and better armed.

The Spanish haven't beaten the Dutch after more than fifty years of terror, Inquisition, and bloodshed. Our allies are safe and strong and something more— they're bleeding the Spanish Empire to death. We'll win because we own the seas and because the Spanish king, in his vain arrogance, won't let an alien people free."

"You own the seas? Our seas too? The ones around our coasts?"

"No, of course not, Toranaga-sama. I didn't mean to sound arrogant. I meant, of course, European seas, though—"

"Good, I'm glad that's clear. You were saying? Though . . . ?"

"Though on *all* the high seas, we will soon be sweeping the enemy away," Blackthorne said clearly.

"You said 'the enemy.' Perhaps we're your enemies too? What then? Will you try to sink our ships and lay waste our shores?"

"I cannot conceive of being enemy to you."

"I can, very easily. What then?"

"If you came against my land I would attack you and try to beat you," Blackthorne said.

"And if your ruler orders you to attack us here?"

"I would advise against it. Strongly. Our Queen would listen. She's—"

"You're ruled by a queen and not a king?"

"Yes, Lord Toranaga. Our Queen is wise. She wouldn't—couldn't make such an unwise order."

"And if she did? Or if your legal ruler did?"

"Then I would commend my soul to God for I would surely die. One way or another."

"Yes. You would. You and all your legions." Toranaga paused for a moment. Then: "How long did it take you to come here?"

"Almost two years. Accurately one year, eleven months, and two days. An approximate sea distance of four thousand leagues, each of three miles."

Father Alvito translated, then added a brief elaboration. Toranaga and Hiro-matsu questioned the priest, and he nodded and replied. Toranaga used his fan thoughtfully.

"I converted the time and distance, Captain-Pilot Blackthorne, into their measures," the priest said politely.

"Thank you."

Toranaga spoke directly again. "How did you get here? By what route?"

"By the Pass of Magellan. If I had my maps and rutters I could show you clearly, but they were stolen—they were removed from my ship with my letters of marque and all my papers. If you—"

Blackthorne stopped as Toranaga spoke brusquely with Hiro-matsu, who was equally perturbed.

"You claim all your papers were removed—stolen?"

"Yes."

"That's terrible, if true. We abhor theft in Nippon—Japan. The punishment for theft is death. The matter will be investigated instantly. It seems incredible that any Japanese would do such a thing, though there are foul bandits and pirates, here and there."

"Perhaps they were misplaced," Blackthorne said. "And put in safekeeping somewhere. But they are valuable, Lord Toranaga. Without my sea charts I would be like a blind man in a maze. Would you like me to explain my route?"

"Yes, but later. First tell me *why* you came all that distance."

"We came to trade, peacefully," Blackthorne repeated, holding on to his impatience. "To trade and go home again. To make you richer and us richer. And to try—"

"You richer and us richer? Which of those is most important?"

"Both partners must profit, of course, and trade must be fair. We're seeking long-term trade; we'll offer better terms than you get from the Portuguese and Spanish and give better service. Our merchants—" Blackthorne stopped at the sound of loud voices outside the room. Hiro-matsu and half the guards were instantly at the doorway and the others moved into a tight knot screening the dais. The samurai on the inner doors readied as well.

Toranaga had not moved. He spoke to Father Alvito.

"You are to come over here, Captain Blackthorne, away from the door," Father Alvito said with carefully contained urgency. "If you value your life, don't move suddenly or say anything." He moved slowly to the left inner door and sat down near it.

Blackthorne bowed uneasily to Toranaga, who ignored him, and walked toward the priest cautiously, deeply conscious that from his point of view the interview was a disaster. "What's going on?" he whispered as he sat.

The nearby guards stiffened menacingly and the priest said something quickly to reassure them. "You'll be a dead man the next time you speak," he said to Blackthorne, and thought, the sooner the better. With measured slowness, he took a handkerchief from his sleeve and wiped the sweat off his hands. It had taken all his training and fortitude to remain calm and genial during the heretic's interview, which had been worse than even he and the Father-Visitor had expected.

"You'll have to be present?" the Father-Visitor had asked last night.

"Toranaga has asked me specifically."

"I think it's very dangerous for you and for all of us. Perhaps you could plead sickness. If you're there you'll have to translate what the pirate says—and from what Father Sebastio writes he's a devil on earth, as cunning as a Jew."

"It's much better I should be there, Eminence. At least I'll be able to intercept Blackthorne's less obvious lies."

"Why has he come here? Why now, when everything was becoming perfect again? Do they really have other ships in the Pacific? Is it possible they've sent a fleet against Spanish Manila? Not that I care one whit for that pestilential city or any of the Spanish colonies in the Philippines, but an enemy fleet in the Pacific! That would have terrible implications for us here in Asia. And if he could get Toranaga's ear, or Ishido's, or any of the more powerful *daimyos*—well, it would be enormously difficult, to say the least."

"Blackthorne's a fact. Fortunately we're in a position to deal with him."

"As God is my judge, if I didn't know better I'd almost believe the Spaniards —or more probably their misguided lackeys, the Franciscans and Benedictines— deliberately guided him here just to plague us."

"Perhaps they did, Eminence. There's nothing the monks won't do to destroy us. But that's only jealousy because we're succeeding where they're failing. Surely God will show them the error of their ways! Perhaps the Englishman will 'remove' himself before he does any harm. His rutters prove him to be what he is. A pirate and leader of pirates!"

"Read them to Toranaga, Martin. The parts where he describes the sacking of the defenseless settlements from Africa to Chile, and the lists of plunder and all the killings."

"Perhaps we should wait, Eminence. We can always produce the rutters. Let's hope he'll damn himself without them."

Father Alvito wiped the palms of his hands again. He could feel Blackthorne's eyes on him. God have mercy on you, he thought. For what you've said today to Toranaga, your life's not worth a counterfeit mite, and worse, your soul's beyond redemption. You're crucified, even without the evidence in your rutters. Should we send them back to Father Sebastio so he can return them to Mura? What would Toranaga do if the papers were never discovered? No, that'd be too dangerous for Mura.

The door at the far end shivered open.

"Lord Ishido wishes to see you, Sire," Naga announced. "He's—he's here in the corridor and he wishes to see you. At once, he says."

"All of you, go back to your places," Toranaga said to his men. He was instantly obeyed. But all samurai sat facing the door, Hiro-matsu at their head, swords eased in their scabbards. "Naga-san, tell Lord Ishido he is always welcome. Ask him to come in."

The tall man strode into the room. Ten of his samurai—Grays—followed, but they remained at the doorway and, at his signal, sat cross-legged.

Toranaga bowed with precise formality and the bow was returned with equal exactitude.

Father Alvito blessed his luck that he was present. The impending clash between the two rival leaders would completely affect the course of the Empire and the future of Mother Church in Japan, so any clue or direct information that might help the Jesuits to decide where to throw their influence would be of immeasurable importance. Ishido was Zen Buddhist and fanatically anti-Christian, Toranaga was Zen Buddhist and openly sympathetic. But most Christian *daimyos* supported Ishido, fearing—with justification, Father Alvito believed—the ascendence of Toranaga. The Christian *daimyos* felt that if Toranaga eliminated Ishido's influence from the Council of Regents, Toranaga would usurp all power for himself. And once he had power, they believed he would implement the Taikō's Expulsion Edicts and stamp out the True Faith. If, however, Toranaga was eliminated, the succession, a weak succession, would be assured and the Mother Church would prosper.

As the allegiance of the Christian *daimyos* wavered, so it was with all the other *daimyos* in the land, and the balance of power between the two leaders fluctuated constantly, so no one knew for certain which side was, in reality, the most powerful. Even he, Father Alvito, the most informed European in the Empire, could not say for certain which side even the Christian *daimyos* would actually support when the clash became open, or which faction would prevail.

He watched Toranaga walk off the dais, through the encircling safety of his men.

"Welcome, Lord Ishido. Please sit there." Toranaga gestured at the single cushion on the dais. "I'd like you to be comfortable."

"Thank you, no, Lord Toranaga." Ishido Kazunari was lean and swarthy and very tough, a year younger than Toranaga. They were ancient enemies. Eighty thousand samurai in and around Osaka Castle did his bidding, for he was Commander of the garrison—and therefore Commander of the Heir's Bodyguard—Chief General of the Armies of the West, Conqueror of Korea, member of the Council of Regents, and formally Inspector General of all the late Taikō's armies, which were legally all the armies of all *daimyos* throughout the realm.

"Thank you, no," he repeated. "I'd be embarrassed to be comfortable while you were not, *neh?* One day I will take your cushion, but not today."

A current of anger went through the Browns at Ishido's implied threat, but Toranaga replied amiably, "You came at a most opportune moment. I was just finishing interviewing the new barbarian. Tsukku-san, please tell him to stand up."

The priest did as he was bidden. He felt Ishido's hostility from across the room. Apart from being anti-Christian, Ishido had always been vigorous in his condemnation of all Europeans and wanted the Empire totally closed to them.

Ishido looked at Blackthorne with pronounced distaste. "I heard he was ugly but I didn't realize how ugly. Rumor has it that he's a pirate. Is he?"

"Can you doubt it? And he's also a liar."

"Then before you crucify him, please let me have him for half a day. The Heir might be amused to see him with his head on first." Ishido laughed roughly. "Or perhaps he should be taught to dance like a bear, then you could exhibit him throughout the Empire: 'The Freak from the East.'"

Though it was true that Blackthorne had, uniquely, come out of the eastern seas—unlike the Portuguese, who always came from the south and hence were called Southern Barbarians—Ishido was blatantly implying that Toranaga, who dominated the eastern provinces, was the true freak.

But Toranaga merely smiled as though he did not understand. "You're a man of vast humor, Lord Ishido," he said. "But I agree the sooner the barbarian's removed the better. He's long-winded, arrogant, loud-mouthed, an oddity, yes, but one of little value, and with no manners whatsoever. Naga-san, send some men and put him with the common criminals. Tsukku-san, tell him to follow them."

"Captain-Pilot, you are to follow those men."

"Where am I going?"

Father Alvito hesitated. He was glad that he had won, but his opponent was brave and had an immortal soul which could yet be saved. "You are to be detained," he said.

"For how long?"

"I don't know, my son. Until Lord Toranaga decides."

CHAPTER 12

As Toranaga watched the barbarian leave the room, he took his mind regretfully off the startling interview and came to grips with the more immediate problem of Ishido.

Toranaga had decided not to dismiss the priest, knowing it would further infuriate Ishido, even though he was equally certain the continued presence of the priest might be dangerous. The less foreigners know, the better. The less anyone knows the better, he thought. Will Tsukku-san's influence on the Christian *daimyos* be for me or against me? Until today I would have trusted him implicitly. But there were some strange moments with the barbarian that I don't yet understand.

Ishido deliberately did not follow the usual courtesies but came instantly to the point. "Again I must ask, what is your answer to the Council of Regents?"

"Again I repeat: As President of the Council of Regents I do not believe any answer is necessary. I've made a few minor family relationships that are unimportant. No answer is required."

"You betrothe your son, Naga-san, to the daughter of Lord Masamune—marry one of your granddaughters to Lord Zataki's son and heir—another granddaughter to Lord Kiyama's son. All the marriages are to feudal lords or their close relations and therefore not minor and absolutely contrary to our Master's orders."

"Our late Master, the Taikō, has been dead a year. Unfortunately. Yes. I regret my brother-in-law's death and would have preferred him alive and still guiding the destiny of the Empire." Toranaga added pleasantly, turning a knife in a constant wound, "If my brother-in-law were alive there's no doubt he would approve these family connections. His instructions applied to marriages that threatened the succession of *his* house. I don't threaten his house or my nephew Yaemon, the Heir. I'm content as Lord of the Kwanto. I seek no more territory. I'm at peace with my neighbors and wish his peace to continue. By the Lord Buddha, I'll not be the first to break the peace."

For six centuries the realm had been seared by constant civil war. Thirty-five years ago, a minor *daimyo* called Goroda had taken possession of Kyoto, abetted mainly by Toranaga. Over the next two decades this warrior had miraculously subdued half of Japan, made a mountain of skulls and declared himself Dictator—still not yet powerful enough to petition the reigning Emperor to grant him the title Shōgun though he was vaguely descended from a branch of the Fujimotos. Then, sixteen years ago, Goroda was assassinated by one of his generals and his power fell into the hands of his chief vassal and most brilliant general, the peasant Nakamura.

In four short years, General Nakamura, helped by Toranaga, Ishido, and others, obliterated Goroda's descendants and brought the whole of Japan under his absolute, sole control, the first time in history that one man had subjugated all the realm. In triumph, he went to Kyoto to bow before Go-Nijo, the Son of Heaven. There, because he was born peasant, Nakamura had had to accept the

142

lesser title of Kwampaku, Chief Adviser, which later he renounced in favor of his son, taking for himself the title Taikō. But every *daimyo* bowed before him, even Toranaga. Incredibly, there had been complete peace for twelve years. Last year the Taikō had died.

"By the Lord Buddha," Toranaga said again. "I'll not be the first to break the peace."

"But you will go to war?"

"A wise man prepares for treachery, *neh?* There are evil men in every province. Some are in high places. We both know the limitless extent of treachery in the hearts of men." Toranaga stiffened. "Where the Taikō left a legacy of unity, now we are split into my East and your West. The Council of Regents is divided. The *daimyos* are at odds. A Council cannot rule a maggot-infested hamlet, let alone an Empire. The sooner the Taikō's son is of age, the better. The sooner there's another Kwampaku the better."

"Or perhaps Shōgun?" Ishido said insinuatingly.

"Kwampaku or Shōgun or Taikō, the power is the same," Toranaga said. "Of what real value is a title? The *power* is the only important thing. Goroda never became Shōgun. Nakamura was more than content as Kwampaku and later Taikō. He *ruled* and that is the important thing. What does it matter that my brother-in-law was once a peasant? What does it matter that my family is ancient? What does it matter that you're low born? You're a general, a liege lord, even one of the Council of Regents."

It matters very much, Ishido thought. You know it. I know it. Every *daimyo* knows it. Even the Taikō knew it. "Yaemon is seven. In seven years he becomes Kwampaku. Until that time—"

"In *eight* years, General Ishido. That's our historic law. When my nephew is fifteen he becomes adult and inherits. Until that time we five Regents rule in his name. That's what our late Master willed."

"Yes. And he also ordered that no hostages were to be taken by Regents against one another. Lady Ochiba, the mother of the Heir, is hostage in your castle at Yedo, against your safety here, and that also violates his will. You formally agreed to obey his covenants as did all the Regents. You even signed the document in your own blood."

Toranaga sighed. "The Lady Ochiba is visiting Yedo where her only sister is in labor. Her sister is married to my son and heir. My son's place is in Yedo while I am here. What's more natural than for a sister to visit a sister at such a time? Isn't she honored? Perhaps I'll have a first grandson, *neh?*"

"The mother of the Heir is the most important lady in the Empire. She should not be in—" Ishido was going to say "enemy hands" but he thought better of it—"in an unusual city." He paused, then added clearly, "The Council would like you to order her home today."

Toranaga avoided the trap. "I repeat, the Lady Ochiba's no hostage and therefore is not under my orders and never was."

"Then let me put it differently. The Council requests her presence in Osaka instantly."

"Who requests this?"

"I do. Lord Sugiyama. Lord Onoshi and Lord Kiyama. Further, we're all agreed we wait here until she's back in Osaka. Here are their signatures."

Toranaga was livid. Thus far he had manipulated the Council so that voting was always split two to three. He had never been able to win a four-to-one against Ishido, but neither had Ishido against him. Four to one meant isolation and disaster. Why had Onoshi defected? And Kiyama? Both implacable enemies even before they had converted to the foreign religion. And what hold had Ishido now over them?

Ishido knew that he had shattered his enemy. But one move remained to make victory complete. So he implemented the plan that he and Onoshi had agreed upon. "We Regents are all agreed that the time has come to finish with those who are planning to usurp my Master's power and kill the Heir. Traitors will be condemned. They will be exhibited in the streets as common criminals, with all their generations, and then they will be executed like common criminals, with all their generations. Fujimoto, Takashima, low born, high born—no matter who. Even Minowara!"

A gasp of rage broke from every Toranaga samurai, for such sacrilege against the semi-regal families was unthinkable; then the young samurai, Usagi, Hiro-matsu's grandson-in-law, was on his feet, flushed with anger. He ripped out his killing sword and leapt at Ishido, the naked blade readied for the two-handed slash.

Ishido was prepared for the death blow and made no move to defend himself. This was what he had planned for, hoped for, and his men had been ordered not to interfere until he was dead. If he, Ishido, were killed here, now, by a Toranaga samurai, the whole Osaka garrison could fall on Toranaga legitimately and slay him, irrespective of the hostage. Then the Lady Ochiba would be eliminated in retaliation by Toranaga's sons and the remaining Regents would be forced to move jointly against the Yoshi clan, who, now isolated, would be stamped out. Only then would the Heir's succession be guaranteed and he, Ishido, would have done his duty to the Taikō.

But the blow did not come. At the last moment Usagi came to his senses and tremulously sheathed the sword.

"Your pardon, Lord Toranaga," he said, kneeling abjectly. "I could not bear the shame of—of having you hear such—such insults. I ask permission—I apologize and—I ask permission to commit seppuku immediately for I cannot live with this shame."

Though Toranaga had remained still, he had been ready to intercept the blow and he knew Hiro-matsu was ready and that others would have been ready also, and that probably Ishido would only have been wounded. He understood, too, why Ishido had been so insulting and inflammatory. I will repay you with an enormity of interest, Ishido, he promised silently.

Toranaga gave his attention to the kneeling youth. "How dare you imply that anything Lord Ishido said was meant in any way as an insult to *me*. Of course he would never be so impolite. How dare you listen to conversations that do not concern you. No, you will not be allowed to commit seppuku. That's an honor. You have no honor and no self-discipline. You will be crucified like a common criminal today. Your swords will be broken and buried in the *eta* village. Your son will be buried in the *eta* village. You head will be put on a spike for all the population to jeer at with a sign on it: 'This man was born samurai by mistake. His name has ceased to be!' "

With a supreme effort Usagi controlled his breathing but the sweat dripped and the shame of it tortured him. He bowed to Toranaga, accepting his fate with outward calm.

Hiro-matsu walked forward and tore both swords from his grandson-in-law's belt.

"Lord Toranaga," he said gravely, "with your permission I will personally see that your orders are carried out."

Toranaga nodded.

The youth bowed a last time then began to get up, but Hiro-matsu pushed him back on the floor. "Samurai walk," he said. "So do men. But you're neither. You will crawl to your death."

Silently Usagi obeyed.

And all in the room were warmed by the strength of the youth's self-discipline now, and the measure of his courage. He will be reborn samurai, they told themselves contentedly.

CHAPTER 13

THAT night Toranaga could not sleep. This was rare for him because normally he could defer the most pressing problem until the next day, knowing that if he was alive the next day he would solve it to the best of his ability. He had long since discovered that peaceful sleep could provide the answer to most puzzles, and if not, what did it really matter? Wasn't life just a dewdrop within a dewdrop?

But tonight, there were too many perplexing questions to ponder.

What will I do about Ishido?

Why has Onoshi defected to the enemy?

How will I deal with the Council?

Have the Christian priests meddled again?

Where will the next assassination attempt come from?

When should Yabu be dealt with?

And what must I do about the barbarian?

Was he telling the truth?

Curious how the barbarian came out of the eastern seas just at this time. Is that an omen? Is it his *karma* to be the spark that will light the powder keg?

Karma was an Indian word adopted by Japanese, part of Buddhist philosophy that referred to a person's fate in this life, his fate immutably fixed because of deeds done in a previous life, good deeds giving a better position in this life's strata, bad deeds the reverse. Just as the deeds of this life would completely affect the next rebirth. A person was ever being reborn into this world of tears until, after enduring and suffering and learning through many lifetimes, he became perfect at long last, going to *nirvana,* the Place of Perfect Peace, never having to suffer rebirth again.

Strange that Buddha or some other god or perhaps just *karma* brought the Anjin-san to Yabu's fief. Strange that he landed at the exact village where Mura, the secret head of the Izu spy system, had been settled so many years ago under the very nose of the Taikō and Yabu's pox-diseased father. Strange that Tsukku-san was here in Osaka to interpret and not in Nagasaki where he'd normally be. That also the chief priest of the Christians is here in Osaka, and also the Captain-General of the Portuguese. Strange that the pilot, Rodrigues, was also available to take Hiro-matsu to Anjiro in time to capture the barbarian alive and take possession of the guns. Then there's Kasigi Omi, son of the man who will give me Yabu's head if I but crook my little finger.

How beautiful life is and how sad! How fleeting, with no past and no future, only a limitless *now.*

Toranaga sighed. One thing is certain: the barbarian will never leave. Neither alive nor dead. He is part of the realm forever.

His ears heard almost imperceptible approaching footsteps and his sword was ready. Each night he changed his sleeping room, his guards, and the password haphazardly, against the assassins that were always waiting. The footsteps stopped outside the shoji. Then he heard Hiro-matsu's voice and the beginning of the password: " 'If the Truth is already clear, what is the use of meditation?' "

" 'And if the Truth is hidden?' " Toranaga said.

146

" 'It's already clear,' " Hiro-matsu answered correctly. The quotation was from the ancient Tantaric Buddhist teacher, Saraha.

"Come in."

Only when Toranaga saw that it was, in truth, his counselor, did his sword relax. "Sit down."

"I heard you weren't sleeping. I thought you might need something."

"No. Thank you." Toranaga observed the deepened lines around the old man's eyes. "I'm glad you're here, old friend," he said.

"You're sure you're all right?"

"Oh, yes."

"Then I'll leave you. Sorry to disturb you, Lord."

"No, please, come in, I'm glad you're here. Sit down."

The old man sat down beside the door, his back straight. "I've doubled the guards."

"Good."

After a while Hiro-matsu said, "About that madman, everything was done as you ordered. Everything."

"Thank you."

"His wife—as soon as she heard the sentence, my granddaughter asked my permission to kill herself, to accompany her husband and her son into the Great Void. I refused and ordered her to wait, pending your approval." Hiro-matsu was bleeding inside. How terrible life is!

"You did correctly."

"I formally ask permission to end my life. What he did put you in mortal danger, but it was my fault. I should have detected his flaw. I failed you."

"You may not commit seppuku."

"Please. I formally ask permission."

"No. You're needed alive."

"I will obey you. But please accept my apologies."

"Your apologies are accepted."

After a time, Toranaga said, "What about the barbarian?"

"Many things, Sire. One: If you hadn't been waiting for the barbarian today you would have been hawking since first light, and Ishido would never have enmeshed you in such a disgusting meeting. You have no choice now but to declare war on him—if you can get out of this castle and back to Yedo."

"Second?"

"And third and forty-third and a hundred and forty-third? I'm nowhere near as clever as you, Lord Toranaga, but even I could see that everything we've been led to believe by the Southern Barbarians is not true." Hiro-matsu was glad to talk. It helped ease the hurt. "But if there are *two* Christian religions which hate each other, and if the Portuguese are part of the bigger Spanish nation and if this new barbarian's country—whatever it was called—wars on both and beats them, and if this same country's an island nation like ours, and the great 'if' of all, if he's telling the truth and if the priest's saying accurately what the barbarian was saying. . . . Well, you can put all these 'ifs' together and make sense out of them, and a plan. I can't, so sorry. I only know what I saw at Anjiro, and aboard the ship. That the Anjin-san is very strong in his head—weak in his body presently, though that would be because of the long voyage—and dominating at sea. I don't understand anything about him. How could he be all of these things yet allow a man to piss on his back? Why did he save Yabu's life after what the man did to him, and also the life of his self-admitted enemy, the Portuguese Rodrigu? My head spins from so many questions as though I'm sodden with saké." Hiro-matsu paused. He was very weary. "But I think we should keep him on land and all like him, if others follow, and kill them all very quickly."

"What about Yabu?"

"Order him to commit seppuku tonight."

"Why?"

"He's got no manners. You foretold what he'd do when I arrived at Anjiro. He was going to steal your property. And he's a liar. Don't bother to see him tomorrow as you've arranged. Instead, let me take him your order now. You'll have to kill him sooner or later. Better now when he's accessible, with none of his own vassals surrounding him. I advise no delay."

There was a soft knock on the inner door. "Tora-chan?"

Toranaga smiled as he always did at that very special voice, with that special diminutive. "Yes, Kiri-san?"

"I've taken the liberty, Lord, of bringing cha for you and your guest. May I please come in?"

"Yes."

Both men returned her bow. Kiri closed the door and busied herself with the pouring. She was fifty-three and substantial, Matron of Toranaga's ladies-in-waiting, Kiritsubo-noh-Toshiko, nicknamed Kiri, the oldest of the ladies of his court. Her hair was gray-flecked, her waist thick, but her face sparkled with an eternal joy. "You shouldn't be awake, no, not at this time of night, Tora-chan! It will be dawn soon and I suppose then you'll be out in the hills with your hawks, *neh?* You need sleep!"

"Yes, Kiri-chan!" Toranaga patted her vast rump affectionately.

"Please don't Kiri-chan me!" Kiri laughed. "I'm an old woman and I need lots of respect. Your other ladies give me enough trouble as it is. Kiritsubo-Toshiko-san, if you please, my Lord Yoshi Toranaga-noh-Chikitada!"

"There, you see, Hiro-matsu. After twenty years she still tries to dominate me."

"So sorry, it's more than thirty years, Tora-sama," she said proudly. "And you were as manageable then as you are now!"

When Toranaga was in his twenties he had been a hostage, too, then of the despotic Ikawa Tadazaki, Lord of Suruga and Totomi, father of the present Ikawa Jikkyu, who was Yabu's enemy. The samurai responsible for Toranaga's good conduct had just taken Kiritsubo as his second wife. She was seventeen then. Together this samurai and Kiri, his wife, had treated Toranaga honorably, given him wise counsel, and then, when Toranaga had rebelled against Tadazuki and joined Goroda, had followed him with many warriors and had fought bravely at his side. Later, in the fighting for the capital, Kiri's husband had been killed. Toranaga had asked her if she would become one of his consorts and she had accepted gladly. In those days she was not fat. But she was equally protective and equally wise. That was her nineteenth year, his twenty-fourth, and she had been a focus of his household ever since. Kiri was very shrewd and very capable. For years now, she had run his household and kept it free of trouble.

As free of trouble as any household with women could ever be, Toranaga thought.

"You're getting fat," he said, not minding that she was fat.

"Lord Toranaga! In front of Lord Toda! Oh, so sorry, I shall have to commit seppuku—or at least, I'll have to shave my head and become a nun, and I thought I was so young and slender!" She burst out laughing. "Actually I agree I have a fat rump but what can I do? I just like to eat and that's Buddha's problem and my *karma, neh?*" She offered the cha. "There. Now I'll be off. Would you like me to send the Lady Sazuko?"

"No, my thoughtful Kiri-san, no, thank you. We'll talk for a little, then I'll sleep."

"Good night, Tora-sama. Sweet dreamlessness." She bowed to him and to Hiro-matsu and then she was gone.

They sipped their tea appreciatively.

Toranaga said, "I'm always sorry we never had a son, Kiri-san and I. Once she conceived but she miscarried. That was when we were at the battle of Nagakudé."

"Ah, that one."

"Yes."

This was just after the Dictator Goroda had been assassinated when General Nakamura—the Taikō-to-be—was trying to consolidate all power into his own hands. At that time the issue was in doubt, as Toranaga supported one of Goroda's sons, the legal heir. Nakamura came against Toranaga near the little village of Nagakudé and his force was mauled and routed and he lost that battle. Toranaga retreated cleverly, pursued by a new army, now commanded for Nakamura by Hiro-matsu. But Toranaga avoided the trap and escaped to his home provinces, his whole army intact, ready to battle again. Fifty thousand men died at Nagakudé, very few of them Toranaga's. In his wisdom, the Taikō-to-be called off the civil war against Toranaga, though he would have won. Nagakudé was the only battle the Taikō had ever lost and Toranaga the only general who had ever beaten him.

"I'm glad we never joined battle, Sire," Hiro-matsu said.

"Yes."

"You would have won."

"No. The Taikō was the greatest general and the wisest, cleverest man that has ever been."

Hiro-matsu smiled. "Yes. Except you."

"No. You're wrong. That's why I became *his* vassal."

"I'm sorry he's dead."

"Yes."

"And Goroda—he was a fine man, *neh?* So many good men dead." Hiro-matsu unconsciously turned and twisted the battered scabbard. "You'll have to move against Ishido. That will force every *daimyo* to choose sides, once and for all. We'll win the war eventually. Then you can disband the Council and become Shōgun."

"I don't seek that honor," Toranaga said sharply. "How many times do I have to say it?"

"Your pardon, Sire. I know. But I feel it would be best for Japan."

"That's treason."

"Against whom, Lord? Against the Taikō? He's dead. Against his last will and testament? That's a piece of paper. Against the boy Yaemon? Yaemon's the son of a peasant who usurped the power and heritage of a general whose heirs he stamped out. We were Goroda's allies, then the Taikō's vassals. Yes. But they're both very dead."

"Would you advise that if you were one of the Regents?"

"No. But then I'm not one of the Regents, and I'm very glad. I'm your vassal only. I chose sides a year ago. I did this freely."

"Why?" Toranaga had never asked him before.

"Because you're a man, because you're Minowara and because you'll do the wise thing. What you said to Ishido was right: we're not a people to be ruled by committee. We need a leader. Whom should I have chosen to serve of the five Regents? Lord Onoshi? Yes, he's a very wise man, and a good general. But he's Christian and a cripple and his flesh is so rotten with leprosy that he stinks from fifty paces. Lord Sugiyama? He's the richest *daimyo* in the land, his family's as ancient as yours. But he's a gutless turncoat and we both know him from eternity. Lord Kiyama? Wise, brave, a great general, and an old comrade. But he's Christian too, and I think we have enough gods of our own in this Land of the Gods not to be so arrogant as to worship only one. Ishido? I've detested that treacherous peasant's offal as long as I've known him and the only reason I never killed him was because he was the Taikō's dog." His leathery face cracked into a smile. "So you see, Yoshi Toranaga-noh-Minowara, you gave me no choice."

"And if I go against your advice? If I manipulate the Council of Regents, even Ishido, and put Yaemon into power?"

"Whatever you do is wise. But all the Regents would like you dead. That's the truth. I advocate immediate war. *Immediate*. Before they isolate you. Or more probably murder you."

Toranaga thought about his enemies. They were powerful and abundant.

It would take him all of three weeks to get back to Yedo, traveling the Tokaidō Road, the main trunk road that followed the coast between Yedo and Osaka. To go by ship was more dangerous, and perhaps more time consuming, except by galley which could travel against wind and tide.

Toranaga's mind ranged again over the plan he had decided upon. He could find no flaw in it.

"I heard secretly yesterday that Ishido's mother is visiting her grandson in Nagoya," he said and Hiro-matsu was at once attentive. Nagoya was a huge city-state that was, as yet, not committed to either side. "The lady should be 'invited' by the Abbot to visit the Johji Temple. To see the cherry blossoms."

"Immediately," Hiro-matsu said. "By carrier pigeon." The Johji Temple was famous for three things: its avenue of cherry trees, the militancy of its Zen Buddhist monks, and its open, undying fidelity to Toranaga, who had, years ago, paid for the building of the temple and maintained its upkeep ever since. "The blossoms will be past their prime but she will be there tomorrow. I don't doubt the venerable lady will want to stay a few days, it's so calming. Her grandson should go too, *neh?*"

"No—just her. That would make the Abbot's 'invitation' too obvious. Next: send a secret cipher to my son, Sudara: 'I leave Osaka the moment the Council concludes this session—in four days.' Send it by runner and confirm it by carrier pigeon tomorrow."

Hiro-matsu's disapproval was apparent. "Then can I order up ten thousand men at once? To Osaka?"

"No. The men here are sufficient. Thank you, old friend. I think I'll sleep now."

Hiro-matsu got up and stretched his shoulders. Then at the doorway, "I may give Fujiko, my granddaughter, permission to kill herself?"

"No."

"But Fujiko's samurai, Lord, and you know how mothers are about their sons. The child was her first."

"Fujiko can have many children. How old is she? Eighteen—barely nineteen? I will find her another husband."

Hiro-matsu shook his head, "She will not accept one. I know her too well. It's her innermost wish to end her life. Please?"

"Tell your granddaughter I do not approve of useless death. Permission is refused."

At length Hiro-matsu bowed, and began to leave.

"How long would the barbarian live in that prison?" Toranaga asked.

Hiro-matsu did not turn back. "It depends how cruel a fighter he is."

"Thank you. Good night, Hiro-matsu." When he was sure that he was alone, he said quietly, "Kiri-san?"

The inner door opened, she entered and knelt.

"Send an immediate message to Sudara: 'All is well.' Send it by racing pigeons. Release three of them at the same time at dawn. At noon do the same again."

"Yes, Lord." She went away.

One will get through, he thought. At least four will fall to arrows, spies, or hawks. But unless Ishido's broken our code, the message will still mean nothing to him.

The code was very private. Four people knew it. His eldest son, Noboru; his second son and heir, Sudara; Kiri; and himself. The message deciphered meant: "Disregard all other messages. Activate Plan Five." By prearrangement, Plan Five contained orders to gather all Yoshi clan leaders and their most trusted inner counselors immediately at his capital, Yedo, and to mobilize for war. The code word that signaled war was "Crimson Sky." His own assassination, or capture, made Crimson Sky inexorable and launched the war—an immediate fanatic assault upon Kyoto led by Sudara, his heir, with *all* the legions, to gain possession of that city and the puppet Emperor. This would be coupled with secret, meticulously planned insurrections in fifty provinces which had been prepared over the years against such eventuality. All targets, passes, cities, castles, bridges, had long since been selected. There were enough arms and men and resolve to carry it through.

It's a good plan, Toranaga thought. But it will fail if I don't lead it. Sudara will fail. Not through want of trying or courage or intelligence, or because of treachery. Merely because Sudara hasn't yet enough knowledge or experience and cannot carry enough of the uncommitted *daimyos* with him. And also because Osaka Castle and the heir, Yaemon, stand inviolate in the path, the rallying point for all the enmity and jealousy that I've earned in fifty-two years of war.

Toranaga's war had begun when he was six and had been ordered as hostage into the enemy camp, then reprieved, then captured by other enemies and pawned again, to be repawned until he was twelve. At twelve, he had led his first patrol and won his first battle.

So many battles. None lost. But so many enemies. And now they're gathering together.

Sudara will fail. You're the only one who could win with Crimson Sky, perhaps. The Taikō could do it, absolutely. But it would be better not to have to implement Crimson Sky.

CHAPTER 14

OR Blackthorne it was a hellish dawn. He was locked in a death battle with a fellow convict. The prize was a cup of gruel. Both men were naked. Whenever a convict was put into this vast, single-storied, wooden cellblock, his clothes were taken away. A clothed man occupied more space and clothes could hide weapons.

The murky and suffocating room was fifty paces long and ten wide and packed with naked, sweating Japanese. Scarcely any light filtered through the boards and beams that made up the walls and low ceiling.

Blackthorne could barely stand erect. His skin was blotched and scratched from the man's broken nails and the wood burns from the walls. Finally, he butted his head into the man's face, grabbed his throat and hammered the man's head against the beams until he was senseless. Then he threw the body aside and charged through the sweating mass to the place he had claimed in the corner, and he readied himself for another attack.

At dawn it had been feeding time and the guards began passing the cups of gruel and water through the small opening. This was the first food and water that had been given them since he was put inside at dusk the previous day. The lining up for food and water had been unusually calm. Without discipline no one would eat. Then this apelike man—unshaven, filthy, lice-ridden—had chopped him over the kidneys and taken his ration while the others waited to see what would happen. But Blackthorne had been in too many seafaring brawls to be beaten with one treacherous blow, so he feigned helplessness, then kicked out viciously and the fight had been joined. Now, in the corner, Blackthorne saw to his amazement that one of the men was offering the cup of gruel and the water that he had presumed lost. He took it and thanked the man.

The corners were the choicest areas. A beam ran lengthwise, along the earthern floor, partitioning the room into two sections. In each section were three rows of men, two rows facing each other, their backs to the wall or beam, the other row between them. Only the weak and the sick took the center row. When the stronger men in the outer rows wanted to stretch their legs they had to do so over those in the middle.

Blackthorne saw two corpses, swollen and flyblown, in one of the middle rows. But the feeble and dying men nearby seemed to ignore them.

He could not see far in the heating gloom. Sun was baking the wood already. There were latrine buckets but the stench was terrible because the sick had befouled themselves and the places in which they hunched.

From time to time guards opened the iron door and names were called out. The men bowed to their comrades and left, but others were soon brought in and the space occupied again. All the prisoners seemed to have accepted their lot and tried, as best they could, to live unselfishly in peace with their immediate neighbors.

One man against the wall began to vomit. He was quickly shoved into the middle row and collapsed, half suffocated, under the weight of legs.

Blackthorne had to close his eyes and fight to control his terror and claustrophobia. Bastard Toranaga! I pray I get the opportunity of putting you inside here one day.

Bastard guards! Last night when they had ordered him to strip he had fought them with a bitter hopelessness, knowing he was beaten, fighting only because he refused to surrender passively. And then he had been forced through the door.

There were four such cell blocks. They were on the edge of the city, in a paved compound within high stone walls. Outside the walls was a roped-off area of beaten earth beside the river. Five crosses were erected there. Naked men and one woman had been bound straddled to the crosspieces by their wrists and ankles, and while Blackthorne had walked on the perimeter following his samurai guards, he saw executioners with long lances thrust the lances crisscross into the victims' chests while the crowd jeered. Then the five were cut down and five more put up and samurai came forward and hacked the corpses into pieces with their long swords, laughing all the while.

Bloody-gutter-festering-bastards!

Unnoticed, the man Blackthorne had fought was coming to his senses. He lay in the middle row. Blood had congealed on one side of his face and his nose was smashed. Suddenly he leapt at Blackthorne, oblivious of the men in his way.

Blackthorne saw him coming at the last moment, frantically parried the onslaught and knocked him in a heap. The prisoners that the man fell on cursed him and one of them, heavyset and built like a bulldog, chopped him viciously on the neck with the side of his hand. There was a dry snap and the man's head sagged.

The bulldog man lifted the half-shaven head by its scraggy, lice-infected topknot and let it fall. He looked up at Blackthorne, said something gutturally, smiled with bare, toothless gums, and shrugged.

"Thanks," Blackthorne said, struggling for breath, thankful that his assailant had not had Mura's skill at unarmed combat. "My namu Anjin-san," he said, pointing at himself. "You?"

"*Ah, so desu!* Anjin-san!" Bulldog pointed at himself and sucked in his breath. "Minikui."

"Minikui-san?"

"*Hai,*" and he added a spate of Japanese.

Blackthorne shrugged tiredly. "*Wakarimasen.*" I don't understand.

"*Ah, so desu!*" Bulldog chattered briefly with his neighbors. Then he shrugged again and Blackthorne shrugged and together they lifted the dead man and put him with the other corpses. When they came back to the corner no one had taken their places.

Most of the inmates were asleep or fitfully trying to sleep.

Blackthorne felt filthy and horrible and near death. Don't worry, he told himself, you've a long way to go before you die. . . . No, I can't live long in this hell hole. There're too many men. Oh, God, let me out! Why is the room swimming up and down, and is that Rodrigues floating up from the depths with moving pincers for eyes? I can't breathe, I can't breathe. I've got to get out of here, please, please, don't put more wood in the fire and what are you doing here, Croocq lad, I thought they let you go. I thought you were back in the village but now we're here in the village and how did I get here—it's so cool and there's that girl, so pretty, down by the docks but why are they dragging her away to the shore, the naked samurai, Omi there laughing? Why down across the sand, blood marks in the sand, all naked, me naked, hags and villagers and children, and there's the cauldron and we're in the cauldron and no, no more wood no more wood, I'm drowning in liquid filth, Oh God Oh God oh God I'm dying

dying dying *"In nomine Patris et Filii et Spiritus Sancti."* That's the Last Sacrament and you're Catholic we're all Catholic and you'll burn or drown in piss and burn with fire the fire the fire. . . .

He dragged himself out of the nightmare, his ears exploding with the peaceful, earth-shattering finality of the Last Sacrament. For a moment he did not know if he was awake or asleep because his disbelieving ears heard the Latin benediction again and his incredulous eyes were seeing a wrinkled old scarecrow of a European stooped over the middle row, fifteen paces away. The toothless old man had long filthy hair and a matted beard and broken nails and wore a foul, threadbare smock. He raised a hand like a vulture's claw and held up the wooden cross over the half-hidden body. A shaft of sun caught it momentarily. Then he closed the dead man's eyes, and mumbled a prayer and glanced up. He saw Blackthorne staring at him.

"Mother of God, art thou real?" the man croaked in coarse, peasant Spanish, crossing himself.

"Yes," Blackthorne said in Spanish. "Who are you?"

The old man groped his way over, mumbling to himself. The other inmates let him pass or step on them or over them without saying a word. He stared down at Blackthorne through rheumy eyes, his face warted. "Oh, Blessed Virgin, the señor is real. Who art thou? I'm . . . I'm Friar . . . Friar Domingo . . . Domingo . . . Domingo of the Sacred . . . the Sacred Order of St. Francis . . . the Order . . . ." and then for a while his words became a jumble of Japanese and Latin and Spanish. His head twitched and he wiped away the ever present spittle that dribbled to his chin. "The señor is real?"

"Yes, I'm real." Blackthorne eased himself up.

The priest muttered another Hail Mary, the tears coursing his cheeks. He kissed the cross repeatedly and would have got down on his knees if there had been space. Bulldog shook his neighbor awake. Both squatted and made just enough room for the priest to sit.

"By the Blessed St. Francis, my prayers have been answered. Thou, thou, thou, I thought that I was seeing another apparition, señor, a ghost. Yes, an evil spirit. I've seen so many—so many—how long is the señor here? It's hard for a body to see in the gloom and my eyes, they're not good. . . . How long?"

"Yesterday. And you?"

"I don't know, señor. A long time. I'm put here in September—it was in the year of our Lord fifteen hundred ninety-eight."

"It's May now. Sixteen hundred."

"Sixteen hundred?"

A moaning cry distracted the monk. He got up and picked his way over the bodies like a spider, encouraging a man here, touching another there, his Japanese fluent. He could not find the dying man so he droned the last rites to that part of the cell and blessed everyone and no one minded.

"Come with me, my son."

Without waiting, the monk hobbled down the cage, through the mass of men, into the gloom. Blackthorne hesitated, not wanting to leave his place. Then he got up and followed. After ten paces he looked back. His place had vanished. It seemed impossible that he had ever been there at all.

He continued down the length of the hut. In the far corner was, incredibly, an open space. Just enough room for a small man to lie down in. It contained a few pots and bowls and an ancient straw mat.

Father Domingo stepped through the men into the space and beckoned him. The surrounding Japanese watched silently, letting Blackthorne pass.

"They are my flock, señor. They are all my sons in the Blessed Lord Jesus.

I've converted so many here—this one's John, and here's Mark and Methuselah. . . ." The priest stopped for breath. "I'm so tired. Tired. I . . . must, I must . . ." His words trailed off and he slept.

At dusk more food arrived. When Blackthorne began to get up, one of the nearby Japanese motioned him to stay and brought him a well-filled bowl. Another man gently patted the priest awake, offering the food.

"*Iyé,*" the old man said, shaking his head, a smile on his face, and pushed the bowl back into the man's hands.

"*Iyé, Farddah-sama.*"

The priest allowed himself to be persuaded and ate a little, then got up, his joints creaking, and handed his bowl to one of those in the middle row. This man touched the priest's hand to his forehead and he was blessed.

"I'm so pleased to see another of my own kind," the priest said, sitting beside Blackthorne again, his peasant voice thick and sibilant. He pointed weakly to the other end of the cell block. "One of my flock said the señor used the word 'pilot,' 'anjin' ? The señor is a pilot?"

"Yes."

"There are others of the señor's crew here?"

"No, I'm alone. Why are you here?"

"If the señor is alone—the señor came from Manila?"

"No. I've never been to Asia before," Blackthorne said carefully, his Spanish excellent. "This was my first voyage as pilot. I was . . . I was outward bound. Why are you here?"

"Jesuits put me here, my son. Jesuits and their filthy lies. The señor was outward bound? Thou art not Spanish, no—nor Portuguese . . ." The monk peered at him suspiciously and Blackthorne was surrounded by his reeking breath. "Was the ship Portuguese? Tell the truth, before God!"

"No, Father. It was not Portuguese. Before God!"

"Oh, Blessed Virgin, thank you! Please forgive me, señor. I was afraid—I'm old and stupid and diseased. Thy ship was Spanish out of where? I'm so glad—where is the señor from originally? Spanish Flanders? Or the Duchy of Brandenburg perhaps? Some part of our dominions in Germania? Oh, it's so good to talk my blessed mother tongue again! Was the señor shipwrecked like us? Then foully thrown into this jail, falsely accused by those devil Jesuits? May God curse them and show them the error of their treachery!" His eyes glittered fiercely. "The señor said he has never been to Asia before?"

"No."

"If the señor has never been to Asia before, then he will be like a child in the wilderness. Yes, there's so much to tell! Does the señor know that Jesuits are merely traders, gun runners, and usurers? That they control all the silk trade here, all trade with China? That the annual Black Ship is worth a million in gold? That they've forced His Holiness, the Pope, to grant them total power over Asia—them and their dogs, the Portuguese? That all other religious are forbidden here? That Jesuits deal in gold, buying and selling for profit—for themselves and the heathen —against the direct orders of His Holiness, Pope Clement, of King Philip, and against the laws of this land? That they secretly smuggled guns into Japan for Christian kings here, inciting them to rebellion? That they meddle in politics and pimp for the kings, lie and cheat and bear false witness against us! That their Father Superior himself sent a secret message to our Spanish Viceroy in Luzon asking him for conquistadores to conquer the land—they begged for a Spanish invasion to cover more Portuguese mistakes. All our troubles can be put at their threshold, señor. It's the Jesuits who have lied and cheated and spread poison against Spain and our beloved King Philip! Their lies put me here and caused twenty-six Holy Fathers to be martyred! They think that just because I was a peasant once, I don't understand . . . but I can read and write, señor, I can read and write! I was one of his Excellency's secretaries, the Viceroy. They think we Franciscans don't understand . . ." At this point he broke into another ranting jumble of Spanish and Latin.

Blackthorne's spirit had been revived, his curiosity agog with what the priest had said. What guns? What gold? What trade? What Black Ship? A million? What invasion? What Christian kings?

Aren't you cheating the poor sick man? he asked himself. He thinks you're friend, not enemy.

I haven't lied to him.

But haven't you implied you're friend?

I answered him directly.

But you volunteered nothing?

No.

Is that fair?

That's the first rule of survival in enemy waters: volunteer nothing.

The monk's tantrum grew apace. The nearby Japanese shifted uneasily. One of them got up and shook the priest gently and spoke to him. Father Domingo gradually came out of his fit, his eyes cleared. He looked at Blackthorne with recognition, replied to the Japanese, and calmed the rest.

"So sorry, señor," he said breathlessly. "They—they thought I was angry against—against the señor. God forgive my foolish rage! It was just—*que va,* Jesuits come from hell, along with heretics and heathens. I can tell you much about them." The monk wiped the spittle off his chin and tried to calm himself. He pressed his chest to ease the pain there. "The señor was saying? Thy ship, it was cast ashore?"

"Yes. In a way. We came aground." Blackthorne replied. He eased his legs carefully. The men who were watching and listening gave him more room. One got up and motioned him to stretch out. "Thanks," he said at once. "Oh, how do you say 'thank you,' Father?"

" *'Domo.'* Sometimes you say *'arigato.'* A woman has to be very polite, señor. She says *'arigato goziemashita.'* "

"Thank you. What's his name?" Blackthorne indicated the man who had got up.

"That's Gonzalez."

"But what's his Japanese name?"

"Ah yes! He's Akabo. But that just means 'porter,' señor. They don't have names. Only samurai have names."

"What?"

"Only samurai have names, first names and surnames. It's their law, señor. Everyone else has to make do with what they are—porter, fisherman, cook, executioner, farmer, and so on. Sons and daughters are mostly just First Daughter, Second Daughter, First Son, and so on. Sometimes they'd call a man 'fisherman who lives near the elm tree' or 'fisherman with bad eyes.' " The monk shrugged and stifled a yawn. "Ordinary Japanese are't allowed names. Whores give themselves names like Carp or Moon or Petal or Eel or Star. It's strange, señor, but it's their law. We give them Christian names, real names, when we baptize them, bringing them salvation and the word of God . . ." His words trailed off and he slept.

"Domo, Akabo-san," Blackthorne said to the porter.

The man smiled shyly and bowed and sucked in his breath.

Later the monk awakened and said a brief prayer and scratched. "Only yesterday, the señor said? He came here only yesterday? What occurred with the señor?"

"When we landed there was a Jesuit there," Blackthorne said. "But you, Father. You were saying they accused you? What happened to you and your ship?"

"Our ship? Did the señor ask about our ship? Was the señor coming from Manila like us? Or—oh, how foolish of me! I remember now, the señor was outward bound from home and never in Asia before. By the Blessed Body of Christ, it's so good to talk to a civilized man again, in my blessed mother's tongue! *Que va,* it's been so long. My head aches, aches, señor. Our ship? We were going home at long last. Home from Manila to Acapulco, in the land of Cortes, in Mexico, thence overland to Vera Cruz. And thence another ship and across the Atlantic, and at long, long last, to *home.* My village is outside Madrid, señor, in the mountains. It is called Santa Veronica. Forty years I've been away, señor. In the New World, in Mexico and in the Philippines. Always with our glorious conquistadores, may the Virgin watch over them! I was in Luzon when we destroyed the heathen native king, Lumalon, and conquered Luzon, and so brought the word of God to the Philippines. Many of our Japan converts fought with us even then, señor. Such fighters! That was in 1575. Mother Church is well planted there, my son, and never a filthy Jesuit or Portuguese to be seen. I came to the Japans for almost two years, then had to leave for Manila again when the Jesuits betrayed us."

The monk stopped and closed his eyes, drifting off. Later he came back again, and, as old people will sometimes do, he continued as though he had never slept. "My ship was the great galleon *San Felipe.* We carried a cargo of spices, gold and silver, and specie to the value of a million and a half silver pesos. One of the great storms took us and cast us onto the shores of Shikoku. Our ship broke her back on the sand bar—on the third day—by that time we had landed our bullion and most of our cargo. Then word came that everything was confiscated, confiscated by the Taikō himself, that we were pirates and . . ." He stopped at the sudden silence.

The iron door of the cell cage had swung open.

Guards began to call names from the list. Bulldog, the man who had befriended Blackthorne, was one of those called. He walked out and did not look back. One of the men in the circle also was chosen. Akabo. Akabo knelt to the monk, who blessed him and made the sign of the cross over him and quickly gave him the Last Sacrament. The man kissed the cross and walked away.

The door closed again.

"They're going to execute him?" Blackthorne asked.

"Yes, his Calvary is outside the door. May the Holy Madonna take his soul swiftly and give him his everlasting reward."

"What did that man do?"

"He broke the law—their law, señor. The Japanese are a simple people. And very severe. They truly have only one punishment—death. By the cross, by strangulation, or by decapitation. For the crime of arson, it is death by burning. They have almost no other punishment—banishment sometimes, cutting the hair from women sometimes. But"—the old man sighed—"but most always it is death."

"You forgot imprisonment."

The monk's nails picked absently at the scabs on his arm. "It's not one of their punishments, my son. To them, prison is just a temporary place to keep the man until they decide his sentence. Only the guilty come here. For just a little while."

"That's nonsense. What about you? You've been here a year, almost two years."

"One day they will come for me, like all the others. This is but a resting place between the hell of earth and the glory of Everlasting Life."

"I don't believe you."

"Have no fear, my son. It is the will of God. I am here and can hear the señor's confession and give him absolution and make him perfect—the glory of Everlasting Life is barely a hundred steps and moments away from that door. Would the señor like me to hear his confession now?"

"No—no, thank you. Not now." Blackthorne looked at the iron door. "Has anyone ever tried to break out of here?"

"Why should they do that? There is nowhere to run—nowhere to hide. The authorities are very strict. Anyone helping an escaped convict or even a man who commits a crime—" He pointed vaguely at the door of the hut. "Gonzalez —Akabo—the man who has—has left us. He's a kaga-man. He told me—"

"What's a kaga-man?"

"Oh, those are the porters, señor, the men that carry the palanquins, or the smaller two-man kaga that's like a hammock swung on a pole. He told us his partner stole a silken scarf from a customer, poor fellow, and because he himself did not report the theft, his life is forfeit also. The señor may believe me, to try to escape or even to help someone to escape, the man would lose his life and all his family. They are very severe, señor."

"So everyone goes to execution like sheep then?"

"There is no other choice. It is the will of God."

Don't get angry, or panic, Blackthorne warned himself. Be patient. You can think of a way. Not everything the priest says is true. He's deranged. Who wouldn't be after so much time?

"These prisons are new to them, señor," the monk was saying. "The Taikō instituted prisons here a few years ago, so they say. Before him there were none. In previous days when a man was caught, he confessed his crime and he was executed."

"And if he didn't confess?"

"Everyone confesses—sooner is better, señor. It is the same in our world, if you are caught."

The monk slept a little, scratching in his sleep and muttering. When he woke up, Blackthorne said, "Please tell me, Father, how the cursed Jesuits put a man of God in this pest hole."

"There is not much to tell, and everything. After the Taikō's men came and took all our bullion and goods, our Captain-General insisted on going to the capital to protest. There was no cause for the confiscation. Were we not servants of His Most Imperial Catholic Majesty, King Philip of Spain, ruler of the greatest and richest empire in the world? The most powerful monarch in the world? Were we not friends? Was not the Taikō asking Spanish Manila to trade direct with Japan, to break the filthy monopoly of the Portuguese? It was all a mistake, the confiscation. It had to be.

"I went with our Captain-General because I could speak a little Japanese—not much in those days. Señor, the *San Felipe* had floundered and come ashore in October of 1597. The Jesuits—one was of the name Father Martin Alvito—they dared to offer to mediate for us, there in Kyoto, the capital. The impertinence! Our Franciscan Father Superior, Friar Braganza, he was in the capital, and he was an ambassador—a real ambassador from Spain to the court of the Taikō! The Blessed Friar Braganza, he had been there in the capital, in Kyoto, for five years, señor. The Taikō himself, personally, had asked our Viceroy in Manila to send Franciscan monks and an ambassador to Japan. So the Blessed Friar Braganza had come. And we, señor, we of the *San Felipe,* we knew that he was to be trusted, not like the Jesuits.

"After many, many days of waiting, we had one interview with the Taikō—he was a tiny, ugly little man, señor—and we asked for our goods back and another ship, or passage on another ship, which our Captain-General offered to pay for handsomely. The interview went well, we thought, and the Taikō dismissed us. We went to our monastery in Kyoto and waited and then, over the next months while we waited for his decision, we continued to bring the word of God to the heathen. We held our services openly, not like thieves in the night as the Jesuits do." Friar Domingo's voice was edged with contempt. "We wore our habits and vestments—we didn't go disguised, like native priests, as they do. We brought the Word to the people, the halt and sick and poor, not like the Jesuits, who consort with princes only. Our congregations increased. We had a hospital for lepers, our own church, and our flock prospered, señor. Greatly. We were about to convert many of their kings and then one day we were betrayed.

"One day in January, we Franciscans, we were all brought before the magistrate and accused under the Taikō's personal seal, señor, accused as violators of their law, as disturbers of their peace, and sentenced to death by crucifixion. There were forty-three of us. Our churches throughout the land were to be destroyed, all our congregations to be torn apart—Franciscan—not Jesuit, señor. Just us, señor. We had been falsely accused. The Jesuits had poured poison in the Taikō's ear that we were conquistadores, that we wanted to invade these shores, when it was Jesuits who begged his Excellency, our Viceroy, to send an army from Manila. I saw the letter myself! From their Father Superior! They're devils who pretend to serve the Church and Christ, but they serve only themselves. They lust for power, power at any cost. They hide behind a net of poverty and piousness, but underneath, they feed like kings and amass fortunes. *Que va,* señor, the truth is that they were jealous of our congregations, jealous of our church, jealous of our truth and way of life. The *daimyo* of Hizen, Dom Francisco—his Japanese name is Harima Tadao but he has been baptized Dom Francisco—he interceded for us. He is just like a king, all *daimyos* are like kings, and he's a Franciscan and he interceded for us, but to no avail.

"In the end, twenty-six were martyred. Six Spaniards, seventeen of our Japanese neophytes, and three others. The Blessed Braganza was one, and there were three boys among the neophytes. Oh, señor, the faithful were there in their thousands that day. Fifty, a hundred thousand people watched the Blessed Martyrdom at Nagasaki, so I was told. It was a bitter cold February day and a bitter year. That was the year of the earthquakes and typhoons and flood and storm and fire, when the Hand of God lay heavy on the Great Murderer and even smashed down his great castle, Fushimi, when He shuddered the earth. It was terrifying but marvelous to behold, the Finger of God, punishing the heathen and the sinners.

"So they were martyred, señor, six good Spaniards. Our flock and our church were laid waste and the hospital closed up." The old man's face drained. "I—I was one of those chosen for martyrdom, but—but it was not to be my honor. They set us marching from Kyoto and when we came to Osaka they put some of us in one of our missions here and the rest—the rest had one of their ears cut off, then they were paraded like common criminals in the streets. Then the Blessed Brethren were set walking westward. For a month. Their blessed journey ended at the hill called Nishizaki, overlooking the great harbor of Nagasaki. I begged the samurai to let me go with them but, señor, he ordered me back to the mission here in Osaka. For no reason. And then, months later, we were put in this cell.

There were three of us—I think it was three, but I was the only Spaniard. The others were neophytes, our lay brothers, Japaners. A few days later the guards called out their names. But they never called out mine. Perhaps it is the will of God, señor, or perhaps those filthy Jesuits leave me alive just to torture me—they who took away my chance at martyrdom among my own. It's hard, señor, to be patient. So very hard . . ."

The old monk closed his eyes, prayed, and cried himself to sleep.

Much as he wished it, Blackthorne could not sleep though night had come. His flesh crawled from the lice bites. His head swarmed with terror.

He knew, with terrible clarity, there was no way to break out. He was overwhelmed with futility and sensed he was on the brink of death. In the darkest part of the night terror swamped him, and, for the first time in his life, he gave up and wept.

"Yes, my son?" the monk murmured. "What is it?"

"Nothing, nothing," Blackthorne said, his heart thundering. "Go back to sleep."

"There's no need to fear. We are all in God's hands," the monk said and slept again.

The great terror left Blackthorne. In its place was a terror that could be lived with. I'll get out of here somehow, he told himself, trying to believe the lie.

At dawn came food and water. Blackthorne was stronger now. Stupid to let go like that, he cautioned himself. Stupid and weak and dangerous. Don't do that again or you'll break and go mad and surely die. They'll put you in the third row and you'll die. Be careful and be patient and guard yourself.

"How are you today, señor?"

"Fine, thank you, Father. And you?"

"Quite well, thank you."

"How do I say that in Japanese?"

"Domo, genki desu."

"Domo, genki desu. You were saying yesterday, Father, about the Portuguese Black Ships—what are they like? Have you seen one?"

"Oh, yes, señor. They're the greatest ships in the world, almost two thousand tons. As many as two hundred men and boys are necessary to sail one, señor, and with crew and passengers her complement would be almost a thousand souls. I'm told these carracks sail well before the wind but lumber when the wind's abeam."

"How many guns do they carry?"

"Sometimes twenty or thirty on three decks."

Father Domingo was glad to answer questions and talk and teach, and Blackthorne was equally glad to listen and learn. The monk's rambling knowledge was priceless and far reaching.

"No, señor," he was saying now. *"Domo* is thank you and *dozo* is please. Water is *mizu.* Always remember that Japaners put a great price on manners and courtesy. Once when I was in Nagasaki— Oh, if I only had ink and a quill and paper! Ah, I know—here, trace the words in the dirt, that will help you to remember them . . ."

"Domo," Blackthorne said. Then, after memorizing a few more words, he asked, "How long've Portuguese been here?"

"Oh, the land was discovered in 1542, señor, the year I was born. There were three men, da Mota, Peixoto, and I can't remember the other name. They were all Portuguese traders, trading the China coasts in a China junk from a port in Siam. Has the señor been to Siam?"

"No."

"Ah, there is much to see in Asia. These three men were trading but they were caught in a great storm, a typhoon, and blown off their course to land safely at Tanegashima at Kyushu. That was the first time a European set foot on Japan's soil, and at once trade began. A few years later, Francis Xavier, one of the founding members of the Jesuits, arrived here. That was in 1549 . . . a bad year for Japan, señor. One of our Brethren should have been first, then we would have inherited this realm, not the Portuguese. Francis Xavier died three years later in Chine, alone and forsaken. . . . Did I tell the señor there's a Jesuit already at the court of the Emperor of China, in a place called Peking? . . . Oh, you should see Manila, señor, and the Philippines! We have four cathedrals and almost three thousand conquistadores and nearly six thousand Japaner soldiers spread through the islands and three hundred Brethren. . . ."

Blackthorne's mind filled with facts and Japanese words and phrases. He asked about life in Japan and *daimyos* and samurai and trade and Nagasaki and war and peace and Jesuits and Franciscans and Portuguese in Asia and about Spanish Manila, and always more about the Black Ship that plied annually from Macao. For three days and three nights Blackthorne sat with Father Domingo and questioned and listened and learned and slept in nightmare, to awaken and ask more questions and gain more knowledge.

Then, on the fourth day, they called out his name.

"Anjin-san!"

CHAPTER 15

I N the utter silence, Blackthorne got to his feet.

"Thy confession, my son, say it quickly."

"I—I don't think—I—" Blackthorne realized through his dulled mind that he was speaking English, so he pressed his lips together and began to walk away. The monk scrambled up, presuming his words to be Dutch or German, and grabbed his wrist and hobbled with him.

"Quickly, señor. I will give the absolution. Be quick, for thine immortal soul. Say it quickly, just that the señor confesses before God all things past and present—"

They were nearing the iron gate now, the monk holding on to Blackthorne with surprising strength.

"Say it now! The Blessed Virgin will watch over you!"

Blackthorne tore his arm away, and said hoarsely in Spanish, "Go with God, Father."

The door slammed behind him.

The day was incredibly cool and sweet, the clouds meandering before a fine southeasterly wind.

He inhaled deep draughts of the clean, glorious air and blood surged through his veins. The joy of life possessed him.

Several naked prisoners were in the courtyard along with an official, jailers with spears, *eta,* and a group of samurai. The offical was dressed in a somber kimono and an overmantle with starched, winglike shoulders and he wore a small dark hat. This man stood in front of the first prisoner and read from a delicate scroll and, as he finished, each man began to plod after his party of jailers toward the great doors of the courtyard. Blackthorne was last. Unlike the others he was given a loin cloth, cotton kimono, and thonged clogs for his feet. And his guards were samurai.

He had decided to run for it the moment he had passed the gate, but as he approached the threshold, the samurai surrounded him more closely and locked him in. They reached the gateway together. A large crowd looked on, clean and spruce, with crimson and yellow and golden sunshades. One man was already roped to his cross and the cross was lifted into the sky. And beside each cross two *eta* waited, their long lances sparkling in the sun.

Blackthorne's pace slowed. The samurai jostled closer, hurrying him. He thought numbly that it would be the better to die now, quickly, so he steadied his hand to lunge for the nearest sword. But he never took the opportunity because the samurai turned away from the arena and walked toward the perimeter, heading for the streets that led to the city and toward the castle.

Blackthorne waited, scarcely breathing, wanting to be sure. They walked through the crowd, who backed away and bowed, and then they were in a street and now there was no mistake.

Blackthorne felt reborn.

When he could speak, he said, "Where are we going?" not caring that the words would not be understood or that they were in English. Blackthorne was quite light-headed. His step hardly touched the ground, the thongs of his clogs were

162

not uncomfortable, the untoward touch of the kimono was not unpleasing. Actually, it feels quite good, he thought. A little draughty perhaps, but on a fine day like this—just the sort of thing to wear on the quarterdeck!

"By God, it's wonderful to speak English again," he said to the samurai. "Christ Jesus, I thought I was a dead man. That's my eighth life gone. Do you know that, old friends? Now I've only one to go. Well, never mind! Pilots have ten lives, at least, that's what Alban Caradoc used to say." The samurai seemed to be growing irritated by his incomprehensible talk.

Get hold of yourself, he told himself. Don't make them touchier than they are.

He noticed now that the samurai were all Grays. Ishido's men. He had asked Father Alvito the name of the man who opposed Toranaga. Alvito had said "Ishido." That was just before he had been ordered to stand up and had been taken away. Are all Grays Ishido's men? As all Browns are Toranaga's?

"Where are we going? There?" He pointed at the castle which brooded above the town. "There, *hai?*"

"*Hai.*" The leader nodded a cannonball head, his beard grizzled.

What does Ishido want with me? Blackthorne asked himself.

The leader turned into another street, always going away from the harbor. Then he saw her—a small Portuguese brig, her blue and white flag waving in the breeze. Ten cannon on the main deck, with bow and stern twenty-pounders. *Erasmus* could take her easily, Blackthorne told himself. What about my crew? What are they doing back there at the village? By the Blood of Christ, I'd like to see them. I was so glad to leave them that day and go back to my own house where Onna—Haku—was, the house of . . . what was his name? Ah yes, Mura-san. And what about that girl, the one in my floor-bed, and the other one, the angel beauty who talked that day to Omi-san? The one in the dream who was in the cauldron too.

But why remember that nonsense? It weakens the mind. 'You've got to be very strong in the head to live with the sea,' Alban Caradoc had said. Poor Alban.

Alban Caradoc had always appeared so huge and godlike, all seeing, all knowing, for so many years. But he had died in terror. It had been on the seventh day of the Armada. Blackthorne was commanding a hundred-ton gaff-rigged ketch out of Portsmouth, running arms and powder and shot and food to Drake's war galleons off Dover as they harried and tore into the enemy fleet which was beating up the channel toward Dunkirk where the Spanish legions lay, waiting to transship to conquer England.

The great Spanish fleet had been ripped by storms and by the more vicious, more sleek, more maneuverable warships that Drake and Howard had built.

Blackthorne had been in a swirling attack near Admiral Howard's flagship *Renown* when the wind had changed, freshened to gale force, the squalls monstrous, and he had had to decide whether to try to beat to windward to escape the broadside that would burst from the great galleon *Santa Cruz* just ahead, or to run before the wind alone, through the enemy squadron, the rest of Howard's ships having already turned about, hacking more northerly.

"Go north to windward!" Alban Caradoc had shouted. He had shipped as second in command. Blackthorne was Captain-Pilot and responsible, and this his first command. Alban Caradoc had insisted on coming to the fight, even though he had no right to be aboard except that he was an Englishman and all Englishmen had the right to be aboard in this darkest time in history.

"Belay there!" Blackthorne had ordered and had swung the tiller southward, heading into the maw of the enemy fleet, knowing the other way would leave them doomed by the guns of the galleon that now towered above them.

So they had gone southerly, racing before the wind, through the galleons. The three-deck cannonade of the *Santa Cruz* passed safely overhead and he got off two broadsides into her, flea bites to so huge a vessel, and then they were scudding through the center of the enemy. The galleons on either side did not wish to fire at this lone ship, for their broadsides might have damaged each other, so the guns stayed silent. Then his ship was through and escaping when a three-deck cannonade from the *Madre de Dios* straddled them. Both their masts careened away like arrows, men enmeshed in the rigging. Half the starboard main deck had vanished, the dead and the dying everywhere.

He had seen Alban Caradoc lying against a shattered gun carriage, so incredibly tiny without legs. He cradled the old seaman whose eyes were almost starting out of his head, his screams hideous. "Oh Christ I don't want to die don't want to die, help help me, help me help me, oh Jesus Christ it's the pain, *helllp!*" Blackthorne knew there was only one thing he could do for Alban Caradoc. He picked up a belaying pin and smashed down with all his force.

Then, weeks later, he had to tell Felicity that her father was dead. He told her no more than that Alban Caradoc had been killed instantly. He did not tell her he had blood on his hands that would never come off. . . .

Blackthorne and the samurai were walking through a wide winding street now. There were no shops, only houses side by side, each within its own land and high fences, the houses and fences and the road itself all staggeringly clean.

This cleanliness was incredible to Blackthorne because in London and the cities and towns of England—and Europe—offal and night soil and urine were cast into the streets, to be scavenged or allowed to pile up until pedestrians and carts and horses could not pass. Only then would most townships perhaps cleanse themselves. The scavengers of London were great herds of swine that were driven through the main thoroughfares nightly. Mostly the rats and the packs of wild dogs and cats and fires did the cleansing of London. And the flies.

But Osaka was so different. How do they do it? he asked himself. No pot holes, no piles of horse dung, no wheel ruts, no filth or refuse of any sort. Just hard-packed earth, swept and clean. Walls of wood and houses of wood, sparkling and neat. And where are the packs of beggars and cripples that fester every township in Christendom? And the gangs of footpads and wild youths that would inevitably be skulking in the shadows?

The people they passed bowed politely, some knelt. Kaga-men hurried along with palanquins or the one-passenger kagas. Parties of samurai—Grays, never Browns—walked the streets carelessly.

They were walking a shop-lined street when his legs gave out. He toppled heavily and landed on his hands and knees.

The samurai helped him up but, for the moment, his strength had gone and he could walk no further.

"*Gomen nasai, dozo ga matsu,*"—I'm sorry, please wait—he said, his legs cramped. He rubbed his knotted calf muscles and blessed Friar Domingo for the priceless things that the man had taught him.

The samurai leader looked down at him and spoke at length.

"*Gomen nasai, nihon go ga hanase-masen,*"—I'm sorry, I don't speak Japanese, Blackthorne replied, slowly but clearly. "*Dozo, ga matsu.*"

"*Ah! So desu,* Anjin-san. *Wakarimasu,*" the man said, understanding him. He gave a short sharp command and one of the samurai hurried away. After a while Blackthorne got up, tried to hobble along, but the leader of the samurai said "*Iyé*" and motioned him to wait.

Soon the samurai came back with four semi-naked kaga-men and their kaga. Samurai showed Blackthorne how to recline in it and to hold on to the strap that hung from the central pole.

The party set off again. Soon Blackthorne recovered his strength and preferred walking again, but he knew he was still weak. I've got to get some rest, he thought. I've no reserve. I must get a bath and some food. Real food.

Now they were climbing wide steps that joined one street to another and entered a new residential section that skirted a substantial wood with tall trees and paths through it. Blackthorne found it vastly enjoyable to be out of the streets, the well-tended sward soft underfoot, the track wandering through the trees.

When they were deep in the wood, another party of thirty-odd Grays approached from around a curve ahead. As they came alongside, they stopped, and after the usual ceremonial of their captains greeting each other, all their eyes turned on Blackthorne. There was a volley of questions and answers and then, as these men began to reassemble to leave, their leader calmly pulled out his sword and impaled the leader of Blackthorne's samurai. Simultaneously the new group fell on the rest of Blackthorne's samurai. The ambush was so sudden and so well planned that all ten Grays were dead almost at the same instant. Not one had even had time to draw his sword.

The kaga-men were on their knees, horrified, their foreheads pressed into the grass. Blackthorne stood beside them. The captain-samurai, a heavyset man with a large paunch, sent sentries to either end of the track. Others were collecting the swords of the dead men. During all of this, the men paid Blackthorne no attention at all, until he began to back away. Immediately there was a hissing command from the captain which clearly meant to stay where he was.

At another command all these new Grays stripped off their uniform kimonos. Underneath they wore a motley collection of rags and ancient kimonos. All pulled on masks that were already tied around their necks. One man collected the gray uniforms and vanished with them into the woods.

They must be bandits, Blackthorne thought. Why else the masks? What do they want with me?

The bandits chattered quietly among themselves, watching him as they cleaned their swords on the clothes of the dead samurai.

"Anjin-san? *Hai?*" The captain's eyes above the cloth mask were round and jet and piercing.

"*Hai,*" Blackthorne replied, his skin crawling.

The man pointed at the ground, clearly telling him not to move. "*Wakarimasu ka?*"

"*Hai.*"

They looked him up and down. Then one of their outpost sentries—no longer gray-uniformed but masked, like all of them—came out of the bushes for an instant, a hundred paces away. He waved and vanished again.

Immediately the men surrounded Blackthorne, preparing to leave. The bandit captain put his eyes on the kaga-men, who shivered like dogs of a cruel master and put their heads deeper into the grass.

Then the bandit leader barked an order. The four slowly raised their heads with disbelief. Again the same command and they bowed and groveled and backed away; then as one, they took to their heels and vanished into the undergrowth.

The bandit smiled contemptuously and motioned Blackthorne to begin walking back toward the city.

He went with them, helplessly. There was no running away.

They were almost to the edge of the wood when they stopped. There were noises ahead and another party of thirty samurai rounded the bend. Browns and Grays, the Browns the vanguard, their leader in a palanquin, a few pack horses following. They stopped immediately. Both groups moved into skirmish positions, eyeing each other hostilely, seventy paces between them. The bandit leader walked into the space between, his movements jerky, and shouted angrily at the other samurai, pointing at Blackthorne and then further back to where the ambush had taken place. He tore out his sword, held it threateningly on high, obviously telling the other party to get out of the way.

All the swords of his men sang out of their scabbards. At his order one of the bandits stationed himself behind Blackthorne, his sword raised and readied, and again the leader harangued the opposition.

Nothing happened for a moment, then Blackthorne saw the man in the palanquin get down and he instantly recognized him. It was Kasigi Yabu. Yabu shouted back at the bandit leader but this man shook his sword furiously, ordering them out of the way. His tirade stopped with finality. Then Yabu gave a curt order, and charged with a screaming battle cry, limping slightly, sword high, his men rushing with him, Grays not far behind.

Blackthorne dropped to escape the sword blow that would have cut him in half, but the blow was ill-timed and the bandit leader turned and fled into the undergrowth, his men following.

The Browns and the Grays were quickly alongside Blackthorne, who scrambled to his feet. Some of the samurai charged after the bandits into the bushes, others ran up the track, and the rest scattered protectively. Yabu stopped at the edge of the brush, shouted orders imperiously, then came back slowly, his limp more pronounced.

"*So desu,* Anjin-san," he said, panting from his exertion.

"*So desu,* Kasigi Yabu-san," Blackthorne replied, using the same phrase which meant something like "well" or "oh really" or "is that the truth." He pointed in the direction that the bandits had run away. *"Domo."* He bowed politely, equal to equal, and said another blessing for Friar Domingo. *"Gomen nasai, nihon go ga hanase-masen"*—I'm sorry, I can't speak Japanese.

"Hai," Yabu said, not a little impressed, and added something that Blackthorne did not understand.

"Tsuyaku ga imasu ka?" Blackthorne asked. Do you have an interpreter?

"Iyé, Anjin-san. *Gomen nasai."*

Blackthorne felt a little easier. Now he could communicate directly. His vocabulary was sparse, but it was a beginning.

Eeeee, I wish I did have an interpreter, Yabu was thinking fervently. By the Lord Buddha!

I'd like to know what happened when you met Toranaga, Anjin-san, what questions he asked and what you answered, what you told him about the village and guns and cargo and ship and galley and about Rodrigu. I'd like to know everything that was said, and how it was said, and where you've been and why you're here. Then I'd have an idea of what was in Toranaga's mind, the way he's thinking. Then I could plan what I'm going to tell him today. As it is now, I'm helpless.

Why did Toranaga see *you* immediately when we arrived, and not *me?* Why no word or orders from him since we docked until today, other than the obligatory, polite greeting and "I look forward with pleasure to seeing you shortly"? Why has he sent for me today? Why has our meeting been postponed twice? Was it because of something you said? Or Hiro-matsu? Or is it just a normal delay caused by all his other worries?

Oh, yes, Toranaga, you've got almost insurmountable problems. Ishido's influence is spreading like fire. And do you know about Lord Onoshi's treachery yet?

Do you know that Ishido has offered me Ikawa Jikkyu's head and province if I secretly join him now?

Why did you pick today to send for me? Which good *kami* put me here to save the Anjin-san's life, only to taunt me because I can't talk directly to him, or even through someone else, to find the key to your secret lock? Why did you put him into prison for execution? Why did Ishido want him out of prison? Why did the bandits try to capture him for ransom? Ransom from whom? And why is the Anjin-san still alive? That bandit should have easily cut him in half.

Yabu noticed the deeply etched lines that had not been in Blackthorne's face the first time he had seen him. He looks starved, thought Yabu. He's like a wild dog. But not one of the pack, the leader of the pack, *neh?*

Oh yes, Pilot, I'd give a thousand koku for a trustworthy interpreter right now.

I'm going to be your master. You're going to build my ships and train my men. I have to manipulate Toranaga somehow. If I can't, it doesn't matter. In my next life I'll be better prepared.

"Good dog!" Yabu said aloud to Blackthorne and smiled slightly. "All you need is a firm hand, a few bones, and a few whippings. First I'll deliver you to Lord Toranaga—after you've been bathed. You stink, Lord Pilot!"

Blackthorne did not understand the words, but he sensed friendliness in them and saw Yabu's smile. He smiled back. "*Wakarimasen*"—I don't understand.

"*Hai,* Anjin-san."

The *daimyo* turned away and glanced after the bandits. He cupped his hands around his mouth and shouted. Instantly all the Browns returned to him. The chief samurai of the Grays was standing in the center of the track and he too called off the chase. None of the bandits were brought back.

When this captain of the Grays came up to Yabu there was much argument and pointing to the city and to the castle, and obvious disagreement between them.

At length Yabu overrode him, his hand on his sword, and motioned Blackthorne to get into the palanquin.

"*Iyé,*" the captain said.

The two men were beginning to square up to one another and the Grays and the Browns shifted nervously.

"Anjin-san *desu shunjin* Toranaga-sama . . ."

Blackthorne caught a word here, another there. *Watakushi* meant "I," *hitachi* added meant "we," *shunjin* meant "prisoner." And then he remembered what Rodrigues had said, so he shook his head and interrupted sharply. "*Shunjin, iyé! Watakushi wa* Anjin-san!"

Both men stared at him.

Blackthorne broke the silence and added in halting Japanese, knowing the words to be ungrammatical and childishly spoken, but hoping they would be understood, "I friend. Not prisoner. Understand please. Friend. So sorry, friend want bath. Bath, understand? Tired. Hungry. Bath." He pointed to the castle donjon. "Go there! Now, please. Lord Toranaga one, Lord Ishido two. Go *now.*"

And with added imperiousness on the last "*ima*" he got awkwardly into the palanquin and lay down on the cushions, his feet sticking far out.

Then Yabu laughed, and everyone joined in.

"*Ah so,* Anjin-sama!" Yabu said with a mocking bow.

"*Iyé,* Yabu-sama. Anjin-*san.*" Blackthorne corrected him contentedly. Yes, you bastard. I know a thing or two now. But I haven't forgotten about you. And soon I'll be walking on your grave.

CHAPTER 16

PERHAPS it would have been better to consult me before removing *my* prisoner from *my* jurisdiction, Lord Ishido," Toranaga was saying.

"The barbarian was in the common prison with common people. Naturally I presumed you'd no further interest in him, otherwise I wouldn't have had him taken out of there. Of course, I never meant to interfere with your private affairs." Ishido was outwardly calm and deferential but inside he was seething. He knew that he had been trapped into an indiscretion. It was true that he should have asked Toranaga first. Ordinary politeness demanded it. Even that would not have mattered at all if he still had the barbarian in his power, in his quarters; he would simply have handed over the foreigner at his leisure, if and when Toranaga had asked for him. But for some of his men to have been intercepted and ignominiously killed, and then for the *daimyo* Yabu and some of Toranaga's men to have taken physical possession of the barbarian from more of his men changed the position completely. He had lost face, whereas his whole strategy for Toranaga's public destruction was to put Toranaga into precisely that position. "Again I apologize."

Toranaga glanced at Hiro-matsu, the apology music to their ears. Both men knew how much inner bleeding it had cost Ishido. They were in the great audience room. By prior agreement, the two antagonists had only five guards present, men of guaranteed reliability. The rest were waiting outside. Yabu was also waiting outside. And the barbarian was being cleaned. Good, Toranaga thought, feeling very pleased with himself. He put his mind on Yabu briefly and decided not to see him today after all, but to continue to play him like a fish. So he asked Hiro-matsu to send him away and turned again to Ishido. "Of course your apology is accepted. Fortunately no harm was done."

"Then I may take the barbarian to the Heir—as soon as he's presentable?"

"I'll send him as soon as I've finished with him."

"May I ask when that will be? The Heir was expecting him this morning."

"We shouldn't be too concerned about that, you and I, *neh?* Yaemon's only seven. I'm sure a seven-year-old boy can possess himself with patience. *Neh?* Patience is a form of discipline and requires practice. Doesn't it? I'll explain the misunderstanding myself. I'm giving him another swimming lesson this morning."

"Oh?"

"Yes. You should learn to swim too, Lord Ishido. It's excellent exercise and could come in very useful during war. All my samurai can swim. I insist that all learn that art."

"Mine spend their time practicing archery, swordsmanship, riding, and shooting."

"Mine add poetry, penmanship, flower arranging, the *cha-no-yu* ceremony. Samurai should be well versed in the arts of peace to be strong for the arts of war."

"Most of my men are already more than proficient in those arts," Ishido said, conscious that his own writing was poor and his learning limited. "Samurai are birthed for war. I understand war very well. That is enough at the moment. That and obedience to our Master's will."

"Yaemon's swimming lesson is at the Hour of the Horse." The day and the night were each split into six equal parts. The day began with the Hour of the Hare, from 5 A.M. to 7 A.M., then the Dragon, from 7 A.M. to 9 A.M. The hours of the Snake, Horse, Goat, Monkey, Cock, Dog, Boar, Rat and Ox followed, and the cycle ended with the Hour of the Tiger between 3 A.M. and 5 A.M. "Would you like to join the lesson?"

"Thank you, no. I'm too old to change my ways," Ishido said thinly.

"I hear the captain of your men was ordered to commit seppuku."

"Naturally. The bandits should have been caught. At least one of them should have been caught. Then we would have found the others."

"I'm astounded that such carrion could operate so close to the castle."

"I agree. Perhaps the barbarian could describe them."

"What would a barbarian know?" Toranaga laughed. "As to the bandits, they were *ronin*, weren't they? *Ronin* are plentiful among your men. Inquiries there might prove fruitful. *Neh?*"

"Inquiries are being pressed. In many directions." Ishido passed over the veiled sneer about *ronin*, the masterless, almost outcast mercenary samurai who had, in their thousands, flocked to the Heir's banner when Ishido had whispered it abroad that he, on behalf of the Heir and the mother of the Heir, would accept their fidelity, would—incredibly—forgive and forget their indiscretions or past, and would, in the course of time, repay their loyalty with a Taikō's lavishness. Ishido knew that it had been a brilliant move. It gave him an enormous pool of trained samurai to draw upon; it guaranteed loyalty, for *ronin* knew they would never get another such chance; it brought into his camp all the angry ones, many of whom had been made *ronin* by Toranaga's conquests and those of his allies. And lastly, it removed a danger to the realm—an increase in the bandit population—for almost the only supportable way of life open to a samurai unlucky enough to become *ronin* was to become a monk or bandit.

"There are many things I don't understand about this ambush," Ishido said, his voice tinged with venom. "Yes. Why, for instance, should bandits try to capture this barbarian for ransom? There are plenty of others in the city, vastly more important. Isn't that what the bandit said? It was ransom he wanted. Ransom from whom? What's the barbarian's value? None. And how did they know where he would be? It was only yesterday that I gave the order to bring him to the Heir, thinking it would amuse the boy. Very curious."

"Very," Toranaga said.

"Then there's the coincidence of Lord Yabu being in the vicinity with some of your men and some of mine at that exact time. Very curious."

"Very. Of course he was there because I had sent for him, and your men were there because we agreed—at your suggestion—that it was good policy and a way to begin to heal the breach between us, that your men accompany mine wherever they go while I'm on this official visit."

"It is also strange that the bandits who were sufficiently brave and well organized to slay the first ten without a fight acted like Koreans when our men arrived. The two sides were equally matched. Why didn't the bandits fight, or take the barbarian into the hills immediately, and not stupidly stay on a main path to the castle? Very curious."

"Very. I'll certainly be taking double guards with me tomorrow when I go hawking. Just in case. It's disconcerting to know bandits are so close to the castle. Yes. Perhaps you'd like to hunt, too? Fly one of your hawks against mine? I'll be hunting the hills to the north."

"Thank you, no. I'll be busy tomorrow. Perhaps the day after? I've ordered twenty thousand men to sweep all the forests, woods, and glades around Osaka. There won't be a bandit within twenty *ri* in ten days. That I can promise you."

Toranaga knew that Ishido was using the bandits as an excuse to increase the number of his troops in the vicinity. If he says twenty, he means fifty. The neck of the trap is closing, he told himself. Why so soon? What new treachery has happened? Why is Ishido so confident? "Good. Then the day after tomorrow, Lord Ishido. You'll keep your men away from my hunting area? I wouldn't want my game disturbed," he added thinly.

"Of course. And the barbarian?"

"He is and always was my property. And his ship. But you can have him when I've finished with him. And afterwards you can send him to the execution ground if you wish."

"Thank you. Yes, I'll do that." Ishido closed his fan and slipped it into his sleeve. "He's unimportant. What is important and the reason for my coming to see you is that—oh, by the way, I heard that the lady, my mother, is visiting the Johji monastery."

"Oh? I would have thought the season's a little late for looking at cherry blossoms. Surely they'd be well past their prime now?"

"I agree. But then if she wishes to see them, why not? You can never tell with the elderly, they have minds of their own and see things differently, *neh?* But her health isn't good. I worry about her. She has to be very careful—she takes a chill very easily."

"It's the same with my mother. You have to watch the health of the old." Toranaga made a mental note to send an immediate message to remind the abbot to watch over the old woman's health very carefully. If she were to die in the monastery the repercussions would be terrible. He would be shamed before the Empire. All *daimyos* would realize that in the chess game for power he had used a helpless old woman, the mother of his enemy, as a pawn, and failed in his responsibility to her. Taking a hostage was, in truth, a dangerous ploy.

Ishido had become almost blind with rage when he had heard that his revered mother was in the Toranaga stronghold at Nagoya. Heads had fallen. He had immediately brought forward plans for Toranaga's destruction, and had taken a solemn resolve to invest Nagoya and obliterate the *daimyo,* Kazamaki—in whose charge she had ostensibly been—the moment hostilities began. Last, a private message had been sent to the abbot through intermediaries, that unless she was brought safely out of the monastery within twenty-four hours, Naga, the only son of Toranaga within reach and any of his women that could be caught, would, unhappily, wake up in the leper village, having been fed by them, watered by them, and serviced by one of their whores. Ishido knew that while his mother was in Toranaga's power he had to tread lightly. But he had made it clear that if she was not let go, he would set the Empire to the torch. "How is the lady, your mother, Lord Toranaga," he asked politely.

"She's very well, thank you." Toranaga allowed his happiness to show, both at the thought of his mother and at the knowledge of Ishido's impotent fury. "She's remarkably fit for seventy-four. I only hope I'm as strong as she is when I'm her age."

You're fifty-eight, Toranaga, but you'll never reach fifty-nine, Ishido promised himself. "Please give her my best wishes for a continued happy life. Thank you again and I'm sorry that you were inconvenienced." He bowed with great politeness, and then, holding in his soaring pleasure with difficulty, he added, "Oh, yes, the important matter I wanted to see you about was that the last formal meeting of the Regents has been postponed. We do not meet tonight at sunset."

Toranaga kept the smile on his face but inside he was rocked. "Oh? Why?"

"Lord Kiyama's sick. Lord Sugiyama and Lord Onoshi have agreed to the delay. So did I. A few days are unimportant, aren't they, on such important matters?"

"We can have the meeting without Lord Kiyama."

"We have agreed that we should not." Ishido's eyes were taunting.

"Formally?"

"Here are our four seals."

Toranaga was seething. Any delay jeopardized him immeasurably. Could he barter Ishido's mother for an immediate meeting? No, because it would take too much time for the orders to go back and forth and he would have conceded a very great advantage for nothing. "When will the meeting be?"

"I understand Lord Kiyama should be well tomorrow, or perhaps the next day."

"Good. I'll send my personal physician to see him."

"I'm sure he'd appreciate that. But his own has forbidden any visitors. The disease might be contagious, *neh?*"

"What disease?"

"I don't know, my Lord. That's what I was told."

"Is the doctor a barbarian?"

"Yes. I understand the chief doctor of the Christians. A Christian doctor-priest for a Christian *daimyo.* Ours are not good enough for so—so important a *daimyo,*" Ishido said with a sneer.

Toranaga's concern increased. If the doctor were Japanese, there were many things he could do. But with a Christian doctor—inevitably a Jesuit priest—well, to go against one of them, or even to interfere with one of them, might alienate all Christian *daimyos,* which he could not afford to risk. He knew his friendship with Tsukku-san would not help him against the Christian *daimyos* Onoshi or Kiyama. It was in Christian interests to present a united front. Soon he would have to approach them, the barbarian priests, to make an arrangement, to find out the price of their cooperation. If Ishido truly has Onoshi and Kiyama with him—and all the Christian *daimyos* would follow these two if they acted jointly— then I'm isolated, he thought. Then my only way left is Crimson Sky.

"I'll visit Lord Kiyama the day after tomorrow," he said, naming a deadline.

"But the contagion? I'd never forgive myself if anything happened to you while you're here in Osaka, my Lord. You are our guest, in my care. I must insist you do not."

"You may rest comfortably, my Lord Ishido, the contagion that will topple me has not yet been born, *neh?* You forget the soothsayer's prediction." When the Chinese embassy had come to the Taikō six years ago to try to settle the Japanese-Korean-Chinese war, a famous astrologer had been among them. This Chinese had forecast many things that had since come true. At one of the Taikō's incredibly lavish ceremonial dinners, the Taikō had asked the soothsayer to predict the deaths of certain of his counselors. The astrologer had said that Toranaga would die by the sword when he was middle-aged. Ishido, the famous conqueror of Korea—or Chosen as Chinese called that land—would die un-diseased, an old man, his feet firm in the earth, the most famous man of his day. But the Taikō himself would die in his bed, respected, revered, of old age, leaving a healthy son to follow him. This had so pleased the Taikō, who was still childless, that he had decided to let the embassy return to China and not kill them as he had planned for their previous insolences. Instead of negotiating for peace as he had expected, the Chinese Emperor, through this embassy, had merely offered to "invest him as King of the Country of Wa," as the Chinese called Japan. So he had sent them home alive and not in the very small boxes that had already been prepared for them, and renewed the war against Korea and China.

"No, Lord Toranaga, I haven't forgotten," Ishido said, remembering very well. "But contagion can be uncomfortable. Why be uncomfortable? You could catch the pox like your son Noboru, so sorry—or become a leper like Lord Onoshi. He's still young, but he suffers. Oh, yes, he suffers."

Momentarily Toranaga was thrown off balance. He knew the ravages of both diseases too well. Noboru, his eldest living son, had caught the Chinese pox when he was seventeen—ten years ago—and all the cures of the doctors, Japanese, Chinese, Korean, and Christian, had not managed to allay the disease which had already defaced him but would not kill him. If I become all powerful, Toranaga promised himself, perhaps I can stamp out that disease. Does it really come from women? How do women get it? How can it be cured? Poor Noboru, Toranaga thought. Except for the pox you'd be my heir, because you're a brilliant soldier, a better administrator than Sudara, and very cunning. You must have done many bad things in a previous life to have had to carry so many burdens in this one.

"By the Lord Buddha, I'd not wish either of those on anyone," he said.

"I agree," Ishido said, believing Toranaga would wish them both on him if he could. He bowed again and left.

Toranaga broke the silence. "Well?"

Hiro-matsu said, "If you stay or leave now, it's the same—disaster, because now you've been betrayed and you are isolated, Sire. If you stay for the meeting —you won't get a meeting for a week—Ishido will have mobilized his legions around Osaka and you'll never escape, whatever happens to the Lady Ochiba in Yedo, and clearly Ishido's decided to risk her to get you. It's obvious you're betrayed and the four Regents will make a decision against you. A four against one vote in Council impeaches you. If you leave, they'll still issue whatever orders Ishido wishes. You're bound to uphold a four-to-one decision. You swore to do it. You cannot go against your solemn word as a Regent."

"I agree."

The silence held.

Hiro-matsu waited, with growing anxiety. "What are you going to do?"

"First I'm going to have my swim," Toranaga said with surprising joviality. "Then I'll see the barbarian."

The woman walked quietly through Toranaga's private garden in the castle toward the little thatched hut that was set so prettily in a glade of maples. Her silk kimono and obi were the most simple yet the most elegant that the most famous craftsmen in China could make. She wore her hair in the latest Kyoto fashion, piled high and held in place with long silver pins. A colorful sunshade protected her very fair skin. She was tiny, just five feet, but perfectly proportioned. Around her neck was a thin golden chain, and hanging from it, a small golden crucifix.

Kiri was waiting on the veranda of the hut. She sat heavily in the shade, her buttocks overflowing her cushion, and she watched the woman approach along the steppingstones which had been set so carefully into the moss that they seemed to have grown there.

"You're more beautiful than ever, younger than ever, Toda Mariko-san," Kiri said without jealousy, returning her bow.

"I wish that were true, Kiritsubo-san," Mariko replied, smiling. She knelt on a cushion, unconsciously arranging her skirts into a delicate pattern.

"It's true. When did we last meet? Two—three years ago? You haven't changed a hair's breadth in twenty years. It must be almost twenty years since we first met. Do you remember? It was at a feast Lord Goroda gave. You were fourteen, just married and rare."

"And frightened."

"No, not you. Not frightened."

"It was sixteen years ago, Kiritsubo-san, not twenty. Yes, I remember it very well." Too well, she thought, heartsick. That was the day my brother whispered that he believed our revered father was going to be revenged on his liege Lord, the Dictator Goroda, that he was going to assassinate him. *His liege Lord!*

Oh, yes, Kiri-san, I remember that day and that year and that hour. It was the beginning of all the horror. I've never admitted to anyone that I knew what was going to happen before it happened. I never warned my husband, or Hiromatsu, his father—both faithful vassals of the Dictator—that treachery was planned by one of his greatest generals. Worse, I never warned Goroda my liege Lord. So I failed in my duty to my liege Lord, to my husband, to his family, which because of my marriage is my only family. Oh, Madonna, forgive me my sin, help me to cleanse myself. I kept silent to protect my beloved father, who desecrated the honor of a thousand years. O my God, O Lord Jesus of Nazareth, save this sinner from eternal damnation. . . .

"It was sixteen years ago," Mariko said serenely.

"I was carrying Lord Toranaga's child that year," Kiri said, and she thought, if Lord Goroda had not been foully betrayed and murdered by your father, my Lord Toranaga would never have had to fight the battle of Nagakudé, I would never have caught a chill there and my child would never have miscarried. Perhaps, she told herself. And perhaps not. It was just *karma, my karma,* whatever happened, *neh?* "Ah, Mariko-san," she said, no malice in her, "that's so long ago, it almost seems like another lifetime. But you're ageless. Why can't I have your figure and beautiful hair, and walk so daintily?" Kiri laughed. "The answer's simple: Because I eat too much!"

"What does it matter? You bask in Lord Toranaga's favor, *neh?* So you're fulfilled. You're wise and warm and whole and happy in yourself."

"I'd rather be thin and still able to eat and be in favor," Kiri said. "But you? You're not happy in yourself?"

"I'm only an instrument for my Lord Buntaro to play upon. If the Lord, my husband, is happy, then of course I'm happy. His pleasure's my pleasure. It's the same with you," Mariko said.

"Yes. But not the same." Kiri moved her fan, the golden silk catching the afternoon sun. I'm so glad I'm not you, Mariko, with all your beauty and brilliance and courage and learning. No! I couldn't bear being married to that hateful, ugly, arrogant, violent man for a day, let alone seventeen years. He's so opposite to his father, Lord Hiro-matsu. Now, there's a wonderful man. But Buntaro? How do fathers have such terrible sons? I wish I had a son, oh, how I wish! But you, Mariko, how have you borne such ill treatment all these years? How have you endured your tragedies? It seems impossible that there's no shadow of them on your face or in your soul. "You're an amazing woman, Toda Buntaro Mariko-san."

"Thank you, Kiritsubo Toshiko-san. Oh Kiri-san, it's so good to see you."

"And you. How is your son?"

"Beautiful—beautiful—beautiful. Saruji's fifteen now, can you imagine it? Tall and strong and just like his father, and Lord Hiro-matsu has given Saruji his own fief and he's—did you know that he's going to be married?"

"No, to whom?"

"She's a granddaughter of Lord Kiyama's. Lord Toranaga's arranged it so well. A very fine match for our family. I only wish the girl herself was—was more attentive to my son, more worthy. Do you know she . . . " Mariko laughed, a little shyly. "There, I sound like every mother-in-law that's ever been. But I think you'd agree, she isn't really trained yet."

"You'll have time to do that."

"Oh, I hope so. Yes. I'm lucky I don't have a mother-in-law. I don't know what I'd do."

"You'd enchant her and train her as you train all your household, *neh?*"

"Eeeee, I wish that was also true." Mariko's hands were motionless in her lap. She watched a dragonfly settle, then dart away. "My husband ordered me here. Lord Toranaga wishes to see me?"

"Yes. He wants you to interpret for him."

Mariko was startled. "With whom?"

"The new barbarian."

"Oh! But what about Father Tsukku-san? Is he sick?"

"No." Kiri played with her fan. "I suppose it's left to us to wonder why Lord Toranaga wants you here and not the priest, as in the first interview. Why is it, Mariko-san, that we have to guard all the monies, pay all the bills, train all the servants, buy all the food and household goods—even most times the clothes of our Lords—but they don't really *tell* us anything, do they?"

"Perhaps that's what our intuition's for."

"Probably." Kiri's gaze was level and friendly. "But I'd imagine that this would all be a very private matter. So you would swear by your Christian God not to divulge anything about this meeting. To anyone."

The day seemed to lose its warmth.

"Of course," Mariko said uneasily. She understood very clearly that Kiri meant she was to say nothing to her husband or to his father or to her confessor. As her husband had ordered her here, obviously at Lord Toranaga's request, her duty to her liege Lord Toranaga overcame her duty to her husband, so she could withhold information freely from him. But to her confessor? Could she say nothing to him? And why was she the interpreter and not Father Tsukku-san? She knew that once more, against her will, she was involved in the kind of political intrigue that had bedeviled her life, and wished again that her family was not ancient and Fujimoto, that she had never been born with the gift of tongues that had allowed her to learn the almost incomprehensible Portuguese and Latin languages, and that she had never been born at all. But then, she thought, I would never have seen my son, nor learned about the Christ Child or His Truth, or about the Life Everlasting.

It is your *karma*, Mariko, she told herself sadly, just *karma*. "Very well, Kiri-san." Then she added with foreboding, "I swear by the Lord my God, that I will not divulge anything said here today, or at any time I am interpreting for my liege Lord."

"I would also imagine that you might have to exclude part of your own feelings to translate exactly what is said. This new barbarian is strange and says peculiar things. I'm sure my Lord picked you above all possibilities for special reasons."

"I am Lord Toranaga's to do with as he wishes. He need never have any fear for my loyalty."

"That was never in question, Lady. I meant no harm."

A spring rain came and speckled the petals and the mosses and the leaves, and disappeared leaving ever more beauty in its wake.

"I would ask a favor, Mariko-san. Would you please put your crucifix under your kimono?"

Mariko's fingers darted for it defensively. "Why? Lord Toranaga has never objected to my conversion, nor has Lord Hiro-matsu, the head of my clan! My husband has—my husband allows me to keep it and wear it."

"Yes. But crucifixes send *this* barbarian mad and my Lord Toranaga doesn't want him mad, he wants him soothed."

Blackthorne had never seen anyone so petite. *"Konnichi wa,"* he said. *"Konnichi,* Toranaga-sama." He bowed as a courtier, nodded to the boy who knelt, wide-eyed, beside Toranaga, and to the fat woman who was behind him. They were all on the veranda that encircled the small hut. The hut contained a single small room with rustic screens and hewn beams and thatched roof, and a kitchen area behind. It was set on pilings of wood and raised a foot or so above a carpet of pure white sand. This was a ceremonial Tea House for the *cha-no-yu* ceremony and built at vast expense with rare materials for that purpose alone, though sometimes, because these houses were isolated, in glades, they were used for trysts and private conversations.

Blackthorne gathered his kimono around him and sat on the cushion that had been placed on the sand below and in front of them. *"Gomen nasai,* Toranagasama, *nihon go ga hanase-masen. Tsuyaku go imasu ka?"*

"I am your interpreter, senhor," Mariko said at once, in almost flawless Portuguese. "But you speak Japanese?"

"No, senhorita, just a few words or phrases," Blackthorne replied, taken aback. He had been expecting Father Alvito to be the interpreter, and Toranaga to be accompanied by samurai and perhaps the *daimyo* Yabu. But no samurai were near, though many ringed the garden.

"My Lord Toranaga asks where—First, perhaps I should ask if you prefer to speak Latin?"

"Whichever you wish, senhorita." Like any educated man, Blackthorne could read, write, and speak Latin, because Latin was the only language of learning throughout the civilized world.

Who is this woman? Where did she learn such perfect Portuguese? And Latin? Where else but from the Jesuits, he thought. In one of their schools. Oh, they're so clever! The first thing they do is build a school.

It was only seventy years ago that Ignatius Loyola had formed the Society of Jesus and now their schools, the finest in Christendom, were spread across the world and their influence bolstered or destroyed kings. They had the ear of the Pope. They had halted the tide of the Reformation and were now winning back huge territories for their Church.

"We will speak Portuguese then," she was saying. "My Master wishes to know where you learned your 'few words and phrases'?"

"There was a monk in the prison, senhorita, a Franciscan monk, and he taught me. Things like, 'food, friend, bath, go, come, true, false, here, there, I, you, please, thank you, want, don't want, prisoner, yes, no,' and so on. It's only a beginning, unfortunately. Would you please tell Lord Toranaga that I'm better prepared now to answer his questions, to help, and more than a little pleased to be out of prison. For which I thank him."

Blackthorne watched as she turned and spoke to Toranaga. He knew that he would have to speak simply, preferably in short sentences, and be careful because, unlike the priest who interpreted simultaneously, this woman waited till he had finished, then gave a synopsis, or a version of what was said—the usual problem of all except the finest interpreters, though even they, as with the Jesuit, allowed their own personalities to influence what was said, voluntarily or involuntarily. The bath and massage and food and two hours of sleep had immeasurably refreshed him. The bath attendants, all women of girth and strength, had pum-

meled him and shampooed his hair, braiding it in a neat queue, and the barber
had trimmed his beard. He had been given a clean loincloth and kimono and sash,
and tabi and thongs for his feet. The futons on which he had slept had been so
clean, like the room. It had all seemed dreamlike and, waking from dreamlessness, he had wondered momentarily which was the dream, this or the prison.

He had waited impatiently, hoping that he would be guided again to Toranaga,
planning what to say and what to reveal, how to outwit Father Alvito and how
to gain ascendance over him. And over Toranaga. For he knew, beyond all doubt,
because of what Friar Domingo had told him about the Portuguese, and Japanese
politics and trade, that he could now help Toranaga, who, in return, could easily
give him the riches he desired.

And now, with no priest to fight, he felt even more confident. I need just a
little luck and patience.

Toranaga was listening intently to the doll-like interpreter.

Blackthorne thought, I could pick her up with one hand and if I put both hands
around her waist, my fingers would touch. How old would she be? Perfect!
Married? No wedding ring. Ah, that's interesting. She's wearing no jewelry of
any kind. Except the silver pins in her hair. Neither is the other woman, the fat
one.

He searched his memory. The other two women in the village had worn no
jewelry either, and he had not seen any on any of Mura's household. Why?

And who's the fat woman? Toranaga's wife? Or the boy's nursemaid? Would
the lad be Toranaga's son? Or grandson, perhaps? Friar Domingo had said that
Japanese had only one wife at one time but as many consorts—legal mistresses
—as they wished.

Was the interpreter Toranaga's consort?

What would it be like to have such a woman in bed? I'd be afraid of crushing
her. No, she wouldn't break. There are women in England almost as small. But
not like her.

The boy was small and straight and round-eyed, his full black hair tied into
a short queue, his pate unshaven. His curiosity seemed enormous.

Without thinking, Blackthorne winked. The boy jumped, then laughed and
interrupted Mariko and pointed and spoke out, and they listened indulgently and
no one hushed him. When he had finished, Toranaga spoke briefly to Blackthorne.

"Lord Toranaga asks why did you do that, senhor?"

"Oh, just to amuse the lad. He's a child like any, and children in my country
would usually laugh if you did that. My son must be about his age now. My son's
seven."

"The Heir is seven," Mariko said after a pause, then translated what he had
said.

"Heir? Does that mean the boy's Lord Toranaga's only son?" Blackthorne
asked.

"Lord Toranaga has instructed me to say that you will please confine yourself
to answering questions only, for the moment." Then she added, "I'm sure, if you
are patient, Pilot-Captain B'ackthon, that you'll be given an opportunity to ask
anything you wish later."

"Very well."

"As your name is very hard to say, senhor, for we do not have the sounds to
pronounce it—may I, for Lord Toranaga, use your Japanese name, Anjin-san?"

"Of course." Blackthorne was going to ask hers but he remembered what she
had said and reminded himself to be patient.

"Thank you. My Lord asks, do you have any other children?"

"A daughter. She was born just before I left my home in England. So she's about two now."

"You have one wife or many?"

"One. That's our custom. Like the Portuguese and Spanish. We don't have consorts—formal consorts."

"Is this your first wife, senhor?"

"Yes."

"Please, how old are you?"

"Thirty-six."

"Where in England do you live?"

"On the outskirts of Chatham. That's a small port near London."

"London is your chief city?"

"Yes."

"He asks, what languages do you speak?"

"English, Portuguese, Spanish, Dutch, and of course, Latin."

"What is 'Dutch'?"

"It's a language spoken in Europe, in the Netherlands. It's very similar to German."

She frowned. "Dutch is a heathen language? German too?"

"Both are non-Catholic countries," he said carefully.

"Excuse me, isn't that the same as heathen?"

"No, senhorita. Christianity is split in two distinct and very separate religions. Catholicism and Protestantism. There are two versions of Christianity. The sect in Japan is Catholic. At the moment both sects are very hostile to each other." He marked her astonishment and felt Toranaga's growing impatience at being left out of the conversation. Be careful, he cautioned himself. She's certainly Catholic. Lead up to things. And be simple. "Perhaps Lord Toranaga doesn't wish to discuss religion, senhorita, as it was partially covered in our first meeting."

"You are a Protestant Christian?"

"Yes."

"And Catholic Christians are your enemies?"

"Most would consider me heretic and their enemy, yes."

She hesitated, turned to Toranaga and spoke at length.

There were many guards around the perimeter of the garden. All well away, all Browns. Then Blackthorne noticed ten Grays sitting in a neat group in the shade, all eyes on the boy. What significance has that? he wondered.

Toranaga was cross-questioning Mariko, then spoke directly at Blackthorne.

"My Lord wishes to know about you and your family," Mariko began. "About your country, its queen and previous rulers, habits, customs, and history. Similarly about all other countries, particularly Portugal and Spain. All about the world you live in. About your ships, weapons, foods, trade. About your wars and battles and how to navigate a ship, how you guided your ship and what happened on the voyage. He wants to understand— Excuse me, why do you laugh?"

"Only because, senhorita, that seems to be just about everything I know."

"That is precisely what my Master wishes. 'Precisely' is the correct word?"

"Yes, senhorita. May I compliment you on your Portuguese, which is flawless."

Her fan fluttered a little. "Thank you, senhor. Yes, my Master wants to learn the *truth* about everything, what is fact and what would be your opinion."

"I'd be glad to tell him. It might take a little time."

"My Master has the time, he says."

Blackthorne looked at Toranaga. "*Wakarimasu.*"

"If you will excuse me, senhor, my Master orders me to say your accent is a little wrong." Mariko showed him how to say it and he repeated it and thanked her. "I am Senhora Mariko Buntaro, not senhorita."

"Yes, senhora." Blackthorne glanced at Toranaga. "Where would he like me to begin?"

She asked him. A fleeting smile sped across Toranaga's strong face. "He says, at the beginning."

Blackthorne knew that this was another trial. What, out of all the limitless possibilities, should he start with? Whom should he talk to? To Toranaga, the boy, or the woman? Obviously, if only men had been present, to Toranaga. But now? Why were the women and the boy present? That must have significance.

He decided to concentrate on the boy and the women. "In ancient times my country was ruled by a great king who had a magic sword called Excalibur and his queen was the most beautiful woman in the land. His chief counselor was a wizard, Merlin, and the king's name was Arthur," he began confidently, telling the legend that his father used to tell so well in the mists of his youth. "King Arthur's capital was called Camelot and it was a happy time of no wars and good harvests and . . ." Suddenly he realized the enormity of his mistake. The kernel of the story was about Guinevere and Lancelot, an adulterous queen and a faithless vassal, about Mordred, Arthur's illegitimate son, who treacherously goes to war against his father, and about a father who kills this son in battle, only to be mortally wounded by him. Oh, Jesus God, how could I be so stupid? Isn't Toranaga like a great king? Aren't these his ladies? Isn't that his son?

"Are you sick, senhor?"

"No—no, I'm sorry—it was just . . ."

"You were saying, senhor, about this king and the good harvest?"

"Yes. It . . . like most countries, our past is clouded with myths and legends, most of which are unimportant," he said lamely, trying to gain time.

She stared at him perplexed. Toranaga's eyes became more piercing and the boy yawned.

"You were saying, senhor?"

"I—well—" Then he had a flash of inspiration. "Perhaps the best thing I could do is draw a map of the world, senhora, as we know it," he said in a rush. "Would you like me to do that?"

She translated this and he saw a glimmer of interest from Toranaga, nothing from the boy or the women. How to involve them?

"My Master says yes. I will send for paper—"

"Thank you. But this will do for the moment. Later, if you'll give me some writing materials I can draw an accurate one."

Blackthorne got off his cushion and knelt. With his finger he began to draw a crude map in the sand, upside down so that they could see better. "The earth's round, like an orange, but this map is like its skin, cut off in ovals, north to south, laid flat and stretched a bit at the top and bottom. A Dutchman called Mercator invented the way to do this accurately twenty years ago. It's the first accurate world map. We can even navigate with it—or his globes." He had sketched the continents boldly. "This is north and this south, east and west. Japan is here, my country's on the other side of the world—there. This is all unknown and unexplored . . ." His hand eliminated everything in North America north of a line from Mexico to Newfoundland, everything in South America apart from Peru and a narrow strip of coast land around that continent, then everything north and east of Norway, everything east of Muscovy, all Asia, all inland Africa, everything south of Java and the tip of South America. "We know the coastlines, but little else. The interiors of Africa, the Americas, and Asia are almost entirely mysteries." He stopped to let her catch up.

She was translating more easily now and he felt their interest growing. The boy stirred and moved a little closer.

"The Heir wishes to know where we are on the map."

"Here. This is Cathay, China, I think. I don't know how far we are off the coast. It took me two years to sail from here to here." Toranaga and the fat woman craned to see better.

"The Heir says but why are we so small on your map?"

"It's just a scale, senhora. On this continent, from Newfoundland here, to Mexico here, is almost a thousand leagues, each of three miles. From here to Yedo is about a hundred leagues."

There was a silence, then they talked amongst themselves.

"Lord Toranaga wishes you to show him on the map how you came to Japan."

"This way. This is Magellan's Pass—or Strait—here, at the tip of South America. It's called that after the Portuguese navigator who discovered it, eighty years ago. Since then the Portuguese and Spanish have kept the way secret, for their exclusive use. We were the first outsiders through the Pass. I had one of their secret rutters, a type of map, but even so, I still had to wait six months to get through because the winds were against us."

She translated what he had said. Toranaga looked up, disbelieving.

"My Master says you are mistaken. All bar—all Portuguese come from the south. That is their route, the only route."

"Yes. It's true the Portuguese favor that way—the Cape of Good Hope, we call it—because they have dozens of forts all along these coasts—Africa and India and the Spice Islands—to provision in and winter in. And their galleon-warships patrol and monopolize the sea lanes. However, the Spanish use Magellan's Pass to get to their Pacific American colonies, and to the Philippines, or they cross here, at the narrow isthmus of Panama, going overland to avoid months of travel. For us it was safer to sail via Magellan's Strait, otherwise we'd have had to run the gauntlet of all those enemy Portuguese forts. Please tell Lord Toranaga I know the position of many of them now. Most employ Japanese troops, by the way," he added with emphasis. "The friar who gave me the information in the prison was Spanish and hostile to the Portuguese and hostile to all Jesuits."

Blackthorne saw an immediate reaction on her face, and when she translated, on Toranaga's face. Give her time, and keep it simple, he warned himself.

"Japanese troops? You mean samurai?"

"*Ronin* would describe them, I imagine."

"You said a 'secret' map? My Lord wishes to know how you obtained it."

"A man named Pieter Suyderhof, from Holland, was the private secretary to the Primate of Goa—that's the title of the chief Catholic priest and Goa's the capital of Portuguese India. You know, of course, that the Portuguese are trying to take over that continent by force. As private secretary to this archbishop, who was also the Portuguese Viceroy at the time, all sorts of documents passed through his hands. After many years he obtained some of their rutters—maps —and copied them. These gave the secrets of the way through Magellan's Pass and also how to get around the Cape of Good Hope, and the shoals and reefs from Goa to Japan via Macao. My rutter was the Magellan one. It was with my papers that I lost from my ship. They are vital to me, and could be of immense value to Lord Toranaga."

"My Master says that he has sent orders to seek them. Continue please."

"When Suyderhof returned to Holland, he sold them to the Company of East India Merchants, which was given the monopoly for Far Eastern exploration."

She was looking at him coldly. "This man was a paid spy?"

"He was paid for his maps, yes. That's their custom, that's how they reward a man. Not with a title or land, only money. Holland's a republic. Of course, senhora, my country and our allies, Holland, are at war with Spain and Portugal and have been for years. You'll understand, senhora, in war it's vital to find out your enemies' secrets."

Mariko turned and spoke at length.

"My Lord says, why would this archbishop employ an enemy?"

"The story Pieter Suyderhof told was that this archbishop, who was a Jesuit, was interested only in trade. Suyderhof doubled their revenue, so he was 'cherished.' He was an extremely clever merchant—Hollanders are usually superior to Portuguese in this—so his credentials weren't checked very closely. Also many men with blue eyes and fair hair, Germans and other Europeans, are Catholic." Blackthorne waited till that was translated, then added carefully, "He was chief spy for Holland in Asia, a soldier of the country, and he put some of his people on Portuguese ships. Please tell Lord Toranaga that without Japan's trade, Portuguese India cannot live for long."

Toranaga kept his eyes on the map while Mariko talked. There was no reaction to what she had said. Blackthorne wondered if she had translated everything.

Then: "My Master would like a detailed world map, on paper, as soon as possible, with all the Portuguese bases marked, and the numbers of *ronin* at each. He says please continue."

Blackthorne knew he had made a giant step forward. But the boy yawned so he decided to change course, still heading for the same harbor. "Our world is not always as it seems. For instance, south of this line, we call it the Equator, the seasons are reversed. When we have summer, they have winter; when we have summer, they're freezing."

"Why is that?"

"I don't know, but it's true. Now, the way to Japan is through either of these two southern straits. We English, we're trying to find a northern route, either northeast over the Siberias, or northwest over the Americas. I've been as far north as this. The whole land's perpetual ice and snow here and it's so cold most of the year that if you don't wear fur mittens, your fingers'll freeze in moments. The people who live there are called Laplanders. Their clothes are made out of fur pelts. The men hunt and the women do all the work. Part of the women's work is to make all the clothes. To do this, most times they have to chew the pelts to soften them before they can stitch them."

Mariko laughed out loud.

Blackthorne smiled with her, feeling more confident now. "It's true, senhora. It's *honto*."

"*Sorewa honto desu ka?*" Toranaga asked impatiently. What's true?

Through more laughter, she told him what had been said. They also began to laugh.

"I lived among them for almost a year. We were trapped in the ice and had to wait for the thaw. Their food is fish, seals, occasionally polar bears, and whales, which they eat raw. Their greatest delicacy is to eat raw whale blubber."

"Oh, come now, Anjin-san!"

"It's true. And they live in small round houses made entirely out of snow and they never bathe."

"What, never?" she burst out.

He shook his head, and decided not to tell her baths were rare in England, rarer even than in Portugal and Spain, which were warm countries.

She translated this. Toranaga shook his head in disbelief.

"My Master says this is too much of an exaggeration. No one could live without baths. Even uncivilized people."

"That's the truth—*honto,*" he said calmly and raised his hand. "I swear by Jesus of Nazareth and by my soul, I swear it is the truth."

She watched him in silence. "Everything?"

"Yes. Lord Toranaga wanted the truth. Why should I lie? My life is in his hands. It is easy to prove the truth—no, to be honest, it would be very hard to prove what I've said—you'd have to go there and see for yourself. Certainly the Portuguese and Spanish, who are my enemies, won't support me. But Lord Toranaga asked for the truth. He can trust me to tell it to him."

Mariko thought a moment. Then she scrupulously translated what he had said. At length:

"Lord Toranaga says, it is unbelievable that any human could live without bathing."

"Yes. But those are the cold lands. Their habits are different from yours, and mine. For instance, in my country, everyone believes baths are dangerous for your health. My grandmother, Granny Jacoba, used to say, 'A bath when you're birthed and another when laid out'll see thee through the Pearly Gates.'"

"That's very hard to believe."

"Some of your customs are very hard to believe. But it is true that I've had more baths in the short time I've been in your country than in as many years before. I admit freely I feel better for them." He grinned. "I no longer believe baths are dangerous. So I've gained by coming here, no?"

After a pause Mariko said, "Yes," and translated.

Kiri said, "He's astonishing—astonishing, *neh?*"

"What's your judgment of him, Mariko-san?" Toranaga asked.

"I'm convinced he's telling the truth, or believes he's telling it. Clearly it would seem that he could, perhaps, have a great value to you, my Lord. We have such a tiny knowledge of the outside world. Is that valuable to you? I don't know. But it's almost as though he's come down from the stars, or up from under the sea. If he's enemy to the Portuguese and the Spanish, then his information, if it can be trusted, could perhaps be vital to your interests, *neh?*"

"I agree," Kiri said.

"What do you think, Yaemon-sama?"

"Me, Uncle? Oh, I think he's ugly and I don't like his golden hair and cat's eyes and he doesn't look human at all," the boy said breathlessly. "I'm glad I wasn't born barbarian like him but samurai like my father, can we go for another swim, please?"

"Tomorrow, Yaemon," Toranaga said, vexed at not being able to talk directly to the pilot.

While they talked among themselves Blackthorne decided that the time had come. Then Mariko turned to him again.

"My Master asks why were you in the north?"

"I was pilot of a ship. We were trying to find a northeast passage, senhora. Many things I can tell you will sound laughable, I know," he began. "For instance, seventy years ago the kings of Spain and Portugal signed a solemn treaty that split ownership of the New World, the undiscovered world, between them. As your country falls in the Portuguese half, officially your country belongs to Portugal—Lord Toranaga, you, everyone, this castle and everything in it were given to Portugal."

"Oh, please, Anjin-san. Pardon me, that's nonsense!"

"I agree their arrogance is unbelievable. But it's true." Immediately she began to translate and Toranaga laughed derisively.

"Lord Toranaga says he could equally well split the heavens between himself and the Emperor of China, *neh?*"

"Please tell Lord Toranaga, I'm sorry, but that's not the same," Blackthorne said, aware that he was on dangerous ground. "This is written into legal documents which give each king the right to claim any non-Catholic land discovered by their subjects and to stamp out the existing government and replace it with Catholic rule." On the map, his finger traced a line north to south that bisected Brazil. "Everything east of this line is Portugal's, everything west is Spain's. Pedro Cabral discovered Brazil in 1500, so now Portugal owns Brazil, has stamped out the native culture and legal rulers, and has become rich from the gold and silver taken out of mines and plundered from native temples. All the rest of the Americas so far discovered is Spanish-owned now—Mexico, Peru, almost this whole south continent. They've wiped out the Inca nations, obliterated their culture, and enslaved hundreds of thousands of them. The conquistadores have modern guns—the natives none. With the conquistadores come the priests. Soon a few princes are converted, and enmities used. Then prince is turned against prince and realm swallowed up piecemeal. Now Spain is the richest nation in our world from the Inca and Mexican gold and silver they've plundered and sent back to Spain."

Mariko was solemn now. She had quickly grasped the significance of Blackthorne's lesson. And so had Toranaga.

"My Master says this is a worthless conversation. How could they give themselves such rights?"

"They didn't," Blackthorne said gravely. "The Pope gave them the rights, the Vicar of Christ on earth himself. In return for spreading the word of God."

"I don't believe it," she exclaimed.

"Please translate what I said, senhora. It is *honto*."

She obeyed and spoke at length, obviously unsettled. Then:

"My Master—my Master says you are—you are just trying to poison him against your enemies. What is the truth? On your own life, senhor."

"Pope Alexander VI set the first line of demarcation in 1493," Blackthorne commenced, blessing Alban Caradoc who had hammered so many facts into him when he was young, and Father Domingo for informing him about Japanese pride and giving him clues to Japanese minds. "In 1506 Pope Julius II sanctioned changes to the Treaty of Tordesillas, signed by Spain and Portugal in 1494, which altered the line a little. Pope Clement VII sanctioned the Treaty of Saragossa in 1529, barely seventy years ago, which drew a second line here"—his finger traced a line of longitude in the sand which cut through the tip of southern Japan. "This gives Portugal the exclusive right to your country, all these countries— from Japan, China to Africa—in the way I have said. To exploit exclusively— *by any means*—in return for spreading Catholicism." Again he waited and the woman hesitated, in turmoil, and he could feel Toranaga's growing irritation at having to wait for her to translate.

Mariko forced her lips to speak and repeated what he had said. Then she listened to Blackthorne again, detesting what she heard. Is this really possible? she asked herself. How could His Holiness say such things? Give our country to the Portuguese? It must be a lie. But the pilot swore by the Lord Jesus.

"The pilot says, Lord," she began, "in—in the days that these decisions were made by His Holiness the Pope, all their world, even the Anjin-san's country was Catholic Christian. The schism had not—not yet occurred. So, so these— these papal decisions would, of course, be binding on—on all nations. Even so, he adds that though the Portuguese have exclusivity to *exploit* Japan, Spain and Portugal are quarreling incessantly about the *ownership* because of the richness of our trade with China."

"What's your opinion, Kiri-san?" Toranaga said, as shocked as the others.

Only the boy toyed with his fan uninterestedly.

"He believes he's telling the truth," Kiri said. "Yes, I think that. But how to prove it—or part of it?"

"How would you prove it, Mariko-san?" Toranaga asked, most perturbed by Mariko's reaction to what had been said, but very glad that he had agreed to use her as interpreter.

"I would ask Father Tsukku-san," she said. "Then, too, I would send someone—a trusted vassal—out into the world to see. Perhaps with the Anjin-san."

Kiri said, "If the priest does not support these statements, it may not necessarily mean this Anjin-san is lying, *neh?*" Kiri was pleased that she had suggested using Mariko as an interpreter when Toranaga was seeking an alternative to Tsukku-san. She knew Mariko was to be trusted and that, once Mariko had sworn by her alien God, she would ever be silent under rigorous questioning by any Christian priest. The less those devils know, the better, Kiri thought. And what a treasure of knowledge this barbarian has!

Kiri saw the boy yawn again and was glad of it. The less the child understands the better, she told herself. Then she said, "Why not send for the leader of the Christian priests and ask about these facts? See what he says. Their faces are open, mostly, and they have almost no subtlety."

Toranaga nodded, his eyes on Mariko. "From what you know about the Southern Barbarians, Mariko-san, would you say that a Pope's orders would be obeyed?"

"Without doubt."

"His orders would be considered as though the voice of the Christian God was speaking?"

"Yes."

"Would all Catholic Christians obey his orders?"

"Yes."

"Even our Christians here?"

"I would think, yes."

"Even you?"

"Yes, Sire. If it was a direct order from His Holiness to me personally. Yes, for my soul's salvation." Her gaze was firm. "But until that time I will obey no man but my liege lord, the head of my family, or my husband. I am Japanese, a Christian yes, but first I am samurai."

"I think it would be good then, that this Holiness stays away from our shores." Toranaga thought for a moment. Then he decided what to do with the barbarian, Anjin-san. "Tell him . . ." He stopped. All their eyes went to the path and to the elderly woman who approached. She wore the cowled habit of a Buddhist nun. Four Grays were with her. The Grays stopped and she came on alone.

CHAPTER 17

THEY all bowed low. Toranaga noticed that the barbarian copied him and did not get up or stare, which all barbarians except Tsukku-san would have done, according to their own custom. The pilot learns quickly, he thought, his mind still blazing from what he had heard. Ten thousand questions were crowding him, but, according to his discipline, he channeled them away temporarily to concentrate on the present danger.

Kiri had scurried to give the old woman her cushion and helped her to sit, then knelt behind her, in motionless attendance.

"Thank you, Kiritsubo-san," the woman said, returning their bow. Her name was Yodoko. She was the widow of the Taikō and now, since his death, a Buddhist nun. "I'm sorry to come uninvited and to interrupt you, Lord Toranaga."

"You're never unwelcome or uninvited, Yodoko-sama."

"Thank you, yes, thank you." She glanced at Blackthorne and squinted to try to see better. "But I think I did interrupt. I can't see who— Is he a barbarian? My eyes are getting worse and worse. It's not Tsukku-san, is it?"

"No, he's the new barbarian," Toranaga said.

"Oh, him!" Yodoko peered closer. "Please tell him I can't see very well, hence my impoliteness."

Mariko did as she was told. "He says many people in his country are short-sighted, Yodoko-sama, but they wear spectacles. He asked if we have them. I told him yes, some of us—from the Southern Barbarians. That you used to wear them but don't anymore."

"Yes. I prefer the mist that surrounds me. Yes, I don't like a lot of what I see nowadays." Yodoko turned back and looked at the boy, pretending to have just seen him. "Oh! My son! So there you are. I was looking for you. How good it is to see the Kwampaku!" She bowed deferentially.

"Thank you, First Mother," Yaemon beamed and bowed back. "Oh, you should have heard the barbarian. He's been drawing us a map of the world and telling us funny things about people who don't bathe at all! Never in their whole lives and they live in snow houses and wear skins like evil *kami.*"

The old lady snorted. "The less they come here the better, I think, my son. I could never understand them and they always smell so horrible. I could never understand how the Lord Taikō, your father, could tolerate them. But then he was a man and you're a man, and you've more patience than a lowly woman. You've a good teacher, Yaemon-sama." Her old eyes flicked back to Toranaga. "Lord Toranaga's got more patience than anyone in the Empire."

"Patience is important for a man, vital for a leader," Toranaga said. "And a thirst for knowledge is a good quality too, eh, Yaemon-sama? And knowledge comes from strange places."

"Yes, Uncle. Oh yes," Yaemon said. "He's right, isn't he, First Mother?"

"Yes, yes. I agree. But I'm glad I'm a woman and don't have to worry about these things, *neh?*" Yodoko hugged the boy, who had come to sit beside her. "So, my son. Why am I here? To fetch the Kwampaku. Why? Because the Kwampaku is late for his food and late for his writing lessons."

"I hate writing lessons and I'm going swimming!"

Toranaga said with mock gravity, "When I was your age I used to hate writing too. But then, when I was twenty, I had to stop fighting battles and go back to school. I hated that worse."

"Go back to school, Uncle? After leaving it forever? Oh, how terrible!"

"A leader has to write well, Yaemon-sama. Not only clearly but beautifully, and the Kwampaku better than anyone else. How else can he write to His Imperial Highness or to the great *daimyos*? A leader has to be better than his vassals in everything, in every way. A leader has to do many things that are difficult."

"Yes, Uncle. It's very difficult to be Kwampaku." Yaemon frowned importantly. "I think I'll do my lessons now and not when I'm twenty because then I'll have important matters of state."

They were all very proud of him. "You're very wise, my son," said Yodoko.

"Yes, First Mother. I'm wise like my father, as my mother says. When's Mother coming home?"

Yodoko peered up at Toranaga. "Soon."

"I hope very soon," Toranaga said. He knew Yodoko had been sent to fetch the boy by Ishido. Toranaga had brought the boy and the guards directly to the garden to further irritate his enemy. Also to show the boy the strange pilot and so deprive Ishido of the pleasure of providing that experience for him.

"It's very wearisome being responsible for my son," Yodoko was saying. "It would be very good to have the Lady Ochiba here in Osaka, home again, then I can get back to the temple, *neh?* How is she, and how is the Lady Genjiko?"

"They're both in excellent health," Toranaga told her, chortling to himself. Nine years ago, in an unusual show of friendship, the Taikō had privately invited him to marry Lady Genjiko, the younger sister of Lady Ochiba, his favorite consort. 'Then our houses will be joined together forever, *neh?*' the Taikō had said.

'Yes, Sire. I will obey though I do not deserve the honor,' Toranaga had replied deferentially, desiring the link with the Taikō. But he knew that though Yodoko, the Taikō's wife, might approve, his consort Ochiba hated him and would use her great influence over the Taikō to prevent the marriage. And, too, it was wiser to avoid having Ochiba's sister as his wife, for that would give her enormous powers over him, not the least of which was the keys to his treasury. But, if she were to marry his son, Sudara, then Toranaga as supreme head of the family would have complete domination. It had taken all his skill to maneuver the marriage between Sudara and Genjiko but it had happened and now Genjiko was priceless to him as a defense against Ochiba, because Ochiba adored her sister.

"My daughter-in-law isn't in labor yet—it was expected to begin yesterday— but I would imagine the Lady Ochiba will leave immediately there's no danger."

"After three girls, it's time Genjiko gave you a grandson, *neh?* I will say prayers for his birth."

"Thank you," Toranaga said, liking her as always, knowing that she meant it, even though he represented nothing but danger to her house.

"I hear your Lady Sazuko's with child?"

"Yes. I'm very fortunate." Toranaga basked in the thought of his newest consort, the youth of her, the strength of her, and the warmth. I hope we have a son, he told himself. Yes, that would be very good. Seventeen's a good age to have a first child, if you've perfect health as she has. "Yes, I'm very fortunate."

"Buddha has blessed you." Yodoko felt a twinge of envy. It seemed so unfair that Toranaga had five sons living and four daughters and five granddaughters already, and, with this child of Sazuko's soon to arrive, and still many strong years left in him and many consorts in his house, he could sire many more sons. But all her hopes were centered on this one seven-year-old child, her child as much as Ochiba's. Yes, he's as much my son, she thought. How I hated Ochiba in the beginning. . . .

She saw them all staring at her and she was startled. "Yes?"

Yaemon frowned. "I said, can we go and have my lessons, First Mother? I said it two times."

"I'm sorry, my son, I was drifting away. That's what happens when you get old. Yes, come along then." Kiri helped her up. Yaemon ran off ahead. The Grays were already on their feet and one of them caught him and affectionately swung him onto his shoulders. The four samurai who had escorted her waited separately.

"Walk with me a little, Lord Toranaga, would you please? I need a strong arm to lean on."

Toranaga was on his feet with surprising agility. She took his arm but did not use his strength. "Yes. I need a strong arm. Yaemon does. And so does the realm."

"I'm always ready to serve you," Toranaga said.

When they were away from the others, she said quietly, "Become sole Regent. Take the power and rule yourself. Until Yaemon becomes of age."

"The Taikō's testament forbids this—even if I wished it, which I don't. The curbs he made preclude one Regent's taking power. I don't seek sole power. I never have."

"Tora-chan," she said, using the nickname the Taikō had given him so long ago, "we have few secrets, you and I. You could do it, if you wished. I will answer for the Lady Ochiba. Take the power for your own lifetime. Become Shōgun and make—"

"Lady, what you say is treason. I-do-not-seek-to-be-Shōgun."

"Of course, but please listen to me a last time. Become Shōgun, make Yaemon your *sole* heir—your sole heir. He could be Shōgun, after you. Isn't his bloodline Fujimoto—through Lady Ochiba back to her grandfather Goroda and through him back to antiquity? Fujimoto!"

Toranaga stared at her. "You think the *daimyos* would agree to such a claim, or that His Highness, the Son of Heaven, could approve the appointment?"

"No. Not for Yaemon by himself. But if you were Shōgun first, and you adopted him, you could persuade them, all of them. We will support you, the Lady Ochiba and I."

"She has agreed to this?" asked Toranaga, astounded.

"No. We've never discussed it. It's my idea. But she will agree. I will answer for her. In advance."

"This is an impossible conversation, Lady."

"You can manage Ishido, and all of them. You always have. I'm afraid of what I hear, Tora-chan, rumors of war, the taking of sides, and the Dark Centuries beginning again. When war begins it will go on forever and eat Yaemon up."

"Yes. I believe that, too. Yes, if it begins it will last forever."

"Then take the power! Do what you wish, to whomever you wish, however you wish. Yaemon's a worthy boy. I know you like him. He has his father's mind and with your guidance, we would all benefit. He should have his heritage."

"I'm not opposing him, or his succession. How many times need I say it?"

"The Heir will be destroyed unless you actively support him."

"I do support him!" Toranaga said. "In every way. That's what I agreed with the Taikō, your late husband."

Yodoko sighed and pulled her habit closer. "These old bones are chilled. So many secrets and battles, treacheries and deaths and victories, Tora-chan. I'm only a woman, and very much alone. I'm glad that I'm dedicated to Buddha now, and that most of my thoughts are toward Buddha and my next life. But in this one I have to protect my son and to say these things to you. I hope you will forgive my impertinence."

"I always seek and enjoy your counsel."

"Thank you." Her back straightened a little. "Listen, while I'm alive neither the Heir nor the Lady Ochiba will ever go against you."

"Yes."

"Will you consider what I proposed?"

"My late Master's will forbids it. I cannot go against the will or my sacred promise as a Regent."

They walked in silence. Then Yodoko sighed. "Why not take her to wife?"

Toranaga stopped in his tracks. "Ochiba?"

"Why not? She's totally worthy as a political choice. A perfect choice for you. She's beautiful, young, strong, her bloodline's the best, part Fujimoto, part Minowara, the sun dances in her, and she has an immense joy of life. You've no official wife now—so why not? This would solve the problem of the succession and stop the realm from being torn apart. You would have other sons by her surely. Yaemon would succeed you, then his sons or her other sons. You could become Shōgun. You would have the power of the realm and the power of a father so you could train Yaemon to your way. You would adopt him formally and he would be as much your son as any you have. Why not marry Lady Ochiba?"

Because she's a wildcat, a treacherous tigress with the face and body of a goddess, who thinks she's an empress and acts like one, Toranaga told himself. You could never trust her in your bed. She'd be just as likely to thread a needle through your eyes when you're asleep as she'd be to caress you. Oh no, not her! Even if I married her in name only—which she'd never agree to—oh no! It's impossible! For all sorts of reasons, not the least of which is that she's hated me and plotted my downfall, and that of my house, ever since she whelped for the first time, eleven years ago.

Even then, even at seventeen, she had committed herself to my destruction. Ah, so soft outwardly, like the first ripe peach of summer, and as fragrant. But inwardly sword steel with a mind to match, weaving her spells, soon making the Taikō mad over her to the exclusion of all others. Yes, she had the Taikō cowed since she was fifteen when he first took her formally. Yes, and don't forget, truly, she pillowed him, even then, not he her, however much he believed it. Yes, even at fifteen, Ochiba knew what she sought and the way to obtain it. Then the miracle happening, giving the Taikō a son at long last, she alone of all the women he had in his life. How many pillow ladies? A hundred at least, him a stoat who sprayed more Joyful Juice into more Heavenly Chambers than ten ordinary men! Yes. And these women of all ages and all castes, casual or consort, from a Fujimoto princess to Fourth Class courtesans. But none ever even became pregnant, though later, many of those that the Taikō dismissed or divorced or married off had children by other men. None, except the Lady Ochiba.

But she gave him his first son at fifty-three, poor little thing, sickly and dying so soon, the Taikō rending his clothes, almost crazy with grief, blaming himself and not her. Then, four years later, miraculously she whelped again, miraculously another son, miraculously healthy this time, she twenty-one now. Ochiba the Peerless, the Taikō had called her.

Did the Taikō father Yaemon or not? Eeeee, I'd give a lot to know the truth. Will we ever know the truth? Probably not, but what would I not give for proof, one way or another.

Strange that the Taikō, so clever about everything else, was not clever about

Ochiba, doting on her and Yaemon to insanity. Strange that of all the women she should have been the mother of his heir, she whose father and stepfather and mother were dead because of the Taikō.

Would she have the cleverness to pillow with another man, to take his seed, then obliterate this same man to safeguard herself? Not once but twice?

Could she be so treacherous? Oh, yes.

Marry Ochiba? Never.

"I'm honored that you would make such a suggestion," Toranaga said.

"You're a *man,* Tora-chan. You could handle such a woman easily. You're the only man in the Empire who could, *neh?* She would make a marvelous match for you. Look how she fights to protect her son's interests now, and she's only a defenseless woman. She'd be a worthy wife for you."

"I don't think she would ever consider it."

"And if she did?"

"I would like to know. Privately. Yes, that would be an inestimable honor."

"Many people believe that only you stand between Yaemon and the succession."

"Many people are fools."

"Yes. But you're not, Toranaga-sama. Neither is the Lady Ochiba."

Nor are you, my Lady, he thought.

CHAPTER 18

I N the darkest part of the night the assassin came over the wall into the garden.
He was almost invisible. He wore close-fitting black clothes and his tabi
were black, and a black cowl and mask covered his head. He was a small
man and he ran noiselessly for the front of the stone inner fortress and stopped
just short of the soaring walls. Fifty yards away two Browns guarded the main
door. Deftly he threw a cloth-covered hook with a very thin silk rope attached
to it. The hook caught on the stone ledge of the embrasure. He shinned up the
rope, squeezed through the slit, and disappeared inside.

The corridor was quiet and candle-lit. He hurried down it silently, opened an
outside door, and went out onto the battlements. Another deft throw and a short
climb and he was into the corridor above. The sentries that were on the corners
of the battlements did not hear him though they were alert.

He pressed into an alcove of stone as other Browns walked by quietly, on
patrol. When they had passed, he slipped along the length of this passageway.
At the corner he stopped. Silently he peered around it. A samurai was guarding
the far door. Candles danced in the quiet. The guard was sitting cross-legged and
he yawned and leaned back against the wall and stretched. His eyes closed
momentarily. Instantly, the assassin darted forward. Soundlessly. He formed a
noose with the silk rope in his hands, dropped it over the guard's neck and jerked
tight. The guard's fingers tried to claw the garrote away but he was already dying.
A short stab with the knife between the vertebrae as deft as a surgeon's and the
guard was motionless.

The man eased the door open. The audience room was empty, the inner doors
unguarded. He pulled the corpse inside and closed the door again. Unhesitatingly
he crossed the space and chose the inner left door. It was wood and heavily
reinforced. The curved knife slid into his right hand. He knocked softly.

" 'In the days of the Emperor Shirakawa . . .' " he said, giving the first part
of the password.

From the other side of the door there was a sibilance of steel leaving a scabbard
and the reply, " ' . . . there lived a wise man called Enraku-ji . . .' "

" ' . . . who wrote the thirty-first sutra.' I have urgent dispatches for Lord
Toranaga."

The door swung open and the assassin lunged forward. The knife went upward
into the first samurai's throat just below the chin and came out as fast and buried
itself identically into the second of the guards. A slight twist and out again. Both
men were dead on their feet. He caught one and let him slump gently; the other
fell, but noiselessly. Blood ran out of them onto the floor and their bodies twitched
in the throes of death.

The man hurried down this inner corridor. It was poorly lit. Then a shoji
opened. He froze, slowly looked around.

Kiri was gaping at him, ten paces away. A tray was in her hands.

He saw that the two cups on the tray were unused, the food untouched. A
thread of steam came from the teapot. Beside it, a candle spluttered. Then the
tray was falling and her hands went into her obi and emerged with a dagger, her
mouth worked but made no sound, and he was already racing for the corner.

At the far end a door opened and a startled, sleep-drenched samurai peered out.

The assassin rushed toward him and tore open a shoji on his right that he sought. Kiri was screaming and the alarm had sounded, and he ran, sure-footed in the darkness, across this anteroom, over the waking women and their maids, into the innermost corridor at the far side.

Here it was pitch dark but he groped along unerringly to find the right door in the gathering furor. He slid the door open and jumped for the figure that lay on the futon. But his knife arm was caught by a viselike grip and now he was thrashing in combat on the floor. He fought with cunning, broke free, and slashed again but missed, entangled with the quilt. He hurled it off and threw himself at the figure, knife poised for the death thrust. But the man twisted with unexpected agility and a hardened foot dug into his groin. Pain exploded in him as his victim darted for safety.

Then samurai were crowding the doorway, some with lanterns, and Naga, wearing only a loincloth, his hair tousled, leapt between him and Blackthorne, sword on high.

"Surrender!"

The assassin feinted once, shouted, *"Namu Amida Butsu—"* In the Name of the Buddha Amida—turned the knife on himself and with both hands thrust it up under the base of his chin. Blood spurted and he slumped to his knees. Naga slashed once, his sword a whirling arc, and the head rolled free.

In the silence Naga picked the head up and ripped off the mask. The face was ordinary, the eyes still fluttering. He held the head, hair dressed like a samurai, by its topknot.

"Does anyone know him?"

No one answered. Naga spat in the face, threw the head angrily to one of his men, tore open the black clothes and lifted the man's right arm, and found what he was looking for. The small tattoo—the Chinese character for Amida, the special Buddha—was etched in the armpit.

"Who is officer of the watch?"

"I am, Lord." The man was white with shock.

Naga leaped at him and the others scattered. The officer made no attempt to avoid the ferocious sword blow which took off his head and part of his shoulder and one arm.

"Hayabusa-san, order all samurai from this watch into the courtyard," Naga said to an officer. "Double guards for the new watch. Get the body out of here. The rest of you are—" He stopped as Kiri came to the doorway, the dagger still in her hand. She looked at the corpse, then at Blackthorne.

"The Anjin-san's not hurt?" she asked.

Naga glanced at the man who towered over him, breathing with difficulty. He could see no wounds or blood. Just a sleep-tousled man who had almost been killed. White-faced but no outward fear. "Are you hurt, Pilot?"

"I don't understand."

Naga went over and pulled the sleeping kimono away to see if the pilot had been wounded.

"Ah, understand now. No. No hurt," he heard the giant say and he saw him shake his head.

"Good," he said. "He seems unhurt, Kiritsubo-san."

He saw the Anjin-san point at the body and say something. "I don't understand you," Naga replied. "Anjin-san, you stay here," and to one of the men he said, "Bring him some food and drink if he wants it."

"The assassin, he was Amida-tattooed, *neh?*" Kiri asked.

"Yes, Lady Kiritsubo."

"Devils—devils."

"Yes."

Naga bowed to her then looked at one of the appalled samurai. "You follow me. Bring the head!" He strode off, wondering how he was going to tell his father. Oh, Buddha, thank you for guarding my father.

"He was a *ronin,*" Toranaga said curtly. "You'll never trace him, Hiro-matsu-san."

"Yes. But Ishido's responsible. He had no honor to do this, *neh?* None. To use these dung-offal assassins. Please, I beg you, let me call up our legions now. I'll stop this once and for all time."

"No." Toranaga looked back at Naga. "You're sure the Anjin-san's not hurt?"

"No, Sire."

"Hiro-matsu-san. You will demote all guards of this watch for failing in their duty. They are forbidden to commit seppuku. They're ordered to live with their shame in front of all my men as soldiers of the lowest class. Have the dead guards dragged by their feet through the castle and city to the execution ground. The dogs can feed off them."

Now he looked at his son, Naga. Earlier that evening, urgent word had arrived from Johji Monastery in Nagoya about Ishido's threat against Naga. Toranaga had at once ordered his son confined to close quarters and surrounded by guards, and the other members of the family in Osaka—Kiri and the Lady Sazuko—equally guarded. The message from the abbot had added that he had considered it wise to release Ishido's mother at once and send her back to the city with her maids. "I dare not risk the life of one of your illustrious sons foolishly. Worse, her health is not good. She has a chill. It's best she should die in her own house and not here."

"Naga-san, you are equally responsible the assassin got in," Toranaga said, his voice cold and bitter. "Every samurai is responsible, whether on watch or off watch, asleep or awake. You are fined half your yearly revenue."

"Yes, Lord," the youth said, surprised that he was allowed to keep anything, including his head. "Please demote me also," he said. "I cannot live with the shame. I deserve nothing but contempt for my own failure, Lord."

"If I wanted to demote you I would have done so. You are ordered to Yedo at once. You will leave with twenty men tonight and report to your brother. You will get there in record time! Go!" Naga bowed and went away, white-faced. To Hiro-matsu he said equally roughly, "Quadruple my guards. Cancel my hunting today, and tomorrow. The day after the meeting of Regents I leave Osaka. You'll make all the preparations, and until that time, I will stay here. I will see no one uninvited. No one."

He waved his hand in angry dismissal. "All of you can go. Hiro-matsu, you stay."

The room emptied. Hiro-matsu was glad that his humiliation was to be private, for, of all of them, as Commander of the Bodyguard, he was the most responsible. "I have no excuse, Lord. None."

Toranaga was lost in thought. No anger was visible now. "If you wanted to hire the services of the secret Amida Tong, how would you find them? How would you approach them?"

"I don't know, Lord."

"Who would know?"

"Kasigi Yabu."

Toranaga looked out of the embrasure. Threads of dawn were mixed with the eastern dark. "Bring him here at dawn."

"You think he's responsible?"

Toranaga did not answer, but returned to his musings.

At length the old soldier could not bear the silence. "Please Lord, let me get out of your sight. I'm so ashamed with our failure—"

"It's almost impossible to prevent such an attempt," Toranaga said.

"Yes. But we should have caught him outside, nowhere near you."

"I agree. But I don't hold you responsible."

"I hold myself responsible. There's something I must say, Lord, for I *am* responsible for your safety until you're back in Yedo. There will be more attempts on you, and all our spies report increased troop movement. Ishido is mobilizing."

"Yes," Toranaga said casually. "After Yabu, I want to see Tsukku-san, then Mariko-san. Double the guards on the Anjin-san."

"Despatches came tonight that Lord Onoshi has a hundred thousand men improving his fortifications in Kyushu," Hiro-matsu said, beset by his anxiety for Toranaga's safety.

"I will ask him about it, when we meet."

Hiro-matsu's temper broke. "I don't understand you at all. I must tell you that you risk everything stupidly. Yes, stupidly. I don't care if you take my head for telling you, but it's the truth. If Kiyama and Onoshi vote with Ishido you will be impeached! You're a dead man—you've risked everything by coming here and you've lost! Escape while you can. At least you'll have your head on your shoulders!"

"I'm in no danger yet."

"Doesn't this attack tonight mean anything to you? If you hadn't changed your room again you'd be dead now."

"Yes, I might, but probably not," Toranaga said. "There were multiple guards outside *my* doors tonight and also last night. And you were on guard to-night as well. No assassin could get near me. Even this one who was so well pre-pared. He knew the way, even the password, *neh?* Kiri-san said she heard him use it. So I think he knew which room I was in. I wasn't his prey. It was the Anjin-san."

"The barbarian?"

"Yes."

Toranaga had anticipated that there would be further danger to the barbarian after the extraordinary revelations of this morning. Clearly the Anjin-san was too dangerous to some to leave alive. But Toranaga had never presumed that an attack would be mounted within his private quarters or so fast. Who's betraying me? He discounted a leakage of information from Kiri, or Mariko. But castles and gardens always have secret places to eavesdrop, he thought. I'm in the center of the enemy stronghold, and where I have one spy, Ishido—and others—will have twenty. Perhaps it was just a spy.

"Double the guards on the Anjin-san. He's worth ten thousand men to me."

After Lady Yodoko had left this morning, he had returned to the gar-den Tea House and had noticed at once the Anjin-san's inner frailty, the over-bright eyes and grinding fatigue. So he had controlled his own excitement and almost overpowering need to probe deeper, and had dismissed him, saying that they would continue tomorrow. The Anjin-san had been given into Kiri's care with instructions to get him a doctor, to harbor his strength, to give him barbarian food if he wished it, and even to let him have the sleeping room that Toranaga himself used most nights. "Give him anything you feel necessary, Kiri-san," he had told her privately. "I need him very fit, very quickly, in mind and body."

Then the Anjin-san had asked that he release the monk from prison today, for the man was old and sick. He had replied that he would consider it and sent the barbarian away with thanks, not telling him that he had already ordered samurai to go to the prison at once and fetch this monk, who was perhaps equally valuable, both to him and to Ishido.

Toranaga had known about this priest for a long time, that he was Spanish and hostile to the Portuguese. But the man had been ordered there by the Taikō so he was the Taikō's prisoner, and he, Toranaga, had no jurisdiction over anyone in Osaka. He had sent the Anjin-san deliberately into that prison not only to pretend to Ishido that the stranger was worthless, but also in the hope that the impressive pilot would be able to draw out the monk's knowledge.

The first clumsy attempt on the Anjin-san's life in the cell had been foiled, and at once a protective screen had been put around him. Toranaga had rewarded his vassal spy, Minikui, a kaga-man, by extracting him safely and giving him four kagas of his own and the hereditary right to use the stretch of the Tokaidō Road—the great trunk road that joined Yedo and Osaka—between the Second and Third Stages, which were in his domains near Yedo, and had sent him secretly out of Osaka the first day. During the following days his other spies had sent reports that the two men were friends now, the monk talking and the Anjin-san asking questions and listening. The fact that Ishido probably had spies in the cell too did not bother him. The Anjin-san was protected and safe. Then Ishido had unexpectedly tried to spirit him out, into alien influence.

Toranaga remembered the amusement he and Hiro-matsu had had in planning the immediate "ambush"—the *"ronin* bandits" being one of the small, isolated groups of his own elite samurai who were secreted in and around Osaka—and in arranging the delicate timing of Yabu who, unsuspecting, had effected the "rescue." They had chuckled together, knowing that once more they had used Yabu as a puppet to rub Ishido's nose in his own dung.

Everything had succeeded beautifully. Until today.

Today the samurai he had sent to fetch the monk had returned empty-handed. "The priest is dead," the man had reported. "When his name was called, he didn't come out, Lord Toranaga. I went in to fetch him, but he was dead. The criminals around him said when the jailers called his name, he just collapsed. He was dead when I turned him over. Please excuse me, you sent me for him and I've failed to do what you ordered. I didn't know if you wanted his head, or his head on his body seeing he was a barbarian, so I brought the body with the head still on. Some of the criminals around him said they were his converts. They wanted to keep the corpse and they tried to keep it so I killed a few and brought the corpse. It's stinking and verminous but it's in the courtyard, Sire."

Why did the monk die? Toranaga asked himself again. Then he saw Hiro-matsu looking at him questioningly. "Yes?"

"I just asked who would want the pilot dead?"

"Christians."

Kasigi Yabu followed Hiro-matsu along the corridor, feeling grand in the dawn. There was a nice salt tang to the breeze, and it reminded him of Mishima, his home city. He was glad that at long last he was to see Toranaga and the waiting was over. He had bathed and dressed with care. Last letters had been written to his wife and to his mother and his final will sealed in case the interview went against him. Today he was wearing the Murasama blade within its battle-honored scabbard.

They turned another corner, then unexpectedly Hiro-matsu opened an iron-bound reinforced door and led the way up the stone steps into the inner central keep of this part of the fortifications. There were many guards on duty and Yabu sensed danger.

The stairs curled upward and ended at an easily defendable redoubt. Guards opened the iron door. He went out onto the battlements. Has Hiro-matsu been told to throw me off, or will I be ordered to jump? he asked himself unafraid.

To his surprise Toranaga was there and, incredibly, Toranaga got up to greet him with a jovial deference he had no right to expect. After all, Toranaga was Lord of the Eight Provinces, whereas he was only Lord of Izu. Cushions had been placed carefully. A teapot was cradled in a sheath of silk. A richly dressed, square-faced girl of little beauty was bowing low. Her name was Sazuko and she was the seventh of Toranaga's official consorts, the youngest, and very pregnant.

"How nice to see you, Kasigi Yabu-san. I'm so sorry to have kept you waiting."

Now Yabu was certain that Toranaga had decided to remove his head, one way or another, for, by universal custom, your enemy is never more polite than when he is planning or has planned your destruction. He took out both his swords and placed them carefully on the stone flags, allowed himself to be led away from them and seated in the place of honor.

"I thought it would be interesting to watch the dawning, Yabu-san. I think the view here is exquisite—even better than from the Heir's donjon. *Neh?*"

"Yes, it is beautiful," Yabu said without reservation, never having been so high in the castle before, sure now that Toranaga's remark about "the Heir" implied that his secret negotiations with Ishido were known. "I'm honored to be allowed to share it with you."

Below them were the sleeping city and harbor and islands, Awaji to the west, the coastline falling off to the east, the growing light in the eastern sky slashing the clouds with flecks of crimson.

"This is my Lady Sazuko. Sazuko, this is my ally, the famous Lord Kasigi Yabu of Izu, the *daimyo* who brought us the barbarian and the treasure ship!" She bowed and complimented him and he bowed and she returned his bow again. She offered Yabu the first cup of tea but he politely declined the honor, beginning the ritual, and asked her to give it to Toranaga, who refused, and pressed him to accept it. Eventually, continuing the ritual, as the honored guest he allowed himself to be persuaded. Hiro-matsu accepted the second cup, his gnarled fingers holding the porcelain with difficulty, the other hand wrapped around the haft of his sword, loose in his lap. Toranaga accepted a third cup and sipped his cha, then together they gave themselves to nature and watched the sunrise. In the silence of the sky.

Gulls mewed. The city sounds began. The day was born.

Lady Sazuko sighed, her eyes wet with tears. "It makes me feel like a goddess being so high, watching so much beauty, *neh?* It's so sad that it's gone forever, Sire. So very sad, *neh?*"

"Yes," Toranaga said.

When the sun was halfway above the horizon, she bowed and left. To Yabu's surprise, the guards left also. Now they were alone. The three of them.

"I was pleased to receive your gift, Yabu-san. It was most generous, the whole ship and everything in it," Toranaga said.

"Whatever I have is yours," Yabu said, still deeply affected by the dawning. I wish I had more time, he thought. How elegant of Toranaga to do this! To give me a lastness of such immensity. "Thank you for this dawn."

"Yes," Toranaga said. "It was mine to give. I'm pleased that you enjoyed my gift, as I enjoyed yours."

There was a silence.

"Yabu-san. What do you know about the Amida Tong?"

"Only what most people know: that it's a secret society of ten—units of ten—a leader and never more than nine acolytes in any one area, women and men. They are sworn by the most sacred and secret oaths of the Lord Buddha Amida, the Dispenser of Eternal Love, to obedience, chastity, and death; to spend their lives training to become a perfect weapon for one kill; to kill only at the order of the leader, and if they fail to kill the person chosen, be it a man, woman, or child, to take their own life at once. They're religious fanatics who are certain they'll go directly from this life to Buddhahood. Not one of them has ever been caught alive." Yabu knew about the attempt on Toranaga's life. All Osaka knew by now and knew also that the Lord of the Kwanto, the Eight Provinces, had locked himself safely inside hoops of steel. "They kill rarely, their secrecy is complete. There's no chance of revenge on them because no one knows who they are, where they live, or where they train."

"If you wanted to employ them, how would you go about it?"

"I would whisper it in three places—in the Heinan Monastery, at the gates of the Amida shrine, and in the Johji Monastery. Within ten days, if you are considered an acceptable employer, you will be approached through intermediaries. It is all so secret and devious that, even if you wished to betray them or catch them, it would never be possible. On the tenth day they ask for a sum of money, in silver, the amount depending on the person to be assassinated. There is no bargaining, you pay what they ask beforehand. They guarantee only that one of their members will attempt the kill within ten days. Legend has it that if the kill is successful, the assassin goes back to their temple and then, with great ceremony, commits ritual suicide."

"Then you think we could never find out who paid for the attack today?"

"No."

"Do you think there will be another?"

"Perhaps. Perhaps not. They contract for one attempt at one time, *neh?* But you'd be wise to improve your security—among your samurai, and also among your women. The Amida women are trained in poison, as well as knife and garrote, so they say."

"Have you ever employed them?"

"No."

"But your father did?"

"I don't know, not for certain. I was told that the Taikō asked him to contact them once."

"Was the attack successful?"

"Anything the Taikō did was successful. One way or another."

Yabu felt someone behind him and presumed it to be the guards coming back secretly. He was measuring the distance to his swords. Do I try to kill Toranaga? he asked himself again. I had decided to and now I don't know. I've changed. Why?

"What would you have to pay them for my head?" Toranaga asked him.

"There is not enough silver in all Asia to tempt me to employ them to do this."

"What would another have to pay?"

"Twenty thousand koku—fifty thousand—a hundred—perhaps more, I don't know."

"Would you pay a hundred thousand koku to become Shōgun? Your bloodline goes back to the Takashimas, *neh?*"

Yabu said proudly, "I would pay nothing. Money's filth—a toy for women to play with or for dung-filled merchants. But if that were possible, which it isn't, I would give my life and the life of my wife and mother and all my kin except my one son, and all my samurai in Izu and all their women and children to be Shōgun one day."

"And what would you give for the Eight Provinces?"

"Everything as before, except the life of my wife and mother and son."

"And for Suruga Province?"

"Nothing," Yabu said with contempt. "Ikawa Jikkyu's worth nothing. If I don't take his head and all his generation in this life I'll do it in another. I piss on him and his seed for ten thousand lifetimes."

"And if I were to give him to you? And all Suruga—and perhaps the next province, Totomi, as well?"

Yabu suddenly tired of the cat-and-mouse game and the talk about the Amida. "You've decided to take my head, Lord Toranaga—very well. I'm ready. I thank you for the dawn. But I've no wish to spoil such elegance with further talk, so let's be done."

"But I haven't decided to take your head, Yabu-san," Toranaga said. "Whatever gave you the thought? Has an enemy poured poison in your ears? Ishido perhaps? Aren't you my favored ally? Do you think that I'd entertain you here, without guards, if I thought you hostile?"

Yabu turned slowly. He had expected to find samurai behind him, swords poised. There was no one there. He looked back at Toranaga. "I don't understand."

"I brought you here so we could talk privately. And to see the dawn. Would you like to rule the provinces of Izu, Suruga, and Totomi—if I do not lose this war?"

"Yes. Very much," Yabu said, his hopes soaring.

"You would become my vassal? Accept me as your liege lord?"

Yabu did not hesitate. "Never," he said. "As ally, yes. As my leader, yes. Lesser than you always, yes. My life and all I possess thrown onto your side, yes. But Izu is mine. I am *daimyo* of Izu and I will never give power over Izu to anyone. I swore that oath to my father, and the Taikō who reaffirmed our hereditary fief, first to my father and then to me. The Taikō confirmed Izu to me and my successors forever. He was our liege lord and I swore never to have another until his heir became of age."

Hiro-matsu twisted his sword slightly in his hand. Why doesn't Toranaga let me get it over with once and for all? It's been agreed. Why all the wearing talk? I ache and I want to piss and I need to lie down.

Toranaga scratched his groin. "What did Ishido offer you?"

"Jikkyu's head—the moment that yours is off. And his province."

"In return for what?"

"Support when war begins. To attack your southern flank."

"Did you accept?"

"You know me better than that."

Toranaga's spies in Ishido's household had whispered that the bargain had been struck, and that it included responsibility for the assassination of his three sons, Noboru, Sudara, and Naga. "Nothing more? Just support?"

"By every means at my disposal," Yabu said delicately.

"Including assassination?"

"I intend to wage the war, when it begins, with all my force. For my ally. In any way I can to guarantee his success. We need a sole Regent in Yaemon's minority. War between you and Ishido is inevitable. It's the only way."

Yabu was trying to read Toranaga's mind. He was scornful of Toranaga's indecision, knowing that he himself was the better man, that Toranaga needed his support, that at length he would vanquish him. But meanwhile what to do? he asked himself and wished Yuriko, his wife, were here to guide him. She would know the wisest course. "I can be very valuable to you. I can help you become sole Regent," he said, deciding to gamble.

"Why should I wish to be sole Regent?"

"When Ishido attacks I can help you to conquer him. When he breaks the peace," Yabu said.

"How?"

He told them his plan with the guns.

"A regiment of five hundred gun-samurai?" Hiro-matsu erupted.

"Yes. Think of the fire power. All elite men, trained to act as one man. The twenty cannon equally together."

"It's a bad plan. Disgusting," Hiro-matsu said. "You could never keep it secret. If we start, the enemy would start also. There would never be an end to such horror. There's no honor in it and no future."

"Isn't this coming war the only one we're concerned with, Lord Hiro-matsu?" Yabu replied. "Aren't we concerned only with Lord Toranaga's safety? Isn't that the duty of his allies and vassals?"

"Yes."

"All Lord Toranaga has to do is win the one great battle. That will give him the heads of all his enemies—and power. I say this strategy will give him victory."

"I say it won't. It's a disgusting plan with no honor."

Yabu turned to Toranaga. "A new era requires clear thinking about the meaning of honor."

A sea gull soared overhead mewing.

"What did Ishido say to your plan?" Toranaga asked.

"I did not discuss it with him."

"Why? If you think your plan's valuable to me, it would be equally valuable to him. Perhaps more so."

"You gave me a dawn. You're not a peasant like Ishido. You're the wisest, most experienced leader in the Empire."

What's the real reason? Toranaga was asking himself. Or have you told Ishido too? "If this plan were to be followed, the men would be half yours and half mine?"

"Agreed. I would command them."

"My appointee would be second-in-command?"

"Agreed. I would need the Anjin-san to train my men as gunners, cannoneers."

"But he would be my property permanently, you would cherish him as you do the Heir? You'd be totally responsible for him and do with him precisely as I say?"

"Agreed."

Toranaga watched the crimson clouds for a moment. This planning is all nonsense, he thought. I will have to declare Crimson Sky myself and lunge for Kyoto at the head of all my legions. One hundred thousand against ten times that number. "Who will be interpreter? I can't detach Toda Mariko-san forever."

"For a few weeks, Sire? I will see that the barbarian learns our language."

"That'd take years. The only barbarians who've ever mastered it are Christian priests, *neh?* They spend years. Tsukku-san's been here almost thirty years, *neh?* He won't learn fast enough, anymore than we can learn their foul languages."

"Yes. But I promise you, this Anjin-san'll learn very quickly." Yabu told them the plan Omi had suggested to him as if it were his own idea.

"That might be too dangerous."

"It would make him learn quickly, *neh?* And then he's tamed."

After a pause, Toranaga said, "How would you maintain secrecy during the training?"

"Izu is a peninsula, security is excellent there. I'll base near Anjiro, well south and away from Mishima and the border for more safety."

"Good. We'll set up carrier pigeon links from Anjiro to Osaka and Yedo at once."

"Excellent. I need only five or six months and—"

"We'll be lucky to have six days!" Hiro-matsu snorted. "Are you saying that your famous espionage net has been swept away, Yabu-san? Surely you've been getting reports? Isn't Ishido mobilizing? Isn't Onoshi mobilizing? Aren't we locked in here?"

Yabu did not answer.

"Well?" Toranaga said.

Yabu said, "Reports indicate all that is happening and more. If it's six days then it's six days and that's *karma.* But I believe you're much too clever to be trapped here. Or provoked into an early war."

"If I agreed to your plan, you would accept me as your leader?"

"Yes. And when you win, I would be honored to accept Suruga and Totomi as part of my fief forever."

"Totomi would depend on the success of your plan."

"Agreed."

"You will obey me? With all your honor?"

"Yes. By *bushido,* by the Lord Buddha, by the life of my mother, my wife, and my future posterity."

"Good," Toranaga said. "Let's piss on the bargain."

He went to the edge of the battlements. He stepped up on the ledge of the embrasure, then onto the parapet itself. Seventy feet below was the inner garden. Hiro-matsu held his breath, aghast at his master's bravado. He saw him turn and beckon Yabu to stand beside him. Yabu obeyed. The slightest touch could have sent them tumbling to their deaths.

Toranaga eased his kimono and loincloth aside, as did Yabu. Together they urinated and mixed their urine and watched it dew the garden below.

"The last bargain I sealed this way was with the Taikō himself," Toranaga said, greatly relieved at being able to empty his bladder. "That was when he decided to give me the Kwanto, the Eight Provinces, as my fief. Of course, at that time the enemy Hojo still owned them, so first I had to conquer them. They were our last remaining opposition. Of course, too, I had to give up my hereditary fiefs of Imagawa, Owari, and Ise at once for the honor. Even so, I agreed and we pissed on the bargain." He straddled the parapet easily, settling his loincloth comfortably as though he stood in the garden itself, not perched like an eagle so far above. "It was a good bargain for both of us. We conquered the Hojo and took over five thousand heads within the year. Stamped him out and all his tribe. Perhaps you're right, Kasigi Yabu-san. Perhaps you can help me as I helped the Taikō. Without me, the Taikō would never have become Taikō."

"I can help to make you sole Regent, Toranaga-sama. But not Shōgun."

"Of course. That's the one honor I don't seek, as much as my enemies say I do." Toranaga jumped down to the safety of the stone flags. He looked back at Yabu who still stood on the narrow parapet adjusting his sash. He was sorely tempted to give him a quick shove for his insolence. Instead he sat down and broke wind loudly. "That's better. How's your bladder, Iron Fist?"

"Tired, Lord, very tired." The old man went to the side and emptied himself thankfully over the battlements too, but he did not stand where Toranaga and

Yabu had stood. He was very glad that he did not also have to seal the bargain with Yabu. That's one bargain I will never honor. Never.

"Yabu-san. This must all be kept secret. I think you should leave within the next two or three days," Toranaga said.

"Yes. With the guns and the barbarian, Toranaga-sama?"

"Yes. You will go by ship." Toranaga looked at Hiro-matsu. "Prepare the galley."

"The ship is ready. The guns and powder are still in the holds," Hiro-matsu replied, his face mirroring his disapproval.

"Good."

You've done it, Yabu wanted to shout. You've got the guns, the Anjin-san, everything. You've got your six months. Toranaga'll never go to war quickly. Even if Ishido assassinates him in the next few days, you've still got everything. Oh, Buddha, protect Toranaga until I'm at sea! "Thank you," he said, his sincerity openly vast. "You'll never have a more faithful ally."

When Yabu was gone, Hiro-matsu wheeled on Toranaga. "That was a bad thing to do. I'm ashamed of that bargain. I'm ashamed that my advice counts for so little. I've obviously outlived my usefulness to you and I'm very tired. That little snot-dung *daimyo* knows he's manipulated you like a puppet. Why, he even had the effrontery to wear his Murasama sword in your presence."

"I noticed," Toranaga said.

"I think the gods have bewitched you, Lord. You openly dismiss such an insult and allow him to gloat in front of you. You openly allow Ishido to shame you in front of all of us. You prevent me and all of us from protecting you. You refuse my granddaughter, a samurai lady, the honor and peace of death. You've lost control of the Council, your enemy has outmaneuvered you, and now you piss on a solemn bargain that is as disgusting a plan as I've ever heard, and you do this with a man who deals in filth, poison, and treachery like his father before him." He was shaking with rage. Toranaga did not answer, just stared calmly at him as though he had said nothing. "By all *kami,* living and dead, you are bewitched." Hiro-matsu burst out, "I question you—and shout and insult you and you only stare at me! You've gone mad or I have. I ask permission to commit seppuku or if you won't allow me that peace I'll shave my head and become a monk—anything, anything, but let me be gone."

"You will do neither. But you will send for the barbarian priest, Tsukku-san."

And then Toranaga laughed.

CHAPTER 19

FATHER ALVITO rode down the hill from the castle at the head of his usual company of Jesuit outriders. All were dressed as Buddhist priests except for the rosary and crucifix they wore at their waists. There were forty outriders, Japanese, all well-born sons of Christian samurai, students from the seminary at Nagasaki who had accompanied him to Osaka. All were well mounted and caparisoned and as disciplined as the entourage of any *daimyo*.

He hurried along in a brisk trot, oblivious of the warm sunshine, through the woods and the city streets toward the Jesuit Mission, a large stone European-style house that stood near the wharves and soared from its clustered outbuildings, treasure rooms, and warehouses, where all of Osaka's silks were bartered and paid for.

The cortege clattered through the tall iron gates set in the high stone walls and into the paved central courtyard and stopped near the main door. Servants were already waiting to help Father Alvito dismount. He slid out of the saddle and threw them the reins. His spurs jingled on the stone as he strode up the cloistered walk of the main building, turned the corner, passed the small chapel, and went through some arches into the innermost courtyard, which contained a fountain and a peaceful garden. The antechamber door was open. He threw off his anxiety, composed himself, and walked in.

"Is he alone?" he asked.

"No, no, he isn't, Martin," Father Soldi said. He was a small, benign, pock-marked man from Naples who had been the Father-Visitor's secretary for almost thirty years, twenty-five of them in Asia. "Captain-General Ferriera's with his Eminence. Yes, the peacock's with him. But his Eminence said you were to go in at once. What's gone wrong, Martin?"

"Nothing."

Soldi grunted and went back to sharpening his quill. " 'Nothing,' the wise Father said. Well, I'll know soon enough."

"Yes," Alvito said, liking the older man. He walked for the far door. A wood fire was burning in a grate, illuminating the fine heavy furniture, dark with age and rich with polish and care. A small Tintoretto of a Madonna and Child that the Father-Visitor had brought with him from Rome, which always pleased Alvito, hung over the fireplace.

"You saw the Ingeles again?" Father Soldi called after him.

Alvito did not answer. He knocked at the door.

"Come in."

Carlo dell'Aqua, Father-Visitor of Asia, personal representative of the General of the Jesuits, the most senior Jesuit and thus the most powerful man in Asia, was also the tallest. He stood six feet three inches, with a physique to match. His robe was orange, his cross exquisite. He was tonsured, white-haired, sixty-one years old, and by birth a Neapolitan.

"Ah, Martin, come in, come in. Some wine?" he said, speaking Portuguese with a marvelous Italian liquidity. "You saw the Ingeles?"

"No, your Eminence. Just Toranaga."

"Bad?"

"Yes."

"Some wine?"

"Thank you."

"How bad?" Ferriera asked. The soldier sat beside the fire in the high-backed leather chair as proudly as a falcon and as colorful—the *fidaglio,* the Captain-General of the *Nao del Trato,* this year's Black Ship. He was in his middle thirties, lean, slight, and formidable.

"I think very bad, Captain-General. For instance, Toranaga said the matter of this year's trade could wait."

"Obviously trade can't wait, nor can I," Ferriera said. "I'm sailing on the tide."

"You don't have your port clearances. I'm afraid you'll have to wait."

"I thought everything was arranged months ago." Again Ferriera cursed the Japanese regulations that required all shipping, even their own, to have incoming and outgoing licenses. "We shouldn't be bound by stupid native regulations. You said this meeting was just a formality—to collect the documents."

"It should have been, but I was wrong. Perhaps I'd better explain—"

"I must return to Macao immediately to prepare the Black Ship. We've already purchased a million ducats' worth of the best silks at February's Canton Fair and we'll be carrying at least a hundred thousand ounces of Chinese gold. I thought I'd made it clear that every penny of cash in Macao, Malacca, and Goa, and every penny the Macao traders and city fathers can borrow is invested in this year's venture. And every penny of yours."

"We're just as aware as you are of its importance," dell'Aqua said pointedly.

"I'm sorry, Captain-General, but Toranaga's President of the Regents and it's the custom to go to him," Alvito said. "He wouldn't discuss this year's trade or your clearances. He said, initially, he did not approve of assassination."

"Who does, Father?" Ferriera said.

"What's Toranaga talking about, Martin?" dell'Aqua asked. "Is this some sort of ruse? Assassination? What has that to do with us?"

"He said: 'Why would you Christians want to assassinate my prisoner, the pilot?' "

"What?"

"Toranaga believes the attempt last night was on the Ingeles, not him. Also he says there was another attempt in prison." Alvito kept his eyes fixed on the soldier.

"What do you accuse me of, Father?" Ferriera said. "An assassination attempt? Me? In Osaka Castle? This is the first time I've ever been in Japan!"

"You deny any knowledge of it?"

"I do not deny that the sooner the heretic's dead the better," Ferriera said coldly. "If the Dutch and English start spreading their filth in Asia we're in for trouble. All of us."

"We're already in trouble," Alvito said. "Toranaga began by saying that he understands from the Ingeles that incredible profits are being made from the Portuguese *monopoly* of the China trade, that the Portuguese are extravagantly overpricing the silks that only the Portuguese can buy in China, paying for them with the sole commodity the Chinese will accept in exchange, Japanese silver—which again the Portuguese are equally ludicrously underpricing. Toranaga said: 'Because hostility exists between China and Japan and all direct trade between us is forbidden and the Portuguese alone have their permission to carry the trade, the pilot's charge of "usury" should be formally replied to—*in writing*—by the Portuguese.' He 'invites' you, Eminence, to provide the Regents with a report on rates of exchange—silver to silk, silk to silver, gold to silver. He added that he does not, of course, object to our making a large profit, providing it comes from the Chinese."

"You will, of course, refuse such an arrogant request," Ferriera said.

"That is very difficult."

"Then provide a false report."

"That would endanger our whole position, which is based on trust," dell'Aqua said.

"Can you trust a Jappo? Of course not. Our profits must remain secret. That God-cursed heretic!"

"I'm sorry to tell you Blackthorne seems to be particularly well informed." Alvito looked involuntarily at dell'Aqua, his guard dropping momentarily.

The Father-Visitor said nothing.

"What else did the Jappo say?" Ferriera asked, pretending that he had not seen the look between them, wishing he knew the full extent of their knowledge.

"Toranaga asks me to provide him, by tomorrow noon, with a map of the world showing the lines of demarcation between Portugal and Spain, the names of the Popes who approved the treaties, and their dates. Within three days he 'requests' a written explanation of our 'conquests' in the New World, and 'purely for my own interest' were his exact words, the amount of gold and silver taken back—he actually used Blackthorne's word 'plundered'—taken back to Spain and Portugal from the New World. And he also requests another map showing the extent of the Empires of Spain and Portugal a hundred years ago, fifty years ago, and today, together with exact positions of our bases from Malacca to Goa—he named them all accurately by the way; they were written on a piece of paper—and also the numbers of Japanese mercenaries employed by us at each of our bases."

Dell'Aqua and Ferriera were appalled. "This must absolutely be refused," the soldier boomed.

"You can't refuse Toranaga," dell'Aqua said.

"I think, your Eminence, you put too much reliance on his importance," Ferriera said. "It seems to me that this Toranaga's just another despot king among many, just another murdering heathen, certainly not to be feared. Refuse him. Without our Black Ship their whole economy collapses. They're begging for our Chinese silks. Without silks there'd be no kimonos. They must have our trade. I say the pox on Toranaga. We can trade with the Christian kings—what were their names? Onoshi and Kiyama—and the other Christian kings of Kyushu. After all, Nagasaki's there, we're there in strength, all trade's done there."

"We can't, Captain," dell'Aqua said. "This is your first visit to Japan so you've no idea of our problems here. Yes, they need us, but we need them more. Without Toranaga's favor—and Ishido's—we'll lose influence over the Christian kings. We'll lose Nagasaki and everything we've built over fifty years. Did you precipitate the attempt on this heretic pilot?"

"I said openly to Rodrigues, and to anyone else who would listen from the very first, that the Ingeles was a dangerous pirate who would infect anyone he came into contact with, and who therefore should be removed in any way possible. You said the same in different words, your Eminence. So did you, Father Alvito. Didn't the matter come up at our conference with Onoshi and Kiyama two days ago? Didn't you say this pirate was dangerous?"

"Yes. But—"

"Father, you will forgive me, but sometimes it is necessary for soldiers to do God's work in the best way they can. I must tell you I was furious with Rodrigues for not creating an 'accident' during the storm. He, of all people, should have known better! By the Body of Christ, look what that devil Ingeles has already done to Rodrigues himself. The poor fool's grateful to him for saving his life when it's the most obvious trick in the world to gain his confidence. Wasn't Rodrigues fooled into allowing the heretic pilot to usurp his own quarterdeck, certainly almost causing his death? As to the castle attempt, who knows what happened? That has to have been ordered by a native, that's a Jappo trick. I'm not sad they tried, only disgusted that they failed. When *I* arrange for his removal, you may rest assured he will be removed."

Alvito sipped his wine. "Toranaga said that he was sending Blackthorne to Izu."

"The peninsula to the east?" Ferriera asked.

"Yes."

"By land or by ship?"

"By ship."

"Good. Then I regret to tell you that all hands may be lost at sea in a regrettable storm."

Alvito said coldly, "And I regret to tell you, Captain-General, that Toranaga said—I'll give you his exact words: 'I am putting a personal guard around the pilot, Tsukku-san, and if any accident befalls him it will be investigated to the limit of my power and the power of the Regents, and if, by chance, a Christian is responsible, or anyone remotely associated with Christians, it's quite possible the Expulsion Edicts would be reexamined and very possible that all Christian churches, schools, places of rest, will be immediately closed.' "

Dell'Aqua said, "God forbid that should happen."

"Bluff," Ferriera sneered.

"No, you're wrong, Captain-General. Toranaga's as clever as a Machiavelli and as ruthless as Attila the Hun." Alvito looked back at dell'Aqua. "It would be easy to blame us if anything happened to the Ingeles."

"Yes."

"Perhaps you should go to the source of your problem," Ferriera said bluntly. "Remove Toranaga."

"This is no time for jokes," the Father-Visitor said.

"What has worked brilliantly in India and Malaya, Brazil, Peru, Mexico, Africa, the Main and elsewhere will work here. I've done it myself in Malacca and Goa a dozen times with the help of Jappo mercenaries, and I've nowhere near your influence and knowledge. We use the Christian kings. We'll help one of them to remove Toranaga if he's the problem. A few hundred conquistadores would be enough. Divide and rule. I'll approach Kiyama. Father Alvito, if you'll interpret—"

"You cannot equate Japanese with Indians or with illiterate savages like the Incas. You cannot divide and rule here. Japan is not like any other nation. Not at all," dell'Aqua said wearily. "I must ask you formally, Captain-General, not to interfere in the internal politics of this country."

"I agree. Please forget what I said. It was indelicate and naïve to be so open. Fortunately storms are normal at this time of the year."

"If a storm occurs, that is in the Hand of God. But you will *not* attack the pilot."

"Oh?"

"No. Nor will you order anyone to do it."

"I am bound by *my* king to destroy the enemies of my king. The Ingeles is an enemy national. A parasite, a pirate, a heretic. If I choose to eliminate him, that is my affair. I am Captain-General of the Black Ship this year, therefore Governor of Macao this year, with viceregal powers over these waters this year, and if I want to eliminate him, or Toranaga or whomever, I will."

"Then you do so over my direct orders to the contrary and thereby risk immediate excommunication."

"This is beyond your jurisdiction. It is a temporal matter, not a spiritual one."

"The position of the Church here is, regrettably, so intermixed with politics and with the silk trade, that everything touches the safety of the Church. And while I live, by my hope of salvation, no one will jeopardize the future of the Mother Church here!"

"Thank you for being so explicit, your Eminence. I will make it my business to become more knowledgeable about Jappo affairs."

"I suggest you do, for all our sakes. Christianity is tolerated here only because all *daimyos* believe absolutely that if they expel us and stamp out the Faith, the Black Ships will never come back. We Jesuits are sought after and have some measure of influence only because we alone can speak Japanese and Portuguese and can interpret and intercede for them on matters of trade. *Unfortunately* for the Faith, what they believe is not true. I'm certain trade would continue, irrespective of our position and the position of the Church, because Portuguese traders are more concerned with their own selfish interests than with the service of our Lord."

"Perhaps the selfish interests of the clerics who wish to force us—even to the extent of asking His Holiness for the legal powers—to force us to sail into whatever port they decide and trade with whatever *daimyo* they prefer, irrespective of the hazards, is equally evident!"

"You forget yourself, Captain-General!"

"I do not forget that the Black Ship of last year was lost between here and Malacca with all hands, with over two hundred tons of gold aboard and five hundred thousand crusados worth of silver bullion, after being delayed unnecessarily into the bad weather season because of your personal requests. Or that this catastrophe almost ruined everyone from here to Goa."

"It was necessary because of the Taikō's death and the internal politics of the succession."

"I do not forget you asked the Viceroy of Goa to cancel the Black Ship three years ago, to send it only when you said, to which port you decided, or that he overruled this as as an arrogant interference."

"That was to curb the Taikō, to bring him an economic crisis in the midst of his stupid war on Korea and China, because of the Nagasaki martyrdoms he had ordered, because of his insane attack on the Church and the Expulsion Edicts he had just published expelling us all from Japan. If you cooperate with us, follow our advice, all Japan would be Christian in a single generation! What is more important—trade or the salvation of souls?"

"My answer is souls. But since you've enlightened me on Jappo affairs let me put Jappo affairs in their correct perspective. Jappo silver alone unlocks Chinese silks and Chinese gold. The immense profits we make and export to Malacca and Goa and thence to Lisbon support our whole Asian Empire, all forts, all missions, all expeditions, all missionaries, all discoveries, and pays for most, if not all of our European commitments, prevents the heretics from overrunning us and keeps them out of Asia, which would provide them with all the wealth they need to destroy us and the Faith at home. What's more important, Father—Spanish, Portuguese, and Italian Christendom, or Jappo Christendom?"

Dell'Aqua glared down at the soldier. "Once and for all, you-will-not-involve-yourself-with-the-internal-politics-here!"

A coal fell from the fire and spluttered on the rug. Ferriera, the nearest, kicked it to safety. "And if I'm to be—to be curbed, what do you propose to do about the heretic? Or Toranaga?"

Dell'Aqua sat down, believing that he had won. "I don't know, at the moment. But even to think of removing Toranaga is ludicrous. He's very sympathetic to us, and very sympathetic to increasing trade"—his voice became more withering—"and therefore to increasing your profits."

"And your profits," Ferriera said, taking the bit again.

"Our profits are committed to the work of Our Lord. As you well know." Dell'Aqua tiredly poured some wine, offered it, placating him. "Come now, Ferriera, let's not quarrel in this fashion. This business of the heretic—terrible, yes. But quarreling avails nothing. We need your counsel and your brains and your strength. You can believe me, Toranaga is vital to us. Without him to restrain the other Regents, this whole country will go back to anarchy again."

"Yes, it's true, Captain-General," Alvito said. "But I don't understand why he's still in the castle and has agreed to a delay in the meeting. It's incredible that he seems to have been outmaneuvered. He must surely know that Osaka's locked tighter than a jealous crusader's chastity belt. He should have left days ago."

Ferriera said, "If he's vital, why support Onoshi and Kiyama? Haven't those two sided with Ishido against him? Why don't you advise them against it? It was discussed only two days ago."

"They told us of their decision, Captain. We did not discuss it."

"Then perhaps you should have, Eminence. If it's so important, why not order them against it? With a threat of excommunication."

Dell'Aqua sighed. "I wish it were so simple. You don't do things like that in Japan. They abhor outside interference in their internal affairs. Even a suggestion on our part has to be offered with extreme delicacy."

Ferriera drained his silver goblet and poured some more wine and calmed himself, knowing that he needed the Jesuits on his side, that without them as interpreters he was helpless. You've got to make this voyage successful, he told himself. You've soldiered and sweated eleven years in the service of the King to earn, rightfully—twenty times over—the richest prize in his power to give, the Captain-Generalship of the annual Black Ship for one year and the tenth part that goes with the honor, a tenth of all silk, of all gold, of all silver, and of all profit from each transaction. You're rich for life now, for thirty lifetimes if you had them, all from this one single voyage. If you accomplish it.

Ferriera's hand went to the haft of his rapier, to the silver cross that formed part of the silver filigree. "By the Blood of Christ, my Black Ship will sail on time from Macao to Nagasaki and then, the richest treasure ship in history, she'll head south with the monsoon in November for Goa and thence home! As Christ is my judge, that's what's going to happen." And he added silently, if I have to burn all Japan and all Macao and all China to do it, by the Madonna!

"Our prayers are with you, of course they are," dell'Aqua replied, meaning it. "We know the importance of your voyage."

"Then what do you suggest? Without port clearances and safe conducts to trade, I'm hamstrung. Can't we avoid the Regents? Perhaps there's another way?"

Dell'Aqua shook his head. "Martin? You're our trade expert."

"I'm sorry, but it's not possible," Alvito said. He had listened to the heated exchange with simmering indignation. Foul-mannered, arrogant, motherless cretin, he had thought, then immediately, oh, God, give me patience, for without this man and others like him, the Church dies here. "I'm sure within a day or two, Captain-General, everything will be sealed. A week at the most. Toranaga has very special problems at the moment. It will be all right, I'm sure."

"I'll wait a week. No more." The undercurrent of menace in Ferriera's tone was frightening. "I'd like to get my hands on that heretic. I'd rack the truth out of him. Did Toranaga say anything about the supposed fleet? An enemy fleet?"

"No."

"I'd like to know that truth, because inbound, my ship will be wallowing like a fat pig, her holds bulging with more silks than have ever been sent at one time. We're one of the biggest ships in the world but I've no escort, so if a single enemy frigate were to catch us at sea—or that Dutch whore, the *Erasmus*—we'd be at her mercy. She'd make me haul down the Imperial flag of Portugal with no trouble at all. The Ingeles had better not get his ship to sea, with gunners and cannon and shot aboard."

"*E vero, è solamente vero,*" dell'Aqua muttered.

Ferriera finished his wine. "When's Blackthorne being sent to Izu?"

"Toranaga didn't say," Alvito replied. "I got the impression it would be soon."

"Today?"

"I don't know. Now the Regents meet in four days. I would imagine it would be after that."

Dell'Aqua said heavily, "Blackthorne must not be interfered with. Neither he nor Toranaga."

Ferriera stood up. "I'll be getting back to my ship. You'll dine with us? Both of you? At dusk? There's a fine capon, a joint of beef and Madeira wine, even some new bread."

"Thank you, you're very kind." Dell'Aqua brightened slightly. "Yes, some good food again would be wonderful. You're very kind."

"You'll be informed the instant I have word from Toranaga, Captain-General," Alvito said.

"Thank you."

When Ferriera had gone and the Visitor was sure that he and Alvito could not be overheard, he said anxiously, "Martin, what else did Toranaga say?"

"He wants an explanation, in writing, of the gun-running incident, and the request for conquistadores."

"*Mamma mia . . .*"

"Toranaga was friendly, even gentle, but—well, I've never seen him like this before."

"What exactly did he say?"

" 'I understand, Tsukku-san, that the previous head of your order of Christians, Father da Cunha, wrote to the governors of Macao, Goa, and the Spanish Viceroy in Manila, Don Sisco y Vivera, in July of 1588 of your counting, asking for an invasion of hundreds of Spanish soldiers with guns to support some Christian *daimyos* in a rebellion which the chief Christian priest was trying to incite against their lawful liege lord, my late master, the Taikō. What were the names of these *daimyos*? Is it true that no soldiers were sent but vast numbers of guns were smuggled into Nagasaki under your Christian seal from Macao? Is it true that the Father-Giant secretly seized these guns when he returned to Japan for the second time, as Ambassador from Goa, in March or April 1590, by your counting, and secretly smuggled them out of Nagasaki on the Portuguese ship, the *Santa Cruz,* back to Macao?' " Alvito wiped the sweat off his hands.

"Did he say anything more?"

"Not of importance, Eminence. I had no chance to explain—he dismissed me at once. The dismissal was polite but it was still a dismissal."

"Where is that cursed Englishman getting his information from?"

"I wish I knew."

"Those dates and names. You're not mistaken? He said them exactly like that?"

"No, Eminence. The names were written on a piece of paper. He showed it to me."

"Blackthorne's writing?"

"No. The names were written phonetically in Japanese, in *hiragana.*"

"We've got to find out who's interpreting for Toranaga. He must be astonishingly good. Surely not one of ours? It can't be Brother Manuel, can it?" he asked bitterly, using Masamanu Jiro's baptismal name. Jiro was the son of a Christian samurai who had been educated by the Jesuits since childhood and, being intelligent and devout, had been selected to enter the seminary to be trained to be a full priest of the four vows, of which there were none from the Japanese yet. Jiro had been with the Society for twenty years, then, incredibly, he left before being ordained and he was now a violent antagonist of the Church.

"No. Manuel's still in Kyushu, may he burn in hell forever. He's still a violent enemy of Toranaga's, he'd never help him. Fortunately, he was never party to any political secrets. The interpreter was the Lady Maria," Alvito said, using Toda Mariko's baptismal name.

"Toranaga told you that?"

"No, your Eminence. But I happen to know that she's been visiting the castle, and she was seen with the Ingeles."

"You're sure?"

"Our information is completely accurate."

"Good," dell'Aqua said. "Perhaps God is helping us in His inscrutable fashion. Send for her at once."

"I've already seen her. I made it my business to meet her by chance. She was delightful as always, deferential, pious as always, but she said pointedly before I had an opportunity to question her, 'Of course, the Empire is a very private land, Father, and some things, by custom, have to stay very private. Is it the same in Portugal, and within the Society of Jesus?' "

"You're her confessor."

"Yes. But she won't say anything."

"Why?"

"Clearly she's been forewarned and forbidden to discuss what happened and what was said. I know them too well. In this, Toranaga's influence would be greater than ours."

"Is her faith so small? Has our training of her been so inept? Surely not. She's as devout and as good a Christian as any woman I've ever met. One day she'll become a nun—perhaps even the first Japanese abbess."

"Yes. But she will say nothing now."

"The Church is in jeopardy. This is important, perhaps too important," dell' Aqua said. "She would understand that. She's far too intelligent not to realize it."

"I beg you, do not put her faith to the test in this. We must lose. She warned me. That's what she was saying as clearly as if it were written down."

"Perhaps it would be good to put her to the test. For her own salvation."

"That's up to you to order or not to order. But I'm afraid that she must obey Toranaga, Eminence, and not us."

"I will think about Maria. Yes," dell'Aqua said. He let his eyes drift to the fire, the weight of his office crushing him. Poor Maria. That cursed heretic! How do we avoid the trap? How do we conceal the truth about the guns? How could a Father Superior and Vice-Provincial like da Cunha, who was so well trained, so experienced, with seven years' practical knowledge in Macao and Japan—how could he make such a hideous mistake?

"How?" he asked the flames.

I can answer, he told himself. It's too easy. You panic or you forget the glory of God or become pride-filled or arrogant or petrified. Who wouldn't have, perhaps, under the same circumstances? To be received by the Taikō at sunset with favor, a triumphal meeting with pomp and ceremony—almost like an act of contrition by the Taikō, who was seemingly on the point of converting. And then to be awakened in the middle of the same night with the Taikō's Expulsion Edicts decreeing that all religious orders were to be out of Japan within twenty days on pain of death, never to return, and worse, that all Japanese converts throughout the land were ordered to recant at once or they would immediately be exiled or put to death.

Driven to despair, the Superior had wildly advised the Kyushu Christian *daimyos*—Onoshi, Misaki, Kiyama and Harima of Nagasaki among them—to rebel to save the Church and had written frantically for conquistadores to stiffen the revolt.

The fire spluttered and danced in the iron grate. Yes, all true, dell'Aqua thought. If only I'd known, if only da Cunha had consulted me first. But how could he? It takes six months to send a letter to Goa and perhaps another six months for one to return and da Cunha did write immediately but he was the Superior and on his own and had to cope at once with the disaster.

Though dell'Aqua had sailed immediately on receiving the letter, with hastily arranged credentials as Ambassador from the Viceroy of Goa, it had taken months to arrive at Macao, only to learn that da Cunha was dead, and that he and all Fathers were forbidden to enter Japan on pain of death.

But the guns had already gone.

Then, after ten weeks, came the news that the Church was not obliterated in Japan, that the Taikō was not enforcing his new laws. Only half a hundred churches had been burned. Only Takayama had been smashed. And word seeped back that though the Edicts would remain officially in force, the Taikō was now prepared to allow things to be as they were, provided that the Fathers were much more discreet in their conversions, their converts more discreet and well behaved, and that there were no more blatant public worship or demonstrations and no burning of Buddhist churches by zealots.

Then, when the ordeal seemed at an end, dell'Aqua had remembered that the guns had gone weeks before, under Father Superior da Cunha's seal, that they still lay in the Jesuit Nagasaki warehouses.

More weeks of agony ensued until the guns were secretly smuggled back to Macao—yes, under my seal this time, dell'Aqua reminded himself, hopefully the secret buried forever. But those secrets never leave you in peace, however much you wish or pray.

How much does the heretic know?

For more than an hour his Eminence sat motionless in his high-backed leather chair, staring sightlessly at the fire. Alvito waited patiently near the bookcase, his hands in his lap. Shafted sunlight danced off the silver crucifix on the wall behind the Father-Visitor. On one side wall was a small oil by the Venetian painter Titian that dell'Aqua had bought in his youth in Padua, where he had been sent by his father to study law. The other wall was lined with his Bibles and his books, in Latin, Portuguese, Italian, and Spanish. And, from the Society's own movable-type press at Nagasaki that he had ordered and brought at so much cost from Goa ten years ago, two shelves of Japanese books and pamphlets: devotional books and catechisms of all sorts, translated with painstaking labor into Japanese by Jesuits; works adapted from Japanese into Latin to try to help Japanese acolytes learn that language; and last, two small books that were beyond price, the first Portuguese-Japanese grammar, Father Sancho Alvarez's life's work, printed six years ago, and its companion, the incredible Portuguese-Latin-Japanese dictionary printed last year in Roman letters as well as *hiragana* script. It had been begun at his order twenty years ago, the first dictionary of Japanese words ever compiled.

Father Alvito picked up the book and caressed it lovingly. He knew that it was a unique work of art. For eighteen years he himself had been compiling such a work and it was still nowhere near finished. But his was to be a dictionary with explanatory supplements and far more detailed—almost an introduction to Japan and the Japanese, and he knew without vanity that if he managed to finish it, it would be a masterpiece compared to Father Alvarez's work, that if his name was ever to be remembered, it would be because of his book and the Father-Visitor, who was the only father he had ever known.

"You want to leave Portugal, my son, and join the service of God?" the giant Jesuit had said the first day he had met him.

"Oh, yes, please, Father," he had replied, craning up at him with desperate longing.

"How old are you, my son?"

"I don't know, Father, perhaps ten, perhaps eleven, but I can read and write, the priest taught me, and I'm alone, I've no one of my own, I belong to no one. . . ."

Dell'Aqua had taken him to Goa and thence to Nagasaki, where he had joined the seminary of the Society of Jesus, the youngest European in Asia, at long last belonging. Then came the miracle of the gift of tongues and the positions of trust as interpreter and trade adviser, first to Harima Tadao, *daimyo* of the fief of Hizen in Kyushu where Nagasaki lay, and then in time to the Taikō himself. He was ordained, and later even attained the privilege of the fourth vow. This was the special vow over and above the normal vows of poverty, chastity, and obedience, given only to the elite of Jesuits, the vow of obedience to the Pope personally—to be his personal tool for the work of God, to go where the Pope personally ordered and do what he personally wanted; to become, as the founder of the Society, the Basque soldier Loyola, designed, one of the Regimini Militantis Ecclesiae, one of the professed, the special private soldiers of God for His elected general on earth, the Vicar of Christ.

I've been so very lucky, Alvito thought. Oh, God, help me to help.

At last dell'Aqua got up and stretched and went to the window. Sun sparkled off the gilded tiles of the soaring central castle donjon, the sheer elegance of the structure belying its massive strength. Tower of evil, he thought. How long will it stand there to remind each one of us? Is it only fifteen—no, it was seventeen years ago that the Taikō put four hundred thousand men to building and excavating, and bled the country to pay for this, his monument, and then, in two short years, Osaka Castle was finished. Incredible man! Incredible people! Yes. And there it stands, indestructible. Except to the Finger of God. He can humble it in an instant, if He wishes. Oh, God, help me to do Thy will.

"Well, Martin, it seems we have work to do." Dell'Aqua began to walk up and down, his voice now as firm as his step. "About the English pilot: If we don't protect him he'll be killed and we risk Toranaga's disfavor. If we manage to protect him he'll soon hang himself. But dare we wait? His presence is a threat to us and there is no telling how much further damage he can do before that happy date. Or we can help Toranaga to remove him. Or, last, we can convert him."

Alvito blinked. "What?"

"He's intelligent, very knowledgeable about Catholicism. Aren't most Englishmen really Catholic at heart? The answer is yes if their king or queen is Catholic, and no if he or she is Protestant. The English are careless about religion. They're fanatic against us at the moment, but isn't that because of the Armada? Perhaps Blackthorne can be converted. That would be the perfect solution—to the Glory of God, and save his heretic soul from a damnation he's certainly going to.

"Next, Toranaga: We'll give him the maps he wants. Explain about 'spheres of influence.' Isn't that really what the lines of demarcation were for, to separate the influence of the Portuguese and our Spanish friends? *Sì, è vero!* Tell him that on the other important matters I will personally be honored to prepare them for him and will give them to him as soon as possible. Because I'll have to check the facts in Macao, could he please grant a reasonable delay? And in the same breath say that you are delighted to inform him that the Black Ship will sail three weeks early, with the biggest cargo of silks and gold ever, that all our assignments of goods and our portion of the cargo and . . ." he thought a moment—"and at least thirty percent of the whole cargo will be sold through Toranaga's personally appointed broker."

"Eminence, the Captain-General won't like sailing early and won't like—"

"It will be your responsibility to get Toranaga's immediate sailing clearance for Ferriera. Go and see him at once with my reply. Let him be impressed with our efficiency, isn't that one of the things he admires? With immediate clearances, Ferriera will concede the minor point of arriving early in the season, and as to the broker, what's the difference to the Captain-General between one native or another? He will still get his percentage."

"But Lords Onoshi and Kiyama and Harima usually split the brokerage of the cargo between them. I don't know if they'd agree."

"Then solve the problem. Toranaga will agree to the delay for a concession. The only concessions he needs are power, influence, and money. What can we give him? We cannot deliver the Christian *daimyos* to him. We—"

"Yet," Alvito said.

"Even if we could, I don't know yet if we should or if we will. Onoshi and Kiyama are bitter enemies, but they've joined against Toranaga because they're sure he'd obliterate the Church—and them—if he ever got control of the Council."

"Toranaga will support the Church. Ishido's our real enemy."

"I don't share your confidence, Martin. We mustn't forget that because Onoshi and Kiyama are Christians, all their followers are Christians in their tens of thousands. We cannot offend them. The only concession we can give to Toranaga is something to do with trade. He's fanatic about trade but has never managed to participate personally. So the concession I suggest might tempt him to grant a delay which perhaps we can extend into a permanent one. You know how the Japanese like this form of solution—the big stick poised, which both sides pretend does not exist, eh?"

"In my opinion it's politically unwise for Lord Onoshi and Lord Kiyama to turn against Toranaga at this time. They should follow the old proverb about keeping a line of retreat open, no? I could suggest to them that an offer to Toranaga of twenty-five percent—so each has an equal share, Onoshi, Kiyama, Harima, and Toranaga—would be a small consideration to soften the impact of their 'temporary' siding with Ishido against him."

"Then Ishido will distrust them and hate us even more when he finds out."

"Ishido hates us immeasurably now. Ishido doesn't trust them any more than they trust him and we don't know yet why they've taken his side. With Onoshi and Kiyama's agreement, we would formally put the proposal as though it was merely *our* idea to maintain impartiality between Ishido and Toranaga. Privately we can inform Toranaga of their generosity."

Dell'Aqua considered the virtues and defects of the plan. "Excellent," he said at length. "Put it into effect. Now, about the heretic. Give his rutters to Toranaga today. Go back to Toranaga at once. Tell him that the rutters were sent to us secretly."

"How do I explain the delay in giving them to him?"

"You don't. Just tell the truth: they were brought by Rodrigues but that neither of us realized the sealed package contained the missing rutters. Indeed, we did not open them for two days. They were in truth forgotten in the excitement about the heretic. The rutters prove Blackthorne to be pirate, thief, and traitor. His own words will dispose of him once and for all, which is surely divine justice. Tell Toranaga the truth—that Mura gave them to Father Sebastio, as indeed happened, who sent them to us knowing we would know what to do with them. That clears Mura, Father Sebastio, everyone. We should tell Mura by carrier pigeon what has been done. I'm sure Toranaga will realize that we have had his interests at heart over Yabu's. Does he know that Yabu's made an arrangement with Ishido?"

"I would say certainly, Eminence. But rumor has it that Toranaga and Yabu are friends now."

"I wouldn't trust that satan's whelp."

"I'm sure Toranaga doesn't. Any more than Yabu has really made any commitment to him."

Suddenly they were distracted by an altercation outside. The door opened and a cowled monk came bare-footed into the room, shaking off Father Soldi. "The blessings of Jesus Christ upon you," he said, his voice rasping with hostility. "May He forgive you your sins."

"Friar Perez—what are you doing here?" dell'Aqua burst out.

"I've come back to this cesspit of a land to proclaim the word of God to the heathen again."

"But you're under Edict never to return on pain of immediate death for inciting to riot. You escaped the Nagasaki martyrdom by a miracle and you were ordered—"

"That was God's will, and a filthy heathen Edict of a dead maniac has nothing to do with me," the monk said. He was a short, lean Spaniard with a long unkempt beard. "I'm here to continue God's work." He glanced at Father Alvito. "How's trade, Father?"

"Fortunately for Spain, very good," Alvito replied icily.

"I don't spend time in the counting house, Father. I spend it with my flock."

"That's commendable," dell'Aqua said sharply. "But spend it where the Pope ordered—outside of Japan. This is *our* exclusive province. And it's also Portuguese territory, not Spanish. Do I have to remind you that three Popes have ordered all denominations out of Japan except us? King Philip also ordered the same."

"Save your breath, Eminence. The work of God surpasses earthly orders. I'm back and I'll throw open the doors of the churches and beseech the multitudes to rise up against the ungodly."

"How many times must you be warned? You can't treat Japan like an Inca protectorate peopled with jungle savages who have neither history nor culture. I forbid you to preach and insist you obey Holy orders."

"We will convert the heathen. Listen, Eminence, there's another hundred of my brothers in Manila waiting for ships here, good Spaniards all, and lots of our glorious conquistadores to protect us if need be. We'll preach openly and we'll wear our robes openly, not skulk about in idolatrous silken shirts like Jesuits!"

"You must not agitate the authorities or you'll reduce Mother Church to ashes!"

"I tell you to your face we're coming back to Japan and we'll stay in Japan. We'll preach the Word in spite of you—in spite of any prelate, bishop, king, or even any pope, for the glory of God!" The monk slammed the door behind him.

Flushed with rage, dell'Aqua poured a glass of Madeira. A little of the wine slopped onto the polished surface of his desk. "Those Spaniards will destroy us all." Dell'Aqua drank slowly, trying to calm himself. At length he said, "Martin, send some of our people to watch him. And you'd better warn Kiyama and Onoshi at once. There's no telling what'll happen if that fool flaunts himself in public."

"Yes, Eminence." At the door Alvito hesitated. "First Blackthorne and now Perez. It's almost too much of a coincidence. Perhaps the Spaniards in Manila knew about Blackthorne and let him come here just to bedevil us."

"Perhaps, but probably not." Dell'Aqua finished his glass and set it down carefully. "In any event, with the help of God and due diligence, neither of them will be permitted to harm the Holy Mother Church—whatever the cost."

CHAPTER 20

I'LL be a God-cursed Spaniard if this isn't the life!"
Blackthorne lay seraphically on his stomach on thick futons, wrapped partially in a cotton kimono, his head propped on his arms. The girl was running her hands over his back, probing his muscles occasionally, soothing his skin and his spirit, making him almost want to purr with pleasure. Another girl was pouring saké into a tiny porcelain cup. A third waited in reserve, holding a lacquer tray with a heaping bamboo basket of deep-fried fish in Portuguese style, another flask of saké, and some chopsticks.

"*Nan desu ka,* Anjin-san?" What is it, Honorable Pilot—what did you say?

"I can't say that in *Nihon-go,* Rako-san." He smiled at the girl who offered the saké. Instead he pointed at the cup. "What's this called? *Namae ka?*"

"*Sabazuki.*" She said it three times and he repeated it and then the other girl, Asa, offered the fish and he shook his head. "*Iyé, domo.*" He did not know how to say "I'm full now" so he tried instead "not hungry now."

"*Ah! Ima hara hette wa oranu,*" Asa explained, correcting him. He said the phrase several times and they all laughed at his pronunciation, but eventually he made it sound right.

I'll never learn this language, he thought. There's nothing to relate the sounds to in English, or even Latin or Portuguese.

"Anjin-san?" Asa offered the tray again.

He shook his head and put his hand on his stomach gravely. But he accepted the saké and drank it down. Sono, the girl who was massaging his back, had stopped, so he took her hand and put it on his neck and pretended to groan with pleasure. She understood at once and continued to massage him.

Each time he finished the little cup it was immediately refilled. Better go easy, he thought, this is the third flask and I can feel the warmth into my toes.

The three girls, Asa, Sono, and Rako, had arrived with the dawn, bringing cha, which Friar Domingo had told him the Chinese sometimes called *t'ee,* and which was the national drink of China and Japan. His sleep had been fitful after the encounter with the assassin but the hot piquant drink had begun to restore him. They had brought small rolled hot towels, slightly scented. When he did not know what they were used for, Rako, the chief of the girls, showed him how to use them on his face and hands.

Then they had escorted him with his four samurai guards to the steaming baths at the far side of this section of the castle and handed him over to the bath attendants. The four guards sweated stoically while he was bathed, his beard trimmed, his hair shampooed and massaged.

Afterwards, he felt miraculously renewed. They gave him another fresh, knee-length cotton kimono and more fresh tabi and the girls were waiting for him again. They led him to another room where Kiri and Mariko were. Mariko said that Lord Toranaga had decided to send the Anjin-san to one of his provinces in the next few days to recuperate and that Lord Toranaga was very pleased with him and there was no need for him to worry about anything for he was in Lord Toranaga's personal care now. Would Anjin-san please also begin to prepare the maps with material that she would provide. There would be other meetings with

213

the Master soon, and the Master had promised that she would be made available soon to answer any questions the Anjin-san might have. Lord Toranaga was very anxious that Blackthorne should learn about the Japanese as he himself was anxious to learn about the outside world, and about navigation and ways of the sea. Then Blackthorne had been led to the doctor. Unlike samurai, doctors wore their hair close-cropped without a queue.

Blackthorne hated doctors and feared them. But this doctor was different. This doctor was gentle and unbelievably clean. European doctors were barbers mostly and uncouth, and as louse-ridden and filthy as everyone else. This doctor touched carefully and peered politely and held Blackthorne's wrist to feel his pulse, looked into his eyes and mouth and ears, and softly tapped his back and his knees and the soles of his feet, his touch and manner soothing. All a European doctor wanted was to look at your tongue and say "Where is the pain?" and bleed you to release the foulnesses from your blood and give you a violent emetic to clean away the foulnesses from your entrails.

Blackthorne hated being bled and purged and every time was worse than before. But this doctor had no scalpels or bleeding bowl nor the foul chemic smell that normally surrounded them, so his heart had begun to slow and he relaxed a little.

The doctor's fingers touched the scars on his thigh interrogatively. Blackthorne made the sound of a gun because a musket ball had passed through his flesh there many years ago. The doctor said *"Ah so desu"* and nodded. More probes, deep but not painful, over his loins and stomach. At length, the doctor spoke to Rako, and she nodded and bowed and thanked him.

"Ichi ban?" Blackthorne had asked, wanting to know if he was all right.

"Hai, Anjin-san."

"Honto ka?"

"Honto."

What a useful word, *honto*—'Is it the truth?' 'Yes, the truth,' Blackthorne thought. *"Domo,* Doctor-san."

"Do itashimashité," the doctor said, bowing. You're welcome—think nothing of it.

Blackthorne bowed back. The girls had led him away and it was not until he was lying on the futons, his cotton kimono loosed, the girl Sono gentling his back, that he remembered he had been naked at the doctor's, in front of the girls and the samurai, and that he had not noticed or felt shame.

"Nan desu ka, Anjin-san?" Rako asked. What is it, Honorable Pilot? Why do you laugh? Her white teeth sparkled and her eyebrows were plucked and painted in a crescent. She wore her dark hair piled high and a pink flowered kimono with a gray-green obi.

"Because I'm happy, Rako-san. But how to tell you? How do I tell you I laughed because I'm happy and the weight's off my head for the first time since I left home. Because my back feels marvelous—all of me feels marvelous. Because I've Toranaga-sama's ear and I've put three fat broadsides into the God-cursed Jesuits and another six into the poxy Portuguese!" Then he jumped up, tied his kimono tight, and began dancing a careless hornpipe, singing a sea shanty to keep time.

Rako and the others were agog. The shoji had slid open instantly and now the samurai guards were equally popeyed. Blackthorne danced and sang mightily until he could contain himself no longer, then he burst out laughing and collapsed. The girls clapped and Rako tried to imitate him, failing miserably, her trailing kimono inhibiting her. The others got up and persuaded him to show them how to do it, and he tried, the three girls standing in a line watching his feet, holding up their kimonos. But they could not, and soon they were all chattering and giggling and fanning themselves.

Abruptly the guards were solemn and bowing low. Toranaga stood in the doorway flanked by Mariko and Kiri and his ever present samurai guards. The girls all knelt, put their hands flat on the floor and bowed, but the laughter did not leave their faces, nor was there any fear in them. Blackthorne bowed politely also, not as low as the women.

"*Konnichi wa* Toranaga-sama," Blackthorne said.

"*Konnichi wa* Anjin-san," Toranaga replied. Then he asked a question.

"My Master says, what were you doing, senhor?" Mariko said.

"It was just a dance, Mariko-san," Blackthorne said, feeling foolish. "It's called a hornpipe. It's a sailors' dance and we sing shanties—songs—at the same time. I was just happy—perhaps it was the saké. I'm sorry, I hope I didn't disturb Toranaga-sama."

She translated.

"My Master says he would like to see the dance and hear the song."

"Now?"

"Of course now."

At once Toranaga sat cross-legged and his small court spread themselves around the room and they looked at Blackthorne expectantly.

There, you fool, Blackthorne told himself. That's what comes of letting your guard down. Now you've got to perform and you know your voice is off and your dancing clumsy.

Even so, he tied his kimono tight and launched himself with gusto, pivoting, kicking, twirling, bouncing, his voice roaring lustily.

More silence.

"My Master says that he's never seen anything like that in his whole life."

"*Arigato goziemashita!*" Blackthorne said, sweating partially from his effort and partially from his embarrassment. Then Toranaga put his swords aside, tucked his kimono high into his belt, and stood beside him. "Lord Toranaga will dance your dance," Mariko said.

"Eh?"

"Please teach him, he says."

So Blackthorne began. He demonstrated the basic step, then repeated it again and again. Toranaga mastered it quickly. Blackthorne was not a little impressed with the agility of the large-bellied, amply buttocked older man.

Then Blackthorne began to sing and to dance and Toranaga joined in, tentatively at first, to the cheers of the onlookers. Then Toranaga threw off his kimono and folded his arms and began to dance with equal verve alongside Blackthorne, who threw off his kimono and sang louder and picked up the tempo, almost overcome by the grotesqueness of what they were doing, but swept along now by the humor of it. Finally Blackthorne did a sort of hop, skip, and jump and stopped. He clapped and bowed to Toranaga and they all clapped for their master, who was very happy.

Toranaga sat down in the center of the room, breathing easily. Immediately Rako sped forward to fan him and the others ran for his kimono. But Toranaga pushed his own kimono toward Blackthorne and took the simple kimono instead.

Mariko said, "My Master says that he would be pleased for you to accept this as a gift." She added, "Here it would be considered a great honor to be given even a very old kimono by one's liege lord."

"*Arigato goziemashita,* Toranaga-sama." Blackthorne bowed low, then said to Mariko, "Yes, I understand the honor he does to me, Mariko-san. Please thank Lord Toranaga with the correct formal words that I unfortunately do not yet know, and tell him I will treasure it and, even more, the honor that he did me in dancing my dance with me."

Toranaga was even more pleased.

With reverence, Kiri and the servant girls helped Blackthorne into their master's kimono and showed Blackthorne how to tie the sash. The kimono was brown silk with the five scarlet crests, the sash white silk.

"Lord Toranaga says he enjoyed the dance. One day he will perhaps show you some of ours. He would like you to learn to speak Japanese as quickly as possible."

"I'd like that too." But even more, Blackthorne thought, I'd like to be in my own clothes, eating my own food in my own cabin in my own ship with my cannon primed, pistols in my belt, and the quarterdeck tilted under a press of sails. "Would you ask Lord Toranaga when I can have my ship back?"

"Senhor?"

"My ship, senhora. Please ask him when I can get my ship back. My crew, too. All her cargo's been removed—there were twenty thousand pieces of eight in the strongbox. I'm sure he'll understand that we're merchants, and though we appreciate his hospitality, we'd like to trade—with the goods we brought with us—and move on homeward. It'll take us almost eighteen months to get home."

"My Master says you have no need to be concerned. Everything will be done as soon as possible. You must first become strong and healthy. You're leaving at dusk."

"Senhora?"

"Lord Toranaga said you were to leave at dusk, senhor. Did I say it wrongly?"

"No, no, not at all, Mariko-san. But an hour or so ago you told me I'd be leaving in a few days."

"Yes, but now he says you will leave tonight." She translated all this to Toranaga, who replied again.

"My Master says it's better and more convenient for you to go tonight. There is no need to worry, Anjin-san, you are in his personal care. He is sending the Lady Kiritsubo to Yedo to prepare for his return. You will go with her."

"Please thank him for me. Is it possible—may I ask if it would be possible to release Friar Domingo? The man has a great deal of knowledge."

She translated this.

"My Master says, so sorry, the man is dead. He sent for him immediately you asked yesterday but he was already dead."

Blackthorne was dismayed. "How did he die?"

"My Master says he died when his name was called out."

"Oh! Poor man."

"My Master says, death and life are the same thing. The priest's soul will wait until the fortieth day and then it will be reborn again. Why be sad? This is the immutable law of nature." She began to say something but changed her mind, adding only, "Buddhists believe that we have many births or rebirths, Anjin-san. Until at length we become perfect and reach nirvana—heaven."

Blackthorne put off his sadness for the moment and concentrated on Toranaga and the present. "May I please ask him if my crew—" He stopped as Toranaga glanced away. A young samurai came hurriedly into the room, bowed to Toranaga, and waited.

Toranaga said, *"Nan ja?"*

Blackthorne understood none of what was said except he thought he caught Father Alvito's nickname "Tsukku." He saw Toranaga's eyes flick across to him and noted the glimmer of a smile, and he wondered if Toranaga had sent for the priest because of what he had told him. I hope so, he thought, and I hope Alvito's in the muck up to his nostrils. Is he or isn't he? Blackthorne decided not to ask

Toranaga though he was tempted greatly.

"*Kare ni matsu yoni,*" Toranaga said curtly.

"*Gyoi.*" The samurai bowed and hurried away. Toranaga turned back to Blackthorne. "*Nan ja,* Anjin-san?"

"You were saying, Captain?" Mariko said. "About your crew?"

"Yes. Can Toranaga-sama take them under his protection too? See that they're well cared for? Will they be sent to Yedo too?"

She asked him. Toranaga stuck his swords in the belt of the short kimono. "My Master says of course their arrangements have already been made. You need have no concern over them. Or over your ship."

"My ship is all right? She's taken care of?"

"Yes. He says the ship is already at Yedo."

Toranaga got up. Everyone began to bow but Blackthorne broke in unexpectedly. "One last thing—" He stopped and cursed himself, realizing that he was being discourteous. Toranaga had clearly terminated the interview and they had all begun to bow but had been stopped by Blackthorne's words and now they were all nonplussed, not knowing whether to complete their bows or to wait, or to start again.

"*Nan ja,* Anjin-san?" Toranaga's voice was brittle and unfriendly, for he too had been momentarily thrown off balance.

"*Gomen nasai,* I'm sorry, Toranaga-sama. I didn't wish to be impolite. I just wanted to ask if the Lady Mariko would be allowed to talk with me for a few moments before I go? It would help me."

She asked him.

Toranaga merely grunted an imperious affirmative and walked out, followed by Kiri and his personal guards.

Touchy bastards, all of you, Blackthorne said to himself. Jesus God, you've got to be so careful here. He wiped his forehead with his sleeve, and saw the immediate distress on Mariko's face. Rako hurriedly proffered a small kerchief that they always seemed to have ready from a seemingly inexhaustible supply, tucked secretly somewhere into the back of their obis. Then he realized that he was wearing "the Master's" kimono and that you don't, obviously, wipe your sweaty forehead with "the Master's" sleeve, by God, so you've committed another blasphemy! I'll never learn, never—Jesus God in Heaven—never!

"Anjin-san?" Rako was offering some saké.

He thanked her and drank it down. Immediately she refilled it. He noticed a sheen of perspiration on all their foreheads.

"*Gomen nasai,*" he said to all of them, apologizing, and he took the cup and offered it to Mariko with good humor. "I don't know if it's a polite custom or not, but would you like some saké? Is that allowed? Or do I have to bang my head on the floor?"

She laughed. "Oh yes, it is quite polite and no, please don't hurt your head. There's no need to apologize to me, Captain. Men don't apologize to ladies. Whatever they do is correct. At least, that is what we ladies believe." She explained what she had said to the girls and they nodded as gravely but their eyes were dancing. "You had no way of knowing, Anjin-san," Mariko continued, then took a tiny sip of the saké and gave him back the cup. "Thank you, but no, I won't have any more saké, thank you. Saké goes straight to my head and to my knees. But you learn quickly—it must be very hard for you. Don't worry, Anjin-san, Lord Toranaga told me that he found your aptitude exceptional. He would never have given you his kimono if he wasn't most pleased."

"Did he send for Tsukku-san?"

"Father Alvito?"

"Yes."

"You should have asked him, Captain. He did not tell me. In that he would be quite wise, for women don't have wisdom or knowledge in political things."

"*Ah, so desu ka?* I wish all our women were equally—wise."

Mariko fanned herself, kneeling comfortably, her legs curled under her. "Your dance was very excellent, Anjin-san. Do your ladies dance the same way?"

"No. Just the men. That was a man's dance, a sailor's dance."

"Since you wish to ask me questions, may I ask you some first?"

"Certainly."

"What is the lady, your wife, like?"

"She's twenty-nine. Tall compared with you. By our measurements, I'm six feet two inches, she's about five feet eight inches, you're about five feet, so she'd be a head taller than you and equally bigger—equally proportioned. Her hair's the color of . . ." He pointed at the unstained polished cedar beams and all their eyes went there, then came back to him again. "About that color. Fair with a touch of red. Her eyes are blue, much bluer than mine, blue-green. She wears her hair long and flowing most of the time."

Mariko interpreted this for the others and they all sucked in their breaths, looked at the cedar beams, back to him once more, the samurai guards also listening intently. A question from Rako.

"Rako-san asks if she is the same as us in her body?"

"Yes. But her hips would be larger and more curved, her waist more pronounced and—well, generally our women are more rounded and have much heavier breasts."

"Are all your women—and men—so much taller than us?"

"Generally yes. But some of our people are as small as you. I think your smallness delightful. Very pleasing."

Asa asked something and all their interests quickened.

"Asa asks, in matters of the pillow, how would you compare your women with ours?"

"Sorry, I don't understand."

"Oh, please excuse me. The pillow—in intimate matters. Pillowing's our way of referring to the physical joining of man and woman. It's more polite than fornication, *neh?*"

Blackthorne squelched his embarrassment and said, "I've, er, I've only had one, er, pillow experience here—that was, er, in the village—and I don't remember it too clearly because, er, I was so exhausted by our voyage that I was half dreaming and half awake. But it, er, seemed to me to be very satisfactory."

Mariko frowned. "You've pillowed only once since you arrived?"

"Yes."

"You must be feeling very constricted, *neh?* One of these ladies would be delighted to pillow with you, Anjin-san. Or all of them, if you wish."

"Eh?"

"Certainly. If you don't want one of them, there's no need to worry, they'd certainly not be offended. Just tell me the sort of lady you'd like and we'll make all the arrangements."

"Thank you," Blackthorne said. "But not now."

"Are you sure? Please excuse me, but Kiritsubo-san has given specific instructions that your health is to be protected and improved. How can you be healthy without pillowing? It's very important for a man, *neh?* Oh, very yes."

"Thank you, but I'm—perhaps later."

"You'd have plenty of time. I would be glad to come back later. There will be plenty of time to talk, if you wish. You'd have at least four sticks of time," she said helpfully. "You don't have to leave until sunset."

"Thanks. But not now," Blackthorne said, flattened by the bluntness and lack of delicacy of the suggestion.

"They'd really like to accommodate you, Anjin-san. Oh! Perhaps—perhaps you would prefer a boy?"

"Eh?"

"A boy. It's just as simple if that's what you wish." Her smile was guileless, her voice matter-of-fact.

"Eh?"

"What's the matter?"

"Are you seriously offering me a boy?"

"Why, yes, Anjin-san. What's the matter? I only said we'd send a boy here if *you* wished it."

"I don't wish it!" Blackthorne felt the blood in his face. "Do I look like a God-cursed sodomite?"

His words slashed around the room. They all stared at him transfixed. Mariko bowed abjectly, kept her head to the floor. "Please forgive me, I've made a terrible error. Oh, I've offended where I was only trying to please. I've never talked to a—to a foreigner other than one of the Holy Fathers before, so I've no way of knowing your—your intimate customs. I was never taught about them, Anjin-san—the Fathers did not discuss them. Here some men want boys sometimes—priests have boys from time to time, ours and some of yours—I foolishly presumed that your customs were the same as ours."

"I'm not a priest and it's not our general custom."

The samurai leader, Kazu Oan, was watching angrily. He was charged with the barbarian's safety and with the barbarian's health and he had seen, with his own eyes, the incredible favor that Lord Toranaga had shown to the Anjin-san, and now the Anjin-san was furious. "What's the matter with him?" he asked challengingly, for obviously the stupid woman had said something to offend his very important prisoner.

Mariko explained what had been said and what the Anjin-san had replied. "I really don't understand what he's irritated about, Oan-san," she told him.

Oan scratched his head in disbelief. "He's like a mad ox just because you offered him a boy?"

"Yes."

"So sorry, but were you polite? Did you use a wrong word, perhaps?"

"Oh, no, Oan-san, I'm quite sure. I feel terrible. I'm obviously responsible."

"It must be something else. What?"

"No, Oan-san. It was just that."

"I'll never understand these barbarians," Oan said exasperatedly. "For all our sakes, please calm him down, Mariko-san. It must be because he hasn't pillowed for such a long time. You," he ordered Sono, "you get more saké, hot saké, and hot towels! You, Rako, rub the devil's neck." The maids fled to obey. A sudden thought: "I wonder if it's because he's impotent. His story about pillowing in the village was vague enough, *neh?* Perhaps the poor fellow's enraged because he can't pillow at all and you brought the subject up?"

"So sorry, I don't think so. The doctor said he's very well endowed."

"If he was impotent—that would explain it, *neh?* It'd be enough to make me shout too. Yes! Ask him."

Mariko immediately did as she was ordered, and Oan was horrified as the blood rushed into the barbarian's face again and a spate of foul-sounding barbarian filled the room.

"He—he said 'no.' " Mariko's voice was barely a whisper.

"All that just meant 'no'?"

"They—they use many descriptive curse words when they get excited."

Oan was beginning to sweat with anxiety for he was responsible. "Calm him down!"

One of the other samurai, an older soldier, said helpfully, "Oan-san, perhaps he's one of those that likes dogs, *neh?* We heard some strange stories in Korea about the Garlic Eaters. Yes, they like dogs and . . . I remember now, yes, dogs and ducks. Perhaps these golden heads are like the Garlic Eaters, they stink like them, hey? Maybe he wants a duck."

Oan said, "Mariko-san, ask him! No, perhaps you'd better not. Just calm—" He stopped short. Hiro-matsu was approaching from the far corner. "Salute," he said crisply, trying to keep his voice from quaking because old Iron Fist, in the best of circumstances a disciplinarian, had been like a tiger with boils on his arse for the last week and today he had been even worse. Ten men had been demoted for untidiness, the entire night watch paraded in ignominy throughout the castle, two samurai ordered to commit seppuku because they were late for their watch, and four night-soil collectors thrown off the battlements for spilling part of a container in the castle garden.

"Is he behaving himself, Mariko-san?" Oan heard Iron Fist ask irritably. He was certain the stupid woman who had caused all this trouble was going to blurt out the truth, which would have surely lifted their heads, rightfully, off their shoulders.

To his relief he heard her say, "Yes, Lord. Everything is fine, thank you."

"You're ordered to leave with Kiritsubo-san."

"Yes, Lord." As Hiro-matsu continued with his patrol, Mariko brooded over why she was being sent away. Was it merely to interpret for Kiri with the barbarian on the voyage? Surely that's not so important? Were Toranaga's other ladies going? The Lady Sazuko? Isn't it dangerous for Sazuko to go by sea now? Am I to go alone with Kiri, or is my husband going also? If he stays—and it would be his duty to stay with his lord—who will look after his house? Why do we have to go by ship? Surely the Tokaidō Road is still safe? Surely Ishido won't harm us? Yes, he would—think of our value as hostages, the Lady Sazuko, Kiritsubo, and the others. Is that why we're to be sent by sea?

Mariko had always hated the sea. Even the sight of it almost made her sick. But if I am to go, I am to go, and there's the end of it. *Karma.* She turned her mind off the inevitable to the immediate problem of the baffling foreign barbarian who was causing her nothing but grief.

When Iron Fist had vanished around the corner, Oan raised his head and all of them sighed. Asa came scurrying down the corridor with the saké, Sono close behind with the hot towels.

They watched while the barbarian was ministered to. They saw the taut mask of his face, and the way he accepted the saké without pleasure and the hot towels with cold thanks.

"Oan-san, why not let one of the women send for the duck?" the old samurai whispered agreeably. "We just put it down. If he wants it everything's fine, if not he'll pretend he hasn't seen it."

Mariko shook her head. "Perhaps we shouldn't take this risk. It seems, Oan-san, his type of barbarian has some aversion to talking about pillowing, *neh?* He *is* the first of his kind to come here, so we'll have to feel our way."

"I agree," Oan said. "He was quite gentle until that was mentioned." He glowered at Asa.

"I'm sorry, Oan-san. You're quite right, it was entirely my fault," Asa said at once, bowing, her head almost to the floor.

"Yes. I shall report the matter to Kiritsubo-san."

"Oh!"

"I really think the Mistress should also be told to take care about discussing pillowing with this man," Mariko said diplomatically. "You're very wise, Oan-san. Yes. But perhaps in a way Asa was a fortunate instrument to save the Lady Kiritsubo and even Lord Toranaga from an awful embarrassment! Just think what would have happened if Kiritsubo-san herself had asked that question in front of Lord Toranaga yesterday! If the barbarian had acted like that in front of him . . ."

Oan winced. "Blood would have flowed! You're quite right, Mariko-san, Asa should be thanked. I will explain to Kiritsubo-san that she was fortunate."

Mariko offered Blackthorne more saké.

"No, thank you."

"Again I apologize for my stupidity. You wanted to ask me some questions?"

Blackthorne had watched them talking among themselves, annoyed at not being able to understand, furious that he couldn't curse them roundly for their insults or bang the guards' heads together. "Yes. You said that sodomy is normal here?"

"Oh, forgive me, may we please discuss other things?"

"Certainly, senhora. But first, so I can understand you, let's finish this subject. Sodomy's normal here, you said?"

"Everything to do with pillowing is normal," she said defiantly, prodded by his lack of manners and obvious imbecility, remembering that Toranaga had told her to be informative about nonpolitical things but to recount to him later all questions asked. Also, she was not to take any nonsense from him, for the Anjin was still a barbarian, a probable pirate, and under a formal death sentence which was presently held in abeyance at Toranaga's pleasure. "Pillowing is quite normal. And as to a man going with another man or boy, what has this got to do with anyone but them? What harm does it do them, or others—or me or you? None!" What am I, she thought, an illiterate outcast without brains? A stupid tradesman to be intimidated by a mere barbarian? No. I'm samurai! Yes, you are, Mariko, but you're also very foolish! You're a woman and you must treat him like any man if he is to be controlled: Flatter him and agree with him and honey him. You forget your weapons. Why does he make you act like a twelve-year-old child?

Deliberately she softened her tone. "But if you think—"

"Sodomy's a foul sin, an evil, God-cursed abomination, and those bastards who practice it are the dregs of the world!" Blackthorne overrode her, still smarting under the insult that she had believed he could be one of those. Christ's blood, how could she? Get hold of yourself, he told himself. You're sounding like a pox-ridden fanatic puritan or a Calvinist! And why are you so fanatic against them? Isn't it because they're ever present at sea, that most sailors have tried it that way, for how else can they stay sane with so many months at sea? Isn't it because you've been tempted and you've hated yourself for being tempted? Isn't it because when you were young you had to fight to protect yourself and once you were held down and almost raped, but you broke away and killed one of the bastards, the knife snapped in his throat, you twelve, and this the first death on your long list of deaths? "It's a God-cursed sin—and absolutely against the laws of God and man!"

"Surely those are Christian words which apply to other things?" she retorted acidly, in spite of herself, nettled by his complete uncouthness. "Sin? Where is the sin in that?"

"You should know. You're Catholic, aren't you? You were brought up by Jesuits, weren't you?"

"A Holy Father educated me to speak Latin and Portuguese and to write Latin and Portuguese. I don't understand the meaning *you* attach to Catholic but I am a Christian, and have been a Christian for almost ten years now, and no, they did not talk to us about pillowing. I've never read your pillow books—only religious books. Pillowing a sin? How could it be? How can anything that gives a human pleasure be sinful?"

"Ask Father Alvito!"

I wish I could, she thought in turmoil. But I am ordered not to discuss anything that is said with anyone but Kiri and my Lord Toranaga. I've asked God and the Madonna to help me but they haven't spoken to me. I only know that ever since you came here, there has been nothing but trouble. I've had nothing but trouble. . . . "If it's a sin as you say, why is it so many of our priests do it and always have? Some Buddhist sects even recommend it as a form of worship. Isn't the moment of the Clouds and the Rain as near to heaven as mortals can get? Priests are not evil men, not all of them. And some of the Holy Fathers have been known to enjoy pillowing this way also. Are they evil? Of course not! Why should they be deprived of an ordinary pleasure if they're forbidden women? It's nonsense to say that anything to do with pillowing is a sin and God-cursed!"

"Sodomy's an abomination, against all law! Ask your confessor!"

You're the one who's the abomination—you, Captain Pilot, Mariko wanted to shout. How dare you be so rude and how can you be so moronic! Against God, you said? What absurdity! Against your evil god, perhaps. You claim to be a Christian but you're obviously not, you're obviously a liar and a cheat. Perhaps you do know extraordinary things and have been to strange places, but you're no Christian and you blaspheme. Are you sent by Satan? Sin? How grotesque!

You rant over normal things and act like a madman. You upset the Holy Fathers, upset Lord Toranaga, cause strife between us, unsettle our beliefs, and torment us with insinuations about what is true and what isn't—knowing that we can't prove the truth immediately.

I want to tell you that I despise you and all barbarians. Yes, barbarians have beset me all my life. Didn't they hate my father because he distrusted them and openly begged the Dictator Goroda to throw them all out of our land? Didn't barbarians pour poison into the Dictator's mind so he began to hate my father, his most loyal general, the man who had helped him even more than General Nakamura or Lord Toranaga? Didn't barbarians cause the Dictator to insult my father, sending my poor father insane, forcing him to do the unthinkable and thus cause all my agonies?

Yes, they did all that and more. But also they brought the peerless Word of God, and in the dark hours of my need when I was brought back from hideous exile to even more hideous life, the Father-Visitor showed me the Path, opened my eyes and my soul and baptized me. And the Path gave me strength to endure, filled my heart with limitless peace, released me from perpetual torment, and blessed me with the promise of Eternal Salvation.

Whatever happens I am in the Hand of God. Oh, Madonna, give me thy peace and help this poor sinner to overcome thine enemy.

"I apologize for my rudeness," she said. "You're right to be angry. I'm just a foolish woman. Please be patient and forgive my stupidity, Anjin-san."

At once Blackthorne's anger began to fade. How can any man be angry for long with a woman if she openly admits she was wrong and he right? "I apologize too, Mariko-san," he said, a little mollified, "but with us, to suggest a man is a bugger, a sodomite, is the worst kind of insult."

Then you're all childish and foolish as well as vile, uncouth, and without manners, but what can one expect from a barbarian, she told herself, and said, outwardly penitent, "Of course you're right. I meant no harm, Anjin-sama, please accept my apologies. Oh yes," she sighed, her voice so delicately honeyed that even her husband in one of his most foul moods would have been soothed, "oh yes, it was my fault entirely. So sorry."

The sun had touched the horizon and still Father Alvito waited in the audience room, the rutters heavy in his hands.

God damn Blackthorne, he thought.

This was the first time that Toranaga had ever kept him waiting, the first time in years that he had waited for any *daimyo,* even the Taikō. During the last eight years of the Taikō's rule, he had been given the incredible privilege of immediate access, just as with Toranaga. But with the Taikō the privilege had been earned because of his fluency in Japanese and because of his business acumen. His knowledge of the inner workings of international trade had actively helped to increase the Taikō's incredible fortune. Though the Taikō was almost illiterate, his grasp of language was vast and his political knowledge immense. So Alvito had happily sat at the foot of the Despot to teach and to learn, and, if it was the will of God, to convert. This was the specific job he had been meticulously trained for by dell'Aqua, who had provided the best practical teachers among all the Jesuits and among the Portuguese traders in Asia. Alvito had become the Taikō's confidant, one of the four persons—and the only foreigner—ever to see all the Taikō's personal treasure rooms.

Within a few hundred paces was the castle donjon, the keep. It towered seven stories, protected by a further multiplicity of walls and doors and fortifications. On the fourth story were seven rooms with iron doors. Each was crammed with gold bullion and chests of golden coins. In the story above were the rooms of silver, bursting with ingots and chests of coins. And in the one above that were the rare silks and potteries and swords and armor—the treasure of the Empire.

At our present reckoning, Alvito thought, the value must be at least fifty million ducats, more than one year's worth of revenue from the entire Spanish Empire, the Portuguese Empire, and Europe together. The greatest personal fortune of cash on earth.

Isn't this the great prize? he reasoned. Doesn't whoever controls Osaka Castle control this unbelievable wealth? And doesn't this wealth therefore give him power over the land? Wasn't Osaka made impregnable just to protect the wealth? Wasn't the land bled to build Osaka Castle, to make it inviolate to protect the gold, to hold it in trust against the coming of age of Yaemon?

With a hundredth part we could build a cathedral in every city, a church in every town, a mission in every village throughout the land. If only we could get it, to use it for the glory of God!

The Taikō had loved power. And he had loved gold for the power it gave over men. The treasure was the gleaning of sixteen years of undisputed power, from the immense, obligatory gifts that all *daimyos,* by custom, were expected to offer yearly, and from his own fiefs. By right of conquest, the Taikō personally owned one fourth of all the land. His personal annual income was in excess of five million koku. And because he was Lord of all Japan with the Emperor's mandate, in theory he owned all revenue of all fiefs. He taxed no one. But all *daimyos,* all samurai, all peasants, all artisans, all merchants, all robbers, all outcasts, all barbarians, even *eta,* contributed voluntarily, in great measure. For their own safety.

So long as the fortune is intact and Osaka is intact and Yaemon the *de facto* custodian, Alvito told himself, Yaemon will rule when he is of age in spite of Toranaga, Ishido, or anyone.

A pity the Taikō's dead. With all his faults, we knew the devil we had to deal with. Pity, in fact, that Goroda was murdered, for he was a real friend to us. But he's dead, and so is the Taikō, and now we have new pagans to bend —Toranaga and Ishido.

Alvito remembered the night that the Taikō had died. He had been invited by the Taikō to keep vigil—he, together with Yodoko-sama, the Taikō's wife, and the Lady Ochiba, his consort and mother of the Heir. They had watched and waited long in the balm of that endless summer's night.

Then the dying began, and came to pass.

"His spirit's gone. He's in the hands of God now," he had said gently when he was sure. He had made the sign of the cross and blessed the body.

"May Buddha take my Lord into his keeping and rebirth him quickly so that he will take back the Empire into his hands once more," Yodoko had said in silent tears. She was a nice woman, a patrician samurai who had been a faithful wife and counselor for forty-four of her fifty-nine years of life. She had closed the eyes and made the corpse dignified, which was her privilege. Sadly she had made an obeisance three times and then she had left him and the Lady Ochiba.

The dying had been easy. For months the Taikō had been sick and tonight the end was expected. A few hours ago he had opened his eyes and smiled at Ochiba and at Yodoko, and had whispered, his voice like a thread: "Listen, this is my death poem:

"Like dew I was born
Like dew I vanish
Osaka Castle and all that I have ever done
Is but a dream
Within a dream."

A last smile, so tender, from the Despot to them and to him. "Guard my son, all of you." And then the eyes had opaqued forever.

Father Alvito remembered how moved he had been by the last poem, so typical of the Taikō. He had hoped because he had been invited that, on the threshold, the Lord of Japan would have relented and would have accepted the Faith and the Sacrament that he had toyed with so many times. But it was not to be. "You've lost the Kingdom of God forever, poor man," he had muttered sadly, for he had admired the Taikō as a military and political genius.

"What if your Kingdom of God's up a barbarian's back passage?" Lady Ochiba had said.

"What?" He was not certain he had heard correctly, revolted by her unexpected hissing malevolence. He had known Lady Ochiba for almost twelve years, since she was fifteen, when the Taikō had first taken her to consort, and she had ever been docile and subservient, hardly saying a word, always smiling sweetly and happy. But now . . .

"I said, 'What if your God's kingdom's in a barbarian's back passage?' "

"May God forgive you! Your Master's dead only a few moments—"

"The Lord my Master's dead, so your influence over him is dead. *Neh?* He wanted you here, very good, that was his right. But now he's in the Great Void and commands no more. Now I command. Priest, you stink, you always have, and your foulness pollutes the air. Now get out of my castle and leave us to our grief!"

The stark candlelight had flickered across her face. She was one of the most beautiful women in the land. Involuntarily he had made the sign of the cross against her evil.

Her laugh was chilling. "Go away, priest, and never come back. Your days are numbered!"

"No more than yours. I am in the hands of God, Lady. Better you take heed of Him, Eternal Salvation can be yours if you believe."

"Eh? You're in the hands of God? The Christian God, *neh?* Perhaps you are. Perhaps not. What will you do, priest, if when you're dead you discover there is no God, that there's no hell and your Eternal Salvation just a dream within a dream?"

"I believe! I believe in God and in the Resurrection and in the Holy Ghost!" he said aloud. "The Christian promises are true. They're true, they're true—I believe!"

"Nan ja, Tsukku-san?"

For a moment he only heard the Japanese and it had no meaning for him. Toranaga was standing in the doorway surrounded by his guards.

Father Alvito bowed, collecting himself, sweat on his back and face. "I am sorry to have come uninvited. I—I was just daydreaming. I was remembering that I've had the good fortune to witness so many things here in Japan. My whole life seems to have been here and nowhere else."

"That's been our gain, Tsukku-san."

Toranaga walked tiredly to the dais and sat on the simple cushion. Silently the guards arranged themselves in a protective screen.

"You arrived here in the third year of Tensho, didn't you?"

"No, Sire, it was the fourth. The Year of the Rat," he replied, using their counting, which had taken him months to understand. All the years were measured from a particular year that was chosen by the ruling Emperor. A catastrophe or a godsend might end an era or begin one, at his whim. Scholars were ordered to select a name of particularly good omen from the ancient books of China for the new era which might last a year or fifty years. Tenshō meant "Heaven Righteousness." The previous year had been the time of the great tidal wave when two hundred thousand had died. And each year was given a number as well as a name—one of the same succession as the hours of the day: Hare, Dragon, Snake, Horse, Goat, Monkey, Cock, Dog, Boar, Rat, Ox and Tiger. The first year of Tensho had fallen in the Year of the Cock, so it followed that 1576 was the Year of the Rat in the Fourth Year of Tensho.

"Much has happened in those twenty-four years, *neh,* old friend?"

"Yes, Sire."

"Yes. The rise of Goroda and his death. The rise of the Taikō and his death. And now?" The words ricocheted off the walls.

"That is in the hands of the Infinite." Alvito used a word that could mean God, and also could mean Buddha.

"Neither the Lord Goroda nor the Lord Taikō believed in any gods, or any Infinite."

"Didn't the Lord Buddha say there are many paths to nirvana, Sire?"

"Ah, Tsukku-san, you're a wise man. How is someone so young so wise?"

"I wish sincerely I was, Sire. Then I could be of more help."

"You wanted to see me?"

"Yes. I thought it important enough to come uninvited."

Alvito took out Blackthorne's rutters and placed them on the floor in front of him, giving the explanations dell'Aqua had suggested. He saw Toranaga's face harden and he was glad of it.

"Proof of his *piracy?"*

"Yes, Sire. The rutters even contain the exact words of their orders, which include: 'if necessary to land in force and claim any territory reached or discovered.' If you wish I can make an exact translation of all the pertinent passages."

"Make a translation of everything. Quickly," Toranaga said.

"There's something else the Father-Visitor thought you should know." Alvito told Toranaga everything about the maps and reports and the Black Ship as had been arranged, and he was delighted to see the pleased reaction.

"Excellent," Toranaga said. "Are you sure the Black Ship will be early? Absolutely sure?"

"Yes," Alvito answered firmly. Oh, God, let it happen as we hope!

"Good. Tell your liege lord that I look forward to reading his reports. Yes. I imagine it will take some months for him to obtain the correct facts?"

"He said he would prepare the reports as soon as possible. We will be sending you the maps as you wanted. Would it be possible for the Captain-General to have his clearances soon? That would help enormously if the Black Ship is to come early, Lord Toranaga."

"You guarantee the ship will arrive early?"

"No man can guarantee the wind and storm and sea. But the ship will leave Macao early."

"You will have them before sunset. Is there anything else? I won't be available for three days, until after the conclusion of the meeting of the Regents."

"No, Sire. Thank you. I pray that the Infinite will keep you safe, as always." Alvito bowed and waited for his dismissal, but instead, Toranaga dismissed his guards.

This was the first time Alvito had ever seen a *daimyo* unattended.

"Come and sit here, Tsukku-san." Toranaga pointed beside him, on the dais.

Alvito had never been invited onto the dais before. Is this a vote of confidence —or a sentence?

"War is coming," Toranaga said.

"Yes," he replied, and he thought, this war will never end.

"The Christian Lords Onoshi and Kiyama are strangely opposed to my wishes."

"I cannot answer for any *daimyo,* Sire."

"There are bad rumors, *neh?* About them, and about the other Christian *daimyos.* "

"Wise men will always have the interests of the Empire at heart."

"Yes. But in the meantime, against my will, the Empire is being split into two camps. Mine and Ishido's. So all interests in the Empire lie on one side or another. There is no middle course. Where do the interests of the Christians lie?"

"On the side of peace. Christianity is a religion, Sire, not a political ideology."

"Your Father-Giant is head of your Church here. I hear you speak—you can speak in this Pope's name."

"We are forbidden to involve ourselves in your politics, Sire."

"You think Ishido will favor you?" Toranaga's voice hardened. "He's totally opposed to your religion. I've always shown you favor. Ishido wants to implement the Taikō's Expulsion Edicts at once and close the land totally to all barbarians. I want an expanding trade."

"We do not control any of the Christian *daimyos.* "

"How do I influence them, then?"

"I don't know enough to attempt to counsel you."

"You know enough, old friend, to understand that if Kiyama and Onoshi stand against me alongside Ishido and the rest of his rabble, all other Christian *daimyos* will soon follow them—then twenty men stand against me for every one of mine."

"If war comes, I will pray you win."

"I'll need more than prayers if twenty men oppose one of mine."

"Is there no way to avoid war? It will never end once it starts."

"I believe that too. Then everyone loses—we and the barbarian and the Christian Church. But if all Christian *daimyos* sided with me now—openly—there would be no war. Ishido's ambitions would be permanently curbed. Even if he raised his standard and revolted, the Regents could stamp him out like a rice maggot."

Alvito felt the noose tightening around his throat. "We are here only to spread the Word of God. Not to interfere in your politics, Sire."

"Your previous leader offered the services of the Christian *daimyos* of Kyushu to the Taikō before we had subdued that part of the Empire."

"He was mistaken to do so. He had no authority from the Church or from the *daimyos* themselves."

"He offered to give the Taikō ships, Portuguese ships, to transport our troops to Kyushu, offered Portuguese soldiers with guns to help us. Even against Korea and against China."

"Again, Sire, he did it mistakenly, without authority from anyone."

"Soon everyone will have to choose sides, Tsukku-san. Yes. Very soon."

Alvito felt the threat physically. "I am always ready to serve you."

"If I lose, will you die with me? Will you commit *jenshi*—will you follow me, or come with me into death, like a loyal retainer?"

"My life is in the hands of God. So is my death."

"Ah, yes. Your Christian God!" Toranaga moved his swords slightly. Then he leaned forward. "Onoshi and Kiyama committed to me, within forty days, and the Council of Regents will repeal the Taikō's Edicts."

How far dare I go? Alvito asked himself helplessly. How far? "We cannot influence them as you believe."

"Perhaps your leader should order them. *Order them!* Ishido will betray you and them. I know him for what he is. So will the Lady Ochiba. Isn't she already influencing the Heir against you?"

Yes, Alvito wanted to shout. But Onoshi and Kiyama have secretly obtained Ishido's sworn commitment in writing to let them appoint all of the Heir's tutors, one of whom will be a Christian. And Onoshi and Kiyama have sworn a Holy Oath that they're convinced you will betray the Church, once you have eliminated Ishido. "The Father-Visitor cannot order them, Lord. It would be an unforgivable interference with your politics."

"Onoshi and Kiyama in forty days, the Taikō's Edicts repealed—and no more of the foul priests. The Regents will forbid them to come to Japan."

"What?"

"You and your priests only. None of the others—the stenching, begging Black Clothes—the barefoot hairies! The ones who shout stupid threats and create nothing but open trouble. Them. You can have all their heads if you want them—the ones who are here."

Alvito's whole being cried caution. Never had Toranaga been so open. One slip now and you'll offend him and make him the Church's enemy forever.

Think what Toranaga's offering! Exclusivity throughout the Empire! The one thing that would guarantee the purity of the Church and her safety while she is growing strong. The one thing beyond price. The one thing no one can provide—not even the Pope! No one—except Toranaga. With Kiyama and Onoshi supporting him openly, Toranaga could smash Ishido and dominate the Council.

Father Alvito would never have believed that Toranaga would be so blunt. Or offer so much. Could Onoshi and Kiyama be made to reverse themselves? Those two hate each other. For reasons only they know they have joined to oppose Toranaga. Why? What would make them betray Ishido?

"I'm not qualified to answer you, Sire, or to speak on such a matter, *neh?* I only tell you our purpose is to save souls," he said.

"I hear my son Naga's interested in your Christian Faith."

Is Toranaga threatening or is he offering? Alvito asked himself. Is he offering to allow Naga to accept the Faith—what a gigantic coup that would be—or is he saying, "Unless you cooperate I will order him to cease"? "The Lord, your son, is one of many nobles who have open minds about religion, Sire."

Alvito suddenly realized the enormity of the dilemma that Toranaga faced. He's trapped—he has to make an arrangement with us, he thought exultantly. He has to try! Whatever we want, he has to give us—if *we* want to make an arrangement with *him*. At long last he openly admits the Christian *daimyos* hold the balance of power! Whatever we want! What else could we have? Nothing at all. Except . . .

Deliberately he dropped his eyes to the rutters that he had laid before Toranaga. He watched his hand reach out and put the rutters safely in the sleeve of his kimono.

"Ah, yes, Tsukku-san," Toranaga said, his voice eerie and exhausted. "Then there's the new barbarian—the pirate. The enemy of your country. They will be coming here soon, in numbers, won't they? They can be discouraged—or encouraged. Like this one pirate. *Neh?*"

Father Alvito knew that now they had everything. Should I ask for Blackthorne's head on a silver platter like the head of St. John the Baptist to seal this bargain? Should I ask for permission to build a cathedral at Yedo, or one within the walls of Osaka Castle? For the first time in his life he felt himself floundering, rudderless in the reach for power.

We want no more than is offered! I wish I could settle the bargain now! If it were up to me alone, I would gamble. I know Toranaga and I would gamble on him. I would agree to try and I'd swear a Holy Oath. Yes, I would excommunicate Onoshi or Kiyama if they would not agree, to gain those concessions for Mother Church. Two souls for tens of thousands, for hundreds of thousands, for millions. That's fair! I would say, Yes, yes, yes, for the Glory of God. But I can settle nothing, as you well know. I'm only a messenger, and part of my message . . .

"I need help, Tsukku-san. I need it now."

"All that I can do, I will do, Toranaga-sama. You have my promise."

Then Toranaga said with finality, "I will wait forty days. Yes. Forty days."

Alvito bowed. He noticed that Toranaga returned the bow lower and more formally than he had ever done before, almost as though he were bowing to the Taikō himself. The priest got up shakily. Then he was outside the room, walking up the corridor. His step quickened. He began to hurry.

Toranaga watched the Jesuit from the embrasure as he crossed the garden, far below. The shoji edged open again but he cursed his guards away and ordered them, on pain of death, to leave him alone. His eyes followed Alvito intently, through the fortified gate, out into the forecourt, until the priest was lost in the maze of innerworks.

And then, in the lonely silence, Toranaga began to smile. And he tucked up his kimono and began to dance. It was a hornpipe.

CHAPTER 21

Just after dusk Kiri waddled nervously down the steps, two maids in attendance. She headed for her curtained litter that stood beside the garden hut. A voluminous cloak covered her traveling kimono and made her appear even more bulky, and a vast, wide-brimmed hat was tied under her jowls.

The Lady Sazuko was waiting patiently for her on the veranda, heavily pregnant, Mariko nearby. Blackthorne was leaning against the wall near the fortified gate. He wore a belted kimono of the Browns and tabi socks and military thongs. In the forecourt, outside the gate, the escort of sixty heavily armed samurai was drawn up in neat lines, every third man carrying a flare. At the head of these soldiers Yabu talked with Buntaro—Mariko's husband—a short, thickset, almost neckless man. Both were attired in chain mail with bows and quivers over their shoulders, and Buntaro wore a horned steel war helmet. Porters and kaga-men squatted patiently in well-disciplined silence near the multitudinous baggage.

The promise of summer floated on the slight breeze, but no one noticed it except Blackthorne, and even he was conscious of the tension that surrounded them all. And too, he was intensely aware that he alone was unarmed.

Kiri plodded over to the veranda. "You shouldn't be waiting in the cold, Sazuko-san. You'll catch a chill! You must remember the child now. These spring nights are still filled with damp."

"I'm not cold, Kiri-san. It's a lovely night and it's my pleasure."

"Is everything all right?"

"Oh, yes. Everything's perfect."

"I wish I weren't going. Yes. I hate going."

"There's no need to worry," Mariko said reassuringly, joining them. She wore a similar wide-brimmed hat, but hers was bright where Kiri's was somber. "You'll enjoy getting back to Yedo. Our Master will be following in a few days."

"Who knows what tomorrow will bring, Mariko-san?"

"Tomorrow is in the hands of God."

"Tomorrow will be a lovely day, and if it isn't, it isn't!" Sazuko said. "Who cares about tomorrow? *Now* is good. You're beautiful and we'll all miss you, Kiri-san, and you, Mariko-san!" She glanced at the gateway, distracted, as Buntaro shouted angrily at one of the samurai, who had dropped a flare.

Yabu, senior to Buntaro, was nominally in charge of the party. He had seen Kiri arrive and strutted back through the gate. Buntaro followed.

"Oh, Lord Yabu—Lord Buntaro," Kiri said with a flustered bow. "I'm so sorry to have kept you waiting. Lord Toranaga was going to come down, but in the end, decided not to. You are to leave now, he said. Please accept my apologies."

"None are necessary." Yabu wanted to be quit of the castle as soon as possible, and quit of Osaka, and back in Izu. He still could hardly believe that he was leaving with his head, with the barbarian, with the guns, with everything. He had sent urgent messages by carrier pigeon to his wife in Yedo to make sure that all was prepared at Mishima, his capital, and to Omi at the village of Anjiro. "Are you ready?"

Tears glittered in Kiri's eyes. "Just let me catch my breath and then I'll get into the litter. Oh, I wish I didn't have to go!" She looked around, seeking

229

Blackthorne, finally catching sight of him in the shadows. "Who is responsible for the Anjin-san? Until we get to the ship?"

Buntaro said testily, "I've ordered him to walk beside my wife's litter. If she can't keep him in control, I will."

"Perhaps, Lord Yabu, you'd escort the Lady Sazuko—"

"Guards!"

The warning shout came from the forecourt. Buntaro and Yabu hurried through the fortified door as all the men swirled after them and others poured from the innerworks.

Ishido was approaching down the avenue between the castle walls at the head of two hundred Grays. He stopped in the forecourt outside the gate and, though no man seemed hostile on either side and no man had his hand on his sword or an arrow in his bow, all were ready.

Ishido bowed elaborately. "A fine evening, Lord Yabu."

"Yes, yes indeed."

Ishido nodded perfunctorily to Buntaro, who was equally offhand, returning the minimum politeness allowable. Both had been favorite generals of the Taikō. Buntaro had led one of the regiments in Korea when Ishido had been in overall command. Each had accused the other of treachery. Only the personal intervention and a direct order of the Taikō had prevented bloodshed and a vendetta.

Ishido studied the Browns. Then his eyes found Blackthorne. He saw the man half bow and nodded in return. Through the gateway he could see the three women and the other litter. His eyes came to rest on Yabu again. "You'd think you were all going into battle, Yabu-san, instead of just being a ceremonial escort for the Lady Kiritsubo."

"Hiro-matsu-san issued orders, because of the Amida assassin. . . ."

Yabu stopped as Buntaro stomped pugnaciously forward and planted his huge legs in the center of the gateway. "We're always ready for battle. With or without armor. We can take on ten men for each one of ours, and fifty of the Garlic Eaters. We never turn our backs and run like snot-nosed cowards, leaving our comrades to be overwhelmed!"

Ishido's smile was filled with contempt, his voice a goad. "Oh? Perhaps you'll get an opportunity soon—to stand against real men, not Garlic Eaters!"

"How soon? Why not tonight? Why not here?"

Yabu moved carefully between them. He also had been in Korea and he knew that there was truth on both sides and that neither was to be trusted, Buntaro less than Ishido. "Not tonight because we're among friends, Buntaro-san," he said placatingly, wanting desperately to avoid a clash that would lock them forever within the castle. "We're among friends, Buntaro-san."

"What friends? I know friends—and I know enemies!" Buntaro whirled back to Ishido. "Where's this man—this real man you talked of, Ishido-san? Eh? Or men? Let him—let them all crawl out of their holes and stand in front of me—Toda Buntaro, Lord of Sakura—if any one of them's got the juice!"

Everyone readied.

Ishido stared back malevolently.

Yabu said, "This is not the time, Buntaro-san. Friends or ene—"

"Friends? Where? In this manure pile?" Buntaro spat into the dust.

One of the Grays' hands flashed for his sword hilt, ten Browns followed, fifty Grays were a split second behind, and now all were waiting for Ishido's sword to come out to signal the attack.

Then Hiro-matsu walked out of the garden shadows, through the gateway into the forecourt, his killing sword loose in his hands and half out of its scabbard.

"You can find friends in manure, sometimes, my son," he said calmly. Hands eased off sword hilts. Samurai on the opposing battlements—Grays and Browns —slackened the tension of their arrow-armed bowstrings. "We have friends all over the castle. All over Osaka. Yes. Our Lord Toranaga keeps telling us so." He stood like a rock in front of his only living son, seeing the blood lust in his eyes. The moment Ishido had been seen approaching, Hiro-matsu had taken up his battle station at the inner doorway. Then, when the first danger had passed, he had moved with catlike quiet into the shadows. He stared down into Buntaro's eyes. "Isn't that so, my son?"

With an enormous effort, Buntaro nodded and stepped back a pace. But he still blocked the way to the garden.

Hiro-matsu turned his attention to Ishido. "We did not expect you tonight, Ishido-san."

"I came to pay my respects to the Lady Kiritsubo. I was not informed until a few moments ago that anyone was leaving."

"Is my son right? We should worry we're not among friends? Are we hostages who should beg favors?"

"No. But Lord Toranaga and I agreed on protocol during his visit. A day's notice of the arrival or departure of high personages was to be given so I could pay the proper respects."

"It was a sudden decision of Lord Toranaga's. He did not consider the matter of sending one of his ladies back to Yedo important enough to disturb you," Hiro-matsu told him. "Yes, Lord Toranaga is merely preparing for his own departure."

"Has that been decided upon?"

"Yes. The day the meeting of the Regents concludes. You'll be informed at the correct time, according to protocol."

"Good. Of course, the meeting may be delayed again. The Lord Kiyama is even sicker."

"Is it delayed? Or isn't it?"

"I merely mentioned that it might be. We hope to have the pleasure of Lord Toranaga's presence for a long time to come, *neh?* He will hunt with me tomorrow?"

"I have requested him to cancel all hunting until the meeting. I don't consider it safe. I don't consider any of this area safe any longer. If filthy assassins can get through your sentries so easily, how much more easy would treachery be outside the walls?"

Ishido let the insult pass. He knew this and the affronts would further inflame his men but it did not suit him to light the fuse yet. He had been glad that Hiro-matsu had interceded for he had almost lost control. The thought of Buntaro's head in the dust, the teeth chattering, had consumed him. "All commanders of the guards on that night have already been ordered into the Great Void as you well know. The Amidas are laws unto themselves, unfortunately. But they will be stamped out very soon. The Regents will be asked to deal with them once and for all. Now, perhaps I may pay my respects to Kiritsubo-san."

Ishido walked forward. His personal bodyguard of Grays stepped after him. They all shuddered to a stop. Buntaro had an arrow in his bow and, though the arrow pointed at the ground, the bow was already bent to its limit. "Grays are forbidden through this gate. That's agreed by protocol!"

"I'm Governor of Osaka Castle and Commander of the Heir's Bodyguard! I have the right to go anywhere!"

Once more Hiro-matsu took control of the situation. "True, you are Commander of the Heir's Bodyguard and you do have the right to go anywhere. But only five men may accompany you through that gate. Wasn't that agreed by you and my Master while he is here?"

"Five or fifty, it makes no difference! This insult is intol—"

"Insult? My son means no insult. He's following orders agreed by his liege Lord and by you. Five men. Five!" The word was an order and Hiro-matsu turned his back on Ishido and looked at his son. "The Lord Ishido does us honor by wishing to pay respect to the Lady Kiritsubo."

The old man's sword was two inches out of its scabbard and no one was sure if it was to slash at Ishido if the fight began or to hack off his son's head if he pointed the arrow. All knew that there was no affection between father and son, only a mutual respect for the other's viciousness. "Well, my son, what do you say to the Commander of the Heir's Bodyguard?"

The sweat was running down Buntaro's face. After a moment he stepped aside and eased the tension off the bow. But he kept the arrow poised.

Many times Ishido had seen Buntaro in the competition lists firing arrows at two hundred paces, six arrows launched before the first hit the target, all equally accurate. He would happily have ordered the attack now and obliterated these two, the father and son, and all the rest. But he knew it would be the act of a fool to start with them and not with Toranaga, and, in any event, perhaps when the real war came Hiro-matsu would be tempted to leave Toranaga and fight with him. The Lady Ochiba had said she would approach old Iron Fist when the time came. She had sworn that he would never forsake the Heir, that she would weld Iron Fist to her, away from Toranaga, perhaps even get him to assassinate his master and so avoid any conflict. What hold, what secret, what knowledge does she have over him? Ishido asked himself again. He had ordered Lady Ochiba to be spirited out of Yedo, if it was possible, before the Regents' meeting. Her life would not be worth a grain of rice after Toranaga's impeachment—which all the other Regents had agreed upon. Impeachment and immediate seppuku, forced if need be. If she escapes, good. If not, never mind. The Heir will rule in eight years.

He strode through the gateway into the garden, Hiro-matsu and Yabu accompanying him. Five guards followed. He bowed politely and wished Kiritsubo well. Then, satisfied that all was as it should be, he turned and left with all his men.

Hiro-matsu exhaled and scratched his piles. "You'd better leave now, Yabu-san. That rice maggot'll give you no more trouble."

"Yes. At once."

Kiri kerchiefed the sweat off her brow. "He's a devil *kami!* I'm afraid for our Master." The tears began to flow. "I don't want to leave!"

"No harm will come to Lord Toranaga, I promise you, Lady," Hiro-matsu said. "You must go. Now!"

Kiri tried to stifle her sobs and unloosed the thick veil that hung from the brim of her wide hat. "Oh, Yabu-sama, would you escort Lady Sazuko inside? Please?"

"Of course."

Lady Sazuko bowed and hurried off, Yabu following. The girl ran up the steps. As she neared the top she slipped and fell.

"The baby!" Kiri shrieked. "Is she hurt?"

All their eyes flashed to the prostrate girl. Mariko ran for her but Yabu reached her first. He picked her up. Sazuko was more startled than hurt. "I'm all right," she said, a little breathlessly. "Don't worry, I'm perfectly all right. It was foolish of me."

When he was sure, Yabu walked back to the forecourt preparing for instant departure.

Mariko came back to the gateway, greatly relieved. Blackthorne was gaping at the garden.

"What is it?" she asked.

"Nothing," he said after a pause. "What did Lady Kiritsubo shout out?"

" 'The baby! Is she hurt?' The Lady Sazuko's with child," she explained. "We were all afraid the fall might have hurt her."

"Toranaga-sama's child?"

"Yes," Mariko said, looking back at the litter.

Kiri was inside the closed translucent curtains now, the veil loosed. Poor woman, Mariko thought, knowing she was only trying to hide the tears. I would be equally terrified to leave my Lord, if I were she.

Her eyes went to Sazuko, who waved once more from the top of the steps, then went inside. The iron door clanged after her. That sounded like a death knell, Mariko thought. Will we ever see them again?

"What did Ishido want?" Blackthorne asked.

"He was—I don't know the correct word. He was investigating—making a tour of inspection without warning."

"Why?"

"He's Commander of the castle," she said, not wishing to tell the real reason.

Yabu was shouting orders at the head of the column and set off. Mariko got into her litter, leaving the curtains partially open. Buntaro motioned Blackthorne to move aside. He obeyed.

They waited for Kiri's litter to pass. Blackthorne stared at the half-seen, shrouded figure, hearing the muffled sobs. The two frightened maids, Asa and Sono, walked alongside. Then he glanced back a last time. Hiro-matsu was standing alone beside the little hut, leaning on his sword. Now the garden was shut from his view as samurai closed the huge fortified door. The great wooden bar fell into place. There were no guards in the forecourt now. They were all on the battlements.

"What's going on?" Blackthorne asked.

"Please, Anjin-san?"

"It looks like they're under siege. Browns against the Grays. Are they expecting trouble? More trouble?"

"Oh, so sorry. It's normal to close the doors at night," Mariko said.

He began to walk beside her as her litter moved off, Buntaro and the remainder of the rear guard taking up their station behind him. Blackthorne was watching the litter ahead, the swaying gait of the bearers and the misted figure inside the curtains. He was greatly unsettled though he tried to hide it. When Kiritsubo had suddenly shrieked, he had looked at her instantly. Everyone else was looking at the prostrate girl on the staircase. His impulse was to look over there as well but he saw Kiritsubo suddenly scuttle with surprising speed inside the little hut. For a moment he thought his eyes were playing him tricks because in the night her dark cloak and dark kimono and dark hat and dark veil made her almost invisible. He watched as the figure vanished for a moment, then reappeared, darted into the litter, and jerked the curtains closed. For an instant their eyes met. It was Toranaga.

CHAPTER 22

THE little cortege surrounding the two litters went slowly through the maze of the castle and through the continual checkpoints. Each time there were formal bows, the documents were meticulously examined afresh, a new captain and group of escorting Grays took over, and then they were passed. At each checkpoint Blackthorne watched with ever increasing misgivings as the captain of the guard came close to scrutinize the drawn curtains of Kiritsubo's litter. Each time the man bowed politely to the half-seen figure, hearing the muffled sobs, and in the course of time, waved them on again.

Who else knows, Blackthorne was asking himself desperately. The maids must know—that would explain why they're so frightened. Hiro-matsu certainly must have known, and Lady Sazuko, the decoy, absolutely. Mariko? I don't think so. Yabu? Would Toranaga trust him? That neckless maniac Buntaro? Probably not.

Obviously this is a highly secret escape attempt. But why should Toranaga risk his life outside the castle? Isn't he safer inside? Why the secrecy? Who's he escaping from? Ishido? The assassins? Or someone else in the castle? Probably all of them, Blackthorne thought, wishing they were safely in the galley and out to sea. If Toranaga's discovered it's going to rain dung, the fight's going to be to the death and no quarter asked or given. I'm unarmed and even if I had a brace of pistols or a twenty pounder and a hundred bully boys, the Grays'd swamp us. I've nowhere to run and nowhere to hide. It's a turd-stuffed fornicator whichever way you count it!

"Are you tiring, Anjin-san?" Mariko asked daintily. "If you like, I'll walk and you can ride."

"Thanks," he replied sourly, missing his boots, the thonged slippers still awkward. "My legs are fine. I was just wishing we were safe at sea, that's all."

"Is the sea ever safe?"

"Sometimes, senhora. Not often." Blackthorne hardly heard her. He was thinking, by the Lord Jesus, I hope I don't give Toranaga away. That would be terrible! It'd be so much simpler if I hadn't seen him. That was just bad luck, one of those accidents that can disrupt a perfectly planned and executed scheme. The old girl, Kiritsubo, she's a great actress, and the young one too. It was only because I couldn't understand what she'd shouted out that I didn't fall for the ruse. Just bad luck I saw Toranaga clearly—bewigged, made up, kimonoed, and cloaked, just like Kiritsubo, but still Toranaga.

At the next checkpoint the new captain of Grays came closer than ever before, the maids tearfully bowing and standing in the way without trying to appear as though they were standing in the way. The captain peered across at Blackthorne and walked over. After an incredulous scrutiny he talked with Mariko, who shook her head and answered him. The man grunted and strolled back to Yabu, returned the documents and waved the procession onward again.

"What did he say?" Blackthorne asked.

"He wondered where you were from—where your home was."

"But you shook your head. How was that an answer?"

"Oh, so sorry, he said—he wondered if the far-distant ancestors of your people were related to the *kami*—the spirit—that lives to the north, on the outskirts of

China. Till quite recently we thought China was the only other civilized place on earth—except for Japan, *neh?* China is so immense it is like the world itself," she said, and closed the subject. The captain had actually asked if she thought this barbarian was descended from Harimwakairi, the *kami* that looked after cats, adding this one certainly stank like a polecat in rut, as the *kami* was supposed to do.

She had replied that she didn't think so, inwardly ashamed of the captain's rudeness, for the Anjin-san did not have a stench like Tsukku-san or the Father-Visitor or usual barbarians. His aroma was almost imperceptible now.

Blackthorne knew she wasn't telling him the truth. I wish I could speak their gibberish, he thought. I wish more I could get off this cursed island, back aboard *Erasmus,* the crew fit and plenty of grub, grog, powder, and shot, our goods traded and away home again. When will that be? Toranaga said soon. Can he be trusted? How did he get the ship to Yedo? Tow it? Did the Portuguese sail her? I wonder how Rodrigues is. Did his leg rot? He should know by now if he's going to live with two legs or one—if the amputation doesn't kill him—or if he's going to die. Jesus God in Heaven, protect me from wounds and all doctors. And priests.

Another checkpoint. For the life of him, Blackthorne could not understand how everyone could remain so polite and patient, always bowing and allowing the documents to be handed over and handed back, always smiling and no sign of irritation whatsoever on either side. They're so different from us.

He glanced at Mariko's face, which was partially obscured by her veil and wide hat. He thought she looked very pretty and he was glad that he had had it out with her over her mistake. At least I won't have any more of that nonsense, he told himself. Bastard queers, they're all blood-mucked bastards!

After he had accepted her apology this morning he had begun to ask about Yedo and Japanese customs and Ishido and about the castle. He had avoided the topic of sex. She had answered at length, but had avoided any political explanations and her replies were informative but innocuous. Soon she and the maids had left to prepare for her departure, and he had been alone with the samurai guards.

Being so closely hemmed in all the time was making him edgy. There's always someone around, he thought. There are too many of them. They're like ants. I'd like the peace of a bolted oak door for a change, the bolt my side and not theirs. I can't wait to get aboard again, out into the air, out to sea. Even in that sow-bellied gut-churner of a galley.

Now as he walked through Osaka Castle, he realized that he would have Toranaga in his own element, at sea, where he himself was king. We'll have time enough to talk, Mariko'll interpret and I'll get everything settled. Trade agreements, the ship, the return of our silver, and payment if he wants to trade for the muskets and powder. I'll make arrangements to come back next year with a full cargo of silk. Terrible about Friar Domingo, but I'll put his information to good use. I'm going to take *Erasmus* and sail her up the Pearl River to Canton and I'll break the Portuguese and China blockade. Give me my ship back and I'm rich. Richer than Drake! When I get home I'll call up all the seadogs from Plymouth to the Zuider Zee and we'll take over the trade of all Asia. Where Drake singed Philip's beard, I'm going to cut off his testicles. Without silk, Macao dies, without Macao, Malacca dies, then Goa! We can roll up the Portuguese Empire like a carpet. 'You want the trade of India, Your Majesty? Afrique? Asia? The Japans? Here's how you can take it in five years!'

'Arise, Sir John!'

Yes, knighthood was within easy reach, at long last. And perhaps more.

Captains and navigators became admirals, knights, lords, even earls. The only way for an Englishman, a commoner, to safety, the true safety of position within the realm, was through the Queen's favor, bless her. And the way to her favor was to bring her treasure, to help her pay for the war against stinking Spain, and that bastard the Pope.

Three years'll give me three trips, Blackthorne gloated. Oh, I know about the monsoon winds and the great storms, but *Erasmus*'ll be closehauled and we'll ship in smaller amounts. Wait a minute—why not do the job properly and forget the small amounts? Why not take this year's Black Ship? Then you have everything!

How?

Easily—if she has no escort and we catch her unawares. But I've not enough men. Wait, there're men at Nagasaki! Isn't that where all the Portuguese are? Didn't Domingo say it was almost like a Portuguese seaport? Rodrigues said the same! Aren't there always seamen in their ships who've been pressed aboard or forced aboard, always some who're ready to jump ship for quick profit on their own, whoever the captain and whatever the flag? With *Erasmus* and our silver I could hire a crew. I know I could. I don't need three years. Two will be enough. Two more years with my ship and a crew, then home. I'll be rich and famous. And we'll part company, the sea and I, at long last. Forever.

Toranaga's the key. How are you going to handle him?

They passed another checkpoint, and turned a corner. Ahead was the last portcullis and last gateway of the castle proper, and beyond it, the final drawbridge and final moat. At the far side was the ultimate strongpoint. A multitude of flares made the night into crimson day.

Then Ishido stepped out of the shadows.

The Browns saw him almost at the same instant. Hostility whipped through them. Buntaro almost leaped past Blackthorne to get nearer the head of the column.

"That bastard's spoiling for a fight," Blackthorne said.

"Senhor? I'm sorry, senhor, what did you say?"

"Just—I said your husband seems—Ishido seems to get your husband very angry, very quickly."

She made no reply.

Yabu halted. Unconcerned he handed the safe conduct to the captain of the gate and wandered over to Ishido. "I didn't expect to see you again. Your guards are very efficient."

"Thank you." Ishido was watching Buntaro and the closed litter behind him.

"Once should be enough to check our pass," Buntaro said, his weapons rattling ominously. "Twice at the most. What are we—a war party? It's insulting."

"No insult is intended, Buntaro-san. Because of the assassin, I ordered tighter security." Ishido eyed Blackthorne briefly and wondered again if he should let him go or hold him as Onoshi and Kiyama wanted. Then he looked at Buntaro again. Offal, he thought. Your head will be on a spike soon. How could such exquisiteness as Mariko stay married to an ape like you?

The new captain was meticulously checking everyone, ensuring that they matched the list. "Everything's in order, Yabu-sama," he said as he returned to the head of the column. "You don't need the pass anymore. We keep it here."

"Good." Yabu turned to Ishido. "We meet soon."

Ishido took a roll of parchment out of his sleeve. "I wanted to ask Lady Kiritsubo if she'd take this with her to Yedo. For my niece. It's unlikely I'll go to Yedo for some time."

"Certainly." Yabu put out his hand.

"Don't trouble yourself, Yabu-san. I'll ask her." Ishido walked toward the litter.

The maids obsequiously intercepted him. Asa held out her hand. "May I take the message, Lord. My Mis—"

"No."

To the surprise of Ishido and everyone nearby, the maids did not move out of the way.

"But my Mis—"

"Move!" Buntaro snarled.

Both maids backed off with abject humility, frightened now.

Ishido bowed to the curtain. "Kiritsubo-san, I wonder if you'd be kind enough to take this message for me to Yedo? To my niece?"

There was a slight hesitation between the sobs and the figure bowed an assent.

"Thank you." Ishido offered up the slim roll of parchment an inch from the curtains.

The sobs stopped. Blackthorne realized Toranaga was trapped. Politeness demanded that Toranaga take the scroll and his hand would give him away.

Everyone waited for the hand to appear.

"Kiritsubo-san?"

Still no movement. Then Ishido took a quick pace forward, jerked the curtains apart and at the same instant Blackthorne let out a bellow and began dancing up and down like a maniac. Ishido and the others whirled on him dumbfounded.

For an instant Toranaga was in full view behind Ishido. Blackthorne thought that perhaps Toranaga could pass for Kiritsubo at twenty paces but here at five, impossible, even though the veil covered his face. And in the never-ending second before Toranaga had tugged the curtains closed again, Blackthorne knew that Yabu had recognized him, Mariko certainly, Buntaro probably, and some of the samurai possibly. He lunged forward, grabbed the roll of parchment and thrust it through a crack in the curtains and turned, babbling, "It's bad luck in my country for a prince to give a message himself like a common bastard . . . bad luck . . ."

It had all happened so unexpectedly and so fast that Ishido's sword was not out until Blackthorne was bowing and raving in front of him like an insane jack-in-the-box, then his reflexes took over and sent the sword slashing for the throat.

Blackthorne's desperate eyes found Mariko. "For Christ's sake, help—bad luck—*bad luck!*"

She cried out. The blade stopped a hair's breadth from his neck. Mariko poured out an explanation of what Blackthorne had said. Ishido lowered his sword, listened for a moment, overrode her with a furious harangue, then shouted with increasing vehemence and hit Blackthorne in the face with the back of his hand.

Blackthorne went berserk. He bunched his great fists and hurled himself at Ishido.

If Yabu hadn't been quick enough to catch Ishido's sword arm Blackthorne's head would have rolled in the dust. Buntaro, a split second later, grabbed Blackthorne, who already had his hands around Ishido's throat. It took four Browns to haul him off Ishido, then Buntaro smashed him hard on the back of the neck, stunning him. Grays leaped to their master's defense, but Browns surrounded Blackthorne and the litters and for a moment it was a standoff, Mariko and the maids deliberately wailing and crying, helping to create further chaos and diversions.

Yabu began placating Ishido, Mariko tearfully repeated over and over in forced semihysteria that the mad barbarian believed he was only trying to save Ishido, the Great Commander—whom he thought was a prince—from a bad *kami*. "And it's the worst insult to touch their faces, just like with us, that's what sent him momentarily mad. He's a senseless barbarian but a *daimyo* in his own land and he was only trying to help you, Lord!"

Ishido ranted and kicked Blackthorne, who was just coming to. Blackthorne heard the tumult with great peace. His eyes cleared. Grays were surrounding them twenty to one, swords drawn, but so far no one was dead and everyone waited in discipline.

Blackthorne saw that all attention was focused on him. But now he knew he had allies.

Ishido spun on him again and came closer, shouting. He felt the grip of the Browns tighten and knew the blow was coming, but this time, instead of trying to fight out of their grasp, which they expected, he started to collapse, then immediately straightened and broke away, laughing insanely, and began a jibbering hornpipe. Friar Domingo had told him that everyone in Japan believed madness was caused only by a *kami* and thus madmen, like all young children and very old men, were not responsible and had special privileges, sometimes. So he capered in a frenzy, singing in time to Mariko, "Help . . . I need help for God's sake . . . can't keep this up much longer . . . help . . ." desperately acting the lunatic, knowing it was the only thing that might save them.

"He's mad—he's possessed," Mariko cried out, at once realizing Blackthorne's ploy.

"Yes," Yabu said, still trying to recover from the shock of seeing Toranaga, not knowing yet if the Anjin-san was acting or if he had really gone mad.

Mariko was beside herself. She didn't know what to do. The Anjin-san saved Lord Toranaga but how did he know? she kept repeating to herself senselessly.

Blackthorne's face was bloodless except for the scarlet weal from the blows. He danced on and on, frantically waiting for help but none came. Then, silently damning Yabu and Buntaro as motherless cowards and Mariko for the stupid bitch she was, he stopped the dance suddenly, bowed to Ishido like a spastic puppet and half walked, half danced for the gateway. "Follow me, follow me!" he shouted, his voice almost strangling him, trying to lead the way like a Pied Piper.

The Grays barred his way. He roared with feigned rage and imperiously ordered them out of the way, immediately switching to hysterical laughter.

Ishido grabbed a bow and arrow. The Grays scattered. Blackthorne was almost through the gateway. He turned at bay, knowing there was no point in running. Helplessly he began his rabid dance again.

"He's mad, a mad dog! Mad dogs have to be dealt with!" Ishido's voice was raw. He armed the bow and aimed.

At once Mariko leapt forward from her protective position near Toranaga's litter and began to walk toward Blackthorne. "Don't worry, Lord Ishido," she cried out. "There's no need to worry—it's a momentary madness—may I be permitted . . ." As she came closer she could see Blackthorne's exhaustion, the set maniacal smile, and she was frightened in spite of herself. "I can help now, Anjin-san," she said hurriedly. "We have to try to—to walk out. I will follow you. Don't worry, he won't shoot us. Please stop dancing now."

Blackthorne stopped instantly, turned and walked quietly onto the bridge. She followed a pace behind him as was custom, expecting the arrows, hearing them.

A thousand eyes watched the giant madman and the tiny woman on the bridge, walking away.

Yabu came to life. "If you want him killed, let me do it, Ishido-sama. It's unseemly for you to take his life. A general doesn't kill with his own hands. Others should do his killing for him." He came very close and he dropped his voice. "Leave him alive. The madness came from your blow. He's a *daimyo* in his own land and the blow—it was as Mariko-san said, *neh?* Trust me, he's valuable to us alive."

"What?"

"He's more valuable alive. Trust me. You can have him dead any time. We need him alive."

Ishido read desperation in Yabu's face, and truth. He put the bow down. "Very well. But one day I'll want him alive. I'll hang him by his heels over the pit."

Yabu swallowed and half bowed. He nervously waved the cortege onward, fearful that Ishido would remember the litter and "Kiritsubo."

Buntaro, pretending deference, took the initiative and started the Browns on their way. He did not question the fact that Toranaga had magically appeared like a *kami* in their midst, only that his master was in danger and almost defenseless. He saw that Ishido had not taken his eyes off Mariko and the Anjin-san, but even so, he bowed politely to him and set himself behind Toranaga's litter to protect his master from any arrows if the fight began here.

The column was approaching the gate now. Yabu fell into place as a lonely rear guard. Any moment he expected the cortege to be halted. Surely some of the Grays must have seen Toranaga, he thought. How soon before they tell Ishido? Won't he think I was part of the escape attempt? Won't this ruin me forever?

Halfway over the bridge Mariko looked back for an instant. "They're following, Anjin-san, both litters are through the gate and they're on the bridge now!"

Blackthorne did not reply or turn back. It required all of his remaining will to stay erect. He had lost his sandals, his face burned from the blow, and his head pounded with pain. The last guards let him through the portcullis and beyond. They also let Mariko pass without stopping. And then the litters.

Blackthorne led the way down the slight hill, past the open ground and across the far bridge. Only when he was in the wooded area totally out of sight of the castle did he collapse.

CHAPTER 23

A NJIN-SAN—Anjin-san!
Semiconscious, he allowed Mariko to help him drink some saké. The
column had halted, the Browns arranged tightly around the curtained
litter, their escorting Grays ahead and behind. Buntaro had shouted at one of
the maids, who had immediately produced the flask from one of the baggage
kagas, told his personal guards to keep everyone away from "Kiritsubo-san's"
litter, then hurried to Mariko. "Is the Anjin-san all right?"

"Yes, yes, I think so," Mariko replied. Yabu joined them.

To try to throw off the captain of the Grays, Yabu said carelessly, "We can
go on, Captain. We'll leave a few men and Mariko-san. When the barbarian's
recovered, she and the men can follow."

"With great deference, Yabu-san, we will wait. I'm charged to deliver you all
safely to the galley. As one party," the captain told him.

They all looked down as Blackthorne choked slightly on the wine. "Thanks,"
he croaked. "Are we safe now? Who else knows that—"

"You're safe now!" she interrupted deliberately. She had her back to the
captain and she cautioned him with her eyes. "Anjin-san, you're safe now and
there's no need to worry. Do you understand? You had some kind of fit. Just
look around—you're safe now!"

Blackthorne did as she ordered. He saw the captain and the Grays and understood. His strength was returning quickly now, helped by the wine. "Sorry,
senhora. It was just panic, I think. I must be getting old. I go mad often and
can never remember afterwards what happened. Speaking Portuguese is exhausting, isn't it?" He switched to Latin. "Canst thou understand?"

"Assuredly."

"Is this tongue 'easier'?"

"Perhaps," she said, relieved that he understood the need for caution, even
using Latin, which was to Japanese an almost incomprehensible and unlearnable
language except to a handful of men in the Empire, all of whom would be Jesuit
trained and most committed to the priesthood. She was the only woman in all
their world who could speak and read and write Latin and Portuguese. "Both
languages are difficult, each hath dangers."

"Who else knoweth the 'dangers'?"

"My husband and he who leads us."

"Art thou sure?"

"Both indicated thusly."

The captain of Grays shifted restlessly and said something to Mariko.

"He asks if thou art yet dangerous, if thy hands and feet should be restrained.
I said no. Thou art cured of thy palsy now."

"Yes," he said, lapsing back into Portuguese. "I have fits often. If someone
hits me in the face it sends me mad. I'm sorry. Never can remember what happens
during them. It's the Finger of God." He saw that the captain was concentrating
on his lips and he thought, caught you, you bastard, I'll bet you understand
Portuguese.

240

Sono the maid had her head bent close to the litter curtains. She listened, and came back to Mariko.

"So sorry, Mariko-sama, but my Mistress asks if the madman is well enough to continue? She asks if you would give him your litter because my Mistress feels we should hurry for the tide. All the trouble that the madman has caused has made her even more upset. But, knowing that the mad are only afflicted by the gods, she will say prayers for his return to health, and will personally give him medicines to cure him once we are aboard."

Mariko translated.

"Yes. I'm all right now." Blackthorne got up and swayed on his feet.

Yabu barked a command.

"Yabu-san says you will ride in the litter, Anjin-san." Mariko smiled when he began to protest. "I'm really very strong and you needn't worry, I'll walk beside you so you can talk if you wish."

He allowed himself to be helped into the litter. At once they started again. The rolling gait was soothing and he lay back depleted. He waited until the captain of the Grays had strode away to the head of the column, then whispered in Latin, warning her, "That centurion understandeth the other tongue."

"Aye. And I believe some Latin also," she whispered back as quietly. She walked for a moment. "In seriousness, thou art a brave man. I thank thee for saving him."

"Thou hadst stronger bravery."

"No, the Lord God hath placed my feet onto the path, and rendered me a little useful. Again I thank thee."

The city by night was a fairyland. The rich houses had many colored lanterns, oil-lit and candle-lit, hanging over their gateways and in their gardens, the shoji screens giving off a delightful translucence. Even the poor houses were mellowed by the shojis. Lanterns lit the way of pedestrians and kagas, and of samurai, who rode horseback.

"We burn oil for lamps in the houses as well as candles, but with the coming of night, most people go to bed," Mariko explained as they continued through the city streets, winding and curling, the pedestrians bowing and the very poor on their knees until they had passed, the sea glittering in the moonlight.

"It's the same with us. How do you cook? Over a wood stove?" Blackthorne's strength had returned quickly and his legs no longer felt like jelly. She had refused to take the litter back, so he lay there, enjoying the air and the conversation.

"We use a charcoal brazier. We don't eat foods like you do, so our cooking is more simple. Just rice and a little fish, raw mostly, or cooked over charcoal with a sharp sauce and pickled vegetables, a little soup perhaps. No meat—never meat. We're a frugal people—we have to be, only so little of our land, perhaps a fifth of our soil, can be cultivated—and we're many. With us it's a virtue to be frugal, even in the amount of food we eat."

"Thou art brave. I thank thee. The arrows flew not, because of the shield of thy back."

"No, Captain of Ships. It cometh from the will of God."

"Thou art brave and thou art beautiful."

She walked in silence for a moment. No one has ever called me beautiful before—no one, she thought. "I am not brave and I am not beautiful. Swords are beautiful. Honor is beautiful."

"Courage is beautiful and thou hast it in abundance."

Mariko did not answer. She was remembering this morning and all the evil words and evil thoughts. How can a man be so brave and so stupid, so gentle and so cruel, so warming and so detestable—all at the same time? The Anjin-san was limitlessly brave to take Ishido's attention off the litter, and completely clever to feign madness and so lead Toranaga out of the trap. How wise of Toranaga to escape this way! But be cautious, Mariko, she warned herself. Think about Toranaga and not about this stranger. Remember his evil and stop the moist warmth in your loins that you have never had before, the warmth courtesans talk about and storybooks and pillowbooks describe.

"Aye," she said. "Courage is beautiful and thou hast it in abundance." Then she turned to Portuguese once more. "Latin is such a tiring language."

"You learned it in school?"

"No, Anjin-san, it was later. After I was married I lived in the far north for quite a long time. I was alone, except for servants and villagers, and the only books I had were Portuguese and Latin—some grammars and religious books, and a Bible. Learning the languages passed the time very well, and occupied my mind. I was very fortunate."

"Where was your husband?"

"At war."

"How long were you alone?"

"We have a saying that time has no single measure, that time can be like frost or lightning or a tear or siege or storm or sunset, or even like a rock."

"That's a wise saying," he told her. Then added, "Your Portuguese is very good, senhora. And your Latin. Better than mine."

"You have a honeyed tongue, Anjin-san!"

"It's *honto!*"

"*Honto* is a good word. The *honto* is that one day a Christian Father came to the village. We were like two lost souls. He stayed for four years and helped me immensely. I'm glad I can speak well," she said, without vanity. "My father wanted me to learn the languages."

"Why?"

"He thought we should know the devil with which we had to deal."

"He was a wise man."

"No. Not wise."

"Why?"

"One day I will tell you the story. It's a sadness."

"Why were you alone for a rock of time?"

"Why don't you rest? We have a long way to go yet."

"Do you want to ride?" Again he began to get up but she shook her head. "No, thank you. Please stay where you are. I enjoy walking."

"All right. But you don't want to talk anymore?"

"If it pleases you we can talk. What do you want to know?"

"Why were you alone for a rock of time?"

"My husband sent me away. My presence had offended him. He was perfectly correct to do this. He honored me by not divorcing me. Then he honored me even more by accepting me and our son back again." Mariko looked at him. "My son is fifteen now. I'm really an old lady."

"I don't believe you, senhora."

"It's *honto.*"

"How old were you when you were married?"

"Old, Anjin-san. Very old."

"We have a saying: Age is like frost or siege or sunset, even sometimes like a rock." She laughed. Everything about her is so graceful, he thought, mesmerized by her. "On you, Venerable Lady, old age sits prettily."

"For a woman, Anjin-san, old age is never pretty."

"Thou art wise as thou art beautiful." The Latin came too easily and though it sounded more formal and more regal, it was more intimate. Watch yourself, he thought.

No one has ever called me beautiful before, she repeated to herself. I wish it were true. "Here it is not wise to notice another man's woman," she said. "Our customs are quite severe. For example, if a married woman is found alone with a man in a room with the door closed—just if they are alone and talking privately—by law her husband or his brother or his father has the right to put her to death instantly. If the girl is unmarried, the father can, of course, always do with her as he pleases."

"That's not fair or civilized." He regretted the slip instantly.

"We find ourselves quite civilized, Anjin-san." Mariko was glad to be insulted again, for it had broken the spell and dispelled the warmth. "Our laws are very wise. There are far too many women, free and unattached, for a man to take one who belongs elsewhere. It's a protection for women, in truth. A wife's duty is solely to her husband. Be patient. You'll see how civilized, how advanced we are. Women have a place, men have a place. A man may have only one official wife at one time—but of course, many consorts—but women here have much more freedom than Spanish or Portuguese ladies, from what I've been told. We can go freely where we please, when we please. We may leave our husbands, if we wish, divorce them. We may refuse to marry in the first place, if we wish. We own our own wealth and property, our bodies and our spirits. We have tremendous powers if we wish. Who looks after all your wealth, your money, in your household?"

"I do, naturally."

"Here the wife looks after everything. Money is nothing to a samurai. It's beneath contempt to a real man. I manage all my husband's affairs. He makes all the decisions. I merely carry out his wishes and pay his bills. This leaves him totally free to do his duty to his lord, which is his sole duty. Oh, yes, Anjin-san, you must be patient before you criticize."

"It wasn't meant as a criticism, senhora. It's just that we believe in the sanctity of life, that no one can lightly be put to death unless a law court—the Queen's law court—agrees."

She refused to allow herself to be soothed. "You say a lot of things I don't understand, Anjin-san. But didn't you say 'not fair and not civilized'?"

"Yes."

"That then is a criticism, *neh?* Lord Toranaga asked me to point out it's unseemly to criticize without knowledge. You must remember our civilization, our culture, is thousands of years old. Three thousand of these are documented. Oh yes, we are an ancient people. As ancient as China. How many years does your culture go back?"

"Not long, senhora."

"Our Emperor, Go-Nijo, is the one hundred and seventh of his unbroken line, right back to Jimmu-tenno, the first earthling, who was descended from the five generations of terrestrial spirits and, before them, the seven generations of celestial spirits who came from Kuni-toko-tachi-noh-Mikoto—the first spirit—who appeared when the earth was split from the heavens. Not even China can claim such a history. How many generations have your kings ruled your land?"

"Our Queen's the third of the Tudor line, senhora. But she's old now and childless so she's the last."

"One hundred and seven generations, Anjin-san, back to divinity," she repeated proudly.

"If you believe that, senhora, how can you also say you're Catholic?" He saw her bridle, then shrug.

"I am only a ten-year Christian and therefore a novice, and though I believe in the Christian God, in God the Father and the Son and the Holy Ghost, with all my heart, our Emperor is directly descended from the gods or from God. He is divine. There are a lot of things I cannot explain or understand. But the divinity of my Emperor is without question. Yes, I am Christian, but first I am a Japanese."

Is this the key to all of you? That first you are Japanese? he asked himself. He had watched her, astonished by what she was saying. Their customs are insane! Money means nothing *to a real man?* That explains why Toranaga was so contemptuous when I mentioned money at the first meeting. One hundred and seven generations? Impossible! Instant death just for being innocently in a closed room with a woman? That's barbarism—an open invitation to murder. They advocate and admire murder! Isn't that what Rodrigues said? Isn't that what Omi-san did? Didn't he just murder that peasant? By Christ's blood, I haven't thought of Omi-san for days. Or the village. Or the pit or being on my knees in front of him. Forget him, listen to her, be patient as she says, ask her questions because she'll supply the means to bend Toranaga to your plan. Now Toranaga is absolutely in your debt. You saved him. He knows it, everyone knows it. Didn't she thank you, not for saving her but for saving him?

The column was moving through the city heading for the sea. He saw Yabu keeping the pace up and momentarily Pieterzoon's screams came soaring into his head. "One thing at a time," he muttered, half to himself.

"Yes," Mariko was saying. "It must be very difficult for you. Our world is so very different from yours. Very different but very wise." She could see the dim figure of Toranaga within the litter ahead and she thanked God again for his escape. How to explain to the barbarian about us, to compliment him for his bravery? Toranaga had ordered her to explain, but how? "Let me tell you a story, Anjin-san. When I was young my father was a general for a *daimyo* called Goroda. At that time Lord Goroda was not the great Dictator but a *daimyo* still struggling for power. My father invited this Goroda and his chief vassals to a feast. It never occurred to him that there was no money to buy all the food and saké and lacquerware and tatamis that such a visit, by custom, demanded. Lest you think my mother was a bad manager, she wasn't. Every groat of my father's revenue went to his own vassal samurai and although, officially, he had only enough for four thousand warriors, by scrimping and saving and manipulating my mother saw that he led five thousand three hundred into battle to the glory of his liege lord. We, the family—my mother, my father's consorts, my brothers and sisters—we had barely enough to eat. But what did that matter? My father and his men had the finest weapons and the finest horses, and they gave of their best to their lord.

"Yes, there was not enough money for this feast, so my mother went to the wigmakers in Kyoto and sold them her hair. I remember it was like molten darkness and hung to the pit of her back. But she sold it. The wigmakers cut it off the same day and gave her a cheap wig and she bought everything that was necessary and saved the honor of my father. It was her duty to pay the bills and she paid. She did her duty. For us duty is all important."

"What did he say, your father, when he found out?"

"What should he say, other than to thank her? It was her duty to find the money. To save his honor."

"She must have loved him very much."

"Love is a Christian word, Anjin-san. Love is a Christian thought, a Christian ideal. We have no word for 'love' as I understand you to mean it. Duty, loyalty, honor, respect, desire, those words and thoughts are what we have, all that we need." She looked at him and in spite of herself, she relived the instant when he had saved Toranaga, and through Toranaga, her husband. Never forget they were both trapped there, they would both be dead now, but for this man.

She made sure that no one was near. "Why did you do what you did?"

"I don't know. Perhaps because . . ." He stopped. There were so many things he could say: 'Perhaps because Toranaga was helpless and I didn't want to get chopped. . . . Because if he was discovered we'd all be caught in the mess. . . . Because I knew that no one knew except me and it was up to me to gamble. . . . Because I didn't want to die—there's too much to do to waste my life, and Toranaga's the only one who can give me back my ship and my freedom.' Instead he replied in Latin, "Because He hath said, render to Caesar the things that are Caesar's."

"Aye," she said, and added in the same language, "aye, that is what I was attempting to say. To Caesar those things, and to God those things. It is thusly with us. God is God and our Emperor is from God. And Caesar is Caesar, to be honored as Caesar." Then, touched by his understanding and the tenderness in his voice, she said, "Thou art wise. Sometimes I think thou understandst more than thou sayest."

Aren't you doing what you swore you would never do? Blackthorne asked himself. Aren't you playing the hypocrite? Yes and no. I owe them nothing. I'm a prisoner. They've stolen my ship and my goods and murdered one of my men. They're heathen—well, some of them are heathen and the rest are Catholics. I owe nothing to heathens and Catholics. But you'd like to bed her and you were complimenting her, weren't you?

God curse all consciences!

The sea was nearer now, half a mile away. He could see many ships, and the Portuguese frigate with her riding lights. She'd make quite a prize. With twenty bully boys I could take her. He turned back to Mariko. Strange woman, from a strange family. Why did she offend Buntaro—that baboon? How could she bed with that, or marry that? What is the "sadness"?

"Senhora," he said, keeping his voice gentle, "your mother must have been a rare woman. To do that."

"Yes. But because of what she did, she will live forever. Now she is legend. She was as samurai as—as my father was samurai."

"I thought only men were samurai."

"Oh, no, Anjin-san. Men and women are equally samurai, warriors with responsibilities to their lords. My mother was true samurai, her dutifulness to her husband exceeded everything."

"She's at your home now?"

"No. Neither she nor my father nor any of my brothers or sisters or family. I am the last of my line."

"There was a catastrophe?"

Mariko suddenly felt tired. I'm tired of speaking Latin and foul-sounding Portuguese and tired of being a teacher, she told herself. I'm not a teacher. I'm only a woman who knows her duty and wants to do it in peace. I want none of that warmth again and none of this man who unsettles me so much. I want none of him.

"In a way, Anjin-san, it was a catastrophe. One day I will tell you about it." She quickened her pace slightly and walked away, nearer to the other litter. The two maids smiled nervously.

"Have we far to go, Mariko-san?" Sono asked.

"I hope not too far," she said reassuringly.

The captain of Grays loomed abruptly out of the darkness on the other side of the litter. She wondered how much that she had said to the Anjin-san had been overheard.

"You'd like a kaga, Mariko-san? Are you getting tired?" the captain asked.

"No, no thank you." She slowed deliberately, drawing him away from Toranaga's litter. "I'm not tired at all."

"The barbarian's behaving himself? He's not troubling you?"

"Oh, no. He seems to be quite calm now."

"What were you talking about?"

"All sorts of things. I was trying to explain some of our laws and customs to him." She motioned back to the castle donjon that was etched against the sky above. "Lord Toranaga asked me to try to get some sense into him."

"Ah yes, Lord Toranaga." The captain looked briefly at the castle, then back to Blackthorne. "Why's Lord Toranaga so interested in him, Lady?"

"I don't know. I suppose because he's an oddity."

They turned a corner, into another street, with houses behind garden walls. There were few people about. Beyond were wharves and the sea. Masts sprouted over the buildings and the air was thick with the smell of seaweed. "What else did you talk about?"

"They've some very strange ideas. They think of money all the time."

"Rumor says his whole nation's made up of filthy merchant pirates. Not a samurai among them. What's Lord Toranaga want with him?"

"So sorry, I don't know."

"Rumor says he's Christian, he claims to be Christian. Is he?"

"Not our sort of Christian, Captain. You're Christian, Captain?"

"My Master's Christian so I am Christian. My Master is Lord Kiyama."

"I have the honor to know him well. He honored my husband by betrothing one of his granddaughters to my son."

"Yes, I know, Lady Toda."

"Is Lord Kiyama better now? I understand the doctors won't allow anyone to see him."

"I haven't seen him for a week. None of us has. Perhaps it's the Chinese pox. God protect him from that, and God curse all Chinese!" He glared toward Blackthorne. "Doctors say these barbarians brought the pest to China, to Macao, and thence to our shores."

"*Sumus omnes in manu Dei,*" she said. We are all in the hands of God.

"*Ita, amen,*" the captain replied without thinking, falling into the trap.

Blackthorne had caught the slip also and he saw a flash of anger on the captain's face and heard him say something through his teeth to Mariko, who flushed and stopped also. He slid out of the litter and walked back to them. "If thou speakest Latin, Centurion, then it would be a kindness if thou wouldst speak a little with me. I am eager to learn about this great country of thine."

"Yes, I can speak thy tongue, foreigner."

"It is not my tongue, Centurion, but that of the Church and of all educated people in my world. Thou speakest it well. How and when did thou learn?"

The cortege was passing them and all the samurai, both Grays and Browns, were watching them. Buntaro, near Toranaga's litter, stopped and turned back. The captain hesitated, then began walking again and Mariko was glad that Blackthorne had joined them. They walked in silence a moment.

"The Centurion speaks the tongue fluidly, splendidly, doesn't he," Blackthorne said to Mariko.

"Yes, indeed. Didst thou learn it in a seminary, Centurion?"

"And thou, foreigner," the captain said coldly, paying her no attention, loathing the recollection of the seminary at Macao that he had been ordered into as a child by Kiyama to learn the languages. "Now that we speak directly, tell me with simplicity why did thou ask this lady: 'Who else knoweth . . .' Who else knoweth what?"

"I recollect not. My mind was wandering."

"Ah, wandering, eh? Then why didst thou say: 'Things of Caesar render to Caesar'?"

"It was just a pleasantry. I was in discussion with this lady, who tells illuminating stories that are sometimes difficult to understand."

"Yes, there is much to understand. What sent thee mad at the gate? And why didst thou recover so quickly from thy fit?"

"That came through the beneficence of God."

They were walking beside the litter once more, the captain furious that he had been trapped so easily. He had been forewarned by Lord Kiyama, his master, that the woman was filled with boundless cleverness: 'Don't forget she carries the taint of treachery throughout her whole being, and the pirate's spawned by the devil Satan. Watch, listen, and remember. Perhaps she'll impeach herself and become a further witness against Toranaga for the Regents. Kill the pirate the moment the ambush begins.'

The arrows came out of the night and the first impaled the captain through the throat and, as he felt his lungs fill with molten fire and death swallowing him, his last thought was one of wonder because the ambush was not to have been here in this street but further on, down beside the wharves, and the attack was not to be against them but against the pirate.

Another arrow had slammed into the litter post an inch from Blackthorne's head. Two arrows had pierced the closed curtains of Kiritsubo's litter ahead, and another had struck the girl Asa in the waist. As she began screaming, the bearers dropped the litters and took to their heels in the darkness. Blackthorne rolled for cover, taking Mariko with him into the lee of the tumbled litter, Grays and Browns scattering. A shower of arrows straddled both litters. One thudded into the ground where Mariko had been the instant before. Buntaro was covering Toranaga's litter with his body as best he could, an arrow stuck into the back of his leather-chainmail-bamboo armor, and then, when the volley ceased, he rushed forward and ripped the curtains apart. The two arrows were imbedded in Toranaga's chest and side but he was unharmed and he jerked the barbs out of the protective armor he wore beneath the kimono. Then he tore off the wide-brimmed hat and the wig. Buntaro searched the darkness for the enemy, on guard, an arrow ready in his bow, while Toranaga fought out of the curtains and, pulling his sword from under the coverlet, leapt to his feet. Mariko started to scramble to help Toranaga but Blackthorne pulled her back with a shout of warning as again arrows bracketed the litters, killing two Browns and a Gray. Another came so close to Blackthorne that it took the skin off his cheek. Another pinned the skirt of his kimono to the earth. The maid, Sono, was beside the writhing girl, who was bravely holding back her screams. Then Yabu shouted and pointed and charged. Dim figures could be seen on one of the tiled roofs. A last volley whooshed out of the darkness, always at the litters. Buntaro and other Browns blocked their path to Toranaga. One man died. A shaft ripped through a joint in Buntaro's shoulder armor and he grunted with pain. Yabu and

Browns and Grays were near the wall now in pursuit but the ambushers vanished into the blackness, and though a dozen Browns and Grays raced for the corner to head them off, all knew that it was hopeless. Blackthorne groped to his feet and helped Mariko up. She was shaken but untouched.

"Thank you," she said, and hurried over to Toranaga to help screen him from Grays. Buntaro was shouting to some of his men to douse the flares near the litters. Then one of the Grays said, "Toranaga!" and though it was spoken quietly everyone heard.

In the flickering light of the flares, the sweat-streaked makeup made Toranaga seem grotesque.

One of the officer Grays bowed hastily. Here, incredibly, was the enemy of his master, free, outside the castle walls. "You will wait here, Lord Toranaga. You," he snapped at one of his men, "report to Lord Ishido at once," and the man raced away.

"Stop him," Toranaga said quietly. Buntaro launched two arrows. The man fell dying. The officer whipped out his two-handed sword and leaped for Toranaga with a screaming battle cry but Buntaro was ready and parried the blow. Simultaneously the Browns and the Grays, all intermixed, jerked out their swords and jumped for space. The street erupted into a swirling melee. Buntaro and the officer were well matched, feinting and slashing. Suddenly a Gray broke from the pack and charged for Toranaga but Mariko immediately picked up a flare, ran forward, and shoved it into the officer's face. Buntaro hacked his assailant in two, then whirled and ripped the second man apart, and cut down another who was trying to reach Toranaga as Mariko darted back out of the way, a sword now in her hands, her eyes never leaving Toranaga or Buntaro, his monstrous bodyguard.

Four Grays banded together and hurled themselves at Blackthorne, who was still rooted near his litter. Helplessly he saw them coming. Yabu and a Brown leaped to intercept, fighting demonically. Blackthorne jumped away, grabbed a flare, and using it as a whirling mace, threw the attackers momentarily off balance. Yabu killed one, maimed another, then four Browns rushed back to dispose of the last two Grays. Without hesitation Yabu and the wounded Brown hurled themselves into the attack once more, protecting Toranaga. Blackthorne ran forward and picked up a long half-sword, half-spear and raced nearer to Toranaga. Toranaga alone stood motionless, his sword sheathed, in the screaming fracas.

The Grays fought courageously. Four joined in a suicidal charge at Toranaga. The Browns broke it and pressed their advantage. The Grays regrouped and charged again. Then a senior officer ordered three to retreat for help and the rest to guard the retreat. The three Grays tore off, and though they were pursued and Buntaro shot one, two escaped.

The rest died.

CHAPTER 24

THEY were hurrying through deserted back streets, circling for the wharf and the galley. There were ten of them—Toranaga leading, Yabu, Mariko, Blackthorne, and six samurai. The rest, under Buntaro, had been sent with the litters and baggage train by the planned route, with instructions to head leisurely for the galley. The body of Asa the maid was in one of the litters. During a lull in the fighting, Blackthorne had pulled the barbed shaft out of her. Toranaga had seen the dark blood that gushed in its wake and had watched, puzzled, as the pilot had cradled her instead of allowing her to die quietly in private dignity, and then, when the fighting had ceased entirely, how gently the pilot had put her into the litter. The girl was brave and had whimpered not at all, just looked up at him until death had come. Toranaga had left her in the curtained litter as a decoy and one of the wounded had been put in the second litter, also as a decoy.

Of the fifty Browns that had formed the escort, fifteen had been killed and eleven mortally wounded. The eleven had been quickly and honorably committed to the Great Void, three by their own hands, eight assisted by Buntaro at their request. Then Buntaro had assembled the remainder around the closed litters and had left. Forty-eight Grays lay in the dust.

Toranaga knew that he was dangerously unprotected but he was content. Everything has gone well, he thought, considering the vicissitudes of chance. How interesting life is! At first I was sure it was a bad omen that the pilot had seen me change places with Kiri. Then the pilot saved me and acted the madman perfectly, and because of him we escaped Ishido. I hadn't planned for Ishido to be at the main gate, only at the forecourt. That was careless. Why was Ishido there? It isn't like Ishido to be so careful. Who advised him? Kiyama? Onoshi? Or Yodoko? A woman, ever practical would—could suspect such a subterfuge.

It had been a good plan—the secret escape dash—and established for weeks, for it was obvious that Ishido would try to keep him in the castle, would turn the other Regents against him by promising them anything, would willingly sacrifice his hostage at Yedo, the Lady Ochiba, and would use any means to keep him under guard until the final meeting of the Regents, where he would be cornered, impeached, and dispatched.

"But they'll still impeach you!" Hiro-matsu had said when Toranaga had sent for him just after dusk last night to explain what was to be attempted and why he, Toranaga, had been vacillating. "Even if you escape, the Regents will impeach you behind your back as easily as they'll do it to your face. So you're bound to commit seppuku when they order it, as they will order it."

"Yes," Toranaga had said. "As President of the Regents I am bound to do that if the four vote against me. But here"—he had taken a rolled parchment out of his sleeve—"here is my formal resignation from the Council of Regents. You will give it to Ishido when my escape is known."

"What?"

"If I resign I'm no longer bound by my Regent's oath. *Neh?* The Taikō never forbade me to resign, *neh?* Give Ishido this, too." He had handed Hiro-matsu the chop, the official seal of his office as President.

"But now you're totally isolated. You're doomed!"

"You're wrong. Listen, the Taikō's testament implanted a council of *five* Regents on the realm. Now there are four. To be legal, before they can exercise the Emperor's mandate, the four have to elect or appoint a new member, a fifth, *neh?* Ishido, Kiyama, Onoshi, and Sugiyama have to *agree, neh?* Doesn't the new Regent have to be acceptable to all of them? Of course! Now, old comrade, who in all the world will those enemies agree to share ultimate power with? Eh? And while they're arguing, no decisions and—"

"We're preparing for war and you're no longer bound and you can drop a little honey here and bile there and those pile-infested dungmakers will eat themselves up!" Hiro-matsu had said with a rush. "Ah, Yoshi Toranaga-noh-Minowara, you're a man among men. I'll eat my arse if you're not the wisest man in the land!"

Yes, it was a good plan, Toranaga thought, and they all played their parts well: Hiro-matsu, Kiri, and my lovely Sazuko. And now they're locked up tight and they will stay that way or they will be allowed to leave. I think they will never be allowed to leave.

I will be sorry to lose them.

He was leading the party unerringly, his pace fast but measured, the pace he hunted at, the pace he could keep up continuously for two days and one night if need be. He still wore the traveling cloak and Kiri's kimono, but the skirts were hitched up out of the way, his military leggings incongruous.

They crossed another deserted street and headed down an alleyway. He knew the alarm would soon reach Ishido and then the hunt would be on in earnest. There's time enough, he told himself.

Yes, it was a good plan. But I didn't anticipate the ambush. That's cost me three days of safety. Kiri was sure she could keep the deception a secret for at least three days. But the secret's out now and I won't be able to slip aboard and out to sea. Who was the ambush for? Me or the pilot? Of course the pilot. But didn't the arrows bracket both litters? Yes, but the archers were quite far away and it would be hard to see, and it would be wiser and safer to kill both, just in case.

Who ordered the attack, Kiyama or Onoshi? or the Portuguese? or the Christian Fathers?

Toranaga turned around to check the pilot. He saw that he was not flagging, nor was the woman who walked beside him, though both were tired. On the skyline he could see the vast squat bulk of the castle and the phallus of the donjon. Tonight was the second time I've almost died there, he thought. Is that castle really going to be my nemesis? The Taikō told me often enough: 'While Osaka Castle lives my line will never die and you, Toranaga Minowara, your epitaph will be written on its walls. Osaka will cause your death, my faithful vassal!' And always the hissing, baiting laugh that set his soul on edge.

Does the Taikō live within Yaemon? Whether he does or not, Yaemon is his legal heir.

With an effort Toranaga tore his eyes away from the castle and turned another corner and fled into a maze of alleys. At length he stopped outside a battered gate. A fish was etched into its timbers. He knocked in code. The door opened at once. Instantly the ill-kempt samurai bowed. "Sire?"

"Bring your men and follow me," Toranaga said and set off again.

"Gladly." This samurai did not wear the Brown uniform kimono, only motley rags of a *ronin,* but he was one of the special elite secret troops that Toranaga had smuggled into Osaka against such an emergency. Fifteen men, similarly clothed, and equally well armed, followed him and quickly fell into place as advance and rear guard, while another ran off to spread the alarm to other secret cadres. Soon Toranaga had fifty troops with him. Another hundred covered his flanks. Another thousand would be ready at dawn should he need them. He relaxed and slackened his pace, sensing that the pilot and the woman were tiring too fast. He needed them strong.

Toranaga stood in the shadows of the warehouse and studied the galley and the wharf and the foreshore. Yabu and a samurai were beside him. The others had been left in a tight knot a hundred paces back down the alley.

A detachment of a hundred Grays waited near the gangway of the galley a few hundred paces away, across a wide expanse of beaten earth that precluded any surprise attack. The galley itself was alongside, moored to stanchions fixed into the stone wharf that extended a hundred yards out into the sea. The oars were shipped neatly, and he could see indistinctly many seamen and warriors on deck.

"Are they ours or theirs?" he asked quietly.

"It's too far to be sure," Yabu replied.

The tide was high. Beyond the galley, night fishing boats were coming in and going out, lanterns serving as their riding and fishing lights. North, along the shore, were rows of beached fishing craft of many sizes, tended by a few fishermen. Five hundred paces south, alongside another stone wharf, was the Portuguese frigate, the *Santa Theresa*. Under the light of flares, clusters of porters were busily loading barrels and bales. Another large group of Grays lolled nearby. This was usual because all Portuguese and all foreign ships in port were, by law, under perpetual surveillance. It was only at Nagasaki that Portuguese shipping moved in and out freely.

If security could be tightened there, the safer we'd all sleep at night, Toranaga told himself. Yes, but could we lock them up and still have trade with China in ever increasing amounts? That's one trap the Southern Barbarians have us in from which there's no escape, not while the Christian *daimyos* dominate Kyushu and the priests are needed. The best we can do is what the Taikō did. Give the barbarians a little, pretend to take it away, try to bluff, knowing that without the China trade, life would be impossible.

"With your permission, Lord, I will attack at once," the samurai whispered.

"I advise against it," Yabu said. "We don't know if our men are aboard. And there could be a thousand men hidden all around here. Those men"—he pointed at the Grays near the Portuguese ship—"those'll raise the alarm. We could never take the ship and get it out to sea before they'd bottled us up. We need ten times the men we've got now."

"General Lord Ishido will know soon," the samurai said. "Then all Osaka'll be swarming with more hostiles than there are flies on a new battlefield. I've a hundred and fifty men with those on our flanks. That'll be enough."

"Not for safety. Not if our sailors aren't ready on the oars. Better to create a diversion, one that'd draw off the Grays—and any that are in hiding. Those, too," Yabu pointed again at the men near the frigate.

"What kind of diversion?" Toranaga said.

"Fire the street."

"That's impossible!" the samurai protested, aghast. Arson was a crime punishable by the public burning of all the family of the guilty person, of every generation of the family. The penalty was the most severe by law because fire was the greatest hazard to any village or town or city in the Empire. Wood and paper were their only building materials, except for tiles on some roofs. Every home, every warehouse, every hovel, and every palace was a tinderbox. "We can't fire the street!"

"What's more important," Yabu asked him, "the destruction of a few streets, or the death of our Master?"

"The fire'd spread, Yabu-san. We can't burn Osaka. There are a million people here—more."

"Is that your answer to my question?"

Ashen, the samurai turned to Toranaga. "Sire, I'll do anything you ask. Is that what you want me to do?"

Toranaga merely looked at Yabu.

The *daimyo* jerked his thumb contemptuously at the city. "Two years ago half of it burned down and look at it now. Five years ago was the Great Fire. How many hundred thousand were lost then? What does it matter? They're only shopkeepers, merchants, craftsmen, and *eta*. It's not as though Osaka's a village filled with peasants."

Toranaga had long since gauged the wind. It was slight and would not fan the blaze. Perhaps. But a blaze could easily become a holocaust that would eat up all the city. Except the castle. Ah, if it would only consume the castle I wouldn't hesitate for a moment.

He turned on his heel and went back to the others. "Mariko-san, take the pilot and our six samurai and go to the galley. Pretend to be almost in panic. Tell the Grays that there's been an ambush—by bandits or *ronin,* you're not sure which. Tell them where it happened, that you were sent ahead urgently by the captain of our escorting Grays to get the Grays here to help, that the battle's still raging, that you think Kiritsubo's been killed or wounded—to please hurry. If you're convicing, this will draw most of them off."

"I understand perfectly, Sire."

"Then, no matter what the Grays do, go on board with the pilot. If our sailors are there and the ship's safe and secure, come back to the gangway and pretend to faint. That's our signal. Do it exactly at the head of the gangway." Toranaga let his eyes rest on Blackthorne. "Tell him what you're going to do, but not that you're going to faint." He turned away to give orders to the rest of his men and special private instructions to the six samurai.

When Toranaga had finished, Yabu drew him aside. "Why send the barbarian? Wouldn't it be safer to leave him here? Safer for you?"

"Safer for him, Yabu-san, but not for me. He's a useful decoy."

"Firing the street would be even safer."

"Yes." Toranaga thought that it was better to have Yabu on his side than on Ishido's. I'm glad I did not make him jump off the tower yesterday.

"Sire?"

"Yes, Mariko-san?"

"I'm sorry, but the Anjin-san asks what happens if the ship's held by the enemy?"

"Tell him there's no need to go with you if he's not strong enough."

Blackthorne kept his temper when she told him what Toranaga had said. "Tell Lord Toranaga that his plan is no good for you, that you should stay here. If all's well I can signal."

"I can't do that, Anjin-san, that's not what our Master has ordered," Mariko told him firmly. "Any plan he makes is bound to be very wise."

Blackthorne realized there was no point in arguing. God curse their bloody-minded, muleheaded arrogance, he thought. But, by the Lord God, what courage they've got! The men and this woman.

He had watched her, standing at the ambush, in her hands the long killing sword that was almost as tall as herself, ready to fight to the death for Toranaga. He had seen her use the sword once, expertly, and though Buntaro had killed the attacker, she had made it easier by forcing the man to back off. There was still blood on her kimono now and it was torn in places and her face was dirty.

"Where did you learn to use a sword?" he had asked while they rushed for the docks.

"You should know that all samurai ladies are taught very early to use a knife to defend their honor and that of their lords," she had said matter-of-factly, and showed him how the stiletto was kept safe in the obi, ready for instant use. "But some of us, a few, are also taught about sword and spear, Anjin-san. Some fathers feel daughters as well as sons must be prepared to do battle for their lords. Of course, some women are more warlike than others and enjoy going into battle with their husbands or fathers. My mother was one of these. My father and mother decided I should know the sword and the spear."

"If it hadn't been for the captain of the Grays being in the way, the first arrow would have gone right through you," he had said.

"Through you, Anjin-san," she corrected him, very sure. "But you did save my life by pulling me to safety."

Now, looking at her, he knew that he would not like anything to happen to her. "Let me go with the samurai, Mariko-san. You stay here. Please."

"That's not possible, Anjin-san."

"Then I want a knife. Better, give me two."

She passed this request to Toranaga, who agreed. Blackthorne slid one under the sash, inside his kimono. The other he tied, haft downwards, to the inside of his forearm with a strip of silk he tore off the hem of his kimono.

"My Master asks do all Englishmen carry knives secretly in their sleeves like that?"

"No. But most seamen do."

"That's not usual here—or with the Portuguese," she said.

"The best place for a spare knife's in your boot. Then you can do wicked damage, very fast. If need be."

She translated this and Blackthorne noticed the attentive eyes of Toranaga and Yabu, and he sensed that they did not like him armed. Good, he thought. Perhaps I can stay armed.

He wondered again about Toranaga. After the ambush had been beaten off and the Grays killed, Toranaga had, through Mariko, thanked him before all the Browns for his "loyalty." Nothing more, no promises, no agreements, no rewards. But Blackthorne knew that those would come later. The old monk had told him that loyalty was the only thing they rewarded. 'Loyalty and duty, señor,' he had said. 'It is their cult, this *bushido*. Where we give our lives to God and His Blessed Son Jesus, and Mary the Mother of God, these animals give themselves to their masters and die like dogs. Remember, señor, for thy soul's sake, they're animals.'

They're not animals, Blackthorne thought. And much of what you said, Father, is wrong and a fanatic's exaggeration.

He said to Mariko, "We need a signal—if the ship's safe or if it isn't."

Again she translated, innocently this time. "Lord Toranaga says that one of our soldiers will do that."

"I don't consider it brave to send a woman to do a man's job."

"Please be patient with us, Anjin-san. There's no difference between men and women. Women are equal as samurai. In this plan a woman would be so much better than a man."

Toranaga spoke to her shortly.

"Are you ready, Anjin-san? We're to go now."

"The plan's rotten and dangerous and I'm tired of being a goddamned sacrificial plucked duck, but I'm ready."

She laughed, bowed once to Toranaga, and ran off. Blackthorne and the six samurai raced after her.

She was very fleet and he did not catch up with her as they rounded the corner and headed across the open space. He had never felt so naked. The moment they appeared, the Grays spotted them and surged forward. Soon they were surrounded, Mariko jabbering feverishly with the samurai and the Grays. Then he too added to the babel in a panting mixture of Portuguese, English, and Dutch, motioning them to hurry, and groped for the gangway to lean against it, not needing to pretend that he was badly winded. He tried to see inside the ship but could make out nothing distinctly, only many heads appearing at the gunwale. He could see the shaven pates of many samurai and many seamen. He could not discern the color of the kimonos.

From behind, one of the Grays was talking rapidly to him, and he turned around, telling him that he didn't understand—to go there, quickly, back up the street where the God-cursed battle was going on. "*Wakarimasu ka?* Get your scuttle-tailed arse to hell out of here! *Wakarimasu ka?* The fight's there!"

Mariko was frantically haranguing the senior officer of the Grays. The officer came back toward the ship and shouted orders. Immediately more than a hundred samurai, all Grays, began pouring off the ship. He sent a few north along the shore to intercept the wounded and help them if necessary. One was sent scurrying off to get help from the Grays near the Portuguese galley. Leaving ten men behind to guard the gangway, he led the remainder in a rush for the street which curled away from the dock, up to the city proper.

Mariko came up to Blackthorne. "Does the ship seem all right to you?" she asked.

"She's floating." With a great effort Blackthorne grasped the gangway ropes and pulled himself on deck. Mariko followed. Two Browns came after her.

The seamen packing the port gunwale gave way. Four Grays were guarding the quarterdeck and two more were on the forepoop. All were armed with bows and arrows as well as swords.

Mariko questioned one of the sailors. The man answered her obligingly. "They're all sailors hired to take Kiritsubo-san to Yedo," she told Blackthorne.

"Ask him . . ." Blackthorne stopped as he recognized the short, squat mate he had made captain of the galley after the storm. "*Konbanwa,* Captain-san!"— Good evening.

"*Konbanwa,* Anjin-san. *Watashi iyé* Captain-san *ima,*" the mate replied with a grin, shaking his head. He pointed at a lithe sailor with an iron-gray stubbly queue who stood alone on the quarterdeck. "*Imasu* Captain-san!"

"*Ah, so desu? Halloa,* Captain-san!" Blackthorne called out and bowed, and lowered his voice. "Mariko-san, find out if there are any Grays below."

Before she could say anything the captain had bowed back and shouted to the mate. The mate nodded and replied at length. Some of the sailors also voiced their agreement. The captain and all aboard were very impressed.

"*Ah, so desu,* Anjin-san!" Then the captain cried out, "*Keirei!*"—Salute! All aboard, except the samurai, bowed to Blackthorne in salute.

Mariko said, "This mate told the captain that you saved the ship during the storm, Anjin-san. You did not tell us about the storm or your voyage."

"There's little to tell. It was just another storm. Please thank the captain and say I'm happy to be aboard again. Ask him if we're ready to leave when the others arrive." And added quietly, "Find out if there are any more Grays below."

She did as she was ordered.

The captain came over and she asked for more information and then, picking up the captain's cue concerning the importance of Blackthorne aboard, she bowed to Blackthorne. "Anjin-san, he thanks you for the life of his ship and says they're ready," adding softly, "About the other, he doesn't know."

Blackthorne glanced ashore. There was no sign of Buntaro or the column to the north. The samurai sent running southward toward the *Santa Theresa* was still a hundred yards from his destination, unnoticed as yet. "What now?" he said, when he could stand the waiting no longer.

She was asking herself, Is the ship safe? Decide.

"That man'll get there any moment," he said, looking at the frigate.

"What?"

He pointed. "That one—the samurai!"

"What samurai? I'm sorry, I can't see that far, Anjin-san. I can see everything on the ship, though the Grays to the front of the ship are misted. What man?"

He told her, adding in Latin, "Now he is barely fifty paces away. Now he is seen. We need assistance gravely. Who giveth the sign? With importance it should be given quickly."

"My husband, is there any sign of him?" she asked in Portuguese.

He shook his head.

Sixteen Grays stand between my Master and his safety, she told herself. Oh Madonna, protect him!

Then, committing her soul to God, frightened that she was making the wrong decision, she went weakly to the head of the gangway and pretended to faint.

Blackthorne was taken unawares. He saw her head crash nastily against the wooden slats. Seamen began to crowd, Grays converged from the dock and from the decks as he rushed over. He picked her up and carried her back, through the men, toward the quarterdeck.

"Get some water—water, *hai?*"

The seamen stared at him without comprehension. Desperately he searched his mind for the Japanese word. The old monk had told it to him fifty times. Christ God, what is it? "Oh—*mizu, mizu, hai?*"

"*Ah, mizu! Hai,* Anjin-san." A man began to hurry away. There was a sudden cry of alarm.

Ashore, thirty of Toranaga's *ronin*-disguised samurai were loping out of the alleyway. The Grays that had begun to leave the dock spun around on the gangway. Those on the quarterdeck and forepoop craned to see better. Abruptly one shouted orders. The archers armed their bows. All samurai, Browns and Grays below, tore out their swords, and most rushed back to the wharf.

"Bandits!" one of the Browns screamed on cue. At once the two Browns on deck split up, one going forward, one aft. The four on land fanned out, intermingling with the waiting Grays.

"Halt!"

Toranaga's *ronin*-samurai charged. An arrow smashed a man in the chest and he fell heavily. Instantly the Brown on the forepoop killed the Gray archer and tried for the other but this samurai was too quick and they locked swords, the Gray shouting a warning of treachery to the others. The Brown on the aft quarterdeck had maimed one of the Grays but the other three dispatched him quickly and they raced for the head of the gangway, seamen scattering. The samurai on the dock below were fighting to the death, the Grays overwhelming the four Browns, knowing that they had been betrayed and that, at any moment, they too would be engulfed by the attackers. The leader of the Grays on deck, a large tough grizzle-bearded man, confronted Blackthorne and Mariko.

"Kill the traitors!" he bellowed, and with a battle cry, he charged.

Blackthorne had seen them all look down at Mariko, still lying in her faint, murder in their eyes, and he knew that if he did not get help soon they were both dead, and that help would not be forthcoming from the seamen. He remembered that only samurai may fight samurai.

He slid his knife into his hand and hurled it in an arc. It took the samurai in the throat. The other two Grays lunged for Blackthorne, killing swords high. He held the second knife and stood his ground over Mariko, knowing that he dare not leave her unprotected. From the corner of his eye he saw the battle for the gangway was almost won. Only three Grays still held the bridge below, only these three kept help from flooding aboard. If he could stay alive for less than a minute he was safe and she was safe. Kill 'em, kill the bastards!

He felt, more than saw, the sword slashing for his throat and leaped backward out of its way. One Gray stabbed after him, the other halted over Mariko, sword raised. At that instant Blackthorne saw Mariko come to life. She threw herself into the unsuspecting samurai's legs, crashing him to the deck. Then, scrambling across to the dead Gray, she grabbed the sword out of his still twitching hand and leaped on the guard with a cry. The Gray had regained his feet, and, howling with rage, he came at her. She backed and slashed bravely but Blackthorne knew she was lost, the man too strong. Somehow Blackthorne avoided another death thrust from his own foe and kicked him away and threw his knife at Mariko's assailant. It struck the man in the back, causing his blow to go wild, and then Blackthorne found himself on the quarterdeck, helplessly at bay, one Gray bounding up the steps after him, the other, who had just won the forepoop fight, racing toward him along the deck. He jumped for the gunwale and the safety of the sea but slipped on the blood-wet deck.

Mariko was staring up, white-faced, at the huge samurai who still had her cornered, swaying on his feet, his life ebbing fast but not fast enough. She hacked at him with all her force but he parried the blow, held her sword, and tore it out of her grasp. He gathered his ultimate strength, and lunged as the *ronin*-samurai burst up the gangway, over the dead Grays. One pounced on Mariko's assailant, another fired an arrow at the quarterdeck.

The arrow ripped into the Gray's back, smashing him off balance, and his sword sliced past Blackthorne into the gunwale. Blackthorne tried to scramble away but the man caught him, brought him crashing to the deck, and clawed for his eyes. Another arrow hit the second Gray in the shoulder and he dropped his sword, screaming with pain and rage, tearing futilely at the shaft. A third arrow twisted him around. Blood surged out of his mouth, and, choking, his eyes staring, he groped for Blackthorne and fell on him as the last Gray arrived for the kill, a short stabbing knife in his hands. He hacked downward, Blackthorne helpless, but a friendly hand caught the knife arm, then the enemy head had vanished from the neck, a fountain of blood spraying upwards. Both corpses were pulled off Blackthorne and he was hauled to his feet. Wiping the blood off his face, he dimly saw that Mariko was stretched out on the deck, *ronin*-samurai milling around her. He shook off his helpers and stumbled toward her, but his knees gave out and he collapsed.

CHAPTER 25

I T took Blackthorne a good ten minutes to regain enough strength to stand
unaided. In that time the *ronin*-samurai had dispatched the badly wounded
and had cast all corpses into the sea. The six Browns had perished, and all
the Grays. They had cleansed the ship and made her ready for instant departure,
sent seamen to their oars and stationed others by the stanchions, waiting to slip
the mooring ropes. All flares had been doused. A few samurai had been sent to
scout north along the shore to intercept Buntaro. The bulk of Toranaga's men
hurried southward to a stone breakwater about two hundred paces away, where
they took up a strong defensive position against the hundred Grays from the
frigate who, having seen the attack, were approaching fast.

When all aboard had been checked and double-checked, the leader cupped his
hands around his lips and hallooed shoreward. At once more *ronin*-disguised
samurai under Yabu came out of the night, and fanned into protective shields,
north and south. Then Toranaga appeared and began to walk slowly toward the
gangway alone. He had discarded the woman's kimono and the dark traveling
cloak and removed the makeup. Now he wore his armor, and over it a simple
brown kimono, swords in his sash. The gap behind him was closed by the last
of his guards and the phalanx moved with measured tread toward the wharf.

Bastard, Blackthorne thought. You're a cruel, cold-gutted, heartless bastard
but you've got majesty, no doubt about that.

Earlier, he had seen Mariko carried below, helped by a young woman, and
he had presumed that she was wounded but not badly, because all badly wounded
samurai are murdered at once if they won't or can't kill themselves, and she's
samurai.

His hands were very weak but he grasped the helm and pulled himself upright,
helped by the seaman, and felt better, the slight breeze taking away the dregs
of nausea. Swaying on his feet, still dulled, he watched Toranaga.

There was a sudden flash from the donjon and the faint echoing of alarm bells.
Then, from the castle walls, fires began to reach for the stars. Signal fires.

Christ Jesus, they must've got the news, they must've heard about Toranaga's
escape!

In the great silence he saw Toranaga looking back and upward. Lights began
to flicker all over the city. Without haste Toranaga turned and came aboard.

From the north distant cries came down on the wind. Buntaro! It must be,
with the rest of the column. Blackthorne searched the far darkness but could see
nothing. Southward the gap between attacking Grays and defending Browns was
closing rapidly. He estimated numbers. About equal at the moment. But for how
long?

"*Keirei!*" All aboard knelt and bowed low as Toranaga came on deck.
Toranaga motioned to Yabu, who followed him. Instantly Yabu took command,
giving orders to cast off. Fifty samurai from the phalanx ran up the gangway to
take defensive positions, facing shoreward, arming their bows.

Blackthorne felt someone tugging at his sleeve.

"Anjin-san!"

"*Hai?*" He stared down into the captain's face. The man uttered a spate of

257

words, pointing at the helm. Blackthorne realized that the captain presumed he held the con and was asking permission to cast off.

"*Hai,* Captain-san," he replied. "Cast off! *Isogi!*" Yes, very quick, he told himself, wondering how he remembered the word so easily.

The galley eased away from the jetty, helped by the wind, the oarsmen deft. Then Blackthorne saw the Grays hit the breakwater away up the shore and the tumultuous assault began. At that moment, out of the darkness from behind a nearby line of beached boats charged three men and a girl embroiled in a running fight with nine Grays. Blackthorne recognized Buntaro and the girl Sono.

Buntaro led the hacking retreat to the jetty, his sword bloody, arrows sticking into the armor on his chest and back. The girl was armed with a spear but she was stumbling, her wind gone. One of the Browns stopped courageously to cover the retreat. The Grays swamped him. Buntaro raced up the steps, the girl beside him with the last Brown, then he turned and hit the Grays like a mad bull. The first two went crashing off the ten-foot wharf; one broke his back on the stones below and the other fell howling, his right arm gone. The Grays hesitated momentarily, giving the girl time to aim her spear, but all aboard knew it was only a gesture. The last Brown rushed past his master and flung himself headlong at the enemy. The Grays cut him down, then charged en masse.

Archers from the ship fired volley after volley, killing or maiming all but two of the attacking Grays. A sword ricocheted off Buntaro's helmet onto his shoulder armor. Buntaro smashed the Gray under the chin with his mailed forearm, breaking his neck, and hurled himself at the last.

This man died too.

The girl was on her knees now, trying to catch her breath. Buntaro did not waste time making sure the Grays were dead. He simply hacked off their heads with single, perfect blows, and then, when the jetty was completely secure, he turned seaward, waved at Toranaga exhausted but happy. Toranaga called back, equally pleased.

The ship was twenty yards from the jetty, the gap still widening.

"Captain-san," Blackthorne called out, gesturing urgently. "Go back to the wharf! *Isogi!*"

Obediently the captain shouted the orders. All oars ceased and began to back water. At once Yabu came hurtling across to the quarterdeck and spoke heatedly to the captain. The order was clear. The ship was not to return.

"There's plenty of time, for Christ's sake. Look!" Blackthorne pointed at the empty beaten earth and at the breakwater where the *ronin* were holding the Grays at bay.

But Yabu shook his head.

The gap was thirty yards now and Blackthorne's mind was shouting, What's the matter with you, that's Buntaro, her husband.

"You can't let him die, he's one of ours," he shouted at Yabu and at the ship. "Him! Buntaro!" He spun round on the captain. "Back there! *Isogi!*" But this time the seaman shook his head helplessly and held the escape course and the oarsmaster continued the beat on the great drum.

Blackthorne rushed for Toranaga, who had his back to him, studying the shore and wharf. At once four bodyguard samurai stepped in the pilot's way, swords on high. He called out, "Toranaga-sama! *Dozo!* Order the ship back! There! *Dozo* —please! Go back!"

"*Iyé,* Anjin-san." Toranaga pointed once at the castle signal flares and once at the breakwater, and turned his back again with finality.

"Why, you shitless coward . . ." Blackthorne began, but stopped. Then he rushed for the gunwale and leaned over it. "Swiiiiimm!" he hollered, making the motions. "Swim, for Christ's sake!"

Buntaro understood. He raised the girl to her feet and spoke to her and half-shoved her toward the wharf edge but she cried out and fell on her knees in front of him. Obviously she could not swim.

Desperately Blackthorne searched the deck. No time to launch a small boat. Much too far to throw a rope. Not enough strength to swim there and back. No life jackets. As a last resort he ran over to the nearest oarsmen, two to each great sweep, and stopped their pull. All oars on the portside were momentarily thrown off tempo, oar crashing into oar. The galley slewed awkwardly, the beat stopped, and Blackthorne showed the oarsmen what he wanted.

Two samurai went forward to restrain him but Toranaga ordered them away.

Together, Blackthorne and four seamen launched the oar like a dart over the side. It sailed for some way then hit the water cleanly, and its momentum carried it to the wharf.

At that moment there was a victory shout from the breakwater. Reinforcements of Grays were streaming down from the city and, though the *ronin*-samurai were holding off the present attackers, it was only a matter of time before the wall was breached.

"Come on," Blackthorne shouted. *"Isogiiii!"*

Buntaro pulled the girl up, pointed at the oar and then out to the ship. She bowed weakly. He dismissed her and turned his full attention to battle, his vast legs set firm on the jetty.

The girl called out once to the ship. A woman's voice answered and she jumped. Her head broke the surface. She flailed for the oar and grabbed it. It bore her weight easily and she kicked for the ship. A small wave caught her and she rode it safely and came closer to the galley. Then her fear caused her to loosen her grip and the oar slipped away from her. She thrashed for an endless moment, then vanished below the surface.

She never came back.

Buntaro was alone now on the wharf and he stood watching the rise and the fall of the battle. More reinforcement Grays, a few cavalry among them, were coming up from the south to join the others and he knew that soon the breakwater would be engulfed by a sea of men. Carefully he examined the north and west and south. Then he turned his back to the battle and went to the far end of the jetty. The galley was safely seventy yards from its tip, at rest, waiting. All fishing boats had long since fled the area and they waited as far away as possible on both sides of the harbor, their riding lights like so many cats' eyes in the darkness.

When he reached the end of the dock, Buntaro took off his helmet and his bow and quiver and his top body armor and put them beside his scabbards. The naked killing sword and the naked short sword he placed separately. Then, stripped to the waist, he picked up his equipment and cast it into the sea. The killing sword he studied reverently, then tossed it with all his force, far out into the deep. It vanished with hardly a splash.

He bowed formally to the galley, to Toranaga, who went at once to the quarterdeck where he could be seen. He bowed back.

Buntaro knelt and placed the short sword neatly on the stone in front of him, moonlight flashing briefly on the blade, and stayed motionless, almost as though in prayer, facing the galley.

"What the hell's he waiting for?" Blackthorne muttered, the galley eerily quiet without the drumbeat. "Why doesn't he jump and swim?"

"He's preparing to commit seppuku."

Mariko was standing nearby, propped by a young woman.

"Jesus, Mariko, are you all right?"

"All right," she said, hardly listening to him, her face haggard but no less beautiful.

He saw the crude bandage on her left arm near the shoulder where the sleeve had been slashed away, her arm resting in a sling of material torn from a kimono. Blood stained the bandage and a dribble ran down her arm.

"I'm so glad—" Then it dawned on him what she had said. "Seppuku? He's going to kill himself? Why? There's plenty of time for him to get here! If he can't swim, look—there's an oar that'll hold him easily. There, near the jetty, you see it? Can't you see it?"

"Yes, but my husband can swim, Anjin-san," she said. "All of Lord Toranaga's officers must—must learn—he insists. But he has decided not to swim."

"For Christ's sake, why?"

A sudden frenzy broke out shoreward, a few muskets went off, and the wall was breached. Some of the *ronin*-samurai fell back and ferocious individual combat began again. This time the enemy spearhead was contained, and repelled.

"Tell him to swim, by God!"

"He won't, Anjin-san. He's preparing to die."

"If he wants to die, for Christ's sake, why doesn't he go there?" Blackthorne's finger stabbed toward the fight. "Why doesn't he help his men? If he wants to die, why doesn't he die fighting, like a *man?*"

Mariko did not take her eyes from the wharf, leaning against the young woman. "Because he might be captured, and if he swam he might also be captured, and then the enemy would put him on show before the common people, shame him, do terrible things. A samurai cannot be captured and remain samurai. That's the worst dishonor—to be captured by an enemy—so my husband is doing what a *man,* a samurai, must do. A samurai dies with dignity. For what is life to a samurai? Nothing at all. All life is suffering, *neh?* It is his right and *duty* to die with honor, before witnesses."

"What a stupid waste," Blackthorne said, through his teeth.

"Be patient with us, Anjin-san."

"Patient for what? For more lies? Why won't you trust me? Haven't I earned that? You lied, didn't you? You pretended to faint and that was the signal. Wasn't it? I asked you and you lied."

"I was ordered . . . it was an order to protect you. Of course I trust you."

"You lied," he said, knowing that he was being unreasonable, but he was beyond caring, abhorring the insane disregard for life and starved for sleep and peace, starved for his own food and his own drink and his own ship and his own kind. "You're all animals," he said in English, knowing they were not, and moved away.

"What was he saying, Mariko-san?" the young woman asked, hard put to hide her distaste. She was half a head taller than Mariko, bigger-boned and square-faced with little, needle-shaped teeth. She was Usagi Fujiko, Mariko's niece, and she was nineteen.

Mariko told her.

"What an awful man! What foul manners! Disgusting, *neh?* How can you bear to be near him?"

"Because he saved our Master's honor. Without his bravery I'm sure Lord Toranaga would have been captured—we'd all have been captured." Both women shuddered.

"The gods protect us from that shame!" Fujiko glanced at Blackthorne, who leaned against the gunwale up the deck, staring at the shore. She studied him a moment. "He looks like a golden ape with blue eyes—a creature to frighten children with. Horrid, *neh?*" Fujiko shivered and dismissed him and looked again at Buntaro. After a moment she said, "I envy your husband, Mariko-san."

"Yes," Mariko replied sadly. "But I wish he had a second to help him." By custom another samurai always assisted at a seppuku, standing slightly behind the kneeling man, to decapitate him with a single stroke before the agony became unbearable and uncontrollable and so shamed the man at the supreme moment of his life. Unseconded, few men could die without shame.

"Karma," Fujiko said.

"Yes. I pity him. That's the one thing he feared—not to have a second."

"We're luckier than men, *neh?"* Samurai women committed seppuku by thrusting their knives into their throats and therefore needed no assistance.

"Yes," Mariko said.

Screams and battle cries came wafting on the wind, distracting them. The breakwater was breached again. A small company of fifty Toranaga *ronin*-samurai raced out of the north in support, a few horsemen among them. Again the breach was ferociously contained, no quarter sought or given, the attackers thrown back and a few more moments of time gained.

Time for what, Blackthorne was asking bitterly. Toranaga's safe now. He's out to sea. He's betrayed you all.

The drum began again.

Oars bit into the water, the prow dipped and began to cut through the waves, and aft a wake appeared. Signal fires still burned from the castle walls above. The whole city was almost awake.

The main body of Grays hit the breakwater. Blackthorne's eyes went to Buntaro. "You poor bastard!" he said in English. "You poor, stupid bastard!"

He turned on his heel and walked down the companionway along the main deck toward the bow to watch for shoals ahead. No one except Fujiko and the captain noticed him leaving the quarterdeck.

The oarsmen pulled with fine discipline and the ship was gaining way. The sea was fair, the wind friendly. Blackthorne tasted the salt and welcomed it. Then he detected the ships crowding the harbor mouth half a league ahead. Fishing vessels yes, but they were crammed with samurai.

"We're trapped," he said out loud, knowing somehow they were enemy.

A tremor went through the ship. All who watched the battle on shore had shifted in unison.

Blackthorne looked back. Grays were calmly mopping up the breakwater, while others were heading unhurried toward the jetty for Buntaro, but four horsemen—Browns—were galloping across the beaten earth from out of the north, a fifth horse, a spare horse, tethered to the leader. This man clattered up the wide stone steps of the wharf with the spare horse and raced its length while the other three slammed toward the encroaching Grays. Buntaro had also looked around but he remained kneeling and, when the man reined in behind him, he waved him away and picked up the knife in both hands, blade toward himself. Immediately Toranaga cupped his hands and shouted, "Buntaro-san! Go with them now—try to escape!"

The cry swept across the waves and was repeated and then Buntaro heard it clearly. He hesitated, shocked, the knife poised. Again the call, insistent and imperious.

With effort Buntaro drew himself back from death and icily contemplated life and the escape that was ordered. The risk was bad. Better to die here, he told himself. Doesn't Toranaga know that? Here is an honorable death. There, almost certain capture. Where do you run? Three hundred *ri,* all the way to Yedo? You're certain to be captured!

He felt the strength in his arm, saw the firm, unshaking, needle-pointed dagger hovering near his naked abdomen, and he craved for the releasing agony of death at long last. At long last a death to expiate all the shame: the shame of his father's kneeling to Toranaga's standard when they should have kept faith with Yaemon, the Taikō's heir, as they had sworn to do; the shame of killing so many men who honorably served the Taikō's cause against the usurper, Toranaga; the shame of the woman, Mariko, and of his only son, both forever tainted, the son because of the mother and she because of her father, the monstrous assassin, Akechi Jinsai. And the shame of knowing that because of them, his own name was befouled forever.

How many thousand agonies have I not endured because of her?

His soul cried out for oblivion. Now so near and easy and honorable. The next life will be better; how could it be worse?

Even so, he put down the knife and obeyed, and cast himself back into the abyss of life. His liege lord had ordered the ultimate suffering and had decided to cancel his attempt at peace. What else is there for a samurai but obedience?

He jumped up, hurled himself into the saddle, jammed his heels into the horse's sides, and, together with the other man, he fled. Other *ronin*-cavalry galloped out of the night to guard their retreat and cut down the leading Grays. Then they too vanished, a few Gray horsemen in pursuit.

Laughter erupted over the ship.

Toranaga was pounding the gunwale with his fist in glee, Yabu and the samurai were roaring. Even Mariko was laughing.

"One man got away, but what about all the dead?" Blackthorne cried out enraged. "Look ashore—there must be three, four hundred bodies there. *Look at them, for Christ's sake!*"

But his shout did not come through the laughter.

Then a cry of alarm from the bow lookout. And the laughter died.

CHAPTER 26

ORANAGA said calmly, "Can we break through them, Captain?" He was watching the grouped fishing boats five hundred yards ahead, and the tempting passage they had left between them.

"No, Sire."

"We've no alternative," Yabu said. "There's nothing else we can do." He glared aft at the massed Grays who waited on the shore and the jetty, their faint, jeering insults riding on the wind.

Toranaga and Yabu were on the forepoop now. The drum had been silenced and the galley wallowed in a light sea. All aboard waited to see what would be decided. They knew that they were bottled tight. Ashore disaster, ahead disaster, to wait disaster. The net would come closer and closer and then they would be captured. If need be, Ishido could wait days.

Yabu was seething. If we'd rushed for the harbor mouth directly we'd boarded instead of wasting useless time over Buntaro, we'd be safely out to sea by now, he told himself. Toranaga's losing his wits. Ishido will believe I betrayed him. There's nothing I can do—unless we can fight our way out, and even then I'm committed to fight for Toranaga against Ishido. Nothing I can do. Except give Ishido Toranaga's head. *Neh?* That would make you a Regent and bring you the Kwanto, *neh?* And then with six months of time and the musket samurai, why not even President of the Council of Regents? Or why not the big prize! Eliminate Ishido and become Chief General of the Heir, Lord Protector and Governor of Osaka Castle, the controlling general of all the legendary wealth in the donjon, with power over the Empire during Yaemon's minority, and afterwards power second only to Yaemon. Why not?

Or even the biggest prize of all. Shōgun. Eliminate Yaemon, then you'll be Shōgun.

All for a single head and some benevolent gods!

Yabu's knees felt weak as his longing soared. So easy to do, he thought, but no way to take the head and escape—yet.

"Order attack stations!" Toranaga commanded at last.

As Yabu gave the orders and samurai began to prepare, Toranaga turned his attention to the barbarian, who was still near the forepoop, where he had stopped when the alarm was given, leaning against the short mainmast.

I wish I could understand him, Toranaga thought. One moment so brave, the next so weak. One moment so valuable, the next so useless. One moment killer, the next coward. One moment docile, the next dangerous. He's man and woman, *Yang* and *Yin*. He's nothing but opposites, and unpredictable.

Toranaga had studied him carefully during the escape from the castle, during the ambush and after it. He had heard from Mariko and the captain and others what had happened during the fight aboard. He had witnessed the astonishing anger a few moments ago and then, when Buntaro had been sent off, he had heard the shout and had seen through veiled eyes the stretched ugliness on the man's face, and then, when there should have been laughter, only anger.

Why not laughter when an enemy's outsmarted? Why not laughter to empty the tragedy from you when *karma* interrupts the beautiful death of a true samurai, when *karma* causes the useless death of a pretty girl? Isn't it only through laughter that we become one with the gods and thus can endure life and can overcome all the horror and waste and suffering here on earth? Like tonight, watching all those brave men meet their fate here, on this shore, on this gentle night, through a *karma* ordained a thousand lifetimes ago, or perhaps even one.

Isn't it only through laughter we can stay human?

Why doesn't the pilot realize he's governed by *karma* too, as I am, as we all are, as even this Jesus the Christ was, for, if the truth were known, it was only his *karma* that made him die dishonored like a common criminal with other common criminals, on the hill the barbarian priests tell about.

All *karma*.

How barbaric to nail a man to a piece of wood and wait for him to die. They're worse than the Chinese, who are pleasured by torture.

"Ask him, Yabu-san!" Toranaga said.

"Sire?"

"Ask him what to do. The pilot. Isn't this a sea battle? Haven't you told me the pilot's a genius at sea? Good, let's see if you're right. Let him prove it."

Yabu's mouth was a tight cruel line and Toranaga could feel the man's fear and it delighted him.

"Mariko-san," Yabu barked. "Ask the pilot how to get out—how to break through those ships."

Obediently Mariko moved away from the gunwale, the girl still supporting her. "No, I'm all right now, Fujiko-san," she said. "Thank you." Fujiko let her go and watched Blackthorne distastefully.

Blackthorne's answer was short.

"He says 'with cannon,' Yabu-san," Mariko said.

"Tell him he'll have to do better than that if he wants to retain his head!"

"We must be patient with him, Yabu-san," Toranaga interrupted. "Mariko-san, tell him politely, 'Regrettably we have no cannon. Isn't there another way to break out? It's impossible by land.' Translate exactly what he replies. Exactly."

Mariko did so. "I'm sorry, Lord, but he says, no. Just like that. 'No.' Not politely."

Toranaga moved his sash and scratched an itch under his armor. "Well then," he said genially, "the Anjin-san says cannon and he's the expert, so cannon it is. Captain, go there!" His blunt, calloused finger pointed viciously at the Portuguese frigate. "Get the men ready, Yabu-san. If the Southern Barbarians won't lend me their cannon, then you will have to take them. Won't you?"

"With very great pleasure," Yabu said softly.

"You were right, he is a genius."

"But you found the solution, Toranaga-san."

"It's easy to find solutions given the answer, *neh?* What's the solution to Osaka Castle, Ally?"

"There isn't one. In that the Taikō was perfect."

"Yes. What's the solution to treachery?"

"Of course, ignominious death. But I don't understand why you should ask me that."

"A passing thought—Ally." Toranaga glanced at Blackthorne. "Yes, he's a clever man. I have great need of clever men. Mariko-san, will the barbarians give me their cannon?"

"Of course. Why shouldn't they?" It had never occurred to her that they would not. She was still filled with anxiety over Buntaro. It would have been so much better to allow him to die back there. Why risk his honor? She wondered why Toranaga had ordered Buntaro away by land at the very last moment. Toranaga could just as easily have ordered him to swim to the boat. It would have been much safer and there was plenty of time. He could even have ordered it when Buntaro had first reached the end of the jetty. Why wait? Her most secret self answered that their lord must have had a very good reason to have waited and to have so ordered.

"And if they don't? Are you prepared to kill Christians, Mariko-san?" Toranaga asked. "Isn't that their most impossible law? Thou shalt not kill?"

"Yes, it is. But for you, Lord, we will go gladly into hell, my husband and my son and I."

"Yes. You're true samurai and I won't forget that you took up a sword to defend me."

"Please do not thank me. If I helped, in any minor way, it was my duty. If anyone is to be remembered, please let it be my husband or my son. They are more valuable to you."

"At the moment you're more valuable to me. You could be even more valuable."

"Tell me how, Sire. And it will be done."

"Put this foreign God away."

"Sire?" Her face froze.

"Put your God away. You have one too many loyalties."

"You mean become apostate, Sire? Give up Christianity?"

"Yes, unless you can put this God where He belongs—in the back of your spirit, not in the front."

"Please excuse me, Sire," she said shakily, "but my religion has never interfered with my loyalty to you. I've always kept my religion a private matter, all the time. How have I failed you?"

"You haven't yet. But you will."

"Tell me what I must do to please you."

"The Christians may become my enemies, *neh?*"

"Your enemies are mine, Lord."

"The priests oppose me now. They may order all Christians to war on me."

"They can't, Sire. They're men of peace."

"And if they continue to oppose me? If Christians war on me?"

"You will never have to fear my loyalty. Never."

"This Anjin-san may speak the truth and your priests with false tongues."

"There are good priests and bad priests, Sire. But you are my liege lord."

"Very well, Mariko-san," Toranaga said. "I'll accept that. You're ordered to become friends with this barbarian, to learn all he knows, to report everything he says, to learn to think like him, to 'confess' nothing about what you're doing, to treat all priests with suspicion, to report everything the priests ask you or say to you. Your God must fit in between, elsewhere—or not at all."

Mariko pushed a thread of hair out of her eyes. "I can do all that, Sire, and still remain Christian. I swear it."

"Good. Swear it by this Christian God."

"Before God I swear it."

"Good." Toranaga turned and called out, "Fujiko-san!"

"Yes, Sire?"

"Did you bring maids with you?"

"Yes, Sire. Two."

"Give one to Mariko-san. Send the other for cha."

"There's saké if you wish."

"Cha. Yabu-san, would you like cha or saké?"

"Cha, please."

"Bring saké for the Anjin-san."

Light caught the little golden crucifix that hung from Mariko's neck. She saw Toranaga stare at it. "You . . . you wish me not to wear it, Sire? To throw it away?"

"No," he said. "Wear it as a reminder of your oath."

They all watched the frigate. Toranaga felt someone looking at him and glanced around. He saw the hard face and cold blue eyes and felt the hate—no, not hate, the suspicion. How dare the barbarian be suspicious of me, he thought.

"Ask the Anjin-san why didn't he just say there're plenty of cannon on the barbarian ship? Get them to escort us out of the trap?"

Mariko translated. Blackthorne answered.

"He says . . ." Mariko hesitated, then continued in a rush, "Please excuse me, he said, 'It's good for him to use his own head.' "

Toranaga laughed. "Thank him for his. It's been most useful. I hope it stays on his shoulders. Tell him that now we're equal."

"He says, 'No, we're not equal, Toranaga-sama. But give me my ship and a crew and I'll wipe the seas clean. Of any enemy.' "

"Mariko-san, do you think he meant me as well as the others—the Spanish and the Southern Barbarians?" The question was put lightly.

The breeze wafted strands of hair into her eyes. She pushed them away tiredly. "I don't know, so sorry. Perhaps, perhaps not. Do you want me to ask him? I'm sorry, but he's a . . . he's very strange. I'm afraid I don't understand him. Not at all."

"We've plenty of time. Yes. In time he'll explain himself to us."

Blackthorne had seen the frigate quietly slip her moorings the moment her escort of Grays had hurried away, had watched her launch her longboat, which had quickly warped the ship away from her berth at the jetty, well out into the stream. Now she lay a few cables offshore in deep water, safe, a light bow anchor holding her gently, broadside to the shore. This was the normal maneuver of all European ships in alien or hostile harbors when a shore danger threatened. He knew, too, that though there was—and had been—no untoward movement on deck, by now all cannon would be primed, muskets issued, grape, cannonball, and chainshot ready in abundance, cutlasses waiting in their racks—and armed men aloft in the shrouds. Eyes would be searching all points of the compass. The galley would have been marked the moment it had changed course. The two stern chasers, thirty pounders, which were pointing directly at them, would be trained on them. Portuguese gunners were the best in the world, after the English.

And they'll know about Toranaga, he told himself with great bitterness, because they're clever and they'd have asked their porters or the Grays what all the trouble was about. Or by now the God-cursed Jesuits who know everything would have sent word about Toranaga's escape, and about me.

He could feel his short hairs curling. Any one of those guns can blow us to hell. Yes, but we're safe because Toranaga's aboard. Thank God for Toranaga.

Mariko was saying, "My Master asks what is your custom when you want to approach a warship?"

"If you had cannon you'd fire a salute. Or you can signal with flags, asking permission to come alongside."

"My Master says, and if you have no flags?"

Though they were still outside cannon range it was almost, to Blackthorne, as if he were already climbing down one of the barrels, though the gunports were still closed. The ship carried eight cannon a side on her main deck, two at the stern and two at the bow. *Erasmus* could take her, he told himself, without a doubt, providing the crew was right. I'd like to take her. Wake up, stop daydreaming, we're not aboard *Erasmus* but this sow-gutted galley and that Portuguese ship's the only hope we have. Under her guns we're safe. Bless your luck for Toranaga.

"Tell the captain to break out Toranaga's flag at the masthead. That'll be enough, senhora. That'll make it formal and tell them who's aboard, but I'd bet they know already."

This was done quickly. Everyone in the galley seemed to be more confident now. Blackthorne marked the change. Even he felt better under the flag.

"My Master says, but how do we tell them we wish to go alongside?"

"Tell him without signal flags he has two choices: he waits outside cannon range and sends a deputation aboard her in a small boat, or we go directly within hailing distance."

"My Master says, which do you advise?"

"Go straight alongside. There's no reason for caution. Lord Toranaga's aboard. He's the most important *daimyo* in the Empire. Of course she'll help us and— Oh Jesu God!"

"Senhor?"

But he did not reply, so she quickly translated what had been said and listened to Toranaga's next question. "My Master asks, the frigate will what? Please explain your thought and the reason you stopped."

"I suddenly realized, he's at war with Ishido now. Isn't he? So the frigate may not be inclined to help him."

"Of course they'll help him."

"No. Which side benefits the Portuguese more, Lord Toranaga or Ishido? If they believe Ishido will, they'll blow us to hell out of the water."

"It's unthinkable that the Portuguese would fire on any Japanese ship," Mariko said at once.

"Believe me, they will, senhora. And I'll bet that frigate won't let us alongside. I wouldn't if I were her pilot. Christ Jesus!" Blackthorne stared ashore.

The taunting Grays had left the jetty now and were spreading out parallel to the shore. No chance there, he thought. The fishing boats still lay malevolently clogging the harbor's neck. No chance there either. "Tell Toranaga there's only one other way to get out of the harbor. That's to hope for a storm. Maybe we could ride it out, where the fishing boats can't. Then we could slip past the net."

Toranaga questioned the captain, who answered at length, then Mariko said to Blackthorne, "My Master asks, do you think there'll be a storm?"

"My nose says yes. But not for days. Two or three. Can we wait that long?"

"Your nose tells you? There is a smell to a storm?"

"No, senhora. It's just an expression."

Toranaga pondered. Then he gave an order.

"We are going to within hailing distance, Anjin-san."

"Then tell him to go directly astern of her. That way we're the smallest target. Tell him they're treacherous—I know how seriously treacherous they are when their interests are threatened. They're worse than the Dutch! If that ship helps Toranaga escape, Ishido will take it out on all Portuguese and they won't risk that."

"My Master says we'll soon have that answer."

"We're naked, senhora. We've no chance against those cannon. If the ship's hostile—even if it's simply neutral—we're sunk."

"My Master says, yes, but it will be your duty to persuade them to be benevolent."

"How can I do that? I'm their enemy."

"My Master says, in war and in peace, a good enemy can be more valuable than a good ally. He says you will know their minds—you will think of a way to persuade them."

"The only sure way's by force."

"Good. I agree, my Master says. Please tell me how you would pirate that ship."

"What?"

"He said, good, I agree. How would you pirate the ship, how would you conquer it? I require the use of their cannon. So sorry, isn't that clear, Anjin-san?"

"And again I say I'm going to blow her out of the water," Ferriera, the Captain-General, declared.

"No," dell'Aqua replied, watching the galley from the quarterdeck.

"Gunner, is she in range yet?"

"No, Don Ferriera," the chief gunner replied. "Not yet."

"Why else is she coming at us if not for hostile reasons, Eminence? Why doesn't she just escape? The way's clear." The frigate was too far from the harbor mouth for anyone aboard to see the encroaching fishing boats crowding in ambush.

"We risk nothing, Eminence, and gain everything," Ferriera said. "We pretend we didn't know Toranaga was aboard. We thought the bandits—bandits led by the pirate heretic—were going to attack us. Don't worry, it will be easy to provoke them once they're in range."

"No," dell'Aqua ordered.

Father Alvito turned back from the gunwale. "The galley's flying Toranaga's flag, Captain-General."

"False colors!" Ferriera added sardonically, "That's the oldest sea trick in the world. We haven't seen Toranaga. Perhaps he isn't aboard."

"No."

"God's death, war would be a catastrophe! It'll hurt, if not ruin, the Black Ship's voyage this year. I can't afford that! I won't have anything interfere with that!"

"Our finances are in a worse position than yours, Captain-General," dell'Aqua rapped. "If we don't trade this year, the Church is bankrupt, is that clear? We've had no funds from Goa or Lisbon for three years and the loss of last year's profit. . . . God give me patience! I know better than you what's at stake. The answer is no!"

Rodrigues was sitting painfully in his seachair, his leg in a splint resting on a padded stool that was lashed safe near the binnacle. "The Captain-General's right, Eminence. Why should she come at us, if not to try something? Why not escape, eh? Eminence, we've a piss-cutting opportunity here."

"Yes, and it is a military decision," Ferriera said.

Alvito turned on him sharply. "No, his Eminence is arbiter in this, Captain-General. We must not hurt Toranaga. We must help him."

Rodrigues said, "You've told me a dozen times that once war starts it'll go on forever. War's started, hasn't it? We've seen it start. That's got to hurt trade. With Toranaga dead the war's over and all our interests are safe. I say blow the ship to hell."

"We even get rid of the heretic," Ferriera added, watching Rodrigues. "You prevent a war for the glory of God, and another heretic goes to torment."

"It would be unwarranted interference in their politics," dell'Aqua replied, avoiding the real reason.

"We interfere all the time. The Society of Jesus is famous for it. We're not simple, thick-headed peasants!"

"I'm not suggesting you are. But while I'm aboard you will not sink that ship."

"Then kindly go ashore."

"The sooner the archmurderer is dead, the better, Eminence," Rodrigues suggested. "Him or Ishido, what's the difference? They're both heathen, and you can't trust either of them. The Captain-General's right, we'll never get an opportunity like this again. And what about our Black Ship?" Rodrigues was pilot with a fifteenth part of all the profit. The real pilot of the Black Ship had died of the pox in Macao three months ago and Rodrigues had been taken off his own ship, the *Santa Theresa,* and given the new post, to his everlasting joy. Pox was the official reason, Rodrigues reminded himself grimly, though many said the other pilot was knifed in the back by a *ronin* in a whorehouse brawl. By God, this is my great chance. Nothing's going to interfere with that!

"I will accept full responsibility," Ferriera was saying. "It's a military decision. We're involved in a native war. My ship's in danger." He turned again to the chief gunner. "Are they in range yet?"

"Well, Don Ferriera, that depends what you wish." The chief gunner blew on the end of the taper, which made it glow and spark. "I could take off her bow now, or her stern, or hit her amidships, whichever you prefer. But if you want a man dead, a particular man, then a moment or two would bring them into killing range."

"I want Toranaga dead. And the heretic."

"You mean the Ingeles, the pilot?"

"Yes."

"Someone will have to point the Jappo out. The pilot I'll recognize, doubtless."

Rodrigues said, "If the pilot's got to die to kill Toranaga and stop the war then I'm for it, Captain-General. Otherwise he should be spared."

"He's a heretic, an enemy of our country, an abomination, and he's already caused us more trouble than a nest of vipers."

"I've already pointed out that first the Ingeles is a pilot and last he's a pilot, one of the best in the world."

"Pilots should have special privileges? Even heretics?"

"Yes, by God. We should use him like they use us. It'd be a God-cursed waste to kill such experience. Without pilots there's no piss-cutting Empire and no trade and no nothing. Without me, by God, there's no Black Ship and no profit and no way home, so my opinion's God-cursed important."

There was a cry from the masthead, "Ho on the quarterdeck, the galley's changing her course!" The galley had been heading straight for them but now she had swung a few points to port, out into the harbor.

Immediately Rodrigues shouted, "Action stations! Starboard watch aloft—all sails ho! Up anchor!" At once all men rushed to obey.

"What's amiss, Rodrigues?"

"I don't know, Captain-General, but we're getting out into open sea. That fat-gutted whore's going to windward."

"What does that matter? We can sink them at any time," Ferriera said. "We've stores still to bring aboard and the Fathers have to go back to Osaka."

"Aye. But no hostile's getting to windward of my ship. That whore doesn't depend on the wind, she can go against it. She might be coming round to hack at us from our bow where we've only one cannon and board us!"

Ferriera laughed contemptuously. "We've twenty cannon aboard! They've none! You think that filthy heathen pig boat would dare to try to attack us? You're simple in the head!"

"Yes, Captain-General, that's why I've still got one. The *Santa Theresa's* ordered to sea!"

The sails were crackling out of their ropes and the wind took them, the spars grinding. Both watches were on deck at battle stations. The frigate began to make way but her going was slow. "Come on, you bitch," Rodrigues urged.

"We're ready, Don Ferriera," the chief gunner said. "I've got her in my sights. I can't hold her for long. Which is this Toranaga? Point him out!"

There were no flares aboard the galley; the only illumination came from the moonlight. The galley was still astern, a hundred yards off, but turned to port now and headed for the far shore, the oars dipping and falling in unbroken rhythm. "Is that the pilot? The tall man on the quarterdeck?"

"Yes," Rodrigues said.

"Manuel and Perdito! Take him and the quarterdeck!" The cannon nearest made slight adjustments. "Which is this Toranaga? Quickly! Helmsmen, two points to starboard!"

"Two points to starboard it is, Gunner!"

Conscious of the sanding bottom and the shoals nearby, Rodrigues was watching the shrouds, ready at any second to override the chief gunner, who by custom had the con on a stern cannonade. "Ho, port maindeck cannon!" the gunner shouted. "Once we've fired we'll let her fall off the wind. Drop all gun ports, prepare for a broadside!" The gun crews obeyed, their eyes going to the officers on the quarterdeck. And the priests. "For the love of God, Don Ferriera, which is this Toranaga?"

"Which is he, Father?" Ferriera had never seen him before.

Rodrigues had recognized Toranaga clearly on the foredeck in a ring of samurai, but he did not want to be the one to put the mark on him. Let the priests do that, he thought. Go on, Father, play the Judas. Why should we always do all the pox-foul work, not that I care a chipped doubloon for that heathen son of a whore.

Both priests were silent.

"Quick, which would Toranaga be?" the gunner asked again.

Impatiently Rodrigues pointed him out. "There, on the poop. The short, thickset bastard in the middle of those other heathen bastards."

"I see him, Senhor Pilot."

The gun crews made last slight adjustments.

Ferriera took the taper out of the gunner's mate's hand.

"Are you trained on the heretic?"

"Yes, Captain-General, are you ready? I'll drop my hand. That's the signal!"

"Good."

"Thou shalt not kill!" It was dell'Aqua.

Ferriera whirled on him. "They're heathens and heretics!"

"There are Christians among them and even if there weren't—"

"Pay no attention to him, Gunner!" the Captain-General snarled. "We fire when you're ready!"

Dell'Aqua went forward to the muzzle of the cannon and stood in the way. His bulk dominated the quarterdeck and the armed sailors that lay in ambush. His hand was on the crucifix. "I say, *Thou shalt not kill!*"

"We kill all the time, Father," Ferriera said.

"I know, and I'm ashamed of it and I beg God's forgiveness for it." Dell'Aqua had never before been on the quarterdeck of a fighting ship with primed guns, and muskets, and fingers on triggers, readying for death. "While I'm here there'll be no killing and I'll not condone killing from ambush!"

"And if they attack us? Try to take the ship?"

"I will beg God to assist us against them!"

"What's the difference, now or later?"

Dell'Aqua did not answer. Thou shalt not kill, he thought, and Toranaga has promised everything, Ishido nothing.

"What's it to be, Captain-General? Now's the time!" the master gunner cried. "Now!"

Ferriera bitterly turned his back on the priests, threw down the taper and went to the rail. "Get ready to repel an attack," he shouted. "If she comes within fifty yards uninvited, you're all ordered to blow her to hell whatever the priests say!"

Rodrigues was equally enraged but he knew that he was as helpless as the Captain-General against the priest. Thou shalt not kill? By the blessed Lord Jesus, what about you? he wanted to shout. What about the auto da fé? What about the Inquisition? What about you priests who pronounce the sentence "guilty" or "witch" or "satanist" or "heretic"? Remember the two thousand witches burned in Portugal alone, the year I sailed for Asia? What about almost every village and town in Portugal and Spain, and the dominions visited and investigated by the Scourges of God, as the cowled Inquisitors proudly called themselves, the smell of burning flesh in their wake? Oh, Lord Jesus Christ, protect us!

He pushed his fear and loathing away and concentrated on the galley. He could just see Blackthorne and he thought, ah Ingeles, it's good to see you, standing there holding the con, so tall and cocky. I was afraid you'd gone to the execution ground. I'm glad you escaped, but even so it's lucky you don't have a single little cannon aboard, for then I'd blow you out of the water, and to hell with what the priests would say.

Oh, Madonna, protect me from a bad priest.

"Ahoy, *Santa Theresa!*"

"Ahoy, Ingeles!"

"Is that you, Rodrigues?"

"Aye!"

"Thy leg?"

"Thy mother!"

Rodrigues was greatly pleased by the bantering laugh that came across the sea that separated them.

For half an hour the two ships had maneuvered for position, chasing, tacking, and falling away, the galley trying to get windward and bottle the frigate on a lee shore, the frigate to gain sea room to sail out of harbor if she desired. But neither had been able to gain an advantage, and it was during this chase that those aboard the frigate had seen the fishing boats crowding the mouth of the harbor for the first time and realized their significance.

"That's why he's coming at us! For protection!"

"Even more reason for us to sink him now he's trapped. Ishido will thank us forever," Ferriera had said.

Dell'Aqua had remained obdurate. "Toranaga's much too important. I insist first we must talk to Toranaga. You can always sink him. He doesn't have cannon. Even I know that only cannon can fight cannon."

So Rodrigues had allowed a stalemate to develop to give them breathing time.

Both ships were in the center of the harbor, safe from fishing ships and safe from each other, the frigate trembling into the wind, ready to fall off instantly, and the galley, oars shipped, drifting broadside to just within calling distance. It was only when Rodrigues had seen the galley ship all oars and turn broadside to his guns that he had turned into the wind to allow her to approach within shouting range and had prepared for the next series of moves. Thank God, the blessed Jesus, Mary, and Joseph, we've cannon and that bastard has none, Rodrigues thought again. The Ingeles is too smart.

But it's good to be opposed by a professional, he told himself. Much safer. Then no one makes a foolhardy mistake and no one gets hurt unnecessarily.

"Permission to come aboard?"

"Who, Ingeles?"

"Lord Toranaga, his interpreter, and guards."

Ferriera said quietly, "No guards."

Alvito said, "He must bring some. It's a matter of face."

"The pox on face. No guards."

"I don't want samurai aboard," Rodrigues agreed.

"Would you agree to five?" Alvito asked. "Just his personal guards? You understand the problem, Rodrigues."

Rodrigues thought a moment, then nodded. "Five are all right, Captain-General. We'll detail five men as your 'personal bodyguards' with a brace of pistols apiece. Father, you fix the details now. Better the Father to arrange the details, Captain-General, he knows how. Go on, Father, but tell us what's being said."

Alvito went to the gunwale and shouted, "You gain nothing by your lies! Prepare your souls for hell—you and your bandits. You've ten minutes, then the Captain-General's going to blow you to eternal torment!"

"We're flying Lord Toranaga's flag, by God!"

"False colors, pirate!"

Ferriera took a step forward. "What are you playing at, Father?"

"Please be patient, Captain-General," Alvito said. "This is only a matter of form. Otherwise Toranaga has to be permanently offended that we've insulted his flag—which we have. That's Toranaga—that's no simple *daimyo!* Perhaps you'd better remember that he personally has more troops under arms than the King of Spain!"

The wind was sighing in the rigging, the spars clattering nervously. Then flares were lit on the quarterdeck and now they could see Toranaga clearly. His voice came across the waves.

"Tsukku-san! How dare you avoid my galley! There are no pirates here—only in those fishing ships at the harbor mouth. I wish to come alongside instantly!"

Alvito shouted back in Japanese, feigning astonishment, "But Lord Toranaga, so sorry, we had no idea! We thought it was just a trick. The Grays said bandit-*ronin* had taken the galley by force! We thought bandits, under the English pirate, were sailing under false colors. I will come immediately."

"No. I will come alongside at once."

"I beg you, Lord Toranaga, allow me to come to escort you. My Master, the Father-Visitor, is here and also the Captain-General. They insist we make amends. Please accept our apologies!" Alvito changed to Portuguese again and shouted loudly to the bosun, "Launch a longboat," and back again to Toranaga in Japanese, "The boat is being launched at once, my Lord."

Rodrigues listened to the cloying humility in Alvito's voice and he thought how much more difficult it was to deal with Japanese than with Chinese. The Chinese understood the art of negotiation, of compromise and concession and reward. But the Japanese were pride-filled and when a man's pride was injured

—any Japanese, not necessarily just samurai—then death was a small price to repay the insult. Come on, get it over with, he wanted to shout.

"Captain-General, I'll go at once," Father Alvito was saying. "Eminence, if you come as well that compliment will do much to appease him."

"I agree."

"Isn't that dangerous?" Ferriera said. "You two could be used as hostages."

Dell'Aqua said, "The moment there's a sign of treachery, I order you, in God's name, to obliterate that ship and all who sail in her, whether we're aboard or not." He strode off the quarterdeck, down onto the main deck, past the guns, the skirts of his robe swinging majestically. At the head of the gangway he turned and made the sign of the cross. Then he clattered down the gangway into the boat.

The bosun cast off. All the sailors were armed with pistols, and a fused keg of powder was under the bosun's seat.

Ferriera leaned over the gunwale and called down quietly, "Eminence, bring the heretic back with you."

"What? What did you say?" It amused dell'Aqua to toy with the Captain-General, whose continual insolence had mortally offended him, for of course he had decided long since to acquire Blackthorne, and he could hear perfectly well. *Che stupido,* he was thinking.

"Bring the heretic back with you, eh?" Ferriera called again.

On the quarterdeck Rodrigues heard the muffled, "Yes, Captain-General," and he thought, what treachery are you about, Ferriera?

He shifted in the chair with difficulty, his face bloodless. The pain in his leg was grinding and it took much of his strength to contain it. The bones were knitting well and, Madonna be praised, the wound was clean. But the fracture was still a fracture and even the slight dip of the ship at rest was troublesome. He took a swallow of grog from the well-used seabag that hung from a peg on the binnacle.

Ferriera was watching him. "Your leg's bad?"

"It's all right." The grog deadened the hurt.

"Will it be all right enough to voyage from here to Macao?"

"Yes. And to fight a sea battle all the way. And to come back in the summer, if that's what you mean."

"Yes, that's what I mean, Pilot." The lips were thin again, drawn into that tight mocking smile. "I need a fit pilot."

"I'm fit. My leg's mending well." Rodrigues shook off the pain. "The Ingeles won't come aboard us willingly. I wouldn't."

"A hundred guineas says you're wrong."

"That's more than I make in a year."

"Payable after we reach Lisbon, from the profits from the Black Ship."

"Done. Nothing'll make him come aboard, not willingly. I'm a hundred guineas richer, by God!"

"Poorer! You forget the Jesuits want him here more than I do."

"Why should they want that?"

Ferriera looked at him levelly and did not answer, wearing the same twisted smile. Then, baiting him, he said, "I'd escort Toranaga out, for possession of the heretic."

"I'm glad I'm your comrade and necessary to you and the Black Ship," Rodrigues said. "I wouldn't want to be your enemy."

"I'm glad we understand one another, Pilot. At long last."

* * *

"I require escort out of the harbor. I need it quickly," Toranaga told dell'Aqua through the interpreter Alvito, Mariko nearby, also listening, with Yabu. He stood on the galley's poopdeck, dell'Aqua below on the main deck, Alvito beside him, but even so their eyes were almost level. "Or, if you wish, your warship can remove the fishing boats from out of my way."

"Forgive me, but that would be an unwarranted hostile act that you would not—could not recommend to the frigate, Lord Toranaga," dell'Aqua said, talking directly to him, finding Alvito's simultaneous translation eerie, as always. "That would be impossible—an open act of war."

"Then what do you suggest?"

"Please come back to the frigate. Let us ask the Captain-General. He will have a solution, now that we know what your problem is. He's the military man, we are not."

"Bring him here."

"It would be quicker for you to go there, Sire. Apart, of course, from the honor you would do us."

Toranaga knew the truth of this. Only moments before they had seen more fishing boats loaded with archers launched from the southern shore and, though they were safe at the moment, it was clear that within the hour the neck of the harbor would be choked with hostiles.

And he knew he had no choice.

"Sorry, Sire," the Anjin-san had explained earlier, during the abortive chase, "I can't get near the frigate. Rodrigues is too clever. I can stop him escaping if the wind holds but I can't trap him, unless he makes a mistake. We'll have to parley."

"Will he make a mistake and will the wind hold?" he had asked through Mariko.

She had replied, "The Anjin-san says, a wise man never bets on the wind, unless it's a trade wind and you're out to sea. Here we're in a harbor where the mountains cause the wind to eddy and flow. The pilot, Rodrigues, won't make a mistake."

Toranaga had watched the two pilots pit their wits against each other and he knew, beyond doubt, that both were masters. And he had come to realize also that neither he nor his lands nor the Empire would ever be safe without possessing modern barbarian ships, and through these ships, control of their own seas. The thought had shattered him.

"But how can I negotiate with them? What possible excuse could they use for such open hostility against me? Now it's my duty to bury them for their insults to my honor."

Then the Anjin-san had explained the ploy of false colors: how all ships used the device to get close to the enemy, or to attempt to avoid an enemy, and Toranaga had been greatly relieved that there might be an acceptable face-saving solution to that problem.

Now Alvito was saying, "I think we should go at once, Sire."

"Very well," Toranaga agreed. "Yabu-san, take command of the ship. Mariko-san, tell the Anjin-san he is to stay on the quarterdeck and to keep the helm, then you come with me."

"Yes, Lord."

It had been clear to Toranaga from the size of the longboat that he could take only five guards with him. But this, too, had been anticipated and the final plan was simple: if he could not persuade the frigate to help, then he and his guards would kill the Captain-General, their pilot, and the priests and barricade themselves in one of the cabins. Simultaneously the galley would be flung at the frigate from her bow as the Anjin-san had suggested and, together, they would try to take the frigate by storm. They would take her or they would not take her, but either way there would be a quick solution.

"It is a good plan, Yabu-san," he had said.

"Please allow me to go in your place to negotiate."

"They would not agree."

"Very well, but once we're out of the trap expel all barbarians from our realm. If you do, you'll gain more *daimyos* than you lose."

"I'll consider it," Toranaga had said, knowing it was nonsense, that he must have the Christian *daimyos* Onoshi and Kiyama on his side, and therefore the other Christian *daimyos,* or by default he would be eaten up. Why would Yabu wish to go to the frigate? What treachery did he plan if there was no help?

"Sire," Alvito was saying for dell'Aqua, "may I invite the Anjin-san to accompany us?"

"Why?"

"It occurred to me that he might like to greet his colleague the anjin Rodrigues. The man has a broken leg and cannot come here. Rodrigues would like to see him again, thank him for saving his life, if you don't mind."

Toranaga could not think of any reason why the Anjin-san should not go. The man was under his protection, therefore inviolate. "If he wishes to do so, very well. Mariko-san, accompany Tsukku-san."

Mariko bowed. She knew her job was to listen and to report and to ensure that everything that was said was reported correctly, without omission. She felt better now, her coiffure and face once more perfect, a fresh kimono borrowed from Lady Fujiko, her left arm in a neat sling. One of the mates, an apprentice doctor, had dressed her wound. The slice into her upper arm had not cut a tendon and the wound itself was clean. A bath would have made her whole, but there were no facilities on the galley.

Together she and Alvito walked back to the quarterdeck. He saw the knife in Blackthorne's sash and the way the soiled kimono seemed to fit. How far has he leeched his way into Toranaga's confidence, he asked himself. "Well met, Captain-Pilot Blackthorne."

"Rot in hell, Father!" Blackthorne replied affably.

"Perhaps we'll meet there, Anjin-san. Perhaps we will. Toranaga said you can come aboard the frigate."

"His orders?"

" 'If you wish,' he said."

"I don't wish."

"Rodrigues would like to thank you again and to see you."

"Give him my respects and say I'll see him in hell. Or here."

"His leg prevents that."

"How is his leg?"

"Healing. Through your help and the grace of God, in a few weeks, God willing, he will walk, though he will limp forever."

"Tell him I wish him well. You'd better be going, Father, time's a-wasting."

"Rodrigues would like to see you. There's grog on the table and a fine roast capon with fresh greens and gravy and new fresh bread, butter hot. It'd be sad, Pilot, to waste such food."

"What?"

"There's new golden bread, Captain-Pilot, fresh hardtack, butter, and a side of beef. Fresh oranges from Goa and even a gallon of Madeira wine to wash it down with, or brandy if you'd prefer. There's beer, too. Then there's Macao capon, hot and juicy. The Captain-General's an epicure."

"God damn you to hell!"

"He will, when it pleases Him. I only tell you what exists."

"What does 'epicure' mean?" Mariko asked.

"It's one who enjoys food and sets a fine table, Senhora Maria," Alvito said, using her baptismal name. He had marked the sudden change on Blackthorne's face. He could almost see the saliva glands working and feel the stomach-churning agony. Tonight when he had seen the repast set out in the great cabin, the gleaming silver and white tablecloth and chairs, real leather-cushioned chairs, and smelt the new breads and butter and rich meats, he himself had been weak with hunger, and he wasn't starved for food or unaccustomed to Japanese cuisine.

It is so simple to catch a man, he told himself. All you need to know is the right bait. "Good-by, Captain-Pilot!" Alvito turned and walked for the gangway. Blackthorne followed.

"What's amiss, Ingeles?" Rodrigues asked.

"Where's the food? Then we can talk. First the food you promised." Blackthorne stood shakily on the main deck.

"Please follow me," Alvito said.

"Where are you taking him, Father?"

"Of course to the great cabin. Blackthorne can eat while Lord Toranaga and the Captain-General talk."

"No. He can eat in my cabin."

"It's easier, surely, to go where the food is."

"Bosun! See that the pilot's fed at once—all that he needs, in my cabin, anything from the table. Ingeles, do you want grog, or wine or beer?"

"Beer first, then grog."

"Bosun, see to it, take him below. And listen, Pesaro, give him some clothes out of my locker, and boots, everything. And stay with him till I call you."

Wordlessly Blackthorne followed Pesaro the bosun, a large burly man, down the companionway. Alvito began to go back to dell'Aqua and Toranaga, who were talking through Mariko near the companionway, but Rodrigues stopped him.

"Father! Just a moment. What did you say to him?"

"Only that you would like to see him and that we had food aboard."

"But I was offering him the food?"

"No, Rodrigues, I didn't say that. But wouldn't you want to offer food to a fellow pilot who was hungry?"

"That poor bastard's not hungry, he's starving. If he eats in that state he'll gorge like a ravenous wolf, then he'll vomit it up as fast as a drunk-gluttoned whore. Now, we wouldn't want one of us, even a heretic, to eat like an animal and vomit like an animal in front of Toranaga, would we, Father? Not in front of a piss-cutting sonofabitch—particularly one as clean-minded as a pox-mucked whore's cleft!"

"You must learn to control the filth of your tongue, my son," Alvito said. "It will send you to hell. You'd better say a thousand Ave Marias and go without food for two days. Bread and water only. A penance to God's Grace to remind you of His Mercy."

"Thank you, Father, I will. Gladly. And if I could kneel I would, and I'd kiss your cross. Yes, Father, this poor sinner thanks you for your God-given patience. I must guard my tongue."

Ferriera called out from the companionway, "Rodrigues, are you coming below?"

"I'll stay on deck while that bitch galley's there, Captain-General. If you need me I'm here." Alvito began to leave. Rodrigues noticed Mariko. "Just a minute, Father. Who's the woman?"

"Donna Maria Toda. One of Toranaga's interpreters."

Rodrigues whistled tonelessly. "Is she good?"

"Very good."

"Stupid to allow her aboard. Why did you say 'Toda'? She's one of old Toda Hiro-matsu's consorts?"

"No. She's the wife of his son."

"Stupid to bring her aboard." Rodrigues beckoned one of the seamen. "Spread the word the woman speaks Portuguese."

"Yes, senhor." The man hurried away and Rodrigues turned back to Father Alvito.

The priest was not in the least intimidated by the obvious anger. "The Lady Maria speaks Latin too—and just as perfectly. Was there anything else, Pilot?"

"No, thank you. Perhaps I'd better get on with my Hail Marys."

"Yes, you should." The priest made the sign of the cross and left. Rodrigues spat into the scuppers and one of the helmsmen winced and crossed himself.

"Go nail yourself to the mast by your green-addled foreskin!" Rodrigues hissed.

"Yes, Captain-Pilot, sorry, senhor. But I get nervous near the good Father. I meant no harm." The youth saw the last grains of sand fall through the neck of the hourglass and he turned it.

"At the half, go below, and take a God-cursed pail and water and a scrubbing brush with you, and clean up the mess in my cabin. Tell the bosun to bring the Ingeles aloft and you make my cabin clean. And it'd better be very clean, or I'll have your guts for garters. And while you're doing it, say Ave Marias for your God-cursed soul."

"Yes, Senhor Pilot," the youth said weakly. Rodrigues was a fanatic, a madman, about cleanliness, and his own cabin was like the ship's Holy Grail. Everything had to be spotless, no matter what the weather.

CHAPTER 27

THERE must be a solution, Captain-General," dell'Aqua said patiently. "Do you want an overt act of war against a friendly nation?" "Of course not."

Everyone in the great cabin knew that they were all in the same trap. Any overt act put them squarely with Toranaga against Ishido, which they should absolutely avoid in case Ishido was the eventual victor. Presently Ishido controlled Osaka, and the capital, Kyoto, and the majority of the Regents. And now, through the *daimyos* Onoshi and Kiyama, Ishido controlled most of the southern island of Kyushu, and with Kyushu, the port of Nagasaki, the main center of all trading, and thus all trade and the Black Ship this year.

Toranaga said through Father Alvito, "What's so difficult? I just want you to blow the pirates out of the harbor mouth, *neh?*"

Toranaga sat uncomfortably in the place of honor, in the high-backed chair at the great table. Alvito sat next to him, the Captain-General opposite, dell'Aqua beside the Captain-General. Mariko stood behind Toranaga and the samurai guards waited near the door, facing the armed seamen. And all the Europeans were conscious that though Alvito translated for Toranaga everything that was said in the room, Mariko was there to ensure that nothing was said openly between them against her Master's interests and that the translation was complete and accurate.

Dell'Aqua leaned forward. "Perhaps, Sire, you could send messengers ashore to Lord Ishido. Perhaps the solution lies in negotiation. We could offer this ship as a neutral place for the negotiations. Perhaps in this way you could settle the war."

Toranaga laughed scornfully. "What war? We're not at war, Ishido and I."

"But, Sire, we saw the battle on the shore."

"Don't be naïve! Who were killed? A few worthless *ronin*. Who attacked whom? Only *ronin*, bandits or mistaken zealots."

"And at the ambush? We understand that Browns fought Grays."

"Bandits were attacking all of us, Browns and Grays. My men merely fought to protect me. In night skirmishes mistakes often happen. If Browns killed Grays or Grays Browns that's a regrettable error. What are a few men to either of us? Nothing. We're not at war."

Toranaga read their disbelief so he added, "Tell them, Tsukku-san, that armies fight wars in Japan. These ridiculous skirmishes and assassination attempts are mere probes, to be dismissed when they fail. War didn't begin tonight. It began when the Taikō died. Even before that, when he died without leaving a grown son to follow him. Perhaps even before that, when Goroda, the Lord Protector, was murdered. Tonight has no lasting significance. None of you understands our realm, or our politics. How could you? Of course Ishido's trying to kill me. So are many other *daimyos*. They've done so in the past and they'll do so in the future. Kiyama and Onoshi have been both friend and enemy. Listen, if I'm killed that would simplify things for Ishido, the real enemy, but only for a moment. I'm in his trap now and if his trap's successful he merely has a momentary advantage. If I escape, there never was a trap. But understand clearly, all of you, that my death will not remove the cause of war nor will it prevent further conflict. Only if Ishido dies will there be no conflict. So there's no open war now. None." He shifted in the chair, detesting the odor in the cabin from the oily foods and unwashed bodies. "But we do have an immediate problem. I want your cannon. I want them now. Pirates beset me at the harbor mouth. I said earlier, Tsukku-san, that soon everyone must choose sides. Now, where do you and your leader and the whole Christian Church stand? And are my Portuguese friends with me or against me?"

Dell'Aqua said, "You may be assured, Lord Toranaga, we all support your interests."

"Good. Then remove the pirates at once."

"That'd be an act of war and there's no profit in it. Perhaps we can make a trade, eh?" Ferriera said.

Alvito did not translate this but said instead, "The Captain-General says, we're only trying to avoid meddling in your politics, Lord Toranaga. We're traders."

Mariko said in Japanese to Toranaga, "So sorry, Sire, that's not correct. That's not what was said."

Alvito sighed. "I merely transposed some of his words, Sire. The Captain-General is not aware of certain politenesses as he is a stranger. He has no understanding of Japan."

"But you do have, Tsukku-san?" Toranaga asked.

"I try, Sire."

"What did he actually say?"

Alvito told him.

After a pause Toranaga said, "The Anjin-san told me the Portuguese were very interested in trade, and in trade they have no manners, or humor. I understand and will accept your explanation, Tsukku-san. But from now on please translate everything exactly as it is said."

"Yes, Lord."

"Tell the Captain-General this: When the conflict is resolved I will expand trade. I am in favor of trade. Ishido is not."

Dell'Aqua had marked the exchange and hoped that Alvito had covered Ferriera's stupidity. "We're not politicians, Sire, we're religious and we represent the Faith and the Faithful. We do support your interests. Yes."

"I agree. I was considering—" Alvito stopped interpreting and his face lit up and he let Toranaga's Japanese get away from him for a moment. "I'm sorry, Eminence, but Lord Toranaga said, 'I was considering asking you to build a temple, a large temple in Yedo, as a measure of my confidence in your interests.' "

For years, ever since Toranaga had become Lord of the Eight Provinces, dell'Aqua had been maneuvering for that concession. And to get it from him now, in the third greatest city in the Empire, was a priceless concession. The Visitor knew the time had come to resolve the problem of the cannon. "Thank him, Martin Tsukku-san," he said, using the code phrase that he had previously agreed upon with Alvito, committing their course of action, with Alvito the standard-bearer, "and say we will try always to be at his service. Oh yes, and ask him what he had in mind about the cathedral," he added for the Captain-General's benefit.

"Perhaps I may speak directly, Sire, for a moment," Alvito began to Toranaga. "My Master thanks you and says what you previously asked is perhaps possible. He will endeavor always to assist you."

"Endeavor is an abstract word, and unsatisfactory."

"Yes, Sire." Alvito glanced at the guards, who, of course, listened without appearing to. "But I remember you saying earlier that it is sometimes wise to be abstract."

Toranaga understood at once. He waved his hand in dismissal to his men. "Wait outside, all of you."

Uneasily they obeyed. Alvito turned to Ferriera. "We don't need your guards now, Captain-General."

When the samurai had gone Ferriera dismissed his men and glanced at Mariko. He wore pistols in his belt and had another in his boot.

Alvito said to Toranaga, "Perhaps, Sire, you would like the Lady Mariko to sit?"

Again Toranaga understood. He thought for a moment, then half nodded and said, without turning around, "Mariko-san, take one of my guards and find the Anjin-san. Stay with him until I send for you."

"Yes, Lord."

The door closed behind her.

Now they were alone. The four of them.

Ferriera said, "What's the offer? What's he offering?"

"Be patient, Captain-General," dell'Aqua replied, his fingers drumming on his cross, praying for success.

"Sire," Alvito began to Toranaga, "the Lord my Master says that everything you asked he will try to do. Within the forty days. He will send you word privately about progress. I will be the courier, with your permission."

"And if he's not successful?"

"It will not be through want of trying, or persuasion, or through want of thought. He gives you his word."

"Before the Christian God?"

"Yes. Before God."

"Good. I will have it in writing. Under his seal."

"Sometimes full agreements, delicate agreements, should not be reduced to writing, Sire."

"You're saying unless I put my agreement in writing, you won't?"

"I merely remembered one of your own sayings that a samurai's honor is certainly more important than a piece of paper. The Visitor gives you his word before God, his word of honor, as a samurai would. Your honor is totally sufficient for the Visitor. I just thought he would be saddened to be so untrusted. Do you wish me to ask for a signature?"

At length Toranaga said, "Very well. His word before the God Jesus, *neh?* His word before his God?"

"I give it on his behalf. He has sworn by the Blessed Cross to try."

"You as well, Tsukku-san?"

"You have equally my word, before my God, by the Blessed Cross, that I will do everything I can to help him persuade the Lords Onoshi and Kiyama to be your allies."

"In return I will do what I previously promised. On the forty-first day you may lay the foundation stone for the biggest Christian temple in the Empire."

"Could that land, Sire, be put aside at once?"

"As soon as I arrive at Yedo. Now. What about the pirates? The pirates in the fishing boats? You will remove them at once?"

"If you had cannon, would you have done that yourself, Sire?"

"Of course, Tsukku-san."

"I apologize for being so devious, Sire, but we have had to formulate a plan. The cannon do not belong to us. Please give me one moment." Alvito turned to dell'Aqua. "Everything is arranged about the cathedral, Eminence." Then to Ferriera he added, beginning their agreed plan: "You will be glad you did not sink him, Captain-General. Lord Toranaga asks if you would carry ten thousand ducats of gold for him when you leave with the Black Ship for Goa, to invest in the gold market in India. We would be delighted to help in the transaction through our usual sources there, placing the gold for you. Lord Toranaga says half the profit is yours." Both Alvito and dell'Aqua had decided that by the time the Black Ship had turned about, in six months, Toranaga either would be reinstated as President of the Regents and therefore more than pleased to permit this most profitable transaction, or he would be dead. "You should easily clear four thousand ducats profit. At no risk."

"In return for what concession? That's more than your annual subsidy from the King of Spain for your whole Society of Jesus in Asia. In return for what?"

"Lord Toranaga says pirates prevent him leaving the harbor. He would know better than you if they're pirates."

Ferriera replied in the same matter-of-fact voice that both knew was only for Toranaga's benefit, "It's ill-advised to put your faith in this man. His enemy holds all the royal cards. All the Christian kings are against him. Certainly the main two, I heard them with my own ears. They said this Jappo's the real enemy. I believe them and not this motherless cretin."

"I'm sure Lord Toranaga knows better than us who are pirates and who are not," dell'Aqua told him unperturbed, knowing the solution as Alvito knew the solution. "I suppose you've no objection to Lord Toranaga's dealing with the pirates himself?"

"Of course not."

"You have plenty of spare cannon aboard," the Visitor said. "Why not give him some privately. Sell him some, in effect. You sell arms all the time. He's buying arms. Four cannon should be more than enough. It would be easy to transship them in the longboat, with enough powder and shot, again privately. Then the matter is solved."

Ferriera sighed. "Cannon, my dear Eminence, are useless aboard the galley. There are no gun ports, no gun ropes, no gun stanchions. They can't use cannon, even if they had the gunners, which they don't."

Both priests were flabbergasted. "Useless?"

"Totally."

"But surely, Don Ferriera, they can adapt . . ."

"That galley's incapable of using cannon without a refit. It would take at least a week."

"*Nan ja?*" Toranaga said suspiciously, aware that something was amiss however much they had tried to hide it.

"What is it, Toranaga asks," Alvito said.

Dell'Aqua knew the sand had run out on them. "Captain-General, please help us. Please. I ask you openly. We've gained enormous concessions for the Faith. You must believe me and yes, you must trust us. You must help Lord Toranaga out of the harbor somehow. I beg you on behalf of the Church. The cathedral alone is an enormous concession. Please."

Ferriera allowed none of the ecstasy of victory to show. He even added a token gravity to his voice. "Since you ask help in the Church's name, Eminence, of course I'll do what you ask. I'll get him out of this trap. But in return I want the Captain-Generalship of next year's Black Ship whether this year's is successful or not."

"That's the personal gift of the King of Spain, his alone. That's not mine to bestow."

"Next: I accept the offer of his gold, but I want your guarantee that I'll have no trouble from the Viceroy at Goa, or here, about the gold or about either of the Black Ships."

"You dare to hold me and the Church to ransom?"

"This is merely a business arrangement between you, me, and this monkey."

"He's no monkey, Captain-General. You'd better remember it."

"Next: Fifteen percent of this year's cargo instead of ten."

"Impossible."

"Next: To keep everything tidy, Eminence, your word before God—now—that neither you nor any of the priests under your jurisdiction will ever threaten me with excommunication unless I commit a future act of sacrilege, which none of this is. And further, your word that you and the Holy Fathers will actively support me and help these two Black Ships—also before God."

"And next, Captain-General? Surely that's not all? Surely there's something else?"

"Last: I want the heretic."

Mariko stared down at Blackthorne from the cabin doorway. He lay in a semicoma on the floor, retching his innards out. The bosun was leaning against the bunk leering at her, the stumps of his yellow teeth showing.

"Is he poisoned, or is he drunk?" she asked Totomi Kana, the samurai beside her, trying without success to close her nostrils to the stench of the food and the vomit, to the stench of the ugly seaman in front of her, and to the ever present stench from the bilges that pervaded the whole ship. "It almost looks as though he's been poisoned, *neh?*"

"Perhaps he has, Mariko-san. Look at that filth!" The samurai waved distastefully at the table. It was strewn with wooden platters containing the remains of a mutilated haunch of roast beef, blood rare, half the carcass of a spitted chicken, torn bread and cheese and spilled beer, butter and a dish of cold bacon-fat gravy, and a half emptied bottle of brandy.

Neither of them had ever seen meat on a table before.

"What d'you want?" the bosun asked. "No monkeys in here, *wakarimasu?* No monkey-sans this-u room-u!" He looked at the samurai and waved him away. "Out! Piss off!" His eyes flowed back over Mariko. "What's your name? Namu, eh?"

"What's he saying, Mariko-san?" the samurai asked.

The bosun glanced at the samurai for a moment then back to Mariko again. "What's the barbarian saying, Mariko-san?"

Mariko took her mesmerized eyes off the table and concentrated on the bosun. "I'm sorry, senhor, I didn't understand you. What did you say?"

"Eh?" The bosun's mouth dropped further open. He was a big fat man with eyes too close together and large ears, his hair in a ratty tarred pigtail. A crucifix hung from the rolls of his neck and pistols were loose in his belt. "Eh? You can talk Portuguese? A Jappo who can talk good Portuguese? Where'd you learn to talk civilized?"

"The—the Christian Father taught me."

"I'll be a God-cursed son of a whore! Madonna, a flower-san who can talk civilized!"

Blackthorne retched again and tried feebly to get off the deck.

"Can you—please can you put the pilot there?" She pointed at the bunk.

"Aye. If this monkey'll help."

"Who? I'm sorry, what did you say? Who?"

"Him! The Jappo. Him."

The words rocked through her and it took all of her will to remain calm. She motioned to the samurai. "Kana-san, will you please help this barbarian. The

Anjin-san should be put there."

"With pleasure, Lady."

Together the two men lifted Blackthorne and he flopped back in the bunk, his head too heavy, mouthing stupidly.

"He should be washed," Mariko said in Japanese, still half stunned by what the bosun had called Kana.

"Yes, Mariko-san. Order the barbarian to send for servants."

"Yes." Her disbelieving eyes went inexorably to the table again. "Do they really eat that?"

The bosun followed her glance. At once he leaned over and tore off a chicken leg and offered it to her. "You hungry? Here, little Flower-san, it's good. It's fresh today—real Macao capon."

She shook her head.

The bosun's grizzled face split into a grin and he helpfully dipped the chicken leg into the heavy gravy and held it under her nose. "Gravy makes it even better. Hey, it's good to be able to talk proper, eh? Never did that before. Go on, it'll give you strength—where it counts! It's Macao capon I tell you."

"No—no, thank you. To eat meat—to eat meat is forbidden. It's against the law, and against Buddhism and Shintoism."

"Not in Nagasaki it isn't!" The bosun laughed. "Lots of Jappos eat meat all the time. They all do when they can get it, and swill our grog as well. You're Christian, eh? Go on, try, little Donna. How d'you know till you try?"

"No, no, thank you."

"A man can't live without meat. That's real food. Makes you strong so you can jiggle like a stoat. Here—" He offered the chicken leg to Kana. "You want?"

Kana shook his head, equally nauseated. "*Iyé!*"

The bosun shrugged and threw it carelessly back onto the table. "*Iyé* it is. What've you done to your arm? You hurt in the fight?"

"Yes. But not badly." Mariko moved it a little to show him and swallowed the pain.

"Poor little thing! What d'you want here, Donna Senhorita, eh?"

"To see the An— to see the pilot. Lord Toranaga sent me. The pilot's drunk?"

"Yes, that and the food. Poor bastard ate too fast 'n drank too fast. Took half the bottle in a gulp. Ingeles're all the same. Can't hold their grog and they've no *cojones.*" His eyes went all over her. "I've never seen a flower as small as you before. And never talked to a Jappo who could talk civilized before."

"Do you call all Japanese ladies and samurai Jappos and monkeys?"

The seaman laughed shortly. "Hey, senhorita, that was a slip of the tongue. That's for usuals, you know, the pimps and whores in Nagasaki. No offense meant. I never did talk to a civilized senhorita before, never knowed there was any, by God."

"Neither have I, senhor. I've never talked to a civilized Portuguese before, other than a Holy Father. We're Japanese, not Jappos, *neh?* And monkeys are animals, aren't they?"

"Sure." The bosun showed the broken teeth. "You speak like a Donna. Yes. No offense, Donna Senhorita."

Blackthorne began mumbling. She went to the bunk and shook him gently. "Anjin-san! Anjin-san!"

"Yes—yes?" Blackthorne opened his eyes. "Oh—hello—I'm sor—I . . ." But the weight of his pain and the spinning of the room forced him to lie back.

"Please send for a servant, senhor. He should be washed."

"There's slaves—but not for that, Donna Senhorita. Leave the Ingeles—what's a little vomit to a heretic?"

"No servants?" she asked, flabbergasted.

"We have slaves—black bastards, but they're lazy—wouldn't trust one to wash him myself," he added with a twisted grin.

Mariko knew she had no alternative. Lord Toranaga might have need of the Anjin-san at once and it was her duty. "Then I need some water," she said. "To wash him with."

"There's a barrel in the stairwell. In the deck below."

"Please fetch some for me, senhor."

"Send him." The bosun jerked a finger at Kana.

"No. You will please fetch it. Now."

The bosun looked back at Blackthorne. "You his doxie?"

"What?"

"The Ingeles's doxie?"

"What's a doxie, senhor?"

"His woman. His mate, you know, senhorita, this pilot's sweetheart, his jigajig. Doxie."

"No. No, senhor, I'm not his doxie."

"His, then? This mon— this samurai's? Or the king's maybe, him that's just come aboard? Tora-something? You one of his?"

"No."

"Nor any aboard's?"

She shook her head. "Please, would you get some water?"

The bosun nodded and went out.

"That's the ugliest, foulest-smelling man I've ever been near," the samurai said. "What was he saying?"

"He—the man asked if—if I was one of the pilot's consorts."

The samurai went for the door.

"Kana-san!"

"I demand the right on your husband's behalf to avenge that insult. At once! As though you'd cohabit with any barbarian!"

"Kana-san! Please close the door."

"You're Toda Mariko-san! How dare he insult you? The insult must be avenged!"

"It will be, Kana-san, and I thank you. Yes. I give you the right. But we are here at Lord Toranaga's order. Until he gives his approval it would not be correct for you to do this."

Kana closed the door reluctantly. "I agree. But I formally ask that you petition Lord Toranaga before we leave."

"Yes. Thank you for your concern over my honor." What would Kana do if he knew all that had been said, she asked herself, appalled. What would Lord Toranaga do? Or Hiro-matsu? Or my husband? Monkeys? Oh, Madonna, give me thy help to hold myself still and keep my mind working. To ease Kana's wrath, she quickly changed the subject. "The Anjin-san looks so helpless. Just like a baby. It seems barbarians can't stomach wine. Just like some of our men."

"Yes. But it's not the wine. Can't be. It's what he's eaten."

Blackthorne moved uneasily, groping for consciousness.

"They've no servants on the ship, Kana-san, so I'll have to substitute for one of the Anjin-san's ladies." She began to undress Blackthorne, awkwardly because of her arm.

"Here, let me help you." Kana was very deft. "I used to do this for my father when the saké took him."

"It's good for a man to get drunk once in a while. It releases all the evil spirits."

"Yes. But my father used to suffer badly the next day."

"My husband suffers very badly. For days."

After a moment, Kana said, "May Buddha grant that Lord Buntaro escapes."

"Yes." Mariko looked around the cabin. "I don't understand how they can live in such squalor. It's worse than the poorest of our people. I was almost fainting in the other cabin from the stench."

"It's revolting. I've never been aboard a barbarian ship before."

"I've never been on the sea before."

The door opened and the bosun set down the pail. He was shocked at Blackthorne's nudity and jerked out a blanket from under the bunk and covered him. "He'll catch his death. Apart from that—shameful to do that to a man, even him."

"What?"

"Nothing. What's your name, Donna Senhorita?" His eyes glittered.

She did not answer. She pushed the blanket aside and washed Blackthorne clean, glad for something to do, hating the cabin and the foul presence of the bosun, wondering what they were talking about in the other cabin. Is our Master safe?

When she had finished she bundled the kimono and soiled loincloth. "Can this be laundered, senhor?"

"Eh?"

"These should be cleaned at once. Could you send for a slave, please?"

"They're a lazy bunch of black bastards, I told you. That'd take a week or more. Throw 'em away, Donna Senhorita, they're not worth breath. Our Pilot-Captain Rodrigues said to give him proper clothes. Here." He opened a sea locker. "He said to give him any from here."

"I don't know how to dress a man in those."

"He needs a shirt 'n trousers 'n codpiece 'n socks and boots 'n sea jacket." The bosun took them out and showed her. Then, together, she and the samurai began to dress Blackthorne, still in his half-conscious stupor.

"How does he wear this?" She held up the triangular, baglike codpiece with its attached strings.

"Madonna, he wears it in front, like this," the bosun said, embarrassed, fingering his own. "You tie it in place over his trousers, like I told. Over his cod."

She looked at the bosun's, studying it. He felt her look and stirred.

She put the codpiece on Blackthorne and settled him carefully in place, and together she and the samurai put the back strings between his legs and tied the strings around his waist. To the samurai she said quietly, "This is the most ridiculous way of dressing I've ever seen."

"It must be very uncomfortable," Kana replied. "Do priests wear them, Mariko-san? Under their robes?"

"I don't know."

She brushed a strand of hair out of her eyes. "Senhor. Is the Anjin-san dressed correctly now?"

"Aye. Except for his boots. They're there. They can wait." The bosun came over to her and her nostrils clogged. He dropped his voice, keeping his back to the samurai. "You want a quickie?"

"What?"

"I fancy you, senhorita, eh? What'd you say? There's a bunk in the next cabin. Send your friend aloft. The Ingeles's out for an hour yet. I'll pay the usual."

"What?"

"You'll earn a piece of copper—even three if you're like a stoat, and you'll straddle the best cock between here and Lisbon, eh? What d'you say?"

The samurai saw her horror. "What is it, Mariko-san?"

Mariko pushed past the bosun, away from the bunk. Her words stumbled. "He . . . he said . . ."

Kana drew out his sword instantly but found himself staring into the barrels of two cocked pistols. Nevertheless he began to lunge.

"Stop, Kana-san!" Mariko gasped. "Lord Toranaga forbade any attack until he ordered it!"

"Go on, monkey, come at me, you stink-pissed shithead! You! Tell this monkey to put up his sword or he'll be a headless sonofabitch before he can fart!"

Mariko was standing within a foot of the bosun. Her right hand was still in her obi, the haft of the stiletto knife still in her palm. But she remembered her duty and took her hand away. "Kana-san, replace your sword. Please. We must obey Lord Toranaga. We must obey him."

With a supreme effort, Kana did as he was told.

"I've a mind to send you to hell, Jappo!"

"Please excuse him, senhor, and me," Mariko said, trying to sound polite. "There was a mistake, a mis—"

"That monkey-faced bastard pulled a sword. That wasn't a mistake, by Jesus!"

"Please excuse it, senhor, so sorry."

The bosun wet his lips. "I'll forget it if you're friendly, Little Flower. Into the next cabin with you, and tell this monk—tell him to stay here and I'll forget about it."

"What—what's your name, senhor?"

"Pesaro. Manuel Pesaro, why?"

"Nothing. Please excuse the misunderstanding, Senhor Pesaro."

"Get in the next cabin. Now."

"What's going on? What's . . ." Blackthorne did not know if he was awake or still in a nightmare, but he felt the danger. "What's going on, by God!"

"This stinking Jappo drew on me!"

"It was a—a mistake, Anjin-san," Mariko said. "I—I've apologized to the Senhor Pesaro."

"Mariko? Is that you—Mariko-san?"

"*Hai,* Anjin-san. *Honto. Honto.* "

She came nearer. The bosun's pistols never wavered off Kana. She had to brush past him and it took an even greater effort not to take out her knife and gut him. At that moment the door opened. The youthful helmsman came into the cabin with a pail of water. He gawked at the pistols and fled.

"Where's Rodrigues?" Blackthorne said, attempting to get his mind working.

"Aloft, where a good pilot should be," the bosun said, his voice grating. "This Jappo drew on me, by God!"

"Help me up on deck." Blackthorne grasped the bunk sides. Mariko took his arm but she could not lift him.

The bosun waved a pistol at Kana. "Tell him to help. And tell him if there's a God in heaven he'll be swinging from the yardarm before the turn."

First Mate Santiago took his ear away from the secret knothole in the wall of the great cabin, the final "Well, that's all settled then" from dell'Aqua ringing in his brain. Noiselessly he slipped across the darkened cabin, out into the corridor, and closed the door quietly. He was a tall, spare man with a lived-in face, and wore his hair in a tarred pigtail. His clothes were neat, and like most seamen, he was barefoot. In a hurry, he shinned up the companionway, ran across the main deck up onto the quarterdeck where Rodrigues was talking to Mariko. He excused himself and leaned down to put his mouth very close to Rodrigues' ear and began to pour out all that he had heard, and had been sent to hear, so that no one else on the quarterdeck could be party to it.

Blackthorne was sitting aft on the deck, leaning against the gunwale, his head resting on his bent knees. Mariko sat straight-backed facing Rodrigues, Japanese fashion, and Kana, the samurai, bleakly beside her. Armed seamen swarmed the decks and crow's nest aloft and two more were at the helm. The ship still pointed into the wind, the air and night clean, the nimbus stronger and rain not far off. A hundred yards away the galley lay broadside, at the mercy of their cannon, oars shipped, except for two each side which kept her in station, the slight tide taking her. The ambushing fishing ships with hostile samurai archers were closer but they were not encroaching as yet.

Mariko was watching Rodrigues and the mate. She could not hear what was being said, and even if she could, her training would have made her prefer to close her ears. Privacy in paper houses was impossible without politeness and consideration; without privacy civilized life could not exist, so all Japanese were trained to hear and not hear. For the good of all.

When she had come on deck with Blackthorne, Rodrigues had listened to the bosun's explanation and to her halting explanation that it was her fault, that she had mistaken what the bosun had said, and that this had caused Kana to pull out his sword to protect her honor. The bosun had listened, grinning, his pistols still leveled at the samurai's back.

"I only asked if she was the Ingeles's doxie, by God, she being so free with washing him and sticking his privates into the cod."

"Put up your pistols, bosun."

"He's dangerous, I tell you. String him up!"

"I'll watch him. Go for'ard!"

"This monkey'd've killed me if I wasn't faster. Put him on the yardarm. That's what we'd do in Nagasaki!"

"We're not in Nagasaki—go for'ard! Now!"

And when the bosun had gone Rodrigues had asked, "What did he say to you, senhora? Actually say?"

"It—nothing, senhor. Please."

"I apologize for that man's insolence to you and to the samurai. Please apologize to the samurai for me, ask his pardon. And I ask you both formally to forget the bosun's insults. It will not help your liege lord or mine to have trouble aboard. I promise you I will deal with him in my own way in my own time."

She had spoken to Kana and, under her persuasion, at length he had agreed.

"Kana-san says, very well, but if he ever sees the bosun Pesaro on shore he will take his head."

"That's fair, by God. Yes. *Domo arigato,* Kana-san," Rodrigues said with a smile, "and *domo arigato goziemashita,* Mariko-san."

"You speak Japanese?"

"Oh no, just a word or two. I've a wife in Nagasaki."

"Oh! You have been long in Japan?"

"This is my second tour from Lisbon. I've spent seven years in these waters all told—here, and back and forth to Macao and to Goa." Rodrigues added, "Pay no attention to him—he's *eta.* But Buddha said even *eta* have a right to life. *Neh?*"

"Of course," Mariko said, the name and face branded forever into her mind.

"My wife speaks some Portuguese, nowhere near as perfectly as you. You're Christian, of course?"

"Yes."

"My wife's a convert. Her father's samurai, though a minor one. His liege lord is Lord Kiyama."

"She is lucky to have such a husband," Mariko said politely, but she asked herself, staggered, how could one marry and live with a barbarian? In spite of her inherent manners, she asked, "Does the lady, your wife, eat meat, like—like that in the cabin?"

"No," Rodrigues replied with a laugh, his teeth white and fine and strong. "And in my house at Nagasaki I don't eat meat either. At sea I do and in Europe. It's our custom. A thousand years ago before the Buddha came it was your custom too, *neh?* Before Buddha lived to point the *Tao,* the Way, all people ate meat. Even here, senhora. Even here. Now of course, we know better, some of us, *neh?"*

Mariko thought about that. Then she said, "Do all Portuguese call us monkeys? And Jappos? Behind our backs?"

Rodrigues pulled at the earring he wore. "Don't you call us barbarians? Even to our face? We're civilized, at least we think so, senhora. In India, the land of Buddha, they call Japanese 'Eastern Devils' and won't allow any to land if they're armed. You call Indians 'Blacks' and nonhuman. What do the Chinese call Japanese? What do you call the Chinese? What do you call the Koreans? Garlic Eaters, *neh?"*

"I don't think Lord Toranaga would be pleased. Or Lord Hiro-matsu, or even the father of your wife."

"The Blessed Jesus said, 'First cast the mote out of your own eye before you cast the beam out of mine.' "

She thought about that again now as she watched the first mate whispering urgently to the Portuguese pilot. It's true: we sneer at other people. But then, we're citizens of the Land of the Gods, and therefore especially chosen by the gods. We alone, of all peoples, are protected by a divine Emperor. Aren't we, therefore, completely unique and superior to all others? And if you are Japanese *and* Christian? I don't know. Oh, Madonna, give me thy understanding. This Rodrigues pilot is as strange as the English pilot. Why are they very special? Is it their training? It's unbelievable what they do, *neh?* How can they sail around the earth and walk the sea as easily as we do the land? Would Rodrigues' wife know the answer? I'd like to meet her, and talk to her.

The mate lowered his voice even more.

"He said what?" Rodrigues exclaimed with an involuntary curse and in spite of herself Mariko tried to listen. But she could not hear what the mate repeated. Then she saw them both look at Blackthorne and she followed their glance, perturbed by their concern.

"What else happened, Santiago?" Rodrigues asked guardedly, conscious of Mariko.

The mate told him in a whisper behind a cupped mouth. "How long'll they stay below?"

"They were toasting each other. And the bargain."

"Bastards!" Rodrigues caught the mate's shirt. "No word of this, by God. On your life!"

"No need to say that, Pilot."

"There's always a need to say it." Rodrigues glanced across at Blackthorne. "Wake him up!"

The mate went over and shook him roughly.

"Whatsamatter, eh?"

"Hit him!"

Santiago slapped him.

"Jesus Christ, I'll . . ." Blackthorne was on his feet, his face on fire, but he swayed and fell.

"God damn you, wake up, Ingeles!" Furiously Rodrigues stabbed a finger at the two helmsmen. "Throw him overboard!"

"Eh?"

"Now, by God!"

As the two men hurriedly picked him up, Mariko said, "Pilot Rodrigues, you mustn't—" but before she or Kana could interfere the two men had hurled Blackthorne over the side. He fell the twenty feet and belly-flopped in a cloud of spray and disappeared. In a moment he surfaced, choking and spluttering, flailing at the water, the ice-cold clearing his head.

Rodrigues was struggling out of his seachair. "Madonna, give me a hand!"

One of the helmsmen ran to help as the first mate got a hand under his armpit. "Christ Jesus, be careful, mind my foot, you clumsy dunghead!"

They helped him to the side. Blackthorne was still coughing and spluttering, but now as he swam for the side of the ship he was shouting curses at those who had cast him overboard.

"Two points starboard!" Rodrigues ordered. The ship fell off the wind slightly and eased away from Blackthorne. He shouted down, "Stay to hell off my ship!" Then urgently to his first mate, "Take the longboat, pick up the Ingeles, and put him aboard the galley. Fast. Tell him . . ." He dropped his voice.

Mariko was grateful that Blackthorne was not drowning. "Pilot! The Anjin-san's under Lord Toranaga's protection. I demand he be picked up at once!"

"Just a moment, Mariko-san!" Rodrigues continued to whisper to Santiago, who nodded, then scampered away. "I'm sorry, Mariko-san, gomen kudasai, but it was urgent. The Ingeles had to be woken up. I knew he could swim. He has to be alert and fast!"

"Why?"

"I'm his friend. Did he ever tell you that?"

"Yes. But England and Portugal are at war. Also Spain."

"Yes. But pilots should be above war."

"Then to whom do you owe duty?"

"To the flag."

"Isn't that to your king?"

"Yes and no, senhora. I owed the Ingeles a life." Rodrigues was watching the longboat. "Steady as she goes—now put her into the wind," he ordered the helmsman.

"Yes, senhor."

He waited, checking and rechecking the wind and the shoals and the far shore. The leadsman called out the fathoms. "Sorry, senhora, you were saying?" Rodrigues looked at her momentarily, then went back once more to check the lie of his ship and the longboat. She watched the longboat too. The men had hauled Blackthorne out of the sea and were pulling hard for the galley, sitting instead of standing and pushing the oars. She could no longer see their faces clearly. Now the Anjin-san was blurred with the other man close beside him, the man that Rodrigues had whispered to. "What did you say to him, senhor?"

"Who?"

"Him. The senhor you sent after the Anjin-san."

"Just to wish the Ingeles well and Godspeed." The reply was flat and noncommittal.

She translated to Kana what had been said.

When Rodrigues saw the longboat alongside the galley he began to breathe again. "Hail Mary, Mother of God . . ."

The Captain-General and the Jesuits came up from below. Toranaga and his guards followed.

"Rodrigues! Launch the longboat! The Fathers are going ashore," Ferriera said.

"And then?"

"And then we put to sea. For Yedo."

"Why there? We were sailing for Macao," Rodrigues replied, the picture of innocence.

"We're taking Toranaga home to Yedo. First."

"We're what? But what about the galley?"

"She stays or she fights her way out."

Rodrigues seemed to be even more surprised and looked at the galley, then at Mariko. He saw the accusation written in her eyes.

"*Matsu,*" the pilot told her quietly.

"What?" Father Alvito asked. "Patience? Why patience, Rodrigues?"

"Saying Hail Marys, Father. I was saying to the lady it teaches you patience."

Ferriera was staring at the galley. "What's our longboat doing there?"

"I sent the heretic back aboard."

"You what?"

"I sent the Ingeles back aboard. What's the problem, Captain-General? The Ingeles offended me so I threw the bugger overboard. I'd have let him drown but he could swim so I sent the mate to pick him up and put him back aboard his ship as he seemed to be in Lord Toranaga's favor. What's wrong?"

"Fetch him back aboard."

"I'll have to send an armed boarding party, Captain-General. Is that what you want? He was cursing and heaping hellfire on us. He won't come back willingly this time."

"I want him back aboard."

"What's the problem? Didn't you say the galley's to stay and fight or whatever? So what? So the Ingeles is hip-deep in shit. Good. Who needs the bugger, anyway? Surely the Fathers'd prefer him out of their sight. Eh, Father?"

Dell'Aqua did not reply. Nor did Alvito. This disrupted the plan that Ferriera had formulated and had been accepted by them and by Toranaga: that the priests would go ashore at once to smooth over Ishido, Kiyama, and Onoshi, professing that they had believed Toranaga's story about the pirates and did not know that he had "escaped" from the castle. Meanwhile the frigate would charge for the harbor mouth, leaving the galley to draw off the fishing boats. If there was an overt attack on the frigate, it would be beaten off with cannon, and the die cast.

"But the boats shouldn't attack us," Ferriera had reasoned. "They have the galley to catch. It will be your responsibility, Eminence, to persuade Ishido that we had no other choice. After all, Toranaga is President of the Regents. Finally, the heretic stays aboard."

Neither of the priests had asked why. Nor had Ferriera volunteered his reason.

The Visitor put a gentle hand on the Captain-General and turned his back on the galley. "Perhaps it's just as well the heretic's there," he said, and he thought, how strange are the ways of God.

No, Ferriera wanted to scream. I wanted to see him drown. A man overboard in the early dawn at sea—no trace, no witnesses, so easy. Toranaga would never be the wiser; a tragic accident, as far as he was concerned. And it was the fate Blackthorne deserved. The Captain-General also knew the horror of sea death to a pilot.

"*Nan ja?*" Toranaga asked.

Father Alvito explained that the pilot was on the galley and why. Toranaga turned to Mariko, who nodded and added what Rodrigues had said previously.

Toranaga went to the side of the ship and gazed into the darkness. More fishing boats were being launched from the north shore and the others would soon be in place. He knew that the Anjin-san was a political embarrassment and this was a simple way the gods had given him if he desired to be rid of the Anjin-san. Do I want that? Certainly the Christian priests will be vastly happier if the Anjin-san vanishes, he thought. And also Onoshi and Kiyama, who feared the man so much that either or both had mounted the assassination attempts. Why such fear?

It's *karma* that the Anjin-san is on the galley now and not safely here. *Neh?* So the Anjin-san will drown with the ship, along with Yabu and the others and the guns, and that is also *karma*. The guns I can lose, Yabu I can lose. But the Anjin-san?

Yes.

Because I still have eight more of these strange barbarians in reserve. Perhaps their collective knowledge will equal or exceed that of this single man. The important thing is to be back in Yedo as quickly as possible to prepare for the war, which cannot be avoided. Kiyama and Onoshi? Who knows if they'll support me. Perhaps they will, perhaps not. But a plot of land and some promises are nothing in the balance if the Christian weight is on my side in forty days.

"It's *karma*, Tsukku-san. *Neh?*"

"Yes, Sire." Alvito glanced at the Captain-General, very satisfied. "Lord Toranaga suggests that nothing is done. It's the will of God."

"Is it?"

The drum on the galley began abruptly. The oars bit into the water with great strength.

"What, in the name of Christ, is he doing?" Ferriera bellowed.

And then, as they watched the galley pulling away from them, Toranaga's pennant came fluttering down from the masthead.

Rodrigues said, "Looks like they're telling every God-cursed fishing boat in the harbor that Lord Toranaga's no longer aboard."

"What's he going to do?"

"I don't know."

"Don't you?" Ferriera asked.

"No. But if I was him I'd head for sea and leave us in the cesspit—or try to. The Ingeles has put the finger on us now. What's it to be?"

"You're ordered to Yedo." The Captain-General wanted to add, if you ram the galley all the better, but he didn't. Because Mariko was listening.

The priests thankfully went ashore in the longboat.

"All sails ho!" Rodrigues shouted, his leg paining and throbbing. "Sou' by sou'west! All hands lay to!"

"Senhora, please tell Lord Toranaga he'd best go below. It'll be safer," Ferriera said.

"He thanks you and says he will stay here."

Ferriera shrugged, went to the edge of the quarterdeck. "Prime all cannon. Load grape! Action stations!"

CHAPTER 28

"*ISOGI!*" Blackthorne shouted, urging the oarsmaster to increase the beat. He looked aft at the frigate that was bearing down on them, close-hauled now under full sail, then for'ard again, estimating the next tack that she must use. He wondered if he had judged right, for there was very little sea room here, near the cliffs, barely a few yards between disaster and success. Because of the wind, the frigate had to tack to make the harbor mouth, while the galley could maneuver at its whim. But the frigate had the advantage of speed. And on the last tack Rodrigues had made it clear that the galley had better stay out of the way when the *Santa Theresa* needed sea room.

Yabu was chattering at him again but he paid no heed. "Don't understand—*wakarimasen,* Yabu-san! Listen, Toranaga-sama said, me, Anjin-san, *ichi-ban ima!* I'm chief Captain-san now! *Wakarimasu ka,* Yabu-san?" He pointed the course on the compass to the Japanese captain, who gesticulated at the frigate, barely fifty yards aft now, overtaking them rapidly on another collision path.

"Hold your course, by God!" Blackthorne said, the breeze cooling his sea-sodden clothes, which chilled him but helped to clear his head. He checked the sky. No clouds were near the bright moon and the wind was fair. No danger there, he thought. God keep the moon bright till we're through.

"Hey, Captain!" he called out in English, knowing it made no difference if he spoke English or Portuguese or Dutch or Latin because he was alone. "Send someone for saké! Saké! *Wakarimasu ka?*"

"*Hai,* Anjin-san."

A seaman was sent scurrying. As the man ran he looked over his shoulder, frightened by the size of the approaching frigate and her speed. Blackthorne held their course, trying to force the frigate to turn before she had gained all space to windward. But she never wavered and came directly at him. At the last second he swung out of her way and then, when her bowsprit was almost over their aft deck, he heard Rodrigues' order, "Bear on the larboard tack! Let go stays'ls, and steady as she goes!" Then a shout at him in Spanish, "Thy mouth in the devil's arse, Ingeles!"

"Thy mother was there first, Rodrigues!"

Then the frigate peeled off the wind to scud now for the far shore, where she would have to turn again to reach into the wind and tack for this side once more before she could turn a last time again and make for the harbor mouth.

For an instant the ships were so close that he could almost touch her, Rodrigues, Toranaga, Mariko, and the Captain-General swaying on the quarterdeck. Then the frigate was away and they were twisting in her wash.

"*Isogi, isogi,* by God!"

The rowers redoubled their efforts and with signs Blackthorne ordered more men on the oars until there were no reserves. He had to get to the mouth before the frigate or they were lost.

The galley was eating up the distance. But so was the frigate. At the far side of the harbor she spun like a dancer and he saw that Rodrigues had added tops'ls and topgallants.

"He's as canny a bastard as any Portuguese born!"

The saké arrived but it was taken out of the seaman's hands by the young woman who had helped Mariko and offered precariously to him. She had stayed gamely on deck, even though clearly out of her element. Her hands were strong, her hair well groomed, and her kimono rich, in good taste and neat. The galley lurched in the chop. The girl reeled and dropped the cup. Her face did not change but he saw the flush of shame.

"*Por nada,*" he said as she groped for it. "It doesn't matter. *Namae ka?*"

"Usagi Fujiko, Anjin-san."

"Fujiko-san. Here, give it to me. *Dozo.*" He held out his hand and took the flask and drank directly from it, gulping the wine, eager to have its heat inside his body. He concentrated on the new course, skirting the shoals that Santiago, on Rodrigues' orders, had told him about. He rechecked the bearing from the headland that gave them a clean, hazardless run to the mouth while he finished the warmed wine, wondering in passing how it had been warmed, and why they always served it warm and in small quantities.

His head was clear now, and he felt strong enough, if he was careful. But he knew he had no reserves to draw upon, just as the ship had no reserves.

"Saké, *dozo,* Fujiko-san." He handed her the flask and forgot her.

On the windward tack the frigate made way too well and she passed a hundred yards ahead of them, bearing for the shore. He heard obscenities coming down on the wind and did not bother to reply, conserving his energy.

"*Isogi,* by God! We're losing!"

The excitement of the race and of being alone again and in command—more by the strength of his will than by position—added to the rare privilege of having Yabu in his power, filled him with unholy glee. "If it wasn't that the ship'd go down and me with her, I'd put her on the rocks just to see you drown, shit-face Yabu! For old Pieterzoon!"

But didn't Yabu save Rodrigues when you couldn't? Didn't he charge the bandits when you were ambushed? And he was brave tonight. Yes, he's a shit-face, but even so he's a brave shit-face and that's the truth.

The flask of saké was offered again. "*Domo,*" he said.

The frigate was keeled over, close-hauled and greatly pleasing to him. "I couldn't do better," he said aloud to the wind. "But if I had her, I'd go through the boats and out to sea and never come back. I'd sail her home, somehow, and leave the Japans to the Japanese and to the pestilential Portuguese." He saw Yabu and the captain staring at him. "I wouldn't really, not yet. There's a Black Ship to catch and plunder to be had. And revenge, eh, Yabu-san?"

"*Nan desu ka,* Anjin-san? *Nan ja?*"

"*Ichi-ban!* Number one!" he replied, waving at the frigate. He drained the flask. Fujiko took it from him.

"Saké, Anjin-san?"

"*Domo, iyé!*"

The two ships were very near the massed fishing boats now, the galley heading straight for the pass that had been deliberately left between them, the frigate on the last reach and turning for the harbor mouth. Here the wind freshened as the protecting headlands fell away, open sea half a mile ahead. Gusts billowed the frigate's sails, the shrouds crackling like pistol shots, froth now at her bow and in her wake.

The rowers were bathed with sweat and flagging. One man dropped. And another. The fifty-odd *ronin*-samurai were already in position. Ahead, archers in the fishing boats either side of the narrow channel were arming their bows. Blackthorne saw small braziers in many of the boats and he knew that the arrows would be fire arrows when they came.

He had prepared for battle as best he could. Yabu had understood that they would have to fight, and had understood fire arrows immediately. Blackthorne had erected protective wooden bulkheads around the helm. He had broken open some of the crates of muskets and had set those who could to arming them with powder and with shot. And he had brought several small kegs of powder up onto the quarterdeck and fused them.

When Santiago, the first mate, had helped him aboard the longboat, he had told him that Rodrigues was going to help, with God's good grace.

"Why?" he had asked.

"My Pilot says to tell you that he had you thrown overboard to sober you up, senhor."

"Why?"

"Because, he said to tell you, Senhor Pilot, because there was danger aboard the *Santa Theresa,* danger for you."

"What danger?"

"You are to fight your own way out, he tells you, if you can. But he will help."

"Why?"

"For the Madonna's sweet sake, hold your heretic tongue and listen, I've little time."

Then the mate had told him about the shoals and the bearings and the way of the channel and the plan. And given him two pistols. "How good a shot are you, my Pilot asks."

"Poor," he had lied.

"Go with God, my Pilot said to tell you finally."

"And him—and you."

"For me I assign thee to hell!"

"Thy sister!"

Blackthorne had fused the kegs in case the cannon began and there was no plan, or if the plan proved false, and also against encroaching hostiles. Even such a little keg, the fuse alight, floated against the side of the frigate would sink her as surely as a seventy-gun broadside. It doesn't matter how small the keg, he thought, providing it guts her.

"*Isogi* for your lives!" he called out and took the helm, thanking God for Rodrigues and the brightness of the moon.

Here at the mouth the harbor narrowed to four hundred yards. Deep water was almost shore to shore, the rock headlands rising sharp from the sea.

The space between the ambushing fishing boats was a hundred yards.

The *Santa Theresa* had the bit between her teeth now, the wind abaft the beam to starboard, strong wake aft, and she was gaining on them fast. Blackthorne held the center of channel and signed to Yabu to be ready. All their *ronin*-samurai had been ordered to squat below the gunwales, unseen, until Blackthorne gave the signal, when it was every man—with musket or sword—to port or to starboard, wherever they were needed, Yabu commanding the fight. The Japanese captain knew that his oarsmen were to follow the drum and the drum master knew that he had to obey the Anjin-san. And the Anjin-san alone was to guide the ship.

The frigate was fifty yards astern, in mid-channel, heading directly for them, and making it obvious that she required the mid-channel path.

*   *   *

Aboard the frigate, Ferriera breathed softly to Rodrigues, "Ram him." His eyes were on Mariko, who stood ten paces off, near the railings, with Toranaga.

"We daren't—not with Toranaga there and the girl."

"Senhora!" Ferriera called out. "Senhora—better to get below, you and your master. It'd be safer for him on the gundeck."

Mariko translated to Toranaga, who thought a moment, then walked down the companionway onto the gundeck.

"God damn my eyes," the chief gunner said to no one in particular. "I'd like to fire a broadside and sink something. It's a God-cursed year since we sunk even a poxed pirate."

"Aye. The monkeys deserve a bath."

On the quarterdeck Ferriera repeated, "Ram the galley, Rodrigues!"

"Why kill your enemy when others're doing it for you?"

"Madonna! You're as bad as the priest! Thou hast no blood in thee!"

"Yes, I have none of the killing blood," Rodrigues replied, also in Spanish. "But thou? Thou hast it. Eh? And Spanish blood perhaps?"

"Are you going to ram him or not?" Ferriera asked in Portuguese, the nearness of the kill possessing him.

"If she stays where she is, yes."

"Then, Madonna, let her stay where she is."

"What had you in mind for the Ingeles? Why were you so angry he wasn't aboard us?"

"I do not like you or trust you now, Rodrigues. Twice you've sided, or seemed to side, with the heretic against me, or us. If there was another acceptable pilot in all Asia, I would beach you, Rodrigues, and I would sail off with my Black Ship."

"Then you will drown. There's a smell of death over you and only I can protect you."

Ferriera crossed himself superstitiously. "Madonna, thou and thy filthy tongue! What right hast thou to say that?"

"My mother was a gypsy and she the seventh child of a seventh child, as I am."

"Liar!"

Rodrigues smiled. "Ah, my Lord Captain-General, perhaps I am." He cupped his hands and shouted, "Action stations!" and then to the helmsman, "Steady as she goes, and if that belly-gutter whore doesn't move, sink her!"

Blackthorne held the wheel firmly, arms aching, legs aching. The oarsmaster was pounding the drum, the oarsmen making a final effort.

Now the frigate was twenty yards astern, now fifteen, now ten. Then Blackthorne swung hard to port. The frigate almost brushed them, heeled over toward them, and then she was alongside. Blackthorne swung hard astarboard to come parallel to the frigate, ten yards from her. Then, together—side by side—they were ready to run the gauntlet between the hostiles.

"Puuuull, pull, you bastards!" Blackthorne shouted, wanting to stay exactly alongside, because only here were they guarded by the frigate's bulk and by her sails. Some musket shots, then a salvo of burning arrows slashed at them, doing no real damage, but several by mistake struck the frigate's lower sails and fire broke out.

All the commanding samurai in the boats stopped their archers in horror. No one had ever attacked a Southern Barbarian ship before. Don't they alone bring the silks which make every summer's humid heat bearable, and every winter's cold bearable, and every spring and fall a joy? Aren't the Southern Barbarians protected by Imperial decrees? Wouldn't burning one of their ships infuriate them so much that they would, rightly, never come back again?

So the commanders held their men in check while Toranaga's galley was under the frigate's wing, not daring to risk the merest chance that one of them would be the cause of the cessation of the Black Ships without General Ishido's direct approval. And only when seamen on the frigate had doused the flames did they breathe easier.

When the arrows stopped, Blackthorne also began to relax. And Rodrigues. The plan was working. Rodrigues had surmised that under his lee the galley had a chance, its only chance. 'But my Pilot says you must prepare for the unexpected, Ingeles,' Santiago had reported.

"Shove that bastard aside," Ferriera said. "God damn it, I ordered you to shove him into the monkeys!"

"Five points to port!" Rodrigues ordered obligingly.

"Five points aport it is!" the helmsman echoed.

Blackthorne heard the command. Instantly he steered port five degrees and prayed. If Rodrigues held the course too long they would smash into the fishing boats and be lost. If he slackened the beat and fell behind, he knew the enemy boats would swamp him whether they believed Toranaga was aboard or not. He must stay alongside.

"Five points starboard!" Rodrigues ordered, just in time. He wanted no more fire arrows either; there was too much powder on deck. "Come on, you pimp," he muttered to the wind. "Put your *cojones* in my sails and get us to hell out of here."

Again Blackthorne had swung five points starboard to maintain station with the frigate and the two ships raced side by side, the galley's starboard oars almost touching the frigate, the port oars almost swamping the fishing boats. Now the captain understood, and so did the oarsmaster and the rowers. They put their final strength into the oars. Yabu shouted a command and the *ronin*-samurai put down their bows and rushed to help and Yabu pitched in also.

Neck and neck. Only a few hundred yards to go.

Then Grays on some of the fishing boats, more intrepid than the others, sculled forward into their path and threw grappling hooks. The prow of the galley swamped the boats. The grappling hooks were cast overboard before they caught. The samurai holding them were drowned. And the stroke did not falter.

"Go more to port!"

"I daren't, Captain-General. Toranaga's no fool and look, there's a reef ahead!"

Ferriera saw the spines near the last of the fishing boats. "Madonna, drive him onto it!"

"Two points port!"

Again the frigate swung over and so did Blackthorne. Both ships aimed for the massed fishing boats. Blackthorne had also seen the rocks. Another boat was swamped and a salvo of arrows came aboard. He held his course as long as he dared, then shouted, "Five points starboard!" to warn Rodrigues, and swung the helm over.

Rodrigues took evasive action and fell away. But this time he held a slight collision course which was not part of the plan.

"Go on, you bastard," Rodrigues said, whipped by the chase and by dread. "Let's weigh your *cojones.* "

Blackthorne had to choose instantly between the spines and the frigate. He blessed the rowers, who still stayed at their oars, and the crew and all aboard who, through their discipline, gave him the privilege of choice. And he chose.

He swung further to starboard, pulled out his pistol and aimed it. "Make way, by God!" he shouted and pulled the trigger. The ball whined over the frigate's quarterdeck just between the Captain-General and Rodrigues.

As the Captain-General ducked, Rodrigues winced. Thou Ingeles son of a milkless whore! Was that luck or good shooting or did you aim to kill?

He saw the second pistol in Blackthorne's hand, and Toranaga staring at him. He dismissed Toranaga as unimportant.

Blessed Mother of God, what should I do? Stick with the plan or change it? Isn't it better to kill this Ingeles? For the good of all? Tell me, yes or no!

Answer thyself, Rodrigues, on thy eternal soul! Art thou not a man?

Listen then: Other heretics will follow this Ingeles now, like lice, whether this one is killed or not killed. I owe him a life and I swear I do not have the killing blood in me—not to kill a pilot.

"Starboard your helm," he ordered and gave way.

"My Master asks why did you almost smash into the galley?"

"It was just a game, senhora, a game pilots play. To test the other's nerves."

"And the pistol shot?"

"Equally a game—to test my nerve. The rocks were too close and perhaps I was pushing the Ingeles too much. We are friends, no?"

"My Master says it is foolish to play such games."

"Please give him my apologies. The important thing is that he is safe and now the galley is safe and therefore I am glad. *Honto.*"

"You arranged this escape, this ruse, with the Anjin-san?"

"It happened that he is very clever and was perfect in his timing. The moon lit his way, the sea favored him, and no one made a mistake. But why the hostiles didn't swamp him, I don't know. It was the will of God."

"Was it?" Ferriera said. He was staring at the galley astern of them and he did not turn around.

They were well beyond the harbor mouth now, safely out into the Osaka Roads, the galley a few cables aft, neither ship hurrying. Most of the galley's oars had been shipped temporarily, leaving only enough to make way calmly while the majority of the oarsmen recuperated.

Rodrigues paid Captain-General Ferriera no heed. He was absorbed instead with Toranaga. I'm glad we're on Toranaga's side, Rodrigues told himself. During the race, he had studied him carefully, glad for the rare opportunity. The man's eyes had been everywhere, watching gunners and guns and the sails and the fire party with an insatiable curiosity, asking questions, through Mariko, of the seamen or the mate: What's this for? How do you load a cannon? How much powder? How do you fire them? What are these ropes for?

"My Master says, perhaps it was just *karma.* You understand *karma,* Captain-Pilot?"

"Yes."

"He thanks you for the use of your ship. Now he will go back to his own."

"What?" Ferriera turned around at once. "We'll be in Yedo long before the galley. Lord Toranaga's welcome to stay aboard."

"My Master says, there's no need to trouble you anymore. He will go onto his own ship."

"Please ask him to stay. I would enjoy his company."

"Lord Toranaga thanks you but he wishes to go at once to his own ship."

"Very well. Do as he says, Rodrigues. Signal her and lower the longboat."

Ferriera was disappointed. He had wanted to see Yedo and wanted to get to know

Toranaga better now that so much of their future was tied to him. He did not believe what Toranaga had said about the means of avoiding war. We're at war on this monkey's side against Ishido whether we like it or not. And I don't like it. "I'll be sorry not to have Lord Toranaga's company." He bowed politely.

Toranaga bowed back, and spoke briefly.

"My Master thanks you." To Rodrigues, she added, "My Master says he will reward you for the galley when you return with the Black Ship."

"I did nothing. It was merely a duty. Please excuse me for not getting up from my chair—my leg, *neh?*" Rodrigues replied, bowing. "Go with God, senhora."

"Thank you, Captain-Pilot. Do thou likewise."

As she groped wearily down the companionway behind Toranaga, she noticed that the bosun Pesaro was commanding the longboat. Her skin crawled and she almost heaved. She willed the spasm away, thankful that Toranaga had ordered them all off this malodorous vessel.

"A fair wind and safe voyage," Ferriera called down to them. He waved once and the salutation was returned and then the longboat cast off.

"Stand down when the longboat's back and that bitch galley's out of sight," he ordered the chief gunner.

On the quarterdeck he stopped in front of Rodrigues. He pointed at the galley. "You'll live to regret keeping him alive."

"That's in the hands of God. The Ingeles is an 'acceptable' pilot, if you could pass over his religion, my Captain-General."

"I've considered that."

"And?"

"The sooner we're in Macao the better. Make record time, Rodrigues." Ferriera went below.

Rodrigues' leg was throbbing badly. He took a swig from the grog sack. May Ferriera go to hell, he told himself. But, please God, not until we reach Lisbon.

The wind veered slightly and a cloud reached for the nimbus of the moon, rain not far off and dawn streaking the sky. He put his full attention on his ship and her sails and the lie of her. When he was completely satisfied, he watched the longboat. And finally the galley.

He sipped more rum, content that his plan had worked so neatly. Even the pistol shot that had closed the issue. And content with his decision.

It was mine to make and I made it.

"Even so, Ingeles," he said with a great sadness, "the Captain-General's right. With thee, heresy has come to Eden."

CHAPTER 29

ANJIN-SAN?"

"*Hai?*" Blackthorne swooped out of a deep sleep.

"Here's some food. And cha."

For a moment he could not remember who he was or where he was. Then he recognized his cabin aboard the galley. A shaft of sunlight was piercing the darkness. He felt greatly rested. There was no drumbeat now and even in his deepest sleep, his senses had told him that the anchor was being lowered and his ship was safe, near shore, the sea gentle.

He saw a maid carrying a tray, Mariko beside her—her arm no longer in a sling—and he was lying in the pilot's bunk, the same that he had used during the Rodrigues voyage from Anjiro village to Osaka and that was now, in a way, almost as familiar as his own bunk and cabin aboard *Erasmus. Erasmus!* It'll be grand to be back aboard and to see the lads again.

He stretched luxuriously, then took the cup of cha Mariko offered.

"Thank you. That's delicious. How's your arm?"

"Much better, thank you." Mariko flexed it to show him. "It was just a flesh wound."

"You're looking better, Mariko-san."

"Yes, I'm better now."

When she had come back aboard at dawn with Toranaga she had been near fainting. "Better to stay aloft," he had told her. "The sickness will leave you faster."

"My Master asks—asks why the pistol shot?"

"It was just a game pilots play," he had told her.

"My Master compliments you on your seamanship."

"We were lucky. The moon helped. And the crew were marvelous. Mariko-san, would you ask the Captain-san if he knows these waters? Sorry, but tell Toranaga-sama I can't keep awake much longer. Or can we hove to for an hour or so out to sea? I've got to sleep."

He vaguely remembered her telling him that Toranaga said he could go below, that the Captain-san was quite capable as they would be staying in coastal waters and not going out to sea.

Blackthorne stretched again and opened a cabin porthole. A rocky shore was two hundred-odd yards away. "Where are we?"

"Off the coast of Totomi Province, Anjin-san. Lord Toranaga wanted to swim and to rest the oarsmen for a few hours. We'll be at Anjiro tomorrow."

"The fishing village? That's impossible. It's near noon and at dawn we were off Osaka. It's impossible!"

"Ah, that was yesterday, Anjin-san. You've slept a day and a night and half another day," she replied. "Lord Toranaga said to let you sleep. Now he thinks a swim would be good to wake you up. After food."

Food was two bowls of rice and charcoal-roasted fish with the dark, salt-bitter, vinegar-sweet sauce that she had told him was made from fermented beans.

"Thank you—yes, I'd like a swim. Almost thirty-six hours? No wonder I feel fine." He took the tray from the maid, ravenous. But he did not eat at once. "Why is she afraid?" he asked.

"She's not, Anjin-san. Just a little nervous. Please excuse her. She's never seen a foreigner close to before."

"Tell her when the moon's full, barbarians sprout horns and fire comes out of our mouths like dragons."

Mariko laughed. "I certainly will not." She pointed to the sea table. "There is tooth powder and a brush and water and fresh towels." Then said in Latin, "It pleasures me to see thou art well. It is as was related on the march, thou hast great bravery."

Their eyes locked and then the moment was allowed to pass. She bowed politely. The maid bowed. The door closed behind them.

Don't think about her, he ordered himself. Think about Toranaga or Anjiro. Why do we stop at Anjiro tomorrow? To off-load Yabu? Good riddance!

Omi will be at Anjiro. What about Omi?

Why not ask Toranaga for Omi's head? He owes you a favor or two. Or why not ask to fight Omi-san. How? With pistols or with swords? You'd have no chance with a sword and it'd be murder if you had a gun. Better to do nothing and wait. You'll have a chance soon and then you'll be revenged on both of them. You bask in Toranaga's favor now. Be patient. Ask yourself what you need from him. Soon we'll be in Yedo, so you've not much time. What about Toranaga?

Blackthorne was using the chopsticks as he had seen the men in the prison use them, lifting the bowl of rice to his lips and pushing the tacky rice from the lip of the bowl into his mouth with the sticks. The pieces of fish were more difficult. He was still not deft enough, so he used his fingers, glad to eat alone, knowing that to eat with his fingers would be very impolite in front of Mariko or Toranaga or any Japanese.

When every morsel was gone he was still famished.

"Got to get more food," he said aloud. "Jesus God in heaven, I'd like some fresh bread and fried eggs and butter and cheese. . . ."

He came on deck. Almost everyone was naked. Some of the men were drying themselves, others sunbathing, and a few were leaping overboard. In the sea alongside the ship, samurai and seamen were swimming or splashing as children would.

"*Konnichi wa,* Anjin-san."

"*Konnichi wa,* Toranaga-sama," he said.

Toranaga, quite naked, was coming up the gangway that had been let down to the sea. "*Sonata wa oyogitamo ka?*" he said, motioning at the sea, slapping the water off his belly and his shoulders, warm under the bright sun.

"*Hai,* Toranaga-sama, *domo,*" Blackthorne said, presuming that he was being asked if he wanted to swim.

Again Toranaga pointed at the sea and spoke shortly, then called Mariko to interpret. Mariko walked down from the poopdeck, shielding her head with a crimson sunshade, her informal white cotton kimono casually belted.

"Toranaga-sama says you look very rested, Anjin-san. The water's invigoration."

"Invigorating," he said, correcting her politely. "Yes."

"Ah, thank you—invigorating. He says please swim then."

Toranaga was leaning carelessly against the gunwale, wiping the water out of his ears with a small towel, and when his left ear would not clear, he hung his head over and hopped on his left heel until it did. Blackthorne saw that Toranaga was very muscular and very taut, apart from his belly. Ill at ease, very conscious of Mariko, he stripped off his shirt and his codpiece and trousers until he was equally naked.

"Lord Toranaga asks if all Englishmen are as hairy as you? The hair so fair?"

"Some are," he said.

"We—our men don't have hair on their chests or arms like you do. Not very much. He says you've a very good build."

"So has he. Please thank him." Blackthorne walked away from her to the head of the gangplank, aware of her and the young woman, Fujiko, who was kneeling on the poop under a yellow parasol, a maid beside her, also watching him. Then, unable to contain his dignity enough to walk naked all the way down to the sea, he dived over the side into the pale blue water. It was a fine dive and the sea chill reached into him exhilaratingly. The sandy bottom was three fathoms down, seaweed waving, multitudes of fish unfrightened by the swimmers. Near the seabed his plummeting stopped and he twisted and played with the fish, then surfaced and began a seemingly lazy, easy, but very fast overarm stroke for the shore that Alban Caradoc had taught him.

The small bay was desolate: many rocks, a tiny pebbled shore, and no sign of life. Mountains climbed a thousand feet to a blue, measureless sky.

He lay on a rock sunning himself. Four samurai had swum with him and were not far away. They smiled and waved. Later he swam back, and they followed. Toranaga was still watching him.

He came up on deck. His clothes were gone. Fujiko and Mariko and two maids were still there. One of the maids bowed and offered him a ridiculously small towel, which he took and began to dry himself with, turning uneasily into the gunwale.

I order you to be at ease, he told himself. You're at ease naked in a locked room with Felicity, aren't you? It's only in public when women are around— when she's around—that you're embarrassed. Why? They don't notice nakedness and that's totally sensible. You're in Japan. You're to do as they do. You will be like them and act like a king.

"Lord Toranaga says you swim very well. Would you teach him that stroke?" Mariko was saying.

"I'd be glad to," he said and forced himself to turn around and lean as Toranaga was leaning. Mariko was smiling up at him—looking so pretty, he thought.

"The way you dived into the sea. We've—we've never seen that before. We always jump. He wants to learn how to do that."

"Now?"

"Yes, please."

"I can teach him—at least, I can try."

A maid was holding a cotton kimono for Blackthorne so, gratefully, he slipped it on, tying it with the belt. Now, completely relaxed, he explained how to dive, how to tuck your head between your arms and spring up and out but to beware of belly flopping.

"It's best to start from the foot of the gangway and sort of fall in head first to begin with, without jumping or running. That's the way we teach children."

Toranaga listened and asked questions and then, when he was satisfied, he said through Mariko, "Good. I think I understand." He walked to the head of the gangway. Before Blackthorne could stop him, Toranaga had launched himself toward the water, fifteen feet below. The belly flop was vicious. No one laughed. Toranaga spluttered back to the deck and tried again. Again he landed flat. Other samurai were equally unsuccessful.

"It's not easy," Blackthorne said. "It took me a long time to learn. Give it a rest and we'll try again tomorrow."

"Lord Toranaga says, 'Tomorrow is tomorrow. Today I will learn how to dive.' "

Blackthorne put his kimono aside and demonstrated again. Samurai aped him. Again they failed. So did Toranaga. Six times.

After another demonstration dive Blackthorne scrambled onto the foot of the gangplank and saw Mariko among them, nude, readying to launch herself into space. Her body was exquisite, the bandage on her upper arm fresh. "Wait, Mariko-san! Better to try from here. The first time."

"Very well, Anjin-san."

She walked down to him, the tiny crucifix enhancing her nudity. He showed her how to bend and to fall forward into the sea, catching her by the waist to turn her over so that her head went in first.

Then Toranaga tried near the waterline and was moderately successful. Mariko tried again and the touch of her skin warmed Blackthorne and he clowned momentarily and fell into the water, directing them from there until he had cooled off. Then he ran up to the deck and stood on the gunwale and showed them a deadman's dive, which he thought might be easier, knowing that it was vital for Toranaga to succeed. "But you've got to keep rigid, *hai?* Like a sword. Then you cannot fail." He fell outward. The dive was clean and he trod water and waited.

Several samurai came forward but Toranaga waved them aside. He held up his arms stiffly, his backbone straight. His chest and loins were scarlet from the belly flops. Then he let himself fall forward as Blackthorne had shown. His head went into the water first and his legs tumbled over him, but it was a dive and the first successful dive of any of them and a roar of approval greeted him when he surfaced. He did it again, this time better. Other men followed, some successful, others not. Then Mariko tried.

Blackthorne saw the taut little breasts and tiny waist, flat stomach and curving legs. A flicker of pain went across her face as she lifted her arms above her head. But she held herself like an arrow and fell bravely outward. She speared the water cleanly. Almost no one except him noticed.

"That was a fine dive. Really fine," he said, giving her a hand to lift her easily out of the water onto the gangway platform. "You should stop now. You might open up the cut on your arm."

"Yes, thank you, Anjin-san." She stood beside him, barely reaching his shoulder, very pleased with herself. "That's a rare sensation, the falling outward and the having to stay stiff, and most of all, the having to dominate your fear. Yes, that was a very rare sensation indeed." She walked up the companionway and put on the kimono that the maid held out for her. Then, drying her face delicately, she went below.

Christ Jesus, that's much woman, he thought.

That sunset Toranaga sent for Blackthorne. He was sitting on the poopdeck on clean futons near a small charcoal brazier upon which small pieces of aromatic wood were smoking. They were used to perfume the air and keep away the dusk gnats and mosquitoes. His kimono was pressed and neat, and the huge, winglike shoulders of the starched overmantle gave him a formidable presence. Yabu, too, was formally dressed, and Mariko. Fujiko was also there. Twenty samurai sat silently on guard. Flares were set into stands and the galley still swung calmly at anchor in the bay.

"Saké, Anjin-san?"

"*Domo,* Toranaga-sama." Blackthorne bowed and accepted the small cup from

Fujiko, lifted it in toast to Toranaga and drained it. The cup was immediately refilled. Blackthorne was wearing a Brown uniform kimono and it felt easier and freer than his own clothes.

"Lord Toranaga says we're staying here tonight. Tomorrow we arrive at Anjiro. He would like to hear more about your country and the world outside."

"Of course. What would he like to know? It's a lovely night, isn't it?" Blackthorne settled himself comfortably, aware of her femininity. Too aware. Strange, I'm more conscious of her now that she's clothed than when she wore nothing.

"Yes, very. Soon it will be humid, Anjin-san. Summer is not a good time." She told Toranaga what she had said. "My Master says to tell you that Yedo is marshy. The mosquitoes are bad in summer, but spring and autumn are beautiful—yes, truly the birth and the dying seasons of the year are beautiful."

"England's temperate. The winter's bad perhaps one winter in seven. And the summer also. Famine about once in six years, though sometimes we get two bad years in a row."

"We have famine too. All famine is bad. How is it in your country now?"

"We've had bad harvests three times in the last ten years and no sun to ripen the corn. But that's the Hand of the Almighty. Now England's very strong. We're prosperous. Our people work hard. We make all our own cloth, all arms—most of the woolen cloth of Europe. A few silks come from France but the quality's poor and they're only for the very rich."

Blackthorne decided not to tell them about plague or the riots or insurrections caused by enclosing the common lands, and the drift of peasants to towns and to cities. Instead he told them about the good kings and queens, sound leaders and wise parliaments and successful wars.

"Lord Toranaga wants to be quite clear. You claim only sea power protects you from Spain and Portugal?"

"Yes. That alone. Command of our seas keeps us free. You're an island nation too, just like us. Without command of your seas, aren't you also defenseless against an outside enemy?"

"My Master agrees with you."

"Ah, you've been invaded too?" Blackthorne saw a slight frown as she turned to Toranaga and he reminded himself to confine himself to answers and not questions.

When she spoke to him again she was more grave. "Lord Toranaga says I should answer your question, Anjin-san. Yes, we've been invaded twice. More than three hundred years ago—it would be 1274 of your counting—the Mongols of Kublai Khan, who had just conquered China and Korea, came against us when we refused to submit to his authority. A few thousand men landed in Kyushu but our samurai managed to contain them, and after a while the enemy withdrew. But seven years later they came again. This time the invasion consisted of almost a thousand Chinese and Korean ships with two hundred thousand enemy troops—Mongols, Chinese, and Korean—mostly cavalry. In all Chinese history, this was the greatest invasion force ever assembled. We were helpless against such an overwhelming force, Anjin-san. Again they began to land at Hakata Bay in Kyushu but before they could deploy all their armies a Great Wind, a *tai-fun,* came out of the south and destroyed the fleet and all it contained. Those left ashore were quickly killed. It was a *kamikazi,* a Divine Wind, Anjin-san," she said with complete belief, "a *kamikazi* sent by the gods to protect this Land of the Gods from the foreign invader. The Mongols never came back and after eighty years or so their dynasty, the Chin, was thrown out of China," Mariko added with great satisfaction. "The gods protected us against them. The gods will always protect us against invasion. After all, this is *their* land, *neh?"*

Blackthorne thought about the huge numbers of ships and men in the invasion; it made the Spanish Armada against England seem insignificant. "We were helped by a storm too, senhora," he said with equal seriousness. "Many believe it was also sent by God—certainly it was a miracle—and who knows, perhaps it was." He glanced at the brazier as a coal spluttered and flames danced. Then he said, "The Mongols nearly engulfed us in Europe, too." He told her how the hordes of Genghis Khan, Kublai Khan's grandfather, had come almost to the gates of Vienna before his onslaught was stopped and then turned back, mountains of skulls in his wake. "People in those days believed Genghis Khan and his soldiers were sent by God to punish the world for its sins."

"Lord Toranaga says he was just a barbarian who was immensely good at war."

"Yes. Even so, in England we bless our luck we're an island. We thank God for that and the Channel. And our navy. With China so close and so powerful —and with you and China at war—I'm surprised you don't have a big navy. Aren't you afraid of another attack?" Mariko did not answer but translated for Toranaga what had been said. When she had finished, Toranaga spoke to Yabu, who nodded and answered, equally serious. The two men conversed for a while. Mariko answered another question from Toranaga, then spoke to Blackthorne once more.

"To control your seas, Anjin-san, how many ships do you need?"

"I don't know exactly, but now the Queen's got perhaps a hundred and fifty ships-of-the-line. Those are ships built only for war."

"My Master asks how many ships a year does your queen build?"

"Twenty to thirty warships, the best and fleetest in the world. But the ships are usually built by private groups of merchants and then sold to the Crown."

"For a profit?"

Blackthorne remembered samurai opinion of profit and money. "The Queen generously gives more than the actual cost to encourage research and new styles of building. Without royal favor this would hardly be possible. For example, *Erasmus,* my ship, is a new class, an English design built under license in Holland."

"Could you build such a ship here?"

"Yes. If I had carpenters, interpreters, and all the materials and time. First I'd have to build a smaller vessel. I've never built one entirely by myself before so I'd have to experiment. . . . Of course," he added, attempting to contain his excitement as the idea developed, "of course, if Lord Toranaga wanted a ship, or ships, perhaps a trade could be arranged. Perhaps he could order a number of warships to be built in England. We could sail them out here for him—rigged as he'd want and armed as he'd want."

Mariko translated. Toranaga's interest heightened. So did Yabu's. "He asks, can our sailors be trained to sail such ships?"

"Certainly, given time. We could arrange for the sailing masters—or one of them—to stay in your waters for a year. Then he could set up a training program for you. In a few years you'd have your own navy. A modern navy. Second to none."

Mariko spoke for a time. Toranaga questioned her again searchingly and so did Yabu.

"Yabu-san asks, second to none?"

"Yes. Better than anything the Spaniards would have. Or the Portuguese."

A silence gathered. Toranaga was evidently swept by the idea though he tried to hide it.

"My Master asks, are you sure this could be arranged?"

"Yes."

"How long would it take?"

"Two years for me to sail home. Two years to build a ship or ships. Two to sail back. Half the cost would have to be paid in advance, the remainder on delivery."

Toranaga thoughtfully leaned forward and put some more aromatic wood on the brazier. They all watched him and waited. Then he talked with Yabu at length. Mariko did not translate what was being said and Blackthorne knew better than to ask, as much as he would dearly have liked to be party to the conversation. He studied them all, even the girl Fujiko, who also listened attentively, but he could gather nothing from any of them. He knew this was a brilliant idea that could bring immense profit and guarantee his safe passage back to England.

"Anjin-san, how many ships could you sail out?"

"A flotilla of five ships at a time would be best. You could expect to lose at least one ship through storm, tempest, or Spanish-Portuguese interference—I'm sure they'd try very hard to prevent your having warships. In ten years Lord Toranaga could have a navy of fifteen to twenty ships." He let her translate that, then he continued, slowly. "The first flotilla could bring you master carpenters, shipwrights, gunners, seamen, and masters. In ten to fifteen years, England could supply Lord Toranaga with thirty modern warships, more than enough to dominate your home waters. And, by that time, if you wanted, you could possibly be building your own replacements here. We'll— " He was going to say "sell" but changed the word. "My Queen would be honored to help you form your own navy, and yes, if you wish, we'll train it and provision it."

Oh yes, he thought exultantly, as the final embellishment to the plan dropped into place, and we'll officer it and provide the Admiral and the Queen'll offer you a binding alliance—good for you and good for us—which will be part of the trade, and then together, friend Toranaga, we will harry the Spaniard and Portuguese dog out of these seas and own them forever. This could be the greatest single trading pact any nation has ever made, he thought gleefully. And with an Anglo-Japanese fleet clearing these seas, we English will dominate the Japan-China silk trade. Then it'll be millions every year!

If I can pull this off I'll turn the course of history. I'll have riches and honors beyond my dream. I'll become an ancestor. And to become an ancestor is just about the best thing a man can try to do, even though he fails in the trying.

"My Master says, it's a pity you don't speak our language."

"Yes, but I'm sure you're interpreting perfectly."

"He says that not as a criticism of me, Anjin-san, but as an observation. It's true. It would be much better for my Lord to talk direct, as I can talk to you."

"Do you have any dictionaries, Mariko-san? And grammars—Portuguese-Japanese or Latin-Japanese grammars? If Lord Toranaga could help me with books and teachers I'd try to learn your tongue."

"We have no such books."

"But the Jesuits have. You said so yourself."

"Ah!" She spoke to Toranaga, and Blackthorne saw both Yabu's and Toranaga's eyes light up, and smiles spread over their faces.

"My Master says you will be helped, Anjin-san."

At Toranaga's orders Fujiko gave Blackthorne and Yabu more saké. Toranaga drank only cha, as did Mariko. Unable to contain himself Blackthorne said, "What does he say to my suggestion? What's his answer?"

"Anjin-san, it would be better to be patient. He will answer in his own time."

"Please ask him now."

Reluctantly Mariko turned to Toranaga. "Please excuse me, Sire, but the Anjin-san asks with great deference, what do you think of his plan? He very humbly and most politely requests an answer."

"He'll have my answer in good time."

Mariko said to Blackthorne, "My Master says he will consider your plan and think carefully about what you have said. He asks you to be patient."

"*Domo,* Toranaga-sama."

"I'm going to bed now. We'll leave at dawn." Toranaga got up. Everyone followed him below, except Blackthorne. Blackthorne was left with the night.

At first promise of dawn Toranaga released four of the carrier pigeons that had been sent to the ship with the main baggage when the ship was being prepared. The birds circled twice, then broke off, two homing for Osaka, two for Yedo. The cipher message to Kiritsubo was an order to be passed on to Hiro-matsu that they should all attempt to leave peacefully at once. Should they be prevented, they were to lock themselves in. The moment the door was forced they were to set fire to that part of the castle and to commit seppuku.

The cipher to his son Sudara, in Yedo, told that he had escaped, was safe, and ordered him to continue secret preparations for war.

"Get to sea, Captain."

"Yes, Lord."

By noon they had crossed the bight between Totomi and Izu provinces and were off Cape Ito, the southernmost point of the Izu peninsula. The wind was fair, the swell modest, and the single mainsail helped their passage.

Then, close by shore in a deep channel between the mainland and some small rock islands, when they had turned north, there was an ominous rumbling ashore.

All oars ceased.

"What in the name of Christ . . ." Blackthorne's eyes were riveted shoreward.

Suddenly a huge fissure snaked up the cliffs and a million tons of rock avalanched into the sea. The waters seemed to boil for a moment. A small wave came out to the galley, then passed by. The avalanche ceased. Again the rumbling, deeper now and more growling, but farther off. Rocks dribbled from the cliffs. Everyone listened intently and waited, watching the cliff face. Sounds of gulls, of surf and wind. Then Toranaga motioned to the drum master, who picked up the beat once more. The oars began. Life on the ship became normal.

"What was that?" Blackthorne said.

"Just an earthquake." Mariko was perplexed. "You don't have earthquakes?"

"No. Never. I've never seen one before."

"Oh, we have them frequently, Anjin-san. That was nothing, just a small one. The main shock center would be somewhere else, even out to sea. Or perhaps this one was just a little one here, all by itself. You were lucky to witness a small one."

"It was as though the whole earth was shaking. I could have sworn I saw . . . I've heard about tremors. In the Holy Land and the Ottomans, they have them sometimes. Jesus!" He exhaled, his heart still thumping roughly. "I could have sworn I saw that whole cliff shake."

"Oh, it did, Anjin-san. When you're on land, it's the most terrible feeling in the whole world. There's no warning, Anjin-san. The tremors come in waves, sometimes sideways, sometimes up and down, sometimes three or four shakes quickly. Sometimes a small one followed by a greater one a day later. There's no pattern. The worst that I was in was at night, six years ago near Osaka, the third day of the Month of the Falling Leaves. Our house collapsed on us, Anjin-san. We weren't hurt, my son and I. We dug ourselves out. The shocks went on for a week or more, some bad, some very bad. The Taikō's great new castle at Fujimi was totally destroyed. Hundreds of thousands of people were lost in that earthquake and in the fires that followed. That's the greatest danger, Anjin-san—the fires that always follow. Our towns and cities and villages die so easily. Sometimes there is a bad earthquake far out to sea and legend has it that this causes the birth of the Great Waves. They are ten or twenty feet high. There is never a warning and they have no season. A Great Wave just comes out of the sea to our shores and sweeps inland. Cities can vanish. Yedo was half destroyed some years ago by such a wave."

"This is normal for you? Every year?"

"Oh, yes. Every year in this Land of the Gods we have earth tremors. And fires and flood and Great Waves, and the monster storms—the *tai-funs*. Nature is very strong with us." Tears gathered at the corners of her eyes. "Perhaps that is why we love life so much, Anjin-san. You see, we have to. Death is part of our air and sea and earth. You should know, Anjin-san, in this Land of Tears, death is our heritage."

BOOK THREE

CHAPTER 30

"Y OU'RE certain everything's ready, Mura?"
"Yes, Omi-san, yes, I think so. We've followed your orders exactly
—and Igurashi-san's."
"Nothing had better go wrong or there'll be another headman by sunset,"
Igurashi, Yabu's chief lieutentant, told him with great sourness, his one eye
bloodshot from lack of sleep. He had arrived yesterday from Yedo with the first
contingent of samurai and with specific instructions.

Mura did not reply, just nodded deferentially and kept his eyes on the ground.

They were standing on the foreshore, near the jetty, in front of the kneeling
rows of silent, overawed, and equally exhausted villagers—every man, woman,
and child, except for the bed-ridden—waiting for the galley to arrive. All wore
their best clothes. Faces were scrubbed, the whole village swept and sparkling
and made wholesome as though this were the day before New Year when, by
ancient custom, all the Empire was cleaned. Fishing boats were meticulously marshaled, nets tidy, ropes coiled. Even the beach along the bay had been
raked.

"Nothing will go wrong, Igurashi-san," Omi said. He had had little sleep this
last week, ever since Yabu's orders had come from Osaka via one of Toranaga's
carrier pigeons. At once he had mobilized the village and every able-bodied man
within twenty *ri* to prepare Anjiro for the arrival of the samurai and Yabu. And
now that Igurashi had whispered the very private secret, for his ears only, that
the great *daimyo* Toranaga was accompanying his uncle and had successfully
escaped Ishido's trap, he was more than pleased he had expended so much money.
"There's no need for you to worry, Igurashi-san. This is my fief and my responsibility."

"I agree. Yes, it is." Igurashi waved Mura contemptuously away. And then
he added quietly, "You're responsible. But without offense, I tell you you've never
seen our Master when something goes wrong. If we've forgotten anything, or
these dung eaters haven't done what they're supposed to, our Master will make
your whole fief and those to the north and south into manure heaps before sunset
tomorrow." He strode back to the head of his men.

This morning the final companies of samurai had ridden in from Mishima,
Yabu's capital city to the north. Now they, too, with all the others, were drawn
up in packed military formation on the foreshore, in the square, and on the
hillside, their banners waving with the slight breeze, upright spears glinting in
the sun. Three thousand samurai, the elite of Yabu's army. Five hundred cavalry.

Omi was not afraid. He had done everything it was possible to do and had
personally checked everything that could be checked. If something went wrong,
then that was just *karma*. But nothing is going to go wrong, he thought excitedly.
Five hundred koku had been spent or was committed on the preparations—more
than his entire year's income before Yabu had increased his fief. He had been
staggered by the amount but Midori, his wife, had said they should spend lavishly,
that the cost was minuscule compared to the honor that Lord Yabu was doing
him. "And with Lord Toranaga here—who knows what great opportunities
you'll have?" she had whispered.

311

She's so right, Omi thought proudly.

He rechecked the shore and the village square. Everything seemed perfect. Midori and his mother were waiting under the awning that had been prepared to receive Yabu and his guest, Toranaga. Omi noticed that his mother's tongue was wagging and he wished that Midori could be spared its constant lash. He straightened a fold in his already impeccable kimono and adjusted his swords and looked seaward.

"Listen, Mura-san," Uo, the fisherman, was whispering cautiously. He was one of the five village elders and they were kneeling with Mura in front of the rest. "You know, I'm so frightened, if I pissed I'd piss dust."

"Then don't, old friend." Mura suppressed his smile.

Uo was a broad-shouldered, rocklike man with vast hands and broken nose, and he wore a pained expression. "I won't. But I think I'm going to fart." Uo was famous for his humor and for his courage and for the quantity of his wind. Last year when they had had the wind-breaking contest with the village to the north he had been champion of champions and had brought great honor to Anjiro.

"Eeeeee, perhaps you'd better not," Haru, a short, wizened fisherman, chortled. "One of the shitheads might get jealous."

Mura hissed, "You're ordered not to call samurai that while even one's near the village." *Oh ko,* he was thinking wearily, I hope we've not forgotten anything. He glanced up at the mountainside, at the bamboo stockade surrounding the temporary fortress they had constructed with such speed and sweat. Three hundred men, digging and building and carrying. The other new house had been easier. It was on the knoll, just below Omi's house, and he could see it, smaller than Omi's but with a tiled roof, a makeshift garden, and a small bath house. I suppose Omi will move there and give Lord Yabu his, Mura thought.

He looked back at the headland where the galley would appear any moment now. Soon Yabu would step ashore and then they were all in the hands of the gods, all *kami,* God the Father, His Blessed Son, and the Blessed Madonna, *oh ko!*

Blessed Madonna, protect us! Would it be too much to ask to put Thy great eye on this special village of Anjiro? Just for the next few days? We need special favor to protect us from our Lord and Master, oh yes! I will light fifty candles and my sons will definitely be brought up in the True Faith, Mura promised.

Today Mura was very glad to be a Christian; he could intercede with the One God and that was an added protection for his village. He had become a Christian in his youth because his own liege lord had been converted and had at once ordered all his followers to become Christians. And when, twenty years ago, this lord was killed fighting for Toranaga against the Taikō, Mura had remained Christian to honor his memory. A good soldier has but one master, he thought. One real master.

Ninjin, a round-faced man with very buck teeth, was especially agitated by the presence of so many samurai. "Mura-san, so sorry, but it's dangerous what you've done—terrible, *neh?* That little earthquake this morning, it was a sign from the gods, an omen. You've made a terrible mistake, Mura-san."

"What is done is done, Ninjin. Forget about it."

"How can I? It's in my cellar and—"

"Some of it's in your cellar. I've plenty myself," Uo said, no longer smiling.

"Nothing's anywhere. Nothing, old friends," Mura said cautiously. "Nothing exists." On his orders, thirty koku of rice had been stolen over the last few days from the samurai commissariat and was now secreted around the village, along with other stores and equipment—and weapons.

"Not weapons," Uo had protested. "Rice yes, but not weapons!"

"War is coming."

"It's against the law to have weapons," Ninjin had wailed.

Mura snorted. "That's a new law, barely twelve years old. Before that we could have any weapons we wanted and we weren't tied to the village. We could go where we wanted, be what we wanted. We could be peasant-soldier, fisherman, merchant, even samurai—some could, you know it's the truth."

"Yes, but now it's different, Mura-san, different. The Taikō ordered it to be different!"

"Soon it'll be as it's always been. We'll be soldiering again."

"Then let's wait," Ninjin had pleaded. "Please. Now it's against the law. If the law changes that's *karma*. The Taikō made the law: no weapons. None. On pain of instant death."

"Open your eyes, all of you! The Taikō's dead! And I tell you, soon Omi-san'll need trained men and most of us have warred, *neh?* We've fished and warred, all in their season. Isn't that true?"

"Yes, Mura-san," Uo had agreed through his fear. "Before the Taikō we weren't tied."

"They'll catch us, they have to catch us," Ninjin had wept. "They'll have no mercy. They'll boil us like they boiled the barbarian."

"Shut up about the barbarian!"

"Listen, friends," Mura had said. "We'll never get such a chance again. It's sent by God. Or by the gods. We must take every knife, arrow, spear, sword, musket, shield, bow we can. The samurai'll think other samurai've stolen them—haven't the shitheads come from all over Izu? And what samurai really trusts another? We must take back our right to war, *neh?* My father was killed in battle—so was his and his! Ninjin, how many battles have you been in—dozens, *neh?* Uo—what about you? Twenty? Thirty?"

"More. Didn't I serve with the Taikō, curse his memory? Ah, before he became Taikō, he was a man. That's the truth! Then something changed him, *neh?* Ninjin, don't forget that Mura-san is headman! And we shouldn't forget his father was headman too! If the headman says weapons, then weapons it has to be."

Now, kneeling in the sun, Mura was convinced that he had done correctly, that this new war would last forever and their world would be again as it had always been. The village would be here, and the boats and some villagers. Because all men—peasant, *daimyo,* samurai, even the *eta*—all men had to eat and the fish were waiting in the sea. So the soldier-villagers would take time out from war from time to time, as always, and they would launch their boats. . . .

"Look!" Uo said and pointed involuntarily in the sudden hush.

The galley was rounding the headland.

Fujiko was kneeling abjectly in front of Toranaga in the main cabin that he had used during the voyage, and they were alone.

"I beg you, Sire," she pleaded. "Take this sentence off my head."

"It's not a sentence, it's an order."

"I will obey, of course. But I cannot do—"

"Cannot?" Toranaga flared. "How dare you argue! I tell you you're to be the pilot's consort and you have the impertinence to argue?"

"I apologize, Sire, with all my heart," Fujiko said quickly, the words gushing. "That was not meant as an argument. I only wanted to say that I cannot do this in the way that you wished. I beg you to understand. Forgive me, Sire, but it's not possible to be happy—or to pretend happiness." She bowed her head to the futon. "I humbly beseech you to allow me to commit seppuku."

"I've said before I do not approve of senseless death. I have a use for you."

"Please, Sire, I wish to die. I humbly beg you. I wish to join my husband and my son."

Toranaga's voice slashed at her, drowning the sounds of the galley. "I've already refused you that honor. You don't merit it, yet. And it's only because of your grandfather, because Lord Hiro-matsu's my oldest friend, that I've listened patiently to your ill-mannered mouthings so far. Enough of this nonsense, woman. Stop acting like a dung-headed peasant!"

"I humbly beg permission to cut off my hair and become a nun. Buddha will—"

"No. I've given you an order. Obey it!"

"Obey?" she said, not looking up, her face stark. Then, half to herself, "I thought I was ordered to Yedo."

"You were ordered to this vessel! You forget your position, you forget your heritage, you forget your duty. You forget your duty! I'm disgusted with you. Go and get ready."

"I want to die, please let me join them, Sire."

"Your husband was born samurai by mistake. He was malformed, so his offspring would be equally malformed. That fool almost ruined me! Join them? What nonsense! You're forbidden to commit seppuku! Now, get out!"

But she did not move.

"Perhaps I'd better send you to the *eta*. To one of their houses. Perhaps that'd remind you of your manners and your duty."

A shudder racked her, but she hissed back defiantly, "At least they'd be Japanese!"

"*I am your liege lord.* You-will-do-as-I-order."

Fujiko hesitated. Then she shrugged. "Yes, Lord. I apologize for my ill manners." She placed her hands flat on the futon and bowed her head low, her voice penitent. But in her heart she was not persuaded and he knew and she knew what she intended to do. "Sire, I sincerely apologize for disturbing you, for destroying your *wa*, your harmony, and for my bad manners. You were right. I was wrong." She got up and went quietly to the door of the cabin.

"If I grant you what you wish," Toranaga said, "will you, in return, do what I want, with all your heart?"

Slowly she looked back. "For how long, Sire? I beg to ask for how long must I be consort to the barbarian?"

"A year."

She turned away and reached for the door handle.

Toranaga said, "Half a year."

Fujiko's hand stopped. Trembling, she leaned her head against the door. "Yes. Thank you, Sire. Thank you."

Toranaga got to his feet and went to the door. She opened it for him and bowed him through and closed it after him. Then the tears came silently.

She was samurai.

Toranaga came on deck feeling very pleased with himself. He had achieved what he wanted with the minimum of trouble. If the girl had been pressed too far she would have disobeyed and taken her own life without permission. But now she would try hard to please and it was important that she become the pilot's consort happily, at least outwardly so, and six months would be more than enough time. Women are much easier to deal with than men, he thought contentedly. So much easier, in certain things.

Then he saw Yabu's samurai massed around the bay and his sense of well-being vanished.

"Welcome to Izu, Lord Toranaga," Yabu said. "I ordered a few men here to act as escort for you."

"Good."

The galley was still two hundred yards from the dock, approaching neatly, and they could see Omi and Igurashi and the futons and the awning.

"Everything's been done as we discussed in Osaka," Yabu was saying. "But why not stay with me for a few days? I'd be honored and it would prove very useful. You could approve the choice of the two hundred and fifty men for the Musket Regiment, and meet their commander."

"Nothing would please me more but I must get to Yedo as quickly as possible, Yabu-san."

"Two or three days? Please. A few days free from worry would be good for you, *neh?* Your health is important to me—to all your allies. Some rest, good food, and hunting."

Toranaga was desperately seeking a solution. To stay here with only fifty guards was unthinkable. He would be totally in Yabu's power, and that would be worse than his situation at Osaka. At least Ishido was predictable and bound by certain rules. But Yabu? Yabu's as treacherous as a shark and you don't tempt sharks, he told himself. And never in their home waters. And never with your own life. He knew that the bargain he had made with Yabu at Osaka had as much substance as the weight of their urine when it had reached the ground, once Yabu believed he could get better concessions from Ishido. And Yabu's presenting Toranaga's head on a wooden platter to Ishido would get Yabu immediately far more than Toranaga was prepared to offer.

Kill him or go ashore? Those were the choices.

"You're too kind," he said. "But I must get to Yedo." I never thought Yabu would have time to gather so many men here. Has he broken our code?

"Please allow me to insist, Toranaga-sama. The hunting's very good nearby. I've falcons with my men. A little hunting after being confined at Osaka would be good, *neh?*"

"Yes, it would be good to hunt today. I regret losing my falcons there."

"But they're not lost. Surely Hiro-matsu will bring them with him to Yedo?"

"I ordered him to release them once we were safely away. By the time they'd have reached Yedo they would have been out of training and tainted. It's one of my few rules: only to fly the falcons that I've trained, and to allow them no other master. That way they make only my mistakes."

"It's a good rule. I'd like to hear the others. Perhaps over food, tonight?"

I need this shark, Toranaga thought bitterly. To kill him now is premature.

Two ropes sailed ashore to be caught and secured. The ropes tightened and screeched under the strain and the galley swung alongside deftly. Oars were shipped. The gangway slid into place and then Yabu stood at its head.

At once the massed samurai shouted their battle cry in unison. *"Kasigi! Kasigi!"* and the roar that they made sent the gulls cawing and mewing into the sky. As one man, the samurai bowed.

Yabu bowed back, then turned to Toranaga and beckoned him expansively. "Let's go ashore."

Toranaga looked out over the massed samurai, over the villagers prostrate in the dust, and he asked himself, Is this where I die by the sword as the astrologer has foretold? Certainly the first part has come to pass: my name is now written on Osaka walls.

He put that thought aside. At the head of the gangway he called out loudly and imperiously to his fifty samurai, who now wore Brown uniform kimonos as he did, "All of you, stay here! You, Captain, you will prepare for instant departure! Mariko-san, you will be staying in Anjiro for three days. Take the pilot and Fujiko-san ashore at once and wait for me in the square." Then he faced the shore and to Yabu's amazement increased the force of his voice. "Now, Yabu-san, I will inspect your regiments!" At once he walked past him and stomped down the gangplank with all the easy confident arrogance of the fighting general he was.

No general had ever won more battles and no one was more cunning except the Taikō, and he was dead. No general had fought more battles, or was ever more patient or had lost so few men. And he had never been defeated.

A rustle of astonishment sped throughout the shore as he was recognized. This inspection was completely unexpected. His name was passed from mouth to mouth and the strength of the whispering, the awe that it generated, gratified him. He felt Yabu following but did not look back.

"Ah, Igurashi-san," he said with a geniality he did not feel. "It's good to see you. Come along, we'll inspect your men together."

"Yes, Lord."

"And you must be Kasigi Omi-san. Your father's an old comrade in arms of mine. You follow, too."

"Yes, Lord," Omi replied, his size increasing with the honor being done to him. "Thank you."

Toranaga set a brisk pace. He had taken them with him to prevent them from talking privately with Yabu for the moment, knowing that his life depended on keeping the initiative.

"Didn't you fight with us at Odawara, Igurashi-san?" he was asking, already knowing that this was where the samurai had lost his eye.

"Yes, Sire. I had the honor. I was with Lord Yabu and we served on the Taikō right wing."

"Then you had the place of honor—where fighting was the thickest. I have much to thank you and your master for."

"We smashed the enemy, Lord. We were only doing our duty." Even though Igurashi hated Toranaga, he was proud that the action was remembered and that he was being thanked.

Now they had come to the front of the first regiment. Toranaga's voice carried loudly. "Yes, you and the men of Izu helped us greatly. Perhaps, if it weren't for you, I would not have gained the Kwanto! Eh, Yabu-sama?" he added, stopping suddenly, giving Yabu publicly the added title, and thus the added honor.

Again Yabu was thrown off balance by the flattery. He felt it was no more than his due, but he had not expected it from Toranaga, and it had never been his intention to allow a formal inspection. "Perhaps, but I doubt it. The Taikō ordered the Beppu clan obliterated. So it was obliterated."

That had been ten years ago, when only the enormously powerful and ancient Beppu clan, led by Beppu Genzaemon, opposed the combined forces of General Nakamura, the Taikō-to-be, and Toranaga—the last major obstacle to Nakamura's complete domination of the Empire. For centuries the Beppu had owned the Eight Provinces, the Kwanto. A hundred and fifty thousand men had ringed their castle-city of Odawara, which guarded the pass that led through the mountains into the incredibly rich rice plains beyond. The siege lasted eleven months. Nakamura's new consort, the patrician Lady Ochiba, radiant and barely eighteen, had come to her lord's household outside the battlements, her infant son in her arms, Nakamura doting on his firstborn child. And with Lady Ochiba had come her younger sister, Genjiko, whom Nakamura proposed giving in marriage to Toranaga.

"Sire," Toranaga had said, "I'd certainly be honored to lock our houses closer together, but instead of me marrying the Lady Genjiko as you suggest, let her marry my son and heir, Sudara."

It had taken Toranaga many days to persuade Nakamura but he had agreed. Then when the decision was announced to the Lady Ochiba, she had replied at once, "With humility, Sire, I oppose the marriage."

Nakamura had laughed. "So do I! Sudara's only ten and Genjiko thirteen. Even so, they're now betrothed and on his fifteenth birthday they'll marry."

"But, Sire, Lord Toranaga's already your brother-in-law, *neh?* Surely that's enough of a connection? You need closer ties with the Fujimoto and the Takashima—even at the Imperial Court."

"They're dungheads at Court, and all in pawn," Nakamura had said in his rough, peasant voice. "Listen, O-chan: Toranaga's got seventy thousand samurai. When we've smashed the Beppu he'll have the Kwanto and more men. My son will need leaders like Yoshi Toranaga, like I need them. Yes, and one day my son will need Yoshi Sudara. Better Sudara should be my son's uncle. Your sister's betrothed to Sudara, but Sudara will live with us for a few years, *neh?*"

"Of course, Sire," Toranaga had agreed instantly, giving up his son and heir as a hostage.

"Good. But listen, first you and Sudara will swear eternal loyalty to my son."

And so it had happened. Then during the tenth month of siege this first child of Nakamura had died, from fever or bad blood or malevolent *kami.*

"May all gods curse Odawara and Toranaga," Ochiba had raved. "It's Toranaga's fault that we're here—he wants the Kwanto. It's his fault our son's dead. He's your real enemy. He wants you to die and me to die! Put him to death—or put him to work. Let him lead the attack, let him pay with his life for the life of our son! I demand vengeance. . . ."

So Toranaga had led the attack. He had taken Odawara Castle by mining the walls and by frontal attack. Then the grief-stricken Nakamura had stamped the city into dust. With its fall and the hunting down of all the Beppu, the Empire was subdued and Nakamura became first Kwampaku and then Taikō. But many had died at Odawara.

Too many, Toranaga thought, here on the Anjiro shore. He watched Yabu. "It's a pity the Taikō's dead, *neh?*"

"Yes."

"My brother-in-law was a great leader. And a great teacher too. Like him, I never forget a friend. Or an enemy."

"Soon Lord Yaemon will be of age. His spirit is the Taikō's spirit. Lord Tora—" But before Yabu could stop the inspection Toranaga had already gone on again and there was little he could do but follow.

Toranaga walked down the ranks, exuding geniality, picking out a man here, another there, recognizing some, his eyes never still as he reached into his memory for faces and names. He had that very rare quality of special generals who inspect so that every man feels, at least for a moment, that the general has looked at him alone, perhaps even talked with him alone among his comrades. Toranaga was doing what he was born to do, what he had done a thousand times: controlling men with his will.

By the time the last samurai was passed, Yabu, Igurashi, and Omi were exhausted. But Toranaga was not, and again, before Yabu could stop him, he had walked rapidly to a vantage point and stood high and alone.

"Samurai of Izu, vassals of my friend and ally, Kasigi Yabu-sama!" he called out in that vast sonorous voice. "I'm honored to be here. I'm honored to see part of the strength of Izu, part of the forces of my great ally. Listen, samurai, dark clouds are gathering over the Empire and threaten the Taikō's peace. We must protect the Taikō's gifts to us against treachery in high places! Let every samurai be prepared! Let every weapon be sharp! Together we will defend his will! And we will prevail! May the gods of Japan both great and small pay attention! May they blast without pity all those who oppose the Taikō's orders!" Then he raised both his arms and uttered their battle cry, *"Kasigi,"* and, incredibly, he bowed to the legions and held the bow.

They all stared at him. Then, *"Toranaga!"* came roaring back at him from the regiments again and again. And the samurai bowed in return.

Even Yabu bowed, overcome by the strength of the moment.

Before Yabu could straighten, Toranaga had set off down the hill once more at a fast pace. "Go with him, Omi-san," Yabu ordered. It would have been unseemly for him to run after Toranaga himself.

"Yes, Lord."

When Omi had gone, Yabu said to Igurashi, "What's the news from Yedo?"

"The Lady Yuriko, your wife, said first to tell you there's a tremendous amount of mobilization over the whole Kwanto. Nothing much on the surface but underneath everything's boiling. She believes Toranaga's preparing for war—a sudden attack, perhaps against Osaka itself."

"What about Ishido?"

"Nothing before we left. That was five days ago. Nor anything about Toranaga's escape. I only heard about that yesterday when your Lady sent a carrier pigeon from Yedo."

"Ah, Zukimoto's already set up that courier service?"

"Yes, Sire."

"Good."

"Her message read: 'Toranaga has successfully escaped from Osaka with our Master in a galley. Make preparations to welcome them at Anjiro.' I thought it best to keep this secret except from Omi-san, but we're all prepared."

"How?"

"I've ordered a war 'exercise,' Sire, throughout Izu. Within three days every road and pass into Izu will be blocked, if that's what you want. There's a mock pirate fleet to the north that could swamp any unescorted ship by day or by night, if that's what you want. And there's space here for you and a guest, however important, if that's what you want."

"Good. Anything else? Any other news?"

Igurashi was reluctant to pass along news the implications of which he did not understand. "We're prepared for anything here. But this morning a cipher came from Osaka: 'Toranaga has resigned from the Council of Regents.' "

"Impossible! Why should he do that?"

"I don't know. I can't think this one out. But it must be true, Sire. We've never had wrong information from this source before."

"The Lady Sazuko?" Yabu asked cautiously, naming Toranaga's youngest consort, whose maid was a spy in his employ.

Igurashi nodded. "Yes. But I don't understand it at all. Now the Regents will impeach him, won't they? They'll order his death. It'd be madness to resign, *neh?*"

"Ishido must have forced him to do it. But how? There wasn't a breath of rumor. Toranaga would never resign on his own! You're right, that'd be the act of a madman. He's lost if he has. It must be false."

Yabu walked down the hill in turmoil and watched Toranaga cross the square toward Mariko and the barbarian, with Fujiko nearby. Now Mariko was walking beside Toranaga, the others waiting in the square. Toranaga was talking quickly and urgently. And then Yabu saw him give her a small parchment scroll and he wondered what it contained and what was being said. What new trickery is Toranaga planning, he asked himself, wishing he had his wife Yuriko here to help him with her wise counsel.

At the dock Toranaga stopped. He did not go onto the ship and into the protection of his men. He knew that it was on the shore that the final decision would be made. He could not escape. Nothing was yet resolved. He watched Yabu and Igurashi approaching. Yabu's untoward impassivity told him very much.

"So, Yabu-san?"

"You will stay for a few days, Lord Toranaga?"

"It would be better for me to leave at once."

Yabu ordered everyone out of hearing. In a moment the two men were alone on the shore.

"I've had disquieting news from Osaka. You've resigned from the Council of Regents?"

"Yes. I've resigned."

"Then you've killed yourself, destroyed your cause, all your vassals, all your allies, all your friends! You've buried Izu and you've murdered me!"

"The Council of Regents can certainly take away your fief, and your life if they want. Yes."

"By all gods, living and dead and yet to be born . . ." Yabu fought to dominate his temper. "I apologize for my bad manners but your—your incredible attitude . . . yes, I apologize." There was no real purpose to be gained in a show of emotion which all knew was unseemly and defacing. "Yes, it is better for you to stay here then, Lord Toranaga."

"I think I would prefer to leave at once."

"Here or Yedo, what's the difference? The Regents' order will come immediately. I imagine you'd want to commit seppuku at once. With dignity. In peace. I would be honored to act as your second."

"Thank you. But no legal order's yet arrived so my head will stay where it is."

"What does a day or two matter? It's inevitable that the order will come. I will make all arrangements, yes, and they will be perfect. You may rely on me."

"Thank you. Yes, I can understand why you would want my head."

"My own head will be forfeit too. If I send yours to Ishido, or take it and ask his pardon, that might persuade him, but I doubt it, *neh?*"

"If I were in your position I might ask for your head. Unfortunately my head will help you not at all."

"I'm inclined to agree. But it's worth trying." Yabu spat violently in the dust. "I deserve to die for being so stupid as to put myself in that dunghead's power."

"Ishido will never hesitate to take your head. But first he'll take Izu. Oh yes, Izu's lost with him in power."

"Don't bait me! I know that's going to happen!"

"I'm not baiting you, my friend," Toranaga told him, enjoying Yabu's loss of face. "I merely said, with Ishido in power you're lost and Izu's lost, because his kinsman Ikawa Jikkyu covets Izu, *neh?* But, Yabu-san, Ishido doesn't have the power. Yet." And he told him, friend to friend, why he had resigned.

"The Council's hamstrung!" Yabu couldn't believe it.

"There isn't any Council. There won't be until there are five members again." Toranaga smiled. "Think about it, Yabu-san. Now I'm stronger than ever, *neh?* Ishido's neutralized—so is Jikkyu. Now you've got all the time you need to train

your guns. Now you own Suruga and Totomi. Now you own Jikkyu's head. In a few months you'll see his head on a spike and the heads of all his kin, and you'll ride in state into your new domains." Abruptly he spun and shouted, "Igurashi-san!" and five hundred men heard the command.

Igurashi came running but before the samurai had gone three paces, Toranaga called out, "Bring an honor guard with you. Fifty men! At once!" He did not dare to give Yabu a moment's respite to detect the enormous flaw in his argument: that if Ishido was hamstrung now and did not have power, then Toranaga's head on a wooden platter would be of enormous value to Ishido and thus to Yabu. Or even better, Toranaga bound like a common felon and delivered alive at the gates of Osaka Castle would bring Yabu immortality and the keys to the Kwanto.

While the honor guard was forming in front of him, Toranaga said loudly, "In honor of this occasion, Yabu-sama, perhaps you would accept this as a token of friendship." Then he took out his long sword, held it flat on both hands, and offered it.

Yabu took the sword as though in a dream. It was priceless. It was a Minowara heirloom and famous throughout the land. Toranaga had possessed this sword for fifteen years. It had been presented to him by Nakamura in front of the assembled majesty of all the important *daimyos* in the Empire, except Beppu Genzaemon, as part payment for a secret agreement.

This had happened shortly after the battle of Nagakudé, long before the Lady Ochiba. Toranaga had just defeated General Nakamura, the Taikō-to-be, when Nakamura was still just an upstart without mandate or formal power or formal title and his reach for absolute power still in the balance. Instead of gathering an overwhelming host and burying Toranaga, which was his usual policy, Nakamura had decided to be conciliatory. He had offered Toranaga a treaty of friendship and a binding alliance, and to cement them, his half sister as wife. That the woman was already married and middle-aged bothered neither Nakamura nor Toranaga at all. Toranaga agreed to the pact. At once the woman's husband, one of Nakamura's vassals—thanking the gods that the invitation to divorce her had not been accompanied by an invitation to commit seppuku—had gratefully sent her back to her half brother. Immediately Toranaga married her with all the pomp and ceremony he could muster, and the same day concluded a secret friendship pact with the immensely powerful Beppu clan, the open enemies of Nakamura, who, at this time, still sat disdainfully in the Kwanto on Toranaga's very unprotected back door.

Then Toranaga had flown his falcons and waited for Nakamura's inevitable attack. But none had come. Instead, astoundingly, Nakamura had sent his revered and beloved mother into Toranaga's camp as a hostage, ostensibly to visit her stepdaughter, Toranaga's new wife, but still hostage nonetheless, and had, in return, invited Toranaga to the vast meeting of all the *daimyos* that he had arranged at Osaka. Toranaga had thought hard and long. Then he had accepted the invitation, suggesting to his ally Beppu Genzaemon that it would be unwise for them both to go. Next, he had set sixty thousand samurai secretly into motion toward Osaka against Nakamura's expected treachery, and had left his eldest son, Noboru, in charge of his new wife and her mother. Noboru had at once piled tinder-dry brushwood to the eaves of their residence and had told them bluntly he would fire it if anything happened to his father.

Toranaga smiled, remembering. The night before he was due to enter Osaka, Nakamura, unconventional as ever, had paid him a secret visit, alone and unarmed.

"Well met, Tora-san."

"Well met, Lord Nakamura."

"Listen: We've fought too many battles together, we know too many secrets, we've shit too many times in the same pot to want to piss on our own feet or on each other's."

"I agree," Toranaga had said cautiously.

"Listen then: I'm within a sword's edge of winning the realm. To get total power I've got to have the respect of the ancient clans, the hereditary fief holders, the present heirs of the Fujimoto, the Takashima, and Minowara. Once I've got power, any *daimyo* or any three together can piss blood for all I care."

"You have my respect—you've always had it."

The little monkey-faced man had laughed richly. "You won at Nagakudé fairly. You're the best general I've ever known, the greatest *daimyo* in the realm. But now we're going to stop playing games, you and I. Listen: tomorrow I want you to bow to me before all the *daimyos, as a vassal.* I want you, Yoshi Toranaga-noh-Minowara a willing vassal. Publicly. Not to tongue my hole, but polite, humble, and respectful. If you're my vassal, the rest'll fart in their haste to put their heads in the dust and their tails in the air. And the few that don't—well, let them beware."

"That will make you Lord of all Japan. *Neh?*"

"Yes. The first in history. And you'll have given it to me. I admit I can't do it without you. But listen: If you do that for me you'll have first place after me. Every honor you want. Anything. There's enough for both of us."

"Is there?"

"Yes. First I take Japan. Then Korea. Then China. I told Goroda I wanted that and that's what I'll have. Then you can have Japan—a province of my China!"

"But now, Lord Nakamura? Now I have to submit, *neh?* I'm in your power, *neh?* You're in overwhelming strength in front of me—and the Beppu threaten my back."

"I'll deal with them soon enough," the peasant warlord had said. "Those sneering carrion refused my invitation to come here tomorrow—they sent my scroll back covered in bird's shit. You want their lands? The whole Kwanto?"

"I want nothing from them or from anyone," he had said.

"Liar," Nakamura had said genially. "Listen, Tora-san: I'm almost fifty. None of my women has ever birthed. I've juice in plenty, always have had, and in my life I must have pillowed a hundred, two hundred women, of all types, of all ages, in every way, but none has ever birthed a child, not even stillborn. I've everything but I've no sons and never will. That's my *karma.* You've four sons living and who knows how many daughters. You're forty-three so you can pillow your way to a dozen more sons as easy as horses shit and that's your *karma.* Also you're Minowara and that's *karma.* Say I adopt one of your sons and make him my heir?"

"Now?"

"Soon. Say in three years. It was never important to have an heir before but now things're different. Our late Master Goroda had the stupidity to get himself murdered. Now the land's mine—could be mine. Well?"

"You'll make the agreements formal, publicly formal, in two years?"

"Yes. In two years. You can trust me—our interests are the same. Listen: In two years, in public; and we agree, you and I, which son. This way we share everything, eh? Our joint dynasty's settled into the future, so no problems there and that's good for you and good for me. The pickings'll be huge. First the Kwanto. Eh?"

"Perhaps Beppu Genzaemon will submit—*if* I submit."

"I can't allow them to, Tora-san. You covet their lands."

"I covet nothing."

Nakamura's laugh had been merry. "Yes. But you should. The Kwanto's worthy of you. It's safe behind mountain walls, easy to defend. With the delta you'll control the richest rice lands in the Empire. You'll have your back to the sea and an income of two million koku. But don't make Kamakura your capital. Or Odawara."

"Kamakura's always been capital of the Kwanto."

"Why shouldn't you covet Kamakura, Tora-san? Hasn't it contained the holy shrine of your family's guardian *kami* for six hundred years? Isn't Hachiman, the *kami* of war, the Minowara deity? Your ancestor was wise to choose the *kami* of war to worship."

"I covet nothing, worship nothing. A shrine is just a shrine and the *kami* of war's never been known to stay in any shrine."

"I'm glad you covet nothing, Tora-san, then nothing will disappoint you. You're like me in that. But Kamakura's no capital for you. There are seven passes into it, too many to defend. And it's not on the sea. No, I wouldn't advise Kamakura. Listen: You'd be better and safer to go farther over the mountains. You need a seaport. There's one I saw once—Yedo—a fishing village now, but you'll make it into a great city. Easy to defend, perfect for trade. You favor trade. I favor trade. Good. So you must have a seaport. As to Odawara, we're going to stamp it out, as a lesson to all the others."

"That will be very difficult."

"Yes. But it'd be a good lesson for all the other *daimyos, neh?*"

"To take that city by storm would be costly."

Again the taunting laugh. "It could be, to you, if you don't join me. I've got to go through your present lands to get at it—did you know you're the Beppu front line? The Beppu pawn? Together you and them could keep me off for a year or two, even three. But I'll get there in the end. Oh, yes. Eeeee, why waste more time on them? They're all dead—except your son-in-law if you want—ah, I know you've an alliance with them, but it's not worth a bowl of horseshit. So what's your answer? The pickings are going to be vast. First the Kwanto—that's yours—then I've all Japan. Then Korea—easy. Then China—hard but not impossible. I know a peasant can't become Shōgun, but 'our' son *will* be Shōgun, and he could straddle the Dragon Throne of China too, or his son. Now that's the end of talk. What's your answer, Yoshi Toranaga-noh-Minowara, vassal or not? Nothing else is of value to me."

"Let's piss on the bargain," Toranaga had said, having gained everything that he had wanted and planned for. And the next day, before the bewildered majesty of the truculent *daimyos,* he had humbly offered up his sword and his lands and his honor and his heritage to the upstart peasant warlord. He had begged to be allowed to serve Nakamura and his house forever. And he, Yoshi Toranaga-noh-Minowara, had bowed his head abjectly into the dust. The Taikō-to-be now had been magnanimous and had taken his lands and had at once gifted him the Kwanto as a fief once it was conquered, ordering total war on the Beppu for their insults to the Emperor. And he had also given Toranaga this sword that he had recently acquired from one of the Imperial treasuries. The sword had been made by the master swordsmith Miyoshi-Go centuries before, and had once belonged to the most famous warrior in history, Minowara Yoshitomo, the first of the Minowara Shōguns.

Toranaga remembered that day. And he recalled other days: a few years later when the Lady Ochiba gave birth to a boy; and another when, incredibly, after the Taikō's first son had conveniently died, Yaemon, the second son, was born.

So was the whole plan ruined. *Karma.*

He saw Yabu holding the sword of his ancestor with reverence.

"Is it as sharp as they say?" Yabu asked.

"Yes."

"You do me great honor. I will treasure your gift." Yabu bowed, conscious that, because of the gift, he would be the first in the land after Toranaga.

Toranaga bowed back, and then, unarmed, he walked for the gangway. It took all his will to hide his fury and not to let his feet falter, and he prayed that Yabu's avariciousness would keep him mesmerized for just a few moments more.

"Cast off!" he ordered, coming onto the deck, and then turned shoreward and waved cheerfully.

Someone broke the silence and shouted his name, then others took up the shout. There was a general roar of approval at the honor done to their lord. Willing hands shoved the ship out to sea. The oarsmen pulled briskly. The galley made way.

"Captain, get to Yedo quickly!"

"Yes, Sire."

Toranaga looked aft, his eyes ranging the shore, expecting danger any instant. Yabu stood near the jetty, still bemused by the sword. Mariko and Fujiko were waiting beside the awning with the other women. The Anjin-san was on the edge of the square where he had been told to wait—rigid, towering, and unmistakably furious. Their eyes met. Toranaga smiled and waved.

The wave was returned, but coldly, and this amused Toranaga very much.

Blackthorne walked cheerlessly up to the jetty.

"When's he coming back, Mariko-san?"

"I don't know, Anjin-san."

"How do we get to Yedo?"

"We stay here. At least, I stay for three days. Then I'm ordered there."

"By sea?"

"By land."

"And me?"

"You are to stay here."

"Why?"

"You expressed an interest in learning our language. And there's work for you to do here."

"What work?"

"I don't know, I'm sorry. Lord Yabu will tell you. My Master left me here to interpret, for three days."

Blackthorne was filled with foreboding. His pistols were in his belt but he had no knives and no more powder and no more shot. That was all in the cabin aboard the galley.

"Why didn't you tell me we were staying here?" he asked. "You just said to come ashore."

"I didn't know you were to remain here also," she replied. "Lord Toranaga told me only a moment ago, in the square."

"Why didn't he tell me then? Tell me himself?"

"I don't know."

"I was supposed to be going to Yedo. That's where my crew is. That's where my ship is. What about them?"

"He just said you were to stay here."

"For how long?"

"He didn't tell me, Anjin-san. Perhaps Lord Yabu will know. Please be patient."

Blackthorne could see Toranaga standing on the quarterdeck, watching shoreward. "I think he knew all along I was to stay here, didn't he?"

She did not answer. How childish it is, she said to herself, to speak aloud what you think. And how extraordinarily clever Toranaga was to have escaped this trap.

Fujiko and the two maids stood beside her, waiting patiently in the shade with Omi's mother and wife, whom she had met briefly, and she looked beyond them to the galley. It was picking up speed now. But it was still within easy arrow range. Any moment now she knew she must begin. Oh, Madonna, let me be strong, she prayed, all her attention centering on Yabu.

"Is it true? Is that true?" Blackthorne was asking.

"What? Oh, I'm sorry, I don't know, Anjin-san. I can only tell you Lord Toranaga is very wise. The wisest man. Whatever his reason, it was good." She studied the blue eyes and hard face, knowing that Blackthorne had no understanding of what had occurred here. "Please be patient, Anjin-san. There's nothing to be afraid of. You're his favored vassal and under his—"

"I'm not afraid, Mariko-san. I'm just tired of being shoved around the board like a pawn. And I'm no one's vassal."

"Is 'retainer' better? Or how would you describe a man who works for another or is retained by another for special . . ." Then she saw the blood soar into Yabu's face.

"The guns—the guns are still on the galley!" he cried out.

Mariko knew the time had come. She hurried over to him as he turned to shout orders at Igurashi.

"Your pardon, Lord Yabu," she said, overriding him, "there's no need to worry about your guns. Lord Toranaga said to ask your pardon for his haste but he has urgent things to do on your joint behalves at Yedo. He said he would return the galley instantly. With the guns. And with extra powder. And also with the two hundred and fifty men you require from him. They'll be here in five or six days."

"What?"

Mariko explained patiently and politely again as Toranaga had told her to do. Then, once Yabu understood, she took out a roll of parchment from her sleeve. "My Master begs you to read this. It concerns the Anjin-san." She formally offered it to him.

But Yabu did not take the scroll. His eyes went to the galley. It was well away now, going very fast. Out of range. But what does that matter, he thought contentedly, now over his anxiety. I'll get the guns back quickly and now I'm out of the Ishido trap and I've Toranaga's most famous sword and soon all the *daimyos* in the land will be aware of my new position in the armies of the East—second to Toranaga alone! Yabu could still see Toranaga and he waved once and the wave was returned. Then Toranaga vanished off the quarterdeck.

Yabu took the scroll and turned his mind to the present. And to the Anjin-san.

Blackthorne was watching thirty paces away and he felt his hackles rise under Yabu's piercing gaze. He heard Mariko speaking in her lilting voice but that did not reassure him. His hand tightened covertly on the pistol.

"Anjin-san!" Mariko called out. "Would you please come over here!"

As Blackthorne approached them, Yabu glanced up from the parchment, nodded in friendly fashion. When Yabu had finished reading he handed the paper back to Mariko and spoke briefly, partly to her, partly to him.

Reverently Mariko offered the paper to Blackthorne. He took it and examined the incomprehensible characters.

"Lord Yabu says you are welcome in this village. This paper is under Lord Toranaga's seal, Anjin-san. You are to keep it. He's given you a rare honor. Lord Toranaga has made you a hatamoto. This is the position of a special retainer of his personal staff. You have his absolute protection, Anjin-san. Lord Yabu, of course, acknowledges this. I will explain later the privileges, but Lord Toranaga has given you also a salary of twenty koku a month. That is about—"

Yabu interrupted her, expansively waving his hand at Blackthorne, then at the village, and spoke at length. Mariko translated. "Lord Yabu repeats that you are welcome here. He hopes you will be content, that everything will be done to make your stay comfortable. A house will be provided for you. And teachers. You will please learn Japanese as quickly as possible, he says. Tonight he will ask you some questions and tell you about some special work."

"Please ask him, what work?"

"May I advise just a little more patience, Anjin-san. Now is not the time, truly."

"All right."

"*Wakarimasu ka,* Anjin-san?" Yabu said. Do you understand?

"*Hai,* Yabu-san. *Domo.*"

Yabu gave orders to Igurashi to dismiss the regiment, then strode over to the villagers, who were still prostrate in the sand.

He stood in front of them in the warm fine spring afternoon, Toranaga's sword still in his hand. His words whipped over them. Yabu pointed the sword at Blackthorne and harangued them a few moments more and ended abruptly. A tremor went through the villagers. Mura bowed and said "*hai*" several times and turned and asked the villagers a question and all eyes went to Blackthorne.

"*Wakarimasu ka?*" Mura called out and they all answered "*hai,*" their voices mixing with the sighing of the waves upon the beach.

"What's going on?" Blackthorne asked Mariko, but Mura shouted, "*Keirei!*" and the villagers bowed low again, once to Yabu and once to Blackthorne. Yabu strode off without looking back.

"What's going on, Mariko-san?"

"He—Lord Yabu told them you are his honored guest here. That you are also Lord Toranaga's very honored vas—retainer. That you are here mostly to learn our tongue. That he has given the village the honor and responsibility of teaching you. The village is responsible, Anjin-san. Everyone here is to help you. He told them that if you have not learned satisfactorily within six months, the village will be burnt, but before that, every man, woman, and child will be crucified."

CHAPTER 31

THE day was dying now, the shadows long, the sea red, and a kind wind blowing.

Blackthorne was coming up the path from the village toward the house that Mariko had earlier pointed out and told him was to be his. She had expected to escort him there but he had thanked her and refused and had walked past the kneeling villagers toward the promontory to be alone and to think.

He had found the effort of thinking too great. Nothing seemed to fit. He had doused salt water over his head to try to clear it but that had not helped. At length he had given up and had walked back aimlessly along the shore, past the jetty, across the square and through the village, up to this house where he was to live now and where, he remembered, there had not been a dwelling before. High up, dominating the opposite hillside, was another sprawling dwelling, part thatch, part tile, within a tall stockade, many guards at the fortified gateway.

Samurai were strutting through the village or standing talking in groups. Most had already marched off behind their officers in disciplined groups up the paths and over the hill to their bivouac encampment. Those samurai that Blackthorne met, he absently greeted and they greeted him in return. He saw no villagers.

Blackthorne stopped outside the gate that was set into the fence. There were more of the peculiar characters painted over the lintel and the door itself was cut out in ingenious patterns designed to hide and at the same time to reveal the garden behind.

Before he could open the door it swung inward and a frightened old man bowed him through.

"*Konbanwa,* Anjin-san." His voice quavered piteously—Good evening.

"*Konbanwa,*" he replied. "Listen, old man, er—*o namae ka?*"

"*Namae watashi wa,* Anjin-sama? *Ah, watashi* Ueki-ya . . . Ueki-ya." The old man was almost slavering with relief.

Blackthorne said the name several times to help remember it and added "san" and the old man shook his head violently. "*Iyé, gomen nasai! Iyé* 'san,' Anjin-sama. Ueki-ya! Ueki-ya!"

"All right, Ueki-ya." But Blackthorne thought, why not "san" like everyone else?

Blackthorne waved his hand in dismissal. The old man hobbled away quickly. "I'll have to be more careful. I have to help them," he said aloud.

A maid came apprehensively onto the veranda through an opened shoji and bowed low.

"*Konbanwa,* Anjin-san."

"*Konbanwa,*" he replied, vaguely recognizing her from the ship. He waved her away too.

A rustle of silk. Fujiko came from within the house. Mariko was with her.

"Was your walk pleasant, Anjin-san?"

"Yes, pleasant, Mariko-san." He hardly noticed her or Fujiko or the house or garden.

"Would you like cha? Or perhaps saké? Or a bath perhaps? The water is hot." Mariko laughed nervously, perturbed by the look in his eyes. "The bath house

326

is not completely finished, but we hope it will prove adequate."

"Saké, please. Yes, some saké first, Mariko-san."

Mariko spoke to Fujiko, who disappeared inside the house once more. A maid silently brought three cushions and went away. Mariko gracefully sat on one.

"Sit down, Anjin-san, you must be tired."

"Thank you."

He sat on the steps of the veranda and did not take off his thongs. Fujiko brought two flasks of saké and a teacup, as Mariko had told her, not the tiny porcelain cup that should have been used.

"Better to give him a lot of saké quickly," Mariko had said. "It would be better to make him quite drunk but Lord Yabu needs him tonight. A bath and saké will perhaps ease him."

Blackthorne drank the proffered cup of warmed wine without tasting it. And then a second. And a third.

They had watched him coming up the hill through the slit of barely opened shojis.

"What's the matter with him?" Fujiko had asked, alarmed.

"He's distressed by what Lord Yabu said—the promise to the village."

"Why should that bother him? He's not threatened. It's not his life that was threatened."

"Barbarians are very different from us, Fujiko-san. For instance, the Anjin-san believes villagers are people, like any other people, like samurai, some perhaps even better than samurai."

Fujiko had laughed nervously. "That's nonsense, *neh?* How can peasants equal samurai?"

Mariko had not answered. She had just continued watching the Anjin-san. "Poor man," she said.

"Poor village!" Fujiko's short upper lip curled disdainfully. "A stupid waste of peasants and fishermen! Kasigi Yabu-san's a fool! How can a barbarian learn our tongue in half a year? How long did the barbarian Tsukku-san take? More than twenty years, *neh?* And isn't he the only barbarian who's ever been able to talk even passable Japanese?"

"No, not the only one, though he's the best I've ever heard. Yes, it's difficult for them. But the Anjin-san's an intelligent man and Lord Toranaga said that in half a year, isolated from barbarians, eating our food, living as we do, drinking cha, bathing every day, the Anjin-san will soon be like one of us."

Fujiko's face had been set. "Look at him, Mariko-san . . . so ugly. So monstrous and alien. Curious to think that as much as I detest barbarians, once he steps through the gate I'm committed and he becomes my lord and master."

"He's brave, very brave, Fujiko. And he saved Lord Toranaga's life and is very valuable to him."

"Yes, I know, and that should make me dislike him less but, so sorry, it doesn't. Even so, I'll try with all my strength to change him into one of us. I pray Lord Buddha will help me."

Mariko had wanted to ask her niece, why the sudden change? Why are you now prepared to serve the Anjin-san and obey Lord Toranaga so absolutely, when only this morning you refused to obey, you swore to kill yourself without permission or to kill the barbarian the moment he slept? What did Lord Toranaga say to change you, Fujiko?

But Mariko had known better than to ask. Toranaga had not taken her into this confidence. Fujiko would not tell her. The girl had been too well trained by her mother, Buntaro's sister, who had been trained by her father, Hiro-matsu.

I wonder if Lord Hiro-matsu will escape from Osaka Castle, she asked herself, very fond of the old general, her father-in-law. And what about Kiri-san and the Lady Sazuko? Where is Buntaro, my husband? Where was he captured? Or did he have time to die?

Mariko watched Fujiko pour the last of the saké. This cup too was consumed like the others, without expression.

"*Dozo*. Saké," Blackthorne said.

More saké was brought. And finished. "*Dozo, saké.*"

"Mariko-san," Fujiko said, "the Master shouldn't have any more, *neh?* He'll get drunk. Please ask him if he'd like his bath now. I will send for Suwo."

Mariko asked him. "Sorry, he says he'll bathe later."

Patiently Fujiko ordered more saké and Mariko added quietly to the maid, "Bring some charcoaled fish."

The new flask was emptied with the same silent determination. The food did not tempt him but he took a piece at Mariko's gracious persuasion. He did not eat it.

More wine was brought, and two more flasks were consumed.

"Please give the Anjin-san my apologies," Fujiko said. "So sorry, but there isn't any more saké in his house. Tell him I apologize for this lack. I've sent the maid to fetch some more from the village."

"Good. He's had more than enough, though it doesn't seem to have touched him at all. Why not leave us now, Fujiko? Now would be a good time to make the formal offer on your behalf."

Fujiko bowed to Blackthorne and went away, glad that custom decreed that important matters were always to be handled by a third party in private. Thus dignity could always be maintained on both sides.

Mariko explained to Blackthorne about the wine.

"How long will it take to get more?"

"Not long. Perhaps you'd like to bathe now. I'll see that saké's sent the instant it arrives."

"Did Toranaga say anything about my plan before he left? About the navy?"

"No. I'm sorry, he said nothing about that." Mariko had been watching for the telltale signs of drunkenness. But to her surprise none had appeared, not even a slight flush, or a slurring of words. With this amount of wine consumed so fast, any Japanese would be drunk. "The wine is not to your taste, Anjin-san?"

"Not really. It's too weak. It gives me nothing."

"You seek oblivion?"

"No—a solution."

"Anything that can be done to help, will be done."

"I must have books and paper and pens."

"Tomorrow I will begin to collect them for you."

"No, tonight, Mariko-san. I must start now."

"Lord Toranaga said he will send you a book—what did you call it?—the grammar books and word books of the Holy Fathers."

"How long will that take?"

"I don't know. But I'm here for three days. Perhaps this may be a help to you. And Fujiko-san is here to help also." She smiled, happy for him. "I'm honored to tell you she is given to you as consort and she—"

"*What?*"

"Lord Toranaga asked her if she would be your consort and she said she would be honored and agreed. She will—"

"But I haven't agreed."

"Please? I'm sorry, I don't understand."

"I don't want her. Either as consort or around me. I find her ugly."

Mariko gaped at him. "But what's that got to do with consort?"

"Tell her to leave."

"But Anjin-san, you can't refuse! That would be a terrible insult to Lord Toranaga, to her, to everyone! What harm has she done you? None at all! Usagi Fujiko's consen—"

"You listen to me!" Blackthorne's words ricocheted around the veranda and the house. "Tell her to leave!"

Mariko said at once, "So sorry, Anjin-san, yes you're right to be angry. But—"

"I'm not angry," Blackthorne said icily. "Can't you . . . *can't* you people get it through your heads I'm tired of being a puppet? I don't want that woman around, I want my ship back and my crew back and that's the end of it! I'm not staying here six months and I detest your customs. It's God-cursed terrible that one man can threaten to bury a whole village just to teach me Japanese, and as to consorts—that's worse than slavery—and it's a goddamned insult to arrange that without asking me in advance!"

What's the matter now? Mariko was asking herself helplessly. What has ugliness to do with consort? And anyway Fujiko's not ugly. How can he be so incomprehensible? Then she remembered Toranaga's admonition: 'Mariko-san, you're personally responsible, firstly that Yabu-san doesn't interfere with my departure after I've given him my sword, and secondly, you're totally responsible for settling the Anjin-san docilely in Anjiro.'

'I'll do my best, Sire. But I'm afraid the Anjin-san baffles me.'

'Treat him like a hawk. That's the key to him. I tame a hawk in two days. You've three.'

She looked away from Blackthorne and put her wits to work. He does seem like a hawk when he's in a rage, she thought. He has the same screeching, senseless ferocity, and when not in rage the same haughty, unblinking stare, the same total selfcenteredness, with exploding viciousness never far away.

"I agree. You're completely right. You've been imposed upon terribly, and you're quite right to be angry," she said soothingly. "Yes, and certainly Lord Toranaga should have asked even though he doesn't understand your customs. But it never occurred to him that you would object. He only tried to honor you as he would a most favored samurai. He made you a hatamoto, that's almost like a kinsman, Anjin-san. There are only about a thousand hatamoto in all the Kwanto. And as to the Lady Fujiko, he was only trying to help you. The Lady Usagi Fujiko would be considered . . . among us, Anjin-san, this would be considered a great honor."

"Why?"

"Because her lineage is ancient and she's very accomplished. Her father and grandfather are *daimyos*. Of course she's samurai, and of course," Mariko added delicately, "you would honor her by accepting her. And she does need a home and a new life."

"Why?"

"She is recently widowed. She's only nineteen, Anjin-san, poor girl, but she lost a husband and a son and is filled with remorse. To be formal consort to you would give her a new life."

"What happened to her husband and son?"

Mariko hesitated, distressed at Blackthorne's impolite directness. But she knew enough about him by now to understand that this was *his* custom and not meant as lack of manners. "They were put to death, Anjin-san. While you're here you will need someone to look after your house. The Lady Fujiko will be—"

"Why were they put to death?"

"Her husband almost caused the death of Lord Toranaga. Please con—"

"Toranaga ordered their deaths?"

"Yes. But he was correct. Ask her—she will agree, Anjin-san."

"How old was the child?"

"A few months, Anjin-san."

"Toranaga had an infant put to death for something the father did?"

"Yes. It's our custom. Please be patient with us. In some things we are not free. Our customs are different from yours. You see, by law, we belong to our liege lord. By law a father possesses the lives of his children and wife and consorts and servants. By law his life is possessed by his liege lord. This is our custom."

"So a father can kill anyone in his house?"

"Yes."

"Then you're a nation of murderers."

"No."

"But your custom condones murder. I thought you were Christian."

"I am, Anjin-san."

"What about the Commandments?"

"I cannot explain, truly. But I am Christian and samurai and Japanese, and these are not hostile to one another. To me, they're not. Please be patient with me and with us. Please."

"You'd put your own children to death if Toranaga ordered it?"

"Yes. I only have one son but yes, I believe I would. Certainly it would be my duty to do so. That's the law—if my husband agreed."

"I hope God can forgive you. All of you."

"God understands, Anjin-san. Oh, He will understand. Perhaps He will open your mind so you can understand. I'm sorry, I cannot explain very well, *neh?* I apologize for my lack." She watched him in the silence, unsettled by him. "I don't understand you either, Anjin-san. You baffle me. Your customs baffle me. Perhaps if we're both patient we can both learn. The Lady Fujiko, for instance. As consort she will look after your house and your servants. And your needs —any of your needs. You must have someone to do that. She will see to the running of your house, everything. You do not need to pillow her, if that concerns you—if you do not find her pleasing. You do not even need to be polite to her, though she merits politeness. She will serve you, as you wish, in any way you wish."

"I can treat her any way I want?"

"Yes."

"I can pillow her or not pillow her?"

"Of course. She will find someone that pleases you, to satisfy your body needs, if you wish, or she will not interfere."

"I can treat her like a servant? A slave?"

"Yes. But she merits better."

"Can I throw her out? Order her out?"

"If she offends you, yes."

"What would happen to her?"

"Normally she would go back to her parents' house in disgrace, who may or may not accept her back. Someone like Lady Fujiko would prefer to kill herself before enduring that shame. But she . . . you should know true samurai are not permitted to kill themselves without their lord's permission. Some do, of course, but they've failed in their duty and aren't worthy to be considered samurai. I would not kill myself, whatever the shame, not without Lord Toranaga's permission or my husband's permission. Lord Toranaga has forbidden her to end her life. If you send her away, she'll become an outcast."

"Why? Why won't her family accept her back?"

Mariko sighed. "So sorry, Anjin-san, but if you send her away, her disgrace will be such that no one will accept her."

"Because she's contaminated? From being near a barbarian?"

"Oh no, Anjin-san, only because she had failed in her duty to you," Mariko said at once. "She is your consort now—Lord Toranaga ordered it and she agreed. You're master of a house now."

"Am I?"

"Oh, yes, believe me, Anjin-san, you have privileges. And as a hatamoto you're blessed. And well off. Lord Toranaga's given you a salary of twenty koku a month. For that amount of money a samurai would normally have to provide his lord with himself and two other samurai, armed, fed, and mounted for the whole year, and of course pay for their families as well. But you don't have to do that. I beg you, consider Fujiko as a person, Anjin-san. I beg you to be filled with Christian charity. She's a good woman. Forgive her her ugliness. She'll be a worthy consort."

"She hasn't a home?"

"Yes. This is her home." Mariko took hold of herself. "I beg you to accept her formally. She can help you greatly, teach you if you wish to learn. If you prefer, think of her as nothing—as this wooden post or the shoji screen, or as a rock in your garden—anything you wish, but allow her to stay. If you won't have her as consort, be merciful. Accept her and then, as head of the house, according to our law, kill her."

"That's the only answer you have, isn't it? Kill!"

"No, Anjin-san. But life and death are the same thing. Who knows, perhaps you'll do Fujiko a greater service by taking her life. It's your right now before all the law. *Your* right. If your prefer to make her outcast, that too is your right."

"So I'm trapped again," Blackthorne said. "Either way she's killed. If I don't learn your language then a whole village is butchered. If I don't do whatever you want, some innocent is always killed. There's no way out."

"There's a very easy solution, Anjin-san. Die. You do not have to endure the unendurable."

"Suicide's crazy—and a mortal sin. I thought you were Christian."

"I've said I am. But for you, Anjin-san, for you there are many ways of dying honorably without suicide. You sneered at my husband for not wanting to die fighting, *neh?* That's not our custom, but apparently it's yours. So why don't you do that? You have a pistol. Kill Lord Yabu. You believe he's a monster, *neh?* Even attempt to kill him and today you'll be in heaven or hell."

He looked at her, hating her serene features, seeing her loveliness through his hate. "It's weak to die like that for no reason. Stupid's a better word."

"You say you're Christian. So you believe in the Jesus child—in God—and in heaven. Death shouldn't frighten you. As to 'no reason,' it is up to you to judge the value or nonvalue. You may have reason enough to die."

"I'm in your power. You know it. So do I."

Mariko leaned over and touched him compassionately. "Anjin-san, forget the village. A thousand million things can happen before those six months occur. A tidal wave or earthquake, or you get your ship and sail away, or Yabu dies, or we all die, or who knows? Leave the problems of God to God and *karma* to *karma*. Today you're here and nothing you can do will change that. Today you're alive and here and honored, and blessed with good fortune. Look at this sunset, it's beautiful, *neh?* This sunset exists. Tomorrow does not exist. There is only *now*. Please look. It is so beautiful and it will never happen ever again, never, not *this* sunset, never in all infinity. Lose yourself in it, make yourself one with nature and do not worry about *karma,* yours, mine, or that of the village."

He found himself beguiled by her serenity, and by her words. He looked westward. Great splashes of purple-red and black were spreading across the sky. He watched the sun until it vanished.

"I wish you were to be consort," he said.

"I belong to Lord Buntaro and until he is dead I cannot think or say what might be thought or said."

Karma, thought Blackthorne.

Do I accept *karma?* Mine? Hers? Theirs?

The night's beautiful.

And so is she and she belongs to another.

Yes, she's beautiful. And very wise: Leave the problems of God to God and *karma* to *karma.* You did come here uninvited. You are here. You are in their power.

But what's the answer?

The answer will come, he told himself. Because there's a God in heaven, a God somewhere.

He heard the tread of feet. Some flares were approaching up the hill. Twenty samurai, Omi at their head.

"I'm sorry, Anjin-san, but Omi-san orders you to give him your pistols."

"Tell him to go to hell!"

"I can't, Anjin-san. I dare not."

Blackthorne kept one hand loosely on the pistol hilt, his eyes on Omi. He had deliberately remained seated on the veranda steps. Ten samurai were within the garden behind Omi, the rest near the waiting palanquin. As soon as Omi had entered uninvited, Fujiko had come from the interior of the house and now stood on the veranda, white-faced, behind Blackthorne. "Lord Toranaga never objected and for days I've been armed around him and Yabu-san."

Mariko said nervously, "Yes, Anjin-san, but please understand, what Omi-san says is true. It's our custom that you cannot go into a *daimyo*'s presence with arms. There's nothing to be af—nothing to concern you. Yabu-san's your friend. You're his guest here."

"Tell Omi-san I won't give him my guns." Then, when she remained silent, Blackthorne's temper snapped and he shook his head. "*Iyé,* Omi-san! *Wakarimasu ka? Iyé!*"

Omi's face tightened. He snarled an order. Two samurai moved forward. Blackthorne whipped out the guns. The samurai stopped. Both guns were pointed directly into Omi's face.

"*Iyé!*" Blackthorne said. And then, to Mariko, "Tell him to call them off or I'll pull the triggers."

She did so. No one moved. Blackthorne got slowly to his feet, the pistols never wavering from their target. Omi was absolutely still, fearless, his eyes following Blackthorne's catlike movements.

"Please, Anjin-san. This is very dangerous. You must see Lord Yabu. You may not go with pistols. You're hatamoto, you're protected and you're also Lord Yabu's guest."

"Tell Omi-san if he or any of his men come within ten feet of me I'll blow his head off."

"Omi-san says politely, 'For the last time you are ordered to give me the guns. Now.' "

"*Iyé.*"

"Why not leave them here, Anjin-san? There's nothing to fear. No one will touch—"

"You think I'm a fool?"

"Then give them to Fujiko-san!"

"What can she do? He'll take them from her—anyone'll take them—then I'm defenseless."

Mariko's voice sharpened. "Why don't you listen, Anjin-san? Fujiko-san is your consort. If you order it she'll protect the guns with her life. That's her duty. I'll never tell you again, but Toda-noh-Usagi Fujiko is samurai."

Blackthorne was concentrating on Omi, hardly listening to her. "Tell Omi-san I don't like orders. I'm Lord Toranaga's guest. I'm Lord Yabu's guest. You 'ask' guests to do things. You don't order them, and you don't march into a man's house uninvited."

Mariko translated this. Omi listened expressionlessly, then replied shortly, watching the unwavering barrels.

"He says, 'I, Kasigi Omi, I would ask for your pistols, and ask you to come with me because Kasigi Yabu-sama orders you into his presence. But Kasigi Yabu-sama orders me to order you to give me your weapons. So sorry, Anjin-san, for the last time I order you to give them to me.'"

Blackthorne's chest was constricted. He knew he was going to be attacked and he was furious at his own stupidity. But there comes a time when you can't take any more and you pull a gun or a knife and then blood is spilled through stupid pride. Most times stupid. If I'm to die Omi will die first, by God!

He felt very strong though somewhat light-headed. Then what Mariko said began to ring in his ears: 'Fujiko's samurai, she is your consort!' And his brain began to function. "Just a moment! Mariko-san, please say this to Fujiko-san. Exactly: 'I'm going to give you my pistols. You are to guard them. No one except me is to touch them.'"

Mariko did as he asked, and behind him, he heard Fujiko say, *"Hai."*

"Wakarimasu ka, Fujiko-san?" he asked her.

"Wakarimasu, Anjin-san," she replied in a thin, nervous voice.

"Mariko-san, please tell Omi-san I'll go with him now. I'm sorry there's been a misunderstanding. Yes, I'm sorry there was a misunderstanding."

Blackthorne backed away, then turned. Fujiko accepted the guns, perspiration beading her forehead. He faced Omi and prayed he was right. "Shall we go now?"

Omi spoke to Fujiko and held out his hand. She shook her head. He gave a short order. The two samurai started toward her. Immediately she shoved one pistol into the sash of her obi, held the other with both hands at arm's length and leveled it at Omi. The trigger came back slightly and the striking lever moved. *"Ugoku na!"* she said. *"Dozo!"*

The samurai obeyed. They stopped.

Omi spoke rapidly and angrily and she listened and when she replied her voice was soft and polite but the pistol never moved from his face, the lever half-cocked now, and she ended, *"Iyé, gomen nasai,* Omi-san!" No, I'm sorry, Omi-san.

Blackthorne waited.

A samurai moved a fraction. The lever came back dangerously, almost to the top of its arc. But her arm remained steady.

"Ugoku na!" she ordered.

No one doubted that she would pull the trigger. Not even Blackthorne. Omi said something curtly to her and to his men. They came back. She lowered the pistol but it was still ready.

"What did he say?" Blackthorne asked.

"Only that he would report this incident to Yabu-san."

"Good. Tell him I will do the same." Blackthorne turned to her. *"Domo,* Fujiko-san." Then, remembering the way Toranaga and Yabu talked to women, he grunted imperiously at Mariko. "Come on, Mariko-san . . . *ikamasho!"* He started for the gate.

"Anjin-san!" Fujiko called out.

"Hai?" Blackthorne stopped. Fujiko was bowing to him and spoke quickly to Mariko.

Mariko's eyes widened, then she nodded and replied, and spoke to Omi, who also nodded, clearly enraged but restraining himself.

"What's going on?"

"Please be patient, Anjin-san."

Fujiko called out, and there was an answer from within the house. A maid came onto the veranda. In her hands were two swords. Samurai swords.

Fujiko took them reverently, offered them to Blackthorne with a bow, speaking softly.

Mariko said, "Your consort rightly points out that a hatamoto is, of course, obliged to wear the two swords of the samurai. More than that, it's his duty to do so. She believes it would not be correct for you to go to Lord Yabu without swords—that it would be impolite. By our law it's *duty* to carry swords. She asks if you would consider using these, unworthy though they are, until you buy your own."

Blackthorne stared at her, then at Fujiko and back to her again. "Does that mean I'm samurai? That Lord Toranaga made me samurai?"

"I don't know, Anjin-san. But there's never been a hatamoto who wasn't samurai. Never." Mariko turned and questioned Omi. Impatiently he shook his head and answered. "Omi-san doesn't know either. Certainly it's the special privilege of a hatamoto to wear swords at all times, even in the presence of Lord Toranaga. It is his duty because he's a completely trustworthy bodyguard. Also only a hatamoto has the right of immediate audience with a lord."

Blackthorne took the short sword and stuck it in his belt, then the other, the long one, the killing one, exactly as Omi was wearing his. Armed, he did feel better. *"Arigato goziemashita,* Fujiko-san," he said quietly.

She lowered her eyes and replied softly. Mariko translated.

"Fujiko-san says, with permission, Lord, because you must learn our language correctly and quickly, she humbly wishes to point out that *'domo'* is more than sufficient for a man to say. *'Arigato,'* with or without *'goziemashita,'* is an unnecessary politeness, an expression that only women use."

"Hai. Domo. Wakarimasu, Fujiko-san." Blackthorne looked at her clearly for the first time with his newfound knowledge. He saw the sweat on her forehead and the sheen on her hands. The narrow eyes and square face and ferret teeth. "Please tell my consort, in this one case I do not consider *'arigato goziemashita'* an unnecessary politeness to her."

Yabu glanced at the swords again. Blackthorne was sitting cross-legged on a cushion in front of him in the place of honor, Mariko to one side, Igurashi beside him. They were in the main room of the fortress.

Omi finished talking.

Yabu shrugged. "You handled it badly, nephew. Of course it's the consort's duty to protect the Anjin-san and his property. Of course he has the right to wear swords now. Yes, you handled it badly. I made it clear the Anjin-san's my honored guest here. Apologize to him."

Immediately Omi got up and knelt in front of Blackthorne and bowed. "I apologize for my error, Anjin-san." He heard Mariko say that the barbarian accepted the apology. He bowed again and calmly went back to his place and sat down again. But he was not calm inside. He was now totally consumed by one idea: the killing of Yabu.

He had decided to do the unthinkable: kill his liege Lord and the head of his clan.

But not because he had been made to apologize publicly to the barbarian. In this Yabu had been right. Omi knew he had been unnecessarily inept, for although Yabu had stupidly ordered him to take the pistols away at once tonight, he knew they should have been manipulated away and left in the house, to be stolen later or broken later.

And the Anjin-san had been perfectly correct to give the pistols to his consort, he told himself, just as she was equally correct to do what she did. And she would certainly have pulled the trigger, her aim true. It was no secret that Usagi Fujiko sought death, or why. Omi knew, too, that if it hadn't been for his earlier decision this morning to kill Yabu, he would have stepped forward into death and then his men would have taken the pistols away from her. He would have died nobly as she would be ordered into death nobly and men and women would have told the tragic tale for generations. Songs and poems and even a Nōh play, all so inspiring and tragic and brave, about the three of them: the faithful consort and faithful samurai who both died dutifully because of the incredible barbarian who came from the eastern sea.

No, Omi's decision had nothing to do with this public apology, although the unfairness added to the hatred that now obsessed him. The main reason was that today Yabu had publicly insulted Omi's mother and wife in front of peasants by keeping them waiting for hours in the sun like peasants, and had then dismissed them without acknowledgment like peasants.

"It doesn't matter, my son," his mother had said. "It's his privilege."

"He's our liege Lord," Midori, his wife, had said, the tears of shame running down her cheeks. "Please excuse him."

"And he didn't invite either of you to greet him and his officers at the fortress," Omi had continued. "At the meal you arranged! The food and saké alone cost one koku!"

"It's our duty, my son. It's our duty to do whatever Lord Yabu wants."

"And the order about Father?"

"It's not an order yet. It's a rumor."

"The message from Father said he'd heard that Yabu's going to order him to shave his head and become a priest, or slit his belly open. Yabu's wife privately boasts it!"

"That was whispered to your father by a spy. You cannot always trust spies. So sorry, but your father, my son, isn't always wise."

"What happens to you, Mother, if it isn't a rumor?"

"Whatever happens is *karma*. You must accept *karma.*"

"No, these insults are unendurable."

"Please, my son, accept them."

"I gave Yabu the key to the ship, the key to the Anjin-san and the new barbarians, and the way out of Toranaga's trap. My help has brought him immense prestige. With the symbolic gift of the sword he's now second to Toranaga in the armies of the East. And what have we got in return? Filthy insults."

"Accept your *karma.*"

"You must, husband, I beg you, listen to the Lady, your mother."

"I can't live with this shame. I will have vengeance and then I will kill myself and these shames will pass from me."

"For the last time, my son, accept your *karma,* I beg you."

"My *karma* is to destroy Yabu."

The old lady had sighed. "Very well. You're a man. You have the right to decide. What is to be is to be. But the killing of Yabu by itself is nothing. We must plan. His son must also be removed, and also Igurashi. Particularly Igurashi. Then your father will lead the clan as is his right."

"How do we do that, Mother?"

"We will plan, you and I. And be patient, *neh?* Then we must consult with your father. Midori, even you may give counsel, but try not to make it valueless, *neh?*"

"What about Lord Toranaga? He gave Yabu his sword."

"I think Lord Toranaga only wants Izu strong and a *vassal* state. Not as an ally. He doesn't want allies any more than the Taikō did. Yabu thinks he's an ally. I think Toranaga detests allies. Our clan will prosper as Toranaga vassals. *Or as Ishido vassals!* Who to choose, eh? And how to do the killing?"

Omi remembered the surge of joy that had possessed him once the decision had been made final.

He felt it now. But none of it showed on his face as cha and wine were offered by carefully selected maids imported from Mishima for Yabu. He watched Yabu and the Anjin-san and Mariko and Igurashi. They were all waiting for Yabu to begin.

The room was large and airy, big enough for thirty officers to dine and wine and talk. There were many other rooms and kitchens for bodyguards and servants, and a skirting garden, and though all were makeshift and temporary, they had been excellently constructed in the time at his disposal and easily defendable. That the cost had come out of Omi's increased fief bothered him not at all. This had been his duty.

He looked through the open shoji. Many sentries in the forecourt. A stable. The fortress was guarded by a ditch. The stockade was constructed of giant bamboos lashed tightly. Big central pillars supported the tiled roof. Walls were light sliding shoji screens, some shuttered, most of them covered with oiled paper as was usual. Good planks for the flooring were set on pilings raised off beaten earth below and these were covered with tatamis.

At Yabu's command, Omi had ransacked four villages for materials to construct this and the other house and Igurashi had brought quality tatamis and futons and things unobtainable in the village.

Omi was proud of his work, and the bivouac camp for three thousand samurai had been made ready on the plateau over the hill that guarded the roads that led to the village and to the shore. Now the village was locked tight and safe by land. From the sea there would always be plenty of warning for a liege lord to escape.

But I have no liege lord. Whom shall I serve now, Omi was asking himself. Ikawa Jukkyu? Or Toranaga directly? Would Toranaga give me what I want in return? Or Ishido? Ishido's so difficult to get to, *neh?* But much to tell him now. . . .

This afternoon Yabu had summoned Igurashi, Omi, and the four chief captains and had set into motion his clandestine training plan for the five hundred gun-samurai. Igurashi was to be commander, Omi was to lead one of the hundreds. They had arranged how to induct Toranaga's men into the units when they arrived, and how these outlanders were to be neutralized if they proved treacherous.

Omi had suggested that another highly secret cadre of three more units of one hundred samurai each should be trained surreptitiously on the other side of the peninsula as replacements, as a reserve, and as a precaution against a treacherous move by Toranaga.

"Who'll command Toranaga's men? Who'll he send as second in command?" Igurashi had asked.

"It makes no difference," Yabu had said. "I'll appoint his five assistant officers, who'll be given the responsibility of slitting his throat, should it be necessary. The code for killing him and all the outlanders will be 'Plum Tree.' Tomorrow, Igurashi-san, you will choose the men. I will approve each personally and none of them is to know, yet, my overall strategy of the musket regiment."

Now as Omi was watching Yabu, he savored the newfound ecstasy of vengeance. To kill Yabu would be easy, but the killing must be coordinated. Only then would his father or his elder brother be able to assume control of the clan, and Izu.

Yabu came to the point. "Mariko-san, please tell the Anjin-san, tomorrow I want him to start training my men to shoot like barbarians and I want to learn everything there is to know about the way that barbarians war."

"But, so sorry, the guns won't arrive for six days, Yabu-san," Mariko reminded him.

"I've enough among my men to begin with," Yabu replied. "I want him to start tomorrow."

Mariko spoke to Blackthorne.

"What does he want to know about war?" he asked.

"He said everything."

"What particularly?"

Mariko asked Yabu.

"Yabu-san says, have you been part of any battles on land?"

"Yes. In the Netherlands. One in France."

"Yabu-san says, excellent. He wants to know European strategy. He wants to know how battles are fought in your lands. In detail."

Blackthorne thought a moment. Then he said, "Tell Yabu-san I can train any number of men for him and I know exactly what he wants to know." He had learned a great deal about the way the Japanese warred from Friar Domingo. The friar had been an expert and vitally concerned. 'After all, señor,' the old man had said, 'that knowledge is essential, isn't it—to know how the heathen war? Every Father must protect his flock. And are not our glorious conquistadores the blessed spearhead of Mother Church? And haven't I been with them in the front of the fighting in the New World and the Philippines and studied them for more than twenty years? I know war, señor, I *know* war. It has been my duty— God's will to know war. Perhaps God has sent you to me to teach you, in case I die. Listen, my flock here in this jail have been my teachers about Japan warfare, señor. So now I know how their armies fight and how to beat them. How they could beat us. Remember, señor, I tell thee a secret on thy soul: Never join Japanese ferocity with modern weapons and modern methods. Or on land they will destroy us.'

Blackthorne committed himself to God. And began. "Tell Lord Yabu I can help him very much. And Lord Toranaga. I can make their armies unbeatable."

"Lord Yabu says, if your information proves useful, Anjin-san, he will increase your salary from Lord Toranaga's two hundred and forty koku to five hundred koku after one month."

"Thank him. But say, if I do all that for him, I request a favor in return: I want him to rescind his decree about the village and I want my ship and crew back in five months."

Mariko said, "Anjin-san, you cannot bargain with him, like a trader."

"Please ask him. As a humble favor. From an honored guest and grateful vassal-to-be."

Yabu frowned and replied at length.

"Yabu-san says that the village is unimportant. The villagers need a fire under their rumps to make them do anything. You are not to concern yourself with them. As to the ship, it's in Lord Toranaga's care. He's sure you'll get it back soon. He asked me to put your request to Lord Toranaga the moment I arrive in Yedo. I'll do this, Anjin-san."

"Please apologize to Lord Yabu, but I must ask him to rescind the decree. Tonight."

"He's just said no, Anjin-san. It would not be good manners."

"Yes, I understand. But please ask him again. It's very important to me . . . a petition."

"He says you must be patient. Don't concern yourself with villagers."

Blackthorne nodded. Then he decided. "Thank you. I understand. Yes. Please thank Yabu-san but tell him I cannot live with this shame."

Mariko blanched. "What?"

"I cannot live with the shame of having the village on my conscience. I'm dishonored. I cannot endure this. It's against my Christian belief. I will have to commit suicide at once."

"Suicide?"

"Yes. That's what I've decided to do."

Yabu interrupted. *Nan ja,* Mariko-san?"

Haltingly she translated what Blackthorne had said. Yabu questioned her and she answered. Then Yabu said, "If it wasn't for your reaction this would be a joke, Mariko-san. Why are you so concerned? Why do you think he means it?"

"I don't know, Sire. He seems . . . I don't know. . . ." Her voice trailed off. "Omi-san?"

"Suicide's against all Christian beliefs, Sire. They never suicide as we do. As a samurai would."

"Mariko-san, you're Christian. Is that true?"

"Yes, Sire. Suicide's a mortal sin, against the word of God."

"Igurashi-san? What do you think?"

"It's a bluff. He's no Christian. Remember the first day, Sire? Remember what he did to the priest? And what he allowed Omi-san to do to him to save the boy?"

Yabu smiled, recollecting that day and the night that had followed. "Yes. I agree. He's no Christian, Mariko-san."

"So sorry, but I don't understand, Sire. What about the priest?"

Yabu told her what had happened the first day between Blackthorne and the priest.

"He desecrated a cross?" she said, openly shocked.

"And threw the pieces into the dust," Igurashi added. "It's all a bluff, Sire. If this thing with the village dishonors him, how can he stay here when Omi-san so dishonored him by pissing on him?"

"What? I'm sorry, Sire," Mariko said, "but again I don't understand."

Yabu said to Omi, "Explain that to her."

Omi obeyed. She was disgusted by what he told her but kept it off her face.

"Afterwards the Anjin-san was completely cowed, Mariko-san." Omi finished, "Without weapons he'll always be cowed."

Yabu sipped some saké. "Say this to him, Mariko-san: suicide's not a barbarian custom. It's against his Christian God. So how can he suicide?"

Mariko translated. Yabu was watching carefully as Blackthorne replied.

"The Anjin-san apologizes with great humility, but he says, custom or not, God or not, this shame of the village is too great to bear. He says that . . . that he's in Japan, he's hatamoto and has the right to live according to our laws." Her hands were trembling. "That's what he said, Yabu-san. The right to live according to our customs—our law."

"Barbarians have no rights."

She said, "Lord Toranaga made him hatamoto. That gives him the right, *neh?*"

A breeze touched the shojis, rattling them.

"How could he commit suicide? Eh? Ask him."

Blackthorne took out the short, needle-sharp sword and placed it gently on the tatami, point facing him.

Igurashi said simply, "It's a bluff! Who ever heard of a barbarian acting like a civilized person?"

Yabu frowned, his heartbeat slowed by the excitement. "He's a brave man, Igurashi-san. No doubt about that. And strange. But this?" Yabu wanted to see the act, to witness the barbarian's measure, to see how he went into death, to experience with him the ecstasy of the going. With an effort he stopped the rising tide of his own pleasure. "What's your counsel, Omi-san?" he asked throatily.

"You said to the village, Sire, 'If the Anjin-san did not learn *satisfactorily.*' I counsel you to make a slight concession. Say to him that whatever he learns within the five months will be 'satisfactory,' but he must, in return, swear by his God never to reveal this to the village."

"But he's not Christian. How will that oath bind him?"

"I believe he's a type of Christian, Sire. He's against the Black Robes and that's what is important. I believe swearing by his own God will be binding. And he should also swear, in this God's name, that he'll apply his mind totally to learning and totally to your service. Because he's clever he will have learned very much in five months. Thus, your honor is saved, his—if it exists or not—is also saved. You lose nothing, gain everything. Very important, you gain his allegiance of his own free will."

"You believe he'll kill himself?"

"Yes."

"Mariko-san?"

"I don't know, Yabu-san. I'm sorry, I cannot advise you. A few hours ago I would have said, no, he will not commit suicide. Now I don't know. He's . . . since Omi-san came for him tonight, he's been . . . different."

"Igurashi-san?"

"If you give in to him now and it's bluff he'll use the same trick all the time. He's cunning as a fox-*kami*—we've all seen how cunning, *neh?* You'll have to say 'no' one day, Sire. I counsel you to say it now—it's a bluff."

Omi leaned forward and shook his head. "Sire, please excuse me, but I must repeat, if you say no you risk a great loss. If it is a bluff—and it may well be—then as a proud man he will become hate-filled at his further humiliation and he won't help you to the limit of his being, which you need. He's asked for something as a hatamoto which he's entitled to, he says he wants to live according to our customs of his own free will. Isn't that an enormous step forward, Sire? That's marvelous for you, and for him. I counsel caution. Use him to your advantage."

"I intend to," Yabu said thickly.

Igurashi said, "Yes, he's valuable and yes, I want his knowledge. But he's got to be controlled—you've said that many times, Omi-san. He's barbarian. That's all he is. Oh, I know he's hatamoto today and yes, he can wear the two swords from today. But that doesn't make him samurai. He's not samurai and never will be."

Mariko knew that of all of them she should be able to read the Anjin-san the most clearly. But she could not. One moment she understood him, the next, he was incomprehensible again. One moment she liked him, the next she hated him. Why?

Blackthorne's haunted eyes looked into the distance. But now there were beads of sweat on his forehead. Is that from fear? thought Yabu. Fear that the bluff will be called? Is he bluffing?

"Mariko-san?"

"Yes, Lord?"

"Tell him . . ." Yabu's mouth was suddenly dry, his chest aching. "Tell the Anjin-san the sentence stays."

"Sire, please excuse me, but I urge you to accept Omi-san's advice."

Yabu did not look at her, only at Blackthorne. The vein in his forehead pulsed. "The Anjin-san says he's decided. So be it. Let's see if he's barbarian—or hatamoto."

Mariko's voice was almost imperceptible. "Anjin-san, Yabu-san says the sentence stays. I'm sorry."

Blackthorne heard the words but they did not disturb him. He felt stronger and more at peace than he had ever been, with a greater awareness of life than he had ever had.

While he was waiting he had not been listening to them or watching them. The commitment had been made. The rest he had left to God. He had been locked in his own head, hearing the same words over and over, the same that had given him the clue to life here, the words that surely had been sent from God, through Mariko as medium: 'There is an easy solution—die. To survive here you must live according to our customs. . . .'

". . . the sentence stays."

So now I must die.

I should be afraid. But I'm not.

Why?

I don't know. I know only that once I truly decided that the sole way to live here as a man is to do so according to their customs, to risk death, to die—perhaps to die—that suddenly the fear of death was gone. 'Life and death are the same . . . Leave *karma* to *karma*.'

I am not afraid to die.

Beyond the shoji, a gentle rain had begun to fall. He looked down at the knife. I've had a good life, he thought.

His eyes came back to Yabu. *"Wakarimasu,"* he said clearly and though he knew his lips had formed the word it was as though someone else had spoken.

No one moved.

He watched his right hand pick up the knife. Then his left also grasped the hilt, the blade steady and pointing at his heart. Now there was only the sound of his life, building and building, soaring louder and louder until he could listen no more. His soul cried out for eternal silence.

The cry triggered his reflexes. His hands drove the knife unerringly toward its target.

Omi had been ready to stop him but he was unprepared for the suddenness and ferocity of Blackthorne's thrust, and as Omi's left hand caught the blade and his right the haft, pain bit into him and blood spilled from his left hand. He fought the power of the thrust with all his strength. He was losing. Then Igurashi helped. Together they halted the blow. The knife was taken away. A thin trickle of blood ran from the skin over Blackthorne's heart where the point of the knife had entered.

Mariko and Yabu had not moved.

Yabu said, "Say to him, say to him whatever he learns is enough, Mariko-san. Order him—no, ask him, ask the Anjin-san to swear as Omi-san said. Everything as Omi-san said."

Blackthorne came back from death slowly. He stared at them and the knife from an immense distance, without understanding. Then the torrent of his life rushed back but he could not grasp its significance, believing himself dead and not alive.

"Anjin-san? Anjin-san?"

He saw her lips move and heard her words but all his senses were concentrated on the rain and the breeze.

"Yes?" His own voice was still far off but he smelled the rain and heard the droplets and tasted the sea salt upon the air.

I'm alive, he told himself in wonder. I'm alive and that's real rain outside and the wind's real and from the north. There's a real brazier with real coals and if I pick up the cup it will have real liquid in it and it will have taste. I'm not dead. I'm alive!

The others sat in silence, waiting patiently, gentle with him to honor his bravery. No man in Japan had ever seen what they had seen. Each was asking silently, what's the Anjin-san going to do now? Will he be able to stand by himself and walk away or will his spirit leave him? How would I act if I were he?

Silently a servant brought a bandage and bound Omi's hand where the blade had cut deeply, staunching the flow of blood. Everything was very still. From time to time Mariko would say his name quietly as they sipped cha or saké, but very sparingly, savoring the waiting, the watching, and the remembering.

For Blackthorne this no life seemed to last forever. Then his eyes saw. His ears heard.

"Anjin-san?"

"*Hai?*" he answered through the greatest weariness he had ever known.

Mariko repeated what Omi had said as though it came from Yabu. She had to say it several times before she was sure that he understood clearly.

Blackthorne collected the last of his strength, victory sweet to him. "My word is enough, as his is enough. Even so, I'll swear by God as he wants. Yes. As Yabu-san will swear by his god in equal honor to keep his side of the bargain."

"Lord Yabu says yes, he swears by the Lord Buddha."

So Blackthorne swore as Yabu wished him to swear. He accepted some cha. Never had it tasted so good. The cup seemed very heavy and he could not hold it for long.

"The rain is fine, isn't it?" he said, watching the raindrops breaking and vanishing, astonished by the untoward clarity of his vision.

"Yes," she told him gently, knowing that his senses were on a plane never to be reached by one who had not gone freely out to meet death, and, through an unknowing *karma,* miraculously come back again.

"Why not rest now, Anjin-san? Lord Yabu thanks you and says he will talk more with you tomorrow. You should rest now."

"Yes. Thank you. That would be fine."

"Do you think you can stand?"

"Yes. I think so."

"Yabu-san asks if you would like a palanquin?"

Blackthorne thought about that. At length he decided that a samurai would walk—would try to walk.

"No, thank you," he said, as much as he would have liked to lie down, to be carried back, to close his eyes and to sleep instantly. At the same time he knew he would be afraid to sleep yet, in case this was the dream of after-death and the knife not there on the futon but still buried in the real him, and this hell, or the beginning of hell.

Slowly he took up the knife and studied it, glorying in the *real* feel. Then he put it in its scabbard, everything taking so much time.

"Sorry I'm so slow," he murmured.

"You mustn't be sorry, Anjin-san. Tonight you're reborn. This is another life, a new life," Mariko said proudly, filled with honor for him. "It's given to few to return. Do not be sorry. We know it takes great fortitude. Most men do not have enough strength left afterwards even to stand. May I help you?"

"No. No, thank you."

"It is no dishonor to be helped. I would be honored to be allowed to help you."

"Thank you. But I—I wish to try. First."

But he could not stand at once. He had to use his hands to get to his knees and then he had to pause to get more strength. Later he lurched up and almost fell. He swayed but did not fall.

Yabu bowed. And Mariko, Omi, and Igurashi.

Blackthorne walked like a drunk for the first few paces. He clutched a pillar and held on for a moment. Then he began again. He faltered, but he was walking away, alone. As a man. He kept one hand on the long sword in his belt and his head was high.

Yabu exhaled and drank deeply of the saké. When he could speak he said to Mariko, "Please follow him. See that he gets home safely."

"Yes, Sire."

When she had gone, Yabu turned on Igurashi. "You-manure-pile-fool!"

Instantly Igurashi bowed his head to the mat in penitence.

"Bluff you said, *neh?* Your stupidity almost cost me a priceless treasure."

"Yes, Sire, you're right, Sire. I beg leave to end my life at once."

"That would be too good for you! Go and live in the stables until I send for you! Sleep with the stupid horses. You're a horse-headed fool!"

"Yes, Sire. I apologize, Sire."

"Get out! Omi-san will command the guns now. Get out!"

The candles flickered and spluttered. One of the maids spilled the tiniest drop of saké on the small lacquered table in front of Yabu and he cursed her eloquently. The others apologized at once. He allowed them to placate him, and accepted more wine. "Bluff? Bluff, he said. Fool! Why do I have fools around me?"

Omi said nothing, screaming with laughter inside.

"But you're no fool, Omi-san. Your counsel's valuable. Your fief's doubled from today. Six thousand koku. For next year. Take thirty *ri* around Anjiro as your fief."

Omi bowed to the futon. Yabu deserves to die, he thought scornfully, he's so easy to manipulate. "I deserve nothing, Sire. I was just doing my duty."

"Yes. But a liege lord should reward faithfulness and duty." Yabu was wearing the Yoshitomo sword tonight. It gave him great pleasure to touch it. "Suzu," he called to one of the maids. "Send Zukimoto here!"

"How soon will war begin?" Omi asked.

"This year. Maybe you have six months, perhaps not. Why?"

"Perhaps the Lady Mariko should stay more than three days. To protect you."

"Eh? Why?"

"She's the mouth of the Anjin-san. In half a month—with her—he can train twenty men who can train a hundred who can train the rest. Then whether he lives or dies doesn't matter."

"Why should he die?"

"You're going to call the Anjin-san again, his next challenge or the one after, Sire. The result may be different next time, who knows? You may want him to die." Both men knew, as Mariko and Igurashi had known, that for Yabu to swear by any god was meaningless and, of course, he had no intention of keeping any promise. "You may want to put pressure on him. Once you have the information, what good is the carcass?"

"None."

"You need to learn barbarian war strategy but you must do it very quickly. Lord Toranaga may send for him, so you must have the woman as long as you can. Half a month should be enough to squeeze his head dry of what he knows, now that you have his complete attention. You'll have to experiment, to adapt their methods to our ways. Yes, it would take at least half a month. *Neh?*"

"And Toranaga-san?"

"He will agree, if it's put correctly to him, Sire. He must. The guns are his as well as yours. And her continuing presence here is valuable in other ways."

"Yes," Yabu said with satisfaction, for the thought of holding her as hostage had also entered his mind on the ship when he had planned to offer Toranaga as a sacrifice to Ishido. "Toda Mariko should be protected, certainly. It would be bad if she fell into evil hands."

"Yes. And perhaps she could be the means of controlling Hiro-matsu, Buntaro, and all their clan, even Toranaga."

"You draft the message about her."

Omi said, offhand, "My mother heard from Yedo today, Sire. She asked me to tell you that the Lady Genjiko has presented Toranaga with his first grandson."

Yabu was at once attentive. Toranaga's grandson! Could Toranaga be controlled through this infant? The grandson assures Toranaga's dynasty, *neh?* How can I get the infant as hostage? "And Ochiba, the Lady Ochiba?" he asked.

"She's left Yedo with all her entourage. Three days ago. By now she's safe in Lord Ishido's territory."

Yabu thought about Ochiba and her sister, Genjiko. So different! Ochiba, vital, beautiful, cunning, relentless, the most desirable woman in the Empire and mother of the Heir. Genjiko, her younger sister, quiet, brooding, flat-faced and plain, with a pitilessness that was legend, even now, that had come down to her from their mother, who was one of Goroda's sisters. The two sisters loved each other, but Ochiba hated Toranaga and his brood, as Genjiko detested the Taikō and Yaemon, his son. Did the Taikō really father Ochiba's son, Yabu asked himself again, as all *daimyos* had done secretly for years. What wouldn't I give to know the answer to that. What wouldn't I give to possess that woman.

"Now that Lady Ochiba's no longer hostage in Yedo . . . that could be good and bad," Yabu said tentatively. "*Neh?*"

"Good, only good. Now Ishido and Toranaga must begin very soon." Omi deliberately omitted the "sama" from those two names. "The Lady Mariko should stay, for your protection."

"See to it. Draft the message to send to Toranaga."

Suzu, the maid, knocked discreetly and opened the door. Zukimoto came into the room. "Sire?"

"Where are all the gifts I ordered brought from Mishima for Omi-san?"

"They're all in the storehouse, Lord. Here's the list. The two horses can be selected from the stables. Do you want me to do that now?"

"No. Omi-san will choose them tomorrow." Yabu glanced at the carefully written list: "Twenty kimonos (second quality); two swords; one suit of armor (repaired but in good condition); two horses; arms for one hundred samurai—one sword, helmet, breastplate, bow, twenty arrows and spear for each man (best quality). Total value: four hundred and twenty-six koku. Also the rock called 'The Waiting Stone'—value: priceless."

"Ah yes," he said in better humor, remembering that night. "The rock I found in Kyushu. You were going to rename it 'The Waiting Barbarian,' weren't you?"

"Yes, Sire, if it still pleases you," Omi said. "But would you honor me tomorrow by deciding where it should go in the garden? I don't think there's a place good enough."

"Tomorrow I'll decide. Yes." Yabu let his mind rest on the rock, and on those far-off days with his revered master, the Taikō, and last on the Night of the Screams. Melancholy seeped into him. Life is so short and sad and cruel, he thought. He eyed Suzu. The maid smiled back hesitantly, oval-faced, slender, and very delicate like the other two. The three had been brought by palanquin from his household in Mishima. Tonight they were all barefoot, their kimonos the very best silk, their skins very white. Curious that boys can be so graceful, he pondered, in many ways more feminine, more sensuous than girls are. Then he noticed Zukimoto. "What're you waiting for? Eh? Get out!"

"Yes, Sire. You asked me to remind you about taxes, Sire." Zukimoto heaved up his sweating bulk and gratefully hurried away.

"Omi-san, you will double all taxes at once," Yabu said.

"Yes, Sire."

"Filthy peasants! They don't work hard enough. They're lazy—all of them! I keep the roads safe from bandits, the seas safe, give them good government, and what do they do? They spend the days drinking cha and saké and eating rice. It's time my peasants lived up to their responsibility!"

"Yes, Sire," Omi said.

Next, Yabu turned to the subject that possessed his mind. "The Anjin-san astonished me tonight. But not you?"

"Oh yes he did, Sire. More than you. But you were wise to make him commit himself."

"You say Igurashi was right?"

"I merely admired your wisdom, Sire. You would have had to say 'no' to him some time. I think you were very wise to say it now, tonight."

"I thought he'd killed himself. Yes. I'm glad you were ready. I planned on you being ready. The Anjin-san's an extraordinary man, for a barbarian, *neh*? A pity he's barbarian and so naïve."

"Yes."

Yabu yawned. He accepted saké from Suzu. "Half a month, you say? Mariko-san should stay at least that, Omi-san. Then I'll decide about her, and about him. He'll need to be taught another lesson soon." He laughed, showing his bad teeth. "If the Anjin-san teaches us, we should teach him, *neh*? He should be taught how to commit seppuku correctly. That'd be something to watch, *neh*? See to it! Yes, I agree the barbarian's days are numbered."

CHAPTER 32

TWELVE days later, in the afternoon, the courier from Osaka arrived. An escort of ten samurai rode in with him. Their horses were lathered and near death. The flags at their spearheads carried the cipher of the all-powerful Council of Regents. It was hot, overcast, and humid.

The courier was a lean, hard samurai of senior rank, one of Ishido's chief lieutenants. His name was Nebara Jozen and he was known for his ruthlessness. His Gray uniform kimono was tattered and mud-stained, his eyes red with fatigue. He refused food or drink and impolitely demanded an immediate audience with Yabu.

"Forgive my appearance, Yabu-san, but my business is urgent," he said. "Yes, I ask your pardon. My Master says first, why do you train Toranaga's soldiers along with your own and, second, why do they drill with so many guns?"

Yabu had flushed at the rudeness but he kept his temper, knowing that Jozen would have had specific instructions and that such lack of manners bespoke an untoward position of power. And too, he was greatly unsettled that there had been another leak in his security.

"You're very welcome, Jozen-san. You may assure your master that I always have his interests at heart," he said with a courteousness that fooled no one present.

They were on the veranda of the fortress. Omi sat just behind Yabu. Igurashi, who had been forgiven a few days before, was nearer to Jozen and surrounding them were intimate guards. "What else does your master say?"

Jozen replied, "My Master will be glad that your interests are his. Now, about the guns and the training: my Master would like to know why Toranaga's son, Naga, is second-in-command. Second-in-command of what? What's so important that a Toranaga son should be here, the Lord General Ishido asks with politeness. That's of interest to him. Yes. Everything his allies do interests him. Why is it, for instance, the barbarian seems to be in charge of training? Training of what? Yes, Yabu-sama, that's very interesting also." Jozen shifted his swords more comfortably, glad that his back was protected by his own men. "Next: The Council of Regents meets again on the first day of the new moon. In twenty days. You are formally invited to Osaka to renew your oath of fidelity."

Yabu's stomach twisted. "I understood Toranaga-sama had resigned?"

"He has, Yabu-san, indeed he has. But Lord Ito Teruzumi's taking his place. My Master will be the new President of the Regents."

Yabu was panic-stricken. Toranaga had said that the four Regents could never agree on a fifth. Ito Teruzumi was a minor *daimyo* of Negato Province in western Honshu but his family was ancient, descended from Fujimoto lineage, so he would be acceptable as a Regent, though he was an ineffectual man, effeminate and a puppet. "I would be honored to receive their invitation," Yabu said defensively, trying to buy time to think.

"My Master thought you might wish to leave at once. Then you would be in Osaka for the formal meeting. He orders me to tell you all the *daimyos* are getting the same invitation. Now. So *all* will have an opportunity to be there in good time on the twenty-first day. A Flower-Viewing Ceremony has been authorized

345

by His Imperial Highness, Emperor Go-Nijo, to honor the occasion." Jozen offered an official scroll.

"This isn't under the seal of the Council of Regents."

"My Master has issued the invitation now, knowing that, as a loyal vassal of the late Taikō, as a loyal vassal of Yaemon, his son and heir and the rightful ruler of the Empire when he becomes of age, you will understand that the new Council will, of course, approve his action. *Neh?*"

"It would certainly be a privilege to witness the formal meeting." Yabu struggled to control his face.

"Good," Jozen said. He pulled out another scroll, opened it, and held it up. "This is a copy of Lord Ito's letter of appointment, accepted and signed and authorized by the other Regents, Lords Ishido, Kiyama, Onoshi, and the Lord Sugiyama." Jozen did not bother to conceal a triumphant look, knowing that this totally closed the trap on Toranaga and any of his allies, and that equally the scroll made him and his men invulnerable.

Yabu took the scroll. His fingers trembled. There was no doubt of its authenticity. It had been countersigned by the Lady Yodoko, the wife of the Taikō, who affirmed that the document was true and signed in her presence, one of six copies that were being sent throughout the Empire, and that this particular copy was for the Lords of Iwari, Mikawa, Totomi, Sugura, Izu, and the Kwanto. It was dated eleven days ago.

"The Lords of Iwari, Mikawa, Suruga and Totomi have already accepted. Here are their seals. You're the last but one on my list. Last is the Lord Toranaga."

"Please thank your master and tell him I look forward to greeting him and congratulating him," Yabu said.

"Good. I'll require it in writing. Now would be satisfactory."

"This evening, Jozen-san. After the evening meal."

"Very well. And now we can go and see the training."

"There is none today. All my men are on forced marches," Yabu said. The moment Jozen and his men had entered Izu, word had been rushed to Yabu, who had at once ordered his men to cease all firing and to continue only silent weapon training well away from Anjiro. "Tomorrow you can come with me—at noon, if you wish."

Jozen looked at the sky. It was late afternoon now. "Good. I could use a little sleep. But I'll come back at dusk, with your permission. Then you and your commander, Omi-san, and the second commander, Naga-san, will tell me, for my Master's interest, about the training, the guns, and everything. And about the barbarian."

"He's—yes. Of course." Yabu motioned to Igurashi. "Arrange quarters for our honored guest and his men."

"Thank you, but that's not necessary," Jozen said at once. "The ground's futon enough for a samurai, my saddle's pillow enough. Just a bath, if you please . . . this humidity, *neh?* I'll camp on the crest—of course, with your permission."

"As you wish."

Jozen bowed stiffly and walked away, surrounded by his men. All were heavily armed. Two bowmen had been left holding their horses.

Once they were well away, Yabu's face contorted with rage. "Who betrayed me? Who? Where's the spy?"

Equally ashen, Igurashi waved the guards out of earshot. "Yedo, Sire," he said. "Must be. Security's perfect here."

"*Oh ko!*" Yabu said, almost rending his clothes. "I'm betrayed. We're isolated. Izu and the Kwanto are isolated. Ishido's won. He's won."

Omi said quickly, "Not for twenty days, Sire. Send a message at once to Lord

Toranaga. Inform him that—"

"Fool!" Yabu hissed. "Of course Toranaga already knows. Where I've one spy he has fifty. He's left me in the trap."

"I don't think so, Sire," Omi said, unafraid. "Iwari, Mikawa, Totomi, and Sugura are all hostile to him, *neh?* And to anyone who's allied to him. They'd never warn him, so perhaps he doesn't know yet. Inform him and suggest—"

"Didn't you hear?" Yabu shouted. "All four Regents agree to Ito's appointment, so the Council's legal again and the Council meets in twenty days!"

"The answer to that is simple, Sire. Suggest to Toranaga that he have Ito Teruzumi or one of the other Regents assassinated at once."

Yabu's mouth dropped open. "What?"

"If you don't wish to do that, send me, let me try. Or Igurashi-san. With Lord Ito dead, Ishido's helpless again."

"I don't know whether you've gone mad, or what," Yabu said helplessly. "Do you understand what you've just said?"

"Sire, I beg you, please, to be patient with me. The Anjin-san's given you priceless knowledge, *neh?* More than we ever dreamed possible. Now Toranaga knows this also, through your reports, and probably from Naga-san's private reports. If we can win enough time, our five hundred guns and the other three hundred will give you absolute battle power, but only once. When the enemy, whoever he is, sees the way you use men and firepower they'll learn quickly. But they'll have lost that first battle. One battle—if it's the right battle—will give Toranaga total victory."

"Ishido doesn't need any battle. In twenty days he has the Emperor's mandate."

"Ishido's a peasant. He's the son of a peasant, a liar, and he runs away from his comrades in battle."

Yabu stared at Omi, his face mottled. "You—do you know what you're saying?"

"That's what he did in Korea. I was there. I saw it, my father saw it. Ishido *did* leave Buntaro-san and us to fight our own way out. He's just a treacherous peasant—the Taikō's dog, certainly. You can't trust peasants. But Toranaga's Minowara. You can trust him. I advise you to consider only Toranaga's interests."

Yabu shook his head in disbelief. "Are you deaf? Didn't you hear Nebara Jozen? Ishido's won. The Council is in power in twenty days."

"*May be* in power."

"Even if Ito. . . . How could you? It's not possible."

"Certainly I could try but I could never do it in time. None of us could, not in twenty days. But Toranaga could." Omi knew he had put himself into the jaws of the dragon. "I beg you to consider it."

Yabu wiped his face with his hands, his body wet. "After this summons, if the Council is convened and I'm not present, I and all my clan are dead, you included. I need two months, at least, to train the regiment. Even if we had them trained now, Toranaga and I could never win against all the others. No, you're wrong, I have to support Ishido."

Omi said, "You don't have to leave for Osaka for ten days—fourteen, if you go by forced march. Tell Toranaga about Nebara Jozen at once. You'll save Izu and the Kasigi house. I beg you. Ishido will betray you and eat you up. Ikawa Jikkyu is his kinsman, *neh?*"

"But what about Jozen?" Igurashi exclaimed. "Eh? And the guns? The grand strategy? He wants to know about everything tonight."

"Tell him. In detail. What is he but a lackey," Omi said, beginning to maneuver them. He knew he was risking everything, but he had to try to protect Yabu from siding with Ishido and ruining any chance they had. "Open your plans to him."

Igurashi disagreed heatedly. "The moment Jozen learns what we're doing, he'll send a message back to Lord Ishido. It's too important not to. Ishido'll steal the plans, then we're finished."

"We trail the messenger and kill him at our convenience."

Yabu flushed. "That scroll was signed by the highest authority in the land! They all travel under the Regents' protection! You must be mad to suggest such a thing! That would make me an outlaw!"

Omi shook his head, keeping confidence on his face. "I believe Yodoko-sama and the others have been duped, as His Imperial Highness has been duped, by the traitor Ishido. We must protect the guns, Sire. We must stop any messenger—"

"Silence! Your advice is madness!"

Omi bowed under the tongue-lash. But he looked up and said calmly, "Then please allow me to commit seppuku, Sire. But first, please allow me to finish. I would fail in my duty if I didn't try to protect you. I beg this last favor as a faithful vassal."

"Finish!"

"There's no Council of Regents *now,* so there is no legal protection now for that insulting, foul-mannered Jozen and his men, unless you honor an illegal document through—" Omi was going to say "weakness" but he changed the word and kept his voice quietly authoritative—"through being duped like the others, Sire. *There is no Council.* They cannot 'order' you to do anything, or anyone. Once it's convened, yes, they can, and then you will have to obey. But now, how many *daimyos* will obey before *legal* orders can be issued? Only Ishido's allies, *neh?* Aren't Iwari, Mikawa, Totomi, and Sugura all ruled by his kinsmen and allied to him openly? That document absolutely means war, yes, but I beg you to wage it on your terms and not Ishido's. Treat this threat with the contempt it deserves! Toranaga's never been beaten in battle. Ishido has. Toranaga avoided being part of the Taikō's ruinous attack on Korea. Ishido didn't. Toranaga's in favor of ships and trade. Ishido isn't. Toranaga will want the barbarian's navy— didn't you advocate it to him? Ishido won't. Ishido will close the Empire. Toranaga will keep it open. Ishido will give Ikawa Jikkyu your hereditary fief of Izu if he wins. Toranaga will give you all Jikkyu's province. You're Toranaga's chief ally. Didn't he give you his sword? Hasn't he given you control of the guns? Don't the guns guarantee one victory, *with surprise?* What does the peasant Ishido give in return? He sends a *ronin*-samurai with no manners, with deliberate orders to shame you in your own province! I say Toranaga Minowara is your only choice. You must go with him." He bowed and waited in silence.

Yabu glanced at Igurashi. "Well?"

"I agree with Omi-san, Sire." Igurashi's face mirrored his worry. "As to killing a messenger—that would be dangerous, no turning back then, Sire. Jozen will certainly send one or two tomorrow. Perhaps they could vanish, killed by bandits—" He stopped in mid-sentence. "Carrier pigeons! There were two panniers of them on Jozen's pack horses!"

"We'll have to poison them tonight," Omi said.

"How? They'll be guarded."

"I don't know. But they've got to be removed or maimed before dawn."

Yabu said, "Igurashi, send men to watch Jozen at once. See if he sends one of his pigeons now—today."

"I suggest you send all our falcons and falconers to the east, also at once," Omi added quickly.

Igurashi said, "He'll suspect treachery if he sees his bird downed, or his birds tampered with."

Omi shrugged. "It must be stopped."

Igurashi looked at Yabu.

Yabu nodded resignedly. "Do it."

When Igurashi came back he said, "Omi-san, one thing occurred to me. A lot of what you said was right, about Jikkyu and Lord Ishido. But if you advise making the messengers 'vanish,' why toy with Jozen at all? Why tell him anything? Why not just kill them all at once?"

"Why not indeed? Unless it might amuse Yabu-sama. I agree your plan's better, Igurashi-san," Omi said.

Both men were looking at Yabu now. "How can I keep the guns secret?" he asked them.

"Kill Jozen and his men," Omi replied.

"No other way?"

Omi shook his head. Igurashi shook his head.

"Maybe I could barter with Ishido," Yabu said, shaken, trying to think of a way out of the trap. "You're correct about the time. I've ten days, fourteen at the most. How to deal with Jozen and still leave time to maneuver?"

"It would be wise to pretend that you're going to Osaka," Omi said. "But there's no harm in informing Toranaga at once, *neh?* One of our pigeons could get to Yedo before dusk. Perhaps. No harm in that."

Igurashi said, "You could tell Lord Toranaga about Jozen arriving, and about the Council meeting in twenty days, yes. But the other, about assassinating Lord Ito, that's too dangerous to put in writing even if . . . Much too dangerous, *neh?*"

"I agree. Nothing about Ito. Toranaga should think of that himself. It's obvious, *neh?*"

"Yes, Sire. Unthinkable but obvious."

Omi waited in the silence, his mind frantically seeking a solution. Yabu's eyes were on him but he was not afraid. His advice had been sound and offered only for the protection of the clan and the family and Yabu, the present leader of the clan. That Omi had decided to remove Yabu and change the leadership had not prevented him from counseling Yabu sagaciously. And he was prepared to die now. If Yabu was so stupid as not to accept the obvious truth of his ideas, then there soon would be no clan to lead anyway. *Karma.*

Yabu leaned forward, still undecided. "Is there any way to remove Jozen and his men without danger to me, and stay uncommitted for ten days?"

"Naga. Somehow bait a trap with Naga," Omi said simply.

At dusk, Blackthorne and Mariko rode up to the gate of his house, outriders following. Both were tired. She rode as a man would ride, wearing loose trousers and over them a belted mantle. She had on a wide-brimmed hat and gloves to protect her from the sun. Even peasant women tried to protect their faces and their hands from the rays of the sun. From time immemorial, the darker the skin the more common the person; the whiter, the more prized.

Male servants took the halters and led the horses away. Blackthorne dismissed his outriders in tolerable Japanese and greeted Fujiko, who waited proudly on the veranda as usual.

"May I serve you cha, Anjin-san," she said ceremoniously, as usual, and "No," he said as usual. "First I will bathe. Then saké and some food." And, as usual, he returned her bow and went through the corridor to the back of the house, out into the garden, along the circling path to the mud-wattled bath house. A servant took his clothes and he went in and sat down naked. Another servant scrubbed him and soaped him and shampooed him and poured water over him to wash away the lather and the dirt. Then, completely clean, gradually—because the water was so hot—he stepped into the huge iron-sided bath and lay down.

"Christ Jesus, that's grand," he exulted, and let the heat seep into his muscles, his eyes closed, the sweat running down his forehead.

He heard the door open and Suwo's voice and "Good evening, Master," followed by many words of Japanese which he did not understand. But tonight he was too tired to try to converse with Suwo. And the bath, as Mariko had explained many times, 'is not merely for cleaning the skin. The bath is a gift to us from God or the gods, a god-bequeathed pleasure to be enjoyed and treated as such.'

"No talk, Suwo," he said. "Tonight wish think."

"Yes, Master. Your pardon, but you should say, 'Tonight I wish to think.' "

"Tonight I wish to think." Blackthorne repeated the correct Japanese, trying to get the almost incomprehensible sounds into his head, glad to be corrected but very weary of it.

"Where's the dictionary-grammar book?" he had asked Mariko first thing this morning. "Has Yabu-sama sent another request for it?"

"Yes. Please be patient, Anjin-san. It will arrive soon."

"It was promised with the galley and the troops. It didn't arrive. Troops and guns but no books. I'm lucky you're here. It'd be impossible without you."

"Difficult, but not impossible, Anjin-san."

"How do I say, 'No, you're doing it wrong! You must all run as a team, stop as a team, aim and fire as a team.'?"

"To whom are you talking, Anjin-san?" she had asked.

And then again he had felt his frustration rising. "It's all very difficult, Mariko-san."

"Oh, no, Anjin-san. Japanese is very simple to speak compared with other languages. There are no articles, no 'the,' 'a,' or 'an.' No verb conjugations or infinitives. All verbs are regular, ending in *masu,* and you can say almost everything by using the present tense only, if you want. For a question just add *ka* after the verb. For a negative just change *masu* to *masen.* What could be easier? *Yukimasu* means I go, but equally you, he, she, it, we, they go, or will go, or even could have gone. Even plural and singular nouns are the same. *Tsuma* means wife, or wives. Very simple."

"Well, how do you tell the difference between I go, *yukimasu,* and they went, *yukimasu?*"

"By inflection, Anjin-san, and tone. Listen: *yukimasu—yukimasu.* "

"But these both sounded exactly the same."

"Ah, Anjin-san, that's because you're thinking in your own language. To understand Japanese you have to think Japanese. Don't forget our language is the language of the infinite. It's all so simple, Anjin-san. Just change your concept of the world. Japanese is just learning a new art, detached from the world. . . . It's all so simple."

"It's all shit," he had muttered in English, and felt better.

"What? What did you say?"

"Nothing. But what you say doesn't make sense."

"Learn the written characters," Mariko had said.

"I can't. It'll take too long. They're meaningless."

"Look, they're really simple pictures, Anjin-san. The Chinese are very clever. We borrowed their writing a thousand years ago. Look, take this character, or symbol, for a pig."

"It doesn't look like a pig."

"Once it did, Anjin-san. Let me show you. Here. Add a 'roof' symbol over a 'pig' symbol and what do you have?"

"A pig and a roof."

"But what does that mean? The new character?"

"I don't know."

" 'Home.' In the olden days the Chinese thought a pig under a roof was home. They're not Buddhists, they're meat eaters, so a pig to them, to peasants, represented wealth, hence a good home. Hence the character."

"But how do you say it?"

"That depends if you're Chinese or Japanese."

"*Oh ko!*"

"*Oh ko,* indeed," she had laughed. "Here's another character. A 'roof' symbol and a 'pig' symbol and a 'woman' symbol. A 'roof' with two 'pigs' under it means 'contentment.' A 'roof' with two 'women' under it equals 'discord.' *Neh?*"

"Absolutely!"

"Of course, the Chinese are very stupid in many things and their women are not trained as women are here. There's no discord in your home, is there?"

Blackthorne thought about that now, on the twelfth day of his rebirth. No. There was no discord. But neither was it a home. Fujiko was only like a trustworthy housekeeper and tonight when he went to his bed to sleep, the futons would be turned back and she would be kneeling beside them patiently, expressionlessly. She would be dressed in her sleeping kimono, which was similar to a day kimono but softer and with only a loose sash instead of a stiff obi at the waist.

"Thank you, Lady," he would say. "Good night."

She would bow and go silently to the room across the corridor, next to the one Mariko slept in. Then he would get under the fine silk mosquito net. He had never known such nets before. Then he would lie back happily, and in the night, hearing the few insects buzzing outside, he would dwell on the Black Ship, how important the Black Ship was to Japan.

Without the Portuguese, no trade with China. And no silks for clothes or for nets. Even now, with the humidity only just beginning, he knew their value.

If he stirred in the night a maid would open the door almost instantly to ask if there was anything he wanted. Once he had not understood. He motioned the maid away and went to the garden and sat on the steps, looking at the moon. Within a few minutes Fujiko, tousled and bleary, came and sat silently behind him.

"Can I get you anything, Lord?"

"No, thank you. Please go to bed."

She had said something he did not understand. Again he had motioned her away so she spoke sharply to the maid, who attended her like a shadow. Soon Mariko came.

"Are you all right, Anjin-san?"

"Yes. I don't know why you were disturbed. Christ Jesus—I'm just looking at the moon. I couldn't sleep. I just wanted some air."

Fujiko spoke to her haltingly, ill at ease, hurt by the irritation in his voice. "She says you told her to go back to sleep. She just wanted you to know that it's not our custom for a wife or consort to sleep while her master's awake, that's all, Anjin-san."

"Then she'll have to change her custom. I'm often up at night. By myself. It's a habit from being at sea—I sleep very lightly ashore."

"Yes, Anjin-san."

Mariko had explained and the two women had gone away. But Blackthorne knew that Fujiko had not gone back to sleep and would not, until he slept. She was always up and waiting whatever time he came back to the house. Some nights he walked the shore alone. Even though he insisted on being alone, he knew that he was followed and watched. Not because they were afraid he was trying to escape. Only because it was their custom for important people always to be attended. In Anjiro he was important.

In time he accepted her presence. It was as Mariko had first said, 'Think of her as a rock or a shoji or a wall. It is her duty to serve you.'

It was different with Mariko.

He was glad that she had stayed. Without her presence he could never have begun the training, let alone explained the intricacies of strategy. He blessed her and Father Domingo and Alban Caradoc and his other teachers.

I never thought the battles would ever be put to good use, he thought again. Once when his ship was carrying a cargo of English wools to Antwerp, a Spanish army had swooped down upon the city and every man had gone to the barricades and to the dikes. The sneak attack had been beaten off and the Spanish infantry outgunned and outmaneuvered. That was the first time he had seen William, Duke of Orange, using regiments like chess pieces. Advancing, retreating in pretended panic to regroup again, charging back again, guns blazing in packed, gut-hurting, ear-pounding salvos, breaking through the Invincibles to leave them dying and screaming, the stench of blood and powder and urine and horses and dung filling you, and a wild frantic joy of killing possessing you and the strength of twenty in your arms.

"Christ Jesus, it's grand to be victorious," he said aloud in the tub.

"Master?" Suwo said.

"Nothing," he replied in Japanese. "I talking—I was just think—just thinking aloud."

"I understand, Master. Yes. Your pardon."

Blackthorne let himself drift away.

Mariko. Yes, she's been invaluable.

After that first night of his almost suicide, nothing had ever been said again. What was there to say?

I'm glad there's so much to do, he thought. No time to think except here in the bath for these few minutes. Never enough time to do everything. Ordered to concentrate on training and teaching and not on learning, but wanting to learn, trying to learn, needing to learn to fulfill the promise to Yabu. Never enough hours. Always exhausted and drained by bedtime, sleeping instantly, to be up at dawn and riding fast to the plateau. Training all morning, then a sparse meal, never satisfying and never meat. Then every afternoon until nightfall—sometimes till very late at night—with Yabu and Omi and Igurashi and Naga and Zukimoto and a few of the other officers, talking about war, answering questions about war. How to wage war. How barbarians war and how Japanese war. On land and at sea. Scribes always taking notes. Many, many notes.

Sometimes with Yabu alone.

But always Mariko there—part of him—talking for him. And for Yabu. Mariko different now toward him, he no longer a stranger.

Other days the scribes reading back the notes, always checking, being meticulous, revising and checking again until now, after twelve days and a hundred hours or so of detailed exhaustive explanation, a war manual was forming. Exact. And lethal.

Lethal to whom? Not to us English or Hollanders, who will come here peacefully and only as traders. Lethal to Yabu's enemies and to Toranaga's enemies, and to our Portuguese and Spanish enemies when they try to conquer Japan. Like they've done everywhere else. In every newly discovered territory. First the priests arrive. Then the conquistadores.

But not here, he thought with great contentment. Never here—now. The manual's lethal and proof against that. No conquest here, given a few years for the knowledge to spread.

"Anjin-san?"

"*Hai,* Mariko-san?"

She was bowing to him. "Yabu-*ko wa kiden no goshusseki o kon-ya wa hitsuyo to senu to oserareru,* Anjin-san."

The words formed slowly in his head: 'Lord Yabu does not require to see you tonight.'

"*Ichi-ban,*" he said blissfully. "*Domo.*"

"*Gomen nasai,* Anjin-san. *Anatawa*—"

"Yes, Mariko-san," he interrupted her, the heat of the water sapping his energy. "I know I should have said it differently but I don't want to speak any more Japanese now. Not tonight. Now I feel like a schoolboy who's been let out of school for the Christmas holiday. Do you realize these'll be the first free hours I've had since I arrived?"

"Yes, yes I do." She smiled wryly. "And do you realize, Senhor Captain-Pilot B'rack'fon, these will be the first free hours I've had since I arrived?"

He laughed. She was wearing a thick cotton bathing robe tied loosely, and a towel around her head to protect her hair. Every evening as soon as his massage began, she would take the bath, sometimes alone, sometimes with Fujiko.

"Here, you have it now," he said, beginning to get out.

"Oh, please, no, I don't wish to disturb you."

"Then share it. It's wonderful."

"Thank you. I can hardly wait to soak the sweat and dust away." She took off her robe and sat on the tiny seat. A servant began to lather her, Suwo waiting patiently near the massage table.

"It *is* rather like a school holiday," she said, as happily.

The first time Blackthorne had seen her naked on the day that they swam he had been greatly affected. Now her nakedness, of itself, did not touch him physically. Living closely in Japanese style in a Japanese house where the walls were paper and the rooms multipurpose, he had seen her unclothed and partially clothed many times. He had even seen her relieving herself.

"What's more normal, Anjin-san? Bodies are normal, and differences between men and women are normal, *neh?*"

"Yes, but it's, er, just that we're trained differently."

"But now you're here and our customs are your customs and normal is normal. *Neh?*"

Normal was urinating or defecating in the open if there were no latrines or buckets, just lifting your kimono or parting it and squatting or standing, everyone else politely waiting and not watching, rarely screens for privacy. Why should one require privacy? And soon one of the peasants would gather the feces and mix it with water to fertilize crops. Human manure and urine were the only substantial source of fertilizer in the Empire. There were few horses and bullocks, and no other animal sources at all. So every human particle was harbored and sold to the farmers throughout the land.

And after you've seen the highborn and the lowborn parting or lifting and standing or squatting, there's not much left to be embarrassed about.

"Is there, Anjin-san?"

"No."

"Good," she had said, very satisfied. "Soon you will like raw fish and fresh seaweed and then you'll really be hatamoto."

The maid poured water over her. Then, cleansed, Mariko stepped into the bath and lay down opposite him with a long-drawn sigh of ecstasy, the little crucifix dangling between her breasts.

"How do you do that?" he said.

"What?"

"Get in so quickly. It's so hot."

"I don't know, Anjin-san, but I asked them to put more firewood on and to heat up the water. For you, Fujiko always makes sure it's—we would call it tepid."

"If this is tepid, then I'm a Dutchman's uncle!"

"What?"

"Nothing."

The water's heat made them drowsy and they lolled a while, not saying a word. Later she said, "What would you like to do this evening, Anjin-san?"

"If we were up in London we'd—" Blackthorne stopped. I won't think about them, he told himself. Or London. That's gone. That doesn't exist. Only here exists.

"If?" She was watching him, aware of the change.

"We'd go to a theater and see a play," he said, dominating himself. "Do you have plays here?"

"Oh, yes, Anjin-san. Plays are very popular with us. The Taikō liked to perform in them for the entertainment of his guests, even Lord Toranaga likes to. And of course there are many touring companies for the common people. But our plays are not quite like yours, so I believe. Here our actors and actresses wear masks. We call the plays 'Nōh.' They're part music, partially danced and mostly very sad, very tragic, historical plays. Some are comedies. Would we see a comedy, or perhaps a religious play?"

"No, we'd go to the Globe Theater and see something by a playwright called Shakespeare. I like him better than Ben Jonson or Marlowe. Perhaps we'd see *The Taming of the Shrew* or *A Midsummer Night's Dream* or *Romeo and Juliet*. I took my wife to *Romeo and Juliet* and she liked it very much." He explained the plots to her.

Mostly Mariko found them incomprehensible. "It would be unthinkable here for a girl to disobey her father like that. But so sad, *neh?* Sad for a young girl and sad for the boy. She was only thirteen? Do all your ladies marry so young?"

"No. Fifteen or sixteen's usual. My wife was seventeen when we were married. How old were you?"

"Just fifteen, Anjin-san." A shadow crossed her brow which he did not notice. "And after the play, what would we do?"

"I would take you to eat. We'd go to Stone's Chop House in Fetter Lane, or the Cheshire Cheese in Fleet Street. They are inns where the food's special."

"What would you eat?"

"I'd rather not remember," he said with a lazy smile, turning his mind back to the present. "I can't remember. Here is where we are and here is where we'll eat, and I enjoy raw fish and *karma* is *karma*." He sank deeper into the tub. "A great word '*karma*.' And a great idea. Your help's been enormous to me, Mariko-san."

"It's my pleasure to be of a little service to you." Mariko relaxed into the warmth. "Fujiko has some special food for you tonight."

"Oh?"

"She bought a—I think you call it a pheasant. It's a large bird. One of the falconers caught it for her."

"A pheasant? You really mean it? *Honto?*"

"*Honto,*" she replied. "Fujiko asked them to hunt for you. She asked me to tell you."

"How is it being cooked?"

"One of the soldiers had seen the Portuguese preparing them and he told Fujiko-san. She asks you to be patient if it's not cooked properly."

"But how is she doing it—how're the cooks doing it?" He corrected himself, for servants alone did the cooking and cleaning.

"She was told that first someone pulls out all the feathers, then—then takes out the entrails." Mariko controlled her squeamishness. "Then the bird's either cut into small pieces and fried with oil, or boiled with salt and spices." Her nose wrinkled. "Sometimes they cover it with mud and put it into the coals of a fire and bake it. We have no ovens, Anjin-san. So it will be fried. I hope that's all right."

"I'm sure it'll be perfect," he said, certain it would be inedible.

She laughed. "You're so transparent, Anjin-san, sometimes."

"You don't understand how important food is!" In spite of himself he smiled. "You're right. I shouldn't be interested in food. But I can't control hunger."

"You'll soon be able to do that. You'll even learn how to drink cha from an empty cup."

"What?"

"This is not the place to explain that, Anjin-san, or the time. For that you must be very awake and very alert. A quiet sunset, or dawning, is necessary. I will show you how, one day, because of what you did. Oh, it is so good to lie here, isn't it? A bath is truly the gift of God."

He heard the servants outside the wall, stoking the fire. He bore the intensifying heat as long as he could, then emerged from the water, half helped by Suwo, and lay back gasping on the thick towel cloth. The old man's fingers probed. Blackthorne could have cried out with pleasure. "That's so good."

"You've changed so much in the last few days, Anjin-san."

"Have I?"

"Oh yes, since your rebirth—yes, very much."

He tried to recall the first night but could remember little. Somehow he had made it back on his own legs. Fujiko and the servants had helped him to bed. After a dreamless sleep, he woke at dawn and went for a swim. Then, drying in the sun, he had thanked God for the strength and the clue that Mariko had given him. Later, walking home, he greeted the villagers, knowing secretly that they were freed of Yabu's curse, as he was freed.

Then, when Mariko had arrived, he had sent for Mura.

"Mariko-san, please tell Mura this: 'We have a problem, you and I. We will solve it together. I want to join the village school. To learn to speak with children.' "

"They haven't a school, Anjin-san."

"None?"

"No. Mura says there's a monastery a few *ri* to the west and the monks could teach you reading and writing if you wish. But this is a village, Anjin-san. The children here need to learn the ways of fish, the sea, making nets, planting and growing rice and crops. There's little time for anything else, except reading and writing. And, too, parents and grandparents teach their own, as always."

"Then how can I learn when you've gone?"

"Lord Toranaga will send the books."

"I'll need more than books."

"Everything will be satisfactory, Anjin-san."

"Yes. Perhaps. But tell the headman that whenever I make a mistake, everyone —everyone, even a child—is to correct me. At once. I order it."

"He says thank you, Anjin-san."

"Does anyone here speak Portuguese?"

"He says no."

"Anyone nearby?"

"*Iyé,* Anjin-san."

"Mariko-san, I've got to have someone when you leave."

"I'll tell Yabu-san what you've said."

"Mura-san, you—"

"He says you must not use 'san' to him or to any villagers. They are beneath you. It's not correct for you to say 'san' to them or anyone beneath you."

Fujiko had also bowed to the ground that first day. "Fujiko-san welcomes you home, Anjin-san. She says you have done her great honor and she begs your forgiveness for being rude on the ship. She is honored to be consort and head of your house. She asks if you will keep the swords as it would please her greatly. They belonged to her father, who is dead. She had not given them to her husband because he had swords of his own."

"Thank her and say I'm honored she's consort," he had said.

Mariko had bowed too. Formally. "You are in a new life now, Anjin-san. We look at you with new eyes. It is our custom to be formal sometimes, with great seriousness. You have opened my eyes. Very much. Once you were just a barbarian to me. Please excuse my stupidity. What you did proves you're samurai. Now you *are* samurai. Please forgive my previous bad manners."

He had felt very tall that day. But his self-inflicted near-death had changed him more than he realized and scarred him forever, more than the sum of all his other near-deaths.

Did you rely on Omi? he asked himself. That Omi would catch the blow? Didn't you give him plenty of warning?

I don't know. I only know I'm glad he *was* ready, Blackthorne answered himself truthfully. That's another life gone!

"That's my ninth life. The last!" he said aloud. Suwo's fingers ceased at once.

"What?" Mariko asked. "What did you say, Anjin-san?"

"Nothing. It was nothing," he replied, ill at ease.

"I hurt you, Master?" Suwo said.

"No."

Suwo said something more that he did not understand.

"*Dozo?*"

Mariko said distantly, "He wants to massage your back now."

Blackthorne turned on his stomach and repeated the Japanese and forgot it at once. He could see her through the steam. She was breathing deeply, her head tilted back slightly, her skin pink.

How does she stand the heat, he asked himself. Training, I suppose, from childhood.

Suwo's fingers pleasured him, and he drowsed momentarily.

What was I thinking about?

You were thinking about your ninth life, your last life, and you were frightened, remembering the superstition. But it is foolish here in this Land of the Gods to be superstitious. Things are different here and this is forever. Today is forever.

Tomorrow many things can happen.
Today I'll abide by their rules.
I will.

The maid brought in the covered dish. She held it high above her head as was custom, so that her breath would not defile the food. Anxiously she knelt and placed it carefully on the tray table in front of Blackthorne. On each little table were bowls and chopsticks, saké cups and napkins, and a tiny flower arrangement. Fujiko and Mariko were sitting opposite him. They wore flowers and silver combs in their hair. Fujiko's kimono was a pale green pattern of fish on a white background, her obi gold. Mariko wore black and red with a thin silver overlay of chrysanthemums and a red and silver check obi. Both wore perfume, as always. Incense burned to keep the night bugs away.

Blackthorne had long since composed himself. He knew that any displeasure from him would destroy their evening. If pheasants could be caught there would be other game, he thought. He had a horse and guns and he could hunt himself, if only he could get the time.

Fujiko leaned over and took the lid off the dish. The small pieces of fried meat were browned and seemed perfect. He began to salivate at the aroma.

Slowly he took a piece of meat in his chopsticks, willing it not to fall, and chewed the flesh. It was tough and dry, but he had been meatless for so long it was delicious. Another piece. He sighed with pleasure. "*Ichi-ban, ichi-ban,* by God!"

Fujiko blushed and poured him saké to hide her face. Mariko fanned herself, the crimson fan a dragonfly. Blackthorne quaffed the wine and ate another piece and poured more wine and ritualistically offered his brimming cup to Fujiko. She refused, as was custom, but tonight he insisted, so she drained the cup, choking slightly. Mariko also refused and was also made to drink. Then he attacked the pheasant with as little gusto as he could manage. The women hardly touched their small portions of vegetables and fish. This didn't bother him because it was a female custom to eat before or afterward so that all their attention could be devoted to the master.

He ate all the pheasant and three bowls of rice and slurped his saké, which was also good manners. He felt replete for the first time in months. During the meal he had finished six flasks of the hot wine, Mariko and Fujiko two between them. Now they were flushed and giggling and at the silly stage.

Mariko chuckled and put her hand in front of her mouth. "I wish I could drink saké like you, Anjin-san. You drink saké better than any man I've ever known. I wager you'd be the best in Izu! I could win a lot of money on you!"

"I thought samurai disapproved of gambling."

"Oh they do, absolutely they do, they're not merchants and peasants. But not all samurai are as strong as others and many—how do you say—many'll bet like the Southern Bar—like the Portuguese bet."

"Do women bet?"

"Oh, yes. Very much. But only with other ladies and in careful amounts and always so their husbands never find out!" She gaily translated for Fujiko, who was more flushed than she.

"Your consort asks do Englishmen bet? Do you like to wager?"

"It's our national pastime." And he told them about horse racing and skittles and bull baiting and coursing and whippets and hawking and bowls and the new stock companies and letters of marque and shooting and darts and lotteries and boxing and cards and wrestling and dice and checkers and dominoes and the time at the fairs when you put farthings on numbers and bet against the wheels of chance.

"But how do you find time to live, to war, and to pillow, Fujiko asks?"

"There's always time for those." Their eyes met for a moment but he could not read anything in hers, only happiness and maybe too much wine.

Mariko begged him to sing the hornpipe song for Fujiko, and he did and they congratulated him and said it was the best they had ever heard.

"Have some more saké!"

"Oh, *you* mustn't pour, Anjin-san, that's woman's duty. Didn't I tell you?"

"Yes. Have some more, *dozo.*"

"I'd better not. I think I'll fall over." Mariko fluttered her fan furiously and the draft stirred the threads of hair that had escaped from her immaculate coiffure.

"You have nice ears," he said.

"So have you. We, Fujiko-san and I, we think your nose is perfect too, worthy of a *daimyo.*"

He grinned and bowed elaborately to them. They bowed back. The folds of Mariko's kimono fell away from her neck slightly, revealing the edge of her scarlet under-kimono and the swell of her breasts, and it stirred him considerably.

"Saké, Anjin-san?"

He held out the cup, his fingers steady. She poured, watching the cup, the tip of her tongue touching her lips as she concentrated.

Fujiko reluctantly accepted some too, though she said that she couldn't feel her legs anymore. Her quiet melancholia had gone tonight and she seemed young again. Blackthorne noticed that she was not as ugly as he had once thought.

Jozen's head was buzzing. Not from saké but from the incredible war strategy that Yabu, Omi, and Igurashi had described so openly. Only Naga, the second-in-command, son of the arch-enemy, had said nothing, and had remained throughout the evening cold, arrogant, stiff-backed, with the characteristic large Toranaga nose on a taut face.

"Astonishing, Yabu-sama," Jozen said. "Now I can understand the reason for secrecy. My Master will understand it also. Wise, very wise. And you, Naga-san, you've been silent all evening. I'd like your opinion. How do you like this new mobility—this new strategy?"

"My father believes that all war possibilities should be considered, Jozen-san," the young man replied.

"But you, what's your opinion?"

"I was sent here only to obey, to observe, to listen, to learn, and to test. Not to give opinions."

"Of course. But as second-in-command—I should say, as an illustrious second-in-command—do you consider the experiment a success?"

"Yabu-sama or Omi-san should answer that. Or my father."

"But Yabu-sama said that everyone tonight was to talk freely. What's there to hide? We are all friends, *neh?* So famous a son of so famous a father must have an opinion. *Neh?*"

Naga's eyes narrowed under the taunt but he did not reply.

"Everyone can speak freely, Naga-san," Yabu said. "What do you think?"

"I think that, with surprise, this idea would win one skirmish or possibly one battle. With surprise, yes. But then?" Naga's voice swept on icily. "Then all sides would use the same plan and vast numbers of men would die unnecessarily, slain without honor by an assailant who won't even know who he has killed. I doubt if my father will actually authorize its use in a real battle."

"He's said that?" Yabu put the question incisively, careless of Jozen.

"No, Yabu-sama. I'm giving my own opinion. Of course."

"But the Musket Regiment—you don't approve of it? It disgusts you?" Yabu asked darkly.

Naga looked at him with flat, reptilian eyes. "With great deference, since you ask my opinion, yes, I find it disgusting. Our forefathers have always known whom they killed or who defeated them. That's *bushido,* our way, the Way of the Warrior, the way of a true samurai. The better man victorious, *neh?* But now this? How do you prove your valor to your lord? How can he reward courage? To charge bullets is brave, yes, but also stupid. Where's the valor in that? Guns are against our samurai code. Barbarians fight this way, peasants fight this way. Do you realize filthy merchants and peasants, even *eta,* could fight this way?" Jozen laughed and Naga continued even more menacingly. "A few fanatic peasants could easily kill any number of samurai with enough guns! Yes, peasants could kill any one of us, even the Lord Ishido, who wants to sit in my father's place."

Jozen bridled. "Lord Ishido doesn't covet your father's lands. He only seeks to protect the Empire for its rightful heir."

"My father's no threat to the Lord Yaemon, or to the Realm."

"Of course, but you were talking about peasants. The Lord Taikō was once a peasant. My Lord Ishido was once a peasant. I was once a peasant. And a *ronin!*"

Naga wanted no quarrel. He knew he was no match for Jozen, whose prowess with sword and ax was renowned. "I wasn't trying to insult your master or you or anyone, Jozen-san. I was merely saying that we samurai must all make very certain that peasants never have guns or none of us will be safe."

"Merchants and peasants'll never worry us," Jozen said.

"I agree," Yabu added, "and Naga-san, I agree with part of what you say. Yes. But guns are modern. Soon all battles will be fought with guns. I agree it's distasteful. But it's the way of modern war. And then it'll be as it always was—the bravest samurai will always conquer."

"No, so sorry, but you're wrong, Yabu-sama! What did this cursed barbarian tell us—the essence of their war strategy? He freely admits that all their armies are conscript and mercenary. *Neh?* Mercenary! No sense of duty to their lords. The soldiers only fight for pay and loot, to rape and to gorge. Didn't he say their armies are *peasant armies?* That's what guns have brought to their world and that's what guns will bring to ours. If I had power, I'd take this barbarian's head tonight and outlaw all guns permanently."

"Is that what your father thinks?" Jozen asked too quickly.

"My father doesn't tell me or anyone what he thinks, as you surely know. I don't speak for my father, no one speaks for him," Naga replied, angry at allowing himself to be trapped into talking at all. "I was sent here to obey, to listen and not to talk. I apologize for talking. I would not have spoken unless you asked me. If I have offended you, or you, Yabu-sama, or you, Omi-san, I apologize."

"There's no need to apologize. I asked your views," Yabu said. "Why should anyone be offended? This is a discussion, *neh?* Among leaders. You'd outlaw guns?"

"Yes. I think you'd be wise to keep a very close check on every gun in your domain."

"All peasants are forbidden weapons of any kind. My peasants and my people are very well controlled."

Jozen smirked at the slim youth, loathing him. "Interesting ideas you have, Naga-san. But you're mistaken about the peasants. They're nothing to samurai but providers. They're no more threat than a pile of dung."

"At the moment!" Naga said, his pride commanding him. "That's why I'd outlaw guns now. You're right, Yabu-san, that a new era requires new methods. But because of what this Anjin-san, this one barbarian, has said, I'd go much further than our present laws. I would issue Edicts that anyone other than a samurai found with a gun or caught trading in guns would immediately forfeit his life and that of every member of his family of every generation. Further, I would prohibit the making or importing of guns. I'd prohibit barbarians from wearing them or from bringing them to our shores. Yes, if I had power—which I do not seek and never will—I'd keep barbarians out of our country totally, except for a few priests and one port for trade, which I'd surround with a high fence and trusted warriors. Last, I'd put this foul-minded barbarian, the Anjin-san, to death at once so that his filthy knowledge will not spread. He's a disease."

Jozen said, "Ah, Naga-san, it must be good to be so young. You know, my Master agrees with much of what you said about the barbarians. I've heard him say many times, 'Keep them out—kick them out—kick their arses away to Nagasaki and keep them bottled there!' You'd kill the Anjin-san, eh? Interesting. My Master doesn't like the Anjin-san either. But for him—" He stopped. "Ah, yes, you've a good thought about guns. I can see that clearly. May I tell that to my Master? Your idea about new laws?"

"Of course." Naga was mollified, and calmer now that he had spoken what had been bottled up from the first day.

"You've given this opinion to Lord Toranaga?" Yabu asked.

"Lord Toranaga has not asked my opinion. I hope one day he will honor me by asking as you have done," Naga replied at once with sincerity, and wondered if any of them detected the lie.

Omi said, "As this is a free discussion, Sire, I say this barbarian is a treasure. I believe we must learn from the barbarian. We must know about guns and fighting ships because they know about them. We must know everything they know as soon as they know it, and even now, some of us must begin to learn to think like they do so that soon we can surpass them."

Naga said confidently, "What could they possibly know, Omi-san? Yes, guns and ships. But what else? How could they destroy us? There's not a samurai among them. Doesn't this Anjin admit openly that even their kings are murderers and religious fanatics? We're millions, they're a handful. We could swamp them with our hands alone."

"This Anjin-san opened my eyes, Naga-san. I've discovered that our land, and China, isn't the whole world, it's only a very small part. At first I thought the barbarian was just a curiosity. Now I don't. I thank the gods for him. I think he's saved us and I know we can learn from him. Already he's given us power over the Southern Barbarians—and over China."

"What?"

"The Taikō failed because their numbers are too great for us, man to man, arrow to arrow, neh? With guns and barbarian skill we could take Peking."

"With barbarian treachery, Omi-san!"

"With barbarian knowledge, Naga-san, we could take Peking. Whoever takes Peking eventually controls China. And whoever controls China can control the world. We must learn not to be ashamed of taking knowledge from wherever it comes."

"I say we need nothing from outside."

"Without offense, Naga-san, I say we must protect this Land of the Gods by any means. It's our prime duty to protect the unique, divine position we have on earth. Only this is the Land of the Gods, *neh?* Only our Emperor is divine. I agree this barbarian should be gagged. But not by death. By permanent isolation here in Anjiro, until we have learned everything he knows."

Jozen scratched thoughtfully. "My Master will be told of your views. I agree the barbarian should be isolated. Also that training should cease at once."

Yabu took a scroll from his sleeve. "Here is a full report on the experiment for Lord Ishido. When Lord Ishido wishes the training to cease, of course, the training will cease."

Jozen accepted the scroll. "And Lord Toranaga? What about him?" His eyes went to Naga. Naga said nothing but stared at the scroll.

Yabu said, "You will be able to ask his opinion directly. He has a similar report. I presume you'll be leaving for Yedo tomorrow? Or would you like to witness the training? I hardly need tell you the men are not yet proficient."

"I would like to see one 'attack.' "

"Omi-san, arrange it. You lead it."

"Yes, Sire."

Jozen turned to his second-in-command and gave him the scroll. "Masumoto, take this to Lord Ishido. You will leave at once."

"Yes, Jozen-san."

Yabu said to Igurashi, "Provide him with guides to the border and fresh horses."

Igurashi left with the samurai immediately.

Jozen stretched and yawned. "Please excuse me," he said, "but it's all the riding I've done in the last few days. I must thank you for an extraordinary evening, Yabu-sama. Your ideas are far-reaching. And yours, Omi-san. And yours, Naga-san. I'll compliment you to the Lord Toranaga and to my Master. Now if you'll excuse me, I'm very tired and Osaka is a long way off."

"Of course," Yabu said. "How was Osaka?"

"Very good. Remember those bandits, the ones that attacked you by land and sea?"

"Of course."

"We took four hundred and fifty heads that night. Many were wearing Toranaga uniforms."

"*Ronin* have no honor. None."

"Some *ronin* have," Jozen said, smarting from the insult. He lived always with the shame of having once been *ronin*. "Some were even wearing our Grays. Not one escaped. They all died."

"And Buntaro-san?"

"No. He—" Jozen stopped. The "no" had slipped out but now that he had said it he did not mind. "No. We don't know for certain—no one collected his head. You've heard nothing about him?"

"No," Naga said.

"Perhaps he was captured. Perhaps they just cut him into pieces and scattered him. My Master would like to know when you have news. All's very good now at Osaka. Preparations for the meeting go forward. There'll be lavish entertainments to celebrate the new era, and of course, to honor *all* the *daimyos.*"

"And Lord Toda Hiro-matsu?" Naga asked politely.

"Old Iron Fist's as strong and gruff as ever."

"He's still there?"

"No. He left with all your father's men a few days before I did."

"And my father's household?"

"I heard that the Lady Kiritsubo and the Lady Sazuko asked to stay with my

Master. A doctor advised the Lady to rest for a month—her health, you know. He thought the journey would not be good for the expected child." To Yabu he added, "She fell down the night you left, didn't she?"

"Yes."

"There's nothing serious, I hope," Naga asked, very concerned.

"No, Naga-san, nothing serious," Jozen said, then again to Yabu, "You've informed Lord Toranaga of my arrival?"

"Of course."

"Good."

"The news you brought us would interest him greatly."

"Yes. I saw a carrier pigeon circle and fly north."

"I have that service now." Yabu did not add that Jozen's pigeon had also been observed, or that falcons had intercepted it near the mountains, or that the message had been decoded: "At Anjiro. All true as reported. Yabu, Naga, Omi, and barbarian here."

"I will leave tomorrow, with your permission, after the 'attack.' You'll give me fresh horses? I must not keep Lord Toranaga waiting. I look forward to seeing him. So does my Master. At Osaka. I hope you'll accompany him, Naga-san."

"If I'm ordered there, I will be there." Naga kept his eyes lowered but he was burning with suppressed fury.

Jozen left and walked with his guards up the hill to his camp. He rearranged the sentries and ordered his men to sleep and got into his small brush lean-to that they had constructed against the coming rain. By candlelight, under a mosquito net, he rewrote the previous message on a thin piece of rice paper and added: "The five hundred guns are lethal. Massed surprise gun attacks planned— full report already sent with Masumoto." Then he dated it and doused the candle. In the darkness he slipped out of his net, removed one of the pigeons from the panniers and placed the message in the tiny container on its foot. Then he stealthily made his way to one of his men and handed him the bird.

"Take it out into the brush," he whispered. "Hide it somewhere where it can roost safely until dawn. As far away as you can. But be careful, there are eyes all around. If you're intercepted say I told you to patrol, but hide the pigeon first."

The man slid away as silently as a cockroach.

Pleased with himself, Jozen looked toward the village below. There were lights on in the fortress and on the opposite slope, in the house that he knew to be Omi's. There were a few also in the house just below, the one presently occupied by the barbarian.

That whelp Naga's right, Jozen thought, waving his hand at a mosquito. The barbarian's a filthy plague.

"Good night, Fujiko-san."

"Good night, Anjin-san."

The shoji closed behind her. Blackthorne took off his kimono and loincloth and put on the lighter sleeping kimono, got under the mosquito net, and lay down.

He blew out the candle. Deep darkness enveloped him. The house was quiet now. The small shutters were closed and he could hear the surf. Clouds obscured the moon.

The wine and laughter had made him drowsy and euphoric and he listened to the surf and felt himself drifting with it, his mind fogged. Occasionally, a dog barked in the village below. I should get a dog, he thought, remembering his own bull terrier at home. Wonder if he's still alive? Grog was his name but Tudor, his son, always called him "Og-Og."

Ah, Tudor, laddie. It's been such a long time.

Wish I could see you all—even write a letter and send it home. Let's see, he thought. How would I begin?

"My darlings: This is the first letter I've been able to send home since we made landfall in Japan. Things are well now that I know how to live according to their ways. The food is terrible but tonight I had pheasant and soon I'll get my ship back again. Where to start my story? Today I'm like a feudal lord in this strange country. I have a house, a horse, eight servants, a housekeeper, my own barber, and my own interpreter. I'm clean-shaven now and shave every day—the steel razors they have here must certainly be the best in the world. My salary's huge—enough to feed two hundred and fifty Japan families for one year. In England that'd be the equivalent of almost a thousand golden guineas a year! Ten times my salary from the Dutch company. . . ."

The shoji began to open. His hand sought his pistol under the pillow and he readied, dragging himself back. Then he caught the almost imperceptible rustle of silk and a waft of perfume.

"Anjin-san?" A thread of whisper, filled with promise.

"*Hai?*" he asked as softly, peering into the darkness, unable to see clearly.

Footsteps came closer. There was the sound of her kneeling and the net was pulled aside and she joined him inside the enclosing net. She took his hand and lifted it to her breast, then to her lips.

"Mariko-san?"

At once fingers reached up in the darkness and touched his lips, cautioning silence. He nodded, understanding the awful risk they were taking. He held her tiny wrist and brushed it with his lips. In the pitch black his other hand sought and caressed her face. She kissed his fingers one by one. Her hair was loose and waist length now. His hands traveled her. The lovely feel of silk, nothing beneath.

Her taste was sweet. His tongue touched her teeth, then rimmed her ears, discovering her. She loosened his robe and let hers fall aside, her breathing more languorous now. She pushed closer, nestling, and pulled the covering over their heads. Then she began to love him, with hands and with lips. With more tenderness and seeking and knowledge than he had ever known.

CHAPTER 33

BLACKTHORNE awoke at dawn. Alone. At first he was sure he had been dreaming, but her perfume still lingered and he knew that it had not been a dream.

A discreet knock.

"*Hai?*"

"*Ohayo,* Anjin-san, *gomen nasai.*" A maid opened the shoji for Fujiko, then carried in the tray with cha and a bowl of rice gruel and sweet rice cakes.

"*Ohayo,* Fujiko-san, *domo,*" he said, thanking her. She always came with his first meal personally, opened the net and waited while he ate, and the maid laid out a fresh kimono and tabi and loincloth.

He sipped the cha, wondering if Fujiko knew about last night. Her face gave nothing away.

"*Ikaga desu ka?*" How are you, Blackthorne asked.

"*Okagasama de genki desu,* Anjin-san. *Anata wa?*" Very well, thank you. And you?

The maid took out his fresh clothes from the concealed cupboard that melted neatly into the rest of the paper-latticed room, then left them alone.

"*Anata wa yoku nemutta ka?*" Did you sleep well?

"*Hai,* Anjin-san, *arigato goziemashita!*" She smiled, put her hand to her head pretending pain, mimed being drunk and sleeping like a stone. "*Anata wa?*"

"*Watashi wa yoku nemuru.*" I slept very well.

She corrected him, "*Watashi wa yoku nemutta.*"

"*Domo. Watashi wa yoku nemutta.*"

"*Yoi! Taihenyoi!*" Good. Very good.

Then from the corridor he heard Mariko call out, "Fujiko-san?"

"*Hai,* Mariko-san?" Fujiko went to the shoji and opened it a crack. He could not see Mariko. And he did not understand what they were saying.

I hope no one knows, he thought. I pray it is secret, just between us. Perhaps it would be better if it had been a dream.

He began to dress. Fujiko came back and knelt to do up the catches on the tabi.

"Mariko-san? *Nan ja?*"

"*Nane mo,* Anjin-san," she replied. It was nothing important.

She went to the *takonama,* the alcove with its hanging scroll and flower arrangement, where his swords were always put. She gave them to him. He stuck them in his belt. The swords no longer felt ridiculous to him, though he wished that he could wear them less self-consciously.

She had told him that her father had been granted the swords for bravery after a particularly bloody battle in the far north of Korea, seven years ago during the first invasion. The Japanese armies had ripped through the kingdom, victorious, slashing north. Then, when they were near the Yalu River, the Chinese hordes had abruptly poured across the border to join battle with the Japanese armies and, through the weight of their incredible numbers, had routed them. Fujiko's father had been part of the rearguard that had covered the retreat back to the mountains north of Seoul, where they had turned and fought the battle to a stalemate. This and the second campaign had been the costliest military expedition ever undertaken. When the Taikō had died last year, Toranaga, on behalf of the Council of Regents, had at once ordered the remnants of their armies home, to the great relief of the vast majority of *daimyos,* who detested the Korean campaign.

Blackthorne walked out to the veranda. He stepped into his thongs and nodded to his servants, who had been assembled in a neat line to bow him off, as was custom.

It was a drab day. The sky was overcast and a warm wet wind came off the sea. The steppingstones that were set into the gravel of the path were wet with the rain that had fallen in the night.

Beyond the gate were the horses and his ten samurai outriders. And Mariko. She was already mounted and wore a pale yellow mantle over pale green silk trousers, a wide-brimmed hat and veil held with yellow ribbons, and gloves. A rain parasol was ready in its saddle-sheath.

"Ohayo," he said formally. *"Ohayo,* Mariko-san."

"Ohayo, Anjin-san. *Ikaga desu ka?"*

"Okagesama de genki desu. Anata wa?"

She smiled. *"Yoi, arigato goziemashita."*

She gave not the faintest hint that anything was different between them. But he expected none, not in public, knowing how dangerous the situation was. Her perfume came over him and he would have liked to kiss her here, in front of everyone.

"Ikimasho!" he said and swung into the saddle, motioning the samurai to ride off ahead. He walked his horse leisurely and Mariko fell into place beside him. When they were alone, he relaxed.

"Mariko."

"Hai?"

Then he said in Latin, "Thou art beautiful and I love thee."

"I thank thee, but so much wine last night makes my head to feel not beautiful today, not in truth, and love is a Christian word."

"Thou art beautiful and Christian, and wine could not touch thee."

"Thank thee for the lie, Anjin-san, yes, thank thee."

"No. I should thank thee."

"Oh? Why?"

"Never 'why,' no 'why.' I thank thee sincerely."

"If wine and meat make thee so warm and fine and gallant," she said, "then I must tell thy consort to move the heaven and the earth to obtain them for thee every evening."

"Yes. I would have everything the same, always."

"Thou art untoward happy today," she said. "Good, very good. But why? Why truly?"

"Because of thee. Thou knowest why."

"I know nothing, Anjin-san."

"Nothing?" he teased.

"Nothing."

He was taken aback. They were quite alone, and safe.

"Why doth 'nothing' take the heart out of thy smile?" she asked.

"Stupidity! Absolute stupidity! I forgot that it is most wise to be cautious. It was only that we were alone and I wanted to speak of it. And, in truth, to say more."

"Thou speakest in riddles. I do not understand thee."

He was nonplussed again. "Thou dost not wish to talk about it? At all?"

"About what, Anjin-san?"

"What passed in the night then?"

"I passed thy door in the night when my maid, Koi, was with thee."

"What!"

"We, your consort and I, we thought she would be a pleasing gift for thee. She pleased thee, did she not?"

Blackthorne was trying to recover. Mariko's maid was her size but younger and never so fair and never so pretty, and yes, it was pitch dark and yes, his head was fogged with wine but no, it was not the maid.

"That's not possible," he said in Portuguese.

"What's not possible, senhor?" she asked in the same language.

He reverted to Latin again, as the outriders were not far away, the wind blowing in their direction. "Please do not joke with me. No one can hear. I know a presence and a perfume."

"Thou thinkest it was me? Oh, it was not, Anjin-san. I would be honored but I could never possibly . . . however much I might want—oh no, Anjin-san. It was not me but Koi, my maid. I would be honored, but I belong to another even though he's dead."

"Yes, but it wasn't your maid." He bit back his anger. "But leave it as thou desirest."

"It was my maid, Anjin-san," she said placatingly. "We anointed her with my perfume and instructed her: no words, only touch. We never thought for a moment thou wouldst consider her to be me! This was not to trick thee but for thine ease, knowing that discussing things of the pillow still embarrasses thee." She was looking at him with wide, innocent eyes. "She pleasured thee, Anjin-san? Thou pleasured her."

"A joke concerning things of great importance is sometimes without humor."

"Things of great import will always be treated with great import. But a maid in the night with a man is without import."

"I do not consider thee without import."

"I thank thee. I say that equally. But a maid in the night with a man is private and without import. It is a gift from her to him and, sometimes, from him to her. Nothing more."

"Never?"

"Sometimes. But this private pillow matter does not have this vast seriousness of thine."

"Never?"

"Only when the woman and man join together against the law. In *this* land."

He reined in, finally comprehending the reason for her denial. "I apologize," he said. "Yes, thou art right and I most very wrong. I should never have spoken. I apologize."

"Why apologize? For what? Tell me, Anjin-san, was this girl wearing a crucifix?"

"No." .

"I always wear it. Always."

"A crucifix can be taken off," he said automatically in Portuguese. "That proves nothing. It could be loaned, like a perfume."

"Tell me a last truth: Did you really see the girl? Really *see* her?"

"Of course. Please let us forget I ever—"

"The night was very dark, the moon overcast. Please, the truth, Anjin-san. Think! Did you really see the girl?"

Of course I saw her, he thought indignantly.

God damn it, think truly. You didn't *see* her. Your head *was* fogged. She could have been the maid but you knew it was Mariko because you wanted Mariko and saw only Mariko in your head, believing that Mariko would want you equally. You're a fool. A God damned fool.

"In truth, no. In truth I should really apologize," he said. "How do I apologize?"

"There's no need to apologize, Anjin-san," she replied calmly. "I've told you many times a man never apologizes, even when he's wrong. You were not wrong." Her eyes teased him now. "My maid needs no apology."

"Thank you," he said, laughing. "You make me feel less of a fool."

"The years flee from you when you laugh. The so-serious Anjin-san becomes a boy again."

"My father told me I was born old."

"Were you?"

"He thought so."

"What's he like?"

"He was a fine man. A shipowner, a captain. The Spanish killed him at a place called Antwerp when they put that city to the sword. They burned his ship. I was six, but I remember him as a big, tall, good-natured man with golden hair. My older brother, Arthur, he was just eight. . . . We had bad times then, Mariko-san."

"Why? Please tell me. Please!"

"It's all very ordinary. Every penny of money was tied into the ship and that was lost . . . and, well, not long after that, my sister died. She starved to death really. There was famine in '71 and plague again."

"We have plague sometimes. The smallpox. You were many in your family?"

"Three of us," he said, glad to talk to take away the other hurt. "Willia, my sister, she was nine when she died. Arthur, he was next—he wanted to be an artist, a sculptor, but he had to become an apprentice stonemason to help support us. He was killed in the Armada. He was twenty-five, poor fool, he just joined a ship, untrained, such a waste. I'm the last of the Blackthornes. Arthur's wife and daughter live with my wife and kids now. My mother's still alive and so's old Granny Jacoba—she's seventy-five and hard as a piece of English oak though she was Irish. At least they were alive when I left more than two years ago."

The ache was coming back. I'll think about them when I start for home, he promised himself, but not until then.

"There'll be a storm tomorrow," he said, watching the sea. "A strong one, Mariko-san. Then in three days we'll have fair weather."

"This is the season of squalls. Mostly it's overcast and rain-filled. When the rains stop it becomes very humid. Then begin the *tai-funs.*"

I wish I were at sea again, he was thinking. Was I ever at sea? Was the ship real? What's reality? Mariko or the maid?

"You don't laugh very much, do you, Anjin-san?"

"I've been seafaring too long. Seamen're always serious. We've learned to watch the sea. We're always watching and waiting for disaster. Take your eyes off the sea for a second and she'll grasp your ship and make her matchwood."

"I'm afraid of the sea," she said.

"So am I. An old fisherman told me once, 'The man who's not afraid of the sea'll soon be drownded for he'll go out on a day he shouldn't. But we be afraid of the sea so we be only drownded now and again.' " He looked at her. "Mariko-San . . ."

"Yes?"

"A few minutes ago you'd convinced me that—well, let's say I was convinced. Now I'm not. What's the truth? The *honto.* I must know."

"Ears are to hear with. Of course it was the maid."

"This maid. Can I ask for her whenever I want?"

"Of course. A wise man would not."

"Because I might be disappointed? Next time?"

"Possibly."

"I find it difficult to possess a maid and lose a maid, difficult to say nothing. . . ."

"Pillowing is a pleasure. Of the body. Nothing has to be said."

"But how do I tell a maid that she is beautiful? That I love her? That she filled me with ecstasy?"

"It isn't seemly to 'love' a maid this way. Not here, Anjin-san. That passion's not even for a wife or a consort." Her eyes crinkled suddenly. "But only toward someone like Kiku-san, the courtesan, who is so beautiful and merits this."

"Where can I find this girl?"

"In the village. It would be my honor to act as your go-between."

"By Christ, I think you mean it."

"Of course. A man needs passions of all kinds. This Lady is worthy of romance—if you can afford her."

"What does that mean?"

"She would be very expensive."

"You don't buy love. That type's worth nothing. 'Love' is without price."

She smiled. "Pillowing always has its price. Always. Not necessarily money, Anjin-san. But a man pays, always, for pillowing in one way, or in another. True love, we call it duty, is of soul to soul and needs no such expression—no physical expression, except perhaps the gift of death."

"You're wrong. I wish I could show you the world as it is."

"I know the world as it is, and as it will be forever. You want this contemptible maid again?"

"Yes. You know I want . . ."

Mariko laughed gaily. "Then she will be sent to you. At sunset. We will escort her, Fujiko and I!"

"Goddamn it—I think you would too!" He laughed with her.

"Ah, Anjin-san, it is good to see you laugh. Since you came back to Anjiro you have gone through a great change. A very great change."

"No. Not so much. But last night I dreamed a dream. That dream was perfection."

"God is perfection. And sometimes so is a sunset or moonrise or the first crocus of the year."

"I don't understand you at all."

She turned back the veil on her hat and looked directly at him. "Once another man said to me, 'I don't understand you at all,' and my husband said, 'Your pardon, Lord, but no man can understand her. Her father doesn't understand her, neither do the gods, nor her barbarian God, not even her mother understands her.' "

"That was Toranaga? Lord Toranaga?"

"Oh, no, Anjin-san. That was the Taikō. Lord Toranaga understands me. He understands everything."

"Even me?"

"Very much you."

"You're sure of that, aren't you?"

"Yes. Oh, very yes."

"Will he win the war?"

"Yes."

"I'm his favored vassal?"

"Yes."

"Will he take my navy?"

"Yes."

"When will I get my ship back?"

"You won't."

"Why?"

Her gravity vanished. "Because you'll have your 'maid' in Anjiro and you'll be pillowing so much you'll have no energy to leave, even on your hands and knees, when she begs you to go aboard your ship, and when Lord Toranaga asks you to go aboard and to leave us all!"

"There you go again! One moment so serious, the next not!"

"That's only to answer you, Anjin-san, and to put certain things in a correct place. Ah, but before you leave us you should see the Lady Kiku. She's worthy of a great passion. She's so beautiful and talented. For her you would have to be extraordinary!"

"I'm tempted to accept that challenge."

"I challenge no one. But if you're prepared to be samurai and not—not foreigner—if you're prepared to treat pillowing for what it is, then I would be honored to act as go-between."

"What does that mean?"

"When you're in good humor, when you're ready for very special amusement, ask your consort to ask me."

"Why Fujiko-san?"

"Because it's your consort's duty to see that you are pleasured. It is our custom to make life simple. We admire simplicity, so *men* and *women* can take pillowing for what it is: an important part of life, certainly, but between a man and a woman there are more vital things. Humility, for one. Respect. Duty. Even this 'love' of yours. Fujiko 'loves' you."

"No she doesn't!"

"She will give you her life. What more is there to give?"

At length he took his eyes off her and looked at the sea. The waves were cresting the shore as the wind freshened. He turned back to her. "Then nothing is to be said?" he asked. "Between us?"

"Nothing. That is wise."

"And if I don't agree?"

"You must agree. You are here. This is your home."

The attacking five hundred galloped over the lip of the hill in a haphazard pack, down onto the rock-strewn valley floor where the two thousand "defenders" were drawn up in a battle array. Each rider wore a musket slung on his back and a belt with pouches for bullets, flints, and a powder horn. Like most samurai, their clothes were a motley collection of kimonos and rags, but their weapons always the best that each could afford. Only Toranaga and Ishido, copying him, insisted that their troops be uniformed and punctilious in their dress. All other *daimyos* considered such outward extravagance a foolish squandering of money, an unnecessary innovation. Even Blackthorne had agreed. The armies of Europe were never uniformed—what king could afford that, except for a personal guard?

He was standing on a rise with Yabu and his aides, Jozen and all his men, and Mariko. This was the first full-scale rehearsal of an attack. He waited uneasily. Yabu was uncommonly tense, and Omi and Naga both had been touchy almost to the point of belligerence. Particularly Naga.

"What's the matter with everyone?" he had asked Mariko.

"Perhaps they wish to do well in front of their lord and his guest."

"Is he a *daimyo* too?"

"No. But important, one of Lord Ishido's generals. It would be good if everything were perfect today."

"I wish I'd been told there was to be a rehearsal."

"What would that have accomplished? Everything you could do, you have done."

Yes, Blackthorne thought, as he watched the five hundred. But they're nowhere near ready yet. Surely Yabu knows that too, everyone does. So if there is a disaster, well, that's *karma,* he told himself with more confidence, and found consolation in that thought.

The attackers gathered speed and the defenders stood waiting under the banners of their captains, jeering at the "enemy" as they would normally do, strung out in loose formation, three or four men deep. Soon the attackers would dismount out of arrow range. Then the most valiant warriors on both sides would truculently strut to the fore to throw down the gauntlet, proclaiming their own lineage and superiority with the most obvious of insults. Single armed conflicts would begin, gradually increasing in numbers, until one commander would order a general attack and then it was every man for himself. Usually the greater number defeated the smaller, then the reserves would be brought up and committed, and again the melee until the morale of one side broke, and the few cowards that retreated would soon be joined by the many and a rout would ensue. Treachery was not unusual. Sometimes whole regiments, following their master's orders, would switch sides, to be welcomed as allies—always welcomed but never trusted. Sometimes the defeated commanders would flee to regroup to fight again. Sometimes they would stay and fight to the death, sometimes they would commit seppuku with ceremony. Rarely were they captured. Some offered their services to the victors. Sometimes this was accepted but most times refused. Death was the lot of the vanquished, quick for the brave and shame-filled for the cowardly. And this was the historic pattern of all skirmishes in this land, even at great battles, soldiers here the same as everywhere, except that here they were more ferocious and many, many more were prepared to die for their masters than anywhere else on earth.

The thunder of the hoofs echoed in the valley.

"Where's the attack commander? Where's Omi-san?" Jozen asked.

"Among the men, be patient," Yabu replied.

"But where's his standard? And why isn't he wearing battle armor and plumes? Where's the commander's standard? They're just like a bunch of filthy no-good bandits!"

"Be patient! All officers are ordered to remain nondescript. I told you. And please don't forget we're pretending a battle is raging, that this is part of a big battle, with reserves and arm—"

Jozen burst out, "Where are their swords? None of them are wearing swords! Samurai without swords? They'd be massacred!"

"Be patient!"

Now the attackers were dismounting. The first warriors strode out from the defending ranks to show their valor. An equal number began to measure up against them. Then, suddenly, the ungainly mass of attackers rushed into five tight-disciplined phalanxes, each with four ranks of twenty-five men, three phalanxes ahead and two in reserve, forty paces back. As one, they charged the enemy. In range they shuddered to a stop on command and the front ranks fired an ear-shattering salvo in unison. Screams and men dying. Jozen and his men ducked reflexively, then watched appalled as the front ranks knelt and began to reload and the second ranks fired over them, with the third and fourth ranks following the same pattern. At each salvo more defenders fell, and the valley was filled with shouts and screams and confusion.

"You're killing your own men!" Jozen shouted above the uproar.

"It's blank ammunition, not real. They're all acting, but imagine it's a real attack with real bullets! Watch!"

Now the defenders "recovered" from the initial shock. They regrouped and whirled back to a frontal attack. But by this time the front ranks had reloaded and, on command, fired another salvo from a kneeling position, then the second rank fired standing, immediately kneeling to reload, then the third and the fourth, as before, and though many musketeers were slow and the ranks ragged, it was easy to imagine the awful decimation trained men would cause. The counterattack faltered, then broke apart, and the defenders retreated in pretended confusion, back up the rise to stop just below the observers. Many "dead" littered the ground.

Jozen and his men were shaken. "Those guns would break any line!"

"Wait. The battle's not over!"

Again the defenders re-formed and now their commanders exhorted them to victory, committed the reserves, and ordered the final general attack. The samurai rushed down the hill, emitting their terrible battle cries, to fall on the enemy.

"Now they'll be stamped into the ground," Jozen said, caught up like all of them in the realism of this mock battle.

And he was right. The phalanxes did not hold their ground. They broke and fled before the battle cries of the true samurai with their swords and spears, and Jozen and his men added their shouts of scorn as the regiments hurtled to the kill. The musketeers were fleeing like the Garlic Eaters, a hundred paces, two hundred paces, three hundred, then suddenly, on command, the phalanxes regrouped, this time in a V formation. Again the shattering salvos began. The attack faltered. Then stopped. But the guns continued. Then they, too, stopped. The game ceased. But all on the rise knew that under actual conditions the two thousand would have been slaughtered.

Now, in the silence, defenders and attackers began to sort themselves out. The "bodies" got up, weapons were collected. There was laughter and groaning. Many men limped and a few were badly hurt.

"I congratulate you, Yabu-sama," Jozen said with great sincerity. "Now I understand what all of you meant."

"The firing was ragged," Yabu said, inwardly delighted. "It will take months to train them."

Jozen shook his head. "I wouldn't like to attack them now. Not if they had real ammunition. No army could withstand that punch—no line. The ranks could never stay closed. And then you'd pour ordinary troops and cavalry through the gap and roll up the sides like an old scroll." He thanked all *kami* that he'd had the sense to see one attack. "It was terrible to watch. For a moment I thought the battle was real."

"They were ordered to make it look real. And now you may review my musketeers, if you wish."

"Thank you. That would be an honor."

The defenders were streaming off to their camps that sat on the far hillside. The five hundred musketeers waited below, near the path that went over the rise and slid down to the village. They were forming into their companies, Omi and Naga in front of them, both wearing swords again.

"Yabu-sama?"

"Yes, Anjin-san?"

"Good, no?"

"Yes, good."

"Thank you, Yabu-sama. I please."

Mariko corrected him automatically. "I am pleased."

"Ah, so sorry. I am pleased."

Jozen took Yabu aside. "This is all out of the Anjin-san's head?"

"No," Yabu lied. "But it's the way barbarians fight. He's just training the men to load and to fire."

"Why not do as Naga-san advised? You've the barbarian's knowledge now. Why risk its spreading? He is a plague. Very dangerous, Yabu-sama. Naga-san was right. It's true—peasants *could* fight this way. Easily. Get rid of the barbarian now."

"If Lord Ishido wants his head, he has only to ask."

"I ask it. Now." Again the truculence. "I speak with his voice."

"I'll consider it, Jozen-san."

"And also, in his name, I *ask* that all guns be withdrawn from those troops at once."

Yabu frowned, then turned his attention to the companies. They were approaching up the hill, their straight, disciplined ranks faintly ludicrous as always, only because such order was unusual. Fifty paces away they halted. Omi and Naga came on alone and saluted.

"It was all right for a first exercise," Yabu said.

"Thank you, Sire," Omi replied. He was limping slightly and his face was dirty, bruised, and powder marked.

Jozen said, "Your troops would have to carry swords in a real battle, Yabu-sama, *neh?* A samurai must carry swords—eventually they'd run out of ammunition, *neh?*"

"Swords will be in their way, in charge and retreat. Oh, they'll wear them as usual to maintain surprise, but just before the first charge they'll get rid of them."

"Samurai will always need swords. In a real battle. Even so, I'm glad you'll never have to use this attack force, or—" Jozen was going to add, "or this filthy, treacherous method of war." Instead he said, "Or we'll all have to give our swords away."

"Perhaps we will, Jozen-san, when we go to war."

"You'd give up your Murasama blade? Or even Toranaga's gift?"

"To win a battle, yes. Otherwise no."

"Then you might have to run very fast to save your fruit when your musket jammed or your powder got wet." Jozen laughed at his own sally. Yabu did not.

"Omi-san! Show him!" he ordered.

At once Omi gave an order. His men slipped out the short sheathed bayonet sword that hung almost unnoticed from the back of their belts and snapped it into a socket on the muzzle of their muskets.

"Charge!"

Instantly the samurai charged with their battle cry, *"Kasigiiiiiii!"*

The forest of naked steel stopped a pace away from them. Jozen and his men were laughing nervously from the sudden, unexpected ferocity. "Good, very good," Jozen said. He reached out and touched one of the bayonets. It was extremely sharp. "Perhaps you're right, Yabu-sama. Let's hope it's never put to the test."

"Omi-san!" Yabu called. "Form them up. Jozen-san's going to review them. Then go back to camp. Mariko-san, Anjin-san, you follow me!" He strode down the rise through the ranks, his aides, Blackthorne, and Mariko following.

"Form up at the path. Replace bayonets!"

Half the men obeyed at once, turned about, and walked down the slope again. Naga and his two hundred and fifty samurai remained where they were, bayonets still threatening.

Jozen bristled. "What's going on?"

"I consider your insults intolerable," Naga said venomously.

"That's nonsense. I haven't insulted you, or anyone! Your bayonets insult my position! Yabu-sama!"

Yabu turned back. Now he was on the other side of the Toranaga contingent. "Naga-san," he called out coldly. "What's the meaning of this?"

"I cannot forgive this man's insults to my father—or to me."

"He's protected. You cannot touch him now! He's under the cipher of the Regents!"

"Your pardon, Yabu-sama, but this is between Jozen-san and myself."

"No. You are under my orders. I order you to tell your men to return to camp."

Not a man moved. The rain began.

"Your pardon, Yabu-san, please forgive me, but this is between him and me and whatever happens I absolve you of responsibility for my action and those of my men."

Behind Naga, one of Jozen's men drew his sword and lunged for Naga's unprotected back. A volley of twenty muskets blew off his head at once. These twenty men knelt and began to reload. The second rank readied.

"Who ordered live ammunition?" Yabu demanded.

"I did. I, Yoshi Naga-noh-Toranaga!"

"Naga-san! I order you to let Nebara Jozen and his men go free. You are ordered to your quarters until I can consult Lord Toranaga about your insubordination!"

"Of course you will inform Lord Toranaga and *karma* is *karma*. But I regret, Lord Yabu, that first this man must die. All of them must die. Today!"

Jozen shrieked, "I'm protected by the Regents! You'll gain nothing by killing me."

"I regain my honor, *neh?*" Naga said. "I repay your sneers at my father and your insults to me. But you would have had to die anyway. *Neh?* I could not have been more clear last night. Now you've seen an attack. I cannot risk Ishido learning all this"—his hand waved at the battlefield—"this horror!"

"He already knows!" Jozen blurted out, blessing his foresight of the previous evening. "He knows already! I sent a message by pigeon secretly at dawn! You gain nothing by killing me, Naga-san!"

Naga motioned to one of his men, an old samurai, who came forward and threw the strangled pigeon at Jozen's feet. Then a man's severed head was also cast upon the ground—the head of the samurai, Masumoto, sent yesterday by Jozen with the scroll. The eyes were still open, the lips drawn back in a hate-filled grimace. The head began to roll. It tumbled through the ranks until it came to rest against a rock.

A moan broke from Jozen's lips. Naga and all his men laughed. Even Yabu smiled. Another of Jozen's samurai leaped for Naga. Twenty muskets blasted him, and the man next to him, who had not moved, also fell in agony, mortally wounded.

The laughter ceased.

Omi said, "Shall I order my men to attack, Sire?" It had been so easy to maneuver Naga.

Yabu wiped the rain off his face. "No, that would achieve nothing. Jozen-san and his men are already dead, whatever I do. That's his *karma,* as Naga-san has his. Naga-san!" he called out. "For the last time, I order you to let them all go!"

"Please excuse me but I must refuse."

"Very well. When it is finished, report to me."

"Yes. There should be an official witness, Yabu-sama. For Lord Toranaga and for Lord Ishido."

"Omi-san, you will stay. You will sign the death certification and make out the dispatch. Naga-san and I will countersign it."

Naga pointed at Blackthorne. "Let him stay too. Also as witness. He's responsible for their deaths. He should witness them."

"Anjin-san, go up there! To Naga-san! Do you understand?"

"Yes, Yabu-san. I understand, but why, please?"

"To be a witness."

"Sorry, don't understand."

"Mariko-san, explain 'witness' to him, that he's to witness what's going to happen—then you follow me." Hiding his vast satisfaction, Yabu turned and left.

Jozen shrieked, "Yabu-sama! Please! Yabuuuuu-samaaaa!"

Blackthorne watched. When it was finished he went home. There was silence in his house and a pall over the village. A bath did not make him feel clean. Saké did not take away the foulness from his mouth. Incense did not unclog the stench from his nostrils.

Later Yabu sent for him. The attack was dissected, moment by moment. Omi and Naga were there with Mariko—Naga as always cold, listening, rarely commenting, still second-in-command. None of them seemed touched by what had happened.

They worked till after sunset. Yabu ordered the tempo of training stepped up. A second five hundred was to be formed at once. In one week another.

Blackthorne walked home alone, and ate alone, beset by his ghastly discovery: *that they had no sense of sin, they were all conscienceless—even Mariko.*

That night he couldn't sleep. He left the house, the wind tugging at him. Gusts were frothing the waves. A stronger squall sent debris clattering against a village hovel. Dogs howled at the sky and foraged. The rice-thatched roofs moved like living things. Shutters were banging and men and women, silent wraiths, fought them closed and barred them. The tide came in heavily. All the fishing boats had been hauled to safety much farther up the beach than usual. Everything was battened down.

He walked the shore then returned to his house, leaning against the press of the wind. He had met no one. Rain squalled and he was soon drenched.

Fujiko waited for him on the veranda, the wind ripping at her, guttering the shielded oil lamp. Everyone was awake. Servants carried valuables to the squat adobe and stone storage building in the back of the garden.

The gale was not menacing yet.

A roof tile twisted loose as the wind squeezed under an eave and the whole roof shuddered. The tile fell and shattered loudly. Servants hurried about, some readying buckets of water, others trying to repair the roof. The old gardener, Ueki-ya, helped by children, was lashing the tender bushes and trees to bamboo stakes.

Another gust rocked the house.

"It's going to blow down, Mariko-san."

She said nothing, the wind clawing at her and Fujiko, wind tears in the corners of their eyes. He looked at the village. Now debris was blowing everywhere. Then the wind poured through a rip in the paper shoji of one dwelling and the whole wall vanished, leaving only a latticed skeleton. The opposite wall crumbled and the roof collapsed.

Blackthorne turned helplessly as the shoji of his room blew out. That wall vanished and so did the opposite one. Soon all the walls were in shreds. He could see throughout the house. But the roof supports held and the tiled roof did not shift. Bedding and lanterns and mats skittered away, servants chasing them.

The storm demolished the walls of all the houses in the village. And some dwellings were obliterated completely. No one was badly hurt. At dawn the wind subsided and men and women began to rebuild their homes.

By noon the walls of Blackthorne's house were remade and half the village was back to normal. The light lattice walls required little work to put up once more, only wooden pegs and lashings for joints that were always morticed and carpentered with great skill. Tiled and thatched roofs were more difficult but he saw that people helped each other, smiling and quick and very practiced. Mura hurried through the village, advising, guiding, chivying, and supervising. He came up the hill to inspect progress.

"Mura, you made . . ." Blackthorne sought the words. "You make it look easy."

"Ah, thank you, Anjin-san. Yes, thank you, but we were fortunate there were no fires."

"You fires oftens?"

"So sorry, 'Do you have fires often?' "

"Do you have fires often?" Blackthorne repeated.

"Yes. But I'd ordered the village prepared. *Prepared,* you understand?"

"Yes."

"When these storms come—" Mura stiffened and glanced over Blackthorne's shoulder. His bow was low.

Omi was approaching in his bouncing easy stride, his friendly eyes only on Blackthorne, as though Mura did not exist. "Morning, Anjin-san," he said.

"Morning, Omi-san. Your house is good?"

"All right. Thank you." Omi looked at Mura and said brusquely, "The men should be fishing, or working the fields. The women too. Yabu-sama wants his taxes. Are you trying to shame me in front of him with laziness?"

"No, Omi-sama. Please excuse me. I will see to it at once."

"It shouldn't be necessary to tell you. I won't tell you next time."

"I apologize for my stupidity." Mura hurried away.

"You're all right today," Omi said to Blackthorne. "No troubles in the night?"

"Good today, thank you. And you?"

Omi spoke at length. Blackthorne did not catch all of it, as he had not understood all of what Omi had said to Mura, only a few words here, a few there.

"So sorry. I don't understand."

"Enjoy? How did you like yesterday? The attack? The 'pretend' battle?"

"Ah, I understand. Yes, I think good."

"And the witnessing?"

"Please?"

"Witnessing! The *ronin* Nebara Jozen and his men?" Omi imitated the bayonet lunge with a laugh. "You witnessed their deaths. Deaths! You understand?"

"Ah, yes. The truth, Omi-san, not like killings."

"*Karma,* Anjin-san."

"*Karma.* Today trainings?"

"Yes. But Yabu-sama wants to talk only. Later. Understand, Anjin-san? Talk only, later," Omi repeatedly patiently.

"Talk only. Understand."

"You're beginning to speak our language very well. Yes. Very well."

"Thank you. Difficult. Small time."

"Yes. But you're a good man and you try very hard. That's important. We'll get you time, Anjin-san, don't worry—I'll help you." Omi could see that most of what he was saying was lost, but he didn't mind, so long as the Anjin-san got the gist. "I want to be your friend," he said, then repeated it very clearly. "Do you understand?"

"Friend? I understand 'friend.' "

Omi pointed at himself then at Blackthorne. "I want to be your friend."

"Ah! Thank you. Honored."

Omi smiled again and bowed, equal to equal, and walked away.

"Friends with him?" Blackthorne muttered. "Has he forgotten? I haven't."

"Ah, Anjin-san," Fujiko said, hurrying up to him. "Would you like to eat? Yabu-sama is going to send for you soon."

"Yes, thank you. Many breakings?" he asked, pointing at the house.

"Excuse me, so sorry, but you should say, 'Was there much breakage?' "

"Was there much breakage?"

"No real damage, Anjin-san."

"Good. No hurtings?"

"Excuse me, so sorry, you should say, 'No one was hurt?' "

"Thank you. No one was hurt?"

"No, Anjin-san. No one was hurt."

Suddenly Blackthorne was sick of being continually corrected, so he terminated the conversation with an order. "I'm hunger. Food!"

"Yes, immediately. So sorry, but you should say, 'I'm *hungry.*' A person has hunger, but is hungry." She waited until he had said it correctly, then went away.

He sat on the veranda and watched Ueki-ya, the old gardener, tidying up the damage and the scattered leaves. He could see women and children repairing the village, and boats going to sea through the chop. Other villagers trudged off to the fields, the wind abating now. I wonder what taxes they have to pay, he asked himself. I'd hate to be a peasant here. Not only here—anywhere.

At first light he had been distressed by the apparent devastation of the village. "That storm'd hardly touch an English house," he had said to Mariko. "Oh, it was a gale all right, but not a bad one. Why don't you build out of stone or bricks?"

"Because of the earthquakes, Anjin-san. Any stone building would, of course, split and collapse and probably hurt or kill the inhabitants. With our style of building there's little damage. You'll see how quickly everything's put back together."

"Yes, but you've fire hazards. And what happens when the Great Winds come? The *tai-funs?*"

"It is very bad then."

She had explained about the *tai-funs* and their seasons—from June until September, sometimes earlier, sometimes later. And about the other natural catastrophes.

A few days ago there had been another tremor. It was slight. A kettle had fallen off the brazier and overturned it. Fortunately the coals had been smothered. One house in the village had caught fire but the fire did not spread. Blackthorne had never seen such efficient fire fighting. Apart from that, no one in the village had paid much attention. They had merely laughed and gone on with their lives.

"Why do people laugh?"

"We consider it very shameful and impolite to show strong feelings, particularly fear, so we hide them with a laugh or a smile. Of course we're all afraid, though we must never show it."

Some of you show it, Blackthorne thought.

Nebara Jozen had shown it. He had died badly, weeping with fear, begging for mercy, the killing slow and cruel. He had been allowed to run, then bayoneted carefully amidst laughter, then forced to run again, and hamstrung. Then he had been allowed to crawl away, then gutted slowly while he screamed, his blood dribbling with the phlegm, then left to die.

Next Naga had turned his attention to the other samurai. At once three of Jozen's men knelt and bared their bellies and put their short knives in front of them to commit ritual seppuku. Three of their comrades stood behind them as their seconds, long swords out and raised, two-handed, all of them now unmolested by Naga and his men. As the samurai who knelt reached out for their knives, they stretched their necks and the three swords flashed down and decapitated them with the single blow. Teeth chattered in the fallen heads, then were still. Flies swarmed.

Then two samurai knelt, the last man standing ready as second. The first of those kneeling was decapitated in the manner of his comrades as he reached for the knife. The other said, "No. I, Hirasaki Kenko, I know how to die—how a samurai should die."

Kenko was a lithe young man, perfumed and almost pretty, pale-skinned, his hair well oiled and very neat. He picked up his knife reverently and partially wrapped the blade with his sash to improve his grip.

"I protest Nebara Jozen-san's death and those of his men," he said firmly, bowing to Naga. He took a last look at the sky and gave his second a last reassuring smile. "*Sayonara,* Tadeo." Then he slid the knife deep into the left side of his stomach. He ripped it full across with both hands and took it out and plunged it deep again, just above his groin, and jerked it up in silence. His lacerated bowels spilled into his lap and as his hideously contorted, agonized face pitched forward, his second brought the sword down in a single slashing arc.

Naga personally picked up this head by the hair knot and wiped off the dirt and closed the eyes. Then he told his men to see that the head was washed, wrapped, and sent to Ishido with full honors, with a complete report on Hirasaki Kenko's bravery.

The last samurai knelt. There was no one left to second him. He too was young. His fingers trembled and fear consumed him. Twice he had done his duty to his comrades, twice cut cleanly, honorably, saving them the trial of pain and the shame of fear. And once he had waited for his dearest friend to die as a samurai should die, self-immolated in pride-filled silence, then again cut cleanly with perfect skill. He had never killed before.

His eyes focused on his own knife. He bared his stomach and prayed for his lover's courage. Tears were gathering but he willed his face into a frozen, smiling mask. He unwound his sash and partially wrapped the blade. Then, because the youth had done his duty well, Naga signaled to his lieutenant.

This samurai came forward and bowed, introducing himself formally. "Osaragi Nampo, Captain of Lord Toranaga's Ninth Legion. I would be honored to act as your second."

"Ikomo Tadeo, First Officer, vassal of Lord Ishido," the youth replied. "Thank you. I would be honored to accept you as my second."

His death was quick, painless, and honorable.

The heads were collected. Later Jozen shrieked into life again. His frantic hands tried helplessly to remake his belly.

They left him to the dogs that had come up from the village.

CHAPTER 34

AT the Hour of the Horse, eleven o'clock in the morning, ten days after the death of Jozen and all his men, a convoy of three galleys rounded the headland at Anjiro. They were crammed with troops. Toranaga came ashore. Beside him was Buntaro.

"First I wish to see an attack exercise, Yabu-san, with the original five hundred," Toranaga said. "At once."

"Could it be tomorrow? That would give me time to prepare," Yabu said affably, but inwardly he was furious at the suddenness of Toranaga's arrival and incensed with his spies for not forewarning him. He had had barely enough time to hurry to the shore with a guard of honor. "You must be tired—"

"I'm not tired, thank you," Toranaga said, intentionally brusque. "I don't need 'defenders' or an elaborate setting or screams or pretended deaths. You forget, old friend, I've acted in enough Nōh plays and staged enough to be able to use my imagination. I'm not a *ronin*-peasant! Please order it mounted at once."

They were on the beach beside the wharf. Toranaga was surrounded by elite guards, and more were pouring off the moored galley. Another thousand heavily armed samurai were crammed into the two galleys that waited just offshore. It was a warm day, the sky cloudless, with a light surf and heat haze on the horizon.

"Igurashi, see to it!" Yabu bottled his rage. Since the first message he had sent concerning Jozen's arrival eleven days ago, there had been the merest trickle of noncommittal reports from Yedo from his own espionage network, and nothing but sporadic and infuriatingly inconclusive replies from Toranaga to his ever more urgent signals: "Your message received and under serious study." "Shocked by your news about my son. Please wait for further instructions." Then, four days ago: "Those responsible for Jozen's death will be punished. They are to remain at their posts but to continue under arrest until I can consult with Lord Ishido." And yesterday, the bombshell: "Today I received the new Council of Regents' formal invitation to the Osaka Flower-Viewing Ceremony. When do you plan to leave? Advise immediately."

"Surely that doesn't mean Toranaga's actually going?" Yabu had asked, baffled.

"He's forcing you to commit yourself," Igurashi had replied. "Whatever you say traps you."

"I agree," Omi had said.

"Why aren't we getting news from Yedo? What's happened to our spies?"

"It's almost as though Toranaga's put a blanket over the whole Kwanto," Omi had told him. "Perhaps he knows who your spies are!"

"Today's the tenth day, Sire," Igurashi had reminded Yabu. "Everything's ready for your departure to Osaka. Do you want to leave or not?"

Now, here on the beach, Yabu blessed his guardian *kami* who had persuaded him to accept Omi's advice to stay until the last possible day, three days hence.

"About your final message, Toranaga-sama, the one that arrived yesterday," he said. "You're surely not going to Osaka?"

"Are you?"

"I acknowledge you as leader. Of course, I've been waiting for your decision."

"My decision is easy, Yabu-sama. But yours is hard. If you go, the Regents will certainly chop you for destroying Jozen and his men. And Ishido is really very angry—and rightly so. *Neh?*"

"I didn't do it, Lord Toranaga. Jozen's destruction—however merited—was against my orders."

"It was just as well Naga-san did it, *neh?* Otherwise you'd certainly have had to do it yourself. I'll discuss Naga-san later, but come along, we'll talk as we walk up to the training ground. No need to waste time." Toranaga set off at his brisk pace, his guards following closely. "Yes, you really are in a dilemma, old friend. If you go, you lose your head, you lose Izu, and of course your whole Kasigi family goes to the execution ground. If you stay, the Council will order the same thing." He looked across at him. "Perhaps you should do what you suggested I do the last time I was in Anjiro. I'll be happy to be your second. Perhaps your head will ease Ishido's ill humor when I meet him."

"My head's of no value to Ishido."

"I don't agree."

Buntaro intercepted them. "Excuse me, Sire. Where do you want the men billeted?"

"On the plateau. Make your permanent camp there. Two hundred guards will stay with me at the fortress. When you've made the arrangements join me. I'll want you to see the training exercise." Buntaro hurried off.

"Permanent camp? You're staying here?" Yabu asked.

"No, only my men. If the attack's as good as I hear, we'll be forming nine assault battalions of five hundred samurai each."

"What?"

"Yes. I've brought another thousand selected samurai for you now. You'll provide the other thousand."

"But there aren't enough guns and the train—"

"So sorry, you're wrong. I've brought a thousand muskets and plenty of powder and shot. The rest will arrive within a week with another thousand men."

"We'll have nine assault battalions?"

"Yes. They'll be one regiment. Buntaro will command."

"Perhaps it would be better if I did that. He'll be—"

"Oh, but you forget the Council meets in a few days. How can you command a regiment if you're going to Osaka? Haven't you prepared to leave?"

Yabu stopped. "We're allies. We agreed you're the leader and we pissed on the bargain. I've kept it, and I'm keeping it. Now I ask, what's your plan? Do we war or don't we?"

"No one's declared war on me. Yet."

Yabu craved to unsheath the Yoshitomo blade and splash Toranaga's blood on the dirt, once and for all, whatever the cost. He could feel the breath of the Toranaga guards all around him but he was beyond caring now. "Isn't the Council your death knell too? You said that yourself. Once they've met, you have to obey. *Neh?*"

"Of course." Toranaga waved his guards back, leaning easily on his sword, his stocky legs wide and firm.

"Then what's your decision? What do you propose?"

"First to see an attack."

"Then?"

"Then to go hunting."

"Are you going to Osaka?"

"Of course."

"When?"

"When it pleases me."

"You mean, *not* when it pleases Ishido."

"I mean when it pleases me."

"We'll be isolated," Yabu said. "We can't fight all Japan, even with an assault regiment, and we can't possibly train it in ten days."

"Yes."

"Then what's the plan?"

"What exactly happened with Jozen and Naga-san?"

Yabu told it truly, omitting only the fact that Naga had been manipulated by Omi.

"And my barbarian? How's the Anjin-san behaving?"

"Good. Very good." Yabu told him about the attempted seppuku on the first night, and how he had neatly bent the Anjin-san to their mutual advantage.

"That was clever," Toranaga said slowly. "I'd never have guessed he'd try seppuku. Interesting."

"It was fortunate I told Omi to be ready."

"Yes."

Impatiently Yabu waited for more but Toranaga remained silent. "This news I sent about Lord Ito becoming a Regent," Yabu said at last. "Did you know about it before I sent word?"

Toranaga did not answer for a moment. "I'd heard rumors. Lord Ito's a perfect choice for Ishido. The poor fool's always enjoyed being shafted while he has his nose up another man's anus. They'll make good bedfellows."

"His vote will destroy you, even so."

"Providing there's a Council."

"Ah, then you do have a plan?"

"I always have a plan—or plans—didn't you know? But you, what's your plan, Ally? If you want to leave, leave. If you want to stay, stay. Choose!" He walked on.

Mariko handed Toranaga a scroll of closely written characters.

"Is this everything?" he asked.

"Yes, Sire," she replied, not liking the stuffiness of the cabin or being aboard the galley again, even moored at the dock. "A lot of what's in the War Manual will be repeated, but I made notes every night and wrote down everything as it happened—or tried to. It's almost like a diary of what was said and happened since you left."

"Good. Has anyone else read it?"

"Not to my knowledge." She used her fan to cool herself. "The Anjin-san's consort and servants have seen me writing it, but I've kept it locked away."

"What are your conclusions?"

Mariko hesitated. She glanced at the cabin door and at the closed porthole.

Toranaga said, "Only my men are aboard and no one's below decks. Except us."

"Yes, Sire. I just remembered the Anjin-san saying there are no secrets aboard a ship. So sorry." She thought a moment, then said confidently, "The Musket Regiment will win one battle. Barbarians could destroy us if they landed in force with guns and cannon. You must have a barbarian navy. Thus far, the Anjin-san's knowledge has been enormously valuable to you, so much so it should be kept secret, only for your ears. In the wrong hands his knowledge would be lethal to you."

"Who shares his knowledge now?"

"Yabu-san knows much but Omi-san more—he's the most intuitive. Igurashi-san, Naga-san, and the troops—the troops of course understand the strategy, not the finer details and none of the Anjin-san's political and general knowledge. Me, more than any. I've written down everything he's said, asked, or commented on, Sire. As best I can. Of course he has only told us about certain things, but his range is vast and his memory near perfect. With patience he can provide you with an accurate picture of the world, its customs and dangers. *If* he's telling the truth."

"Is he?"

"I believe so."

"What's your opinion of Yabu?"

"Yabu-san's a violent man with no scruples whatsoever. He honors nothing but his own interests. Duty, loyalty, tradition, mean nothing to him. His mind has flashes of great cunning, even brilliance. He's equally dangerous as ally or enemy."

"All commendable virtues. What's to be said against him?"

"A bad administrator. His peasants would revolt if they had weapons."

"Why?"

"Extortionate taxes. Illegal taxes. He takes seventy-five parts from every hundred of all rice, fish, and produce. He's begun a head tax, land tax, boat tax—every sale, every barrel of saké, everything's taxed in Izu."

"Perhaps I should employ him or his quartermaster for the Kwanto. Well, what he does here's his own business, his peasants'll never get weapons so we've nothing to worry about. I could still use this as a base if need be."

"But Sire, sixty parts is the legal limit."

"It was the legal limit. The Taikō made it legal but he's dead. What else about Yabu?"

"He eats little, his health appears good, but Suwo, the masseur, thinks he has kidney trouble. He has some curious habits."

"What?"

She told him about the Night of the Screams.

"Who told you about that?"

"Suwo. Also Omi-san's wife and mother."

"Yabu's father used to boil his enemies too. Waste of time. But I can understand his need to do it occasionally. His nephew, Omi?"

"Very shrewd. Very wise. Completely loyal to his uncle. A very capable, impressive vassal."

"Omi's family?"

"His mother is—is suitably firm with Midori, his wife. The wife is samurai, gentle, strong, and very good. All are loyal vassals of Yabu-san. Presently Omi-san has no consorts though Kiku, the most famous courtesan in Izu, is almost like a consort. If he could buy her contract I think he'd bring her into his house."

"Would he help me against Yabu if I wanted him to?"

She pondered that. Then shook her head. "No, Sire. I don't think so. I think he's his uncle's vassal."

"Naga?"

"As good a samurai as a man could be. He saw at once the danger of Jozen-san and his men to you, and locked things up until you could be consulted. As much as he detests the Musket Battalion he trains the companies hard to make them perfect."

"I think he was very stupid—to be Yabu's puppet."

She adjusted a fold in her kimono, saying nothing.

Toranaga fanned himself. "Now the Anjin-san?"

She had been expecting this question and now that it had come, all the clever observations she was going to make vanished from her head.

"Well?"

"You must judge from the scroll, Sire. In certain areas he's impossible to explain. Of course, his training and heritage have nothing in common with ours. He's very complex and beyond our—beyond *my* understanding. He used to be very open. But since his attempted seppuku, he's changed. He's more secretive." She told him what Omi had said and had done on that first night. And about Yabu's promise.

"Ah, Omi stopped him—not Yabu-san?"

"Yes."

"And Yabu followed Omi's advice?"

"Exactly, Sire."

"So Omi's the adviser. Interesting. But surely the Anjin-san doesn't expect Yabu to keep the promise?"

"Yes, absolutely."

Toranaga laughed. "How childish!"

"Christian 'conscience' is deeply set in him, so sorry. He cannot avoid his *karma,* one part of which is that he's totally to be governed through this hatred of a death, or deaths, of what he calls 'innocents.' Even Jozen's death affected him deeply. For many nights his sleep was disturbed and for days he hardly talked to anyone."

"Would this 'conscience' apply to all barbarians?"

"No, though it should to all Christian barbarians."

"Will he lose this 'conscience'?"

"I don't think so. But he's as defenseless as a doll until he does."

"His consort?"

She told him everything.

"Good." He was pleased that his choice of Fujiko and his plan had worked so well. "Very good. She did very well over the guns. What about his habits?"

"Mostly normal, except for an astounding embarrassment over pillow matters and a curious reluctance to discuss the most normal functions." She also described his unusual need for solitude, and his abominable taste in food. "In most other things he's attentive, reasonable, sharp, an adept pupil, and very curious about us and our customs. It's all in my report, but briefly, I've explained something of our way of life, a little of us and our history, about the Taikō and the problems besetting our Realm now."

"Ah, about the Heir?"

"Yes, Sire. Was that wrong?"

"No. You were told to educate him. How's his Japanese?"

"Very good, considering. In time he'll speak our language quite well. He's a good pupil, Sire."

"Pillowing?"

"One of the maids," she said at once.

"He chose her?"

"His consort sent her to him."

"And?"

"It was mutually satisfactory, I understand."

"Ah! Then she had no difficulty."

"No, Sire."

"But he's in proportion?"

"The girl said, 'Oh very yes.' 'Lavish' was the word she used."

"Excellent. At least in that his *karma's* good. That's the trouble with a lot of men—Yabu for one, Kiyama for another. Small shafts. Unfortunate to be born with a small shaft. Very. Yes." He glanced at the scroll, then closed his fan with a snap. "And you, Mariko-san? What about you?"

"Good, thank you, Sire. I'm very pleased to see you looking so well. May I offer you congratulations on the birth of your grandson."

"Thank you, yes. Yes, I'm pleased. The boy's well formed and appears healthy."

"And the Lady Genjiko?"

Toranaga grunted. "She's as strong as always. Yes." He pursed his lips, brooding for a moment. "Perhaps you could recommend a foster mother for the child." It was custom for sons of important samurai to have foster mothers so that the natural mother could attend to her husband and to the running of his house, leaving the foster mother to concentrate on the child's upbringing, making him strong and a credit to the parents. "I'm afraid it won't be easy to find the right person. The Lady Genjiko's not the easiest mistress to work for, *neh?*"

"I'm sure you'll find the perfect person, Sire. I'll certainly give it some thought," Mariko replied, knowing that to offer such advice would be foolish, for no woman born could possibly satisfy both Toranaga and his daughter-in-law.

"Thank you. But you, Mariko-san, what about you?"

"Good, Sire, thank you."

"And your Christian conscience?"

"There's no conflict, Sire. None. I've done everything you would wish. Truly."

"Have any priests been here?"

"No, Sire."

"You have need of one?"

"It would be good to confess and take the Sacrament and be blessed. Yes, truthfully, I would like that—to confess the things permitted and to be blessed."

Toranaga studied her closely. Her eyes were guileless. "You've done well, Mariko-san. Please continue as before."

"Yes, Sire, thank you. One thing—the Anjin-san needs a grammar book and dictionary badly."

"I've sent to Tsukku-san for them." He noticed her frown. "You don't think he'll send them?"

"He would obey, of course. Perhaps not with the speed you'd like."

"I'll soon know that." Toranaga added ominously, "He has only thirteen days left."

Mariko was startled. "Sire?" she asked, not understanding.

"Thirteen? Ah," Toranaga said nonchalantly, covering his momentary lapse, "when we were aboard the Portuguese ship he asked permission to visit Yedo. I agreed, providing it was within forty days. There are thirteen left. Wasn't forty days the time this *bonze,* this prophet, this Moses spent on the mountain collecting the commands of 'God' that were etched in stone?"

"Yes, Sire."

"Do you believe that happened?"

"Yes. But I don't understand how or why."

"A waste of time discussing 'God-things.' *Neh?*"

"If you seek facts, yes, Sire."

"While you were waiting for this dictionary, have you tried to make one?"

"Yes, Toranaga-sama. I'm afraid it's not very good. Unfortunately there seems to be so little time, so many problems. Here—everywhere," she added pointedly.

He nodded agreement, knowing that she would dearly like to ask many things:

about the new Council and Lord Ito's appointment and Naga's sentence and if war would be immediate. "We're fortunate to have your husband back with us, *neh?*"

Her fan stopped. "I never thought he'd escape alive. Never. I've said a prayer and burnt incense to his memory daily." Buntaro had told her this morning how another contingent of Toranaga samurai had covered his retreat from the beach and he had made the outskirts of Osaka without trouble. Then, with fifty picked men and spare horses, disguised as bandits, he hastily took to the hills and lesser paths in a headlong dash for Yedo. Twice his pursuers caught up with him but there were not enough of the enemy to contain him and he fought his way through. Once he was ambushed and lost all but four men, and escaped again and went deeper into the forest, traveling by night, sleeping during the day. Berries and spring water, a little rice snatched from lonely farmhouses, then galloping on again, hunters always at his heels. It had taken him twenty days to reach Yedo. Two men had survived with him.

"It was almost a miracle," she said. "I thought I was possessed by a *kami* when I saw him here beside you on the beach."

"He's clever. Very strong and very clever."

"May I ask what news of Lord Hiro-matsu, Sire? And Osaka? Lady Kiritsubo and the Lady Sazuko?"

Noncommittal, Toranaga informed her that Hiro-matsu had arrived back at Yedo the day before he had left, though his ladies had decided to stay at Osaka, the Lady Sazuko's health being the reason for their delay. There was no need to elaborate. Both he and Mariko knew that this was merely a face-saving formula and that General Ishido would never allow two such valuable hostages to leave now that Toranaga was out of his grasp.

"*Shigata ga nai,*" he said. "*Karma, neh?*" There's nothing that can be done. That's *karma,* isn't it?

"Yes."

He picked up the scroll. "Now I must read this. Thank you, Mariko-san. You've done very well. Please bring the Anjin-san to the fortress at dawn."

"Sire, now that my Master is here, I will have—"

"Your husband has already agreed that while I'm here you're to remain where you are and act as interpreter, your prime duty being to the Anjin-san for the next few days."

"But Sire, I must set up house for my Lord. He'll need servants and a house."

"That will be a waste of money, time, and effort at the moment. He'll stay with the troops—or at the Anjin-san's house—whichever pleases him." He noticed a flash of irritation. "*Nan ja?*"

"My place should be with my Master. To serve him."

"Your place is where I want it to be. *Neh?*"

"Yes, please excuse me. Of course."

"Of course."

She left.

He read the scroll carefully. And the War Manual. Then he reread parts of the scroll. He put them both away safely and posted guards on the cabin and went aloft.

It was dawn. The day promised warmth and overcast. He canceled the meeting with the Anjin-san, as he had intended, and rode to the plateau with a hundred guards. There he collected his falconers and three hawks and hunted for twenty *ri.* By noon he had bagged three pheasants, two large woodcock, a hare, and a brace of quail. He sent one pheasant and the hare to the Anjin-san, the rest to the fortress. Some of his samurai were not Buddhists and he was tolerant of their eating habits. For himself he ate a little cold rice with fish paste, some pickled seaweed with slivers of ginger. Then he curled up on the ground and slept.

Now it was late afternoon and Blackthorne was in the kitchen, whistling merrily. Around him were the chief cook, assistant cook, the vegetable preparer, fish preparer, and their assistants, all smiling but inwardly mortified because their master was here in their kitchen with their mistress, also because she had told them he was going to honor them by showing them how to prepare and cook in his style. And last because of the hare.

He had already hung the pheasant under the eaves of an outhouse with careful instructions that no one, *no one* was to touch it but him. "Do they understand, Fujiko-san? No touching but me?" he asked with mock gravity.

"Oh, yes, Anjin-san. They all understand. So sorry, excuse me, but you should say 'No one's to touch it except me.' "

"Now," he was saying to no one in particular, "the gentle art of cooking. Lesson One."

"*Dozo gomen nasai?*" Fujiko asked.

"*Miru!*" Watch.

Feeling young again—for one of his first chores had been to clean the game he and his brother poached at such huge risk from the estates around Chatham—he selected a long, curving knife. The *sushi* chef blanched. This was his favorite knife, with an especially honed edge to ensure that the slivers of raw fish were always sliced to perfection. All the staff knew this and they sucked in their breaths, smiling even more to hide their embarrassment for him, as he increased the size of his smile to hide his own shame.

Blackthorne slit the hare's belly and neatly turned out the stomach sac and entrails. One of the younger maids heaved and fled silently. Fujiko resolved to fine her a month's wages, wishing at the same time that she too could be a peasant and so flee with honor.

They watched, glazed, as he cut off the paws and feet, then pushed the forelegs back into the pelt, easing the skin off the legs. He did the same with the back legs and worked the pelt around to bring the naked back legs out through the belly slit, and then, with a deft jerk, he pulled the pelt over the head like a discarded winter coat. He lay the almost skinned animal on the chopping table and decapitated it, leaving the head with its staring, pathetic eyes still attached to the pelt. He turned the pelt right side out again, and put it aside. A sigh went through the kitchen. He did not hear it as he concentrated on slicing off the legs into joints and quartering the carcass. Another maid fled unnoticed.

"Now I want a pot," Blackthorne said with a hearty grin.

No one answered him. They just stared with the same fixed smiles. He saw a large iron cauldron. It was spotless. He picked it up with bloody hands and filled it with water from a wooden container, then hung the pot over the brazier, which was set into the earthen floor in a pit surrounded by stone. He added the pieces of meat.

"Now some vegetables and spices," he said.

"*Dozo?*" Fujiko asked throatily.

He did not know the Japanese words so he looked around. There were some carrots, and some roots that looked like turnips in a wooden basket. These he cleaned and cut up and added to the soup with salt and some of the dark soya sauce.

"We should have some onions and garlic and port wine."

"*Dozo?*" Fujiko asked again helplessly.

"*Kotaba shirimasen.* " I don't know the words.

She did not correct him, just picked up a spoon and offered it. He shook his head. "Saké," he ordered. The assistant cook jerked into life and gave him the small wooden barrel.

"*Domo.* " Blackthorne poured in a cupful, then added another for good measure. He would have drunk some from the barrel but he knew that it would be bad manners, to drink it cold and without ceremony, and certainly not here in the kitchen.

"Christ Jesus, I'd love a beer," he said.

"*Dozo goziemashita,* Anjin-san?"

"*Kotaba shirimasen*—but this stew's going to be great. *Ichi-ban, neh?*" He pointed at the hissing pot.

"*Hai,*" she said without conviction.

"*Okuru tsukai arigato* Toranaga-sama," Blackthorne said. Send a messenger to thank Lord Toranaga. No one corrected the bad Japanese.

"*Hai.*" Once outside Fujiko rushed for the privy, the little hut that stood in solitary splendor near the front door in the garden. She was very sick.

"Are you all right, Mistress?" her maid, Nigatsu, said. She was middle-aged, roly-poly, and had looked after Fujiko all her life.

"Go away! But first bring me some cha. No—you'll have to go into the kitchen . . . oh oh oh!"

"I have cha here, Mistress. We thought you'd need some so we boiled the water on another brazier. Here!"

"Oh, you're so clever!" Fujiko pinched Nigatsu's round cheek affectionately as another maid came to fan her. She wiped her mouth on the paper towel and sat gratefully on cushions on the veranda. "Oh, that's better!" And it was better in the open air, in the shade, the good afternoon sun casting dark shadows and butterflies foraging, the sea far below, calm and iridescent.

"What's going on, Mistress? We didn't dare even to peek."

"Never mind. The Master's—the Master's—never mind. His customs are weird but that's our *karma.* "

She glanced away as her chief cook came unctuously through the garden and her heart sank a little more. He bowed formally, a taut, thin little man with large feet and very buck teeth. Before he could utter a word Fujiko said through a flat smile, "Order new knives from the village. A new rice-cooking pot. A new chopping board, new water containers—all utensils you think necessary. Those that the Master used are to be kept for his private purposes. You will set aside a special area, construct another kitchen if you wish, where the Master can cook if he so desires—until you are proficient."

"Thank you, Fujiko-sama," the cook said. "Excuse me for interrupting you, but, so sorry, please excuse me, I know a fine cook in the next village. He's not a Buddhist and he's even been with the army in Korea so he'd know all about the—how to—how to cook for the Master so much better than I."

"When I want another cook I will tell you. When I consider you inept or malingering I will tell you. Until that time you will be chief cook here. You accepted the post for six months," she said.

"Yes, Mistress," the cook said with outward dignity, though quaking inside, for Fujiko-noh-Anjin was no mistress to trifle with. "Please excuse me, but I was engaged to cook. I am proud to cook. But I never accepted to—to be butcher. *Eta* are butchers. Of course we can't have an *eta* here but this other cook isn't a Buddhist like me, my father, his father before him and his before him, Mistress, and they never, never. . . . Please, this new cook will—"

"You will cook here as you've always cooked. I find your cooking excellent, worthy of a master cook in Yedo. I even sent one of your recipes to the Lady Kiritsubo in Osaka."

"Oh? Thank you. You do me too much honor. Which one, Mistress?"

"The tiny, fresh eels and jellyfish and sliced oysters, with just the right touch of soya, that you make so well. Excellent! The best I've ever tasted."

"Oh, thank you, Mistress," he groveled.

"Of course your soups leave much to be desired."

"Oh, so sorry!"

"I'll discuss those with you later. Thank you, cook," she said, experimenting with a dismissal.

The little man stood his ground gamely. "Please excuse me, Mistress, but *oh ko,* with complete humbleness, if the Master—when the Master—"

"When the Master tells you to cook or to butcher or whatever, you will rush to do it. Instantly. As any loyal servant should. Meanwhile, it may take you a great deal of time to become proficient so perhaps you'd better make temporary arrangements with this other cook to visit you on the rare days the Master might wish to eat in his own fashion."

His honor satisfied, the cook smiled and bowed. "Thank you. Please excuse my asking for enlightenment."

"Of course you pay for the substitute cook from your own salary."

When they were alone again, Nigatsu chortled behind her hand. "Oh, Mistress-chan, may I compliment you on your total victory and your wisdom? Chief cook almost broke wind when you said that he was going to have to pay too!"

"Thank you, Nanny-san." Fujiko could smell the hare beginning to cook. What if he asks me to eat it with him, she was thinking, and almost wilted. Even if he doesn't I'll still have to serve it. How can I avoid being sick? You will not be sick, she ordered herself. It's your *karma.* You must have been completely dreadful in your previous life. Yes. But remember everything is fine now. Only five months and six days more. Don't think of that, just think about your Master, who is a brave, strong man, though one with ghastly eating habits . . .

Horses clattered up to the gate. Buntaro dismounted and waved the rest of his men away. Then, accompanied only by his personal guard, he strode through the garden, dusty and sweat-soiled. He carried his huge bow and on his back was his quiver. Fujiko and her maid bowed warmly, hating him. Her uncle was famous for his wild, uncontrollable rages which made him lash out without warning or pick a quarrel with almost anyone. Most of the time only his servants suffered, or his women. "Please come in, Uncle. How kind of you to visit us so soon," Fujiko said.

"Ah, Fujiko-san. Do— What's that stench?"

"My Master's cooking some game Lord Toranaga sent him—he's showing my miserable servants how to cook."

"If he wants to cook, I suppose he can, though . . ." Buntaro wrinkled his nose distastefully. "Yes, a master can do anything in his own house, within the law, unless it disturbs the neighbors."

Legally such a smell could be cause for complaint and it could be very bad to inconvenience neighbors. Inferiors never did anything to disturb their superiors. Otherwise heads would fall. That was why, throughout the land, samurai lived cautiously and courteously near samurai of equal rank if possible, peasants next to peasants, merchants in their own streets, and *eta* isolated outside. Omi was their immediate neighbor. He's superior, she thought. "I hope sincerely no one's disturbed," she told Buntaro uneasily, wondering what new evil he was concocting. "You wanted to see my Master?" She began to get up but he stopped her.

"No, please don't disturb him, I'll wait," he said formally and her heart sank. Buntaro was not known for his manners and politeness from him was very dangerous.

"I apologize for arriving like this without first sending a messenger to request an appointment," he was saying, "but Lord Toranaga told me I might perhaps be allowed to use the bath and have quarters here. From time to time. Would you ask the Anjin-san later, if he would give his permission?"

"Of course," she said, continuing the usual pattern of etiquette, loathing the idea of having Buntaro in her house. "I'm sure he will be honored, Uncle. May I offer you cha or saké while you wait?"

"Saké, thank you."

Nigatsu hurriedly set a cushion on the veranda and fled for the saké, as much as she would have liked to stay.

Buntaro handed his bow and quiver to his guard, kicked off his dusty sandals, and stomped onto the veranda. He pulled his killing sword out of his sash, sat cross-legged, and laid the sword on his knees.

"Where's my wife? With the Anjin-san?"

"No, Buntaro-sama, so sorry, she was ordered to the fortress where—"

"*Ordered?* By whom? By Kasigi Yabu?"

"Oh, no, by Lord Toranaga, Sire, when he came back from hunting this afternoon."

"Oh, Lord Toranaga?" Buntaro simmered down and scowled across the bay at the fortress. Toranaga's standard flew beside Yabu's.

"Would you like me to send someone for her?"

He shook his head. "There's time enough for her." He exhaled, looked across at his niece, daughter of his youngest sister. "I'm fortunate to have such an accomplished wife, *neh?*"

"Yes, Sire. Yes you are. She's been enormously valuable to interpret the Anjin-san's knowledge."

Buntaro stared at the fortress, then sniffed the wind as the smell of the cooking wafted up again. "It's like being at Nagasaki, or back in Korea. They cook meat all the time there, boil it or roast it. Stink—you've never smelled anything like it. Koreans're animals, like cannibals. The garlic stench even gets into your clothes and hair."

"It must have been terrible."

"The war was good. We could have won easily. And smashed through to China. And civilized both countries." Buntaro flushed and his voice rasped. "But we didn't. We failed and had to come back with our shame because we were betrayed. Betrayed by filthy traitors in high places."

"Yes, that's so sad, but you're right. Very right, Buntaro-sama," she said soothingly, telling the lie easily, knowing no nation on earth could conquer China, and no one could civilize China, which had been civilized since ancient times.

The vein on Buntaro's forehead was throbbing and he was talking almost to himself. "They'll pay. All of them. The traitors. It's only a matter of waiting beside a river long enough for the bodies of your enemies to float by, *neh?* I'll wait and I'll spit on their heads soon, very soon. I've promised myself that." He looked at her. "I hate traitors and adulterers. And all liars!"

"Yes, I agree. You're so right, Buntaro-sama," she said, chilled, knowing there was no limit to his ferocity. When Buntaro was sixteen he had executed his own mother, one of Hiro-matsu's lesser consorts, for her supposed infidelity while his father, Hiro-matsu, was at war fighting for the Dictator, Lord Goroda. Then, years later, he had killed his own eldest son by his first wife for supposed insults and sent her back to her family, where she died by her own hand, unable to bear the shame. He had done terrible things to his consorts and to Mariko. And he had quarreled violently with Fujiko's father and had accused him of cowardice in Korea, discrediting him to the Taikō, who had at once ordered him to shave his head and become a monk, to die debauched, so soon, eaten up by his own shame.

It took all of Fujiko's will to appear tranquil. "We were so proud to hear that you had escaped the enemy," she said.

The saké arrived. Buntaro began to drink heavily.

When there had been the correct amount of waiting, Fujiko got up. "Please excuse me for a moment." She went to the kitchen to warn Blackthorne, to ask his permission for Buntaro to be quartered in the house, and to tell him and the servants what had to be done.

"Why here?" Blackthorne asked irritably. "Why to stay here? Is necessary?"

Fujiko apologized and tried to explain that, of course, Buntaro could not be refused. Blackthorne returned moodily to his cooking and she came back to Buntaro, her chest aching.

"My Master says he's honored to have you here. His house is your house."

"What's it like being consort to a barbarian?"

"I would imagine horrible. But to the Anjin-san, who is hatamoto and therefore samurai? I suppose like to other men. This is the first time I've been consort. I prefer to be a wife. The Anjin-san's like other men, though yes, some of his ways are very strange."

"Who'd have thought one of our house would be consort to a barbarian—even a hatamoto."

"I had no choice. I merely obeyed Lord Toranaga, and grandfather, the leader of our clan. It's a woman's place to obey."

"Yes." Buntaro finished his cup of saké and she refilled it. "Obedience's important for a woman. And Mariko-san's obedient, isn't she?"

"Yes, Lord." She looked into his ugly, apelike face. "She's brought you nothing but honor, Sire. Without the Lady, your wife, Lord Toranaga could never have got the Anjin-san's knowledge."

He smiled crookedly. "I hear you stuck pistols in Omi-san's face."

"I was only doing my duty, Sire."

"Where did you learn to use guns?"

"I had never handled a gun until then. I didn't know if the pistols were loaded. But I would have pulled the triggers."

Buntaro laughed. "Omi-san thought that too."

She refilled his cup. "I never understood why Omi-san didn't try to take them away from me. His lord had ordered him to take them, but he didn't."

"I would have."

"Yes, Uncle. I know. Please excuse me, I would still have pulled the triggers."

"Yes. But you would have missed!"

"Yes, probably. Since then I've learned how to shoot."

"He taught you?"

"No. One of Lord Naga's officers."

"Why?"

"My father would never allow his daughters to learn sword or spear. He thought, wisely I believe, we should devote our time to learning gentler things. But sometimes a woman needs to protect her master and his house. The pistol's a good weapon for a woman, very good. It requires no strength and little practice. So now I can perhaps be a little more use to my Master, for I will surely blow any man's head off to protect him, and for the honor of our house."

Buntaro drained his cup. "I was proud when I heard you'd opposed Omi-san as you did. You were correct. Lord Hiro-matsu will be proud too."

"Thank you, Uncle. But I was only doing an ordinary duty." She bowed formally. "My Master asks if you would allow him the honor of talking with you now, if it pleases you."

He continued the ritual. "Please thank him but first may I bathe? If it pleases him, I'll see him when my *wife* returns."

CHAPTER 35

LACKTHORNE waited in the garden. Now he wore the Brown uniform kimono that Toranaga had given him with swords in his sash and a loaded pistol hidden under the sash. From Fujiko's hurried explanations and subsequently from the servants, he had gathered that he had to receive Buntaro formally, because the samurai was an important general and hatamoto, and was the first guest in the house. So he had bathed and changed quickly and had gone to the place that had been prepared.

He had seen Buntaro briefly yesterday, when he arrived. Buntaro had been busy with Toranaga and Yabu the rest of the day, together with Mariko, and Blackthorne had been left alone to organize the hurried attack demonstration with Omi and Naga. The attack was satisfactory.

Mariko had returned to the house very late. She had told him briefly about Buntaro's escape, the days of being hunted by Ishido's men, eluding them, and at last breaking through the hostile provinces to reach the Kwanto. "It was very difficult, but perhaps not too difficult, Anjin-san. My husband is very strong and very brave."

"What's going to happen now? Are you leaving?"

"Lord Toranaga orders that everything's to remain as it was. Nothing's to be changed."

"You're changed, Mariko. A spark's gone out of you."

"No. That's your imagination, Anjin-san. It's just my relief that he's alive when I was certain he was dead."

"Yes. But it's made a difference, hasn't it?"

"Of course. I thank God my Master wasn't captured—that he lived to obey Lord Toranaga. Will you excuse me, Anjin-san. I'm tired now. I'm sorry, I'm very very tired."

"Is there anything I can do?"

"What should you do, Anjin-san? Except to be happy for me and for him. Nothing's changed, really. Nothing is finished because nothing began. Everything's as it was. My husband's alive."

Don't you wish he were dead? Blackthorne asked himself in the garden. No.

Then why the hidden pistol? Are you filled with guilt?

No. Nothing began.

Didn't it?

No.

You thought you were taking her. Isn't that the same as taking her in fact?

He saw Mariko walk into the garden from the house. She looked like a porcelain miniature following half a pace behind Buntaro, his burliness seeming even greater by comparison. Fujiko was with her, and the maids.

He bowed. "*Yokoso oide kudasareta,* Buntaro-san." Welcome to my house, Buntaro-san.

They all bowed. Buntaro and Mariko sat on the cushions opposite him. Fujiko seated herself behind him. Nigatsu and the maid, Koi, began to serve tea and saké. Buntaro took saké. So did Blackthorne.

"*Domo,* Anjin-san. *Ikaga desu ka?*"

"*Ii. Ikaga desu ka?*"

"*Ii. Kowa jozuni shabereru yoni natta na.*" Good. You're beginning to speak Japanese very well.

Soon Blackthorne became lost in the conversation, for Buntaro was slurring his words, speaking carelessly and rapidly.

"Sorry, Mariko-san, I didn't understand that."

"My husband wishes to thank you for trying to save him. With the oar. You remember? When we were escaping from Osaka."

"*Ah, so desu! Domo.* Please tell him I still think we should have put back to shore. There was time enough. The maid drowned unnecessarily."

"He says that was *karma.*"

"That was a wasted death," Blackthorne replied, and regretted the rudeness. He noticed that she did not translate it.

"My husband says that the assault strategy is very good, very good indeed."

"*Domo.* Tell him I'm glad he escaped unharmed. And that he's to command the regiment. And of course, that he's welcome to stay here."

"*Domo,* Anjin-san. Buntaro-sama says, yes, the assault plan is very good. But for himself he will always carry his bow and swords. He can kill at a much greater range, with great accuracy, and faster than a musket."

"Tomorrow I will shoot against him and we will see, if he likes."

"You will lose, Anjin-san, so sorry. May I caution you not to attempt that," she said.

Blackthorne saw Buntaro's eyes flick from Mariko to him and back again. "Thank you, Mariko-san. Say to him that I would like to see him shoot."

"He asks, can you use a bow?"

"Yes, but not as a proper bowman. Bows are pretty much out of date with us. Except the crossbow. I was trained for the sea. There we use only cannon, musket, or cutlass. Sometimes we use fire arrows but only for enemy sails in close quarters."

"He asks, how are they used, how do you make them, these fire arrows? Are they different from ours, like the ones used against the galley at Osaka?"

Blackthorne began to explain and there were the usual tiring interruptions and probing requestionings. By now he was used to their incredibly inquisitive minds about any aspect of war, but found it exhausting to talk through an interpreter. Even though Mariko was excellent, what she actually said was rarely exact. A long reply would always be shortened, some of what was spoken would, of course, be changed slightly, and misunderstandings occurred. So explanations had to be repeated unnecessarily.

But without Mariko, he knew that he could never have become so valuable. It's only knowledge that keeps me from the pit, he reminded himself. But that's no problem, because there's much to tell yet and a battle to win. A real battle to win. You're safe till then. You've a navy to plan. And then home. Safe.

He saw Buntaro's swords and the guard's swords and he felt his own and the oiled warmth of his pistol and he knew, truthfully, he would never be safe in this land. Neither he nor anyone was safe, not even Toranaga.

"Anjin-san, Buntaro-sama asks if he sends you men tomorrow, could you show them how to make these arrows?"

"Where can we get pitch?"

"I don't know." Mariko cross-questioned him on where it was usually found and what it looked like or smelled like, and on possible alternatives. Then she spoke to Buntaro at length. Fujiko had been silent all the while, her eyes and ears trained, missing nothing. The maids, well commanded by a slight motion of Fujiko's fan to an empty cup, constantly replenished the saké flasks.

"My husband says he will discuss this with Lord Toranaga. Perhaps pitch exists somewhere in the Kwanto. We've never heard of it before. If not pitch, we have thick oils—whale oils—which might substitute. He asks do you sometimes use war rockets, like the Chinese?"

"Yes. But they're not considered of much value except in siege. The Turks used them when they came against the Knights of St. John in Malta. Rockets are used mostly to cause fire and panic."

"He asks please give him details about this battle."

"It was forty years ago, in the greatest—" Blackthorne stopped, his mind racing. This had been the most vital siege in Europe. Sixty thousand Islamic Turks, the cream of the Ottoman Empire, had come against six hundred Christian knights supported by a few thousand Maltese auxiliaries, at bay in their vast castle complex at St. Elmo on the tiny island of Malta in the Mediterranean. The knights had successfully withstood the six-month siege and, incredibly, had forced the enemy to retreat in shame. This victory had saved the whole Mediterranean seaboard, and thus Christendom, from being ravaged at whim by the infidel hordes.

Blackthorne had suddenly realized that this battle gave him one of the keys to Osaka Castle: how to invest it, how to harry it, how to break through the gates, and how to conquer it.

"You were saying, senhor?"

"It was forty years ago, in the greatest inland sea we have in Europe, Mariko-san. The Mediterranean. It was just a siege, like any siege, not worth talking about," he lied. Such knowledge was priceless, certainly not to be given away lightly and absolutely not now. Mariko had explained many times that Osaka Castle stood inexorably between Toranaga and victory. Blackthorne was certain that the solution to Osaka might well be his passport out of the Empire, with all the riches he would need in this life.

He noticed that Mariko seemed troubled. "Senhora?"

"Nothing, senhor." She began to translate what he had said. But he knew that she knew he was hiding something. The smell of the stew distracted him.

"Fujiko-san!"

"*Hai,* Anjin-san?"

"*Shokuji wa madaka? Kyaku wa . . . sazo kufuku de oro, neh?*" When's dinner? The guests may be hungry.

"*Ah, gomen nasai, hi ga kurete kara ni itashimasu.*"

Blackthorne saw her point at the sun and realized that she had said "after sunset." He nodded and grunted, which passed in Japan for a polite "thank you, I understand."

Mariko turned again to Blackthorne. "My husband would like you to tell him about a battle you've been in."

"They're all in the War Manual, Mariko-san."

"He says he's read it with great interest, but it contains only brief details. Over the next days he wishes to learn everything about all your battles. One now, if it pleases you."

"They're all in the War Manual. Perhaps tomorrow, Mariko-san." He wanted time to examine his blinding new thought about Osaka Castle and *that* battle, and he was tired of talking, tired of being cross-questioned, but most of all he wanted to eat.

"Please, Anjin-san, would you tell it again, just once, for my husband?"

He heard the careful pleading under her voice so he relented. "Of course. Which do you think he'd like?"

"The one in the Netherlands. Near 'Zeeland'—is that how you pronounce it?"

"Yes," he said.

So he began to tell the story of this battle which was like almost every other battle in which men died, most of the time because of the mistakes and stupidity of the officers in command.

"My husband says it's not so here, Anjin-san. Here the commanding officers have to be very good or they die very quickly."

"Of course, my criticisms applied to European leaders only."

"Buntaro-sama says he will tell you about our wars and our leaders, particularly the Lord Taikō, over the days. A fair exchange for your information," she said noncommittally.

"*Domo.*" Blackthorne bowed slightly, feeling Buntaro's eyes grind into him. What do you really want from me, you son of a bitch?

Dinner was a disaster. For everyone.

Even before they had left the garden to go to the veranda to eat, the day had become ill-omened.

"Excuse me, Anjin-san, but what's that?" Mariko pointed. "Over there. My husband asks, what's that?"

"Where? Oh, there! That's a pheasant," Blackthorne said. "Lord Toranaga sent it to me, along with a hare. We're having that for dinner, English-style—at least I am, though there'd be enough for everyone."

"Thank you, but . . . we, my husband and I, we don't eat meat. But why is the pheasant hanging there? In this heat, shouldn't it be put away and prepared?"

"That's the way you prepare pheasant. You hang it to mature the meat."

"What? Just like that? Excuse me, Anjin-san," she said, flustered, "so sorry. But it'll go rotten quickly. It still has its feathers and it's not been . . . cleaned."

"Pheasant meat's dry, Mariko-san, so you hang it for a few days, perhaps a couple of weeks, depending on the weather. Then you pluck it, clean it, and cook it."

"You—you leave it in the air? To rot? Just like—"

"*Nan ja?*" Buntaro asked impatiently.

She spoke to him apologetically and he sucked in his breath, then got up and peered at it and prodded it. A few flies buzzed, then settled back again. Hesitantly Fujiko spoke to Buntaro and he flushed.

"Your consort said you ordered that no one was to touch it but you?" Mariko asked.

"Yes. Don't you hang game here? Not everyone's Buddhist."

"No, Anjin-san. I don't think so."

"Some people believe you should hang a pheasant by the tail feathers until it drops off, but that's an old wives' tale," Blackthorne said. "By the neck's the right way, then the juices stay where they belong. Some people let it hang until it drops off the neck but personally, I don't like meat that gamy. We used to—" He stopped for she had gone a slight shade of green.

"*Nan desu ka,* Mariko-san?" Fujiko asked quickly.

Mariko explained. They all laughed nervously and Mariko got up, weakly patting the sheen off her forehead. "I'm sorry, Anjin-san, would you excuse me a moment . . ."

Your food's just as strange, he wanted to say. What about yesterday, the raw squid—white, slimy, almost tasteless chewy meat with nothing but soya sauce to wash it down? Or the chopped octopus tentacles, again raw, with cold rice and seaweed? How about fresh jellyfish with yellow-brown, souped *torfu*—fermented beancurds—that looked like a bowl of dog puke? Oh yes, served beautifully in a fragile, attractive bowl, but still looking like puke! Yes, by God, enough to make any man sick!

Eventually they went to the veranda room and, after the usual interminable bowings and small talk and cha and saké, the food began to arrive. Small trays of clear fish soup and rice and raw fish, as always. And then his stew.

He lifted the lid of the pot. The steam rose and golden globules of fat danced on the shimmering surface. The rich, mouth-watering gravy-soup was heavy with meat juices and tender chunks of flesh. Proudly he offered it but they all shook their heads and begged him to eat.

"Domo," he said.

It was good manners to drink soup directly from the small lacquered bowls and to eat anything solid in the soup with chopsticks. A ladle was on the tray. Hard put to stop his hunger, he filled the bowl and began to eat. Then he saw their eyes.

They were watching with nauseated fascination which they unsuccessfully tried to hide. His appetite began to slip away. He tried to dismiss them but could not, his stomach growling. Hiding his irritation, he put down the bowl and replaced the lid and told them gruffly it was not to his taste. He ordered Nigatsu to take it away.

"Should it be thrown away then, Fujiko asks," Mariko said hopefully.

"Yes."

Fujiko and Buntaro relaxed.

"Would you like more rice?" Fujiko asked.

"No, thank you."

Mariko waved her fan, smiled encouragingly, and refilled his saké cup. But Blackthorne was not soothed and he resolved in the future to cook in the hills in private, to eat in private, and to hunt openly.

To hell with them, he thought. If Toranaga can hunt, so can I. When am I going to see him? How long do I have to wait?

"The pox on waiting and the pox on Toranaga!" he said aloud in English and felt better.

"What, Anjin-san?" Mariko asked in Portuguese.

"Nothing," he replied. "I was just wondering when I'd see Lord Toranaga."

"He didn't tell me. Very soon, I imagine."

Buntaro was slurping his saké and soup loudly as was custom. This began to annoy Blackthorne. Mariko talked cheerfully with her husband, who grunted, hardly acknowledging her. She was not eating, and it further irked him that both she and Fujiko were almost fawning on Buntaro and also that he himself had to put up with this unwanted guest.

"Tell Buntaro-sama that in my country a host toasts the honored guest." He lifted his cup with a grim smile. "Long life and happiness!" He drank.

Buntaro listened to Mariko's explanation. He nodded in agreement, lifted his cup in return, smiled through his teeth, and drained it.

"Health!" Blackthorne toasted again.

And again.

And again.

"Health!"

This time Buntaro did not drink. He put down the full cup and looked at Blackthorne out of his small eyes. Then Buntaro called to someone outside. The shoji slid open at once. His guard, ever present, bowed and handed him the immense bow and quiver. Buntaro took it and spoke vehemently and rapidly to Blackthorne.

"My husband—my husband says you wanted to see him shoot, Anjin-san. He thinks tomorrow is too far away. Now is a good time. The gateway of your house, Anjin-san. He asks which post do you choose?"

"I don't understand," Blackthorne said. The main gate would be forty paces away, somewhere across the garden, but now completely masked by the closed shoji wall to his right.

"The left or the right post? Please choose." Her manner was urgent.

Warned, he looked at Buntaro. The man seemed detached, oblivious of them, a squat ugly troll who sat gazing into the distance.

"Left," he said, fascinated.

"Hidari!" she said.

At once Buntaro slid an arrow from the quiver and, still sitting, set up the bow, raised it, drew back the bowstring to eye level and released the shaft with savage, almost poetic liquidity. The arrow slashed toward Mariko's face, touched a strand of her hair in passing, and disappeared through the shoji paper wall. Another arrow was launched almost before the first had vanished, and then another, each one coming within an inch of impaling Mariko. She remained calm and motionless, kneeling as she had always been.

A fourth arrow and then a last. The silence was filled with the echo of the twanging bowstring. Buntaro sighed and came back slowly. He put the bow across his knees. Mariko and Fujiko sucked in their breaths and smiled and bowed and complimented Buntaro and he nodded and bowed slightly. They looked at Blackthorne. He knew that what he had witnessed was almost magical. All the arrows had gone through the same hole in the shoji.

Buntaro handed the bow back to his guard and picked up his tiny cup. He stared at it a moment, then raised it to Blackthorne, drained it and spoke harshly, his brutish self again.

"He—my husband asks, politely, please go and look."

Blackthorne thought a moment, trying to still his heart. "There's no need. Of course he hit the target."

"He says he would like you to be sure."

"I'm sure."

"Please, Anjin-san. You would honor him."

"I don't need to honor him."

"Yes. But may I please quietly add my request."

Again the plea was in her eyes.

"How do I say, 'That was marvelous to watch'?"

She told him. He said the words and bowed. Buntaro bowed perfunctorily in return.

"Ask him please to come with me to see the arrows."

"He says that he would like you to go by yourself. He does not wish to go, Anjin-san."

"Why?"

"If he has been accurate, senhor, you should see that by yourself. If not, you should see that alone too. Then neither you nor he can be embarrassed."

"And if he's missed?"

"He hasn't. But by our custom accuracy under such impossible circumstances is unimportant compared to the grace that the archer shows, the nobility of movement, his strength to shoot sitting, or the detachment about the winning or losing."

The arrows were within an inch of each other in the middle of the left post. Blackthorne looked back at the house and he could see, forty-odd paces away, the small neat hole in the paper wall that was a spark of light in the darkness.

It's almost impossible to be so accurate, he thought. From where Buntaro was sitting he couldn't see the garden or the gate, and it was black night outside. Blackthorne turned back to the post and raised the lantern higher. With one hand he tried to pull out an arrow. The steel head was buried too deep. He could have snapped the wooden shaft but he did not wish to.

The guard was watching.

Blackthorne hesitated. The guard came forward to help but he shook his head, "*Iyé, domo,*" and went back inside.

"Mariko-san, please tell my consort that I would like the arrows left in the post forever. All of them. To remind me of a master archer. I've never seen such shooting." He bowed to Buntaro.

"Thank you, Anjin-san." She translated and Buntaro bowed and thanked him for the compliment.

"Saké!" Blackthorne ordered.

They drank more. Much more. Buntaro quaffed his carelessly now, the wine taking him. Blackthorne watched him covertly then let his attention wander away as he wondered how the man had managed to line up and fire the arrows with such incredible accuracy. It's impossible, he thought, yet I saw him do it. Wonder what Vinck and Baccus and the rest are doing right now. Toranaga had told him the crew were now settled in Yedo, near *Erasmus.* Christ Jesus, I'd like to see them and get back aboard.

He glanced across at Mariko, who was saying something to her husband. Buntaro listened, then to Blackthorne's surprise, he saw the samurai's face become contorted with loathing. Before he could avert his eyes Buntaro had looked at him.

"*Nan desu ka?*" Buntaro's words sounded almost like an accusation.

"*Nani-mo,* Buntaro-san." Nothing. Blackthorne offered everyone saké, hoping to cover his lapse. Again the women accepted, but just sipped their wine sparingly. Buntaro finished his cup at once, his mood ugly. Then he harangued Mariko lengthily.

In spite of himself, Blackthorne spoke out. "What's the matter with him? What's he saying?"

"Oh, I'm sorry, Anjin-san. My husband was asking about you, about your wife and consorts. And about your children. And about what happened since we left Osaka. He—" She stopped, changing her mind, and added in a different voice, "He's most interested in you and your views."

"I'm interested in him and his views, Mariko-san. How did you meet, you and he? When were you married? Did—" Buntaro overrode him with a flurry of impatient Japanese.

At once Mariko translated what had been said. Buntaro reached over and sloshed two teacups full of saké, offered one to Blackthorne and waved at the women to take the others.

"He—my husband says sometimes saké cups are too small." Mariko poured the other teacups full. She sipped one, Fujiko the other. There was another, more bellicose harangue and Mariko's smile froze on her face, Fujiko's also.

"*Iyé, dozo gomen nasai,* Buntaro-sama," Mariko began.

"*Ima!*" Buntaro ordered.

Nervously Fujiko started to talk but Buntaro shut her up with one look.

"*Gomen nasai,*" Fujiko whispered in apology. "*Dozo, gomen nasai.*"

"What did he say, Mariko-san?"

She appeared not to hear Blackthorne. "*Dozo gomen nasai,* Buntaro-sama, *watashi—*"

Her husband's face reddened. "*IMA!*"

"So sorry, Anjin-san, but my husband orders me to tell—to answer your questions—to tell you about myself. I told him that I did not think that family matters should be discussed so late at night, but he orders it. Please be patient." She took a large sip of the saké. Then another. The strands of hair that were loose over her ears waved in the slight current made by Fujiko's fan. She drained the cup and put it down. "My maiden name is Akechi. I am the daughter of General Lord Akechi Jinsai, the assassin. My father treacherously assassinated his liege lord, the Dictator Lord Goroda."

"God in heaven! Why'd he do that?"

"Whatever the reason, Anjin-san, it is insufficient. My father committed the worst crime in our world. My blood's tainted, as is the blood of my son."

"Then why—" He stopped.

"Yes, Anjin-san?"

"I was only going to say that I understand what that means . . . to kill a liege lord. I'm surprised that you were left alive."

"My husband honored me—"

Again Buntaro viciously interrupted her and she apologized and explained what Blackthorne had asked. Contemptuously Buntaro waved her on.

"My husband honored me by sending me away," she continued in the same gentle way. "I begged to be allowed to commit seppuku but he denied me that privilege. It was . . . I must explain, seppuku is his privilege to give, or Lord Toranaga's. I still humbly ask it once a year on the anniversary of the day of the treachery. But in his wisdom, my husband has always refused me." Her smile was lovely. "My husband honors me every day, every moment, Anjin-san. If I were he I would not be able to even talk to such a . . . befouled person."

"That's why—that's why you're the last of your line?" he asked, remembering what she had said about a catastrophe on the march from Osaka Castle.

Mariko translated the question for Buntaro and then turned back again. "*Hai,* Anjin-san. But it wasn't a catastrophe, not for them. They were caught in the hills, my father and his family, by Nakamura, the general who became the Taikō. It was Nakamura who led the armies of vengeance and slaughtered all my father's forces, twenty thousand men, every one. My father and his family were trapped, but my father had time to help them all, my four brothers and three sisters, my—my mother and his two consorts. Then he committed seppuku. In that he was samurai and they were samurai," she said. "They knelt bravely before him, one by one, and he slew them one by one. They died honorably. And he died honorably. My father's two brothers and one uncle had sided with him in his treachery against their liege lord. They were also trapped. And they died with equal honor. Not one Akechi was left alive to face the hate and derision of the enemy except me—no, please forgive me, Anjin-san, I'm wrong—my father and his brothers and uncle, they were the real enemy. Of the enemy, only I am left alive, a living witness to filthy treachery. I, Akechi Mariko, was left alive because I was married and so belonged to my husband's family. We lived at Kyoto then. I was at Kyoto when my father died. His treachery and rebellion lasted only thirteen days, Anjin-san. But as long as men live in these islands, the name Akechi will be foul."

"How long had you been married when that happened?"

"Two months and three days, Anjin-san."

"And you were fifteen then?"

"Yes. My husband honored me by not divorcing me or casting me out as he should have done. I was sent away. To a village in the north. It was cold there, Anjin-san, in Shonai Province. So cold."

"How long were you there?"

"Eight years. The Lord Goroda was forty-nine when he committed seppuku to prevent capture. That was almost sixteen years ago, Anjin-san, and most of his descen—"

Buntaro interrupted again, his tongue a whip.

"Please excuse me, Anjin-san," Mariko said. "My husband correctly points out it should have been enough for me to say that I am the daughter of a traitor, that long explanations are unnecessary. Of course some explanations are necessary," she added carefully. "Please excuse my husband's bad manners and I beg you to remember what I said about ears to hear with and the Eightfold Fence. Forgive me, Anjin-san, I am ordered away. You may not leave until he leaves, or passes out with drink. Do not interfere." She bowed to Fujiko. *"Dozo gomen nasai."*

"Do itashimashité."

Mariko bowed her head to Buntaro and left. Her perfume lingered.

"Saké!" Buntaro said and smiled evilly.

Fujiko filled the teacup.

"Health," Blackthorne said, in turmoil.

For more than an hour he toasted Buntaro until he felt his own head swimming. Then Buntaro passed out and lay in the shattered mess of the teacups. The shoji opened instantly. The guard came in with Mariko. They lifted Buntaro, helped by servants who seemed to appear out of nowhere, and carried him to the room opposite. Mariko's room. Assisted by the maid, Koi, she began to undress him. The guard slid the shoji closed and sat outside it, his hand on the haft of his loosened sword.

Fujiko waited, watching Blackthorne. Maids came and tidied up the disorder. Wearily Blackthorne ran his hands through his long hair and retied the ribbon of his queue. Then he lurched up and went out onto the veranda, his consort following.

The air smelled good and cleansed him. But not enough. He sat ponderously on the stoop and drank in the night.

Fujiko knelt behind him and leaned forward. *"Gomen nasai,* Anjin-san," she whispered, nodding back at the house. *"Wakarimasu ka?"* Do you understand?

"Wakarimasu, shigata ga nai." Then, seeing her untoward fear, he stroked her hair.

"Arigato, arigato, Anjin-sama."

"Anatawa suimin ima, Fujiko-san," he said, finding the words with difficulty. You sleep now.

"Dozo gomen nasai, Anjin-sama, *suimin, neh?"* she said, motioning him toward his own room, her eyes pleading.

"Iyé. Watashi oyogu ima." No, I'm going for a swim.

"Hai, Anjin-sama." Obediently she turned and called out. Two of the servants came running. Both were young men from the village, strong and known to be good swimmers.

Blackthorne did not object. Tonight he knew his objections would be meaningless.

"Well, anyway," he said aloud as he lurched down the hill, the men following, his brain dulled with drink, "anyway, I've put him to sleep. He can't hurt her now."

Blackthorne swam for an hour and felt better. When he came back Fujiko was waiting on the veranda with a pot of fresh cha. He accepted some, then went to bed and was instantly asleep.

The sound of Buntaro's voice, teeming with malice, awoke him. His right hand was already grasping the hilt of the loaded pistol he always kept under the futon, and his heart was thundering in his chest from the suddenness of his waking.

Buntaro's voice stopped. Mariko began to talk. Blackthorne could only catch a few words but he could feel the reasonableness and the pleading, not abject or whining or even near tears, just her usual firm serenity. Again Buntaro erupted.

Blackthorne tried not to listen.

"Don't interfere," she had told him and she was wise. He had no rights, but Buntaro had many. "I beg you to be careful, Anjin-san. Remember what I told you about ears to hear with and the Eightfold Fence."

Obediently he lay back, his skin chilled with sweat, and forced himself to think about what she had said.

"You see, Anjin-san," she had told him that very special evening when they were finishing the last of many last flasks of saké and he had been joking about the lack of privacy everywhere—people always around and paper walls, ears and eyes always prying, "here you have to learn to create your own privacy. We're taught from childhood to disappear within ourselves, to grow impenetrable walls behind which we live. If we couldn't, we'd all certainly go mad and kill each other and ourselves."

"What walls?"

"Oh, we've a limitless maze to hide in, Anjin-san. Rituals and customs, taboos of all kinds, oh yes. Even our language has nuances you don't have which allow us to avoid, politely, any question if we don't want to answer it."

"But how do you close your ears, Mariko-san? That's impossible."

"Oh, very easy, with training. Of course, training begins as soon as a child can talk, so very soon it's second nature to us—how else could we survive? First you begin by cleansing your mind of *people,* to put yourself on a different plane. Sunset watching is a great help or listening to the rain—Anjin-san, have you noticed the different sounds of rain? If you really *listen,* then the present vanishes, *neh? Listening* to blossoms falling and to rocks growing are exceptionally good exercises. Of course, you're not supposed to *see* the things, they're only signs, messages to your *hara,* your center, to remind you of the transcience of life, to help you gain *wa,* harmony, Anjin-san, perfect harmony, which is the most sought-after quality in all Japanese life, all art, all . . ." She had laughed. "There, you see what so much saké does to me." The tip of her tongue touched her lips so enticingly. "I will whisper a secret to you: Don't be fooled by our smiles and gentleness, our ceremonial and our bowing and sweetnesses and attentions. Beneath them all we can be a million *ri* away, safe and alone. For that's what we seek—oblivion. One of our first poems ever written—it's in the Kojiko, our first history book that was written down about a thousand years ago—perhaps that will explain what I'm saying:

> '*Eight cumulus arise*
> *For the lovers to hide within.*
> *The Eightfold Fence of Izumo Province*
> *Enclose those Eightfold clouds—*
> *Oh how marvelous, that Eightfold Fence!*'

We would certainly go mad if we didn't have an Eightfold Fence, oh very yes!"

Remember the Eightfold Fence, he told himself, as the hissing fury of Buntaro continued. I don't know anything about her. Or him, really. Think about the Musket Regiment or home or Felicity or how to get the ship or about Baccus or Toranaga or Omi-san. What about Omi? Do I need revenge? He wants to be my friend and he's been good and kind since the pistols and . . .

The sound of the blow tore into his head. Then Mariko's voice began again, and there was a second blow and Blackthorne was on his feet in an instant, the shoji open. The guard stood facing him balefully in the corridor outside Mariko's door, sword ready.

Blackthorne was preparing to launch himself at the samurai when the door at the far end of the corridor opened. Fujiko, her hair loose and flowing over the sleeping kimono, approached, the sound of ripping cloth and another clout seemingly not touching her at all. She bowed politely to the guard and stood between them, then bowed meekly to Blackthorne and took his arm, motioning him back into the room. He saw the taut readiness of the samurai. He had only one pistol and one bullet at the moment so he retreated. Fujiko followed and shut the shoji behind her. Then, very afraid, she shook her head warningly, and touched a finger to her lips and shook her head again, her eyes pleading with him.

"*Gomen nasai, wakarimasu ka?*" she breathed.

But he was concentrating on the wall of the adjoining room that he could smash in so easily.

She looked at the wall also, then put herself between him and the wall, and sat, motioning him to do the same.

But he could not. He stood readying himself for the charge that would destroy them all, goaded by a whimper that followed another blow.

"*Iyé!*" Fujiko shook in terror.

He waved her out of the way.

"*Iyé, iyé,*" she begged again.

"*IMA!*"

At once Fujiko got up and motioned him to wait as she rushed noiselessly for the swords that lay in front of the *takonama,* the little alcove of honor. She picked up the long sword, her hands shaking, drew it out of the scabbard, and prepared to follow him through the wall. At that instant there was a final blow and a rising torrent of rage. The other shoji slammed open, and unseen, Buntaro stamped away, followed by the guard. There was silence in the house for a moment, then the sound of the garden gate crashing closed.

Blackthorne went for his door. Fujiko darted in the way but he shoved her aside and pulled it open.

Mariko was still on her knees in one corner of the next room, a livid welt on her cheek, her hair disheveled, her kimono in tatters, bad bruises on her thighs and lower back.

He rushed over to pick her up but she cried out, "Go away, please go away, Anjin-san!"

He saw the trickle of blood from the corner of her mouth. "Jesus, how bad are you—"

"I told you not to interfere. Please go away," she said in the same calm voice that belied the violence in her eyes. Then she saw Fujiko, who had stayed at the doorway. She spoke to her. Fujiko obediently took Blackthorne's arm to lead him away but he tore out of her grasp. "Don't! *Iyé!*"

Mariko said, "Your presence here takes away my face and gives me no peace or comfort and shames me. Go away!"

"I want to help. Don't you understand?"

"Don't you understand? You have no rights in this. This is a private quarrel between husband and wife."

"That's no excuse for hitting—"

"Why don't you listen, Anjin-san? He can beat me to death if he wishes. He has the right and I wish he would—even that! Then I wouldn't have to endure the shame. You think it's easy to live with my shame? Didn't you hear what I told you? *I'm Akechi Jinsai's daughter!*"

"That's not your fault. You did nothing!"

"It is my fault and I am my father's daughter." Mariko would have stopped there. But, looking up and seeing his compassion, his concern, and his love, and knowing how he so honored truth, she allowed some of her veils to fall.

"Tonight was my fault, Anjin-san," she said. "If I would weep as he wants, beg forgiveness as he wants, cringe and be petrified and fawn as he wants, open my legs in pretended terror as he desires, do all these womanly things that my duty demands, then he'd be like a child in my hand. But I will not."

"Why?"

"Because that's my revenge. To repay him for leaving me alive after the treachery. To repay him for sending me away for eight years and leaving me alive all that time. And to repay him for ordering me back into life and leaving me alive." She sat back painfully and arranged her tattered kimono closer around her. "I'll never give myself to him again. Once I did, freely, even though I detested him from the first moment I saw him."

"Then why did you marry him? You've said women here have rights of refusal, that they don't have to marry against their wishes."

"I married him to please Lord Goroda, and to please my father. I was so young I didn't know about Goroda then, but if you want the truth, Goroda was the cruelest, most loathsome man that was ever born. He drove my father to treachery. That's the real truth! Goroda!" She spat the name. "But for him we'd all be alive and honored. I pray God that Goroda's committed to hell for all eternity." She moved carefully, trying to ease the agony in her side. "There's only hatred between my husband and me, that's our *karma*. It would be so easy for him to allow me to climb into the small place of death."

"Why doesn't he let you go? Divorce you? Even grant you what you want?"

"Because he's a man." A ripple of pain went through her and she grimaced. Blackthorne was on his knees beside her, cradling her. She pushed him away, fought for control. Fujiko, at the doorway, watched stoically.

"I'm all right, Anjin-san. Please leave me alone. You mustn't. You must be careful."

"I'm not afraid of him."

Wearily she pushed the hair out of her eyes and stared up searchingly. Why not let the Anjin-san go to meet his *karma,* Mariko asked herself. He's not of our world. Buntaro will kill him so easily. Only Toranaga's personal protection has shielded him so far. Yabu, Omi, Naga, Buntaro—any one of them could be provoked so easily into killing him.

He's caused nothing but trouble since he arrived, *neh?* So has his knowledge. Naga's right: the Anjin-san can destroy our world unless he's bottled up.

What if Buntaro knew the truth? Or Toranaga? About the pillowing. . . .

"Are you insane?" Fujiko had said that first night.

"No."

"Then why are you going to take the maid's place?"

"Because of the saké and for amusement, Fujiko-chan, and for curiosity," she had lied, hiding the real reason: because he excited her, she wanted him, she had never had a lover. If it was not tonight it would never be, and it had to be the Anjin-san and only the Anjin-san.

So she had gone to him and had been transported and then, yesterday, when the galley arrived, Fujiko had said privately, "Would you have gone if you'd known your husband was alive?"

"No. Of course not," she had lied.

"But now you're going to tell Buntaro-sama, *neh?* About pillowing with the Anjin-san?"

"Why should I do that?"

"I thought that might be your plan. If you tell Buntaro-sama at the right time his rage will burst over you and you'll be gratefully dead before he knows what he's done."

"No, Fujiko-san, he'll never kill me. Unfortunately. He'll send me to the *eta* if he has excuse enough—if he could get Lord Toranaga's approval—but he'll never kill me."

"Adultery with the Anjin-san—would that be enough?"

"Oh yes."

"What would happen to your son?"

"He would inherit my disgrace, if I am disgraced, *neh?*"

"Please tell me if you ever think Buntaro-sama suspects what happened. While I'm consort, it's my duty to protect the Anjin-san."

Yes, it is, Fujiko, Mariko had thought then. And that would give you the excuse to take open vengeance on your father's accuser that you are desperate for. But your father was a coward, so sorry, poor Fujiko. Hiro-matsu was there, otherwise your father would be alive now and Buntaro dead, for Buntaro is hated far more than they ever despised your father. Even the swords you prize so much, they were never given as a battle honor, they were bought from a wounded samurai. So sorry, but I'll never be the one to tell you, even though that also is the truth.

"I'm not afraid of him," Blackthorne was saying again.

"I know," she said, the pain taking her. "But please, I beg you, be afraid of him for me."

Blackthorne went for the door.

Buntaro was waiting for him a hundred paces away in the center of the path that led down to the village—squat, immense, and deadly. The guard stood beside him. It was an overcast dawn. Fishing boats were already working the shoals, the sea calm.

Blackthorne saw the bow loose in Buntaro's hands, and the swords, and the guard's swords. Buntaro was swaying slightly and this gave him hope that the man's aim would be off, which might give him time to get close enough. There was no cover beside the path. Beyond caring, he cocked both pistols and bore down on the two men.

To hell with cover, he thought through the haze of his blood lust, knowing at the same time that what he was doing was insane, that he had no chance against the two samurai or the long-range bow, that he had no rights whatsoever to interfere. And then, while he was still out of pistol range, Buntaro bowed low, and so did the guard. Blackthorne stopped, sensing a trap. He looked all around but there was no one near. As though in a dream, he saw Buntaro sink heavily onto his knees, put his bow aside, his hands flat on the ground, and bow to him as a peasant would bow to his lord. The guard did likewise.

Blackthorne stared at them, dazed. When he was sure his eyes were not tricking him, he came forward slowly, pistols ready but not leveled, expecting treachery. Within easy range he stopped. Buntaro had not moved. Custom dictated that he should kneel and return the salutation because they were equals or near equals but he could not understand why there should be such unbelievable deferential ceremony in a situation like this where blood was going to flow.

"Get up, you son of a bitch!" Blackthorne readied to pull both triggers.

Buntaro said nothing, did nothing, but kept his head bowed, his hands flat. The back of his kimono was soaked with sweat.

"*Nan ja?*" Blackthorne deliberately used the most insulting way of asking "What is it?" wanting to bait Buntaro into getting up, into beginning, knowing that he could not shoot him like this, with his head down and almost in the dust.

Then, conscious that it was rude to stand while they were kneeling and that the "*nan ja*" was an almost intolerable and certainly unnecessary insult, Blackthorne knelt and, holding onto the pistols, put both hands on the ground and bowed in return.

He sat back on his heels. "*Hai?*" he asked with forced politeness.

At once Buntaro began mumbling. Abjectly. Apologizing. For what and exactly why, Blackthorne did not know. He could only catch a word here and another there and saké many times, but clearly it was an apology and a humble plea for forgiveness. Buntaro went on and on. Then he ceased and put his head down into the dust again.

Blackthorne's blinding rage had vanished by now. "*Shigata ga nai,*" he said huskily, which meant, "it can't be helped," or "there's nothing to be done," or "what could you do?" not knowing yet if the apology was merely ritual, prior to attack. "*Shigata ga nai. Hakkiri wakaranu ga shinpai surukotowanai.*" It can't be helped. I don't understand exactly—but don't worry.

Buntaro looked up and sat back. "*Arigato—arigato,* Anjin-sama. *Domo gomen nasai.*"

"*Shigata ga nai,*" Blackthorne repeated and, now that it was clear the apology was genuine, he thanked God for giving him the miraculous opportunity to call off the duel. He knew that he had no rights, he had acted like a madman, and that the only way to resolve the crisis with Buntaro was according to rules. And that meant Toranaga.

But why the apology, he was asking himself frantically. Think! You've got to learn to think like them.

Then the solution rushed into his brain. It must be because I'm hatamoto, and Buntaro, the guest, disturbed the *wa,* the harmony of my house. By having a violent open quarrel with his wife in *my* house, he insulted *me,* therefore he's totally in the wrong and he has to apologize whether he means it or not. An apology's obligatory from one samurai to another, from a guest to a host. . . .

Wait! And don't forget that by their custom, all men are allowed to get drunk, are expected to get drunk sometimes, and when drunk they are not, within reason, responsible for their actions. Don't forget there's no loss of face if you get stinking drunk. Remember how unconcerned Mariko and Toranaga were on the ship when I was stupefied. They were amused and not disgusted, as we'd be.

And aren't you really to blame? Didn't you start the drinking bout? Wasn't it your challenge?

"Yes," he said aloud.

"*Nan desu ka,* Anjin-san?" Buntaro asked, his eyes bloodshot.

"*Nani mo. Watashi no kashitsu desu.*" Nothing. It was my fault.

Buntaro shook his head and said that no, it was only his fault and he bowed and apologized again.

"Saké," Blackthorne said with finality and shrugged. "*Shigata ga nai.* Saké!"

Buntaro bowed and thanked him again. Blackthorne returned it and got up. Buntaro followed, and the guard. Both bowed once more. Again it was returned.

At length Buntaro turned and reeled away. Blackthorne waited until he was out of arrow range, wondering if the man was as drunk as he appeared to be. Then he went back to his own house.

Fujiko was on the veranda, once more within her polite, smiling shell. What are you really thinking, he asked himself as he greeted her, and was welcomed back.

Mariko's door was closed. Her maid stood beside it.

"Mariko-san?"

"Yes, Anjin-san?"

He waited but the door stayed closed. "Are you all right?"

"Yes, thank you." He heard her clear her throat, then the weak voice continued. "Fujiko has sent word to Yabu-san and to Lord Toranaga that I'm indisposed today and won't be able to interpret."

"You'd better see a doctor."

"Oh, thank you, but Suwo will be very good. I've sent for him. I've . . . I've just twisted my side. Truly I'm all right, there's no need for you to worry."

"Look, I know a little about doctoring. You're not coughing up blood, are you?"

"Oh, no. When I slipped I just knocked my cheek. Really, I'm quite all right."

After a pause, he said, "Buntaro apologized."

"Yes. Fujiko watched from the gate. I thank you humbly for accepting his apology. Thank you. And Anjin-san, I'm so sorry that you were disturbed . . . it's unforgivable that your harmony . . . please accept my apologies too. I should never have let my mouth run away with me. It was very impolite—please forgive me also. The quarrel was my fault. Please accept my apology."

"For being beaten?"

"For failing to obey my husband, for failing to help him to sleep contentedly, for failing him, and my host. Also for what I said."

"You're sure there's nothing I can do?"

"No—no, thank you, Anjin-san. It's just for today."

But Blackthorne did not see her for eight days.

CHAPTER 36

"I INVITED you to hunt, Naga-san, not to repeat views I've already heard," Toranaga said.

"I beg you, Father, for the last time: stop the training, outlaw guns, destroy the barbarian, declare the experiment a failure and have done with this obscenity."

"No. For the last time." The hooded falcon on Toranaga's gloved hand shifted uneasily at the unaccustomed menace in her master's voice and she hissed irritably. They were in the brush, beaters and guards well out of earshot, the day sweltering and dank and overcast.

Naga's chin jutted. "Very well. But it's still my duty to remind you that you're in danger here, and to demand again, with due politeness, now for the last time, that you leave Anjiro today."

"No. Also for the last time."

"Then take my head!"

"I already have your head!"

"Then take it today, now, or let me end my life, since you won't take good advice."

"Learn patience, puppy!"

"How can I be patient when I see you destroying yourself? It's my duty to point it out to you. You stay here hunting and wasting time while your enemies are pulling the whole world down on you. The Regents meet tomorrow. Four-fifths of all *daimyos* in Japan are either at Osaka already or on the way there. You're the *only* important one to refuse. Now you'll be impeached. Then nothing can save you. At the very least you should be home at Yedo surrounded by the legions. Here you're naked. We can't protect you. We've barely a thousand men, and hasn't Yabu-san mobilized all Izu? He's got more than eight thousand men within twenty *ri*, another six closing his borders. You know spies say he has a fleet waiting northward to sink you if you try to escape by galley! You're his prisoner again, don't you see that? One carrier pigeon from Ishido and Yabu can destroy you, whenever he wants. How do you know he isn't planning treachery with Ishido?"

"I'm sure he's considering it. I would if I were he, wouldn't you?"

"No, I wouldn't."

"Then you'd soon be dead, which would be absolutely merited, but so would all your family, all your clan and all your vassals, which would be absolutely unforgivable. You're a stupid, truculent fool! You won't use your mind, you won't listen, you won't learn, you won't curb your tongue or your temper! You let yourself be manipulated in the most childish way and believe that everything can be solved with the edge of your sword. The only reason I don't take your stupid head or let you end your present worthless life is because you're young, because I used to think you had some possibilities, your mistakes are not malicious, there's no guile in you and your loyalty's unquestioned. But if you don't quickly learn patience and self-discipline, I'll take away your samurai status and order you and all your generations into the peasant class!" Toranaga's right fist slammed his saddle and the falcon let out a piercing, nervous scream. *"Do you understand?"*

Naga was in shock. In his whole life Naga had never seen his father shout with rage or lose his temper, or even heard of him doing so. Many times he had felt the bite of his tongue but with justification. Naga knew he made many mistakes, but always his father had turned it so that what he'd done no longer seemed as stupid as it had at first. For instance, when Toranaga had shown him how he had fallen into Omi's—or Yabu's—trap about Jozen, he had had to be physically stopped from charging off at once to murder them both. But Toranaga had ordered his private guards to pour cold water over Naga until he was rational, and had calmly explained that he, Naga, had helped his father immeasurably by eliminating Jozen's menace. "But it would have been better if you'd known you were being manipulated into the action. Be patient, my son, everything comes with patience," Toranaga had counseled. "Soon you'll be able to manipulate them. What you did was very good. But you must learn to reason what's in a man's mind if you're to be of any use to yourself—or to your lord. I need leaders. I've fanatics enough."

Always his father had been reasonable and forgiving but today. . . . Naga leapt off his horse and knelt abjectly. "Please forgive me, Father. I never meant to make you angry . . . it's only because I'm frantic with worry over your safety. Please excuse me for disturbing the harmony—"

"*Hold your tongue!*" Toranaga bellowed, causing his horse to shy.

Frantically Toranaga held on with his knees and pulled the reins tighter in his right hand, the horse skittering. Off balance, his falcon began to bate—to jump off his fist, her wings fluttering wildly, screaming her ear-shattering *hek-ek-ek-ek-ek*—infuriated by the unaccustomed and unwelcome agitation surrounding her. "There, my beauty, there . . ." Toranaga desperately tried to settle her and gain control of the horse as Naga jumped for the horse's head. He caught the bridle and just managed to stop the horse from bolting. The falcon was screaming furiously. At length, reluctantly, she settled back on Toranaga's expert glove, held firmly by her thong jesses. But her wings still pulsated nervously, the bells on her feet jangling shrilly.

"*Hek-ek-ek-ek-eeeeekk!*" she shrieked a final time.

"There, there, my beauty. There, everything's all right," Toranaga said soothingly, his face still mottled with rage, then turned on Naga, trying to keep the animosity out of his tone for the falcon's sake. "If you've ruined her condition today, I'll—I'll—"

At that instant one of the beaters hallooed warningly. Immediately Toranaga slipped off the falcon's hood with his right hand, gave her a moment to adjust to her surroundings, then launched her.

She was long-winged, a peregrine, her name Tetsu-ko—Lady of Steel—and she whooshed up into the sky, circling to her station six hundred feet above Toranaga, waiting for her prey to be flushed, her nervousness forgotten. Then, turning on the downwind pass, she saw the dogs sent in and the covey of pheasant scattered in a wild flurry of wing beatings. She marked her prey, heeled over and stooped—closed her wings and dived relentlessly—her talons ready to hack.

She came hurtling down but the old cock pheasant, twice her size, side-slipped and, in panic, tore arrow-straight for the safety of a copse of trees, two hundred paces away. Tetsu-ko recovered, opened her wings, charging headlong after her quarry. She gained altitude and then, once more vertically above the cock, again stooped, hacked viciously, and again missed. Toranaga excitedly shouted encouragement, warning of the danger ahead, Naga forgotten.

With a frantic clattering of wings, the cock was streaking for the protection of the trees. The peregrine, again whirling high above, stooped and came slashing down. But she was too late. The wily pheasant vanished. Careless of her own safety, the falcon crashed through the leaves and branches, ferociously seeking her victim, then recovered and flashed into the open once more, screeching with rage, to rush high above the copse.

At that moment, a covey of partridge was flushed and whirred away, staying close to the ground seeking safety, darting this way and that, cunningly following the contours of the earth. Tetsu-ko marked one, folded her wings, and fell like a stone. This time she did not miss. One vicious hack of her hind talons as she passed broke the partridge's neck. The bird crashed to the ground in a bursting cloud of feathers. But instead of following her kill to the earth or binding it to her and landing with it, she soared screaming into the sky, climbing higher and ever higher.

Anxiously Toranaga took out the lure, a small dead bird tied to a thin rope, and whirred it around his head. But Tetsu-ko was not tempted back. Now she was a tiny speck in the sky and Toranaga was sure that he had lost her, that she had decided to leave him, to go back to the wilds, to kill at her whim and not at his whim, to eat when she wanted and not when he decided, and to fly where the winds bore her or fancy took her, masterless and forever free.

Toranaga watched her, not sad, but just a little lonely. She was a wild creature and Toranaga, like all falconers, knew he was only a temporary earthbound master. Alone he had climbed to her eyrie in the Hakoné mountains and taken her from the nest as a fledgling, and trained her, cherished her, and given her her first kill. Now he could hardly see her circling there, riding the thermals so gloriously, and he wished, achingly, that he too could ride the empyrean, away from the iniquities of earth.

Then the old cock pheasant casually broke from the trees to feed once more. And Tetsu-ko stooped, plummeting from the heavens, a tiny streamlined weapon of death, her claws ready for the coup de grace.

The cock pheasant died instantly, feathers bursting from him on impact, but she held on, falling with him to let go, her wings slashing the air to brake violently at the very last second. Then she closed her wings and settled on her kill.

She held it in her claws and began to pluck it with her beak prior to eating. But before she could eat Toranaga rode up. She stopped, distracted. Her merciless brown eyes, ringed with yellow ceres, watched as he dismounted, her ears listening to his cooing praise of her skill and bravery, and then, because she was hungry and he the giver of food and also because he was patient and made no sudden movement but knelt gently, she allowed him to come closer.

Toranaga was complimenting her softly. He took out his hunting knife and split the pheasant's head to allow Tetsu-ko to feed on the brains. As she began to feast on this tidbit, at *his* whim, he cut off the head and she came effortlessly onto his fist, where she was accustomed to feed.

All the time Toranaga praised her and when she'd finished this morsel he stroked her gently and complimented her lavishly. She bobbed and hissed her contentment, glad to be safely back on the fist once more where she could eat, for of course, ever since she had been taken from the nest, the fist was the only place she had ever been allowed to feed, her food always given to her by Toranaga personally. She began to preen herself, ready for another death.

Because Tetsu-ko had flown so well, Toranaga decided to let her gorge and fly her no more today. He gave her a small bird that he had already plucked and opened for her. When she was halfway through her meal he slipped on her hood. She continued to feed contentedly through the hood. When she had finished and began to preen herself again, he picked up the cock pheasant, bagged it, and beckoned his falconer, who had waited with the beaters. Exhilarated, they discussed the glory of the kill and counted the bag. There was a hare, a brace of quail, and the cock pheasant. Toranaga dismissed the falconer and the beaters, sending them back to camp with all the falcons. His guards waited downwind.

Now he turned his attention to Naga. "So?"

Naga knelt beside his horse, bowed. "You're completely correct, Sire—what you said about me. I apologize for offending you."

"But not for giving me bad advice?"

"I—I beg you to put me with someone who can teach me so that I'll never do that. I never want to give you bad advice, never."

"Good. You'll spend part of every day talking with the Anjin-san, learning what he knows. He can be one of your teachers."

"Him?"

"Yes. That may teach you some discipline. And if you can get it through that rock you have between your ears to *listen,* you'll certainly learn things of value to you. You might even learn something of value to me."

Naga stared sullenly at the ground.

"I want you to know everything he knows about guns, cannon, and warfare. You'll become my expert. Yes. And I want you to be very expert."

Naga said nothing.

"And I want you to become his friend."

"How can I do that, Sire?"

"Why don't *you* think of a way? Why don't you use *your* head?"

"I'll try. I swear I'll try."

"I want you to do better than that. You're ordered to succeed. Use some 'Christian charity.' You should've learned enough to do that. *Neh?*"

Naga scowled. "That's impossible to learn, much as I tried. It's the truth! All Tsukku-san talked was dogma and nonsense that would make any man vomit. Christian's for peasants, not samurai. Don't kill, don't take more than one woman, and fifty other stupidities! I obeyed you then and I'll obey you now—I always obey! Why not just let me do the things I can, Sire? I'll become Christian if that's what you want but I can't believe it—it's all manure and . . . I apologize for speaking. I'll become the Anjin-san's friend. I will."

"Good. And remember he's worth twenty thousand times his own weight in raw silk and he's got more knowledge than you'll have in twenty lifetimes."

Naga held himself in check and nodded dutifully in agreement.

"Good. You'll be leading two of the battalions, Omi-san two, and one will be held in reserve under Buntaro."

"And the other four, Sire?"

"We haven't guns enough for them. That was a feint to put Yabu off the scent," Toranaga said, throwing his son a morsel.

"Sire?"

"That was just an excuse to bring another thousand men here. Don't they arrive tomorrow? With two thousand men I can hold Anjiro and escape, if need be. *Neh?*"

"But Yabu-san can still—" Naga bit back the comment, knowing that once more he was sure to make a mistaken judgment. "Why is it I'm so stupid?" he asked bitterly. "Why can't I see things like you do? Or like Sudara-san? I want to help, to be of use. I don't want to provoke you all the time."

"Then learn patience, my son, and curb your temper. Your time will come soon enough."

"Sire?"

Toranaga was suddenly weary of being patient. He looked up at the sky. "I think I'll sleep for a while."

At once Naga took off the saddle and the horse blanket and laid them on the ground as a samurai bed. Toranaga thanked him and watched him place sentries. When he was sure that everything was correct and safe, he lay down and closed his eyes.

But he did not want to sleep, only to think. He knew it was an extremely bad sign that he had lost his temper. You're fortunate it was only in front of Naga, who doesn't know any better, he told himself. If that had happened near Omi, or Yabu, they'd have realized at once that you're almost frantic with worry. And such knowledge might easily inspire them to treachery. You were fortunate this time. Tetsu-ko put everything into proportion. But for her you might have let others see your rage and that would have been insanity.

What a beautiful flight! Learn from her: Naga's got to be treated like a falcon. Doesn't he scream and bate like the best of them? Naga's only problem is that he's being flown at the wrong game. His game is combat and sudden death, and he'll have that soon enough.

Toranaga's anxiety began to return. What's going on in Osaka? I miscalculated badly about the *daimyos*—who would accept and who would reject the summons. Why haven't I heard? Am I betrayed? So many dangers around me. . . .

What about the Anjin-san? He's falcon too. But he isn't broken to the fist yet, as Yabu and Mariko claim. What's his prey? His prey is the Black Ship and the Rodrigues-anjin and the ugly, arrogant little Captain-General who's not long for this earth, and all the Black Robe priests and all the Stinking Hairy priests, all Portuguese and all Spaniards and Turkmen, whoever they are, and Islamers, whoever they are, not forgetting Omi and Yabu and Buntaro and Ishido and me.

Toranaga turned over to get more comfortable and smiled to himself. But the Anjin-san's not a long-winged falcon, a hawk of the lure, that you fly free above you to stoop at a particular quarry. He's more like a short-winged hawk, a hawk of the fist, that you fly direct from the fist to kill anything that moves, say a goshawk that'll take partridge or a hare three times her own weight, rats, cats, dogs, woodcock, starlings, rooks, overtaking them with fantastic short bursts of speed to kill with a single crush of her talons; the hawk that detests the hood and won't accept it, just sits on your wrist, arrogant, dangerous, self-sufficient, pitiless, yellow-eyed, a fine friend and foul-tempered if the mood's on her.

Yes, the Anjin-san's a short-wing. Whom do I fly him at?

Omi? Not yet.

Yabu? Not yet.

Buntaro?

Why did the Anjin-san really go after Buntaro with pistols? Because of Mariko, of course. But have they pillowed? They've had plenty of opportunity. I think yes. "Lavish" she said that first day. Good. Nothing wrong in their pillowing —Buntaro was believed dead—providing it's a perpetual secret. But the Anjin-san was stupid to risk so much over another man's woman. Aren't there always a thousand others, free and unattached, equally pretty, equally small or big or fine or tight or highborn or whatever, without the hazard of belonging elsewhere? He acted like a stupid, jealous barbarian. Remember the Rodrigues-anjin? Didn't he duel and kill another barbarian according to their custom, just to take a low-class merchant's daughter that he then married in Nagasaki? Didn't the Taikō let this murder go unavenged, against my advice, because it was only a barbarian death and not one of ours? Stupid to have two laws, one for us, one for them. There should be only one. There must be only one law.

No, I won't fly the Anjin-san at Buntaro, I need that fool. But whether those two pillowed or not, I hope the thought never occurs to Buntaro. Then I would have to kill Buntaro quickly, for no force on earth would stop him from killing the Anjin-san and Mariko-san and I need them more than Buntaro. Should I eliminate Buntaro now?

The moment Buntaro had sobered up, Toranaga had sent for him. "How dare you put your interest in front of mine! How long will Mariko-san be unable to interpret?"

"The doctor said a few days, Sire. I apologize for all the trouble!"

"I made it very clear I needed her services for another twenty days. Don't you remember?"

"Yes. I'm sorry."

"If she'd displeased you, a few slaps on the buttocks would've been more than enough. All women need that from time to time, but more is loutish. You've selfishly jeopardized the training and acted like a bovine peasant. Without her I can't talk to the Anjin-san!"

"Yes. I know, Lord, I'm sorry. It's the first time I've hit her. It's just —sometimes she drives me insane, so much that—that I can't seem to see."

"Why don't you divorce her then? Or send her away? Or kill her, or order her to cut her throat when I've no further use for her?"

"I can't. I can't, Lord," Buntaro had said. "She's—I've wanted her from the first moment I saw her. When we were married, the first time, she was everything a man could want. I thought I was blessed—you remember how every *daimyo* in the realm wanted her! Then . . . then I sent her away to protect her after the filthy assassination, pretending to be disgusted with her for her safety, and then, when the Taikō told me to bring her back years later, she excited me even more. The truth is I expected her to be grateful, and took her as a man will, and didn't care about the little things a woman wants, like poems and flowers. But she'd changed. She was as faithful as ever, but just ice, always asking for death, for me to kill her." Buntaro was frantic. "I can't kill her or allow her to kill herself. She's tainted my son and makes me detest other women but I can't rid myself of her. I've . . . I've tried being kind but always the ice is there and it drives me mad. When I came back from Korea and heard she'd converted to this nonsense Christian religion I was amused, for what does any stupid religion matter? I was going to tease her about it but before I knew what was happening, I had my knife at her throat and swore I'd cut her if she didn't renounce it. Of course she wouldn't renounce it, what samurai would under such a threat, *neh?* She just looked up at me with those eyes of hers and told me to go on. 'Please cut me, Lord,' she said. 'Here, let me hold my head back for you. I pray God I'll bleed to death,' she said. I didn't cut her, Sire. I took her. But I did cut off the hair and ears of some of her ladies who had encouraged her to become Christian and turned them out of the castle. And I did the same to her foster mother, and cut off her nose as well, vile-tempered old hag! And then Mariko said, because . . . because I'd punished her ladies, the next time I came to her bed uninvited she'd commit seppuku, in any way she could, at once . . . in spite of her duty to you, in spite of her duty to the family, even in spite of the—the commandments of her Christian God!" Tears of rage were running down his cheeks unheeded. "I can't kill her, much as I want to. I can't kill Akechi Jinsai's daughter, much as she deserves it. . . ."

Toranaga had let Buntaro rant on until he was spent, then dismissed him, ordering him to stay totally away from Mariko until he considered what was to be done. He dispatched his own doctor to examine her. The report was favorable: bruises but no internal damage.

For his own safety, because he expected treachery and the sand of time was running out, Toranaga decided to increase the pressure on all of them. He ordered Mariko into Omi's house with instructions to rest, to stay within the confines of the house and completely out of the Anjin-san's way. Next he had summoned the Anjin-san and pretended irritation when it was clear they could hardly converse at all, dismissing him peremptorily. All training was intensified. Cadres were sent on forced marches. Naga was ordered to take the Anjin-san along and walk him into the ground. But Naga didn't walk the Anjin-san into the ground.

So he tried himself. He led a battalion eleven hours over the hills. The Anjin-san kept up, not with the front rank, but still he kept up. Back again at Anjiro, the Anjin-san said in his almost incomprehensible gibberish, hardly able to stand, "Toranaga-sama, I walk can. I guns training can. So sorry, no possibles two at same timings, *neh?*"

Toranaga smiled now, lying under the overcast waiting for the rain, warmed by the game of breaking Blackthorne to the fist. He's a short-wing all right. Mariko's equally tough, equally intelligent, but more brilliant, and she's got a ruthlessness that he'll never have. She's like a peregrine, like Tetsu-ko. The best. Why is it the female hawk, the falcon, is always bigger and faster and stronger than the male, always better than the male?

They're all hawks—she, Buntaro, Yabu, Omi, Fujiko, Ochiba, Naga and all my sons and my daughters and women and vassals, and all my enemies—all hawks, or prey for hawks.

I must get Naga into position high over his quarry and let him stoop. Who should it be? Omi or Yabu?

What Naga had said about Yabu was true.

"So, Yabu-san, what have you decided?" he had asked, the second day.

"I'm not going to Osaka until you go, Sire. I've ordered all Izu mobilized."

"Ishido will impeach you."

"He'll impeach you first, Sire, and if the Kwanto falls, Izu falls. I made a solemn bargain with you. I'm on your side. The Kasigi honor their bargains."

"I'm equally honored to have you as an ally," he had lied, pleased that Yabu had once more done what he had planned for him to do. The next day Yabu had assembled a host and asked him to review it and then, in front of all his men, knelt formally and offered himself as vassal.

"You acknowledge me your feudal lord?" Toranaga had said.

"Yes. And all the men of Izu. And Lord, please accept this gift as a token of filial duty." Still on his knees, Yabu had offered his Murasama sword. "This is the sword that murdered your grandfather."

"That's not possible!"

Yabu had told him the history of the sword, how it had come down to him over the years and how, only recently, he had learned of its true identity. He summoned Suwo. The old man told what he had witnessed when he himself was little more than a boy.

"It's true, Lord," Suwo had said proudly. "No man saw Obata's father break the sword or cast it into the sea. And I swear by my hope of samurai rebirth that I served your grandfather, Lord Chikitada. I served him faithfully until that day he died. I was there, I swear it."

Toranaga had accepted the sword. It seemed to quiver with malevolence in his hand. He had always scoffed at the legend that certain swords possessed a killing urge of their own, that some swords needed to leap out of the scabbard to drink blood, but now Toranaga believed it.

He shuddered, remembering that day. Why do Murasama blades hate us? One killed my grandfather. Another almost cut off my arm when I was six, an unexplained accident, no one near but still my sword arm was slashed and I nearly bled to death. A third decapitated my first-born son.

"Sire," Yabu had said, "such a befouled blade shouldn't be allowed to live, *neh?* Let me take it out to sea and drown it so that this sword at least can never threaten you or your descendants."

"Yes—yes," he had muttered, thankful that Yabu had made the suggestion. "Do it now!" And only when the sword had sunk out of sight, into the very deep, witnessed by his own men, had his heart begun to pump normally. He had thanked Yabu, ordered taxes to be stabilized at sixty parts for peasants, forty for their lords, and had given him Izu as his fief. So everything was as before, except that now all power in Izu belonged to Toranaga, if he wished to take it back.

Toranaga turned over to ease the ache in his sword arm and settled again more comfortably, enjoying the nearness of the earth, gaining strength from it as always.

That blade's gone, never to return. Good, but remember what the old Chinese soothsayer foretold, he thought: that you would die by the sword. But whose sword and is it to be by my own hand or another's?

I'll know when I know, he told himself without fear.

Now sleep. *Karma* is *karma*. Be thou of Zen. Remember, in tranquillity, that the Absolute, the Tao, is within thee, that no priest or cult or dogma or book or saying or teaching or teacher stands between Thou and It. Know that Good and Evil are irrelevant, I and Thou irrelevant, Inside and Outside irrelevant as are Life and Death. Enter into the Sphere where there is no fear of death nor hope of afterlife, where thou art free of the impediments of life or the needs of salvation. Thou art thyself the Tao. Be thou, *now,* a rock against which the waves of life rush in vain. . . .

The faint shout brought Toranaga out of his meditation and he leaped to his feet. Naga was excitedly pointing westward. All eyes followed his point.

The carrier pigeon was flying in a direct line for Anjiro from the west. She fluttered into a distant tree to rest for a moment, then took off once more as rain began to fall.

Far to the west, in her wake, was Osaka.

CHAPTER 37

THE handler at the pigeon coop held the bird gently but firmly as Toranaga stripped off his sodden clothes. He had galloped back through the downpour. Naga and other samurai anxiously crowded the small doorway, careless of the warm rain which still fell in torrents, drumming on the tiled roof.

Carefully Toranaga dried his hands. The man offered the pigeon. Two tiny, beaten-silver cylinders were attached to each of her legs. One would have been usual. Toranaga had to work hard to keep the nervous tremble out of his fingers. He untied the cylinders and took them over to the light of the window opening to examine the minute seals. He recognized Kiri's secret cipher. Naga and the others were watching tensely. His face revealed nothing.

Toranaga did not break the seals at once, much as he wanted to. Patiently he waited until a dry kimono was brought. A servant held a large oiled-paper umbrella for him and he walked to his own quarters in the fortress. Soup and cha were waiting. He sipped them and listened to the rain. When he felt calm, he posted guards and went into an inner room. In privacy he broke the seals. The paper of the four scrolls was very thin, the characters tiny, the message long and in code. Decoding was laborious. When it was completed, he read the message and then reread it twice. Then he let his mind range.

Night came. The rain stopped. Oh, Buddha, let the harvest be good, he prayed. This was the season when the paddy fields were being flooded and, throughout the land, the pale green rice seedlings were being planted into the weedless, almost liquid fields to be harvested in four or five months, depending on the weather. And, throughout the land, the poor and the rich, *eta* and emperor, servant and samurai, all prayed that just the right amount of rain and sun and humidity came correctly in its season. And every man, woman, and child counted the days to harvest.

We'll need a great harvest this year, thought Toranaga.

"Naga! Naga-san!"

His son came running. "Yes, Father?"

"At the first hour after dawn fetch Yabu-san and his chief advisers to the plateau. Also Buntaro and our three senior captains. And Mariko-san. Bring them all to the plateau at dawn. Mariko-san can serve cha. Yes. And I want the Anjin-san standing by at the camp. Guards to ring us at two hundred paces."

"Yes, Father." Naga turned to obey. Unable to contain himself he blurted out, "Is it war? Is it?"

Because Toranaga needed a harbinger of optimism throughout the fortress, he did not berate his son for the ill-disciplined impertinence.

"Yes," he said. "Yes—but on my terms."

Naga closed the shoji and rushed off. Toranaga knew that, although Naga's face and manner would now be outwardly composed, nothing would disguise the excitement in his walk or the fire behind his eyes. So rumor and counterrumor would rush through Anjiro to spread quickly throughout Izu and beyond, if the fires were fed properly.

"I'm committed now," he said aloud to the flowers that stood serenely in the *takonama,* shadows flickering in the pleasant candlelight.

414

Kiri had written: "Sire, I pray Buddha you are well and safe. This is our last carrier pigeon so I also pray Buddha guides her to you—traitors killed all the others last night by firing the coop and this one escaped only because she's been sick and I was nursing her privately.

"Yesterday morning Lord Sugiyama suddenly resigned, exactly as planned. But before he could make good his escape, he was trapped on the outskirts of Osaka by Ishido's *ronin*. Unhappily some of Sugiyama's family were also caught with him—I heard he was betrayed by one of his people. Rumor has it that Ishido offered him a compromise: that if Lord Sugiyama delayed his resignation until after the Council of Regents convened (tomorrow), so that you could be legally impeached, in return Ishido guaranteed that the Council would formally give Sugiyama the whole of the Kwanto and, as a measure of good faith, Ishido would release him and his family at once. Sugiyama refused to betray you. Immediately Ishido ordered *eta* to convince him. They tortured Sugiyama's children, then his consort, in front of him, but he still would not abandon you. They were all given bad deaths. His, the final one, was very bad.

"Of course, there were no witnesses to this treachery and it's all hearsay but I believe it. Of course Ishido disclaimed any knowledge of the murders or participation in them, vowing that he'll hunt down the 'murderers.' At first Ishido claimed that Sugiyama had never actually resigned, therefore, in his opinion, the Council could still meet. I sent copies of Sugiyama's resignation to the other Regents, Kiyama, Ito, and Onoshi, and sent another openly to Ishido and circulated four more copies among the *daimyos*. (How clever of you, Tora-chan, to have known that extra copies would be necessary.) So, from yesterday, exactly as you planned with Sugiyama, the Council is legally no more—in this you've succeeded completely.

"Good news: Lord Mogami safely turned back outside the city with all his family and samurai. Now he's openly your ally, so your far-northern flank is secure. The Lords Maeda, Kukushima, Asano, Ikeda, and Okudiara all quietly slipped out of Osaka last night to safety—also the Christian Lord Oda.

"Bad news is that the families of Maeda, Ikeda, and Oda and a dozen other important *daimyos* did not escape and are now hostage here, as are those of fifty or sixty lesser uncommitted lords.

"Bad news is that yesterday your half brother, Zataki, Lord of Shinano, publicly declared for the Heir, Yaemon, against you, accusing you of plotting with Sugiyama to overthrow the Council of Regents by creating chaos, so now your northeastern border is breached and Zataki and his fifty thousand fanatics will oppose you.

"Bad news is that almost every *daimyo* accepted the Emperor's 'invitation.'

"Bad news is that not a few of your friends and allies here are incensed that you did not give them prior knowledge of your strategy so they could prepare a line of retreat. Your old friend, the great Lord Shimazu, is one. I heard this afternoon that he's openly demanded that all lords should be ordered by the Emperor to kneel before the boy, Yaemon, now.

"Bad news is that that Lady Ochiba is brilliantly spinning her web, promising fiefs and titles and court rank to the uncommitted. Tora-chan, it's a great pity she's not on your side, she's a worthy enemy. The Lady Yodoko alone advocates prayer and calm but no one listens, and the Lady Ochiba wants to precipitate war now while she feels you're weak and isolated. So sorry, my Lord, but you're isolated and, I think, betrayed.

"Worst of all is that now the Christian Regents, Kiyama and Onoshi, are openly together and violently opposed to you. They issued a joint statement this morning deploring Sugiyama's 'defection,' saying that his action has put the realm into confusion, that 'we must all be strong for the sake of the Empire. The Regents have supreme responsibility. We must be ready to stamp out, together, any lord or group of lords who wish to overthrow the Taikō's will, or the legal succession.' (Does this mean they plan to meet as a Council of four Regents?) One of our Christian spies in the Black Robes' headquarters here whispered that the priest Tsukku-san secretly left Osaka five days ago, but we don't know if he went to Yedo or to Nagasaki, where the Black Ship is expected. Did you know it will be very early this season? Perhaps within twenty or thirty days?

"Sire: I've always hesitated about giving quick opinions based on hearsay, rumors, spies, or a woman's intuition (there, you see, Tora-chan, I have learned from you!) but time is short and I may not be able to speak to you again: First, too many families are trapped here. Ishido will never let them go (as he will never let us go). These hostages are an immense danger to you. Few lords have Sugiyama's sense of duty or fortitude. Very many, I think, will now go with Ishido, however reluctantly, because of these hostages. Next, I think that Maeda will betray you, also probably Asano. I tally of all two hundred and sixty-four *daimyos* in our land, only twenty-four who are certain to follow you, another fifty possibly. That's not nearly enough. Kiyama and Onoshi will sway all or most of the Christian *daimyos* and I believe they will not join you now. Lord Mori, the richest and greatest of all, is against you personally, as always, and he'll pull Asano, Kobayakawa, and perhaps Oda into his net. With your half brother Lord Zataki against you, your position is terribly precarious. I counsel you to declare Crimson Sky at once and rush for Kyoto. It's your only hope.

"As to the Lady Sazuko and myself, we're well and content. The child quickens nicely and if it's the child's *karma* to be born, thus will it happen. We're safe in our corner of the castle, the door tightly locked, the portcullis down. Our samurai are filled with devotion to you and to your cause and if it is our *karma* to depart this life then we will depart serenely. Your Lady misses you greatly, very greatly. For myself, Tora-chan, I long to see you, to laugh with you, and to see your smile. My only regret in death would be that I could no longer do these things, and watch over you. If there is an afterlife and God or Buddha or *kami* exist, I promise I will somehow bend them all to your side . . . though first I may beseech them to make me slender and young and fruitful for you, yet leave me my enjoyment of food. Ah, that would indeed be heaven, to be able to eat and eat and yet be perpetually young and thin!

"I send you my laughter. May Buddha bless thee and thine."

Toranaga read them the message, except the private part about Kiri and the Lady Sazuko. When he had finished they looked at him and each other incredulously, not only because of what the message said but also because he was so openly taking them all into his confidence.

They were seated on mats set in a semicircle around him in the center of the plateau, without guards, safe from eavesdroppers. Buntaro, Yabu, Igurashi, Omi, Naga, the Captains, and Mariko. Guards were posted two hundred paces away.

"I want some advice," Toranaga said. "My counselors are in Yedo. This matter is urgent and I want all of you to act in their place. What's going to happen and what I should do. Yabu-san?"

Yabu was in turmoil. Every path seemed to lead to disaster. "First, Sire, just exactly what is 'Crimson Sky'?"

"It's the code name for my final battle plan, a single violent rush at Kyoto with all my legions, relying on mobility and surprise, to take possession of the capital from the evil forces that now surround it, to wrest the person of the

Emperor from the filthy grasp of those who've duped him, led by Ishido. Once the Son of Heaven's safely released from their clutches, then to petition him to revoke the mandate granted the present Council, who are clearly traitorous, or dominated by traitors, and grant me his mandate to form a new Council which would put the interests of the realm and the Heir before personal ambition. I would lead eighty to one hundred thousand men, leaving my lands unprotected, my flanks unguarded, and a retreat unsecured." Toranaga saw them staring at him flabbergasted. He did not mention the cadres of elite samurai who had been so furtively planted in many of the important castles and provinces over the years, and who were to explode simultaneously into revolt to create the chaos essential to the plan.

Yabu burst out, "But you'd have to fight every pace of the way. Ikawa Jikkyu strangles the Tokaidō for a hundred *ri.* Then more Ishido strongholds straddle the rest!"

"Yes. But I plan to rush northwest along the Koshu-kaidō, then stab down on Kyoto and stay away from the coast lands."

At once many shook their heads and began to speak but Yabu overrode them. "But, Sire, the message said your kinsman Zataki-san's already gone over to the enemy! Now your road north is blocked too. His province is athwart the Koshu-kaidō. You'll have to fight through all Shinano—that's mountainous and very hard, and his men are fanatically loyal. You'll be carved to pieces in those mountains."

"That's the only way, the only way I have a chance. I agree there are too many hostiles on the coastal road."

Yabu glanced at Omi, wishing he could consult with him, loathing the message and the whole Osaka mess, hating being first to speak, and utterly detesting the vassal status he had accepted at Omi's pleading.

"It's your only chance, Yabu-sama," Omi had urged. "The only way you'll avoid Toranaga's trap and leave yourself room to maneuver—"

Igurashi had interrupted furiously. "Better to fall on Toranaga today while he's got few men here! Better to kill him and take his head to Ishido while there's time."

"Better to wait, better to be patient—"

"What happens if Toranaga orders our Master to give up Izu?" Igurashi had shouted. "As liege lord to vassal, Toranaga has that right!"

"He'll never do it. He needs our Master more than ever now. Izu guards his southern door. He can't have Izu hostile! He must have our Master on his—"

"What if he orders Lord Yabu out?"

"We rebel! We kill Toranaga if he's here or fight any army he sends against us. But he'll never do that, don't you see? As his vassal, Toranaga must protect—"

Yabu had let them argue and then at length he had seen Omi's wisdom. "Very well. I agree! And offering him my Murasama sword to fix the bargain's genius, Omi-san," he had gloated, taken wholeheartedly by the cunning of the plan. "Yes. Genius. His Yoshitomo blade more than takes its place. And of course, I'm more valuable to Toranaga now than ever before. Omi's right, Igurashi. I've no choice. I'm committed to Toranaga from now on. A vassal!"

"Until war comes," Omi had said deliberately.

"Of course. Of course only until war comes! Then I can change sides—or do a dozen things. You're right, Omi-san, again!"

Omi's the best counselor I've ever had, he told himself. But the most dangerous. Omi's clever enough to take Izu if I die. But what does that matter. We're all dead.

"You're blocked completely," he told Toranaga. "You're isolated."

"Is there any alternative?" Toranaga asked.

"Excuse me, Sire," Omi said, "but how long would it take to ready this attack?"

"It's ready now."

"Izu's ready too, Sire," Yabu said. "Your hundred and my sixteen thousand and the Musket Regiment—is that enough?"

"No. Crimson Sky's a desperation plan—everything risked on one attack."

"You have to risk it, as soon as the rains cease and we can war," Yabu insisted. "What choice have you got? Ishido will form a new Council at once, they still have the mandate. So you'll be impeached, today or tomorrow or the next day. Why wait to be eaten up? Listen, maybe the Regiment could blast a way through the mountains! Let it be Crimson Sky! All men thrown into one great attack. It's the Way of the Warrior—it's worthy of samurai, Toranaga-sama. The guns, our guns, will blow Zataki out of our way and if you succeed or fail, what does it matter? The try will live forever!"

Naga said, "Yes. But we'll win—we will!" A few of the captains nodded their agreement, relieved that war had come. Omi said nothing.

Toranaga was looking at Buntaro. "Well?"

"Lord, I beg you to excuse me from giving an opinion. I and my men do whatever you decide. That's my only duty. My opinion is no value to you because I do what you alone decide."

"Normally I'd accept that but not today!"

"War then. What Yabu-san says is right. Let's go to Kyoto. Today, tomorrow, or when the rains stop. Crimson Sky! I'm tired of waiting."

"Omi-san?" Toranaga asked.

"Yabu-sama is correct, Sire. Ishido will bend the Taikō's will to appoint a new Council very soon. The new Council will have the Emperor's mandate. Your enemies will applaud and most of your friends will hesitate and so betray you. The new Council will impeach you at once. Then—"

"Then it's Crimson Sky?" Yabu interrupted.

"If Lord Toranaga orders it, then it is. But I don't think the impeachment order has any value at all. You can forget it!"

"Why?" Toranaga asked, as all attention went to Omi.

"I agree with you, Sire. Ishido's evil, *neh?* Any *daimyos* who agree to serve him are equally evil. True men know Ishido for what he is, and also know that the Emperor's been duped again." Omi was prudently treading through the quicksands that he knew could swallow him. "I think he made a lasting mistake murdering Lord Sugiyama. Because of those foul murders, I think now all *daimyos* will suspect treachery from Ishido, and very few outside of Ishido's immediate grasp will bow to the orders of his 'Council.' You're safe. For a time."

"For how much time?"

"The rains are with us for two months, about. When the rains cease Ishido will plan to send Ikawa Jikkyu and Lord Zataki against you simultaneously, to catch you in a pincer, and Ishido's main army will support them over the Tokaidō Road. Meanwhile, until the rains stop, every *daimyo* who bears a grudge against any other *daimyo* will only pay Ishido lip service until he makes the first move, then I think they'll forget him and they'll all take revenge or grab territory at their whim. The Empire will be torn as it was before the Taikō. But you, Sire, between Yabu-sama and yourself, jointly, with luck you have enough strength to hold the passes to the Kwanto and to Izu against the first wave and beat it off. I don't think Ishido could mount another attack—not a great one. When Ishido and the others have expended their energies, together you and Lord Yabu can cautiously come from behind our mountains and gradually take the Empire into your own hands."

"When will that be?"

"In the time of your children, Sire."

"You say fight a defensive battle?" Yabu asked scornfully.

"I think jointly you're both safe behind the mountains. You wait, Toranaga-sama. You wait until you have more allies. You hold the passes. This can be done! General Ishido's evil, but not stupid enough to commit all his force to one battle. He'll stay skulking inside Osaka. So for the time being, we mustn't use our regiment. We must tighten security and keep them as a secret weapon, poised and ever ready, until you come from behind your mountains—but now I don't think I will ever see them used." Omi was conscious of the eyes watching him. He bowed to Toranaga. "Please excuse me for talking at length, Sire."

Toranaga studied him, then glanced at his son. He saw the youth's pent-up excitement and knew it was time to cast him at his prey. "Naga-san?"

"What Omi-san said is true," Naga told him at once, exultantly. "Most of it. But I say use the two months to gather allies, to isolate Ishido even more, and when the rains cease, attack without warning—Crimson Sky."

Toranaga asked, "You disagree with Omi-san's opinion about a lengthy war?"

"No. But isn't this—" Naga stopped.

"Go on, Naga-san. Speak openly!"

Naga held his tongue, his face white.

"You're ordered to continue!"

"Well, Sire, it occurred to me that—" Again he stopped, then said in a gush, "Isn't this your great opportunity to become Shōgun? If you succeed in taking Kyoto and get the mandate, why form a Council? Why not petition the Emperor to make you Shōgun? It would be best for you and best for the realm." Naga tried to keep the fear out of his voice for he was speaking treason against Yaemon and most samurai here—Yabu, Omi, Igurashi, and Buntaro particularly—were open loyalists. "I say you should be Shōgun!" He turned defensively on the others. "If this opportunity is let go. . . . Omi-san, you're right about a long war, but I say Lord Toranaga must take power, to give power! A long war will ruin the Empire, split it into a thousand fragments again! Who wants that? Lord Toranaga must be Shōgun. To gift the Empire on to Yaemon, to Lord Yaemon, the realm must be secured first! There'll never be another opportunity. . . ." His words trailed off. He squared his back, frightened because he had said it, glad that he had said publicly what he had been thinking forever.

Toranaga sighed. "I have never sought to become Shōgun. How many times do I have to say it? I support my nephew Yaemon and the Taikō's will." He looked at them all, one by one. Lastly at Naga. The youth winced. But Toranaga said kindly, calling him back to the lure, "Your zeal and youth alone excuse you. Unfortunately, many much older and wiser than you think that's my ambition. It isn't. There's only one way to settle that nonsense and that's put Lord Yaemon into power. And that I intend to do."

"Yes, Father. Thank you. Thank you," Naga replied in despair.

Toranaga shifted his eyes to Igurashi. "What's your counsel?"

The one-eyed samurai scratched. "Me, I'm only a soldier, not a counselor, but I wouldn't advise Crimson Sky, not if we can war on our terms like Omi-san says. I fought in Shinano years ago. That's bad country, and then Lord Zataki was with us. I wouldn't want to war in Shinano again and never if Zataki was hostile. And if Lord Maeda's suspect, well, how can you plan a battle if your biggest ally may betray you? Lord Ishido'll put two, three hundred thousand men against you and still keep a hundred holding Osaka. Even with the guns we've not enough men to attack. But behind the mountains using the guns, you could hold out forever if it happens like Omi-san says. We could hold the passes. You've enough rice—doesn't the Kwanto supply half the Empire? Well, a third at least—and we could send you all the fish you need. You'd be safe. Let Lord Ishido and devil Jikkyu come at us if it's to happen like Omi-san said, that soon the enemy'll be feeding on each other. If not, keep Crimson Sky ready. A man can die for his lord only once in this life."

"Has anyone anything to add?" Toranaga asked. No one answered him. "Mariko-san?"

"It's not my place to speak here, Sire," she replied. "I'm sure everything has been said that should have been said. But may I be allowed to ask for all your counselors here, what do *you* think will happen?"

Toranaga chose his words deliberately. "I believe that what Omi-san forecast will happen. With one exception: the Council won't be impotent. The Council will wield enough influence to gather an invincible allied force. When the rains cease it will be thrown against the Kwanto, bypassing Izu. The Kwanto will be gobbled up, then Izu. Only after I'm dead will the *daimyos* fight among themselves."

"But why, Sire?" Omi ventured.

"Because I've too many enemies, I own the Kwanto, I've warred for more than forty years and never lost a battle. They're all afraid of me. I *know* that first the vultures will pack together to destroy me. Later they'll destroy themselves, but first they'll join to destroy me if they can. Know very clearly, all of you, I'm the only real threat to Yaemon, even though I'm no threat at all. That's the irony of it. They all believe I want to be Shōgun. I don't. This is another war that's not necessary at all!"

Naga broke the silence. "Then what are you going to do, Sire?"

"Eh?"

"What are you going to do?"

"Obviously, Crimson Sky," Toranaga said.

"But you said they'd eat us up?"

"They would—*if* I gave them any time. But I'm not going to give them any time. We go to war at once!"

"But the rains—what about the rains?"

"We will arrive in Kyoto wet. Hot and stinking and wet. Surprise, mobility, audacity, and timing win wars, *neh?* Yabu-san was right. The guns will blast a way through the mountains."

For an hour they discussed plans and the feasibility of large-scale war in the rainy season—an unheard-of strategy. Then Toranaga sent them away, except Mariko, telling Naga to order the Anjin-san here. He watched them walk off. They had all been outwardly enthusiastic once the decision had been announced, Naga and Buntaro particularly. Only Omi had been reserved and thoughtful and unconvinced. Toranaga discounted Igurashi for he knew that, rightly, the soldier would do only what Yabu ordered, and he dismissed Yabu as a pawn, treacherous certainly, but still a pawn. Omi's the only one worthwhile, he thought. I wonder if he's worked out yet what I'm really going to do?

"Mariko-san. Find out, tactfully, how much the courtesan's contract would cost."

She blinked. "Kiku-san, Sire?"

"Yes."

"Now, Sire? At once?"

"Tonight would do excellently." He looked at her blandly. "Her contract's not necessarily for me, perhaps for one of my officers."

"I would imagine the price would depend on whom, Sire."

"I imagine it will. But set a price. The girl of course has the right of refusal, if she wishes, when the samurai's named, but tell her mama-san owner that I don't expect the girl will have the bad manners to mistrust my choice for her. Tell the owner also that Kiku is a Lady of the First Class of Mishima and not Yedo or Osaka or Kyoto," Toranaga added genially, "so I expect to pay Mishima prices and not Yedo or Osaka or Kyoto prices."

"Yes, Sire, of course."

Toranaga moved his shoulder to ease the ache, shifting his swords.

"May I massage it for you, Sire? Or send for Suwo?"

"No, thank you. I'll see Suwo later." Toranaga got up and relieved himself with great pleasure, then sat down again. He wore a short, light silk kimono, blue patterned, and the simple straw sandals. His fan was blue and decorated with his crest.

The sun was low, rain clouds building heavily.

"It's vast to be alive," he said happily. "I can almost hear the rain waiting to be born."

"Yes," she said.

Toranaga thought a moment. Then he said as a poem:

> *"The sky*
> *Scorched by the sun,*
> *Weeps*
> *Fecund tears."*

Mariko obediently put her mind to work to play the poem game with him, so popular with most samurai, spontaneously twisting the words of the poem that he had made up, adapting them, making another from his. After a moment she replied:

> *"But the forest*
> *Wounded by the wind,*
> *Weeps*
> *Dead leaves."*

"Well said! Yes, very well said!" Toranaga looked at her contentedly, enjoying what he saw. She was dressed in a pale green kimono with patterns of bamboo, a dark green obi and orange sunshade. There was a marvelous sheen to the blue-black hair, which was piled high under her wide-brimmed hat. He remembered nostalgically how they had all—even the Dictator Goroda himself—wanted her when she was thirteen and her father, Akechi Jinsai, had first presented this, his eldest daughter, at Goroda's court. And how Nakamura, the Taikō-to-be, had begged the Dictator to give her to him, and then how Goroda had laughed, and publicly called him his randy little monkey general, and told him to "stick to fighting battles, peasant, don't fight to stick patrician holes!" Akechi Jinsai had openly scorned Nakamura, his rival for Goroda's favor, the main reason why Nakamura had delighted in smashing him. And why also Nakamura had delighted in watching Buntaro squirm for years, Buntaro who had been given the girl to cement an alliance between Goroda and Toda Hiro-matsu. I wonder, Toranaga asked himself mischievously, looking at her, I wonder if Buntaro were dead, would she consent to be one of my consorts? Toranaga had always preferred experienced women, widows or divorced wives, but never too pretty or too wise or too young or too well-born, so never too much trouble and always grateful.

He chuckled to himself. I'd never ask her because she's everything I don't want in a consort—except that her age is perfect.

"Sire?" she asked.

"I was thinking about your poem, Mariko-san," he said, even more blandly. Then added:

"Why so wintery?
Summer's
Yet to come, and the fall of
Glorious autumn."

She said in answer:

"If I could use words
Like falling leaves,
What a bonfire
My poems would make!"

He laughed and bowed with mock humility. "I concede victory, Mariko-sama. What will the favor be? A fan? Or a scarf for your hair?"

"Thank you, Sire," she replied. "Yes, whatever pleases you."

"Ten thousand koku yearly to your son."

"Oh, Sire, we don't deserve such favor!"

"You won a victory. Victory and duty must be rewarded. How old is Saruji now?"

"Fifteen—almost fifteen."

"Ah, yes—he was betrothed to one of Lord Kiyama's granddaughters recently, wasn't he?"

"Yes, Sire. It was in the Eleventh month last year, the Month of the White Frost. He's presently at Osaka with Lord Kiyama."

"Good. Ten thousand koku, beginning at once. I will send the authority with tomorrow's mail. Now, enough of poems, please give me your opinion."

"My opinion, Sire, is that we are all safe in your hands, as the land is safe in your hands."

"I want you to be serious."

"Oh, but I am, Sire. I thank you for the favor to my son. That makes everything perfect. I believe whatever you do will be right. By the Madon—yes, by the Madonna, I swear I believe that."

"Good. But I still want your opinion."

Immediately she replied, without a care in the world, as an equal to an equal. "First, you should bring Lord Zataki secretly back to your side. I'd surmise you either know how to do this already, or more probably, you have a secret agreement with your half brother, and you prompted his mythical 'defection' in the first place to lull Ishido into a false position. Next: You'll never attack first. You never have, you've always counseled patience, and you only attack when you're sure to win, so publicly ordering Crimson Sky at once is only another diversion. Next, timing: My opinion is you should do what you will do, pretend to order Crimson Sky but never commit it. This will throw Ishido into confusion because, obviously, spies here and in Yedo will report your plan, and he'll have to scatter his force like a covey of partridge, in filthy weather, to prepare for a threat that'll never materialize. Meanwhile you'll spend the next two months gathering allies, to undermine Ishido's alliances and break up his coalition, which you must do by any means. And of course, you must tempt Ishido out of Osaka Castle. If you don't, Sire, he will win, or at least, you will lose the Shōgunate. You—"

"I've already made my position clear on that," Toranaga rapped, no longer amused. "And you forget yourself."

Mariko said carelessly and happily, "I have to talk secrets today, Sire, because of the hostages. They're a knife in your heart."

"What about them?"

"Be patient with me please, Sire. I may never be able to talk to you in what the Anjin-san would call an 'open English private way' ever again—you're never alone like we're alone now. I beg you to excuse my bad manners." Mariko gathered her wits and, astoundingly, continued to speak as an equal. "My absolute opinion is that Naga-san was right. You must become Shōgun, *or you will have failed in your duty to the Empire and to the Minowara.*"

"How dare you say such a thing!"

Mariko remained quite serene, his open anger touching her not at all. "I counsel you to marry the Lady Ochiba. It's eight years before Yaemon's old enough, legally, to inherit—that's an eternity! Who knows what could happen in eight months, let alone eight years."

"Your whole family can be obliterated in eight days!"

"Yes, Sire. But that has nothing to do with you and your duty, and the realm. Naga-san's right. You must take the power to give power." With mock gravity she added breathlessly, "And now may your faithful counselor commit seppuku or should I do it later?" and she pretended to swoon.

Toranaga gawked at her incredible effrontery, then he roared with laughter and pounded his fist on the ground. When he could talk, he choked out, "I'll never understand you, Mariko-san."

"Ah, but you do, Sire," she said, patting the perspiration off her forehead. "You're kind to let this devoted vassal make you laugh, to listen to her requests, to say what must be said, had to be said. Forgive me my impertinence, please."

"Why should I, eh? Why?" Toranaga smiled, genial now.

"Because of the hostages, Sire," she said simply.

"Ah, them!" He too became serious.

"Yes. I must go to Osaka."

"Yes," he said. "I know."

CHAPTER 38

A CCOMPANIED by Naga, Blackthorne trudged disconsolately down the hill
toward the two figures who sat on the futons in the center of the ring
of guards. Beyond the guards were the rising foothills of the mountains
that soared to a clouded sky. The day was sultry. His head was aching from the
grief of the last few days, from worrying about Mariko, and from being unable
to talk except in Japanese for so long. Now he recognized her and some of his
misery left him.

Many times he had gone to Omi's house to see Mariko or to inquire about her.
Samurai had always turned him away, politely but firmly. Omi had told him
as a *tomodashi,* a friend, that she was all right. Don't worry, Anjin-san. Do
you understand? Yes, he had said, understanding only that he could not see
her.

Then he had been sent for by Toranaga and had wanted to tell him so much
but because of his lack of words had failed to do anything other than irritate him.
Fujiko had gone several times to see Mariko. When she came back she always
said that Mariko was well, adding the inevitable, *"Shinpai suruna,* Anjin-san.
Wakarimasu?" Don't worry—do you understand?

With Buntaro it had been as though nothing had ever happened. They mouthed
polite greetings when they met during the day. Apart from occasionally using
the bath house, Buntaro was like any other samurai in Anjiro, neither friendly
nor unfriendly.

From dawn to dusk Blackthorne had been chased by the accelerated training.
He had had to suppress his frustration as he tried to teach, and strove to learn
the language. By nightfall he was always exhausted. Hot and sweating and
rain-soaked. And alone. Never had he felt so alone, so aware of not belonging
in this alien world.

Then there was the horror that began three days ago. It had been a very long
humid day. At sunset he had wearily ridden home and had instantly felt trouble
permeating his house. Fujiko had greeted him nervously.

"Nan desu ka?"

She had replied quietly, at length, eyes lowered.

"Wakarimasen." I don't understand. *"Nan desu ka?"* he asked again, impatiently, his fatigue making him irritable.

Then she had beckoned him into the garden. She pointed at the eaves but the
roof seemed sound enough to him. More words and signs and it finally dawned
on him that she was pointing to where he had hung the pheasant.

"Oh, I'd forgotten about that! *Watashi . . ."* But he couldn't remember how
to say it so he just shrugged wearily. *"Wakarimasu. Nan desu kiji ka?"* I understand. What about the pheasant?

Servants were peering at him from doors and windows, clearly petrified. She
spoke again. He concentrated but her words did not make sense.

"Wakarimasen, Fujiko-san." I don't understand, Fujiko-san.

She took a deep breath, then shakily imitated someone removing the pheasant,
carrying it away, and burying it.

"Ahhhh! *Wakarimasu,* Fujiko-san. *Wakarimasu!* Was it getting high?" he

424

asked. As he did not know the Japanese word he held his nose and pantomimed stench.

"*Hai, hai,* Anjin-san. *Dozo gomen nasai, gomen nasai.*" She made the sound of flies and, with her hands, painted a picture of a buzzing cloud.

"*Ah so desu! Wakarimasu.*" Once upon a time he would have apologized and, if he had known the words, he would have said, I'm so sorry for the inconvenience. Instead he just shrugged, eased the ache in his back, and mumbled, "*Shigata ga nai,*" wanting only to slide into the ecstasy of the bath and massage, the only joy that made life possible. "The hell with it," he said in English, turning away. "If I'd been here during the day I'd've noticed it. The hell with it!"

"*Dozo,* Anjin-san?"

"*Shigata ga nai,*" he repeated louder.

"*Ah so desu, arigato goziemashita.*"

"*Tare toru desu ka?*" Who took it?

"Ueki-ya."

"Oh, that old bugger!" Ueki-ya, the gardener, the kind, toothless old man who tended the plants with loving hands and made his garden beautiful. "*Yoi. Motte kuru* Ueki-ya." Good, fetch him.

Fujiko shook her head. Her face had become chalky white.

"Ueki-ya *shinda desu, shinda desu!*" she whispered.

"Ueki-ya *ga shindato? Donoyoni? Doshité? Doshité shindanoda?*" How? Why? How did he die?

Her hand pointed at the place where the pheasant had been and she spoke many gentle incomprehensible words. Then she mimed the single cut of a sword.

"*Jesus Christ God!* You put that old man to death over a stinking, God-cursed pheasant?"

At once all the servants rushed to the garden and fell on their knees. They put their heads into the dirt and froze, even the children of the cook.

"What the piss-hell's going on?" Blackthorne was almost berserk.

Fujiko waited stoically until they were all there, then she too went down on her knees and bowed, as a samurai and not as a peasant. "*Gomen nasai, dozo gomen na—*"

"The pox on your *gomen nasai!* What right've you to do that? Ehhhhh?" and he began to swear at her foully. "Why in the name of Christ didn't you ask me first? Eh?"

He fought for control, aware that all of his servants knew he legally could hack Fujiko and all of them to pieces here in the garden for causing him so much displeasure, or for no reason at all, and that not even Toranaga himself could interfere with his handling of his own household.

He saw one of the children was trembling with terror and panic. "Jesus Christ in heaven, give me strength . . ." He held on to one of the posts to steady himself. "It's not your fault," he choked out, not realizing he wasn't speaking Japanese. "It's hers! It's you! You murdering bitch!"

Fujiko looked up slowly. She saw the accusing finger and the hatred on his face. She whispered a command to her maid, Nigatsu.

Nigatsu shook her head and began to beg.

"*Ima!*"

The maid fled. She returned with the killing sword, tears streaming her face. Fujiko took the sword and offered it to Blackthorne with both hands. She spoke and though he did not know all the words he knew that she was saying, "I'm responsible, please take my life because I've displeasured you."

"*IYÉ!*" He grabbed the sword and threw it away. "You think that'll bring Ueki-ya back to life?"

Then, suddenly, he realized what he had done, and what he was doing now. "Oh, Jesus God . . ."

He left them. In despair he went to the outcrop above the village near the shrine that was beside the ancient gnarled cypress tree and he wept.

He wept because a good man was dead unnecessarily and because he knew now that he had murdered him. "Lord God forgive me. I'm responsible—not Fujiko. I killed him. I ordered that no one was to touch the pheasant but me. I asked her if everyone understood and she said yes. I ordered it with mock gravity but that doesn't matter now. I gave the orders, knowing their law and knowing their customs. The old man broke my stupid order so what else could Fujiko-san do? I'm to blame."

In time the tears were spent. It was deep night now. He returned to his house.

Fujiko was waiting for him as always, but alone. The sword was across her lap. She offered it to him. *"Dozo—dozo,* Anjin-san."

"Iyé," he said, taking the sword as a sword should be taken. *"Iyé,* Fujiko-san. *Shigata ga nai, neh? Karma, neh?"* His hand touched her in apology. He knew that she had had to bear all the worst of his stupidity.

Her tears spilled. *"Arigato, arigato go—goziemashita,* Anjin-san," she said brokenly. *"Gomen nasai . . ."*

His heart went out to her.

Yes, Blackthorne thought with great sadness, yes it did, but that doesn't excuse you or take away her humiliation—or bring Ueki-ya back to life. You were to blame. You should have known better. . . .

"Anjin-san!" Naga said.

"Yes? Yes, Naga-san?" He pulled himself out of his remorse and looked down at the youth who walked beside him. "Sorry, what you say?"

"I said I hoped to be your friend."

"Ah, thank you."

"Yes, and perhaps you'd—" There was a jumble of words Blackthorne did not understand.

"Please?"

"Teach, *neh?* Understand 'teach'? Teach about world?"

"Ah, yes, so sorry. Teach what, please?"

"About foreign lands—outside lands. The world, *neh?"*

"Ah, understand now. Yes, try."

They were near the guards now. "Begin tomorrow, Anjin-san. Friends, *neh?"*

"Yes, Naga-san. Try."

"Good." Very satisfied, Naga nodded. When they came up to the samurai Naga ordered them out of the way, motioning Blackthorne to go on alone. He obeyed, feeling very alone in the circle of men.

"Ohayo, Toranaga-sama. *Ohayo,* Mariko-san," he said, joining them.

"Ohayo, Anjin-san. *Dozo suwaru."* Good day, Anjin-san, please sit down.

Mariko smiled at him. *"Ohayo,* Anjin-san. *Ikaga desu ka?"*

"Yoi, domo." Blackthorne looked back at her, so glad to see her. "Thy presence fills me with joy, great joy," he said in Latin.

"And thine—it is so good to see thee. But there is a shadow on thee. Why?"

"Nan ja?" Toranaga asked.

She told him what had been said. Toranaga grunted, then spoke.

"My Master says you're looking careworn, Anjin-san. I must agree too. He asks what's troubling you."

"It's nothing. *Domo,* Toranaga-sama. *Nane mo."* It's nothing.

"Nan ja?" Toranaga asked directly. *"Nan ja?"*

Obediently Blackthorne replied at once. "Ueki-ya," he said helplessly. *"Hai,* Ueki-ya."

"Ah so desu!" Toranaga spoke at length to Mariko.

"My Master says there is no need to be sad about Old Gardener. He asks me to tell you that it was all officially dealt with. Old Gardener understood completely what he was doing."

"I don't understand."

"Yes, it would be very difficult for you, but you see, Anjin-san, the pheasant was rotting in the sun. Flies were swarming terribly. Your health, your consort's health, and that of your whole house was being threatened. Also, so sorry, there had been some very private, cautious complaints from Omi-san's head servant —and others. One of our most important rules is that the individual may never disturb the *wa,* the harmony of the group, remember? So something had to be done. You see, decay, the stench of decay, is revolting to us. It's the worst smell in the world to us, so sorry. I tried to tell you but—well, it's one of the things that sends us all a little mad. Your head servant—"

"Why didn't someone come to me at once? Why didn't someone just tell me?" Blackthorne asked. "The pheasant was meaningless to me."

"What was there to tell? You'd given orders. You are head of the house. They didn't know your customs or what to do, other than to solve the dilemma according to our custom." She spoke to Toranaga for a moment, explaining what Blackthorne had said, then turned back again. "Is this distressing you? Do you wish me to continue?"

"Yes, please, Mariko-san."

"Are you sure?"

"Yes."

"Well then, your head servant, Small Tooth Cook, called a meeting of your servants, Anjin-san. Mura, the village headman, was asked to attend officially. It was decided that village *eta* could not be asked to take it away. This was only a house problem. One of the servants had to take it and bury it, even though you'd given absolute orders it was not to be moved. Obviously your consort was duty bound to see your orders were obeyed. Old Gardener asked to be allowed to carry it away. Lately he'd been living and sleeping in great pain from his abdomen and he found kneeling and weeding and planting very tiring, and could not do his work to his own satisfaction. Third Cook Assistant also offered, saying he was very young and stupid and he was sure his life counted for nothing against such a grave matter. At length Old Gardener was allowed the honor. Truly it was a great honor, Anjin-san. With great solemnity they all bowed to him and he to them and happily he took the thing away and buried it to the great relief of all.

"When he came back he went directly to Fujiko-san and told her what he'd done, that he'd disobeyed your law, *neh?* She thanked him for removing the hazard, then told him to wait. She came to me for advice and asked me what she should do. The matter had been done formally so it would have to be dealt with formally. I told her I didn't know, Anjin-san. I asked Buntaro-san but he didn't know either. It was complicated, because of you. So he asked Lord Toranaga. Lord Toranaga saw your consort himself." Mariko turned back to Toranaga and told him where she had reached in the story, as he had requested.

Toranaga spoke rapidly. Blackthorne watched them, the woman so petite and lovely and attentive, the man compact, rock-hard, his sash tight over his large belly. Toranaga did not talk with his hands like many, but kept them still, his left hand propped on his thigh, the other always on his sword hilt.

"Hai, Toranaga-sama. *Hai."* Mariko glanced at Blackthorne and continued

as formally. "Our Master asks me to explain that, so sorry, if you'd been Japanese there would have been no difficulty, Anjin-san. Old Gardener would simply have gone to the burial ground to receive his release. But, please excuse me, you're a foreigner, even though Lord Toranaga made you hatamoto—one of his personal vassals—and it was a matter of deciding whether you were legally samurai or not. I'm honored to tell you that he ruled you are samurai and you do have samurai rights. So everything was resolved at once and made easy. A crime had been committed. Your orders had been deliberately disobeyed. The law is clear. There is no option." She was grave now. "But Lord Toranaga knows of your sensitivity to killing, so to save you pain, he personally ordered one of his samurai to send Old Gardener into the Void."

"But why didn't someone ask me first? That pheasant meant nothing to me."

"The pheasant has nothing do with it, Anjin-san," she explained. "You're head of a house. The law says no member of your house may disobey you. Old Gardener deliberately broke the law. The whole world would fall to pieces if people were allowed to flout the law. Your—"

Toranaga broke in and spoke to her. She listened, answered some questions, then again he motioned her to continue.

"*Hai.* Lord Toranaga wants me to assure you that he personally saw that Old Gardener got the quick, painless, and honorable death he merited. He even loaned the samurai his own sword, which is very sharp. And I should tell you that Old Gardener was very proud that in his failing days he was able to help your house, Anjin-san, proud that he helped to establish your samurai status before all. Most of all he was proud of the honor being paid to him. Public executioners were not used, Anjin-san. Lord Toranaga wants me to make that very clear to you."

"Thank you, Mariko-san. Thank you for making it clear." Blackthorne turned to Toranaga, bowed most correctly. "*Domo,* Toranaga-sama, *domo arigato. Wakarimasu. Domo.*"

Toranaga bowed back agreeably. "*Yoi,* Anjin-san. *Shinpai suru monojanai, neh? Shigata ga nai, neh?*" Good. Now don't worry, eh? What could you do, eh?

"*Nané mo.*" Nothing. Blackthorne answered the questions Toranaga put to him about the musket training, but nothing that they were saying reached him. His mind was tottering under the impact of what he had been told. He had abused Fujiko before all his servants and abused the trust of all his household, when Fujiko had done only what was correct and so had they.

Fujiko was blameless. They're all blameless. Except me.

I cannot undo what's been done. Neither to Ueki-ya nor to her. Or to them. How can I live with this shame?

He sat cross-legged in front of Toranaga, the slight sea breeze tugging at his kimono, swords in his sash. Dully he listened and answered and nothing was important. War is coming, she was saying. When, he was asking. Very soon, she was saying, so you are to leave at once with me, you are to accompany me part of the way, Anjin-san, because I'm going to Osaka, but you're going on to Yedo by land to prepare your ship for war. . . .

Suddenly the silence was colossal.

Then the earth began to shake.

He felt his lungs about to burst, and every fiber of his being screamed panic. He tried to stand but could not and saw all the guards were equally helpless. Toranaga and Mariko desperately held onto the ground with their hands and feet. The rumbling, catastrophic roar was coming from earth and sky. It surrounded them, building and building until their eardrums were ready to split. They became part of the frenzy. For an instant the frenzy stopped, the shock continuing. He felt his vomit rising, his unbelieving mind shrieking that this was land where it was firm and safe and not sea where the world tilted every moment. He spat to clear the foul taste away, clutching the trembling earth, retching again and again.

An avalanche of rocks started from the mountain to the north and howled down into the valley below, adding to the tumult. Part of the samurai camp vanished. He groped to his hands and knees, Toranaga and Mariko doing the same. He heard himself shouting but no sound seemed to be coming from his lips or from theirs.

The tremor stopped.

The earth was firm again, firm as it had always been, firm as it always should be. His hands and knees and body were trembling uncontrollably. He tried to still them and catch his breath.

Then again the earth cried out. The second quake began. It was more violent. Then the earth ripped open at the far end of the plateau. This gaping fissure rushed toward them at an incredible speed, passed five paces away, and tore onward. His disbelieving eyes saw Toranaga and Mariko teetering on the brink of the cleft where there should have been solid ground. As though in a nightmare he saw Toranaga, nearest to the maw, begin to topple into it. He came out of his stupor, lunged forward. His right hand grabbed Toranaga's sash, the earth trembling like a leaf in the wind.

The cleft was twenty paces deep and ten across and stank of death. Mud and rocks poured down, dragging Toranaga and him with it. Blackthorne fought for handhold and foothold, raving at Toranaga to help, almost pulled down into the abyss. Still partially stunned, Toranaga hacked his toes into the face of the wall and, half dragged and half carried by Blackthorne, clawed his way out. They both lay gasping in safety.

At that moment there was another shock.

The earth split again. Mariko screamed. She tried to scramble out of the way but this new fissure swallowed her. Frantically Blackthorne crawled for the edge, the after-shocks throwing him off balance. On the brink he stared down. She shivered on a ledge a few feet below as the ground reeled and the sky looked down. The chasm was thirty paces deep, ten wide. The lip crumbled away under him sickeningly. He let himself slide down, mud and stones almost blinding him, and caught hold of her, pulling her to the safety of another ledge. Together they fought for balance. A new shock. The ledge mostly gave way and they were lost. Then Toranaga's iron hand caught his sash, stopping their slide into hell.

"For Christ's sake . . ." Blackthorne cried, his arms almost torn from their sockets as he held on to her and fought for holds with his feet and free hand. Toranaga grappled him until they were on a narrow shelf again, then the sash broke. A moment's respite from the tremors gave Blackthorne time to get her onto the shelf, debris raining on them. Toranaga leapt to safety, shouting for him to hurry. The chasm howled and began to close, Blackthorne and Mariko still deep in its gullet. Toranaga could no longer help. Blackthorne's terror lent him inhuman strength and somehow he managed to rip Mariko out of the tomb and shove her upward. Toranaga clutched her wrist and hauled her over the lip. Blackthorne scrambled after her but reeled backward as part of his wall fell away. The far wall screeched sickeningly as it approached. Mud and stones tumbled off it. For a moment he thought he was trapped but he tore himself free and groped half out of his grave. He lay on the shuddering brink, his lungs gulping air, unable to crawl away, legs in the cleft. The gap was closing. Then it stopped— six paces across the mouth, eight deep.

All rumbling ceased. The earth firmed. The silence gathered.

On their hands and knees, helpless, they waited for the horror to begin again. Blackthorne started to get up, sweat dripping.

"Iyé." Toranaga motioned him to stay down, his face a mess, a cruel gash on his temple where his head had smashed against a rock.

They were all panting, their chests heaving, bile in their mouths. Guards were picking themselves up. Some began running toward Toranaga.

"Iyé!" he shouted. *"Maté!"* Wait!

They obeyed and went down on their hands and knees again. The waiting seemed to go on forever. Then a bird screeched out of a tree and took to the air screaming. Another bird followed. Blackthorne shook his head to clear the sweat from his eyes. He was seeing his broken, bleeding fingernails gripping the tufts of grass. Then in the grass an ant moved. Another and another. They began to forage.

Still frightened he sat back on his heels. "When's it safe?"

Mariko did not answer. She was mesmerized by the cleft in the ground. He scrambled over to her. "Are you all right?"

"Yes—yes," she said breathlessly. Her face was daubed with mud. Her kimono was ripped and filthy. Both sandals and one tabi were missing. And her parasol. He helped her away from the lip. She was still numbed.

Then he looked at Toranaga. *"Ikaga desu ka?"*

Toranaga was unable to speak, his chest grinding, his arms and legs raw with abrasions. He pointed. The fissure which had almost swallowed him now was just a narrow ditch in the soil. Northward the ditch yawned into a ravine again but it was not as wide as it once had been, nor as deep.

Blackthorne shrugged. *"Karma."*

Toranaga belched loudly, then hawked and spat and belched again. This helped his voice to work and a torrent of abuse poured over the ditch, his blunt fingers stabbed at it, and though Blackthorne could not understand all the words, Toranaga was clearly saying as a Japanese would, "The pox on the *karma,* the pox on the quake, the pox on the ditch—I've lost my swords and the pox on that!'

Blackthorne burst into laughter, his relief at being alive and the stupidity of it all consuming him. A moment, then Toranaga laughed too, and their hilarity swept into Mariko.

Toranaga got to his feet. Gingerly. Then, warmed by the joy of life, he began clowning on the ditch, burlesquing himself and the quake. He stopped and beckoned Blackthorne to join him and straddled the ditch, opened his loincloth and, laughter taking him again, told Blackthorne to do the same. Blackthorne obeyed and both men tried to urinate into the ditch. But nothing came, not even a dribble. They tried very hard, which increased their laughter and blocked them even more. At length they succeeded and Blackthorne sat down to collect his strength, leaning back on his hands. When he had recovered a little he turned to Mariko. "Is the earthquake over for good, Mariko-san?"

"Until the next shock, yes." She continued to brush the mud off her hands and kimono.

"Is it always like that?"

"No. Sometimes it's very slight. Sometimes there's another series of shocks after a stick of time or a day or half a stick or half a day. Sometimes there's only one shock—you never know, Anjin-san. It's over until it begins again. *Karma, neh?"*

Guards were watching them without moving, waiting for Toranaga's order. To the north fires were raging in the crude lean-to bivouac. Samurai were fighting the fires and digging at the rock avalanche to find the buried. To the east, Yabu, Omi, and Buntaro stood with other guards beside the far end of the fissure, untouched except for bruises, also waiting to be summoned. Igurashi had vanished. The earth had gorged on him.

Blackthorne let himself drift. His self-contempt had vanished and he felt utterly serene and whole. Now his mind dwelt proudly on being samurai, and going to Yedo, and his ship, and war, and the Black Ship, and back to samurai again. He glanced at Toranaga and would have liked to ask him a dozen questions, but he noticed that the *daimyo* was lost in his own thoughts and he knew it would be impolite to disturb him. There's plenty of time, he thought contentedly, and looked over at Mariko. She was tending her hair and face, so he did not watch. He lay full length and looked up at the sky, the earth feeling warm on his back, waiting patiently.

Toranaga spoke, serious now. *"Domo,* Anjin-san, *neh? Domo."*

"Dozo, Toranaga-sama. *Nané mo. Hombun, neh?"* Please, Toranaga-sama, it was nothing. Duty.

Then, not knowing enough words and wanting it accurate, Blackthorne said, "Mariko-san, would you explain for me: I seem to understand now what you meant and Lord Toranaga meant about *karma* and the stupidity of worrying about what *is.* A lot seems clearer. I don't know why—perhaps it's because I've never been so terrified, maybe that's cleaned my head, but I seem to think clearer. It's—well, like Old Gardener. Yes, that was all my fault and I'm truly sorry, but that was a mistake, not a deliberate choice on my part. It *is.* So nothing can be done about it. A moment ago we were all almost dead. So all that worry and heartache was a waste, wasn't it? *Karma.* Yes, I know *karma* now. Do you understand?"

"Yes." She translated to Toranaga.

"He says, 'Good, Anjin-san. *Karma* is the beginning of knowledge. Next is patience. Patience is very important. The strong are the patient ones, Anjin-san. Patience means holding back your inclination to the seven emotions: hate, adoration, joy, anxiety, anger, grief, fear. If you don't give way to the seven, you're *patient,* then you'll soon understand all manner of things and be in harmony with Eternity.'"

"You believe that, Mariko-san?"

"Yes. Very much. I try, also, to be patient, but it's hard."

"I agree. That's also *wa,* your harmony, your 'tranquillity,' *neh?"*

"Yes."

"Tell him I thank him truly for what he did for Old Gardener. I didn't before, not from my heart. Tell him that."

"There's no need, Anjin-san. He knew before that you were just being polite."

"How did he know?"

"I told you he is the wisest man in the world."

He grinned.

"There," she said, "your age has fallen off you again," and added in Latin, "Thou art thyself again, and better than before!"

"But thou art beautiful, as always."

Her eyes warmed and she averted them from Toranaga. Blackthorne saw this and marked her caution. He got to his feet and stared down into the jagged cleft. Carefully he jumped into it and disappeared.

Mariko scrambled up, momentarily afraid, but Blackthorne quickly came back to the surface. In his hands was Fujiko's sword. It was still scabbarded, though muddied and scarred. His short stabbing sword had disappeared.

He knelt in front of Toranaga and offered his sword as a sword should be offered. *"Dozo,* Toranaga-sama," he said simply. *"Kara* samurai *ni* samurai, *neh?"* Please, Lord Toranaga, from a samurai to a samurai, eh?

"Domo, Anjin-san." The Lord of the Kwanto accepted the sword and shoved it into his sash. Then he smiled, leaned forward, and clapped Blackthorne once

on the shoulder, hard. *"Tomo, neh?"* Friend, eh?

"Domo." Blackthorne glanced away. His smile faded. A cloud of smoke was drifting over the rise above where the village would be. At once he asked Toranaga if he could leave, to make sure Fujiko was all right.

"He says, yes, Anjin-san. And we are to see him at the fortress at sunset for the evening meal. There are some things he wishes to discuss with you."

Blackthorne went back to the village. It was devastated, the course of the road bent out of recognition, the surface shattered. But the boats were safe. Many fires still burned. Villagers were carrying buckets of sand and buckets of water. He turned the corner. Omi's house was tilted drunkenly on its side. His own was a burnt-out ruin.

CHAPTER 39

FUJIKO had been injured. Nigatsu, her maid, was dead. The first shock had collapsed the central pillars of the house, scattering the coals of the kitchen fire. Fujiko and Nigatsu had been trapped by one of the fallen beams and the flames had turned Nigatsu into a torch. Fujiko had been pulled free. One of the cook's children had also been killed, but the rest of his servants had suffered only bruises and some twisted limbs. They all were overjoyed to find that Blackthorne was alive and unhurt.

Fujiko was lying on a salvaged futon near the undamaged garden fence, half conscious. When she saw also that Blackthorne was unscathed she almost wept. "I thank Buddha you're not hurt, Anjin-san," she said weakly.

Still partially in shock, she tried to get up but he bade her not to move. Her legs and lower back were badly burned. A doctor was already tending her, wrapping bandages soaked in cha and other herbs around her limbs to soothe them. Blackthorne hid his concern and waited until the doctor had finished, then said privately, "Fujiko-san, *yoi ka?*" Lady Fujiko will be all right?

The doctor shrugged. "*Hai.*" His lips came back from his protruding teeth again. "*Karma, neh?*"

"*Hai.*" Blackthorne had seen enough burned seamen die to know that any bad burn was dangerous, the open wound almost always rotting within a few days and nothing to stop the infection spreading. "I don't want her to die."

"*Dozo?*"

He said it in Japanese and the doctor shook his head and told him that the Lady would surely be all right. She was young and strong.

"*Shigata ga nai,*" the doctor said and ordered maids to keep her bandages moist, gave Blackthorne herbs for his own abrasions, told him he would return soon, then scuttled up the hill toward Omi's wrecked house above.

Blackthorne stood at his main gate, which was unharmed. Buntaro's arrows were still embedded in the left post. Absently he touched one. *Karma* that she was burned, he thought sadly.

He went back to Fujiko and ordered a maid to bring cha. He helped her to drink and held her hand until she slept, or appeared to sleep. His servants were salvaging whatever they could, working quickly, helped by a few villagers. They knew the rains would be coming soon. Four men were trying to erect a temporary shelter.

"*Dozo,* Anjin-san." The cook was offering him fresh tea, trying to keep the misery off his face. The little girl had been his favorite daughter.

"*Domo,*" Blackthorne replied. "*Sumimasen.*" I'm sorry.

"*Arigato,* Anjin-san. *Karma, neh?*"

Blackthorne nodded, accepted the tea, and pretended not to notice the cook's grief, lest he shame him. Later a samurai came up the hill bringing word from Toranaga that Blackthorne and Fujiko were to sleep in the fortress until the house was rebuilt. Two palanquins arrived. Blackthorne lifted her gently into one of them and sent her with maids. He dismissed his own palanquin, telling her he'd follow soon.

The rain began but he paid it no heed. He sat on a stone in the garden that had given him so much pleasure. Now it was a shambles. The little bridge was broken, the pond shattered, and the streamlet had vanished.

"Never mind," he said to no one. "The rocks aren't dead."

Ueki-ya had told him that a garden must be settled around its rocks, that without them a garden is empty, merely a place of growing.

One of the rocks was jagged and ordinary but Ueki-ya had planted it so that if you looked at it long and hard near sunset, the reddish glow glinting off the veins and crystal buried within, you could see a whole range of mountains with lingering valleys and deep lakes and, far off, a greening horizon, night gathering there.

Blackthorne touched the rock. "I name you Ueki-ya-sama," he said. This pleased him and he knew that if Ueki-ya were alive, the old man would have been very pleased also. Even though he's dead, perhaps he'll know, Blackthorne told himself, perhaps his *kami* is here now. Shintoists believed that when they died they became a *kami*. . . .

'What is a *kami*, Mariko-san?'

'*Kami* is inexplicable, Anjin-san. It is like a spirit but not, like a soul but not. Perhaps it is the insubstantial essence of a thing or person . . . you should know a human becomes a *kami* after death but a tree or rock or plant or painting is equally a *kami. Kami* are venerated, never worshiped. They exist between heaven and earth and visit this Land of the Gods or leave it, all at the same time.'

'And Shinto? What's Shinto?'

'Ah, that is inexplicable too, so sorry. It's like a religion, but isn't. At first it even had no name—we only called it Shinto, the Way of the *Kami,* a thousand years ago, to distinguish it from Butsudo, the Way of Buddha. But though it's indefinable Shinto is the essence of Japan and the Japanese, and though it possesses neither theology nor godhead nor faith nor system of ethics, it is our justification for existence. Shinto is a nature cult of myths and legends in which no one believes wholeheartedly, yet everyone venerates totally. A person *is* Shinto in the same way he is *born* Japanese.'

'Are you Shinto too—as well as Christian?'

'Oh yes, oh very yes, of course. . . .'

Blackthorne touched the stone again. "Please, *kami* of Ueki-ya, please stay in my garden."

Then, careless of the rain, he let his eyes take him into the rock, past the lush valleys and serene lake and to the greening horizon, darkness gathering there.

His ears told him to come back. He looked up. Omi was watching him, squatting patiently on his haunches. It was still raining and Omi wore a newly pressed kimono under his rice-straw raincoat, and a wide, conical bamboo hat. His hair was freshly shampooed.

"*Karma,* Anjin-san," he said, motioning at the smoldering ruins.

"*Hai. Ikaga desu ka?*" Blackthorne wiped the rain off his face.

"*Yoi.*" Omi pointed up at his house. "*Watakushi no yuya wa hakaisarete imasen ostukai ni narimasen-ka?*" My bath wasn't damaged. Would you care to use it?

"*Ah so desu! Domo,* Omi-san, *hai, domo.*" Gratefully Blackthorne followed Omi up the winding path, into his courtyard. Servants and village artisans under Mura's supervision were already hammering and sawing and repairing. The central posts were already back in place and the roof almost resettled.

With signs and simple words and much patience, Omi explained that his servants had managed to douse the fires in time. Within a day or two, he told

Blackthorne, the house would be up again, as good as it was, so not to worry. Yours will take longer, a week, Anjin-san. Don't worry, Fujiko-san is a fine manager. She'll have all costs arranged with Mura in no time and your house'll be better than ever. I hear she was burned? Well, this happens sometimes, but not to worry, our doctors are very expert with burns—they have to be, *neh?* Yes, Anjin-san, it was a bad quake, but not that bad. The rice fields were hardly touched and the so essential irrigation system was undamaged. And the boats weren't damaged and that's very important too. Only a hundred and fifty-four samurai were killed in the avalanche, that's not many, *neh?* As to the village, a week and you'll hardly know there was a quake. Five peasants were killed and a few children—nothing! Anjiro was very lucky, *neh?* I hear you pulled Toranaga-sama out of a death trap. We're all grateful to you, Anjin-san. Very. If we'd lost him . . . Lord Toranaga said he accepted your sword—you're lucky, that's a great honor. Yes. Your *karma's* strong, very good, very rich. Yes, we thank you very much. Listen, we'll talk more after you've bathed. I'm glad to have you as a friend.

Omi called out for the bath attendants. *"Isogi!"* Hurry up!

The servants escorted Blackthorne to the bath house, which was set within a tiny maple grove and joined to the main house by a neat winding walk, usually roofed. The bath was much more luxurious than his own. One wall was cracked badly but villagers were already replastering it. The roof was sound although a few tiles were missing and rain leaked in here and there, but that did not matter.

Blackthorne stripped and sat on the tiny seat. The servants lathered him and shampooed him in the rain. When he was cleansed he went inside and immersed himself in the steaming bath. All his troubles melted away.

Fujiko's going to be all right. I'm a lucky man—lucky I was there to pull Toranaga out, lucky to save Mariko, and lucky he was there to pull us out.

Suwo's magic renewed him as usual. Later he let Suwo dress his bruises and cuts and put on the clean loincloth and kimono and tabi that had been left for him, and went out. The rain had stopped.

A temporary lean-to had been erected in one corner of the garden. It had a neat raised floor and was furnished with clean futons and a little vase with a flower arrangement. Omi was waiting for him and in attendance was a toothless, hard-faced old woman.

"Please sit down, Anjin-san," Omi said.

"Thank you, and thanks for the clothes," he replied in halting Japanese.

"Please don't mention it. Would you like cha or saké?"

"Cha," Blackthorne decided, thinking that he had better keep his head clear for his interview with Toranaga. "Thank you."

"This is my mother," Omi said formally, clearly idolizing her.

Blackthorne bowed. The old woman simpered and sucked in her breath.

"It's my honor, Anjin-san," she said.

"Thank you, but I'm honored." Blackthorne repeated automatically the succession of formal politenesses that Mariko had taught him.

"Anjin-san, we were so sorry to see your house in flames."

"What could one do? That's *karma, neh?*"

"Yes, *karma.*" The old woman looked away and scowled. "Hurry up! The Anjin-san wants his cha warm!"

The girl standing beside the maid who carried the tray took Blackthorne's breath away. Then he remembered her. Wasn't this the girl he'd seen with Omi, the first time, when he was passing through the village square on his way to the galley?

"This is my wife," Omi said tersely.

"I'm honored," Blackthorne said as she took her place, knelt, and bowed.

"You must forgive her slowness," Omi's mother said. "Is the cha warm enough for you?"

"Thank you, it's very good." Blackthorne had noted that the old woman had not used the wife's name as she should have. But then, he was not surprised because Mariko had told him already about the dominating position of a girl's mother-in-law in Japanese society.

"Thank God it's not the same in Europe," he had told her.

"A wife's mother-in-law can do no wrong—after all, Anjin-san, the parents choose the wife in the first place and what father would choose without first consulting his own wife? Of course, the daughter-in-law has to obey, and the son always does what his mother and father want."

"Always?"

"Always."

"What if the son refuses?"

"That's not possible. Everyone has to obey the head of the house. A son's first duty is to his parents. Of course. Sons are given everything by their mothers—life, food, tenderness, protection. She succors them all their lives. So of course it's right that a son should heed his mother's wishes. The daughter-in-law—she has to obey. That's her duty."

"It's not the same with us."

"It's hard to be a good daughter-in-law, very hard. You just have to hope that you live long enough to have sons to become one yourself."

"And your mother-in-law?"

"Ah, she's dead, Anjin-san. She died many years ago. I never knew her. Lord Hiro-matsu, in his wisdom, never took another wife."

"Buntaro-san's his only son?"

"Yes. My husband has five living sisters, but no brothers." She had joked, "In a way we're related now, Anjin-san. Fujiko's my husband's niece. What's the matter?"

"I'm surprised you never told me, that's all."

"Well, it's complicated, Anjin-san." Then Mariko had explained that Fujiko was actually an adopted daughter of Numata Akinori, who had married Buntaro's youngest sister, and that Fujiko's real father was a grandson of the Dictator Goroda by his eighth consort, that Fujiko had been adopted by Numata when an infant at the Taikō's orders because the Taikō wanted closer ties between the descendants of Hiro-matsu and Goroda. . . .

"What?"

Mariko had laughed, telling him that, yes, Japanese family relationships were very complicated because adoption was normal, that families exchanged sons and daughters often, and divorced and remarried and intermarried all the time. With so many legal consorts and the ease of divorce—particularly if at the order of a liege lord—all families soon become incredibly tangled.

"To unravel Lord Toranaga's family links accurately would take days, Anjin-san. Just think of the complications: Presently he has seven *official* consorts living, who have given him five sons and three daughters. Some of the consorts were widows or previously married with other sons and daughters—some of these Toranaga adopted, some he did not. In Japan you don't ask if a person is adopted or natural. Truly, what does it matter? Inheritance is always at the whim of the head of the house, so adopted or not it is the same, *neh?* Even Toranaga's mother was divorced. Later she remarried and had three more sons and two daughters by her second husband, all of whom are also now married! Her eldest son from her second marriage is Zataki, Lord of Shinano."

Blackthorne had mulled that. Then he had said, "Divorce isn't possible for us. Not possible."

"So the Holy Fathers tell us. So sorry, but that's not very sensible, Anjin-san. Mistakes happen, people change, that's *karma, neh?* Why should a man have to bear a foul wife, or a wife a foul man? Foolish to be stuck forever, man or woman, *neh?*"

"Yes."

"In this we are very wise and the Holy Fathers unwise. This was one of the two great reasons the Taikō would not embrace Christianity, this foolishness about divorce—and the sixth Commandment, 'Thou shalt not kill.' The Father-Visitor sent all the way to Rome begging dispensation for Japanese about divorce. But His Holiness the Pope, in his wisdom, said no. If His Holiness had said yes, I believe the Taikō would have converted, the *daimyos* would be following the True Faith now, and the land would be Christian. The matter of 'killing' would have been unimportant because no one pays any attention to that really, Christians least of all. Such a little concession, for so much, *neh?*"

"Yes," Blackthorne had said. How sensible divorce seemed here. Why was it a mortal sin at home, opposed by every priest in Christendom, Catholic or Protestant, in the name of God?

"What's Toranaga's wife like?" he had asked, wanting to keep her talking. Most of the time she avoided the subject of Toranaga and his family history and it was important for Blackthorne to know everything.

A shadow had crossed Mariko's face. "She's dead. She was his second wife and she died ten or eleven years ago. She was the Taikō's stepsister. Lord Toranaga was never successful with his wives, Anjin-san."

"Why?"

"Oh, the second was old and tired and grasping, worshiping gold, though pretending not to, like her brother, the Taikō himself. Barren and bad-tempered. It was a political marriage, of course. I had to be one of her ladies-in-waiting for a time. Nothing would please her and none of the youths or men could unwind the knot in her Golden Pavilion."

"What?"

"Her Jade Gate, Anjin-san. With their Turtle Heads—their Steaming Shafts. Don't you understand? Her . . . thing."

"Oh! I understand. Yes."

"No one could unwind her knot . . . could satisfy her."

"Not even Toranaga?"

"He never pillowed her, Anjin-san," she had said, quite shocked. "Of course, after the marriage he had nothing to do with her, other than give her a castle and retainers and the keys to his treasure house—why should he? She was quite old, she'd been married twice before, but her brother, the Taikō, had dissolved the marriages. A most unpleasant woman—everyone was most relieved when she went into the Great Void, even the Taikō, and all her stepdaughters-in-law and all of Toranaga's consorts secretly burnt incense with great joy."

"And Toranaga's first wife?"

"Ah, the Lady Tachibana. That was another political marriage. Lord Toranaga was eighteen, she fifteen. She grew up to be a terrible woman. Twenty years ago Toranaga had her put to death because he discovered she was secretly plotting to assassinate their liege lord, the Dictator Goroda, whom she hated. My father often told me he thought they were all lucky to retain their heads—he, Toranaga, Nakamura, and all the generals—because Goroda was merciless, relentless, and particularly suspicious of those closest to him. That woman could have ruined them all, however innocent they were. Because of her plot against Lord Goroda, her only son, Nobunaga, was also put to death, Anjin-san. She killed her own son. Think of that, so sad, so terrible. Poor Nobunaga—he was Toranaga's favorite son and his official heir—brave, a general in his own right, and totally loyal. He was innocent but she still embroiled him in her plot. He was only nineteen when Toranaga ordered him to commit seppuku."

"Toranaga killed his own son? And his wife?"

"Yes, he ordered them onward, but he had no choice, Anjin-san. If he hadn't, Lord Goroda would correctly have presumed Toranaga to be part of the plot himself and would have ordered him instantly to slit his belly. Oh yes, Toranaga was lucky to escape Goroda's wrath and wise to send her onward quickly. When she was dead her daughter-in-law and all Toranaga's consorts were very much ecstatic. Her son had had to send his first wife home in disgrace on her orders for some imagined slight—after bearing him two children. The girl committed seppuku—did I tell you ladies commit seppuku by slitting their throats, Anjin-san, and not their stomachs like men?—but she went to death gratefully, glad to be freed from a life of tears, as the next wife prayed for death, her life made equally miserable by her mother-in-law. . . ."

Now, looking at Midori's mother-in-law, the tea dribbling down her chin, Blackthorne knew that this old hag had power of life or death, divorce or degradation over Midori, provided her husband, the head of their house, agreed. And, whatever they decided, Omi would obey. How terrible, he told himself.

Midori was as graceful and youthful as the old woman was not, her face oval, her hair rich. She was more beautiful than Mariko, but without her fire and strength, pliant as a fern and fragile as gossamer.

"Where are the small foods? Of course the Anjin-san must be hungry, *neh?*" the old woman said.

"Oh, so sorry," Midori replied at once. "Fetch some instantly," she said to the maid. "Hurry! So sorry, Anjin-san!"

"So sorry, Anjin-san," the old woman said.

"Please don't apologize," Blackthorne said to Midori, and instantly knew that it was a mistake. Good manners decreed that he should acknowledge only the mother-in-law, particularly if she had an evil reputation. "So sorry," he said. "I not hungry. Tonight I eat must with Lord Toranaga."

"*Ah so desu!* We heard you saved his life. You should know how grateful we are—all his vassals!" the old woman said.

"It was duty. I did nothing."

"You did everything, Anjin-san. Omi-san and Lord Yabu appreciate your action as much as all of us."

Blackthorne saw the old woman looking at her son. I wish I could fathom you, you old bitch, he thought. Are you as evil as that other one, Tachibana?

Omi said, "Mother, I'm fortunate to have the Anjin-san as a friend."

"We're all fortunate," she said.

"No, I'm fortunate," Blackthorne replied. "I fortunate have friends as family of Kasigi Omi-san." We're all lying, Blackthorne thought, but I don't know why you are. I'm lying for self-protection and because it's custom. But I've never forgotten. . . . Wait a moment. In all honesty, wasn't that *karma?* Wouldn't you have done what Omi did? That was long ago—in a previous life, *neh?* It's meaningless now.

A group of horsemen clattered up the rise, Naga at their head. He dismounted and strode into the garden. All the villagers stopped working and went onto their knees. He motioned them to continue.

"So sorry to disturb you, Omi-san, but Lord Toranaga sent me."

"Please, you're not disturbing me. Please join us," Omi said. Midori at once gave up her cushion, bowing very low. "Would you like cha or saké, Naga-sama?"

Naga sat. "Neither, thank you. I'm not thirsty."

Omi pressed him politely, going through the interminable necessary ritual, even though it was obvious that Naga was in a hurry. "How is the Lord Toranaga?"

"Very good. Anjin-san, you did us a great service. Yes. I thank you personally."

"It was duty, Naga-san. But I did little. Lord Toranaga pulled me from— pulled me from earth also."

"Yes. But that was afterward. I thank you very much."

"Naga-san, is there something I can do for Lord Toranaga?" Omi asked, etiquette finally allowing him to come to the point.

"He would like to see you after the evening meal. There is to be a full conference of all officers."

"I would be honored."

"Anjin-san, you are to come with me now, if it pleases you."

"Of course. It is my honor."

More bows and salutations and then Blackthorne was on a horse and they were cantering down the hill. When the phalanx of samurai came to the square, Naga reined in.

"Anjin-san!"

"Hai?"

"I thank you with all my heart for saving Lord Toranaga. Allow me to be your friend . . ." and some words Blackthorne did not catch.

"So sorry, I don't understand. *'Karite iru'?"*

"Ah, so sorry. *'Karite iru'*—one man *karite iru* another man things—like 'debt.' You understand 'debt'?"

"Owe" jumped into Blackthorne's head. *"Ah so desu! Wakarimasu."*

"Good. I only said that I owed you a debt."

"It was my duty, *neh?"*

"Yes. Even so, I owe you a life."

"Toranaga-sama says all cannon powder and shot were put back on your ship, Anjin-san, here at Anjiro before it left for Yedo. He asks you how long would it take you to get ready for sea?"

"That depends on her state, if the men've careened her and cared for her, the mast replaced and so on. Does Lord Toranaga know how she is?"

"The ship seems in order, he says, but he's not a seaman so he couldn't be sure. He has not been on it since it was first towed into Yedo harbor when he gave instructions for it to be cared for. Presuming the ship is seaworthy, *neh,* he asks how long would it take you to ready for war?"

Blackthorne's heart missed a beat. "On whom do I war, Mariko-san?"

"He asks, on whom would you wish to war?"

"This year's Black Ship," Blackthorne replied at once, making a sudden decision, desperately hoping that this was the correct moment to place before Toranaga the plan he'd secretly developed over the days. He was gambling that saving Toranaga's life this morning gave him a special privilege that would help him over the rough spots.

Mariko was taken by surprise. "What?"

"The Black Ship. Tell Lord Toranaga that all he has to do is give me his letters of marque. I'll do the rest. With my ship and just a little help . . . we split the cargo, all silks and bullion."

She laughed. Toranaga did not.

"My—my Master says that would be an unforgivable act of war against a friendly nation. The Portuguese are essential to Japan."

"Yes, they are—at the moment. But I believe they're his enemy as well as mine and whatever service they provide, we can do better. At less cost."

"He says, perhaps. But he does not believe China will trade with you. Neither the English nor the Netherlanders are in strength in Asia yet and we need the silks now and a continuing supply."

"He's right, of course. But in a year or two that will change and he'll have his proof then. So here's another suggestion. I'm already at war with the Portuguese. Outside the three-mile limit are international waters. Legally, with my present letters of marque, I can take her as a prize and I can sail her to any port and sell her and her cargo. With my ship and a crew it'll be easy. In a few weeks or months I could deliver the Black Ship and all she contains to Yedo. I could sell her in Yedo. Half the value'll be his—a port tax."

"He says what happens at sea between you and your enemies is of little concern to him. The sea belongs to all. But this land is ours, and here our laws govern and our laws may not be broken."

"Yes." Blackthorne knew his course was dangerous, but his intuition told him the timing was perfect and that Toranaga would take the bait. And Mariko. "It was only a suggestion. He asked me on whom I'd like to war. Please excuse me but sometimes it's good to plan against any eventuality. In this I believe Lord Toranaga's interests are mine."

Mariko translated this. Toranaga grunted and spoke shortly.

"Lord Toranaga values sensible suggestions, Anjin-san, like your point about a navy, but this is ludicrous. Even if both your interests were the same, which they're not, how could you and nine men attack such a huge vessel with nearly a thousand persons aboard?"

"I wouldn't. I have to get a new crew, Mariko-san. Eighty or ninety men, trained seamen and gunners. I'll find them at Nagasaki on Portuguese ships." Blackthorne pretended not to notice her intake of breath or the way her fan stopped. "There've got to be a few Frenchies, an Englishman or two if I'm lucky, some Germans or Hollanders—they'll be renegades mostly, or pressed aboard. I'd need a safe conduct to Nagasaki, some protection, and a little silver or gold. There are always seamen in enemy fleets who'll sign on for ready cash and a share of prize money."

"My Master says anyone in command who'd trust such carrion in an attack would be mad."

Blackthorne said, "I agree. But I have to have a crew to put to sea."

"He asks if it would be possible to train samurai and our seamen to be gunners and sailors?"

"Easily. In time. But that could take months. They'd certainly be ready by next year. There'd be no chance to go against this year's Black Ship."

"Lord Toranaga says, 'I don't plan to attack the Black Ship of the Portuguese, this year or next. They're not my enemies and I am not at war with them.' "

"I know. But I am at war with them. Please excuse me. Of course, this is only a discussion, but I'll have to get some men to put to sea, to be of service to Lord Toranaga if he wishes."

They were sitting in Toranaga's private quarters that overlooked the garden. The fortress had hardly been touched by the quake. The night was humid and airless and the smoke from the coils of incense rose lazily to banish the mosquitoes.

"My Master wants to know," Mariko was saying, "if you had your ship now, and the few crew members that arrived with you, would you sail it to Nagasaki to get these further men you require?"

"No. That would be too dangerous. I'd be so hopelessly undermanned that the Portuguese would capture me. It would be much better to get the men first, bring them back to home waters, to Yedo, *neh?* Once I'm full-crewed and armed, the enemy's got nothing in these seas to touch me."

"He does not think you and ninety men could take the Black Ship."

"I can outsail her and sink her with *Erasmus*. Of course, Mariko-san, I know this is all conjecture, but if I was permitted to attack my enemy, the moment I was crewed I'd sail on the tide for Nagasaki. If the Black Ship was already in port, I'd show my battle flags and stand out to sea to blockade her. I'd let her finish trading and then, when the wind was ripe for her homeward voyage, I'd pretend to need supplies and let her slip out of port. I'd catch her a few leagues out because we've the speed on her and my cannon would do the rest. Once she's struck her colors I put a prize crew aboard and bring her back to Yedo. She'll have upwards of three, almost four hundred tons of gold bullion aboard."

"But why won't her captain scuttle his ship once you've beaten him, if you beat him, before you can go aboard?"

"Usually . . ." Blackthorne was going to say, "Usually the crew mutiny if the captain's a fanatic, but I've never known one that mad. Most times you make a deal with the captain—spare their lives, give them a small share and safe berth to the nearest port. But this time I'll have Rodrigues to deal with and I know him and know what he'll do." But he thought better about that, or about revealing his whole plan. Best to leave barbarian ways to barbarians, he told himself. "Usually the defeated ship gives up, Mariko-san," he said instead. "It's a custom —one of our customs of war at sea—saving unnecessary loss of life."

"Lord Toranaga says, so sorry Anjin-san, that's a disgusting custom. If he had ships there would be no surrender." Mariko sipped some cha, then continued, "And if the ship is not yet in port?"

"Then I sweep the sea lanes to catch her a few leagues out in international waters. She'll be easier to take heavy laden and wallowing, but harder to bring into Yedo. When's she expected to dock?"

"My Lord does not know. Perhaps within thirty days, he says. The ship will be early this year."

Blackthorne knew he was so near the prize, so very near. "Then it's blockade her and take her at the end of the season." She translated and Blackthorne thought he saw disappointment momentarily cross Toranaga's face. He paused, as though he were considering alternatives, then he said, "If this was Europe, there'd be another way. You could sail in by night and take her by force. A surprise attack."

Toranaga's grip tightened on his sword hilt.

"He says you'd dare to war on *our* land against *your* enemies?"

Blackthorne's lips were dry. "No. Of course this is still surmise, but if a state of war existed between him and the Portuguese, and Lord Toranaga wanted them hurt, this would be the way to do it. If I had two or three hundred well-disciplined fighters, a good crew, and *Erasmus,* it would be easy to go alongside the Black Ship and board her, drag her out to sea. He could choose the time of the surprise attack—if this was Europe."

There was a long silence.

"Lord Toranaga says, this is not Europe and no state of war exists or will ever exist between him and the Portuguese."

"Of course. One last point, Mariko-san: Nagasaki is not within Lord Toranaga's control, is it?"

"No, Anjin-san. Lord Harima owns the port and the hinterland."

"But don't the Jesuits in practice control the port and all trade?" Blackthorne marked her reluctance to translate but kept up the pressure. "Isn't that the *honto,* Mariko-san? And isn't Lord Harima Catholic? Isn't most of Kyushu Catholic? And therefore don't the Jesuits in some measure control the whole island?"

"Christianity's a religion. The *daimyos* control their own lands, Anjin-san," Mariko said for herself.

"But I was told Nagasaki's really Portuguese soil. I'm told they act as though it is. Didn't Lord Harima's father sell the land to the Jesuits?"

Mariko's voice sharpened. "Yes. But the Taikō took the land back. No foreigner's allowed to own land here now."

"But didn't the Taikō allow his Edicts to lapse, so today nothing happens there without Jesuit approval? Don't Jesuits control all shipping in Nagasaki and all trade? Don't Jesuits negotiate all trade for you and act as intermediaries?"

"You're very well informed about Nagasaki, Anjin-san," she said pointedly.

"Perhaps Lord Toranaga should take control of the port from the enemy. Perhaps—"

"They're your enemy, Anjin-san, not ours," she said, taking the bait at last. "The Jesuits are—"

"*Nan ja?*"

She turned apologetically to Toranaga and explained what had been said between them. When she had finished he spoke severely, a clear reprimand. "*Hai,*" she said several times and bowed, chastened.

Mariko said, "Lord Toranaga reminds me my opinions are valueless and that an interpreter should interpret only, *neh?* Please excuse me."

Once Blackthorne would have apologized for trapping her. Now it did not occur to him. But since he had made his point, he laughed and said, "*Hai, kawaii Tsukkuko-sama!*" Yes, pretty Lady Interpreter!

Mariko smiled wryly, furious at herself for being trapped, her mind in conflict over her divided loyalties.

"*Yoi,* Anjin-san," Toranaga said, once more genial.

"Mariko-san *kawaii desu yori* Tsukku-san *anamsu ka nori masen, neh?*" And Mariko's much prettier than old Mr. Tsukku, isn't she, and so much more fragrant?

Toranaga laughed. "*Hai.*"

Mariko blushed and poured tea, a little mollified. Then Toranaga spoke. Seriously.

"Our Master says, why were you asking so many questions—or making statements—about Lord Harima and Nagasaki?"

"Only to show that the port of Nagasaki is in fact controlled by *foreigners.* By the *Portuguese.* And by my law, I have the legal right to attack the enemy anywhere."

"But this is not 'anywhere,' he says. This is the Land of the Gods and such an attack is unthinkable."

"I agree wholeheartedly. But if ever Lord Harima became hostile, or the Jesuits who lead the Portuguese become hostile, this is the way to hunt them."

"Lord Toranaga says neither he nor any *daimyo* would ever permit an attack by one foreign nation on another on Japanese soil, or the killing by them of *any* of our people. Against enemies of the Emperor, that is a different matter. As to getting fighters and crew, it would be easy for a man to get any number if he spoke Japanese. There are many *wako* in Kyushu."

"*Wako,* Mariko-san?"

"Oh, so sorry. We call corsairs '*wako,*' Anjin-san. They used to have many lairs around Kyushu but they were mostly stamped out by the Taikō. Survivors can still be found, unfortunately. *Wako* terrorized the coasts of China for centuries. It was because of them that China closed her ports to us." She explained to Toranaga what had been said. He spoke again, more emphatically. "He says he will never allow or plan or permit you to make a land attack, though it would be correct for you to harry your Queen's enemy on the high seas. He repeats, this is not anywhere. This is the Land of the Gods. You should be patient as he told you before."

"Yes. I intend to try to be patient in his fashion. I only want to hit the enemy because they *are* the enemy. I believe with all my heart they're his enemy too."

"Lord Toranaga says the Portuguese tell him *you* are his enemy, and Tsukku-san and the Visitor-General are absolutely sure of it."

"If I were able to capture the Black Ship at sea and bring her as a legal prize into Yedo, under the flag of England, would I be permitted to sell her and all she contains in Yedo, according to our custom?"

"Lord Toranaga says that depends."

"If war comes may I be allowed to attack the enemy, Lord Toranaga's enemy, in the best way that I can?"

"He says that is the duty of a hatamoto. A hatamoto is, of course, under his personal orders at all times. My Master wants me to make clear that things in Japan will never be solved by any method other than by Japanese method."

"Yes. I understand completely. With due humility I'd like to point out the more I know about his problems, the more I might be able to help."

"He says a hatamoto's duty is always to help his lord, Anjin-san. He says I am to answer any reasonable questions you have later."

"Thank you. May I ask him, would he like to have a navy of his own? As I suggested on the galley?"

"He has already said he would like a navy, a modern navy, Anjin-san, manned by his own men. What *daimyo* wouldn't?"

"Then say this: If I were lucky enough to take the enemy ship, I'd bring her to Yedo to refit and count the prize. Then I'd transship my half of the bullion to *Erasmus* and sell the Black Ship back to the Portuguese, or offer her to Toranaga-sama as a gift, or burn her, whatever he wishes. Then I'd sail home. Within a year I'd turn around and bring back four warships, as a gift from the Queen of England to Lord Toranaga."

"He asks where would be your profit in this?"

"The *honto* is, there would be plenty left over for me, Mariko-san, after the ships were paid for by Her Majesty. Further, I'd like to take one of his most trusted counselors with me as an Ambassador to my Queen. A treaty of friendship between our countries might be of interest to him."

"Lord Toranaga says that would be much too generous of your Queen. He adds, but if such a thing miraculously happened and you came back with the new ships, who would train his sailors and samurai and captains to man them?"

"I will, initially, if that pleases him. I'd be honored, then others could follow."

"He says what is 'initially'?"

"Two years."

Toranaga smiled fleetingly.

"Our Master says two years would not be enough 'initially.' However, he adds, it's all an illusion. He's not at war with the Portuguese or Lord Harima of Nagasaki. He repeats, what you do outside Japanese waters in your own ship with your own crew is your own *karma*." Mariko seemed disturbed. "Outside our waters you are foreigner, he says. But here you are samurai."

"Yes. I know the honor he has done to me. May I ask how a samurai borrows money, Mariko-san?"

"From a moneylender, Anjin-san. Where else? From a filthy merchant money-lender." She translated for Toranaga. "Why should you need money?"

"Are there moneylenders in Yedo?"

"Oh yes. Moneylenders are everywhere, *neh?* Isn't it the same in your country? Ask your consort, Anjin-san, perhaps she would be able to help you. That is part of her duty."

"You said we're leaving for Yedo tomorrow?"

"Yes, tomorrow."

"Unfortunately Fujiko-san won't be able to travel then."

Mariko talked with Toranaga.

"Lord Toranaga says he will send her by galley, when it leaves. He says what do you need to borrow money for?"

"I'll have to get a new crew, Mariko-san—to sail anywhere, to serve Lord Toranaga, however he'd wish it. Is that permitted?"

"A crew from Nagasaki?"

"Yes."

"He will give you an answer when you reach Yedo."

"*Domo,* Toranaga-sama. Mariko-san, when I get to Yedo where do I go? Will there be someone to guide me?"

"Oh, you must never worry about things like that, Anjin-san. You are one of Lord Toranaga's hatamoto." There was a knock on the inner door.

"Come in."

Naga opened the shoji and bowed. "Excuse me, Father, but you wanted to be told when all your officers were present."

"Thank you, I'll be there shortly." Toranaga thought a moment, then motioned to Blackthorne, his manner friendly. "Anjin-san, go with Naga-san. He will show you to your place. Thank you for your views."

"Yes, Sire. Thank you for listen. Thank you for your words. Yes. I try hard be patient and perfect."

"Thank you, Anjin-san." Toranaga watched him bow and go away. When they were alone, he turned to Mariko. "Well, what do you think?"

"Two things, Sire. First, his hatred of Jesuits is measureless, even surpassing his loathing of Portuguese, so he is a scourge for you to use against either or both, if you want a scourge. We know he is brave, so he would boldly press home any attack from the sea. Second, money is still his goal. In his defense, from what I've learned, money is the only real means the barbarians have to lasting power. They buy lands and position—even their Queen's a merchant and 'sells' land to her lords, and buys ships and lands, probably. They're not so different from us, Lord, except in that. And also in that they do not understand power, or that war is life and life is death."

"Are the Jesuits my enemy?"

"I do not believe so."

"The Portuguese?"

"I believe they're concerned only with profits, land, and spreading the word of God."

"Are Christians my enemy?"

"No, Sire. Though some of your enemies may be Christian—Catholic or Prot-estant."

"Ah, you think the Anjin-san's my enemy?"

"No, Sire. No, I believe he honors you and, in time, will become a real vassal."

"What about our Christians? Who are enemy?"

"Lords Harima, Kiyama, Onoshi, and any other samurai who turns against you."

Toranaga laughed. "Yes, but do the priests control them, as the Anjin-san implies?"

"I do not think so."

"Will those three go against me?"

"I don't know, Sire. In the past, they've all been both hostile and friendly to you. But if they side with Ishido it would be very bad."

"I agree. Yes. You're a valued counselor. It's difficult for you being Catholic Christian, being friends with an enemy, listening to enemy ideas."

"Yes, Sire."

"He trapped you, *neh?*"

"Yes. But in truth he had the right. I was not doing what you had ordered. I was putting myself between his pure thoughts and you. Please accept my apologies."

"It will continue to be difficult. Perhaps even more so."

"Yes, Sire. But it's better to know both sides of the coin. Much of what he said has been found to be true—for instance, about the world being split by Spaniards and Portuguese, about the priests smuggling guns—however impossible it is to believe. You need never fear about my loyalty, Sire. However bad it becomes, I will always do my duty to you."

"Thank you. Well, it's been very interesting, what the Anjin-san said, *neh?* Interesting but nonsense. Yes, thank you, Mariko-san, you're a valued counselor. Shall I order you divorced from Buntaro?"

"Sire?"

"Well?"

Oh to be free, her spirit sang. Oh, Madonna, to be free!

Remember who you are, Mariko, remember what you are. And remember that "love" is a barbarian word.

Toranaga was watching her in the great silence. Outside, mosquitoes strayed into the spirals of incense smoke to dart away to safety. Yes, he brooded, she's a falcon. But what prey do I cast her against?

"No, Sire," Mariko said at last. "Thank you, Sire, but no."

"The Anjin-san's a strange man, *neh?* His head is filled with dreams. Ridiculous to consider attacking our friends the Portuguese, or their Black Ship. Nonsense to believe what he says about four ships or twenty."

Mariko hesitated. "If he says a navy is possible, Sire, then I believe it's possible."

"I don't agree," Toranaga said emphatically. "But you're right that he's a balance against the others, him and his fighting ship. How curious—but how illuminating! It's as Omi said: At the moment we need the barbarians, to learn from them. And there's much yet to learn, particularly from him, *neh?*"

"Yes."

"It's time to open up the Empire, Mariko-san. Ishido will close it as tight as an oyster. If I were President of the Regents again, I'd make treaties with any nation, so long as it's friendly. I'd send men to learn from other nations, yes and I'd send ambassadors. This man's queen would be a good beginning. For a queen perhaps I should send a woman ambassador, if she were clever enough."

"She would have to be very strong and very clever, Sire."

"Yes. It would be a dangerous journey."

"All journeys are dangerous, Sire," Mariko said.

"Yes." Again Toranaga switched without warning. "If the Anjin-san sailed away with his ship weighed with gold, would he come back? He himself?"

After a long time she said, "I don't know."

Toranaga decided not to press her now. "Thank you, Mariko-san," he said in friendly dismissal. "I want you to be present at the meeting, to translate what I say for the Anjin-san."

"Everything, Sire?"

"Yes. And tonight when you go to the Tea House to buy Kiku's contract, take the Anjin-san with you. Tell his consort to make the arrangements. He needs rewarding, *neh?*"

"*Hai.*"

When she was at the shoji Toranaga said, "Once the issue between Ishido and myself is settled, I will order you divorced."

Her hand tightened on the screen. She nodded slightly in acknowledgment. But she did not look back. The door closed after her.

Toranaga watched the smoke for a moment, then got up and walked into the garden to the privy and squatted. When he had finished and had used the paper, he heard a servant slide the container away from beneath the hole to replace it with a clean one. The mosquitoes were droning and he slapped them absently. He was thinking of falcons and hawks, knowing that even the greatest falcons make mistakes, as Ishido had made a mistake, and Kiri, and Mariko, and Omi, and even the Anjin-san.

The hundred and fifty officers were aligned in neat rows, Yabu, Omi, and Buntaro in front. Mariko knelt near Blackthorne to the side. Toranaga marched in with his personal guards and sat on the lonely cushion, facing them. He acknowledged their bows, then informed them briefly of the essence of the dispatch and laid before them, for the first time publicly, his ultimate battle plan. Again he withheld the part that related to the secret and carefully planned insurrections, and also the fact that the attack would take the northern and not the southern coastal road. And, to general acclaim—for all his warriors were glad that at last there was an end to uncertainty—he told them that when the rains ceased he would issue the code words "Crimson Sky" which would launch them on their attack. "Meanwhile I expect Ishido illegally to convene a new Council of Regents. I expect to be falsely impeached. I expect war to be declared on me, against the law." He leaned forward, his left fist characteristically bunched on his thigh, the other tight on his sword. "Listen. I uphold the Taikō's testament and acknowledge my nephew Yaemon as Kwampaku and heir to the Taikō. I desire no other lands. I want no other honors. But if traitors attack me I must defend myself. If traitors dupe His Imperial Highness and attempt to assume power in the land, it is my duty to defend the Emperor and banish evil. *Neh?*"

A roar of approval greeted this. Battle cries of "Kasigi" and "Toranaga" poured through the room to be echoed throughout the fortress.

"The Attack Regiment will be prepared to embark on the galleys for Yedo, Toda Buntaro-san commanding, Kasigi Omi-san second-in-command, within five days. Lord Kasigi Yabu, you will please mobilize Izu and order six thousand men to the frontier passes in case the traitor Ikawa Jikkyu swoops south to cut our lines of communication. When the rains cease, Ishido will attack the Kwanto. . . ."

Omi, Yabu, and Buntaro all silently agreed with Toranaga's wisdom of withholding information about this afternoon's decision to launch the attack in the rainy season, at once.

That will create a sensation, Omi told himself, his bowels churning at the thought of warring in the rains through the mountains of Shinano.

"Our guns will force a way through," Yabu had said so enthusiastically this afternoon.

"Yes," Omi had agreed, having no confidence in the plan but no alternative to offer. It's madness, he told himself, though he was delighted that he had been promoted to second-in-command. I don't understand how Toranaga can conceive that there's any chance of success in the northern route.

There isn't any, he told himself again, and half closed his ears to Toranaga's stirring exhortation in order to allow himself to concentrate once more on the problem of his revenge. Certainly the attack on Shinano will give you a dozen opportunities to manipulate Yabu into the front line at no risk to yourself. War, any war, will be to your advantage, provided the war's not lost. . . .

Then he heard Toranaga say, "Today I was almost killed. Today the Anjin-san pulled me out of the earth. That's the second time, perhaps even the third, that he's saved my life. My life is nothing against the future of my clan, and who is to say whether I would have lived or died without his help? But though it is *bushido* that vassals should never expect a reward for any service, it is the duty of a liege lord to grant favors from time to time."

Amid general acclaim, Toranaga said, "Anjin-san, sit here! Mariko-san, you as well."

Jealously Omi watched the towering man rise and kneel at the spot to which Toranaga had motioned, beside him, and there was not a man in the room who did not wish that he himself had had the good fortune to have done what the barbarian had done.

"The Anjin-san is given a fief near the fishing village of Yokohama to the south of Yedo worth two thousand koku yearly, the right to recruit two hundred samurai retainers, full rights as samurai and hatamoto to the house of Yoshi Toranaga-noh-Chikitada-Minowara. Further, he is to receive ten horses, twenty kimonos, together with full battle equipment for his vassals—the rank of Chief Admiral and Pilot of the Kwanto." Toranaga waited until Mariko had translated, then he called out, "Naga-san!"

Obediently Naga brought the silk-covered package to Toranaga. Toranaga threw off the cover. There were two matching swords, one short, the other a killing sword. "Noticing that the earth had swallowed my swords and that I was unarmed, the Anjin-san went down into the crevasse again to find his own to give to me. Anjin-san, I give these in return. They were made by the master craftsman, Yori-ya. Remember, the sword is the soul of the samurai. If he forgets it, or loses it, *he will never be excused.* "

To even greater acclaim and private envy Blackthorne took the swords, bowed correctly, and put them in his sash, then bowed again.

"Thank you, Toranaga-sama. You do me too much honor. Thank you."

He began to move away but Toranaga bade him stay. "No, sit down here, beside me, Anjin-san." Toranaga looked back at the militant, fanatic faces of his officers.

"Fools!" he wanted to shout. "Don't you understand that war, whether now or after the rains, would only be disastrous? Any war with Ishido-Ochiba-Yae-mon and their present allies must end in slaughter of all my armies, all of you, and the obliteration of me and all my line? Don't you understand I've no chance except to wait and hope that Ishido strangles himself?"

Instead he incited them even more, for it was essential to throw his enemy off balance.

"Listen, samurai: Soon you'll be able to prove your valor, man to man, as our forefathers proved theirs. I will destroy Ishido and all his traitors and first will be Ikawa Jikkyu. I hereby give all his lands, both provinces of Suruga and Totomi worth three hundred thousand koku, to my faithful vassal Lord Kasigi Yabu, and, with Izu, confirm him and his line as their overlords."

A thunderous acclamation. Yabu was flushed with elation.

Omi was banging the floor, shouting just as ecstatically. Now his prize was limitless, for by custom, Yabu's heir would inherit all his lands.

How to kill Yabu without waiting for war?

Then his eyes fixed on the Anjin-san, who was cheering lustily. Why not let the Anjin-san do it for you, he asked himself, and laughed aloud at the idiotic thought. Buntaro leaned over and clapped him on the shoulder, amiably misinterpreting the laughter as happiness for Yabu. "Soon you'll get the fief you merit, *neh?*" Buntaro shouted over the tumult. "You deserve recognition too. Your ideas and counsel are valuable."

"Thank you, Buntaro-san."

"Don't worry—we can get through any mountains."

"Yes." Buntaro was a ferocious battle general and Omi knew they were well matched: Omi the bold strategist, Buntaro the fearless attack leader.

If anyone can get us through the mountains, he can.

There was another burst of cheering as Toranaga ordered saké to be brought, ending the formal meeting.

Omi drank his saké and watched Blackthorne drain another cup, his kimono neat, swords correct, Mariko still talking. You've changed very much, Anjin-san, since that first day, he thought contentedly. Many of your alien ideas are still set firm, but you're almost becoming civilized—

"What's the matter, Omi-san?"

"Nothing—nothing, Buntaro-san . . ."

"You looked as though an *eta* had shoved his buttocks in your face."

"Nothing like that—not at all! Eeeee, just the opposite. I had the beginnings of an idea. Drink up! Hey, Peach-Blossom, bring more saké, my Lord Buntaro's cup is empty!"

CHAPTER 40

I AM instructed to inquire if Kiku-san would be free this evening," Mariko said. "Oh, so sorry, Lady Toda, but I'm not sure," Gyoko, the Mama-san, said ingratiatingly. "May I ask if the honored client would require Lady Kiku for the evening or part of it, or perhaps until tomorrow, if she's not already engaged?"

The Mama-san was a tall, elegant woman in her early fifties with a lovely smile. But she drank too much saké, her heart was an abacus, and she possessed a nose that could smell a single piece of silver from fifty *ri*.

The two women were in an eight-mat room adjoining Toranaga's private quarters. It had been set aside for Mariko, and overlooked, on the other side, a small garden which was enclosed by the first of the inner wall defenses. It was raining again and the droplets sparkled in the flares.

Mariko said genteelly, "That would be a matter for the client to decide. Perhaps an arrangement could be made now which would cover every eventuality."

"So sorry, please excuse me that I don't know her availability at once. She's so sought after, Lady Toda. I'm sure you understand."

"Oh, yes, of course. We're really very fortunate to have such a lady of quality here in Anjiro." Mariko had accented the "Anjiro." She had sent for Gyoko instead of visiting her, as she might possibly have done. And when the woman had arrived, just late enough to make a distinct point, but not enough to be rude, Mariko had been glad of the opportunity to lock horns with so worthy an adversary.

"Was the Tea House damaged very much?" she asked.

"No, fortunately, apart from some valuable pottery and clothes, though it will cost a small fortune to repair the roof and resettle the garden. It's always so expensive to get things done quickly, don't you find?"

"Yes. It's very trying. In Yedo, Mishima, or even in this village."

"It's so important to have tranquil surroundings, *neh?* Would the client perhaps honor us at the Tea House? Or would he wish Kiku-san to visit him here, if she is available?"

Mariko pursed her lips, thinking. "The Tea House."

"*Ah, so desu!*" The Mama-san's real name was Heiko-ichi—First Daughter of the Wall Maker. Her father and his before him had been specialists in making garden walls. For many years she had been a courtesan in Mishima, the capital of Izu, attaining Second Class Rank. But the gods had smiled upon her and, with gifts from her patron, coupled with an astute business sense, she had made enough money to buy her own contract in good time, and so become a manager of ladies with a Tea House of her own when she was no longer sought after for the fine body and saucy wit with which the gods had endowed her. Now she called herself Gyoko-san, Lady Luck. When she was a fledgling courtesan of fourteen, she had been given the name Tsukaiko—Lady Snake Charmer. Her owner had explained to her that that special part of man could be likened to a snake, that a snake was lucky, and if she could become a snake charmer in that sense, then she would be hugely successful. Also the name would make clients laugh, and laughter was essential to this business. Gyoko had never forgotten about laughter.

"Saké, Gyoko-san?"

"Thank you, yes, thank you, Lady Toda."

The maid poured. Then Mariko dismissed her.

They drank silently for a moment. Mariko refilled the cups.

"Such lovely pottery. So elegant," Gyoko said.

"It's very poor. I'm so sorry we have to use it."

"If I can make her available, would five koban be acceptable?" A koban was a gold coin that weighed eighteen grams. One koban equaled three koku of rice.

"So sorry, perhaps I didn't make myself clear. I didn't wish to buy all the Tea House in Mishima, only the lady's services for an evening."

Gyoko laughed. "Ah, Lady Toda, your reputation is well merited. But may I point out that Kiku-san is of the First Class Rank. The Guild gave her that honor last year."

"True, and I'm sure that rank is merited. But that was in Mishima. Even in Kyoto—but of course you were making a joke, so sorry."

Gyoko swallowed the vulgarity that was on her tongue and smiled benignly. "Unfortunately I would have to reimburse clients who, I seem to remember, have already booked her. Poor child, four of her kimonos were ruined when water doused the fires. Hard times are coming to the land, Lady, I'm sure you understand. Five would not be unreasonable."

"Of course not. Five would be fair in Kyoto, for a week of carousing, with two ladies of First Rank. But these are not normal times and one must make allowances. Half a koban. Saké, Gyoko-san?"

"Thank you, thank you. The saké's so good—the quality is so good, so very good. Just one more if you please, then I must be off. If Kiku-san is not free this evening I'd be delighted to arrange one of the other ladies—Akeko perhaps. Or perhaps another day would be satisfactory? The day after tomorrow perhaps?"

Mariko did not answer for a moment. Five koban was outrageous—as much as you'd pay for a famous courtesan of First Class in Yedo. Half a koban would be more than reasonable for Kiku. Mariko knew prices of courtesans because Buntaro used courtesans from time to time and had even bought the contract of one, and she had had to pay the bills, which had, of course, rightly come to her. Her eyes gauged Gyoko. The woman was sipping her saké calmly, her hand steady.

"Perhaps," Mariko said. "But I don't think so, neither another lady nor another night. . . . No, if tonight cannot be arranged I'm afraid that the day after tomorrow would be too late, so sorry. And as to another of the ladies . . ." Mariko smiled and shrugged.

Gyoko set her cup down sadly. "I did hear that our glorious samurai would be leaving us. Such a pity! The nights are so pleasant here. In Mishima we do not get the sea breeze as you do here. I shall be sorry to leave too."

"Perhaps one koban. If this arrangement is satisfactory I would then like to discuss how much her contract would cost."

"Her contract!"

"Yes. Saké?"

"Thank you, yes. Contract—her contract? Well, that's another thing. Five thousand koku."

"That's impossible!"

"Yes," Gyoko agreed, "but Kiku-san's like my own daughter. She *is* my own daughter, better than my own daughter. I've trained her since she was six. She's the most accomplished Lady of the Willow World in all Izu. Oh, I know, in Yedo you have greater ladies, more witty, more worldly, but that's only because Kiku-san hasn't had the good fortune to mix with the same quality of persons. But even now, none can match her singing or her samisen playing. I swear it by all the gods. Give her a year in Yedo, with the right patron and correct sources of knowledge, and she'll compete satisfactorily with any courtesan in the Empire. Five thousand koku is a small sum to pay for such a flower." Perspiration beaded the woman's forehead. "You must excuse me, but I've never considered selling her contract before. She's barely eighteen, blemishless, the only Lady of First Class Rank that I've been privileged to manage. I really don't think I could ever sell her contract even at the price mentioned. No, I think I will have to reconsider, so sorry. Perhaps we could discuss this tomorrow. Lose Kiku-san? My little Kiku-chan?" Tears gathered in the corners of her eyes and Mariko thought, if those are real tears, then you, Gyoko, you've never spread yourself open to a Princely Pestle.

"So sorry. *Shigata ga nai, neh?*" Mariko said courteously and let the woman moan and weep and refilled her cup every so often and then again. How much is the contract really worth, she was asking herself. Five hundred koku would be fantastically more than fair. It depends on the anxiety of the man, who's not anxious in this case. Certainly Lord Toranaga isn't. Who's he buying for? Omi? Probably. But why did Toranaga order the Anjin-san here?

"You agree, Anjin-san?" she had asked him earlier with a nervous laugh, over the boisterousness of the drunken officers.

"You're saying that Lord Toranaga's arranged a lady for me? Part of my reward?"

"Yes. Kiku-san. You can hardly refuse. I—I am ordered to interpret."

"Ordered?"

"Oh, I'll be happy to interpret for you. But, Anjin-san, you really can't refuse. It would be terribly impolite after so many honors, *neh?*" She had smiled up at him, daring him, so proud and delighted with Toranaga's incredible generosity. "Please. I've never seen the inside of a Tea House before—I'd adore to look myself and talk with a real Lady of the Willow World."

"What?"

"Oh, they're called that because the ladies are supposed to be as graceful as willows. Sometimes it's the Floating World, because they're likened to lilies floating in a lake. Go on, Anjin-san, please agree."

"What about Buntaro-sama?"

"Oh, he knows I'm to arrange it for you. Lord Toranaga told him. It's all very official of course. I'm ordered. So are you! Please!" Then she had said in Latin, so glad that no one else in Anjiro spoke the language, "There is another reason that I will tell thee later."

"Ah—tell it to me now."

"Later. But agree, with amusement. Because I ask thee."

"Thou—how can I refuse thee?"

"But with amusement. It must be with amusement. Thy promise!"

"With laughter. I promise. I will attempt it. I promise thee nothing other than I will attempt the crest."

Then she had left him to make the arrangements.

"Oh, I'm distraught at the very thought of selling my beauty's contract," Gyoko was groaning. "Yes, thank you, just a little more saké, then I really must go." She drained the cup and held it out wearily for an immediate refill. "Shall we say two koban for this evening—a measure of my desire to please a Lady of such merit?"

"One. If this is agreed, perhaps we could talk more about the contract this evening, at the Tea House. So sorry to be precipitous, but time, you understand . . ." Mariko waved a hand vaguely toward the conference room. "Affairs of state—Lord Toranaga—the future of the realm—you understand, Gyoko-san."

"Oh, yes, Lady Toda, of course." Gyoko began to get up. "Shall we agree to one and a half for the evening? Good, then that's set—"

"One."

"*Oh ko,* Lady, the half is a mere token and hardly merits discussion," Gyoko wailed, thanking the gods for her acumen and keeping feigned anguish on her face. One and a half koban would be a triple fee. But, more than the money, this was, at long last, the first invitation from one of the real nobility of all Japan for which she had been angling, for which she would gladly have advised Kiku-san to do everything for nothing, twice. "By all the gods, Lady Toda, I throw myself on your mercy, one and a half koban. Please, think of my other children who have to be clothed and trained and fed for years, who do not become as priceless as Kiku-san but have to be cherished as much as she."

"One koban, in gold, tomorrow. *Neh?*"

Gyoko lifted the porcelain flask and poured two cups. She offered one to Mariko, drained the other, and refilled her own immediately. "One," she said, almost gagging.

"Thank you, you're so kind and thoughtful. Yes, times are hard." Mariko sipped her wine demurely. "The Anjin-san and I will be at the Tea House shortly."

"Eh? Whatwasthatyousaid?"

"That the Anjin-san and I will be at the Tea House shortly. I am to interpret for him."

"The barbarian?" Kiku gasped.

"The barbarian. And he'll be here any moment unless we stop him—with her, the cruelest, most grasping harpy I've ever met, may she be reborn a back-passage whore of the Fifteenth Rank."

In spite of her fear, Kiku laughed outright. "Oh, Mama-san, please don't fret so! She seemed such a lovely lady and one whole koban—you really made a marvelous arrangement! There, there, we've lots of time. First some saké will take away all your heartburn. Ako, quick as a hummingbird!"

Ako vanished.

"Yes, the client's the Anjin-san." Gyoko almost choked again.

Kiku fanned her and Hana, the little apprentice, fanned her and held sweet-smelling herbs near her nose. "I thought she was negotiating for Lord Buntaro—or Lord Toranaga himself. Of course when she said the Anjin-san I asked her at once why didn't his own consort, Lady Fujiko, negotiate as correct manners insisted, but all she said was that his Lady was badly sick with burns and she herself had been ordered to talk to me by Lord Toranaga himself."

"Oh! Oh, that I should be so fortunate to serve the great Lord!"

"You will, child, you will if we scheme. But the barbarian! What will all your other customers think? What will they say? Of course I left it undecided, telling Lady Toda that I didn't know if you were free, so you can still refuse if you wish, without offense."

"What can other customers say? Lord Toranaga ordered this. There's nothing to be done, *neh?*" Kiku concealed her apprehension.

"Oh, you can easily refuse. But you must be quick, Kiku-chan. *Oh ko,* I should have been more clever—I should have."

"Don't worry, Gyoko-sama. Everything will be all right. But we must think clearly. It's a big risk, *neh?*"

"Yes. Very."

"We can never turn back if we accept."

"Yes. I know."

"Advise me."

"I cannot, Kiku-chan. I feel I was trapped by *kami.* This must be your decision."

Kiku weighed all the horrors. Then weighed the good. "Let us gamble. Let us accept him. After all he is samurai, and hatamoto, and Lord Toranaga's favored vassal. Don't forget what the fortune-teller said: that I would help you to become rich and famous forever. I pray I may be allowed to do that to repay all your kindnesses."

Gyoko stroked Kiku's lovely hair. "Oh, child, you're so good, thank you, thank you. Yes, I think you're wise. I agree. Let him visit us." She pinched her cheek affectionately. "You always were my favorite! But I would have demanded double for the barbarian admiral if I'd known."

"But we got double, Mama-san."

"We should have had triple!"

Kiku patted Gyoko's hand. "Don't worry—this is the beginning of your good fortune."

"Yes, and it's true the Anjin-san is no ordinary barbarian but a samurai and hatamoto barbarian. Lady Toda told me he's been given a fief of two thousand koku and made Admiral of all Toranaga's ships and he bathes like a civilized person and no longer stinks. . . ."

Ako arrived breathlessly and poured the wine without spilling a drop. Four cups disappeared in quick succession. Gyoko began to feel better. "Tonight must be perfect. Yes. If Lord Toranaga ordered it, of course it has to be. He wouldn't order it personally unless it was important to him personally, *neh?* And the Anjin-san's really like a *daimyo.* Two thousand koku yearly—by all *kami,* we should have so much good fortune! Kiku-san, listen!" She leaned closer and Ako leaned closer, all eyes. "I asked the Lady Toda, seeing that she spoke their vile language, if she knew of any strange customs or ways, stories or dances or positions or songs or instruments or potents that the Anjin-san would prefer."

"Ah, that would be very helpful, very," Kiku said, frightened that she had agreed, wishing that she had had the wisdom to refuse.

"She told me nothing! She speaks their language but knows nothing about their pillow habits. I asked her if she'd ever asked him about that and she said yes, but with disastrous results." Gyoko related the occurrence in Osaka Castle. "Can you imagine how embarrassing that must have been!"

"At least, we know not to suggest boys to him—that's something."

"Apart from that, there's only the maid in his household to go by!"

"Do we have time to send for the maid?"

"I went there myself. Straight from the fortress. Not even a month's salary opened the girl's mouth, stupid little weevil!"

"Was she presentable?"

"Oh yes, for an untrained servant amateur. All she would add was that the Master was virile and not heavy, that he pillowed most abundantly in the most ordinary position. And that he was generously endowed."

"That doesn't help much, Mama-san."

"I know. Perhaps the best thing to do is to have everything ready, just in case, *neh?* Everything."

"Yes. I'll just have to be most cautious. It's very important that everything should be perfect. It will be very difficult—if not impossible—to entertain him correctly if I can't talk to him."

"Lady Toda said she'd interpret for you and for him."

"Ah, how kind of her. That will help greatly, though it's certainly not the same."

"True, true. More saké, Ako—gracefully, child, pour it gracefully. But Kiku-san, you're a courtesan of the First Rank. Improvise. The barbarian admiral saved Lord Toranaga's life today, and sits in his shadow. Our future depends on you! I know you will succeed beautifully. Ako!"

"Yes, Mistress!"

"Make sure that the futons are perfect, that everything's perfect. See that the flowers—no. I'll do the flowers myself! And Cook, where's Cook?" She patted Kiku on the knee. "Wear the golden kimono, with the green one under it. We must impress the Lady Toda tonight very much." She rushed off to begin to get the house in order, all the Ladies and maids and apprentices and servants happily bustling, cleaning and helping, so proud of the good fortune that had come to their house.

When all was settled, the schedule of the other girls rearranged, Gyoko went to her own room and lay down for a moment to gather her strength. She had not told Kiku yet about the offer of the contract.

I will wait and see, she thought. If I can make the arrangement I require, then perhaps I will let my lovely Kiku go. But never before I know to whom. I'm glad I had the foresight to make that clear to Lady Toda before I left. Why are you crying, you silly old woman? Are you drunk again? Get your wits about you! What's the value of unhappiness to you?

"Hana-chan!"

"Yes, Mother-sama?" The child came running to her. Just turned six, with big brown eyes and long, lovely hair, she wore a new scarlet silk kimono. Gyoko had bought her two days ago through the local child broker and Mura.

"How do you like your new name, child?"

"Oh, very much, very much. I'm honored, Mother-sama!"

The name meant "Little Blossom"—as Kiku meant "Chrysanthemum"—and Gyoko had given it to her on the first day. "I'm your mother now," Gyoko had told her kindly but firmly when she paid the price and took possession, marveling that such a potential beauty could come out of such crude fisherfolk as the rotund Tamasaki woman. After four days of intense bargaining, she had paid a koban for the child's services until the age of twenty, enough to feed the Tamasaki family for two years. "Fetch me some cha, then my comb and some fragrant tea leaves to take the saké off my breath."

"Yes, Mother-sama." She rushed off blindly, breathlessly, anxious to please, and collided into Kiku's gossamer skirts at the doorway.

"Oh, oh, oh, so sorryyyy . . ."

"You must be careful, Hana-chan."

"So sorry, so sorry, Elder Sister . . ." Hana-chan was almost in tears.

"Why are you sad, Little Blossom? There, there," Kiku said, brushing away the tears tenderly. "We put away sadness in this house. Remember, we of the Willow World, we never need sadness, child, for what good would that do? Sadness never pleases. Our duty is to please and to be gay. Run along, child, but gently, gently, be graceful." Kiku turned and showed herself to the older woman, her smile radiant. "Does this please you, Mistress-san?"

Blackthorne looked at her and muttered, "Hallelujah!"

"This is Kiku-san," Mariko said formally, elated by Blackthorne's reaction.

The girl came into the room with a swish of silk and knelt and bowed and said something Blackthorne did not catch.

"She says that you are welcome, that you honor this house."

"*Domo,*" he said.

"*Do itashemasite.* Saké, Anjin-san?" Kiku said.

"*Hai, domo.*"

He watched her perfect hands find the flask unerringly, make sure the temperature was correct, then pour into the cup that he lifted toward her, as Mariko had shown him, with more grace than he thought possible.

"You promise you will behave like a Japanese, truly?" Mariko had asked as they set out from the fortress, she riding the palanquin, he walking beside, down the track that curled to the village and to the square that fronted the sea. Torchbearers strode ahead and behind. Ten samurai accompanied them as an honor guard.

"I'll try, yes," Blackthorne said. "What do I have to do?"

"The first thing you must do is to forget what *you* have to do and merely remember that this night is only for *your* pleasure."

Today has been the best day of my life, he was thinking. And tonight—what about tonight? He was excited by the challenge and determined to try to be Japanese and enjoy everything and not be embarrassed.

"What—what does the evening—well—cost?" he had asked.

"That's very un-Japanese, Anjin-san," she had chided him. "What has that to do with anything? Fujiko-san agreed that the arrangement was satisfactory."

He had seen Fujiko before he left. The doctor had visited her and had changed the bandages and given her herb medicines. She was proud of the honors and new fief and had rattled on nicely, showing no pain, glad that he was going to the Tea House—of course, Mariko-san had consulted her and everything had been arranged, how good Mariko-san was! How sorry she was to have the burns so that she couldn't make the arrangements for him herself. He had touched Fujiko's hand before he left, liking her. She had thanked him and apologized again, and sent him on his way hoping that he would have a wonderful evening.

Gyoko and maids had been waiting ceremoniously at the gate of the Tea House to greet them.

"This is Gyoko-san, she's the Mama-san here."

"So honored, Anjin-san, so honored."

"Mama-san? You mean mama? Mother? That's the same in English, Mariko-san. Mama—mommy—mother."

"Oh! It's almost the same, but, so sorry, 'mama-san' just means 'stepmother' or 'foster parent,' Anjin-san. Mother is '*haha-san*' or '*oba-san.*'"

In a moment Gyoko excused herself and hurried away. Blackthorne smiled at Mariko. She had been like a child, gazing at everything. "Oh, Anjin-san, I've always wanted to see the inside of one of these places. Men are so very lucky! Isn't it beautiful? Isn't it marvelous, even in a tiny village? Gyoko-san must have had it refurbished completely by master craftsmen! Look at the quality of the woods and—oh, you're so kind to allow me to be with you. I'll never have another opportunity . . . look at the flowers . . . what an exquisite arrangement . . . and oh, look out into the garden. . . ."

Blackthorne was very glad and very sorry that a maid was in the room and the shoji door open, for even here in a tea house it would be unthinkable and lethal for Mariko to be alone with him in a room.

"Thou art beautiful," he said in Latin.

"And thou." Her face was dancing. "I am very proud of thee, Admiral of Ships. And Fujiko—oh, she was so proud she could hardly lie still!"

"Her burns seemed bad."

"Have no fear. The doctors are well practiced and she is young and strong and confident. Tonight put everything from thy mind. No more questions about Ishido or Ikawa Jikkyu, or battles or codewords or fiefs or ships. Tonight no cares—tonight only magic things for thee."

"Thou art magic for me."

She fluttered her fan and poured the wine and said nothing. He watched her, then they smiled together. "Because others are here and tongues wag, we must still be cautious. But oh, I am so happy for thee," she said.

"Thou. What was the other reason? You said there was another reason you wanted me to be here tonight?"

"Ah yes, the other reason." The same heavy perfume drifted around him. "It is an ancient custom we have, Anjin-san. When a lady who belongs to someone else cares for another man, and wishes to give him something of consequence that it is forbidden to give, then she will arrange for another to take her place—a gift—the most perfect courtesan that she can afford."

"You said 'when a lady *cares for* someone else.' Do you mean 'love'?"

"Yes. But only for tonight."

"Thou."

"Thou, Anjin-san."

"Why tonight, Mariko-san, why not before?"

"Tonight is a magic night and *kami* walk with us. I desire thee."

Then Kiku was at the doorway. "Hallelujah!" And he was welcomed and served saké.

"How do I say that the Lady's especially pretty?"

Mariko told him and he repeated the words. The girl laughed gaily, accepted the compliment, and returned it.

"Kiku-san asks if you would like her to sing or dance for you."

"What is thy preference?"

"This Lady is here for thy pleasure, samurai, not mine."

"And thou? Thou art here also for my pleasure?"

"Yes, in a way—in a very private way."

"Then please ask her to sing."

Kiku clapped her hands gently and Ako brought the samisen. It was long, shaped something like a guitar, and three-stringed. Ako set it in position on the floor and gave the ivory plectrum to Kiku.

Kiku said, "Lady Toda, please tell our honored guest that first I will sing 'The Song of the Dragonfly.' "

"Kiku-san, I would be honored if tonight, here, you would call me Mariko-san."

"You are too kind to me, Madam. Please excuse me. I could not possibly be so impolite."

"Please."

"I will if it pleases you, though. . . ." Her smile was lovely. "Thank you, Mariko-sama."

She strummed a chord. From the moment that the guests had walked through the gateway into her world, all her senses had been tuned. She had secretly watched them while they were with Gyoko-san and when they were alone, searching for any clue how to pleasure him or to impress the Lady Toda.

She had not been prepared for what soon became obvious: clearly the Anjin-san desired the Lady Toda, though he hid it as well as any civilized person could hide it. This in itself was not surprising, for the Lady Toda was most beautiful and accomplished and, most important, she alone could talk with him. What astounded her was that she was certain the Lady Toda desired him equally, if not more.

The barbarian samurai and the Lady samurai, patrician daughter of the assassin Akechi Jinsai, wife of Lord Buntaro! Eeeee! Poor man, poor woman. So sad. Surely this must end in tragedy.

Kiku felt near to tears as she thought of the sadness of life, the unfairness. Oh, how I wish I were born samurai and not a peasant so that I could become even a consort to Omi-sama, not just a temporary toy. I would gladly give my hope of rebirth in return for that.

Put away sadness. Give pleasure, that is your duty.

Her fingers strummed a second chord, a chord filled with melancholy. Then she noticed that though Mariko was beguiled by her music the Anjin-san was not.

Why? Kiku knew that it was not her playing, for she was sure that it was almost perfect. Such mastery as hers was given to few.

A third, more beautiful chord, experimentally. There's no doubt, she told herself hastily, it doesn't please him. She allowed the chord to die away and began to sing unaccompanied, her voice soaring with the sudden changes of tempo that took years to perfect. Again Mariko was entranced, he was not, so at once Kiku stopped. "Tonight is not for music or singing," she announced. "Tonight is for happiness. Mariko-san, how do I say, 'please excuse me' in his language?"

"*Per favor.*"

"*Per favor,* Anjin-san, tonight we must laugh only, *neh?*"

"*Domo,* Kiku-san. *Hai.*"

"It's difficult to entertain without words, but not impossible, *neh?* Ah, I know!" She jumped up and began to do comic pantomimes—*daimyo,* kaga-man, fisherman, hawker, pompous samurai, even an old farmer collecting a full pail—and she did them all so well and so humorously that soon Mariko and Blackthorne were laughing and clapping. Then she held up her hand. Mischievously she began to mimic a man peeing, holding himself or missing, grabbing, searching for the insignificant or weighed down by the incredible, through all the stages of his life, beginning first as a child just wetting the bed and howling, to a young man in a hurry, to another having to hold back, another with size, another with smallness to the point of "where has it gone," and at length to a very old man groaning in ecstasy at being able to pee at all.

Kiku bowed to their applause and sipped cha, patting the sheen from her forehead. She noticed that he was easing his shoulders and back. "Oh, *per favor, senhor!*" and she knelt behind him and began to massage his neck.

Her knowing fingers instantly found the pleasure points. "Oh God, that's . . . *hai* . . . just there!"

She did as he asked. "Your neck will be better soon. Too much sitting, Anjin-san!"

"That very good, Kiku-san. Make Suwo almost bad!"

"Ah, thank you. Mariko-san, the Anjin-san's shoulders are so vast, would you help me? Just do his left shoulder while I do his right? So sorry, but hands are not strong enough."

Mariko allowed herself to be persuaded and did as she was asked. Kiku hid her smile as she felt him tighten under Mariko's fingers and she was very pleased with her improvisations. Now the client was being pleasured through her artistry and knowledge, and being maneuvered as he should be maneuvered.

"Is that better, Anjin-san?"

"Good, very good, thank you."

"Oh, you're very welcome. It's my pleasure. But the Lady Toda is so much more deft than I." Kiku could feel the attraction between them though they tried to conceal it. "Now a little food perhaps?" It came at once.

"For you, Anjin-san," she said proudly. The dish contained a small pheasant, cut into tiny pieces, barbecued over charcoal with a sweet soya sauce. She helped him.

"It delicious, delicious," he said. And it was.

"Mariko-san?"

"Thank you." Mariko took a token piece but did not eat it.

Kiku took a fragment in her chopsticks and chewed it with relish. "It's good, *neh?*"

"No, Kiku-san, it very good! Very good."

"Please, Anjin-san, have some more." She took a second morsel. "There's plenty."

"Thank you. Please. How did—how this?" He pointed to the thick brown sauce.

Mariko interpreted for her. "Kiku says it's sugar and soya with a little ginger. She asks do you have sugar and soya in your country?"

"Sugar in beet, yes, soya no, Kiku-san."

"Oh! How can one live without soya?" Kiku became solemn. "Please tell the Anjin-san that we have had sugar here since one thousand years. The Buddhist monk Ganjin brought it to us from China. All our best things have come from China, Anjin-san. Cha came to us about five hundred years ago. The Buddhist monk Eisai brought some seeds and planted them in Chikuzen Province, where I was born. He also brought us Zen Buddhism."

Mariko translated with equal formality, then Kiku let out a peal of laughter. "Oh so sorry, Mariko-sama, but you both looked so grave. I was just pretending to be solemn about cha—as if it mattered! It was only to amuse you."

They watched Blackthorne finish the pheasant. "Good," he said. "Very good. Please thank Gyoko-san."

"She will be honored." Kiku poured more saké for both of them. Then, knowing it was time, she said innocently, "May I ask what happened today at the earthquake? I hear the Anjin-san saved the life of Lord Toranaga? I would consider it an honor to know firsthand."

She settled back patiently, letting Blackthorne and Mariko enjoy the telling, adding an "oh," or "what happened then?" or pouring saké, never interrupting, being the perfect listener.

And, when they finished, Kiku marveled at their bravery and at Lord Toranaga's good fortune. They talked for a while, then Blackthorne got up and the maid was told to show him the way.

Mariko broke a silence. "You've never eaten meat before, Kiku-san, have you?"

"It is my duty to do whatever I can to please him, for just a little while, *neh?*"

"I never knew how perfect a lady could be. I understand now why there must always be a Floating World, a Willow World, and how lucky men are, how inadequate I am."

"Oh, that was never my purpose, never, Mariko-sama. And not our purpose. We are here only to please, for a fleeting moment."

"Yes. I just meant I admire you so much. I would like you for my sister."

Kiku bowed. "I would not be worthy of that honor." There was warmth between them. Then she said, "This is a very secret place and everyone is to be trusted, there are no prying eyes. The pleasure room in the garden is very dark if one wants it dark. And darkness keeps all secrets."

"The only way to keep a secret is to be alone and whisper it down an empty well at high noon, *neh?*" Mariko said lightly, needing time to decide.

"Between sisters there's no need for wells. I have dismissed my maid until the dawn. Our pleasure room is a very private place."

"There you must be alone with him."

"I can always be alone, always."

"You're so kind to me, Kiku-chan, so very thoughtful."

"It is a magic night, *neh?* And very special."

"Magic nights end too soon, Little Sister. Magic nights are for children, *neh?* I am not a child."

"Who knows what happens on a magic night? Darkness contains everything."

Mariko shook her head sadly and touched her tenderly. "Yes. But for him, if it contained you that would be everything."

Kiku let the matter rest. Then she said, "I am a gift to the Anjin-san? He did not ask for me himself?"

"If he had seen you, how could he not ask for you? Truthfully, it's his honor that you welcome him. I understand that now."

"But he did see me once, Mariko-san. I was with Omi-san when he passed on his way to the ship to go to Osaka the first time."

"Oh, but the Anjin-san said that he saw Midori-san with Omi-san. It was you? Beside the palanquin?"

"Yes, in the square. Oh yes, it was me, Mariko-san, not the Lady, the wife of Omi-sama. He said *'konnichi wa'* to me. But of course, he would not remember. How could he remember? That was during a previous life, *neh?*"

"Oh, he remembered her—the beautiful girl with the green parasol. He said the most beautiful girl he had ever seen. He told me about her many times." Mariko studied her even more closely. "Yes, Kiku-san, you could easily be mistaken for her on such a day, under a parasol."

Kiku poured saké and Mariko was entranced by her unconscious elegance. "My parasol was sea green," she said, very pleased that he had remembered.

"How did the Anjin-san look then? Very different? The Night of the Screams must have been terrible."

"Yes, yes it was. And he was older then, the skin of his face stretched. . . . But we become too serious, Elder Sister. Ah, you don't know how honored I am to be allowed to call you that. Tonight is a night of pleasure only. No more seriousness, *neh?*"

"Yes. I agree. Please forgive me."

"Now, to more practical matters, would you please give me some advice?"

"Anything," Mariko said, as friendly.

"In this matter of the pillow, do people of his nation prefer any instruments or positions that you are aware of? So sorry to ask, but perhaps you might be able to guide me."

It took all of Mariko's training to remain unabashed. "No, not that I know. The Anjin-san is very sensitive about anything to do with pillowing."

"Could he be asked in an oblique way?"

"I don't think you can ask a foreign person like that. Certainly not the Anjin-san. And—so sorry, I don't know what the, er, instruments are—except, of course, a *harigata*."

"Ah!" Again Kiku's intuition guided her and she asked artlessly, "Would you care to see them? I could show them all to you, perhaps with him there, then he need not be asked. We can see from his reaction."

Mariko hesitated, her own curiosity swamping her judgment. "If it could be done with humor . . ."

They heard Blackthorne approaching. Kiku welcomed him back and poured wine. Mariko quaffed hers, glad that she was no longer alone, uneasily sure that Kiku could read her thoughts.

They chatted and played silly games and then, when Kiku judged that the time was correct, she asked them if they would like to see the garden and the pleasure rooms.

They walked out into the night. The garden sparkled in the torchlights where the raindrops still lingered. The path meandered beside a tiny pool and gurgling waterfall. At the end of the path was the small isolated house in the center of the bamboo grove. It was raised off manicured ground and had four steps up to the encircling veranda. Everything about the two-roomed dwelling was tasteful and expensive. The best woods, best carpentry, best tatami, best silk cushions, most elegant hangings in the *takonama*.

"It's so lovely, Kiku-san," Mariko said.

"The Tea House in Mishima is much nicer, Mariko-san. Please be comfortable, Anjin-san! *Per favor,* does this please you, Anjin-san?"

"Yes, very much."

Kiku saw that he was still bemused with the night and the saké but totally conscious of Mariko. She was very tempted to get up and go into the inner room where the futons were turned back and step out onto the veranda again and leave. But if she did, she knew that she would be in violation of the law. More than that, she felt that such an action would be irresponsible, for she knew in her heart Mariko was ready and almost beyond caring.

No, she thought, I mustn't push her into such a tragic indiscretion, much as it might be valuable to my future. I offered but Mariko-san willed herself to refuse. Wisely. Are they lovers? I do not know. That is their *karma.*

She leaned forward and laughed conspiratorially. "Listen, Elder Sister, please tell the Anjin-san that there are some pillow instruments here. Does he have them in his country?"

"He says, no, Kiku-san. So sorry, he's never heard of any."

"Oh! Would it amuse him to see them? They're in the next room, I can fetch them—they're really very exciting."

"Would you like to see them, Anjin-san? She says they're really very funny." Mariko deliberately changed the word.

"Why not," Blackthorne said, his throat constricted, his whole being charged with an awareness of their perfume and their femininity. "You—you use instruments to pillow with?" he asked.

"Kiku-san says sometimes, Anjin-san. She says—and this is true—it's our custom always to try to prolong the moment of the 'Clouds and the Rain' because we believe for that brief instant we mortals are one with the gods." Mariko watched him. "So it's very important to make it last as long as possible, *neh?* Almost a duty, *neh?*"

"Yes."

"Yes. She says to be one with the gods is very essential. It's a good belief and very possible, don't you think, to believe that? The Cloudburst feeling is so unearthly and godlike. Isn't it? So any means to stay one with the gods for as long as possible is our duty, *neh?*"

"Very. Oh, yes."

"Would you like saké, Anjin-san?"

"Thank you."

She fanned herself. "This about the Cloudburst and the Clouds and the Rain or the Fire and the Torrent, as we sometimes call it, is very Japanese, Anjin-san. Very important to be Japanese in pillow things, *neh?*"

To her relief, he grinned and bowed to her like a courtier. "Yes. Very. I'm Japanese, Mariko-san. *Honto!*"

Kiku returned with the silk-lined case. She opened it and took out a substantial life-size penis made of ivory, and another made of softer material, elastic, that Blackthorne had never seen before. Carelessly she set them aside.

"These of course, are ordinary *harigata,* Anjin-san," Mariko said unconcernedly, her eyes glued on the other objects.

"Is that a fact?" Blackthorne said, not knowing what else to say. "Mother of God!"

"But it's just an ordinary *harigata,* Anjin-san. Surely your women have them!"

"Certainly not! No, they don't," he added, trying to remember about the humor.

Mariko couldn't believe it. She explained to Kiku, who was equally surprised. Kiku spoke at length, Mariko agreeing.

"Kiku-san says that's very strange. I must agree, Anjin-san. Here almost every girl uses one for ordinary relief without a second thought. How else can a girl stay healthy when she's restricted where a man is not? Are you sure, Anjin-san? You're not teasing?"

"No—I'm, er, sure our women don't have them. That would be—Jesus, that— well, no, we—they—don't have them."

"Without them life must be very difficult. We have a saying that a *harigata's* like a man but better because it's exactly like his best part but without his worst parts. *Neh?* And it's also better because all men aren't—don't have a sufficiency, as *harigatas* do. Also they're devoted, Anjin-san, and they'll never tire of you, like a man does. And too, they can be as rough or smooth— Anjin-san, you promised, remember? With humor!"

"You're right!" Blackthorne grinned. "By God, you're right. Please excuse me." He picked up the *harigata* and studied it closely, whistling tonelessly. Then he held it up. "You were saying, Teacher-san? It can be rough?"

"Yes," she said cheerfully. "It can be as rough or as smooth as you desire, and *harigatas* very particularly have far more endurance than any man and they never wear out!"

"Oh, that's a point!"

"Yes. Don't forget, not every woman is fortunate enough to belong to a virile man. Without one of these to help release ordinary passions and normal needs, an ordinary woman soon becomes poisoned in body, and that will certainly very soon destroy her harmony, thus hurt her and those around her. Women don't have the freedom men have—to a greater or lesser degree, and rightly, *neh?* The world belongs to men, and rightly, *neh?*"

"Yes." He smiled. "And no."

"I pity your women, so sorry. They must be the same as ours. When you go home you must instruct them, Anjin-san. Ah, yes, tell your Queen, she will understand. We are very sensible in matters of the pillow."

"I'll mention it to Her Majesty." Blackthorne put the *harigata* aside with feigned reluctance. "What's next?"

Kiku produced a string of four large round beads of white jade that were spaced along a strong silken thread. Mariko listened intently to Kiku's explanation, her eyes getting wider than ever before, her fan fluttering, and looked down at the beads in wonder as Kiku came to an end. "*Ah so desu!* Well, Anjin-san," she began firmly, "these are called *konomi-shinju,* Pleasure Pearls, and the senhor or senhora may use them. Saké, Anjin-san?"

"Thank you."

"Yes. Either the lady or the man may use them and the beads are carefully placed in the back passage and then, at the moment of the Clouds and the Rain, the beads are pulled out slowly, one by one."

"What?"

"Yes." Mariko laid the beads on the cushion in front of him. "The Lady Kiku says the timing's very important, and that always a . . . I don't know what you would call it, ah yes, always an oily salve should be used . . . for comfort, Anjin-san." She looked up at him and added, "She says also that Pleasure Pearls can be found in many sizes and that, if used correctly, they can precipitate a very considerable result indeed."

He laughed uproariously and spluttered in English, "I'll bet a barrel of doubloons against a piece of pig shit you can believe that!"

"So sorry, I didn't understand, Anjin-san."

When he could talk, he said in Portuguese, "I'll bet a mountain of gold to a blade of grass, Mariko-san, the result is very considerable indeed." He picked up the beads and examined them, whistling without noticing it. "Pleasure Pearls, eh?" After a moment he put them down. "What else is there?"

Kiku was pleased that her experiment was succeeding. Next she showed them a *himitsu-kawa,* the Secret Skin. "It's a pleasure ring, Anjin-san, that the man wears to keep himself erect when he's depleted. With this, Kiku-san says, the man can gratify the woman after he's passed his pinnacle, or his desire has flagged." Mariko watched him. *"Neh?"*

"Absolutely." Blackthorne beamed. "The Good Lord protect me from either, and from not giving gratification. Please ask Kiku-san to buy me three—just in case!"

Next he was shown the *hiro-gumbi,* Weary Armaments, thin dried stalks of a plant that, when soaked and wrapped around the Peerless Part, swell up and make it appear strong. Then there were all kinds of potents—potents to excite or increase excitement—and all kinds of salves—salves to moisten, to swell, to strengthen.

"Never to weaken?" he asked, to more hilarity.

"Oh no, Anjin-san, that would be unearthly!"

Then Kiku laid out other rings for the man to wear, ivory or elastic or silken rings with nodules or bristles or ribbons or attachments and appendages of every kind, made of ivory or horsehair or seeds or even tiny bells.

"Kiku-san says almost any of these will turn the shyest lady wanton."

Oh God, how would I like thee wanton, he thought. "But these're only for the man to wear, *neh?*" he asked.

"The more excited the lady is, the more the man's enjoyment, *neh?*" Mariko was saying. "Of course, giving pleasure to the woman is equally the man's duty, isn't it, and with one of these, if, unhappily, he's small or weak or old or tired, he can still pleasure her with honor."

"You've used them, Mariko-san?"

"No, Anjin-san, I've never seen them before. These are . . . wives are not for pleasure but for childbearing and for looking after the house and the home."

"Wives don't expect to be pleasured?"

"No. It would not be usual. That is for the Ladies of the Willow World." Mariko fanned herself and explained to Kiku what had been said. "She says, surely it's the same in your world? That the man's duty is to pleasure the lady as it is her duty to pleasure him?"

"Please tell her, so sorry, but it's not the same, just about the opposite."

"She says that is very bad. Saké?"

"Please tell her we're taught to be ashamed of our bodies and pillowing and nakedness and . . . and all sorts of stupidities. It's only being here that's made me realize it. Now that I'm a little civilized I know better."

Mariko translated. He drained his cup. It was refilled immediately by Kiku, who leaned over and held her long sleeve with her left hand so that it would not touch the low lacquered table as she poured with her right.

"Domo."

"Do itashimashite, Anjin-san."

"Kiku-san says we should all be honored that you say such things. I agree, Anjin-san. You make me feel very proud. I was very proud of you today. But surely it's not as bad as you say."

"It's worse. It's difficult to understand, let alone explain, if you've never been there or weren't brought up there. You see—in truth . . ." Blackthorne saw them watching him, waiting patiently, multihued, so lovely and clean, the room so stark and uncluttered and tranquil. All at once his mind began to contrast it with the warm, friendly stench of his English home, rushes on the earth floor, smoke from the open brick fire rising to the roof hole—only three of the new fireplaces with *chimneys* in his whole village, and those only for the very wealthy. Two small bedrooms and then the one large untidy room of the cottage for eating, living, cooking, and talking. You walked into the cottage in your seaboots, summer or winter, mud unnoticed, dung unnoticed, and sat on a chair or bench, the oak table cluttered like the room, three or four dogs and the two children—his son and his dead brother Arthur's girl—climbing and falling and playing higgledy piggledy, Felicity cooking, her long dress trailing in the rushes and dirt, the skivvy maid sniffing and getting in the way and Mary, Arthur's widow, coughing in the next room he'd built for her, near death as always, but never dying.

Felicity. Dear Felicity. A bath once a month perhaps, and then in summer, very private, in the copper tub, but washing her face and hands and feet every day, always hidden to the neck and wrists, swathed in layers of heavy woolens all year long that were unwashed for months or years, reeking like everyone, lice-infested like everyone, scratching like everyone.

And all the other stupid beliefs and superstitions, that cleanliness could kill, open windows could kill, water could kill and encourage flux or bring in the plague, that lice and fleas and flies and dirt and disease were God's punishments for sins on earth.

Fleas, flies, and fresh rushes every spring, but every day to church and twice on Sundays to hear the Word pounded into you: Nothing matters, only God and salvation.

Born in sin, living in shame, Devil's brood, condemned to Hell, praying for salvation and forgiveness, Felicity so devout and filled with fear of the Lord and terror of the Devil, desperate for Heaven. Then going home to food. A haunch of meat from the spit and if a piece fell on the floor you'd pick it up and brush the dirt off and eat it if the dogs didn't get it first, but you'd throw them the bones anyway. Castings on the floor. Leavings pushed onto the floor to be swept up perhaps and thrown into the road perhaps. Sleeping most of the time in your dayclothes and scratching like a contented dog, always scratching. Old so young and ugly so young and dying so young. Felicity. Now twenty-nine, gray, few teeth left, old, lined, and dried up.

"Before her time, poor bloody woman. My God, how unnecessary!" he cried out in rage. "What a stinking bloody waste!"

"Nan desu ka, Anjin-san?" both women said in the same breath, their contentment vanishing.

"So sorry . . . it was just . . . you're all so clean and we're filthy and it's all such a waste, countless millions, me too, all my life . . . and only because we don't know any better! Christ Jesus, what a waste! It's the priests—they're the educated and the educators, priests own all the schools, do all the teaching, always in the name of God, filth in the name of God . . . . It's the truth!"

"Oh yes, of course," Mariko said soothingly, touched by his pain. "Please don't concern yourself now, Anjin-san. That's for tomorrow. . . ."

Kiku wore a smile but she was furious with herself. You should have been more careful, she told herself. Stupid stupid stupid! Mariko-san warned you! Now you've allowed the evening to be ruined, and the magic's gone gone gone!

In truth, the heavy, almost tangible sexuality that had touched all of them had disappeared. Perhaps that's just as well, she thought. At least Mariko and the Anjin-san are protected for one more night.

Poor man, poor lady. So sad. She watched them talking, then sensed a change in tone between them.

"Now I must leave thee," Mariko was saying in Latin.

"Let us leave together."

"I beg thee stay. For thy honor and hers. And mine, Anjin-san."

"I do not want this thy gift," he said. "I want thee."

"I am thine, believe it, Anjin-san. Please stay, I beg thee, and know that tonight I am thine."

He did not insist that she stay.

After she had gone he lay back and put his arms under his head and stared out of the window at the night. Rain splattered the tiles, the wind gusted caressingly from the sea.

Kiku was kneeling motionless in front of him. Her legs were stiff. She would have liked to lie down herself but she did not wish to break his mood by the slightest movement. You are not tired. Your legs do not ache, she told herself. Listen to the rain and think of lovely things. Think of Omi-san and the Tea House in Mishima, and that you're alive and that yesterday's earthquake was just another earthquake. Think of Toranaga-sama and the incredibly extravagant price that Gyoko-san had dared to ask initially for your contract. The soothsayer was right, it is your good fortune to make her rich beyond dreams. And if that part is true, why not all the rest? That one day you will marry a samurai you honor and have a son by him, that you will live and die in old age, part of his household, wealthy and honored, and that, miracle of miracles, your son will grow to equal estate—samurai—as will his sons.

Kiku began to glow at her incredible, wonderful future.

After a time Blackthorne stretched luxuriously, a pleasing weariness upon him. He saw her and smiled.

"*Nan desu ka,* Anjin-san?"

He shook his head kindly, got up and opened the shoji to the next room. There was no maid kneeling beside the netted futons. He and Kiku were alone in the exquisite little house.

He went into the sleeping room and began to take off his kimono. She hurried to help. He undressed completely, then put on the light silk sleeping kimono she held out for him. She opened the mosquito netting and he lay down.

Then Kiku changed also. He saw her take off the obi and the outer kimono and the scarlet-edged lesser kimono of palest green, and finally the underskirt. She put on her peach-colored sleeping kimono, then removed the elaborate formal wig and loosed her hair. It was blue-black and fine and very long.

She knelt outside the net. "*Dozo,* Anjin-san?"

"*Domo,*" he said.

"*Domo arigato goziemashita,*" she whispered.

She slipped under the net and lay beside him. The candles and oil lamps burned brightly. He was glad of the light because she was so beautiful.

His desperate need had vanished, though the ache remained. I don't desire you, Kiku-chan, he thought. Even if you were Mariko it would be the same. Even though you're the most beautiful woman I've ever seen, more beautiful even than Midori-san, who I thought was more beautiful than any goddess. I don't desire you. Later perhaps but not now, so sorry.

Her hand reached out and touched him. *"Dozo?"*

"Iyé," he said gently, shaking his head. He held her hand, then slipped an arm under her shoulders. Obediently she nestled against him, understanding at once. Her perfume mingled with the fragrance of the sheets and futons. So clean, he thought, everything's so incredibly clean.

What was it Rodrigues had said? 'The Japans're heaven on earth, Ingeles, if you know where to look,' or 'This is paradise, Ingeles.' I don't remember. I only know it's not there, across the sea, where I thought it was. It's not there.

Heaven on earth is here.

CHAPTER 41

THE courier galloped down the road in darkness toward the sleeping village. The sky was tinged with dawn and the night fishing boats that had been netting near the shoals were just coming in. He had ridden without rest from Mishima over the mountain passes and bad roads, commandeering fresh horses wherever he could.

His horse pounded through the village streets—covert eyes watching him now—across the square and up the road to the fortress. His standard carried Toranaga's cipher and he knew the current password. Nevertheless he was challenged and identified four times before he was allowed entrance and audience with the officer of the watch.

"Urgent dispatches from Mishima, Naga-san, from Lord Hiro-matsu."

Naga took the scroll and hurried inside. At the heavily guarded shoji he stopped. "Father?"

"Yes?"

Naga slid back the door and waited. Toranaga's sword slipped back into its scabbard. One of the guards brought an oil lamp.

Toranaga sat up in his mosquito net and broke the seal. Two weeks ago he had ordered Hiro-matsu with an elite regiment secretly to Mishima, the castle city on the Tokaidō Road that guarded the entrance to the pass leading across the mountains to the cities of Atami and Odawara on the east coast of Izu. Atami was the gateway to Odawara to the north. Odawara was the key to the defense of the whole Kwanto.

Hiro-matsu wrote: "Sire, your half brother, Zataki, Lord of Shinano, arrived here today from Osaka asking for safe conduct to see you at Anjiro. He travels formally with a hundred samurai and bearers, under the cipher of the 'new' Council of Regents. I regret to tell you the Lady Kiritsubo's news is correct. Zataki's turned traitor and is openly flaunting his allegiance to Ishido. What she did not know is that Zataki is now a Regent in place of Lord Sugiyama. He showed me his official appointment, correctly signed by Ishido, Kiyama, Onoshi, and Ito. It was all I could do to restrain my men at his arrogance and obey your orders to let any messenger from Ishido pass. I wanted to kill this dung eater myself. Traveling with him is the barbarian priest, Tsukku-san, who arrived by sea at the port of Numazu, coming from Nagasaki. He asked permission to visit you so I sent him with the same party. I've sent two hundred of my men to escort them. They'll arrive within two days at Anjiro. When do you return to Yedo? Spies say Jikkyu's mobilizing secretly and news comes from Yedo that the northern clans are ready to throw in with Ishido now that Zataki's Shinano is against you. I beg you to leave Anjiro at once—retreat by sea. Let Zataki follow you to Yedo, where we can deal with him properly."

Toranaga slammed his fist against the floor.

"Naga-san. Fetch Buntaro-san, Yabu-san, and Omi-san here at once."

They arrived very quickly. Toranaga read them the message. "We'd better cancel all training. Send the Musket Regiment, every man, into the mountains. We don't want any security leaks now."

Omi said, "Please excuse me, Sire, but you might consider intercepting the

466

party over the mountains. Say at Yokosé. Invite Lord Zataki"—he chose the title carefully—"to take the waters at one of the nearby spas, but have the meeting at Yokosé. Then, after he's delivered his message, he and all his men can be turned back, escorted to the frontier, or destroyed, just as you wish."

"I don't know Yokosé."

Yabu said importantly, "It's beautiful, almost in the center of Izu, Sire, over the mountains in a valley cleft. It's beside the river Kano. The Kano flows north, eventually through Mishima and Numazo to the sea, *neh?* Yokosé's at a cross-roads—the roads go north-south and east-west. Yes, Yokosé'd be a good place to meet, Sire. Shuzenji Spa's nearby—very hot, very good—one of our best. You should visit it, Sire. I think Omi-san's made a good suggestion."

"Could we defend it easily?"

Omi said quickly, "Yes, Sire. There's a bridge. The land falls steeply from the mountains. Any attackers would have to fight up a snaking road. Both passes can be held with few men. You could never be ambushed. We have more than enough men to defend you and butcher ten times their number—if need be."

"We butcher them whatever happens, *neh?*" Buntaro said with contempt. "But better there than here. Sire, please let me make the place safe. Five hundred archers, no musketeers—all horsemen. Added to the men my father sent, we'll have more than enough."

Toranaga checked the date on the dispatch. "They'll reach the crossroads when?"

Yabu looked at Omi for confirmation. "Tonight at the earliest?"

"Yes. Perhaps not until dawn tomorrow."

"Buntaro-san, leave at once," Toranaga said. "Contain them at Yokosé but keep them the other side of the river. I'll leave at dawn tomorrow with another hundred men. We should be there by noon. Yabu-san, you take charge of our Musket Regiment for the moment and guard our retreat. Put it in ambush across the Heikawa Road, on the skyline, so we can fall back through you if necessary."

Buntaro started to leave but stopped as Yabu said uneasily, "How can there be treachery, Sire? They've only a hundred men."

"I expect treachery. Lord Zataki wouldn't put his head into my hands without a plan, for, of course, I'll take his head if I can," Toranaga said. "Without him to lead his fanatics we'll have a far better chance to get through his mountains. But why's he risking everything? Why?"

Omi said tentatively, "Could he be ready to turn ally again?"

They all knew the longstanding rivalry that had existed between the half brothers. A friendly rivalry up till now.

"No, not him. I never trusted him before. Would any of you trust him now?"

They shook their heads.

Yabu said, "Surely there's nothing to disturb you, Sire. Lord Zataki's a Regent, yes, but he's only a messenger, *neh?*"

Fool, Toranaga wanted to shout, don't you understand anything? "We'll soon know. Buntaro-san, go at once."

"Yes, Sire. I'll choose the meeting place carefully, but don't let him within ten paces. I was with him in Korea. He's too quick with his sword."

"Yes."

Buntaro hurried away. Yabu said, "Perhaps Zataki can be tempted to betray Ishido—some prize perhaps? What's his bait? Even without his leadership the Shinano mountains are cruel."

"The bait's obvious," Toranaga said. "The Kwanto. Isn't that what he wants, has always wanted? Isn't that what all my enemies want? Isn't that what Ishido himself wants?"

They did not answer him. There was no need.

Toranaga said gravely, "May Buddha help us. The Taikō's peace has ended. War is beginning."

Blackthorne's sea ears had heard the urgency in the approaching hoofs and they had whispered danger. He had come out of sleep instantly, ready to attack or retreat, all his senses tuned. The hoofs passed, then headed up the hill toward the fortress, to die away again.

He waited. No sound of a following escort. Probably a lone messenger, he thought. From where? Is it war already?

Dawn was imminent. Now Blackthorne could see a small part of the sky. It was overcast and laden with rain, the air warm with a tang of salt in it, billowing the net from time to time. A mosquito whined faintly outside. He was very pleased to be within, safe for the moment. Enjoy the safety and the tranquillity while it lasts, he told himself.

Kiku was sleeping next to him, curled up like a kitten. Sleep-tousled, she seemed more beautiful to him. He carefully relaxed back into the softness of the quilts on the tatami floor.

This is so much better than a bed. Better than any bunk—my God, how much better! But soon to be back aboard, *neh?* Soon to fall on the Black Ship and take her, *neh?* I think Toranaga's agreed even though he hasn't said so openly. Hasn't he just agreed in Japanese fashion? *'Nothing can ever be solved in Japan except by Japanese methods.'* Yes, I believe that's the truth.

I wanted to be better informed. Didn't he tell Mariko to translate everything and explain about his political problems?

I wanted money to buy my new crew. Didn't he give me two thousand koku?

I asked for two or three hundred corsairs. Hasn't he given me two hundred samurai with all the power and rank I need? Will they obey me? Of course. He made me samurai and hatamoto. So they'll obey to the death and I'll bring them aboard *Erasmus,* they'll be my boarding party and I will lead the attack.

How unbelievably lucky I am! I've everything I want. Except Mariko. But I even have her. I have her secret spirit and her love. And I possessed her body last night, the magic night that never existed. We loved without loving. Is that so different?

There's no love between Kiku and me, just a desire that blossomed. It was grand for me. I hope it was also grand for her. I tried to be Japanese wholely and do my duty, to please her as she pleased me.

He remembered how he had used a pleasure ring. He had felt most awkward and shy and had turned away to put it on, petrified that his strength would vanish, but it had not. And then, when it was in place, they had pillowed again. Her body shuddered and twisted and the tremoring had lifted him to a more urgent plane than any he had ever known.

Afterwards, when he could breathe again, he began to laugh and she had whispered, Why do you laugh, and he had answered, I don't know except you make me happy.

I've never laughed at that moment, ever before. It made everything perfect. ·
I do not love Kiku-san—I cherish her. I love Mariko-san without reservation and I like Fujiko-san completely.

Would you pillow with Fujiko? No. At least, I don't think I could.

Isn't that your duty? If you accept the privileges of samurai and require others to treat you totally as samurai with all that that means, you must accept the responsibilities and duties, *neh?* That's only fair, *neh?* And honorable, *neh?* It's your duty to give Fujiko a son.

And Felicity. What would she say to that?

And when you sail away, what about Fujiko-san and what about Mariko-san? Will you truly return here, leaving the knighthood and the even greater honors that you'll surely be granted, provided you come back laden with treasure? Will you sail outward bound once more into the hostile deep, to smash through the freezing horror of Magellan's Pass, to endure storm and sea and scurvy and mutiny for another six hundred and ninety-eight days to make a second landfall here? To take up this life again?

Decide!

Then he remembered what Mariko had told him about compartments of the mind: 'Be Japanese, Anjin-san, you must, to survive. Do what we do, surrender yourself to the rhythm of *karma* unashamed. Be content with the forces beyond your control. Put all things into their own separate compartments and yield to *wa*, the harmony of life. Yield, Anjin-san, *karma* is *karma, neh?*'

Yes. I'll decide when the time comes.

First I have to get the crew. Next I capture the Black Ship. Then I sail halfway around the earth to England. Then I'll buy and equip the warships. And then I'll decide. *Karma* is *karma*.

Kiku stirred, then buried herself deeper into the quilts, nestling closer. He felt the warmth of her through their silk kimonos. And he was kindled.

"Anjin-chan," she murmured, still in sleep.

"Hai?"

He did not awaken her. He was content to cradle her and rest, enraptured by the serenity that the yielding had given him. But before he went into sleep, he blessed Mariko for teaching him.

"Yes, Omi-sama, certainly," Gyoko said. "I'll fetch the Anjin-san at once. Please excuse me. Ako, come with me." Gyoko sent Ako for tea, then bustled out into the garden wondering what vital news the galloping night messenger had brought, for she too had heard the hoofs. And why is Omi so strange today, she asked herself. Why so cold, rough, and dangerous? And why did he come himself on so menial a task? Why not send any samurai?

Ah, who knows? Omi's a man. How can you understand them, particularly samurai? But something's wrong, terribly wrong. Did the messenger bring a declaration of war? I suppose so. If it's war, then it's war and war never hurt our business. *Daimyos* and samurai will still need entertaining, as always—more so in war—and in war, money means less than ever to them. Good good good.

She smiled to herself. Remember the war days forty-odd years ago when you were seventeen and the toast of Mishima? Remember all the laughter and pillowing and proud nights that melted into days? Remember serving Old Baldy himself, Yabu's father, the nice old gentleman who boiled criminals like his son after him? Remember how hard you had to work to make him soft—unlike the son! Gyoko chuckled. We pillowed three days and three nights, then he became my patron for a whole year. Good times—a good man. Oh, how we pillowed!

War or peace, never mind! *Shigata ga nai?* There's enough invested with the moneylenders and rice merchants, a little here, a little there. Then there's the saké factory in Odawara, the Tea House in Mishima's thriving, and today Lord Toranaga's going to buy Kiku's contract!

Yes, interesting times ahead, and how fantastically interesting the previous night had been. Kiku had been brilliant, the Anjin-san's outburst mortifying.

Kiku had made as deft a recovery as any courtesan in the land. And then, when the Lady Toda had left them, Kiku's artistry had made everything perfect and the night blissful.

Ah, men and women. So predictable. Especially men.

Babies always. Vain, difficult, terrible, petulant, pliant, horrible—marvelous most rarely—but all born with that single incredible redeeming feature that we in the trade refer to as the Jade Root, Turtle Head, Yang Peak, Steaming Shaft, Male Thruster, or simply Piece of Meat.

How insulting! Yet how apt!

Gyoko chuckled and asked herself for the ten thousandth time, by all gods living and dead and yet to be born, what in the world would we do in this world without the Piece of Meat?

She hurried on again, her footsteps just loud enough to announce her presence. She mounted the polished cedar steps. Her knock was practiced.

"Anjin-san—Anjin-san, so sorry but Lord Toranaga's sent for you. You're ordered to the fortress at once."

"What? What did you say?"

She repeated it in simpler language.

"Ah! Understand! All right—I there quick," she heard him say, with his funny accent.

"So sorry, please excuse me. Kiku-san?"

"Yes, Mama-san?" In a moment the shoji slid open. Kiku smiled at her, the kimono clinging and her hair prettily disarrayed. "Good morning, Mama-san, did you have pleasant dreams?"

"Yes, yes, thank you. So sorry to disturb you. Kiku-chan, do you wish for fresh cha?"

"Oh!" Kiku's smile disappeared. This was the code sentence that Gyoko could freely use in front of any client which told Kiku that her most special client, Omi-san, was in the Tea House. Then Kiku could always finish her story or song or dance more quickly, and go to Omi-san, if she wished. Kiku pillowed with very few, though she entertained many—if they paid the fee. Very, very few could afford all her services.

"What is it?" Gyoko asked narrowly.

"Nothing, Mama-san. Anjin-san," Kiku called out gaily, "so sorry, would you like cha?"

"Yes, please."

"It will be here at once," Gyoko said. "Ako! Hurry up, child."

"Yes, Mistress." Ako brought in the tray of tea and two cups and poured, and Gyoko left, again apologizing for disturbing him.

Kiku gave Blackthorne the cup herself. He drank it thirstily, then she helped him to dress. Ako laid out a fresh kimono for her. Kiku was most attentive but she was consumed with the knowledge that soon she would have to accompany the Anjin-san outside the gateway to bow him homeward. It was good manners. More than that, it was her privilege and duty. Only courtesans of the First Rank were ever allowed to go beyond the threshold to bestow that rare honor; all others had to stay within the courtyard. It was unthinkable for her not to finish the night as was expected—that would be a terrible insult to her guest and yet . . .

For the first time in her life, Kiku did not wish to bow one guest homeward in front of another guest.

I can't, not the Anjin-san in front of Omi-san.

Why? she asked herself. Is it because the Anjin-san's barbarian and you're ashamed that all the world will know you've been possessed by a barbarian? No. All Anjiro knows already and a man is like any other, most of the time. This man is samurai, hatamoto, and Admiral of Lord Toranaga's ships! No, nothing like that.

What is it then?

It's because I found in the night that I was shamed by what Omi-san did to him. As we should all be shamed. Omi-san should never have done that. The Anjin-san is branded and my fingers seemed to feel the brand through the silk of his kimono. I burn with shame for him, a good man to whom that should not have been done.

Am I defiled?

No, of course not, just shamed before him. And shamed before Omi-san for being ashamed.

Then in the reaches of her mind she heard Mama-san saying again, 'Child, child, leave man things to men. Laughter is our balm against them, and the world and the gods and even old age.'

"Kiku-san?"

"Yes, Anjin-san?"

"Now I go."

"Yes. Let us go together," she said.

He took her face tenderly in his rough hands and kissed her. "Thank you. No words enough to thank."

"It is I who should thank you. Please allow me to thank you, Anjin-san. Let us leave now."

She allowed Ako to put the finishing touches to her hair, which she left hanging loosely, tied the sash of the fresh kimono, and went with him.

Kiku walked beside him as was her privilege, not a few steps behind as a wife or consort or daughter or servant was obliged to. He put his hand on her shoulder momentarily and this was distasteful to her for they were not in the privacy of a room. Then she had a sudden, horrible premonition that he would kiss her publicly—which Mariko had mentioned was barbarian custom—at the gate. Oh, Buddha let that not happen, she thought, almost faint with fright.

His swords were in the reception room. By custom, all weapons were left under guard, outside the pleasure rooms, to avoid lethal quarrels with other clients, and also to prevent any lady from ending her life. Not all Ladies of the Willow World were happy or fortunate.

Blackthorne put his swords into his sash. Kiku bowed him through to the veranda, where he stepped into his thongs, Gyoko and others assembled to bow him away, an honored guest. Beyond the gateway was the village square and the sea. Many samurai were there milling about, Buntaro among them. Kiku could not see Omi, though she was certain he would be watching somewhere.

The Anjin-san seemed immensely tall, she so small beside him. Now they were crossing the courtyard. Both saw Omi at the same time. He was standing near the gateway.

Blackthorne stopped. "Morning, Omi-san," he said as a friend and bowed as a friend, not knowing that Omi and Kiku were more than friends. How could he know, she thought. No one has told him—why should they tell him? And what does that matter anyway?

"Good morning, Anjin-san." Omi's voice was friendly too, but she saw him bow with only sufficient politeness. Then his jet eyes turned to her again and she bowed, her smile perfect. "Good morning, Omi-san. This house is honored."

"Thank you, Kiku-san. Thank you."

She felt his searching gaze but pretended not to notice, keeping her eyes demurely lowered. Gyoko and the maids and the courtesans who were free watched from the veranda.

"I go fortress, Omi-san," Blackthorne was saying. "All's well?"

"Yes. Lord Toranaga's sent for you."

"Go now. Hope see you soon."

"Yes."

Kiku glanced up. Omi was still staring at her. She smiled her best smile and looked at the Anjin-san. He was watching Omi intently; then feeling her eyes, he turned to her and smiled back. It seemed to her a strained smile. "So sorry, Kiku-san, Omi-san, must go now." He bowed to Omi. It was returned. He went through the gate. She followed, hardly breathing. Movement stopped in the square. In the silence she saw him turn back, and for a hideous moment, she knew he was going to embrace her. But to her enormous relief he did not, and just stood there waiting as a civilized person would wait.

She bowed with all the tenderness she could muster, Omi's gaze boring into her.

"Thank you, Anjin-san," she said and smiled at him alone. A sigh went through the square. "Thank you," then added the time-honored, "Please visit us again. I will count the moments until we meet again."

He bowed with just the right amount of carelessness, strode off arrogantly as a samurai of quality would. Then, because he had treated her very correctly, and to repay Omi for the unnecessary coldness in his bow, instead of going back into her house at once, she stayed where she was and looked after the Anjin-san to give him greater honor. She waited until he was at the last corner. She saw him look back. He waved once. She bowed very low, now delighted with the attention in the square, pretending not to notice it. And only when he was truly gone did she walk back. With pride and with great elegance. And until the gate was closed every man watched her, feeding on such beauty, envious of the Anjin-san, who must be much man for her to wait like that.

"You're so pretty," Omi said.

"I wish that were true, Omi-san," she said with a second-best smile. "Would you like some cha, Omi-sama? Or food?"

"With you, yes."

Gyoko joined them unctuously. "Please excuse my bad manners, Omi-sama. Do take food with us now, please. Have you had a first meal?"

"No—not yet, but I'm not hungry." Omi glanced across at Kiku. "Have you eaten yet?"

Gyoko interrupted expansively, "Allow us to bring you something that won't be too inadequate, Omi-sama. Kiku-san, when you've changed you will join us, *neh?*"

"Of course, please excuse me, Omi-sama, for appearing like this. So sorry." The girl ran off, pretending a happiness she did not feel, Ako in tow.

Omi said shortly, "I would like to be with her tonight, for food and entertainment."

"Of course, Omi-sama," Gyoko replied with a low bow, knowing that she would not be free. "You honor my house and do us too much honor. Kiku-san is so fortunate that you favor her."

"Three thousand koku?" Toranaga was scandalized.

"Yes, Sire," Mariko said. They were on the private veranda in the fortress. Rain had begun already but did not reduce the heat of the day. She felt listless and very tired and longed for autumn coolness. "I'm sorry, but I could not negotiate the woman down any further. I talked until just before dawn. So sorry, Sire, but you did order me to conclude an arrangement last night."

"But three thousand, Mariko-san! That's usury!" Actually, Toranaga was glad to have a new problem to take his mind away from the worry that beset him. The Christian priest Tsukku-san traveling with Zataki, the upstart Regent, augured nothing but trouble. He had examined every avenue of escape, every route of retreat and attack that any man could imagine and the answer was always the same: If Ishido moves quickly, I'm lost.

I've got to find time. But how?

If I were Ishido I'd start now, before the rains stop.

I'd get men into position just as the Taikō and I did to destroy the Beppu. The same plan will always win—it's so simple! Ishido can't be so stupid as not to see that the only real way to defend the Kwanto is to own Osaka, and all the lands between Yedo and Osaka. As long as Osaka's unfriendly, the Kwanto's in danger. The Taikō knew it, why else did he give it to me? Without Kiyama, Onoshi, and the barbarian priests. . . .

With an effort Toranaga put tomorrow into its own compartment and concentrated totally on this impossible amount of money. "Three thousand koku's out of the question!"

"I agree, Sire. You're correct. It's my fault entirely. I thought even five hundred would be excessive but the Gyoko woman would come no lower. There is one concession though."

"What?"

"Gyoko begged the honor of reducing the price to two thousand five hundred koku if you would honor her by agreeing to see her privately for one stick of time."

"A Mama-san would give up five hundred koku just to speak to me?"

"Yes, Sire."

"Why?" he asked suspiciously.

"She told me her reason, Sire, but humbly begged that she be allowed to explain to you herself. I believe her proposal would be interesting to you, Sire. And five hundred koku . . . it would be a saving. I'm appalled that I couldn't make a better arrangement, even though Kiku-san is of the First Rank and completely merits that status. I know I've failed you."

"I agree," Toranaga said sourly. "Even one thousand would be too much. This is Izu not Kyoto!"

"You're quite right, Sire. I told the woman that the price was so ridiculous I could not possibly agree to it myself, even though you'd given me direct orders to complete the bargain last night. I hope you will forgive my disobedience, but I said that I would first have to consult with Lady Kasigi, Omi-san's mother, who's the most senior lady here, before the arrangement was confirmed."

Toranaga brightened, his other worries forgotten. "Ah, so it's arranged but not arranged?"

"Yes, Sire. Nothing is binding until I can consult with the Lady. I said I'd give an answer at noon today. Please forgive my disobedience."

"You should have concluded the arrangement as I ordered!" Toranaga was secretly delighted that Mariko had cleverly given him the opportunity to agree or disagree without any loss of face. It would have been unthinkable for him personally to quibble over a mere matter of money. But *oh ko,* three thousand koku. . . . "You say the girl's contract's worth enough rice to feed a thousand families for three years?"

"Worth every grain of rice, to the right man."

Toranaga eyed her shrewdly. "Oh? Tell me about her and what happened."

She told him everything—except her feeling for the Anjin-san and the depth of his feeling toward her. Or about Kiku's offer to her.

"Good. Yes, very good. That was clever. Yes," Toranaga said. "He must have pleased her very much for her to stand at the gateway like that the first time." Most of Anjiro had been waiting for that moment, to see how the two of them would act, the barbarian and the Willow Lady of the First Rank.

"Yes."

"The three koku invested was well worth it for him. His fame will run before him now."

"Yes," Mariko agreed, more than a little proud of Blackthorne's success. "She's an exceptional lady, Sire."

Toranaga was intrigued by Mariko's confidence in her arrangement. But five hundred koku for the contract would have been more fair. Five hundred koku was more than most Mama-sans made in a lifetime, so for one of them even to consider giving away five hundred. . . . "Worth every grain, you say? I can hardly believe that."

"To the right man, Sire. I believe that. But I could not judge who would be the right man."

There was a knock on the shoji.

"Yes?"

"The Anjin-san's at the main gate, Sire."

"Bring him here."

"Yes, Sire."

Toranaga fanned himself. He had been watching Mariko covertly and had seen the momentary light in her face. He had deliberately not warned her that he had sent for him.

What to do? Everything that is planned still applies. But now I need Buntaro and the Anjin-san and Omi-san more than ever. And Mariko, very much.

"Good morning, Toranaga-sama."

He returned Blackthorne's bow and noted the sudden warmth when the man saw Mariko. There were formal greetings and replies, then he said, "Mariko-san, tell him that he is to leave with me at dawn. You also. You will continue on to Osaka."

A chill went through her. "Yes, Sire."

"I go Osaka, Toranaga-sama?" Blackthorne asked.

"No, Anjin-san. Mariko-san, tell him I'm going to the Shuzenji Spa for a day or two. You both will accompany me there. You'll go on to Osaka. He will journey with you to the border, then go on to Yedo alone."

He watched them narrowly as Blackthorne spoke to her, rapidly and urgently.

"So sorry, Toranaga-sama, but the Anjin-san humbly asks if he could borrow me for a few more days. He says, please excuse me, that my presence with him would greatly speed up the matter of his ship. Then, if it pleases you, he would immediately take one of your coastal ships and ferry me to Osaka, going on to Nagasaki himself. He suggests this might save time."

"I haven't decided anything about his ship, yet. Or about a crew. He may not need to go to Nagasaki. Make that very clear. No, nothing is decided. But I'll consider the request about you. You'll get my decision tomorrow. You can go now. . . . Oh yes, lastly, Mariko-san, tell him that I want his genealogy. He can write it down and you'll translate it, affirming its correctness."

"Yes, Sire. Do you want it at once?"

"No. When he arrives at Yedo will be time enough."

Mariko explained to Blackthorne.

"Why does he want that?" he asked.

Mariko stared at him. "Of course all samurai have to have their births and deaths recorded, Anjin-san, as well as their fiefs and land grants. How else can a liege lord keep everything balanced? Isn't it the same in your country? Here, by law, all our citizens are in official records, even *eta:* births, deaths, marriages. Every hamlet or village or city street has its official scroll. How else can you be sure where and to whom you belong?"

"We don't write it down. Not always. And not officially. Everyone's recorded? Everyone?"

"Oh yes, even *eta,* Anjin-san. It's important, *neh?* Then no one can pretend to be what he is not, wrongdoers can be caught more easily, and men and women or parents can't cheat in marriage, *neh?*"

Blackthorne put that aside for later consideration and played another card in the game he had joined with Toranaga that he hoped would lead to the death of the Black Ship.

Mariko listened attentively, questioned him a moment, then turned to Toranaga. "Sire, the Anjin-san thanks you for your favor and your many gifts. He asks if you would honor him by choosing his two hundred vassals for him. He says your guidance in this would be worth anything."

"Is it worth a thousand koku?" Toranaga asked at once. He saw her surprise and the Anjin-san's. I'm glad you're still transparent, Anjin-san, for all your veneer of civilization, he thought. If I were a gambling person, I'd wager that that wasn't your idea—to ask for my guidance.

"Hai," he heard Blackthorne say firmly.

"Good," he replied crisply. "Since the Anjin-san's so generous, I'll accept his offer. One thousand koku. That will help some other needy samurai. Tell him his men will be waiting for him in Yedo. I'll see you at dawn tomorrow, Anjin-san."

"Yes. Thank you, Toranaga-sama."

"Mariko-san, consult with the Lady Kasigi at once. Since you approved the amount I imagine she'll agree to your arrangement however hideous it seems, though I'd suppose she'll need until dawn tomorrow to give such a ridiculous sum her full consideration. Send some menial to order the Gyoko woman here at sunset. She can bring the courtesan with her. Kiku-san can sing while we talk, *neh?*"

He dismissed them, delighted to have saved fifteen hundred koku. People are so extravagant, he thought benignly.

"Will that leave me enough to get a crew?" Blackthorne asked.

"Oh, yes, Anjin-san. But he hasn't agreed to allow you to go to Nagasaki yet," Mariko said. "Five hundred koku would be more than enough to live on for a year, and the other five hundred will give you about one hundred and eighty koban in gold to buy seamen. That's a very great deal of money."

Fujiko lifted herself painfully and spoke to Mariko.

"Your consort says that you shouldn't worry, Anjin-san. She can give you letters of credit to certain moneylenders who will advance you all that you'll need. She'll arrange everything."

"Yes, but haven't I got to pay all my retainers? How do I pay for a house, Fujiko-san, my household?"

Mariko was shocked. "Please, so sorry, but this is of course not your worry. Your consort has told you that she will take care of everything. She—"

Fujiko interrupted and the two women spoke together for a moment.

"Ah so desu, Fujiko-san!" Mariko turned back to Blackthorne. "She says you must not waste time thinking about it. She begs you please to spend your time worrying only about Lord Toranaga's problems. She has money of her own which

she can draw upon, should it be necessary."

Blackthorne blinked. "She'll lend me her own money?"

"Oh, no, Anjin-san, of course she'll *give* it to you, if you need it, Anjin-san. Don't forget your problem's only this year," Mariko explained. "Next year you're rich, Anjin-san. As to your retainers, for one year they'll get two koku each. Don't forget Toranaga-sama's giving you all their arms and horses, and two koku's enough to feed them and their horses and families. And don't forget, too, you gave Lord Toranaga half your year's income to ensure that they would be chosen by him personally. That's a tremendous honor, Anjin-san."

"You think so?"

"Oh certainly. Fujiko-san agrees wholeheartedly. You were most shrewd to think of that."

"Thank you." Blackthorne allowed a little of his pleasure to show. You're getting your wits back again and you're beginning to think like them, he told himself happily. Yes, that was clever to co-opt Toranaga. Now you'll get the best men possible, and you could never have done it alone. What's a thousand koku against the Black Ship? So yet another of the things Mariko had said was true: that one of Toranaga's weaknesses was that he was a miser. Of course, she had not said so directly, only that Toranaga made all his incredible wealth go further than any *daimyo* in the kingdom. This clue, added to his own observations—that Toranaga's clothes were as simple as his food, and his style of living little different from that of an ordinary samurai—had given him another key to unlock Toranaga.

Thank God for Mariko and old Friar Domingo!

Blackthorne's memory took him back to the jail and he thought how close he had been to death then, and how close he was to death now, even with all his honors. What Toranaga gives, he can take away. You think he's your friend, but if he'll assassinate a wife and murder a favorite son, how would you value his friendship or your life? I don't, Blackthorne told himself, renewing his pledge. That's *karma*. I can do nothing about *karma* and I've been living near death all my life, so nothing's new. I yield to *karma* in all its beauty. I accept *karma* in all its majesty. I trust *karma* to get me through the next six months. Then, by this time next year, I'll be scudding through Magellan's Pass, bound for London Town, out of *his* reach. . . .

Fujiko was talking. He watched her. The bandages were still discolored. She was lying painfully on the futons, a maid fanning her.

"She'll arrange everything for you by dawn, Anjin-san," Mariko said. "Your consort suggests you take two horses and a baggage horse. One man servant and one maid—"

"A man servant'll be enough."

"So sorry, the maid servant must go to serve you. And of course a cook and a cook helper."

"Won't there be kitchens that we—I can use?"

"Oh, yes. But you still have to have your own cooks, Anjin-san. You're a hatamoto."

He knew there was no point in arguing. "I'll leave everything to you."

"Oh, that's so wise of you, Anjin-san, very wise. Now I must go and pack, please excuse me." Mariko left happily. They had not talked much, just enough in Latin for each to know that though the magic night had never come to pass and was, like the other night, never to be discussed, both would live in their imaginations forever.

"Thou."

"Thou."

"I was so proud when I heard she stood at the gate for such a long time. Thy face is immense now, Anjin-san."

"For a moment I almost forgot what thou hadst told me. Involuntarily I was within a hair's distance of kissing her in public."

"Oh ko, Anjin-san, that would have been terrible!"

"Oh ko, thou art right! If it had not been for thee I would be faceless—a worm wriggling in the dust."

"Instead, thou art vast and famous and thy prowess undoubted. Didst thou enjoy one of those curious devices?"

"Ah, fair Lady, in my land we have an ancient custom: A man does not discuss the intimate habits of one lady with another."

"We have the same custom. But I asked if it was enjoyed, not used. Yes, we very much have the same custom. I am glad that the evening was to thy liking." Her smile was warming. "To be Japanese in Japan is wise, *neh?"*

"I cannot thank thee enough for teaching me, for guiding me, for opening my eyes," he said. "For—" He was going to say, for loving me. Instead he added, "for being."

"I have done nothing. Thou art thyself."

"I thank thee, for everything—and thy gift."

"I am glad thy pleasure was great."

"I am sad thy pleasure was nil. I am so glad that thou art also ordered to the Spa. But why to Osaka?"

"Oh, I am not ordered to Osaka. Lord Toranaga allows me to go. We have property and family business matters that must be seen to. Also, my son is there now. Then too, I can carry private messages to Kiritsubo-san and the Lady Sazuko."

"Isn't that dangerous? Remember thy words—war is coming and Ishido is the enemy. Did not Lord Toranaga say the same?"

"Yes. But there is no war yet, Anjin-san. And samurai do not war on their women, unless women war on them."

"But thou? What about the bridge at Osaka, across the moat? Did thou not go with me to dupe Ishido? He would have killed me. And remember thy sword at the fight on the ship."

"Ah, that was only to protect the life of my liege Lord, and my own life, when it was threatened. That was my duty, Anjin-san, nothing more. There is no danger for me. I have been lady-in-waiting to Lady Yodoko, the Taikō's widow, even the Lady Ochiba, mother of the Heir. I'm honored to be their friend. I'm quite safe. That's why Toranaga-sama allows me to go. But for thee in Osaka there is no safety, because of Lord Toranaga's escape, and of what was done to Lord Ishido. So thou must never land there. Nagasaki will be safe for thee."

"Then he has agreed that I may go?"

"No. Not yet. But when he does it will be safe. He has power in Nagasaki."

He wanted to ask, greater than the Jesuits'? Instead he said only, "I pray Lord Toranaga orders thee by ship to Osaka." He saw her tremble slightly. "What troubles thee?"

"Nothing, except . . . except that the sea does not please me."

"Will he order it thus?"

"I don't know. But . . . ." She changed back into the mischievous teaser, and into Portuguese. "But for your health we should bring Kiku-san along with us, *neh?* Tonight, are you going again into her Vermilion Chamber?"

He laughed with her. "That'd be fine, though—" Then he stopped, as with sudden clarity he remembered Omi's look. "You know, Mariko-san, when I was at the gate I'm sure I saw Omi-san looking at her in a very special way, as a lover would look. A jealous lover. I didn't know they were lovers."

"I understand he's one of her customers, a favored customer, yes. But why should that concern you?"

"Because it was a very private look. Very special."

"He has no special claim on her, Anjin-san. She's a courtesan of the First Rank. She's free to accept or reject whom she pleases."

"If we were in Europe, and I pillowed his girl—you understand, Mariko-san?"

"I think I understand, Anjin-san, but why should that concern you? You're not in Europe, Anjin-san, he has no formal claim on her. If she wants to accept you and him, or even reject you or reject him, what has that to do with anything?"

"I'd say he was her lover, in our sense of the word. That's got everything to do with it, *neh?*"

"But what has that to do with her profession, or pillowing?"

Eventually he had thanked her again and left it at that. But his head and his heart told him to beware. It's not as simple as you think, Mariko-san, even here. Omi believes Kiku-san's more than special, even if she doesn't feel the same. Wish I'd known he was her lover. I'd rather have Omi a friend than an enemy. Could Mariko be right again? That pillowing has nothing to do with loving for them?

God help me, I'm so mixed up. Part Eastern now, mostly Western. I've got to act like them and think like them to stay alive. And much of what they believe is so much better than our way that it's tempting to want to become one of them totally, and yet . . . home is there, across the sea, where my ancestors were birthed, where my family lives, Felicity and Tudor and Elizabeth. *Neh?*

"Anjin-san?"

"Yes, Fujiko-san?"

"Please don't worry about money. I can't bear to see you worried. I'm so sorry that I cannot go to Yedo with you."

"Soon see in Yedo, *neh?*"

"Yes. The doctor says I'm healing well and Omi's mother agrees."

"When doctor here?"

"Sunset. So sorry I cannot go with you tomorrow. Please excuse me."

He wondered again about his duty to his consort. Then he put that thought back into its compartment as a new one rushed forward. He examined this idea and found it fine. And urgent. "I go now, come back soon. You rest—understand?"

"Yes. Please excuse me for not getting up, and for . . . so sorry."

He left her and went to his own room. He took a pistol out of its hiding place, checked the priming, and stuck it under his kimono. Then he walked alone to Omi's house. Omi was not there. Midori welcomed him and offered cha, which he politely refused. Her two-year-old infant was in her arms. She said, so sorry, but Omi would return soon. Would the Anjin-san like to wait? She seemed ill at ease, though polite and attentive. Again he refused and thanked her, saying he would come back later, then he went below to his own house.

Villagers had already cleared the ground, preparing to rebuild everything. Nothing had been salvaged from the fire except cooking utensils. Fujiko would not tell him the cost of rebuilding. It was very cheap, she had said. Please don't concern yourself.

"*Karma,* Anjin-sama," one of the villagers said.

"Yes."

"What could one do? Don't worry, your house will soon be ready—better than before."

Blackthorne saw Omi walking up the hill, taut and stern. He went to meet him.

When Omi saw him, he seemed to lose some of his fury. "Ah, Anjin-san," he said cordially. "I hear you're also leaving with Toranaga-sama at dawn. Very good, we can ride together."

Despite Omi's apparent friendliness, Blackthorne was very much on guard.

"Listen, Omi-san, now I go there." He pointed toward the plateau. "Please you go with me, yes?"

"There's no training today."

"Understand. Please you go with me, yes?"

Omi saw that Blackthorne's hand was on the hilt of his killing sword in the characteristic way, steadying it. Then his sharp eyes noticed the bulge under the sash and he realized at once from its partially outlined shape that it was a concealed pistol. "A man who's allowed the two swords should be able to use them, not just wear them, *neh?*" he asked thinly.

"Please? I don't understand."

Omi said it again, more simply.

"Ah, understand. Yes. It better."

"Yes. Lord Yabu said—now that you're completely samurai—that you should begin to learn much that we take for granted. How to act as a second at a seppuku, for example—even to prepare for your own seppuku as we're all obliged to do. Yes, Anjin-san, you should learn to use the swords. Very necessary for a samurai to know how to use and honor his sword, *neh?*"

Blackthorne did not understand half the words. But he knew what Omi was saying. At least, he corrected himself uneasily, I know what he's saying on the surface.

"Yes. True. Important," he told him. "Please, one day you teaches—sorry, you teach perhaps? Please? I honored."

"Yes—I'd like to teach you, Anjin-san."

Blackthorne's hackles rose at the implied threat in Omi's voice. Watch it, he admonished himself. Don't start imagining things. "Thank you. Now walk there, please? Little time. You go with? Yes?"

"Very well, Anjin-san. But we'll ride. I'll join you shortly." Omi walked off up the hill, into his own courtyard.

Blackthorne ordered a servant to saddle his horse and mounted awkwardly from the right side, as was custom in Japan and China. Don't think there'd be much future in letting him teach me swordsmanship, he told himself, his right hand nudging the concealed pistol safer, its pleasing warmth reassuring. This confidence vanished when Omi reappeared. With him were four mounted samurai.

Together they all cantered up the broken road toward the plateau. They passed many samurai companies in full marching gear, armed, under their officers, spear pennants fluttering. When they crested the rise, they saw that the entire Musket Regiment was drawn up outside the camp in route order, each man standing beside his armed horse, a baggage train in the rear, Yabu, Naga, and their officers in the van. The rain began to fall heavily.

"All troops go?" Blackthorne asked, perturbed, and reined in his horse.

"Yes."

"Go Spa with Toranaga-sama, Omi-san?"

"I don't know."

Blackthorne's sense of survival warned him to ask no more questions. But one needed to be answered. "And Buntaro-sama?" he asked indifferently. "He with us tomorrow, Omi-san?"

"No. He's already gone. This morning he was in the square when you left the Tea House. Didn't you see him, near the Tea House?"

Blackthorne could read nothing untoward in Omi's face. "No. Not see, so sorry. He go Spa too?"

"I suppose so. I'm not sure." The rain dripped off Omi's conical hat, which was tied under his chin. His eyes were almost hidden. "Now, why did you want me to come here with you?"

"Show place, like I say." Before Omi could say anything more, Blackthorne spurred his horse forward. With his most careful sea sense he took accurate bearings from memory and went quickly to the exact point over the crevasse. He dismounted and beckoned Omi. "Please."

"What is it, eh?" Omi's voice was edged.

"Please, here Omi-san. Alone."

Omi waved his guards away and spurred forward until he towered over Blackthorne. *"Nan desu ka?"* he asked, his hand seemingly tightening on his sword.

"This place Toranaga-sama . . ." Blackthorne could not think of the words, so explained partially with his hands. "Understand?"

"Here you pulled him out of the earth, *neh?* So?"

Blackthorne looked at him, then deliberately down at his sword, then stared up at him again saying nothing more. He wiped the rain out of his face.

"Nan desu ka?" Omi repeated more irritably.

Still Blackthorne didn't answer. Omi stared down at the crevasse and again at Blackthorne's face. Then his eyes lit up. *"Ah, so desu! Wakarimasu!"* Omi thought a moment then called out to one of the guards, "Get Mura here at once. With twenty men and shovels!"

The samurai galloped off. Omi sent the others back to the village, then dismounted and stood beside Blackthorne. "Yes, Anjin-san," he said, "that's an excellent thought. A good idea."

"Idea? What idea?" Blackthorne asked innocently. "Just show place—think you want know place, *neh?* So sorry—don't understand."

Omi said, "Toranaga-sama lost his swords here. Swords very valuable. He'll be happy to get them back. Very happy, *neh?"*

"Ah so! No my idea, Omi-san," Blackthorne said. "Omi-san idea."

"Of course. Thank you, Anjin-san. You're a good friend and your mind's fast. I should have thought of that myself. Yes, you're a good friend and we'll all need friends for the next few months. War's with us now whether we want it or not."

"Please? So sorry. I don't understand, speak too fast. Please excuse."

"Glad we're friends—you and me. Understand?"

"Hai. You say war? War now?"

"Soon. What can we do? Nothing. Don't worry, Toranaga-sama will conquer Ishido and his traitors. That's the truth, understand? No worry, *neh?"*

"Understand. I go now, my house. All right?"

"Yes. See you at dawn. Again thank you."

Blackthorne nodded. But he did not leave. "She's pretty, *neh?"*

"What?"

"Kiku-san." Blackthorne's legs were slightly apart and he was poised to jump back and pull out the pistol, and aim it and fire it. He remembered with total clarity the unbelievable, effortless speed that Omi had used to decapitate the first villager so long ago, and he was ready as best he could be. He reasoned his only safety was to precipitate the matter of Kiku. Omi would never do it. Omi would consider such bad manners unthinkable. And, filled with shame at his own weakness, Omi would lock his very un-Japanese jealousy away into a secret compartment. Because it was so alien and shame-filled, this jealousy would fester until, when it was least expected, Omi would explode blindly and ferociously.

"Kiku-san?" Omi said.

"*Hai.*" Blackthorne could see that Omi was rocked. Even so he was glad he had chosen the time and the place. "She's pretty, *neh?*"

"Pretty?"

"*Hai.*"

The rain increased. The heavy drops spattered the mud. Their horses shivered uncomfortably. Both men were soaked but the rain was warm and it ran off them.

"Yes," Omi said. "Kiku-san is very pretty," and followed it with a torrent of words Blackthorne did not fathom.

"No words enough now, Omi-san—not enough to speak clear now," Blackthorne said. "Later yes. Not now. Understand?"

Omi seemed not to hear. Then he said, "There's plenty of time, Anjin-san, plenty of time to talk about her, and about you and me and *karma*. But I agree, now is not the time, *neh?*"

"Think understand. Yes. Yesterday not know Omi-san and Kiku-san good friends," he said, pressing the attack.

"She's not my property."

"Now know you and her very friends. Now—"

"Now leave. This matter is closed. The woman is nothing. Nothing."

Stubbornly Blackthorne stayed where he was. "Next time I—"

"This conversation is over! Didn't you hear? Finished!"

"*Iyé! Iyé*, by God!"

Omi's hand went for his sword. Blackthorne leaped back two paces without realizing it. But Omi did not draw his sword and Blackthorne did not pull out his pistol. Both men readied, though neither wanted to begin.

"What do you want to say, Anjin-san?"

"Next time, first I ask—about Kiku-san. If Omi-san say yes—yes. If no—no! Understand? Friend to friend, *neh?*"

Omi relaxed his sword hand slightly. "I repeat—she's not my property. Thank you for showing me this place, Anjin-san. Good-by."

"Friend?"

"Of course." Omi walked over to Blackthorne's horse and held the bridle. Blackthorne swung into the saddle.

He looked down at Omi. If he could have got away with it he knew he would have blown the samurai's head off right now. That would be his safest course. "Good-by, Omi-san, and thank you."

"Good-by, Anjin-san." Omi watched Blackthorne ride off and did not turn his back until he was over the rise. He marked the exact place in the crevasse with some stones and then, in turmoil, squatted on his haunches to wait, oblivious of the deluge.

Soon Mura and the peasants arrived, bespattered with mud.

"Toranaga-sama fell into the crevasse exactly at this point, Mura. His swords are buried here. Bring them to me before sunset."

"Yes, Omi-sama."

"If you'd had any brains, if you were interested in me, your liege Lord, you would have done it already."

"Please excuse my stupidity."

Omi rode off. They watched him briefly, then spread themselves out in a circle around the stones, and began to dig.

Mura dropped his voice. "Uo, you'll go with the baggage train."

"Yes, Mura-san. But how?"

"I'll offer you to the Anjin-san. He won't know any different."

"But his consort, *oh ko,* she will," Uo whispered back.

"She's not going with him. I hear her burns are bad. She's to go by ship to

Yedo later. You know what to do?"

"Seek out the Holy Father privately, answer any questions."

"Yes." Mura relaxed and began to talk normally. "You can go with the Anjin-san, Uo, he'll pay well. Make yourself useful, but not too useful or he'll take you all the way to Yedo."

Uo laughed. "Hey, I hear Yedo's so rich everyone pisses into silver pots—even *eta*. And the women have skins like sea foam with no pubics at all."

"Is that true, Mura-san?" another villager asked. "They've no short hair?"

"Yedo was just a stinking little fishing village, nothing as good as Anjiro, when I was there the first time," Mura told them, without stopping digging. "That was with Toranaga-sama when we were all hunting down the Beppu. We took more than three thousand heads between us. As to pubics, all the girls I've known had them, except one from Korea, but she said she'd had them plucked, one by one."

"What some women will do to attract us, heh?" someone said.

"Yes. But I'd like to see that," Ninjin said toothlessly. "Yes, I'd like to see a Jade Gate without a bush."

"I'd gamble a boatload of fish against a bucket of shit that it hurt to pull out those hairs." Uo whistled.

"When I'm a *kami* I'm going to inhabit Kiku-san's Heavenly Pavilion! They say she was born perfumed and hairless!"

Amid laughter, Uo asked, "Did it make any difference, Mura-san, to attack the Jade Gate without the bush?"

"It was the nearest I ever got. Eeeeh! I got closer and deeper than ever before and that's important, *neh?* So I know it's always better for the girl to take off the bush though some are superstitious about it and some complain of the itch. It's still closer for you and so closer for her—and getting close makes all the difference, *neh?*" They laughed and put their backs into the digging. The pit grew under the rain.

"I'll wager the Anjin-san got plenty close last night for her to stand at the gateway like that! Eeee, what wouldn't I give to have been him." Uo wiped the sweat off his brow. Like all of them he wore only a loincloth and a bamboo, conical hat, and was barefoot.

"Eeee! I was there, Uo, in the square, and I saw it all. I saw her smile and I felt it down through my Fruit and into my toes."

"Yes," another said. "I have to admit just her smile made me stiff as an oar."

"But not as big as the Anjin-san, eh, Mura-san?" Uo chuckled. "Go on, please tell us the story again."

Happily Mura obliged and told about the first night and the bath house. His story had improved in the many tellings, but none of them minded.

"Oh, to be so vast!" Uo mimed carrying a giant erection before him, and laughed so much he slipped in the mud.

"Who'd have thought the barbarian stranger'd ever get from the pit to paradise?" Mura leaned on his shovel a moment, collecting his breath. "I'd never have believed it—like an ancient legend. *Karma, neh?*"

"Perhaps he was one of us—in a previous life—and he's come back with the same mind but a different skin."

Ninjin nodded. "That's possible. Must be—because from what the Holy Father said I thought he'd be burning in the Devil's Hell Furnace long since. Didn't the Father say he'd put a special curse on him? I heard him bring down the vengeance of the great Jesus *kami* himself on the Anjin-san and, *oh ko,* even I was very frightened." He crossed himself and the others hardly noticed. "But the Jesus Christ Madonna God punishes His enemies very strangely if you ask me."

Uo said, "Well, I'm not a Christian, as well you know, but, so sorry, it seems to me the Anjin-san's a good man, please excuse me, and better than the Christian Father who stank and cursed and frightened everyone. And he's been good to us, *neh?* He treats his people well—some say he's Lord Toranaga's friend, must be with all his honors, *neh?* And don't forget Kiku-san honored him with her Golden Gully."

"It's golden all right. I heard the night cost him five koban!"

"Fifteen koku for one night?" Ninjin spluttered. "Eeeeeee, how lucky the Anjin-san is! His *karma's* vast for an enemy of God the Father, Son, and Madonna."

Mura said, "He paid one koban—three koku. But if you think that's a lot . . ." He stopped and looked around conspiratorially to make sure there were no eavesdroppers, though of course in this rain he knew there would be none—and even if there were, what did that matter?

They all stopped and moved closer. "Yes, Mura-san?"

"I just had it whispered to me she's going to be Lord Toranaga's consort. He bought her contract this morning. *Three thousand koku.*"

It was a mind-boggling figure, more than their whole village earned in fish and rice in twenty years. Their respect for her increased, if that were possible. And for the Anjin-san, who was therefore the last man on earth to enjoy her as a courtesan of the First Rank.

"Eeee!" Uo mumbled, hard put to talk. "So much money—I don't know whether I want to vomit or piss or fart."

"Do none," said Mura laconically. "Dig. Let's find the swords."

They obeyed, each lost in his own thoughts. Inexorably, the pit was deepening.

Soon Ninjin, whipped by worry, could contain himself no longer, and he stopped digging. "Mura-san, please excuse me, but what have you decided about the new taxes?" he asked. The others stopped.

Mura kept on digging at his methodical, grinding pace. "What's there to decide? Yabu-sama says pay, so we pay, *neh?*"

"But Toranaga-sama cut our taxes to four parts out of ten and he's our liege Lord now."

"True. But Lord Yabu was given back Izu—and Suruga and Totomi as well— and made overlord again, so who is our liege Lord?"

"Toranaga-sama. Surely, Mura-san, Tora—"

"Are you going to complain to him, Ninjin? Eh? Wake up, Yabu-sama's overlord as he always was. Nothing's changed. And if he puts up taxes we pay more taxes. Finish!"

"But that'll take all our winter stocks. All of them." Ninjin's voice was an infuriating whine but all knew the truth of what he said. "Even with the rice we stole—"

"The rice we've saved," Uo hissed at him, correcting him.

"Even with that, there won't be enough to last through winter. We'll have to sell a boat or two—"

"We sell no boats," Mura said. He jabbed his shovel into the mud and wiped the sweat out of his eyes, retied the string of his hat more firmly. Then he began to dig again. "Work, Ninjin. That will take your mind off tomorrow."

"How do we last the winter, Mura-san?"

"We still have to get through the summer."

"Yes," Ninjin agreed bitterly. "We've paid more than two years' taxes in advance, and still it's not enough."

"*Karma,* Ninjin," Uo said.

"War's coming. Perhaps we'll get a new lord who'll be fairer, *neh?*" another said.

"He can't be worse—no one can be worse."

"Don't wager on that," Mura told them all. "You're alive—you can be very dead very quickly and then no more Golden Gullies, with or without the forest." His shovel hit a rock and he stopped. "Give me a hand, Uo, old friend."

Together they fought the rock out of the mud. Uo whispered anxiously, "Mura-san, what if the Holy Father asks about the weapons?"

"Tell him. And tell him we're ready—that Anjiro's ready."

CHAPTER 42

THEY came to Yokosé by noon. Buntaro had already intercepted Zataki the previous evening and, as Toranaga had ordered, had welcomed him with great formality. "I asked him to camp outside the village, to the north, Sire, until the meeting place could be prepared," Buntaro said. "The formal meeting's to take place here this afternoon, if it pleases you." He added humorlessly, "I thought the Hour of the Goat would be auspicious."

"Good."

"He wanted to meet you tonight but I overruled that. I told him you'd be 'honored' to meet today or tomorrow, whichever he wished, but not after dark."

Toranaga grunted approval but did not yet dismount from his lathered horse. He wore a breastplate, helmet, and light bamboo armor, like his equally travel-stained escort. Again he looked around carefully. The clearing had been well chosen with no chance for ambush. There were no trees or houses within range that could hide archers or musketeers. Just east of the village the land was flat and somewhat higher. North, west, and south were guarded by the village and by the wooden bridge that spanned the fast-flowing river. Here at the narrows the water was swirling and rock-infested. Eastward, behind him and his weary, sweated riders, the track climbed steeply up the pass to the misted crest, five *ri* away. Mountains towered all around, many volcanic, and most with their peaks sleeping in the overcast. In the center of the clearing a twelve-mat dais had been especially erected on low pilings. A tall rush canopy covered it. Haste did not show in the craftsmanship. Two brocade cushions faced each other on the tatamis.

"I've men there, there, and there," Buntaro continued, pointing with his bow at all the overlooking outcrops. "You can see for many *ri* in all directions, Sire. Good defensive positions—the bridge and the whole village are covered. Eastward your retreat's secured by more men. Of course, the bridge is locked tight with sentries and I've left an 'honor guard' of a hundred men at his camp."

"Lord Zataki's there now?"

"No, Sire. I selected an inn for him and his equerries on the outskirts of the village, to the north, worthy of his rank, and invited him to enjoy the baths there. That inn's isolated and secured. I implied you'd be going on to Shuzenji Spa tomorrow and he'd be your guest." Buntaro indicated a neat, single-story inn on the edge of the clearing that faced the best view, near to a hot spring that bubbled from the rock into a natural bath. "That inn's yours, Sire." In front of the inn was a group of men, all on their knees, their heads very low, bowing motionlessly toward them. "They're the headman and village elders. I didn't know if you wanted to see them at once."

"Later." Toranaga's horse neighed wearily and cast its head about, the bridles jingling. He gentled him, and now completely satisfied with the security, he signed to his men and dismounted. One of Buntaro's samurai caught his reins—the samurai, like Buntaro and all of them, armored, battle-armed, and ready.

Toranaga stretched gratefully and limbered up to ease the cramped muscles in his back and legs. He had led the way from Anjiro in a single forced march, stopping only to change mounts. The rest of the baggage train under Omi's command—palanquins and bearers—was still far behind, strung out on the road that came down from the crest. The road from Anjiro had snaked along the coast, then branched. They had taken the west road inland and climbed steadily through luxuriant forests teeming with game, Mount Omura to their right, the peaks of the volcanic Amagi Range on their left soaring almost five thousand feet. The ride had exhilarated him—at last some action! Part of the journey had been through such good hawking country that he promised himself, one day, he would hunt all Izu.

"Good. Yes, very good," he said over the bustle of his men dismounting and chattering and sorting themselves out. "You've done well."

"If you want to honor me, Sire, I beg you to allow me to obliterate Lord Zataki and his men at once."

"He insulted you?"

"No—on the contrary—his manners were worthy of a courtier, but the flag he travels under's a treason against you."

"Patience. How often do I have to tell you?" Toranaga said, not unkindly.

"I'm afraid forever, Sire," Buntaro replied gruffly. "Please excuse me."

"You used to be his friend."

"He used to be your ally."

"He saved your life at Odawara."

"We were on the same side at Odawara," Buntaro said bleakly, then burst out, "How can he do this to you, Sire? Your own brother! Haven't you favored him, fought on the same side—all his life?"

"People change." Toranaga put his full attention on the dais. Delicate silk curtains had been hung from the rafters over the platform for decoration. Ornamental brocade tassels that matched the cushions made a pleasing frieze and larger ones were on the four corner posts. "It's much too rich and gives the meeting too much importance," he said. "Make it simple. Remove the curtains, all the tassels and cushions, return them to the merchants, and if they won't give the quartermaster back the money, tell him to sell them. Get four cushions, not two—simple, chaff-filled."

"Yes, Sire."

Toranaga's gaze fell on the spring and he wandered over to it. The water, steaming and sulphurous, hissed as it came from a cleft in the rocks. His body ached for a bath. "And the Christian?" he asked.

"Sire?"

"Tsukku-san, the Christian priest?"

"Oh him! He's somewhere in the village, but the other side of the bridge. He's forbidden this side without your permission. Why? Is it important? He said something about how he'd be honored to see you, when convenient. Do you want him here now?"

"Was he alone?"

Buntaro's lip curled. "No. He had an escort of twenty acolytes, all tonsured like him—all Kyushu men, Sire, all well-born and all samurai. All well mounted but no weapons. I had them searched. Thoroughly."

"And him?"

"Of course him—him more than any. There were four carrier pigeons among his luggage. I confiscated them."

"Good. Destroy them. . . . Some fool did it in error, so sorry, *neh?*"

"I understand. You want me to send for him now?"

"Later. I'll see him later."

Buntaro frowned. "Was it wrong to search him?"

Toranaga shook his head, and absently looked back at the crest, lost in thought.

Then he said, "Send a couple of men we can trust to watch the Musket Regiment."

"I've already done that, Sire." Buntaro's face lit up with grim satisfaction. "And Lord Yabu's personal guards contain some of our ears and eyes. He won't be able to fart without your knowing it, if that's your wish."

"Good." The head of the baggage train, still far distant, rounded a bend in the curling track. Toranaga could see the three palanquins, Omi mounted in the lead as ordered, the Anjin-san beside him now, also riding easily.

He turned his back on them. "I've brought your wife with me."

"Yes, Sire."

"She's asking my permission to go to Osaka."

Buntaro stared at him, but said nothing. Then he squinted back at the barely discernible figures.

"I gave her my approval—providing, of course, that you also approve."

"Whatever you approve, Sire, I approve," Buntaro said.

"I can allow her to go by land from Mishima or she can accompany the Anjin-san to Yedo, and go by sea to Osaka from there. The Anjin-san's agreed to be responsible for her—if you approve."

"It would be safer by sea." Buntaro was smoldering.

"This all depends on Lord Zataki's message. If Ishido's formally declared war on me, then of course I must forbid it. If not, your wife can go on tomorrow or the day after, if you approve."

"Whatever you decide I agree to."

"This afternoon pass over your duties to Naga-san. This is a good moment to make peace between you and your wife."

"Please excuse me, Sire. I should stay with my men. I beg you to leave me with my men. Until you're safely away."

"Tonight you will pass over your duties to my son. You and your wife will join me at my evening meal. You will stay at the inn. You will make a peace."

Buntaro stared at the ground. Then he said, even more stonily, "Yes, Sire."

"You're ordered to attempt a peace," said Toranaga. He was in a mind to add "an honorable peace is better than war, *neh?*" But that wasn't true and might have begun a philosophic argument and he was tired and wanted no arguments, just a bath and a rest. "Now fetch the headman!"

The headman and elders fell over themselves in their haste to bow before him, welcoming him in the most extravagant way. Toranaga told them bluntly that the bill they would present to his quartermaster when he left would of course be fair and reasonable. *"Neh?"*

"Hai," they chorused humbly, blessing the gods for their unexpected good fortune and the fat pickings that this visit would inevitably bring them. With many more bows and compliments, saying how proud and honored they were to be allowed to serve the greatest *daimyo* in the Empire, the sprightly old headman ushered him into the inn.

Toranaga inspected it completely through coveys of bowing, smiling maids of all ages, the pick of the village. There were ten rooms around a nondescript garden with a small cha house in the center, kitchens in the back, and to the west, nestling the rocks, a large bath house fed from the living springs. The whole inn was neatly fenced—a covered walk led to the bath—and it was easy to defend.

"I don't need the whole inn, Buntaro-san," he said, standing again on the veranda. "Three rooms will be sufficient—one for myself, one for the Anjin-san, and one for the women. You take a fourth. There's no need to pay for the rest."

"My quartermaster tells me he made a very good arrangement for the whole inn, Sire, day by day, better than half price, and it's still out of season. I approved the cost because of your security."

"Very well," Toranaga agreed reluctantly. "But I want to see the bill before we leave. There's no need to waste money. You'd better fill the rooms with guards, four to a room."

"Yes, Sire." Buntaro had already decided to do that. He watched Toranaga stride off with two personal guards, surrounded by four of the prettiest maids, to go to his room in the east wing. Dully, he was wondering, what women? What women needed the room? Fujiko? Never mind, he thought tiredly, I'll know soon enough.

A maid fluttered past. She smiled brightly at him and he smiled back mechanically. She was young and pretty and soft-skinned and he had pillowed with her last night. But the joining had given him no pleasure and though she was deft and enthusiastic and well-trained, his lust soon vanished—he had never felt desire for her. Eventually, for the sake of good manners, he had pretended to reach the pinnacle, as she had pretended, and then she had left him.

Still brooding, he walked out of the courtyard to stare up at the road.

Why Osaka?

At the Hour of the Goat the sentries on the bridge stood aside. The cortege began to cross. First were heralds carrying banners bedecked with the all-powerful cipher of the Regents, then the rich palanquin, and finally more guards.

Villagers bowed. All were on their knees, secretly agog at such richness and pomp. The headman had cautiously asked if he should assemble all their people to honor the occasion. Toranaga had sent a message that those who were not working could watch, with their masters' permission. So the headman, with even more care, had selected a deputation that included mostly the old and the obedient young, just enough to make a show—though every adult would have liked to be present—but not enough to go against the great *daimyo*'s orders. All who could were watching surreptitiously from vantage points in windows and doors.

Saigawa Zataki, Lord of Shinano, was taller than Toranaga, and younger by five years, with the same breadth of shoulders and prominent nose. But his stomach was flat, the stubble of his beard black and heavy, his eyes mere slits in his face. Though there seemed to be an uncanny resemblance between the half brothers when they were apart, now that they were together they were quite dissimilar. Zataki's kimono was rich, his armor glittering and ceremonial, his swords well used.

"Welcome, brother." Toranaga stepped off the dais and bowed. He wore the simplest of kimonos and soldier's straw sandals. And swords. "Please excuse me for receiving you so informally, but I came as quickly as I could."

"Please excuse me for disturbing you. You look well, brother. Very well." Zataki got out of the palanquin and bowed in return, beginning the interminable, meticulous formalities of the ceremonial that now ruled both of them.

"Please take this cushion, Lord Zataki."

"Please excuse me, I would be honored if you would be seated first, Lord Toranaga."

"You're so kind. But please, honor me by sitting first."

They continued playing the game that they had played so many times before, with each other and with friends and enemies, climbing the ladder of power, enjoying the rules that governed each movement and each phrase, that protected their individual honor so that neither could ever make a mistake and endanger himself or his mission.

At length they were seated opposite each other on the cushions, two sword lengths away. Buntaro was behind and to the left of Toranaga. Zataki's chief aide, an elderly gray-haired samurai, was behind and to his left. Around the dais, twenty paces away, were seated ranks of Toranaga samurai, all deliberately still costumed in the clothing they'd journeyed in, but their weapons in perfect condition. Omi was seated on the earth at the edge of the dais, Naga at the opposite side. Zataki's men were dressed formally and richly, their vast, wing-shouldered overmantles belted with silver buckles. But they were equally well armed. They settled themselves, also twenty paces away.

Mariko served ceremonial cha and there was innocuous, formal conversation between the two brothers. At the correct time Mariko bowed and left, Buntaro achingly aware of her and vastly proud of her grace and beauty. And then, too soon, Zataki said brusquely, "I bring orders from the Council of Regents."

A sudden hush fell on the square. Everyone, even his own men, was aghast at Zataki's lack of manners, at the insolent way he had said "orders" and not "message," and at his failure to wait for Toranaga to ask, "How can I be of service?" as ceremonial demanded.

Naga shot a quick glance away from Zataki's sword arm to his father. He saw the flush on Toranaga's neck that was an infallible sign of impending explosion. But Toranaga's face was tranquil, and Naga was amazed as he heard the controlled reply: "So sorry, you have orders? For whom, Brother? Surely you have a message?"

Zataki ripped two small scrolls out of his sleeve. Buntaro's hand almost flashed for his waiting sword at the unexpected suddenness, for ritual called for all movements to be slow and deliberate. Toranaga had not moved.

Zataki broke the seal of the first scroll and read in a loud, chilling voice: "By order of the Council of Regents, in the name of Emperor Go-Niji, the Son of Heaven: We greet our illustrious vassal Yoshi Toranaga-noh-Minowara and invite him to make obeisance before us in Osaka forthwith, and invite him to inform our illustrious ambassador, the Regent, Lord Saigawa Zataki, if our invitation is accepted or refused—forthwith."

He looked up and in an equally loud voice continued, "It's signed by all Regents and sealed with the Great Seal of the Realm." Haughtily he placed the scroll in front of him. Toranaga signaled to Buntaro, who went forward, bowed low to Zataki, picked up the scroll, turned to Toranaga, bowed again. Toranaga accepted the scroll, and motioned Buntaro back to his place.

Toranaga studied the scroll interminably.

"All the signatures are genuine," Zataki said. "Do you accept or refuse?"

In a subdued voice, so that only those on the dais and Omi and Naga could hear him, Toranaga said, "Why shouldn't I take your head for your foul manners?"

"Because I'm my mother's son," Zataki replied.

"That won't protect you if you continue this way."

"Then she'll die before her time."

"What?"

"The Lady, our mother, is in Takato." Takato was the landlocked, impregnable fortress and capital city of Shinano, Zataki's province. "I regret her body will stay there forever."

"Bluff! You honor her as much as I do."

"On her immortal spirit, Brother, as much as I honor her, I detest what you're doing to the realm even more."

"I seek no more territory and no—"

"You seek to overthrow the succession."

"Wrong again, and I'll always protect my nephew from traitors."

"You seek the Heir's downfall, that is what I believe, so I've decided to stay alive and lock Shinano and the northern route against you, *whatever the cost,* and I'll continue to do that until the Kwanto's in friendly hands—*whatever the cost.* "

"In *your* hands, Brother?"

"Any safe hands—which excludes yours. Brother."

"You trust Ishido?"

"I trust no one, you've taught me that. Ishido's Ishido, but his loyalty's unquestioned. Even you'll admit that."

"I'll admit that Ishido's trying to destroy me and split the realm, that he's usurped power and that he's breaking the Taikō's will."

"But you did plot with Lord Sugiyama to wreck the Council of Regents. *Neh?*"

The vein in Zataki's forehead was throbbing like a black worm. "What can you say? One of his counselors admitted the treason: that you plotted with Sugiyama for him to accept Lord Ito in your place, then to resign the day before the first meeting and escape by night, and so throw the realm into confusion. I heard the confession—Brother."

"Were you one of the murderers?"

Zataki flushed. "Overzealous *ronin* killed Sugiyama, not I, nor any of Ishido's men!"

"Curious that you took his place as Regent so quickly, *neh?*"

"No. My lineage is as ancient as yours. But I didn't order the death, nor did Ishido—he swore it on his honor as a samurai. So do I. *Ronin* killed Sugiyama, but he deserved to die."

"By torture, dishonored in a filthy cellar, his children and consorts hacked up in front of him?"

"That's a rumor spread by filthy malcontents—perhaps by *your* spies—to discredit Lord Ishido and through him the Lady Ochiba and the Heir. There's no proof of that."

"Look at their bodies."

"The *ronin* set fire to the house. There are no bodies."

"So convenient, *neh?* How can you be so gullible? You're not a stupid peasant!"

"I refuse to sit here and listen to this manure. Give me your answer now. And then either take my head and she dies or let me go." Zataki leaned forward. "Within moments of my head leaving my shoulders, ten carrier pigeons will be racing north for Takato. I have trustworthy men north, east, and west, a day's march away, out of your reach, and if they fail there are more in safety across your borders. If you take my head or have me assassinated or if I die in Izu— *whatever the reason*—she dies also. Now, either take my head or let's finish the giving of the scrolls and I'll leave Izu at once. Choose!"

"Ishido murdered Lord Sugiyama. In time I can get you proof. That's important, *neh?* I only need a little—"

"You've no more time! Forthwith, the message said. Of course you refuse to obey, good, so it's done. Here." Zataki put the second scroll on the tatamis. "Here's your formal impeachment and order to commit seppuku, which you'll treat with equal contempt—may Lord Buddha forgive you! Now everything's done. I'll leave at once, and the next time we meet will be on a battlefield and by the Lord Buddha, before sunset on the same day, I've promised myself I'll see your head on a spike."

Toranaga kept his eyes on his adversary. "Lord Sugiyama was your friend and mine. Our comrade, as honorable a samurai as ever lived. The truth about his death should be of importance to you."

"Yours has more importance, Brother."

"Ishido's sucked you in like a starving infant at its mother's tit."

Zataki turned to his counselor. "On your honor as a samurai, have I posted men and what is the message?"

The gray-haired, dignified old samurai, chief of Zataki's confidants and well known to Toranaga as an honorable man, felt sickened and ashamed by the blatant display of hatred, as was everyone within hearing. "So sorry, Lord," he said in a choked whisper, bowing to Toranaga, "but my Master is of course telling the truth. How could this be questioned? And, please excuse me, but it is my duty, with all honor and humility, to point out to both of you that such . . . such astonishing and shameful lack of politeness between you is not worthy of your rank or the solemnity of this occasion. If your vassals—if they could have heard—I doubt if either of you could have held them back. You forget your duty as samurai and your duty to your men. Please excuse me"—he bowed to both of them—"but it had to be said." Then he added, "All messages were the same, Lord Toranaga, and under the official seal of Lord Zataki: 'Put the Lady, my mother, to death at once.' "

"How can I prove I'm not trying to overthrow the Heir?" Toranaga asked his brother.

"Immediately abdicate all your titles and power to your son and heir, Lord Sudara, and commit seppuku today. Then I and all my men—to the last man— will support Sudara as Lord of the Kwanto."

"I'll consider what you've said."

"Eh?"

"I'll consider what you've said." Toranaga repeated it more firmly. "We'll meet tomorrow at this time, if it pleases you."

Zataki's face twisted. "Is this another of your tricks? What's there to meet about?"

"About what you said, and about this." Toranaga held up the scroll that was in his hand. "I'll give you my answer tomorrow."

"Buntaro-san!" Zataki motioned at the second scroll. "Please give this to your master."

"No!" Toranaga's voice reverberated around the clearing. Then, with great ceremony, he added loudly, "I am honored formally to accept the Council's message and will submit my answer to their illustrious ambassador, my brother, the Lord of Shinano, tomorrow at this time."

Zataki stared at him suspiciously. "What possible ans—"

"Please excuse me, Lord," the old samurai interrupted quietly with grave dignity, again keeping the conversation private, "so sorry, but Lord Toranaga is perfectly correct to suggest this. It is a solemn choice you have given him, a choice not contained in the scrolls. It is fair and honorable that he should be given the time he requires."

Zataki picked up the second scroll and shoved it back into his sleeve. "Very well. I agree. Lord Toranaga, please excuse my bad manners. Lastly, please tell me where Kasigi Yabu is? I've a scroll for him. Only one in his case."

"I'll send him to you."

The falcon closed her wings and fell a thousand feet out of the evening sky and smashed into the fleeing pigeon with a burst of feathers, then caught it in her talons and carried it earthward, still falling like a stone, and then, a few feet off the ground, she released her now dead prey, braked frantically and landed on it perfectly. *"Ek-ek-ek-eeekk!"* she shrieked, fluttering her neck feathers in pride, her talons ripping off the pigeon's head in her ecstasy of conquest.

Toranaga, with Naga as his equerry, galloped up. The *daimyo* slid off his horse.

He called her gently to fist. Obediently she stepped up onto his glove. At once she was rewarded with a morsel of flesh from a previous kill. He slipped on her hood, tightening the thongs with his teeth. Naga picked up the pigeon and put it into the half-full game bag that hung from his father's saddle, then turned and beckoned to the distant beaters and guards.

Toranaga got back into the saddle, the falcon comfortably on his glove, held by her thin leather jesses. He looked up into the sky, measuring the light still remaining.

In the late afternoon the sun had broken through, and now in the valley, the day dying fast, the sun long since bedded by the western crest, it was cool and pleasant. The clouds were northward, pushed there by the dominant wind, hovering over the mountain peaks and hiding many. At this altitude, land-locked, the air was clean and sweet.

"We should have a good day tomorrow, Naga-san. Cloudless, I'd imagine. I think I'll hunt with the dawn."

"Yes, Father." Naga watched him, perplexed, afraid to ask questions as always, yet wanting to know everything. He could not fathom how his father could be so detached after such a hideous meeting. To bow Zataki away with the due ceremony then, at once, to summon his hawks and beaters and guards and halloo them away to the rolling hills beyond the forest, seemed to Naga to be an unearthly display of self-control. Just the thought of Zataki made Naga's flesh crawl now, and he knew that the old counselor was right: if one tenth of the conversation had been overheard, samurai would have leapt to defend their lord's honor. If it weren't for the threat that hung over his revered grandmother's head, he would have rushed at Zataki himself. I suppose that's why my father is what he is, and is where he is, he thought. . . .

His eyes picked out horsemen breaking from the forest below and galloping up toward them over the rolling foothills. Beyond the dark green of the forest, the river was a twisted ribbon of black. The lights in the inns blinked like fireflies. "Father!"

"Eh? Ah yes, I see them now. Who are they?"

"Yabu-san, Omi-san and . . . eight guards."

"Your eyes are better than mine. Ah yes, now I recognize them."

Naga said without thinking, "I wouldn't have let Yabu-san go alone to Lord Zataki without—" He stopped and stuttered, "Please excuse me."

"Why wouldn't you have sent Yabu-san alone?"

Naga cursed himself for opening his mouth and quailed under Toranaga's gaze. "Please excuse me, because then I'd never know what secret arrangement they would have made. He could, Father, easily. I would have kept them apart—please excuse me. I don't trust him."

"If Yabu-san and Zataki-san plan treachery behind my back, they'll do it whether I send a witness or not. Sometimes it's wiser to give a quarry extra line—that's how to catch a fish, *neh?*"

"Yes, please excuse me."

Toranaga realized that his son didn't understand, would never understand, would always be merely a hawk to hurl at an enemy, swift, sharp, and deadly.

"I'm glad you understand, my son," he said to encourage him, knowing his good qualities, and valuing them. "You're a good son," he added, meaning it.

"Thank you, Father," Naga said, filled with pride at the rare compliment. "I only hope you'll forgive my stupidities and teach me to serve you better."

"You're not stupid." Yabu's stupid, Toranaga almost added. The less people know the better, and it's not necessary to stretch your mind, Naga. You're so young—my youngest but for your half brother, Tadateru. How old is he? Ah, seven, yes, he'd be seven.

He watched the approaching horsemen a moment. "How's your mother, Naga?"

"As always, the happiest lady in the world. She'll still only let me see her once a year. Can't you persuade her to change?"

"No," said Toranaga. "She'll never change."

Toranaga always felt a glow when he thought of Chano-Tsuboné, his eighth official consort and Naga's mother. He laughed to himself as he remembered her earthy humor, her dimpled cheeks and saucy bottom, the way she wriggled and the enthusiasm of her pillowing.

She had been the widow of a farmer near Yedo who had attracted him twenty years ago. She had stayed with him three years, then asked to be allowed to return to the land. He had allowed her to go. Now she lived on a good farm near where she was born—fat and content, a dowager Buddhist nun honored by all and beholden to none. Once in a while he would go to see her and they would laugh together, without reason, friends.

"Ah, she's a good woman," Toranaga said.

Yabu and Omi rode up and dismounted. Ten paces away they stopped and bowed.

"He gave me a scroll," Yabu said, enraged, brandishing it. " '. . . We invite you to leave Izu at once for Osaka, today, and present yourself at Osaka Castle for an audience, or all your lands are now forfeit and you are hereby declared outlaw.' " He crushed the scroll in his fist and threw it on the ground. "Today!"

"Then you'd better leave at once," Toranaga said, suddenly in a foul humor at Yabu's truculence and stupidity.

"Sire, I beg you," Omi began hastily, dropping abjectly to his knees, "Lord Yabu's your devoted vassal and I beg you humbly not to taunt him. Forgive me for being so rude, but Lord Zataki . . . Forgive me for being so rude."

"Yabu-san, please excuse the remark—it was meant kindly," Toranaga said, cursing his lapse. "We should all have a sense of humor about such messages, *neh?*" He called up his falconer, gave him the bird from his fist, dismissed him and the beaters. Then he waved all samurai except Naga out of earshot, squatting on his haunches, and bade them do the same. "Perhaps you'd better tell me what happened."

Yabu said, "There's almost nothing to tell. I went to see him. He received me with the barest minimum of courtesy. First there were 'greetings' from Lord Ishido and a blunt invitation to ally myself secretly with him, to plan your immediate assassination, and to murder every Toranaga samurai in Izu. Of course I refused to listen, and at once—at once—without any courtesy whatsoever, he handed me that!" His finger stabbed belligerently toward the scroll. "If it hadn't been for your direct order protecting him I'd have hacked him to pieces at once! I demand you rescind that order. I cannot live with this shame. I must have revenge!"

"Is that everything that happened?"

"Isn't that enough?"

Toranaga passed over Yabu's rudeness and scowled at Omi. "You're to blame, *neh?* Why didn't you have the intelligence to protect your Lord better? You're supposed to be an adviser. You should have been his shield. You should have drawn Lord Zataki into the open, tried to find out what Ishido had in mind, what the bribe was, what plans they had. You're supposed to be a valued counselor. You're given a perfect opportunity and you waste it like an unpracticed dullard!"

Omi bent his head. "Please excuse me, Sire."

"I might, but I don't see why Lord Yabu should. Now your lord's accepted the scroll. Now he's committed. Now he has to act one way or the other."

"What?" said Yabu.

"Why else do you think I did what I did? To delay—of course, to delay," said Toranaga.

"But one day? What's the value of one day?" Yabu asked.

"Who knows? A day for you is one less for the enemy." Toranaga's eyes snapped back to Omi. "Was the message from Ishido verbal or in writing?"

Yabu answered instead. "Verbal, of course."

Toranaga kept his penetrating gaze on Omi. "You've failed in your duty to your lord and to me."

"Please excuse—"

"What exactly did you say?"

Omi did not reply.

"Have you forgotten your manners as well? What did you say?"

"Nothing, Sire. I said nothing."

"What?"

Yabu blustered, "He said nothing to Zataki because he wasn't present. Zataki asked to speak to me alone."

"Oh?" Toranaga hid his glee that Yabu had had to admit what he had already surmised and that part of the truth was now in the open. "Please excuse me, Omi-san. I naturally presumed you were present."

"It was my error, Sire. I should have insisted. You're correct, I failed to protect my Lord," Omi said. "I should have been more forceful. Please excuse me. Yabu-sama, please excuse me."

Before Yabu could answer, Toranaga said, "Of course you're forgiven, Omi-san. If your lord overruled you, that's his privilege. You did overrule him, Yabu-sama?"

"Yes—yes, but I didn't think it mattered. You think I . . ."

"Well, the harm's done now. What do you plan to do?"

"Of course, dismiss the message for what is it, Sire." Yabu was disquieted. "You think I could have avoided taking it?"

"Of course. You could have negotiated with him for a day. Maybe more. Weeks even," Toranaga added, turning the knife deeper into the wound, maliciously delighted that Yabu's own stupidity had thrust him onto the hook, and not at all concerned with the treachery Yabu had undoubtedly been bribed into, cajoled into, flattered into, or frightened into. "So sorry, but you're committed. Never mind, it's as you said, 'The sooner everyone chooses sides the better.'" He got up. "There's no need to go back to the regiment tonight. Both of you join me at the evening meal. I've arranged an entertainment." For everyone, he added under his breath, with a great deal of satisfaction.

Kiku's skillful fingers strummed a chord, the plectrum held firmly. Then she began to sing and the purity of her voice filled the hushed night. They sat spellbound in the large room that was open to the veranda and the garden beyond, entranced by the extraordinary effect she made under the flickering torches, the gold threads of her kimono catching the light as she leaned over the samisen.

Toranaga glanced around momentarily, aware of the night currents. On one side of him, Mariko sat between Blackthorne and Buntaro. On the other, Omi and Yabu, side by side. The place of honor was still empty. Zataki had been invited, but of course he had regretfully declined due to ill health, though he had been seen galloping the northern hills and was presently pillowing with his legendary strength. Naga and very carefully chosen guards were all around, Gyoko hovering somewhere in the background. Kiku-san knelt on the veranda facing them, her back to the garden—tiny, alone, and very rare.

Mariko was right, Toranaga thought. The courtesan's worth the money. His spirit was beguiled by her, his anxiety about Zataki lessened. Shall I send for her again tonight or shall I sleep alone? His manhood stirred as he remembered last night.

"So, Gyoko-san, you wished to see me?" he had asked in his private quarters at the fortress.

"Yes, Sire."

He lit the measured length of incense. "Please proceed."

Gyoko had bowed, but he hardly had eyes for her. This was the first time he had seen Kiku closely. Nearness improved her exquisite features, as yet unmarked by the rigors of her profession. "Please play some music while we talk," he said, surprised that Gyoko was prepared to talk in front of her.

Kiku had obeyed at once, but her music then was nothing like tonight. Last night it was to soothe, an accompaniment to the business at hand. Tonight was to excite, to awe, and to promise.

"Sire," Gyoko had begun formally, "first may I humbly thank you for the honor you do me, my poor house, and Kiku-san, the first of my Ladies of the Willow World. The price I have asked for contract is insolent I know, impossible I am sure, not agreed to until dawn tomorrow when both the Lady Kasigi and the Lady Toda in their wisdom will decide. If it were a matter for you, you would have decided long ago, for what is contemptible money to any samurai, let alone to the greatest *daimyo* in the world?"

Gyoko had paused for effect. He had not taken the bait, but moved his fan slightly, which could be interpreted as irritation at her expansiveness, acceptance of the compliment, or an absolute rejection of the asking price, depending on her inner mood. Both knew very clearly who really approved the amount.

"What is money? Nothing but a means of communication," she continued, "like Kiku-san's music. What in fact do we of the Willow World do but communicate and entertain, to enlighten the soul of man, to lighten his burden. . . ." Toranaga had stifled a caustic response, reminding himself the woman had bought one stick of time for five hundred koku and five hundred koku merited an attentive audience. So he let her continue and listened with one ear, and let the other enjoy the flow of perfect music that tugged at his innermost being, gentling him into a sense of euphoria. Then he was rudely yanked back into the world of reality by something Gyoko had just said. "What?"

"I was merely suggesting that you should take the Willow World under your protection and change the course of history."

"How?"

"By doing what you have always done, Sire, by concerning yourself with the future of the whole Empire—before your own."

He let the ludicrous exaggeration pass and told himself to close his ears to the music—that he had fallen into the first trap by telling Gyoko to bring the girl, the second by letting himself feast on her beauty and perfume, and the third by allowing her to play seductively while the mistress talked.

"The Willow World? What about the Willow World?"

"Two things, Sire. First, the Willow World is presently intermingled with the real world to the detraction of both. Second, our ladies cannot truly rise to the perfection all men have the right to expect."

"Oh?" A thread of Kiku's perfume, one he had never known before, wafted across him. It was perfectly chosen. Involuntarily he looked at her. A half-smile was on her lips for him alone. Languidly she dropped her eyes and her fingers stroked the strings and he felt them on him intimately.

He tried to concentrate. "So sorry, Gyoko-san. You were saying?"

"Please excuse me for not being clear, Sire. First: The Willow World should be separate from the real one. My Tea House in Mishima is on one street in the south, others are scattered over the whole city. It is the same in Kyoto and Nara, and the same throughout all the Empire. Even in Yedo. But I thought that Yedo could set the pattern of the world."

"How?" His heart missed a beat as a perfect chord fell into place.

"All other crafts wisely have streets of their own, areas of their own. We should be allowed our own place, Sire. Yedo is a new city; you might consider setting aside a special section for your Willow World. Bring all Tea Houses within the walls of this area and forbid any Tea Houses, however modest, outside."

Now his mind concentrated totally, for here was a vast idea. It was so good that he berated himself for not thinking of it himself. All Tea Houses and all courtesans within a fence, and therefore remarkably easy to police, to watch, and to tax, and all their customers equally easy to police, to watch, and to spy upon. The simplicity staggered him. He knew also the powerful influence wielded by the Ladies of the First Rank.

But his face betrayed none of his enthusiasm. "What's the advantage in that, Gyoko-san?"

"We would have our own guild, Sire, with all the protection that a guild means, a real guild in one place, not spread out, so to speak, a guild that all would obey. . . ."

"*Must* obey?"

"Yes, Sire. Must obey, for the good of all. The guild would be responsible that prices were fair and that standards were maintained. Why, in a few years, a Lady of the Second Class in Yedo would equal one in Kyoto and so on. If the scheme was valuable in Yedo why not in every city in your domain?"

"But those owners who are within the fence dominate everything. They're monopolists, *neh?* They can charge usurious entrance fees, *neh,* can lock the doors against many who have an equal right to work in the Willow World, *neh?*"

"Yes, it could be so, Sire. And it will happen in some places, and in some times. But strict laws can easily be made to ensure fairness, and it would seem the good outweighs the bad, for us and for our honored customers and clients. Second: Ladies of—"

"Let us finish your first point, Gyoko-san," Toranaga said dryly. "So that's a point against your suggestion, *neh?*"

"Yes, Sire. It's possible. But any *daimyo* could easily order it otherwise. And he has to deal with only one guild in one place. You, Sire, you would have no trouble. Each area would of course be responsible for the peace of the area. And for taxes."

"Ah yes, taxes! It would certainly be much easier to collect taxes. That's a very good point in its favor."

Gyoko's eyes were on the incense stick. More than half had vanished. "You, in your wisdom, might decree that our Willow World should be the only world, within the whole world, that is never to be taxed, for all time. Never, never, never." She looked up at him clearly, her voice guileless. "After all, Sire, isn't our world also called the 'Floating World,' isn't our only offering beauty, isn't a large part of beauty youth? Isn't something so fleeting and transient as youth a gift from the gods, and sacred? Of all men, Sire, you must know how rare and fleeting youth is, a woman is."

The music died. His eyes were pulled to Kiku-san. She was watching him intently, a small frown on her brow.

"Yes," he said honestly. "I know how fleeting that can be." He sipped his cha. "I will consider what you've said. Second?"

"Second." Gyoko collected her wits. "Second and last, Sire, you could put your chop on the Willow World forever. Consider some of our Ladies: Kiku-san, for instance, has studied singing and dancing and the samisen since she was six. Every waking moment she was working very hard to perfect her art. Admittedly she's rightfully become a Lady of the First Class, as her unique artistry merits. But she's still a courtesan and some clients expect to enjoy her on the pillow as well as through her art. I believe two classes of Ladies should be created. First, courtesans, as always—amusing, happy, physical. Second, a new class, perhaps *gei-sha* could describe them: Art Persons—persons dedicated solely to art. *Gei-shas* would not be expected to go to the pillow as part of their duty. They would solely be entertainers, dancers, singers, musicians—specialists—and so give themselves exclusively to this profession. Let *gei-shas* entertain the minds and spirits of men with their beauty and grace and their artistry. Let courtesans satisfy the body with beauty, grace, and equal artistry."

Again he was struck by the simplicity and the far-reaching possibilities of her idea. "How would you select a *gei-sha?*"

"By her aptitude. At puberty her owner would decide the way of her future. And the guild could approve, or reject, the apprentice, *neh?*"

"It is an extraordinary idea, Gyoko-san."

The woman bowed and shivered. "Please excuse my long-windedness, Sire, but this way, when beauty fades and the body thickens, still the girl can have a rare future and a real value. She won't have to go down the road that all courtesans today must travel. I plead for the artists among them, my Kiku-san for one. I petition you to grant the favored few a future and the position they merit in the land. To learn to sing and to dance and to play requires practice and practice over the years. The pillow needs youth and there is no aphrodisiac like youth. *Neh?*"

"No." Toranaga watched her. "*Gei-shas* may not pillow?"

"That would not be part of a *gei-sha's* duty, whatever the money offered. *Gei-shas* would never be *obliged* to pillow, Sire. If a *gei-sha* wished to pillow with a particular man, it would be her private concern—or perhaps it should be arranged with the permission of her mistress, the price to be only as high as that man can afford. A courtesan's duty would be to pillow with artistry—*gei-shas* and the apprentice *gei-shas* would be untouchable. Please excuse me for talking so long." Gyoko bowed and Kiku bowed. The barest fraction of incense remained.

Toranaga questioned them for twice the allotted time, pleased with the opportunity to learn about their world, probing their ideas and hopes and fears. What he learned excited him. He docketed the information for future use, then he sent Kiku into the garden. "Tonight, Gyoko-san, I would like her to stay, if she would care to, until dawn—if she's free. Would you please ask her? Of course I realize that she may be tired now. After all, she's played so superbly for such a long time and I'll quite understand. But perhaps she would consider it. I'd be grateful if you would ask her."

"Of course, Sire, but I know she would be honored by your invitation. It's our duty to serve in any way we can, *neh?*"

"Yes. But she is, as you so rightly point out, most special. I'll quite understand if she's too tired. Please ask her in a moment." He gave Gyoko a small leather bag containing ten koban, regretting the ostentation, but knowing his position demanded it. "Perhaps this would compensate you for such an exhausting evening, and be a small token of my thanks for your ideas."

"It's our duty to serve, Sire," Gyoko said. He saw her trying to stop her fingers from counting through the soft leather, and fail. "Thank you, Sire. Please excuse me, I will ask her." Then, strangely and unexpectedly, tears filled her eyes. "Please accept the thanks of a vulgar old woman for your courtesy and for listening. It's just that for all the giving of pleasure, our only reward is a river of tears. In truth, Lord, it is difficult to explain how a woman feels . . . please excuse me. . . ."

"Listen, Gyoko-san, I understand. Don't worry. I'll consider everything you've said. Oh yes, you'll both leave with me shortly after dawn. A few days in the mountains will make a pleasant change. I would imagine the contract price will be approved, *neh?*"

Gyoko bowed her thanks, then she brushed her tears away and said firmly, "May I therefore ask the name of the honored person for whom her contract will be bought?"

"Yoshi Toranaga-noh-Minowara."

Now under the Yokosé night, the air sweetly cool, Kiku-san's music and voice possessing their minds and hearts, Toranaga let his mind wander. He remembered the pride-filled glow that had swamped Gyoko's face and he wondered again at the bewildering gullibility of people. How baffling it was that even the most cunning and clever people would frequently see only what they wanted to see, and would rarely look beyond the thinnest of facades. Or they would ignore reality, dismissing it as the facade. And then, when their whole world fell to pieces and they were on their knees slitting their bellies or cutting their throats, or cast out into the freezing world, they would tear their topknots or rend their clothes and bewail their *karma,* blaming gods or *kami* or luck or their lords or husbands or vassals—anything or anyone—but never themselves.

So very strange.

He looked at his guests and saw they were still watching the girl, locked in their secrets, their minds expanded by her artistry—all except the Anjin-san, who was edgy and fidgeting. Never mind, Anjin-san, Toranaga thought with amusement, it's only your lack of civilization. Yes, never mind, that will come in time, and even that doesn't matter so long as you obey. At the moment I need your touchiness and your anger and your violence.

Yes, you're all here. You Omi, and Yabu and Naga and Buntaro, and you Mariko and Kiku-san and even Gyoko, all my Izu hawks and falcons, all trained and very ready. All here except one—the Christian priest. And soon it'll be your turn, Tsukku-san. Or perhaps mine.

Father Martin Alvito of the Society of Jesus was enraged. Just when he knew he should be preparing for his meeting with Toranaga, at which he would need all his wits, he was faced with this new abomination that could not wait. "What have you got to say for yourself?" he lashed out at the cowled Japanese acolyte who knelt abjectly in front of him. The other Brothers stood around the small room in a semicircle.

"Please forgive me, Father. I have sinned," the man stammered in complete misery. "Please forgive—"

"I repeat: It is for Almighty God in His wisdom to forgive, not me. You've committed a mortal sin. You've broken your Holy Oath. Well?"

The reply was barely audible. "I'm sorry, Father." The man was thin and frail. His baptismal name was Joseph and he was thirty. His fellow acolytes, all Brothers of the Society, ranged from eighteen to forty. All were tonsured, all of noble samurai birth from provinces in Kyushu, all rigorously trained for the priesthood though none yet ordained.

"I confessed, Father," Brother Joseph said, keeping his head bowed.

"You think that's enough?" Impatiently Alvito turned away and walked to the window. The room was ordinary, the mats fair, the paper shoji screens poorly repaired. The inn was seedy and third class but the best that he could find in Yokosé, the rest taken by samurai. He stared out into the night, half listening to Kiku's distant voice soaring over the noise of the river. Until the courtesan finished Alvito knew he would not be sent for by Toranaga. "Filthy whore," he said, half to himself, the wailing discordance of Japanese singing annoying him more than usual, intensifying his anger at Joseph's betrayal.

"Listen, Brothers," Alvito said to the rest, turning back to them. "We are in judgment over Brother Joseph, who went with a whore of this town last night, breaking his Holy Oath of chastity, breaking his Holy Oath of obedience, desecrating his immortal soul, his position as a Jesuit, his place in the Church and all that that stands for. Before God I ask each of you—have you done likewise?"

They all shook their heads.

"Have you ever done likewise?"

"No, Father."

"You, sinner! Before God, you admit your sin?"

"Yes, Father, I've already con—"

"Before God, is this the first time?"

"No, this was not the first time," Joseph said. "I—I went with another four nights ago—in Mishima."

"But . . . but yesterday we said Mass! What about your confession yesterday and the night before and the one before that, you didn't— Yesterday we said Mass! For the love of God, you took the Eucharist unconfessed, with full knowledge of a mortal sin?"

Brother Joseph was gray with shame. He had been with the Jesuits since he was eight. "It was the—it was the first time, Father. Only four days ago. I've been sinless all my life. Again I was tempted—and, the Blessed Madonna forgive me, this time I failed. I'm thirty. I'm a man—we're all men. Please, the Lord Jesus Father forgave sinners—why can't you forgive me? We're all men—"

"We're all priests!"

"We're not real priests! We're not professed—we're not even ordained! We're not real Jesuits. We can't take the fourth vow like you, Father," Joseph said sullenly. "Other Orders ordain their brethren but not the Jesuits. Why shouldn't—"

"Hold your tongue!"

"I won't!" Joseph flared. "Please excuse me, Father, but why shouldn't some of us be ordained?" He pointed at one of the Brothers, a tall, round-faced man who watched serenely. "Why shouldn't Brother Michael be ordained? He's studied since he was twelve. Now he's thirty-six and a perfect Christian, almost a saint. He's converted thousands but he's still not been ordained though—"

"In the name of God, you will—"

"In the name of God, Father, why can't one of us be ordained? Someone has to dare to ask you!" Joseph was on his feet now. "I've been training for sixteen years, Brother Matteo for twenty-three, Juliao more, all our lives—countless years. We know the prayers and catechisms and hymns better than you, and Michael and I even speak Latin as well as Portu—"

"Stop!"

"—Portuguese, and we do most of the preaching and debating with the Buddhists and all the other idolaters and do most of the converting. *We* do! In the name of God and the Madonna, what's wrong with us? Why aren't we good enough for Jesuits? Is it just because we're not Portuguese or Spanish, or because we're not hairy or round-eyed? In the name of God, Father, why isn't there an ordained Japanese Jesuit?"

"Now you will hold your tongue!"

"We've even been to *Rome,* Michael, Juliao, and me," Joseph burst out. "You've never been to Rome or met the Father-General or His Holiness the Pope as we've done—"

"Which is another reason you should know better than to argue. You're vowed to chastity, poverty, and *obedience.* You were chosen among the many, favored out of the many, and now you've let your soul get so corrupted that—"

"So sorry, Father, but I don't think we were favored to spend eight years going there and coming back if after all our learning and praying and preaching and waiting not one of us is ordained even though it's been promised. I was twelve when I left. Juliao was elev—"

"I forbid you to say any more! I *order* you to stop." Then in the awful silence Alvito looked at the others, who lined the walls, watching and listening closely. "You will all be ordained in time. But you, Joseph, before God you will—"

"Before God," Joseph erupted, "in whose time?"

"In God's time," Alvito slammed back, stunned by the open rebellion, his zeal blazing. "Get-down-on-your-knees!"

Brother Joseph tried to stare him down but he could not, then his fit passing, he exhaled, sank to his knees, and bowed his head.

"May God have mercy on you. You are self-confessed to hideous mortal sin, guilty of breaking your Holy vow of chastity, your Holy vow of obedience to your superiors. And guilty of unbelievable insolence. How dare you question our General's orders or the policy of the Church? You have jeopardized your immortal soul. You are a disgrace to your God, your Company, your Church, your family, and your friends. Your case is so serious it will have to be dealt with by the Visitor-General himself. Until that time you will not take communion, you will not be confessed or hear confession or any part in any service. . . ." Joseph's shoulders began shaking with the agony of remorse that possessed him. "As initial penance you are forbidden to talk, you will have only rice and water for thirty days, you will spend every night for the next thirty nights on your knees in prayer to the Blessed Madonna for forgiveness for your hideous sins, and further you will be scourged. Thirty lashes. Take off your cassock."

The shoulders stopped trembling. Joseph looked up. "I accept everything you've ordered, Father," he said, "and I apologize with all my heart, with all my soul. I beg your forgiveness as I will beg His forgiveness forever. But I will not be lashed like a common criminal."

"You-will-be-scourged!"

"Please excuse me, Father," Joseph said. "In the name of the Blessed Madonna, it's not the pain. Pain is nothing to me, death is nothing to me. That I'm damned and will burn in hellfire for all eternity may be my *karma,* and I will endure it. But I'm samurai. I'm of Lord Harima's family."

"Your pride sickens me. It's not for the pain you're to be punished, but to remove your disgusting pride. Common criminal? Where is your humility? Our Lord Jesus Christ endured mortification. And he died with common criminals."

"Yes. That's our major problem here, Father."

"What?"

"Please excuse my bluntness, Father, but if the King of Kings had not died like a common criminal on the cross, samurai could accept—"

"Stop!"

"—Christianity more easily. The Society's wise to avoid preaching Christ crucified like the other Orders—"

Like an avenging angel, Alvito held up his cross as a shield in front of him. "In the name of God, keep silent and obey or-you-are-excommunicated! Seize him and strip him!"

The others came to life and moved forward, but Joseph sprang to his feet. A knife appeared in his hand from under his robes. He put his back to the wall. Everyone stopped in his tracks. Except Brother Michael. Brother Michael came forward slowly and calmly, his hand outstretched. "Please give me the knife, Brother," he said gently.

"No. Please excuse me."

"Then pray for me, Brother, as I pray for you." Michael quietly reached up for the weapon.

Joseph darted a few paces back, then readied for a death thrust. "Forgive me, Michael."

Michael continued to approach.

"Michael, stop! Leave him alone," Alvito commanded.

Michael obeyed, inches from the hovering blade.

Then Alvito said, ashen, "God have mercy on you, Joseph. You are excommunicated. Satan has possessed your soul on earth as he will possess it after death. Get thee gone!"

"I renounce the Christian God! I'm Japanese—I'm Shinto. My soul's my own now. I'm not afraid," Joseph shouted. "Yes, we've pride—unlike barbarians. We're Japanese, we're not barbarians. Even our peasants are not barbarians."

Gravely Alvito made the sign of the cross as protection for all of them and fearlessly turned his back on the knife. "Let us pray together, Brothers. Satan is in our midst."

The others also turned away, many sadly, some still in shock. Only Michael remained where he was, looking at Joseph. Joseph ripped off his rosary and cross. He was going to hurl it away but Michael held out his hand again. "Please, Brother, please give it to me—it is such a simple gift," he said.

Joseph looked at him a long moment, then he gave it to him. "Please excuse me."

"I will pray for you," Michael said.

"Didn't you hear? I've renounced God!"

"I will pray that God will not renounce you, Uraga-noh-Tadamasa-san."

"Forgive me, Brother," Joseph said. He stuck the knife in his sash, jerked the door open, and walked blindly along the corridor out onto the veranda. People watched him curiously, among them Uo the fisherman, who was waiting patiently in the shadows. Joseph crossed the courtyard and went toward the gate. A samurai stood in his way.

"Halt!"

Joseph stopped.

"Where are you going, please?"

"I'm sorry, please excuse me, I—I don't know."

"I serve Lord Toranaga. So sorry, I couldn't help hearing what went on in there. The whole inn must have heard. Shocking bad manners . . . shocking for your leader to shout like that and disturb the peace. And you too. I'm on duty here. I think it's best you see the officer of my watch."

"I think—thank you, I'll go the other way. Please excuse—"

"You'll go nowhere, so sorry. Except to see my officer."

"What? Oh—yes. Yes, I'm sorry, of course." Joseph tried to make his brain work.

"Good. Thank you." The samurai turned as another samurai approached from the bridge and saluted.

"I'm to fetch the Tsukku-san for Lord Toranaga."

"Good. You're expected."

CHAPTER 43

ORANAGA watched the tall priest approach across the clearing, the flickering light of the torches making the lean face starker than usual above the blackness of his beard. The priest's orange Buddhist robe was elegant and a rosary and cross hung at his waist.

Ten paces away Father Alvito stopped, knelt, and bowed deferentially, beginning the customary formalities.

Toranaga was sitting alone on the dais, guards in a semicircle around him, well out of hearing. Only Blackthorne was nearby and he lolled against the platform as he had been ordered, his eyes boring into the priest. Alvito appeared not to notice him.

"It is good to see you, Sire," Father Alvito said when it was polite to do so.

"And to see you, Tsukku-san." Toranaga motioned the priest to make himself comfortable on the cushion that had been placed on a tatami on the ground in front of the platform. "It's a long time since I saw you."

"Yes, Sire, there's much to tell." Alvito was deeply conscious that the cushion was on the earth and not on the dais. Also, he was acutely aware of the samurai swords that Blackthorne now wore so near to Toranaga and the way he slouched with such indifference. "I bring a confidential message from my superior, the Father-Visitor, who greets you with deference."

"Thank you. But first, tell me about you."

"Ah, Sire," Alvito said, knowing that Toranaga was far too discerning not to have noticed the remorse that beset him, much as he had tried to throw it off. "Tonight I'm too aware of my own failings. Tonight I'd like to be allowed to put off my earthly duties and go into a retreat to pray, to beg for God's favor." He was shamed by his own lack of humility. Although Joseph's sin had been terrible, Alvito had acted with haste and anger and stupidity. It was his fault that a soul had been outcast, to be lost forever. "Our Lord once said, 'Please, Father, let this cup pass from me.' But even He had to retain the cup. We, in the world, we have to try to follow in His footsteps as best we can. Please excuse me for allowing my problem to show."

"What was your 'cup,' old friend?"

Alvito told him. He knew there was no reason to hide the facts for, of course, Toranaga would hear them very soon if he did not already know them, and it was much better to hear the truth than a garbled version. "It's so very sad to lose a Brother, terrible to make one an outcast, however terrible the crime. I should have been more patient. It was my fault."

"Where is he now?"

"I don't know, Sire."

Toranaga called a guard. "Find the renegade Christian and bring him to me at noon tomorrow." The samurai hurried away.

"I beg mercy for him, Sire," Alvito said quickly, meaning it. But he knew whatever he said would do little to dissuade Toranaga from a path already chosen. Again he wished the Society had its own secular arm empowered to arrest and punish apostates, like elsewhere in the world. He had repeatedly recommended that this be created but he had always been overruled, here in Japan, and also

503

in Rome by the General of the Order. Yet without our own secular arm, he thought tiredly, we'll never be able to exercise real discipline over our Brethren and our flock.

"Why aren't there ordained priests within your Society, Tsukku-san?"

"Because, Sire, not one of our acolytes is yet sufficiently well trained. For instance, Latin is an absolute necessity because our Order requires any Brother to travel anywhere in the world at any time, and Latin, unfortunately, is very difficult to learn. Not one is trained yet, or ready."

Alvito believed this with all his heart. He was also bitterly opposed to a Japanese-ordained Jesuit clergy, in opposition to the Father-Visitor. "Eminence," he had always said, "I beg you, don't be fooled by their modest and decorous exterior. Underneath they're all unreliable characters, and their pride and Japaneseness will always dominate in the end. They'll never be true servants of the Society, or reliable soldiers of His Holiness, the Vicar of Christ on earth, obedient to him alone. Never."

Alvito glanced momentarily at Blackthorne then back to Toranaga, who said, "But two or three of these apprentice priests speak Latin, *neh,* and Portuguese? It's true what that man said, *neh?* Why haven't they been chosen?"

"So sorry, but the General of our Society doesn't consider them sufficiently prepared. Perhaps Joseph's tragic fall is an example."

"Bad to break a solemn oath," Toranaga said. He remembered the year the three boys had sailed off from Nagasaki in a Black Ship to be feted in the court of the Spanish king and the court of the High Priest of the Christians, the same year Goroda had been assassinated. Nine years later they had returned but all their time away had been carefully controlled and monitored. They had left as naïve, youthful Christian zealots and returned just as narrow-minded and almost as ill-informed as when they had left. Stupid waste, Toranaga thought, waste of an incredible opportunity which Goroda had refused to take advantage of, as much as he had advised it.

"No, Tora-san, we need the Christians against the Buddhists," Goroda had said. "Many Buddhist priests and monks are soldiers, *neh?* Most of them are. The Christians aren't, *neh?* Let the Giant Priest have the three youths he wants— they're only Kyushu stumbleheads, *neh?* I tell you to encourage Christians. Don't bother me with a ten-year plan, but burn every Buddhist monastery within reach. Buddhists are like flies on carrion, and Christians nothing but a bag of fart."

Now they're not, Toranaga thought with growing irritation. Now they're hornets.

"Yes," he said aloud. "Very bad to break an oath and shout and disturb the harmony of an inn."

"Please excuse me, Sire, and forgive me for mentioning my problems. Thank you for listening. As always your concern makes me feel better. May I be permitted to greet the pilot?"

Toranaga assented.

"I must congratulate you, Pilot," Alvito said in Portuguese. "Your swords suit you."

"Thank you, Father, I'm learning to use them," Blackthorne replied. "But, sorry to say, I'm not very good with them yet. I'll stick to pistols or cutlasses or cannon when I have to fight."

"I pray that you may never have to fight again, Pilot, and that your eyes will be opened to God's infinite mercy."

"Mine are open. Yours are fogged."

"For your own soul's sake, Pilot, keep your eyes open, and your mind open.

Perhaps you may be mistaken. Even so, I must think you for saving Lord Toranaga's life."

"Who told you that?"

Alvito did not reply. He turned back to Toranaga.

"What was said?" Toranaga asked, breaking a silence.

Alvito told him, adding, "Though he's the enemy of my faith and a pirate, I'm glad he saved you, Sire. God moves in mysterious ways. You've honored him greatly be making him samurai."

"He's hatamoto also." Toranaga was pleasured by the priest's fleeting amazement. "Did you bring a dictionary?"

"Yes, Sire, with several of the maps you wanted, showing some of the Portuguese bases en route from Goa. The book's in my luggage. May I send someone for it, or may I give it to him later myself?"

"Give it to him later. Tonight, or tomorrow. Did you also bring the report?"

"About the alleged guns that were supposed to be brought from Macao? The Father-Visitor is preparing it, Sire."

"And the numbers of Japanese mercenaries employed at each of your new bases?"

"The Father-Visitor has requested an up-to-date report from all of them, Sire, which he will give you as soon as they're complete."

"Good. Now tell me, how did you know about my rescue?"

"Hardly a thing that happens to Toranaga-noh-Minowara is not the subject of rumor and legend. Coming from Mishima we heard that you were almost swallowed up in an earthquake, Sire, but that the 'Golden Barbarian' had pulled you out. Also, that you'd done the same for him and a lady—I presume the Lady Mariko?"

Toranaga nodded briefly. "Yes. She's here in Yokosé." He thought a moment, then said, "Tomorrow she would like to be confessed, according to your customs. But only those things that are nonpolitical. I would imagine that excludes everything to do with me, and my various hatamoto, *neh?* I explained that to her also."

Alvito bowed his understanding. "With your permission, could I say Mass for all the Christians here, Sire? It would be very descrete, of course. Tomorrow?"

"I'll consider it." Toranaga continued to talk about inconsequential matters for a while, then he said, "You have a message for me? From your Chief Priest?"

"With humility, Sire, I beg to say that it was a private message."

Toranaga pretended to think about that, even though he had determined exactly how the meeting would proceed and had already given the Anjin-san specific instructions how to act and what to say. "Very well." He turned to Blackthorne, "Anjin-san, you can go now and we'll talk more later."

"Yes, Sire," Blackthorne replied. "So sorry, the Black Ship. Arrive Nagasaki?"

"Ah, yes. Thank you," he replied, pleased that the Anjin-san's question didn't sound rehearsed. "Well, Tsukku-san, has it docked yet?"

Alvito was startled by Blackthorne's Japanese and greatly perturbed by the question. "Yes, Sire. It docked fourteen days ago."

"Ah, fourteen?" said Toranaga. "You understand, Anjin-san?"

"Yes. Thank you."

"Good. Anything else you can ask Tsukku-san later, *neh?*"

"Yes, Sire. Please excuse me." Blackthorne got up and bowed and wandered off.

Toranaga watched him go. "A most interesting man—for a pirate. Now, first tell me about the Black Ship."

"It arrived safely, Sire, with the greatest cargo of silk that has ever been."

Alvito tried to sound enthusiastic. "The arrangement made between the Lords Harima, Kiyama, Onoshi, and yourself is in effect. Your treasury will be richer with tens of thousands of koban by this time next year. The quality of silks is the finest, Sire. I've brought a copy of the manifest for your quartermaster. The Captain-General Ferriera sends his respects, hoping to see you in person soon. That was the reason for my delay in coming to see you. The Visitor-General sent me post haste from Osaka to Nagasaki to make certain everything was perfect. Just as I was leaving Nagasaki we heard you'd left Yedo for Izu, so I came here as quickly as I could, by ship to Port Nimazu with one of our fastest cutters, then by road. At Mishima I fell in with Lord Zataki and asked permission to join him."

"Your ship's still at Nimazu?"

"Yes, Sire. It will wait for me there."

"Good." For a moment Toranaga wondered whether or not to send Mariko by that ship to Osaka, then decided to deal with that later. "Please give the manifest to the quartermaster tonight."

"Yes, Sire."

"And the arrangement about this year's cargo is sealed?"

"Yes. Absolutely."

"Good. Now the other part. The important part."

Alvito's hands went dry. "Neither Lord Kiyama nor Lord Onoshi will agree to forsake General Ishido. I'm sorry. They will not agree to join your banner now in spite of our strongest suggestion."

Toranaga's voice became low and cruel. "I already pointed out I required more than suggestions!"

"I'm sorry to bring bad news in this part, Sire, but neither would agree to publicly come over to—"

"Ah, publicly, you say? What about privately—secretly?"

"Privately they were both as adamant as pub—"

"You talked to them separately or together?"

"Of course together, and separately, most confidentially, but nothing we suggested would—"

"You only 'suggested' a course of action? Why didn't you order them?"

"It's as the Father-Visitor said, Sire, we can't order any *daimyo* or any—"

"Ah, but you can *order* one of your Brethren? *Neh?*"

"Yes. Sire."

"Did you threaten to make them outcast, too?"

"No, Sire."

"Why?"

"Because they've committed no mortal sin." Alvito said it firmly, as he and dell'Aqua had agreed, but his heart was fluttering and he hated to be the bearer of terrible tidings, which were even worse now because the Lord Harima, who legally owned Nagasaki, had told them privately that all his immense wealth and influence were going to Ishido. "Please excuse me, Sire, but I don't make divine rules, any more than you made the code of *bushido,* the Way of the Warrior. We, we have to comply with what—"

"You make a poor fool outcast for a natural act like pillowing, but when two of your converts behave unnaturally—yes, even treacherously—when I seek your help, urgent help—and I'm your friend—you only make 'suggestions.' You understand the seriousness of this, *neh?*"

"I'm sorry, Lord. Please excuse me but—"

"Perhaps I won't excuse you, Tsukku-san. It's been said before: Now everyone has to choose a side," Toranaga said.

"Of course we are on your side, Sire. But we cannot order Lord Kiyama or Lord Onoshi to do anything—"

"Fortunately I can order my Christian."

"Sire?"

"I can order the Anjin-san freed. With his ship. With his cannon."

"Beware of him, Sire. The Pilot's diabolically clever, but he's a heretic, a pirate and not to be trust—"

"Here the Anjin-san's a samurai and hatamoto. At sea perhaps he's a pirate. If he's a pirate, I imagine he'll attract many other corsairs and *wako* to him— many of them. What a foreigner does on the open sea's his own business, *neh?* That's always been our policy. *Neh?*"

Alvito kept quiet and tried to make his brain function. No one had planned on the Ingeles' becoming so close to Toranaga.

"Those two Christian *daimyos* will make no commitments, not even a secret one?"

"No, Sire. We tried ev—"

"No concession, none?"

"No, Sire—"

"No barter, no arrangement, no compromise, nothing?"

"No, Sire. We tried every inducement and persuasion. Please believe me." Alvito knew he was in the trap and some of his desperation showed. "If it were me, yes, I would threaten them with excommunication, though it would be a false threat because I'd never carry it through, not unless they had committed a mortal sin and wouldn't confess or be penitent and submit. But even a threat for temporal gain would be very wrong of me, Sire, a mortal sin. I'd risk eternal damnation."

"Are you saying if they sinned against your creed, then you'd cast them out?"

"Yes. But I'm not suggesting that could be used to bring them to your side, Sire. Please excuse me but they . . . they're totally opposed to you at the moment. I'm sorry but that's the truth. They both made it very clear, together and in private. Before God I pray they change their minds. We gave you our words to try, before God, the Father-Visitor and I. We fulfilled our promise. Before God we failed."

"Then I shall lose," Toranaga said. "You know that, don't you? If they stand allied with Ishido, all the Christian *daimyos* will side with him. Then I have to lose. Twenty samurai against one of mine. *Neh?*"

"Yes."

"What's their plan? When will they attack me?"

"I don't know, Sire."

"Would you tell me if you did?"

"Yes—yes I would."

I doubt it, Toranaga thought, and looked away into the night, the burden of his worry almost crushing him. Is it to be Crimson Sky after all, he asked himself helplessly? The stupid, bound-to-fail lunge at Kyoto?

He hated the shameful cage that he was in. Like the Taikō and Goroda before him, he had to tolerate the Christian priests because the priests were as inseparable from the Portuguese traders as flies from a horse, holding absolute temporal and spiritual power over their unruly flock. Without the priests there was no trade. Their good will as negotiators and middle men in the Black Ship operation was vital because they spoke the language and were trusted by both sides, and, if ever the priests were completely forbidden the Empire, all barbarians would obediently sail away, never to return. He remembered the one time the Taikō had tried to get rid of the priests yet still encourage trade. For two years there was no Black Ship. Spies reported how the giant chief of the priests, sitting like a poisonous black spider in Macao, had ordered no more trade in reprisal for the Taikō's Expulsion Edicts, knowing that at length the Taikō must humble himself. In the third year he had bowed to the inevitable and invited the priests back, turning a blind eye to his own Edicts and to the treason and rebellion the priests had advocated.

There's no escape from that reality, Toranaga thought. None. I don't believe what the Anjin-san says—that trade is as essential to barbarians as it is to us, that their greed will make them trade, no matter what we do to the priests. The risk is too great to experiment and there's no time and I don't have the power. We experimented once and failed. Who knows? Perhaps the priests could wait us out ten years; they're ruthless enough. If the priests order no trade, I believe there will be no trade. We could not wait ten years. Even five years. And if we expel all barbarians it must take twenty years for the English barbarian to fill up the gap, if the Anjin-san is telling the whole truth and if—and it is an immense if—if the Chinese would agree to trade with them against the Southern Barbarians. I don't believe the Chinese will change their pattern. *They never have.* Twenty years is too long. Ten years is too long.

There's no escape from that reality. Or the worst reality of all, the specter that secretly petrified Goroda and the Taikō and is now rearing its foul head again: that the fanatical, fearless Christian priests, if pushed too far, will put all their influence and their trading power and sea power behind one of the great Christian *daimyos.* Further, they would engineer an invasion force of iron-clad, equally fanatic conquistadores armed with the latest muskets to support this one Christian *daimyo—like they almost did the last time.* By themselves, any number of invading barbarians and their priests are no threat against our overwhelming joint forces. We smashed the hordes of Kublai Khan and we can deal with any invader. But allied to one of our own, a great Christian *daimyo* with armies of samurai, and given civil wars throughout the realm, this could, ultimately, give this one *daimyo* absolute power over all of us.

Kiyama or Onoshi? It's obvious now, that has to be the priest's scheme. The timing's perfect. But which *daimyo?*

Both, initially, helped by Harima of Nagasaki. But who'll carry the final banner? Kiyama—because Onoshi the leper's not long for this earth and Onoshi's obvious reward for supporting his hated enemy and rival, Kiyama, would be a guaranteed, painless, everlasting life in the Christian heaven with a permanent seat at the right hand of the Christian God.

They've four hundred thousand samurai between them now. Their base is Kyushu and that island's safe from my grasp. Together those two could easily subjugate the whole island, then they have limitless troops, limitless food, all the ships necessary for an invasion, all the silk, and Nagasaki. Throughout the land there are perhaps another five or six hundred thousand Christians. Of these, more than half—the Jesuit Christian converts—are samurai, all salted nicely among the forces of all *daimyos,* a vast pool of potential traitors, spies, or assassins—*should the priests order it.* And why shouldn't they? They'd get what they want above life itself: absolute power over all our souls, thus over the soul of this Land of the Gods—to inherit our earth and all that it contains—just as the Anjin-san has explained has already happened fifty times in this New World of theirs. . . . They convert a king, then use him against his own kind, until all the land is swallowed up.

It's so easy for them to conquer us, this tiny band of barbarian priests. How many are there in all Japan? Fifty or sixty? But they've the power. And they *believe.* They're prepared to die gladly for their beliefs, with pride and with bravery, with the name of their God on their lips. We saw that at Nagasaki when the Taikō's experiment proved a disastrous mistake. Not one of the priests recanted, tens of thousands witnessed the burnings, tens of thousands were converted, and this "martyrdom" gave the Christian religion immense prestige that Christian priests have fed on ever since.

For me, the priests have failed, but that won't deter them from their relentless course. That's reality, too.

So, it's Kiyama.

Is the plan already settled, with Ishido a dupe and the Lady Ochiba and Yaemon also? Has Harima already thrown in with them secretly? Should I launch the Anjin-san at the Black Ship and Nagasaki immediately?

What shall I do?

Nothing more than usual. Be patient, seek harmony, put aside all worries about I or Thou, Life or Death, Oblivion or Afterlife, Now or Then, and set a new plan into motion. What plan, he wanted to shout in desperation. There isn't one!

"It saddens me that those two stay with the real enemy."

"I swear we tried, Sire." Alvito watched him compassionately, seeing the heaviness of his spirit.

"Yes. I believe that. I believe you and the Father-Visitor kept your solemn promise, so I will keep mine. You may begin to build your temple at Yedo at once. The land has been set aside. I cannot forbid the priests, the other Hairies, entrance to the Empire, but at least I can make them unwelcome in my domain. The new barbarians will be equally unwelcome, if they ever arrive. As to the Anjin-san . . ." Toranaga shrugged. "But how long all this . . . well, that's *karma, neh?*"

Alvito was thanking God fervently for His mercy and favor at the unexpected reprieve. "Thank you, Sire," he said, hardly able to talk. "I know you'll not regret it. I pray that your enemies will be scattered like chaff and that you may reap the rewards of Heaven."

"I'm sorry for my harsh words. They were spoken in anger. There's so much. . . ." Toranaga got up ponderously. "You have my permission to say your service tomorrow, old friend."

"Thank you, Sire,"Alvito said, bowing low, pitying the normally majestic man. "Thank you with all my heart. May the Divinity bless you and take you into His keeping."

Toranaga trudged into the inn, his guards following. "Naga-san!"

"Yes, Father," the youth said, hurrying up.

"Where's the Lady Mariko?"

"There, Sire, with Buntaro-san." Naga pointed to the small, lantern-lit cha house inside its enclosure in the garden, the shadowed figures within. "Shall I interrupt the *cha-no-yu?*" A *cha-no-yu* was a formal, extremely ritualized Tea Ceremony.

"No. That must never be interfered with. Where are Omi and Yabu-san?"

"They're at their inn, Sire." Naga indicated the sprawling low building on the other side of the river, near the far bank.

"Who chose that one?"

"I did, Sire. Please excuse me, you asked me to find them an inn on the other side of the bridge. Did I misunderstand you?"

"The Anjin-san?"

"He's in his room, Sire. He's waiting in case you want him."

Again Toranaga shook his head. "I'll see him tomorrow." After a pause, he said in the same faraway voice, "I'm going to take a bath now. Then I don't wish to be disturbed till dawn except . . ."

Naga waited uneasily, watching his father stare sightlessly into space, greatly disconcerted by his manner. "Are you all right, Father?"

"What? Oh, yes—yes, I'm all right. Why?"

"Nothing—please excuse me. Do you still want to hunt at dawn?"

"Hunt? Ah yes, that's a good idea. Thank you for suggesting it, yes, that would be very good. See to it. Well, good night . . . Oh yes, the Tsukku-san has my permission to give a private service tomorrow. All Christians may go. You go also."

"Sire?"

"On the first day of the New Year you will become a Christian."

"Me!"

"Yes. Of your own free will. Tell Tsukku-san privately."

"Sire?"

Toranaga wheeled on him. "Are you deaf? Don't you understand the simplest thing anymore?"

"Please excuse me. Yes, Father. I understand."

"Good." Toranaga fell back into his distracted attitude, then wandered off, his personal bodyguard in tow. All samurai bowed stiffly, but he took no notice of them.

An officer came up to Naga, equally apprehensive. "What's the matter with our Lord?"

"I don't know, Yoshinaka-san." Naga looked back at the clearing. Alvito was just leaving, heading toward the bridge, a single samurai escorting him. "Must be something to do with *him.*"

"I've never seen Lord Toranaga walk so heavily. Never. They say—they say that barbarian priest's a magician, a wizard. He must be to speak our tongue so well, *neh?* Could he have put a spell on our Lord?"

"No. Never. Not my father."

"Barbarians make my spine shake too, Naga-san. Did you hear about the row—Tsukku-san and his band shouting and quarreling like ill-mannered *eta?*"

"Yes. Disgusting. I'm sure that man must have destroyed my father's harmony."

"If you ask me, an arrow in that priest's throat would save our Master a lot of trouble."

"Yes."

"Perhaps we should tell Buntaro-san about Lord Toranaga? He's our senior officer."

"I agree—but later. My father said clearly I was not to interrupt the *cha-no-yu.* I'll wait till he's finished."

In the peace and quiet of the little house, Buntaro fastidiously opened the small earthenware tea caddy of the T'ang Dynasty and, with equal care, took up the bamboo spoon, beginning the final part of the ceremony. Deftly he spooned up exactly the right amount of green powder and put it into the handleless porcelain cup. An ancient cast-iron kettle was singing over the charcoal. With the same tranquil grace Buntaro poured the bubbling water into the cup, replaced the kettle on its tripod, then gently beat the powder and water with the bamboo whisk to blend it perfectly.

He added a spoonful of cool water, bowed to Mariko, who knelt opposite him, and offered the cup. She bowed and took it with equal refinement, admiring the green liquid, and sipped three times, rested, then sipped again, finishing it. She offered the cup back. He repeated the symmetry of the formal cha-making and again offered it. She begged him to taste the cha himself, as was expected of her.

He sipped, and then again, and finished it. Then he made a third cup and a fourth. More was politely refused.

With great care, ritually he washed and dried the cup, using the peerless cotton cloth, and laid both in their places. He bowed to her and she to him. The *cha-no-yu* was finished.

Buntaro was content that he had done his best and that now, at least for the moment, there was peace between them. This afternoon there had been none.

He had met her palanquin. At once, as always, he had felt coarse and uncouth in contrast to her fragile perfection—like one of the wild, despised, barbaric Hairy Ainu tribesmen that once inhabited the land but were now driven to the far north, across the straits, to the unexplored island of Hokkaido. All of his well-thought-out words, had left him and he clumsily invited her to the *cha-no-yu,* adding, "It's years since we . . . I've never given one for you but tonight will be convenient." Then he had blurted out, never meaning to say it, knowing that it was stupid, inelegant, and a vast mistake, "Lord Toranaga said it was time for us to talk."

"But you do not, Sire?"

In spite of his resolve he flushed and his voice rasped, "I'd like harmony between us, yes, and more. I've never changed, *neh?"*

"Of course, Sire, and why should you? If there's any fault it's not your place to change but mine. If any fault exists, it's because of me, please excuse me."

"I'll excuse you," he said, towering over her there beside the palanquin, deeply conscious that others were watching, the Anjin-san and Omi among them. She was so lovely and tiny and unique, her hair piled high, her lowered eyes seemingly so demure, yet for him filled now with that same black ice that always sent him into a blind, impotent frenzy, making him want to kill and shout and mutilate and smash and behave the way a samurai never should behave.

"I've reserved the cha house for tonight," he told her. "For tonight, after the evening meal. We're ordered to eat the evening meal with Lord Toranaga. I would be honored if you would be my guest afterwards."

"It's I who am honored." She bowed and waited with the same lowered eyes and he wanted to smash her to death into the ground, then go off and plunge his knife crisscross into his belly and let the eternal pain cleanse the torment from his soul.

He saw her look up at him discerningly.

"Was there anything else, Sire?" she asked, so softly.

The sweat was running down his back and thighs, staining his kimono, his chest hurting like his head. "You're—you're staying at the inn tonight." Then he had left her and made careful dispositions for the whole baggage train. As soon as he could, he had handed his duties over to Naga and strode off with a pretended truculence down the river bank, and when he was alone, he had plunged naked into the torrent, careless of his safety, and fought the river until his head had cleared and the pounding ache had gone.

He had lain on the bank collecting himself. Now that she had accepted he had to begin. There was little time. He summoned his strength and walked back to the rough garden gate that was within the mother garden and stood there for a moment rethinking his plan. Tonight he wanted everything to be perfect. Obviously the hut was imperfect, like its garden—an uncouth provincial attempt at a real cha house. Never mind, he thought, now completely absorbed in his task, it will have to do. Night will hide many faults and lights will have to create the form it lacks.

Servants had already brought the things he had ordered earlier—tatamis, pottery oil lamps, and cleaning utensils—the very best in Yokosé, everything brand-new but modest, discreet and unpretentious.

He stripped off his kimono, laid down his swords, and began to clean. First the tiny reception room and kitchen and veranda. Then the winding path and the flagstones that were let into the moss, and finally the rocks and skirting garden. He scrubbed and broomed and brushed until everything was spotless, letting himself swoop into the humility of manual labor that was the beginning of the *cha-no-yu,* where the host alone was required to make everything faultless. The first perfection was absolute cleanliness.

By dusk he had finished most of the preparations. Then he had bathed meticulously, endured the evening meal, and the singing. As soon as he could he had changed again into more somber clothes and hurried back to the garden. He latched the gate. First he put the taper to the oil lamps. Then, carefully, he sprinkled water on the flagstones and the trees that were now splashed here and there with flickering light, until the tiny garden was a fairyland of dewdrops dancing in the warmth of the summer's breeze. He repositioned some of the lanterns. Finally satisfied, he unlatched the gate and went to the vestibule. The carefully selected pieces of charcoal that had been placed punctiliously in a pyramid on white sand were burning correctly. The flowers seemed correct in the *takonama.* Once more he cleaned the already impeccable utensils. The kettle began to sing and he was pleased with the sound that was enriched by the little pieces of iron he had placed so diligently in the bottom.

All was ready. The first perfection of the *cha-no-yu* was cleanliness, the second, complete simplicity. The last and greatest, suitability to the particular guest or guests.

He heard her footsteps on the flagstones, the sound of her dipping her hands ritually in the cistern of fresh river water and drying them. Three soft steps up to the veranda. Two more to the curtained doorway. Even she had to bend to come through the tiny door that was made deliberately small to humble everyone. At a *cha-no-yu* all were equal, host and guest, the most high *daimyo* and merest samurai. Even a peasant if he was invited.

First she studied her husband's flower arrangement. He had chosen the blossom of a single white wild rose and put a single pearl of water on the green leaf, and set it on red stones. Autumn is coming, he was suggesting with the flower, talking through the flower, do not weep for the time of fall, the time of dying when the earth begins to sleep; enjoy the time of beginning again and experience the glorious cool of the autumn air on this summer evening . . . soon the tear will vanish and the rose, only the stones will remain—soon you and I will vanish and only the stones will remain.

He watched her, apart from himself, now deep in the near trance that a cha-master sometimes was fortunate enough to experience, completely in harmony with his surroundings. She bowed to the flower in homage and came and knelt opposite him. Her kimono was dark brown, a thread of burnt gold at the seams enhancing the white column of her throat and face; her obi the darkest of greens that matched the underkimono; her hair simple and upswept and unadorned.

"You are welcome," he said with a bow, beginning the ritual.

"It is my honor," she replied, accepting her role.

He served the tiny repast on a blemishless lacquered tray, the chopsticks placed just so, the slivers of fish on rice that he had prepared a part of the pattern, and to complete the effect, a few wild flowers that he had found near the river bank scattered in perfect disarray. When she had finished eating and he, in his turn, had finished eating, he lifted the tray, every movement formalized—to be observed and judged and recorded—and took it through the low doorway into the kitchen.

Then alone, at rest, Mariko watched the fire critically, the coals a glowing mountain on a sea of stark white sand below the tripod, her ears listening to the hissing sound of the fire melding with the sighing of the barely simmering kettle above, and, from the unseen kitchen, the sibilance of cloth on porcelain and water cleaning the already clean. In time her eyes wandered to the raw twisted rafters and to the bamboos and the reeds that formed the thatch. The shadows cast by the few lamps he had placed seemingly at random made the small large and the insignificant rare, and the whole a perfect harmony. After she had seen everything and measured her soul against it, she went again into the garden, to the shallow basin that, over eons, nature had formed in the rock. Once more she purified her hands and mouth with the cool, fresh water, drying them on a new towel.

When she had settled back into her place he said, "Perhaps now you would take cha?"

"It would be my honor. But please do not put yourself to so much trouble on my account."

"It is my honor. You are my guest."

So he had served her. And now there was the ending.

In the silence, Mariko did not move for a moment, but stayed in her tranquillity, not wishing yet to acknowledge the ending or disturb the peace surrounding her. But she felt the growing strength of his eyes. The *cha-no-yu* was ended. Now life must begin again.

"You did it perfectly," she whispered, her sadness overwhelming her. A tear slid from her eyes and the falling ripped the heart from his chest.

"No—no. Please excuse me . . . you are perfect . . . it was ordinary," he said, startled by such unexpected praise.

"It was the best I've ever seen," she said, moved by the stark honesty in his voice.

"No. No, please excuse me, if it was fair it was because of you, Mariko-san. It was only fair—you made it better."

"For me it was flawless. Everything. How sad that others, more worthy than I, couldn't have witnessed it also!" Her eyes glistened in the flickering light.

"You witnessed it. That is everything. It was only for you. Others wouldn't have understood."

She felt the hot tears now on her cheeks. Normally she would have been ashamed of them but now they did not trouble her. "Thank you, how can I thank you?"

He picked up a sprig of wild thyme and, his fingers trembling, leaned over and gently caught one of her tears. Silently he looked down at the tear and the branchlet dwarfed by his huge fist. "My work—any work—is inadequate against the beauty of this. Thank you."

He watched the tear on the leaf. A piece of charcoal fell down the mountain and, without thinking, he picked up the tongs and replaced it. A few sparks danced into the air from the mountaintop and it became an erupting volcano.

Both drifted into a sweet melancholia, joined by the simplicity of the single tear, content together in the quiet, joined in humility, knowing that what had been given had been returned in purity.

Later he said, "If our duty did not forbid it, I would ask you to join me in death. Now."

"I would go with you. Gladly," she answered at once. "Let us go to death. Now."

"We can't. Our duty is to Lord Toranaga."

She took out the stiletto that was in her obi and reverently placed it on the tatami. "Then please allow me to prepare the way."

"No. That would be failing in our duty."

"What is to be, will be. You and I cannot turn the scale."

"Yes. But we may not go before our Master. Neither you nor I. He needs every trustworthy vassal for a little longer. Please excuse me, I must forbid it."

"I would be pleased to go tonight. I'm prepared. More than that, I totally desire to go beyond. Yes. My soul is brimming with joy." A hesitant smile. "Please excuse me for being selfish. You're perfectly right about our duty."

The razor-sharp blade glistened in the candlelight. They watched it, lost in contemplation. Then he broke the spell.

"Why Osaka, Mariko-san?"

"There are things to be done there which only I can do."

His frown deepened as he watched the light from a guttering wick catch the tear and become refracted into a billion colors.

"What things?"

"Things that concern the future of our house which must be done by me."

"In that case you must go." He looked at her searchingly. "But you alone?"

"Yes. I wish to make sure all family arrangements are perfect between us and Lord Kiyama for Saruji's marriage. Money and dowry and lands and so on. There's his increased fief to formalize. Lord Hiro-matsu and Lord Toranaga require it done. I am responsible for the house."

"Yes," he said slowly, "that's your duty." His eyes held hers. "If Lord Toranaga says you can go, then go, but it's not likely you'll be permitted there. Even so . . . you must return quickly. Very quickly. It would be unwise to stay in Osaka a moment longer than necessary."

"Yes."

"By sea would be quicker than by road. But you've always hated the sea."

"I still hate the sea."

"Do you have to be there quickly?"

"I don't think half a month or a month would matter. Perhaps, I don't know. I just feel I should go at once."

"Then we will leave the time and the matter of the going to Lord Toranaga—if he permits you to go at all. With Lord Zataki here, and the two scrolls, that can only mean war. It will be too dangerous to go."

"Yes. Thank you."

Glad that that was now finished, he looked around the little room contentedly, unconcerned now that his ugly bulk dominated the space, each of his thighs broader than her waist, his arms thicker than her neck. "This has been a fine room, better than I'd dared to hope. I've enjoyed being here. I'm reminded again that a body's nothing but a hut in the wilderness. Thank you for being here. I'm so glad you came to Yokosé, Mariko-san. If it hadn't been for you I would never have given a *cha-no-yu* here and never felt so one with eternity."

She hesitated, then shyly picked up the T'ang cha caddy. It was a simple, covered jar without adornment. The orange-brown glaze had run just short, leaving an uneven rim of bare porcelain at the bottom, dramatizing the spontaneity of the potter and his unwillingness to disguise the simplicity of his materials. Buntaro had bought it from Sen-Nakada, the most famous cha-master who had ever lived, for twenty thousand koku. "It's so beautiful," she murmured, enjoying the touch of it. "So perfect for the ceremony."

"Yes."

"You were truly a master tonight, Buntaro-san. You gave me so much happiness." Her voice was low and intent and she leaned forward a little. "Everything was perfect for me, the garden and how you used artistry to overcome the flaws with light and shadow. And this"—again she touched the cha caddy. "Everything perfect, even the character you'd written on the towel, *ai*—affection. For me tonight, affection was the perfect word." Again tears spilled down her cheeks. "Please excuse me," she said, brushing them away.

He bowed, embarrassed by such praise. To hide it he began to wrap the caddy in its silken sheaths. When he had finished, he set it into its box and placed it carefully in front of her. "Mariko-san, if our house has money problems, take this. Sell it."

"Never!" It was the only possession, apart from his swords and longbow, that he prized in life. "That would be the last thing I would ever sell."

"Please excuse me, but if pay for my vassals is a problem, take it."

"There's enough for all of them, with care. And the best weapons and the best horses. In that, our house is strong. No, Buntaro-san, the T'ang is yours."

"We've not much time left to us. Who should I will it to? Saruji?"

She looked at the coals and the fire consuming the volcano, humbling it. "No. Not until he's a worthy cha-master, equaling his father. I counsel you to leave the T'ang to Lord Toranaga, who's worthy of it, and ask him before he dies to judge if our son will ever merit receiving it."

"And if Lord Toranaga loses and dies before winter, as I'm certain he'll lose?"

"What?"

"Here in this privacy I can tell you quietly that truth, without pretense. Isn't an important part of the *cha-no-yu* to be without pretense? Yes, he will lose, unless he gets Kiyama and Onoshi—*and* Zataki."

"In that case, set down in your will that the T'ang should be sent with a cortege to His Imperial Highness, petition him to accept it. Certainly the T'ang merits divinity."

"Yes. That would be the perfect choice." He studied the knife then added gloomily, "Ah, Mariko-san, there's nothing to be done for Lord Toranaga. His *karma*'s written. He wins or he loses. And if he wins or loses there'll be a great killing."

"Yes."

Brooding, he took his eyes off her knife and contemplated the wild thyme sprig, the tear still pure. Later he said, "If he loses, before I die—or if I'm dead—I or one of my men will kill the Anjin-san."

Her face was ethereal against the darkness. The soft breeze moved threads of her hair, making her seem even more statuelike. "Please excuse me, may I ask why?"

"He's too dangerous to leave alive. His knowledge, his ideas that I've heard even fifth hand . . . he'll infect the realm, even Lord Yaemon. Lord Toranaga's already under his spell, *neh?*"

"Lord Toranaga enjoys his knowledge," Mariko said.

"The moment Lord Toranaga dies, that also is the Anjin-san's death order. But I hope our Lord's eyes are opened before that time." The guttering lamp spluttered and went out. He glanced up at her. "Are you under his spell?"

"He's a fascinating man. But his mind's so different from ours . . . his values . . . yes, so different in so many ways that it's almost impossible to understand him at times. Once I tried to explain a *cha-no-yu* to him, but it was beyond him."

"It must be terrible to be born barbarian—terrible," Buntaro said.

"Yes."

His eyes dropped to the blade of her stiletto. "Some people think the Anjin-san was Japanese in a previous life. He's not like other barbarians and he . . . he tries hard to speak and act like one of us though he fails, *neh?*"

"I wish you'd seen him almost commit seppuku Buntaro-san. I . . . it was extraordinary. I saw death visit him, to be turned away by Omi's hand. If he was Japanese previously, I think that would explain many things. Lord Toranaga thinks he's very valuable to us now."

"It's time you stopped training him and became Japanese again."

"Sire?"

"I think Lord Toranaga's under his spell. And you."

"Please excuse me, but I don't think I am."

"That other night in Anjiro, the one that went bad, on that night I felt you were with him, against me. Of course it was an evil thought, but I felt it."

Her gaze left the blade. She looked at him steadily and did not reply. Another lamp spluttered briefly and went out. Now only one light remained in the room.

"Yes, I hated him that night," Buntaro continued in the same calm voice, "and wanted him dead—and you and Fujiko-san. My bow whispered to me, like it does sometimes, asking for a killing. And when, the next dawn, I saw him coming down the hill with those cowardly little pistols in his hands, my arrows begged to drink his blood. But I put his killing off and humbled myself, hating my bad manners more than him, shamed by my bad manners and the saké." His tiredness showed now. "So many shames to bear, you and I. *Neh?*"

"Yes."

"You don't want me to kill him?"

"You must do what you know to be your duty," she said. "As I will always do mine."

"We stay at the inn tonight," he said.

"Yes."

And then, because she had been a perfect guest and the *cha-no-yu* the best he had ever achieved, he changed his mind and gave her back time and peace in equal measure that he had received from her. "Go to the inn. Sleep." he said. His hand picked up the stiletto and offered it. "When the maples are bare of leaves—or when you return from Osaka—we will begin again. As husband and wife."

"Yes. Thank you."

"Do you agree freely, Mariko-san?"

"Yes. Thank you."

"Before your God?"

"Yes. Before God."

Mariko bowed and accepted the knife, replaced it in its hiding place, bowed again and left.

Her footsteps died away. Buntaro looked down at the branchlet still in his fist, the tear still trapped in a tiny leaf. His fingers trembled as they gently laid the sprig on the last of the coals. The pure green leaves began to twist and char. The tear vanished with a hiss.

Then, in silence, he began to weep with rage, suddenly sure in his innermost being that she had betrayed him with the Anjin-san.

Blackthorne saw her come out of the garden and walk across the well-lit courtyard. He caught his breath at the whiteness of her beauty. Dawn was creeping into the eastern sky.

"Hello, Mariko-san."

"Oh—hello Anjin-san! You—so sorry, you startled me—I didn't see you there. You're up late."

"No. *Gomen nasai,* I'm on time." He smiled and motioned to the morning that was not far off. "It's a habit I picked up at sea, to wake just before dawn, in good time to go aloft to get ready to shoot the sun." His smile deepened. "It's you who're up late!"

"I didn't realize that it was . . . that night was gone." Samurai were posted at the gates and all doorways, watching curiously, Naga among them. Her voice became almost imperceptible as she switched to Latin. "Guard thine eyes, I beg thee. Even the darkness of night contains harbingers of doom."

"I beg forgiveness."

They glanced away as horses clattered up to the main gate. Falconers and the hunting party and guards. Dispiritedly Toranaga came from within.

"Everything's ready, Sire," Naga said. "May I come with you?"

"No, no, thank you. You get some rest. Mariko-san, how was the *cha-no-yu?*"

"Most beautiful, Sire. Most very beautiful."

"Buntaro-san's a master. You're fortunate."

"Yes, Sire."

"Anjin-san! Would you like to go hunting? I'd like to learn how you fly a falcon."

"Sire?"

Mariko translated at once.

"Yes, thank you," Blackthorne said.

"Good." Toranaga waved him to a horse. "You come with me."

"Yes, Sire."

Mariko watched them leave. When they had trotted up the path, she went to her room. Her maid helped her undress, remove her makeup, and take down her hair. Then she told the maid to stay in the room, that she was not to be disturbed until noon.

"Yes, mistress."

Mariko lay down and closed her eyes and allowed her body to fall into the exquisite softness of the down quilts. She was exhausted and elated. The *cha-no-yu* had pushed her to a strange height of peacefulness, cleansing her, and from there, the sublime, joy-filled decision to go into death had sent her to a further pinnacle never attained before. Returning from the summit into life once more had left her with an eerie, unbelievable awareness of the beauty of being alive. She had seemed to be outside herself as she answered Buntaro patiently, sure her answers and her performance had been equally perfect. She curled up in the bed, so glad that peace existed now . . . until the leaves fell.

Oh, Madonna, she prayed fervently, I thank thee for thy mercy in granting me my glorious reprieve. I thank thee and worship thee with all my heart and with all my soul and for all eternity.

She repeated an Ave Maria in humility and then, asking forgiveness, in accordance to her custom and in obedience to her liege lord, for another day she put her God into a compartment of her mind.

What would I have done, she mused just before sleep took her, if Buntaro had asked to share my bed?

I would have refused.

And then, if he had insisted, as is his right?

I would have kept my promise to him. Oh, yes. Nothing's changed.

CHAPTER 44

A T the Hour of the Goat the cortege crossed the bridge again. Everything was as before, except that now Zataki and his men were lightly dressed for traveling—or skirmishing. They were all heavily armed and, though very well disciplined, all were spoiling for the death fight, if it came. They seated themselves neatly opposite Toranaga's forces, which heavily outnumbered them. Father Alvito was to one side among the onlookers. And Blackthorne.

Toranaga welcomed Zataki with the same calm formality, prolonging the ceremonious seating. Today the two *daimyos* were alone on the dais, the cushions farther apart under a lower sky. Yabu, Omi, Naga, and Buntaro were on the earth surrounding Toranaga and four of Zataki's fighting counselors spaced themselves behind him.

At the correct time, Zataki took out the second scroll. "I've come for your formal answer."

"I agree to go to Osaka and to submit to the will of the Council," replied Toranaga evenly, and bowed.

"You're going to submit?" Zataki began, his face twisting with disbelief. "You, Toranaga-noh-Minowara, you're going—"

"Listen," Toranaga interrupted in his resonant commanding voice that richocheted around the clearing without seeming to be loud. "The Council of Regents should be obeyed! Even though it's illegal, it *is* constituted and no single *daimyo* has the right to tear the realm apart, however much truth is on his side. The realm takes precedence. If one *daimyo* revolts, it is the duty of all to stamp him out. I swore to the Taikō I'd never be the first to break the peace, and I won't, even though evil is in the land. *I accept the invitation. I will leave today.*"

Aghast, each samurai was trying to foretell what this unbelievable about-face would mean. All were achingly certain that most, if not all, would be forced to become *ronin,* with all that that implied—loss of honor, of revenue, of family, of future.

Buntaro knew that he would accompany Toranaga on his last journey and share his fate—death with all his family, of all generations. Ishido was too much his own personal enemy to forgive, and anyway, who would want to stay alive when his own lord gave up the true fight in such cowardly fashion. *Karma,* Buntaro thought bitterly. Buddha give me strength! Now I'm committed to take Mariko's life and our son's life before I take my own. When? When my duty's done and our lord is safely and honorably gone into the Void. He will need a faithful second, *neh?* All gone, like autumn leaves, all the future and the present, Crimson Sky and destiny. It's just as well, *neh?* Now Lord Yaemon will surely inherit. Lord Toranaga must be secretly tempted in his most private heart to take power, however much he denies it. Perhaps the Taikō will live again through his son and, in time, we'll war on China again and win this time, to stand at the summit of the world as is our divine duty. Yes, the Lady Ochiba and Yaemon won't sell us out next time as Ishido and his cowardly supporters did the last. . . .

Naga was bewildered. No Crimson Sky? No honorable war? No fighting to the death in the Shinano mountains or on the Kyoto plains? No honorable death

518

in battle heroically defending the standard of his father, no mounds of enemy dead to straddle in a last glorious stand, or in a divine victory? No charge even with the filthy guns? None of that—just a seppuku, probably hurried, without pomp or ceremony or honor and his head stuck on a spike for common people to jeer at. Just a death and the end of the Yoshi line. For of course every one of them would die, his father, all his brothers and sisters and cousins, nephews and nieces and aunts and uncles. His eyes focused on Zataki. Blood lust began to flood his brain. . . .

Omi was watching Toranaga with half-seeing eyes, hatred devouring him. Our Master's gone mad, he thought. How can he be so stupid? We've a hundred thousand men and the Musket Regiment and fifty thousand more around Osaka! Crimson Sky's a million times better than a lonely stinking grave!

His hand was heavy on his sword hilt and, for an ecstatic moment, he imagined himself leaping forward to decapitate Toranaga, to hand the head to the Regent Zataki and so end the contemptuous charade. Then to die by his own hand with honor, here, before everyone. For what was the point of living now? Now Kiku was beyond his reach, her contract bought and owned by Toranaga who had betrayed them all. Last night his body had been on fire during her singing and he knew her song had been secretly for him, and him alone. Unrequited fire—him and her. Wait—why not a suicide together? To die beautifully together, to be together for all eternity. Oh, how wonderful that would be! To mix our souls in death as a never-ending witness to our adoration of life. But first the traitor Toranaga, *neh?*

With an effort Omi dragged himself back from the brink.

Everything's gone wrong, he thought. No peace in my house, always anger and quarreling, and Midori always in tears. No nearer my revenge on Yabu. No private, secret arrangement with Zataki, with or without Yabu, negotiated over the hours last night. No deal of any kind. Nothing right anymore. Even when Mura found the swords, both were so mutilated by the earth's force that I know Toranaga hated me for showing them to him. And now finally this—this cowardly, traitorous surrender!

It's almost as though I'm bedeviled—in an evil spell. Cast by the Anjin-san? Perhaps. But everything's still lost. No swords and no revenge and no secret escape route and no Kiku and no future. Wait. There's a future with her. Death's a future and past and present and it'll be so clean and simple. . . .

"You're giving up? We're not going to war?" Yabu bellowed, aware that his death and the death of his line were now guaranteed.

"I accept the Council's invitation," Toranaga replied. "As you will accept the Council's invitation!"

"I won't do—"

Omi came out of his reverie with enough presence of mind to know that he had to interrupt Yabu and protect him from the instant death that any confrontation with Toranaga would bring. But he deliberately froze his lips, shouting to himself with glee at this heaven-sent gift, and waited for Yabu's disaster to overtake him.

"You won't do what?" Toranaga asked.

Yabu's soul shrieked danger. He managed to croak, "I—I—of course your vassals will obey. Yes—if you decide—whatever you decide I—I will do."

Omi cursed and allowed the glazed expression to return, his mind still withered by Toranaga's totally unexpected capitulation.

Angrily Toranaga let Yabu stutter on, increasing the strength of the apology. Then contemptuously he cut him short. "Good." He turned back to Zataki but he did not relax his vigil. "So, Brother, you can put away the second scroll.

There's nothing more—" From the corner of his eye he saw Naga's face change and he wheeled on him. "Naga!"

The youth almost leapt out of his skin, but his hand left his sword. "Yes, Father?" he stammered.

"Go and fetch my writing materials! Now!" When Naga was well out of sword range Toranaga exhaled, relieved that he had prevented the attack on Zataki before it had begun. His eyes studied Buntaro carefully. Then Omi. And last Yabu. He thought the three of them were now sufficiently controlled not to make any foolish move that would precipitate an immediate riot and a great killing.

Once again he addressed Zataki. "I'll give you my formal written acceptance at once. This will prepare the Council for my state visit." He lowered his voice and spoke for Zataki's ears alone. "Inside Izu you're safe, Regent. Outside it you're safe. Until my mother's out of your grasp you're safe. Only until then. This meeting is over."

"Good. 'State visit'?" Zataki was openly contemptuous. "What hypocrisy! I never thought I'd see the day when Yoshi Toranaga-noh-Minowara would kowtow to General Ishido. You're just—"

"Which is more important, Brother?" Toranaga said. "The continuity of my line—or the continuity of the realm?"

Gloom hung over the valley. It was pouring now, the base of the clouds barely three hundred feet from the ground, obscuring completely the way back up the pass. The clearing and the inn's forecourt were filled with shoving, ill-tempered samurai. Horses stamped their feet irritably. Officers were shouting orders with unnecessary harshness. Frightened porters were rushing about readying the departing column. Barely an hour remained to darkness.

Toranaga had written the flowery message and signed it, sending it by messenger to Zataki, over the entreaties of Buntaro, Omi, and Yabu, in private conference. He had listened to their arguments silently.

When they had finished, he said, "I want no more talk. I've decided my path. Obey!"

He had told them he was returning to Anjiro immediately to collect the rest of his men. Tomorrow he would head up the east coast road toward Atami and Odawara, thence over the mountain passes to Yedo. Buntaro would command his escort. Tomorrow the Musket Regiment was to embark on the galleys at Anjiro and put to sea to await him at Yedo, Yabu in command. The following day Omi was ordered to the frontier via the central road with all available Izu warriors. He was to assist Hiro-matsu, who was in overall command, and was to make sure that the enemy, Ikawa Jikkyu, did nothing to interfere with normal traffic. Omi was to base himself in Mishima for the time being, to guard that section of the Tokaidō Road, and to prepare palanquins and horses in sufficient quantity for Toranaga and the considerable entourage that was necessary to a formal state visit. "Alert all stations along the road and prepare them equally. You understand?"

"Yes, Sire."

"Make sure that everything's perfect!"

"Yes, Sire. You may rely on me." Even Omi had winced under the baleful glare.

When everything was ready for his departure, Toranaga came out from his rooms onto the veranda. Everyone bowed. Sourly he motioned them to continue and sent for the innkeeper. The man fawned as he presented the bill on his knees. Toranaga checked it item by item. The bill was very fair. He nodded and threw it at his paymaster for payment, then summoned Mariko and the Anjin-san. Mariko was given permission to go to Osaka. "But first you'll go directly from here to Mishima. Give this private dispatch to Hiro-matsu-san, then continue on to Yedo with the Anjin-san. You're responsible for him until you arrive. You'll probably go by sea to Osaka—I'll decide that later. Anjin-san! Did you get the dictionary from the priest-san?"

"Please? So sorry, I don't understand."

Mariko had translated.

"Sorry. Yes, I book got."

"When we meet in Yedo, you'll speak better Japanese than you do now. *Wakarimasu ka?*"

"*Hai. Gomen nasai.*"

Despondently Toranaga stomped out of the courtyard, a samurai holding a large umbrella for him against the rain. As one, all samurai, porters, and villagers again bowed. Toranaga paid no attention to them, just got into his roofed palanquin at the head of the column and closed the curtains.

At once, the six seminaked bearers raised the litter and started off at a loping trot, their horny bare feet splashing the puddles. Mounted escorting samurai rode ahead, and another mounted guard surrounded the palanquin. Spare porters and the baggage train followed, all hurrying, all tense and filled with dread. Omi led the van. Buntaro was to command the rearguard. Yabu and Naga had already left for the Musket Regiment that was still athwart the road in ambush to await Toranaga at the crest; it would fall in behind to form a rearguard. "Rearguard against whom?" Yabu had snarled at Omi in the few moments of privacy they had had before he galloped off.

Buntaro strode back to the high, curved gateway of the inn, careless of the downpour. "Mariko-san!"

Obediently she hurried to him, her orange oiled-paper umbrella beaten by the heavy drops. "Yes, Sire?"

His eyes raced over her under the brim of his bamboo hat, then went to Blackthorne, who watched from the veranda. "Tell him . . ." He stopped.

"Sire?"

He stared down at her. "Tell him I hold him responsible for you."

"Yes, Sire," she said. "But, please excuse me, I am responsible for me."

Buntaro turned and measured the distance to the head of the column. When he glanced back his face showed a trace of his torment. "Now there'll be no falling leaves for our eyes, *neh?*"

"That is in the hands of God, Sire."

"No, that's in Lord Toranaga's hands," he said with disdain.

She looked up at him without wavering under his stare. The rain beat down. Droplets fell from the rim of her umbrella like a curtain of tears. Mud splattered the hem of her kimono. Then he said, "*Sayonara*—until I see you at Osaka."

She was startled. "Oh, so sorry, won't I see you at Yedo? Surely you'll be there with Lord Toranaga, you'll arrive about the same time, *neh?* I'll see you then."

"Yes. But at Osaka, when we meet there or when you return from there, then we begin again. That's when I'll truly see you, *neh?*"

"Ah, I understand. So sorry."

"*Sayonara*, Mariko-san," he said.

"*Sayonara*, my Lord." Mariko bowed. He returned her obeisance peremptorily and strode through the quagmire to his horse. He swung into the saddle and galloped away without looking back.

"Go with God," she said, staring after him.

* * *

Blackthorne saw her eyes following Buntaro. He waited in the lee of the roof, the rain lessening. Soon the head of the column vanished into the clouds, then Toranaga's palanquin, and he breathed easier, still shattered by Toranaga and the whole ill-omened day.

This morning the hawking had begun so well. He had chosen a tiny, long-wing falcon, like a merlin, and flew her very successfully at a lark, the stoop and soaring chase blown southward beyond a belt of trees by the freshening wind. Leading the charge as was his privilege, he careered through the forest along a well-beaten path, itinerant peddlers and farmers scattering. But a weather-beaten oil seller with an equally threadbare horse blocked the way and cantankerously wouldn't budge. In the excitement of the chase Blackthorne had shouted at the man to move, but the peddler would not, so he cursed him roundly. The oil seller replied rudely and shouted back and then Toranaga was there and Toranaga pointed at his own bodyguard and said, "Anjin-san, give him your sword a moment," and some other words he did not understand. Blackthorne obeyed at once. Before he realized what was happening, the samurai lunged at the peddler. His blow was so savage and so perfect that the oil seller had walked on a pace before falling, divided in two at the waist.

Toranaga had pounded his pommel with momentary delight, then fell back into his melancholy as the other samurai had cheered. The bodyguard cleansed the blade carefully, using his silken sash to protect the steel. He sheathed the sword with satisfaction and returned it, saying something that Mariko explained later. "He just said, Anjin-san, that he was proud to be allowed to test such a blade. Lord Toranaga is suggesting you should nickname the sword 'Oil Seller,' because such a blow and such sharpness should be remembered with honor. Your sword has now become legend, *neh?*"

Blackthorne recalled how he had nodded, hiding his anguish. He was wearing "Oil Seller" now—Oil Seller it would be forevermore—the same sword that Toranaga had presented to him. I wish he'd never given it to me, he thought. But it wasn't all their fault, it was mine too. I shouted at the man, he was rude in return, and samurai *may not* be treated rudely. What other course was there? Blackthorne knew there was none. Even so, the killing had taken the joy out of the hunt for him, though he had to hide that carefully because Toranaga had been moody and difficult all day.

Just before noon, they had returned to Yokosé, then there was Toranaga's meeting with Zataki and then after a steaming bath and massage, suddenly Father Alvito was standing in his way like a vengeful wraith, two hostile acolytes in attendance. "Christ Jesus, get away from me!"

"There's no need to be afraid, or to blaspheme." Alvito had said.

"God curse you and all priests!" Blackthorne said, trying to get hold of himself, knowing that he was deep in enemy territory. Earlier he'd seen half a hundred Catholic samurai trickling over the bridge to the Mass that Mariko had told him was being held in the forecourt of Alvito's inn. His hand sought the hilt of his sword, but he was not wearing it with his bathrobe, or carrying it as was customary, and he cursed his stupidity, hating to be unarmed.

"May God forgive you your blasphemy, Pilot. Yes. May He forgive you and open your eyes. I bear you no malice. I came to bring you a gift. Here, here's a gift from God, Pilot."

Blackthorne took the package suspiciously. When he opened it and saw the Portuguese-Latin-Japanese dictionary/grammar, a thrill rushed through him. He leafed through a few pages. The printing was certainly the best he had ever seen, the quality and detail of the information staggering. "Yes, this is a gift from God all right, but Lord Toranaga ordered you to give it to me."

"We obey only God's orders."

"Toranaga asked you to give it to me?"

"Yes. It was his request."

"And a Toranaga 'request' isn't an order?"

"That depends, Captain-Pilot, on who you are, what you are, and how great your faith." Alvito motioned at the book. "Three of our Brethren spent twenty-seven years preparing that."

"Why are you giving it to me?"

"We were asked to."

"Why didn't you avoid Lord Toranaga's request? You're more than cunning enough to do that."

Alvito shrugged. Quickly Blackthorne flicked through all the pages, checking. Excellent paper, the printing very clear. The numbers of the pages were in sequence.

"It's complete," Alvito said, amused. "We don't deal with half books."

"This is much too valuable to give away. What do you want in return?"

"He asked us to give it to you. The Father-Visitor agreed. So you are given it. It was only printed this year, at long last. It's beautiful, isn't it? We only ask you to cherish it, to treat the book well. It's worth treating well."

"It's worth guarding with a life. This is priceless knowledge, like one of your rutters. But this is better. What do you want for it?"

"We ask nothing in return."

"I don't believe you." Blackthorne weighed it in his hand, even more suspiciously. "You must know this makes me equal to you. It gives me all your knowledge and saves us ten, maybe twenty years. With this I'll soon be speaking as well as you. Once I can do that, I can teach others. This is the key to Japan, neh? Language is the key to anywhere foreign, neh? In six months I'll be able to talk direct to Toranaga-sama."

"Yes, perhaps you will. If you have six months."

"What does that mean?"

"Nothing more than what you already know. Lord Toranaga will be dead long before six months is up."

"Why? What news did you bring him? Ever since he talked with you he's been like a bull with half its throat ripped out. What did you say, eh?"

"My message was private, from his Eminence to Lord Toranaga. I'm sorry —I'm merely a messenger. But General Ishido controls Osaka, as you surely know, and when Toranaga-sama goes to Osaka everything is finished for him. And for you."

Blackthorne felt ice in his marrow. "Why me?"

"You can't escape your fate, Pilot. You helped Toranaga against Ishido. Have you forgotten? You put your hands violently on Ishido. You led the dash out of Osaka harbor. I'm sorry, but being able to speak Japanese, or your swords and samurai status won't help you at all. Perhaps it's worse now that you're samurai. Now you'll be ordered to commit seppuku and if you refuse . . ." Alvito had added in the same gentle voice, "I told you before, they are a simple people."

"We English are simple people, too," he said, with no little bravado. "When we're dead we're dead, but before that we put our trust in God and keep our powder dry. I've a few tricks left, never fear."

"Oh, I don't fear, Pilot. I fear nothing, not you nor your heresy, nor your guns. They're all spiked—as you're spiked."

"That's karma—in the hands of God—call it what you will," Blackthorne told him, rattled. "But by the Lord God, I'll get my ship back and then, in a couple of years, I'll lead a squadron of English ships out here and blow you all to hell out of Asia."

Alvito spoke again with his vast unnerving calm. "That's in the hands of God, Pilot. But here the die is cast and nothing of what you say will happen. Nothing." Alvito had looked at him as though he were already dead. "May God have mercy on you, for as God is *my* judge, Pilot, I believe you'll never leave these islands."

Blackthorne shivered, remembering the total conviction with which Alvito had said that.

"You're cold, Anjin-san?"

Mariko was standing beside him on the veranda now, shaking out her umbrella in the dusk. "Oh, sorry, no, I'm not cold—I was just wandering." He glanced up at the pass. The whole column had vanished into the cloud bank. The rain had abated a little and had become mild and soft. Some villagers and servants splashed through the puddles, homeward bound. The forecourt was empty, the garden waterlogged. Oil lanterns were coming on throughout the village. No longer were there sentries on the gateway, or at both sides of the bridge. A great emptiness seemed to dominate the twilight.

"It's much prettier at night, isn't it?" she said.

"Yes," he replied, totally aware that they were alone together, and safe, if they were careful and if she wanted as he wanted.

A maid came and took her umbrella, bringing dry tabi socks. She knelt and began to towel Mariko's feet dry.

"Tomorrow at dawn we'll begin our journey, Anjin-san."

"How long will it take us?"

"A number of days, Anjin-san. Lord Toranaga said—"Mariko glanced off as Gyoko padded obsequiously from inside the inn. "Lord Toranaga told me there was plenty of time."

Gyoko bowed low. "Good evening, Lady Toda, please excuse me for interrupting you."

"How are you, Gyoko-san?"

"Fine, thank you, though I wish this rain would stop. I don't like this mugginess. But then, when the rains stop, we have the heat and that's so much worse, *neh?* But the autumn's not far away. . . . Ah, we're so lucky to have autumn to look forward to, and heavenly spring, *neh?*"

Mariko did not answer. The maid fastened the tabi for her and got up. "Thank you," Mariko said, dismissing her. "So, Gyoko-san? There's something I can do for you?"

"Kiku-san asked if you would like her to serve you at dinner, or to dance or sing for you tonight. Lord Toranaga left instructions for her to entertain you, if you wished."

"Yes, he told me, Gyoko-san. That would be very nice, but perhaps not tonight. We have to leave at dawn and I'm very tired. There'll be other nights, *neh?* Please give her my apologies, and, oh yes, please tell her I'm delighted to have the company of you both on the road." Toranaga had ordered Mariko to take the two women with her, and she had thanked him, pleased to have them as a formal chaperone.

"You're too kind," Gyoko said with honey on her tongue. "But it's our honor. We're still to go to Yedo?"

"Yes. Of course. Why?"

"Nothing, Lady Toda. But, in that case, perhaps we could stop in Mishima for a day or two? Kiku-san would like to gather up some clothes—she doesn't feel adequately gowned for Lord Toranaga, and I hear the Yedo summer's very sultry and mosquitoed. We should collect her wardrobe, bad as it is."

"Yes. Of course. You'll both have more than enough time."

Gyoko did not look at Blackthorne, though both were very conscious of him. "It's—it's tragic about our Master, *neh?*"

"Karma," Mariko replied evenly. Then she added with a woman's sweet viciousness, "But nothing's changed, Gyoko-san. You'll be paid the day you arrive, in silver, as the contract says."

"Oh, so sorry," the older woman told her, pretending to be shocked. "So sorry, Lady Toda, but money? That was farthest from my mind. Never! I was only concerned with our Master's future."

"He's master of his own future," Mariko said easily, believing it no more. "But your future's good, isn't it—whatever happens. You're rich now. All your worldly troubles are over. Soon you'll be a power in Yedo with your new guild of courtesans, whoever rules the Kwanto. Soon you'll be the greatest of all Mama-sans, and whatever happens, well, Kiku-san's still your protégée and her youth's not touched, neither is her *karma. Neh?*"

"My only concern is for Lord Toranaga," Gyoko answered with practiced gravity, her anus twitching at the thought of two thousand five hundred koku so nearly in her strong room. "If there is any way I could help him I would—"

"How generous of you, Gyoko-san! I'll tell him of your offer. Yes, a thousand koku off the price would help very much. I accept on his behalf."

Gyoko fluttered her fan, put a gracious smile on her face, and just managed not to wail aloud at her imbecility for jumping into a trap like a saké-besotted novice. "Oh no, Lady Toda, how could money help so generous a patron? No, clearly money's no help to him," she babbled, trying to recover. "No, money's no help. Better information or a service or—"

"Please excuse me, what information?"

"None, none at the moment. I was just using that as a figure of speech, so sorry. But money—"

"Ah, so sorry, yes. Well, I'll tell him of your offer. And of your generosity. On his behalf, thank you."

Gyoko bowed at the dismissal and scuttled back into the inn.

Mariko's little laugh trickled out.

"What are you laughing at, Mariko-san?"

She told him what had been said. "Mama-sans must be the same the world over. She's just worried about her money."

"Will Lord Toranaga pay even though . . ." Blackthorne stopped. Mariko waited guilelessly. Then, under her gaze, he continued, "Father Alvito said when Lord Toranaga goes to Osaka, he's finished."

"Oh, yes. Yes, Anjin-san, that's most very true," Mariko said with a brightness she did not feel. Then she put Toranaga and Osaka into their compartments and was tranquil again. "But Osaka's many leagues away and countless sticks of time in the future, and until that time when what is to be *is,* Ishido doesn't know, the good Father doesn't truly know, we don't know, no one knows what will truly happen. *Neh?* Except the Lord God. But He won't tell us, will He? Until perhaps it has already come to pass. *Neh?*"

"Hai!" He laughed with her. "Ah, you're so wise."

"Thank you. I have a suggestion, Anjin-san. During the journey time, let us forget all outside problems. All of them."

"Thou," he said in Latin. "It is good to see thee."

"And thee. Extraordinary care in front of both women during our journey is very necessary, *neh?*"

"Depend on it, Lady."

"I do. In truth I do very much."

"Now we are almost alone, *neh?* Thou and I."

"Yes. But what was is not and never happened."

"True. Yes. Thou art correct again. And beautiful."

A samurai strode through the gateway and saluted her. He was middle-aged with graying hair, his face pitted, and he walked with a slight limp. "Please excuse me, Lady Toda, but we'll leave at dawn, *neh?*"

"Yes, Yoshinaka-san. But it doesn't matter if we're delayed till noon, if you wish. We've plenty of time."

"Yes. As you prefer, let us leave at noon. Good evening, Anjin-san. Please allow me to introduce myself. I'm Akira Yoshinaka, captain of your escort."

"Good evening, Captain."

Yoshinaka turned back to Mariko. "I'm responsible for you and him, Lady, so please tell him I've ordered two men to sleep in his room by night as his personal guards. Then there'll be ten sentries on duty nightly. They'll be all around you. I've a hundred men in all."

"Very well, Captain. But, so sorry, it would be better not to station any men in the Anjin-san's room. It's a very serious custom of theirs to sleep alone, or alone with one lady. My maid will probably be with him, so he'll be protected. Please keep the guards around but not too close, then he won't be unsettled."

Yoshinaka scratched his head and frowned. "Very well, Lady. Yes, I'll agree to that, though my way's more sensible. Then, so sorry, then please ask him not to go on any of these night walks of his. Until we get to Yedo I'm responsible and when I'm responsible for very important persons I get very nervous." He bowed stiffly and went away.

"The Captain asks you not to walk off by yourself during our journey. If you get up at night, always take a samurai with you, Anjin-san. He says this would help him."

"All right. Yes, I'll do that." Blackthorne was watching him leave. "What else did he say? I caught something about sleeping? I couldn't understand him very—" He stopped. Kiku came from within. She wore a bathrobe with a towel decorously swathed around her hair. Barefoot, she sauntered toward the hotspring bath house, half bowed to them, and waved gaily. They returned her salutation.

Blackthorne took in her long legs and the sinuousness of her walk until she disappeared. He felt Mariko's eyes watching him closely and looked back at her. "No," he said blandly and shook his head.

She laughed. "I thought it might be difficult—might be uncomfortable for you, to have her just as a traveling companion after such a special pillowing."

"Uncomfortable, no. On the contrary, very pleasant. I've very pleasant memories. I'm glad she belongs to Lord Toranaga now. That makes everything easy, for her and for him. And everyone." He was going to add, everyone except Omi, but thought better of it. "After all, to me she was only a very special, glorious gift. Nothing more. *Neh?*"

"She was a gift, yes."

He wanted to touch Mariko. But he did not. Instead he turned and stared up at the pass, not sure what he read behind her eyes. Night obscured the pass now. And the clouds. Water dripped nicely from the roof. "What else did the Captain say?"

"Nothing of importance, Anjin-san."

CHAPTER 45

THEIR journey to Mishima took nine days, and every night, for part of the night, they were together. Secretly. Unwittingly Yoshinaka assisted them. At each inn he would naturally choose adjacent rooms for all of them. "I hope you do not object, Lady, but this will make security much easier," he would always say, and Mariko would agree and take the center room, Kiku and Gyoko to one side, Blackthorne to the other. Then, in the dark of the night she would leave her maid, Chimmoko, and go to him. With adjoining rooms, coupled with the usual chatter and night sounds and singing and carousing of other travelers with their swarms of ever-present, anxious-to-please maids, the alert outward-guarding sentries were none the wiser. Only Chimmoko was privy to the secret.

Mariko was aware that eventually Gyoko, Kiku, and all the women in their party would know. But this did not worry her. She was samurai and they were not. Her word would carry against theirs, unless she was caught blatantly, and no samurai, not even Yoshinaka, would normally dare to open her door by night, uninvited. As far as everyone was concerned Blackthorne shared his bed with Chimmoko, or one of the maids in the inn. It was no one's business but his. So only a woman could betray her, and if she was betrayed, her betrayer and all the women of the party would die an even more vulgar and more lingering death than hers for so disgusting a betrayal. Then too, if she wished, before they reached Mishima or Yedo, all knew she could have them put to death at her whim for the slightest indiscretion, real or alleged. Mariko was sure Toranaga would not object to a killing. Certainly he would applaud Gyoko's and, in her private heart, Mariko was sure he would not object even to Kiku's. Two and a half thousand koku could buy many a courtesan of the First Rank.

So she felt safe from the women. But not from Blackthorne, much as she loved him now. He was not Japanese. He had not been trained from birth to build the inner, impenetrable fences behind which to hide. His face or manner or pride would betray them. She was not afraid for herself. Only for him.

"At long last I know what love means," she murmured the first night. And because she no longer fought against love's onslaught but yielded to its irresistibility, her terror for his safety consumed her. "I love thee, so I'm afraid for thee," she whispered, holding onto him, using Latin, the language of lovers.

"I love thee. Oh, how I love thee."

"I've destroyed thee, my love, by beginning. We're doomed now. I've destroyed thee—that is the truth."

"No, Mariko, somehow something will happen to make everything right."

"I should never have begun. The fault is mine."

"Do not worry, I beg thee. *Karma* is *karma.*"

At length she pretended to be persuaded and melted into his arms. But she was sure he would be his own nemesis. For herself she was not afraid.

The nights were joyous. Tender and each one better than before. The days were easy for her, difficult for him. He was constantly on guard, determined for her sake not to make a mistake. "There will be no mistake," she said while they were riding together, safely apart from the rest, now keeping up a pretense of absolute

527

confidence after her lapse of the first night. "Thou art strong. Thou art samurai and there will be no mistake."

"And when we get to Yedo?"

"Let Yedo take care of Yedo. I love thee."

"Yes. I love thee too."

"Then why so sad?"

"Not sad, Lady. Just that silence is painful. I wish to shout my love from the mountaintops."

They delighted in their privacy and their certainty they were still safe from prying eyes.

"What will happen to them, Gyoko-san?" Kiku asked softly in their palanquin on the first day of the journey.

"Disaster, Kiku-san. There's no hope for their future. He hides it well, but she . . . ! Her adoration shouts from her face. Look at her! Like a young girl! Oh, how foolish she is!"

"But oh, how beautiful, *neh?* How lucky to be so fulfilled, *neh?*"

"Yes, but even so I wouldn't wish their deaths on anyone."

"What will Yoshinaka do when he discovers them?" Kiku asked.

"Perhaps he won't. I pray he won't. Men are such fools and so stupid. They can't see the simplest things about women, thanks be to Buddha, bless his name. Let's pray they're not discovered until we've gone about our business in Yedo. Let's pray we're not held responsible. Oh very yes! And this afternoon when we stop, let's find the nearest shrine and I'll light ten incense sticks as a god-favor. By all gods I'll even endow a temple to all gods with three koku yearly for ten years if we escape and if I get my money."

"But they're so beautiful together, *neh?* I've never seen a woman blossom so."

"Yes, but she'll wither like a broken camellia when she's accused before Buntaro-san. Their *karma* is their *karma* and there's nothing we can do about them. Or about Lord Toranaga—or even Omi-san. Don't cry, child."

"Poor Omi-san."

Omi had overtaken them on the third day. He had stayed at their inn, and after the evening meal he had spoken privately to Kiku, asking her formally to join him for all eternity.

"Willingly, Omi-san, willingly," she had answered at once, allowing herself to cry, for she liked him very much. "But my duty to Lord Toranaga who favored me, and to Gyoko-san who formed me, forbids it."

"But Lord Toranaga's forfeited his rights to you. He's surrendered. He's finished."

"But his contract isn't, Omi-san, much as I wish it. His contract's legal and binding. Please excuse me, I must refuse—"

"Don't answer now, Kiku-san. Think about it. Please, I beg you. Tomorrow give me your answer," he said and left her.

But her tearful answer had been the same. "I can't be so selfish, Omi-san. Please forgive me. My duty to Lord Toranaga and to Gyoko-san—I can't, much as I'd wish it. Please forgive me."

He had argued. More private tears flowed. They had sworn perpetual adoration and then she had sent him away with a promise: "If the contract's broken, or Lord Toranaga dies and I'm freed, then I'll do whatever you want, I'll obey whatever you order." And so he had left the inn and rode on ahead to Mishima filled with foreboding, and she had dried her tears and repaired her makeup. Gyoko complimented her. "You're so wise, child. Oh, how I wish the Lady Toda had half your wisdom."

Yoshinaka led leisurely from inn to inn along the course of the river Kano as it meandered northward to the sea, falling in with the delays that always seemed to happen, not caring about time. Toranaga had told him privately there was no need to hurry, providing he delivered his charges safely to Yedo by the new moon. "I'd prefer them there later than sooner, Yoshinaka-san. You understand?"

"Yes, Sire," he had replied. Now he blessed his guarding *kami* for giving him the respite. At Mishima with Lord Hiro-matsu—or at Yedo with Lord Toranaga—he would have to make his obligatory report, verbally and in writing. Then he would have to decide whether he should tell what he thought, not what he had been so careful not to see. Eeeeee, he told himself appalled, surely I'm mistaken. The Lady Toda? Her and any man, let alone the barbarian!

Isn't it your duty to see? he asked himself. To obtain proof. To catch them behind closed doors, bedded together. You'll be condemned yourself for collusion if you don't, *neh?* It'd be so easy, even though they're very careful.

Yes, but only a fool would bring such tidings, he thought. Isn't it better to play the dullard and pray no one betrays them and so betrays you? Her life's ended, we're all doomed, so what does it matter? Turn your eyes away. Leave them to their *karma*. What does it matter?

With all his soul, the samurai knew it mattered very much.

"Ah, good morning, Mariko-san. How beautiful the day is," Father Alvito said, walking up to them. They were outside the inn, ready to start the day's journey. He made the sign of the cross over her. "May God bless you and keep you in His hands forever."

"Thank you, Father."

"Good morning, Pilot. How are you today?"

"Good, thank you. And you?"

Their party and the Jesuits had leapfrogged each other on the march. Sometimes they had stayed at the same inn. Sometimes they journeyed together.

"Would you like me to ride with you this morning, Pilot? I'd be happy to continue the Japanese lessons, if you've a mind."

"Thank you. Yes, I'd like that."

On the first day, Alvito had offered to try to teach Blackthorne the language.

"In return for what?" Blackthorne had asked warily.

"Nothing. It would help me pass the time, and to tell you the truth, at the moment I'm saddened by life and feel old. Also perhaps to apologize for my harsh words."

"I expect no apology from you. You've your way, I've mine. We can never meet."

"Perhaps—but on our journey we could share things, *neh?* We're travelers on the same road. I'd like to help you."

"Why?"

"Knowledge belongs to God. Not to man. I'd like to help you as a gift—nothing in return."

"Thanks, but I don't trust you."

"Then, if you insist, in return tell me about your world, what you've seen and where you've been. Anything you like, but only what you like. The real truth. Truly, it would fascinate me and it would be a fair exchange. I came to Japan when I was thirteen or fourteen, and I've seen nothing of the world. We could even agree to a truce for the journey, if you wish."

"But no religion or politics and no Papist doctrines?"

"I am what I am, Pilot, but I will try."

So they began to exchange knowledge cautiously. For Blackthorne it seemed an unfair trade. Alvito's erudition was enormous, he was a masterly teacher, whereas Blackthorne thought he related only things that any pilot would know. "But that's not true," Alvito had said. "You're a unique pilot, you've done incredible things. One of half a dozen on earth, *neh?*"

Gradually a truce did happen between them and this pleased Mariko.

"This is friendship, Anjin-san, or the beginning of it," Mariko said.

"No. Not friendship. I distrust him as much as ever, as he does me. We're perpetual enemies. I've forgotten nothing, nor has he. This is a respite, temporary, probably for a special purpose he'd never tell if I were to ask. I understand him and there's no harm, so long as I don't drop my guard."

While he spent time with Alvito, she would ride lazily with Kiku and Gyoko and talk about pillowing and about ways to please men and about the Willow World. In return she told them about her world, sharing what she had witnessed or been part of or learned, about the Dictator Goroda, the Taikō, and even Lord Toranaga, judicious stories about the majestic ones that no commoner would ever know.

A few leagues south of Mishima the river curled away to the west, to fall placidly to the coast and the large port of Numazu, and they left the ravinelike country and pushed across the flat rice paddy plains along the wide busy road that headed northward. There were many streams and tributaries to ford. Some were shallow. Some were deep and very wide and they had to be poled across in flat barges. Very few were spanned. Usually they were all carried across on the shoulders of porters from the plenty that were always stationed nearby for this special purpose, chattering and bidding for that privilege.

This was the seventh day from Yokosé. The road forked and here Father Alvito said he had to leave them. He would take the west path, to return to his ship for a day or so, but he would catch them up and join them again on the road from Mishima to Yedo, if that was permitted. "Of course, you're both welcome to come with me if you wish."

"Thank you but, so sorry, there are things I must do in Mishima," Mariko said.

"Anjin-san? If Lady Mariko's going to be busy, you'd be welcome by yourself. Our cook's very good, the wine's fair. As God is my judge, you'd be safe, and free to come and go as you wish. Rodrigues is aboard."

Mariko saw that Blackthorne wanted to leave her. How can he? she asked herself with a great sadness. How can he want to leave me when time is so short? "Please go, Anjin-san," she said. "It would be nice for you—and good to see the Rodrigues, *neh?*"

But Blackthorne did not go, much as he wanted to. He didn't trust the priest. Not even for Rodrigues would he put his head in that trap. He thanked Alvito and they watched him ride away.

"Let's stop now, Anjin-san," Mariko said, even though it was barely noon. "There's no hurry, *neh?*"

"Excellent. Yes, I'd like that."

"The Father's a good man but I'm glad he's gone."

"So am I. But he's not a good man. He's a priest."

She was taken aback by his vehemence. "Oh, so sorry, Anjin-san, please excuse me for say—"

"It's not important, Mariko-chan. I told you—nothing's forgotten. He'll always be after my hide." Blackthorne went to find Captain Yoshinaka.

Troubled, she looked down the western fork.

The horses of Father Alvito's party moved through the other travelers unhurriedly. Some passersby bowed to the small cortege, some knelt in humility, many were curious, many hard-faced. But all moved politely out of the way. Except even the lowest samurai. When Father Alvito met a samurai he moved to the left or to the right and his acolytes followed him.

He was glad to be leaving Mariko and Blackthorne, glad of the break. He had urgent dispatches to send to the Father-Visitor that he had been unable to send because his carrier pigeons had been destroyed in Yokosé. There were so many problems to solve: Toranaga, Uo the fisherman, Mariko, and the pirate. And Joseph, who continued to dog his footsteps.

"What's he doing there, Captain Yoshinaka?" he had blurted out the first day, when he noticed Joseph among the guards, wearing a military kimono and, awkwardly, swords.

"Lord Toranaga ordered me to take him to Mishima, Tsukku-san. There I'm to turn him over to Lord Hiro-matsu. Oh, so sorry, does the sight of him offend you?"

"No—no," he had said unconvincingly.

"Ah, you're looking at his swords? There's no need to worry. They're only hilts, they've no blades. It's Lord Toranaga's orders. Seems as the man was ordered into your Order so young it's not clear if he should have real swords or not, much as he's entitled to wear them, much as he wants them. Seems he joined your Order as a child, Tsukku-san. Even so, of course we can't have a samurai without swords, *neh?* Uraga-noh-Tadamasa's certainly samurai though he's been a barbarian priest for twenty years. Our Master's wisely made this compromise."

"What's going to happen to him?"

"I'm to hand him over to Lord Hiro-matsu. Maybe he'll be sent back to his uncle for judgment, maybe he'll stay with us. I only obey orders, Tsukku-san."

Father Alvito went to speak with Joseph but Yoshinaka had stopped him politely. "So sorry, but my Master also ordered him kept to himself. Away from everyone. Particularly Christians. Until Lord Harima gives a judgment, my Master said. Uraga-san's Lord Harima's vassal, *neh?* Lord Harima's Christian too. *Neh?* Lord Toranaga says a Christian *daimyo* should deal with the Christian renegade. After all, Lord Harima's his uncle and leader of the house and it was he who ordered him into your keeping in the first place."

Though it was forbidden, Alvito had tried again that night to talk to Joseph privately, to beg him to withdraw his sacrilege and kneel in penance to the Father-Visitor, but the youth had coldly walked away, without listening, and after that, Joseph was always sent far ahead.

Somehow, Holy Madonna, we've got to bring him back to the mercy of God, Alvito thought in anguish. What can I do? Perhaps the Father-Visitor will know how to handle Joseph. Yes, and he'll know what to do about Toranaga's incredible decision to submit, which in their secret conferences they had discarded as an impossibility. "No—that's totally against Toranaga's character," dell'Aqua had said. "He'll go to war. When the rains cease, perhaps before, if he can get Zataki to recant and betray Ishido. My forecast is he'll wait as long as he can and try to force Ishido to make the first move—his usual waiting game. Whatever happens, so long as Kiyama and Onoshi support Ishido and Osaka, the Kwanto will be overrun and Toranaga destroyed."

"And Kiyama and Onoshi? They'll keep their enmity buried, for the common good?"

"Yes. They're totally convinced a Toranaga victory would be the Holy Church's death knell. Now that Harima will side with Ishido, I'm afraid Toranaga's a broken dream."

Civil war again, Alvito thought. Brother against brother, father against son, village against village. Anjiro ready to revolt, armed with stolen muskets, so Uo the fisherman had whispered. And the other frightening news: a secret Musket Regiment almost ready! A modern, European-style cavalry unit of more than two thousand muskets, adapted to Japanese warfare. Oh, Madonna, protect the faithful and curse that heretic. . . .

Such a pity Blackthorne is twisted and mind-deformed. He could be such a valuable ally. I never would have thought that but it's true. He's incredibly wise in the ways of the sea and the world. Brave and cunning, honest within his heresy, straight and guileless. Never needs to be told something twice, his memory astonishing. He's taught me so much about the world. And about himself. Is that wrong, Alvito wondered sadly as he turned to wave at Mariko a last time. Is it wrong to learn about your enemy, and in return, to teach? No. Is it wrong to turn a blind eye to mortal sin?

Three days out from Yokosé, Brother Michael's observation had shattered him. "You believe they're lovers?"

"What is God but love? Isn't that the Lord Jesus' word?" Michael had replied. "I only mentioned I saw their eyes touching each other and that it was so beautiful to see. About their bodies I don't know, Father, and in truth I don't care. Their souls touch and I seem to be more aware of God because of it."

"You must be mistaken about them. She'd never do that! It's against her whole heritage, against her law and the law of God. She's a devout Christian. She knows adultery's a hideous sin."

"Yes, that is what we teach. But her marriage was Shinto, not consecrated before the Lord our God, so is it adultery?"

"Do you also question the Word? Are you infected by Joseph's heresy?"

"No, Father, please excuse me, never the Word. Only what man has made of it."

From then on he had watched more closely. Clearly the man and woman liked each other greatly. Why shouldn't they? Nothing wrong in that! Constantly thrown together, each learning from the other, the woman ordered to put away her religion, the man having none, or only a patina of the Lutheran heresy as dell'Aqua had said was true of all Englishmen. Both strong, vital people, however ill-matched.

At confession she said nothing. He did not press her. Her eyes told him nothing and everything, but never was there anything real to judge. He could hear himself explaining to dell'Aqua, 'Michael must have been mistaken, Eminence.'

'But did she commit adultery? Was there any proof?'

'Thankfully, no proof.'

Alvito reined in and turned back momentarily. He saw her standing on the slight rise, the Pilot talking to Yoshinaka, the old madam and her painted whore lying in their palanquin. He was tormented by the fanatic zeal welling up inside him. For the first time he dared to ask, Have you whored with the Pilot, Mariko-san? Has the heretic damned your soul for all eternity? You, who were chosen in life to be a nun and probably our first native abbess? Are you living in foul sin, unconfessed, desecrated, hiding your sacrilege from your confessor, and thus are you too befouled before God?

He saw her wave. This time he did not acknowledge it but turned his back, jabbed his spurs into his horse's flanks, and hurried away.

That night their sleep was disturbed.

"What is it, my love?"

"Nothing, Mariko-chan. Go back to sleep."

But she did not. Nor did he. Long before she had to, she slipped back into her own room, and he got up and sat in the courtyard studying the dictionary under candlelight until dawn. When the sun came and the day warmed, their night cares vanished and they continued their journey peacefully. Soon they reached the great trunk road, the Tokaidō, just east of Mishima, and travelers became more numerous. The vast majority were, as always, on foot, their belongings on their backs. There were a few pack horses on the road and no carriages at all.

"Oh, carriage—that's something with wheels, *neh?* They're of no use in Japan, Anjin-san. Our roads are too steep and always crisscrossed with rivers and streams. Wheels would also ruin the surface of the roads, so they are forbidden to everyone except the Emperor, and he travels only a few cermonial *ri* in Kyoto on a special road. We don't need wheels. How can you carry vehicles over a river or stream—and there are too many, far too many to bridge. There are perhaps sixty streams to cross between here and Yedo, Anjin-san. How many have we already had to cross? Dozens, *neh?* No, we all walk or ride horseback. Of course horses and palanquins particularly are allowed only for important persons, *daimyos* and samurai, and not even all samurai."

"What? Even if you can afford one you can't hire one?"

"Not unless you've the correct rank, Anjin-san. That's very wise, don't you think? Doctors and the very old can travel by horse or palanquin, or the very sick, if they get permission in writing from their liege lord. Palanquins or horses wouldn't be right for peasants and commoners, Anjin-san. That could teach them lazy habits, *neh?* It's much more healthy for them to walk."

"Also it keeps them in their place. *Neh?*"

"Oh, yes. But that all makes for peace and orderliness and *wa.* Only merchants have money to waste, and what are they but parasites who create nothing, grow nothing, make nothing but feed off another's labor? Definitely *they* should all walk, *neh?* In this we are very wise."

"I've never seen so many people on the move," Blackthorne said.

"Oh, this is nothing. Wait till we get nearer Yedo. We adore to travel, Anjin-san, but rarely alone. We like to travel in groups."

But the crowds did not inhibit their progress. The Toranaga cipher that their standards carried, Toda Mariko's personal rank, and the brusque efficiency of Akira Yoshinaka and the runners he sent ahead to proclaim who followed, ensured the best private rooms every night at the best inn, and an uninterrupted passage. All other travelers and samurai quickly stood aside and bowed very low, waiting until they had passed.

"Do they all have to stop and kneel like that to everyone?"

"Oh, no, Anjin-san. Only to *daimyos* and important persons. And to most samurai—yes, that would be a very wise practice for any commoner. It's polite to do so, Anjin-san, and necessary, *neh?* Unless the common people respect the samurai and themselves, how can the law be upheld and the realm be governed? Then too, it's the same for everyone. We stopped and bowed and allowed the Imperial messenger to pass, didn't we? Everyone must be polite, *neh?* Lesser *daimyos* have to dismount and bow to more important ones. Ritual governs our lives, but the realm is obedient."

"Say two *daimyos* are equal and they meet?"

"Then both would dismount and bow equally and go their separate ways."

"Say Lord Toranaga and General Ishido met?"

Mariko turned smoothly to Latin. "Who are they, Anjin-san? Those names I know not, not today, not between thee and me."

"Thou art correct. Please excuse me."

"Listen, my love, let us make a promise that if the Madonna smiles on us and we escape from Mishima, only at Yedo, at First Bridge, only when it is completely forced upon us let us leave our private world. Please?"

"What special danger's in Mishima?"

"There our Captain must submit a report to the Lord Hiro-matsu. There I must see him also. He is a wise man, very vigilant. It would be easy for us to be betrayed."

"We have been cautious. Let us petition God that thy fears are without merit."

"For myself I am not concerned—only for thee."

"And I for thee."

"Then do we promise, one to another, to stay within our private world?"

"Yes. Let us pretend it is the real world—our only world."

"There's Mishima, Anjin-san." Mariko pointed across the last stream.

The sprawling castle city which housed nearly sixty thousand people was mostly obscured by morning's low-lying mist. Only a few house tops and the stone castle were discernible. Beyond were mountains that ran down to the western sea. Far to the northwest was the glory of Mount Fuji. North and east the mountain range encroached on the sky. "What now?"

"Now Yoshinaka's been asked to find the liveliest inn within ten *ri*. We'll stay there two days. It will take me at least that to complete my business. Gyoko and Kiku-san will be leaving us for that time."

"Then?"

"Then we go on. What does your weather sense tell you about Mishima?"

"That it's friendly and safe," he replied. "After Mishima, what then?"

She pointed northeast, unconvinced. "Then we'll go that way. There's a pass that curls up through the mountains toward Hakoné. It's the most grueling part of the whole Tokaidō Road. After that the road falls away to the city of Odawara, which is much bigger than Mishima, Anjin-san. It's on the coast. From there to Yedo is only a matter of time."

"How much time?"

"Not enough."

"You're wrong, my love, so sorry," he said. "There's all the time in the world."

CHAPTER 46

ENERAL Toda Hiro-matsu accepted the private dispatch that Mariko offered. He broke Toranaga's seals. The scroll told briefly what had happened at Yokosé, confirmed Toranaga's decision to submit, ordered Hiro-matsu to hold the frontier and the passes to the Kwanto against *any* intruder until he arrived (but to expedite any messenger from Ishido or from the east) and gave instructions about the renegade Christian and about the Anjin-san. Wearily the old soldier read the message a second time. "Now tell me everything you saw at Yokosé, or heard, affecting Lord Toranaga."

Mariko obeyed.

"Now tell me what you think happened."

Again she obeyed.

"What occurred at the *cha-no-yu* between you and my son?"

She told him everything, exactly as it happened.

"My son said our Master would lose? *Before* the second meeting with Lord Zataki?"

"Yes, Sire."

"You're sure?"

"Oh, yes, Sire."

There was a long silence in the room high up in the castle donjon that dominated the city. Hiro-matsu got to his feet and went to the arrow embrasure in the thick stone wall, his back and joints aching, his sword loose in his hands. "I don't understand."

"Sire?"

"Neither my son, nor our Master. We can smash through any armies Ishido puts into the field. And as to the decision to submit. . . ."

She toyed with her fan, watching the evening sky, star-filled and pleasing.

Hiro-matsu studied her. "You're looking very well, Mariko-san, younger than ever. What's your secret?"

"I haven't one, Sire," she replied, her throat suddenly dry. She waited for her world to shatter but the moment passed and the old man turned his shrewd eyes back to the city below.

"Now tell me what happened since you left Osaka. Everything you saw or heard or were part of," he said.

It was far into the night by the time she had finished. She related everything clearly, except the extent of her intimacy with the Anjin-san. Even here she was careful not to hide her liking for him, her respect for his intelligence and bravery. Or Toranaga's admiration for his value.

For a while Hiro-matsu continued to wander up and down, the movement easing his pain. Everything dovetailed with Yoshinaka's report and Omi's report —and even Zataki's tirade before that *daimyo* had stormed off to Shinano. Now he understood many things that had been unclear and had enough information to make a calculated decision. Some of what she related disgusted him. Some made him hate his son even more; he could understand his son's motives, but that made no difference. The rest of what she said forced him to resent the barbarian and sometimes to admire him. "You saw him pull our Lord to safety?"

535

"Yes. Lord Toranaga would be dead now, Sire, but for him. I'm quite certain. Three times he has saved our Master: escaping from Osaka Castle, aboard the galley in Osaka harbor, and absolutely at the earthquake. I saw the swords Omi-san had dug up. They were twisted like noodle dough and just as useless."

"You think the Anjin-san really meant to commit seppuku?"

"Yes. By the Lord God of the Christians, I believe he made that commitment. Only Omi-san prevented it. And, Sire, I believe totally he's worthy to be samurai, worthy to be hatamoto."

"I didn't ask for that opinion."

"Please excuse me, Sire, truly you didn't. But that question was still in the front of your mind."

"You've become a thought reader as well as barbarian trainer?"

"Oh, no, please excuse me, Sire, of course not," she said in her nicest voice. "I merely answer the leader of my clan to the best of my very poor ability. Our Master's interests are first in my mind. Your interests are second only to his."

"Are they?"

"Please excuse me, but that shouldn't be necessary to ask. Command me, Sire. I'll do your bidding."

"Why so proud, Mariko-san?" he asked testily. "And so right? Eh?"

"Please excuse me, Sire. I was rude. I don't deserve such—"

"I know! No woman does!" Hiro-matsu laughed. "But even so, there are times when we need a woman's cold, cruel, vicious, cunning, practical wisdom. They're so much cleverer than we are, *neh?*"

"Oh, no, Sire," she said, wondering what was really in his mind.

"It's just as well we're alone. If that was repeated in public they'd say old Iron Fist's overripe, that it's time for him to put down his sword, shave his head, and begin to say prayers to Buddha for the souls of the men he's sent into the Void. And they'd be right."

"No, Sire. It's as the Lord, your son, said. Until our Master's fate is set, you may not retreat. Neither you, nor the Lord my husband. Nor I."

"Yes. Even so, I'd be very pleased to lay down my sword and seek the peace of Buddha for myself and those I have killed."

He stared at the night for a time, feeling his age, then looked at her. She was pleasing to see, more than any woman he had ever known.

"Sire?"

"Nothing, Mariko-san. I was remembering the first time I saw you."

That was when Hiro-matsu had secretly mortgaged his soul to Goroda to obtain this slip of a girl for his own son, the same son who had slaughtered his own mother, the one woman Hiro-matsu had ever really adored. Why did I get Mariko for him? Because I wanted to spite the Taikō, who desired her also. To spite a rival, nothing more.

Was my consort truly unfaithful? the old man asked himself, reopening the perpetual sore. Oh gods, when I look you in the face I'll demand an answer to that question. I want a yes or no! I demand the truth! I think it's a lie, but Buntaro said she was alone with that man in the room, disheveled, her kimono loose, and it was months before I returned. It could be a lie, *neh?* Or the truth, *neh?* It must be the truth—surely no son would behead his own mother without being sure?

Mariko was observing the lines of Hiro-matsu's face, his skin stretched and scaled with age, and the ancient muscular strength of his arms and shoulders. What are you thinking? she wondered, liking him. Have you seen through me yet? Do you know about me and the Anjin-san now? Do you know I quiver with love for him? That when I have to choose between him and thee and Toranaga, I will choose him?

Hiro-matsu stood near the embrasure looking down at the city below, his fingers kneading the scabbard and the haft of his sword, oblivious of her. He was brooding about Toranaga and what Zataki had said a few days ago in bitter disgust, disgust that he had shared.

"Yes, of course I want to conquer the Kwanto and plant my standard on the walls of Yedo Castle now and make it my own. I never did before but now I do," Zataki had told him. "But this way? There's no honor in it! No honor for my brother or you or me! Or anyone! Except Ishido, and that peasant doesn't know any better."

"Then support Lord Toranaga! With your help Tora—"

"For what? So my brother can become Shōgun and stamp out the Heir?"

"He's said a hundred times he supports the Heir. I believe he does. And we'd have a Minowara to lead us, not an upstart peasant and the hellcat Ochiba, *neh?* Those incompetents will have eight years of rule before Yaemon's of age if Lord Toranaga dies. Why not give Lord Toranaga the eight years—*he's Minowara!* He's said a thousand times he'll hand over power to Yaemon. Is your brain in your arse? Toranaga's not Yaemon's enemy or yours!"

"No Minowara would kneel to that peasant! He's pissed on his honor and all of ours. Yours and mine!"

They had argued, and cursed each other, and in privacy, had almost come to blows. "Go on," he had taunted Zataki, "draw your sword, traitor! You're traitor to your brother who's head of your clan!"

"I'm head of my own clan. We share the same mother, but not father. Toranaga's father sent my mother away in disgrace. I'll not help Toranaga—but if he abdicates and slits his belly I'll support Sudara. . . ."

There's no need to do that, Hiro-matsu told the night, still enraged. There's no need to do that while I'm alive, or meekly to submit. I'm General-in-Chief. It's my duty to protect my master's honor and house, even from himself. So now *I* decide:

Listen, Sire, please excuse me, but this time I disobey. With pride. This time I betray you. Now I'm going to co-opt your son and heir, the Lord Sudara, and his wife, the Lady Genjiko, and together we'll order Crimson Sky when the rains cease, and then war begins. And until the last man in the Kwanto dies, facing the enemy, I'll hold you safe in Yedo Castle, whatever you say, whatever the cost.

Gyoko was delighted to be home again in Mishima among her girls and ledgers and bills of lading, her debts receivable, mortgage deeds, and promissory notes.

"You've done quite well," she told her chief accountant.

The wizened little man bobbed a thank you and hobbled away. Balefully she turned to her chief cook. "Thirteen silver *chogin,* two hundred copper *momne* for one week's food?"

"Oh, please excuse me, Mistress, but rumors of war have sent prices soaring to the sky," the fat man said truculently. "Everything. Fish and rice and vegetables—even soya sauce has doubled since last month and saké's worse. Work work work in that hot, airless kitchen that must certainly be improved. Expensive! Ha! In one week I've served one hundred and seventy-two guests, fed ten courtesans, eleven hungry apprentice courtesans, four cooks, sixteen maids, and fourteen men servants! Please excuse me, Mistress, so sorry, but my grandmother's very sick so I must ask for ten days' leave to . . ."

Gyoko rent her hair just enough to make her point but not enough to mar her appearance and sent him away saying she was ruined, ruined, that she'd have to close the most famous Tea House in Mishima without such a perfect head cook and that it would all be his fault—his fault that she'd have to cast all her devoted girls and faithful but unfortunate retainers into the snow. "Don't forget winter's coming," she wailed as a parting shot.

Then contentedly alone, she added up the profits against the losses and the profits were twice what she expected. Her saké tasted better than ever and if food prices were up, so was the cost of saké. At once she wrote to her son in Odawara, the site of their saké factory, telling him to double their output. Then she sorted out the inevitable quarrels of the maids, sacked three, hired four more, sent for her courtesan broker, and bid heavily for the contracts of seven more courtesans she admired.

"And when would you like the honored ladies to arrive, Gyoko-san?" the old woman simpered, her own commission considerable.

"At once. At once. Go on, run along."

Next she summoned her carpenter and settled plans for the extension of this tea house, for the extra rooms for the extra ladies.

"At long last the site on Sixth Street's up for sale, Mistress. Do you want me to close on that now?"

For months she had been waiting for that particular corner location. But now she shook her head and sent him away with instructions to option four hectares of wasteland on the hill, north of the city. "But don't do it all yourself. Use intermediaries. Don't be greedy. And I don't want it aired that you're buying for me."

"But four hectares? That's—"

"At least four, perhaps five, over the next five months. But options only—understand? They're all to be put in these names."

She handed him the list of safe appointees and hurried him off, in her mind's eye seeing the walled city within a city already thriving. She chortled with glee.

Next every courtesan was sent for and complimented or chided or howled at or wept with. Some were promoted, some degraded, pillow prices increased or decreased. Then, in the midst of everything, Omi was announced.

"So sorry, but Kiku-san's not well," she told him. "Nothing serious! It's just the change of weather, poor child."

"I insist on seeing her."

"So sorry, Omi-san, but surely you don't *insist?* Kiku-san belongs to your liege Lord, *neh?*"

"I know whom she belongs to," Omi shouted. "I want to see her, that's all."

"Oh, so sorry, of course, you have every right to shout and curse, so sorry, please excuse me. But, so sorry, she's not well. This evening—or perhaps later —or tomorrow—what can I do, Omi-san? If she becomes well enough perhaps I could send word if you'll tell me where you're staying. . . ."

He told her, knowing that there was nothing he could do, and stormed off wanting to hack all Mishima to pieces.

Gyoko thought about Omi. Then she sent for Kiku and told her the program she'd arranged for her two nights in Mishima. "Perhaps we can persuade our Lady Toda to delay four or five nights, child. I know half a dozen here who'll pay a father's ransom to have you entertain them at private parties. Ha! Now that the great *daimyo's* bought you, none can touch you, not ever again, so you can sing and dance and mime and be our first *gei-sha!*"

"And poor Omi-san, Mistress? I've never heard him so cross before, so sorry he shouted at you."

"Ha! What's a shout or two when we consort with *daimyos* and the richest of the rich rice and silk brokers at long last. Tonight I'll tell Omi-san where you'll be the last time you sing, but much too soon so he'll have to wait. I'll arrange a nearby room. Meanwhile he'll have lots of saké . . . and Akiko to serve him. It won't hurt to sing a sad song or two to him afterwards—we're still not sure about Toranaga-sama, *neh?* We still haven't had a down payment, let alone the balance."

"Please excuse me, wouldn't Choko be a better choice? She's prettier and younger and sweeter. I'm sure he would enjoy her more."

"Yes, child. But Akiko's strong and very experienced. When this sort of madness is on men they're inclined to be rough. Rougher than you'd imagine. Even Omi-san. I don't want Choko damaged. Akiko likes danger and needs some violence to perform well. She'll take the sting out of his Beauteous Barb. Run along now, your prettiest kimono and best perfumes. . . ."

Gyoko shooed Kiku away to get ready and once more hurled herself into finishing the management of her house. Then, everything completed—even the formal cha invitation tomorrow to the eight most influential Mama-sans in Mishima to discuss a matter of great import—she sank gratefully into a perfect bath, "Ahhhhhhhhh!"

At the perfect time, a perfect massage. Perfume and powder and makeup and coiffure. New loose kimono of rare frothy silk. Then, at the perfect moment, her favorite arrived. He was eighteen, a student, son of an impoverished samurai, his name Inari.

"Oh, how lovely you are—I rushed here the moment your poem arrived," he said breathlessly. "Did you have a pleasant journey? I'm so happy to welcome you back! Thank you, thank you for the presents—the sword is perfect and the kimono! Oh, how good you are to me!"

Yes, I am, she told herself, though she stoutly denied it to his face. Soon she was lying beside him, sweaty and languorous. Ah, Inari, she thought bemused, your Pellucid Pestle's not built like the Anjin-san's but what you lack in size you surely make up with cataclysmic vigor!

"Why do you laugh?" he asked sleepily.

"Because you make me happy," she sighed, delighted that she'd had the great good fortune to be educated. She chatted easily, complimented him extravagantly, and petted him to sleep, her hands and voice out of long habit smoothly achieving all that was necessary of their own volition. Her mind was far away. She was wondering about Mariko and her paramour, rethinking the alternatives. How far dare she press Mariko? Or whom should she give them away to, or threaten her with, subtly of course—Toranaga, Buntaro, or whom? The Christian priest? Would there be any profit in that? Or Lord Kiyama—certainly any scandal connecting the great Lady Toda with the barbarian would ruin her son's chance of marrying Kiyama's granddaughter. Would that threat bend her to my will? Or should I do nothing—is there more profit in that somehow?

Pity about Mariko. Such a lovely lady! My, but she'd make a sensational courtesan! Pity about the Anjin-san. My, but he's a clever one—I could make a fortune out of him too.

How can I best use this secret, most profitably, before it's no longer a secret and those two are destroyed?

Be careful, Gyoko, she admonished herself. There's not much time left to decide about this, or about the other new secrets: about the guns and arms hidden by the peasants in Anjiro for instance, or about the new Musket Regiment—its numbers, officers, organization, and number of guns. Or about Toranaga, who, the last night in Yokosé, pillowed Kiku pleasantly, using a classic "six shallow and five deep" rhythm for the hundred thrusts with the strength of a thirty-year-old and slept till dawn like a babe. That's not the pattern of a man distraught with worry, *neh?*

What about the agony of the tonsured virgin priest who, naked and on his knees, prayed first to his bigot Christian God, begging forgiveness for the sin he was about to commit with the girl, and the other sin, a real one, that he had done in Osaka—strange secret things of the "confessional" that were whispered to him by a leper, then treacherously passed on by him to Lord Harima. What would Toranaga make of that? Endlessly pouring out what was whispered and passed onward, and then the praying with tight-closed eyes—before the poor demented fool spread the girl wide with no finesse and, later, slunk off like a foul night creature. So much hatred and agony and twisted shame.

What about Omi's second cook, who whispered to a maid who whispered to her paramour who whispered to Akiko that he'd overheard Omi and his mother plotting the death of Kasigi Yabu, their liege lord? Ha! That knowledge made public would set a cat among all the Kasigi pigeons! So would Omi's and Yabu's secret offer to Zataki if whispered into Toranaga's ear—or the words Zataki muttered in his sleep that his pillow partner memorized and sold to me the next day for a whole silver *chojin*, words that implied General Ishido and Lady Ochiba ate together, slept together, and that Zataki himself had heard them grunting and groaning and crying out as Yang pierced Yin even up to the Far Field! Gyoko smiled to herself smugly. Shocking, *neh*, people in such high places!

What about the other strange fact that at the moment of the Clouds and the Rain, and a few times before, the Lord Zataki had unconsciously called his pillow partner "Ochiba." Curious, *neh?*

Would the oh-so-necessary-to-both-sides Zataki change his song if Toranaga offered him Ochiba as bait? Gyoko chuckled, warmed by all the lovely secrets, all so valuable in the right ears, that men had spilled out with their Joyful Juice. "He'd change," she murmured confidently. "Oh, very yes."

"What?"

"Nothing, nothing Inari-chan. Did you sleep well?"

"What?"

She smiled and let him slide back into sleep. Then, when he was ready, she put her hands and lips on him for his pleasure. And for hers.

"Where's the Ingeles now, Father?"

"I don't know exactly, Rodrigues. Yet. It would be one of the inns south of Mishima. I left a servant to find out which." Alvito gathered up the last of the gravy with a crust of new bread.

"When will you know?"

"Tomorrow, without fail."

"*Que va,* I'd like to see him again. Is he fit?" Rodrigues asked levelly.

"Yes." The ship's bell sounded six times. Three o'clock in the afternoon.

"Did he tell you what happened to him since he left Osaka?"

"I know parts of it. From him and others. It's a long story and there's much to tell. First I'll deal with my dispatches, then we'll talk."

Rodrigues leaned back in his chair in the small stern cabin. "Good. That'd be very good." He saw the sharp features of the Jesuit, the sharp brown eyes flecked with yellow. Cat's eyes. "Listen, Father," he said, "the Ingeles saved my ship and my life. Sure he's enemy, sure he's heretic, but he's a pilot, one of the best that's ever been. It's not wrong to respect an enemy, even to like one."

"The Lord Jesus forgave his enemies but they still crucified Him." Calmly Alvito returned the pilot's gaze. "But I like him too. At least, I understand him better. Let's leave him for the moment."

Rodrigues nodded agreeably. He noticed the priest's plate was empty so he reached across the table and moved the platter closer. "Here, Father, have some more capon. Bread?"

"Thank you. Yes, I will. I didn't realize how hungry I was." The priest gratefully tore off another leg and took more sage and onion and bread stuffing, then poured the last of the rich gravy over it.

"Wine?"

"Yes, thank you."

"Where are the rest of your people, Father?"

"I left them at an inn near the wharf."

Rodrigues glanced out of the stern bay windows that overlooked Nimazu, the wharfs and the port and, just to starboard, the mouth of the Kano, where the water was darker than the rest of the sea. Many fishing boats were plying back and forth. "This servant you left, Father—you can trust him? You're sure he'll find us?"

"Oh, yes. They'll certainly not move for two days at least." Alvito had already decided not to mention what he, or more truthfully he reminded himself, what Brother Michael suspected, so he just added, "Don't forget they're traveling in state. With Toda Mariko's rank, and Toranaga's banners, they're very much in state. Everyone within four leagues would know about them and where they're staying."

Rodrigues laughed. "The Ingeles in state? Who'd have believed that? Like a poxy *daimyo!*"

"That's not the half of it, Pilot. Toranaga's made him samurai and hatamoto."

"What?"

"Now Pilot-Major Blackthorne wears the two swords. With his pistols. And now he's Toranaga's confidant, to a certain extent, and protégé."

"The Ingeles?"

"Yes." Alvito let the silence hang in the cabin and went back to eating.

"Do you know the why of it?" Rodrigues asked.

"Yes, in part. All in good time, Pilot."

"Just tell me the why. Briefly. Details later, please."

"The Anjin-san saved Toranaga's life for the third time. Twice during the escape from Osaka, the last in Izu during an earthquake." Alvito chomped lustily on the thigh meat. A thread of juice ran into his black beard.

Rodrigues waited but the priest said no more. Thoughtfully his eyes dropped to the goblet cradled in his hands. The surface of the deep red wine caught the light. After a long pause, he said, "It wouldn't be good for us, that piss-cutting Ingeles close to Toranaga. Not at all. Not him. Eh?"

"I agree."

"Even so, I'd like to see him." The priest said nothing. Rodrigues let him clean his plate in silence, then offered more, the joy gone out of him. The last of the carcass and the final wing were accepted, and another goblet of wine. Then, to finish, some fine French cognac that Father Alvito got from a cupboard.

"Rodrigues? Would you care for a glass?"

"Thank you." The seaman watched Alvito pour the nut-brown liquor into the crystal glass. All the wine and cognac had come from the Father-Visitor's private stock as a parting gift to his Jesuit friend.

"Of course, Rodrigues, you're welcome to share it with the Father," dell'Aqua had said. "Go with God, may He watch over you and bring you safely to port and home again."

"Thank you, Eminence."

Yes, thank you, Eminence, but no God-cursed thanks, Rodrigues told himself bitterly, no thanks for getting my Captain-General to order me aboard this pigboat under this Jesuit's command and out of my Gracia's arms, poor darling. Madonna, life's so short, too short and too treacherous to waste being chaperone to gut-stinking priests, even Alvito who's more of a man than any and, because of that, more dangerous. Madonna, give me some help!

"Oh! You reave, Rod-san? Reave so soon? Oh, so sorry. . . ."

"Soon come back, my darling."

"Oh, so sorry . . . we miss, ritt'e one and I."

For a moment he had considered taking her aboard the *Santa Filipa,* but instantly dismissed the thought, knowing it to be perilous for her and for him and for the ship. "So sorry, back soon."

"We wait, Rod-san. Please excuse my sad, so sorry."

Always the hesitant, heavily accented Portuguese she tried so hard to speak, insisting that she be called by her baptismal name Gracia and not by the lovely-sounding Nyan-nyan, which meant Kitten and suited her so well and pleased him better.

He had sailed away from Nagasaki, hating to leave, cursing all priests and captain-generals, wanting an end to summer and autumn so he could up-anchor the Black Ship, her holds weighed now with bullion, to head for home at long last, rich and independent. But then what? The perpetual question swamped him. What about *her*—and the child? Madonna, help me to answer that with peace.

"An excellent meal, Rodrigues," Alvito said, toying with a crumb on the table. "Thank you."

"Good." Rodrigues was serious now. "What's your plan, Father? We should—" He stopped in mid-sentence and glanced out of the windows. Then, dissatisfied, he got up from the table and limped painfully over to a land side porthole and peered out.

"What is it, Rodrigues?"

"Thought I felt the tide change. Just want to check our sea room." He opened the cover further and leaned out, but still couldn't see the bow anchor. "Excuse me a moment, Father."

He went on deck. Water lapped the anchor chain that angled into the muddy water. No movement. Then a thread of wake appeared and the ship began to ease off safely, to take up her new station with the ebb. He checked her lie, then the lookouts. Everything was perfect. No other boats were near. The afternoon was fine, the mist long since gone. They were a cable or so offshore, far enough out to preclude a sudden boarding, and well away from the sea lanes that fed the wharves.

His ship was a lorcha, a Japanese hull adapted to modern Portuguese sails and rigging: swift, two-masted, and sloop-rigged. It had four cannon amidships, two small bow chasers and two stern chasers. Her name was the *Santa Filipa* and she carried a crew of thirty.

His eyes went to the city, and to the hills beyond. "Pesaro!"

"Yes, senhor?"

"Get the longboat ready. I'm going ashore before dusk."

"Good. She'll be ready. When're you back?"

"Dawn."

"Even better! I'll lead the shore party—ten men."

"No shore leave, Pesaro. It's *kinjiru!* Madonna, is your brain addled?" Rodrigues straddled the quarterdeck and leaned against the gunwale.

"Not right that all should suffer," said the bosun, Pesaro, his great calloused hands flexing. "I'll lead the party and promise there'll be no trouble. We've been cooped up for two weeks now."

"The port authorities here said *kinjiru,* so sorry, but still goddamned *kinjiru!*

Remember? This isn't Nagasaki!"

"Yes, by the blood of Christ Jesus, and more's the pity!" The heavy-set man scowled. "It was only one Jappo that got chopped."

"One chopped dead, two knifed badly, a lot of wounded, and a girl hurt before the samurai stopped the riot. I warned you all before you went ashore: 'Nimazu's not Nagasaki—so behave yourselves!' Madonna! We were lucky to get away with just one of our seamen dead. They'd have been within the law to chop all five of you."

"Their law, Pilot, not ours. God-cursed monkeys! It was only a whorehouse brawl."

"Yes, but your men started it, the authorities have quarantined my ship, and you're all benched. You included!" Rodrigues moved his leg to ease the pain. "Be patient, Pesaro. Now that the Father's back we'll be off."

"On the tide? At dawn? Is that an order?"

"No, not yet. Just get the longboat ready. Gomez will come with me."

"Let me come as well, eh? *Per favor,* Pilot. I'm sick to death of being stuck in this pox-cursed bucket."

"No. And you'd better not go ashore tonight. You or any."

"And if you're not back by dawn?"

"You rot here at anchor till I do. Clear?"

The bosun's scowl deepened. He hesitated, then backed down. "Yes, yes, that's clear, by God."

"Good." Rodrigues went below.

Alvito was asleep but he awoke the moment the pilot opened the cabin door. "Ah, all's well?" he asked, replete now in mind and body.

"Yes. It was just the turn." Rodrigues gulped some wine to take the foul taste out of his mouth. It was always like that after a near-mutiny. If Pesaro had not yielded instantly, once again Rodrigues would have had to blow a hole in a man's face or put him in irons or order fifty lashes or keelhaul the man or perform any one of a hundred obscenities essential by sea law to maintain discipline. Without discipline any ship was lost. "What's the plan now, Father? We sail at dawn?"

"How are the carrier pigeons?"

"In good health. We've still six—four Nagasakis, two Osakas."

The priest checked the angle of the sun. Four or five hours to sunset. Plenty of time to launch the birds with the first coded message long since planned: "Toranaga surrenders to Regents' order. I'm going first to Yedo, then Osaka. I will accompany Toranaga to Osaka. He says we can still build the cathedral at Yedo. Detailed dispatch with Rodrigues."

"Would you please ask the handler to prepare two Nagasakis and one Osaka immediately," Alvito said. "Then we'll talk. I won't be sailing back with you. I'm going on to Yedo by road. It'll take me most of the night and tomorrow to write a detailed dispatch which you'll carry to the Father-Visitor, for his hands only. Will you sail as soon as I've finished?"

"All right. If it's too near dusk I'll wait till dawn. There are shoals and shifting sands for ten leagues."

Alvito assented. The twelve extra hours would make no difference. He knew it would have been far better if he'd been able to send off the news from Yokosé, God curse the heathen devil who destroyed my birds there! Be patient, he told himself. What's the hurry? Isn't that a vital rule of our Order? Patience. All comes to him who waits—and works. What does twelve hours matter, or even eight days? Those won't change the course of history. The die was cast in Yokosé.

"You'll travel with the Ingeles?" Rodrigues was asking. "Like before?"

"Yes. From Yedo I'll make my own way back to Osaka. I'll accompany

Toranaga. I'd like to you to stop at Osaka with a copy of my dispatch, in case the Father-Visitor's there, or has left Nagasaki before you arrive and is on the way there. You can give it to Father Soldi, his secretary—only him."

"All right. I'll be glad to leave. We're hated here."

"With God's mercy we can change all that, Rodrigues. With God's good grace we'll convert all the heathens here."

"Amen to that. Yes." The tall man eased his leg with the throb lessened momentarily. He stared out of the windows. Then he got up impatiently. "I'll fetch the pigeons myself. Write your message, then we'll talk. About the Ingeles." He went to the deck and selected the birds from the panniers. When he returned the priest had already used the special needle-sharp quill and ink to inscribe the same coded message on the tiny slivers of paper. Alvito armed the tiny cylinders, sealed them, and launched the birds. The three circled once, then headed westward in convoy into the afternoon sun.

"Shall we talk here or below?"

"Here. It's cooler." Rodrigues motioned the quarterdeck watch amidships out of earshot.

Alvito sat on the seachair. "First about Toranaga."

He told the Pilot briefly what had happened in Yokosé, omitting the incident with Brother Joseph and his suspicions about Mariko and Blackthorne. Rodrigues was as stunned by the surrender as he had been. "No war? It's a miracle! Now we're truly safe, our Black Ship's safe, the Church is rich, we're rich . . . thanks be to God, the saints, and the Madonna! That's the best news you could've brought, Father. We're safe!"

"If God wills it. One thing Toranaga said disturbed me. He put it this way: 'I can order my Christian freed—the Anjin-san. With his ship, and with his cannon.' "

Rodrigues' vast good humor left him. "*Erasmus* is still in Yedo? She's still in Toranaga's control?"

"Yes. Would it be serious if the Ingeles were loosed?"

"Serious? That ship would blast hell out of us if she caught our Black Ship twixt here and Macao with him aboard, armed, with a half-decent crew. We've only the small frigate to run interference and she's no match for *Erasmus!* Nor are we. She could dance around us and we'd have to strike our colors."

"Are you certain?"

"Yes. Before God—she'd be a killer." Angrily Rodrigues bunched a fist. "But wait a moment—the Ingeles said he'd arrived here with no more than twelve men, and not all seamen, many of them merchants and most sick. That few couldn't handle her. The only place he could get a crew would be at Nagasaki—or Macao. He might get enough at Nagasaki! There're those who'd . . . he'd better be kept away from there, and Macao!"

"Say he had a native crew?"

"You mean some of Toranaga's cutthroats? Or *wako?* You mean if Toranaga's surrendered, all his men become *ronin, neh?* If the Ingeles had enough time he could train 'em. Easy. Christ Jesus . . . please excuse me, Father, but if the Ingeles got samurai or *wako.* . . . Can't risk that—he's too good. We all saw that in Osaka! Him loose in that piss-cutter in Asia with a samurai crew. . . ."

Alvito watched him, even more concerned now. "I think I'd better send another message to the Father-Visitor. He should be informed if it's this urgent. He'll know what to do."

"I know what to do!" Rodrigues' fist smashed down on the gunwale. He got to his feet and turned his back. "Listen, Father, hear my confession: The first night—the very first time he stood alongside me on the galley out to sea, when

we were going from Anjiro—my heart told me to kill him, then again during
the storm. The Lord Jesus help me, that was the time I sent him for'ard and
deliberately swerved into the wind without warning, him without a lifeline, to
murder him, but the Ingeles didn't go overboard like anyone else would've done.
I thought that was the Hand of God, and knew it for certain when later he
overruled me and saved my ship, and then when my ship was safe and the wave
took me and I was drowning, my last thought was that that also was God's
punishment on me for an attempted murder. You don't do that to a pilot—he'd
never do that to me! I deserved it that time and then, when I found myself alive
and him bending over me, helping me drink, I was so ashamed and again I begged
God's forgiveness and swore a Holy oath to try to make it up to him. Madonna!"
he burst out in torment, "that man saved me though he *knew* I tried to murder
him. I saw it in his eyes. He saved me and helped me live and now I've got to
kill him."

"Why?"

"The Captain-General was right: God help us all if the Ingeles puts to sea in
Erasmus, armed, with a half-decent crew."

Blackthorne and Mariko were sleeping in the nocturnal peace of their little
house, one of a cluster that made up the Inn of the Camellias, which was on 9th
Street South. There were three rooms in each. Mariko had taken one room for
herself and Chimmoko, Blackthorne another, and the third that let onto the front
door and veranda had been left empty for living and eating and talking.

"You think this is safe?" Blackthorne had asked anxiously. "Not to have
Yoshinaka, or more maids or guards sleeping there?"

"No, Anjin-san. Nothing's truly safe. But it will be pleasant to be alone. This
inn's thought to be the prettiest and most famous in Izu. It is pretty, *neh?*"

And it was. Each tiny house was set on elegant pilings with circling verandas
and four steps up, made from the finest woods, everything polished and gleaming.
Each was separate, fifty paces from its neighbors and surrounded by manicured
gardens within the greater garden within the high bamboo wall. There were
streamlets, and lily ponds and waterfalls and blossom trees in abundance with
day perfumes and night perfumes, sweet smelling and luxurious. Clean stone
footpaths, delicately roofed, led to the central baths, cold and hot and very hot,
fet by natural springs. Multicolored lanterns and happy servants and maids and
never a cross word to disturb the tree bells and bubbling water and singing birds
in their aviaries.

"Of course I did ask for two houses, Anjin-san, one for you and one for me.
Unfortunately, only one was available, so sorry. But Yoshinaka-san isn't displeased. On the contrary, he was relieved as he wouldn't have to split his men.
He has posted sentries on every path so we are quite safe and can't be disturbed
as in other places. Why should we be disturbed? What could possibly be wrong
with a room here and a room there and Chimmoko to share my bed?"

"Nothing. I've never seen such a beautiful place. How clever you are, and how
beautiful."

"Ah, how kind you are to me, Anjin-san. First bathe, then the evening food
and lots of saké."

"Good. Very good."

"Put down your dictionary, Anjin-san, please."

"But you're always encouraging me."

"If you put your book down I—I'll tell you a secret."

"What?"

"I've invited Yoshinaka-san to eat with us. And some ladies. To entertain us."

"Ah!"

"Yes. After I leave you, you will select one, *neh?*"

"But that might disturb your sleep, so sorry."

"I promise I will sleep very heavily, my love. Seriously, a change might be good for thee."

"Yes, but next year, not now."

"Be serious."

"I am."

"Ah, then in that case, if by chance you politely changed your mind and sent her away soon—*after* Yoshinaka-san has left with his partner—ah, who knows what the night *kami* might find for thee then?"

"What?"

"I went shopping today."

"Oh? And what did you buy?"

"Ah!"

She had bought an assortment of the pillow devices that Kiku had shown them, and much later, when Yoshinaka had left and Chimmoko was guarding on the veranda, she offered them to him with a deep bow. Half in jest, he accepted with equal formality, and together they selected a pleasure ring.

"That looks very prickly, Anjin-san, *neh?* Are you sure you don't mind?"

"No, not if you don't, but stop laughing or you'll ruin everything. Put out the candles."

"Oh no, please, I want to watch."

"For the love of God, stop laughing, Mariko!"

"But you're laughing too."

"Never mind, put the light out or. . . . There, now look what you've done."

"Oh!"

"Stop laughing! It's no good putting your head in the futons. . . ."

Then later, trouble.

"Mariko . . ."

"Yes, my love?"

"I can't find it."

"Oh! Let me help you."

"Ah, it's all right. I've got it. I was lying on it."

"Oh. You're—you're sure you don't mind?"

"No, but it's a bit, well, not exactly uplifting, all this talking about it and having to wait. Is it?"

"Oh, I don't mind. It was my fault for laughing. Oh, Anjin-san, I love you so, please excuse me."

"You're excused."

"I love to touch thee."

"I've never known anything like your touch."

"What are you doing, Anjin-san?"

"I'm putting it on."

"Is it difficult?"

"Yes. Stop laughing!"

"Oh, I'm so sorry, perhaps you—"

"Stop laughing!"

"Please forgive me. . . ."

Afterwards she went to sleep instantly, totally spent. He did not. For him it had been fine, but not perfect. He'd been too worried about her. He'd decided this time was for *her* pleasure, and not his.

Yes, that was for her, he thought, loving her. But one thing was perfect: I know I've truly satisfied her. For once I'm absolutely sure.

He slept. Later the sound of voices and quarreling, and, mixed with it, Portuguese, began to filter through his slumber. For a moment he thought he was dreaming, then he recognized the voice. "Rodrigues!"

Mariko murmured, still locked in sleep.

At the sound of footsteps on the path he lurched to his knees in controlled panic. He lifted her as if she were a doll, went for the shoji, and stopped just as it was opened from the outside. It was Chimmoko. The maid's head was lowered and her eyes discreetly closed. He rushed past her with Mariko in his arms and laid her gently in her own quilts, still half asleep, and ran silently for his own room again, the sweat chill on him though the night was warm. He groped into a kimono and hurried out again to the veranda. Yoshinaka had reached the second step.

"*Nan desu ka,* Yoshinaka-san?"

"*Gomen nasai,* Anjin-san," Yoshinaka said. He pointed to the flares at the far gate of the inn, adding many words that Blackthorne did not understand. But the gist of it was that that man there, the barbarian, he wants to see you and I told him to wait and he said he wouldn't wait, acting like a *daimyo* which he isn't, and tried to push past, which I stopped. He said he was your friend. Is he?

"Heya, Ingeles! It's me, Vasco Rodrigues!"

"Hey, Rodrigues!" Blackthorne shouted back happily. "Be right with you. *Hai,* Yoshinaka-san. *Kare wa watashi no ichi yujin desu.*" He's my friend.

"*Ah so desu!*"

"*Hai. Domo.*"

Blackthorne ran down the steps to go to the gateway. Behind him he heard Mariko's voice, "*Nan ja,* Chimmoko?" and a whisper back and then she called out with authority, "Yoshinaka-san!"

"*Hai,* Toda-sama!"

Blackthorne glanced around. The samurai walked up the steps and crossed toward Mariko's room. Her door was closed. Chimmoko stood outside it. Now her own crumpled bedding was near the door where she would always sleep, correctly, should her mistress not wish her to be in the room with her. Yoshinaka bowed to the door and began to report. Blackthorne walked along the path with growing elation, barefoot, his eyes on the Portuguese, the width of the welcoming smile, the light from the flares dancing off his earrings and the buckle of his jaunty hat.

"Hey, Rodrigues! It's great to see you. How's your leg? How'd you find me?"

"Madonna, you've grown, Ingeles, filled out! Yes, fit and healthy and acting like a piss-cutting *daimyo!*" Rodrigues gave him a bear hug and he returned it.

"How's your leg?"

"Hurts like shit but it works and I found you by asking where the great Anjin-san was—the big barbarian bandit bastard with the blue eyes!"

They laughed together, swapping obscenities, careless of the samurai and servants that surrounded them. In a moment Blackthorne sent a servant for saké and led the way back. Both strolled with their sailor's gait, Rodrigues' right hand, by habit, on his rapier's hilt, the other thumb hooked into his wide belt near his pistol. Blackthorne was a few inches taller but the Portuguese had even wider shoulders and a barrel-chested power to him.

Yoshinaka was waiting on the veranda.

"*Domo arigato,* Yoshinaka-san," Blackthorne said, thanking the samurai again, and motioned Rodrigues to one of the cushions. "Let's talk here."

Rodrigues put a foot on the steps but stopped as Yoshinaka moved in front of him, pointed at the rapier and the pistol, then held out his left hand, palm upwards. *"Dozo!"*

The Portuguese frowned up at him. *"Iyé, samurai-sama, domo ari—"*

"Dozo!"

"Iyé, samurai-sama, iyé!" Rodrigues repeated more sharply. *"Watashi yujin* Anjin-san, *neh?"*

Blackthorne moved forward a step, still amazed at the suddenness of the confrontation. *"Yoshinaka-san, shigata ga nai, neh?"* he said with a smile. *"Rodrigues yujin, wata—"*

"Gomen nasai, Anjin-san. *Kinjiru!"* Yoshinaka rapped an order. Instantly samurai leapt forward, surrounding Rodrigues threateningly, and again he held out his hand. *"Dozo!"*

"These shit-filled whores're touchy, Ingeles," Rodrigues said through a toothy smile. "Call 'em off, eh? I've never had to give up my arms before."

"Don't, Rodrigues!" he said quickly, sensing his friend's imminent decision, then to Yoshinaka, *"Domo, gomen nasai,* Rodrigues *yujin, watash—"*

"Gomen nasai, Anjin-san. *Kinjiru.* Then roughly to the Portuguese, *"Ima!"*

Rodrigues snarled back, *"Iyé! Wakarimasu ka?"*

Blackthorne hastily stepped between them. "Hey, Rodrigues, what does it matter, *neh?* Let Yoshinaka-san have them. It's nothing to do with you or me. It's because of the lady, Toda Mariko-sama. She's in there. You know how touchy they are about weapons near *daimyos* or their wives. We'll argue all night, you know how they are, eh? What's the difference.?"

The Portuguese forced a smile back on his face. "Sure. Why not? *Hai. Shigata ga nai,* samurai-sama. *So desu!"*

He bowed like a courtier without sincerity, slid his rapier and scabbard from its clasp and took out his pistol, and offered them. Yoshinaka motioned to a samurai, who took the weapons and ran off to the gateway, where he put them down and stood guard over them. Rodrigues started to mount the steps, but again Yoshinaka politely and firmly asked him to stop. Other samurai came forward to search him. Furious, Rodrigues leaped back. *"IYÉ! Kinjiru,* by God! What the—"

The samurai fell on him, pinned his arms tight, and searched him thoroughly. They found two knives in the tops of his boots, another strapped to his left forearm, two small pistols—one concealed in the lining of his coat, one under his shirt—and a small pewter hip flask.

Blackthorne examined the pistols. Both were primed. "Was the other primed too?"

"Yes. Of course. This land's hostile, haven't you noticed, Ingeles? Tell them to let go of me!"

"This isn't the usual way to visit a friend by night. *Neh?"*

"I tell you this land's hostile. I'm always armed like this. Aren't you normally? Madonna, tell these bastards to let me go."

"Is that the lot? Everything?"

"Of course—tell 'em to let me go, Ingeles!"

Blackthorne gave the pistols to a samurai and stepped forward. His fingers felt carefully around the inside of Rodrigues' wide leather belt. A stiletto slid from its secret sheath, very thin, very springy, made of the best Damascus steel. Yoshinaka swore at the samurai who had made the search. They apologized but Blackthorne only watched Rodrigues.

"Any more?" he asked, the stiletto loose in his hand.

Rodrigues stared back at him stonily.

"I'll tell 'em where to look—and how to look, Rodrigues. How a Spaniard would—some of them. Eh?"

"*Me cago en la leche, che cabron!*"

"*Que va, leche!* Hurry up!" Still no answer. Blackthorne went forward with the knife. "*Dozo,* Yoshinaka-san. *Watash—*"

Rodrigues said hoarsely, "In my hat band," and Blackthorne stopped.

"Good," he said and reached for the wide-brimmed hat.

"You would, wouldn't you—teach them?"

"Wouldn't you?"

"Be careful of the feather, Ingeles, I cherish that."

The band was wide and stiff, the feather jaunty like the hat. Inside the band was a thin stiletto, smaller, specially designed, the fine steel easily molding the curve. Yoshinaka barked out another vicious reprimand to the samurai.

"Before God, that's all, Rodrigues?"

"Madonna—I told you."

"Swear it."

Rodrigues complied.

"Yoshinaka-san, *ima ichi-ban. Domo,*" Blackthorne said. He's all right now. Thank you.

Yoshinaka gave the order. His men released the Portuguese. Rodrigues rubbed his limbs to ease the pain. "Is it all right to sit down, Ingeles?"

"Yes."

Rodrigues wiped off the sweat with a red kerchief, then picked up the pewter flask and sat cross-legged on one of the cushions. Yoshinaka remained nearby on the veranda. All but four samurai went back to their posts. "Why are they so touchy? Why are you so touchy, Ingeles? I've never had to give up my weapons before. Am I an assassin?"

"I asked you if that was all your weapons and you lied."

"I wasn't listening. Madonna! Would you—held like a common criminal?" Rodrigues added sourly, "Eh, what's it matter, Ingeles, what's anything matter? The night's spoiled. . . . Hey, but wait, Ingeles! Why should anything be allowed to spoil a great evening? I forgive them. And I forgive you, Ingeles. You were right and I was wrong. I apologize. It's good to see you." He unscrewed the stopper and offered the flask. "Here—here's some fine brandy."

"You first."

Rodrigues' face became ashen. "Madonna—do you think I bring poison?"

"No. You drink first."

Rodrigues drank.

"Again!"

The Portuguese obeyed, then wiped his mouth with the back of his hand. Blackthorne accepted the flask. "*Salud!*" He tipped it back and pretended to swallow, secretly keeping his tongue over the opening to prevent the liquor from going into his mouth, much as he wanted the drink. "Ah!" he said. "That was good. Here!"

"Keep it, Ingeles. It's a present."

"From the good Father? Or from you?"

"From me."

"Before God?"

"God and the Virgin, thou and thy 'before God'!" Rodrigues said. "It was a gift from me and the Father! He owns all the liquor aboard the *Santa Filipa* but the Eminence said I could share it and the flask's one of a dozen aboard. It's a gift. Where are your manners?"

Blackthorne pretended to drink again and offered it back. "Here, have another."

Rodrigues felt the liquor all the way to his toes and was glad that, after accepting the full flask from Alvito, he had privately emptied it and washed it out carefully and refilled it with brandy from his own bottle. Madonna, forgive me, he prayed, forgive me for doubting the Holy Father. Oh, Madonna, God, and Lord Jesus, for the love of God, come to earth again and change this world where sometimes we dare not even trust priests.

"What's the matter?"

"Nothing, Ingeles. I was just thinking that this world's a foul pisscutter when you can't trust anyone nowadays. I came in friendship and now there's a hole in the world."

"Did you?"

"Yes."

"Armed like that?"

"I'm always armed like that. That's why I'm alive. *Salud!*" The big man raised the flask gloomily and sipped again. "Piss on the world, piss on everything."

"Are you saying, piss on me?"

"Ingeles, this is me, Vasco Rodrigues, Pilot of the Portuguese Navy, not a flyblown samurai. I've exchanged many insults with you, all in friendship. Tonight I came to see my friend and now I have no friend. So sad."

"Yes."

"I shouldn't be sad but I am. Being friends with thee complicated my life extraordinarily." Rodrigues got up and eased his back, then sat down again. "I hate sitting on these God-cursed cushions! Chairs are for me. Aboard. Well, *salud*, Ingeles."

"When you swerved into wind and I was amidships, that was to put me overboard. Wasn't it?"

"Yes," Rodrigues answered at once. He got to his feet. "Yes, I'm glad you asked me for that is on my conscience terribly. I'm glad to apologize to you in life for I could not bring myself to confess it to you. Yes, Ingeles. I don't ask forgiveness or understanding or anything. But I am glad to confess that shame to your face."

"You think I'd do that to you?"

"No. But then if the time came. . . . You never know till your own time of trial."

"You came here to kill me?"

"No. I don't think so. I don't think that was first in my mind, though for my people and my country we both know it would be better for you to be dead. So sad, but so true. How foolish is life, eh, Ingeles?"

"I don't want you dead, Pilot. Just your Black Ship."

"Listen, Ingeles," said Rodrigues without anger. "If we meet at sea, you in your ship, armed, me in mine, look to your life. That's all I came to promise you—only that. I thought it would be possible to tell you that as a friend and still remain your friend. Except for a sea meeting, I am forever in your debt. *Salud!*"

"I hope to catch your Black Ship at sea. *Salud,* Pilot."

Rodrigues stalked off. Yoshinaka and the samurai followed him. At the gateway the Portuguese collected his arms. Soon he was swallowed by the night.

Yoshinaka waited until the sentries sorted themselves out. When he was satisfied that all was secure he limped off to his own quarters. Blackthorne sat back on one of the cushions and in a moment that he had sent for saké happily padded up with the tray. She poured one cup and would have stayed to serve him but he dismissed her. Now he was alone. The night sounds surrounded him again, the rustling and the waterfall and the movements of the night birds.

Everything was as before, but everything had changed.

Sadly he reached out to refill his cup but there was a sibilance of silk and Mariko's hand held the flask. She poured for him, the other cup for herself.

"*Domo,* Mariko-san."

"*Do itashimashité,* Anjin-san." She settled herself on the other cushion. They sipped the hot wine.

"He was going to kill you, *neh?*"

"I don't know, not for sure."

"What did it mean—to search like a Spaniard?"

"Some of them strip their prisoners then probe in private places. And not gently. They call it to search *con significa,* with significance. Sometimes they use knives."

"Oh." She sipped and listened to the water among the stones. "It's the same here, Anjin-san. Sometimes. That's why it's never wise to be captured. If you're captured you've dishonored yourself so completely that anything the captor does. . . . It's best not to be captured. *Neh?*"

He stared at the lanterns moving in the cool sweet breeze. "Yoshinaka was right—I was wrong. The search was necessary. It was your idea, *neh?* You told Yoshinaka to search him?"

"Please excuse me, Anjin-san, I hope that didn't create an embarrassment for you. It was just that I was afraid for you."

"I thank thee," he said, using Latin again, though he was sorry there had been a search. Without the search he would still have a friend. Perhaps, he cautioned himself.

"Thou art welcome," she said. "But it was only my duty."

Mariko was wearing a night kimono and overkimono of blue, her hair braided loosely, falling to her waist. She looked back at the far gateway which could be seen through the trees. "You were very clever about the liquor, Anjin-san. I almost pinched myself with anger at forgetting to warn Yoshinaka about that. You were most shrewd to make him drink twice. Do you use poison a lot in your countries?"

"Sometimes. Some people do. It's a filthy way."

"Yes, but very effective. It happens here too."

"Terrible, isn't it, not being able to trust anyone."

"Oh, no, Anjin-san, so sorry," she answered. "That's just one of life's most important rules—no more, no less."

BOOK FOUR

CHAPTER 47

*E*RASMUS glittered in the high noon sun beside the Yedo wharf, resplendent.

"Jesus God in Heaven, Mariko, look at her! Have you ever seen anything like her? Look at her lines!"

His ship was beyond the closed, encircling barriers a hundred paces away, moored to the dock with new ropes. The whole area was heavily guarded, more samurai were on deck, and signs everywhere said this was a forbidden area except with Lord Toranaga's personal permission.

Erasmus had been freshly painted and tarred, her decks were spotless, her hull caulked and her rigging repaired. Even the foremast that had been carried away in the storm had been replaced with the last of the spares she carried in her hold, and stepped to a perfect angle. All rope ends were neatly coiled, all cannon gleaming under a protective sheen of oil behind their gun ports. And the ragged Lion of England fluttered proudly over all.

"Ahoy!" he shouted joyfully from outside the barriers, but there was no answering call. One of the sentries told him there were no barbarians aboard today.

"*Shigata ga nai,*" Blackthorne said. "*Domo.*" He curbed his soaring impatience to go aboard at once and beamed at Mariko. "It's as if she's just come out of a refit at Portsmouth dockyard, Mariko-san. Look at her cannon—the lads must've worked like dogs. She's beautiful, *neh?* Can't wait to see Baccus and Vinck and the others. Never thought I'd find her like that. Christ Jesus, she looks so pretty, *neh?*"

Mariko was watching him and not the ship. She knew she was forgotten now. And replaced.

Never mind, she told herself. Our journey's over.

This morning they had arrived at the last of the turnpikes on the outskirts of Yedo. Once more their travel papers were checked. Once more they were passed through with politeness, but this time a new honor guard was waiting for them.

"They're to take us to the castle, Anjin-san. You'll stay there, and this evening we're to meet Lord Toranaga."

"Good, then there's plenty of time. Look, Mariko-san, the docks aren't more than a mile off, *neh?* My ship's there somewhere. Would you ask the Captain Yoshinaka if we can go there, please?"

"He says, so sorry, but he has no instructions to do that, Anjin-san. He is to take us to the castle."

"Please tell him . . . perhaps I'd better try. *Taicho-san! Okashira, sukoshi no aida watakushi wa ikitai no desu. Watakushi no funega asoko ni arimasu.*" Captain, I want to go there now for a little while. My ship's there.

"*Iyé,* Anjin-san, *gomen nasai. Ima . . .*"

Mariko had listened approvingly and with amusement as Blackthorne had argued courteously and insisted firmly, and then, reluctantly, Yoshinaka had allowed them to detour, but just for a moment, *neh?* and only because the Anjin-san claimed hatamoto status, which gave certain inalienable rights, and had pointed out that a quick examination was important to Lord Toranaga, that

555

it would certainly save their lord's immensely valuable time and was vital to his meeting tonight. Yes, the Anjin-san may look for a moment, but so sorry, it is of course forbidden to go on the ship without papers signed personally by Lord Toranaga, and it must only be for a moment because we are expected, so sorry.

"*Domo,* Taicho-san," Blackthorne had said expansively, more than a little pleased with his increased understanding of the correct ways to persuade and his growing command of the language.

Last night and most of yesterday they had spent at an inn barely two *ri* southward down the road, Yoshinaka allowing them to dawdle as before.

Oh, that was such a lovely night, she thought.

There had been so many lovely days and nights. All perfect except the first day after leaving Mishima, when Father Tsukku-san caught up with them again and the precarious truce between the two men was ripped asunder. Their quarrel had been sudden, vicious, fueled by the Rodrigues incident and too much brandy. Threat and counterthreat and curses and then Father Alvito had spurred on ahead for Yedo, leaving disaster in his wake, the joy of the journey ruined.

"We must not let this happen, Anjin-san."

"But that man had no right—"

"Oh yes, I agree. And of course you're correct. But please, if you let this incident destroy your harmony, you will be lost and so will I. Please, I implore you to be Japanese. Put this incident away—that's all it is, one incident in ten thousand. You must not allow it to wreck your harmony. Put it away into a compartment."

"How? How can I do that? Look at my hands! I'm so God-cursed angry I can't stop them shaking!"

"Look at this rock, Anjin-san. Listen to it growing."

"What?"

"Listen to the rock grow, Anjin-san. Put your mind on that, on the harmony of the rock. Listen to the *kami* of the rock. Listen my love, for thy life's sake. And for mine."

So he had tried and had succeeded just a little and the next day, friends again, lovers again, at peace again, she continued to teach, trying to mold him—without his knowing he was being molded—to the Eightfold Fence, building inner walls and defenses that were his only path to harmony. And to survival.

"I'm so glad the priest has gone and won't come back, Anjin-san."

"Yes."

"It would have been better if there had been no quarrel. I'm afraid for you."

"Nothing's different—he always was my enemy, always will be. *Karma* is *karma.* But don't forget nothing exists outside us. Not yet. Not him or anyone. Not until Yedo. *Neh?*"

"Yes. You are so wise. And right again. I'm so happy to be with thee. . . ."

Their road from Mishima left the flat lands quickly and wound up the mountain to Hakoné Pass. They rested there two days atop the mountain, joyous and content, Mount Fuji glorious at sunrise and sunset, her peak obscured by a wreath of clouds.

"Is the mountain always like that?"

"Yes, Anjin-san, most always shrouded. But that makes the sight of Fuji-san, clear and clean, so much more exquisite, *neh?* You can climb all the way to the top if you wish."

"Let's do that now!"

"Not now, Anjin-san. One day we will. We must leave something to the future, *neh?* We'll climb Fuji-san in autumn. . . ."

Always there were pretty, private inns down to the Kwanto plains. And always rivers and streams and rivulets to cross, the sea on the right now. Their party had meandered northward along the busy, bustling Tokaidō, across the greatest rice bowl in the Empire. The flat alluvial plains were rich with water, every inch cultivated. The air was hot and humid now, heavy with the stench of human manure that the farmers moistened with water and ladled onto the plants with loving care.

"Rice gives us food to eat, Anjin-san, tatamis to sleep on, sandals to walk with, clothes to shut out the rain and the cold, thatch to keep our houses warm, paper for writing. Without rice we cannot exist."

"But the stink, Mariko-san!"

"That's a small price to pay for so much bounty, *neh?* Just do as we do, open your eyes and ears and mind. Hear the wind and the rain, the insects and the birds, listen to the plants growing, and in your mind, see your generations following unto the end of time. If you do that, Anjin-san, soon you smell only the loveliness of life. It requires practice . . . but you become very Japanese, *neh?*"

"Ah, thank you, m'lady! But I do confess I'm beginning to like rice. Yes. I certainly prefer it to potatoes, and you know another thing—I don't miss meat as much as I did. Isn't that strange? And I'm not as hungry as I was."

"I am more hungry than I've ever been."

"Ah, I was talking about food."

"Ah, so was I. . . ."

Three days away from Hakoné Pass her monthly time began and she had asked him to take one of the maids of the inn. "It would be wise, Anjin-san."

"I'd prefer not to, so sorry."

"Please, I ask thee. It is a safeguard. A discretion."

"Because you ask, then yes. But tomorrow, not tonight. Tonight let us sleep in peace."

Yes, Mariko thought, that night we slept peacefully and the next dawn was so lovely that I left his warmth and sat on the veranda with Chimmoko and watched the birth of another day.

"Ah, good morning, Lady Toda." Gyoko had been standing at the garden entrance, bowing to her. "A gorgeous dawn, *neh?*"

"Yes, beautiful."

"Please may I interrupt you? Could I speak to you privately—alone? About a business matter."

"Of course." Mariko had left the veranda, not wishing to disturb the Anjin-san's sleep. She sent Chimmoko for cha and ordered blankets to be put on the grass, near the little waterfall.

When it was correct to begin and they were alone, Gyoko said, "I was considering how I could be of the most help to Toranaga-sama."

"The thousand koku would be more than generous."

"Three secrets might be more generous."

"One might be, Gyoko-san, if it was the right one."

"The Anjin-san is a good man, *neh?* His future must be helped too, *neh?*"

"The Anjin-san has his own *karma,*" she replied, knowing that the time of bargaining had come, wondering what she must concede, if she dared to concede anything. "We were talking about Lord Toranaga, *neh?* Or is one of the secrets about the Anjin-san?"

"Oh no, Lady. It's as you say. The Anjin-san has his own *karma,* as I'm sure he has his own secrets. It's just occurred to me that the Anjin-san is one of Lord Toranaga's favored vassals, so any protection our Lord has in a way helps his vassals, *neh?*"

"I agree. Of course, it's the duty of vassals to pass on *any* information that could help their lord."

"True, Lady, very true. Ah, it's such an honor for me to serve you. *Honto.* May I tell you how honored I am to have been allowed to travel with you, to talk with you, and eat and laugh with you, and occasionally to act as a modest counselor, however ill-equipped I am, for which I apologize. And finally to say that your wisdom is as great as your beauty, and your bravery as vast as your rank."

"Ah, Gyoko-san, please excuse me, you're too kind, too thoughtful. I am just a wife of one of my Lord's generals. You were saying? Four secrets?"

"Three, Lady. I was wondering if you'd intercede with Lord Toranaga for me. It would be unthinkable for me to whisper directly to him what I know to be true. That would be very bad manners because I wouldn't know the right words to choose, or how to put the information before him, and in any event, in a matter of any importance, our custom to use a go-between is so much better, *neh?*"

"Surely Kiku-san would be a better choice? I've no way of knowing when I'll be sent for or how long it would be before I'll have an audience with him, or even if he'd be interested in listening to anything I might have to tell him."

"Please excuse me, Lady, but you would be extraordinarily better. You could judge the value of the information, she couldn't. You possess his ear, she other things."

"I'm not a counselor, Gyoko-san. Nor a valuer."

"I'd say they're worth a thousand koku."

"So desu ka?"

Gyoko made perfectly sure no one was listening, then told Mariko what the renegade Christian priest had muttered aloud that the Lord Onoshi had whispered to him in the confessional that he had related to his uncle, Lord Harima; then what Omi's second cook had overhead of Omi's and his mother's plot against Yabu; and lastly, all she knew about Zataki, his apparent lust for the Lady Ochiba, and about Ishido and Lady Ochiba.

Mariko had listened intently without comment—although breaking the secrecy of the confessional shocked her greatly—her mind hopping at the swarm of possibilities this information unlocked. Then she cross-questioned Gyoko carefully, to make sure she understood clearly what she was being told and to etch it completely in her own memory.

When she was satisfied that she knew everything that Gyoko was prepared to divulge at the moment—for, obviously, so shrewd a bargainer would always hold much in reserve—she sent for fresh cha.

She poured Gyoko's cup herself, and they sipped demurely. Both wary, both confident.

"I've no way of knowing how valuable this information is, Gyoko-san."

"Of course, Mariko-sama."

"I imagine this information—and the thousand koku—would please Lord Toranaga greatly."

Gyoko bit back the obscenity that flared behind her lips. She had expected a substantial reduction in the beginning bid. "So sorry, but money has no significance to such a *daimyo,* though it is a heritage to a peasant like myself—a thousand koku makes me an ancestress, *neh?* One must always know what one is, Lady Toda. *Neh?*" Her tone was barbed.

"Yes. It's good to know what you are, and who you are, Gyoko-san. That is one of the rare gifts a woman has over a man. A woman always knows. Fortunately I know what I am. Oh very yes. Please come to the point."

Gyoko did not flinch under the threat but slammed back into attack with corresponding impolite brevity. "The point is we both know life and understand death—and both believe treatment in hell and everywhere else depends on money."

"Do we?"

"Yes. So sorry, I believe a thousand koku is too much."

"Death is preferable?"

"I've already written my death poem, Lady:

> *When I die,*
> *don't burn me,*
> *don't bury me,*
> *just throw my body on a field to fatten some empty-bellied dog. "*

"That could be arranged. Easily."

"Yes. But I've long ears and a safe tongue, which could be more important." Mariko poured more cha. For herself. "So sorry, have you?"

"Oh yes, oh very yes. Please excuse me but it's no boast that I was trained well, Lady, in that and many other things. I'm not afraid to die. I've written my will, and detailed instructions to my kin in case of a sudden death. I've made my peace with the gods long since and forty days after I'm dead I know I'll be reborn. And if I'm not"—the woman shrugged—"then I'm a *kami. "*Her fan was stationary. "So I can afford to reach for the moon, *neh?* Please excuse me for mentioning it but I'm like you: I fear nothing. But unlike you in this life—I've nothing to lose."

"So much talk of evil things, Gyoko-san, on such a pleasant morning. It is pleasant, *neh?"* Mariko readied to bury her fangs. "I'd much prefer to see you alive, living into honored old age, one of the pillars of your new guild. Ah, that was a very tender idea. A good one, Gyoko-san."

"Thank you, Lady. Equally I'd like you safe and happy and prospering in the way that you'd wish. With all the toys and honors you'd require."

"Toys?" Mariko repeated, dangerous now.

Gyoko was like a trained dog on the scent near the kill. "I'm only a peasant, Lady, so I wouldn't know what honors you wish, what toys would please you. *Or your son. "*

Unnoticed by either of them the slim wooden haft of Mariko's fan snapped between her fingers. The breeze had died. Now the hot wet air hung in the garden that looked out on a waveless sea. Flies swarmed and settled and swarmed again.

"What—what honors or toys would you wish? For yourself?" Mariko stared with malevolent fascination at the older woman, clearly aware now that she must destroy this woman or her son would perish.

"Nothing for myself. Lord Toranaga's given me honors and riches beyond my dreams. But for *my* son? Ah yes, he could be given a helping hand."

"What help?"

"Two swords."

"Impossible."

"I know, Lady. So sorry. So easy to grant, yet so impossible. War's coming. Many will be needed to fight."

"There'll be no war now. Lord Toranaga's going to Osaka."

"Two swords. That's not much to ask."

"That's impossible. So sorry, that's not mine to give."

"So sorry, but I haven't asked *you* for anything. But that's the only thing that would please me. Yes. Nothing else." A dribble of sweat fell from Gyoko's face onto her lap. "I'd like to offer Lord Toranaga five hundred koku from the contract price, as a token of my esteem in these hard times. The other five hundred will go to my son. A samurai needs a heritage, *neh?*"

"You sentence your son to death. All Toranaga samurai will die or become *ronin* very soon."

"*Karma.* My son already has sons, Lady. They will tell their sons that once we were samurai. That's all that matters, *neh?*"

"It's not mine to give."

"True. So sorry. But that's all that would satisfy me."

Irritably, Toranaga shook his head. "Her information's interesting—perhaps—but not worth making her son samurai."

Mariko replied, "She seems to be a loyal vassal, Sire. She said she'd be honored if you'd deduct a further five hundred koku from the contract fee for some needy samurai."

"That's not generosity. No, not at all. That's merely guilt over the original usurious asking price."

"Perhaps it's worth considering, Sire. Her idea about the guild, about *gei-sha* and the new classes of courtesans, will have far-reaching effects, *neh?* It would do no harm, perhaps."

"I don't agree. No. Why should she be rewarded? There's no reason for granting her that honor. Ridiculous! She surely didn't ask you for it, did she?"

"It would have been more than a little impertinent for her to do that, Sire. I have made the suggestion because I believe she could be very valuable to you."

"She'd better be more valuable. Her secrets are probably lies too. These days I get nothing but lies." Toranaga rang a small bell and an equerry appeared instantly at the far door.

"Sire?"

"Where's the courtesan Kiku?"

"In your quarters, Sire."

"Is the Gyoko woman with her?"

"Yes, Sire."

"Send them both out of the castle. At once! Send them back to. . . . No, lodge them at an inn—a third-class inn—and tell them to wait there until I send for them." Toranaga said testily, as the man vanished, "Disgusting! Pimps wanting to be samurai? Filthy peasants don't know their place anymore!"

Mariko watched him sitting on his cushion, his fan waving desultorily. She was jarred by the change in him. Gloom, irritation, and petulance, where before there had always been only buoyant confidence. He had listened to the secrets with interest, but not with the excitement she had expected. Poor man, she thought with pity, he's given up. What's the good of any information to him? Perhaps he's wise to cast things of the world aside and prepare for the unknown. Better you should do that yourself too, she thought, dying inside a bit more. Yes, but you can't, not yet, somehow you've got to protect your son.

They were on the sixth floor of the tall fortified donjon and the windows overlooked the whole city on three quarters of the compass. Sunset was dark tonight, the thread of moon low on the horizon, the dank air stifling, though here, almost a hundred feet above the floor of the castle battlements, the room gathered every breath of wind. The room was low and fortified and took up half the whole floor, other rooms beyond.

Toranaga picked up the dispatch that Hiro-matsu had sent with Mariko and read it again. She noticed his hand tremble.

"What's he want to come to Yedo for?" Impatiently Toranaga tossed the scroll aside.

"I don't know, Sire, so sorry. He just asked me to give you this dispatch."

"Did you talk to the Christian renegade?"

"No, Sire. Yoshinaka-san said you'd given orders against anyone doing that."

"How was Yoshinaka on the journey?"

"Very capable, Sire," she said, patiently answering the question for a second time. "Very efficient. He guarded us very well and delivered us on time exactly."

"Why didn't the priest Tsukku-san come back with you all the way?"

"On the road from Mishima, Sire, he and the Anjin-san quarreled," Mariko told him, not knowing what Father Alvito might have already told Toranaga, if in fact Toranaga had sent for him yet. "The Father decided to travel on alone."

"What was the quarrel about?"

"Partially over me, my soul, Sire. Mostly because of their religious enmity and because of the war between their rulers."

"Who started it?"

"They were equally to blame. It began over a flask of liquor." Mariko told him what had passed with Rodrigues, then continued, "The Tsukku-san had brought a second flask as a gift, wanting, so he said, to intercede for Rodrigues-san, but the Anjin-san said, shockingly bluntly, that he didn't want any 'Papist liquor,' preferred saké, and he didn't trust priests. The—the Holy Father flared up, was equally shockingly blunt, saying he had never dealt in poison, never would, and could never condone such a thing."

"Ah, poison? Do they use poison as a weapon?"

"The Anjin-san told me some of them do, Sire. This led to more violent words and then they were hacking at each other over religion, my soul, about Catholics and Protestants . . . I left to fetch Yoshinaka-san as soon as I could and he stopped the quarrel."

"Barbarians cause nothing but trouble. Christians cause nothing but trouble. *Neh?*"

She did not answer him. His petulance unsettled her. It was so unlike him and there seemed to be no reason for such a breakdown in his legendary self-control. Perhaps the shock of being beaten is too much for him, she thought. Without him we're all finished, my son's finished, and the Kwanto will soon be in other hands. His gloom was infecting her. She had noticed in the streets and in the castle the pall that seemed to hang over the whole city—a city that was famous for its gaiety, brash good humor, and delight with life.

"I was born the year the first Christians arrived and they've bedeviled the land ever since," Toranaga said. "For fifty-eight years nothing but trouble. *Neh?*"

"I'm sorry they offend you, Sire. Was there anything else? With your permi—"

"Sit down. I haven't finished yet." Toranaga rang the bell again. The door opened. "Send Buntaro-san in."

Buntaro walked in. Grim-faced, he knelt and bowed. She bowed to him, numb, but he did not acknowledge her.

A while ago Buntaro had met their cortege at the castle gate. After a brief greeting, he had told her she was to go at once to Lord Toranaga. The Anjin-san would be sent for later.

"Buntaro-san, you asked to see me in your wife's presence as soon as possible?"

"Yes, Sire."

"What is it you want?"

"I humbly beg permission to take the Anjin-san's head," Buntaro said.

"Why?"

"Please excuse me but I . . . I don't like the way he looks at my wife. I wanted . . . I wanted to say it in front of her, the first time, before you. Also, he insulted me at Anjiro and I can no longer live with this shame."

Toranaga glanced at Mariko, who seemed to be frozen in time. "You accuse her of encouraging him?"

"I . . . I ask permission to take his head."

"You accuse her of encouraging him? Answer the question!"

"Please excuse me, Sire, but if I thought that I'd be duty bound to take her head the same instant," Buntaro replied stonily, his eyes on the tatamis. "The barbarian's a constant irritation to my harmony. I believe he's a harassment to you. Let me remove his head, I beg you." He looked up, his heavy jowls unshaven, eyes deeply shadowed. "Or let me take my wife now and tonight we'll go before you—to prepare the way."

"What do you say to that, Mariko-san?"

"He is my husband. Whatever he decides, that will I do—unless you overrule him, Sire. This is my duty."

Toranaga looked from man to woman. Then his voice hardened, and for a moment he was like the Toranaga of old. "Mariko-san, you will leave in three days for Osaka. You will prepare *that* way for me, and wait for me there. Buntaro-san, you will accompany me as commander of my escort when I leave. After you have acted as my second, you or one of your men may do the same with the Anjin-san—with or without his approval."

Buntaro cleared his throat. "Sire, please order Crim—"

"Hold your tongue! You forget yourself! I've told you *no* three times! The next time you have the impertinence to offer unwanted advice you will slit your belly in a Yedo cesspool!"

Buntaro's head was on the tatamis. "I apologize, Sire. I apologize for my impertinence."

Mariko was equally appalled by Toranaga's ill-mannered, shameful outburst, and she bowed low also, to hide her own embarrassment. In a moment Toranaga said, "Please excuse my temper. Your plea is granted, Buntaro-san, but only after you've acted as my second."

"Thank you, Sire. Please excuse me for offending you."

"I ordered you both to make peace with one another. Have you done so?"

Buntaro nodded shortly. Mariko too.

"Good. Mariko-san, you will come back with the Anjin-san tonight, in the Hour of the Dog. You may go now."

She bowed and left them.

Toranaga stared at Buntaro. "Well? *Do you* accuse her?"

"It . . . it is unthinkable she'd betray me, Sire," Buntaro answered sullenly.

"I agree." Toranaga waved a fly away with his fan, seeming very tired. "Well, you may have the Anjin-san's head soon. I need it on his shoulders a little longer."

"Thank you, Sire. Again please excuse me for irritating you."

"These are irritating times. Foul times." Toranaga leaned forward. "Listen, I want you to go to Mishima at once to relieve your father for a few days. He asks permission to come here to consult with me. I don't know what. . . . Anyway, I must have someone in Mishima I can trust. Would you please leave at dawn—but by way of Takato."

"Sire?" Buntaro saw that Toranaga was keeping calm only with an enormous effort, and in spite of his will, his voice was trembling.

"I've a private message for my mother in Takato. You're to tell no one you're going there. But once you're clear of the city, cut north."

"I understand."

"Lord Zataki may prevent you from delivering it—may try to. You are to give it only into her hands. You understand? To her alone. Take twenty men and gallop there. I'll send a carrier pigeon to ask safe conduct from him."

"Your message will be verbal or in writing, Lord?"

"In writing."

"And if I can't deliver it?"

"You must deliver it, of course you must. That's why I picked you! But . . . if you're betrayed like I've . . . if you're betrayed, destroy it before you commit suicide. The moment I hear such evil news, the Anjin-san's head is off his shoulders. And if . . . what about Mariko-san? What about your wife, if something goes wrong?"

"Please dispatch her, Sire, before you die. I would be honored if. . . . She merits a worthy second."

"She won't die dishonorably, you have my promise. I'll see to it. Personally. Now please come back at dawn for the dispatch. Don't fail me. Only into my mother's hands."

Buntaro thanked him again and left, ashamed of Toranaga's outward show of fear.

Now alone, Toranaga took out a kerchief and wiped the sweat off his face. His fingers were trembling. He tried to control them but couldn't. It had taken all his strength to continue acting the stupid dullard, to hide his unbounding excitement over the secrets, which, fantastically, promised the long-hoped-for reprieve.

"A possible reprieve, only possible—if they're true," he said aloud, hardly able to think, the astoundingly welcome information that Mariko had brought from the Gyoko woman still shrieking in his brain.

Ochiba, he was gloating, . . . so that harpy's the lure to bring my brother tumbling out of his mountain eyrie. *My brother wants Ochiba.* But now it's equally obvious he wants more than her, and more than just the Kwanto. He wants the realm. He detests Ishido, loathes Christians, and is now sick with jealousy over Ishido's well-known lust for Ochiba. So he'll fall out with Ishido, Kiyama, and Onoshi. Because what my treacherous brother really wants is to be Shōgun. He's Minowara, with all the lineage necessary, all the ambition, but not the mandate. Or the Kwanto. First he must get the Kwanto to get the rest.

Toranaga rubbed his hands with glee at all the wonderful new possible ploys this newfound knowledge gave him against his brother.

And Onoshi the leper! A drop of honey in Kiyama's ear at the right time, he thought, and the guts of the renegade's treason twisted a little, improved modestly, and Kiyama might gather his legions and go after Onoshi with fire and sword at once. 'Gyoko's quite sure, Sire. The acolyte Brother Joseph said Lord Onoshi had whispered in the confessional that he had made a secret treaty with Ishido against a fellow Christian *daimyo* and wanted absolution. The treaty solemnly agreed that in return for support now, Ishido promised the day you are dead that this fellow Christian would be impeached for treason and invited into the Void, the same day, forcibly if necessary, and Onoshi's son and heir would inherit all lands. The Christian was not named, Sire.'

Kiyama or Harima of Nagasaki? Toranaga asked himself. It doesn't matter. For me it must be Kiyama.

He got up shakily, in spite of his jubilation, and groped to one of the windows, leaned heavily on the wooden sill. He peered at the moon, and the sky beyond. The stars were dull. Rain clouds were building.

"Buddha, all gods, any gods, let my brother take the bait—and let that woman's whisperings be true!"

No shooting star appeared to show the message was acknowledged by the gods. No wind sprang up, no sudden cloud blanketed the crescent moon. Even if there had been a heavenly sign he would have dismissed it as a coincidence.

Be patient. Consider facts only. Sit down and think, he told himself.

He knew the strain was beginning to tell on him but it was vital that none of his intimates or vassals—thus none of the legion of loose-mouthed fools or spies of Yedo—suspect for an instant that he was only feigning capitulation and play-acting the role of a beaten man. At Yokosé he had realized at once that to accept the second scroll from his brother was his death knell. He had decided his only tiny chance of survival was to convince everyone, even himself, that he had absolutely accepted defeat, though in reality it was only a cover to gain time, continuing his lifelong pattern of negotiation, delay, and seeming retreat, always waiting patiently until a chink in the armor appeared over a jugular, then stabbing home viciously, without hesitation.

Since Yokosé he had waited out the lonely watches of the nights and the days, each one harder to bear. No hunting or laughing, no plotting or planning or swimming or banter or dancing and singing in Nōh plays that had delighted him all his life. Only the same lonely role, the most difficult in his life: gloom, surrender, indecision, apparent helplessness, with self-imposed semistarvation.

To help pass the time he had continued to refine the Legacy. This was a series of private secret instructions to his successors that he had formulated over the years on how best to rule after him. Sudara had already sworn to abide by the Legacy, as every heir to the mantle would be required to do. In this way the future of the clan would be assured—may be assured, Toranaga reminded himself as he changed a word or added a sentence or eliminated a paragraph, providing I escape this present trap.

The Legacy began: "The duty of a lord of a province is to give peace and security to the people and does not consist of shedding luster on his ancestors or working for the prosperity of his descendants. . . ."

One of the maxims was: "Remember that fortune and misfortune should be left to heaven and natural law. They are not to be bought by prayer or any cunning device to be thought of by any man or self-styled saint."

Toranaga eliminated ". . . or self-styled saint," and changed the sentence to end ". . . by any man whatsoever."

Normally he would enjoy stretching his mind to write clearly and succinctly, but during the long days and nights it had taken all of his self-discipline to continue playing such an alien role.

That he had succeeded so well pleased him yet dismayed him. How could people be so gullible?

Thank the gods they are, he answered himself for the millionth time. By accepting "defeat" you have twice avoided war. You're still trapped, but now, at long last, your patience has brought its reward and you have a new chance.

Perhaps you've got a chance, he corrected himself. Unless the secrets are false and given by an enemy to enmesh you further.

His chest began to ache, he became weak and dizzy, so he sat down and breathed deeply as the Zen teachers had taught him years ago. 'Ten deep, ten slow, ten deep, ten slow, send your mind into the Void. There is no past or future, hot or cold, pain or joy—from nothing, into nothing. . . .'

Soon he started to think clearly again. Then he went to his desk and began to write. He asked his mother to act as intermediary between himself and his half-brother and to present an offer for the future of their clan. First, he petitioned his brother to consider a marriage with the Lady Ochiba: ". . . of course it would be unthinkable for me to do this, brother. Too many *daimyos* would be enraged at my 'vaulting ambition.' But such a liaison with you would cement the peace of the realm, and confirm the succession of Yaemon—no one doubting your loyalty, though some in error doubt mine. You could certainly get a more eligible wife, but she could hardly get a better husband. Once the traitors to His Imperial

Highness are removed, and I resume my rightful place as President of the Council of Regents, I will invite the Son of Heaven to request the marriage if you will agree to take on such a burden. I sincerely feel this sacrifice is the only way we can both secure the succession and do our sworn duty to the Taikō. Second, you're offered all the domains of the Christian traitors Kiyama and Onoshi, who are presently plotting, with the barbarian priests, a treasonous war against all non-Christian *daimyos,* supported by a musket-armed invasion of barbarians *as they did before against our liege lord, the Taikō.* Further, you're offered all the lands of any other Kyushu Christians who side with the traitor Ishido against me in the final battle. (Did you know that upstart peasant has had the impertinence to let it be known that once I am dead and he *rules* the Regents, he plans to dissolve the Council and marry the mother of the Heir himself?)

"And in return for the above, just this, brother: a secret treaty of alliance now, guaranteed safe passage for my armies through the Shinano mountains, a joint attack under my generalship against Ishido at a time and manner of my choosing. Last, as a measure of my trust I will at once send my son Sudara, his wife the Lady Genjiko, and their children, including my only grandson, to you in Takato. . . ."

This isn't the work of a defeated man, Toranaga told himself as he sealed the scroll. Zataki will know that instantly. Yes, but now the trap's baited. Shinano's athwart my only road, and Zataki's the initial key to the Osaka plains.

Is it true that Zataki wants Ochiba? I risk so much over the supposed whispers of a straddled maid and grunting man. Could Gyoko be lying for her own advantage, that impertinent bloodsucker! Samurai? So that's the real key to unlock all her secrets.

She must have proof about Mariko and the Anjin-san. Why else would Mariko put such a request to me? Toda Mariko and the barbarian! The barbarian and Buntaro! Eeeee, life is strange.

Another twinge over his heart wracked him. After a moment he wrote the message for a carrier pigeon and plodded up the stairs to the loft above. Carefully he selected a Takato pigeon from one of the many panniers and slid the tiny cylinder home. Then he put the pigeon on the perch in the open box that would allow her to fly off at first light.

The message asked his mother to request safe passage for Buntaro, who had an important dispatch for her and his brother. And he had signed it like the offer, Yoshi Toranaga-noh-Minowara, claiming that mantle for the first time in his life.

"Fly safe and true, little bird," he said, caressing her with a fallen feather. "You carry a heritage of ten thousand years."

Once more his eyes went to the city below. The smallest bar of light appeared on the west horizon. Down by the docks he could see the pinpricks of flares that surrounded the barbarian ship.

There's another key, he thought, and he began to rethink the three secrets. He knew he had missed something.

"I wish Kiri were here," he said to the night.

Mariko was kneeling in front of her polished metal mirror. She looked away from her face. In her hands was the dagger, catching the flickering oil light.

"I should use thee," she said, filled with grief. Her eyes sought the Madonna and Child in the niche beside the lovely spray of flowers, and filled with tears. "I know suicide's a mortal sin, but what can I do? How can I live with this shame? It's better for me to do it before I'm betrayed."

The room was quiet like the house. This was their family house, built within the innermost ring of defenses and the wide moat around the castle, where only the most favored and trusted hatamoto were allowed to live. Circling the house was a bamboo-walled garden and a tiny stream ran through it, tapped from the abundance of waters surrounding the castle.

She heard footsteps. The front gate creaked open and there was the sound of servants rushing to greet the master. Quickly she put the knife away in her obi and dried her tears. Soon there were footsteps and she opened her door, bowing politely.

In ill humor, Buntaro told her Toranaga had changed his mind again, that now he was ordered to Mishima temporarily. "I'll leave at dawn. I wanted to wish you a safe journey—" He stopped and peered at her. "Why are you crying?"

"Please excuse me, Sire. It's just because I'm a woman and life seems so difficult for me. And because of Toranaga-sama."

"He's a broken reed. I'm ashamed to say it. Terrible, but that's what he's become. We should go to war. Far better to go to war than to know the only future I've got is to see Ishido's filthy face laughing at my *karma!*"

"Yes, so sorry. I wish there was something I could do to help. Would you like saké or cha?"

Buntaro turned and bellowed at a servant who was waiting in the passageway. "Get saké! Hurry up!"

Buntaro walked into her room. Mariko closed the door. Now he stood at the window looking up at the castle walls and the donjon beyond.

"Please don't worry, Sire," she said placatingly. "The bath's ready and I've sent for your favorite."

He kept his eyes on the donjon, seething. Then he said, "He should resign in Lord Sudara's favor if he's not got the stomach for leadership anymore. Lord Sudara's his son and legal heir, *neh? Neh?*"

"Yes, Sire."

"Yes. Or even better, he should do as Zataki suggested. Commit seppuku. Then we'd have Zataki and his armies fighting with us. With them and the muskets we could smash through to Kyoto, I know we could. Even if we failed, better that than give up like filthy, cowardly Garlic Eaters! Our Master's forfeited all rights. *Neh? NEH?*" He whirled on her.

"Please excuse me—it's not for me to say. He's our liege lord."

Buntaro turned back again, brooding, to stare at the donjon. Lights flickered on all levels. Particularly the sixth. "My advice to his Council is to invite him to depart, and if he won't—to help him. There's precedent enough! There are many who share my opinion, but not Lord Sudara, not yet. Maybe he does secretly, who knows about him, what he's really thinking? When you meet his wife, when you meet Lady Genjiko, talk to her, persuade her. Then she'll persuade him—she leads him by the nose, *neh?* You're friends, she'll listen to you. Persuade her."

"I think that would be very bad to do, Sire. That's treason."

"I order you to talk to her!"

"I will obey you."

"Yes, you'll obey an order, won't you?" he snarled. "Obey? Why are you always so cold and bitter? Eh?" He picked up her mirror and shoved it up to her face. "Look at yourself!"

"Please excuse me if I displease you, Sire." Her voice was level and she stared past the mirror to his face. "I don't wish to anger you."

He watched her for a moment then sullenly tossed the mirror back onto the lacquered table. "I didn't accuse you. If I thought that I'd . . . I wouldn't hesitate."

Mariko heard herself spit back, unforgivably, "Wouldn't hesitate to do what? Kill me, Sire? Or leave me alive to shame me more?"

"I didn't accuse you, only him!" Buntaro bellowed.

"But I accuse you!" she shrieked in return. "And you *did* accuse me!"

"Hold your tongue!"

"You shamed me in front of our lord! You accused me and you won't do your duty! You're afraid! *You're* a coward! A filthy, garlic-eating coward!"

His sword came out of its scabbard, and she gloried in the fact that at least she had dared to push him over the brink.

But the sword remained poised in the air. "I . . . I have your . . . I have your promise before your . . . your God, in Osaka. Before we . . . we go into death . . . I have your promise and I . . . I hold you to that!"

Her baiting laugh was shrill and vicious. "Oh yes, mighty Lord. I'll be your cushion just once more, but your welcome will be dry, bitter, and rancid!"

He hacked blindly with all his two-handed strength at a corner post and the blade sliced almost totally through the foot-thick seasoned beam. He tugged but the sword held fast. Almost berserk, he twisted it and fought it and then the blade snapped. With a final curse he hurled the broken haft through the flimsy wall and staggered drunkenly for the door. The quavering servant stood there with the tray and saké. Buntaro smashed it out of his hands. Instantly the servant knelt, put his head on the floor, and froze.

Buntaro leaned on the shattered door frame. "Wait . . . wait till Osaka."

He groped out of the house.

For a time, Mariko remained immobile, seemingly in a trance. Then the color began to return to her cheeks. Her eyes focused. Silently she returned to her mirror. She studied her reflection for a moment. Then, quite calmly, she finished applying her makeup.

Blackthorne ran up the stairs two at a time, his guard with him. They were on the main staircase within the donjon and he was glad to be unencumbered by his swords. He had formally surrendered them in the courtyard to the first guards, who had also searched him politely but thoroughly. Torches lit the staircase and the landings. On the fourth landing he stopped, almost bursting with pent-up excitement, and called back, "Mariko-san, are you all right?"

"Yes—yes. I'm fine, thank you, Anjin-san."

He began to climb again, feeling light and very strong, until he reached the final landing on the sixth floor. This level was heavily guarded like all the others. His escorting samurai went over to those clustering at the final iron-fortified door and bowed. They bowed back and motioned Blackthorne to wait.

The ironwork and woodwork in the entire castle were excellent. Here in the donjon all the windows, though delicate and soaring, doubled as stations for bowmen, and there were heavy, iron-covered shutters ready to swing into place for further protection.

Mariko rounded the last angle of the easily defensible staircase and reached him.

"You all right?" he asked.

"Oh yes, thank you," she answered, slightly out of breath. But she still possessed the same curious serenity and detachment that he had at once noticed when he had met her in the courtyard but had never seen before.

Never mind, he thought confidently, it's just the castle and Toranaga and Buntaro and being here in Yedo. I know what to do now.

Ever since he had seen *Erasmus* he had been filled with an immense joy. He had truly never expected to find his ship so perfect, so clean and cared for, and ready. There's hardly reason to stay in Yedo now, he had thought. I'll just take a quick look below to test the bilges, an easy dive over the side to check the keel, then guns, powder room, ammunition and shot and sails. During the journey to Yedo he'd planned how to use heavy silk or cotton cloth for sails; Mariko had told him that canvas did not exist in Japan. Just get the sails commissioned, he chortled, and any other spares we need, then off to Nagasaki like a lightning bolt.

"Anjin-san!" The samurai was back.

"Hai?"

"Dozo."

The fortified door swung open silently. Toranaga was seated at the far end of the square room on a section of raised tatamis. Alone.

Blackthorne knelt and bowed low, his hands flat. *"Konbanwa,* Toranaga-sama. *Ikaga desu ka?"*

"Okagesana de genki desu. Anata wa?"

Toranaga seemed older and lackluster, and much thinner than before. *Shigata ga nai,* Blackthorne told himself. Toranaga's *karma* won't touch *Erasmus*—she's going to be his savior, by God.

He answered Toranaga's standard inquiries in simple but well-accented Japanese, using a simplified technique he had developed with Alvito's help. Toranaga complimented him on the improvement and began to speak faster.

Blackthorne used one of the stock phrases he had worked out with Alvito and Mariko: "Please excuse me, Lord, as my Japanese is not good, would you please speak slower and use simple words, as I have to use simple words—please excuse me for putting you to so much trouble."

"All right. Yes, certainly. Tell me, how did you like Yokosé?"

Blackthorne replied, keeping up with Toranaga, his answers halting, his vocabulary still very limited, until Toranaga asked a question, the key words of which he missed entirely. *"Dozo? Gomen nasai,* Toranaga-sama," he said apologetically. *"Wakarimasen."* I don't understand.

Toranaga repeated what he had said, in simpler language. Blackthorne glanced at Mariko. "So sorry, Mariko-san, what's *'sonkei su beki umi'?"*

" 'Seaworthy,' Anjin-san."

"Ah! *Domo."* Blackthorne turned back. The *daimyo* had asked if he could quickly make sure whether his ship was completely seaworthy, and how long that would take. He replied, "Yes, easy. Half day, Lord."

Toranaga thought a moment, then told him to do that tomorrow and report back in the afternoon, during the Hour of the Goat. *"Wakarimasu?"*

"Hai."

"Then you can see your men," Toranaga added.

"Sire?"

"Your vassals. I sent for you to tell you tomorrow you'll have your vassals."

"Ah, so sorry. I understand. Samurai vassals. Two hundred men."

"Yes. Good night, Anjin-san. I'll see you tomorrow."

"Please excuse me, Lord, may I respectfully ask three things?"

"What?"

"First: Possible see my crew now please? Save time, *neh?* Please."

Toranaga agreed and gave a curt order to one of the samurai to guide Blackthorne. "Take a ten-man guard with you. Take the Anjin-san there and bring him back to the castle."

"Yes, Lord."

"Next, Anjin-san?"

"Please possible talk alone? Little time. Please excuse my rudeness." Blackthorne tried not to show his anxiety as Toranaga asked Mariko what this was all about. She replied truthfully that she only knew the Anjin-san had something private to say but she had not asked him what it was.

"You're certain it'll be all right for me to ask him, Mariko-san?" Blackthorne had said as they began to climb the stairs.

"Oh yes. Providing you wait till he's finished. But be sure you know exactly what you're going to say, Anjin-san. He's . . . he's not as patient as he is normally." She had not asked him what he had wanted to ask, and he had not volunteered anything.

"Very well, Anjin-san," Toranaga was saying. "Please wait outside, Mariko-san. She bowed and left. "Yes?"

"So sorry, hear Lord Harima of Nagasaki now enemy."

Toranaga was startled for he had heard about Harima's public commitment to Ishido's standard only when he himself had reached Yedo. "Where did you get that information?"

"Please?"

Toranaga repeated the question slower.

"Ah! Understand. Hear about Lord Harima at Hakoné. Gyoko-san tell us. Gyoko-san hear in Mishima."

"That woman's well informed. Perhaps too well informed."

"Sire?"

"Nothing. Go on. What about Lord Harima?"

"Sire, may I respectfully say: my ship, big weapon over Black Ship, *neh?* If I take Black Ship very quick—priests very anger because no money Christian work here—no money also Portuguese other lands. Last year no Black Ship here, so no money, *neh?* If now take Black Ship quick, very quick, and also next year, all priest has great fear. That's the truth, Sire. Think priests *must* bend if threatens. Priests like this for Toranaga-sama!" Blackthorne snapped his hand shut to make his point.

Toranaga had listened intently, watching his lips as he was doing the same. "I follow you, but to what end, Anjin-san?"

"Sire?"

Toranaga fell into the same pattern of using few words. "To obtain what? To catch what? To get what?"

"Lord Onoshi, Lord Kiyama, and Lord Harima."

"So you want to interfere in our politics like the priests? You think you know how to rule us as well, Anjin-san?"

"So sorry, please excuse me, I don't understand."

"It doesn't matter." Toranaga thought for a long time, then said, "Priests say they've no power to order Christian *daimyos.*"

"No true, Sire, please excuse me. Money *big* power over priests. It's the truth, Sire. If no Black Ship this year, and also next year no Black Ship, ruin. Very, very bad for priests. It's the truth, Sire. Money *is* power. Please consider: If Crimson Sky at same time or before, I attack Nagasaki. Nagasaki enemy now, *neh?* I take Black Ship and attack sea roads between Kyushu and Honshu. Maybe threat enough to make enemy into friend?"

"No. The priests will stop trade. I am not at war with the priests or Nagasaki. Or anyone. I am going to Osaka. There will be no Crimson Sky. *Wakarimasu?*"

"*Hai.*" Blackthorne was not perturbed. He knew that now Toranaga clearly understood that this possible tactic would certainly draw off a large proportion of Kiyama-Onoshi-Harima forces, all of whom were Kyushu-based. And *Erasmus* could certainly wreck any large-scale seaborne transfer of troops from that island to the main one. Be patient, he cautioned himself. Let Toranaga consider it. Maybe it'll be as Mariko says: There is a long time between now and Osaka, and who knows what might happen? Prepare for the best but do not fear the worst.

"Anjin-san, why not say this in front of Mariko-san? She will tell priests? You think that?"

"No, Sire. Only want to try talk direct. Not woman's business to war. One last ask, Toranaga-sama." Blackthorne launched himself on a chosen course. "Custom hatamoto ask favor, sometimes. Please excuse me, Sire, may I respectfully say now possible ask?"

Toranaga's fan stopped waving. "What favor?"

"Know divorce easy if lord say. Ask Toda Mariko-sama wife." Toranaga was dumbstruck and Blackthorne was afraid he'd gone too far. "Please excuse me for my rudeness," he added.

Toranaga recovered quickly. "Mariko-san agrees?"

"No, Toranaga-sama. Secret *my.* Never say to her, anyone. Secret my only. Not say to Toda Mariko-san. Never. *Kinjiru, neh?* But know angers between husband wife. Divorce easy in Japan. This my secret only. Ask Lord Toranaga only. Very secret. Never Mariko-san. Please excuse me if I've offended you."

"That's a presumptuous request for a stranger. Unheard of! Because you're hatamoto I'm duty bound to consider it, though you're forbidden to mention it to her under any circumstances, either to her or to her husband. Is that clear?"

"Please?" Blackthorne asked, not understanding at all, hardly able to think.

"Very bad ask and thought, Anjin-san. Understand?"

"Yes Sire, so sor—"

"Because Anjin-san hatamoto I'm not angry. Will consider. Understand?"

"Yes, I think so. Thank you. Please excuse my bad Japanese, so sorry."

"No talk to her, Anjin-san, about divorce. Mariko-san or Buntaro-san. *Kinjiru, wakarimasu?*"

"Yes, Lord. Understand. Only secret you, I. Secret. Thank you. Please excuse my rudeness and thank you for your patience." Blackthorne bowed perfectly and, almost in a dream, he walked out. The door closed behind him. On the landing everyone was watching him quizzically.

He wanted to share his victory with Mariko. But he was inhibited by her distracted serenity and the presence of the guards. "I'm sorry to keep you waiting" was all he said.

"It was my pleasure," she answered, as noncommittal.

They started down the staircase again. Then, after a flight of stairs, she said, "Your simple way of talking is strange though quite understandable, Anjin-san."

"I was lost too many times. Knowing you were there helped me tremendously."

"I did nothing."

In the silence they walked on, Mariko behind him slightly as was correct custom. At each level they passed through a samurai cordon, then, rounding a bend in the stairs, the trailing hem of her kimono caught in the railings and she stumbled. He caught her, steadying her, and the sudden close touch pleased both of them. "Thank you," she said, flustered, as he put her down again.

They continued on, much closer than they had been tonight.

Outside in the torchlit forecourt, samurai were everywhere. Once more their passes were checked and now they were escorted with their flare-carrying porters through the donjon main gate, along a passage that meandered, mazelike, between high, battlemented stone walls to the next gate that led to the moat and the innermost wooden bridge. In all, there were seven rings of moats within the castle complex. Some were man-made, some adapted from the streams and rivers that abounded. While they headed for the main gate, the south gate, Mariko told him that, when the fortress was completed the year after next, it would house a hundred thousand samurai and twenty thousand horses, with all necessary provisions for one year.

"Then it will be the biggest in the world," Blackthorne said.

"That was Lord Toranaga's plan." Her voice was grave. *"Shigata ga nai, neh?"* At last they came to the final bridge. "There, Anjin-san, you can see the castle's the hub of Yedo, *neh?* The center of a web of streets that angle out to become the city. Ten years ago there was only a little fishing village here. Now, who knows? Three hundred thousand? Two? Four? Lord Toranaga hasn't counted his people yet. But they're all here for one purpose only: to serve the castle that protects the port and the plains that feed the armies."

"Nothing else?" he asked.

"No."

There's no need to be worried, Mariko, and look so solemn, he thought happily. I've solved all that. Toranaga will grant all my requests.

At the far side of the flare-lit Ichi-bashi—First Bridge—that led to the city proper, she stopped. "I must leave you now, Anjin-san."

"When can I see you?"

"Tomorrow. At the Hour of the Goat. I'll wait in the forecourt for you."

"I can't see you tonight? If I'm back early?"

"No, so sorry, please excuse me. Not tonight." Then she bowed formally. *"Konbanwa,* Anjin-san."

He bowed. As a samurai. He watched her going back across the bridge, some of the flare-carriers going with her, insects milling the stationary flares that were stuck in holders on stanchions. Soon she was swallowed up by the crowds and the night.

Then, his excitement increasing, he put his back to the castle and set off after the guide.

CHAPTER 48

T HE barbarians live there, Anjin-san." The samurai motioned ahead.
Ill at ease, Blackthorne squinted into the darkness, the air breathless and sultry. "Where? That house? There?"
"Yes. That's right, so sorry. You see it?"
Another nest of hovels and alleys was a hundred paces ahead, beyond this bare patch of marshy ground, and dominating them was a large house etched vaguely against the jet sky.

Blackthorne looked around for a moment to get his approximate bearings, using his fan against the encroaching bugs. Very soon, once they had left First Bridge, he had become lost in the maze.

Their way had led through innumerable streets and alleys, initially toward the shore, skirting it eastward for a time, over bridges and lesser bridges, then northward again along the bank of another stream which meandered through the outskirts, the land low-lying and moist. The farther from the castle, the meaner were the roads, the poorer the dwellings. The people were more obsequious, and fewer glimmers of light came from the shojis. Yedo was a sprawling mass which seemed to him to be made up of hamlets separated merely by roads or streams.

Here on the southeastern edge of the city it was quite marshy and the road oozed putridly. For some time the stench had been thickening perceptibly, a miasma of seaweed and feces and mud flats, and overlying these an acrid sweet smell he could not place, but that seemed familiar.

"Stinks like Billingsgate at low tide," he muttered, killing another night pest that had landed on his cheek. His whole body was clammy with sweat.

Then he heard the faintest snatch of a rollicking sea shanty in Dutch and all discomfort was forgotten. "Is that Vinck?"

Elated, he hurried toward the sound, porters lighting his way carefully, samurai following.

Now, nearer, he saw that the single-story building was part Japanese, part European. It was raised on pilings and surrounded by a high rickety bamboo fence in a plot of its own, and much newer than the hovels that clustered near. There was no gate in the fence, just a hole. The roof was thatch, the front door stout, the walls rough-boarded, and the windows covered with Dutch-style shutters. Here and there were flecks of light from the cracks. The singing and banter increased but he could not recognize any voices yet. Flagstones led straight to the steps of the veranda through an unkempt garden. A short flagpole was roped to the gateway. He stopped and stared up at it. A limp, makeshift Dutch flag hung there listlessly and his pulse quickened at the sight of it.

The front door was thrown open. A shaft of light spilled onto the veranda. Baccus van Nekk stumbled drunkenly to the edge, eyes half shut, pulled his codpiece aside, and urinated in a high, curving jet.

"Ahhhhh," he murmured with a groaning ecstasy. "Nothing like a piss."

"Isn't there?" Blackthorne called out in Dutch from the gateway. "Why don't you use a bucket?"

"Eh?" Van Nekk blinked myopically into the darkness at Blackthorne, who stood with the samurai under the flares. "JesusGodinheavensamurai!" He gathered himself with a grunt and bowed awkwardly from the waist. *"Gomen nasai,* samurai-sama. *Ichibon gomen nasai* to all monkey-samas." He straightened, forced a painful smile, and muttered half to himself, "I'm drunker'n I thought. Thought the bastard sonofawhore spoke Dutch! *Gomen nasai, neh?"* he called out again, reeling off toward the back of the house, scratching and groping at the codpiece.

"Hey, Baccus, don't you know better than to foul your own nest?"

"What?" Van Nekk jerked around and stared blindly toward the flares, desperately trying to see clearly. "Pilot?" he choked out. "Is that you, Pilot? God damn my eyes, I can't see. Pilot, for the love of God, is that you?"

Blackthorne laughed. His old friend looked so naked there, so foolish, his penis hanging out. "Yes, it's me!" Then to the samurai who watched with thinly covered contempt, *"Matte kurasai."* Wait for me, please.

"Hai, Anjin-san."

Blackthorne came forward and now in the shaft of light he could see the litter of garbage everywhere in the garden. Distastefully he stepped out of the clogs and ran up the steps. "Hello, Baccus, you're fatter than when we left Rotterdam, *neh?"* He clapped him warmly on the shoulders.

"Lord Jesus Christ, is that truly you?"

"Yes, of course it's me."

"We'd given you up for dead, long ago." Van Nekk reached out and touched Blackthorne to make sure he was not dreaming. "Lord Jesus, my prayers are answered. Pilot, what happened to you, where've you come from? It's a miracle! Is it truly you?"

"Yes. Now please put your cod in place and let's go inside," Blackthorne told him, conscious of his samurai.

"What? Oh! Oh sorry, I . . ." Van Nekk hastily complied and tears began to run down his cheeks. "Oh Jesus, Pilot . . . I thought the gin devils were playing me tricks again. Come on, but let me announce you, hey?"

He led the way back, weaving a little, much of his drunkenness evaporated with his joy. Blackthorne followed. Van Nekk held the door open for him, then shouted over the raucous singing, "Lads! Look what Father Christmas's brought us!" He slammed the door shut after Blackthorne for added effect.

Silence was instantaneous.

It took a moment for Blackthorne's eyes to adjust to the light. The fetid air was almost choking him. He saw them all gaping at him as though he were a devil-wraith. Then the spell broke and there were shouts of welcome and joy and everyone was squeezing and punching him on the back, all talking at the same time. "Pilot, where've you come from—Have a drink—Christ, is it possible—Piss in my hat, it's great to see you—We'd given you up for dead—No, we're all right at least mostly all right—Get out of the chair, you whore, the Pilot-sama's to sit in the best sodding chair—Hey, grog, *neh,* quickGodcursed quick! Goddamn my eyes get out of the way I want to shake his hand. . . ."

Finally Vinck hollered, "One at a time, lads! Give him a chance! Give the Pilot the chair and a drink, for God's sake! Yes, I thought he was samurai too. . . ."

Someone shoved a wooden goblet into Blackthorne's hand. He sat in the rickety chair and they all raised their cups and the flood of questions began again.

Blackthorne looked around. The room was furnished with benches and a few crude chairs and tables and illuminated by candles and oil lamps. A huge saké keg stood on the filthy floor. One of the tables was covered with dirty plates and a haunch of half-roasted meat, crusted with flies.

Six bedraggled women cowered on their knees, bowing to him, backed against a wall.

His men, all beaming, waited for him to start: Sonk the cook, Johann Vinck bosun's mate and chief gunner, Salamon the mute, Croocq the boy, Ginsel sailmaker, Baccus van Nekk chief merchant and treasurer, and last Jan Roper, the other merchant, who sat apart as always, with the same sour smile on his thin, taut face.

"Where's the Captain-General?" Blackthorne asked.

"Dead, Pilot, he's dead. . . ." Six voices answered and overrode each other, jumbling the tale until Blackthorne held up his hand. "Baccus?"

"He's dead, Pilot. He never came out of the pit. Remember he was sick, eh? After they took you away, well, that night we heard him choking in the darkness. Isn't that right, lads?"

A chorus of yeses, and van Nekk added, "I was sitting beside him, Pilot. He was trying to get the water but there wasn't any and he was choking and moaning. I'm not too clear about the time—we were all frightened to death—but eventually he choked and then, well, the death rattle. It was bad, Pilot."

Jan Roper added, "It was terrible, yes. But it was God's punishment."

Blackthorne looked from face to face. "Anybody hit him? To quieten him?"

"No—no, oh no," van Nekk answered. "He just croaked. He was left in the pit with the other one—the Japper, you remember him, the one who tried to drown himself in the bucket of piss? Then the Lord Omi had them bring Spellberger's body out and they burned it. But that other poor bugger got left below. Lord Omi just gave him a knife and he slit his own God-cursed belly and they filled in the pit. You remember him, Pilot?"

"Yes. What about Maetsukker?"

"Best you tell that, Vinck."

"Little Rat Face rotted, Pilot," Vinck began, and the others started shouting details and telling the tale until Vinck bellowed, "Baccus asked me, for Chrissake! You'll all get your turn!"

The voices died down and Sonk said helpfully, "You tell it, Johann."

"Pilot, it was his arm started rotting. He got nicked in the fight—you remember the fight when you got knocked out? Christ Jesus, that seems so long ago! Anyway, his arm festered. I bled him the next day and the next, then it started going black. I told him I'd better lance it or the whole arm'd have to come off—told him a dozen times, we all did, but he wouldn't. On the fifth day the wound was stinking. We held him down and I sliced off most of the rot but it weren't no good. I knew it wasn't no good but some of us thought it worth a try. The yellow bastard doctor came a few times but he couldn't do nothing either. Rat Face lasted a day or two, but the rot was too deep and he raved a lot. We had to tie him up toward the end."

"That's right, Pilot," Sonk said, scratching comfortably. "We had to tie him up."

"What happened to his body?" Blackthorne asked.

"They took it up the hill and burned it, too. We wanted to give him and the Captain-General a proper Christian burial but they wouldn't let us. They just burned them."

A silence gathered. "You haven't touched your drink, Pilot!"

Blackthorne raised it to his lips and tasted. The cup was filthy and he almost retched. The raw spirit seared his throat. The stench of unbathed bodies and rancid, unwashed clothing almost overpowered him.

"How's the grog, Pilot?" van Nekk asked.

"Fine, fine."

"Tell him about it, Baccus, go on!"

"Hey! I made a still, Pilot." Van Nekk was very proud and the others were beaming too. "We make it by the barrel now. Rice and fruit and water and let it ferment, wait a week or so and then, with the help of a little magic. . . ." The rotund man laughed and scratched happily. " 'Course it'd be better to keep it a year or so to mellow, but we drink it faster than . . ." His words trailed off. "You don't like it?"

"Oh, sorry, it's fine—fine." Blackthorne saw lice in van Nekk's sparse hair.

Jan Roper said challengingly, "And you, Pilot? You're fine, aren't you? What about you?"

Another flood of questions which died as Vinck shouted, "Give him a chance!" Then the leathery-faced man burst out happily, "Christ, when I saw you standing at the door I thought you was one of the monkeys, honest—honest!"

Another chorus of agreement and van Nekk broke in, "That's right. Damned silly kimonos—you look like a woman, Pilot—or one of those half-men! God-cursed fags, eh! Lot of Jappers are fags, by God! One was after Croocq . . ." There was much shouting and obscene banter, then van Nekk continued, "You'll want your proper clothes, Pilot. Listen, we've got yours here. We came to Yedo with *Erasmus*. They towed her here and we were allowed to bring our clothes ashore with us, nothing else. We brought yours—they allowed us to do that, to keep for you. We brought a kit bag—all your sea clothes. Sonk, fetch 'em, hey?"

"Sure I'll fetch them, but later, eh, Baccus? I don't want to miss nothing."

"All right."

Jan Roper's thin smile was taunting. "Swords and kimonos—like a real heathen! Perhaps you prefer heathen ways now, Pilot?"

"The clothes are cool, better than ours," Blackthorne replied uneasily. "I'd forgotten I was dressed differently. So much has happened. These were all I had so I got used to wearing them. I never thought much about it. They're certainly more comfortable."

"Are those real swords?"

"Yes, of course, why?"

"We're not allowed weapons. Any weapons!" Jan Roper scowled. "Why do they allow you to have 'em? Just like any heathen samurai?"

Blackthorne laughed shortly. "You haven't changed, Jan Roper, have you? Still holier than thou? Well, all in good time about my swords, but first the best news of all. Listen, in a month or so we'll be on the high seas again."

"Jesus God, you mean it, Pilot?" Vinck said.

"Yes."

There was a great roaring cheer and another welter of questions and answers. "I told you we'd get away—I told you God was on our side! Let him talk—let the Pilot talk . . ." Finally Blackthorne held up his hand.

He motioned at the women, who still knelt motionless, more abject now under his attention. "Who're they?"

Sonk laughed. "Them's our doxies, Pilot. Our whores, and cheap, Christ Jesus, they hardly cost a button a week. We got a whole house of 'em next door—and there's plenty more in the village—"

"They rattle like stoats," Croocq butted in, and Sonk said, "That's right, Pilot. 'Course they're squat and bandy but they've lots of vigor and no pox. You want one, Pilot? We've our own bunks, we're not like the monkeys, we've all our own bunks and rooms—"

"You try Big-Arse Mary, Pilot, she's the one for you," Croocq said.

Jan Roper's voice overrode them. "The Pilot doesn't want one of our harlots.

He's got his own. Eh, Pilot?"

Their faces glowed. "Is that true, Pilot? You got women? Hey, tell us, eh? These monkeys're the best that's ever been, eh?"

"Tell us about your doxies, Pilot!" Sonk scratched at his lice again.

"There's a lot to tell," Blackthorne said. "But it should be private. Less ears the better, *neh?* Send the women away, then we can talk privately."

Vinck jerked a thumb at them. "Piss off, *hai?*"

The women bowed and mumbled thanks and apologies and fled, closing the door quietly.

"First about the ship. It's unbelievable. I want to thank you and congratulate you—all the work. When we get home I'm going to insist you get triple shares of all the prize money for all that work and there's going to be a prize beyond . . ." He saw the men look at each other, embarrassed. "What's the matter?"

Van Nekk said uncomfortably, "It wasn't us, Pilot. It was King Toranaga's men. They did it. Vinck showed 'em how, but we didn't do anything."

"What?"

"We weren't allowed back aboard after the first time. None of us has been aboard except Vinck, and he goes once every ten days or so. We did nothing."

"He's the only one," Sonk said. "Johann showed 'em."

"But how'd you talk to them, Johann?"

"There's one of the samurai who talks Portuguese and we talk in that—enough to understand each other. This samurai, his name's Sato-sama, he was put in charge when we came here. He asked who were officers or seamen among us. We said that'd be Ginsel, but he's a gunner mostly, me and Sonk who—"

"Who's the worst pissing cook that—"

"Shut your God-cursed mouth, Croocq!"

"Shit, you can't cook ashore let alone afloat, by God!"

"Please be quiet, you two!" Blackthorne said. "Go on, Johann."

Vinck continued. "Sato-sama asked me what was wrong with the ship and I told him she had to be careened and scraped and repaired all over. Well, I told him all I knew and they got on with it. They careened her good and cleaned the bilges, scrubbed them like a prince's shit house—at least, samurai were bosses and other monkeys worked like demons, hundreds of the buggers. Shit, Pilot, you've never seen workers like 'em!"

"That's true," Sonk said. "Like demons!"

"I did everything the best I could against the day. . . . Jesus, Pilot, you really think we can get away?"

"Yes, if we're patient and if we—"

"If God wills it, Pilot. Only then."

"Yes. Perhaps you're right," Blackthorne replied, thinking, what's it matter that Roper's a fanatic? I need him—all of them. And the help of God. "Yes. We need the help of God," he said and turned back to Vinck. "How's her keel?"

"Clean and sound, Pilot. They've done her better'n I'd've thought possible. Those bastards are as clever as any carpenters, shipwrights, and ropemakers in all Holland. Rigging's perfect—everything."

"Sails?"

"They made a set out of silk—tough as canvas. With a spare set. They took ours down and copied 'em exact, Pilot. Cannon are perfect as possible—all back aboard and there's powder and shot a-plenty. She's ready to sail on the tide, tonight if need be. 'Course she hasn't been to sea so we won't know about the sails till we're in a gale, but I'll bet my life her seams're as tight as when she was first slipped into the Zuider Zee—better 'cause the timbers're seasoned now, thanks be to God!" Vinck paused for breath. "When are we off?"

"A month. About."

They nudged each other, brimming with elation, and loudly toasted the Pilot and the ship.

"How about enemy shipping? There any hereabouts? What about prizes, Pilot?" Ginsel asked.

"Plenty—beyond your dreams. We're all rich."

Another shout of glee. "It's about time."

"Rich, eh? I'll buy me a castle."

"Lord God Almighty, when I get home . . ."

"Rich! Hurrah for the Pilot!"

"Plenty of Papists to kill? Good," Jan Roper said softly. "Very good."

"What's the plan, Pilot?" van Nekk asked, and they all stopped talking.

"I'll come to that in a minute. Do you have guards? Can you move around freely, when you want? How often—"

Vinck said quickly, "We can move anywheres in the village area, perhaps as much as half a league around here. But we're not allowed in Yedo and not—"

"Not across the bridge," Sonk broke in happily. "Tell him about the bridge, Johann!"

"Oh, for the love of God, I was coming to the bridge, Sonk. For God's sake, don't keep interrupting. Pilot, there's a bridge about half a mile southwest. There're a lot of signs on it. That's as far as we're allowed. We're not to go over that. 'Kinjiru,' by God, the samurai say. You understand kinjiru, Pilot?"

Blackthorne nodded and said nothing.

"Apart from that we can go where we like. But only up to the barriers. There's barriers all around about half a league away. Lord God . . . can you believe it, home soon!"

"Tell him about the doc, eh, and about the—"

"The samurai send a doctor once in a while, Pilot, and we have to take our clothes off and he looks at us. . . ."

"Yes. Enough to make a man shit to have a bastard heathen monkey look at you naked like that."

"Apart from that, Pilot, they don't bother us except—"

"Hey, don't forget the doc gives us some God-rotting filthy powdered 'char' herbs we're supposed to steep in hot water but we toss 'em out. When we're sick, good old Johann bleeds us and we're fit."

"Yes," Sonk said. "We throw the char out."

"Apart from that, except for—"

"We're lucky here, Pilot, not like at first."

"That's right. At first—"

"Tell him about the inspection, Baccus!"

"I was coming to that—for God's sake, be patient—give a fellow a chance. How can I tell him anything with you all gabbing. Pour me a drink!" van Nekk said thirstily and continued. "Every ten days a few samurai come here and we line up outside and he counts us. Then they give us sacks of rice and cash, copper cash. It's plenty for everything, Pilot. We swap rice for meat and stuff—fruit or whatever. There's plenty of everything and the women do whatever we want. At first we—"

"But it wasn't like that at first. Tell him about that, Baccus!"

Van Nekk sat on the floor. "God give me strength!"

"You feeling sick, poor old lad?" Sonk asked solicitously. "Best not drink any more or you'll get the devils back, hey? He gets the devils, Pilot, once a week. We all do."

"Are you going to keep quiet while I tell the Pilot?"

"Who, me? I haven't said a thing. I'm not stopping you. Here, here's your drink!"

"Thanks, Sonk. Well, Pilot, first they put us in a house to the west of the city—"

"Down near the fields it was."

"Damnit, then you tell the story, Johann!"

"All right. Christ, Pilot, it was terrible. No grub or liquor and those God-cursed paper house're like living in a field—a man can't take a piss or pick his nose, nothing without someone watching, eh? Yes, and the slightest noise'd bring the neighbors down on us, and samurai'd be at the stoop and who wants those bastards around, eh? They'd be shaking their God-cursed swords at us, shouting and hollering, telling us to keep quiet. Well, one night someone knocked over a candle and the monkeys were all pissed off to hell with us! Jesus God, you should've heard them! They came swarming out of the woodwork with buckets of water, God-cursed mad, hissing and bowing and cursing. . . . It was only one poxy wall that got burned down. . . . Hundreds of 'em swarmed over the house like cockroaches. Bastards! You've—"

"Get on with it!"

"You want to tell it?"

"Go on, Johann, don't pay any attention to him. He's only a shit-filled cook."

"What!"

"Oh, shut up! For God's sake!" Van Nekk hurriedly took up the tale once more. "The next day, Pilot, they marched us out of there and put us into another house in the wharf area. That was just as bad. Then some weeks later, Johann stumbled onto this place. He was the only one of us allowed out, because of the ship, at that time. They'd collect him daily and bring him back at sunset. He was out fishing—we're only a few hundred yards upstream from the sea. . . . Best you tell it, Johann."

Blackthorne felt an itch on his bare leg and he rubbed it without thinking. The irritation got worse. Then he saw the mottled lump of a flea bite as Vinck continued proudly, "It's like Baccus said, Pilot. I asked Sato-sama if we could move and he said, yes, why not. They'd usually let me fish from one of their little skiffs to pass the time. It was my nose that led me here, Pilot. The old nose led me: blood!"

Blackthorne said, "A slaughterhouse! A slaughterhouse and tanning! That's . . ." He stopped and blanched.

"What's up? What is it?"

"This is an *eta* village? Jesus Christ, these people're *eta?*"

"What's wrong with eters?" van Nekk asked. "Of course they're eters."

Blackthorne waved at the mosquitoes that infested the air, his skin crawling. "Damn bugs. They're—they're rotten, aren't they? There's a tannery here, isn't there?"

"Yes. A few streets up, why?"

"Nothing. I didn't recognize the smell, that's all."

"What about eters?"

"I . . . I didn't realize, stupid of me. If I'd seen one of the men I'd've known from their short hairstyle. With the women you'd never know. Sorry. Go on with the story, Vinck."

"Well, then they said—"

Jan Roper interrupted, "Wait a minute, Vinck! What's wrong, Pilot? What about eters?"

"It's just that Japanese think of them as different. They're the executioners, and work the hides and handle corpses." He felt their eyes, Jan Roper's particularly. "*Eta* work hides," he said, trying to keep his voice careless, "and kill all the old horses and oxen and handle dead bodies."

"But what's wrong with that, Pilot? You've buried a dozen yourself, put 'em in shrouds, washed 'em—we all have, eh? We butcher our own meat, always have. Ginsel here's been hangman. . . . What's wrong with all that?"

"Nothing," Blackthorne said, knowing it to be true yet feeling befouled even so.

Vinck snorted. "Eters're the best heathen we've seen here. More like us than the other bastards. We're God-cursed lucky to be here, Pilot, fresh meat's no problem, or tallow—they give us no trouble."

"That's right. If you've lived with eters, Pilot . . ."

"Jesus Christ, the Pilot's had to live with the other bastards all the time! He doesn't know any better. How about fetching Big-Arse Mary, Sonk?"

"Or Twicklebum?"

"Shit, not her, not that old whore. The Pilot'll want a special. Let's ask mama-san. . . ."

"I bet he's starving for real grub! Hey, Sonk, cut him a slice of meat."

"Have some more grog . . ."

"Three cheers for the Pilot . . ."

In the happy uproar van Nekk clapped Blackthorne on the shoulders. "You're home, old friend. Now you're back, our prayers 're answered and all's well in the world. You're home, old friend. Listen, take my bunk. I insist. . . ."

Cheerily Blackthorne waved a last time. There was an answering shout from the darkness the far side of the little bridge. Then he turned away, his forced heartiness evaporated, and he walked around the corner, the samurai guard of ten men surrounding him.

On the way back to the castle his mind was locked in confusion. Nothing was wrong with *eta* and everything was wrong with *eta,* those are my crew there, my own people, and these are heathen and foreign and enemy. . . .

Streets and alleys and bridges passed in a blur. Then he noticed that his own hand was inside his kimono and he was scratching and he stopped in his tracks.

"Those goddamned filthy . . ." He undid his sash and ripped off his sopping kimono and, as though it were defiled, hurled it in a ditch.

"*Dozo, nan desu ka,* Anjin-san?" one of the samurai asked.

"*Nani mo!*" Nothing, by God! Blackthorne walked on, carrying his swords.

"*Ah! Eta! Wakarimasu! Gomen nasai!*" The samurai chatted among themselves but he paid them no attention.

That's better, he was thinking with utter relief, not noticing that he was almost naked, only that his skin had stopped crawling now that the flea-infested kimono was off.

Jesus God, I'd love a bath right now!

He had told the crew about his adventures, but not that he was samurai and hatamoto, or that he was one of Toranaga's protégés, or about Fujiko. Or Mariko. And he had not told them that they were going to land in force at Nagasaki and take the Black Ship by storm, or that he would be at the head of the samurai. That can come later, he thought wearily. And all the rest.

Could I ever tell them about Mariko-san?

His wooden clogs clattered on the wooden slats of First Bridge. Samurai sentries, also half-naked, lolled until they saw him, then they bowed politely as he passed, watching him intently, because this was the incredible barbarian who was astonishingly favored by Lord Toranaga, to whom Toranaga had, unbelievably, granted the never-given-before-to-a-barbarian honor of hatamoto and samurai.

At the main south gate of the castle another guide waited for him. He was escorted to his quarters within the inner ring. He had been allocated a room in one of the fortified though attractive guest houses, but he politely refused to go back there at once. "First bath please," he told the samurai.

"Ah, I understand. That's very considerate of you. The bath house is this way, Anjin-san. Yes, it's a hot night, *neh?* And I hear you've been down to the Filthy Ones. The other guests in the house will appreciate your thoughtfulness. I thank you on their behalf."

Blackthorne did not understand all the words but he gathered the meaning. 'Filthy Ones.' That describes my people and me—us, not them, poor people.

"Good evening, Anjin-san," the chief bath attendant said. He was a vast, middle-aged man with immense belly and biceps. A maid had just awakened him to announce another late customer was arriving. He clapped his hands. Bath maids arrived. Blackthorne followed them into the scrubbing room and they cleansed him and shampooed him and he made them do it a second time. Then he walked through to the sunken bath, stepped into the piping-hot water and fought the heat, then gave himself to its mind-consuming embrace.

In time strong hands helped him out and molded fragrant oil into his skin and untwisted his muscles and his neck, then led him to a resting room, and gave him a laundered, sun-fresh cotton kimono. With a long-drawn-out sigh of pleasure, he lay down.

"*Dozo gomen nasai*—cha, Anjin-san?"

"*Hai. Domo.*"

The cha arrived. He told the maid he would stay here tonight and not trouble to go to his own quarters. Then, alone and at peace, he sipped the cha, feeling it purify him; '. . . filthy-looking char herbs . . .' he thought disgustedly.

"Be patient, don't let it disturb your harmony," he said aloud. "They're just poor ignorant fools who don't know any better. You were the same once. Never mind, now you can show them, *neh?*"

He put them out of his mind and reached for his dictionary. But tonight, for the first night since he had possessed the book, he laid it carefully aside and blew out the candle. I'm too tired, he told himself.

But not too tired to answer a simple question, his mind said: Are they really ignorant fools, or is it you who are fooling yourself?

I'll answer that later, when it's time. Now the answer's unimportant. Now I only know I don't want them near me.

He turned over and put that problem into a compartment and went to sleep.

He awoke refreshed. A clean kimono and loincloth and tabi were laid out. The scabbards of his swords had been polished. He dressed quickly. Outside the house samurai were waiting. They got off their haunches and bowed.

"We're your guard today, Anjin-san."

"Thank you. Go ship now?"

"Yes. Here's your pass."

"Good. Thank you. May I ask your name please?"

"Musashi Mitsutoki."

"Thank you, Musashi-san. Go now?"

They went down to the wharves. *Erasmus* was moored tightly in three fathoms over a sanding bottom. The bilges were sweet. He dived over the side and swam under the keel. Seaweed was minimal and there were only a few barnacles. The rudder was sound. In the magazine, which was dry and spotless, he found a flint and struck a spark to a tiny test mound of gunpowder. It burned instantly, in perfect condition.

Aloft at the foremast peak he looked for telltale cracks. None there or on the climb up, or around any of the spars that he could see. Many of the ropes and halyards and shrouds were joined incorrectly, but that would only take half a watch to change.

Once more on the quarterdeck he allowed himself a great smile. "You're sound as a . . . as a what?" He could not think of a sufficiently great 'what' so he just laughed and went below again. In his cabin he felt alien. And very alone. His swords were on the bunk. He touched them, then slid Oil Seller out of its scabbard. The workmanship was marvelous and the edge perfect. Looking at the sword gave him pleasure, for it was truly a work of art. But a deadly one, he thought as always, twisting it in the light.

How many deaths have you caused in your life of two hundred years? How many more before you die yourself? Do some swords have a life of their own as Mariko says? Mariko. What about her. . . .

Then he caught sight of his sea chest reflected in the steel and this took him out of his sudden melancholy.

He sheathed Oil Seller, careful to avoid fingering the blade, for custom said that even a single touch might mar such perfection.

As he leaned against the bunk, his eyes went to his empty sea chest.

"What about rutters? And navigation instruments?" he asked his image in the copper sea lamp that had been scrupulously polished like everything else. He saw himself answer, "You buy them at Nagasaki, along with your crew. And you snatch Rodrigues. Yes. You snatch him before the attack. *Neh?*"

He watched his smile grow. "You're very sure Toranaga will let you go, aren't you?"

"Yes," he answered with complete confidence. "If he goes to Osaka or not, I'll get what I want. And I'll get Mariko too."

Satisfied, he stuck his swords in his sash and walked up on deck and waited until the doors were resealed.

When he got back to the castle it was not yet noon so he went to his own quarters to eat. He had rice and two helpings of fish that had been broiled over charcoal with soya by his own cook as he had taught the man. A small flask of saké, then cha.

"Anjin-san?"

"*Hai?*"

The shoji opened. Fujiko smiled shyly and bowed.

CHAPTER 49

I'D forgotten about you," he said in English. "I was afraid you were dead."

"*Dozo goziemashita,* Anjin-san, *nan desu ka?*"

"*Nani mo,* Fujiko-san," he told her, ashamed of himself. "*Gomen nasai. Hai. Gomen nasai. Ma-suware odoroita honto ni mata aete ureshi.*" Please excuse me . . . a surprise, *neh?* Good to see you. Please sit down.

"*Domo arigato goziemashita,*" she said, and told him in her thin, high voice how pleased she was to see him, how much his Japanese had improved, how well he looked, and how most very glad she was to be here.

He watched her kneel awkwardly on the cushion opposite. "Legs . . ." He sought the word "burns" but couldn't remember it, so he said instead, "Legs fire hurt. Bad?"

"No. So sorry. But it still hurts a little to sit," Fujiko said, concentrating, watching his lips. "Legs hurt, so sorry."

"Please show me."

"So sorry, please, Anjin-san, I don't wish to trouble you. You have other problems. I'm—"

"Don't understand. Too fast, sorry."

"Ah, sorry. Legs all right. No trouble," she pleaded.

"Trouble. You are consort, *neh?* No shame. Show now!"

Obediently she got up. Clearly she was uncomfortable, but once she was upright, she began to untie the strings of her obi.

"Please call maid," he ordered.

She obeyed. At once the shoji slid open and a woman he did not recognize rushed to assist her.

First the stiff obi was unwound. The maid put Fujiko's sheathed dagger and obi to one side.

"What's your name?" he asked the maid brusquely, as a samurai should.

"Oh, please excuse me, Sire, so very sorry. My name is Hana-ichi."

He grunted an acknowledgment. Miss First Blossom, now there's a fine name! All maids, by custom, were called Miss Brush or Crane or Fish or Second Broom or Fourth Moon or Star or Tree or Branch, and so on.

Hana-ichi was middle-aged and very concerned. I'll bet she's a family retainer, he told himself. Perhaps a vassal of Fujiko's late husband. Husband! I'd forgotten about him as well, and the child who was murdered—as the husband was murdered by fiend Toranaga who's not a fiend but a *daimyo* and a good, perhaps great leader. Yes. Probably the husband deserved his fate if the real truth were known, *neh?* But not the child, he thought. There's no excuse for that.

Fujiko allowed her green patterned outer kimono to fall aside loosely. Her fingers trembled as she untied the thin silken sash of the yellow, under kimono and let that fall aside also. Her skin was light and the part of her breasts he could see within the folds of silk showed that they were flat and small. Hana-ichi knelt and untied the strings of the underskirt that reached from her waist to the floor to enable her mistress to step out of it.

"*Iyé,*" he ordered. He walked over and lifted the hem. The burns began at the backs of her calves. "*Gomen nasai,*" he said.

582

She stood motionless. A tear of sweat trickled down her cheek, spoiling her makeup. He pulled the skirt higher. The skin was burned all up the backs of her legs but it seemed to be healing perfectly. Scar tissue had formed already and there was no infection, and no suppurations, only a little clean blood where the new scar tissue had broken at the backs of her knees as she had knelt.

He moved her kimonos aside and loosed the underskirt waist band. The burns stopped at the top of her legs, bypassed her rump where the beam had pinned her down and protected her, then began again in the small of her back. A swathe of burn, half a hand span, girdled her waist. Scar tissue was already settling into permanent crinkles. Unsightly, but healing perfectly.

"Doctor very good. Best I ever see!" He let her kimonos fall back. "Best, Fujiko-san! The scars, what does it matter, *neh?* Nothing. I see many fire hurts, understand? Want see, then sure good or not good. Doctor very good. Buddha watch Fujiko-san." He put his hands on her shoulders and looked into her eyes. "No worry now. *Shigata ga nai, neh?* You understand?"

Her tears spilled. "Please excuse me, Anjin-san. I'm so embarrassed. Please excuse my stupidity for being there, caught there like a half-witted *eta.* I should have been with you, guarding you—not stuck with servants in the house. There's nothing for me in the house, nothing, no reason to be in a house. . . ."

He let her talk on though he understood almost nothing of what she said, holding her compassionately. I've got to find out what the doctor used, he thought excitedly. That's the quickest and the best healing I've ever seen. Every master of every one of Her Majesty's ships should know that secret—yes, and truly, every captain of every ship in Europe. Wait a moment, wouldn't every master pay golden guineas for that secret? You could make a fortune! Yes. But not that way, he told himself, never that. Never out of a sailor's agony.

She's lucky though that it was only the backs of her legs and her back and not her face. He looked down at her face. It was still as square and flat as ever, her teeth just as sharp and ferretlike, but the warmth that flowed from her eyes compensated for the ugliness. He gave her another hug. "Now. No weep. Order!"

He sent the maid for fresh cha and saké and many cushions and helped her recline on them, as much as at first it embarrassed her to obey. "How can I ever thank you?" she said.

"No thanks. Give back—" Blackthorne thought a moment but he couldn't remember the Japanese words for "favor" or "remember," so he pulled out the dictionary and looked them up. "Favor: *o-negai*" . . . "remember: *omoi dasu.*" *"Hai, mondoso o-negai! Omi desu ka?"* Give back favor. Remember? He held up his fists mimicking pistols and pointing them. "Omi-san, remember?"

"Oh, of course," she cried out. Then, in wonder, she asked to look at the book. She had never seen Roman writing before, and the column of Japanese words into Latin and into Portuguese and vice versa were meaningless to her, but she quickly grasped its purpose. "It's a book of all our . . . so sorry. Word book, *neh?"*

"Hai."

" *'Hombun'?"* she asked.

He showed her how to find the word in Latin and in Portuguese. *"Hombun:* duty." Then added in Japanese, "I understand duty. Samurai duty, *neh?"*

"Hai." She clapped her hands as if she had been shown a magic toy. But it is magic, isn't it, he told himself, a gift from God. This unlocks her mind and Toranaga's mind and soon I'll speak perfectly.

She gave him other words and he told her English or Latin or Portuguese, always understanding the words she chose and always finding them. The dictionary never failed.

He looked up a word. *"Majutsu desu, neh?"* It's magic, isn't it?

"Yes, Anjin-san. The book's magic." She sipped her cha. "Now I can talk to you. Really talk to you."

"Little. Only slow, understand?"

"Yes. Please be patient with me. Please excuse me."

The huge donjon bell sounded the Hour of the Goat and the temples in Yedo echoed the time change.

"I go now. Go Lord Toranaga." He put the book into his sleeve.

"I'll wait here please, if I may."

"Where stay?"

She pointed. "Oh, there, my room's next door. Please excuse my abruptness—"

"Slowly. Talk slowly. Talk simply!"

She repeated it slowly, with more apologies. "Good," he said. "Good. I'll see you later."

She began to get up but he shook his head and went into the courtyard. The day was overcast now, the air suffocating. Guards awaited him. Soon he was in the donjon forecourt. Mariko was there, more slender than ever, more ethereal, her face alabaster under her rust-gold parasol. She wore somber brown, edged with green.

"Ohayo, Anjin-san. *Ikaga desu ka?"* she asked, bowing formally.

He told her that he was fine, happily keeping up their custom of talking in Japanese for as long as he could, turning to Portuguese only when he was tired or when they wished to be more secretive.

"Thou . . ." he said cautiously as they walked up the stairs of the donjon.

"Thou," Mariko echoed, and went immediately into Portuguese with the same gravity as last night. "So sorry, please, no Latin today, Anjin-san, today Latin cannot sit well—Latin cannot serve the purpose it was made for, *neh?"*

"When can I talk to you?"

"That's very difficult, so sorry. I have duties. . . ."

"There's nothing wrong, is there?"

"Oh no," she replied. "Please excuse me, what could be wrong? Nothing's wrong."

They climbed another flight in silence. On the next level their passes were checked as always, guards leading and following them. Rain began heavily and this eased the humidity.

"It'll rain for hours," he said.

"Yes. But without the rains there's no rice. Soon the rains will stop altogether, in two or three weeks, then it will be hot and humid until the autumn." She looked out of the windows at the enveloping cloudburst. "You'll enjoy the autumn, Anjin-san."

"Yes." He was watching *Erasmus,* far distant, down beside the wharf. Then the rains obscured his ship and he climbed a little way. "After we've talked with Lord Toranaga we'll have to wait till this has passed. Perhaps there'd be somewhere here we could talk?"

"That might be difficult," she said vaguely, and he found this odd. She was usually decisive and implemented his polite "suggestions" as the orders they would normally be considered. "Please excuse me, Anjin-san, but things are difficult for me at the moment, and there are many things I have to do." She stopped momentarily and shifted her parasol to her other hand, holding the hem of her skirt. "How was your evening? How were your friends, your crew?"

"Fine. Everything was fine," he said.

"But not 'fine'?" she asked.

"Fine—but very strange." He looked back at her. "You notice everything, don't you?"

"No, Anjin-san. But you didn't mention them and you've been thinking about them greatly this last week or so. I'm no magician. So sorry."

After a pause, he said, "You're sure you're all right? There's no problem with Buntaro-san, is there?"

He had never discussed Buntaro with her or mentioned his name since Yokosé. By agreement that specter was never conjured up by either of them since the first moment. "This is my only request, Anjin-san," she had whispered the first night. "Whatever happens during our journey to Mishima or, Madonna willing, to Yedo, this has nothing to do with anyone but us, *neh?* Nothing is to be mentioned between us about what really *is. Neh?* Nothing. Please?"

"I agree. I swear it."

"And I do likewise. Finally, our journey ends at Yedo's First Bridge."

"No."

"There must be an ending, my darling. At First Bridge our journey ends. Please, or I will die with agony over fear for you and the danger I have put you in. . . ."

Yesterday morning he had stood at the threshold of First Bridge, a sudden weight on his spirit, in spite of his elation over *Erasmus.*

"We should cross the bridge now, Anjin-san," she had said.

"Yes. But it is only a bridge. One of many. Come along, Mariko-san. Walk beside me across *this* bridge. Beside me, please. Let us walk together," then added in Latin, "and believe that thou art carried and that we go hand in hand into a new beginning."

She stepped out of her palanquin and walked beside him until they reached the other side. There she got back into the curtained litter and they went up the slight rise. Buntaro was waiting at the castle gate.

Blackthorne remembered how he had prayed for a lightning bolt to come out of the sky.

"There's no problem with him, is there?" he asked again as they came to the final landing.

She shook her head.

Toranaga said, "Ship very ready, Anjin-san? No mistake?"

"No mistake, Sire. Ship perfect."

"How many extra men—how many more want for ship. . . ." Toranaga glanced at Mariko. "Please ask him how many extra crew he'll need to sail the ship properly. I want to be quite sure he understands what I want to know."

"The Anjin-san says, to sail her a minimum of thirty seamen and twenty gunners. His original crew was one hundred and seven, including cooks and merchants. To sail and fight in these waters, the complement of two hundred samurai would be enough."

"And he believes the other men he needs could be hired in Nagasaki?"

"Yes, Sire."

Toranaga said distastefully, "I certainly wouldn't trust mercenaries."

"Please excuse me, do you wish me to translate that, Sire?"

"What? Oh no, never mind that."

Toranaga got up, still pretending peevishness, and looked out of the windows at the rain. The whole city was obscured by the downpour. Let it rain for months, he thought. All gods, make the rain last until New Year. When will Buntaro see my brother? "Tell the Anjin-san I'll give him his vassals tomorrow. Today's terrible. This rain will go on all day. There's no point in getting soaked."

"Yes, Sire," he heard her say and smiled ironically to himself. Never in his whole life had weather prevented him from doing anything. That should certainly convince her, or any other doubters, that I've changed permanently for the worse, he thought, knowing he could not yet diverge from his chosen course. "Tomorrow or the next day, what does it matter? Tell him when I'm ready I'll send for him. Until then he's to wait in the castle."

He heard her pass on the orders to the Anjin-san.

"Yes, Lord Toranaga, I understand," Blackthorne replied for himself. "But may I respectfully ask: Possible go Nagasaki quick? Think important. So sorry."

"I'll decide that later," Toranaga said brusquely, not making it easy for him. He motioned him to leave. "Good-by, Anjin-san. I'll decide your future soon." He saw that the man wanted to press the point but politely didn't. Good, he thought, at least he's learning some manners! "Tell the Anjin-san there's no need for him to wait for you, Mariko-san. Good-by, Anjin-san."

Mariko did as she was ordered. Toranaga turned back to contemplate the city and the cloudburst. He listened to the sound of the rain. The door closed behind the Anjin-san. "What was the quarrel about?" Toranaga asked, not looking at her.

"Sire?"

His ears, carefully tuned, had caught the slightest tremble in her voice. "Of course between Buntaro and yourself, or have you had another quarrel that concerns me?" he added with biting sarcasm, needing to precipitate the matter quickly. "With the Anjin-san perhaps, or my Christian enemies, or the Tsukku-san?"

"No, Sire. Please excuse me. It began as always, like most quarrels, Sire, between husband and wife. Really over nothing. Then suddenly, as always, all the past gets spewed up and it infects the man and the woman if the mood's on them."

"And the mood was on you?"

"Yes. Please excuse me. I provoked my husband unmercifully. It was my fault entirely. I regret, Sire, in those times, so sorry, people say wild things."

"Come on, hurry up, what wild things?" She was like a doe at bay. Her face was chalky. She knew that spies must have already whispered to him what was shouted in the quiet of their house.

She told him everything that had been said as best she could remember it. Then she added, "I believe my husband's words were spoken in wild rage which I provoked. He's loyal—I know he's loyal. If anyone is to be punished it's me, Sire. I did provoke the madness."

Toranaga sat again on the cushion, his back ramrod, his face granite. "What did the Lady Genjiko say?"

"I haven't spoken to her, Sire."

"But you intend to, or intended to, *neh?*"

"No, Sire. With your permission I intend to leave at once for Osaka."

"You will leave when I say and not before and treason is a foul beast wherever it's to be found!"

She bowed under the whiplash of his tongue. "Yes, Sire. Please forgive me. The fault is mine."

He rang a small hand bell. The door opened. Naga stood there. "Yes, Sire?"

"Order the Lord Sudara here with the Lady Genjiko at once."

"Yes, Sire." Naga turned to go.

"Wait! Then summon my Council, Yabu and all—and all senior generals.

They're to be here at midnight. And clear this floor. All guards! You come back with Sudara!"

"Yes, Sire." Whitefaced, Naga closed the door after him.

Toranaga heard men clattering down the stairs. He went to the door and opened it. The landing was clear. He slammed the door and bolted it. He picked up another bell and rang it. An inner door at the far end of the room opened. This door was hardly noticeable, so cleverly had it been melded with the woodwork. A middle-aged heavy-set woman stood there. She wore a cowled Buddhist nun's habit. "Yes, Great Lord?"

"Cha please, Chano-chan," he said. The door closed. Toranaga's eyes went back to Mariko. "So you think he's loyal?"

"I know it, Sire. Please forgive me, it was my fault, not his," she said, desperate to please. "I provoked him."

"Yes, you did that. Disgusting. Terrible. Unforgivable!" Toranaga took out a paper kerchief and wiped his brow. "But fortunate," he said.

"Sire?"

"If you hadn't provoked him, perhaps I might never have learned of any treason. And if he'd said all that without provocation, there'd be only one course of action. As it is," he continued, "you give me an alternative."

"Sire?"

He did not answer. He was thinking, I wish Hiro-matsu were here, then there'd be at least one man I could trust completely. "What about you? What about your loyalty?"

"Please, Sire, you must know you have that."

He did not reply. His eyes were unrelenting.

The inner door opened and Chano, the nun, came confidently into the room without knocking, a tray in her hands. "Here you are, Great Lord, it was ready for you." She knelt as a peasant, her hands were rough like a peasant's, but her self-assurance was enormous and her inner contentment obvious. "May Buddha bless you with his peace." Then she turned to Mariko, bowed as a peasant would bow, and settled back comfortably. "Perhaps you'd honor me by pouring, Lady. You'll do it prettily without spilling it, *neh?*" Her eyes gleamed with private amusement.

"With pleasure, Oku-san," Mariko said, giving her the religious Mother title, hiding her surprise. She had never seen Naga's mother before. She knew most of Toranaga's other official ladies, having seen them at official ceremonies, but she was on good terms only with Kiritsubo and Lady Sazuko.

Toranaga said, "Chano-chan, this is the Lady Toda Mariko-noh-Buntaro."

"*Ah, so desu,* so sorry, I thought you were one of my Great Lord's honored ladies. Please excuse me, Lady Toda, may the blessings of Buddha be upon thee."

"Thank you," Mariko said. She offered the cup to Toranaga. He accepted it and sipped.

"Pour for Chano-san and yourself," he said.

"So sorry, not for me, Great Lord, with your permission, but my back teeth're floating from so much cha and the bucket's a long way away for these old bones."

"The exercise would do you good," Toranaga said, glad that he had sent for her when he returned to Yedo.

"Yes, Great Lord. You're right—as you always were." Chano turned her genial attention again to Mariko. "So you're Lord Akechi Jinsai's daughter."

Mariko's cup hesitated in the air. "Yes. Please excuse me . . ."

"Oh, that's nothing to wish to be excused about, child." Chano laughed kindly, and her stomach heaved up and down. "I didn't place you without your name, please excuse me, but the last time I saw you was at your wedding."

"Oh?"

"Oh, yes, I saw you at your wedding, but you didn't see me. I spied you from behind a screen. Yes, you and all the great ones, the Dictator, and Nakamura, the Taikō-to-be, and all the nobles. Oh, I was much too shy to mix in that company. But that was such a good time for me. The best of my life. That was the second year my Great Lord favored me and I was heavy with child—though still the peasant I've always been." Her eyes crinkled and she added, "You're very little different from those days, still one of Buddha's chosen."

"Ah, I wish that were true, Oku-san."

"It's true. Did you know you were one of Buddha's chosen?"

"I'm not, Oku-san, much as I would like to be."

Toranaga said, "She's Christian."

"Ah, Christian—what does that matter to a woman, Christian or Buddha, Great Lord? Not a lot sometimes, though some god's necessary to a woman." Chano chuckled gleefully. "We women need a god, Great Lord, to help us deal with men, *neh?*"

"And we men need patience, godlike patience, to deal with women, *neh?*"

The woman laughed, and it warmed the room and, for an instant, lessened some of Mariko's foreboding. "Yes, Great Lord," Chano continued, "and all because of a Heavenly Pavilion that has no future, little warmth, and a sufficiency of hell."

Toranaga grunted. "What do you say to that, Mariko-san?"

"The Lady Chano is wise beyond her youth," Mariko said.

"Ah, Lady, you say pretty things to an old fool," the nun told her. "I remember you so well. Your kimono was blue with the loveliest pattern of cranes on it I've ever seen. In silver." Her eyes went back to Toranaga. "Well, Great Lord, I just wanted to sit for a moment. Please excuse me now."

"There's time yet. Stay where you are."

"Yes, Great Lord," Chano said, ponderously getting to her feet, "I would obey as always but nature calls. So please be kind to an old peasant, I'd hate to disgrace you. It's time to go. Everything's ready, there's food and saké when you wish it, Great Lord."

"Thank you."

The door closed noiselessly behind her. Mariko waited until Toranaga's cup was empty, then she filled it again.

"What are you thinking?"

"I was waiting, Sire."

"For what, Mariko-san?"

"Lord, I'm hatamoto. I've never asked a favor before. I wish to ask a favor as a hata—"

"I don't wish you to ask any favor as a hatamoto," Toranaga said.

"Then a lifetime wish."

"I'm not a husband to grant that."

"Sometimes a vassal may ask a liege—"

"Yes, sometimes, but not now! Now you will hold your tongue about any lifetime wish or favor or request or whatever." A lifetime wish was a favor that, by ancient custom, a wife might ask of her husband, or a son of a father—and occasionally a husband of a wife—without loss of face, on the condition that if the wish was granted, the person agreed never again to ask another favor in this life. By custom, no questions about the favor might be asked, nor was it ever to be mentioned again.

There was a polite knock at the door.

"Unbolt it," Toranaga said.

She obeyed. Sudara entered, followed by his wife, the Lady Genjiko, and Naga.

"Naga-san. Go down to the second landing below and prevent anyone from coming up without my orders."

Naga stalked off.

"Mariko-san, shut the door and sit down there." Toranaga pointed at a spot slightly in front of him facing the others.

"I've ordered you both here because there are private, urgent family matters to discuss."

Sudara's eyes involuntarily went to Mariko, then back to his father. The Lady Genjiko's did not waver.

Toranaga said roughly, "She's here, my son, for two reasons: the first is because I want her here and the second because I want her here!"

"Yes, Father," Sudara replied, ashamed of his father's discourtesy to all of them. "May I please ask why I have offended you?"

"Is there any reason why I should be offended?"

"No, Sire, unless my zeal for your safety and my reluctance to allow you to depart this earth is cause for offense."

"What about treason? I hear you're daring to assume my place as leader of our clan!"

Sudara's face blanched. So did the Lady Genjiko's. "I have never done that in thought or word or deed. Neither has any member of my family or anyone in my presence."

"That is true, Sire," Lady Genjiko said with equal strength.

Sudara was a proud, lean man with cold, narrow eyes and thin lips that never smiled. He was twenty-four years old, a fine general and the second of Toranaga's five living sons. He adored his children, had no consorts, and was devoted to his wife.

Genjiko was short, three years older than her husband, and dumpy from the four children she had already borne him. But she had a straight back and all of her sister Ochiba's proud, ruthless protectiveness over her own brood, together with the same latent ferocity inherited from their grandfather, Goroda.

"Whoever accused my husband is a liar," she said.

"Mariko-san," Toranaga said, "ask the Lady Genjiko what your husband ordered you to say!"

"My Lord Buntaro asked me, ordered me, to persuade you that the time had come for Lord Sudara to assume power, that others in the Council shared my husband's opinion, that if our Lord Toranaga did not wish to give over power, it—it should be taken from him forcibly."

"Never has either of us entertained that thought, Father," Sudara said. "We're loyal and I would never con—"

"If I gave you power what would you do?" Toranaga asked.

Genjiko replied at once, "How can Lord Sudara know when he has never considered such an unholy possibility? So sorry, Sire, but it's not possible for him to answer because that's never been in his mind. How could it be in his mind? And as to Buntaro-san, obviously the *kami* have taken possession of him."

"Buntaro claimed that others share his opinion."

"Who?" Sudara asked venomously. "Tell me who and they'll die within moments."

"You tell me who!"

"I don't know any, Sire, or I'd have reported it to you."

"You wouldn't have killed them first?"

"Your first law is to be patient, your second is to be patient. I've always followed your orders. I would have waited and reported it. If I've offended you, order me to commit seppuku. I do not merit your anger, Lord, I've committed no treason. I cannot bear your anger washing over me."

The Lady Genjiko concurred. "Yes, Sire. Please excuse me but I humbly agree with my husband. He is blameless and so are all our people. We're faithful—whatever we have is yours, whatever we are you've made, whatever you order we'll do."

"So! You're loyal vassals, are you? Obedient? You always obey orders?"

"Yes, Sire."

"Good. Then go and put your children to death. Now."

Sudara took his eyes off his father and looked at his wife. Her head moved slightly and she nodded her agreement.

Sudara bowed to Toranaga. His hand tightened on his sword hilt and he got up. He closed the door quietly behind him. There was a great silence in his wake. Genjiko looked once at Mariko, then stared at the floor.

Bells tolled the middle of the Hour of the Goat. The air in the room seemed to thicken. Rain stopped briefly then began again, heavier than before.

Just after the bells tolled the next hour there was a knock.

"Yes?"

The door opened. Naga said, "Please excuse me, Sire, my brother . . . Lord Sudara wants to come up again."

"Let him—then return to your post."

Sudara came in and knelt and bowed. He was soaking, his hair matted from the rain. His shoulders shook slightly. "My—my children are. . . . You've already taken my children, Sire."

Genjiko wavered and almost pitched forward. But she dominated her weakness and stared at her husband. "You—you didn't kill them?"

Sudara shook his head and Toranaga said grimly, "Your children are in my quarters, on the floor below. I ordered Chano-san to fetch them after you'd been ordered here. I needed to be sure of you both. Foul times require foul tests." He rang the hand bell.

"You—you withdraw your or—your order, Sire?" Genjiko asked, desperately trying to maintain a cold dignity.

"Yes. My order's withdrawn. This time. It was necessary to know *you*. And my heir."

"Thank you, thank you, Sire." Sudara lowered his head abjectly.

The inner door opened. "Chano-san, bring my grandchildren here for a moment," Toranaga said.

Soon three somberly clad foster mothers and the wet nurse brought the children. The girls were four, three, and two, and the infant son, a few weeks old, was asleep in the arms of his wet nurse. All the girls wore scarlet kimonos with scarlet ribbons in their hair. The foster mothers knelt and bowed to Toranaga and their wards copied them importantly and put their heads to the tatamis—except the youngest girl, whose head needed assistance from a gentle though firm hand.

Toranaga bowed back gravely. Then, their duty done, the children rushed into his embrace—except the littlest one, who toddled into her mother's arms.

At midnight Yabu strutted arrogantly across the flare-lit donjon forecourt. Toranaga's elite corps of personal guards were everywhere. The moon was vague and misted and the stars barely visible.

"Ah, Naga-san, what's the reason for all this?"

"I don't know, Lord, but everyone's ordered to the conference chamber. Please excuse me, but you must leave your swords with me."

Yabu flushed at this unheard-of breach of etiquette. "Are you—" He changed his mind, sensing the youth's chilling tenseness and the restless nervousness of the nearby guards. "On whose orders please, Naga-san?"

"My father's, Lord. So sorry, you can please yourself if you don't wish to go to the conference, but I have to advise you that you are ordered there without swords and, so sorry, that is the way you will appear. Please excuse me, but I have no choice."

Yabu saw the pile of swords already in the lee of the guardhouse beside the huge main gate. He weighed the dangers of a refusal and found them formidable. Reluctantly he relinquished his arms. Naga bowed politely, equally embarrassed, as he accepted them. Yabu went inside. The huge room was embrasured, stone floored, and wooden beamed.

Soon the fifty senior generals were gathered, twenty-three counselors, and seven friendly *daimyos* from minor northern provinces. All were keyed up and fidgeted uncomfortably.

"What's all this about?" Yabu asked as he sourly took his place.

A general shrugged. "It's probably about the trek to Osaka."

Another looked around hopefully. "Perhaps it's a change of plan, *neh?* He's going to order Crimson—"

"So sorry, but your head's in the clouds. He's decided. Our Lord's decided —it's Osaka and nothing else! Hey, Yabu-sama, when did you get here?"

"Yesterday. I've been stuck at a filthy little fishing village called Yokohama for more than two weeks, south of here, with my troops. The port's fine but the bugs! Stinking mosquitoes and bugs—they were never so bad in Izu."

"You're up to date with all the news?"

"You mean all the bad news? The move's still in six days, *neh?*"

"Yes, terrible. Shameful!"

"True, but tonight's worse," another general said grimly. "I've never been without swords before. Never."

"It's an insult," Yabu said deliberately. All those nearby looked at him.

"I agree," General Kiyoshio replied, breaking the silence. Serata Kiyoshio was the grizzled, tough Commander of the Seventh Army. "I've never been without swords in public before. Makes me feel like a stinking merchant! I think . . . eeeeee, orders are orders but some orders should not be given."

"That's quite right," someone said. "What would old Iron Fist have done if he'd been here?"

"He'd have slit his belly before he gave up his swords! He'd have done it tonight in the forecourt!" a young man said. He was Serata Tomo, the general's eldest son, second-in-command of the Fourth Army. "I wish Iron Fist were here! He could get sense . . . he'd have slit his belly first."

"I considered it." General Kiyoshio cleared his throat harshly. "Someone has to be responsible—and do his duty! Someone has to make the point that liege lord means responsibility and duty!"

"So sorry, but you'd better watch your tongue," Yabu advised.

"What's the use of a tongue in a samurai's mouth if he's forbidden to be samurai?"

"None," Isamu, an old counselor, replied. "I agree. Better to be dead."

"So sorry, Isamu-san, but that's our immediate future anyway," the young Serata Tomo said. "We're staked pigeons to a certain dishonored hawk!"

"Please hold your tongues!" Yabu said, hiding his own satisfaction. Then he added carefully, "He's our liege lord and until Lord Sudara or the Council takes open responsibility he stays liege lord and he is to be obeyed. *Neh?*"

General Kiyoshio studied him, his hand unconsciously feeling for his sword hilt. "What have you heard, Yabu-sama?"

"Nothing."

"Buntaro-san said that—" the counselor began.

General Kiyoshio interrupted thinly. "Please excuse me, Isamu-san, but what General Buntaro said or what he didn't say is unimportant. What Yabu-sama says is true. A liege lord is a liege lord. Even so, a samurai has rights, a vassal has rights. Even *daimyos. Neh?*"

Yabu looked back at him, gauging the depth of that invitation. "Izu is Lord Toranaga's province. I'm no longer *daimyo* of Izu—only overlord for him." He glanced around the huge room. "Everyone's here, *neh?*"

"Except Lord Noboru," a general said, mentioning Toranaga's eldest son, who was universally loathed.

"Yes. Just as well. Never mind, General, the Chinese sickness'll finish him soon and we'll be done with his foul humor forever," someone said.

"And stench."

"When's he coming back?"

"Who knows? We don't even know why Toranaga-sama sent him north. Better he stays there, *neh?*"

"If you had that sickness, you'd be as foul-humored as he is, *neh?*"

"Yes, Yabu-san. Yes, I would. Pity he's poxed, he's a good general—better than the Cold Fish," General Kiyoshio added, using Sudara's private nickname.

"Eeeee," the counselor whistled. "There're devils in the air tonight to make you so careless with your tongue. Or is it saké?"

"Perhaps it's the Chinese sickness," General Kiyoshio replied with a bitter laugh.

"Buddha protect me from that!" Yabu said. "If only Lord Toranaga would change his mind about Osaka!"

"I'd slit my belly now if that'd convince him," the young man said.

"No offense, my son, but your head's in the clouds. He'll never change."

"Yes, Father. But I just don't understand him. . . ."

"We're all to go with him? In the same contingent?" Yabu asked after a moment.

Isamu, the old counselor, said, "Yes. We're to go as an escort. With two thousand men with full ceremonial equipment and trappings. It'll take us thirty days to get there. We've six days left."

General Kiyoshio said, "That's not much time. Is it, Yabu-sama?"

Yabu did not reply. There was no need. The general did not require an answer. They settled into their own thoughts.

A side door opened. Toranaga came in. Sudara followed. Everyone bowed stiffly. Toranaga bowed back and sat facing them, Sudara as heir presumptive slightly in front of him, also facing the others. Naga came in from the main door and closed it.

Only Toranaga wore swords.

"It's been reported that some of you speak treason, think treason, and plan treason," he said coldly. No one answered or moved. Slowly, relentlessly, Toranaga looked from face to face.

Still no movement. Then General Kiyoshio spoke. "May I respectfully ask, Sire, what do you mean by 'treason'?"

"Any questioning of an order, or a decision, or a position of any liege lord, at any time, is treason," Toranaga slammed back at him.

The general's back stiffened. "Then I'm guilty of treason."

"Then go out and commit seppuku at once."

"I will, Sire," the soldier said proudly, "but first I claim the right of free speech before your loyal vassals, officers, and coun—"

"You've forfeited all rights!"

"Very well. Then I claim it as a dying wish—as hatamoto—and in return for twenty-eight years of faithful service!"

"Make it very short."

"I will, Sire," General Kiyoshio replied icily. "I beg to say, first: Going to Osaka and bowing to the peasant Ishido is treason against your honor, the honor of your clan, the honor of your faithful vassals, your special heritage, and totally against *bushido*. Second: I indict you for this treason and say you've therefore forfeited your right to be our liege lord. Third: I petition that you immediately abdicate in Lord Sudara's favor and honorably depart this life—or shave your head and retire to a monastery, whichever you prefer."

The general bowed stiffly, then sat back on his haunches. Everyone waited, hardly breathing now that the unbelievable had become a reality.

Abruptly Toranaga hissed, "What are you waiting for?"

General Kiyoshio stared back at him. "Nothing, Sire. Please excuse me." His son began to get up.

"No. You're ordered to stay here!" he said.

The general bowed a last time to Toranaga, got up, and walked out with immense dignity. Some stirred nervously and a swell moved through the room but Toranaga's harshness dominated again: "Is there anyone else who admits treason? Anyone else who dares to break *bushido,* anyone who dares to accuse his liege lord of treason?"

"Please excuse me, Sire," Isumi, the old counselor, said calmly. "But I regret to say that if you go to Osaka it is treason against your heritage."

"The day I go to Osaka you will depart this earth."

The gray-haired man bowed politely. "Yes, Sire."

Toranaga looked them over. Pitilessly. Someone shifted uneasily and eyes snapped onto him. The samurai, a warrior who years ago had lost his wish to fight and had shaved his head to become a Buddhist monk and was now a member of Toranaga's civil administration, said nothing, almost wilting with an untoward fear he tried desperately to hide.

"What're you afraid of, Numata-san?"

"Nothing, Sire," the man said, his eyes downcast.

"Good. Then go and commit seppuku because you're a liar and your fear's an infectious stench."

The man whimpered and stumbled out. Dread stalked them all now. Toranaga watched. And waited.

The air became oppressive, the slight crackling of the torch flames seemed strangely loud. Then, knowing it was his duty and responsibility, Sudara turned and bowed. "Please, Sire, may I respectfully make a statement?"

"What statement?"

"Sire, I believe there is no . . . no more treason here, and that there will be no more trea—"

"I don't share your opinion."

"Please excuse me, Sire, you know I will obey you. We will all obey you. We seek only the best for your—"

"The best is *my* decision. What I decide *is* best."

Helplessly Sudara bowed his acquiescence and became silent. Toranaga did not look away from him. His gaze was remorseless. "You are no longer my heir."

Sudara paled. Then Toranaga shattered the tension in the room: "*I am liege lord here.*"

He waited a moment, then, in utter silence, he got up and arrogantly marched out. The door closed behind him. A great sigh went through the room. Hands sought sword hilts impotently. But no one left his place.

"This . . . this morning I . . . I heard from our commander-in-chief," Sudara began at last. "Lord Hiro-matsu will be here in a few days. I will . . . talk to him. Be silent, be patient, be loyal to our liege Lord. Let us go and pay our respects to General Serata Kiyoshio. . . ."

Toranaga was climbing the stairs, a great loneliness upon him, his footsteps reverberating in the emptiness of the tower. Near the top he stopped and leaned momentarily against the wall, his breathing heavy. The ache was gripping his chest again and he tried to rub it away. "It's just lack of exercise," he muttered. "That's all, just lack of exercise."

He went on. He knew he was in great jeopardy. Treason and fear were contagious and both had to be cauterized without pity the moment they appeared. Even then you could never be sure they were eradicated. The struggle he was locked into was not a child's game. The weak had to be food for the strong, the strong pawns for the very strong. If Sudara publicly claimed his mantle he was powerless to prevent it. Until Zataki answered, he had to wait.

Toranaga shut and bolted his door and walked to a window. Below, he could see his generals and counselors silently streaming away to their homes outside the donjon walls. Beyond the castle walls, the city lay in almost total darkness. Above, the moon was pallid and misted. It was a brooding, darkling night. And, it seemed to him, doom walked the heavens.

CHAPTER 50

BLACKTHORNE was sitting alone in the morning sun in a corner of the garden outside his guest house daydreaming, his dictionary in his hand. It was a fine cloudless day—the first for many weeks—and the fifth day since he had last seen Toranaga. All that time he had been confined to the castle, unable to see Mariko or visit his ship or crew, or explore the city, or go hunting or riding. Once a day he went swimming in one of the moats with other samurai, and to pass the time he taught some to swim and some to dive. But this did not make the waiting easier.

"So sorry, Anjin-san, but it's the same for everyone," Mariko had said yesterday when he met her by chance in his section of the castle. "Even Lord Hiromatsu's been kept waiting. It's two days since he arrived and he still hasn't seen Lord Toranaga. No one has."

"But this is important, Mariko-chan. I thought he understood every day's vital. Isn't there some way I can get a message to him?"

"Oh yes, Anjin-san. That's simple. You just write. If you tell me what you want to say I'll write it for you. Everyone has to write for an interview, those are his present orders. Please be patient, that's all we can do."

"Then please ask for an interview. I'd appreciate it. . . ."

"That's no trouble, it's my pleasure."

"Where have you been? It's four days since I saw you."

"Please excuse me but I've had to do so many things. It's—it's a little difficult for me, so many preparations. . . ."

"What's going on? This whole castle's been like a hive about to swarm for almost a week now."

"Oh, so sorry. Everything's fine, Anjin-san."

"Is it? So sorry, a general and a senior administrator commit seppuku in the donjon forecourt. That's usual? Lord Toranaga locks himself away in the ivory tower, keeping people waiting without apparent reason—that's also usual? What about Lord Hiro-matsu?"

"Lord Toranaga is our lord. Whatever he does is right."

"And you, Mariko-san? Why haven't I seen you?"

"Please excuse me, so sorry, but Lord Toranaga ordered me to leave you to your studies. I'm visiting your consort now, Anjin-san. I'm not supposed to visit you."

"Why should he object to that?"

"Merely, I suppose, so that you are obliged to speak our tongue. It's only been a few days, *neh?*"

"When are you leaving for Osaka?"

"I don't know. I expected to go three days ago but Lord Toranaga hasn't signed my pass yet. I've arranged everything—porters and horses—and daily I submit my travel papers to his secretary for signing, but they're always sent back. 'Submit them tomorrow.'"

"I thought I was going to take you to Osaka by sea. Didn't he say I was to take you by sea?"

"Yes. Yes, he did, but—well, Anjin-san, you never know with our liege Lord. He changes plans."

"Has he always been like that?"

"Yes and no. Since Yokosé he's been filled with—how do you say it—melancholy, *neh?*—yes, melancholy, and very different. He—yes, he's different now."

"Since First Bridge you've been filled with melancholy and very different. Yes, you're different now."

"First Bridge was an end and a beginning, Anjin-san, and our promise. *Neh?*"

"Yes. Please excuse me."

She had bowed sadly and left, and then, once safely away, not turning back, she had whispered, "Thou . . ." The word lingered in the corridor with her perfume.

At the evening meal he had tried to question Fujiko. But she also knew nothing of importance or would not, or could not, explain what was amiss at the castle. *"Dozo gomen nasai, Anjin-san."*

He went to bed seething. Seething with frustration over the delays, and the nights without Mariko. It was always bad knowing she was so near, that Buntaro was gone from the city, and now, because of the "Thou . . ." that her desire was still as intense as his. A few days ago he had gone to her house on the pretext that he needed help with Japanese. The samurai guard had told him, so sorry, she was not at home. He had thanked them, then wandered listlessly to the main south gate. He could see the ocean. Because the land was so flat, he could see nothing of the wharves or docks though he thought he could distinguish the tall masts of his ship in the distance.

The ocean beckoned him. It was the horizon more than the deep, the need for a fair wind washing him, eyes squinting against its strength, tongue tasting its salt, the deck heeled over, and aloft the spars and rigging and halyards creaking and groaning under the press of sails that, from time to time, would cackle with glee as the stalwart breeze shifted a point or two.

And it was freedom more than the horizon. Freedom to go to any quarter in any weather at any whim. To stand on his quarterdeck and to be *arbiter,* as here Toranaga alone was *arbiter.*

Blackthorne looked up at the topmost part of the donjon. Sun glinted off its shapely tiled curves. He had never seen movement there, though he knew that every window below the topmost floor was guarded.

Gongs sounded the hour change. For the first time his mind told him this was the middle of the Hour of the Horse, and not eight bells of this watch—high noon.

He put his dictionary into his sleeve, glad that it was time for the first real meal.

Today it was rice and quick-broiled prawns and fish soup and pickled vegetables.

"Would you like some more, Anjin-san?"

"Thank you, Fujiko. Yes. Rice, please. And some fish. Good—very . . ." He looked up the word for "delicious" and said it several times to memorize it. "Yes, delicious, *neh?*"

Fujiko was pleased. "Thank you. This fish from north. Water colder north, understand? Its name is *'kurima-ebi.'* "

He repeated the name and put it into his memory. When he had finished and their trays were taken away, she poured more cha and took a package out of her sleeve.

"Here money, Anjin-san." She showed him the gold coins. "Fifty koban. Worth one hundred fifty koku. You want it, *neh?* For sailors. Please excuse me, do you understand?"

"Yes, thank you."

"You're welcome. Enough?"

"Yes. Think so. Where get?"

"Toranaga-sama's chief . . ." Fujiko sought a simple way to say it. "I go important Toranaga man. Headman. Like Mura, *neh?* Not samurai—only moneyman. Sign my name for you."

"Ah, understand. Thank you. My money? My koku?"

"Oh, yes."

"This house. Food. Servants. Who pay?"

"Oh, I pay. From your—from koku one year."

"Is that enough, please? Enough koku?"

"Oh, yes. Yes, I believe so," she said.

"Why worry? Worry in face?"

"Oh, please excuse me, Anjin-san. I'm not worried. No worry . . ."

"Pain? Burn pain?"

"No pain. See." Fujiko carefully got off the thick cushions he insisted she use. She knelt directly onto the tatamis with no sign of discomfort, then sat back on her heels and settled herself. "There, all better."

"Eeeee, very good," he said, pleased for her. "Show, eh?"

She got up carefully and lifted the hem of her skirts and allowed him to look at the backs of her legs. The scar tissue had not split and there were no suppurations. "Very good," he said. "Yes, soon like baby skin, *neh?*"

"Thank you, yes. Soft. Thank you, Anjin-san."

He noticed the slight change in her voice but did not comment. That night he did not dismiss her.

The pillowing was satisfactory. No more. For him there was no afterglow, no joyous lassitude. It was just a mating. So wrong, he thought, yet not wrong, *neh?*

Before she left him she knelt and bowed again to him and put her hands on his forehead. "I thank you with all my heart. Please sleep now, Anjin-san."

"Thank you, Fujiko-san. I sleep later."

"Please sleep now. It is my duty and would give me great pleasure."

The touch of her hand was warm and dry and not pleasing. Nonetheless he pretended to sleep. She caressed him ineptly though with great patience. Then, quietly, she went back to her own room. Now alone again, glad to be alone, Blackthorne propped his head on his arms and looked up into the darkness.

He had decided about Fujiko during the journey from Yokosé to Yedo. "It is your duty," Mariko had told him, lying in his arms.

"I think that'd be a mistake, *neh?* If she gets with child, well, it'll take me four years to sail home and come back again and, in that time, God knows what could happen." He remembered how Mariko had trembled then.

"Oh, Anjin-san, that is very much time."

"Three then. But you'll be aboard with me. I'll take you back with—"

"Thy promise, my darling! Nothing that *is, neh?*"

"Thou art right. Yes. But with Fujiko, so many bad things could happen. I don't think she would want my child."

"You do not know that. I do not understand you, Anjin-san. *It is your duty.* She could always prevent a child, *neh?* Don't forget, she *is* your consort. In truth, you take away her face if you don't invite her to the pillow. After all, Toranaga himself ordered her into your house."

"Why did he do that?"

"I don't know. It doesn't matter. He ordered it, therefore it is the best for you and best for her. It has been good, *neh?* She's done her duty as best she can, *neh?* Please excuse me, but don't you think you should do yours?"

"Enough of your lectures! Love me and do not talk anymore."

"How should I love thee? Ah, like Kiku-san told me today?"

"How is that?"

"Like this."

"That is very good—so very good."

"Oh, I forgot, please light the lamp, Anjin-san. I have something to show thee."

"Later, now I—"

"Oh, please excuse me, it should be now. I bought it for you. It's a pillow book. The pictures are very funny."

"I don't want to look at a pillow book now."

"But, so sorry, Anjin-san, perhaps one of the pictures would excite you. How can you learn about pillowing without a pillow book?"

"I'm excited already."

"But Kiku-san said it's a very first best way of choosing positions. There are forty-seven. Some of them look astonishing and very difficult, but she said it was important to try all. . . . Why do you laugh?"

"You're laughing—why shouldn't I laugh too?"

"But I was laughing because you were chuckling and I felt your stomach shaking and you won't let me up. Please let me up. Anjin-san!"

"Ah, but you can't be cross, Mariko my darling. There's no woman in the world who can be really even a little cross like this. . . ."

"But Anjin-san, please, you must let me up. I want to show you."

"All right. If that—"

"Oh, no, Anjin-san, I didn't want—you mustn't—can't you just reach out—please not yet—oh, please don't leave me—oh, how I love thee like this. . . ."

Blackthorne remembered that loving. Mariko excited him more than Kiku had, and Fujiko was nothing compared to either. And Felicity?

Ah, Felicity, he thought, focusing on his great problem. I must be mad to love Mariko, and Kiku. And yet . . . the truth about Felicity is that now she can't compare even with Fujiko. Fujiko was clean. Poor Felicity. I'll never be able to tell her, but the memory of her and me rutting like a pair of stoats in the hay or under rancid covers makes my skin crawl now. Now I know better. Now I could teach her but would she wish to learn? And how could we ever get clean and stay clean and live clean?

Home is filth piled on filth, but that's where my wife is and where my children are and where I belong.

"Don't think about *that* home, Anjin-san," Mariko had once said when the dark mists were on him. "Real home is here—the other's ten million times ten million sticks away. Here is reality. You'll send yourself mad if you try to get *wa* out of such impossibilities. Listen, if you want peace you must learn to drink cha from an empty cup."

She had shown him how. "You *think* reality into the cup, you think the cha there—the warm, pale-green drink of the gods. If you concentrate hard. . . . Oh, a Zen teacher could show you, Anjin-san. It is most difficult but so easy. How I wish I was clever enough to show it to you, for then all things in the world can be yours for the asking . . . even the most unobtainable gift—perfect tranquillity."

He had tried many times, but he could never sip the drink when it wasn't there.

"Never mind, Anjin-san. It takes such a long time to learn but you will, sometime."

"Can you?"

"Rarely. Only in moments of great sadness or loneliness. But the taste of the unreal cha seems to give a meaning to life. It is hard to explain. I've done it once or twice. Sometimes you gain *wa* just by trying."

Now, lying in the dark of the castle, sleep so far away, he lit the candle with the flint and concentrated on the little porcelain cup that Mariko had given him which now he always kept beside his bed. For an hour he tried. But he could not purify his mind. Inevitably the same thoughts kept chasing each other: I want to leave, I want to stay. I'm afraid of going back, I'm afraid to remain. I hate both and want both. And then there are the *"eters."*

If it was up to me alone I wouldn't leave, not yet. But others are involved and they're not eters and I signed on as Pilot: *'By the Lord God I promise to take the fleet out and through the Grace of God bring her home again.'* I want Mariko. I want to see the land Toranaga's given me and I need to stay here, to enjoy the fruit of my great luck for just a little longer. Yes. But also duty's involved and that transcends everything, *neh?*

With the dawn Blackthorne knew that though he pretended he had put off the decision again, in reality, he had decided. Irrevocably.

God help me, first and last I'm Pilot.

Toranaga uncurled the tiny slip of paper that arrived two hours after dawn. The message from his mother said simply: "Your brother agrees, my son. His letter of confirmation will leave today by hand. The state visit of Lord Sudara and his family must begin within ten days."

Toranaga sat down weakly. The pigeons fluttered in their roosts then settled back once more. Morning sun filtered into the loft pleasingly though rain clouds were building. Gathering his strength, he hurried down the steps into his quarters below to begin.

"Naga-san!"

"Yes, father?"

"Send Hiro-matsu-san here. After him, my secretary."

"Yes, Father."

The old general came quickly. His joints were creaking from the climb and he bowed low, his sword loose in his hands as ever, his face fiercer than ever, older than ever, and even more resolute.

"You're welcome, old friend."

"Thank you, Lord." Hiro-matsu looked up. "I'm saddened to see the cares of the world are in your face."

"And I'm saddened to see and hear so much treason."

"Yes. Treason is a terrible thing."

Toranaga saw the firm old eyes measuring him. "You can speak freely."

"Have you ever known me not to, Sire?" The old man was grave.

"Please excuse me for keeping you waiting."

"Please excuse me for troubling you. What is your pleasure, Sire? Please give me your decision about the future of your house. Is it finally Osaka—bending to that manure pile?"

"Have you ever known me to make a final decision about anything?"

Hiro-matsu frowned, then thoughtfully straightened his back to ease the ache in his shoulders. "I've always known you to be patient and decisive and you've always won. That's why I can't understand you now. It's not like you to give up."

"Isn't the realm more important than *my* future?"

"No."

"Ishido and the other Regents are still legal rulers according to the Taikō's will."

"I am the vassal of Yoshi Toranaga-noh-Minowara and I acknowledge no one else."

"Good. The day after tomorrow is my chosen day to leave for Osaka."

"Yes. I've heard that."

"You'll be in command of the escort, Buntaro second-in-command."

The old general sighed. "I know that too, Sire. But since I've been back, Sire, I've talked to your senior advisers and gener—"

"Yes. I know. And what is their opinion?"

"That you should not leave Yedo. That your orders should be temporarily overruled."

"By whom?"

"By me. By my orders."

"That's what they wish? Or that is what you've decided?"

Hiro-matsu put his sword on the floor nearer to Toranaga and, now defenseless, looked directly at him. "Please excuse me, Sire, I wish to ask you what I should do. My duty seems to tell me I should take command and prevent your leaving. This will at once force Ishido to come against us. Yes, of course we will lose, but that seems to be the only honorable way."

"But stupid, *neh?*"

The general's iron-gray brows knotted. "No. We die in battle, with honor. We regain *wa*. The Kwanto is a spoil of war, but we'll not see the new master in this life. *Shigata ga nai.*"

"I've never enjoyed expending men uselessly. I've never lost a battle and see no reason why I should begin now."

"Losing one battle is no dishonor, Sire. Is surrender honorable?"

"You are all agreed in this treason?"

"Sire, please excuse me, I asked individuals for a military opinion only. There's no treason or plot."

"You still listened to treason."

"Please excuse me, but if I agree, as your commander-in-chief, then it no longer becomes treason but legal state policy."

"Taking decisions away from your liege lord is treason."

"Sire, there are too many precedents for deposing a lord. You've done it, Goroda did it, the Taikō—we've all done that and worse. A victor never commits treason."

"You've decided to depose me?"

"I ask for your help in the decision."

"You're the one person I thought I could trust!"

"By all gods I only wish to be your most devoted vassal. I'm only a soldier. I wish to do my duty to you. I think only of you. I merit your trust. If it will help, take my head. If it will convince you to fight, I gladly give you my life, my clan's life blood, today—in public or private or whatever way you wish—isn't that what our friend General Kiyoshio did? I'm sorry but I do not understand why I should permit you to throw away a lifetime of effort."

"Then you refuse to obey my orders to head the escort that will leave for Osaka the day after tomorrow?"

A cloud passed over the sun and both men looked out of the windows. "It'll rain again soon," Toranaga said.

"Yes. There's been too much rain this year, *neh?* The rains must stop soon or the harvest'll be ruined."

They looked at each other.

"Well?"

Iron Fist said simply, "I formally ask you, Sire, do you order me to escort you from Yedo, the day after tomorrow, to begin the trek to Osaka?"

"As there seems to be advice from all my counselors to the contrary, I'll accept their opinion, and yours, and delay my departure."

Hiro-matsu was totally unprepared for this. "Eh? You won't be leaving?"

Toranaga laughed, the mask fell off, and he was the old Toranaga again. "I never intended to go to Osaka. Why should I be so stupid?"

"What?"

"My agreement at Yokosé was nothing more than a trick to gain time," Toranaga said affably. "Ishido took the bait. The fool expects me in Osaka within a few weeks. Zataki also took that bait. And you and all my valiant, untrusting vassals also took the bait. With no real concession whatsoever I've gained a month, put Ishido and his filthy allies in turmoil. I hear they're already scrambling for the Kwanto. Kiyama's been promised it as well as Zataki."

"You never intended to go?" Hiro-matsu shook his head, then as the clarity of the idea suddenly hit him, his face broke into a delighted grin. "It's all a ruse?"

"Of course. Listen, everyone had to be taken in, *neh?* Zataki, everyone, even you! Or spies would have told Ishido and he would have moved against us at once and no good fortune on earth or gods in heaven could have prevented disaster to me."

"That's true . . . ah, Lord, forgive me. I'm so stupid. I deserve to lose my head! So it was all nonsense, always nonsense. But . . . but what about General Kiyoshio?"

"He said he was guilty of treason. I don't need treasonous generals, only obedient vassals."

"But why attack Lord Sudara? Why withdraw your favor from him?"

"Because it pleases me to do so," Toranaga said harshly.

"Yes. Please excuse me. That's your sole privilege. I beg you to forgive me for doubting you."

"Why should I forgive you for being you, old friend? I needed you to do what you did and say what you said. Now I need you more than ever. I must have someone I can trust. That's why I'm taking you into my confidence. This has got to be secret between us."

"Oh Sire. You make me so happy. . . ."

"Yes," Toranaga said. "That's the only thing I'm afraid of."

"Sire?"

"You're commander-in-chief. You alone can neutralize this stupid, brooding mutiny while I'm waiting. I trust you and must trust you. My son can't hold my generals in check, though he'd never show outward joy at the secret—if he knew it—but your face is the gateway to your soul, old friend."

"Then let me take my life after I've settled the generals."

"That's no help. *You* must hold them together pending my pretended departure, *neh?* You'll just have to guard your face and your sleep like never before. You're the only one in all the world who knows—you're the only one I must trust, *neh?*"

"Forgive me for my stupidity. I won't fail. Explain to me what I must do."

"Say to my generals what's true—that you persuaded me to take *your* advice, which is also theirs, *neh?* I formally order my departure postponed for seven days. Later I'll postpone it again. Sickness, this time. You're the only one to know."

"Then? Then it will be Crimson Sky?"

"Not as originally planned. Crimson Sky was always a last plan, *neh?*"

"Yes. What about the Musket Regiment? Could it blast a path through the mountains?"

"Part of the way. But not all the way to Kyoto."

"Have Zataki assassinated."

"That might be possible. But Ishido and his allies are still invincible." Toranaga told him the arguments of Omi, Yabu, Igurashi, and Buntaro the day of the earthquake. "At that time I ordered Crimson Sky as another feint to throw Ishido into confusion . . . and also had the right parts of the discussion whispered into the wrong ears. But the fact is, Ishido's force is still invincible."

"How can we split them up? What about Kiyama and Onoshi?"

"No, those two are implacably against me. All the Christians will be against me—except my Christian, and I will soon put him and his ship to very good use. Time is what I need most. I've allies and secret friends throughout the Empire and if I have time. . . . Every day I gain weakens Ishido further. That's my battle plan. Every day of delay is important. Listen, after the rains, Ishido will come against the Kwanto, a simultaneous pincer, Ikawa Jikkyu spearheading the south, Zataki in the north. We contain Jikkyu at Mishima, then fall back to the Hakoné Pass and Odawara, where we make our final stand. In the north we'll hold Zataki fast in the mountains along the Hosho-kaidō Road somewhere near Mikawa. It's true what Omi and Igurashi said: We can hold off the first attack and there *shouldn't* be another great invasion. We fight and we wait behind our mountains. We fight and delay and wait and then when the fruit is ripe for plucking—Crimson Sky."

"Eeeeee, let that day be soon!"

"Listen, old friend, only you can hold my generals in check. With time and the Kwanto secure, completely secure, we can weather the first attack and then Ishido's alliances will begin to break up. Once that happens Yaemon's future is assured and the Taikō's testament inviolate."

"You will not take sole power, Sire?"

"For the last time: 'The law may upset reason but reason may never upset the law, or our whole society will shred like an old tatami. The law may be used to confound reason, reason must certainly not be used to overthrow the law.' The Taikō's will is law."

Hiro-matsu bowed an acceptance. "Very well, Sire. I will never mention it again. Please excuse me. Now—" He let his smile show. "Now, what must I do?"

"Pretend that you've persuaded me to delay. Just keep them all in your iron fist."

"How long must I keep up the pretense?"

"I don't know."

"I don't trust myself, Sire. I may make a mistake, not meaning to. I think I can keep the joy off my face for a few days. With your permission my 'aches' should become so bad that I'll be confined to bed—no visitors, *neh?*"

"Good. Do that in four days. Let some of the pain show from today on. That won't be difficult, *neh?*"

"No, Sire. So sorry. I'm glad the battle begins this year. Next . . . I may not be able to help."

"Nonsense. But it will be this year whether I say yes or no. In sixteen days I will leave Yedo for Osaka. By that time you will have given your 'reluctant approval' and you will lead the march. Only you and I know there will be further delays and that long before I reach my borders I'll turn back to Yedo."

"Please forgive me for doubting you. If it wasn't that I must remain alive to help your plans I could not live with my shame."

"No need for shame, old friend. If you hadn't been convinced, Ishido and

Zataki would have seen through the trick. Oh, by the way, how was Buntaro-san when you saw him?"

"Seething, Sire. It will be good to have a battle for him to fight."

"He suggested removing me as liege lord?"

"If he'd said that to me I would have removed his head! At once!"

"I'll send for you in three days. Ask to see me daily but I'll refuse until then."

"Yes, Sire." The old general bowed abjectly. "Please forgive this old fool. You've given my life purpose again. Thank you." He left.

Toranaga took out the little slip of paper from his sleeve and reread the message from his mother with enormous satisfaction. With the northern route possibly open and Ishido possibly betrayed there, his odds had enormously improved. He put the message to the flame. The paper curled into ash. Contentedly, he pounded the ash to dust. Now, who should be the new commander-in-chief? he asked himself.

At noon, Mariko walked across the donjon forecourt, through the silent ranks of brooding guards, and went inside. Toranaga's secretary was waiting for her in one of the anterooms on the ground floor. "So sorry to send for you, Lady Toda," he said listlessly.

"It's my pleasure, Kawanabi-san."

Kawanabi was a sharp-featured, elderly samurai with a shaven head. Once he had been a Buddhist priest. For years now he had handled all of Toranaga's correspondence. Normally he was bright and enthusiastic. Today, like most people in the castle, he was greatly unsettled. He handed her a small scroll. "Here are your travel documents for Osaka, duly signed. You are to leave tomorrow and get there as soon as possible."

"Thank you." Her voice sounded tiny to her.

"Lord Toranaga says he may have some private dispatches for you to take to Lady Kiritsubo and Lady Koto. Also for General Lord Ishido and Lady Ochiba. They'll be delivered to you tomorrow at dawn if . . . so sorry, if they're ready, I'll see they're delivered to you."

"Thank you."

From a number of scrolls that were stacked with pedantic neatness on his low desk, Kawanabi selected an official document. "I'm directed to give you this. It is the increase in your son's fief as promised by Lord Toranaga. Ten thousand koku yearly. It's dated from the last day of last month and . . . well, here it is."

She accepted it, read it, and checked the official chops. Everything was perfect. But it gave her no happiness. Both believed it was an empty paper now. If her son's life was spared he would become *ronin*. "Thank you. Please thank Lord Toranaga for the honor he does us. May I be allowed to see him before I go?"

"Oh, yes. When you leave here now you're asked to go to the barbarian ship. You're requested to wait for him there."

"I'm—I'm to interpret?"

"He didn't say. I would presume so, Lady Toda." The secretary squinted at a list in his hand. "Captain Yoshinaka's been ordered to lead your escort to Osaka, if it pleases you."

"I would be honored to be in his charge again. Thank you. May I ask how Lord Toranaga is?"

"He seems well enough, but for an active man like him to coop himself up for days on end. . . . What can I say?" He spread his hands helplessly. "So sorry. At least today he saw Lord Hiro-matsu and agreed to a delay. He's also agreed to deal with a few other things . . . rice prices must be stabilized now in case of a bad harvest. . . . But there's so much to do and . . . it's just not like him, Lady Toda. These are terrible times, *neh?* And terrible omens: The soothsayers say the harvest will be ruined this year."

"I will not believe them—until harvest time."

"Wise, very wise. But not many of us will see harvest time. I'm to go with him to Osaka." Kawanabi shivered and leaned forward nervously. "I heard a rumor that the plague's begun again between Kyoto and Osaka—smallpox. Is that another heavenly sign that the gods are turning their faces from us?"

"It's not like you to believe rumors or heavenly signs, Kawanabi-san, or to pass on rumors. You know what Lord Toranaga thinks of that."

"I know. So sorry. But, well . . . no one seems to be normal these days, *neh?*"

"Perhaps the rumor's not true—I pray it's not true." She shook off her foreboding. "Has the new date for the departure been set?"

"I understood Lord Hiro-matsu to say that it was postponed for seven days. I'm so glad our commander-in-chief returned and so glad he persuaded. . . . I wish the whole departure was put off forever. Better fight here than be dishonored there, *neh?*"

"Yes," she agreed, knowing there was no point any longer in pretending that this was not foremost in everyone's mind. "Now that Lord Hiro-matsu's back, perhaps our Lord will see that surrender's not the best course."

"Lady, for your ears alone. Lord Hiro-matsu—" He stopped, looked up, and put a smile on his face. Yabu strode into the room, swords jingling. "Ah, Lord Kasigi Yabu, how nice to see you." He bowed and Mariko bowed and there were pleasantries and then he said, "Lord Toranaga's expecting you, Sire. Please go up at once."

"Good. What does he want to see me about?"

"So sorry, Sire, he didn't tell me—only that he wished to see you."

"How is he?"

Kawanabi hesitated. "No change, Sire."

"His departure—has a new date been fixed?"

"I understand it'll be in seven days."

"Perhaps Lord Hiro-matsu'll put it off even more, *neh?*"

"That would be up to our Lord, Sire."

"Of course." Yabu walked out.

"You were saying about Lord Hiro-matsu?"

"Only for your ears, Lady—as Buntaro-san's not here," the secretary whispered. "When old Iron Fist came from seeing Lord Toranaga, he had to rest for the best part of an hour. He was in very great pain, Lady."

"Oh! It would be terrible if something happened to him now!"

"Yes. Without him there'd be a revolt, *neh?* This delay solves nothing, does it? It's only a truce. The real problem—I'm—I'm afraid since Lord Sudara acted as formal second to General Kiyoshio, every time Lord Sudara's name has been mentioned our Lord gets very angry. . . . It's only Lord Hiro-matsu who's persuaded him to delay and that's the only thing that . . ." Tears started running down the secretary's cheeks. "What's happening, Lady? He's lost control, *neh?*"

"No," she said firmly, without conviction. "I'm sure everything will be all right. Thank you for telling me. I'll try to see Lord Hiro-matsu before I leave."

"Go with God, Lady."

She was startled. "I didn't know you were Christian, Kawanabi-san."

"I'm not, Lady. But I know it is your custom."

She walked out into the sun, greatly concerned over Hiro-matsu, at the same time blessing God that her waiting was over and tomorrow she would escape. She went toward the palanquin and escort waiting for her.

"Ah, Lady Toda," Gyoko said, stepping out of the shadows, intercepting her.

"Ah, good morning, Gyoko-san, how nice to see you. I hope you're well?" she said pleasantly, a sudden chill rushing through her.

"Not well at all, I'm afraid, so sorry. So very sad. It seems we're not in our Lord's favor, Kiku-san and I. Ever since we got here we've been confined to a filthy third-class hotel I wouldn't put an eighth-class male courtesan in."

"Oh, so sorry. I'm sure there must be some mistake."

"Ah yes, a mistake. I certainly hope so, Lady. At long last today I've been given permission to come to the castle, at long last there's an answer to my petition to see the Great Lord, at long last I'm permitted to bow before the Great Lord again—later today." Gyoko smiled at her crookedly. "I heard you were also coming to see the lord-secretary, so I thought I'd wait to greet you. I hope you don't mind."

"It's a pleasure to see you, Gyoko-san. I would have visited you and Kiku-san, or asked you both to visit me, but unfortunately that hasn't been possible."

"Yes—so sad. These are sad times. Difficult for nobles. Difficult for peasants. Poor Kiku-san's quite sick with worry to be out of our Lord's favor."

"I'm sure she's not, Gyoko-san. He—Lord Toranaga has many pressing problems, *neh?*"

"True—true. Perhaps we could take some cha now, Lady Toda. I would be honored to be allowed to talk to you for a moment."

"Ah, so sorry, but I'm ordered to go on official business. Otherwise I would have been honored."

"Ah yes, you've to go to the Anjin-san's ship now. Ah, I forgot, so sorry. How is the Anjin-san?"

"I believe he is well," Mariko said, furious that Gyoko knew her private business. "I've seen him only once—and then just for a few moments—since we arrived."

"An interesting man. Yes, very. Sad not to see one's friends, *neh?*"

Both women wore smiles, their voices polite and carefree, both conscious of the impatient samurai watching and listening to them.

"I heard the Anjin-san visited his friends—his crew. How did he find them?"

"He never told me, Gyoko-san. As I said, I only saw him for a moment. So sorry, but I must go . . ."

"Sad not to see one's friends. Perhaps I could tell you about them. For instance, that they live in an *eta* village."

"What?"

"Yes. It seems his friends asked permission to live there, preferring it to civilized areas. Curious, *neh?* Not like the Anjin-san, who's different. The rumor is they say it's more like home to them—the *eta* village. Curious, neh . . ."

Mariko was remembering how strange the Anjin-san had been on the stairs that day. That explains it, she thought. *Eta!* Madonna, poor man. How ashamed he must have been. "I'm sorry, Gyoko-san, what did you say?"

"Just that it's curious the Anjin-san's so different from the others."

"What're they like? Have you seen them? The others?"

"No, Lady. I wouldn't go there. What should I have to do with them? Or with *eta?* I must think of my clients and my Kiku-san. And my son."

"Ah yes, your son."

Gyoko's face saddened under her parasol but her eyes remained flinty brown like her kimono. "Please excuse me, but I suppose you've no idea why we should be out of favor with Lord Toranaga?"

"No. I'm sure you're mistaken. The contract was settled, *neh?* According to the agreement?"

"Oh yes, thank you. I've a letter of credit on the Mishima rice merchants, payable on demand. Less the amount we agreed. But money was furthest from my mind. What's money when you've lost the favor of your patron—whoever he or she is. *Neh?*"

"I'm sure you retain his favor."

"Ah, favors! I was worried about your favor, too, Lady Toda."

"You always have my goodwill. And friendship, Gyoko-san. Perhaps we could talk another time, I really must go now, so sorry. . . ."

"Ah yes, how kind you are. I'd enjoy that." Gyoko added in her most honeyed voice as Mariko began to turn away, "But will you have time? You go tomorrow, *neh?* To Osaka?"

Mariko felt a sudden ice barb in her chest as the trap closed.

"Is there anything wrong, Lady?"

"No . . . no, Gyoko-san. Will . . . during the Hour of the Dog tonight . . . would that be convenient?"

"You're too kind, Lady. Oh, yes, as you're going to see our Master now, before me, would you intercede for us? We need such a little favor. *Neh?*"

"I would be glad to." Mariko thought a moment. "Some favors can be asked but, even so, are not granted."

Gyoko stiffened slightly. "Ah! You've already asked him the . . . asked him to favor us?"

"Of course—why shouldn't I?" Mariko said carefully. "Isn't Kiku-san a favorite? And aren't you a devoted vassal? Haven't you been granted favors in the past?"

"My requests are always so little. Everything I said before still applies, Lady. Perhaps more so."

"About empty-bellied dogs?"

"About long ears and safe tongues."

"Ah yes. And secrets."

"It would be so easy to satisfy me. My Lord's favor—and my Lady's—is not much to ask, *neh?*"

"No. If an opportunity occurs. . . . I can promise nothing."

"Until this evening, Lady."

They bowed to each other and no samurai was any the wiser. Mariko got into the palanquin to more bows, hiding the trembles that beset her, and the cortege left. Gyoko stared after her.

"You, woman," a young samurai said roughly as he passed. "What're you waiting for? Go about your business."

"Ha!" Gyoko said disdainfully to the amusement of others. "Woman, is it, puppy? If I went about your business I might have a very hard time finding it, hey, even though you're not yet man enough to have thatch!"

The others laughed. With a toss of her head she walked on fearlessly.

"Hello," Blackthorne said.

"Good afternoon, Anjin-san. You look happy!"

"Thank you. It's the sight of such a lovely lady, *neh?*"

"Ah, thank you," Mariko replied. "How is your ship?"

"First class. Would you like to come aboard? I'd like to show you around."

"Is that permitted? I was ordered here to meet Lord Toranaga."

"Yes. We're all waiting for him now." Blackthorne turned and spoke to the senior samurai on the wharf. "Captain, I take Lady Toda there. Show ship. When Lord Toranaga arrive—you call, *neh?*"

"As you wish, Anjin-san."

Blackthorne led the way off the jetty. Samurai were manning the barriers and security was tighter than ever, ashore and on deck. First he went to the quarter-deck. "This is mine, all mine," he said with pride.

"Are any of your crew here?"

"No—none. Not today, Mariko-san." He pointed out everything as quickly as he could, then guided her below. "This is the main cabin." The aft bay windows overlooked the foreshore. He closed the door. Now they were totally alone.

"This is your cabin?" she asked.

He shook his head, watching her. She went into his arms. He held her tight. "Oh, how I have missed thee."

"And I have missed thee. . . ."

"There's so much to tell thee. And to ask thee," he said.

"I've nothing to tell thee. Except that I love thee with all my heart." She shivered in his arms, trying to throw off her terror that Gyoko or someone would denounce them. "I'm so afraid for thee."

"Don't be afraid, Mariko my darling. Everything's going to be all right."

"That's what I tell myself. But today it's impossible to accept *karma* and the will of God."

"You were so distant the last time."

"This is Yedo, my love. And beyond First Bridge."

"It *was* because of Buntaro-san. Wasn't it?"

"Yes," she said simply. "That and Toranaga's decision to surrender. It's such a dishonorable uselessness. . . . I never thought I'd ever say that out loud but I have to say it. So sorry." She nestled closer into the protection of his shoulder.

"When he goes to Osaka, you're finished, too?"

"Yes. The Toda clan are too powerful and important. In any event I would not be left alive."

"Then you must come with me. We'll escape. We'll—"

"So sorry, but there's no escape."

"Unless Toranaga allows it, *neh?*"

"Why should he allow it?"

Quickly Blackthorne told her what he had said to Toranaga, but not that he had also asked for her. "I know I can force the priests to bring Kiyama or Onoshi to his side, if he'll allow me to take *this* Black Ship," he finished excitedly, "and I know I can do that!"

"Yes," she said, glad for the sake of the Church that he was hobbled by Toranaga's decision. Again she examined the logic of his plan and found it flawless. "It should work, Anjin-san. Now that Harima's hostile, there would be no reason why Toranaga-sama shouldn't order an attack if he were going to war, and not surrendering."

"If Lord Kiyama or Lord Onoshi, or both of them, joined him, would that tip the scale toward him?"

"Yes," she said. "With Zataki and time." She had already explained the strategic importance of Zataki's control of the northern route. "But Zataki's opposed to Toranaga-sama."

"Listen, I can strangle the priests. So sorry, but they *are* my enemy though they are your priests. I can dominate them on his behalf—on mine too. Will you help me to help him?"

She stared up at him. "How?"

"Help me to persuade him to give me the chance, and persuade him to delay going to Osaka."

There was the sound of horses and voices raised on the jetty. Distracted, they went to the windows. Samurai were pulling aside one of the barriers. Father Alvito spurred forward into the clearing.

"What does he want?" Blackthorne muttered sourly.

They watched the priest as he dismounted and pulled out a scroll from his sleeve and gave it to the senior samurai. The man read it. Alvito looked up at the ship.

"Whatever it is, is official," she said in a small voice.

"Listen, Mariko-san, I'm not against the Church. The Church isn't evil, it's the priests. And they're not all bad. Alvito isn't, though he's fanatic. I swear to God I believe the Jesuits will bow to Lord Toranaga if I get their Black Ship and threaten next year's, because they've got to have money—Portugal and Spain have got to have money. Toranaga's more important. Will you help me?"

"Yes. Yes, I'll help you, Anjin-san. But, please excuse me, I cannot betray the Church."

"All I ask is that you talk to Toranaga, or help me to talk to him if you think that's better."

A distant bugle sounded. They looked out of the windows again. Everyone was staring west. The head of a procession of samurai around a curtained litter approached from the direction of the castle.

The cabin door opened. "Anjin-san, you will come now, please," the samurai said.

Blackthorne led the way on deck and down to the jetty. His nod to Alvito was coldly polite. The priest was equally glacial.

To Mariko, Alvito was kind. "Hello, Mariko-san. How nice to see you."

"Thank you, Father," she said, bowing low.

"May the blessings of God be upon you." He made the sign of the cross over her. *"In nomine Patris et Filii et Spiritus Sancti."*

"Thank you, Father."

Alvito glanced at Blackthorne. "So, Pilot? How is your ship?"

"I'm sure you already know."

"Yes, I know." Alvito looked *Erasmus* over, his face taut. "May God curse her and all who sail in her if she's used against Faith and Portugal!"

"Is that why you came here? To spread more venom?"

"No, Pilot," Alvito said. "I was asked here to meet Lord Toranaga. I find your presence as distasteful as you find mine."

"Your presence isn't distasteful, Father. It's just the evil you represent."

Alvito flushed and Mariko said quickly, "Please. It is bad to quarrel this way in public. I beg you both to be more circumspect."

"Yes, please excuse me. I apologize, Mariko-san." Father Alvito turned away and looked at the curtained litter coming through the barrier, Toranaga's pennant fluttering, and uniformed samurai before and after, hemming in a straggling, motley group of samurai.

The palanquin stopped. The curtains parted. Yabu stepped out. Everyone was startled. Nonetheless they bowed. Yabu returned the salutation arrogantly.

"Ah, Anjin-san," Yabu said. "How are you?"

"Good, thank you, Sire. And you?"

"Good, thank you. Lord Toranaga's sick. He asked me to come in his place. You understand?"

"Yes. Understand," Blackthorne replied, trying to cover his disappointment at Toranaga's nonarrival. "So sorry Lord Toranaga sick."

Yabu shrugged, acknowledged Mariko deferentially, pretended not to notice Alvito, and studied the ship for a moment. His smile was twisted as he turned back to Blackthorne. *"So desu,* Anjin-san. Your ship's different from the last time

I saw it, *neh?* Yes, the ship's different, you're different, everything's different —even our world's different! *Neh?*"

"So sorry, I don't understand, Sire. Please excuse me but your words very fast. As my—" Blackthorne began the stock phrase but Yabu interrupted gutturally, "Mariko-san, please translate for me."

She did so.

Blackthorne nodded and said slowly, "Yes. Different, Yabu-sama."

"Yes, very different—you're no longer barbarian but samurai, and so is your ship, *neh?*"

Blackthorne saw the smile on the thick lips, the pugnacious stance, and suddenly he was back at Anjiro, back on the beach on his knees, Croocq in the cauldron, Pieterzoon's screams ringing in his ears, the stench of the pit in his nostrils, and his mind was shouting, 'So unnecessary all that—all the suffering and terror and Pieterzoon and Spillbergen and Maetsukker and the jail and *eta* and trapped and all your fault!'

"Are you all right, Anjin-san?" Mariko asked, apprehensive at the look in his eyes.

"What? Oh—oh, yes. Yes, I'm all right."

"What's the matter with him?" Yabu said.

Blackthorne shook his head, trying to clear it and wash the hatred off his face. "So sorry. Please excuse me. I'm—I—it's nothing. Head bad—no sleep. So sorry." He stared back into Yabu's eyes, hoping he had covered his dangerous lapse. "Sorry Toranaga-sama sick—hope no trouble Yabu-sama."

"No, no trouble." Yabu was thinking, yes trouble, you're nothing but trouble and I've had nothing but trouble ever since you and your filthy ship arrived on my shores. Izu gone, my guns gone, all honor gone, and now my head forfeit because of a coward. "No trouble, Anjin-san," he said so nicely. "Toranaga-sama asked me to hand over your vassals to you as he promised." His eyes fell on Alvito. "So, Tsukku-san! Why are you enemy to Toranaga-sama?"

"I'm not, Kasigi Yabu-sama."

"Your Christian *daimyos* are, *neh?*"

"Please excuse me, Sire, but we are priests only, we're not responsible for the political views of those who worship the True Faith, nor do we exercise control over those *daimyos* who—"

"The *True Faith* of this Land of the Gods is Shinto, together with the Tao, the Way of Buddha!"

Alvito did not answer. Yabu turned contemptuously away and snapped an order. The ragged group of samurai began to line up in front of the ship. Not one was armed. Some had their hands bound.

Alvito stepped forward and bowed. "Perhaps you will excuse me, Sire. I was to see Lord Toranaga. As he isn't coming—"

"Lord Toranaga wanted you here to interpret for him with the Anjin-san," Yabu interrupted with deliberate bad manners, as Toranaga had told him to do. "Yes, to interpret as you alone can do so cleverly, speaking directly and at once, *neh?* Of course you have no objection to doing for me what Lord Toranaga required, before you go?"

"No, of course not, Sire."

"Good. Mariko-san! Lord Toranaga asks that you see the Anjin-san's responses are equally correctly translated." Alvito reddened but held onto his temper.

"Yes, Sire," Mariko said, hating Yabu.

Yabu snapped another order. Two samurai went to the litter and returned with the ship's strongbox, heavy between them. "Tsukku-san, now you will begin:

Listen, Anjin-san, firstly, Lord Toranaga's asked me to return this. It's your property, *neh?* Open it," he ordered the samurai. The box was brimful with silver coins. "This is as it was taken off the ship."

"Thank you." Blackthorne was hardly able to believe his eyes, for this gave him power to buy the very best crew, without promises.

"It is to be put in the ship's strong room."

"Yes, of course."

Yabu waved those samurai aboard. Then, to Alvito's growing fury as he continued with the almost simultaneous translating, Yabu said, "Next: Lord Toranaga says you are free to go, or to stay. When you are in our land you are samurai, hatamoto, and governed by samurai law. At sea, beyond our shores, you are as you were before you came here and governed by barbarian laws. You are granted the right for your lifetime to dock at any port in Lord Toranaga's control without search by port authorities. Last, these two hundred men are your vassals. He asked me to formally hand them over, with arms, as he promised."

"I can leave when and how I want?" Blackthorne asked with disbelief.

"Yes, Anjin-san, you can leave as Lord Toranaga has agreed."

Blackthorne stared at Mariko but she avoided his eyes, so he looked again at Yabu. "Could I leave tomorrow?"

"Yes, if you want to." Yabu added, "About these men. They're all *ronin.* All from the northern provinces. They've all agreed to swear eternal allegiance to you and your seed. All are good warriors. None has committed a crime that could be proved. All became *ronin* because their liege lords were killed, died, or were deposed. Many fought on ships against *wako.* " Yabu smiled in his vicious way. "Some may have been *wako*—you understand 'wako'?"

"Yes, Sire."

"Those who are bound are probably bandits or *wako.* They came forward as a band and volunteered to serve you fearlessly in return for a pardon for any past crimes. They've sworn to Lord Noboru—who handpicked all these men for you on Lord Toranaga's orders—that they've never committed any crime against Lord Toranaga or any of his samurai. You can accept them individually, or as a group, or refuse them. You understand?"

"I can refuse any of them?"

"Why should you do that?" Yabu asked. "Lord Noboru picked them carefully."

"Of course, so sorry," Blackthorne told Yabu wearily, conscious of the *daimyo*'s growing ill humor. "I quite understand. But those who are bound—what happens if I refuse them?"

"Their heads will be hacked off. Of course. What's that got to do with anything?"

"Nothing. So sorry."

"Follow me." Yabu stalked over to the litter.

Blackthorne glanced at Mariko. "I can *leave.* You heard it!"

"Yes."

"That means. . . . It's almost like a dream. He said—"

"Anjin-san!"

Obediently Blackthorne hurried over to Yabu. Now the litter served as a dais. A clerk had set up a low table on which were scrolls. A little farther off, samurai guarded a pile of short swords and long swords, spears, shields, axes, bows and arrows, that porters were unloading from pack horses. Yabu motioned Blackthorne to sit beside him, Alvito just in front and Mariko on his other side. The clerk called out names. Each man came forward, bowed with great formality, gave his name and lineage, swore allegiance, signed his scroll, and sealed it with a drop of blood that the clerk ritually pricked from his finger. Each knelt to Blackthorne a final time, then got up and hurried to the armorer. First he was handed a killing sword, then the short one. Each accepted both blades with reverence and examined them meticulously, expressing pride at their quality, and shoved them into his sash with savage glee. Then he was issued other weapons and a war shield. When the men took up their new places, fully armed now, samurai again and no longer *ronin,* they were stronger and straighter and looked even more fierce.

Last were the thirty bound *ronin.* Blackthorne insisted on personally cutting the bonds of each. One by one they swore allegiance as had all the others: "On my honor as a samurai, I swear your enemies are my enemies, and total obedience."

After each man had sworn, he collected his weapons.

Yabu called out, "Uraga-noh-Tadamasa!"

The man stepped forward. Alvito was heartsick. Uraga—Brother Joseph—had been standing unnoticed among the samurai grouped nearby. He was unarmed and wore a simple kimono and bamboo hat. Yabu smirked at Alvito's discomposure and turned to Blackthorne.

"Anjin-san. This is Uraga-noh-Tadamasa. Samurai, now *ronin.* You recognize him? Understand 'recognize'?"

"Yes. Understand. Yes, recognize."

"Good. Once Christian priest, *neh?*"

"Yes."

"Now not. Understand? Now *ronin.* "

"Understand, Yabu-sama."

Yabu watched Alvito. Alvito was staring fixedly at the apostate, who stared back with hatred. "Ah, Tsukku-san, you recognize him too?"

"Yes. I recognize him, Sire."

"Are you ready to translate again—or haven't you any stomach for it anymore?"

"Please continue, Sire."

"Good." Yabu waved a hand at Uraga. "Listen, Anjin-san, Lord Toranaga gives this man to you, if you want him. Once he was a Christian priest—a novice priest. Now he's not. Now he's denounced the false foreign god and has reverted to the True Faith of Shinto and—" He stopped as the Father stopped. "Did you say it exactly, Tsukku-san? *True Faith* of Shinto?"

The priest did not answer. He exhaled, then said it exactly, adding, "That's what *he* said, Anjin-san, may God forgive him." Mariko let that pass without comment, hating Yabu even more, promising herself vengeance on him one day soon.

Yabu watched them, then he continued, "So Uraga-san's a Christian that was. Now he's prepared to serve you. He can speak barbarian and the private tongue of the priests and he was one of the four samurai youths sent to your lands. He even met the chief Christian of all the Christians, so they say—but now he hates them all, just like you, *neh?*" Yabu was watching Alvito, baiting him, his eyes flicking back and forth to Mariko, who was listening as intently. "You hate Christians, Anjin-san, *neh?*"

"Most Catholics are my enemy, yes," he answered, completely aware of Mariko, who was staring stonily into the distance. "Spain and Portugal are enemies of my country, yes."

"Christians are our enemies too. Eh, Tsukku-san?"

"No, Sire. And Christianity gives you the key to immortal life."

"Does it, Uraga-san?" Yabu said.

Uraga shook his head. His voice was raw. "I no longer think so, Sire. No."

"Tell the Anjin-san."

"Senhor Anjin-san," Uraga said, his accent thick but his Portuguese words correct and easily understandable, "I do not think this Catholicism is the lock—so sorry, is the key to immortality."

"Yes," Blackthorne said. "I agree."

"Good," Yabu continued. "So Lord Toranaga offers this *ronin* to you, Anjin-san. He's renegade but from good samurai family. Uraga swears, if you'll accept him, he'll be your secretary, translator, and do anything you want. You'll have to give him swords. What else, Uraga? Tell him."

"Senhor, please excuse me. First . . ." Uraga took off his hat. His hair was a stubble now, his pate shaven in samurai style, but he had no queue yet. "First, I'm shamed my hair is not correct and I have no queue as a samurai should have. But my hair will grow and I am not less samurai for that." He put his hat back on his head. He told Yabu what he had said, and those *ronin* who were near and could hear also listened attentively as he continued, "Second, please excuse me greatly but I cannot use swords—or any weapons. I've—I've never been trained in them. But I will learn, believe me I will learn. Please excuse my shame. I swear absolute allegiance to you and beg you to accept me . . ." Sweat trickled down his face and back.

Blackthorne said compassionately, "*Shigata ga nai, neh? Ukeru anatawa desu,* Uraga-san." What does that matter? I accept you, Uraga-san.

Uraga bowed, then explained to Yabu what he had said. No one laughed. Except Yabu. But his laughter was cut short by the beginning of an altercation between the last two *ronin* over the selection of the remaining swords. "You two, shut up," he shouted.

Both men spun around and one snarled, "You're not my master! Where are your manners? Say please, or shut up yourself!"

Instantly Yabu leaped to his feet and rushed the offending *ronin,* his sword on high. Men scattered, and the *ronin* fled. Near the side of the wharf the man jerked out his sword and abruptly turned to the attack with a fiendish battle cry. At once all his friends darted to his rescue, swords ready, and Yabu was trapped. The man charged. Yabu avoided a violent sword thrust, hacked back, and missed as the pack surged forward for the kill. Too late Toranaga samurai rushed forward, knowing Yabu was a dead man.

"*Stop!*" Blackthorne shouted in Japanese. Everyone froze at the power of his voice. "*Go there!*" He pointed to where the men had been lined up before. "*Now! Order!*"

For a moment all the men on the wharf remained motionless. Then they started to move. The spell broke. Yabu darted at the man who had insulted him. The *ronin* jumped back, sidestepped, his sword held violently above his head, two-handed, waiting fearlessly for the next attack. His friends hesitated.

"*Go there! Now! Order!*"

Reluctantly but obediently, the rest of the men backed out of the way, sheathed their swords. Yabu and the man circled each other slowly.

"You!" Blackthorne shouted. "Stop! Sword down! *I order!*"

The man kept his furious eyes on Yabu but he heard the order and wet his lips. He feinted left, then right. Yabu retreated and the man slipped out of his grasp and rushed nearer to Blackthorne and put his sword down in front of him. "I obey, Anjin-san. I didn't attack him." As Yabu charged, he leaped out of the way and retreated fearlessly, more fleet than Yabu, younger than Yabu, taunting him.

"Yabu-san," Blackthorne called out. "So sorry—think mistake, *neh?* Perhaps—"

But Yabu spouted a flood of Japanese and rushed the man, who fled again without fear.

Alvito was now coldly amused. "Yabu-san said there's no mistake, Anjin-san. This *cabron* has to die, he says. No samurai could accept such an insult!"

Blackthorne felt all their eyes on him as he desperately tried to decide what to do. He watched Yabu stalk the man. Just to the left a Toranaga samurai aimed his bow. The only noise was that of the two men panting and running and shouting at one another. The *ronin* backed, then turned and ran away, around the clearing, sidestepping, weaving, all the time keeping up a guttural hissing flood of invective.

Alvito said, "He's baiting Yabu, Anjin-san. He says: 'I'm samurai—I don't kill unarmed men like you—you're not a samurai, you're a manure-stinking peasant—ah, so that's it, you're not samurai, you're *eta, neh?* Your mother was *eta,* your father was *eta,* and—' " The Jesuit stopped as Yabu let out a bellow of rage and pointed at one of the men and shouted something. "Yabu says: 'You! Give him his sword.' "

The *ronin* hesitated and looked at Blackthorne for the order.

Yabu turned to Blackthorne and shouted, "Give him his sword!"

Blackthorne picked up the sword. "Yabu-san, ask not fight," he said, wishing him dead. "Please ask not fight—"

"Give him the sword!"

An angry murmur went through Blackthorne's men. He held up his hand. "Silence!" He looked at his *ronin* vassal. "Come here. Please!" The man watched Yabu, feinted left then right, and each time Yabu hacked at him in wild rage but the man managed to slip away and race to Blackthorne. This time Yabu did not follow. He just waited and watched like a mad bull readying his charge. The man bowed to Blackthorne and took the sword. Then he turned on Yabu and, with a howling battle cry, flung himself to the attack. Swords clashed and clashed again. Now the two men circled in the silence. There was another frantic exchange, the swords singing. Then Yabu stumbled and the *ronin* charged in for the easy kill. But Yabu neatly sidestepped and struck. The man's hands, still gripping the sword, were sliced off. For a moment the *ronin* stood there howling, staring at his stumps, then Yabu hacked off his head.

There was silence. Then a roar of applause surrounded Yabu. Yabu slashed once more at the twitching corpse. Then, honor vindicated, he picked up the head by the topknot, spat carefully in the face, and tossed it aside. Quietly he walked back to Blackthorne and bowed.

"Please excuse my bad manners, Anjin-san. Thank you for giving him his sword," he said, his voice polite, Alvito translating. "I apologize for shouting. Thank you for allowing me to blood my sword honorably." His eyes dropped to the heirloom Toranaga had given him. Carefully he examined its edge. It was still perfect. He undid his silk sash to cleanse the blood away. "Never touch a blade with your fingers, Anjin-san, that will ruin it. A blade must feel only silk or the body of an enemy." He stopped and looked up. "May I politely suggest you allow your vassals to test their blades? It will be a good omen for them."

Blackthorne turned to Uraga. "Tell them."

When Yabu returned to his house it was late in the day. Servants took his sweat-soiled clothes and gave him a fresh lounging kimono and put his feet into clean tabi. Yuriko, his wife, was waiting for him in the cool of the veranda with cha and saké, piping hot, the way he liked to drink it.

"Saké, Yabu-san?" Yuriko was a tall thin woman with gray-streaked hair. Her dark kimono of poor quality set off her fair skin nicely.

"Thank you, Yuriko-san." Yabu drank the wine gratefully, enjoying the sweet, harsh rasp as it slid down his parched throat.

"It went well, I hear."

"Yes."

"How impertinent of that *ronin!*"

"He served me well, Lady, very well. I feel fine now. I've blooded Toranaga's sword and made it really mine." Yabu finished the cup and she refilled it. His hand fondled his sword hilt. "But you wouldn't have enjoyed the fight. He was a child—he fell into the first trap."

She touched him tenderly. "I'm glad he did, husband."

"Thank you, but I hardly got up a sweat." Yabu laughed. "You should have seen the priest though! It would have made you warm to see that barbarian sweating—I've never seen him so angry. He was so angry it almost choked him to hold it in. Cannibal! They're all cannibals. Pity there's no way to stamp them out before we depart this earth."

"Do you think the Anjin-san could?"

"He's going to try. With ten of those ships and ten of him, I could control the seas from here to Kyushu. With only him I could hurt Kiyama, Onoshi, and Harima and smash Jikkyu and keep Izu! We only need a little time and every *daimyo*'ll be fighting his own special enemy. Izu would be safe and mine again! I don't understand why Toranaga's going to let the Anjin-san go. That's another stupid waste!" He bunched his fist and slammed it on the tatamis. The maid flinched but said nothing. Yuriko did not make the slightest move. A smile flickered across her face.

"How did the Anjin-san take his freedom, and his vassals?" she asked.

"He was so happy he was like an old man dreaming he had a four-pronged Yang. He—oh yes . . ." Yabu frowned, remembering. "But there was one thing I still don't understand. When those *wako* first surrounded me I was a dead man. No doubt about it. But the Anjin-san stopped them and gave me back my life. No reason for him to do that, *neh?* Just before, I'd seen the hate written all over him. So naïve to pretend otherwise—as if I'd trust him."

"He gave you your life?"

"Oh yes. Strange, *neh?*"

"Yes. Many strange things are going on, husband." She dismissed the maid, then asked quietly, "What did Toranaga really want?"

Yabu bent forward and whispered, "I think he wants me to become commander-in-chief."

"Why should he do that? Is Iron Fist dying?" Yuriko asked. "What about Lord Sudara? Or Buntaro? Or Lord Noboru?"

"Who knows, Lady? They're all out of favor, *neh?* Toranaga changes his mind so often no one can predict what he'll do now. First he asked me to go in his place to the wharf and told how he wanted everything said, then he talked about Hiro-matsu, how old he was getting, and asked what I really thought about the Musket Regiment."

"Could he be readying Crimson Sky again?"

"That's always ready. But he hasn't got the Fruit for it. That will need leadership and skill. Once he had it, not now. Now he's a shadow of the Minowara he was. I was shocked at how he looked. So sorry, I made a mistake. I should have gone with Ishido."

"I think you chose correctly."

"What?"

"First have your bath, then I think I have a present for you."

"What present?"

"Your brother Mizuno is coming after the evening meal."

"That's a present?" Yabu bristled. "What would I want with that fool?"

"Special information or wisdom, even from a fool, can be just as valuable as from a counselor, *neh?* Sometimes more so."

"What information?"

"First your bath. And food. You'll need a cool head tonight, Yabu-chan."

Yabu would have pressed her but the bath tempted him, and in truth, he was filled with a pleasing lassitude he had not felt in many a day. Part of it was due to Toranaga's deference this morning, part to the generals' deference over the last few days. But most of it was due to the killing, the ripple of joy that had rushed from sword to arm to head. Ah, to kill so cleanly, man to man—in front of *men*—that's a joy given to so few, so rarely. Rare enough to be appreciated and savored.

So he left his wife and relaxed further into his joy. He allowed hands to tend his body and then, refreshed and renewed, he went to a veranda room. The last rays of sunset bedecked the sky. The moon was low, crescent, and thin. One of his personal maids served his evening meal delicately. He ate sparingly and in silence. A little soup and fish and pickled vegetables.

The girl smiled invitingly. "Shall I turn down the futons now, Sire?"

Yabu shook his head. "Later. First tell my wife I wish to see her."

Yuriko arrived, wearing a neat but old kimono.

"So desu ka?"

"Your brother's waiting. We should see him alone. See him first, Sire, then we'll talk, you and I—also alone. Please be patient, *neh?*"

Kasigi Mizuno, Yabu's younger brother and Omi's father, was a small man with bulbous eyes, high forehead, and thin hair. His swords did not seem to suit him and he could barely handle them. Even with bow and arrow he was not much better.

Mizuno bowed and complimented Yabu on his skill this afternoon, for the news of the exploit had quickly spread around the castle, further enhancing Yabu's reputation as a fighter. Then, anxious to please, he came to the point. "I received a coded letter today from my son, Sire. The lady Yuriko thought I'd better give it to you personally." He handed the scroll to Yabu, with the decoding. The message from Omi read: "Father, please tell Lord Yabu quickly and privately: first Lord Buntaro came to Mishima, *secretly via Takato.* One of his men let this slip during a drunken evening that I'd arranged in their honor. Second: During this secret visit at Takato, which lasted three days, Buntaro saw Lord Zataki twice and the Lady, Zataki's mother, three times. Third: Before Lord Hiro-matsu left Mishima he told his new consort, the Lady Oko, not to worry because 'while I'm alive Lord Toranaga will never leave the Kwanto.' Fourth: that . . ."

Yabu looked up. "How can Omi-san possibly know what Iron Fist said privately to his consort? We don't have spies in his house."

"We have now, Sire. Please read on."

"Fourth: that Hiro-matsu is resolved to commit treason, *if necessary,* and will confine Toranaga in Yedo, *if necessary,* and will order Crimson Sky over Toranaga's refusal with or without Lord Sudara's assent, *if necessary.* Fifth: that these are truths that can be believed. Lady Oko's personal maid is the daughter of my wife's foster mother and was introduced into the Lady Oko's service here at Mishima when, regrettably, her own maid *curiously* acquired a wasting malaise.

Sixth: Buntaro-san is like a madman, brooding and angry—today he challenged and slaughtered a samurai purposelessly, cursing the name of the Anjin-san. Last: Spies report that Ikawa Jikkyu has massed ten thousand men in Suruga, ready to sweep across our borders. Please give Lord Yabu my greetings. . . ." The rest of the message was inconsequential.

"Jikkyu, eh! Must I go to my death with that devil unrevenged!"

"Please be patient, Sire," Yuriko said. "Tell him, Mizuno-san."

"Sire," the little man began. "For months we've tried to put your plan into effect, the one you suggested when the barbarian first arrived. You remember, with all those silver coins, you mentioned that a hundred or even five hundred in the hands of the right cook would eliminate Ikawa Jikkyu once and for all." Mizuno's eyes seemed to grow even more froglike. "It seems that Mura, headman of Anjiro, has a cousin who has a cousin whose brother now is the best cook in Suruga. I heard today he's been accepted into Jikkyu's household. He's been given two hundred on account and the whole price is five hun—"

"We haven't got that money! Impossible! How can I raise five hundred—I'm so in debt now I can't even raise one hundred!"

"Please excuse me, Sire. So sorry, but the money's already set aside. Not all the barbarian coins remained in the strongbox. A thousand coins strayed before it was officially counted. So sorry."

Yabu gawked at him. "How?"

"It seems Omi-san was ordered to do that in your name. The money was brought here secretly to the Lady Yuriko, from whom permission was asked and granted before risking your displeasure."

Yabu thought about that a long time. "Who ordered it?"

"I did. After seeking permission."

"Thank you, Mizuno-san. And thank you, Yuriko-san." Yabu bowed to both. "So! Jikkyu, eh? At long last!" He clapped his brother warmly on the shoulder and the smaller man was almost pathetic in his fawning pleasure. "You did very well, brother. I'll send you some bolts of silk from the treasury. How is the lady, your wife?"

"Well, Sire, very well. She asked you to accept her best wishes."

"We must have food together. Good—good. Now about the rest of the report—what are your views?"

"Nothing, Sire. I would be most interested in what you think it means."

"First—" Yabu stopped as he caught his wife's look, cautioning him, and changed what he was going to say, "First and last, it means that Omi-san, your son, is loyal and an excellent vassal. If I had control of the future I'd promote him—yes, he deserves promotion, *neh?*"

Mizuno was unctuously delighted. Yabu was patient with him, chatting with him, again complimenting him and, as soon as was polite, he dismissed him.

Yuriko sent for cha. When they were quite alone again he said, "What does the rest mean?"

Her face mirrored her excitement now, "Please excuse me, Sire, but I want to give you a new idea: *Toranaga is playing us all for fools and has no intention, and never had any intention, of going to Osaka to surrender.*"

"Nonsense!"

"Let me give you facts. . . . Oh, Sire, you don't know how fortunate you are in your vassal Omi and that stupid brother who stole a thousand coins. Proof of my theory could be as follows: Buntaro-san, a trusted intimate, is sent to Zataki secretly. Why? Obviously to carry a new offer. What would tempt Zataki? The Kwanto—only that. So the offer is the Kwanto—in return for allegiance, once Toranaga is again *President of the Council of Regents—a new one with the new mandate.* He can afford to give it then, *neh?"* She waited, then went on painstakingly. "If he persuades Zataki to betray Ishido, he's a quarter of the way to the capital, Kyoto. How can the pact with his brother be cemented? Hostages! I heard this afternoon Lord Sudara, the Lady Genjiko, and their daughters *and* their son are going to visit their revered grandmother at Takato within ten days."

"All of them?"

"Yes. Next Toranaga gives the Anjin-san back his ship, as good as new, with all the cannon and powder, two hundred fanatics and all that money, surely enough to buy more barbarian mercenaries, *wako* scum out of Nagasaki. Why? To allow him to attack and take the Black Ship of the barbarians. No Black Ship, no money, and immense trouble for the Christian priests who control Kiyama, Onoshi, and all traitorous Christian *daimyos.*"

"Toranaga'd never dare to do that! The Taikō tried and failed and he was all powerful. The barbarians will sail away in fury. We'll never trade again."

"Yes. If *we* did it. But this time it's barbarian against barbarian, *neh?* It's nothing to do with us. And say the Anjin-san attacks Nagasaki and puts it to the torch—isn't Harima now hostile, and Kiyama and Onoshi, and, because of them, most Kyushu *daimyos?* Say the Anjin-san burns a few of their other ports, harries their shipping, and at the same time—"

"And at the same time Toranaga launches Crimson Sky!" Yabu exploded.

"Yes. Oh yes," Yuriko agreed happily. "Dosn't this explain Toranaga? Doesn't this intrigue fit him like a skin? Isn't he doing what he's always done, just waiting like always, playing for time like always, a day here a day there and soon a month has passed and again he has an overwhelming force to sweep all opposition aside? He's gained almost a month since Zataki brought the summons to Yokosé."

Yabu could feel his pulse roaring in his ears. "Then we're safe?"

"No, but we're not lost. I believe it's no surrender." She hesitated. "But everyone was deceived. Oh, he's so clever, *neh?* Everyone fooled like us. Until tonight. Omi gave me the clues. We all forgot Toranaga is a great Nōh actor who can wear his own face as a mask if need be. *Neh?"*

Yabu tried to marshal his thoughts but could not. "But Ishido still has all Japan against us!"

"Yes. Less Zataki. And there must be other secret alliances. Toranaga and you can hold the passes until the time."

"Ishido has Osaka Castle and the Heir and the Taikō's wealth."

"Yes. But he'll stay skulking inside. Someone will betray him."

"What should I do?"

"The opposite to Toranaga. Let him do the waiting, you must force the pace."

"How?"

"The first thing, Sire, is this: Toranaga's forgotten the one thing you noticed this afternoon. The Tsukku-san's total fury. Why? Because the Anjin-san threatens the Christian future, *neh?* So you've got to put the Anjin-san under your protection at once, because those priests or their puppets will murder him within hours. Next: The Anjin-san needs you to protect and guide him, to help him get his new crew at Nagasaki. Without you and your men he has to fail. Without him and his ship and his cannon and more barbarians, Nagasaki won't burn, and that must happen or Kiyama, Onoshi, and Harima and the filthy priests won't be distracted enough to temporarily withdraw their support from Ishido. Meanwhile, Toranaga, now miraculously supported by Zataki and his fanatics, with you leading the Musket Regiment, sweeps through the Shinano passes down to the Kyota plains."

"Yes. Yes, you are right, Yuriko-chan! It has to be that way. Oh, you are so clever, so wise!"

"Wisdom and Luck are no good without the means to put a plan into effect, Sire. You alone can do that—you're the leader, the fighter, the battle-general that Toranaga *must* have. You must see him tonight."

"I can't go to Toranaga and tell him I've seen through his ruse, *neh?*"

"No, but you'll beg him to allow you to go with the Anjin-san, that you must leave at once. We can think of a plausible reason."

"But if the Anjin-san attacks Nagasaki and the Black Ship, won't they stop trading and sail away?"

"Yes. Possibly. But that's next year. By next year Toranaga will be a Regent, President of the Regents. And you his commander-in-chief."

Yabu came down from the clouds. "No," he said firmly. "Once he has power he'll order me to commit seppuku."

"Long before that you will have the Kwanto."

His eyes blinked. "How?"

"Toranaga will never actually give his half brother the Kwanto. Zataki's a perpetual threat. Zataki's a wild man, pride-filled, *neh?* It will be so easy for Toranaga to maneuver Zataki into begging for the foremost place in the battle. If Zataki doesn't get killed . . . perhaps a stray bullet or arrow? Probably a bullet. You must lead the Musket Regiment in the battle, Sire."

"Why shouldn't I receive a stray bullet equally?"

"You may, Sire. But you're not Toranaga's kinsman and therefore no threat to his power. You will become his most devoted *vassal.* He needs fighting generals. You'll earn the Kwanto, and that should be your only goal. He'll give it to you when Ishido's betrayed because he'll take Osaka for himself."

"Vassal? But you said to wait and soon I'd nev—"

"Now I counsel you to support him with all your strength. Not to follow his orders blindly like old Iron Fist, but cleverly. Don't forget, Yabu-chan, during battle, as in any battle, soldiers make mistakes, stray bullets do happen. So long as you lead the Regiment, you can choose, too—any time, *neh?*"

"Yes," he said, awed by her.

"Remember, Toranaga's worth following. He's Minowara, Ishido's a peasant. Ishido's the fool. I can see that now. Ishido should be hammering at the gates of Odawara right now, rain or no rains. Didn't Omi-san say that months ago too? Isn't Odawara undermanned? Isn't Toranaga isolated?"

Yabu pounded his fist on the floor with delight. "Then it's war after all! How clever you are to have seen through him! Ah, so he's been playing the fox all the time, *neh?*"

"Yes," she said, greatly satisfied.

Mariko had come to the same astonishing conclusion, though not from all the same facts. Toranaga must be pretending, playing a secret game, she reasoned. That's the only possible explanation for his incredible conduct—giving the Anjin-san the ship, the money, all the cannon, and freedom in front of Tsukku-san. Now the Anjin-san will absolutely go against the Black Ship. He will take it, and threaten the one next year, and therefore he'll maul the Holy Church terribly and force the Holy Fathers to compel Kiyama and Onoshi to betray Ishido. . . .

But why? If that's true, she thought, perplexed, and Toranaga's considering such a long-range plan, then of course he can't go to Osaka and bow before Ishido, *neh?* He must. . . . Ah! What about today's delay that Hiro-matsu persuaded Toranaga to make? Oh, Madonna on high, Toranaga never intended to surrender! It's *all* a trick.

Why? To gain time.

To accomplish what? To wait and weave a thousand more tricks, and it doesn't matter what, only that Toranaga's once more what he always was, the almighty puppeteer.

How long before Ishido's impatience shatters and he raises the battle standard and moves against us? One month—at the most two. No more. So by the ninth month of this Fifth Year of Keichō, *the* battle for the Kwanto begins!

But what's Toranaga gained in two months? I don't know—I only know that now my son has a chance to inherit his ten thousand koku, and to live and breed, and that now perhaps my father's line will not perish from the earth.

She relished her newfound knowledge, toying with it, examining it, finding her logic flawless. But what to do between now and then? she asked herself. Nothing more than you've already done—and decided to do. *Neh?*

"Mistress?"

"Yes, Chimmoko?"

"Gyoko-san is here. She has an appointment, she says."

"Ah yes. I forget to tell you. First heat saké, then bring it, and her, here."

Mariko reflected on the afternoon. She remembered his arms around her, so safe and warm and strong. 'Can I see you tonight?' he had asked very cautiously, after Yabu and Tsukku-san had left.

'Yes,' she had said impulsively. 'Yes, my darling. Oh, how happy I am for thee. Tell Fujiko-san . . . ask her to send for me after the Hour of the Boar.'

In the quiet of her house her throat tightened. So much foolishness and danger.

She checked her makeup and coiffure in her mirror and tried to compose herself. Footsteps approached. The shoji slid open. "Ah, Lady," Gyoko said, bowing deeply. "How kind of you to see me."

"You're welcome, Gyoko-san."

They drank saké, Chimmoko pouring for them.

"Such lovely pottery, Lady. So beautiful."

They made polite conversation, then Chimmoko was sent away.

"So sorry, Gyoko-san, but our Master did not arrive this afternoon. I haven't seen him, though I hope to before I leave."

"Yes, I heard Yabu-san went to the jetty in his place."

"When I see Toranaga-sama I will ask him once more. But I expect his answer will be the same." Mariko poured saké for both of them. "So sorry, he will not grant my request."

"Yes, I believe you. Not unless there is great pressure."

"There's no pressure that I can use. So sorry."

"So sorry too, Lady."

Mariko put down her cup. "Then you've decided that some tongues are not safe."

Gyoko said harshly, "If I were going to whisper secrets about you, would I tell you to your face? Do you think I'd be so naïve?"

"Perhaps you'd better go, so sorry, but I have so much to do."

"Yes, Lady, and so have I!" Gyoko replied, her voice rough. "Lord Toranaga asked me, *to my face,* what I knew about you and the Anjin-san. This afternoon. I told him there was nothing between you. I said, 'Oh yes, Sire, I've heard the foul rumors too, but there's no truth in them. I swear it on the head of my son, Sire, and his sons. If anyone would know, surely it would be me. You may believe it's all a malicious lie—gossip, jealous gossip, Sire. . . .' Oh yes, Lady, you may believe I was suitably shocked, my acting perfect, and he was convinced." Gyoko quaffed the saké, and added bitterly, "Now we are all ruined if he gets proof—which wouldn't be difficult to get. *Neh?*"

"How?"

"Put the Anjin-san to the test—Chinese methods. Chimmoko—Chinese methods. Me—Kiku-san—Yoshinaka . . . so sorry, even you, Lady—Chinese methods."

Mariko took a deep breath. "May—may I ask you—why you took such a risk?"

"Because in certain situations women must protect each other against men. Because I actually saw nothing. Because you've done me no harm. Because I like you and the Anjin-san and believe you both have your own *karmas*. And because I'd rather have you alive and a friend than dead, and it's exciting to watch you three moths circling the flame of life."

"I don't believe you."

Gyoko laughed softly. "Thank you, Lady." Controlled now, she said with complete sincerity, "Very well, I'll tell you the real reason. I need your help. Yes, Toranaga-sama won't grant my request but perhaps you can think of a way. You're the only chance I've ever had, that I'll ever have in this lifetime, and I can't release it lightly. There, now you know. Please, I humbly beg you to help me with my request." She put both hands on the futons and bowed low. "Please excuse my impertinence, Lady Toda, but all that I have will be put at your side if you will help me." Then she settled back on her heels, adjusted the folds of her kimono, and finished the saké.

Mariko tried to think straight. Her intuition told her to trust the woman but her mind was still partially befogged with her newfound insight into Toranaga and her relief that Gyoko had not denounced her as she had expected, so she decided to put that decision aside for later consideration. "Yes, I will try. You must give me time, please."

"I can give you better than that. Here's a fact: You know Amida Tong? The assassins?"

"What about them?"

"Remember the one in Osaka Castle, Lady? He went against the Anjin-san—not Toranaga-sama. Lord Kiyama's chief steward gave two thousand koku for that attempt."

"Kiyama? But why?"

"He's Christian, *neh*? The Anjin-san was the enemy even then, *neh*? If then, what about now? Now that the Anjin-san's samurai, and free, with his ship."

"Another Amida? Here?"

Gyoko shrugged. "Who knows? But I wouldn't give an *eta*'s loincloth for the Anjin-san's life if he's careless outside the castle."

"Where is he now?"

"In his quarters, Lady. You're going to visit him soon, *neh?* Perhaps it'd be as well to warn him."

"You seem to know everything that's going on, Gyoko-san!"

"I keep my ears open, Lady, and my eyes."

Mariko curbed her anxiety over Blackthorne. "Did you tell Toranaga-sama?"

"Oh yes, I told him that." The corners of Gyoko's eyes crinkled and she sipped her saké. "As a matter of fact, I don't think he was surprised. That's interesting, don't you think?"

"Perhaps you were mistaken."

"Perhaps. In Mishima I heard a rumor that there was a poison plot against Lord Kiyama. Terrible, *neh?*"

"What plot?"

Gyoko told her the details.

"Impossible! One Christian *daimyo* would never do that to another!"

Mariko filled the cups.

"May I ask what else was said, by you and by him?"

"Part of it, Lady, was my plea to get back into his favor and out of that flea-sack inn, and to that he agreed. Now we're to have proper quarters within the castle, near the Anjin-san, in one of the guest houses and I may come and go as I wish. He asked Kiku-san to entertain him tonight and that's another improvement, though nothing will get him out of his melancholia. *Neh?*" Gyoko was watching Mariko speculatively. Mariko kept her face guileless, and merely nodded. The other woman sighed and continued, "Yes, he's very sad. Pity. Part of the time was spent on the three secrets. He asked me to repeat what I knew, what I'd told you."

Ah, Mariko thought, as another clue fell neatly into its slot. Ochiba? So that was Zataki's bait. And Toranaga's also got a cudgel over Omi's head if needed, and a weapon to use against Onoshi with Harima, or even Kiyama.

"You smile, Lady?"

Oh yes, Mariko wanted to say, wanting to share her elation with Gyoko. How valuable your information must have been to our Master, she wanted to tell Gyoko. How he should reward you! You should be made a *daimyo* yourself! And how fantastic Toranaga-sama is to have listened, apparently so unconcernedly. How marvelous he is!

But Toda Mariko-noh-Buntaro only shook her head and said calmly, "I'm sorry your information didn't cheer him up."

"Nothing I said improved his humor, which was dull and defeated. Sad, *neh?*"

"Yes, so sorry."

"Yes." Gyoko sniffed. "Another piece of information before I go, to interest you, Lady, to cement our friendship. It's very possible the Anjin-san is very fertile."

"What?"

"Kiku-san's with child."

"The Anjin-san?"

"Yes. Or Lord Toranaga. Possibly Omi-san. All were within the correct time span. Of course she took precautions after Omi-san as usual, but as you know, no method is perfect, nothing is ever guaranteed, mistakes happen, *neh?* She believes she forgot after the Anjin-san but she's not sure. That was the day the courier arrived at Anjiro, and in the excitement of leaving for Yokosé and of Lord Toranaga's buying her contract—it's understandable, *neh?*" Gyoko lifted her hands, greatly perturbed. "After Lord Toranaga, at my suggestion, she did the reverse. Also we both lit incense sticks and prayed for a boy."

Mariko studied the pattern on her fan. "Who? Who do you think?"

"That's the trouble, Lady. I don't know. I'd be grateful for your advice."

"This beginning must be stopped. Of course. There's no risk to her."

"I agree. Unfortunately, Kiku-san does not agree."

"What? I'm astonished, Gyoko-san! Of course she must. Or Lord Toranaga must be told. After all, it happened before he—"

"*Perhaps* it happened before him, Lady."

"Lord Toranaga will have to be told. Why is Kiku-san so disobedient and foolish?"

"*Karma,* Lady. She wants a child."

"Whose child?"

"She won't say. All she said was that any one of the three had advantages."

"She'd be wise to let this one go and be sure next time."

"I agree. I thought you should know in case. . . . There are many, many days before anything shows or before a miscarriage would be a danger to her. Perhaps she will change her mind. In this I cannot force her. She's no longer my property, though for the time being I'm trying to look after her. It would be splendid if the child was Lord Toranaga's. But say it had blue eyes. . . . A last piece of advice, Lady: Tell the Anjin-san to trust this Uraga-noh-Tadamasa only so far, and never in Nagasaki. Never there. That man's final allegiance will always be to his uncle, Lord Harima."

"How do you find out these things, Gyoko-san?"

"Men need to whisper secrets, Lady. That's what makes them different from us—they *need* to share secrets, but we women only reveal them to gain an advantage. With a little silver and a ready ear—and I have both—it's all so easy. Yes. Men need to *share* secrets. That's why we're superior to them and they'll always be in our power."

CHAPTER 51

I N the darkness just before dawn, the portcullis of a side gate lifted noiselessly and ten men hurried out across the narrow drawbridge of the innermost moat. The iron grille closed after them. At the far side of the bridge the alert sentries deliberately turned their backs and allowed the men to pass unchallenged. All wore dark kimonos and conical hats and held their swords tightly: Naga, Yabu, Blackthorne, Uraga-noh-Tadamasa, and six samurai. Naga led, Yabu beside him, and he took them unerringly through a maze of side turnings, up and down staircases and along little-used passages. Whenever they met patrols or sentries—ever alert—Naga held up a silver cipher and the party was allowed to pass unhindered and unquestioned.

By devious byways he brought them to the main south gate, which was the sole way across the castle's first great moat. Here a company of samurai awaited them. Silently these men surrounded Naga's party, screening them, and they all hurried across the bridge. Still they were not challenged. They continued on, down the slight rise toward First Bridge, keeping as close as they could to the shadows of the flares that abounded near the castle. Once across First Bridge they turned south and vanished into the labyrinth of alleys, heading for the sea.

Just outside the cordon surrounding the *Erasmus* wharf the accompanying samurai stopped and motioned the ten forward, then saluted and turned about and melted into the darkness again.

Naga led the way through the barriers. They were admitted onto the jetty without comment. There were more flares and guards here than before.

"Everything's ready?" Yabu asked, taking charge now.

"Yes, Sire," the senior samurai replied.

"Good. Anjin-san, did you understand?"

"Yes, thank you, Yabu-san."

"Good. You'd better hurry."

Blackthorne saw his own samurai drawn up in a loose square to one side, and he waved Uraga across to them as had been prearranged. His eyes raced over his ship, checking and rechecking as he hurried aboard and jubilantly stood on *his* quarterdeck. The sky was still dark with no sign of dawn yet. All signs indicated a fair day with calm seas.

He looked back at the wharf. Yabu and Naga were deep in conversation. Uraga was explaining to his vassals what was going on. Then the barriers were opening again and Baccus van Nekk and the rest of the crew, all obviously apprehensive, stumbled into the clearing, surrounded by caustic guards.

Blackthorne went to the gunwale and called out, "Hey! Come aboard!"

When his men saw him they seemed less fearful, and began to hurry, but their guards cursed them and they stopped in their tracks.

"Uraga-san!" Blackthorne shouted. "Tell them to let my men aboard. *At once.*"

Uraga obeyed with alacrity. The samurai listened and bowed toward the ship and released the crew.

Vinck was first aboard, Baccus groping his way last. The men were still frightened, but none came up onto the quarterdeck which was Blackthorne's domain alone.

"Great Jesus, Pilot," Baccus panted, above the hubbub of questions. "What's going on?"

"What's amiss, Pilot?" Vinck echoed with the others. "Christ, one moment we was asleep, then all hell broke loose, the door burst open an' the monkeys were marching us here. . . ."

Blackthorne held up his hand. "Listen!" When there was silence he began quietly, "We're taking *Erasmus* to a safe harbor across the—"

"We've not men enough, Pilot," Vinck broke in anxiously. "We'll nev—"

"Listen, Johann! We're going to be towed. The other ship'll be here any moment. Ginsel, go for'ard—you'll swing the lead. Vinck, take the helm, Jan Roper and Baccus stand by the forewinch, Salamon and Croocq aft. Sonk—go below and check our stores. Break out some grog if you can find any. Lay to!"

"Wait a minute, Pilot!" Jan Roper said. "What's all the hurry? Where're we going and why?"

Blackthorne felt a surge of indignation at being questioned, but he reminded himself that they were entitled to know, they were not vassals and not *eta* but his crew, his shipmates, and, in some respects, almost partners. "This is the beginning of the storm season. *Tai-funs* they call them—Great Storms. This berth isn't safe. Across the harbor, a few leagues south, is their best and safest anchorage. It's near a village called Yokohama. *Erasmus* will be safe there and can ride out any storm. Now lay to!"

No one moved.

Van Nekk said, "Only a few leagues, Pilot?"

"Yes."

"What then? And, well, what's the hurry?"

"Lord Toranaga agreed to let me do it now," Blackthorne answered, telling half the truth. "The sooner the better, I thought. He might change his mind again, *neh?* At Yokohama . . ." He looked away as Yabu came stomping aboard with his six guards. The men fled out of his way.

"Jesus," Vinck choked out. "It's him! It's the bastard who gave Pieterzoon his!"

Yabu came up near to the quarterdeck, smiling broadly, oblivious of the terror that infected the crew as they recognized him. He pointed out to sea. "Anjin-san, look! There! Everything's perfect, *neh?*"

A galley like some monstrous sea caterpillar was sweeping silently toward them from the western darkness.

"Good, Yabu-sama! You want stand here?"

"Later, Anjin-san." Yabu walked off to the head of the gangway.

Blackthorne turned back to his men. "Lay for'ard. On the double—and watch your tongues. Speak only gutter Dutch—there's one aboard who understands Portuguese! I'll talk to you when we're under way! Move!"

The men scattered, glad to get away from Yabu's presence. Uraga and twenty of Blackthorne's samurai loped aboard. The others were forming up on the jetty to board the galley.

Uraga said, "These your personal guards, if it pleases you, senhor."

"My name's Anjin-san, not senhor," Blackthorne said.

"Please excuse me, Anjin-san." Uraga began to come up the steps.

"Stop! Stay below! No one ever comes onto the quarterdeck without my permission! Tell them."

"Yes, Anjin-san. Please excuse me."

Blackthorne went to the side to watch the galley docking, just to the west of them. "Ginsel! Go ashore and watch 'em take our hawsers! See they're secured properly. Look lively now!"

Then, his ship in control, Blackthorne scrutinized the twenty men. "Why are they all chosen from the bound group, Uraga-san?"

"They're a clan, sen— Anjin-san. Like brothers, Sire. They beg for the honors of defending you."

"*Anatawa—anatawa—anatawa—*" Blackthorne pointed out ten men at random and ordered them ashore, to be replaced from his other vassals, also to be selected by Uraga at random. And he told Uraga to make it clear *all* his vassals were to be like brothers or they could commit seppuku now.

"*Wakarimasu?*"

"*Hai,* Anjin-san. *Gomen nasai.*"

Soon the bow hawsers were secured aboard the other craft. Blackthorne inspected everything, checked the wind again using all his sea sense, knowing that even within the benign waters of the vast Yedo harbor, their journey could be dangerous if a sudden squall began.

"Cast off!" he shouted. "*Ima,* Captain-san!"

The other captain waved and let his galley ease away from the jetty. Naga was aboard the craft, which was packed with samurai and the rest of Blackthorne's vassals. Yabu stood beside Blackthorne on the quarterdeck of *Erasmus*. She heeled slightly and a tremor went through her as she was taken by the weight of a current. Blackthorne and all the crew were filled with jubilation, their excitement at being once more at sea overriding their anxieties. Ginsel was leaning over the side of the tiny, roped starboard platform, swinging the lead, calling out the fathoms. The jetty began to fall away.

"Ahoy ahead, *Yukkuri sei!*" Slow down!

"*Hai,* Anjin-san," came the answering shout. Together the two ships felt their way out into the harbor stream, riding lights at their mastheads.

"Good, Anjin-san," Yabu said. "Very good!"

Yabu waited until they were well out to sea, then he took Blackthorne aside. "Anjin-san," he said warily. "You saved my life yesterday. Understand? Calling off those *ronin*. Remember?"

"Yes. Only my duty."

"No, not duty. At Anjiro, you remember that other man, the seaman . . . remember?"

"Yes, I remember."

"*Shigata ga nai, neh? Karma, neh?* That was before samurai or hatamoto. . . ." Yabu's eyes were glittering in the light of the sea lantern and he touched Blackthorne's sword and spoke softly and clearly. ". . . Before Oil Seller, *neh?* As samurai to samurai ask forget all before. Start new. Tonight. Please? Understand?"

"Yes, understand."

"You need me, Anjin-san. Without me, no barbarian *wako*. You can't get them alone. Not from Nagasaki. Never. I can get them—help you get them. Now we fight same side. Toranaga's side. Same side. Without me, no *wako,* understand?"

Blackthorne watched the galley ahead for a moment and checked the deck and his seamen. Then he looked down on Yabu. "Yes. Understand."

"You understand 'hate'—the word 'hate'?"

"Yes."

"Hate comes from fear. I do not fear you. You need not fear me. Never again. I want what you want: your new ships here, you here, captain of new ships. I can help you very much. First the Black Ship . . . ah yes, Anjin-san," he said, seeing the joy flood across Blackthorne's face, "I will persuade Lord Toranaga. You know I'm a fighter, *neh?* I'll lead the charge. I'll take the Black Ship for you on land. Together you and I are stronger than one. *Neh?*"

"Yes. Possible get more men? More than two hundred my?"

"If you need two thousand men . . . five thousand! Don't worry, you lead ship—I'll lead the fight. Agree?"

"Yes. Fair trade. Thank you. I agree."

"Good, very good, Anjin-san," Yabu said contentedly. He knew this mutual partnership would benefit them both however much the barbarian hated him. Again Yuriko's logic had been flawless.

Earlier that evening he had seen Toranaga and asked permission to go at once to Osaka to prepare the way for him. "Please excuse me but I thought the matter urgent enough. After all, Sire," Yabu had said deferentially as he and his wife had planned, "you should have someone of rank there to make sure that all your arrangements are perfect. Ishido's a peasant and doesn't understand ceremony, *neh?* The arrangement must be perfect or you should not go, *neh?* It could take weeks, *neh?*"

He had been delighted with the ease with which Toranaga had been persuaded. "Then there's also the barbarian ship, Sire. Better to put it at Yokohama at once in case of *tai-fun.* I'll supervise that myself, with your permission, before I go. The Musket Regiment can be its guards, give them something to do. Then I'll go on directly to Osaka with the galley. By sea'd be better and quicker, *neh?*"

"Very well, yes, if you think that wise, Yabu-san, do it. But take Naga-san with you. Leave him in charge at Yokohama."

"Yes, Sire." Then Yabu had told Toranaga about Tsukku-san's anger; how, if Lord Toranaga wanted the Anjin-san to live long enough to obtain men at Nagasaki in case Toranaga wanted the ship to put to sea, then perhaps this should be done at once without hesitation. "The priest was very angry—I think angry enough to set his converts against the Anjin-san!"

"You're sure?"

"Oh yes, Sire. Perhaps I should put the Anjin-san under my protection for the moment." Then, as though it were a sudden thought, Yabu added, "The simplest thing would be to take the Anjin-san with me. I can start arrangements at Osaka—continue to Nagasaki, get the new barbarians, then complete the arrangements on my return."

"Do whatever you think fit," Toranaga had said. "I'll leave it to you to decide, my friend. What does it matter, *neh?* What does anything matter?"

Yabu was happy that, at long last, he could act. Only Naga's presence had not been planned, but that did not matter, and truly, it would be wise to have him at Yokohama.

Yabu was watching the Anjin-san—the tall, arrogant stance, feet slightly apart, swaying so easily with the pitch and toss of the waves, seemingly part of the ship, so huge and strong and different. So different from when ashore. Consciously Yabu began to take up a similar stance, aping him carefully.

"I want more than the Kwanto, Yuriko-san," he had whispered to his wife just before he had left their house. "Just one more thing. I want command of the sea. I want to be Lord High Admiral. We'll put the whole revenue of the Kwanto behind Omi's plan to *escort* the barbarian to his home, to buy more ships and bring them back again. Omi will go with him, *neh?*"

"Yes," she had said, as happily. "We can trust him."

The wharf at Yedo was deserted now. The last of the samurai guards were disappearing into the byways heading back toward the castle. Father Alvito came out of the shadows, Brother Michael beside him. Alvito looked seaward. "May God curse her and all who sail in her."

"Except one, Father. One of our people sails with the ship. And Naga-san. Naga-san's sworn to become Christian in the first month of next year."

"If there ever is a next year for him," Alvito said, filled with gloom. "I don't know about Naga, perhaps he means it, perhaps not. That ship's going to destroy us and there's nothing we can do."

"God will help us."

"Yes, but meanwhile we're Soldiers of God and we have to help Him. The Father-Visitor must be warned at once, and the Captain-General. Have you found a carrier pigeon for Osaka yet?"

"No, Father, not for any amount of money. Nor even one for Nagasaki. Months ago Toranaga-sama ordered them *all* into his keeping."

Alvito's gloom deepened. "There must be someone with one! Pay anything that's necessary. The heretic will wound us terribly, Michael."

"Perhaps not, Father."

"Why are they moving the ship? Of course for safety, but more to put it out of our reach. Why has Toranaga given the heretic two hundred *wako* and his bullion back? Of course to use as a strike force, and the specie's to buy more pirates—gunners and seamen. Why give Blackthorne freedom? To harry us through the Black Ship. God help us, Toranaga's forsaken us too!"

"We've forsaken him, Father."

"There's nothing we can do to help him! We've tried everything with the *daimyos*. We're helpless."

"Perhaps if we prayed harder, perhaps God would show us a way."

"I pray and pray, but . . . perhaps God has forsaken us, Michael, rightly. Perhaps we're not worthy of His mercy. I know I'm not."

"Perhaps the Anjin-san won't find gunners or seamen. Perhaps he'll never arrive at Nagasaki."

"His silver will buy him all the men he needs. Even Catholics—even Portuguese. Men foolishly think more about this world than the next. They won't open their eyes. They sell their souls all too easily. Yes. I pray Blackthorne never arrives there. *Or his emissaries.* Don't forget, there's no need at all for him to go there. The men could be bought and brought to him. Come along, let's go home now." Dispiritedly, Alvito led the way toward the Jesuit Mission which was a mile or so westward, near the docks, behind one of the large warehouses that normally housed the season's silks and rice and formed part of the market complex the Jesuits governed on behalf of buyer and seller.

They walked a while along the shore, then Alvito stopped and looked seaward again. Dawn was breaking. He could see nothing of the ships. "What chance of our message being delivered?" Yesterday, Michael had discovered that one of Blackthorne's new vassals was a Christian. When the news had flared through the underground network of Yedo last night that something was going to happen with the Anjin-san and his ship, Alvito had hastily scrawled a ciphered message for dell'Aqua, giving all the latest news, and had begged the man to deliver it secretly if ever he reached Osaka.

"The message will arrive." Brother Michael added quietly, "Our man knows he sails with the enemy."

"May God watch him and give him strength and curse Uraga." Alvito looked across at the younger man. "Why? Why did he become apostate?"

"He told you, Father," Brother Michael said. "He wanted to be a priest—ordained in our Society. That wasn't much to ask, for a proud servant of God."

"He was too proud, Brother. God in His wisdom tempted him and found him wanting."

"Yes. I pray I am not found wanting when my turn comes."

Alvito wandered past their Mission toward the large plot of land that had been set aside by Toranaga for the cathedral that should soon rise from the earth to the glory of God. The Jesuit could already see it in his mind, tall, majestic yet delicate, dominating the city, peerless bells cast in Macao or Goa or even Portugal ringing the changes, the vast bronze doors ever wide to the faithful nobility. He could smell the incense and hear the sound of the Latin chants.

But war will destroy that dream, he told himself. War will come again to plague this land and it will be as it ever was.

"Father!" Brother Michael whispered, cautioning him.

A woman was ahead of them, looking at the beginning foundations that already were marked out and partially dug. Beside her were two maids. Alvito waited motionlessly, peering in the half-light. The woman was veiled and richly dressed. Then Brother Michael moved slightly. His foot touched a stone and sent it clattering against an iron shovel, unseen in the gloaming. The woman turned, startled. Alvito recognized her.

"Mariko-san? It's me—Father Alvito."

"Father? Oh, I was—I was just coming to see you. I'm leaving shortly but I wanted to talk to you before I left."

Alvito came up to her. "I'm so glad to see you, Mariko-san. Yes. I heard you were leaving. I tried to see you several times but, at the moment, I'm still forbidden the castle." Wordlessly, Mariko looked back at the beginnings of the cathedral. Alvito glanced at Brother Michael, who was also bewildered that a lady of such importance would be so scantily attended, wandering here so early and unannounced.

"You're here just to see me, Mariko-san?"

"Yes. And to see the ship leave."

"What can I do for you?"

"I wish to be confessed."

"Then let it be here," he said. "Let yours be the first in this place though the ground is barely hallowed."

"Please excuse me, but could you say Mass here, Father?"

"There's no church or altar or vestments or the Eucharist. I could do that in our chapel if you'll foll—"

"Could we drink cha from an empty cup, Father? Please," she asked in a tiny voice. "So sorry to ask. There's so little time."

"Yes," he agreed, at once understanding her.

So he walked to where the altar perhaps would be one day within the magnificent nave, under a vaulting roof. Today, the lightening sky was the roof, and birds and the sound of the surf the majestic choir. He began to chant the solemn beauty of the Mass and Brother Michael helped, and together they brought the Infinite to earth.

But before the giving of the make-believe Sacrament he stopped and said, "Now I must hear thy confession, Maria." He motioned Brother Michael away and sat on a rock within an imaginary confessional and closed his eyes. She knelt. "Before God, do—"

"Before I begin, Father, I beg a favor."

"From me or from God, Maria?"

"I beg a favor, before God."

"What is thy favor?"

"The Anjin-san's life in return for knowledge."

"His life is not mine to give or to withhold."

"Yes. So sorry, but an order could be spread among *all* Christians that his life is not to be taken as a sacrifice to God."

"The Anjin-san is the enemy. A terrible enemy of our Faith."

"Yes. Even so I beg for his life. In return—in return perhaps I can be of great help."

"How?"

"Is my favor granted, Father? Before God?"

"I cannot grant such a favor. It's not mine to give or to withhold. You cannot barter with God."

Mariko hesitated, kneeling on the hard earth before him. Then she bowed and began to get up. "Very well. Then please excuse—"

Alvito said, "I will put the request before the Father-Visitor."

"That's not enough, Father, please excuse me."

"I will put it before him and beg him in God's name to consider your petition."

"If what I tell you is very valuable, will you, before God, swear that you will do everything in your power, everything to succor *him* and guard *him,* providing it is not directly against the Church?"

"Yes. If it is not against the Church."

"And, so sorry, you agree to put my request before the Father-Visitor?"

"Before God, yes."

"Thank you, Father. Listen then. . . ." She told him her reasoning about Toranaga and the hoax.

Suddenly everything was falling into place for Alvito. "You're right, you must be right! God forgive me, how could I have been so stupid?"

"Please listen again, Father, here are more facts." She whispered the secrets about Zataki and Onoshi.

"It's not possible!"

"There's also a rumor that Lord Onoshi plans to poison Lord Kiyama."

"Impossible!"

"Please excuse me, very possible. They're ancient enemies."

"Who told you all this, Maria?"

"The rumor is that Onoshi will poison Lord Kiyama during the Feast of the Blessed Saint Bernard this year," Mariko said tiredly, deliberately not answering the question. "Onoshi's son will be the new lord of all Kiyama's lands. General Ishido has agreed to this, providing my Master has already gone into the Great Void."

"Proof, Mariko-san? Where's the proof?"

"So sorry, I have none. But Lord Harima's party to the knowledge."

"How do you know this? How does Harima know? You say he's part of the plot?"

"No, Father. Just party to the secret."

"Impossible! Onoshi's too close-mouthed and much too clever. If he'd planned that, no one would ever know. You must be mistaken. Who gave you this information?"

"I cannot tell you, so sorry, please excuse me. But I believe it to be true."

Alvito let his mind rush over the possibilities. And then: "Uraga! Uraga was Onoshi's confessor! Oh, Mother of God, Uraga broke the sanctity of the confessional and told his liege lord. . . ."

"Perhaps this secret's not true, Father. But I believe it to be true. Only God knows the real truth, *neh?*"

Mariko had not put her veils aside and Alvito could see nothing of her face. Above, dawn was spreading over the sky. He looked seaward. Now he could see the two ships on the horizon heading southwest, the galley's oars dipping in unison, the wind fair and the sea calm. His chest hurt and his head echoed with the enormity of what he had been told. He prayed for help and tried to sort fact from fancy. In his heart he knew the secrets were true and her reasoning flawless.

"You're saying that Lord Toranaga will outmaneuver Ishido—that he'll win?"

"No, Father. No one will win, but without your help Lord Toranaga will lose. Lord Zataki's not to be trusted. Zataki must always be a major threat to my Lord. Zataki will know this and that all Toranaga's promises are empty because Toranaga must try to eliminate him eventually. If I were Zataki I'd destroy Sudara and the Lady Genjiko and all their children the moment they gave themselves into my hands, and at once I'd move against Toranaga's northern defenses. I'd hurl my legions against the north, which would pull Ishido, Ikawa Jikkyu, and all the others out of their stupid lethargy. Toranaga can be eaten up too easily, Father."

Alvito waited a moment, then he said, "Lift your veils, Maria."

He saw that her face was stark. "Why have you told me all this?"

"To save the Anjin-san's life."

"You commit treason for him, Maria? You, Toda Mariko-noh-Buntaro, daughter of the General Lord Akechi Jinsai, you commit treason because of a foreigner? You ask me to believe that?"

"No, so sorry, also—also to protect the Church. First to protect the Church, Father. . . . I don't know what to do. I thought you might. . . . Lord Toranaga is the Church's only hope. Perhaps you can somehow help him . . . to protect the Church. Lord Toranaga must have help now, he's a good and wise man and the Church will prosper with him. I *know* Ishido's the real enemy."

"Most Christian *daimyos* believe Toranaga will obliterate the Church and the Heir if ever he conquers Ishido and gets power."

"He may, but I doubt it. He will treat the Church fairly. He always has. Ishido is violently anti-Christian. So is the Lady Ochiba."

"All the great Christians are against Toranaga."

"Ishido's a peasant. Toranaga-sama is fair and wise and wants trade."

"There has to be trade, whoever rules."

"Lord Toranaga has always been your friend, and if you're honest with him, he always will be with you." She pointed to the foundations. "Isn't this a measure of his fairness? He gave this land freely—even when you failed him and he'd lost everything—even your friendship."

"Perhaps."

"Last, Father, only Toranaga-sama can prevent perpetual war, you must know that. As a woman I ask that there be no everlasting war."

"Yes, Maria. He's the only one who could do that, perhaps."

His eyes drifted away from her. Brother Michael was kneeling, lost in prayer, the two servants nearer the shore, waiting patiently. The Jesuit felt overwhelmed yet uplifted, exhausted yet filled with strength. "I'm glad that you have come here and told me this. I thank thee. For the Church and for me, a servant of the Church. I will do everything that I have agreed."

She bowed her head and said nothing.

"Will you carry a dispatch, Mariko-san? To the Father-Visitor."

"Yes. If he is at Osaka."

"A private dispatch?"

"Yes."

"The dispatch is verbal. You will tell him everything you said to me and what I said to you. Everything."

"Very well."

"I have your promise? Before God?"

"You have no need to say that to me, Father. I have agreed."

He looked into her eyes, firm and strong and committed. "Please excuse me,

Maria. Now let me hear thy confession."

She dropped her veils again. "Please excuse me, Father, I'm not worthy even to confess."

"Everyone is worthy in the sight of God."

"Except me. I'm not worthy, Father."

"You must confess, Maria. I cannot go on with your Mass—you must come before Him cleansed."

She knelt. "Forgive me, Father, for I have sinned but I can only confess that I am not worthy to confess," she whispered, her voice breaking.

Compassionately Father Alvito put his hand lightly on her head. "Daughter of God, let me beg God's forgiveness for thy sins. Let me in His name absolve thee and make thee whole in His sight." He blessed her, and then he continued her Mass in this imaginary cathedral, under the breaking sky . . . the service more real and more beautiful than it had ever been, for him and for her.

Erasmus was anchored in the best storm harbor Blackthorne had ever seen, far enough from shore to give her plenty of sea room, yet close enough for safety. Six fathoms of clear water over a strong seabed were below, and except for the narrow neck of the entrance, high land all around that would keep any fleet snug from the ocean's wrath.

The day's journey from Yedo had been uneventful though tiring. Half a *ri* northward the galley was moored to a pier near Yokohama fishing village, and now they were alone aboard, Blackthorne and all his men, both Dutch and Japanese. Yabu and Naga were ashore inspecting the Musket Regiment and he had been told to join them shortly. Westward the sun was low on the horizon and the red sky promised another fine day tomorrow.

"Why now, Uraga-san?" Blackthorne was asking from the quarterdeck, his eyes red-rimmed from lack of sleep. He had just ordered the crew and everyone to stand down, and Uraga had asked him to delay for a moment to find out if there were any Christians among the vassals. "Can't it wait until tomorrow?"

"No, Sire, so sorry." Uraga was looking up at him in front of the assembled samurai vassals, the Dutch crew gathering into a nervous knot near the quarterdeck railing. "Please excuse me, but it is most important you find out at once. You are their most enemy. Therefore you must know, for your protection. I only wish to protect you. Not take long, *neh?*"

"Are they all on deck?"

"Yes, Sire."

Blackthorne went closer to the railing and called out in Japanese, "Is anyone Christian?" There was no answer. "I order any Christian come forward." No one moved. So he turned back to Uraga. "Set ten deck guards, then dismiss them."

"With your permission, Anjin-san." From under his kimono Uraga brought out a small painted icon that he had brought from Yedo and threw it face upward on the deck. Then, deliberately, he stamped on it. Blackthorne and the crew were greatly disquieted by the desecration. Except Jan Roper. "Please. Make every vassal do same," Uraga said.

"Why?"

"I know Christians." Uraga's eyes were half hidden by the brim of his hat. "Please, Sire. Important every man do same. Now, tonight."

"All right," Blackthorne agreed reluctantly.

Uraga turned to the assembled vassals. "At my suggestion our Master requires each of us to do this."

The samurai were grumbling among themselves and one interrupted, "We've already said that we're not Christians, *neh?* What does stamping on a barbarian god picture prove? Nothing!"

"Christians are our Master's enemy. Christians are treacherous—but Christians are Christian. Please excuse me, I know Christians—to my shame I forsook our real gods. So sorry, but I believe this is necessary for our Master's safety."

At once a samurai in front declared, "In that case, there's nothing more to be said." He came forward and stamped on the picture. "I worship no barbarian religion! Come on, the rest of you, do what's asked!"

They came forward one by one. Blackthorne watched, despising the ceremony.

Van Nekk said worriedly, "Doesn't seem right."

Vinck looked up at the quarterdeck. "Sodding bastards. They'll all cut our throats with never a thought. You sure you can trust 'em, Pilot?"

"Yes."

Ginsel said, "No Catholic'd ever do that, eh, Johann? That Uraga-sama's clever."

"What's it matter if those buggers're Papist or not, they're all shit-filled samurai."

"Yes," Croocq said.

"Even so, it's not right to do that," van Nekk repeated.

The samurai continued to stamp the icon into the deck one by one, and moved into loose groups. It was a tedious affair and Blackthorne was sorry he had agreed to it, for there were more important things to do before dusk. His eyes went to the village and the headlands. Hundreds of the thatch lean-tos of the Musket Regiment camp spotted the foothills. So much to do, he thought, anxious to go ashore, wanting to see the land, glorying in the fief Toranaga had given him which contained Yokohama. Lord God on high, he told himself, I'm lord of one of the greatest harbors in the world.

Abruptly a man bypassed the icon, tore out his sword, and leaped at Blackthorne. A dozen startled samurai jumped courageously in his way, screening the quarterdeck as Blackthorne spun around, a pistol cocked and aimed. Others scattered, shoving, stumbling, milling in the uproar. The samurai skidded to a halt, howling with rage, then changed direction and hacked at Uraga, who somehow managed to avoid the thrust. The man whirled as other samurai lunged at him, fought them off ferociously for a moment, then rushed for the side and threw himself overboard.

Four who could swim dropped their killing swords, put their short stabbing knives in their mouths, and jumped after him, the rest and the Dutchmen crowding the side.

Blackthorne jumped for the gunwale. He could see nothing below; then he caught sight of swirling shadows in the water. A man came up for air and went down again. Soon four heads surfaced. Between them was the corpse, a knife in his throat.

"So sorry, Anjin-san, it was his own knife," one called up over the roars of the others.

"Uraga-san, tell them to search him, then leave him to the fish."

The search revealed nothing. When all were back on deck, Blackthorne pointed at the icon with his cocked pistol. "All samurai—once more!" He was obeyed instantly and he made sure that every man passed the test. Then, because of Uraga, and to praise him, he ordered his crew to do the same. There was the beginning of a protest.

"Come on," Blackthorne snarled. "Hurry up, or I'll put my foot on your backs!"

"No need to say that, Pilot," van Nekk said. "We're not stinky pagan wogs!"

"They're not stinky pagan wogs! They're samurai, by God!"

They stared up at him. Anger, whipped by fear, rippled through them. Van Nekk began to say something but Ginsel butted in.

"Samurai're heathen bastards and they—or men like 'em—murdered Pieterzoon, our Captain-General, and Maetsukker!"

"Yes, but without these samurai we'll never get home—understand?"

Now all the samurai were watching. Ominously they moved nearer Blackthorne protectively. Van Nekk said, "Let it rest, eh? We're all a bit touchy and overtired. It was a long night. We're not our own masters here, none of us. Nor's the Pilot. The Pilot knows what he's doing—he's the leader, he's Captain-General now."

"Yes, he is. But it's not right for him to take their side over us, and by the Lord God, he's not a king—we're equal to him," Jan Roper hissed. "Just because he's armed like them and dressed like them and can talk to the sods doesn't make him king over us. We've rights and that's our law and his law, by the Lord God, even though he's English. He swore Holy Oaths to abide by the rules—didn't you, Pilot!"

"Yes," Blackthorne said. "It's our law in our seas—where we're masters and in the majority. Now we're not. So do what I tell you to do and do it fast."

Muttering, they obeyed.

"Sonk! Did you find any grog?"

"Nosirnotagodcurseddribble!"

"I'll get saké sent aboard." Then, in Portuguese, Blackthorne added, "Uragasan, you'll come ashore with me and bring someone to scull. You four," he said in Japanese, pointing at the men who had dived over the side, "you four now captains. Understand? Take fifty men each."

"*Hai,* Anjin-san."

"What's your name?" he asked one of them, a tall, quiet man with a scarred cheek.

"Nawa Chisato, Lord."

"You're captain today. All ship. Until I return."

"Yes, Lord."

Blackthorne went to the gangway. A skiff was tied below.

"Where're you going, Pilot?" van Nekk said anxiously.

"Ashore. I'll be back later."

"Good, we'll all go!"

"By God I'll come with—"

"And me. I'm go—"

"Christ Jesus, don't leave me be—"

"No! I'm going alone!"

"But for God's sake what about us!" van Nekk cried out. "What are we going to do? Don't leave us, Pilot. What are—"

"You just wait!" Blackthorne told them. "I'll see food and drink's sent aboard."

Ginsel squared up to Blackthorne. "I thought we were going back tonight. Why aren't we going back tonight?"

"How long we going to stay here, Pilot, and how long—"

"Pilot, what about Yedo?" Ginsel asked louder. "How long we going to stay here, with these God-cursed monkeys?"

"Yes, monkeys, by God," Sonk said happily. "What about our gear and our own folk?"

"Yes, what about our eters, Pilot? Our people and our doxies?"

"They'll be there tomorrow." Blackthorne pushed down his loathing. "Be patient, I'll be back as soon as I can. Baccus, you're in charge." He turned to go.

"I'm going with you," Jan Roper said truculently, following him. "We're in harbor so we take precedence and I want some arms."

Blackthorne turned on him and a dozen swords left their scabbards, ready to kill Jan Roper. "One more word out of you and you're a dead man." The tall, lean merchant flushed and came to a halt. "You curb your tongue near these samurai because any one of them'll take your head before I can stop them just because of your goddamned bad manners—let alone anything else! They're touchy, and near you I'm getting touchy, and you'll get arms when you need them. Understand?"

Jan Roper nodded sullenly and backed off. The samurai were still menacing but Blackthorne quieted them, and ordered them, on pain of death, to leave his crew alone. "I'll be back soon." He walked down the gangway and got into the skiff, Uraga and another samurai following. Chisato, the captain, went up to Jan Roper, who quailed under the menace, bowed, and backed away.

When they were well away from the ship Blackthorne thanked Uraga for catching the traitor.

"Please, no thanks. It was only duty."

Blackthorne said in Japanese so that the other man could understand, "Yes, duty. But your koku change now. Now not twenty, now one hundred a year."

"Oh, Sire, thank you. I don't deserve it. I was only doing my duty and I must—"

"Speak slowly. Don't understand."

Uraga apologized and said it slower.

Blackthorne praised him again, then settled more comfortably in the stern of the boat, his exhaustion overcoming him. He forced his eyes open and glanced back at his ship to reassure himself she was well placed. Van Nekk and the others were at the gunwale and he was sorry that he had brought them aboard though he knew he had had no option. Without them the journey would not have been safe.

Mutinous scum, he thought. What the hell do I do about them? All my vassals know about the *eta* village and they're all as disgusted as. . . . Christ Jesus, what a mess! *Karma, neh?*

He slept. As the skiff nosed into the shore near the pier he awoke. At first he could not remember where he was. He had been dreaming he was back in the castle in Mariko's arms, just like last night.

Last night they had been lying in half-sleep after loving, Fujiko a party to the loving, Chimmoko on guard, when Yabu and his samurai had pounded on the door post. The evening had begun so pleasingly. Fujiko had also discreetly invited Kiku, and never had he seen her more beautiful and exuberant. As bells ended the Hour of the Boar, Mariko had punctually arrived. There had been merriment and saké but soon Mariko had shattered the spell.

"So sorry, but you're in great danger, Anjin-san." She explained, and when she had added what Gyoko had said about not trusting Uraga, both Kiku and Fujiko were equally perturbed.

"Please don't worry. I'll watch him, never fear," he had reassured them.

Mariko had continued, "Perhaps you should watch Yabu-sama too, Anjin-san."

"What?"

"This afternoon I saw the hatred in your face. So did he."

"Never mind," he had said. *"Shigata ga nai, neh?"*

"No. So sorry, it was a mistake. Why did you call your men off when they had Yabu-sama surrounded at first? Surely that was a bad mistake too. They would have killed him quickly and your enemy would have been dead without risk to you."

"That wouldn't have been right, Mariko-san. So many men against one. Not fair."

Mariko had explained to Fujiko and Kiku what he had said. "Please excuse me, Anjin-san, but we all believe that is a very dangerous way of thinking and beg you to forsake it. It's quite wrong and very naïve. Please excuse me for being so blunt. Yabu-san will destroy you."

"No. Not yet. I'm still too important to him. And to Omi-san."

"Kiku-san says, please tell the Anjin-san to beware of Yabu—and this Uraga. The Anjin-san may find it difficult to judge 'importance' here, *neh?*"

"Yes, I agree with Kiku-san," Fujiko had said.

Later Kiku had left to go and entertain Toranaga. Then Mariko broke the peace in the room again. "Tonight I must say *sayonara,* Anjin-san. I am leaving at dawn."

"No, there's no need now," he had said. "That can all be changed now. I'll see Toranaga tomorrow. Now that I've permission to leave, I'll take you to Osaka. I'll get a galley, or coastal boat. At Nagasa—"

"No, Anjin-san. So sorry, I must leave as ordered." No amount of persuasion would touch her.

He had felt Fujiko watching him in the silence, his heart aching with the thought of Mariko leaving. He had looked across at Fujiko. She asked them to excuse her for a moment. She closed the shoji behind her and they were alone and they knew that Fujiko would not return, that they were safe for a little time. Their loving was urgent and violent. Then there were voices and footsteps and barely enough time to become composed before Fujiko joined them through the inner door and Yabu strode in, bringing Toranaga's orders for an immediate, secret departure. ". . . Yokohama, then Osaka for a brief stop, Anjin-san, on again to Nagasaki, back to Osaka, and home here again! I've sent for your crew to report to the ship."

Excitement had rushed through him at this heaven-sent victory. "Yes, Yabu-san. But Mariko-san—Mariko-san go Osaka also, *neh?* Better with us—quicker, safer, *neh?*"

"Not possible, so sorry. Must hurry. Come along! Tide—understand 'tide,' Anjin-san?"

"*Hai,* Yabu-san. But Mariko-san go Osaka—"

"So sorry, she has orders like we have orders. Mariko-san! Explain to him. Tell him to hurry!"

Yabu had been inflexible, and so late at night it was impossible to go to Toranaga to ask him to rescind the order. There had been no time or privacy to talk any more with Mariko or Fujiko, other than to say formal good-bys. But they would meet soon in Osaka. "Very soon, Anjin-san," Mariko had said. . . .

"Lord God, don't let me lose her," Blackthorne said, the sea gulls cawing above the beach, their cries intensifying his loneliness.

"Lose who, Sire?"

Blackthorne came back into reality. He pointed at the distant ship. "We call ships *her*—we think of ships as female, not male. *Wakarimasu ka?*"

"*Hai.*"

Blackthorne could still see the tiny figures of his crew and his insoluble dilemma confronted him once more. You've got to have them aboard, he said to himself, and more like them. And the new men'll not take kindly to samurai either, and they'll be Catholic as well, most of them. God in heaven, how to control them all? Mariko was right. Near Catholics I'm a dead man.

"Even me, Anjin-san," she had said last night.

"No, Mariko-chan. Not you."

"You said we're your enemy, this afternoon."

"I said most Catholics are my enemies."

"They will kill you if they can."

"Yes. But thou . . . will we truly meet in Osaka?"

"Yes. I love thee. Anjin-san, remember, beware of Yabu-san. . . ."

They were all right about Yabu, Blackthorne thought, whatever he says, whatever he promises. I made a bad mistake calling my men off when he was trapped. That bastard'll cut my throat as soon as I've outlived my usefulness, however much he pretends otherwise. And yet Yabu's right too: I need him. I'll never get into Nagasaki and out again without protection. He could surely help to persuade Toranaga. With him leading two thousand more fanatics, we could lay waste all Nagasaki and maybe even Macao. . . .

Madonna! Alone I'm helpless.

Then he remembered what Gyoko had told Mariko about Uraga, about not trusting him. Gyoko was wrong about him, he thought. What else is she wrong about?

BOOK FIVE

CHAPTER 52

ONCE more in the crowded Osaka sea roads after the long journey by galley, Blackthorne again felt the same crushing weight of the city as when he had first seen it. Great swathes had been laid waste by the *tai-fun* and some areas were still fire-blackened, but its immensity was almost untouched and still dominated by the castle. Even from this distance, more than a league, he could see the colossal girth of the first great wall, the towering battlements, all dwarfed by the brooding malevolence of the donjon.

"Christ," Vinck said nervously, standing beside him on the prow, "doesn't seem possible to be so big. Amsterdam'd be a flyspeck alongside it."

"Yes. The storm's hurt the city but not that badly. Nothing could touch the castle."

The *tai-fun* had slammed out of the southwest two weeks ago. They had had plenty of warning, with lowering skies and squalls and rain, and had rushed the galley into a safe harbor to wait out the tempest. They had waited five days. Beyond the harbor the ocean had been whipped to froth and the winds were more violent and stronger than anything Blackthorne had ever experienced.

"Christ," Vinck said again. "Wish we were home. We should've been home a year ago."

Blackthorne had brought Vinck with him from Yokohama and sent the others back to Yedo, leaving *Erasmus* safely harbored and guarded under Naga's command. His crew had been happy to go—as he had been happy to see the last of them. There had been more quarreling that night and a violent argument over the ship's bullion. The money was company money, not his. Van Nekk was treasurer of the expedition and chief merchant and, jointly with the Captain-General, had legal jurisdiction over it. After it had been counted and recounted and found correct, less a thousand coins, van Nekk supported by Jan Roper had argued about the amount that he could take with him to get new men.

"You want far too much, Pilot! You'll have to offer them less!"

"Christ Jesus! Whatever it takes we have to pay. I must have seamen and gunners." He had slammed his fist on the table of the great cabin. "How else are we going to get home?"

Eventually he had persuaded them to let him take enough, and was disgusted that they had made him lose his temper with their pettifogging. The next day he had shipped them back to Yedo, a tenth of the treasure split up among them as back pay, the rest under guard on the ship.

"How do we know it'll be safe here?" Jan Roper asked, scowling.

"Stay and guard it yourself then!"

But none of them had wanted to stay aboard. Vinck had agreed to come with him.

"Why him, Pilot?" van Nekk had asked.

"Because he's a seaman and I'll need help."

Blackthorne had been glad to see the last of them. Once at sea he began to change Vinck to Japanese ways. Vinck was stoic about it, trusting Blackthorne, having sailed too many years with him not to know his measure. "Pilot, for you I'll bathe and wash every day but I'll be God-cursed afore I wear a poxy nighty!"

Within ten days Vinck was happily swinging the lead half-naked, his wide leather belt over his paunch, a dagger stuck in a sheath at his back and one of Blackthorne's pistols safely within his clean though ragged shirt.

"We don't have to go to the castle, do we, Pilot?"

"No."

"Christ Jesus—I'd rather stay away from there."

The day was fine, a high sun shimmering off the calm sea. The rowers were still strong and disciplined.

"Vinck—that's where the ambush was!"

"Christ Jesus, look at those shoals!"

Blackthorne had told Vinck about the narrowness of his escape, the signal fires on those battlements, the piles of dead ashore, the enemy frigate bearing down on him.

"Ah, Anjin-san." Yabu came to join them. "Good, *neh?*" He motioned at the devastation.

"Bad, Yabu-sama."

"It's enemy, *neh?*"

"People are not enemy. Only Ishido and samurai enemy, *neh?*"

"The castle is enemy," Yabu replied, reflecting his disquiet, and that of all those aboard. "Here everything is enemy."

Blackthorne watched Yabu move to the bow, the wind whipping his kimono away from his hard torso.

Vinck dropped his voice. "I want to kill that bastard, Pilot."

"Yes. I've not forgotten about old Pieterzoon either, don't worry."

"Nor me, God be my judge! Beats me how you talk their talk. What'd he say?"

"He was just being polite."

"What's the plan?"

"We dock and wait. He goes off for a day or two and we keep our heads down and wait. Toranaga said he'd send messages for the safe conducts we'd need but even so, we're going to keep our heads down and stay aboard." Blackthorne scanned the shipping and the waters for dangers but found none. Still, he said to Vinck, "Better call the fathoms now, just in case!"

"Aye!"

Yabu watched Vinck swinging the lead for a moment, then strolled back to Blackthorne. "Anjin-san, perhaps you'd better take the galley and go on to Nagasaki. Don't wait, eh?"

"All right," Blackthorne said agreeably, not rising to the bait.

Yabu laughed. "I like you, Anjin-san! But so sorry, alone you'll soon die. Nagasaki's very bad for you."

"Osaka bad—everywhere bad!"

"*Karma.*" Yabu smiled again. Blackthorne pretended to share the joke.

They had had variations of the same conversation many times during the voyage. Blackthorne had learned much about Yabu. He hated him even more, distrusted him even more, respected him more, and knew their *karmas* were interlocked.

"Yabu-san's right, Anjin-san," Uraga had said. "He can protect you at Nagasaki, I cannot."

"Because of your uncle, Lord Harima?"

"Yes. Perhaps I'm already declared outlaw, *neh?* My uncle's Christian— though I think a rice Christian."

"What's that?"

"Nagasaki is his fief. Nagasaki has great harbor on the coast of Kyushu but not the best. So he quickly sees the light, *neh?* He becomes Christian, and orders all his vassals Christian. He ordered me Christian and into the Jesuit School, and then had me sent as one of the Christian envoys to the Pope. He gave land to the Jesuits and—how would you say it—fawns on them. But his heart is only Japanese."

"Do the Jesuits know what you think?"

"Yes, of course."

"Do they believe that about rice Christians?"

"They don't tell *us,* their converts, what they truly believe, Anjin-san. Or even themselves most times. They are trained to have secrets, to use secrets, to welcome them, but never to reveal them. In that they're very Japanese."

"You'd better stay here in Osaka, Uraga-san."

"Please excuse me, Sire, I am your vassal. If you go to Nagasaki, I go."

Blackthorne knew that Uraga was becoming an invaluable aid. The man was revealing so many Jesuit secrets: the how and why and when of their trade negotiations, their internal workings and incredible international machinations. And he was equally informative about Harima and Kiyama and how the Christian *daimyos* thought, and why, probably, they would stay sided with Ishido. God, I know so much now that'd be priceless in London, he thought, and so much still to learn. How can I pass on the knowledge? For instance that China's trade, just in silk to Japan, is worth ten million in gold a year, and that, even now, the Jesuits have one of their professed priests at the Court of the Emperor of China in Peking, honored with courtly rank, a confidant of the rulers, speaking Chinese perfectly. If only I could send a letter—if only I had an envoy.

In return for all the knowledge Blackthorne began to teach Uraga about navigation, about the great religious schism, and about Parliament. Also he taught him and Yabu how to fire a gun. Both were apt pupils. Uraga's a good man, he thought. No problem. Except he's ashamed of his lack of a samurai queue. That'll soon grow.

There was a warning shout from the forepoop lookout.

"Anjin-san!" The Japanese captain was pointing ahead at an elegant cutter, oared by twenty men, that approached from the starboard quarter. At the masthead was Ishido's cipher. Alongside it was the cipher of the Council of Regents, the same that Nebara Jozen and his men had traveled under to Anjiro, to their deaths.

"Who is it?" Blackthorne asked, feeling a tension throughout the ship, all eyes straining into the distance.

"I can't see yet, so sorry," the captain said.

"Yabu-san?"

Yabu shrugged. "An official."

As the cutter came closer, Blackthorne saw an elderly man sitting under the aft canopy, wearing ornate ceremonial dress with the winged overmantle. He wore no swords. Surrounding him were Ishido's Grays.

The drum master ceased the beat to allow the cutter to come alongside. Men rushed to help the official aboard. A Japanese pilot jumped after him and after numerous bows took formal charge of the galley.

Yabu and the elderly man were also formal and painstaking. At length they were seated on cushions of unequal rank, the official taking the most favored position on the poop. Samurai, Yabu's and Grays, sat cross-legged or knelt on the main deck surrounding them in even lesser places. "The Council welcomes you, Kasigi Yabu, in the name of His Imperial Highness," the man said. He was small and stocky, somewhat effete, a senior adviser to the Regents on protocol who also had Imperial Court rank. His name was Ogaki Takamoto, he was a Prince of the Seventh Rank, and his function was to act as one of the intermediaries between the Court of His Imperial Highness, the Son of Heaven, and the Regents. His teeth were dyed black in the manner that all courtiers of the Imperial Court had, by custom, affected for centuries.

"Thank you, Prince Ogaki. It's a privilege to be here on Lord Toranaga's behalf," Yabu said, vastly impressed with the honor being done to him.

"Yes, I'm sure it is. Of course, you're here on your own behalf also, *neh?*" Ogaki said dryly.

"Of course," Yabu replied. "When does Lord Toranaga arrive? So sorry, but the *tai-fun* delayed me for five days and I've had no news since I left."

"Ah, yes, the *tai-fun.* Yes, the Council were so happy to hear that the storm did not touch you." Ogaki coughed. "As to your master, I regret to tell you that he hasn't even reached Odawara yet. There have been interminable delays, and some sickness. Regrettable, *neh?*"

"Oh yes, very—nothing serious, I trust?" Yabu asked quickly, immensely glad to be party to Toranaga's secret.

"No, fortunately nothing serious." Again the dry cough. "Lord Ishido understands that your master reaches Odawara tomorrow."

Yabu was suitably surprised. "When I left, twenty-one days ago, everything was ready for his immediate departure, then Lord Hiro-matsu became sick. I know Lord Toranaga was gravely concerned but anxious to begin his journey—as I'm anxious to begin preparations for his arrival."

"Everything's prepared," the small man said.

"Of course the Council will have no objections if I check the arrangements, *neh?*" Yabu was expansive. "It's essential the ceremony be worthy of the Council and occasion, *neh?*"

"Worthy of His Imperial Majesty, the Son of Heaven. It's *his* summons now."

"Of course but . . ." Yabu's sense of well-being died. "You mean . . . you mean His Imperial Highness will be there?"

"The Exalted has agreed to the Regents' humble request to accept *personally* the obeisance of the new Council, all major *daimyos,* including Lord Toranaga, his family, and vassals. The senior advisers of His Imperial Highness were asked to choose an auspicious day for such a—such a ritual. The twenty-second day of this month, in this, the fifth year of the era Keichō."

Yabu was stupefied. "In—in *nineteen* days?"

"At noon." Fastidiously Ogaki took out a paper kerchief from his sleeve and delicately blew his nose. "Please excuse me. Yes, at noon. The omens were perfect. Lord Toranaga was informed by Imperial messenger fourteen days ago. His immediate humble acceptance reached the Regents three days ago." Ogaki took out a small scroll. "Here is *your* invitation, Lord Kasigi Yabu, to the ceremony."

Yabu quailed as he saw the Imperial seal of the sixteen-petal chrysanthemum and knew that *no one,* not even Toranaga, could possibly refuse such a summons. A refusal would be an unthinkable insult to the Divinity, an open rebellion, and as *all* land belonged to the reigning Emperor, would result in immediate forfeiture of all land, coupled with an Imperial invitation to commit seppuku at once, issued on *his* behalf by the Regents, also sealed with the Great Seal. Such an invitation would be absolute and would have to be obeyed.

Yabu frantically tried to recover his composure.

"So sorry, are you unwell?" Ogaki asked solicitously.

"So sorry," Yabu stuttered, "but never in my wildest dreams. . . . No one could have imagined the Exalted would—would so honor us, *neh?*"

"I agree, oh yes. Extraordinary!"

"Astonishing . . . that His Imperial Highness would—would consider leaving

Kyoto and—and come to Osaka."

"I agree. Even so, on the twenty-second day, the Exalted and the Imperial Regalia will be here." The Imperial Regalia, without which no succession was valid, were the Three Sacred Treasures, considered divine, that all believed had been brought to earth by the god Ninigi-noh-Mikoto and passed on by him personally to his grandson, Jimmu Tenno, the first human Emperor, and by him personally to his successor down to the present holder, the Emperor Go-Nijo: the Sword, the Jewel, and the Mirror. The Sacred Sword and the Jewel always traveled in state with the Emperor whenever he had to stay overnight away from the palace; the Mirror was kept within the inner sanctuary at the great Shinto shrine of Ise. The Sword, the Mirror, and the Jewel belonged to the Son of Heaven. They were divine symbols of legitimate authority, of his divinity, that when *he* was on the move, the divine throne moved with *him*. And thus that with *him* went all power.

Yabu croaked, "It's almost impossible to believe that preparations for *his* arrival could be made in time."

"Oh, the Lord General Ishido, on behalf of the Regents, petitioned the Exalted the moment he first heard from Lord Zataki at Yokosé that Lord Toranaga had agreed, equally astonishingly, to come to Osaka and bow to the inevitable. Only the great honor that your master does the Regents prompted them to petition the Son of Heaven to grace the occasion with the Presence." Again the dry cough. "Please excuse me, you would perhaps give me your formal acceptance in writing as soon as is convenient?"

"May I do it at once?" Yabu asked, feeling very weak.

"I'm sure the Regents would appreciate that."

Feebly Yabu sent for writing materials. *Nineteen* kept pounding in his brain. Nineteen days! Toranaga can delay only nineteen days and then he must be here too. Time enough for me to get to Nagasaki and safely back to Osaka, but not time enough to launch the seaborne attack on the Black Ship and take it, so not time enough to pressure Harima, Kiyama, or Onoshi, or the Christian priests, therefore not time enough to launch Crimson Sky, therefore Toranaga's whole scheme is just another illusion . . . oh oh oh!

Toranaga's failed. I should have known that he would. The answer to my dilemma is clear: Either I blindly trust Toranaga to squeeze out of this net and I help the Anjin-san as planned to get the men to take the Black Ship even more rapidly, or I've got to go to Ishido and tell him everything I know and try to barter for my life and for Izu.

Which?

Paper and brush and ink arrived. Yabu put his anguish aside for a moment and concentrated on writing as perfectly and beautifully as he could. It was unthinkable to reply to the Presence with a cluttered mind. When he had finished his acceptance, he had made the critical decision: He would follow Yuriko's advice completely. At once the weight tumbled off his *wa* and he felt greatly cleansed. He signed his name with an arrogant flourish.

How to be Toranaga's best vassal? So simple: Remove Ishido from this earth. How to do that, yet leave enough time to escape?

Then he heard Ogaki say, "Tomorrow you are invited to a formal reception given by the General Lord Ishido to honor the birthday of the Lady Ochiba."

Still travel-worn, Mariko embraced Kiri first, then hugged the Lady Sazuko, admired the baby, and hugged Kiri again. Personal maids fussed and bustled around them, bringing cha and saké and taking away the trays again, hurrying in and out with cushions and sweet-smelling herbs, opening and closing the shojis overlooking the inner garden in their section of Osaka Castle, waving fans, chattering, and weeping also.

At length Kiri clapped her hands, dismissed the maids, and groped heavily for her special cushion, overcome with excitement and happiness. She was very flushed. Hastily Mariko and the Lady Sazuko fanned her and ministered to her, and only after three large cups of saké was she able to catch her breath again.

"Oh, that's better," she said. "Yes, thank you, child, yes, I'll have some more! Oh, Mariko-chan, you're really here?"

"Yes, yes. Really here, Kiri-san."

Sazuko, looking much younger than her seventeen years, said, "Oh, we've been so worried with only rumors and—"

"Yes, nothing but rumors, Mariko-chan," Kiri interrupted. "Oh, there's so much I want to know, I feel faint."

"Poor Kiri-san, here, have some saké," Sazuko said solicitously. "Perhaps you should loosen your obi and—"

"I'm perfectly all right now! Please don't fuss, child." Kiri exhaled and folded her hands over her ample stomach. "Oh Mariko-san, it's so good to see a friendly face again from outside Osaka Castle."

"Yes," Sazuko echoed, nestling closer to Mariko, and said in a torrent, "whenever we go out of our gate Grays swarm around us like we were queen bees. We're not allowed to leave the castle, except with the Council's permission—none of the ladies are, even Lord Kiyama's—and the Council almost never meets and they hem and haw so there's never any permission and the doctor still says I'm not to travel yet but I'm fine and the baby's fine and. . . . But first tell us—"

Kiri interrupted, "First tell us how our Master is."

The girl laughed, her vivacity undiminished. "I was going to ask that, Kiri-san!"

Mariko replied as Toranaga had ordered. "He's committed to his course—he's confident and content with his decision." She had rehearsed herself many times during her journey. Even so the strength of the gloom she created almost made her want to blurt out the truth. "So sorry," she said.

"Oh!" Sazuko tried not to sound frightened.

Kiri heaved herself to a more comfortable position. *"Karma* is *karma, neh?"*

"Then—then there's no change—no hope?" the girl asked.

Kiri patted her hand. "Believe that *karma* is *karma,* child, and Lord Toranaga is the greatest, wisest man alive. That is enough, the rest is illusion. Mariko-chan, do you have messages for us?"

"Oh, so sorry. Yes, here." Mariko took the three scrolls from her sleeve. "Two for you, Kiri-chan—one from our Master, one from Lord Hiro-matsu. This is for you, Sazuko, from your Lord, but he told me to tell you he misses you and wants to see his newest son. He made me remember to tell you three times. He misses you very much and oh so wants to see his youngest son. He misses you very . . ."

Tears were spilling down the girl's cheeks. She mumbled an apology and ran out of the room clutching the scroll.

"Poor child. It's so very hard for her here." Kiri did not break the seals of her scrolls. "You know about His Imperial Majesty being present?"

"Yes." Mariko was equally grave. "A courier from Lord Toranaga caught up with me a week ago. The message gave no details other than that, and named the day he will arrive here. Have you heard from him?"

"Not directly—nothing private—not for a month now. How is he? Really?"

"Confident." She sipped some saké. "Oh, may I pour for you?"

"Thank you."

"Nineteen days isn't much time, is it, Kiri-chan?"

"It's time enough to go to Yedo and back again if you hurry, time enough to live a lifetime if you want, more than enough time to fight a battle or lose an Empire—time for a million things, but not enough time to eat all the rare dishes or drink all the saké. . . ." Kiri smiled faintly. "I'm certainly not going to diet for the next twenty days. I'm—" She stopped. "Oh, please excuse me—listen to me prattling on and you haven't even changed or bathed. There'll be plenty of time to talk later."

"Oh, please don't concern yourself. I'm not tired."

"But you must be. You'll stay at your house?"

"Yes. That's where the General Lord Ishido's pass permits me to go." Mariko smiled wryly. "His welcome was flowery!"

Kiri scowled. "I doubt if *he'd* be welcome even in hell."

"Oh? So sorry, what now?"

"Nothing more than before. I know he ordered the Lord Sugiyama murders and tortures though I've no proof. Last week one of Lord Oda's consorts tried to sneak out with her children, disguised as a street cleaner. Sentries shot them 'by mistake.' "

"How terrible!"

"Of course, great 'apologies'! Ishido claims security is all important. There was a trumped-up assassination attempt on the Heir—that's his excuse."

"Why don't the ladies leave openly?"

"The Council has ordered wives and families to wait for their husbands, who *must* return for the Ceremony. The great Lord General feels 'the responsibility of their safety too gravely to allow them to wander.' The castle's locked tighter than an old oyster."

"So is the outside, Kiri-san. There are many more barriers than before on the Tokaidō, and Ishido's security's very strong within fifty *ri*. Patrols everywhere."

"Everyone's frightened of him, except us and our few samurai, and we're no more trouble to him than a pimple on a dragon's rump."

"Even our doctors?"

"Them too. Yes, they still advise us not to travel, even if it were permitted, which it will never be."

"Is the Lady Sazuko fit—is the baby fit, Kiri-san?"

"Yes, you can see that for yourself. And so am I." Kiri sighed, the strain showing now, and Mariko noticed there was much more gray in her hair than before. "Nothing's changed since I wrote to Lord Toranaga at Anjiro. We're hostages and we'll stay hostages with all the rest until The Day. Then there'll be a resolution."

"Now that His Imperial Highness is arriving . . . that makes everything final, *neh?*"

"Yes. It would seem so. Go and rest, Mariko-chan, but eat with us tonight. Then we can talk, *neh?* Oh, by the way, one piece of news for you. Your famous barbarian hatamoto—bless him for saving our Master, we heard about that—he docked safely this morning, with Kasigi Yabu-san."

"Oh! I was so worried about them. They left the day before I did by sea. We were also caught in part of the *tai-fun*, near Nagoya, but it wasn't that bad for us. I was afraid at sea. . . . Oh, that's a relief."

"It wasn't too bad here except for the fires. Many thousands of homes burned but barely two thousand dead. We heard today that the main force of the storm hit Kyushu, on the east coast, and part of Shikoku. Tens of thousands died. No one yet knows the full extent of the damage."

"But the harvest?" Mariko asked quickly.

"Much of it's flattened here—fields upon fields. The farmers hope that it will recover but who knows? If there's no damage to the Kwanto during the season, their rice may have to support the whole Empire this year and next."

"It would be far better if Lord Toranaga controlled such a harvest than Ishido. *Neh?*"

"Yes. But, so sorry, nineteen days is not time enough to take in a harvest, with all the prayers in the world."

Mariko finished her saké. "Yes."

Kiri said, "If their ship left the day before you, you must have hurried."

"I thought it best not to dawdle, Kiri-chan. It's no pleasure for me to travel."

"And Buntaro-san? He's well?"

"Yes. He's in charge of Mishima and all the border at the moment. I saw him briefly coming here. Do you know where Kasigi Yabu-sama's staying? I have a message for him."

"In one of the guest houses. I'll find out which and send you word at once." Kiri accepted more wine. "Thank you, Mariko-chan. I heard the Anjin-san's still on the galley."

"He's a very interesting man, Kiri-san. He's become more than a little useful to our Master."

"I heard that. I want to hear everything about him and the earthquake and all your news. Oh yes, there's a formal reception tomorrow evening for Lady Ochiba's birthday, given by Lord Ishido. Of course you'll be invited. I heard that the Anjin-san's going to be invited too. The Lady Ochiba wanted to see what he looks like. You remember the Heir met him once. Wasn't that the first time you saw him too?"

"Yes. Poor man, so he's to be shown off, like a captive whale?"

"Yes." Kiri added placidly, "With all of us. We're all captives, Mariko-chan, whether we like it or not."

Uraga hurried furtively down the alley toward the shore, the night dark, the sky clear and starlit, the air pleasant. He was dressed in the flowing orange robe of a Buddhist priest, his inevitable hat, and cheap straw sandals. Behind him were warehouses and the tall, almost European bulk of the Jesuit Mission. He turned a corner and redoubled his pace. Few people were about. A company of Grays carrying flares patrolled the shore. He slowed as he passed them courteously, though with a priest's arrogance. The samurai hardly noticed him.

He went unerringly along the foreshore, past beached fishing boats, the smells of the sea and shore heavy on the slight breeze. It was low tide. Scattered over the bay and sanding shelves were night fishermen, like so many fireflies, hunting with spears under their flares. Ahead two hundred paces were the wharves and jetties, barnacle encrusted. Moored to one of them was a Jesuit lorcha, the flags of Portugal and the Company of Jesus fluttering, flares and more Grays near the gangway. He changed direction to skirt the ship, heading back into the city a few blocks, then cut down Nineteenth Street, turned into twisting alleys, and came out on to the road that followed the wharves once more.

"You! Halt!"

The order came out of the darkness. Uraga stopped in sudden panic. Grays came forward into the light and surrounded him. "Where're you going, priest?"

"To the east of the city," Uraga said haltingly, his mouth dry. "To our Nichiren shrine."

"Ah, you're Nichiren, *neh?*"

Another samurai said roughly, "I'm not one of those. I'm Zen Buddhist like the Lord General."

"Zen—ah yes, Zen's the best," another said. "Wish I could understand that. It's too hard for my old head."

"He's sweating a lot for a priest, isn't he? Why are you sweating?"

"You mean priests don't sweat?"

A few laughed and someone held a flare closer.

"Why should they sweat?" the rough man said. "All they do is sleep all day and pillow all night—nuns, boys, dogs, themselves, anything they can get—and all the time stuff themselves with food they've never labored for. Priests are parasites, like fleas."

"Eh, leave him alone, he's just—"

"Take off your hat, priest."

Uraga stiffened. "Why? And why taunt a man who serves Buddha? Buddha's doing you no—"

The samurai stepped forward pugnaciously. "I said take off your hat!"

Uraga obeyed. His head was newly shaven as a priest's should be and he blessed whatever *kami* or spirit or gift from Buddha had prompted him to take that added precaution in case he was caught breaking curfew. All the Anjin-san's samurai had been ordered confined to the vessel by the port authorities, pending instructions from higher up. "There's no cause to have foul manners," he flared with a Jesuit's unconscious authority. "Serving Buddha's an honorable life, and becoming a priest is honorable and should be the final part of every samurai's old age. Or do you know nothing of *bushido?* Where are your manners?"

"What? You're samurai?"

"Of course I'm samurai. How else would I dare to talk to samurai about bad manners?" Uraga put on his hat. "It would be better for you to be patrolling than accosting and insulting innocent priests!" He walked off haughtily, his knees weak.

The samurai watched him for a time, then one spat. "Priests!"

"He was right," the senior samurai said sourly. "Where are your manners?"

"So sorry. Please excuse me."

Uraga walked along the road, very proud of himself. Nearer the galley he became wary again and waited a moment in the lee of a building. Then, gathering himself together, he walked into the flare-lit area.

"Good evening," he said politely to the Grays who lolled beside the gangplank, then added the religious blessing, *"Namu Amida Butsu,"* In the Name of the Buddha Amida.

"Thank you. *Namu Amida Butsu.*" The Grays let him pass without hindrance. Their orders were that the barbarian and all samurai were forbidden ashore except for Yabu and his honor guard. No one had said anything about the Buddhist priest who traveled with the ship.

Greatly tired now, Uraga came onto the main deck.

"Uraga-san," Blackthorne called out softly from the quarterdeck. "Over here."

Uraga squinted to adjust his eyes to the darkness. He saw Blackthorne and he smelt the stale, brassy body aroma and knew that the second shadow there had to be the other barbarian with the unpronounceable name who could also speak Portuguese. He had almost forgotten what it was like to be away from the barbarian odor that was part of his life. The Anjin-san was the only one he had met who did not reek, which was one reason why he could serve him.

"Ah, Anjin-san," he whispered and picked his way over to him, briefly greeting the ten guards who were scattered around the deck.

He waited at the foot of the gangway until Blackthorne motioned him up onto the quarterdeck. "It went very—"

"Wait," Blackthorne cautioned him as softly and pointed. "Look ashore. Over there, near the warehouse. See him? No, north a little—there, you see him now?" A shadow moved briefly, then merged into the darkness again.

"Who was it?"

"I've been watching you ever since you came into the road. He's been dogging you. You never saw him?"

"No, Sire," Uraga replied, his foreboding returning to him. "I saw no one, felt no one."

"He didn't have swords, so he wasn't samurai. A Jesuit?"

"I don't know. I don't think so—I was most careful there. Please excuse me that I didn't see him."

"Never mind." Blackthorne glanced at Vinck. "Go below now, Johann. I'll finish this watch and wake you at dawn. Thanks for waiting."

Vinck touched his forelock and went below. The dank smell left with him. "I was getting worried about you," Blackthorne said. "What happened?"

"Yabu-sama's messenger was slow, Anjin-san. Here is my report: I went with Yabu-sama and waited outside the castle from noon till just after dark when—"

"What were you doing all that time? Exactly?"

"Exactly, Sire? I chose a quiet place near the marketplace in sight of First Bridge, and I put my mind into meditation—the Jesuit practice, Anjin-san, but not about God, only about you and Yabu-sama and your future, Sire." Uraga smiled. "Many passersby put coins into my begging bowl. I let my body rest and my mind roam, though I watched the First Bridge all the time. Yabu-sama's messenger came after dark and pretended to pray with me until we were quite alone. The messenger whispered this: 'Yabu-sama says that he will be staying in the castle tonight and that he will return tomorrow morning. There is to be an official function in the castle tomorrow night that you will be invited to, given by General Lord Ishido. Finally, you should consider 'seventy.' " Uraga peered at him. "The samurai repeated that twice, so I presume it's private code, Sire."

Blackthorne nodded but did not volunteer that this was one of many prearranged signals between Yabu and himself. "Seventy" meant that he should ensure the ship was prepared for an instant retreat to sea. But with all his samurai, seamen, and rowers confined aboard, the ship was ready. And as everyone was very aware they were in enemy waters and all were greatly troubled, Blackthorne knew it would require no effort to get the ship headed out to sea.

"Go on, Uraga-san."

"That was all except I was to tell you Toda Mariko-san arrived today."

"Ah! Did she. . . . Isn't that a very fast time to make the land journey here from Yedo?"

"Yes, Sire. Actually, while I was waiting, I saw her company go across the bridge. It was in the afternoon, the middle of the Hour of the Goat. The horses were lathered and muddy and the bearers very tired. Yoshinaka-san led them."

"Did any of them see you?"

"No, Sire. No, I don't think so."

"How many were there?"

"About two hundred samurai, with porters and baggage horses. Twice that number of Grays escorting them. One of the baggage horses had panniers of carrier pigeons."

"Good. Next?"

"As soon as I was able, I left. There's a noodle shop near the Mission that many merchants, rice and silk brokers, Mission people use. I—I went there and ate and listened. The Father-Visitor is again in residence here. Many more converts in Osaka area. Permission has been granted for a huge Mass in twenty days, in honor of Lords Kiyama and Onoshi."

"Is that important?"

"Yes, and astonishing for such a service to be permitted openly. It is to celebrate the Feast of Saint Bernard. Twenty days is the day after the Obeisance Ceremony before the Exalted."

Yabu had told Blackthorne about the Emperor through Uraga. The news had swept through the whole ship, increasing everyone's premonition of disaster.

"What else?"

"In the marketplace many rumors. Most ill-omened. Yodoko-sama, the Taikō's widow, is very sick. That's bad, Anjin-san, because her counsel is always listened to and always reasonable. Some say Lord Toranaga is already near Nagoya, others say he's not yet reached Odawara, so no one knows what to believe. All agree the harvest will be terrible this year, here in Osaka, which means the Kwanto becomes even more greatly important. Most people think civil war will begin as soon as Lord Toranaga's dead, at which time the great *daimyos* will begin to fight among themselves. The price of gold is very high and interest rates up to seventy percent which—"

"That's impossibly high, you must be mistaken." Blackthorne got up and eased his back, then leaned wearily against the gunwale. Politely Uraga and all samurai got up too. It would have been bad manners for them to sit while their master stood.

"Please excuse me, Anjin-san," Uraga was saying, "it's never less than fifty percent, and usually sixty-five to seventy, even eighty. Almost twenty years ago the Father-Visitor petitioned the Holy Fa—petitioned the Pope, to allow us—to allow the Society to lend at ten percentage. He was right that his suggestion—it was approved, Anjin-san—would bring lusters to Christianity and many converts for, of course, only Christians could get loans, which were always modest. You don't pay such highs in your country?"

"Rarely. That's usury! You understand 'usury'?"

"I understand the word, yes. But usury would not begin for us under one hundred percentage. I was going to tell you also now rice is very expensive and that's a bad omen—it's double what it was when I was here a few weeks ago. Land is cheap. Now would be a good time to buy land here. Or a house. In the *tai-fun* and fires perhaps ten thousand homes die, and two, three thousand people. That's all, Anjin-san."

"That's very good. You've done very well. You've missed your real vocation!"

"Sire?"

"Nothing," Blackthorne said, not yet knowing how far he could tease Uraga. "You've done very well."

"Thank you, Sire."

Blackthorne thought a moment, then asked him about the function tomorrow and Uraga advised him as best he could. Finally Uraga told him about his escape from the patrol.

"Would your hair have given you away?" Blackthorne asked.

"Oh yes. Enough for them to take me to their officer." Uraga wiped the sweat off his forehead. "So sorry, it's hot, *neh?*"

"Very," Blackthorne agreed politely, and let his mind sift the information. He glanced seaward, unconsciously checking the sky and sea and wind. Everything was fine and orderly, the fishing boats complacently drifting with the tide, near and far, a spearman in the prow of each under a lantern stabbing down from time to time, and most always bringing up a fine bream or mullet or red snapper that curled and twisted on the spike.

"One last thing, Sire. I went to the Mission—all around the Mission. The guards were very alert and I could never get in there—at least, I don't think so, not unless I went past one of them. I watched for a while, but before I left I saw Chimmoko, Lady Toda's maid, go in."

"You're sure?"

"Yes. Another maid was with her. I think—"

"Lady Mariko? Disguised?"

"No, Sire. I'm sure it was not—this second maid was too tall."

Blackthorne looked seaward again and murmured, half to himself, "What's the significance of that?"

"Lady Mariko is Chris—she's Catholic, *neh?* She knows the Father-Visitor very well. It was he who converted her. Lady Mariko is the most very important Lady, the most famous in the realm, after the three highest nobility: the Lady Ochiba, the Lady Genjiko, and Yodoko-sama, the wife of the Taikō."

"Mariko-san might want Confession? Or a Mass? Or a conference? She sent Chimmoko to arrange them?"

"Any or all, Anjin-san. All ladies of the *daimyos,* both of friends to the Lord General and of those who might oppose him, are confined very much to the castle, *neh?* Once in, they stay in, like fish in a golden bowl, waiting to be speared."

"Leave it! Enough of your doom talk."

"So sorry. Even so, Anjin-san, I think now the Lady Toda will come out no more. Until the nineteenth day."

"I told you to leave it! I understand about hostages and a last day." It was quiet on deck, all their voices muted. The guard was resting easily, waiting out their watch. Small water lapped the hull and the ropes creaked pleasantly.

After a moment, Uraga said, "Perhaps Chimmoko brought a summons—a request for the Father-Visitor to go to her. She was surely under guard when she crossed First Bridge. Surely Toda Mariko-noh-Buntaro-noh-Jinsai was under guard from the first moments she crossed from Lord Toranaga's borders. *Neh?* "

"Can we know if the Father-Visitor goes to the castle?"

"Yes. That is easy."

"How to know what's said—or what's done?"

"That is very hard. Very sorry, but they would speak Portuguese or Latin, *neh?* And who speaks both but you and me? I would be recognized by both." Uraga motioned at the castle and at the city. "There are many Christians there. Any would gain great favor by removing you, or me—*neh?* "

Blackthorne did not answer. No answer was needed. He was seeing the donjon etched against the stars and he remembered Uraga telling him about the legendary, limitless treasure it protected, the Taikō's plunder-levy of the Empire. But now his mind was on what Toranaga might be doing and thinking and planning, and exactly where Mariko was and what was the use of going on to Nagasaki. 'Then you're saying the nineteenth day is the last day, a death day, Yabu-san?' he had repeated, almost nauseated by the knowledge that the trap was sprung on Toranaga. And therefore on him and *Erasmus.*

'*Shigata ga nai!* We go quickly Nagasaki and back again. Quick, understand? Only four days to get men. Then come back.'

'But why? When Toranaga here, all die, *neh?* ' he had said. But Yabu had gone ashore, telling him that the day after tomorrow they would leave. In a ferment he had watched him go, wishing that he had brought *Erasmus* and not the galley. If he had had *Erasmus* he knew that he would have somehow bypassed Osaka and headed straight for Nagasaki, or even more probably, he would have limped off over the horizon to find some snug harbor and taken time out from eternity to train his vassals to work the ship.

You're a fool, he flayed himself. With the few crew you've got now you couldn't have docked her here, let alone found that harbor to wait out the devil storm. You'd be dead already.

"No worry, Sire. *Karma*," Uraga was saying.

"Aye. *Karma*." Then Blackthorne heard danger seaward and his body moved before his mind ordered it and he was twisting as the arrow swooshed past, missed him fractionally to shudder into the bulkhead. He lunged at Uraga to pull him down to safety as another arrow of the same volley hissed into Uraga's throat, impaling him, and then they were both cowering in safety on the deck, Uraga shrieking and samurai shouting and peering over the gunwale out to sea. Grays from the shore guard poured aboard. Another volley came out of the night from the sea and everyone scattered for cover. Blackthorne crawled to the gunwale and peeped through a scupper and saw a nearby fishing boat dousing its flare to vanish into the darkness. All the boats were doing the same, and for a split second he saw scullers pulling away frantically, light glinting off swords and bows.

Uraga's shrieking subsided into a burbling, gut-shattering agony as Grays rushed on to the quarterdeck, bows ready, the whole ship now in an uproar. Vinck came on deck fast, pistol ready, ducked over as he ran. "Christ, what's going on—you all right, Pilot?"

"Yes. Watch out—they're in the fishing boats!" Blackthorne slithered back to Uraga, who was clawing at the shaft, blood seeping from his nose and mouth and ears.

"Jesus," Vinck gasped.

Blackthorne took hold of the arrow's barb with one hand and put his other on the warm, pulsing flesh and pulled with all his strength. The arrow came out cleanly but in its wake blood gushed in a pumping stream. Uraga began to choke.

Now Grays and Blackthorne's own samurai surrounded them. Some had brought shields and they covered Blackthorne, heedless of their own safety. Others quaked in safety though the danger was over. Others were raging at the night, firing at the night, ordering the vanished fishing boats back.

Blackthorne held Uraga in his arms helplessly, knowing there was something he should do but not knowing what, knowing nothing could be done, the frantic sick-sweet-death smell clogging his nostrils, his brain shrieking as always, 'Christ Jesus, thank God it's not my blood, not mine, thank God.'

He saw Uraga's eyes begging, the mouth working with no sound but choking, the chest heaving, then he saw his own fingers move of themselves and they made the sign of the cross before the eyes and he felt Uraga's body shuddering, fluttering, the mouth howling soundlessly, reminding him of any one of the impaled fish.

It took Uraga a hideous time to die.

CHAPTER 53

Now Blackthorne was walking in the castle with his honor guard of twenty vassals surrounded by ten times that number of escorting Grays. Proudly he wore a new uniform, Brown kimono with the five Toranaga ciphers and, for the first time, a formal, huge-winged overmantle. His golden wavy hair was tied in a neat queue. The swords that Toranaga had given him jutted from his sash correctly. His feet were encased in new tabi and thonged sandals.

Grays in abundance were at every intersection, covering every battlement, in a vast show of Ishido strength, for every *daimyo* and general and every samurai officer of importance in Osaka had been invited tonight to the Great Hall that the Taikō had built within the inner ring of fortifications. The sun was down and night arriving quickly.

It's terrible luck to lose Uraga, Blackthorne was thinking, still not knowing if the attack had been against Uraga or himself. I've lost the best source of knowledge I could ever have.

"At noon you go castle, Anjin-san," Yabu had said this morning, when he had returned to the galley. "Grays come for you. You understand?"

"Yes, Yabu-sama."

"Quite safe now. Sorry about attack. *Shigata ga nai!* Grays take you safe place. Tonight you stay in castle. Toranaga part of castle. Also next day we go Nagasaki."

"We have permission?" he had asked.

Yabu shook his head with exasperation. "Pretend go Mishima to collect Lord Hiro-matsu. Also Lord Sudara and family. Understand?"

"Yes."

"Good. Sleep now, Anjin-san. Don't worry about attack. Now all boats ordered stay away from here. It's *kinjiru* here now."

"I understand. Please excuse me, what happens tonight? Why me to castle?"

Yabu had smiled his twisted smile and told him he was on show, that Ishido was curious to see him again. "As a guest you'll be safe," and he had left the galley once more.

Blackthorne had gone below, leaving Vinck on watch, but the moment he was deeply asleep Vinck was tugging him awake and he rushed on deck again.

A small Portuguese twenty-cannon frigate was barreling into harbor, the bit between her teeth, heeled over under a full press of canvas.

"Bastard's in a hurry," Vinck said, quaking.

"Got to be Rodrigues. No one else'd come in with all that sail."

"If I was you, Pilot, I'd get us the hell away from here on the tide, or without the tide. Christ Jesus, we're like moths in a grog bottle. Let's get out—"

"We stay! Can't you get it through your head? We stay until we're allowed to leave. We stay until Ishido says we can go even if the Pope and the King of Spain come ashore together with the whole God-cursed Armada!"

Again he had gone below but sleep had avoided him. At noon, Grays arrived. Heavily escorted, he went with them to the castle. They wound through the city passing the execution ground, the five crosses still there, figures still being tied

652

up and taken down, each cross with its two spearsmen, the crowd watching. He had relived that agony and the terror of the ambush, and the feel of his hand on the hilt of his sword, the kimono about him, his own vassals with him, did not lessen his dread.

The Grays had guided him to Toranaga's part of the castle that he had visited the first time, where Kiritsubo and the Lady Sazuko and her child were still ensconsed, along with the remainder of Toranaga's samurai. There he had had a bath and found the new clothes that had been laid out for him.

"Is Lady Mariko here?"

"No, Sire, so sorry," the servant had told him.

"Then where can I find her, please? I have urgent message."

"So sorry, Anjin-san, I don't know. Please excuse me."

None of the servants would help him. All said, "So sorry, I don't know."

He had dressed, then referred to his dictionary, remembering key words that he would need and prepared as best he could. Then he went into the garden to watch the rocks growing. But they never grew.

Now he was walking across the innermost moat. Flares were everywhere.

He shook off his anxiety and stepped out onto the wooden bridge. Other guests with Grays were all around heading the same way. He could feel them watching him covertly.

His feet took him under the final portcullis and his Grays led through the maze again up to the huge door. Here they left him. So did his own men. They went to one side with other samurai to await him. He went forward into the flare-lit maw.

It was an immense, high-raftered room with a golden ornamented ceiling. Gold-paneled columns supported the rafters, which were made of rare and polished woods and cherished like the hangings on the walls. Five hundred samurai and their ladies were there, wearing all the colors of the rainbow, their fragrances mingling with incense perfume from the precious woods that smoked on tiny wall braziers. Blackthorne's eyes raced over the crowd to find Mariko, or Yabu, or any friendly face. But he found none. To one side was a line of guests who waited to bow before the raised platform at the far end. The courtier, Prince Ogaki Takamoto, was standing there. Blackthorne recognized Ishido—tall, lean, and autocratic—also beside the platform, and he remembered vividly the blinding power of the man's blow on his face, and then his own fingers knotting around the man's throat.

On the platform, alone, was the Lady Ochiba. She sat comfortably on a cushion. Even from this distance he could see the exquisite richness of her kimono, gold threads on the rarest blue-black silk. "The Most High," Uraga had called her in awe, telling him much about her and her history during their journey.

She was slight, almost girlish in build, with a luminous glow to her fair skin. Her sloe eyes were large under painted, arched brows, her hair set like a winged helmet.

The procession of guests crept forward. Blackthorne was standing to one side in a pool of light, a head taller than those nearby. Politely he stepped aside to get out of the way of some passing guests and saw Ochiba's eyes turn to him. Now Ishido was looking at him too. They said something to each other and her fan moved. Their eyes returned to him. Uneasily he went toward a wall to become less conspicuous but a Gray barred his way. *"Dozo,"* this samurai said politely, motioning at the line.

"Hai, domo," Blackthorne said and joined it.

Those in front bowed and others that came after him bowed. He returned their bows. Soon all conversation died. Everyone was looking at him.

Embarrassed, the men and women ahead in the line moved out of his way. Now no one was between him and the platform. He stood rigid momentarily. Then, in the utter silence, he walked forward.

In front of the platform he knelt and bowed formally, once to her and once to Ishido as he had seen others do. He got up again, petrified that his swords would fall or that he would slip and be disgraced, but everything went satisfactorily and he began to back away.

"Please wait, Anjin-san," she said.

He waited. Her luminosity seemed to have increased, and her femininity. He felt the extraordinary sensuality that surrounded her, without conscious effort on her part.

"It is said that you speak our language?" Her voice was unaccountably personal.

"Please excuse me, Highness," Blackthorne began, using his time-tried stock phrase, stumbling slightly in his nervousness. "So sorry, but I have to use short words and respectfully ask you to use very simple words to me so that I may have the honor of understanding you." He knew that without doubt his life could easily depend on his answers. All attention in the room was on them now. Then he noticed Yabu moving carefully through the throng, coming closer. "May I respectfully congratulate you on your birthday and pray that you live to enjoy a thousand more."

"These are hardly simple words, Anjin-san," Lady Ochiba said, very impressed.

"Please excuse me, Highness. I learn that last night. The right way to say, *neh?*"

"Who taught you that?"

"Uraga-noh-Tadamasa, my vassal."

She frowned, then glanced at Ishido, who bent forward and spoke, too rapidly for Blackthorne to catch anything other than the word "arrows."

"Ah, the renegade Christian priest who was killed last night on your ship?"

"Highness?"

"The man—samurai who was killed, *neh?* Last night on ship. You understand?"

"Ah, so sorry. Yes, him." Blackthorne glanced at Ishido, then back at her. "Please excuse me, Highness, your permission greet the Lord General?"

"Yes, you have that permission."

"Good evening, Lord General," Blackthorne said with studied politeness. "Last time meet, I very terrible mad. So sorry."

Ishido returned the bow perfunctorily. "Yes, you were. And very impolite. I hope you won't get mad tonight or any other night."

"Very mad that night, please excuse me."

"That madness is usual among barbarians, *neh?*"

Such public rudeness to a guest was very bad. Blackthorne's eyes flashed to Lady Ochiba for an instant and he discerned surprise in her too. So he gambled. "Ah, Lord General, you are most very right. Barbarian always same madness. But, so sorry, now I am samurai—hatamoto—this great, so very great honor to me. *I am no longer barbarian.*" He used his quarterdeck voice which carried without shouting and filled all the corners of the room. "Now I understand samurai manners—and little *bushido*. And *wa*. I am no longer barbarian, please excuse. *Neh?*" He spoke the last word as a challenge, unafraid. He knew that Japanese understood masculinity and pride, and honored them.

Ishido laughed. "So, samurai Anjin-san," he said, jovial now. "Yes, I accept your apology. Rumors about your courage are true. Good, very good. I should apologize also. Terrible that filthy *ronin* could do such a thing, you understand? Attack in night?"

"Yes, I understand, Sire. Very bad. Four men dead. One of my, three Grays."

"Listen, bad, very bad. Don't worry, Anjin-san. No more." Thoughtfully Ishido glanced at the room. Everyone understood him very clearly. "Now I order guards. Understand? Very careful guards. No more assassin attacks. None. You very carefully guarded now. Quite safe in castle."

"Thank you. So sorry for trouble."

"No trouble. You important, *neh?* You samurai. You have special samurai place with Lord Toranaga. I don't forget—never fear."

Blackthorne thanked Ishido again and turned to the Lady Ochiba. "Highness, in my land we has Queen—have Queen. Please excuse my bad Japanese. . . . Yes, my land rule by Queen. In my land we have custom always must give lady birthday gift. Even Queen." From the pocket in his sleeve he took out the pink camellia blossom that he had cut off a tree in the garden. He laid it in front of her, fearful he was overreaching himself. "Please excuse me if not good manners to give."

She looked at the flower. Five hundred people waited breathlessly to see how she would respond to the daring and the gallantry of the barbarian—and the trap he had, perhaps, unwittingly placed her in.

"I am not a Queen, Anjin-san," she said slowly. "Only the mother of the Heir and widow of the Lord Taikō. I cannot accept your gift as a Queen for I am not a Queen, could never be a Queen, do not pretend to be a Queen, and do not wish to be a Queen." Then she smiled at the room and said to everyone, "But as a lady on her birthday, perhaps I may have your permission to accept the Anjin-san's gift?"

The room burst into applause. Blackthorne bowed and thanked her, having understood only that the gift was accepted. When the crowd was silent again, Lady Ochiba called out, "Mariko-san, your pupil does you credit, *neh?*"

Mariko was coming through the guests, a youth beside her. Near them he recognized Kiritsubo and the Lady Sazuko. He saw the youth smile at a young girl then, self-consciously, catch up with Mariko. "Good evening, Lady Toda," Blackthorne said, then added dangerously in Latin, intoxicated by his success, "The evening is more beautiful because of thy presence."

"Thank you, Anjin-san," she replied in Japanese, her cheeks coloring. She walked up to the platform, but the youth stayed within the circle of onlookers. Mariko bowed to Ochiba. "I have done little, Ochiba-sama. It's all the Anjin-san's work and the word book that the Christian Fathers gave him."

"Ah yes, the word book!" Ochiba made Blackthorne show it to her and, with Mariko's help, explain it elaborately. She was fascinated. So was Ishido. "We must get copies, Lord General. Please order them to give us a hundred of the books. With these, our young men could soon learn barbarian, *neh?*"

"Yes. It's a good idea, Lady. The sooner we have our own interpreters, the better." Ishido laughed. "Let Christians break their own monopoly, *neh?*"

An iron-gray samurai in his sixties who stood in the front of the guests said, "Christians own no monopoly, Lord General. We ask the Christian Fathers—in fact we insist that they be interpreters and negotiators because they're the only ones who can talk to both sides and are trusted by both sides. Lord Goroda began the custom, *neh?* And then the Taikō continued it."

"Of course, Lord Kiyama, I meant no disrespect to *daimyos* or samurai who have become Christian. I referred only to the monopoly of the Christian priests," Ishido said. "It would be better for us if our people and not foreign priests—any priests for that matter—controlled our trade with China."

Kiyama said, "There's never been a case of fraud, Lord General. Prices are fair, the trade is easy and efficient, and the Fathers control their own people. Without the Southern Barbarians there's no silk, no China trade. Without the Fathers we could have much trouble. Very much trouble, so sorry. Please excuse me for mentioning it."

"Ah, Lord Kiyama," the Lady Ochiba said, "I'm sure Lord Ishido is honored that you correct him, isn't that so, Lord General? What would the Council be without Lord Kiyama's advice?"

"Of course," Ishido said.

Kiyama bowed stiffly, not unpleased. Ochiba glanced at the youth and fluttered her fan. "How about you, Saruji-san? Perhaps you would like to learn barbarian?"

The boy blushed under their scrutiny. He was slim and handsome and tried hard to be more manly than his almost fifteen years. "Oh, I hope I wouldn't have to do that, Ochiba-sama, oh no—but if it is ordered I will try. Yes, I'd try very hard."

They laughed at his ingenuousness. Mariko said proudly in Japanese, "Anjin-san, this is my son, Saruji." Blackthorne had been concentrating on their conversation, most of which was too fast and too vernacular for him to comprehend. But he had heard "Kiyama," and an alarm went off. He bowed to Saruji and the bow was formally returned. "He's a very fine man, *neh*? Lucky have such a fine son, Mariko-sama." His veiled eyes were looking at the youth's right hand. It was permanently twisted. Then he remembered that once Mariko had told him her son's birth had been prolonged and difficult. Poor lad, he thought. How can he use a sword? He took his eyes away. No one had noticed the direction of his glance except Saruji. He saw embarrassment and pain in the youth's face.

"Lucky have fine son," he said to Mariko. "But surely impossible, Mariko-sama, you have big son—not enough years, *neh*?"

Ochiba said, "Are you always so gallant, Anjin-san? Do you always say such clever things?"

"Please?"

"Ah, always so clever? Compliments? Do you understand?"

"No, so sorry, please excuse me." Blackthorne's head was aching from concentration. Even so, when Mariko told him what had been said he replied with mock gravity, "Ah, so sorry, Mariko-sama. If Saruji-san is truly your son, please tell the Lady Ochiba I did not know that ladies here were married at ten."

She translated. Then added something that made them laugh.

"What did you say?"

"Ah!" Mariko noticed Kiyama's baleful eyes on Blackthorne. "Please excuse me, Lord Kiyama, may I introduce the Anjin-san to you?"

Kiyama acknowledged Blackthorne's very correct bow politely. "They say you claim to be a Christian?"

"Please?"

Kiyama did not deign to repeat it so Mariko translated.

"Ah, so sorry, Lord Kiyama," Blackthorne said in Japanese. "Yes. I'm Christian—but different sect."

"Your sect is not welcome in my lands. Nor in Nagasaki—or Kyushu, I'd imagine—or in any lands of any *Christian daimyos.*"

Mariko kept her smile in place. She was wondering if Kiyama had personally ordered the Amida assassin, and also the attack last night. She translated, taking the edge off Kiyama's discourtesy, everyone in the room listening intently.

"I'm not a priest, Lord," Blackthorne said, direct to Kiyama. "If I in your land—only trade. No priest talk or teach. Respectfully ask trade only."

"I do not want *your* trade. I do not want *you* in my lands. *You* are forbidden my lands on pain of death. Do you understand?"

"Yes, I understand," Blackthorne said. "So sorry."

"Good." Kiyama haughtily turned to Ishido. "We should exclude this sect and these barbarians completely from the Empire. I will propose this at the Council's next meeting. I must say openly that I think Lord Toranaga was ill-advised to make any foreigner, particularly *this* man samurai. It's a very dangerous precedent."

"Surely that's unimportant! All the mistakes of the present Lord of the Kwanto will be corrected very soon. *Neh?*"

"Everyone makes mistakes, Lord General," Kiyama said pointedly. "Only God is all-seeing and perfect. The only *real* mistake Lord Toranaga has ever made is to put his own interests before those of the Heir."

"Yes," Ishido said.

"Please excuse me," Mariko said. "But that's not true. I'm sorry, but you're both mistaken about my Master."

Kiyama turned on her. Politely. "It's perfectly correct for you to take that position, Mariko-san. But, please let's not discuss that tonight. So, Lord General, where is Lord Toranaga now? What's your latest news?"

"By yesterday's carrier pigeon, I heard he was at Mishima. Now I'm getting daily reports on his progress."

"Good. Then in two days he'll leave his own borders?" Kiyama asked.

"Yes. Lord Ikawa Jikkyu is ready to welcome him as his position merits."

"Good." Kiyama smiled at Ochiba. He was very fond of her. "On that day, Lady, in honor of the occasion, perhaps you would ask the Heir if he would allow the Regents to bow before him?"

"The Heir would be honored, Sire," she replied, to applause. "And afterwards perhaps you and everyone here would be his guests at a poetry competition. Perhaps the Regents would be the judges?"

There was more applause.

"Thank you, but please, perhaps you and Prince Ogaki and some of the ladies would be the judges."

"Very well, if you wish."

"Now, Lady, what's the theme to be? And the first line of the poem?" Kiyama asked, very pleased, for he was renowned for his poetry as well as his swordsmanship and ferocity in war.

"Please, Mariko-san, would you answer Lord Kiyama?" Ochiba said, and again many there admired her adroitness—she was an indifferent poetess where Mariko was renowned.

Mariko was glad the time had come to begin. She thought a moment. Then she said, "It should be about *today,* Lady Ochiba, and the first line: 'On a leafless branch . . .' "

Ochiba and all of them complimented her on her choice. Kiyama was genial now, and said, "Excellent, but we'll have to be very good to compete with you, Mariko-san."

"I hope you will excuse me, Sire, but I won't be competing."

"Of course you'll compete!" Kiyama laughed. "You're one of the best in the realm! It wouldn't be the same if you didn't."

"So sorry, Sire, please excuse me, but I will not be here."

"I don't understand."

Ochiba said, "What do you mean, Mariko-chan?"

"Oh, please excuse me, Lady," Mariko said, "but I'm leaving Osaka tomorrow—with the Lady Kiritsubo and the Lady Sazuko."

Ishido's smile vanished. "Leaving for where?"

"To meet our liege Lord, Sire."

"He—Lord Toranaga will be here in a few days, *neh?*"

"It's months since the Lady Sazuko has seen her husband, and my Lord Toranaga hasn't yet had the pleasure of seeing his newest son. Naturally the Lady Kiritsubo will accompany us. It's been equally long since he's seen the Mistress of his Ladies, *neh?*"

"Lord Toranaga will be here so soon that to go to meet him isn't necessary."

"But *I* think it is necessary, Lord General."

Ishido said crisply, "You've only just arrived and we've been looking forward to your company, Mariko-san. The Lady Ochiba particularly. I agree again with Lord Kiyama, of course you must compete."

"So sorry, but I will not be here."

"Obviously you're tired, Lady. You've just arrived. Certainly this is hardly the time to discuss such a private matter." Ishido turned to Ochiba. "Perhaps, Lady Ochiba, you should greet the remainder of the guests?"

"Yes—yes, of course," Ochiba said, flustered. At once the line began to form up obediently and nervous conversation began, but the silence fell again as Mariko said, "Thank you, Lord General. I agree, but this isn't a private matter and there's nothing to discuss. I am leaving tomorrow to pay my respects to my liege Lord, *with* his ladies."

Ishido said coldly, "You are here, Lady, at the personal invitation of the Son of Heaven, together with the welcome of the Regents. Please be patient. Your lord will be here very soon now."

"I agree, Sire. But His Imperial Majesty's invitation is for the twenty-second day. It does not order me—or anyone—confined to Osaka until that time. Or does it?"

"You forget your manners, Lady Toda."

"Please excuse me, that was the last thing I intended. So sorry, I apologize." Mariko turned to Ogaki, the courtier. "Lord, does the Exalted's invitation require me to stay here until He arrives?"

Ogaki's smile was set. "The invitation is for the twenty-second day of this month, Lady. It requires your presence then."

"Thank you, Sire." Mariko bowed and faced the platform again. "It requires my presence then, Lord General. Not before. So I shall leave tomorrow."

"Please be patient, Lady. The Regents have welcomed you and there are many preparations on which they'll need your assistance, against the Exalted's arrival. Now, Lady Ochi—"

"So sorry, Sire, but the orders of my liege Lord take precedence. I must leave tomorrow."

"You will not leave tomorrow and you are asked, no, begged, Mariko-san, to take part in the Lady Ochiba's competition. Now, Lady—"

"Then I am confined here—against my will?"

Ochiba said, "Mariko-san, let's leave the matter now, please?"

"So sorry, Ochiba-sama, but I am a simple person. I've said openly I have orders from my liege Lord. If I cannot obey them I must know why. Lord General, am I *confined* here until the twenty-second day? If so, by whose orders?"

"You are an honored guest," Ishido told her carefully, willing her to submit. "I repeat, Lady, your lord will be here soon enough."

Mariko felt his power and she fought to resist it. "Yes, but so sorry, again I respectfully ask: Am I confined to Osaka for the next eighteen days and if so, on whose orders?"

Ishido kept his eyes riveted on her. "No, you are not confined."

"Thank you, Sire. Please excuse me for speaking so directly," Mariko said. Many of the ladies in the room turned to their neighbors, and some whispered openly what all those held against their will in Osaka were thinking: 'If she can go, so can I, *neh?* So can you, *neh?* I'm going tomorrow—oh, how wonderful!'

Ishido's voice cut through the undercurrent of whispering. "But, Lady Toda, since you've chosen to speak in this presumptuous fashion, I feel it is my duty to ask the Regents for a formal rejection—in case others might share your misunderstanding." He smiled mirthlessly in the frozen hush. "Until that time you will hold yourself in readiness to answer their questions and receive the ruling."

Mariko said, "I would be honored, Sire, but my duty is to my liege Lord."

"Of course. But this will only be for a few days."

"So sorry, Sire, but my duty is to my liege Lord for the next few days."

"You will possess yourself with patience, Lady. It will take but a little time. This matter is ended. Now, Lord Ki—"

"So sorry, but I cannot delay my departure for a little time."

Ishido bellowed, "You refuse to obey the Council of Regents?"

"No, Sire," Mariko said proudly. "Not unless they trespass on my duty to my liege Lord, which is a samurai's paramount duty!"

"You-will-hold-yourself-ready-to-meet-the-Regents-with-filial-patience!"

"So sorry, I am ordered by my liege Lord to escort his ladies to meet him. At once." She took a scroll out of her sleeve and handed it to Ishido formally.

He tore it open and scanned it. Then he looked up and said, "Even so, you will wait for a ruling from the Regents."

Mariko looked hopefully to Ochiba but there was only bleak disapproval there. She turned to Kiyama. Kiyama was equally silent, equally unmoved.

"Please excuse me, Lord General, but there's no war," she began. "My Master's obeying the Regents, so for the next eighteen—"

"This matter is closed!"

"This matter is closed, Lord General, when you have the manners to let me finish! I'm no peasant to be trodden on. I'm Toda Mariko-noh-Buntaro-noh-Hiromatsu, daughter of the Lord Akechi Jinsai, my line's Takashima and we've been samurai for a thousand years and I say I will never be captive or hostage or confined. For the next eighteen days and until *the day,* by fiat of the Exalted, I am free to go as I please—*as is anyone."*

"Our—our Master, the Taikō, was once a peasant. Many—many samurai are peasants, were peasants. Every *daimyo* was, once, in the past, peasant. Even the first Takashima. Everyone was peasant once. Listen carefully: You-*will*-await the-pleasure-of-the-Regents."

"No. So sorry, my first duty is obedience to my liege Lord."

Enraged, Ishido began to walk toward her.

Although Blackthorne had understood almost nothing of what had been said, his right hand slid unnoticed into his left sleeve to prepare the concealed throwing knife.

Ishido stood over her. "You-will—"

At that moment there was a movement at the doorway. A tear-stained maid weaved through the throng and ran up to Ochiba. "Please excuse me, Mistress," she whimpered, "but it's Yodoko-sama—she's asking for you, she's. . . . You must hurry, the Heir's already there. . . ."

Worriedly Ochiba looked back at Mariko and at Ishido, then at the faces staring up at her. She half bowed to her guests and hurried away. Ishido hesitated. "I'll deal with you later, Mariko-san," he said, then followed Ochiba, his footsteps heavy on the tatamis.

In his wake the whispering began to ebb and flow again. Bells tolled the hour change.

Blackthorne walked over to Mariko. "Mariko-san," he asked, "what's happening?"

She continued to stare sightlessly at the platform. Kiyama took his cramped hand off his sword hilt and flexed it. "Mariko-san!"

"Yes? Yes, Sire?"

"May I suggest you go back to your house. Perhaps I may be permitted to talk to you later—say, at the Hour of the Boar?"

"Yes, yes, of course. Please—please excuse me but I had to. . . ." Her words trailed away.

"This is an ill-omened day, Mariko-san. May God take you into His keeping." Kiyama turned his back on her and spoke to the room with authority. "I suggest we return to our homes to wait . . . to wait and to pray that the Infinite may take the Lady Yodoko quickly and easily and with honor into His peace, if her time has come." He glanced at Saruji, who was still transfixed. "You come with me." He walked out. Saruji began to follow, not wanting to leave his mother, but impelled by the order and intimidated by the attention on him.

Mariko made a half bow to the room and started to leave. Kiri licked her dry lips. Lady Sazuko was beside her, tremulously apprehensive. Kiri took the Lady Sazuko's hand and together the two women followed Mariko. Yabu stepped forward with Blackthorne and they strode out behind them, very conscious that they were the only samurai present wearing Toranaga's uniform.

Outside, Grays awaited them.

"But what in the name of all gods possessed you to take such a stand? Stupid, *neh?*" Yabu stormed at her.

"So sorry," Mariko said, hiding the true reason, wishing Yabu would leave her in peace, furious at his foul manners. "It just happened, Sire. One moment it was a birthday celebration and then . . . I don't know. Please excuse me, Yabu-sama. Please excuse me, Anjin-san."

Again Blackthorne began to say something but once more Yabu overrode him and he leaned back against the window post, completely aggravated, his head throbbing from the effort of trying to understand.

"So sorry, Yabu-sama," Mariko said, and thought, how tiresome men are, they need everything explained in such detail. They can't even see the hairs on their own eyelids.

"You've started a storm that'll swallow us all! Stupid, *neh?*"

"Yes, but it's not right we should be locked up and Lord Toranaga did give me orders that—"

"Those orders are mad! Devils must have taken possession of his head! You'll have to apologize and back down. Now security's going to be tighter than a gnat's arsehole. Ishido will certainly cancel our permits to leave and you've ruined everything." He looked across at Blackthorne. "Now what do we do?"

"Please?"

The three of them had just arrived in the main reception room of Mariko's house that was within the outermost ring of fortifications. Grays had escorted them there and many more than usual were now stationed outside her gate. Kiri and the Lady Sazuko had gone to their own quarters with another "honor" guard of Grays, and Mariko had promised to join them after her meeting with Kiyama.

"But the guards won't let you, Mariko-san," Sazuko had said, distraught.

"Don't worry," she had said. "Nothing's changed. Inside the castle we can move freely, though with escorts."

"They'll stop you! Oh, why did you—"

"Mariko-san's right, child," Kiri had said, unafraid. "Nothing's changed. We'll see you soon, Mariko-chan." Then Kiri had led the way inside their castle wing and Browns had closed the fortified gate and Mariko had breathed again and come to her own house with Yabu and Blackthorne.

Now she was remembering how, when she was standing there alone, carrying the banner alone, she had seen Blackthorne's right hand readying the throwing knife and she had become stronger because of it. Yes, Anjin-san, she thought. You're the only one I knew I could count on. You were there when I needed you.

Her eyes went to Yabu, who sat cross-legged opposite her, grinding his teeth. That Yabu had taken a public stand in her support by following her out had surprised her. Because of his support, and because losing her own temper with him would achieve nothing, she dismissed his truculent insolence and began to play him. "Please excuse my stupidity, Yabu-sama," she said, her voice now penitent and overlaid with tears. "Of course you're right. So sorry, I'm just a stupid woman."

"I agree! Stupid to oppose Ishido in his own nest, *neh?*"

"Yes, so sorry, please excuse me. May I offer you saké or cha?" Mariko clapped her hands. At once the inner door opened and Chimmoko appeared, her hair disheveled, her face frightened and puffed from weeping. "Bring cha and saké for my guests. And food. And make yourself presentable! How dare you appear like that! What do you think this is, a peasant cottage? You shame me before Lord Kasigi!"

Chimmoko fled in tears.

"So sorry, Sire. Please excuse her insolence."

"Eh, that's unimportant, *neh?* What about Ishido? Eeeee Lady . . . your shaft about 'peasant,' that hit the mark, that hurt the mighty Lord General. You've made such an enemy there now! Eeeee, that took his Fruit and squeezed them before everyone!"

"Oh, do you think so? Oh, please excuse me, I didn't mean to insult *him.*"

"Eh, he *is* a peasant, always has been, always will be, and he's always hated those of us who are real samurai."

"Oh, how clever of you, Lord, to know that. Oh, thank you for telling me." Mariko bowed and appeared to brush away a tear and added, "May I please say that I feel so protected now—your strength. . . . If it hadn't been for you, Lord Kasigi, I think I would have fainted."

"Stupid to attack Ishido in front of everyone," Yabu said, slightly mollified.

"Yes. You're right. It's such a pity all our leaders aren't as strong and as clever as you, Sire, then Lord Toranaga wouldn't be in such trouble."

"I agree. But you've still put us into a latrine up to our noses."

"Please excuse me. Yes, it's all my fault." Mariko pretended to hold back tears bravely. She looked down and whispered, "Thank you, Sire, for accepting my apologies. You're so generous."

Yabu nodded, believing the praise merited, her servility necessary, and himself peerless. She apologized again, and soothed and cajoled him. Soon he was pliant. "May I please explain my stupidity to the Anjin-san? Perhaps he can suggest a way out of. . . ." She let her words fade away penitently.

"Yes. Very well."

Mariko bowed her grateful thanks, turned to Blackthorne, and spoke in Portuguese. "Please listen, Anjin-san, listen and don't ask questions for the moment.

So sorry, but first I had to calm this ill-tempered baasterd—is that how you say it?" Quickly she told him what had been said, and why Ochiba had hurried off.

"That's bad," he said, his gaze searching her. *"Neh?"*

"Yes. Lord Yabu asks for your counsel. What should be done to overcome the mess my stupidity's put you both into?"

"What stupidity?" Blackthorne was watching her and her disquiet increased. She looked down at the mats. He spoke directly to Yabu. "Don't know yet, Sire. Now understand—now think."

Yabu replied sourly, "What's there to think about? We're locked in."

Mariko translated without looking up.

"That's true, isn't it, Mariko-san?" Blackthorne said. "That's always been true."

"Yes, so sorry."

He turned away to stare into the night. Flares were placed in brackets on the stone walls that surrounded the front garden. Light flickered off the leaves and plants that had been watered for just that purpose. Westward was the iron-banded gate, guarded by a few Browns.

"Thou," she heard him say, without turning back. "I must speak with thee in private."

"Thou. Yes and I to thee," she replied, keeping her face from Yabu, also not trusting herself. "Tonight I will find thee." She looked up at Yabu. "The Anjin-san agrees with you, Sire, about my stupidity, so sorry."

"But what's the good of that now?"

"Anjin-san," she said, her voice matter-of-fact, "later tonight I'm going to Kiritsubo-san. I know where your quarters are. I'll find you."

"Yes. Thank you." He still kept his back to her.

"Yabu-sama," she said humbly, "tonight I'm going to Kiritsubo-san. She's wise—perhaps she'll have a solution."

"There's only one solution," Yabu said with a finality that unnerved her, his eyes coals. "Tomorrow you will apologize. And you will stay."

Kiyama arrived punctually. Saruji was with him and her heart sank.

When the formal greetings were completed, Kiyama said gravely, "Now, please explain why, Mariko-chan."

"There's no war, Sire. We shouldn't be confined—nor treated as hostages—so I can go as I please."

"You don't have to be at war to have hostages. You know that. The Lady Ochiba was hostage in Yedo against your master's safety here and no one was at war. Lord Sudara and his family are hostage with his brother today, and they're not at war. *Neh?"*

She kept her eyes lowered.

"There are many here who are hostages against the dutiful obedience of their lords to the Council of Regents, the legal rulers of the realm. That's wise. It's an ordinary custom. *Neh?"*

"Yes, Sire."

"Good. Now please tell me the real reason."

"Sire?"

Kiyama said testily. "Don't play games with me! I'm no peasant either! I want to know why you did what you did tonight."

Mariko raised her eyes. "So sorry, but the Lord General simply annoyed me with his arrogance, Sire. I do have orders. There's no harm in taking Kiri and Lady Sazuko away for a few days to meet our Master."

"You know very well that's impossible. Lord Toranaga must know that as well."

"So sorry, but my Master gave me orders. A samurai doesn't question his lord's orders."

"Yes. But I question them because they're nonsense. Your master doesn't deal in nonsense, or make mistakes. And I insist I have the right to question you as well."

"Please excuse me, Sire, there's nothing to discuss."

"But there is. There's Saruji to discuss. Also the fact that I've known you all your life, have honored you all your life. Hiro-matsu-sama is my oldest living friend and your father was a cherished friend and an honored ally of mine, until the last fourteen days of his life."

"A samurai doesn't question the orders of a liege lord."

"Now you can do only one of two things, Mariko-chan. You apologize and stay, or you try to leave. If you try to leave you will be stopped."

"Yes. I understand."

"You will apologize tomorrow. I will call a meeting of the Regents and they will give a ruling about this whole matter. Then you will be allowed to go with Kiritsubo and the Lady Sazuko."

"Please excuse me, how long will that take?"

"I don't know. A few days."

"So sorry, I don't have a few days, I am ordered to leave at once."

"Look at me!" She obeyed. "I, Kiyama Ukon-noh-Odanaga, Lord of Higo, Satsuma, and Osumi, a Regent of Japan, from the line Fujimoto, chief Christian *daimyo* of Japan, I *ask* you to stay."

"So sorry. My liege Lord forbids me to stay."

"Don't you understand what I'm telling you?"

"Yes, Sire. But I have no choice, please excuse me."

He motioned toward her son. "The betrothal between my granddaughter and Saruji . . . I can hardly allow this to go forward if you're disgraced."

"Yes, yes, Sire," Mariko replied, misery in her eyes. "I understand that." She saw the desperation in the boy. "So sorry, my son. But I must do my duty."

Saruji started to say something but changed his mind and then, after a moment, he said, "Please excuse me, Mother, but isn't . . . isn't your duty to the Heir more important than your duty to Lord Toranaga? The Heir's our real liege lord, *neh?*"

She thought about that. "Yes, my son. And no. Lord Toranaga has jurisdiction over me, the Heir does not."

"Then doesn't that mean Lord Toranaga has jurisdiction over the Heir, too?"

"No, so sorry."

"Please excuse me, Mother, I don't understand, but it seems to me if the Heir gives an order, he must overrule our Lord Toranaga."

She did not reply.

"Answer him," Kiyama barked.

"Was that your thought, my son? Or did someone put it into your head?"

Saruji frowned, trying to remember. "We—Lord Kiyama and—and his Lady—we discussed it. And the Father-Visitor. I don't remember. I think I thought of it myself. The Father-Visitor said I was correct, didn't he, Sire?"

"He said the Heir is more important than Lord Toranaga in the realm. Legally. Please answer him directly, Mariko-san."

Mariko said, "If the Heir was a man, of age, Kwampaku, legal ruler of this realm like the Taikō, his father, was, then I would obey him over Lord Toranaga in this. But Yaemon's a child, actually and legally, and therefore not capable.

SHŌGUN (664) BOOK V

Legally. Does that answer you?"

"But—but he's still the Heir, *neh?* The Regents listen to him—Lord Toranaga honors him. What's . . . what's a year, a few years mean, Mother? If you don't apol— Please excuse me, but I'm afraid for you." The youth's mouth was trembling.

Mariko wanted to reach out and embrace him and protect him. But she did not. *"I'm* not afraid, my son. I fear nothing on this earth. I fear only God's judgment," she said, turning to Kiyama.

"Yes," Kiyama said. "I know that. May the Madonna bless you for it." He paused. "Mariko-san, will you apologize publicly to the Lord General?"

"Yes, gladly, providing he publicly withdraws all troops from my path and gives me, the Lady Kiritsubo, and the Lady Sazuko written permission to leave tomorrow."

"Will you obey an order from the Regents?"

"Please excuse me, Sire, in this matter, no."

"Will you honor a request from them?"

"Please excuse me, in this matter, no."

"Will you agree to a request from the Heir and the Lady Ochiba?"

"Please excuse me, what request?"

"To visit them, to stay with them for a few days, while we resolve this affair."

"Please excuse me, Sire, but what is there to resolve?"

Kiyama's restraint broke and he shouted, "The future and good order of the realm for one thing, the future of the Mother Church for another, and you for another! It's clear your close contact with the barbarian has infected you and addled your brain as I knew it would!"

Mariko said nothing, just stared back at him.

With an effort Kiyama brought himself back into control.

"Please excuse my . . . my temper. And my bad manners," he said stiffly. "My only excuse is that I'm gravely concerned." He bowed with dignity. "I apologize."

"It was my fault, Sire. Please excuse me for destroying your harmony and causing you trouble. But I have no alternative."

"Your son's given you one, I've given you several."

She did not answer him.

The air in the room had become stifling for all of them although the night was cool and a breeze fanned the flares.

"You're resolved then?"

"I have no choice, Sire."

"Very well, Mariko-san. There's nothing more to be said. Other than to say again I order you not to force the issue—and I ask it."

She bowed her head.

"Saruji-san, please wait for me outside," Kiyama ordered.

The youth was distraught, barely able to speak. "Yes, Sire." He bowed to Mariko. "Please excuse me, Mother."

"May God keep you in His hands for all eternity."

"And thou."

"Amen to that," Kiyama said.

"Good night, my son."

"Good night, Mother."

When they were alone Kiyama said, "The Father-Visitor's very worried."

"About me, Sire?"

"Yes. And about the Holy Church—and the barbarian. And about the barbarian ship. First tell me about him."

"He's a unique man, very strong and very intelligent. At sea he's . . . he *belongs* there. He seems to become part of a ship and the sea, and, out to sea, there's no man who can approach him in bravery and cunning."

"Even the Rodrigues-san?"

"The Anjin-san overcame him twice. Once here and once on our way to Yedo." She told him about Rodrigues arriving in the night during their stay near Mishima and about the concealed weapons and all that she had overheard. "If their ships were equal, the Anjin-san would win. Even if they were not, I think he'd win."

"Tell me about his ship."

She obeyed.

"Tell me about his vassals."

She told him as it had happened.

"Why would Lord Toranaga give him his ship, money, vassals, and freedom?"

"My Master never told me, Sire."

"Please give me your opinion."

"So that he can loose the Anjin-san against his enemies," Mariko said at once, then added without apology, "Since you ask me, in this case the Anjin-san's particular enemies are the same as my Lord's: the Portuguese, the Holy Fathers prompting the Portuguese, and the Lords Harima, Onoshi, and yourself, Sire."

"Why should the Anjin-san consider us his special enemies?"

"Nagasaki, trade, and your coastal control of Kyushu, Sire. And because you are the chief Catholic *daimyos.*"

"The Church isn't Lord Toranaga's enemy. Nor the Holy Fathers."

"So sorry, but I think Lord Toranaga believes the Holy Fathers support the Lord General Ishido, as you do."

"I support the Heir. I'm against your Master because he does not and he will ruin our Church."

"I'm sorry, but that's not true. Sire, my Master's so superior to the Lord General. You've fought twenty more times as his ally than against him, you know he can be trusted. Why side with his avowed enemy? Lord Toranaga's always wanted trade, and he's simply not anti-Christian like the Lord General and the Lady Ochiba."

"Please excuse me, Mariko-san, but before God, I believe Lord Toranaga secretly detests our Christian Faith, secretly loathes our Church, and secretly is committed to destroying the succession and obliterating the Heir and the Lady Ochiba. His lodestone is the Shōgunate—only that! He secretly wants to be Shōgun, is planning to become Shōgun, and everything is pointed to that sole end."

"Before God, Sire, I do not believe it."

"I know—but that doesn't make you right." He watched her a moment, then said, "By your own admission this Anjin-san and his ship are very dangerous to the Church, *neh?* The Rodrigues agrees with you that if the Anjin-san caught the Black Ship at sea it would be very bad."

"Yes, I believe that too, Sire."

"That would hurt our Mother Church very much, *neh?*"

"Yes."

"But you still won't help the Church against this man?"

"He is not against the Church, Sire, not really against the Fathers, though he distrusts them. He's only against the enemies of his Queen. And the Black Ship is his goal—for profit."

"But he opposes the True Faith and is therefore a heretic. *Neh?*"

"Yes. But I don't believe everything we've been told by the Fathers is true. And much has never been told to us. Tsukku-san admitted many things. My liege

Lord ordered me to become the Anjin-san's confidant and friend, to teach him our language and customs, to learn from him what could be of value to us. And I've found—"

"You mean valuable to Toranaga. *Neh?*"

"Sire, obedience to a liege lord is the pinnacle of a samurai's life. Isn't obedience what you require from all your vassals?"

"Yes. But heresy is terrible and it seems you are allied with the barbarian against your Church and infected by him. I pray God will open your eyes, Mariko-san, before you lose your own salvation. Now, last, the Father-Visitor said you have some private information for me."

"Sire?" This was completely unexpected.

"He said there was a message from the Tsukku-san a few days ago. A special messenger from Yedo. You have some information about—about my allies."

"I asked to see the Father-Visitor tomorrow morning."

"Yes. He told me. Well?"

"Please excuse me, after I've seen him tomorrow, I—"

"Not tomorrow, now! The Father-Visitor said it had to do with Lord Onoshi and concerned the Church and you were to tell me at once. Before God that's what he said. Have things come to such a filthy pass that you won't even trust me?"

"So sorry. I made an agreement with the Tsukku-san. He asked me to speak openly to the Father-Visitor, that's all, Sire."

"The Father-Visitor said you were to tell me now."

Mariko realized she had no alternative. The die was cast. She told him about the plot against his life. All that she knew. He, too, scoffed at the rumor until she told him exactly where the information had come from.

"*His confessor?* Him?"

"Yes. So sorry."

"I regret Uraga's dead," Kiyama said, even more mortified that the night attack on the Anjin-san had been such a fiasco—as the other ambush had been—and now had killed the one man who could prove his enemy Onoshi was a traitor. "Uraga will burn in hellfire forever for that sacrilege. Terrible what he did. He deserves excommunication and hellfire, but even so, he did me a service by telling it—if it's true." Kiyama looked at her, an old man suddenly. "I can't believe Onoshi would do that. Or that Lord Harima would be a party to it."

"Yes. Could you—could you ask Lord Harima if it's true?"

"Yes, but he'd never reveal something like that. I wouldn't, would you? So sad, *neh?* So terrible are the ways of man."

"Yes."

"I will not believe it, Mariko-san. Uraga's dead so we can never get proof. I will take precautions but . . . but I cannot believe it."

"Yes. One thought, Sire. Isn't it very strange, the Lord General putting a guard on the Anjin-san?"

"Why strange?"

"Why protect him? When he detests him? Very strange, *neh?* Could it be that now the Lord General also sees the Anjin-san as a possible weapon against the Catholic *daimyos?*"

"I don't follow you."

"If, God forbid, you died, Sire, Lord Onoshi becomes supreme in Kyushu, *neh?* What could the Lord General do to curb Onoshi? Nothing—except, perhaps, use the Anjin-san."

"It's possible," Kiyama said slowly.

"There's only one reason to protect the Anjin-san—to use him. Where? Only against the Portuguese—and thus the Kyushu Christian *daimyos. Neh?*"

"It's possible."

"I believe the Anjin-san's as valuable to you as to Onoshi or Ishido or my Master. Alive. His knowledge is enormous. Only knowledge can protect us from barbarians, even Portuguese."

Kiyama said scornfully, "We can crush them, expel them any time we like. They're gnats on a horse, nothing more."

"If the Holy Mother Church conquers and all the land becomes Christian as we pray it will, what then? Will *our* laws survive? Will *bushido* survive? Against the Commandments? I suggest it won't—like elsewhere in the Catholic world— not when the Holy Fathers are supreme, not unless we are prepared."

He did not answer her.

Then she said, "Sire, I beg you, ask the Anjin-san what has happened elsewhere in the world."

"I will not. I think he's bewitched you, Mariko-san. I believe the Holy Fathers. I think your Anjin-san is taught by Satan, and I beg you to realize his heresy has already infected you. Three times you used 'Catholic' when you meant Christian. Doesn't that imply you agree with him there are two Faiths, two equally true versions of the True Faith? Isn't your threat tonight a knife in the belly of the Heir? And against the interests of the Church?" He got up. "Thank you for your information. Go with God."

Mariko took a small, thin, sealed scroll of paper from her sleeve. "Lord Toranaga asked me to give you this."

Kiyama looked at the unbroken seal. "Do you know what's in it, Mariko-san?"

"Yes. I was ordered to destroy it and pass on the message verbally if I was intercepted."

Kiyama broke the seal. The message reiterated Toranaga's wish for peace between them, his complete support of the Heir and the succession, and briefly gave the information about Onoshi. It ended, "I don't have proof about Lord Onoshi but Uraga-noh-Tadamasa will have that and, deliberately, he has been made available to you in Osaka for questioning if you wish. However I do have proof that Ishido has also betrayed the secret agreement between you and him giving the Kwanto to your descendants, once I am dead. The Kwanto has been secretly promised to my brother, Zataki, in return for betraying me, as he has already done. Please excuse me, old comrade, but you have been betrayed too. Once I am dead, you and your line will be isolated and destroyed, as will the whole Christian Church. I beg you to reconsider. Soon you will have proof of my sincerity."

Kiyama reread the message and she watched him as she had been ordered. 'Watch him so carefully, Mariko-san,' Toranaga had told her. 'I'm not sure of his agreement with Ishido about the Kwanto. Spies have reported it but I'm not sure. You'll know from what he does—or doesn't do—if you give him the message at the right time.'

She had seen Kiyama react. So that's also true, she thought.

The old *daimyo* looked up and said flatly, "And you are the proof of his sincerity, *neh?* The burnt offering, the sacrificial lamb?"

"No, Sire."

"I don't believe you. And I don't believe him. The Onoshi treason, perhaps. But the rest . . . Lord Toranaga's just up to his old tricks of mixing half-truths and honey and poison. I'm afraid it's you who've been betrayed, Mariko-san."

CHAPTER 54

W E'LL leave at noon."

"No, Mariko-san." Lady Sazuko was almost in tears.

"Yes," Kiri said. "Yes, we'll leave as you say."

"But they'll stop us," the young girl burst out. "It's all so useless."

"No," Mariko told her, "you're wrong, Sazuko-chan, it's very necessary."

Kiri said, "Mariko-san's right. We have orders." She suggested details of their leaving. "We could easily be ready by dawn if you want."

"Noon is when we should leave. That's what *he* said, Kiri-chan," Mariko replied.

"We'll need very few things, *neh?*"

"Yes."

Sazuko said, "Very few! So sorry, but it's all so silly, they'll stop us!"

"Perhaps they won't, child," Kiri said. "Mariko says they'll let us go. Lord Toranaga thinks they'll let us go. So presume that they will. Go and rest. Go on. I must talk to Mariko-san."

The girl went away, greatly troubled.

Kiri folded her hands. "Yes, Mariko-san?"

"I'm sending a cipher by carrier pigeon telling Lord Toranaga what happened tonight. It will go at first light. Ishido's men will certainly try to destroy the rest of my carrier birds tomorrow if there's trouble and I can't bring them here. Is there any message you want to send at once?"

"Yes. I'll write it now. What do you think's going to happen?"

"Lord Toranaga's sure they'll let us go, if I'm strong."

"I don't agree. And, please excuse me, I don't think you put much faith in the attempt either."

"You're wrong. Oh, of course they may stop us tomorrow and if they do there'll be the most terrible quarrel and threats but they'll all mean nothing." Mariko laughed. "Oh, such threats, Kiri-san, and they'll go on all day and all night. But at noon the next day we'll be allowed to go."

Kiri shook her head. "If we're allowed to escape, every other hostage in Osaka will leave too. Ishido will be weakened badly and he'll lose face. He can't afford that."

"Yes." Mariko was very satisfied. "Even so, he's trapped."

Kiri watched her. "In eighteen days our Master'll be here, *neh?* He must be here."

"Yes."

"So sorry, then why is it so important for us to leave at once?"

"He thinks it important enough, Kiri-san. Enough to order it."

"Ah, then he has a plan?"

"Doesn't he always have many plans?"

"Once the Exalted One agreed to be present, then our Master was trapped, *neh?*"

"Yes."

Kiri glanced at the shoji door. It was closed. She leaned forward and said softly,

668

"Then why did he ask me secretly to put that thought into the Lady Ochiba's head?"

Mariko's confidence began to fade. "He told you to do that?"

"Yes. From Yokosé, after he'd seen Lord Zataki for the first time. Why did he spring the trap himself?"

"I don't know."

Kiri bit her lips. "I wish I knew. We'll soon know, but I don't think you're telling me everything you know, Mariko-chan."

Mariko began to bridle but Kiri touched her, again cautioning her to silence, and whispered. "His dispatch to me told me to trust you completely so let's say no more than that. I do trust you, Mariko-chan, but that doesn't stop my mind from working. *Neh?*"

"Please excuse me."

"I'm so proud of you," Kiri said in a normal voice. "Yes, standing up like that to Ishido and all of them. I wish I had your courage."

"It is easy for me. Our Master said we were to leave."

"It's very dangerous, what we do, I think. Even so, how can I help?"

"Give me your support."

"You have that. You've always had that."

"I'll stay here with you till dawn, Kiri. But first I have to talk to the Anjin-san."

"Yes. I'd better go with you."

The two women left Kiri's apartments, an escort of Browns with them, passing other Browns who bowed, clearly enormously proud of Mariko. Kiri led down corridors, across the expanse of the great audience room, and into the corridor beyond. Browns were on guard here, and Grays. When they saw Mariko, all bowed, Browns and Grays equally honoring her. Both Kiri and Mariko were taken aback to find Grays in their domain. They hid their discomfiture and said nothing.

Kiri motioned at a door.

"Anjin-san?" Mariko called out.

"Hai?" The door opened. Blackthorne stood there. Behind him in the room were two more Grays. "Hello, Mariko-san."

"Hello." Mariko glanced at the Grays. "I have to talk to the Anjin-san privately."

"Please talk to him, Lady," their captain said with great deference. "Unfortunately we are ordered by Lord Ishido personally on pain of immediate death not to leave him alone."

Yoshinaka, tonight's officer-of-the-watch, strode up. "Excuse me, Lady Toda, I had to agree to these twenty guards for the Anjin-san. It was Lord Ishido's personal request. So sorry."

"As Lord Ishido is only concerned with the Anjin-san's safety, they're welcome," she said, not at all pleased inside.

Yoshinaka said to the captain of the Grays, "I will be responsible for him while the Lady Toda's with him. You can wait outside."

"So sorry," this samurai said firmly. "I and my men have no alternative but to watch with our own eyes."

Kiri said, "I will be glad to stay. Of course someone's necessary."

"So sorry, Kiritsubo-san, we must be present. Please excuse me, Lady Toda," the captain continued uncomfortably, "but none of us speaks the barbarian."

"No one suggests you would be so impolite as to listen," said Mariko, near anger. "But barbarian customs are different from ours."

Yoshinaka said, "Obviously the Grays must obey their lord. You were totally correct tonight that a samurai's first duty is to his liege lord, Lady Toda, and totally correct to point it out in public."

"Perfectly correct, Lady," the captain of the Grays agreed with the same measure of pride. "There's no other reason for a samurai's life, *neh?*"

"Thank you," she said, warmed by their respect.

"We should also honor the Anjin-san's customs if we can, Captain," Yoshinaka said. "Perhaps I have a solution. Please follow me." He led the way back to the audience room. "Please, Lady, would you take the Anjin-san and sit there." He pointed to the far dais. "The Anjin-san's guards can stay by the doors and do their duty to their liege lord, we can do ours, and you may talk as you wish, according to the Anjin-san's customs. *Neh?*"

Mariko explained to Blackthorne what Yoshinaka had said, then continued prudently in Latin, "They will never leave thee tonight. We have no alternative—except I can order them killed at once if that is thy wish."

"My wish is to talk to thee privately," Blackthorne replied. "But not at the cost of lives. I thank thee for asking me."

Mariko turned to Yoshinaka. "Very well, thank you, Yoshinaka-san. Would you please send someone for incense braziers to keep away the mosquitoes."

"Of course. Please excuse me, Lady, is there any further news of the Lady Yodoko?"

"No, Yoshinaka-san. We heard she's still resting easily, without pain." Mariko smiled at Blackthorne. "Shall we go and sit there, Anjin-san?"

He followed her. Kiri went back to her own quarters and the Grays stood at the doors of the audience room. The captain of the Grays was near Yoshinaka, a few paces away from the others. "I don't like this," he whispered roughly.

"Is the Lady Toda to pull out his sword and kill him? No offense, but where are your wits?"

Yoshinaka limped away to check the other posts. The captain looked at the dais. Mariko and the Anjin-san were seated opposite each other, well lit by flares. He could not hear what they were saying. He focused on their lips but was still no wiser, though his eyes were very good and he could speak Portuguese. I suppose they're talking the Holy Fathers' language again, he told himself. Hideous language, impossible to learn.

Still, what does it matter? Why shouldn't she talk to the heretic in private if that's her pleasure? Neither are long for this earth. So very sad. Oh, Blessed Madonna, take her forever into thy keeping for her bravery.

"Latin is safer, Anjin-san." Her fan sent a droning mosquito skittering.

"They can hear us from here?"

"No, I do not believe so, not if we keep our voices softened and talk as thou hast taught me with so little movement of the mouth."

"Good. What occurred with Kiyama?"

"I love thee."

"Thou . . ."

"I have missed thee."

"And I thee. How can we meet alone?"

"Tonight it is not possible. Tomorrow night will be possible, my love. I have a plan."

"Tomorrow? But what about thy departure?"

"Tomorrow they may stop me, Anjin-san—please do not worry. The next day we will all be free to leave as we wish. Tomorrow night, if I am stopped, I will be with thee."

"How?"

"Kiri will help me. Do not ask me how or what or why. It will be easy—"
She stopped as maids brought the little braziers. Soon the curling threads of
smoke repelled the night creatures. When they were safe again they talked about
their journey, content just being together, loving without touching, always skirting Toranaga and the importance of tomorrow. Then he said, "Ishido's my
enemy. Why are there so many guards around me?"

"To protect thee. But also to hold thee tight. I think Ishido might also want
to use thee against the Black Ship, and Nagasaki and the Lord Kiyama and Lord
Onishi."

"Ah, yes, I had thought that too."

She saw his eyes searching her. "What is it, Anjin-san?"

"Contrary to what Yabu believes, I believe thou art not stupid, that everything
tonight was said deliberately, planned deliberately—on Toranaga's orders."

She smoothed a crease in her brocade kimono. "He gave me orders. Yes."

Blackthorne turned to Portuguese, "He's betrayed you. You're a decoy. Do
you know that? You're just bait for one of his traps."

"Why do you say that?"

"You're the bait. So am I. It's obvious, isn't it? Yabu's bait. Toranaga sent
us all here as a sacrifice."

"No, you're wrong, Anjin-san. So sorry, but you're wrong."

In Latin he said, "I tell thee that thou art beautiful and I love thee, but thou
art a liar."

"No one has ever said that to me before."

"Thou hast also said no one ever said 'I love thee' before."

She looked down at her fan. "Let us talk of other things."

"What does Toranaga gain by sacrificing us?"

She did not answer.

"Mariko-san, I have the right to ask thee. I'm not afraid. I just want to know
what he gains."

"I don't know."

"Thou! Swear by thy love and thy God."

"Even thee?" She replied bitterly in Latin. "Thou also with thy 'Swear before
God' and questions and questions and questions?"

"It is thy life and my life and I cherish *both*. Again, *what does he gain?*"

Her voice became louder. "Listen thou, yes, I chose the time and yes, I am
not a stupid woman and—"

"Be cautious, Mariko-chan, please keep thy voice down or that would be very
stupid."

"So sorry. Yes, it was done deliberately and in public as Toranaga wished."

"Why?"

"Because Ishido's a peasant and he must let us go. The challenge had to be
before his peers. The Lady Ochiba approves our going to meet Lord Toranaga.
I talked to her and she is not opposed. There's nothing to trouble thyself about."

"I do not like to see fire in thee. Or venom. Or crossness. Where is thy
tranquillity? And where are thy manners? Perhaps thou should learn to watch
the rocks growing. *Neh?*"

Mariko's anger vanished and she laughed. "Ah, thee! Thou art right. Please
forgive me." She felt refreshed, herself again. "Oh, how I love thee, and honor
thee, and I was so proud of thee tonight I almost kissed thee, there in front of
them as is thy custom."

"Madonna, that would have set fire in their tinderboxes, *neh?*"

"If I were alone with thee I would kiss thee until thy cries for mercy filled the
universe."

"I thank thee, Lady, but thou art there and I am here and the world's between us."

"Ah, but there's no world between us. My life is full because of thee."

In a moment he said, "And Yabu's orders to you—to apologize and stay?"

"They may not be obeyed, so sorry."

"Because of Toranaga's orders?"

"Yes. But not his orders truly—it is also my wish. All this was my suggestion to him. It is I who begged to be allowed to come here, my darling. Before God that is the truth."

"What will happen tomorrow?"

She told him what she had told Kiri, adding, "Everything is going to be better than planned. Isn't Ishido *already* thy patron? I swear I do not know how Lord Toranaga can be so clever. Before I left he told me that would happen, might happen. He knew that Yabu has no power in Kyushu. Only Ishido or Kiyama could protect thee there. We are not decoys. We are in his protection. We're quite safe."

"What about the nineteen days—eighteen now? Toranaga *must* be here, *neh?*"

"Yes."

"Then isn't this as Ishido says, a waste of time?"

"Truly I don't know. I only know that nineteen, eighteen, or even three days can be an eternity."

"Or tomorrow?"

"Tomorrow also. Or the next day."

"And if Ishido will not let thee go tomorrow?"

"This is the only chance we have. All of us. Ishido must be humbled."

"Thou art certain?"

"Yes, before God, Anjin-san."

Blackthorne clawed out of a nightmare again but the moment he was truly awake the dream vanished. Grays were staring at him through the mosquito net in the light of early dawn.

"Good morning," he said to them, hating to have been watched while he slept.

He came from under the net and went out into the corridor, down staircases, until he came to the garden toilet. Guards, both Browns and Grays, accompanied him. He hardly noticed them.

The dawn was smoky. The sky to the east was already burnt clean of the haze. The air smelled salt and wet from the sea. Flies already swarmed. It'll be hot today, he thought.

Footsteps approached. Through the door opening he saw Chimmoko. She waited patiently, chatting with the guards, and when he came out she bowed and greeted him.

"Where Mariko-san?" he asked.

"With Kiritsubo-san, Anjin-san."

"Thank you. When leave?"

"Soon, Sire."

"Say to Mariko-san like say good morning before leave." He said it again although Mariko had already promised to find him before she went back to her home to collect her belongings.

"Yes, Anjin-san."

He nodded as a samurai should and left her and went to wash and bathe. It was not custom to have a hot bath in the morning. But every morning he would always go there and pour cold water all over himself. "Eeeee, Anjin-san," his guards or watchers would always say, "that surely is most very good for your health."

He dressed and went to the battlements that overlooked the forecourt of this castle wing. He wore a Brown kimono and swords, his pistol concealed under his sash. Browns on sentry duty welcomed him as one of them, though very disquieted by his Grays. Other Grays teemed on the battlements opposite, over-looking them, and outside their gate.

"Many Grays, many more than usual. Understand, Anjin-san?" Yoshinaka said, coming out onto the balcony.

"Yes."

The captain of the Grays moved up to them. "Please don't go too near the edge, Anjin-san. So sorry."

The sun was on the horizon. It's warmth felt good on Blackthorne's skin. There were no clouds in the sky and the breeze was dying.

The captain of the Grays pointed at Blackthorne's sword. "Is that Oil Seller, Anjin-san?"

"Yes, Captain."

"May I be allowed to see the blade?"

Blackthorne drew the sword part way from its scabbard. Custom decreed a sword should not be totally drawn unless it was to be used.

"Eeee, beautiful, *neh?*" the captain said. The others, Browns and Grays, crowded round, equally impressed.

Blackthorne shoved the sword back, not displeased. "Honor to wear Oil Seller."

"Can you use a sword, Anjin-san?" the captain asked.

"No, Captain. Not as samurai. But I learn."

"Ah, yes. That's very good."

In the forecourt two stories below, Browns were exercising, still in shadow. Blackthorne watched them. "How many samurai here, Yoshinaka-san?"

"Four hundred and three, Anjin-san, including two hundred that came with me."

"And out there?"

"Grays?" Yoshinaka laughed. "Lots—very many."

The Grays' captain showed his teeth with his grin. "Almost one hundred thousand. You understand, Anjin-san, 'one hundred thousand'?"

"Yes. Thank you."

They all looked away as a phalanx of porters and pack horses and three palanquins rounded the far corner and approached under guard from the end of the access to this cul-de-sac. The avenue was still deeply shadowed and dark between the tall guarded walls. Flares still burned in wall sockets. Even from this distance they could see the nervousness of the porters. Grays across from them seemed more hushed and attentive, and so did the Browns on guard.

The tall gates opened to admit the party, their escorting Grays staying outside with their comrades, then closed again. The great iron bar clanged back into the large brackets that were set deep into the granite walls. No portcullis guarded this gateway.

Yoshinaka said, "Anjin-san, please excuse me. I must see all is well. All ready, *neh?*"

"I wait here."

"Yes." Yoshinaka left.

The Grays' captain went to the parapet and watched below. Christ Jesus,

Blackthorne was thinking, I hope she's right and Toranaga's right. Not long now, eh? He measured the sun and muttered vaguely to himself in Portuguese, "Not long to go."

Unconsciously the captain grunted his agreement and Blackthorne realized the man understood him clearly *in Portuguese,* was therefore Catholic and another possible assassin. His mind rushed back to last night, and he remembered that everything he had said to Mariko had been in Latin. Was it all in Latin? Mother of God, what about her saying ". . . I can order them killed?" Was that in Latin? Does he speak Latin, too, like that other captain, the one who was killed during the first escape from Osaka?

The sun was gathering strength now and Blackthorne took his eyes off the captain of Grays. If you didn't murder me in the night maybe you'll never do it, he thought, putting this Catholic into a compartment.

He saw Kiri come out into the forecourt below. She was supervising maids bearing panniers and chests for the pack horses. She looked tiny, standing on the main steps where Sazuko had pretended to slip, initiating Toranaga's escape. Just to the north was the lovely garden and tiny rustic house where he'd first seen Mariko and Yaemon, the Heir. His mind journeyed with the noon cortege out of the castle, curling through the maze, then safely out, through the woods, and down to the sea. He prayed that she would be safe and everyone safe. Once they were away, Yabu and he would leave and go to the galley and out to sea.

From here on the battlements the sea seemed so near. The sea beckoned. And the horizon.

"*Konbanwa,* Anjin-san."

"Mariko-san!" She was as radiant as ever.

"*Konbanwa,*" he said, then in Latin, nonchalantly, "Beware of this Gray man—he understands," continuing instantly in Portuguese to give her time to cover, "yes, I don't understand how you can be so beautiful after so little sleep." He took her arm and put her back to the captain, guiding her nearer the parapet. "Look, there's Kiritsubo-san!"

"Thank you. Yes—yes, I'm . . . thank you."

"Why don't you wave to Kiritsubo-san?"

She did as she was asked and called out her name. Kiri saw them and waved back.

After a moment, relaxed again and in control, Mariko said, "Thank you, Anjin-san. You're very clever and very wise." She greeted the captain casually and wandered to a ledge and sat down, first making sure that the seat was clean. "It's going to be a fine day, *neh?*"

"Yes. How did you sleep?"

"I didn't, Anjin-san. Kiri and I chatted the last of the night away and I saw the dawn come. I love dawns. You?"

"My rest was disturbed but—"

"Oh, so sorry."

"I'm fine now—really. You're leaving now?"

"Yes, but I'll be back at noon to collect Kiri-san and the Lady Sazuko." She turned her face away from the captain and said in Latin, "Thou. Remember the Inn of the Blossoms?"

"Assuredly. How could I forget?"

"If there is a delay . . . tonight will be thus—as perfect and as peace-filled."

"Ah, that that could be possible. But I would prefer thee safely on thy way."

Mariko continued in Portuguese. "Now I must go, Anjin-san. You will please excuse me?"

"I'll take you to the gate."

"No, please. Watch me from here. You and the *captain* can watch from here, *neh?*"

"Of course," Blackthorne said at once, understanding. "Go with God."

"And thee."

He stayed on the parapet. While he waited sunlight fell into the forecourt, thrusting the shadows away. Mariko appeared below. He saw her greet Kiri and Yoshinaka and they chatted together, no enemy Grays near them. Then they bowed. She looked up at him, shading her eyes, and waved gaily. He waved back. The gates were pushed aside and, with Chimmoko a few discreet paces behind her, she walked out, accompanied by her escort of ten Browns. The gates swung closed once more. For a moment she was lost from view. When she reappeared, fifty Grays from the swarm outside their walls had surrounded them as a further honor guard. The cortege marched away down the sunless avenue. He watched her until she had turned the far corner. She never looked back.

"Go eat now, Captain," he said.

"Yes, of course, Anjin-san."

Blackthorne went to his own quarters and ate rice, pickled vegetables, and broiled chunks of fish, followed by early fruit from Kyushu—crisp small apples, apricots, and hard-fleshed plums. He savored the tart fruit and the cha.

"More, Anjin-san?" the servant asked.

"No, thank you." He offered fruits to his guards and they were accepted gratefully, and when they had finished, he went back to the sunny battlements again. He would have liked to examine the priming of his concealed pistol but he thought it better not to draw attention to it. He had checked it once in the night as best he could under the sheet, under the mosquito net. But without actually seeing, he could not be sure of the tamping or the flint.

There's nothing more you can do, he thought. You're a puppet. Be patient, Anjin-san, your watch ends at noon.

He gauged the height of the sun. It will be the beginning of the two-hour period of the Snake. After the Snake comes the Horse. In the middle of the Horse is high noon.

Temple bells throughout the castle and the city tolled the beginning of the Snake and he was pleased with his accuracy. He noticed a small stone on the battlement floor. He went forward and picked up the stone and placed it carefully on a ledge of an embrasure in the sun, then leaned back once more, propping his feet comfortably, and stared at it.

Grays were watching his every movement. The captain frowned. After a while he said, "Anjin-san, what's the significance of the stone?"

"Please?"

"The stone. Why stone, Anjin-san?"

"Ah! I watch stone grow."

"Oh so sorry, I understand," the captain replied apologetically. "Please excuse me for disturbing you."

Blackthorne laughed to himself, and turned his gaze back to the stone. "Grow, you bastard," he said. But as much as he cursed it, ordered it, or cajoled it, it would not grow.

Do you really expect to see a rock growing? he asked himself. No, of course not, but it passes the time and promotes tranquillity. You can't have enough *wa*. *Neh?*

Eeeeee, where's the next attack coming from? There's no defense against an assassin if the assassin is prepared to die. Is there?

*   *   *

Rodrigues checked the priming of a musket he had taken at random from the rack beside the stern cannon. He found the flint was worn and pitted and therefore dangerous. Without a word he hurled the musket at the gunner. The man just managed to catch it before the stock smashed into his face.

"Madonna, Senhor Pilot," the man cried out, "there's no need—"

"Listen, you motherless turd, the next time I find anything wrong with a musket or cannon during your watch, you'll get fifty lashes and lose three months' pay. Bosun!"

"Yes, Pilot?" Pesaro, the bosun, heaved his bulk nearer and scowled at the young gunner.

"Turn out both watches! Check every musket and cannon, everything. Only God knows when we'll need 'em."

"I'll see to it, Pilot." The bosun shoved his face at the gunner. "I'll piss in your grog tonight, Gomez, for all the extra work an' you'd better lap it up with a smile. Get to work!"

There were eight small cannon amidships on the main deck, four port and four starboard and a bowchaser. Enough to beat off any uncannoned pirates but not enough to press home an attack. The small frigate was two-masted, called the *Santa Luz.*

Rodrigues waited until the crews were at their tasks, then turned away and leaned on the gunwale. The castle glinted dully in the sun, the color of old pewter, except for the donjon with its blue and white walls and golden roofs. He spat into the water and watched the spittle to see if it would reach the jetty pilings as he hoped or go into the sea. It went into the sea. "Piss," he muttered to no one, wishing he had his own frigate, the *Santa Maria,* under him right now. God-cursed bad luck that she's in Macao just when we need her.

"What's amiss, Captain-General?" he had asked a few days ago at Nagasaki when he'd been routed out of his warm bed in his house that overlooked the city and the harbor.

"I've got to get to Osaka at once," Ferriera had said, plumed and arrogant as any bantam cock, even at this early hour. "An urgent signal's arrived from dell'Aqua."

"What's the matter now?"

"He didn't say—just that it was vital to the future of the Black Ship."

"Madonna, what mischief're they up to now? What's vital? Our ship's as sound as any ship afloat, her bottom's clean and rigging perfect. Trade's better than we ever imagined and on time, the monkeys're behaving themselves, pigarse Harima's confident, and—" He stopped as the thought exploded in his brain. *"The Ingeles! He's put to sea?"*

"I don't know. But if he has . . ."

Rodrigues had stared out of the great harbor mouth, half expecting to see *Erasmus* already blockading there, showing the hated flag of England, waiting there like a rabid dog against the day they'd have to put to sea for Macao and home. "Jesu, Mother of God and all saints, let that not happen!"

"What's our fastest way? Lorcha?"

"The *Santa Luz,* Captain-General. We can sail within the hour. Listen, the Ingeles can do nothing without men. Don't forget—"

"Madonna, you listen, he can speak their jibberish now, eh? Why can't he use monkeys, eh? There are enough Jappo pirates to crew him twenty times over."

"Yes, but not gunners and not sailors as he'd need 'em—he's not got time to train Jappos. By next year maybe, but not against us."

"Why in the name of the Madonna and the saints the priests gave him one of their dictionaries I'll never know. Meddling bastards! They must've been possessed by the Devil! It's almost as though the Ingeles is protected by the Devil!"

"I tell you he's just clever!"

"There are many who've been here for twenty years and can't speak a word of Jappo gibberish, but the Ingeles can, eh? I tell you he's given his soul to Satan, and in return for the black arts he's protected. How else do you explain it? How many years've you been trying to talk their tongue and you even live with one? *Leche,* he could easily use Jappo pirates."

"No, Captain-General, he's got to get men from here and we're waiting for him and you've already put anyone suspect in irons."

"With twenty thousand cruzados in silver and a promise about the Black Ship, he can buy all the men he needs, including the jailers and the God-cursed jail around them. *Cabron!* Perhaps he can buy you, too."

"Watch your tongue!"

"You're the motherless, milkless Spaniard, Rodrigues! It's your fault he's alive, you're responsible. Twice you let him escape!" The Captain-General had squared up to him in rage. "You should have killed him when he was in your power."

"Perhaps, but that's froth on my life's wake," Rodrigues had said bitterly. "I went to kill him when I could."

"Did you?"

"I've told you twenty times. Have you no ears! Or is Spanish dung as usual in your ears as well as in your mouth!" His hand had reached for his pistol and the Captain-General had drawn his sword, then the frightened Japanese girl was between them. "Prees, Rod-san, no angers—no quarre', prees! Christian, prees!"

The blinding rage had fallen off both of them, and Ferriera had said, "I tell you before God, the Ingeles must be Devil-spawned—I almost killed you, and you me, Rodrigues. I see it clearly now. He's put a spell on all of us—particularly you!"

Now in the sunshine at Osaka, Rodrigues reached for the crucifix he wore around his neck and he prayed a desperate prayer that he be protected from all warlocks and his immortal soul kept safe from Satan.

Isn't the Captain-General right, isn't that the only answer, he reasoned again, filled with foreboding. The Ingeles' life is charmed. Now he's an intimate of the archfiend Toranaga, now he's got his ship back and the money back and *wako,* in spite of everything, and he does speak like one of them and that's impossible so quickly even with the dictionary, but he did get the dictionary and priceless help. Jesus God and Madonna, take the Evil Eye off me!

"Why'd you give the Ingeles the dictionary, Father?" he had asked Alvito at Mishima. "Surely you should have delayed that?"

"Yes, Rodrigues," Father Alvito had told him confidently, "and I needn't have gone out of my way to help him. But I'm convinced there's a chance of converting him. I'm so sure. Toranaga's finished now. . . . It's just one man and a soul. I have to try to save him."

Priests, Rodrigues thought. *Leche* on all priests. But not on dell'Aqua and Alvito. Oh, Madonna, I apologize for all my evil thoughts about him and the Father Alvito. Forgive me and bury the Ingeles somehow before I have him in my sights. I do not wish to kill him because of my Holy Oath, even though, before Thee, I know he must die quickly. . . .

The duty helmsman turned the hourglass and rang eight bells. It was high noon.

CHAPTER 55

MARIKO was walking up the crowded sunlit avenue toward the gates in the cul-de-sac. Behind her was a body guard of ten Browns. She wore a pale green kimono and white gloves and a wide-brimmed dark green traveling hat tied with a golden net scarf under her chin, and she shaded herself with an iridescent sun shade. The gates swung open and stayed open.

It was very quiet in the avenue. Grays lined both sides and all the battlements. She could see the Anjin-san on their own battlements, Yabu beside him, and in the courtyard the waiting column with Kiri there, and the Lady Sazuko. All the Browns were in full ceremonials in the forecourt under Yoshinaka, except twenty who stood on the battlements with Blackthorne and two to each window overlooking the forecourt.

Unlike the Grays, none of the Browns had armor or carried bows. Swords were their only weapons.

Many women, samurai women, were also watching, some from the windows of other fortified houses that lined the avenue, and some from battlements. Others stood in the avenue among the Grays, a few gaily dressed children with them. All of the women carried sunshades though some wore samurai swords, as was their right if they wished.

Kiyama was near the gate with half a hundred of his own men, not Grays.

"Good day, Sire," Mariko said to him, and bowed. He bowed back and she passed through the archway.

"Hello, Kiri-chan, Sazuko-chan. How pretty you both look! Is everything ready?"

"Yes," they replied with false cheeriness.

"Good." Mariko got into her open palanquin and sat, stiff-backed. "Yoshinaka-san! Please begin."

At once the captain limped forward and shouted the orders. Twenty Browns formed up as a vanguard and moved off. Porters picked up Mariko's curtainless palanquin and followed the Browns through the gate, Kiri's and Lady Sazuko's close behind, the young girl holding her infant in her arms.

When Mariko's palanquin came into the sunlight outside their walls, a captain of Grays stepped forward between the vanguard and the palanquin, and stood directly in her way. The vanguard stopped abruptly. So did the porters.

"Please excuse me," he said to Yoshinaka, "but may I see your papers?"

"So sorry, Captain, but we require none," Yoshinaka replied in the great silence.

"So sorry, but the Lord General Ishido, Governor of the Castle, Captain of the Heir's Bodyguard, with the approval of the Regents, has instituted orders throughout the castle which have to be complied with."

Mariko said formally, "I am Toda Mariko-noh-Buntaro and I have been ordered by my liege Lord, Lord Toranaga, to escort his ladies to meet him. Kindly let us pass."

"I would be glad to, Lady," the samurai said proudly, planting his feet, "but without papers *our* liege Lord says no one may leave Osaka Castle. Please excuse me."

Mariko said, "Captain, what is your name please?"

"Sumiyori Danzenji, Lady, Captain of the Fourth Legion, and my line is as ancient as your own."

"So sorry, Captain Sumiyori, but if you do not move out of the way I will order you killed."

"You will not pass without papers!"

"Please kill him, Yoshinaka-san."

Yoshinaka leaped forward without hesitation, his sword a whirling arc, and he struck at the off-balanced Gray. His blade bit deep into the man's side and was jerked out instantly, and the second more vicious blow took off the man's head, which rolled in the dust a little way before stopping.

Yoshinaka wiped his blade clean and sheathed it. "Lead on!" he ordered the vanguard. "Hurry up!" The vanguard formed up again and, their footsteps echoing, they marched off. Then, out of nowhere, an arrow thwanged into Yoshinaka's chest. The cortege lurched to a stop. Yoshinaka tore at the shaft silently for a moment, then his eyes glazed and he toppled.

A small moan broke from Kiri's lips. A puff of air tugged at the ends of Mariko's gossamer scarf. Somewhere in the avenue a child's cries were hushed. Everyone waited breathlessly.

"Miyai Kazuko-san," Mariko called out. "Please take charge."

Kazuko was young and tall and very proud, clean-shaven, with deep-set cheeks, and he came from the grouped Browns near Kiyama who stood beside the gateway. He strode past Kiri's and Sazuko's litters to stand beside Mariko's and bowed formally. "Yes, Lady. Thank you."

"You!" He shouted to the men ahead. "Move off!" Taut, some fearful, all frantic, they obeyed and once again the procession began, Kazuko walking beside Mariko's litter. Then, a hundred paces in front of them, twenty Grays moved out of the massed ranks of samurai and stood silently across the roadway. The twenty Browns closed the gap. Then someone faltered and the vanguard trickled to a stop.

"Clear them out of the way!" Kazuko shouted.

Immediately one Brown leaped forward, and the others followed and the killing became swift and cruel. Each time a Gray fell, another would calmly walk out of the waiting pack to join his comrades in the killing. It was always fair, always evenly matched, man to man, now fifteen against fifteen, now eight against eight, a few wounded Grays thrashing in the dirt, now three Browns against two Grays and another Gray strode out, and soon it was one to one, the last Brown, blood-stained and wounded, already victor of four duels. The last Gray dispatched him easily and stood alone among the bodies and looked at Miyai Kazuko.

All the Browns were dead. Four Grays lay wounded, eighteen dead.

Kazuko went forward, unsheathing his sword in the enormous hush.

"Wait," Mariko said. "Please wait, Kazuko-san."

He stopped but kept his eyes on the Gray, spoiling for the fight. Mariko stepped out of the palanquin and went back to Kiyama. "Lord Kiyama, I formally ask you please to order those men out of the way."

"So sorry, Toda-sama, the castle orders must be obeyed. The orders are legal. But if you wish, I will call a meeting of the Regents and ask for a ruling."

"I am samurai. My orders are clear, in keeping with *bushido* and sanctified by our code. They must be obeyed and overrule legally any man-made ordinance. The law may upset reason, but reason may not overthrow the law. If I am not permitted to obey, I will not be able to live with that shame."

"I will call an immediate meeting."

"Please excuse me, Sire, what you do is your own business. I am concerned only with my Lord's orders and my own shame." She turned and went quietly back to the head of the column. "Kazuko-san! I order you please to lead us out of the castle!"

He walked forward. "I am Miyai Kazuko, Captain, from the line Serata, of Lord Toranaga's Third Army. Please get out of the way."

"I am Biwa Jiro, Captain, of Lord General Ishido's garrison. My life is worthless, even so you will not pass," the Gray said.

With the sudden roaring battle cry of "Toranagaaaaaa!" Kazuko rushed to the fray. Their swords shrieked as the blows and counterblows were parried. The two men circled. The Gray was good, very good, and so was Kazuko. Their swords rang out in the clash. No one else moved.

Kazuko conquered but he was very badly wounded and he stood over his enemy, swaying on his feet, and with his good arm he shook his sword at the sky, bellowing his war cry, gloating in his victory, "Toranagaaaaa!" There was no cheering at his conquest. All knew it would be unseemly in the ritual that enveloped them now.

Kazuko forced one foot forward, then another, and, stumbling, he ordered, "Follow me!" his voice crumbling.

No one saw where the arrows came from but they slaughtered him. And the mood of the Browns changed from fatalism to ferocity at this insult to Kazuko's manhood. He was already dying fast, and would have fallen soon, alone, still doing his duty, still leading them out of the castle. Another officer of the Browns ran forward with twenty men to form a new vanguard and the rest swarmed around Mariko, Kiri, and Lady Sazuko.

"Forward!" the officer snarled.

He stepped off and the twenty silent samurai came after him. Like somnambulists, the porters picked up their burdens and stumbled around the bodies. Then ahead, a hundred paces, twenty more Grays with an officer moved silently from the hundreds that waited. The porters stopped. The vanguard quickened their pace.

"Halt!" The officers bowed curtly to each other and said their lineage.

"Please get out of the way."

"Please show me your papers."

This time the Browns hurtled forward at once with cries of "Toranagaaaaaa!" to be answered by "Yaemoooooonn!" and the carnage began. And each time a Gray fell, another would walk out coolly until all the Browns were dead.

The last Gray wiped his blade clean and sheathed it and stood alone barring the path. Another officer came forward with twenty Browns from the company behind the litters.

"Wait," Mariko ordered. Ashen, she stepped out of her palanquin and put her sunshade aside and picked up Yoshinaka's sword, unsheathed it, and walked forward alone.

"You know who I am. Please get out of my way."

"I am Kojima Harutomo, Sixth Legion, Captain. Please excuse me, you may not pass, Lady," the Gray said with pride.

She darted forward but her blow was contained. The Gray backed and stayed on the defensive though he could have killed her without effort. He retreated slowly down the avenue, she following, but he made her work for every foot. Hesitantly the column started after her. Again she tried to bring the Gray to battle, cutting, thrusting, always attacking fiercely, but the samurai slid away, avoiding her blows, holding her off, not attacking, allowing her to exhaust herself. But he did this gravely, with dignity, giving her every courtesy, giving her the honor that was her due. She attacked again but he parried the onslaught that would have overcome a lesser swordsman, and backed another pace. The perspiration streamed from her. A Brown started forward to help but his officer quietly ordered him to stop, knowing that no one could interefere. Samurai on both sides waited for the signal, craving the release to kill.

In the crowd, a child was hiding his eyes in his mother's skirts. Gently she pried him away and knelt. "Please watch, my son," she murmured. "You are samurai."

Mariko knew she could not last much longer. She was panting now from her exertions and could feel the brooding malevolence surrounding her. Then ahead and all around, Grays began to ease away from the walls and the noose around the column quickly tightened. A few Grays walked out to try to surround her and she stopped advancing, knowing that she could, too easily, be trapped and disarmed and captured, which would destroy everything at once. Now Browns moved up to assist her and the rest took positions around the litters. The mood in the avenue was ominous now, every man committed, the sweet smell of blood in their nostrils. The column was strung out from the gateway and Mariko saw how easy it would be for the Grays to cut them all off if they wished and leave them stranded in the roadway.

"Wait!" she called out. Everyone stopped. She half-bowed to her assailant, then, head high, turned her back on him and walked back to Kiri. "So . . . so sorry, but it is not possible to fight through these men, at the moment," she said, her chest heaving. "We . . . we must go back for a moment." Sweat was streaking her face as she went down the line of men. When she came to Kiyama, she stopped and bowed. "Those men have prevented me from doing my duty, from obeying my liege Lord. I cannot live with shame, Sire. I will commit seppuku at sunset. I formally beg you to be my second."

"No. You will not do this."

Her eyes flashed and her voice rang out fearlessly. "Unless we are allowed to obey our liege Lord, *as is our right,* I will commit seppuku at sunset!"

She bowed and walked toward the gateway. Kiyama bowed to her and his men did likewise. Then all in the avenue and on the battlements and at the windows, all bowed to her in homage. She went through the archway, across the forecourt into the garden. Her footsteps took her to the secluded, rustic little cha house. She went inside and, once alone, she wept silently for all the men who had died.

CHAPTER 56

B EAUTIFUL, *neh?*" Yabu pointed below at the dead.
"Please?" Blackthorne asked.
"It was a poem. You understand 'poem'?"
"I understand word, yes."
"It was a poem, Anjin-san. Don't you see that?"

If Blackthorne had had the words he would have said, No, Yabu-san. But I did see clearly for the first time what was really in her mind, the moment she gave the first order and Yoshinaka killed the first man. Poem? It was a hideous, courageous, senseless, extraordinary ritual, where death's as formalized and inevitable as at a Spanish Inquisition, and all the deaths merely a prelude to Mariko's. Everyone's committed now, Yabu-san—you, me, the castle, Kiri, Ochiba, Ishido, everyone—all because *she* decided to do what she decided was necessary. And when did she decide? Long ago, *neh?* Or, more correctly, Toranaga made the decision for her.

"So sorry, Yabu-san, not words enough," he said.

Yabu hardly heard him. There was quiet on the battlements and in the avenue, everyone as motionless as statues. Then the avenue began to come alive, voices hushed, movements subdued, the sun beating down, as each came out of his trance.

Yabu sighed, filled with melancholia. "It was a poem, Anjin-san," he said again, and left the battlements.

When Mariko had picked up the sword and gone forward alone, Blackthorne had wanted to leap down into the arena and rush at her assailant to protect her, to blow the Gray's head off before she was slain. But, with everyone, he had done nothing. Not because he was afraid. He was no longer afraid to die. Her courage had shown him the uselessness of that fear and he had come to terms with himself long ago, on that night in the village with the knife.

I meant to drive the knife into my heart that night.

Since then my fear of death's been obliterated, just as she said it would be. 'Only by living at the edge of death can you understand the indescribable joy of life.' I don't remember Omi stopping the thrust, only feeling reborn when I awoke the next dawn.

His eyes watched the dead, there in the avenue. I could have killed that Gray for her, he thought, and perhaps another and perhaps several, but there would always have been another and my death would not have tipped the scale a fraction. I'm not afraid to die, he told himself. I'm only appalled there's nothing I can do to protect her.

Grays were picking up bodies now, Browns and Grays treated with equal dignity. Other Grays were streaming away, Kiyama and his men among them, women and children and maids all leaving, dust in the avenue rising under their feet. He smelled the acrid, slightly fetid death-smell mixed with the salt breeze, his mind eclipsed by her, the courage of her, the indefinable warmth that her fearless courage had given him. He looked up at the sun and measured it. Six hours to sunset.

He headed for the steps that led below.

"Anjin-san? Where go please?"

He turned back, his own Grays forgotten. The captain was staring at him. "Ah, so sorry. Go there!" He pointed to the forecourt.

The captain of Grays thought a moment, then reluctantly agreed. "All right. Please you follow me."

In the forecourt Blackthorne felt the Browns' hostility towards his Grays. Yabu was standing beside the gates watching the men come back. Kiri and the Lady Sazuko were fanning themselves, a wet nurse feeding the infant. They were sitting on hastily laid out coverlets and cushions that had been placed in the shade on a veranda. Porters were huddled to one side, squatting in a tight, frightened group around the baggage and pack horses. He headed for the garden but the guards shook their heads. "So sorry, this is out of bounds for the moment, Anjin-san."

"Yes, of course," he said, turning away. The avenue was clearing now, though five-hundred-odd Grays still stayed, settling themselves, squatting or sitting cross-legged in a wide semicircle, facing the gates. The last of the Browns stalked back under the arch.

Yabu called out, "Close the gates and bar them."

"Please excuse me, Yabu-san," the officer said, "but the Lady Toda said they were to be left open. We are to guard them against all men but the gates are to be left open."

"You're sure?"

The officer bridled. He was a neat, bent-faced man in his thirties with a jutting chin, mustached and bearded. "Please excuse me—of course I am sure."

"Thank you. I meant no offense, *neh?* Are you the senior officer here?"

"The Lady Toda honored me with her confidence, yes. Of course, you are senior to me."

"I am in command but you are in charge."

"Thank you, Yabu-san, but the Lady Toda commands here. You are senior officer. I would be honored to be second to you. If you will permit it."

Yabu said balefully, "It's permitted, Captain. I know very well who commands us here. Your name, please?"

"Sumiyori Tabito."

"Wasn't the first Gray 'Sumiyori' also?"

"Yes, Yabu-san. He was my cousin."

"When you are ready, Captain Sumiyori, please call a meeting of all officers."

"Certainly, Sire. With *her* permission."

Both men looked away as a lady hobbled into the forecourt. She was elderly and samurai and leaned painfully on a cane. Her hair was white but her back was straight and she went over to Kiritsubo, her maid holding a sunshade over her.

"Ah, Kiritsubo-san," she said formally. "I am Maeda Etsu, Lord Maeda's mother, and I share the Lady Toda's views. With her permission I would like to have the honor of waiting with her."

"Please sit down, you're welcome," Kiri said. A maid brought another cushion and both maids helped the old lady to sit.

"Ah, that's better—so much better," Lady Etsu said, biting back a groan of pain. "It's my joints, they get worse every day. Ah, that's a relief. Thank you."

"Would you like cha?"

"First cha, then saké, Kiritsubo-san. Lots of saké. Such excitement's thirsty work, *neh?*"

Other samurai women were detaching themselves from the crowds that were leaving and they came back through the ranks of the Grays into the pleasing shade. A few hesitated and three changed their minds, but soon there were fourteen ladies on the veranda and two had brought children with them.

"Please excuse me, but I am Achiko, Kiyama Nagamasa's wife, and I want to go home too," a young girl was saying timidly, holding her little son's hand. "I want to go home to my husband. May I beg permission to wait too, please?"

"But Lord Kiyama will be furious with you, Lady, if you stay here."

"Oh, so sorry, Kiritsubo-san, but Grandfather hardly knows me. I'm only wife to a very minor grandson. I'm sure he won't care and I haven't seen my husband for months and I don't care either what they say. Our Lady's right, *neh?*"

"Quite right, Achiko-san," old Lady Etsu said, firmly taking charge. "Of course you're welcome, child. Come and sit by me. What's your son's name? What a fine boy you've got."

The ladies chorused their agreement and another boy who was four piped up plaintively, "Please, I'm a fine boy too, *neh?*" Someone laughed and all the ladies joined in.

"You are indeed," Lady Etsu said and laughed again.

Kiri wiped away a tear. "There, that's better, I was getting far too serious, *neh?*" She chuckled. "Ah, Ladies, I'm so honored to be allowed to greet you in *her* name. You must all be starving, and you're so right, Lady Etsu, this is all thirsty work!" She sent maids for food and drink and introduced those ladies who needed introducing, admiring a fine kimono here or a special parasol there. Soon they were all chattering and happy and fluttering like so many parakeets.

"How can a man understand women?" Sumiyori said blankly.

"Impossible!" Yabu agreed.

"One moment they're frightened and in tears and the next. . . . When I saw the Lady Mariko pick up Yoshinaka's sword, I thought I'd die with pride."

"Yes. Pity that last Gray was so good. I'd like to have seen her kill. She'd have killed a lesser man."

Sumiyori rubbed his beard where the drying sweat irritated him. "What would you have done if you'd been him?"

"I would have killed her then charged the Browns. Too much blood there. It was all I could do not to slaughter all the Grays near me on the battlement."

"It's good to kill sometimes. Very good. Sometimes it's very special and then it's better than a lusting woman."

There was a burst of laughter from the ladies as the two little boys started strutting up and down importantly, their scarlet kimonos dancing. "It's good to have children here again. I thank all gods mine are at Yedo."

"Yes." Yabu was looking at the women speculatively.

"I was wondering the same," Sumiyori said quietly.

"What's your answer?"

"There's only one now. If Ishido lets us go, fine. If Lady Mariko's seppuku is wasted, then . . . then we'll help those ladies into the Void and begin the killing. They won't want to live."

Yabu said, "Some may want to."

"You can decide that later, Yabu-san. It would benefit our Master if they all commit seppuku here. And the children."

"Yes."

"Afterward we'll man the walls and then open the gates at dawn. We'll fight till noon. That'll be enough. Then those who are left will come back inside and set fire to this part of the castle. If I'm alive then I'd be honored if you'd be my second."

"Of course."

Sumiyori grinned. "This's going to blow the realm apart, *neh?* All this killing and her seppuku. It'll spread like fire—it'll eat up Osaka, *neh?* You think that'll delay the Exalted? Would that be our Master's plan?"

"I don't know. Listen, Sumiyori-san, I'm going back to my house for a moment. Fetch me as soon as the Lady comes back." He walked over to Blackthorne, who sat musing on the main steps. "Listen, Anjin-san," Yabu said furtively, "perhaps I have a plan. Secret, *neh?* 'Secret,' you understand?"

"Yes. Understand." Bells tolled the hour change. The time rang in all their heads, the beginning of the Hour of the Monkey, six bells of the afternoon watch, three of the clock. Many turned to the sun and, without thinking, measured it.

"What plan?" Blackthorne asked.

"Talk later. Stay close by. Say nothing, understand?"

"Yes."

Yabu stalked out of the gateway with ten Browns. Twenty Grays attached themselves and together they went down the avenue. His guest house was not far around the first corner. The Grays stayed outside his gate. Yabu motioned the Browns to wait in the garden and he went inside alone.

"It's impossible, Lord General," Ochiba said. "You can't let a lady of her rank commit seppuku. So sorry, but you've been trapped."

"I agree," Lord Kiyama said forcefully.

"With due humility, Lady," Ishido said, "whatever I said or didn't say, doesn't matter an *eta*'s turd to her. She'd already decided, at least Toranaga had."

"Of course he's behind it," Kiyama said as Ochiba recoiled at Ishido's uncouthness. "So sorry, but he's outsmarted you again. Even so you can't let her commit seppuku!"

"Why?"

"Please, so sorry, Lord General, we must keep our voices down," Ochiba said. They were waiting in the spacious antechamber of Lady Yodoko's sick room in the inner quarters of the donjon, on the second floor. "I'm sure it wasn't your fault and there must be a solution."

Kiyama said quietly, "You cannot let her continue her plan, Lord General, because that will inflame every lady in the castle."

Ishido glared at him. "You seem to forget a couple were shot by mistake and that didn't create a ripple among them—except to stop any more escape attempts."

"That was a terrible mistake, Lord General," Ochiba said.

"I agree. But we are at war, Toranaga's not yet in our hands, and until he's dead you and the Heir are in total danger."

"So sorry—I'm not worried for myself—only for my son," Ochiba said. "They've all got to be back here in eighteen days. I advise you to let them all go."

"That's an unnecessary risk. So sorry. We're not certain she means it."

"She does," Kiyama told him contemptuously, despising Ishido's truculent presence in the opulent, overrich quarters that reminded him so clearly of the Taikō, his friend and revered patron. "She's *samurai.*"

"Yes," Ochiba said. "So sorry, but I agree with Lord Kiyama. Mariko-san will do what she says. Then there's that hag Etsu! Those Maedas are a proud lot, *neh?*"

Ishido walked over to the window and looked out. "They can all burn as far as I'm concerned. The Toda woman's Christian, *neh?* Isn't suicide against her religion? A special sin?"

"Yes, but she'll have a second—so it won't be suicide."

"And if she doesn't?"

"What?"

"Say she's disarmed and has no second?"

"How could you do that?"

"Capture her. Confine her with carefully chosen maids until Toranaga's across our borders." Ishido smiled. "Then she can do what she wants. I'd be even delighted to help her."

"How could you capture her?" Kiyama asked. "She'd always have time to seppku, or to use her knife."

"Perhaps. But say she could be captured and disarmed and held for a few days. Isn't the 'few days' vital? Isn't that why she's insisting on going today, before Toranaga crosses over our borders and castrates himself?"

"Could it be done?" Lady Ochiba asked.

"Possibly," Ishido said.

Kiyama pondered this. "In eighteen days Toranaga must be here. He could delay at the border for at the most another four days. She would have to be held for a week at the most."

"Or forever," Ochiba said. "Toranaga's delayed so much, I sometimes think he'll never come."

"He has to by the twenty-second day," Ishido said. "Ah, Lady, that was a brilliant, brilliant idea."

"Surely that was your idea, Lord General?" Ochiba's voice was soothing though she was very tired from a sleepless night. "What about Lord Sudara and my sister? Are they with Toranaga now?"

"No, Lady. Not yet. They will be brought here by sea."

"She is not to be touched," Ochiba said. "Or her child."

"Her child is direct heir of Toranaga, who's heir to the Minowaras. My duty to *the* Heir, Lady, makes me point this out again."

"My sister is not to be touched. Nor is her son."

"As you wish."

She said to Kiyama, "Sire, how good a Christian is Mariko-san?"

"Pure," Kiyama replied at once. "You mean about suicide being a sin? I—I think she would honor that or her eternal soul is forfeit, Lady. But I don't know if . . ."

"Then there's a simpler solution," Ishido said without thinking. "Command the High Priest of the Christians to order her to stop harassing the legal rulers of the Empire!"

"He doesn't have the power," Kiyama said. Then he added, his voice even more barbed, "That's political interference—something you've always been bitterly against, and rightly."

"It seems Christians interfere only when it suits them," Ishido said. "It was only a suggestion."

The inner door opened and a doctor stood there. His face was grave and exhaustion aged him. "So sorry, Lady, she's asking for you."

"Is she dying?" Ishido asked.

"She's near death, Lord General, yes, but when, I don't know."

Ochiba hurried across the large room and through the inner door, her blue kimono clinging, the skirts swaying gracefully. Both men watched her. The door closed. For a moment the two men avoided each other's eyes, then Kiyama said, "You really think Lady Toda could be captured?"

"Yes," Ishido told him, watching the door.

* * *

Ochiba crossed this even more opulent room and knelt beside the futons. Maids and doctors surrounded them. Sunlight seeped through the bamboo shutters and skittered off the gold and red inlaid carvings of the beams and posts and doors. Yodoko's bed was surrounded by decorative inlaid screens. She seemed to be sleeping, her bloodless face settled within the hood of her Buddhist robe, her wrists thin, the veins knotted, and Ochiba thought how sad it was to become old. Age was so unfair to women. Not to men, only to women. Gods protect me from old age, she prayed. Buddha protect my son and put him safely into power and protect me only as long as I'm capable of protecting him and helping him.

She took Yodoko's hand, honoring her. "Lady?"

"O-chan?" Yodoko whispered, using her nickname.

"Yes, Lady?"

"Ah, how pretty you are, so pretty, you always were." The hand went up and caressed the beautiful hair and Ochiba was not offended by the touch but pleased as always, liking her greatly. "So young and beautiful and sweet-smelling. How lucky the Taikō was."

"Are you in pain, Lady? Can I get you something?"

"Nothing—nothing, I just wanted to talk." The old eyes were sunken but had lost none of their shrewdness. "Send the others away."

Ochiba motioned them to leave and when they were alone she said, "Yes, Lady?"

"Listen, my darling, make the Lord General let her go."

"He can't, Lady, or all the other hostages will leave and we'll lose strength. The Regents all agree," Ochiba said.

"Regents!" Yodoko said with a thread of scorn. "Do *you* agree?"

"Yes, Lady, and last night you said she was not to go."

"Now you must let her go or others will follow her seppuku and you and our son will be befouled because of Ishido's mistake."

"The Lord General's loyal, Lady. Toranaga isn't, so sorry."

"You can trust Lord Toranaga—not him."

Ochiba shook her head. "So sorry, but I'm convinced Toranaga's committed to become Shōgun and will destroy our son."

"You're wrong. He's said it a thousand times. Other *daimyos* are trying to use him for their own ambitions. They always have. Toranaga was the Taikō's favorite. Toranaga has always honored the Heir. Toranaga's Minowara. Don't be swayed by Ishido, or the Regents. They've their own *karmas,* their own secrets, O-chan. Why not let her go? It's all so simple. Forbid her the sea, then she can always be delayed somewhere inside our borders. She's still in your General's net, and Kiri and all the others, *neh?* She'll be surrounded by Grays. Think like the Taikō would or like Toranaga would. You and our son are being pulled into . . ." The words trailed off and her eyelids began to flutter. The old lady gathered her remaining strength and continued, "Mariko-san could never object to guards. I know she means what she says. Let her go."

"Of course that was considered, Lady," Ochiba said, her voice gentle and patient, "but outside the castle Toranaga has secret bands of samurai, hidden in and around Osaka, we don't know how many, and he has allies—we're not sure who. She might escape. Once she goes, all the others would follow her at once and we'd lose a great security. You agreed, Yodoko-chan, don't you remember? So sorry, but I asked you last night, don't you remember?"

"Yes, I remember, child," Yodoko said, her mind wandering. "Oh, how I wish the Lord Taikō were here again to guide you." The old lady's breathing was becoming labored.

"Can I give you some cha or saké?"

"Cha, yes please, some cha."

She helped the old one to drink. "Thank you, child." The voice was feebler now, the strain of conversation speeding the dying. "Listen, child, you must trust Toranaga. Marry him, barter with him for the succession."

"No—no," Ochiba said, shocked.

"Yaemon could rule after him, then the fruit of your new marriage after our son. The sons of our son will honorably swear eternal fidelity to this new Toranaga line."

"Toranaga's always hated the Taikō. You know that, Lady. Toranaga is the source of all the trouble. For years, *neh?* Him!"

"And you? What about your pride, child?"

"He's the enemy, our enemy."

"You've two enemies, child. Your pride and the need to have a man to compare to our husband. Please be patient with me, you're young and beautiful and fruitful and deserve a husband. Toranaga's worthy of you, you of him. Toranaga is the only chance Yaemon has."

"No, he's the enemy."

"He was our husband's greatest friend and most loyal vassal. Without . . . without Toranaga . . . don't you see . . . it was Toranaga's help . . . don't you see? You could manage . . . manage him. . . ."

"So sorry, but I hate him—he disgusts me, Yodoko-chan."

"Many women. . . . What was I saying? Oh yes, many women marry men who disgust them. Praise be to Buddha I never had to suffer that. . . ." The old woman smiled briefly. Then she sighed. It was a long, serious sigh and went on for too long and Ochiba thought the end had come. But the eyes opened a little and a tiny smile appeared again. *"Neh?"*

"Yes."

"Will you. Please?"

"I will think about it."

The old fingers tried to tighten. "I beg you, promise me you'll marry Toranaga and I will go to Buddha knowing that the Taikō's line will live forever, like his name . . . his name will live for. . . ."

The tears ran freely down Ochiba's face as she cradled the listless hand.

Later the eyes trembled and the old woman whispered, "You must let Akechi Mariko go. Don't . . . don't let her reap vengeance on us for what the Taikō did . . . did to . . . to her . . . to her father. . . ."

Ochiba was caught unaware. "What?"

There was no answer. Later Yodoko began mumbling, ". . . Dear Yaemon, hello, my darling son, how . . . you're such a fine boy, but you've so many enemies, so foolish so. . . . Aren't you just an illusion too, isn't . . . ."

A spasm racked her. Ochiba held onto the hand and caressed it. *"Namu Amida Butsu,"* she whispered in homage.

There was another spasm, then the old woman said clearly, "Forgive me, O-chan."

"There is nothing to forgive, Lady."

"So much to forgive. . . ." The voice became fainter, and the light began to fade from her face. "Listen . . . prom—promise about . . . about Toranaga, Ochiba-sama . . . important . . . please . . . you can trust him. . . ." The old eyes were beseeching her, willing her.

Ochiba did not want to obey yet knew that she should obey. Her mind was unsettled by what had been said about Akechi Mariko, and still resounded with the Taikō's words, repeated ten thousand times, "You can trust Yodoko-sama, O-chan. She's the Wise One—never forget it. She's right most times and you can always trust her with your life, and my son's life and mine. . . ."

Ochiba conceded. "I prom—" She stopped abruptly.

The light of Yodoko-sama flickered a final time and went out.

"Namu Amida Butsu." Ochiba touched the hand to her lips, and she bowed and laid the hand back on the coverlet and closed the eyes, thinking about the Taikō's death, the only other death she had witnessed so closely. That time Lady Yodoko had closed the eyes as was a wife's privilege and it had been in this same room, Toranaga waiting outside, as Ishido and Kiyama were now outside, continuing a vigil that had begun the day before.

"But why send for Toranaga, Lord?" she had asked. "You should rest."

"I'll rest when I'm dead, O-chan," the Taikō had said. "I must settle the succession. Finally. While I've the strength."

So Toranaga had arrived, strong, vital, exuding power. The four of them were alone then, Ochiba, Yodoko, Toranaga and Nakamura, the Taikō, the Lord of Japan lying on his deathbed, all of them waiting for the orders that would be obeyed.

"So, Tora-san," the Taikō had said, welcoming him with the nickname Goroda had given Toranaga long ago, the deep-set eyes peering up out of the tiny, withered simian face that was set on an equally tiny body—a body that had had the strength of steel until a few months ago when the wasting began. "I'm dying. From nothing, into nothing, but you'll be alive and my son's helpless."

"Not helpless, Sire. All the *daimyos* will honor your son as they honor you."

The Taikō laughed. "Yes, they will. Today. While I'm alive—ah yes! But how do I make sure Yaemon will rule after me?"

"Appoint a Council of Regents, Sire."

"Regents!" the Taikō said scornfully. "Perhaps I should make you my heir and let you judge if Yaemon's worthy to follow you."

"I would not be worthy to do that. Your son should follow you."

"Yes, and Goroda's sons should have followed him."

"No. They broke the peace."

"And you stamped them out on my orders."

"You held the Emperor's mandate. They rebelled against your lawful mandate, Sire. Give me your orders now, and I will obey them."

"That's why I called you here."

Then the Taikō said, "It's a rare thing to have a son at fifty-seven and a foul thing to die at sixty-three—if he's an only son and you've got no kin and you're Lord of Japan. *Neh?"*

"Yes," Toranaga said.

"Perhaps it would've been better if I'd never had a son, then I could pass the realm on to you as we agreed. You've more sons than a Portugee's got lice."

"Karma."

The Taikō had laughed and a string of spittle, flecked with blood, seeped out of his mouth. With great care Yodoko wiped the spittle away and he smiled up at his wife. "Thank you, Yo-chan, thank you." Then the eyes turned onto Ochiba herself and Ochiba had smiled back but his eyes weren't smiling now, just probing, wondering, pondering the never-dared-to-be-asked question that she was sure was forever in his mind: Is Yaemon really my son?

"Karma, O-chan. *Neh?"* It was gently said but Ochiba's fear that he would ask her directly racked her and tears glistened in her eyes.

"No need for tears, O-chan. Life's only a dream within a dream," the old man said. He lay for a moment musing, then he peered at Toranaga again, and with a sudden, unexpected warmth for which he was famous, said, "Eeeeee, old friend, what a life we've had, *neh?* All the battles? Fighting side by side—together unbeatable. We did the impossible, *neh?* Together we humbled the mighty and spat on their upturned arses while they groveled for more. Us—we did it, a peasant and a Minowara!" The old man chuckled. "Listen, a few more years and I'd have smashed the Garlic Eaters properly. Then with Korean legions and our own Japanese legions, a sharp thrust up to Peking and me on the Dragon Throne of China. Then I'd have given you Japan, which you want, and I'd have what I want." The voice was strong, belying the inner fragility. "A peasant can straddle the Dragon Throne with face and honor—not like here. *Neh?*"

"China and Japan are different, yes, Sire."

"Yes. They're wise in China. There the first of a dynasty's always a peasant or the son of a peasant, and the throne's always taken by force with bloody hands. No hereditary caste there—isn't that China's strength?" Again the laugh. "Force and bloody hands and peasant—that's me. *Neh?*"

"Yes. But you're also samurai. You changed the rules here. You're first of a dynasty."

"I always liked you, Tora-san." The old man sipped cha contentedly. "Yes— think of it, me on the Dragon Throne—think of that! Emperor of China, Yodoko Empress, and after her Ochiba the Fair, and after me Yaemon, and China and Japan forever joined together as they should be. Ah, it would have been so easy! Then with our legions and Chinese hordes I'd stab northwest and south and, like tenth-class whores, the empires of all the earth would lie panting in the dirt, their legs spread wide for us to take what we want. We're unbeatable—you and I were unbeatable—Japanese're unbeatable, of course we are—we know the whole point of life. *Neh?*"

"Yes."

The eyes glittered strangely. "What is it?"

"Duty, discipline, and death," Toranaga replied.

Again a chuckle, the old man seemingly tinier than ever, more wizened than ever, and then, with an equal suddenness for which he was also famous, all the warmth left him. "The Regents?" he asked, his voice venomous and firm. "Whom would you pick?"

"Lords Kiyama, Ishido, Onoshi, Toda Hiro-matsu, and Sugiyama."

The Taikō's face twisted with a malicious grin. "You are the cleverest man in the Empire—after me! Explain to my ladies why you'd pick those five."

"Because they all hate each other, but combined, they can rule effectively and stamp out any opposition."

"Even you?"

"No, not me, Sire." Then Toranaga looked at Ochiba and spoke directly to her. "For Yaemon to inherit power you have to weather another nine years. To do that, above all else, you must maintain the Taikō's peace. I pick Kiyama because he's the chief Christian *daimyo,* a great general, and a most loyal vassal. Next, Sugiyama because he's the richest *daimyo* in the land, his family ancient, he heartily detests Christians, and has the most to gain if Yaemon gets power. Onoshi because he detests Kiyama, offsets his power, is also Christian, but a leper who grasps at life, will live for twenty years and hates all the others with a monstrous violence, particularly Ishido. Ishido because he'll be sniffing out plots—because he's a peasant, detests hereditary samurai, and is violently opposed to Christians. Toda Hiro-matsu because he's honest, obedient, and faithful, as constant as the sun and like the sudden best sword of a master sword-smith. He should be president of the Council."

"And you?"

"I will commit seppuku with my eldest son, Noboru. My son Sudara's married to the Lady Ochiba's sister, so he's no threat, could never be a threat. He could inherit the Kwanto, if it pleases you, providing he swears perpetual allegiance to your house."

No one was surprised that Toranaga had offered to do what was obviously in the Taikō's mind, for Toranaga alone among the *daimyos* was the real threat. Then she had heard her husband say, "O-chan, what is your counsel?"

"Everything that the Lord Toranaga has said, Sire," she had answered at once, "except that you should order my sister divorced from Sudara who should commit seppuku. The Lord Noboru should be Lord Toranaga's heir and should inherit the two provinces of Musashi and Shimoosa, and the rest of the Kwanto should go to your heir, Yaemon. I counsel this to be ordered today."

"Yodoko-sama?"

To her astonishment, Yodoko had said, "Ah, Tokichi, you know I adore you with all my heart and the O-chan, and Yaemon as my own son. I say make Toranaga sole Regent."

"What?"

"If you order him to die, I think you kill our son. Only Lord Toranaga has skill enough, prestige enough, cunning enough to inherit *now*. Put Yaemon into his keeping until he's of age. Order Lord Toranaga to adopt our son formally. Let Yaemon be coached by Lord Toranaga and inherit *after* Toranaga."

"No—this must not be done," Ochiba had protested.

"What do you say to that, Tora-san?" the Taikō asked.

"With humility I must refuse, Sire. I cannot accept that and beg to be allowed to commit seppuku and go before you."

"You will be sole Regent."

"I've never refused to obey you since we made our bargain. But this order I refuse."

Ochiba remembered how she had tried to will the Taikō to let Toranaga obliterate himself as she knew the Taikō had already decided. But the Taikō had changed his mind and, at length, had accepted part of what Yodoko had advised, and made the compromise that Toranaga would be a Regent and President of the Regents. Toranaga had sworn eternal faith to Yaemon but now he was still spinning the web that embroiled them all, like this crisis Mariko had precipitated. "I know it was on his orders," Ochiba muttered, and now Lady Yodoko had wanted her to submit to him totally.

Marry Toranaga? Buddha protect me from that shame, from having to welcome him and feel his weight and his spurting life.

Shame?

Ochiba, what is the truth? she asked herself. The truth is that you wanted him once—before the Taikō, *neh?* Even during, *neh?* Many times in your secret heart. *Neh?* The Wise One was right again about pride being your enemy and about needing a man, a husband. Why not accept Ishido? He honors you and wants you and he's going to win. He would be easy to manage. *Neh?* No, not that uncouth bog trotter! Oh, I know the filthy rumors spread by enemies—filthy impertinence! I swear I'd rather lie with my maids and put my faith in a *harigata* for another thousand lifetimes than abuse my Lord's memory with Ishido. Be honest, Ochiba. Consider Toranaga. Don't you really hate him just because he might have seen you on that dream day?

It had been more than six years ago in Kyushu when she and her ladies had been out hawking with the Taikō and Toranaga. Their party was spread over a wide area and she had been galloping after one of her falcons, separated from the others. She was in the hills in a wood and she'd suddenly come upon this peasant gathering berries beside the lonely path. Her first weakling son had been dead almost two years and there were no more stirrings in her womb, though she had tried every position or trick or regimen, every superstition or potion or prayer, desperate to satisfy her lord's obsession for an heir.

The meeting with the peasant had been so sudden. He gawked up at her as though she were a *kami* and she at him because he was the image of the Taikō, small and monkeylike, but he had youth.

Her mind had shouted that here was the gift from the gods she had prayed for, and she had dismounted and taken his hand and together they went a few paces into the wood and she became like a bitch in heat.

Everything had had a dreamlike quality to it, the frenzy and lust and coarseness, lying on the earth, and even today she could still fell his gushing liquid fire, his sweet breath, his hands clutching her marvelously. Then she had felt his full dead weight and abruptly his breath became putrid and everything about him vile except the wetness, so she had pushed him off. He had wanted more but she had hit him and cursed him and told him to thank the gods she did not turn him into a tree for his insolence, and the poor superstitious fool had cowered on his knees begging her forgiveness—of course she was a *kami,* why else would such beauty squirm in the dirt for such as him?

Weakly she had climbed into the saddle and walked the horse away, dazed, the man and the clearing soon lost, half wondering if all had been a dream and the peasant a real *kami,* praying that he was a *kami,* his essence god-given, that it would make another son for the glory of her Lord and give him the peace that he deserved. Then, just the other side of the wood, Toranaga had been waiting for her. Had he seen her, she wondered in panic.

"I was worried about you, Lady," he had said.

"I'm—I'm perfectly all right, thank you."

"But your kimono's all torn—there's bracken down your back and in your hair. . . ."

"My horse threw me—it's nothing." Then she had challenged him to a race home to prove that nothing was wrong, and had set off like the wild wind, her back still smarting from the brambles that sweet oils soon soothed and, the same night, she had pillowed with her Lord and Master and, nine months later, she had birthed Yaemon to his eternal joy. And hers.

"Of course our husband is Yaemon's father," Ochiba said with complete certainty to the husk of Yodoko. "He fathered both my children—the other was a dream."

Why delude yourself? It was not a dream, she thought. It happened. That man was not a *kami.* You rutted with a peasant in the dirt to sire a son *you* needed as desperately as the Taikō to bind him to you. He would have taken another consort, *neh?*

What about your first-born?

"*Karma,*" Ochiba said, dismissing that latent agony as well.

"Drink this, child," Yodoko had said to her when she was sixteen, a year after she had become the Taikō's formal consort. And she had drunk the strange, warming herb cha and felt so sleepy and the next evening when she awoke again she remembered only strange erotic dreams and bizarre colors and an eerie timelessness. Yodoko had been there when she awakened, as when she had gone to sleep, so considerate, and as worried over the harmony of their lord as she had been. Nine months later she had birthed, the first of all the Taikō's women to do so. But the child was sickly and that child died in infancy.

Karma, she thought.

Nothing had ever been said between herself and Yodoko. About what had happened, or what might have happened, during that vast deep sleep. Nothing, except "Forgive me. . . ." a few moments ago, and, "There is nothing to forgive."

You're blameless, Yodoko-sama, and nothing occurred, no secret act or anything. And if there did, rest in peace, Old One, now that secret lies buried with you. Her eyes were on the empty face, so frail and pathetic now, just as the Taikō had been so frail and pathetic at his ending, *his* question also never asked. *Karma* that he died, she thought dispassionately. If he'd lived another ten years I'd be Empress of China, but now . . . now I'm alone.

"Strange that you died before I could promise, Lady," she said, the smell of incense and the musk of death surrounding her. "I would have promised but you died before I promised. Is that my *karma* too? Do I obey a request and an unspoken promise? What should I do?"

My son, my son, I feel so helpless.

Then she remembered something the Wise One had said: 'Think like the Taikō would—or Toranaga would.'

Ochiba felt new strength pour through her. She sat back in the stillness and, coldly, began to obey.

In a sudden hush, Chimmoko came out of the small gates to the garden and walked over to Blackthorne and bowed. "Anjin-san, please excuse me, my Mistress wishes to see you. If you will wait a moment I will escort you."

"All right. Thank you." Blackthorne got up, still deep in his reverie and his overpowering sense of doom. The shadows were long now. Already part of the forecourt was sunless. The Grays prepared to move with him.

Chimmoko went over to Sumiyori. "Please excuse me, Captain, but my Lady asks you to please prepare everything."

"Where does she want it done?"

The maid pointed at the space in front of the arch. "There, Sire."

Sumiyori was startled. "It's to be public? Not in private with just a few witnesses? She's doing it for all to see?"

"Yes."

"But, well . . . if it's to be here. . . . Her—her . . . what about her second?"

"She believes the Lord Kiyama will honor her."

"And if he doesn't?"

"I don't know, Captain. She—she hasn't told me." Chimmoko bowed and walked across to the veranda to bow again. "Kiritsubo-san, my Mistress says, so sorry, she'll return shortly."

"Is she all right?"

"Oh yes," Chimmoko said proudly.

Kiri and the others were composed now. When they had heard what had been said to the captain they had been equally perturbed. "Does she know other ladies are waiting to greet her?"

"Oh yes, Kiritsubo-san. I—I was watching, and I told her. She said that she's so honored by their presence and she will thank them in person soon. Please excuse me."

They all watched her go back to the gates and beckon Blackthorne. The Grays began to follow but Chimmoko shook her head and said her mistress had not bidden them. The captain allowed Blackthorne to leave.

It was like a different world beyond the garden gates, verdant and serene, the sun on the treetops, birds chattering and insects foraging, the brook falling sweetly into the lily pond. But he could not shake off his gloom.

Chimmoko stopped and pointed at the little *cha-no-yu* house. He went forward alone. He slipped his feet out of his thongs and walked up the three steps. He had to stoop, almost to his knees, to go through the tiny screened doorway. Then he was inside.

"Thou," she said.

"Thou," he said.

She was kneeling, facing the doorway, freshly made up, lips crimson, immaculately coiffured, wearing a fresh kimono of somber blue edged with green, with a lighter green obi and a thin green ribbon for her hair.

"Thou art beautiful."

"And thou." A tentative smile. "So sorry it was necessary for thee to watch."

"It was my duty."

"Not duty," she said. "I did not expect—or plan for—so much killing."

"*Karma.*" Blackthorne pulled himself out of his trance and stopped talking Latin. "You've been planning all this for a long time—your suicide. *Neh?*"

"My life's never been my own, Anjin-san. It's always belonged to my liege Lord, and, after him, to my Master. That's our law."

"It's a bad law."

"Yes. And no." She looked up from the mats. "Are we going to quarrel about things that may not be changed?"

"No. Please excuse me."

"I love thee," she said in Latin.

"Yes. I know that now. And I love thee. But death is thy aim, Mariko-san."

"Thou art wrong, my darling. The life of my Master is my aim. And thy life. And truly, Madonna forgive me, or bless me for it, there are times when thy life is more important."

"There's no escape now. For anyone."

"Be patient. The sun has not yet set."

"I have no confidence in this sun, Mariko-san." He reached out and touched her face. "*Gomen nasai.*"

"I promised thee tonight would be like the Inn of the Blossoms. Be patient. I know Ishido and Ochiba and the others."

"*Que va* on the others," he said in Portuguese, his mood changing. "You mean that you're gambling that Toranaga knows what he's doing. *Neh?*"

"*Que va* on thy ill humor," she replied gently. "This day's too short."

"Sorry—you're right again. Today's no time for ill humor." He watched her. Her face was streaked with shadow bars cast by the sun through the bamboo slats. The shadows climbed and vanished as the sun sank behind a battlement.

"What can I do to help thee?" he asked.

"Believe there is a tomorrow."

For a moment he caught a glimpse of her terror. His arms went out to her and he held her and the waiting was no longer terrible.

Footsteps approached.

"Yes, Chimmoko?"

"It's time, Mistress."

"Is everything ready?"

"Yes, Mistress."

"Wait for me beside the lily pond." The footsteps went away. Mariko turned back to Blackthorne and kissed him gently.

"I love thee," she said.

"I love thee," he said.

She bowed to him and went through the doorway. He followed.

Mariko stopped by the lily pond and undid her obi and let it fall. Chimmoko helped her out of her blue kimono. Beneath it Mariko wore the most brilliant white kimono and obi Blackthorne had ever seen. It was a formal death kimono. She untied the green ribbon from her hair and cast it aside, then, completely in white, she walked on and did not look at Blackthorne.

Beyond the garden, all the Browns were drawn up in a formal three-sided square around eight tatamis that had been laid out in the center of the main gateway. Yabu and Kiri and the rest of the ladies were seated in a line in the place of honor, facing south. In the avenue the Grays were also drawn up ceremoniously, and mingling with them were other samurai and samurai women. At a sign from Sumiyori everyone bowed. She bowed to them. Four samurai came forward and spread a crimson coverlet over the tatamis.

Mariko walked to Kiritsubo and greeted her and Sazuko and all the ladies. They returned her bow and spoke the most formal of greetings. Blackthorne waited at the gates. He watched her leave the ladies and go to the crimson square and kneel in the center, in front of the tiny white cushion. Her right hand brought out her stiletto dagger from her white obi and she placed it on the cushion in front of her. Chimmoko came forward and, kneeling too, offered her a small, pure white blanket and cord. Mariko arranged the skirts of her kimono perfectly, the maid helping her, then tied the blanket around her waist with the cord. Blackthorne knew this was to prevent her skirts being blooded and disarranged by her death throes.

Then, serene and prepared, Mariko looked up at the castle donjon. Sun still illuminated the upper story, glittering off the golden tiles. Rapidly the flaming light was mounting the spire. Then it disappeared.

She looked so tiny sitting there motionless, a splash of white on the square of crimson.

Already the avenue was dark and servants were lighting flares. When they finished, they fled as quickly and as silently as they had arrived.

She reached forward and touched the knife and straightened it. Then she gazed once more through the gateway to the far end of the avenue but it was as still and as empty as it had ever been. She looked back at the knife.

"Kasigi Yabu-sama!"

"Yes, Toda-sama?"

"It seems Lord Kiyama has declined to assist me. Please, I would be honored if you would be my second."

"It is my honor," Yabu said. He bowed and got to his feet and stood behind her, to her left. His sword sang as it slid from its scabbard. He set his feet firmly and with two hands raised the sword. "I am ready, Lady," he said.

"Please wait until I have made the second cut."

Her eyes were on the knife. With her right hand she made the sign of the cross over her breast, then leaned forward and took up the knife without trembling and touched it to her lips as though to taste the polished steel. Then she changed her grip and held the knife firmly with her right hand under the left side of her throat. At that moment flares rounded the far end of the avenue. A retinue approached. Ishido was at their head.

She did not move the knife.

Yabu was still a coiled spring, concentrated on the mark. "Lady," he said, "do you wait or are you continuing? I wish to be perfect for you."

Mariko forced herself back from the brink. "I—we wait . . . we . . . I . . . ." Her hand lowered the knife. It was shaking now. As slowly, Yabu released himself. His sword hissed back into the scabbard and he wiped his hands on his sides.

Ishido stood at the gateway. "It's not sunset yet, Lady. The sun's still on the horizon. Are you so keen to die?"

"No, Lord General. Just to obey my Lord. . . ." She held her hands together to stop their shaking.

A rumble of anger went through the Browns at Ishido's arrogant rudeness and Yabu readied to leap at him, but stopped as Ishido said loudly, "The Lady Ochiba begged the Regents on behalf of the Heir to make an exception in your case. We agreed to her request. Here are permits for you to leave at dawn tomorrow." He shoved them into the hands of Sumiyori, who was nearby.

"Sire?" Mariko said, without understanding, her voice threadbare.

"You are free to leave. At dawn."

"And—and Kiritsubo-san and the Lady Sazuko?"

"Isn't that also part of your 'duty?' Their permits are there also."

Mariko tried to concentrate. "And . . . and her son?"

"Him too, Lady," Ishido's scornful laugh echoed. "And all your men."

Yabu stammered, "Everyone has safe conducts?"

"Yes, Kasigi Yabu-san," Ishido said. "You're senior officer, *neh?* Please go at once to my secretary. He is completing all your passes, though why honored guests would wish to leave I don't know. It's hardly worth it for seventeen days. *Neh?*"

"And me, Lord General?" old Lady Etsu asked weakly, daring to test the totality of Mariko's victory, her heart racing and painful. "May—may I please leave also?"

"Of course, Lady Maeda. Why should we keep anyone against her will? Are we jailers? Of course not! If the Heir's welcome is so offensive that you wish to leave, then leave, though how you intend to travel four hundred *ri* home and another four hundred *ri* here in seventeen days I don't understand."

"Please ex—excuse me, the—the Heir's welcome isn't offen—"

Ishido interrupted icily. "If you wish to leave, apply for a permit in the normal way. It'll take a day or so but we'll see you safely on your way." He addressed the others: "Any ladies may apply, any samurai. I've said before, it's stupid to leave for seventeen days, it's insulting to flout the Heir's welcome, the Lady Ochiba's welcome, and the Regents' welcome . . ."—his ruthless gaze went back to Mariko—"or to pressure them with threats of seppuku, which for a lady should be done in private and not as an arrogant public spectacle. *Neh?* I don't seek the death of women, only enemies of the Heir, but if women are openly his enemy, then I'll soon spit on their corpses too."

Ishido turned on his heel, shouted an order at the Grays, and walked off. At once captains echoed the order and all the Grays began to form up and move off from the gateway, except for a token few who stayed in honor of the Browns.

"Lady," Yabu said huskily, wiping his damp hands again, a bitter vomit taste in his mouth from the lack of fulfillment, "Lady, it's over now. You've . . . you've won. You've won."

"Yes—yes," she said. Her strengthless hands sought the knots of the white cord. Chimmoko went forward and undid the knots and took away the white blanket, then stepped away from the crimson square. Everyone watched Mariko, waiting to see if she could walk away.

Mariko was trying to grope to her feet. She failed. She tried a second time. Again she failed. Impulsively Kiri moved to help her but Yabu shook his head and said, "No, it's her privilege," so Kiri sat back, hardly breathing.

Blackthorne, beside the gates, was still turmoiled by his boundless joy at her reprieve and he remembered how his own will had been stretched that night of his near-seppuku, when he had had to get up as a man and walk home as a man unsupported, and became samurai. And he watched her, despising the need for this courage, yet understanding it, even honoring it.

He saw her hands go to the crimson again, and again she pushed and this time Mariko forced herself upright. She wavered and almost fell, then her feet moved and slowly she tottered across the crimson and reeled helplessly toward the main door. Blackthorne decided that she had done enough, had endured enough, had proved enough, so he came forward and caught her in his arms and lifted her up just as her mind left her.

For a moment he stood there in the arena alone, proud that he was alone and that *he* had decided. She lay like a broken doll in his arms. Then he carried her inside and no one moved or barred his path.

CHAPTER 57

THE attack on the Browns' stronghold began in the darkest reaches of the night, two or three hours before dawn. The first wave of ten *ninja*—the infamous Stealthy Ones—came over the roofs of the battlements opposite, now unguarded by Grays. They threw cloth-covered grappling hooks on ropes over to the other roof and swung across the chasm like so many spiders. They wore tight-fitting clothes of black and black tabi and black masks. Their hands and faces were also blackened. These men were lightly armed with chain knives and shuriken—small, star-shaped, needle-sharp, poison-tipped throwing barbs and discs that were the size of a man's palm. On their backs were slung haversacks and short thin poles.

Ninja were mercenaries. They were artists in stealth, specialists in the disreputable—in espionage, infiltration, and sudden death.

The ten men landed noiselessly. They re-coiled the grapples, and four of them hooked the grapples again onto a projection and immediately swung downward to a veranda twenty feet below. Once they had reached it, as noiselessly, their comrades unhooked the grapples, dropped them down, and moved across the tiles to infiltrate another area.

A tile cracked under one man's foot and they all froze. In the forecourt, three stories and sixty feet below, Sumiyori stopped on his rounds and looked up. His eyes squinted into the darkness. He waited without moving, his mouth open a fraction to improve his hearing, his eyes sweeping slowly. The roof with the *ninja* was in shadow, the moon faint, the stars heavy in the thick humid air. The men stayed absolutely still, even their breathing controlled and imperceptible, seemingly as inanimate as the tiles upon which they stood.

Sumiyori made another circuit with his eyes and with his ears, and then another, and, still not sure, he walked out into the forecourt to see more clearly. Now the four *ninja* on the veranda were also within his field of vision but they were as motionless as the others and he did not notice them either.

"Hey," he called to the guards on the gateway, the doors tight barred now, "you see anything—hear anything?"

"No, Captain," the alert sentries said. "The roof tiles are always chattering, shifting a bit—it's the damp or the heat, perhaps."

Sumiyori said to one of them, "Go up there and have a look. Better still, tell the top-floor guards to make a search just in case."

The soldier hurried off. Sumiyori stared up again, then half shrugged and, reassured, continued his patrol. The other samurai went back to their posts, watching outward.

On the rooftop and on the veranda the *ninja* waited in their frozen positions. Not even their eyes moved. They were schooled to remain immobile for hours if need be—just one part of their perpetual training. Then the leader motioned to them and at once they again moved to the attack. Their grapples and ropes took them quietly to another veranda where they could slide through the narrow windows in the granite walls. Below this top floor, all other windows—defense positions for bowmen—were so narrow that they could not be entered from outside. At another signal the two groups entered simultaneously.

Both rooms were in darkness, with ten Browns sleeping in neat lines. They were put to death quickly and almost noiselessly, a single knife thrust in the throat for most, the raiders' trained senses taking them unerringly to their targets, and in moments the last of the Browns was thrashing desperately, his warning shout garroted just as it had begun. Then, the rooms secured, the doors secured, the leader took out a flint and tinder and lit a candle and carried it, cupped carefully, to the window and signaled three times into the night. Behind him his men were making doubly sure that every Brown was quite dead. The leader repeated the signal, then came away from the window and motioned with his hand, speaking to them in sign language with his fingers.

At once the raiders undid their haversacks and readied their attack weapons—short, sickle-shaped, double-edged knives with a chain attached to the haft, weighted at the end of the chain, and shuriken and throwing knives. At another order, selected men unsheathed the short poles. These were telescoped spears and blow pipes that sprang into full length with startling speed. And as each man completed his preparations he knelt, settled himself facing the door, and, seemingly without conscious effort, became totally motionless. Now the last man was ready. The leader blew out the candle.

When the city bells toned the middle of the Hour of the Tiger—four of the clock, an hour before dawn—the second wave of *ninja* infiltrated. Twenty slid silently out of a large, disused culvert that once had serviced the rivulets of the garden. All these men wore swords. Like so many shadows, they swarmed into position among the shrubs and bushes, became motionless and almost invisible. At the same time another group of twenty came up from the ground by ropes and grapples to attack the battlement that overlooked the forecourt and garden.

Two Browns were on the battlements, carefully watching the empty roofs across the avenue. Then one of the Browns glanced around and saw the grapples behind them and he began to point in alarm. His comrade opened his mouth to shout a warning when the first *ninja* made the embrasure and, with a whipping snap of his wrist, sent a barbed shuriken whirling into this samurai's face and mouth, hideously strangling the shout, and hurled himself forward at the other samurai, his outstretched hand now a lethal weapon, the thumb and forefinger extended, and he stabbed for the jugular. The impact paralyzed the samurai, another vicious blow broke his neck with a dry crack, and the *ninja* jumped at the first agonized samurai, who was clawing at the barbs embedded deeply in his mouth and face, the poison already working.

With a final supreme effort, the dying samurai ripped out his short stabbing sword and struck. His blow sliced deep and the *ninja* gasped but this did not stop the rush and his hand slammed into the Brown's throat, snapping the man's head back and dislocating his spine. The samurai was dead on his feet.

The *ninja* was bleeding badly but he made no sound and still held onto the dead Brown, lowering him carefully to the stone flags, sinking to his knees beside him. All the *ninja* had climbed up the ropes now and stood on the battlement. They bypassed their wounded comrade until the battlement was secured. The wounded man was still on his knees beside the dead Browns, holding his side. The leader examined the wound. Blood was spurting in a steady stream. He shook his head and spoke with his fingers and the man nodded and dragged himself painfully to a corner, the blood leaving a wide trail. He made himself comfortable, leaning against the stone, and took out a shuriken. He scratched the back of one hand several times with the poison barbs, then found his stiletto, put the point at the base of his throat and, two-handed, with all his strength, he thrust upward.

The leader made sure this man was dead then went back to the fortified door that led inside. He opened it cautiously. At that moment they heard footsteps approaching and at once melted back into ambush position.

In the corridor of this, the west wing, Sumiyori was approaching with ten Browns. He dropped two off near the battlement door and, not stopping, walked on. These two reliefs went out on to the battlement as Sumiyori turned the far corner and went down a flight of circular steps. At the bottom was another checkpoint and the two tired samurai bowed and were replaced.

"Pick up the others and go back to your quarters. You'll be wakened at dawn," Sumiyori said.

"Yes, Captain."

The two samurai walked back up the steps, glad to be off duty. Sumiyori continued on down the next corridor, replacing sentries. At length he stopped outside a door and knocked, the last two guards with him.

"Yabu-san?"

"Yes?" The voice was sleepy.

"So sorry, it's the change of the guard."

"Ah, thank you. Please come in."

Sumiyori opened the door but warily stayed on the threshold. Yabu was touseled, propped in the coverlets on one elbow, his other hand on his sword. When he was sure it was Sumiyori he relaxed and yawned. "Anything new, Captain?"

Sumiyori relaxed also and shook his head, came in and closed the door. The room was large and neat and another bed of futons was laid and turned back invitingly. Arrow slit windows overlooked the avenue and city, a sheer drop of thirty feet below. "Everything's quiet. *She's* sleeping now. . . . At least her maid, Chimmoko, said she was." He went to the low bureau where an oil lamp sputtered and poured himself cold cha from a pot. Beside it was their pass, formally stamped, that Yabu had brought back from Ishido's office.

Yabu yawned again and stretched luxuriously. "The Anjin-san?"

"He was awake the last time I checked. That was at midnight. He asked me not to check again until just before dawn—something about his customs. I didn't understand clearly everything he said, but there's no harm, there's a very tight security everywhere, *neh?* Kiritsubo-san and the other ladies are quiet, though she's been up, Kiritsubo-san, most of the night."

Yabu got out of bed. He wore only a loincloth. "Doing what?"

"Just sitting at a window, staring out. Nothing to see out there. I suggested she'd better get some sleep. She thanked me politely and agreed and stayed where she was. Women, *neh?*"

Yabu flexed his shoulders and elbows and scratched vigorously to get his blood flowing. He began to dress. "She should rest. She's got a long way to go today."

Sumiyori set the cup down. "I think it's all a trick."

"What?"

"I don't think Ishido means it."

"We have signed permits. There they are. Every man's listed. You checked the names. How can he go back on a public commitment to us or to Lady Toda? Impossible, *neh?*"

"I don't know. Your pardon, Yabu-san, but I still think it's a trick."

Yabu knotted his sash slowly. "What kind of trick?"

"We'll be ambushed."

"Outside the castle?"

Sumiyori nodded. "Yes, that's what I think."

"He wouldn't dare."

"He'll dare. He'll ambush us or delay us. I can't see him letting *her* go, or Lady

Kiritsubo, or Lady Sazuko or the babe. Even old Lady Etsu and the others."

"No, you're wrong."

Sumiyori shook his head sadly. "I think it would've been better if she'd cut deep and you'd struck. This way nothing's resolved."

Yabu picked up his swords and stuck them in his belt. Yes, he was thinking, I agree with you. Nothing's resolved and she failed in her duty. You know it, I know it, and so does Ishido. Disgraceful! If she'd cut, then we would have all lived forever. As it is now . . . she came back from the brink and dishonored us and dishonored herself. *Shigata ga nai, neh?* Stupid woman!

But to Sumiyori he said, "I think you're wrong. She conquered Ishido. Lady Toda won. Ishido won't dare to ambush us. Go to sleep, I'll wake you at dawn."

Again Sumiyori shook his head. "No, thank you, Yabu-san, I think I'll go the rounds again." He went to a window and peered out. "Something's not right."

"Everything's fine. Get some—wait a moment! What was that? Did you hear something?"

Yabu came up to Sumiyori and pretended to search the darkness, listening intently, and then, without warning, he whipped out his short sword and with the same flashing, spontaneous movement, buried the blade into Sumiyori's back, clapping his other hand over the man's mouth to stop the shriek. The captain died instantly. Yabu held him carefully at arm's length with immense strength so that none of the blood stained him, and carried the body over to the futons, arranging it in a sleeping position. Then he pulled out his sword and began to clean it, furious that Sumiyori's intuition had forced the unplanned killing. Even so, Yabu thought, I can't have him prowling around now.

Earlier, when Yabu was returning from Ishido's office with their safe conduct pass, he had been waylaid privately by a samurai he had never seen before.

"Your co-operation's invited, Yabu-san."

"To what and by whom?"

"By someone you made an offer to yesterday."

"What offer?"

"In return for safe conducts for you and the Anjin-san, you'd see *she* was disarmed during the ambush on your journey. . . . Please don't touch your sword, Yabu-san, there are four archers waiting for an invitation!"

"How dare you challenge me? What ambush?" he had bluffed, feeling weak at the knees, for there was no doubt now that the man was Ishido's intermediary. Yesterday afternoon he had made the secret offer through his own intermediaries, in a desperate attempt to salvage something from the wreckage Mariko had caused to his plans for the Black Ship and the future. At the time he had known that it was a wild idea. It would have been difficult, if not impossible, to disarm her and stay alive, therefore fraught with danger to both sides, and when Ishido, through intermediaries, had turned it down he was not surprised.

"I know nothing of any ambush," he had blustered, wishing that Yuriko were there to help him out of the morass.

"Even so, you're invited to one, though not the way you planned it."

"Who are you?"

"In return you get Izu, the barbarian and his ship—the moment the chief enemy's head is in the dust. Providing, of course, she's captured alive and you stay in Osaka until *the day* and swear allegiance."

"Whose head?" Yabu had said, trying to get his brain working, realizing only now that Ishido had used the request for him to fetch the safe conducts merely as a ruse so the secret offer could be made safely and negotiated.

"Is it yes or no?" the samurai asked.

"Who are you and what are you talking about?" He had held up the scroll.

"Here's Lord Ishido's safe conduct. Not even the Lord General can cancel these after what's happened."

"That's what many say. But, so sorry, bullocks will shit gold dust before you or any are allowed to insult the Lord Yaemon. . . . Please take your hand away from your sword!"

"Then watch your tongue!"

"Of course, so sorry. You agree?"

"I'm overlord of Izu now, and promised Totomi and Suruga," Yabu had said, beginning to bargain. He knew that though he was trapped, as Mariko was trapped, so equally was Ishido trapped, because the dilemma Mariko had precipitated still existed.

"Yes, so you are," the samurai had said. "But I'm not permitted to negotiate. Those are the terms. Is it yes or no? . . ."

Yabu finished cleaning his sword and arranged the sheet over the seemingly sleeping figure of Sumiyori. Then he toweled the sweat off his face and hands, composed his rage, blew out the candle, and opened the door. The two Browns were waiting some paces down the corridor. They bowed.

"I'll wake you at dawn, Sumiyori-san," Yabu said to the darkness. Then, to one of the samurai, "You stand guard here. No one's to go in. No one! Make sure the captain's not disturbed—he needs rest."

"Yes, Sire."

The samurai took up his new post and Yabu strode off down the corridor with the other guard, went up a flight of steps to the main central section of this floor and crossed it, heading for the audience room and inner apartments that were in the east wing. Soon he came to the cul-de-sac corridor of the audience room. Guards bowed and allowed him to enter. Other samurai opened the door to the corridor and complex of private quarters. He knocked at a door.

"Anjin-san?" he said quietly.

There was no answer. He pulled the shoji open. The room was empty, the inner shoji ajar. He frowned, then motioned to his accompanying guard to wait, and hurried across the room into the dimly lit inner corridor. Chimmoko intercepted him, a knife in her hand. Her rumpled bed was in this passageway outside one of the rooms.

"Oh, so sorry, Sire, I was dozing," she said apologetically, lowering her knife. But she did not move out of his path.

"I was looking for the Anjin-san."

"He and my Mistress are talking, Sire, with Kiritsubo-san and the Lady Achiko."

"Please ask him if I could see him a moment."

"Certainly, Sire." Chimmoko politely motioned Yabu back into the other room, waited until he was there, and pulled the inner shoji closed. The guard in the main corridor watched inquisitively.

In a moment the shoji opened again and Blackthorne came in. He was dressed and wore a short sword.

"Good evening, Yabu-san," he said.

"So sorry to disturb you, Anjin-san. I just want see—make sure all right, understand?"

"Yes, thank you. No worry."

"Lady Toda all right? Not sick?"

"Fine now. Very tired but fine. Soon dawn, *neh?*"

Yabu nodded. "Yes. Just want make sure all right. Understand?"

"Yes. This afternoon you say 'plan,' Yabu-san. Remember? Please what secret plan?"

"No secret, Anjin-san," Yabu said, regretting that he had been so open at that time. "You misunderstood. Say only must have plan . . . very difficult escape Osaka, *neh?* Must escape or . . ." Yabu drew a knife across his throat. "Understand?"

"Yes. But now have pass, *neh?* Now safe go out Osaka. *Neh?*"

"Yes. Soon leave. On boat very good. Soon get men at Nagasaki. Understand?"

"Yes."

Very friendly, Yabu went away. Blackthorne closed the door after him and walked back to the inner passageway, leaving his inner door ajar. He passed Chimmoko and went into the other room. Mariko was propped in futons, appearing more diminutive than ever, more delicate and more beautiful. Kiri was kneeling on a cushion. Achiko was curled up asleep to one side.

"What did he want, Anjin-san?" Mariko said.

"Just to see we were all right."

Mariko translated for Kiri.

"Kiri says, did you ask him about the 'plan'?"

"Yes. But he shrugged the question off. Perhaps he changed his mind. I don't know. Perhaps I was mistaken but I thought this afternoon he had something planned, or was planning something."

"To betray us?"

"Of course. But I don't know how."

Mariko smiled at him. "Perhaps you were mistaken. We're safe now."

The young girl, Achiko, mumbled in her sleep and they glanced at her. She had asked to stay with Mariko, as had old Lady Etsu, who was sleeping soundly in an adjoining room. The other ladies had left at sunset to go to their own homes. All had sent formal requests for permission to depart at once. With the failing light, rumors had rushed through the castle that nearly one hundred and five would also apply tomorrow. Kiyama had sent for Achiko, his granddaughter-in-law, but she refused to leave Mariko. At once the *daimyo* had disowned her and demanded possession of the child. She had given up her child. Now the girl was in the midst of a nightmare but it passed and she slept peacefully again.

Mariko looked at Blackthorne. "It's so wonderful to be at peace, *neh?*"

"Yes," he said. Since she had awakened and found herself alive and not dead, her spirit had clung to his. For the first hour they had been alone, she lying in his arms.

"I'm so glad thou art alive, Mariko. I saw thee dead."

"I thought I was. I still cannot believe Ishido gave in. Never in twenty lifetimes. . . . Oh, how I love thy arms about me, and thy strength."

"I was thinking that this afternoon from the first moment of Yoshinaka's challenge I saw nothing but death—yours, mine, everyone's. I saw into your plan, so long in the making, *neh?*"

"Yes. Since the day of the earthquake, Anjin-san. Please forgive me but I didn't—I didn't want to frighten you. I was afraid you wouldn't understand. Yes, from that day I knew it was my *karma* to bring the hostages out of Osaka. Only I could do that for Lord Toranaga. And now it's done. But at what a cost, *neh?* Madonna forgive me."

Then Kiri had arrived and they had had to sit apart but that had not mattered to either of them. A smile or a look or word was enough.

Kiri went over to the slit windows. Out to sea were flecks of light from the inshore fishing boats. "Dawn soon," she said.

"Yes," Mariko said. "I'll get up now."

"Soon. Not yet, Mariko-sama," Kiri told her. "Please rest. You need to gather your strength."

"I wish Lord Toranaga was here."

"Yes."

"Have you prepared another message about . . . about our leaving?"

"Yes, Mariko-sama, another pigeon will leave with the dawn. Lord Toranaga will hear of your victory today," Kiri said. "He'll be so proud of you."

"I'm so glad he was right."

"Yes," Kiri said. "Please forgive me for doubting you and doubting him."

"In my secret heart I doubted him too. So sorry."

Kiri turned back to the window and looked out over the city. Toranaga's wrong, she wanted to shriek. We'll never leave Osaka, however much we pretend. It's our *karma* to stay—*his* karma *to lose.*

In the west wing Yabu stopped at the guardroom. The replacement sentries were ready. "I'm going to make a snap inspection."

"Yes, Sire."

"The rest of you wait for me here. You, come with me."

He went down the main staircase followed by a single guard. At the foot of the staircase in the main foyer were other guards, and outside was the forecourt and garden. A cursory look showed all in order. Then he came back into the fortress, and after a moment, changed direction. To his guard's surprise, he went down the steps into the servants' quarters. The servants dragged themselves out of sleep, hastily putting their heads onto the flagstones. Yabu hardly noticed them. He led the way deeper into the bowels of the fortress, down steps, along little-used arched corridors, the stone sides damp now and mildewed, though well lit. There were no guards here in the cellars for there was nothing to protect. Soon they began to climb again, nearing the outer walls.

Yabu halted suddenly. "What was that?"

The Brown samurai stopped, and listened, and died. Yabu cleaned his sword and pulled the crumpled body into a dark corner, then rushed for a hardly noticed, heavily barred, small iron door set into one of the walls that Ishido's intermediary had told him about. He fought back the rusted bolts. The last one clanged free. The door swung open. A draught of cool air from outside, then a spear stabbed for his throat and stopped just in time. Yabu didn't move, almost paralyzed. *Ninja* stared back at him from the inky darkness beyond the door, weapons poised.

Yabu held up a shaky hand and made a sign as he had been told to do. "I'm Kasigi Yabu," he said.

The black-garbed, hooded, almost invisible leader nodded but kept the spear ready for the lunge. He motioned to Yabu. Yabu obediently backed off a pace. Then, very warily, the leader walked into the center of the corridor. He was tall and heavyset, with wide flat eyes behind his mask. He saw the dead Brown and with a flick of his wrist he sent his spear flashing into the corpse, then retrieved it with the light chain attached to the end. Silently he re-coiled the chain, waiting, listening intently for any danger.

At length satisfied, he motioned at the darkness. Instantly twenty men poured out and rushed for the flight of steps, the long-forgotten back way to the floors above. These men carried assault tools. They were armed with chain knives, swords, and shuriken. And in the center of their black hoods was a red spot.

The leader did not watch them go, but kept his eyes on Yabu and began a slow finger count with his left hand. "One . . . two . . . three . . ." Yabu felt many men watching him from the passage beyond the door. He could see no one.

Now the red-spot attackers were going up the stairs two at a time, and at the top of this flight they stopped. A door barred their path. They waited a moment then cautiously tried to open it. It was stuck. A man with an assault tool, a short steel bar, hooked at one end and chiseled at the other, came forward and jimmied it open. Beyond was another mildewed passage and they hurried along it silently. At the next corner they stopped. The first man peered around, then beckoned the others into another corridor. At the far end a sliver of light shone through a spyhole in the heavy wooden paneling that covered this secret door. He put an eye to it. He could see the breadth of the audience chamber, two Browns and two Grays wearily on sentry duty, guarding the door to the complex of quarters. He looked around, nodded to the others. One of the men was still counting with his fingers, timed to the leader's count two floors below. All their eyes went to the count.

Below in the cellar, the leader's fingers still continued in tempo, ticking off the moments, his eyes never wavering from Yabu. Yabu was watching and waiting, the smell of his own fear-sweat dank in his nostrils. The fingers stopped and the leader's fist closed up sharply. He pointed down the corridor. Yabu nodded and turned and went back the way he had come, walking slowly. Behind him the inexorable count began again. "One . . . two . . . three . . ."

Yabu knew the terrible risk he was taking but he had had no alternative and he cursed Mariko once more for forcing him onto Ishido's side. Part of his bargain was that he had to open this secret door.

"What's behind the door?" he had asked supiciously.

"Friends. This is the sign and the password is to say your name."

"Then they kill me, *neh?*"

"No. You're too valuable, Yabu-san. You've got to make sure the infiltration is covered. . . ."

He had agreed but he had never bargained for *ninja,* the hated and feared semilegendary mercenaries who owed allegiance only to their secret, closely knit family units, who handed down their secrets only to blood kin—how to swim vast distances under water and scale almost smooth walls, how to make themselves invisible and stand for a day and a night without moving, and how to kill with their hands or feet or any and all weapons including poison, fire, and explosives. To *ninja,* violent death for pay was their only purpose in life.

Yabu managed to keep his pace measured as he walked away from the *ninja* leader along the corridor, his chest still hurting from the shock that the attack force was *ninja* and not *ronin.* Ishido must be mad, he told himself, all his senses teetering, expecting a spear or arrow or garrote any moment. Now he was almost at the corner. Then he turned it and, safe once more, he took to his heels and bounded up the stairs, three at a time. At the top, he raced down the arched corridor, then turned the corner heading toward the servants' quarters.

The leader's fingers still ticked off the moments, then the count stopped. He made a more urgent sign to the darkness, and rushed after Yabu. Twenty *ninja* followed him from the darkness and another fifteen took up defensive positions at both ends of the corridor to guard this escape route that led through a maze of forgotten cellars and passages honeycombing the castle to one of Ishido's secret bolt holes under the moat, thence to the city.

Yabu was running fast now and he stumbled in the passageway, just managing to keep his footing, and burst through the servants' quarters, scattering pots and pans and gourds and casks.

"*Ninjaaaaaa!*" he bellowed, which was not part of his agreement, but his own ruse to protect himself should he be betrayed. Hysterically the men and women scattered and took up the shout and tried to vanish under benches and tables as he raced across and out the other side, up more steps into one of the main corridors to meet the first of the Browns' guards, who already had out their swords.

"Sound the alarm!" Yabu shouted. "*Ninja*—there are *ninja* among the servants!"

One samurai fled for the main staircase, the second rushed forward bravely to stand alone at the top of the winding steps that led below, sword raised. Seeing him, the servants came to a halt, then, moaning with terror, blindly huddled into the stones, their arms over their heads. Yabu ran on toward the main doorway and through it to stand on the steps. "Sound the alarm! We're under attack!" he shouted as he had agreed to do, to signal the diversion outside which would cover the main attack through the secret door into the audience chamber, to kidnap Mariko and hurry her away before anyone was wiser.

Samurai on the gates and in the forecourt whirled around, not knowing where to guard, and at that moment the raiders in the garden swarmed out of their hiding places and engulfed the Browns outside. Yabu retreated into the foyer as other Browns came rushing down from the guardroom above to support the men outside.

A captain raced up to him. "What's going on?"

"*Ninja*—outside and among the servants. Where's Sumiyori?"

"I don't know—in his room."

Yabu leapt for the stairs as other men poured down. At that moment the first of the *ninja* from the cellars dashed past the servants to the attack. Barbed shuriken disposed of the lone defender, spears killed the servants. Then this force of raiders was in the main corridor, creating a violent shouting diversion, the milling frantic Browns not knowing where the next attack would spring from.

On the top floor the waiting *ninja* had ripped open their doors at the first alarm and rushed the last of the Browns who were hurrying below, killing them. With poison darts and shuriken, the *ninja* pressed their onslaught. The Browns were quickly overwhelmed, and the attackers jumped over the corpses to reach the main corridor on the floor below. A furious charge of Brown reinforcements was repulsed by the *ninja*, who whirled their weighted chains and cast them at the samurai, either strangling them or entangling their swords to make it easier to impale them with the double-edged knife. Shuriken flashed through the air and the Browns here were decimated. A few *ninja* were cut down but they crawled on like rabid animals and stopped attacking only when death took them completely.

In the garden the first rush of the defending reinforcements was easily thwarted as Browns poured from the main doorway. But another wave of Browns courageously mounted a second charge and swept the invaders back by sheer force of numbers. At a shouted order the raiders retreated, their jet-black clothes making them difficult targets. Exultantly the Browns rushed after them, into ambush, and were slaughtered.

The red-spot attackers were still lying in wait outside the audience room, their leader's eye to the spyhole. He could see the anxious Browns and Blackthorne's Grays, who were guarding the fortified door to the corridor, listening anxiously to the mounting holocaust below. The door opened and other guards, Browns and Grays, crowded the opening and then, no longer able to stand the waiting, officers of both groups ordered all their men out of the audience room to take up defensive positions at the far end of the corridor. Now the way was clear, the door of the inner corridor open, only the captain of Grays beside it, and he also was leaving. The red-spot leader saw a woman hurry up to the threshold, the tall barbarian with her, and he recognized his prey, other women collecting behind them.

Impatient to complete the mission and so relieve the pressure on his clansmen below, and whipped by his killing lust, the red-spot leader gave the signal and burst through his door an instant too soon.

Blackthorne saw him coming and automatically drew his pistol from under his kimono and fired. The back of the leader's head disappeared, momentarily stopping the charge. Simultaneously, the captain of Grays rushed back and attacked with a mindless ferocity and cut down one *ninja*. Then the pack fell on the Gray and he died but these few seconds gave Blackthorne enough time to pull Mariko to safety and slam the door. Frantically he grabbed the iron bar and slid it into place just as *ninja* hurled themselves against it and others fanned out to hold the main doorway.

"Christ Jesus! What's go—"

"*Ninjaaaaaa!*" Mariko shouted as Kiri and Lady Sazuko and Lady Etsu and Chimmoko and Achiko and the other maids poured hysterically from their rooms, blows hammering on the door.

"Quick, this way!" Kiri screamed over the uproar and fled into the interior.

The women followed, helter-skelter, two of them helping old Lady Etsu. Blackthorne saw the door rocking under the furious blows of the assault jimmies. Now the wood was splintering. Blackthorne ran back into his room for his powder horn and swords.

In the audience room the *ninja* had already disposed of the six Browns and Grays at the main outer door and had overhelmed the rest in the corridor beyond. But they had lost two dead, and two were wounded before the fight was complete, the outer doors closed and barred, and this whole section secure.

"Hurry up," the new red-spot leader snarled. The men with the crowbars needed no urging as they ripped at the door. For a moment the leader stood over the corpse of his brother, then kicked it furiously, knowing his brother's impatience had destroyed their surprise attack. He rejoined his men, who circled the door.

In the corridor Blackthorne was reloading rapidly, the door shrieking under the blows. First the powder, tamp it carefully . . . *one of the door panels cracked* . . . next the paper plug to hold the charge tight and next the lead ball and another plug . . . *one of the door hinges snapped and the tip of the jimmy came through* . . . next, blow the dust carefully away from the flint. . . .

"Anjin-san!" Mariko cried out from somewhere in the inner rooms. "Hurry!"

But Blackthorne paid no attention. He walked up to the door and put the nozzle to a splintered crack, stomach high, and pulled the trigger. From the other side of the door there was a scream and the assault on the door ceased. He retreated and began to reload. First powder, tamp it carefully . . . *again the whole door shook as men tore at it with shoulders and raging fists and feet and weapons* . . . next the holding paper and next the ball and next another paper . . . *the door bellowed and shuddered and one of the bolts sprang away and clattered to the floor.* . . .

Kiri was hurrying down an inner passageway, gasping for breath, the others half-dragging Lady Etsu with them, Sazuko crying, "What's the point, there's nowhere to go. . . ." but Kiri ran on, stumbling into another room and across it and she pulled a section of the shoji wall aside. A hidden iron-fortified door was set into the stone wall beyond. She pulled it open. The hinges were well oiled.

"This . . . this is my Master's sec—secret haven," she panted and started to go inside but stopped. "Where's Mariko?"

Chimmoko turned and rushed back.

In the first corridor Blackthorne blew the dust carefully away from the flint and walked forward again. The door was near collapsing but still offered cover. Again he pulled the trigger. Again a scream and a moment's respite, then the blows commenced, another bolt flew off and the whole door teetered. He began to reload.

"Anjin-san!" Mariko was there at the far end beckoning him frantically so he snatched up his weapons and rushed toward her. She turned and fled, guiding him. The door shattered and the *ninja* tore after them.

Mariko was running fast, Blackthorne on her heels. She sped across a room, tripped over her skirts and fell. He grabbed her up and together they bolted across another room. Chimmoko ran up to them. "Hurry!" she shrieked, waiting for them to pass. She followed for a moment, then, unnoticed, she turned back and stood in the path, her knife out.

Ninja came rushing into the room. Chimmoko hurled herself, knife outstretched, at the first man. He parried the blow and flung her aside like a toy, charging after Blackthorne and Mariko. The last man broke Chimmoko's neck with his foot and rushed on.

Mariko was running fast but not fast enough, her skirts inhibiting her, Blackthorne trying to help. They crossed a room, then turned right, into another, and he saw the doorway, Kiri and Sazuko waiting there terrified, Achiko and maids succoring the old women in the room behind them. He shoved Mariko to safety. Then he turned at bay, his uncharged pistol in one hand, sword in the other, expecting Chimmoko. When she didn't appear at once, he began to go back but heard the approaching charge of the *ninja*. He stopped and leaped backward into the room as the first *ninja* appeared. He slammed the door, and spears and shuriken screeched off the iron. Again he barely had time to shove the bolts home before the attackers hurtled against it.

Numbly he thanked God for their escape and then, when he saw the strength of the door and knew that jimmies could not break it easily and that they were safe for the moment, he thanked God again. Trying to catch his breath, he looked around. Mariko was on her knees gulping for air. There were six maids, Achiko, Kiri and Sazuko, and the old lady, who lay gray-faced, almost unconscious. The room was small and stone-walled and another side door let out onto a small battlement veranda. He groped over to a window and looked out. This corner abutment overhung the avenue and forecourt, and he could hear sounds of the battle wafting up from below, screams and shouts and a few hysterical battle cries. Several Grays and unattached samurai were already beginning to collect in the avenue and on the opposite battlements. The gates below were locked against them and held by the *ninja*.

"What the hell's going on?" Blackthorne said, his chest aching.

No one answered him and he went back and knelt beside Mariko and shook her gently. "What's going on?" But she could not answer yet.

Yabu was running down a wide corridor in the west wing toward his sleeping quarters. He turned a corner and skidded to a stop. Ahead a large number of samurai were being pressed back by a ferocious counterattack of raiders who had rushed down from the top floor.

"What's going on?" Yabu shouted over the din, for no raiders were supposed to be here, only below.

"They're all over us," a samurai panted. "These came from above. . . ."

Yabu cursed, realizing he had been duped and not told the whole of the attack plan. "Where's Sumiyori?"

"He must be dead. They've overwhelmed that section, Sire. You were lucky to escape yourself. They must have struck shortly after you left. What are *ninja* attacking for?"

A flurry of shouts distracted them. At the far end, Browns launched another counterattack around a corner, covering samurai who fought with spears. The spearmen drove the *ninja* back, and the Browns charged in pursuit. But a cloud of shuriken enveloped this wave and soon they were screaming and dying, blocking the passageway, the poison convulsing them. Momentarily the rest of the Browns retreated out of range to regroup.

Yabu, unendangered, shouted, "Get bowmen!" Men rushed off to obey.

"What's the attack all about? Why are they in force?" the samurai asked again, blood streaking his face from a cheek wound. Normally the detested *ninja* attacked singly or in small groups, to vanish as quickly as they appeared once their mission was accomplished.

"I don't know," Yabu said, this whole section of the castle now in uproar, the Browns still uncoordinated, still off-balance from the terrifying swiftness of the onslaught.

"If—if Toranaga-sama were here I could understand Ishido ordering a sudden attack but—but why now?" the samurai said. "There's no one or noth—" He stopped as the realization struck him. "Lady Toda!"

Yabu tried to override him, but the man bellowed, "They're after *her,* Yabu-san! They must be after Lady Toda!" He led a rush for the east wing. Yabu hesitated, then followed.

To get to the east wing they had to cross the central landing that the *ninja* now held in strength. Samurai dead were everywhere. Goaded by the knowledge that their revered leader was in danger, the first impetuous charge broke through the cordon. But these men were cut down swiftly. Now more of their comrades had taken up the shouts and the news spread rapidly and the Browns redoubled their efforts. Yabu rushed up to direct the fight, staying in safety as much as he dared. A *ninja* ripped open his haversack and lit a fused gourd from a wall flare and hurled it over the Browns. It shattered against a wall and exploded, scattering fire and smoke, and at once this *ninja* led a counterattack that threw the Browns into a burning, disordered rout. Under cover of the smoke *ninja* reinforcements poured up from the floor below.

"Retreat and regroup!" Yabu shouted in one of the corridors leading off the main landing, wanting to delay as much as he dared, presuming that Mariko was already captured and being carried to the cellar escape below, expecting at any moment the overdue clarion call that signaled success and ordered all *ninja* to break off the attack and retreat. Then a force of Browns from above hurtled in a suicidal attack from a staircase and broke the cordon. They died but others also disobeyed Yabu and charged. More bombs were thrown, setting fire to the wall hangings. Flames began to lick the walls, sparks ignited the tatamis. A sudden gush of fire trapped one of the *ninja,* turning him into a screaming human torch. Then a samurai's kimono caught and he threw himself onto another *ninja* and they burned together. A blazing samurai was using his sword like a battle-ax to cut a way through the ambushers. Ten samurai followed and, though two died in their tracks and three fell mortally wounded, the rest broke out and tore for the east wing. Soon another ten followed. Yabu led the next charge safely as the remaining *ninja* made an orderly retreat to the ground floor and their escape route below. The battle for possession of the cul-de-sac in the east wing began.

* * *

In the small room they were staring at the door. They could hear the attackers scraping at the hinges and at the floor. Then there was a sudden hammering and a harsh, muffled voice from outside.

Two of the maids began to sob.

"What did he say?" Blackthorne asked.

Mariko licked her dry lips. "He—he said, to open the door and surrender or he'd—he'd blow it up."

"Can they do that, Mariko-san?"

"I don't know. They . . . they can use gunpowder, of course, and—" Mariko's hand went to her sash but came out empty. "Where's my knife?"

All the women went for their daggers. Kiri had none. Sazuko none. Nor Achiko or Lady Etsu. Blackthorne had armed his pistol and had his long sword. The short sword had fallen during his frantic dash for safety.

The muffled voice became angrier and more demanding, and all eyes in the room looked at Blackthorne. But Mariko knew she was betrayed and her time had come.

"He said, if we open the door and surrender, everyone will go free except you." Mariko brushed a strand of hair out of her eyes. "He said they want you as a hostage, Anjin-san. That's all they want. . . ."

Blackthorne walked forward to open the door, but Mariko stood pathetically in his way.

"No, Anjin-san, it's a trick," she said. "So sorry, they don't want you, they want me! Don't believe them, I don't believe them."

He smiled at her and touched her briefly and reached for one of the bolts.

"It's not you, it's me—it's a trick! I swear it! Don't believe them, please," she said, and grabbed his sword. It was half out of its scabbard before he realized what she was doing and had caught her hand.

"No!" he ordered. "Stop it!"

"Don't give me into their hands! I've no knife! Please, Anjin-san!" She tried to fight out of his grasp but he lifted her out of the way and put his hand on the top bolt. *"Dozo,"* he said to the others as Mariko desperately tried to stop him. Achiko came forward, pleading with her, and Mariko tried to push her away and cried out, "Please, Anjin-san, it's a trick—for the love of God!"

His hand jerked the top bolt open.

"They want me alive," Mariko shouted wildly. "Don't you see? To capture me, don't you see? They want me alive and then it's all for nothing—tomorrow Toranaga's got to cross the border—I beg you, it's a trick, before God. . . ."

Achiko had her arms around Mariko, pleading with her, pulling her away, and she motioned him to open the door. *"Isogi, isogi,* Anjin-san. . . ."

Blackthorne opened the central bolt.

"For the love of God, don't make all the dying useless! Help me! Remember your vow!"

Now the reality of what she was saying reached him, and in panic he shoved home the bolts. "Why should—"

A ferocious pounding on the door interrupted him, iron clanging on iron, then the voice began, a short violent crescendo. All sound outside ceased. The women fled for the far wall and cowered against it.

"Get away from the door," Mariko shouted, rushing after them. "He's going to explode the door!"

"Delay him, Mariko-san," Blackthorne said and leaped for the side door that led to the battlements. "Our men'll be here soon. Work the bolts, say they're stuck—anything." He strained at the top bolt on the side door but it was rusted tight. Obediently Mariko ran to the door and pretended feeble attempts to shift the central bolt, pleading with the *ninja* outside. Then she began to rattle the lower bolt. Again the voice, more insistent, and Mariko redoubled her weeping pleas.

Blackthorne smashed the butt of his hand against the top catch again and again but it would not shift. The women watched helplessly. Finally this bolt clanged open noisily. Mariko tried to cover the sound and Blackthorne attacked the final bolt. His hands were raw and bloody now. The *ninja* leader outside renewed his fiery warning. In desperation Blackthorne grabbed his sword and used the haft as a cudgel, careless of the noise now. Mariko drowned the sounds as best she could. The bolt seemed welded shut.

Outside the door, the red-spot leader was almost mad with rage. This secret refuge was totally unexpected. His orders from the clan leader were to capture Toda Mariko alive, make sure she was weaponless, and hand her over to Grays who were waiting at the end of the tunnel from the cellars. He knew that time was running out. He could hear the raging battle in the corridor, outside the audience room, and knew disgustedly that they would have been safe below, their mission accomplished, but for this secret rat hole and his overanxious fool of a brother who had begun the rush prematurely.

Karma to have such a brother!

He held a lighted candle in his hand and he had laid a trail of powder to the small kegs they had brought in their haversacks to blow up the secret entrance to the cellars to secure their retreat. But he was in a dilemma. To blow the door was the only way to get through. But the Toda woman was just on the other side of the door and the explosion would surely kill everyone inside and spoil his mission, making all their losses futile.

Footsteps raced toward him. It was one of his own men. "Be quick!" the man whispered. "We can't hold them off much longer!" He raced away.

The red-spot leader decided. He waved his men to cover and shouted a warning through the door. "Get away! I'm blowing the door!" He put the candle to the trail and jumped to safety. The powder spluttered, caught, and snaked for the kegs.

Blackthorne yanked the side door open. Sweet night air rushed in. The women poured onto the veranda. Old Lady Etsu fell but he caught her and pushed her through, whirled for Mariko, but she had pressed back against the iron and called out firmly, "I, Toda Mariko, protest this shameful attack and by my death—"

He lunged for her but the explosion blew him aside as the door wrenched loose from its hinges and blasted into the room and shrieked off a far wall. The detonation knocked Kiri and the others off their feet outside on the battlement, but they were mostly unhurt. Smoke gushed into the room, the *ninja* following instantly. The buckled iron door came to rest in a corner.

The red-spot leader was on his knees beside Mariko as others fanned out protectively. He saw at once that she was broken and dying fast. *Karma,* he thought and jumped to his feet again. Blackthorne was lying stunned, a trickle of blood seeping from his ears and nose, trying to grope back into life. His pistol, bent and useless, was in a corner.

The red-spot leader went forward a pace and stopped. Achiko moved into the doorway.

The *ninja* looked at her, recognizing her. Then he stared down at Blackthorne, despising him for the gun and the cowardice in shooting blindly through the door, killing one of his men and wounding another. He looked back at Achiko and reached for his knife. She charged blindly. His knife took her in the left breast. She was dead as she crumpled and he went forward without anger and withdrew his knife from the twitching body, fulfilling the last part of his orders from above—he presumed from Ishido, though it could never be proved—that if they failed and the Lady Toda managed to kill herself, he was to leave her untouched and not take her head; he was to protect the barbarian and leave all the other women unharmed, except for Kiyama Achiko. He did not know why he had been ordered to kill her, but it had been ordered and paid for, so she was dead.

He signaled the retreat. One of his men put a curved horn to his lips and blew a strident call that echoed through the castle and through the night. The leader made a last check on Mariko. A last check on the girl. And a last check on the barbarian he wanted dead so much. Then he turned on his heel and led the retreat through the rooms and passageways into the audience room. *Ninja* defending the main doorway waited till all the red-spot raiders were through the escape route, then they hurled more smoke and fire bombs into the corridor and rushed for safety. The leader of the red-spots covered them. He waited until all were safe, then scattered handfuls of hardly noticeable deadly caltrops on the floor—small, spiked metal balls tipped with poison. He fled as Browns burst through the smoke into the audience room. Some charged after him and another phalanx hurtled for the corridor. His pursuers screamed as the caltrop needles ripped into the soles of their feet and they began to die.

In the small room, the only sound was Blackthorne's lungs struggling for air. On the battlement Kiri lurched to her feet, her kimono torn and her hands and arms raw with abrasions. She stumbled back and saw Achiko and cried out, then reeled for Mariko and sank to her knees beside her. Another explosion somewhere in the castle rocked the dust a fraction, and there were more screams and distant shouts of "Fire." Smoke billowed into the room. Sazuko and some of the maids got to their feet. Sazuko was bruised about the face and shoulders and her wrist was broken. She saw Achiko, eyes and mouth open in death terror, and she whimpered.

Numbly, Kiri looked across at her and motioned at Blackthorne. The young girl stumbled toward Kiri and saw Mariko. She began to cry. Then she got control of herself and went back to Blackthorne and tried to help him up. Maids rushed to assist her. He held onto them and fought to his feet, then swayed and fell, coughing and retching, the blood still oozing from his ears. Browns burst into the room. They looked around, aghast.

Kiri stayed on her knees beside Mariko. A samurai lifted her up. Others crowded around. They parted as Yabu came into the room, his face ashen. When he saw Blackthorne was still alive, much of his anxiety left him.

"Get a doctor! Quick!" he ordered and knelt beside Mariko. She was still alive, but fading rapidly. Her face was hardly touched but her body was terribly mutilated. Yabu ripped off his kimono and covered her to the neck.

"Hurry the doctor," he rasped, then went over to Blackthorne. He helped him sit against the wall.

"Anjin-san! Anjin-san!"

Blackthorne was still in shock, his ears ringing, eyes hardly seeing, his face a mass of bruises and powder burns. Then his eyes cleared and he saw Yabu, the image twisting drunkenly, the smell of gunsmoke choking him and he didn't know where he was or who he was, only that he was aboard ship in battle and his ship was hurt and needed him. Then he saw Mariko and he remembered.

He lurched up, Yabu helping him, and tottered over to her.

She seemed at peace, sleeping. He knelt heavily and moved the kimono aside. Then he put it back again. Her pulse was almost imperceptible. Then it ceased.

He stayed looking at her, swaying, almost falling, then a doctor was there and the doctor shook his head and said something but Blackthorne could not hear or understand. He only knew that death had come to her, and that he too was dead.

He made the sign of the cross over her and said the sacred Latin words that were necessary to bless her and he prayed for her though no sound came from his mouth. The others watched him. When he had done what he had to do, he fought to his feet again and stood upright. Then his head seemed to burst with red and purple light and he collapsed. Kind hands caught him and helped him to the floor and let him rest.

"Is he dead?" Yabu asked.

"Almost. I don't know about his ears, Yabu-sama," the doctor said. "He may be bleeding inside."

A samurai said nervously, "We'd better hurry, get them out of here. The fire may spread and we'll be trapped."

"Yes," Yabu said. Another samurai called him urgently from the battlements and he went outside.

Old Lady Etsu was lying against the battlement, cradled by her maid, her face gray, eyes rheumy. She peered up at Yabu, focusing with difficulty. "Kasigi Yabu-san?"

"Yes, Lady."

"Are you senior officer here?"

"Yes, Lady."

The old woman said to the maid. "Please help me up."

"But you should wait, the doc—"

"Help me up!"

Samurai on the battlement veranda watched her stand, supported by the maid. "Listen," she said, her voice hoarse and frail in the silence. "I, Maeda Etsu, wife of Maeda Arinosi, Lord of Nagato, Iwami, and Aki, I attest that Toda Mariko-sama cast away her life to save herself from dishonorable capture by these hideous and shameful men. I attest that . . . that Kiyama Achiko chose to attack the *ninja,* casting away her life rather than risk the dishonor of being captured . . . that but for the barbarian samurai's bravery Lady Toda would have been captured and dishonored, and all of us, and we who are alive owe him gratitude, and also our Lords owe him gratitude for protecting us from that shame. . . . I accuse the Lord General Ishido of mounting this dishonorable attack . . . and of betraying the Heir and the Lady Ochiba . . ." The old lady wavered and almost fell, and the maid sobbed and held her more strongly. "And . . . and Lord Ishido has betrayed them and the Council of Regents. I ask you all to bear witness that I can no longer live with this shame. . . ."

"No—no mistress," the maid wept, "I won't let you—"

"Go away! Kasigi Yabu-san, please help me. Go away, woman!"

Yabu took Lady Etsu's weight, which was negligible, and ordered the maid away. She obeyed.

Lady Etsu was in great pain and breathing heavily. "I attest to the truth of this by my own death," she said in a small voice and looked up at Yabu. "I would be honored if . . . if you would be my second. Please help me onto the battlements."

"No, Lady. There's no need to die."

She turned her face away from the others and whispered to him, "I'm dying already, Yabu-sama. I'm bleeding from inside—something's broken inside—the explosion. . . . Help me to do my duty. . . . I'm old and useless and pain's been my bedfellow for twenty years. Let my death also help our Master, *neh?*" There was a glint in the old eyes. *"Neh?"*

Gently he lifted her and stood proudly beside her on the abutment, the fore-court far below. He helped her to stand. Everyone bowed to her.

"I have told the truth. I attest to it by my death," she said, standing alone, her voice quavering. Then she closed her eyes thankfully and let herself fall forward to welcome death.

CHAPTER 58

THE Regents were meeting in the Great Room on the second level of the donjon. Ishido, Kiyama, Zataki, Ito, and Onoshi. The dawn sun cast long shadows and the smell of fire still hung heavy in the air.

Lady Ochiba was present, also greatly perturbed.

"So sorry, Lord General, I disagree," Kiyama was saying in his tight brittle voice. "It's impossible to dismiss Lady Toda's seppuku and my granddaughter's bravery and Lady Maeda's testimony and formal death—along with one hundred and forty-seven Toranaga dead and that part of the castle almost gutted! It just can't be dismissed."

"I agree," Zataki said. He had arrived yesterday morning from Takato and when he had the details of Mariko's confrontation with Ishido he had been secretly delighted. "If she'd been allowed to go yesterday as I advised, we wouldn't be in this snare now."

"It's not as serious as you think." Ishido's mouth was a hard line and Ochiba loathed him at that moment, loathed him for failing and for trapping them all in this crisis. "The *ninja* were only after loot," Ishido said.

"The barbarian is loot?" Kiyama scoffed. "They'd mount such a vast attack for one barbarian?"

"Why not? He could be ransomed, *neh?*" Ishido stared back at the *daimyo,* who was flanked by Ito Teruzumi and Zataki. "Christians in Nagasaki would pay highly for him, dead or alive. *Neh?*"

"That's possible," Zataki agreed. "That's the way barbarians fight."

Kiyama said tightly, "Are you suggesting, formally, that Christians planned and paid for this foul attack?"

"I said it was possible. And it is possible."

"Yes. But unlikely," Ishido interposed, not wanting the precarious balance of the Regents wrecked by an open quarrel now. He was still apoplectic that spies had not forewarned him about Toranaga's secret lair, and still did not understand how it could have been constructed with such secrecy and not a breath of rumor about it. "I suggest *ninja* were after loot."

"That's very sensible and most correct," Ito said with a malicious glint in his eyes. He was a small, middle-aged man, resplendently attired with ornamental swords, even though he had been routed out of bed like all of them. He was made up like a woman and his teeth were blackened. "Yes, Lord General. But perhaps the *ninja* didn't mean to ransom him in Nagasaki but in Yedo, to Lord Toranaga. Isn't he still his lackey?"

Ishido's brow darkened at the mention of the name. "I agree we should spend our time discussing Lord Toranaga and not *ninja.* Probably he ordered the attack, *neh?* He's treacherous enough to do that."

"No, he'd never use *ninja,*" Zataki said. "Treachery yes, but not those filth. Merchants would do that—or barbarians. Not Lord Toranaga."

Kiyama watched Zataki, hating him. "Our Portuguese friends could not, would not, instigate such an interference in our affairs. Never!"

"Would you believe they and or their priests would conspire with one of the

715

Christian Kyushu *daimyos* to war on non-Christians—the war supported by a foreign invasion?"

"Who? Tell me. Do you have proof?

"Not yet, Lord Kiyama. But the rumors are still there and one day I'll get proof." Zataki turned back to Ishido. "What can we do about this attack? What's the way out of the dilemma?" he asked, then glanced at Ochiba. She was watching Kiyama, then her eyes moved to Ishido, then back to Kiyama again, and he had never seen her more desirable.

Kiyama said, "We're all agreed it's evident Lord Toranaga plotted that we should be snared by Toda Mariko-sama, however brave she was, however duty bound and honorable, God have mercy on her."

Ito adjusted a fold in the skirts of his impeccable kimono. "But don't you agree this would be a perfect stratagem for Lord Toranaga, to attack his own vassals like that? Oh, Lord Zataki, I know he'd never use *ninja,* but he is very clever at getting others to take his ideas and believe them as their own. *Neh?*"

"Anything's possible. But *ninja* wouldn't be like him. He's too clever to use them. Or get anyone to do that. They're not to be trusted. And why force Mariko-sama? Far better to wait and let us make the mistake. We were trapped. *Neh?*"

"Yes. We're still trapped." Kiyama looked at Ishido. "And whoever ordered the attack was a fool, and did us no service."

"Perhaps the Lord General's correct, that it's not as serious as we think," Ito said. "But so sad—not an elegant death for her, poor lady."

"That was her *karma* and we're not trapped." Ishido stared back at Kiyama. "It was fortunate she had that bolt hole to run to, otherwise those vermin would have captured her."

"But they didn't capture her, Lord General, and she committed a form of seppuku and so did the others and now, if we don't let everyone go, there'll be more protest deaths and we cannot afford that," Kiyama said.

"I don't agree. Everyone should stay here—at least until Toranaga-sama crosses into our domains."

Ito smiled. "That will be a memorable day."

"You don't think he will?" Zataki asked.

"What I think has no value, Lord Zataki. We'll soon know what he's going to do. Whatever it is makes no difference. Toranaga must die, if the Heir is to inherit." Ito looked at Ishido. "Is the barbarian dead yet, Lord General?"

Ishido shook his head and watched Kiyama. "It would be bad luck for him to die now, or to be maimed—a brave man like that. *Neh?*"

"I think he's a plague and the sooner he dies the better. Have you forgotten?"

"He could be useful to us. I agree with Lord Zataki—and you—Toranaga's no fool. There's got to be a good reason for Toranaga's cherishing him. *Neh?*"

"Yes, you're right again," Ito said. "The Anjin-san did well for a barbarian, didn't he? Toranaga was right to make him samurai." He looked at Ochiba. "When he gave you the flower, Lady, I thought that was a poetic gesture worthy of a courtier."

There was general agreement.

"What about the poetry competition now, Lady?" Ito asked.

"It should be canceled, so sorry," Ochiba said.

"Yes," Kiyama agreed.

"Had you decided on your entry, Sire?" she asked.

"No," he answered. "But now I could say:

'On a withered branch
The tempest fell. . . .
Dark summer's tears.' "

"Let it be her epitaph. She was samurai," Ito said quietly. "I share this summer's tears."

"For me," Ochiba said, "for me I would have preferred a different ending:

'On a withered branch
The snow listened. . . .
Winter's silence.'

But I agree, Lord Ito. I too think we will all share in this dark summer's tears."

"No, so sorry, Lady, but you're wrong," Ishido said. "There will be tears all right, but Toranaga and his allies will shed them." He began to bring the meeting to a close. "I'll start an inquiry into the *ninja* attack at once. I doubt if we'll ever discover the truth. Meanwhile, for security and personal safety, all passes will regretfully be canceled and everyone regretfully forbidden to leave until the twenty-second day."

"No," Onoshi the leper, the last of the Regents, said from his lonely place across the room where he lay, unseen, behind the opaque curtains of his litter. "So sorry, but that's exactly what you can't do. Now you must let everyone go. Everyone."

"Why?"

Onoshi's voice was malevolent and unafraid. "If you don't, you dishonor the bravest Lady in the realm, you dishonor the Lady Kiyama Achiko and the Lady Maeda, God have mercy on their souls. When this filthy act is common knowledge, only God the Father knows what damage it will cause the Heir—and all of us, if we're not careful."

Ochiba felt a chill rush through her. A year ago, when Onoshi had come to pay his respects to the dying Taikō, the guards had insisted the litter curtains be opened in case Onoshi had weapons concealed, and she had seen the ravaged half-face—noseless, earless, scabbed—the burning, fanatic eyes, the stump of the left hand and the good right hand grasping the short stabbing sword.

Lady Ochiba prayed that neither she nor Yaemon would ever catch leprosy. She, too, wanted an end to this conference, for she had to decide now what to do—what to do about Toranaga and what to do about Ishido.

"Second," Onoshi was saying, "if you use this filthy attack as an excuse to hold anyone here, you imply you never intended to let them go even though you gave your solemn written undertaking. Third: you—"

Ishdio interrupted, "The whole Council agreed to issue the safe conducts!"

"So sorry, the whole Council agreed to the wise suggestion of the Lady Ochiba to offer safe conducts, presuming, with her, that few would take advantage of the opportunity to leave, and even if they did delays would occur."

"You suggest Toranaga's women and Toda Mariko wouldn't have left and that others wouldn't have followed?"

"What happened to those women wouldn't swerve Lord Toranaga a jot from his purpose. We've got to worry about our allies! Without the *ninja* attack and the three seppukus this whole nonsense would have been stillborn!"

"I don't agree."

"Third and last: If you don't let everyone go now, after what Lady Etsu said publicly, you'll be convicted by most *daimyos* of ordering the attack—though not publicly—and we all risk the same fate, and then there'll be lots of tears."

"I don't need to rely on *ninja.*"

"Of course," Onoshi agreed, his voice poisonous. "Neither do I, nor does anyone here. But I feel it is my duty to remind you that there are two hundred and sixty-four *daimyos,* that the Heir's strength lies on a coalition of perhaps two hundred, and that the Heir cannot afford to have you, his most loyal standard-bearer and commander-in-chief, presumed guilty of such filthy methods and such monstrous inefficiency as the attack failed."

"You say I ordered that attack?"

"Of course not, so sorry. I merely said you will be convicted by default if you don't let everyone leave."

"Is there anyone here who thinks I ordered it?" No one challenged Ishido openly. There was no proof. Correctly, he had not consulted them and had talked only in vague innuendos, even to Kiyama and Ochiba. But they all knew and all were equally furious that he had had the stupidity to fail—all except Zataki. Even so, Ishido was still master of Osaka, and governor of the Taikō's treasure, so he could not be touched or removed.

"Good," Ishido said with finality. "The *ninja* were after loot. We'll vote on the safe conducts. I vote they be canceled."

"I disagree," Zataki said.

"So sorry, I oppose also," said Onoshi.

Ito reddened under their scrutiny. "I have to agree with Lord Onoshi, at the same time, well . . . it's all very difficult, *neh?*"

"Vote," Ishido said grimly.

"I agree with you, Lord General."

Kiyama said, "So sorry, I don't."

"Good," Onoshi said. "That's settled, but I agree with you, Lord General, we've other pressing problems. We have to know what Lord Toranaga will do now. What's your opinion?"

Ishido was staring at Kiyama, his face set. Then he said, "What's your answer to that?"

Kiyama was trying to clear his head of all his hates and fears and worries, to make a final choice—Ishido or Toranaga. This had to be the time. He remembered vividly Mariko talking about Onoshi's supposed treachery, about Ishido's supposed betrayal and Toranaga's supposed proof of that betrayal, about the barbarian and his ship—and about what might happen to the Heir and the Church if Toranaga dominated the land and what might happen to their law if the Holy Fathers dominated the land. And overlaying that was the Father-Visitor's anguish about the heretic and his ship, and what would happen if the Black Ship was lost, and the Captain-General's God-sworn conviction that the Anjin-san was Satan spawned, Mariko bewitched as the Rodrigues was bewitched. Poor Mariko, he thought sadly, to die like that after so much suffering, without absolution, without last rites, without a priest, to spend eternity away from God's sweet heavenly grace. Madonna have mercy on her. So many summer's tears.

And what about Achiko? Did the *ninja* leader single her out or was that just another killing? How brave she was to charge and not to cringe, poor child. Why is the barbarian still alive? Why didn't the *ninja* kill him? They should have been ordered to, if this filthy attack was conceived by Ishido, as of course it must have been. Shameful of Ishido to fail—disgusting to fail. Ah, but what courage Mariko had, how clever she was to ensnare us in her courageous web! And the barbarian.

If I'd been he I would never have been able to delay the *ninja* with so much courage, or to protect Mariko from the hideous shame of capture—and Kiritsubo and Sazuko and the Lady Etsu, yes, and even Achiko. But for him and the secret sanctuary, Lady Mariko would have been captured. And all of them. It's my samurai duty to honor the Anjin-san for being samurai. *Neh?*

God forgive me, I did not go to Mariko-chan to be her second, which was my Christian duty. The heretic helped her and lifted her up as the Christ Jesus helped others and lifted them up, but I, I forsook her. Who's the Christian?

I don't know. Even so, *he* has to die.

"What about Toranaga, Lord Kiyama?" Ishido said again. "What about the enemy?"

"What about the Kwanto?" Kiyama asked, watching him.

"When Toranaga's destroyed I propose that the Kwanto be given to one of the Regents."

"Which Regent?"

"You," Ishido answered blandly, then added, "or perhaps Zataki, Lord of Shinano." This Kiyama thought wise, for Zataki was needed very much while Toranaga was alive and Ishido had already told him, a month ago, that Zataki had demanded the Kwanto as payment for opposing Toranaga. Together they had agreed Ishido should promise it to him, both knowing this to be an empty promise. Both were agreed Zataki should forfeit his life and his province for such impertinence, as soon as convenient.

"Of course I'm hardly the right choice for that honor," Kiyama said, carefully assessing who in the room were for him and who against.

Onoshi tried to conceal his disapproval. "That suggestion's certainly a valuable one, worthy of discussion, *neh?* But that's for the future. What's the present Lord of the Kwanto going to do now?"

Ishido was still looking at Kiyama. "Well?"

Kiyama felt Zataki's hostility though nothing showed on his enemy's face. Two against me, he thought, and Ochiba, but she has no vote. Ito will always vote with Ishido, so I win—if Ishido means what he says. Does he? he asked himself, studying the hard face in front of him, probing for the truth. Then he decided and he said openly what he had concluded. "Lord Toranaga will never come to Osaka."

"Good," Ishido said. "Then he's isolated, outlawed, and the Imperial invitation to commit seppuku is already prepared for the Exalted's signature. And that's the end of Toranaga and all his line. *Forever.*"

"Yes. If the Son of Heaven comes to Osaka."

"What?"

"I agree with Lord Ito," Kiyama continued, preferring him as an ally and not an enemy. "Lord Toranaga is the wiliest of men. I think he's even cunning enough to stop the Exalted's arrival."

"Impossible!"

"What if the visit's postponed?" Kiyama asked, suddenly enjoying Ishido's discomfort, detesting him for failing.

"The Son of Heaven will be here as planned!"

"And if the Son of Heaven isn't?"

"I tell you He will be!"

"And if He isn't?"

Lady Ochiba asked, "How could Lord Toranaga do that?"

"I don't know. But if the Exalted wanted his visit delayed for a month . . . there's nothing we could do. Isn't Lord Toranaga a past master at subversion? I'd put nothing past him—even subverting the Son of Heaven."

There was dead silence in the room. The enormity of that thought, and its repercussions, enveloped them.

"Please excuse me but . . . but what's the answer then?" Ochiba spoke for them all.

"War!" Kiyama said. "We mobilize today—secretly. We wait until the visit's postponed, as it will be. That's our signal that Toranaga has subverted the Most High. The same day we march against the Kwanto, during the rainy season."

Suddenly the floor began to quiver.

The first earthquake was slight and lasted only for a few moments but it made the timbers cry out.

Now there was another tremor. Stronger. A fissure ripped up a stone wall and stopped. Dust pattered down from the rafters. Joists and beams and tiles shrieked and tiles scattered off a roof and pitched into the forecourt below.

Ochiba felt faint and nauseous and she wondered if it was her *karma* to be buried in the rubble today. She hung onto the trembling floor and waited with everyone in the castle, and with all the city and the ships in the harbor, for the real shock to come.

But it did not come. The quake ended. Life began again. The joy of living rushed back into them, and their laughter echoed through the castle. Everyone seemed to know that this time—for this hour, for this day—the holocaust would pass them by.

"*Shigata ga nai,*" Ishido said, still convulsed. "*Neh?*"

"Yes," Ochiba said gloriously.

"Let's vote," Ishido said, relishing his existence. "I vote for war!"

"And I!"

"And I!"

"And I!"

"And I!"

When Blackthorne regained consciousness he knew that Mariko was dead, and he knew how she had died and why she had died. He was lying on futons, Grays guarding him, a raftered ceiling overhead, dazzling sunshine hurting him, the silence weird. A doctor was studying him. The first of his great fears left him.

I can see.

The doctor smiled and said something, but Blackthorne could not hear him. He started to get up but a blinding pain set off a violent ringing in his ears. The acrid taste of gunpowder was still in his mouth and his entire body was hurting.

For a moment he lost consciousness again, then he felt gentle hands lift his head and put a cup to his lips and the bitter-sweet tang of the jasmine-scented herb cha took away the taste of gunpowder. He forced his eyes open. Again the doctor said something and again he could not hear and again terror began to well, but he stopped it, his mind remembering the explosion and seeing her dead and, before she had died, giving her an absolution he was not qualified to give. Deliberately he pushed that memory away and made himself dwell on the other explosion—the time he was blown overboard after old Alban Caradoc had lost his legs. That time he had also had the same ringing in his ears and the same pain and soundlessness, but his hearing had returned after a few days.

There's no need to worry, he told himself. Not yet.

He could see the length of the sun's shadows and the color of the light. It's a little after dawn, he thought, and blessed God again that his sight was undamaged.

He saw the doctor's lips move but no sound came through the ringing turbulence.

Carefully he felt his face and mouth and jaws. No pain there and no wounds. Next his throat and arms and chest. No wounds yet. Now he willed his hands lower, over his loins, to his manhood. But he was not mutilated there as Alban Caradoc had been, and he blessed God that he had not been harmed there and left alive to know, as poor Alban Caradoc had known.

He rested a moment, his head aching abominably. Then he felt his legs and feet. Everything seemed all right. Cautiously he put his hands over his ears and pressed, then half opened his mouth and swallowed and half yawned to try to clear his ears. But this only increased the pain.

You will wait a day and half a day, he ordered himself, and ten times that time if need be and, until then, you will not be afraid.

The doctor touched him, his lips moving.

"Can't hear, so sorry," Blackthorne said calmly, hearing his words only in his head.

The doctor nodded and spoke again. Now Blackthorne read on the man's lips, *I understand. Please sleep now.*

But Blackthorne knew that he would not sleep. He had to plan. He had to get up and leave Osaka and go to Nagasaki—to get gunners and seamen to take the Black Ship. There was nothing more to think about, nothing more to remember. There was no more reason to play at being samurai or Japanese. Now he was released, all debts and friendships were canceled. Because she was gone.

Again he lifted his head and again the blinding pain. He dominated it and sat up. The room spun and he vaguely remembered that in his dreams he had been back at Anjiro in the earthquake when the earth had twisted and he leaped into it to save Toranaga and her from being swallowed by the earth. He could still feel the cold, clammy wetness and smell the death stench coming from the fissure, Toranaga huge and monstrous and laughing in his dream.

He forced his eyes to see. The room stopped spinning and the nausea passed. "Cha, *dozo,*" he said, the taste of gunpowder back again. Hands helped him to drink and then he held out his arms and they helped him to stand. Without them he would have fallen. His body was one great hurt, but now he was sure that nothing was broken inside or out, except his ears, and that rest and massage and time would cure him. He thanked God again that he was not blinded or mutilated and left alive. The Grays helped him to sit again and he lay back a moment. He did not notice that the sun moved a quadrant from the time he lay back to the time he opened his eyes.

Curious, he thought, measuring the sun's shadow, not realizing he had slept. I could have sworn it was near dawn. My eyes are playing me tricks. It's nearer the end of the forenoon watch now. That reminded him of Alban Caradoc and his hands moved over himself once more to make sure he had not dreamed that he was unhurt.

Someone touched him and he looked up. Yabu was peering down at him and speaking.

"So sorry," Blackthorne said slowly. "Can't hear yet, Yabu-san. Soon all right. Ears hurt, do you understand?"

He saw Yabu nod and frown. Yabu and the doctor talked together and then, with signs, Yabu made Blackthorne understand that he would return soon and to rest until he did. He left.

"Bath, please, and massage," Blackthorne said.

Hands lifted him and took him there. He slept under the soothing fingers, his body wallowing in the ecstasy of warmth and tenderness and the sweet-smelling oils that were rubbed into his flesh. And all the while his mind planned.

While he slept Grays came and lifted the litter bed and carried it to the inner quarters of the donjon, but he did not awaken, drugged with fatigue and by the healing, sleep-filled potion.

"He'll be safe now, Lady," Ishido said.

"From Kiyama?" Ochiba asked.

"From all Christians." Ishido motioned to the guards to be very alert and led the way out of the room to the hallway, thence to a garden basking in the sun.

"Is that why the Lady Achiko was killed? Because she was Christian?"

Ishido had ordered it in case she was an assassin planted by her grandfather Kiyama to kill Blackthorne. "I've no idea," he said.

"They hang together like bees in a swarm. How can anyone believe their religious nonsense?"

"I don't know. But they'll all be stamped out soon enough."

"How, Lord General? How do you do that when so much depends on their goodwill?"

"Promises—until Toranaga's dead. Then they'll fall on each other. We divide and rule. Isn't that what Toranaga does, what the Lord Taikō did? Kiyama wants the Kwanto, *neh?* For the Kwanto he'll obey. So he's promised it, in a future time. Onoshi? Who knows what that madman wants . . . except to spit on Toranaga's head and Kiyama's before he dies."

"And what if Kiyama finds out about your promise to Onoshi—that all Kiyama lands are his—or that you mean to keep your promise to Zataki and not to him?"

"Lies, Lady, spread by enemies." Ishido looked at her. "Onoshi wants Kiyama's head. Kiyama wants the Kwanto. So does Zataki."

"And you, Lord General? What is it you want?"

"First the Heir safely fifteen, then safely ruler of the realm. And you and him safe and protected until that time. Nothing more."

"Nothing?"

"No, Lady."

Liar, Ochiba thought. She broke off a fragrant flower and smelled the perfume, and, pleased by it, offered it to him. "Lovely, *neh?*"

"Yes, lovely," Ishido said, taking it. "Thank you."

"Yodoko-sama's funeral was beautiful. You're to be congratulated, Lord General."

"I'm sorry she's dead," Ishido said politely. "Her counsel was always valuable."

They strolled a while. "Have they left yet? Kiritsubo-san and the Lady Sazuko and her son?" Ochiba asked.

"No. They'll leave tomorrow. After Lady Toda's funeral. Many will leave tomorrow, which is bad."

"So sorry, but does it matter? Now that we all agree Toranaga-sama's not coming here?"

"I think so. But it's not important, not while we hold Osaka Castle. No, Lady, we have to be patient as Kiyama suggested. We wait until the day. Then we march."

"Why wait? Can't you march now?"

"It will take time to gather our hosts."

"How many will oppose Toranaga?"

"Three hundred thousand men. At least three times Toranaga's number."

"And my garrison?"

"I'll leave eighty thousand elite within the walls, another fifty at the passes."

"And Zataki?"

"He'll betray Toranaga. In the end he'll betray him."

"You don't find it curious that Lord Sudara, my sister, and all her children are visiting Takato?"

"No. Of course Zataki's pretended to make some secret arrangement with his half brother. But it's only a trick, nothing more. He will betray him."

"He should—he has the same rotten bloodline," she said with distaste. "But I would be most upset if anything happened to my sister and her children."

"Nothing will, Lady. I'm sure."

"If Zataki was prepared to assassinate his own mother . . . *neh?* You're certain he won't betray you?"

"No. Not in the end. Because he hates Toranaga more than he does me, Lady, and he honors you and desires the Kwanto above all else." Ishido smiled at the floors soaring above them. "As long as the castle's ours and the Kwanto exists to give away, there's nothing to fear."

"This morning I was afraid," she said, holding a flower to her nose, enjoying the perfume, wanting it to erase the aftertaste of fear that still lingered. "I wanted to rush away but then I remembered the soothsayer."

"Eh? Oh, him. I'd forgotten about him," Ishido said with grim amusement. This was the soothsayer, the Chinese envoy, who had foretold that the Taikō would die in his bed leaving a healthy son after him, that Toranaga would die by the sword in middle age, that Ishido would die in old age, the most famous general in the realm, his feet firm in the earth. And that the Lady Ochiba would end her days at Osaka Castle, surrounded by the greatest nobles in the Empire.

"Yes," Ishido said again, "I'd forgotten about him. Toranaga's middle-aged, *neh?*"

"Yes." Again Ochiba felt the depth of his look and her loins melted at the thought of a real man on her, in her, surrounding her, taking her, giving her a new life within. This time an honorable birthing, not like the last one, when she had wondered in horror what the child would be like and look like.

How foolish you are, Ochiba, she told herself, as they walked the shaded, fragrant paths. Put away those silly nightmares—that's all they ever were. You were thinking about *a man.*

Suddenly Ochiba wished that Toranaga was here beside her and not Ishido, that Toranaga was master of Osaka Castle and master of the Taikō's treasure, Protector of the Heir and Chief General of the Armies of the West, and not Ishido. Then there would be no problems. Together they would possess the realm, all of it, and now, today, at this moment, she would beckon him to bed or to an inviting glade and tomorrow or the next day they would marry, and whatever happened in the future, today she would possess and be possessed and be at peace.

Her hand reached out and she pulled a branchlet toward her, breathing the sweet, rich gardenia fragrance.

Put away dreams, Ochiba, she told herself. Be a realist like the Taikō—or Toranaga.

"What are you going to do with the Anjin-san?" she asked.

Ishido laughed. "Hold him safe—let him take the Black Ship perhaps, or use him as a threat against Kiyama and Onoshi if need be. They both hate him, *neh?* Oh yes, he's a sword at their throats—and at their filthy Church."

"In the chess game of the Heir against Toranaga, how would you judge the Anjin-san's value, Lord General? A pawn? A knight, perhaps?"

"Ah, Lady, in the Great Game barely a pawn," Ishido said at once. "But in the game of the Heir against the Christians, a castle, easily a castle, perhaps two."

"You don't think the games are interlocked?"

"Yes, interlocked, but the Great Game will be settled by *daimyo* against *daimyo,* samurai against samurai, and sword against sword. Of course, in both games, you're the queen."

"No, Lord General, please excuse me, not a queen," she said, glad that he realized it. Then, to be safe, she changed the subject. "Rumor has it that the Anjin-san and Mariko-san pillowed together."

"Yes. Yes, I heard that too. You wish to know the truth about it?"

Ochiba shook her head. "It would be unthinkable that that had happened."

Ishido was watching her narrowly. "You think there'd be a value in destroying her honor? Now? And along with her, Buntaro-san?"

"I meant nothing, Lord General, nothing like that. I was just wondering—just a woman's foolishness. But it's as Lord Kiyama said this morning—dark summer's tears, sad, so sad, *neh?*"

"I preferred your poem, Lady. I promise you Toranaga's side will have the tears."

"As to Buntaro-san, perhaps neither he nor Lord Hiro-matsu will fight for Lord Toranaga at *the* battle."

"That's fact?"

"No, Lord General, not fact, but possible."

"But there's something you can do perhaps?"

"Nothing, except petition their support for the Heir—and all Toranaga's generals, once the battle is committed."

"It's committed now, a north-south pincer movement and the final onslaught at Odawara."

"Yes, but not actually. Not until army opposes army on the battlefield." Then she asked, "So sorry, but are you sure it's wise for the Heir to lead the armies?"

"I will lead the armies, but the Heir must be present. Then Toranaga cannot win. Even Toranaga will never attack the Heir's standard."

"Wouldn't it be safer for the Heir to stay here—because of assassins, the Amidas. . . . We can't risk his life. Toranaga has a long arm, *neh?*"

"Yes. But not that long and the Heir's personal standard makes our side lawful and Toranaga's unlawful. I know Toranaga. In the end he'll respect the law. And that alone will put his head on a spike. He's dead, Lady. Once he's dead I will stamp out the Christian Church—all of it. Then you and the Heir will be safe."

Ochiba looked up at him, an unspoken promise in her eyes. "I will pray for success—and your safe return."

His chest tightened. He had waited so long. "Thank you, Lady, thank you," he said, understanding her. "I will not fail you."

She bowed and turned away. What impertinence, she was thinking. As if I'd take a peasant to husband. Now, should I really discard Toranaga?

Dell'Aqua was kneeling at prayer in front of the altar in the ruins of the little chapel. Most of the roof was caved in and part of one wall, but the earthquake had not damaged the chancel and nothing had touched the lovely stained glass window, or the carved Madonna that was his pride.

The afternoon sun was slanting through the broken rafters. Outside, workmen were already shifting rubble from the garden, repairing and talking and, mixed with their chattering, dell'Aqua could hear the cries of the gulls coming ashore and he smelled a tang to the breeze, part salt and part smoke, seaweed and mud flats. The scent bore him home to his estate outside Naples where, mixed with sea smells, would be the perfume of lemons and oranges and warm new breads cooking, and pasta and garlic and *abbacchio* roasting over the coals, and, in the great villa, the voices of his mother and brothers and sisters and their children, all happy and jolly and alive, basking in golden sunshine.

Oh, Madonna, let me go home soon, he prayed. I've been away too long. From home and from the Vatican. Madonna, take thy burden off me. Forgive me but I'm sick to death of Japanese and Ishido and killing and raw fish and Toranaga and Kiyama and rice Christians and trying to keep Thy Church alive. Give me Thy strength.

And protect us from Spanish bishops. Spaniards do not understand Japan or Japanese. They will destroy what we have begun for Thy glory. And forgive Thy servant, the Lady Maria, and take her into Thy keeping. Watch over. . . .

He heard someone come into the nave. When he had finished his prayers, he got up and turned around.

"So sorry to interrupt you, Eminence," Father Soldi said, "but you wanted to know at once. There's an express cipher from Father Alvito. From Mishima. The pigeon's just arrived."

"And?"

"He just says he'll see Toranaga today. Last night was impossible because Toranaga was away from Mishima but he's supposed to return at noon today. The cipher's dated dawn this morning."

Dell'Aqua tried to stifle his disappointment, then looked at the clouds and the weather, seeking reassurance. News of the *ninja* attack and Mariko's death had been sent off to Alvito at dawn, the same message by two pigeons for safety.

"The news will be there by now," Soldi said.

"Yes. Yes, I hope so."

Dell'Aqua led the way out of the chapel, along the cloisters, toward his offices. Soldi, small and birdlike, had to hurry to keep up with the Father-Visitor's great strides. "There's something else of extreme importance, Eminence," Soldi said. "Our informants report that just after dawn the Regents voted for war."

Dell'Aqua stopped. "War?"

"It seems they're convinced now Toranaga will never come to Osaka, or the Emperor. So they've decided jointly to go against the Kwanto."

"No mistake?"

"No, Eminence. It's war. Kiyama has just sent word through Brother Michael which confirms our other source. Michael's just come back from the castle. The vote was unanimous."

"How soon?"

"The moment they know for certain that the Emperor's not coming here."

"The war will never stop. God have mercy on us! And bless Mariko—at least Kiyama and Onoshi were forewarned of Toranaga's perfidy."

"What about Onoshi, Eminence? What about his perfidy against Kiyama?"

"I've no proof of that, Soldi. It's too farfetched. I can't believe Onoshi would do that."

"But if he does, Eminence?"

"It's not possible just now, even if it was planned. Now they need each other."

"Until the demise of Lord Toranaga. . . ."

"You don't have to remind me about the enmity of those two, or the lengths they'll go to—God forgive both of them." He walked on again.

Soldi caught up with him. "Should I send this information to Father Alvito?"

"No. Not yet. First I have to decide what to do. Toranaga will learn of it soon enough from his own sources. God take this land into His keeping and have mercy on all of us."

Soldi opened the door for the Father-Visitor. "The only other matter of importance is that the Council has formally refused to let us have the Lady Maria's body. She's to have a state funeral tomorrow and we are not invited."

"That's to be expected, but it's splendid that they want to honor her like that. Send one of our people to fetch part of her ashes—that will be allowed. The ashes will be buried in hallowed ground at Nagasaki." He straightened a picture automatically and sat behind his desk. "I'll say a Requiem for her here—the full Requiem there with all the pomp and ceremony we can muster when her remains are formally interred. She'll be buried in cathedral grounds as a most blessed daughter of the Church. Arrange a plaque, employ the finest artists, calligrapher —everything must be perfect."

"Yes, Eminence."

"Her blessed courage and self-sacrifice will be an enormous encouragement to our flock. Very important, Soldi."

"And Kiyama's granddaughter, Sire? The authorities will let us have her body. He insisted."

"Good. Then her remains should be sent to Nagasaki at once. I'll consult Kiyama about how important he wishes to make her funeral."

"You will conduct the service, Eminence?"

"Yes, providing it's possible for me to leave here."

"Lord Kiyama would be very pleased with that honor."

"Yes—but we must make sure her service doesn't detract from the Lady Maria's. Maria's is politically very, very important."

"Of course, Eminence. I quite understand."

Dell'Aqua studied his secretary. "Why don't you trust Onoshi?"

"Sorry, Eminence—probably it's because he's a leper and petrifies me. I apologize."

"Apologize to him, Soldi, he's not to blame for his disease," dell'Aqua said. "We've no proof about the plot."

"The other things the Lady said were true. Why not this?"

"We have no proof. It's all surmise."

"Yes, surmise."

Dell'Aqua moved the glass decanter, watching the refracting light. "At my prayers I smelled the orange blossoms and new breads and, oh, how I wanted to go home."

Soldi sighed. "I dream of *abbacchio,* Eminence, and of meats *pizzaiola* and a flagon of Lacrima Christi and . . . God forgive me the hungers of hunger! Soon we can go home, Eminence. Next year. By next year everything will be settled here."

"Nothing will be settled by next year. This war will hurt us. It will hurt the Church and the faithful terribly."

"No, Eminence. Kyushu will be Christian whoever wins," Soldi said confidently, wanting to cheer up his superior. "This island can wait for God's good time. There's more than enough to do in Kyushu, Eminence, isn't there? Three million souls to convert, half a million of the faithful to minister to. Then there's Nagasaki and trade. They must have trade. Ishido and Toranaga will tear themselves to pieces. What does that matter? They're both anti-Christ, pagans and murderers."

"Yes. But unfortunately what happens in Osaka and Yedo controls Kyushu. What to do, what to do?" Dell'Aqua pushed his melancholy away. "What about the Ingeles? Where's he now?"

"Still under guard in the donjon."

"Leave me for a while, old friend, I have to think. I have to decide what to do. Finally. The Church is in great danger." Dell'Aqua looked out the windows into the forecourt. Then he saw Friar Perez approaching.

Soldi went to the door to intercept the monk. "No," the Father-Visitor said. "I'll see him now."

"Ah, Eminence, good afternoon," Friar Perez said, scratching unconsciously. "You wanted to see me?"

"Yes. Please fetch the letter, Soldi."

"I heard your chapel was destroyed," the monk said.

"Damaged. Please sit down." Dell'Aqua sat in his high-backed chair behind the desk, the monk opposite him. "No one was hurt, thanks be to God. Within a few days it'll be new again. What about your Mission?"

"Untouched," the monk said with open satisfaction. "There were fires all around us after the tremors and many died but we weren't touched. The Eye of God watches over us." Then he added cryptically, "I hear heathens were murdering heathens in the castle last night."

"Yes. One of our most important converts, the Lady Maria, was killed in the melee."

"Ah yes, I got reports too. 'Kill him, Yoshinaka,' the Lady Maria said, and started the bloodbath. I heard she even tried to kill a few herself, before she committed suicide."

Dell'Aqua flushed. "You don't understand anything about the Japanese after all this time, and you even speak a little of their language."

"I understand heresy, stupidity, killing, and political interference, and I speak the pagan tongue very well. I understand a lot about these heathens."

"But not about manners."

"The word of God requires none. It is *the Word*. Oh, yes. I also understand about adultery. What do you think of adultery—and harlots, Eminence?"

The door opened. Soldi offered dell'Aqua the Pope's letter, then left them.

The Father-Visitor gave the paper to the monk, savoring his victory. "This is from His Holiness. It arrived yesterday by special messenger from Macao."

The monk took the Papal Order and read it. This commanded, with the formal agreement of the King of Spain, that all priests of all religious orders were in future to travel to Japan *only* via Lisbon, Goa, and Macao, that all were forbidden on pain of immediate excommunication to go from Manila direct to Japan, and that lastly, all priests, other than Jesuits, were to leave Japan *at once* for Manila whence they could, if their superiors wished, return to Japan, but only via Lisbon, Goa, and Macao.

Friar Perez scrutinized the seal and the signature and the date, reread the Order carefully, then laughed derisively and shoved the letter on the desk. "I don't believe it!"

"That's an Order from His Holiness the—"

"It's another heresy against the Brethren of God, against us, or any mendicants who carry the Word to the heathen. With this device we're forbidden Japan forever, because the Portuguese, abetted by certain people, will prevaricate forever and never grant us passage or visas. *If* this is genuine it only proves what we've been saying for years: Jesuits can subvert even the Vicar of Christ in Rome!"

Dell'Aqua held onto his temper. "You're ordered to leave. Or you will be excommunicated."

"Jesuit threats are meaningless, Eminence. You don't speak with the Tongue of God, you never have, you never will. You're not soldiers of Christ. You serve a Pope, Eminence, a man. You're politicians, men of the earth, men of the fleshpots with your pagan silks and lands and power and riches and influence. The Lord Jesus Christ came to earth in the guise of a simple man who scratched and went barefoot and stank. I will never leave—nor will my Brothers!"

Dell'Aqua had never been so angry in his life. "You-will-leave-Japan!"

"Before God, I won't! But this is the last time I'll come here. If you want me in future, come to our Holy Mission, come and minister to the poor and the sick and the unwanted, like Christ did. Wash their feet like Christ did, and save your own soul before it's too late."

"You are commanded on pain of excommunication to leave Japan at once."

"Come now, Eminence, I'm not excommunicated and never will be. Of course I accept the document, unless it's out of date. This is dated September 16, 1598, almost two years ago. It must be checked, it's far too important to accept at once—and that will take four years at least."

"Of course it's not out of date!"

"You're wrong. As God is my judge, I believe it is. In a few weeks, at the most a few months, we'll have an Archbishop of Japan at long last. A Spanish Bishop! The letters I have from Manila report the Royal Warrant's expected by every mail."

"Impossible! This is Portuguese territory and *our* province!"

"It was Portuguese. It was Jesuit. But that's all changed now. With the help of our Brothers and Divine Guidance, the King of Spain has overthrown your General in Rome."

"That's nonsense. Lies and rumors. On your immortal soul, obey the commands of the Vicar of Christ."

"I will. I will write to him today, I promise you. Meanwhile, expect a Spanish Bishop, a Spanish Viceroy, and a new Captain of the Black Ship—also a Spaniard! That's also to be part of the Royal Warrant. We have friends in high places too and, at long last, they have vanquished the Jesuits, once and for all! Go with God, Eminence." Friar Perez got up, opened the door, and went away.

In the outer office Soldi watched him leave, then hastily came back into the room. Frightened by dell'Aqua's color, he hurried to the decanter and poured some brandy. "Eminence?"

Dell'Aqua shook his head and continued to stare sightlessly into the distance. For the past year there there had been disquieting news from their delegates to the Court of Philip of Spain at Madrid about the growing influence of the enemies of the Society.

"It's not true, Eminence. Spaniards can't come here. It can't be true."

"It can be true, easily. Too easily." Dell'Aqua touched the Papal Order. "This Pope may be dead, our General dead . . . even the King of Spain. Meanwhile . . ." He got to his feet and stood at his full height. "Meanwhile we'll prepare for the worst and pray for help and do the best we can. Send Brother Michael to fetch Kiyama here at once."

"Yes, Eminence. But Kiyama's never been here before. Surely it's unlikely he would come now?"

"Tell Michael to use any words necessary, but he's to bring Kiyama here before sunset. Next, send the war news to Martin at once, to be passed to Toranaga at once. You write the details but I want to send a private cipher with it. Next, send someone to fetch Ferriera here."

"Yes, Eminence. But about Kiyama, surely Michael won't be able—"

"Tell Michael to order him here, in God's name if necessary! We're Soldiers of Christ, we're going to war—to God's war! Hurry up!"

CHAPTER 59

"ANJIN-san?"

Blackthorne heard his name in his dream. It came from very far away, echoing forever. *"Hai?"* he answered.

Then he heard the name repeated and a hand touched him, his eyes opened and focused in the half-light of dawn, his consciousness flooded back and he sat upright. The doctor was again kneeling beside his bed. Kiritsubo and the Lady Ochiba stood nearby, staring down at him. Grays were all around the large room. Oil lanterns flickered warmly.

The doctor spoke to him again. The ringing was still in his ears and the voice faint, but there was no mistake now. He could hear once more. Involuntarily his hands went to his ears and he pressed them to clear them. At once pain exploded in his head and set off sparks and colored lights and a violent throbbing.

"Sorry," he muttered, waiting for the agony to lessen, willing it to lessen. "Sorry, ears hurt, *neh?* But I hear now—understand, Doctor-san? Hear now—little. Sorry, what say?" He watched the man's lips to help himself hear.

"The Lady Ochiba and Kiritsubo-sama want to know how you are."

"Ah!" Blackthorne looked at them. Now he noticed that they were formally dressed. Kiritsubo wore all white, except for a green head scarf. Ochiba's kimono was dark green, without pattern or adornment, her long shawl white gossamer. "Better, thank you," he said, his soul disquieted by the white. "Yes, better." Then he saw the quality of the light outside and realized that it was near dawn and not twilight. "Doctor-san, please I sleep a day and night?"

"Yes, Anjin-san. A day and a night. Lie back, please." The doctor took Blackthorne's wrist with his long fingers and pressed them against the pulse, listening with his fingertips to the nine pulses, three on the surface, three in the middle, and three deep down, as Chinese medicine taught from time immemorial.

All in the room waited for the diagnosis. Then the doctor nodded, satisfied. "Everything seems good, Anjin-san. No bad hurt, understand? Much head pain, *neh?*" He turned and explained in more detail to the Lady Ochiba and Kiritsubo.

"Anjin-san," Ochiba said. "Today Mariko-sama's funeral. You understand 'funeral'?"

"Yes, Lady."

"Good. Her funeral's just after dawn. It is your privilege to go if you wish. You understand?"

"Yes. Think so. Yes, please, I go also."

"Very well." Ochiba spoke to the doctor, telling him to look after his patient very carefully. Then, with a polite bow to Kiritsubo and a smile at Blackthorne, she left.

Kiri waited till she was gone. "All right, Anjin-san?"

"Head bad, Lady. So sorry."

"Please excuse me, I wanted to say thank you. Do you understand?"

"Duty. Only duty. Fail. Mariko-sama dead, *neh?*"

Kiri bowed to him in homage. "Not fail. Oh, no, not fail. Thank you, Anjin-san. For her and me and for the others. Say more later. Thank you." Then she too went away.

Blackthorne took hold of himself and got to his feet. The pain in his head was monstrous, making him want to cry out. He forced his lips into a tight line, his chest aching badly, his stomach churning. In a moment the nausea passed but left a filthy taste in his mouth. He eased his feet forward and walked over to the window and held on to the sill, fighting not to retch. He waited, then walked up and down, but this did not take away the pain in his head or the nausea.

"I all right, thank you," he said, and sat again gratefully.

"Here, drink this. Make better. Settle *hara.*" The doctor had a benign smile. Blackthorne drank and gagged on the brew that smelled like ancient bird droppings and mildewed kelp mixed with fermenting leaves on a hot summer's day. The taste was worse.

"Drink. Better soon, so sorry."

Blackthorne gagged again but forced it down.

"Soon better, so sorry."

Women servants came and combed and dressed his hair. A barber shaved him. Hot towels were brought for his hands and face, and he felt much better. But the pain in his head remained. Other servants helped him to dress in the formal kimono and winged overmantle. There was a new short stabbing sword. "Gift, Master. Gift from Kiritsubo-sama," a woman servant said.

Blackthorne accepted it and stuck it in his belt with his killing sword, the one Toranaga had given him, its haft chipped and almost broken where he had smashed at the bolt. He remembered Mariko standing with her back against the door, then nothing till he was kneeling over her and watching her die. Then nothing until now.

"So sorry, this is the donjon, *neh?*" he said to the captain of Grays.

"Yes, Anjin-san." The captain bowed deferentially, squat like an ape and just as dangerous.

"Why am I here, please?"

The captain smiled and sucked in his breath politely. "The Lord General ordered it."

"But why here?"

The samurai said, "It was the Lord General's orders. Please excuse me, you understand?"

"Yes, thank you," Blackthorne said wearily.

When he was finally ready he felt dreadful. Some cha helped him for a while, then sickness swept through him and he vomited into the bowl a servant held for him, his chest and head pierced with red hot needles at every spasm.

"So sorry," the doctor said patiently. "Here, please drink."

He drank more of the brew but it did not help him.

By now dawn was spreading across the sky. Servants beckoned him and helped him to walk out of the large room, his guards going in front, the remainder following. They went down the staircase and out into the forecourt. A palanquin was waiting with more guards. He got into it thankfully. At an order from his captain of Grays the porters picked up the shafts and, the guards hovering protectively, they joined the procession of litters and samurai and ladies on foot, winding through the maze, out of the castle. All were dressed in their best. Some of the women wore somber kimonos with white head scarves, others wore all white except for a colored scarf.

Blackthorne was aware that he was being watched. He pretended not to notice and tried to keep his back stiff and his face emotionless, and prayed that the sickness would not return to shame him. His pain increased.

The cortege wound through the castle strongpoints, past thousands of samurai drawn up in silent ranks. No one was challenged, no papers demanded. The mourners went through checkpoint after checkpoint, under portcullises and across the five moats without stopping. Once through the main gate, outside the main fortifications, he noticed his Grays become more wary, their eyes watching everyone nearby, keeping close to him, guarding him very carefully. This lessened his anxiety. He had not forgotten that he was a marked man. The procession curled across a clear space, went over a bridge, then took up station in the square beside the river bank.

This space was three hundred paces by five hundred paces. In the center was a pit fifteen paces square and five deep, filled with wood. Over the pit was a high matted roof dressed with white silk and surrounding it were walls of white linen sheets, hung from bamboos, that pointed exactly East, North, West, and South, a small wooden gate in the middle of each wall.

"The gates are for the soul to go through, Anjin-san, in its flight to heaven," Mariko had told him at Hakoné.

"Let's go for a swim or talk of other things. Happy things."

"Yes, of course, but first please may I finish because this is a very happy thing. Our funeral is most very important to us so you should learn about it, Anjin-san, neh? Please?"

"All right. But why have four gates? Why not just one?"

"The soul must have a choice. That's wise—oh, we are very wise, neh? Did I tell thee today that I love thee?" she had said. "We are a very wise nation to allow the soul a choice. Most souls choose the south gate, Anjin-san. That's the important one, where there are tables with dried figs and fresh pomegranates and other fruits, radishes and other vegetables, and the sheaves of rice plantlets if the season is correct. And always a bowl of fresh cooked rice, Anjin-san, that's most important. You see, the soul might want to eat before leaving."

"If it's me, put a roast pheasant or—"

"So sorry, no flesh—not even fish. We're serious about that, Anjin-san. Also on the table there'll be a small brazier with coals burning nicely with precious woods and oils in it to make everything smell sweet. . . ."

Blackthorne felt his eyes fill with tears.

"I want my funeral to be near dawn," she had always said so serenely. "I love the dawn most of all. And, if it could also be in the autumn . . ."

My poor darling, he thought. You knew all along there'd never be an autumn.

His litter stopped in a place of honor in the front rank, near the center, and he was close enough to see tears on the water-sprinkled fruits. Everything was there as she had said. Around were hundreds of palanquins and the square was packed with a thousand samurai and their ladies on foot, all silent and motionless. He recognized Ishido and, beside him, Ochiba. Neither looked at him. They sat on their sumptuous litters and stared at the white linen walls that rustled in the gentling breeze. Kiyama was on the other side of Ochiba, Zataki nearby, with Ito. Onoshi's closed litter was also there. All had echelons of guards. Kiyama's samurai wore crosses. And Onoshi's.

Blackthorne looked around, seeking Yabu, but he could find him nowhere, nor were there any Browns or a friendly face. Now Kiyama was gazing at him stonily and when he saw the look in the eyes he was glad for his guards. Nonetheless he bowed slightly. But Kiyama's gaze never altered, nor was his politeness acknowledged. After a moment, Kiyama looked away and Blackthorne breathed easier.

The sound of drums and bells and metal beating on metal tore the air. Discordant. Piercing. All eyes went to the main gateway to the castle. Then, out of the maw came an ornate roofed palanquin, borne by eight Shinto priests, a high priest sitting on it like a graven Buddha. Other priests beat metal drums before and after this litter, and then came two hundred orange-robed Buddhist priests and more white-clad Shinto priests, and then her bier.

The bier was rich and roofed, all in white, and she was dressed in white and propped sitting, her head slightly forward, her face made up and hair meticulous. Ten Browns were her pallbearers. Before the bier two priestlings strew tiny paper rose petals that the wind took and scattered, signifying that life was as ephemeral as a flower, and after them two priests dragged two spears backwards, indicating that she was samurai and duty strong as the steel blades were strong. After them came four priests with unlit torches. Saruji, her son, followed next, his face as white as his kimono. Then Kiritsubo and the Lady Sazuko, both in white, their hair loosed but draped in gossamer green. The girl's hair fell below her waist, Kiri's was longer. Then there was a space, and last was the remainder of the Toranaga garrison. Some of the Browns were wounded and many limped.

Blackthorne saw only her. She seemed to be in prayer and there was not a mark on her. He kept himself rigid, knowing what an honor this public ceremony, with Ishido and Ochiba as chief witnesses, was for her. But that did not lighten his misery.

For more than an hour, the high priest chanted incantations and the drums clamored. Then in a sudden silence, Saruji stepped forward and took an unlit torch and went to each of the four gates, East, North, West, and South, to make sure they were unobstructed.

Blackthorne saw that the boy was trembling, his eyes downcast as he came back to the bier. Then he lifted the white cord attached to it and guided the pallbearers through the south gate. The whole litter was placed carefully on the wood. Another solemn incantation, then Saruji touched the oil-soaked torch to the coals of the brazier. It blazed at once. He hesitated, then went back through the south gate alone and cast the torch into the pyre. The oil-impregnated wood caught. Quickly it became a furnace. Soon the flames were ten feet high. Saruji was forced back by the heat, then he fetched sweet-scented woods and oils and threw them into the fire. The tinder-dry roof exploded. The linen walls caught. Now the whole pit area was a raging, pyrogenic mass—swirling, crackling, unquenchable.

The roof posts collapsed. A sigh went through the onlookers. Priests came forward and put more wood onto the pyre and the flames rose further, the smoke billowing. Now only the four small gates remained. Blackthorne saw the heat scorching them. Then they too burst into flames.

Then Ishido, the chief witness, got out of his palanquin and walked forward and made the ritual offering of precious wood. He bowed formally and sat again in his litter. At his order, the porters lifted him and he went back to the castle. Ochiba followed him. Others began to leave.

Saruji bowed to the flames a last time. He turned and walked over to Blackthorne. He stood in front of him and bowed. "Thank you, Anjin-san," he said. Then he went away with Kiri and Lady Sazuko.

"All finished, Anjin-san," the captain of Grays said with a grin. "*Kami* safe now. We go castle."

"Wait. Please."

"So sorry, orders, *neh?*" the captain said anxiously, the others guarding closely.

"Please wait."

Careless of their anxiety, Blackthorne got out of the litter, the pain almost blinding him. The samurai spread out, covering him. He walked to the table and picked up some of the small pieces of camphor wood and threw them into the furnace. He could see nothing through the curtain of flames.

"In nomine Patris et Filii et Spiritus Sancti," he muttered in benediction and made a small sign of the cross. Then he turned and left the fire.

When he awoke his head was much better but he felt drained, the dull ache still throbbing behind his temples and across the front of his head.

"How feel, Anjin-san?" the doctor said with his toothy smile, the voice still faint. "Sleep long time."

Blackthorne lifted himself on an elbow and gazed sleepily at the sun's shadows. Must be almost five of the clock in the afternoon now, he thought. I've slept better than six hours. "Sleep all day, *neh?*"

The doctor smiled. "All yesterday and night and most of today. Understand?"

"Understand. Yes." Blackthorne lay back, a sheen of sweat on his skin. Good, he thought. The best thing I could have done, no wonder I feel better.

His bed of soft quilts was screened now on three sides with exquisite movable partitions, their panel paintings landscapes and seascapes, and inlaid with ivory. Sunlight came through windows opposite and flies swarmed, the room vast and pleasant and quiet. Outside were castle sounds, now mixed with horses trotting past, bridles jingling, their hoofs unshod. The slight breeze bore the aroma of smoke. Don't know if I'd want to be burned, he thought. But wait a minute, isn't that better than being put in a box and buried and then the worms. . . . Stop it, he ordered himself, feeling himself drifting into a downward spiral. There's nothing to worry about, *karma* is *karma* and when you're dead, you're dead, and you never know anything then—and anything's better than drowning, water filling you, your body becoming foul and blotted, the crabs. . . . Stop it!

"Drink, please." The doctor gave him more of the foul brew. He gagged but kept it down.

"Cha, please." The woman servant poured it for him and he thanked her. She was a moon-faced woman of middle age, slits for eyes and a fixed empty smile. After three cups his mouth was bearable.

"Please, Anjin-san, how ears?"

"Same. Still distance . . . distance, understand? Very distance."

"Understand. Eat, Anjin-san?"

A small tray was set with rice and soup and charcoaled fish. His stomach was queasy but he remembered that he had hardly eaten for two days so he sat up and forced himself to take some rice and he drank the fish soup. This settled his stomach so he ate more and finished it all, using the chopsticks now as extensions of his fingers, without conscious effort. "Thank you. Hungry."

"Yes," the doctor said. He put a linen bag of herbs on the low table beside the bed. "Make cha with this, Anjin-san. Once every day until all gone. Understand?"

"Yes. Thank you."

"It has been an honor to serve you." The old man motioned to the servant, who took away the empty tray, and after another bow followed her and left by the same inner door. Now Blackthorne was alone. He lay back on the futons feeling much better.

"I was just hungry," he said aloud. He was wearing only a loincloth. His formal clothes were in a careless pile where he had left them and this surprised him, though a clean Brown kimono was beside his swords. He let himself drift, then suddenly he felt an alien presence. Uneasily he sat up and glanced around. Then he got onto his knees and looked over the screens, and before he knew it, he was standing, his head splitting from the sudden panicked movement as he saw the tonsured Japanese Jesuit staring at him, kneeling motionlessly beside the main doorway, a crucifix and rosary in his hand.

"Who are you?" he asked through his pain.

"I'm Brother Michael, senhor." The coal-dark eyes never wavered. Blackthorne moved from the screens and stood over his swords. "What d'you want with me?"

"I was sent to ask how you are," Michael said quietly in clear though accented Portugese.

"By whom?"

"By the Lord Kiyama."

Suddenly Blackthorne realized they were totally alone. "Where are my guards?"

"You don't have any, senhor."

"Of course I've guards! I've twenty Grays. Where are my Grays?"

"There were none here when I arrived, senhor. So sorry. You were still sleeping then." Michael motioned gravely outside the door. "Perhaps you should ask those samurai."

Blackthorne picked up his sword. "Please get away from the door."

"I'm not armed, Anjin-san."

"Even so, don't come near me. Priests make me nervous."

Obediently Michael got to his feet and moved away with the same unnerving calm. Outside two Grays lolled against the balustrade of the landing.

"Afternoon," Blackthorne said politely, not recognizing either of them.

Neither bowed. "Afternoon, Anjin-san," one replied.

"Please, where my other guards?"

"All guards taken away Hour of the Hare, this morning. Understand Hour of Hare? We're not your guards, Anjin-san. This is our ordinary post."

Blackthorne felt the cold sweat trickling down his back. "Guards taken away—who order?"

Both samurai laughed. The tall one said, "Here, inside the donjon, Anjin-san, only the Lord General gives orders—or the Lady Ochiba. How do you feel now?"

"Better, thank you."

The taller samurai called out down the hall. In a few moments an officer came out of a room with four samurai. He was young and taut. When he saw Blackthorne his eyes lit up. "Ah, Anjin-san. How do you feel?"

"Better, thank you. Please excuse me, but where my guards?"

"I am ordered to tell you, when you wake up, that you're to go back to your ship. Here's your pass." The captain took the paper from his sleeve and gave it to him and pointed contemptuously at Michael. "This fellow's to be your guide."

Blackthorne tried to get his head working, his brain screeching danger. "Yes. Thank you. But first, please must see Lord Ishido. Very important."

"So sorry. Your orders are to go back to the ship as soon as you wake up. Do you understand?"

"Yes. Please excuse me, but very important I see Lord Ishido. Please tell your captain. Now. Must see Lord Ishido before leave. Very important, so sorry."

The samurai scratched at the pockmarks on his chin. "I will ask. Please dress." He strode off importantly to Blackthorne's relief. The four samurai remained. Blackthorne went back and dressed quickly. They watched him. The priest waited in the corridor.

Be patient, he told himself. Don't think and don't worry. It's a mistake. Nothing's changed. You've still the power you always had.

He put both swords in his sash and drank the rest of the cha. Then he saw the pass. The paper was stamped and covered with characters. There's no mistake about that, he thought, the fresh kimono already sticking to him.

"Hey, Anjin-san," one of the samurai said, "hear you kill five *ninja*. Very, very good, *neh?*"

"So sorry, two only. Perhaps three." Blackthorne twisted his head from side to side to ease the ache and dizziness.

"I heard there were fifty-seven *ninja* dead—one hundred and sixteen Browns. Is that right?"

"I don't know. So sorry."

The captain came back into the room. "Your orders are to go to your ship, Anjin-san. This priest is your guide."

"Yes. Thank you. But first, so sorry, must see Lady Ochiba. Very, very important. Please ask your—"

The captain spun on Michael and spoke gutturally and very fast. *"Neh?"* Michael bowed, unperturbed, and turned to Blackthorne. "So sorry, senhor. He says his superior is asking his superior, but meanwhile you are to leave at once and follow me—to the galley."

"Ima!" the captain added for emphasis.

Blackthorne knew he was a dead man. He heard himself say, "Thank you, Captain. Where my guards, please?"

"You haven't any guards."

"Please send my ship. Please fetch my own vassals from—"

"Order go ship now! Understand, *neh?*" The words were impolite and very final. "Go ship!" the captain added with a crooked smile, waiting for Blackthorne to bow first.

Blackthorne noticed this and it all became a nightmare, everything slowed and fogged, and he desperately wanted to empty himself and wipe the sweat off his face and bow, but he was sure that the captain would hardly bow back, perhaps not even politely and never as an equal, so he would be shamed before all of them. It was clear that he had been betrayed and sold out to the Christian enemy, that Kiyama and Ishido and the priests were part of the betrayal, and for whatever reason, whatever the price, there was nothing now that he could do except wipe off the sweat and bow and leave and *they* would be waiting for him.

Then Mariko was with him and he remembered *her* terror and all that she had meant and all that she had done and all that she had taught him. He forced his hand onto the broken hilt of his sword and set his feet truculently apart, knowing that his fate was decided, his *karma* fixed, and that if he had to die he preferred to die now with pride than later.

"I'm John Blackthorne, Anjin-san," he said, his absolute commitment lending him a strange power and perfect rudeness. "General of Lord Toranaga ship. All ship. Samurai and hatamoto! Who are you?"

The captain flushed. "Saigo Masakatsu of Kaga, Captain, of Lord Ishido's garrison."

"I'm hatamoto—are you hatamoto?" Blackthorne asked, even more rudely, not even acknowledging the name of his opponent, only seeing him with an enormous, unreal clarity—seeing every pore, every stubbled whisker, every fleck of color in the hostile brown eyes, every hair on the back of the man's hand gripping the sword hilt.

"No, not hatamoto."

"Are you samurai—or *ronin?*" The last word hissed out and Blackthorne felt men behind him but he did not care. He was only watching the captain, waiting for the sudden, death-dealing blow that summoned up all *hara-gei*, all the innermost source of energy, and he readied to return the blow with equal blinding force in a mutual, honorable death, and so defeat his enemy.

To his astonishment he saw the captain's eyes change, and the man shriveled and bowed, low and humble. The man held the bow, leaving himself defenseless. "Please—please excuse my bad manners. I—I was *ronin* but—but the Lord General gave me a second chance. Please excuse my bad manners, Anjin-san." The voice was laced with shame.

It was all unreal and Blackthorne was still ready to strike, expecting to strike, expecting death and not a conquest. He looked at the other samurai. As one man they bowed and held the bow with their captain, granting him victory.

After a moment Blackthorne bowed stiffly. But not as an equal. They held their bow until he turned and walked along the corridor, Michael following, out onto the main steps, down the steps into the forecourt. He could feel no pain now. He was filled only with an enormous glow. Grays were watching him, and the group of samurai that escorted him and Michael to the first checkpoint kept carefully out of his sword range. One man was hurriedly sent ahead.

At the next checkpoint the new officer bowed politely as an equal and he bowed back. The pass was examined meticulously but correctly. Another escort took them to the next checkpoint where everything was repeated. Thence over the innermost moat, and the next. No one interfered with them. Hardly any samurai paid attention to him.

Gradually he noticed his head was scarcely aching. His sweat had dried. He unknotted his fingers from his sword hilt and flexed them a moment. He stopped at a fountain which was set in a wall and drank and splashed water on his head.

The escorting Grays stopped and waited politely, and all the time he was trying to work out why he had lost favor and the protection of Ishido and Lady Ochiba. Nothing's changed, he thought frantically. He looked up and saw Michael staring at him. "What do you want?"

"Nothing, senhor," Michael said politely. Then a smile spread and it was filled with warmth. "Ah, senhor, you did me a great service back there, making that foul-mannered *cabron* drink his own urine. Oh, that was good to see! Thou," he added in Latin. "I thank thee."

"I did nothing for you," Blackthorne said in Portuguese, not wanting to talk Latin.

"Yes. But peace be upon you, senhor. Know that God moves in mysterious ways. It was a service for all *men*. That *ronin* was shamed and he deserved it. It is a filthy thing to abuse *bushido.*"

"You're samurai too?"

"Yes, senhor, I have that honor," Michael said. "My father is cousin to Lord Kiyama and my clan is of Hizen Province in Kyushu. How did you know he was *ronin?*"

Blackthorne tried to remember. "I'm not sure. Perhaps because he said he was from Kaga and that's a long way off and Mariko—Lady Toda said Kaga's far north. I don't know—I don't remember really what I said."

The officer of the escort came back to them. "Please excuse me, Anjin-san, but is this fellow bothering you?"

"No. No, thank you." Blackthorne set off again. The pass was checked again, with courtesy, and they went on.

The sun was lowering now, still a few hours to sunset, and dust devils whirled in tiny spirals in the heated air currents. They passed many stables, all horses facing out—lances and spears and saddles ready for instant departure, samurai grooming the horses and cleaning equipment. Blackthorne was astounded by their number.

"How many horse, Captain?" he asked.

SHŌGUN (737) BOOK V

"Thousands, Anjin-san. Ten, twenty, thirty thousand here and elsewhere in the castle."

When they were crossing the next to last moat, Blackthorne beckoned Michael. "You're guiding me to the galley?"

"Yes. That's what I was told to do, senhor."

"Nowhere else?"

"No, senhor."

"By whom?"

"Lord Kiyama. And the Father-Visitor, senhor."

"Ah, him! I prefer Anjin-san, not senhor—Father."

"Please excuse me, Anjin-san, but I'm not a Father. I'm not ordained."

"When does that happen?"

"In God's time," Michael said confidently.

"Where's Yabu-san?"

"I don't know, so sorry."

"You're just taking me to my ship, nowhere else?"

"Yes, Anjin-san."

"And then I'm free? Free to go where I want?"

"I was told to ask how you were, then to guide you to the ship, nothing more. I'm just a messenger, a guide."

"Before God?"

"I'm just a guide, Anjin-san."

"Where did you learn to speak Portuguese so well? And Latin?"

"I was one of the four . . . the four acolytes sent by the Father-Visitor to Rome. I was thirteen, Uraga-noh-Tadamasa twelve."

"Ah! Now I remember. Uraga-san told me you were one of them. You were his friend. You know he's dead?"

"Yes. I was sickened to hear about it."

"Christians did that."

"Murderers did that, Anjin-san. Assassins. They will be judged, never fear."

After a moment, Blackthorne said, "How did you like Rome?"

"I detested it. We all did. Everything about it—the food and the filth and ugliness. They're all *eta* there—unbelievable! It took us eight years to get there and back and oh how I blessed the Madonna when at last I got back."

"And the Church? The Fathers?"

"Detestable. Many of them," Michael said calmly. "I was shocked with their morals and mistresses and greed and pomp and hypocrisy and lack of manners —and their two standards, one for the flock and one for the shepherds. It was all hateful . . . and yet I found God among some of them, Anjin-san. So strange. I found the Truth, in the cathedrals and cloisters and among the Fathers." Michael looked at him guilelessly, a tenderness permeating him. "It was rare, Anjin-san, very rarely that I found a glimmer—that's true. But I did find the Truth and God and know that Christianity is the only path to life everlasting . . . please excuse me, Catholic Christianity."

"Did you see the auto-da-fé—or Inquisition—or jails—witch trials?"

"I saw many terrible things. Very few men are wise—most are sinners and great evil happens on earth in God's name. But not of God. This world is a vale of tears and only a preparation for Everlasting Peace." He prayed silently for a moment, then, refreshed, he looked up. "Even some heretics can be good, *neh?*"

"Maybe," Blackthorne replied, liking him.

The last moat and last gate, the main south gate. The last checkpoint, and his paper was taken away. Michael walked under the last portcullis. Blackthorne followed. Outside the castle a hundred samurai were waiting. Kiyama's men. He saw their crucifixes and their hostility and he stopped. Michael did not. The officer motioned Blackthorne onward. He obeyed. The samurai closed up behind him and around him, locking him in their midst. Porters and tradesmen on this main road scattered and bowed and groveled until they were passed. A few held up pathetic crosses and Michael blessed them, leading the way down the slight slope, past the burial ground where the pit no longer smoked, across a bridge and into the city, heading for the sea. Grays and other samurai were coming up from the city among the pedestrians. When they saw Michael they scowled and would have forced him onto the side if it hadn't been for the mass of Kiyama samurai.

Blackthorne followed Michael. He was beyond fear, though not beyond wishing to escape. But there was no place to run, or to hide. On land. His only safety was aboard *Erasmus,* beating out to sea, a full crew with him, provisioned and armed.

"What happens at the galley, Brother?"

"I don't know, Anjin-san."

Now they were in the city streets, nearing the sea. Michael turned a corner and came into an open fish market. Pretty maids and fat maids and old ladies and youths and men and buyers and sellers and children all gaped at him, then began bowing hastily. Blackthorne followed the samurai through the stalls and panniers and bamboo trays of all kinds of fish, sea-sparkling fresh, laid out so cleanly—many swimming in tanks, prawns and shrimps, lobster and crabs and crayfish. Never so clean in London, he thought absently, neither the fish nor those who sold them. Then he saw a row of food stalls to one side, each with a small charcoal brazier, and he caught the full perfume of broiling crayfish.

"Jesus!" Without thinking, he changed direction. Immediately the samurai barred his way. "*Gomen nasai, kinjiru,*" one of them said.

"*Iyé!*" Blackthorne replied as roughly. "*Watashi tabetai desu, neh? Watashi Anjin-san, neh?*" I'm hungry. I'm the Anjin-san!

Blackthorne began to push through them. The senior officer hurried to intercept. Quickly Michael stepped back and talked placatingly, though with authority, and asked permission and, reluctantly, it was granted.

"Please, Anjin-san," he said, "the officer says eat if you wish. What would you like?"

"Some of those, please." Blackthorne pointed at the giant prawns that were headless and split down their length, all pink and white fleshed, the shells crisped to perfection. "Some of those." He could not tear his eyes off them. "Please tell the officer I haven't eaten for almost two days and I'm suddenly famished. So sorry."

The fish seller was an old man with three teeth and leathery skin and he wore only a loincloth. He was puffed with pride that his stall had been chosen and he picked out the five best prawns with nimble chopsticks and laid them neatly on a bamboo tray and set others to sizzle.

"*Dozo,* Anjin-sama!"

"*Domo.*" Blackthorne felt his stomach growling. He wanted to gorge. Instead he picked one up with the fresh wooden chopsticks, dipped it in the sauce, and ate with relish. It was delicious.

"Brother Michael?" he asked, offering the plate. Michael took one, but only for good manners. The officer refused, though he thanked him.

Blackthorne finished that plate and had two more. He could have eaten another two but decided not to for good manners and also because he didn't want to strain his stomach.

"*Domo,*" he said, setting down the plate with a polite obligatory belch. "*Bimi desu!*" Delicious.

The man beamed and bowed and the stallkeepers nearby bowed and then Blackthorne realized to his horror that he had no money. He reddened.

"What is it?" Michael asked.

"I, er, I haven't any money with me—or, er, anything to give the man. I've—could you lend me some please?"

"I haven't any money, Anjin-san. We don't carry money."

There was an embarrassed silence. The seller grinned, waiting patiently. Then, with equal embarrassment, Michael turned to the officer and quietly asked him for money. The officer was coldly furious with Blackthorne. He spoke brusquely to one of his men who came forward and paid the stallkeeper handsomely, to be thanked profusely, as, pink and sweating, Michael turned and led again. Blackthorne caught up with him. "Sorry about that but it . . . it never occurred to me! That's the first time I've bought anything here. I've never had money, as crazy as it sounds, and I never thought . . . I've never used money. . . ."

"Please, forget it, Anjin-san. It was nothing."

"Please tell the officer I'll pay him when I get to the ship."

Michael did as he was asked. They walked in silence for a while, Blackthorne getting his bearings. At the end of this street was the beach, the sea calm and dullish under the sunset light. Then he saw where they were and pointed left, to a wide street that ran east-west. "Let's go that way."

"This way is quicker, Anjin-san."

"Yes, but your way we've got to pass the Jesuit Mission and the Portuguese lorcha. I'd rather make a detour and go the long way round."

"I was told to go this way."

"Let's go the other way." Blackthorne stopped. The officer asked what was the matter and Michael explained. The officer waved them onward—Michael's way.

Blackthorne weighed the results of refusing. He would be forced, or bound and carried, or dragged. None of these suited him, so he shrugged and strode on.

They came out onto the wide road that skirted the beach. Half a *ri* ahead were the Jesuit wharves and warehouses and a hundred paces farther he could see the Portuguese ship. Beyond that, another two hundred paces, was his galley. It was too far away to see men aboard yet.

Blackthorne picked up a stone and sent it whistling out to sea. "Let's walk along the beach for a while."

"Certainly, Anjin-san." Michael went down the sand. Blackthorne walked in the shallows, enjoying the cool of the sea, the soughing of the slight surf.

"It's a fine time of the day, *neh?*"

"Ah, Anjin-san," Michael said with sudden, open friendliness, "there are many times, Madonna forgive me, I wish I wasn't a priest but just the son of my father, and this is one of them."

"Why?"

"I'd like to spirit you away, you and your strange ship at Yokohama, to Hizen, to our great harbor of Sasebo. Then I would ask you to barter with me—I'd ask you to show me and our sea captains the ways of your ship and your ways of the sea. In return I'd offer you the best teachers in the realm, teachers of *bushido, cha-no-yu, hara-gei, ki, zazen* meditation, flower arranging, and all the special unique knowledges that we possess."

"I'd like that. Why don't we do it now?"

"It's not possible today. But you already know so much and in such a short time, *neh?* Mariko-sama was a great teacher. You are a worthy samurai. And you have a quality that's rare here: unpredictability. The Taikō had it, Toranaga-sama has it too. You see, usually we're a very predictable people."

"Are you?"

"Yes."

"Then predict a way I can escape the trap I'm in."

"So sorry, there isn't one, Anjin-san," Michael said.

"I don't believe that. How did you know my ship is at Yokohama?"

"That's common knowledge."

"Is it?"

"Almost everything about you—and your defense of Lord Toranaga, and the Lady Maria, Lady Toda—is well known. And honored."

"I don't believe that either." Blackthorne picked up another flat stone and sent it skimming over the waves. They went on, Blackthorne humming a sea shanty, liking Michael very much. Soon their way was blocked by a breakwater. They skirted it and came up onto the road once more. The Jesuit warehouse and Mission were tall and brooding now under the reddening sky. He saw the orange-robed Lay Brothers guarding the arched stone gateway and sensed their hostility. But it did not touch him. His head began to ache again.

As he had expected, Michael headed for the Mission gates. He readied himself, resolved that they would have to beat him into unconsciousness before he went inside and they forced him to give up his weapons.

"You're just guiding me to my galley, eh?"

"Yes, Anjin-san." To his astonishment Michael motioned him to stop outside the gateway. "Nothing's changed. I was told to inform the Father-Visitor as we passed. So sorry, but you'll have to wait a moment."

Thrown off guard, Blackthorne watched him enter the gates alone. He had expected that the Mission was to be the end of his journey. First an Inquisition and trial, with torture, then handed over to the Captain-General. He looked at the lorcha a hundred paces away. Ferriera and Rodrigues were on the poop and armed seamen crowded the main deck. Past the ship, the wharf road curled slightly and he could just see his galley. Men were watching from the gunwales and he thought he recognized Yabu and Vinck among them but could not be sure. There seemed to be a few women aboard also but who they were he did not know. Surrounding the galley were Grays. Many Grays.

His eyes returned to Ferriera and Rodrigues. Both were heavily armed. So were the seamen. Gun crews lounged near the two small shore-side cannon, but in reality they were manning them. He recognized the great bulk of Pesaro, the bosun, moving down the companionway with a group of men. His eyes followed them, then his blood chilled. A tall stake was driven into the packed earth on the farside wharf. Wood was piled around the base.

"Ah, Captain-Pilot, how are you?"

Dell'Aqua was coming through the gates, dwarfing Michael beside him. Today the Father-Visitor was wearing a Jesuit robe, his great height and luxuriant gray-white beard giving him the ominous regality of a biblical patriarch, every inch an Inquisitor, outwardly benign, Blackthorne thought. He stared up into the brown eyes, finding it strange to look up at any man, and even stranger to see compassion in the eyes. But he knew there would be no pity behind the eyes and he expected none. "Ah, Father-Visitor, how are you?" he replied, the prawns now leaden in his stomach, sickening him.

"Shall we go on?"

"Why not?"

So the Inquisition's to be aboard, Blackthorne thought, desperately afraid, wishing he had pistols in his belt. You'd be the first to die, Eminence.

"You stay here, Michael," dell'Aqua said. Then he glanced toward the Portuguese frigate. His face hardened and he set off.

Blackthorne hesitated. Michael and the surrounding samurai were watching him oddly.

"*Sayonara,* Anjin-san," Michael said. "Go with God."

Blackthorne nodded briefly and started to walk through the samurai, waiting for them to fall on him to take away his swords. But they let him through unmolested. He stopped and looked back, his heart racing.

For a moment he was tempted to draw his sword and charge. But there was no escape that way. They wouldn't fight him. Many had spears so they would catch him and disarm him, and bind him and hand him on. I won't go bound, he promised himself. His only path was forward and there his swords were helpless against guns. He would charge the guns but they would just maim him in the knees and bind him. . . .

"Captain Blackthorne, come along," dell'Aqua called out.

"Yes, just a moment please." Blackthorne beckoned Michael. "Listen, Brother, down by the beach you said I was a worthy samurai. Did you mean it?"

"Yes, Anjin-san. That and everything."

"Then I beg a favor, as a samurai," he said quietly but urgently.

"What favor?"

"To die as a samurai."

"Your death isn't in my hands. It's in the Hand of God, Anjin-san."

"Yes. But I ask that favor of you." Blackthorne waved at the distant stake. "That's no way. That's filthy."

Perplexed, Michael peered toward the lorcha. Then he saw the stake for the first time. "Blessed Mother of God . . ."

"Captain Blackthorne, please come along," dell'Aqua called again.

Blackthorne said, more urgently, "Explain to the officer. He's got enough samurai here to insist, *neh?* Explain to him. You've been to Europe. You know how it is there. It's not much to ask, *neh?* Please, I'm samurai. One of them could be my second."

"I . . . I will ask." Michael went back to the officer and began to talk softly and urgently.

Blackthorne turned and centered his attention on the ship. He walked forward. Dell'Aqua waited till he was alongside and set off again.

Ahead, Blackthorne saw Ferriera strut off the poop, down along the main deck, pistols in his belt, rapier at his side. Rodrigues was watching him, right hand on the butt of a long-barreled dueling piece. Pesaro and ten seamen were already on the jetty, leaning on bayoneted muskets. And the long shadow of the stake reached out toward him.

Oh, God, for a brace of pistols and ten jolly Jack Tars and one cannon, he thought, as the gap closed inexorably. Oh, God, let me not be shamed. . . .

"Good evening, Eminence," Ferriera said, his eyes seeing only Blackthorne. "So, Inge—"

"Good evening, Captain-General." Dell'Aqua pointed angrily at the stake. "Is this your idea?"

"Yes, Eminence."

"Go back aboard your ship!"

"This is a military decision."

"*Go aboard your ship!*"

"*No!* Pesaro!" At once the bosun and the bayoneted shore party came on guard and advanced toward Blackthorne. Ferriera slid out the pistol. "So, Ingeles, we meet again."

"That's something that pleases me not at all." Blackthorne's sword came out of its scabbard. He held it awkwardly with two hands, the broken haft hurting him.

"Tonight you will be pleased in hell," Ferriera said thickly.

"If you had any courage you'd fight—man to man. But you're not a man, you're a coward, a Spanish coward without balls."

"Disarm him!" Ferriera ordered.

At once the ten men went forward, bayonets leveled. Blackthorne backed away but he was surrounded. Bayonets stabbed for his legs and he slashed at an assailant, but as the man retreated another attacked from behind. Then dell'Aqua came to his senses and shouted, "Put down your guns! Before God, I order you to stop!"

The seamen were flustered. All muskets were zeroed in on Blackthorne, who stood helplessly at bay, sword high.

"Get back, all of you," dell'Aqua called out. "Get back! Before God, get back! Are you animals?"

Ferriera said, "I want that man!"

"I know, and I've already told you you can't have him! Yesterday and today! Are you deaf? God give me patience! Order your men aboard!"

"I order you to turn around and go away!"

"You order *me?*"

"Yes, I order you! I'm Captain-General, Governor of Macao, Chief Officer of Portugal in Asia, and that man's a threat to the State, the Church, the Black Ship, and Macao!"

"Before God, I'll excommunicate you and all your crew if this man's harmed. You hear?" Dell'Aqua spun on the musketeers, who backed off, frightened. Except Pesaro. Pesaro stood his ground defiantly, his pistol loose in his hand, waiting for Ferriera's order. "Get on that ship and out of the way!"

"You're making a mistake," Ferriera stormed. "He's a *threat!* I'm Military Commander in Asia and I say—"

"This is a Church matter, not a military de—"

Blackthorne was dazed, hardly able to think or to see, his head once more exploding with pain. Everything had happened so fast, one moment guarded, the next not, one moment betrayed to the Inquisition, the next escaped, then to be betrayed again and now defended by the Chief Inquisitor. Nothing made sense.

Ferriera was shouting, "I caution you again! As God's my judge, you're making a mistake and I'll inform Lisbon!"

"Meanwhile order your men aboard or I'll remove you as Captain-General of the Black Ship!"

"You don't have that power!"

"Unless you order your men aboard and order the Ingeles unharmed *at once,* I declare you excommunicated—and any man who serves under you, in any command, excommunicated, and curse you and all who serve you, in the Name of God!"

"By the Madonna—" Ferriera stopped. He was not afraid for himself but now his Black Ship was jeopardized and he knew most of his crew would desert him unless he obeyed. For a moment he contemplated shooting the priest, but that would not take away the curse. So he conceded. "Very well—back aboard, everyone! Stand down!"

Obediently the men scattered, glad to be away from the priest's wrath. Blackthorne was still bewildered, half wondering if his head was tricking him. Then, in the melee, Pesaro's hatred burst. He aimed. Dell'Aqua saw the covert movement and leaped forward to protect Blackthorne with his own bulk. Pesaro pulled the trigger but at that moment arrows impaled him, the pistol fired harmlessly, and he collapsed screaming.

Blackthorne spun around and saw six Kiyama archers, fresh arrows already in their bows. Standing near them was Michael. The officer spoke harshly. Pesaro gave a last shriek, his limbs contorted, and he died.

Michael trembled as he broke the silence. "The officer says, so sorry, but he was afraid for the Father-Visitor's life." Michael was begging God to forgive him for giving the signal to fire. But Pesaro had been warned, he reasoned. And it is my duty to see the Father-Visitor's orders are obeyed, that his life is protected, that assassins are stamped out and no one excommunicated.

Dell'Aqua was on his knees beside the corpse of Pesaro. He made the sign of the cross and said the sacred words. The Portuguese around him were watching the samurai, craving the order to kill the murderers. The rest of Kiyama's men were hastening from the Mission gate where they had remained, and a number of Grays were streaming back from the galley area to investigate. Through his almost blinding rage Ferriera knew he could not afford a fight here and now. "Everyone back aboard! Bring Pesaro's body!" Sullenly the shore party began to obey.

Blackthorne lowered his sword but did not sheathe it. He waited stupefied, expecting a trick, expecting to be captured and dragged aboard.

On the quarterdeck Rodrigues said quietly, "Stand by to repel boarders, but carefully, by God!" Instantly men slipped to action stations. "Cover the Captain-General! Prepare the longboat. . . ."

Dell'Aqua got up and turned on Ferriera, who stood arrogantly at the companionway, prepared to defend his ship. "You're responsible for that man's death!" the Father-Visitor hissed. "Your fanatic, vengeful lust and unho—"

"Before you say something publicly you may regret, Eminence, you'd better think carefully," Ferriera interrupted. "I bowed to your order even though I knew, before God, you were making a terrible mistake. You heard me order my men back! Pesaro disobeyed you, not me, and the truth is you're responsible if anyone is. You prevented him and us from doing our duty. That Ingeles is the enemy! It was a military decision, by God! I'll inform Lisbon." His eyes checked the battle readiness of his ship and the approaching samurai.

Rodrigues had moved to the main deck gangway. "Captain-General, I can't get out to sea with this wind and this tide."

"Get a longboat ready to haul us out if need be."

"It's being done."

Ferriera shouted at the seamen carrying Pesaro, telling them to hurry. Quickly all were back aboard. The cannon were manned, though discreetly, and everyone had two muskets nearby. Left and right, samurai were massing on the wharf but they made no overt move to interfere.

Still on the dock Ferriera said peremptorily to Michael, "Tell them all to disperse! There's no trouble here—nothing for them to do. There was a mistake, a bad one, but they were right to shoot the bosun. Tell them to disperse." He hated to say it and wanted to kill them all but he could almost smell the peril on the wharf and he had no option now but to retreat.

Michael did as he was ordered. The officers did not move.

"You'd better go on, Eminence," Ferriera said bitterly. "But this is not the last of it—you'll regret saving him!"

Dell'Aqua too felt the explosiveness surrounding them. But it did not touch him. He made the sign of the cross and said a small benediction, then he turned away. "Come along, Pilot."

"Why are you letting me go?" Blackthorne asked, the pain in his head agonizing, still not daring to believe it.

"Come along, Pilot!"

"But why are you letting me go? I don't understand."

"Nor do I," Ferriera said. "I'd like to know the *real* reason too, Eminence. Isn't he still a threat to us and the Church?"

Dell'Aqua stared at him. Yes, he wanted to say, to wipe the arrogance off the popinjay's face in front of him. But the bigger threat is the immediate war and how to buy time for you and fifty years of Black Ships, and whom to choose: Toranaga or Ishido. You understand nothing of our problems, Ferriera, or the stakes involved, or the delicacy of our position here or the dangers.

"Please Lord Kiyama, reconsider. I suggest you should choose Lord Toranaga," he had told the *daimyo* yesterday, through Michael as interpreter, not trusting his own Japanese, which was only fair.

"This is unwarranted interference in Japanese affairs and outside your jurisdiction. And, too, the barbarian must die."

Dell'Aqua had used all his diplomatic skill but Kiyama had been adamant and had refused to commit himself or change his position. Then, this morning, when he had gone to Kiyama to tell him that, through God's will, the Ingeles was neutralized, there had been a glimmer of hope.

"I've considered what you said," Kiyama had told him. "I will not ally myself with Toranaga. Between now and the battle I will watch both contenders very carefully. At the correct time I will choose. And now I consent to let the barbarian go . . . not because of what you've told me but because of the Lady Mariko, to honor her . . . and because the Anjin-san is *samurai.* . . ."

Ferriera was still staring back at him. "Isn't the Ingeles still a threat?"

"Have a safe journey, Captain-General, and Godspeed. Pilot, I'm taking you to your galley. . . . Are you all right?"

"It's . . . my head it's . . . I think the explosion. . . . You're really letting me go? Why?"

"Because the Lady Maria, the Lady Mariko, asked us to protect you." Dell'-Aqua started off again.

"But that's no reason! You wouldn't do that just because she asked you."

"I agree," Ferriera said. Then he called out, "Eminence, why not tell him the whole truth?"

Dell'Aqua did not stop. Blackthorne began to follow but he did not turn his back to the ship, still expecting treachery. "Doesn't make sense. You know I'm going to destroy you. I'll take your Black Ship."

Ferriera laughed scornfully. "With what, Ingeles? *You have no ship!*"

"What do you mean?"

"You have no ship. She's dead. If she wasn't, I'd never let you go, whatever his Eminence threatened."

"It's not true . . ."

Through the fog in his head Blackthorne heard Ferriera say it again and laugh louder, and add something about an accident and the Hand of God and your ship's burned to her spine, so you'll never harm *my* ship now, though you're still heretic and enemy, and still a threat to the Faith. Then he saw Rodrigues clearly, pity on his face, and the lips spelled out, Yes, it's true, Ingeles.

"It's not true, can't be true."

Then the Inquisitor priest was saying from a million leagues away, "I received a message this morning from Father Alvito. It seems an earthquake caused a tidal wave, the wave . . .”

But Blackthorne was not listening. His mind was crying out, Your ship’s dead, you’ve let her down, your ship’s dead, you’ve no ship no ship no ship. . . .

“It’s not true! You’re lying, my ship’s in a safe harbor and guarded by four thousand men. She’s safe!”

Someone said, “But not from God,” and then the Inquisitor was talking again, “The tidal wave heeled your ship. They say that oil lamps on deck were upset and the fire spread. Your ship’s gutted. . . .”

“Lies! What about the deck watch? There’s always a deck watch! It’s impossible,” he shouted, but he knew that somehow the price for his life had been his ship.

“You’re beached, Ingeles,” Ferriera was goading him. “You’re marooned. You’re here forever, you’ll never get passage on one of our ships. You’re beached forever. . . .”

It went on and on and he was drowning. Then his eyes cleared. He heard the cry of the gulls and smelled the stink of the shore and saw Ferriera, he saw his enemy and knew it was all a lie to drive him mad. He knew it absolutely and that the priests were part of the plot. “God take you to hell!” he shouted and rushed at Ferriera, his sword raised high. But only in his dream was it a rush. Hands caught him easily and took his swords away and set him walking between two Grays, through all the others, until he was at the companionway of the galley and they gave him back his swords and let him go.

It was difficult for him to see or to hear, his brain hardly working now in the pain, but he was certain it was all a trick to drive him mad and that it would succeed if he did not make a great effort. Help me, he prayed, someone help me, then Yabu was beside him and Vinck and his vassals and he could not distinguish the languages. They guided him aboard, Kiri there somewhere and Sazuko, a child crying in a maid’s arms, the remnants of the Browns’ garrison crowding the deck, rowers and seamen.

Smell of sweat, fear sweat. Yabu was talking at him. And Vinck. It took a long time to concentrate. “Pilot, why in Christ’s name did they let you go?”

“I . . . they . . .” He could not say the words.

Then somehow he found himself on the quarterdeck and Yabu was ordering the Captain-san to put to sea before Ishido changed his mind about letting them all leave, and before the Grays on the dock changed their minds about permitting the galley to go, telling the Captain full speed for Nagasaki . . . Kiri saying, so sorry, Yabu-sama, please first Yedo, we must go to Yedo. . . .

The oars of the shallow draft vessel eased off the wharf, against the tide and against the wind, and went out into the stream, gulls crying in the wake, and Blackthorne pulled himself out of his daze enough to say coherently, “No. So sorry. Go Yokohama. Must Yokohama.”

“First get men at Nagasaki, Anjin-san, understand? Important. First men! Have plan,” Yabu said.

“No. Go Yokohama. My ship . . . my ship danger.”

“What danger?” Yabu demanded.

“Christians say . . . say fire!”

“What!!”

“For the love of Christ, Pilot, what’s amiss?” Vinck cried out.

Blackthorne pointed shakily toward the lorcha. “They told me . . . they told me *Erasmus* is lost, Johann. Our ship’s lost . . . fired.” Then he burst out, “Oh, God, let it all be a lie!”

BOOK SIX

CHAPTER 60

H E stood in the shallows and looked out at the charred skeleton of his ship
aground and heeled over, awash in the small surf, seventy yards seaward, masts gone, decks gone, everything gone, except for the keel and
the ribs of her chest that jutted to the sky.

"The monkeys tried to beach her," Vinck said sullenly.

"No. The tide took her there."

"For Christ's sweet sake, why say that, Pilot? If you've a God-cursed fire and
you're near the God-cursed shore you beach her to fight it there! Jesus, even these
piss-arsed bastards know that!" Vinck spat on the sand. "Monkeys! You should
never've left her to them. What're we going to do now? How we going to get
home? You should've left her at Yedo safe, an' us safe, with our eters."

The whine in Vinck's voice irritated Blackthorne. Everything about Vinck
irritated him now. Three times in the last week he had almost told his vassals
to knife Vinck quietly and throw him overboard to put him out of his misery
when the weeping and bewailing and accusations had become too much. But he
had always curbed his temper and gone aloft or below to seek out Yabu. Near
Yabu, Vinck made no sound, petrified of him, and rightly. Aboard it had been
easy to contain himself. Here, shamed before his ship's nakedness, it was not easy.

"Perhaps they beached her, Johann," he said, weary unto death.

"You bet the muck-eating bastards beached her! But they didn't put out the
fire, God curse them all to hell! Should never've let Jappos on her, stinking,
piss-arsed monkeys. . . ."

Blackthorne shut his ears and concentrated on the galley. She was moored
downwind to the wharf, a few hundred paces away, by Yokohama village. The
lean-tos of the Musket Regiment were still scattered about the foreshore and
foothills, men drilling, hurrying, a pall of anxiety over all of them. It was a warm
sunny day with a fair wind blowing. His nose caught a scent of mimosa perfume.
He could see Kiri and Lady Sazuko in conversation under orange sunshades on
the forepoop and he wondered if the perfume came from them. Then he watched
Yabu and Naga walking up and down the wharf, Naga talking and Yabu listening, both very tense. Then he saw them look across at him. He sensed their
restlessness.

When the galley had rounded the point two hours ago, Yabu had said, "Why
go look closer, Anjin-san? Ship dead, *neh?* All finished. Go Yedo! Get ready for
war. No time now."

"So sorry—stop here. Must look close. Please."

"Go Yedo! Ship dead—finished. *Neh?*"

"You want, you go. I swim."

"Wait. Ship dead, *neh?*"

"So sorry, please stop. Little time. Then Yedo."

At length Yabu had agreed and they had docked and Naga had met them. "So
sorry, Anjin-san. *Neh?*" Naga had said, his eyes bleary from sleeplessness.

"Yes, so sorry. Please what happen?"

"So sorry, don't know. Not *honto.* I was not here, understand? I was ordered
Mishima few days. When come back, men say earthquake at night—all happen

749

at night, understand? You understand 'earthquake,' Anjin-san?"

"Understand. Yes. Please continue."

"So little earthquake. At night. Some men say tidal wave arrive, some say not tidal wave but just one big wave, storm wave. There was a storm that night, *neh?* Little *tai-fun.* You understand *'tai-fun'?"*

"Yes."

"Ah, so sorry. Very dark night. They say big wave come. They say oil lamps on deck break. Ship catch fire, *neh?* Everything fire, quick, very—"

"But guards, Naga-san? Where deck men?"

"Very dark. Fire very quick, understand? So sorry. *Shigata ga nai, neh?"* he added hopefully.

"Where deck men, Naga-san? I leave guard. *Neh?"*

"When I returned one day later, very sorry, *neh?* Ship finished, still burning there in shallows—near shore. Ship finished. I get all men from ship and all shore patrol of that night. I ask them to report. No one is sure what happened." Naga's face darkened. "I order them to salvage—to bring everything possible, understand? Everything. All up there now in camp." He pointed to the plateau. "Under guard. My guards. Then I put them to death and rushed back to Mishima to report to Lord Toranaga."

"All of them? All to death?"

"Yes—they failed in their duty."

"What Lord Toranaga say?"

"Very angry. Very right to be angry, *neh?* I offer seppuku. Lord Toranaga refuse permission. Eeeeee! Lord Toranaga very angry, Anjin-san." Naga waved a nervous hand around the foreshore. "Whole regiment in disgrace, Anjin-san. Everyone. All chief officers here in disgrace, Anjin-san. Sent to Mishima. Fifty-eight seppuku already."

Blackthorne had thought about that number and he wanted to shriek, five thousand or fifty thousand can't repay the loss of my ship! "Bad," his mouth was saying. "Yes, very bad."

"Yes. Better go Yedo. Today. War today, tomorrow, next day. Sorry."

Then Naga had spoken intently with Yabu for a few moments, and Blackthorne, dull-witted, hating the foul-sounding words, hating Naga and Yabu and all of them, could barely follow him though he saw Yabu's unease increase. Naga turned again to him with an embarrassed finality. "So sorry, Anjin-san. Nothing more I could do. *Honto, neh?"*

Blackthorne had forced himself to nod. *"Honto. Domo,* Naga-san. *Shigata ga nai."* He had made some excuse and left them to walk down to his ship, to be alone, no longer trusting himself to contain his insane rage, knowing that there was nothing he could do, that he would never know any more of the truth, that whatever the truth he had lost his ship, that the priests had somehow managed to pay men, or cajole men, or threaten them into this filthy desecration. He had fled from Yabu and Naga, walking slowly and erect, but before he could escape the wharf, Vinck had rushed after him and begged not to be left behind. Seeing the man's abject cringing fear, he had agreed and allowed him to follow. But he had closed his mind to him.

Then, suddenly, down by the shore, they had come on the grisly remains of the heads. More than a hundred, hidden from the wharf by dunes and stuck on spears. Seabirds rose up in a white shrieking cloud as they approached, and settled back to continue ravaging and quarreling once they had hurried past.

Now he was studying the hulk of his ship, one thought obsessing him: Mariko had seen the truth and had whispered the truth to Kiyama or to the priests: 'Without his ship the Anjin-san's helpless against the Church. I ask you to leave him alive, just kill the ship. . . .'

He could hear her saying it. She was right. It was such a simple solution to the Catholics' problem. Yes. But any one of them could have thought of the same thing. And how did they breach the four thousand men? Whom did they bribe? How?

It doesn't matter who. Or how. They've won.

God help me, without my ship I'm dead. I can't help Toranaga and his war will swallow us up.

"Poor ship," he said. "Forgive me—so sad to die so uselessly. After all those leagues."

"Eh?" Vinck said.

"Nothing," he said. Poor ship, forgive me. It was never my bargain with her or anyone. Poor Mariko. Forgive her too.

"What did you say, Pilot?"

"Nothing. I was just thinking out loud."

"You said something. I heard you say something, for Christ's sake!"

"For Christ's sake, shut up!"

"Eh? Shut up, is it? We're marooned with these piss eaters for the rest of our lives! Eh?"

"Yes!"

"We're to grovel to these God-cursed heathen shitheads for the rest of our muck-eating lives and how long'll that be when all they talk about's war war war? Eh?"

"Yes."

"Yes, is it?" Vinck's whole body trembling, and Blackthorne readied. "It's your fault. You said to come to the Japans and we come and how many died coming here? You're to blame!"

"Yes. Sorry, but you're right!"

"Sorry are you, Pilot? How're we going to get home? That's your God-cursed job, to get us home! How you going to do that? Eh?"

"I don't know. Another of our ships'll get here, Johann. We've just got to wait anoth—"

"Wait? How long're we to wait? Five muck-plagued years, twenty? Christ Jesus, you said yourself all these shitheads're at war *now!*" Vinck's mind snapped. "They're going to chop off our heads and stick them like those there and the birds'll eat us. . . ." A paroxysm of insane laughter shook him and he reached into his ragged shirt. Blackthorne saw the pistol butt and it would have been easy to smash Vinck to the ground and take the pistol but he did nothing to defend himself. Vinck waved the pistol in his face, dancing around him with drooling, lunatic glee. Blackthorne waited unafraid, hoping for the bullet, then Vinck took to his heels down the beach, the seabirds scudding into the air, mewing and cawing out of his path. Vinck ran for a frantic hundred paces or more, then collapsed, ending up on his back, his legs still moving, arms waving, mouthing obscenities. After a moment he turned on his belly with a last shriek, facing Blackthorne, and froze. There was a silence.

When Blackthorne came up to Vinck the pistol was leveled at him, the eyes staring with demented antagonism, the lips pulled back from his teeth. Vinck was dead.

Blackthorne closed the eyes and picked him up and slung him over his shoulder and walked back. Samurai were running toward him, Naga and Yabu at their head.

"What happened, Anjin-san?"

"He went mad."

"Is that so? Is he dead?"

"Yes. First burial, then Yedo. All right?"

"*Hai.*"

Blackthorne sent for a shovel and asked them to leave him for a while and he buried Vinck above the water line on a crest that overlooked the wreck. He said a service over the grave and planted a cross in the grave that he fashioned out of two pieces of driftwood. It was so easy to say the service. He had spoken it too many times. On this voyage alone over a hundred times for his own crew since they'd left Holland. Only Baccus van Nekk and the boy Croocq survived now; the others had come from other ships—Salamon the mute, Jan Roper, Sonk the cook, Ginsel the sailmaker. Five ships and four hundred and ninety-six men. And now Vinck. All gone now except the seven of us. And for what?

To circumnavigate the globe? To be the first?

"I don't know," he said to the grave. "But that won't happen now."

He made everything tidy. "*Sayonara,* Johann." Then he walked down to the sea and swam naked to the wreck to purify himself. He had told Naga and Yabu that this was their custom after burying one of their men on land. The captain had to do it in private if there was no one else and the sea was the purifier before their God, which was the Christian God but not quite the same as the Jesuit Christian God.

He hung on to one of the ship's ribs and saw that barnacles were already clustering, sand already silting over the keel plate, three fathoms below. Soon the sea would claim her and she would vanish. He looked around aimlessly. Nothing to salvage, he told himself, expecting nothing.

He swam ashore. Some of his vassals waited with fresh clothes. He dressed and put his swords in his sash and walked back. Near the wharf one of his vassals pointed. "Anjin-san!"

A carrier pigeon, pursued by a hawk, was clattering wildly for the safety of the home coop in the village. The coop was in the attic of the tallest building, set back from the seashore on a slight rise. With a hundred yards to go, the hawk on station, high above its prey, closed its wings and plummeted. The stoop hit with a burst of feathers but it was not perfect. The pigeon fell screeching as though mortally wounded, then, near the ground, recovered and fled for home. She scrambled through a hole in the coop to safety, the hawk *ek-ek-ek-ing* with rage a few paces behind, and everyone cheered, except Blackthorne. Even the pigeon's cleverness and bravery did not touch him. Nothing touched anymore.

"Good, *neh?*" one of his vassals said, embarrassed by his master's dourness.

"Yes." Blackthorne went back to the galley. Yabu was there and the Lady Sazuko, Kiri and the captain. Everything was ready. "Yabu-san. *Ima* Yedo *ka?*" he asked.

But Yabu did not answer and no one noticed him. All eyes were on Naga, who was hurrying toward the village. A pigeon handler came out of the building to meet him. Naga broke the seal and read the slip of paper. "Galley and all aboard to stay at Yokohama until I arrive." It was signed Toranaga.

The horsemen came rapidly over the lip of the hill in the early sun. First were the fifty outriders and scouts of the advance guard led by Buntaro. Next came the banners. Then Toranaga. After him was the bulk of the war party under the command of Omi. Following them were Father Alvito Tsukku-san and ten acolytes in a tight group and, after them, a small rear guard, among them hunters with falcons on their gloves, all hooded except one great yellow-eyed goshawk.

All samurai were heavily armed and wore chain cuirasses and cavalry battle armor.

Toranaga rode easily, his spirit lightened now, a newer and stronger man, and he was glad to be near the end of his journey. It was two and a half days since he had sent the order to Naga to keep the galley at Yokohama and had left Mishima on this forced march. They had come very fast, picking up fresh horses every twenty *ri* or so. At one station where horses were not available the samurai in charge was removed, and his stipend given to another, and he was invited to commit seppuku or shave his head and become a priest. The samurai chose death.

The fool had been warned, Toranaga thought, the whole Kwanto's mobilized and on a war footing. Still, that man wasn't a total waste, he told himself. At least the news of that example will flash the length of my domains and there'll be no more unnecessary delays.

So much yet to do, he thought, his mind frantic with facts and plans and counterplans. In four days it will be *the day,* the twenty-second day of eighth month, the Month for Viewing the Moon. Today, at Osaka, the courtier Ogaki Takamoto formally goes to Ishido and regretfully announces that the Son of Heaven's visit to Osaka has to be delayed for a few days due to ill health.

It had been so easy to manipulate the delay. Although Ogaki was a Prince of the Seventh Rank and descended from the Emperor Go-Shoko, the ninety-fifth of the dynasty, he was impoverished like all members of the Imperial Court. The Court possessed no revenue of its own. Only samurai possessed revenue and, for hundreds of years, the Court had had to exist on a stipend—always carefully controlled and lean—granted it by the Shōgun, Kwampaku, or ruling Junta of the day. So Toranaga had humbly and very cautiously assigned ten thousand koku yearly to Ogaki, through intermediaries, to donate to needy relatives as Ogaki himself wished, saying with due humility that, being Minowara and therefore also descended from Go-Shoko, he was delighted to be of service and trusted that the Exalted would take care of his precious health in so treacherous a climate as Osaka's, particularly around the twenty-second day.

Of course there was no guarantee that Ogaki could persuade or dissuade the Exalted, but Toranaga had surmised that the advisers to the Son of Heaven, or the Son of Heaven himself, would welcome an excuse to delay—hopefully, at length to cancel. Only once in three centuries had a ruling Emperor ever left his sanctuary at Kyoto. That had been four years ago at the invitation of the Taikō to view the cherry blossoms near Osaka Castle, coincident with his resigning the Kwampaku title in favor of Yaemon—and so, by implication, putting the Imperial Seal on the succession.

Normally no *daimyo,* even Toranaga, would have dared to make such an offer to any member of the Court because it insulted and usurped the prerogative of a superior—in this case the Council—and would instantly be construed as treason, as it rightly was. But Toranaga knew he was already indicted for treason.

Tomorrow Ishido and his allies will move against me. How much more time have I left? Where should *the* battle be? Odawara? Victory depends only on the time and the place, and not on the number of men. They'll outnumber me three to one at the very least. Never mind, he thought, *Ishido's coming out of Osaka Castle!* Mariko pried him out. In the chess game for power I sacrificed my queen but Ishido's lost two castles.

Yes. But you lost more than a queen in the last play. You lost a ship. A pawn can become a queen—but not a ship!

They were riding downhill in a quick, bone-jarring trot. Below was the sea. They turned a corner on the path and there was Yokohama village, with the wreck just offshore. He could see the plateau where the Musket Regiment were drawn up in battle review with their horses and equipment, muskets in their holsters, other samurai, equally well armed, lining his route as an honor guard nearer the shore. On the outskirts of the village the villagers were kneeling in neat rows waiting to honor him. Beyond them was the galley, the sailors waiting with their captain. On either side of the wharf, fishing boats were beached in meticulous array and he made a mental note to reprimand Naga. He had ordered the regiment ready for instant departure, but to stop fishermen or peasants from fishing or working the fields was irresponsible.

He turned in his saddle and called up a samurai, ordering him to tell Buntaro to go ahead and see that all was safe and prepared. "Then go to the village and dismiss all the villagers to their work, except the headman."

"Yes, Sire." The man dug in his spurs and galloped away.

Now Toranaga was near enough to the plateau to distinguish faces. The Anjin-san and Yabu, then Kiri and the Lady Sazuko. His excitement quickened.

Buntaro was galloping down the track, his great bow and two full quivers on his back, half a dozen samurai close behind him. They swung off the track and came out onto the plateau. Instantly he saw Blackthorne and his face became even sterner. Then he reined in and looked around cautiously. A roofed reviewing stand bearing a single cushion was facing the regiment. Another, smaller and lower, was nearby. Kiri and the Lady Sazuko waited under it. Yabu, as the most senior officer, was at the head of the regiment, Naga on his right, the Anjin-san on his left. All seemed safe, and Buntaro waved the main party onward. The advance guard trotted up, dismounted, and spread protectively around the reviewing stand. Then Toranaga rode into the arena. Naga lifted the battle standard on high. At once the four thousand men shouted, "Toranagaaaaaaa!" and bowed.

Toranaga did not acknowledge their salute. In absolute silence he took stock. He noticed that Buntaro was covertly watching the Anjin-san. Yabu was wearing the sword he had given him, but was very nervous. The Anjin-san's bow was correct and motionless, the haft of his sword broken. Kiri and his youngest consort were kneeling, their hands flat on the tatamis, their faces demurely lowered. His eyes softened momentarily, then he gazed disapprovingly at the regiment. Every man was still bowing. He did not bow back, just nodded curtly and he felt the tremor that went through the samurai as they straightened up again. Good, he thought, dismounting nimbly, glad that they feared his vengeance. A samurai took his reins and led his horse away as he turned his back on the regiment and, sweat stained like all of them in the humidity, he walked over to his ladies. "So, Kiri-san, welcome home!"

She bowed again joyously. "Thank you, Sire. I never thought I'd have the pleasure of seeing you ever again."

"Nor I, Lady." Toranaga let a glimmer of his happiness show. He glanced at the young girl. "So, Sazuko-san? Where's my son?"

"With his wet nurse, Sire," she replied breathlessly, basking in his open favor.

"Please send someone to fetch our child at once."

"Oh please, Sire, with your permission, may I bring him to you myself?"

"Yes, yes, if you wish." Toranaga smiled and watched her go for a moment, liking her greatly. Again he looked at Kiri. "Is everything all right with you?" he asked for her ears alone.

"Yes, Lord. Oh, yes—and seeing you so strong fills me with gladness."

"You've lost weight, Kiri-chan, and you're younger than ever."

"Ah, so sorry, Sire, it's not true. But thank you, thank you."

He grinned at her. "Whatever it is then, it suits you. Tragedy—loneliness—being forsaken. . . . I'm pleased to see you, Kiri-chan."

"Thank you, Sire. I'm so happy that *her* obedience and sacrifice unlocked Osaka. It would please *her* greatly, Sire, to know she was successful."

"First I have to deal with this rabble, then later we'll talk. There's lots to talk about, *neh?*"

"Yes, oh yes!" Her eyes sparkled. "The Son of Heaven will be delayed, *neh?*"

"That would be wise. *Neh?*"

"I have a private message from Lady Ochiba."

"Ah? Good! But it will have to wait." He paused. "The Lady Mariko, she died honorably? By choice and not by accident or mistake?"

"Mariko-sama *chose* death. It was seppuku. If she hadn't done what she did, they would have captured her. Oh, Sire, she was so marvelous all those evil days. So brave. And the Anjin-san. If it hadn't been for him, she would have been captured and shamed. We would all have been captured and shamed."

"Ah yes, the *ninja*." Toranaga exhaled, his eyes became jet and she shivered in spite of herself. "Ishido's got much to answer for, Kiri-chan. Please excuse me." He stalked over to the reviewing stand and sat, stern and menacing again. His guards surrounded him.

"Omi-san!"

"Yes, Sire?" Omi came forward and bowed, seeming older than before, leaner now.

"Escort the Lady Kiritsubo to her quarters, and make sure mine are adequate. I'll stay here tonight."

Omi saluted and walked off and Toranaga was glad to see that the sudden change of plan produced not even a flicker in Omi's eyes. Good, he thought, Omi's learning, or his spies have told him I've secretly ordered Sudara and Hiro-matsu here so I could not possibly leave until tomorrow.

Now he turned his full attention on the regiment. At his signal Yabu came forward and saluted. He returned the salutation politely. "So, Yabu-san! Welcome back."

"Thank you, Sire. May I say how happy I am you avoided Ishido's treachery."

"Thank you. And you too. Things did not go well at Osaka. *Neh?*"

"No. My harmony is destroyed, Sire. I had hoped to lead the retreat from Osaka bringing you both your ladies safely, and your son, and also the Lady Toda, the Anjin-san, and seamen for his ship. Unfortunately, so sorry, we were both betrayed—there and here."

"Yes." Toranaga looked at the wreck below that was washed by the sea. Anger flickered across his face and everyone readied for the outburst. But none came. *"Karma,"* he said. "Yes, *karma*, Yabu-san. What can one do against the elements? Nothing. Negligence is another thing. Now, about Osaka, I want to hear everything that happened, in detail—as soon as the regiment's dismissed and I've bathed."

"I have a report for you in writing, Sire."

"Good. Thank you, but first I'd prefer you to tell it to me."

"Is it true the Exalted won't go to Osaka?"

"What the Exalted decides is up to the Exalted."

"Do you wish to review the regiment before I dismiss them?" Yabu asked formally.

"Why should I give them that honor? Don't you know they're in disgrace, the elements notwithstanding?" he added thinly.

"Yes, Sire. So sorry. Terrible." Yabu was trying unsuccessfully to read Toranaga's mind. "I was appalled when I heard what had happened. It seems almost impossible."

"I agree." Toranaga's face darkened and he looked at Naga and beyond him to the massed ranks. "I still fail to understand how there could be such incompetence. I needed that ship!"

Naga was agitated. "Please excuse me, Sire, but do you wish me to make another inquiry?"

"What can you do now that you haven't already done?"

"I don't know, Sire, nothing Sire, please excuse me."

"Your investigation was thorough, *neh?*"

"Yes, Sire. Please forgive my stupidity."

"It wasn't your fault. You weren't here. Or in command." Impatiently Toranaga turned back to Yabu. "It's curious, even sinister, that the shore patrol, the camp patrol, the deck patrol, and the commander were all Izu men on that night—except for the Anjin-san's few *ronin.* "

"Yes, Sire. Curious, but not sinister, so sorry. You were perfectly correct to hold the officers responsible, as Naga-san was to punish the others. So sorry, I made my own investigations as soon as I arrived but I've no more information, nothing to add. I agree it's *karma—karma* helped somehow by manure-eating Christians. Even so, I apologize."

"Ah, you say it was sabotage?"

"There's no evidence, Sire, but a tidal wave and simple fire seem too easy an explanation. Certainly any fire should have been doused. Again I apologize."

"I accept your apologies but, meanwhile, please tell me how I replace that ship. I need *that* ship!"

Yabu could feel acid in his stomach. "Yes, Sire. I know. So sorry, it cannot be replaced, but the Anjin-san told us during the voyage that soon other fighting ships from his country will come here."

"How soon?"

"He doesn't know, Sire."

"A year? Ten years? I've barely got ten days."

"So sorry, I wish I knew. Perhaps you should ask him, Sire."

Toranaga looked directly at Blackthorne for the first time. The tall man was standing alone, the light gone from his face. "Anjin-san!"

"Yes, Sire?"

"Bad, *neh?* Very bad." Toranaga pointed at the wreck below. *"Neh?"*

"Yes, very bad, Sire."

"How soon other ships come?"

"My ships, Sire?"

"Yes."

"When—when Buddha says."

"Tonight we talk. Go now. Thank you for Osaka. Yes. Go to galley—or village. Talk tonight. Understand?"

"Yes. Talk tonight, yes, understand, Sire. Thank you. When tonight, please?"

"I'll send a messenger. Thank you for Osaka."

"My duty, *neh?* But I do little. Toda Mariko-sama give everything. Everything for Toranaga-sama."

"Yes." Gravely Toranaga returned the bow. The Anjin-san began to leave, but stopped. Toranaga glanced at the far end of the plateau. Tsukku-san and his acolytes had just ridden in and were dismounting there. He had not granted the priest an interview at Mishima—though he had sent word to him at once about the ship's destruction—and had deliberately kept him waiting, pending the outcome of Osaka and the safe arrival of the galley at Anjiro. Only then had he decided to bring the priest here with him to allow the confrontation to happen, at the right time.

Blackthorne began to head for the priest.

"No, Anjin-san. Later, not now. Now go village!" he ordered.

"But, Sire! That man kill my ship! He's the enemy!"

"You will go there!" Toranaga pointed to the village below. "You will wait there please. Tonight we will talk."

"Sire, please, that man—"

"No. You will go to the galley," Toranaga said. "You will go now. Please." This is better than breaking any falcon to the fist, he thought excitedly, momentarily distracted, putting his will to bear on Blackthorne. It's better because the Anjin-san's just as wild and dangerous and unpredictable, always an unknown quantity, unique, unlike any man I've ever known.

From the corner of his eyes he noticed Buntaro had moved into the Anjin-san's path, ready and anxious to force obedience. How foolish, Toranaga thought in passing, and so unnecessary. He kept his eyes on Blackthorne. And dominated him.

"Yes. Go now, Lord Toranaga. So sorry. Go now," Blackthorne said. He wiped the sweat off his face and started to go.

"Thank you, Anjin-san," Toranaga said. He did not allow his triumph to show. He watched Blackthorne obediently walk away—violent, strong, murderous, but controlled now by the will of Toranaga.

Then he changed his mind. "Anjin-san!" he called out, deciding it was time to release the jesses and let the killer fly free. The final test. "Listen, go there if you wish. I think it better not to kill the Tsukku-san. But if you want to kill him—kill. Better not to kill." He said it slowly and carefully, and repeated it. *"Wakarimasu ka?"*

"Hai."

Toranaga looked into the incredibly blue eyes that were filled with an unthinking animosity and he wondered if this wild bird, cast at its prey, would kill or not kill at his whim alone and return to the fist without eating. *"Wakarimasu ka?"*

"Hai."

Toranaga waved his hand in dismissal. Blackthorne turned and stalked off northward. Toward the Tsukku-san. Buntaro moved out of his way. Blackthorne did not seem to notice anyone except the priest. The day seemed to become more sultry.

"So, Yabu-san. What's he going to do?" Toranaga asked.

"Kill. Of course he'll kill if he can catch him. The priest deserves to die, *neh?* All Christian priests deserve to die, *neh?* All Christians. I'm sure they were behind the sabotage—the priests and Kiyama, though I can't prove it."

"You'll gamble your life he'll kill Tsukku-san?"

"No, Sire," Yabu said hastily. "No. I wouldn't. So sorry. He's barbarian—they're both barbarian."

"Naga-san?"

"If it were me, I'd kill the priest and all of them, now that I had your permission. I've never known anyone openly to hate so much. The last two days the Anjin-san's been like an insane man, walking up and down, muttering, staring at the wreck, sleeping there curled up on the sand, hardly eating. . . ." Naga looked after Blackthorne again. "I agree it wasn't just nature that destroyed the ship. I know the priests, somehow they were behind it—I can't prove it either, but somehow. . . I don't believe it happened because of the storm."

"Choose!"

"He'll explode. Look at his walk. . . . I think he'll kill—I hope he'll kill."

"Buntaro-san?"

Buntaro turned back, his heavy jowls unshaven, his brawny legs planted, his fingers on his bow. "You advised him not to kill the Tsukku-san so you do not want the priest dead. If the Anjin-san kills or doesn't kill matters nothing to me, Sire. I care only what matters to you. May I stop him if he begins to disobey you? I can do it easily from this range."

"Could you guarantee to wound him only?"

"No, Sire."

Toranaga laughed softly and broke the spell. "The Anjin-san won't kill him. He'll shout and rave or hiss like a snake and rattle his sword and the Tsukku-san will be swollen up with 'holy' zeal, completely unafraid, and he'll hiss back saying, 'It was an Act of God. I never touched your ship!' Then the Anjin-san will call him a liar and the Tsukku-san will be filled with more zeal and repeat the claim and swear to the truth in his God's name and he'll probably curse him back and they'll hate each other for twenty lifetimes. No one will die. At least, not now."

"How do you know all that, Father?" Naga exclaimed.

"I don't know it for certain, my son. But that's what I think will happen. It's always important to take time to study men—important men. Friends and enemies. To understand them. I've watched both of them. They're both very important to me. *Neh,* Yabu-san?"

"Yes, Sire," Yabu said, suddenly disquieted.

Naga shot a quick glance after Blackthorne. The Anjin-san was still walking with the same unhurried stride, now seventy paces away from the Tsukku-san, who waited at the head of his acolytes, the breeze moving their orange robes.

"But, Father, neither is a coward, *neh?* Why doesn't—how can they back away now with honor?"

"He won't kill for three reasons. First, because the Tsukku-san's unarmed and won't fight back, even with his hands. It's against their code to kill an unarmed man—that's a dishonor, a sin against their Christian God. Second, because he's Christian. Third, because I decided it was not the time."

Buntaro said, "Please excuse me, but I can understand the third, even the first, but isn't the real reason for their hate that both believe the other man's not Christian but evil—a Satan worshiper? Isn't that what they call it?"

"Yes, but this Jesus God of theirs taught or was supposed to have taught that you forgive your enemy. That's being Christian."

"That's stupid, *neh?*" Naga said. "To forgive your enemy is stupid."

"I agree." Toranaga looked at Yabu. "It is foolish to forgive an enemy. *Neh,* Yabu-san?"

"Yes," Yabu agreed.

Toranaga looked northward. The two figures were very close and now, privately, Toranaga was cursing his impetuousness. He still needed both men very much, and there had been no need to risk either of them. He had launched the Anjin-san for personal excitement, not to kill, and he regretted his stupidity. Now he waited, caught up as all of them. But it happened as he had forecast and the clash was short and sharp and spite-filled, even from this distance, and he fanned himself, greatly relieved. He would have dearly liked to have understood what had actually been said, to know if he had been correct. Soon they saw the Anjin-san stride away. Behind him, the Tsukku-san mopped his brow with a colored paper handkerchief.

"Eeeee!" Naga uttered in admiration. "How can we lose with you in command?"

"Too easily, my son, if that is my *karma*." Then his mood changed. "Naga-san, order all samurai who came back with the galley from Osaka to my quarters."

Naga hurried away.

"Yabu-san. I'm pleased to welcome you back safely. Dismiss the regiment—after the evening meal we'll talk. May I send for you?"

"Of course. Thank you, Sire." Yabu saluted and went off.

Now alone but for guards that he waved out of hearing, Toranaga studied Buntaro. Buntaro was unsettled, as a dog would be when stared at. When he could bear it no longer, he said, "Sire?"

"Once you asked for his head, *neh? Neh?*"

"Yes—yes, Sire."

"Well?"

"He—he insulted me at Anjiro. I'm—I'm still shamed."

"I order that shame dismissed."

"Then it's dismissed, Sire. But she betrayed me with him and that cannot be dismissed, not while he's alive. I've proof. I want him dead. Now. He . . . please, his ship's gone, what use is he now to you, Sire? I ask it as a lifetime favor."

"What proof?"

"Everyone knows. On the way from Yokosé. I talked to Yoshinaka. Everyone knows," he added sullenly.

"Yoshinaka *saw* her and him together? He accused her?"

"No. But what he said . . ." Buntaro looked up, in agony. "I know, that is enough. Please, I beg it as a lifetime favor. I've never asked anything of you, *neh?*"

"I need him alive. But for him the *ninja* would have captured her, and shamed her, and therefore you."

"A lifetime wish," Buntaro said. "I ask it. His ship's gone—he's, he's done what you wanted. Please."

"I have proof he did not shame you with her."

"So sorry, what proof?"

"Listen. This is for your ears alone—as I agreed with her. I ordered her to become his friend." Toranaga bore down on him. "They were friends, yes. The Anjin-san worshiped her, but he never shamed you with her, or she with him. At Anjiro, just before the earthquake, when she first suggested going to Osaka to free all the hostages—by challenging Ishido publicly and then forcing a crisis by committing seppuku, whatever he tried to do—on that day I de—"

"That was planned then?"

"Of course. Will you never learn? On that day I ordered her divorced from you."

"Sire?"

"Divorced. Isn't the word clear?"

"Yes, but—"

"Divorced. She'd driven you insane for years, you'd treated her foully for years. What about your treatment of her foster mother and ladies? Didn't I tell you I needed her to interpret the Anjin-san, yet you lost your temper and beat her—the truth is you almost killed her that time, *neh? Neh?*"

"Yes—please excuse me."

"The time had come to finish that marriage. I ordered it finished. Then."

"She asked for divorce?"

"No. I decided and I ordered it. But your wife begged me to revoke the order. I refused. Then your wife said she would commit seppuku at once without my permission before she would allow you to be shamed in that way. I ordered her to obey. She refused." Toranaga continued angrily, "Your wife forced me, her *liege lord,* to withdraw my legal order and made me agree to make my order absolute only after Osaka—both of us knowing that Osaka for her meant death. Do you understand?"

"Yes—yes, I understand that."

"At Osaka the Anjin-san saved her honor and the honor of my ladies and my youngest son. But for him, they and *all* the hostages at Osaka would still be in Osaka, I'd be dead or in Ikawa Jikkyu's hands, probably in chains like a common felon!"

"Please excuse me . . . but why did she do that? She hated me—why should she delay divorce? Because of Saruji?"

"For your honor. She understood duty. Your wife was so concerned for your honor—even after her death—that part of my agreement was that this was to be a private affair between her and you and myself. No one else would ever know, not the Anjin-san, her son, anyone—not even her Christian priest confessor."

"What?"

Toranaga explained it again. At length Buntaro understood clearly and Toranaga dismissed him and then, at long last alone for the moment, he got up and stretched, exhausted by all his labor since he had arrived. The sun was still high though it was afternoon now. His thirst was great. He accepted cold cha from his personal bodyguard, then walked down to the shore. He stripped off his sopping kimono and swam, the sea feeling glorious to him, refreshing him. He swam underwater but did not stay submerged too long, knowing that his guards would be anxious. He surfaced and floated on his back, looking up into the sky, gathering strength for the long night ahead.

Ah, Mariko, he thought, what a wondrous lady you are. Yes, *are,* because you will certainly live forever. Are you with your Christian God in your Christian heaven? I hope not. That would be a terrible waste. I hope your spirit's just awaiting Buddha's forty days for rebirth somewhere here. I pray your spirit comes into my family. Please. But again as a lady—not as a man. We could not afford to have you as a man. You're much too special to waste as a man.

He smiled. It had happened at Anjiro just as he had told Buntaro, though she had never forced him to rescind his order. "How could she force me to do anything I didn't want?" he said to the sky. She had *asked* him dutifully, correctly, not to make the divorce public until after Osaka. But, he assured himself, she would certainly have committed seppuku if I'd refused her. She would have insisted, *neh?* Of course she would have insisted and that would have ruined everything. By agreeing in advance I merely saved her unnecessary shame and argument, and myself unnecessary trouble—and by keeping it private now, as I'm sure she would have wished it, everyone gains further. I'm glad I conceded, he thought benignly, then laughed aloud. A slight wave chopped over him and he took a mouthful of sea water and choked.

"Are you all right, Sire?" an anxious guard, swimming nearby, called out.

"Yes. Of course yes." Toranaga retched again and spat out the phlegm, treading water, and thought, that will teach you to be smug. That's your second mistake today. Then he saw the wreck. "Come on, I'll race you!" he called out to his guard.

A race with Toranaga meant a race. Once one of his generals had deliberately allowed him to win, hoping to gain favor. That mistake cost the man everything.

The guard won. Toranaga congratulated him and held onto one of the ribs and waited until his breathing was normal, then he looked around, his curiosity enormous. He swam down and inspected the keel of *Erasmus.* When he was satisfied he went ashore and returned to the camp, refreshed and ready.

A temporary house had been set up for him in a good position under a wide thatched roof that was supported with strong bamboo posts. Shoji walls and partitions were set on a raised deck flooring of wood and tatamis. Sentries were already stationed, and rooms were also there for Kiri and Sazuko and servants and cooks, joined by a complex of simple paths, raised on temporary pilings.

He saw his child for the first time. Obviously the Lady Sazuko would never have been so impolite as to bring her son back to the plateau at once, fearing that she might intrude in important matters—as she would have done—even though he had happily given her that opportunity.

The child pleased him greatly. "He's a fine boy," he boasted, holding the infant with practiced assurance. "And, Sazuko, you're younger and more attractive than ever. We must have more children at once. Motherhood suits you."

"Oh, Sire," she said, "I was afraid I'd never see you again, and never be able to show you your newest son. How are we going to escape the trap . . . Ishido's armies. . . ."

"Look what a fine boy he is! Next week I'll build a shrine in his honor and endow it with . . ." He stopped and halved the figure he'd first thought of and then halved that again. ". . . with twenty koku a year."

"Oh, Sire, how generous you are!"

Her smile was guileless. "Yes," he said. "That's enough for a miserable parasite priest to say a few *Namu Amida Butsu, neh?*"

"Oh, yes, Sire. Will the shrine be near the castle in Yedo? Oh, wouldn't it be wonderful if it could be on a river or stream?"

He agreed reluctantly even though such a choice plot would cost more than he had wanted to spend on such frippery. But the boy's fine, I can afford to be generous this year, he thought.

"Oh, thank you, Sire . . ." The Lady Sazuko stopped. Naga was hurrying over to where they sat on a shaded veranda.

"Please excuse me, Father, but your Osaka samurai? How do you want to see them, singly or all together?"

"Singly."

"Yes, Sire. The priest Tsukku-san would like to see you when convenient."

"Tell him I'll send for him as soon as possible." Again Toranaga began to talk with his consort but, politely and at once, she asked to be excused, knowing that he wanted to deal with the samurai immediately. He asked her to stay but she begged to be allowed to go and he agreed.

He interviewed the men carefully, sifting their stories, calling a samurai back occasionally, cross-checking. By sunset he knew clearly what had happened, or what they all thought had happened. Then he ate lightly and quickly, his first meal today, and summoned Kiri, sending all guards out of hearing.

"First tell me what you did, what you saw, and what you witnessed, Kiri-chan."

Night had fallen before he was satisfied, even though she was perfectly prepared.

"Eeeeeee," he said. "That was a near thing, Kiri-chan. Too near."

"Yes," Kiri replied, her hands folded in her ample lap. Then she added with great tenderness, "All gods, great and small, were guarding you, Sire, and us. Please excuse me that I doubted the outcome, doubted you. The gods were watching over us."

"It seems that way, yes, very much." Toranaga watched the night. The flames of the flares were being wafted by the slight sea breeze that also blew away the night insects and made the evening more comfortable. A fine moon rode the sky and he could see the dark marks on its face and he wondered absently if the dark was land and the rest ice and snow, and why the moon was there, and who lived there. Oh, there are so many things I'd like to know, he thought.

"Can I ask a question, Tora-chan?"

"What question, Lady?"

"Why did Ishido let us go? Really? He needn't have, *neh?* If I'd been him I wouldn't have done it—never. Why?"

"First tell me the Lady Ochiba's message."

"The Lady Ochiba said, 'Please tell Lord Toranaga that I respectfully wish there was some way that his differences with the Heir could be resolved. As a token of the Heir's affection, I'd like to tell Toranaga-sama the Heir has said many times he does not want to lead any armies against his uncle, the Lord of the Kwan—' "

"She said that!"

"Yes. Oh yes."

"Surely she must know—and Ishido—that if Yaemon holds the standard against me I must lose!"

"That's what she said, Sire."

"*Eeeeeee!*" Toranaga bunched his great calloused fist and banged it on the tatamis. "If that's a real offer and not a trick I'm halfway to Kyoto, and one pace beyond."

"Yes," Kiri said.

"What's the price?"

"I don't know. She said nothing more, Sire. That was all the message—apart from good wishes to her sister."

"What can I give Ochiba that she doesn't have already? Osaka's hers, the treasure's hers, Yaemon's always been Heir of the realm for me. This war's unnecessary. Whatever happens, in eight years Yaemon becomes Kwampaku and inherits the earth, this earth. There's nothing left to give her."

"Perhaps she wants marriage?"

Toranaga shook his head emphatically. "No, not her. That woman would never marry me."

"It's the perfect solution, Sire, for her."

"She'd never consider it. Ochiba my wife? Four times she begged the Taikō to invite me Onward."

"Yes. But that was when he was alive."

"I will do anything that would cement the realm, keep the peace, and make Yaemon Kwampaku. Is that what she wants?"

"It would confirm the succession. That's her lodestone."

Again Toranaga stared at the moon, but now his mind was concentrating on the puzzle, reminded again of what Lady Yodoko had said at Osaka. When no immediate answer was forthcoming he put it aside to continue with the more important present. "I think she's up to her tricks again. Did Kiyama tell you that the barbarian ship had been sabotaged?"

"No, Sire."

Toranaga frowned. "That's surprising, because he must have known about it then. I told Tsukku-san as soon as I heard—he went through the motions of sending a carrier bird at once, though it would only have confirmed what they already must have known."

"Their treachery should be punished, *neh?* On the instigators as well as the fools who allowed it."

"With patience they'll get their reward, Kiri-san. I hear the Christian priests claim it was an 'Act of God.' "

"Such hypocrisy! Stupid, *neh?*"

"Yes." Very stupid in one way, Toranaga thought, not in another. "Well, thank you, Kiri-san. Again I'm delighted you're safe. We'll stay here tonight. Now, please excuse me. Send for Yabu-san and when he arrives, bring cha and saké and then leave us alone."

"Yes, Sire. May I ask my question now?"

"The same question?"

"Yes, Sire. Why did Ishido let us go?"

"The answer is, Kiri-chan, I don't know. He made a mistake."

She bowed and went away contentedly.

It was almost the middle of the night before Yabu left. Toranaga bowed him away as an equal and thanked him again for everything. He had invited him to the secret Council of War tomorrow, had confirmed him as General of the Musket Regiment, and confirmed his Overlordship of Totomi and Suruga in writing —once they were conquered and secured.

"Now the regiment's absolutely vital, Yabu-san. You're to be solely responsible for its strategy and training. Omi-san can be liaison between us. Use the Anjin-san's knowledge—anything. *Neh?*"

"Yes, that will be perfect, Sire. May I humbly thank you."

"You did me a geat service bringing my ladies, my son, and the Anjin-san back safely. Terrible about the ship—*karma*. Perhaps another one will arrive soon. Good night, my friend."

Toranaga sipped his cha. He was feeling very tired now.

"Naga-san?"

"Sire?"

"Where's the Anjin-san?"

"By the wreck with some of his vassals."

"What's he doing there?"

"Just staring at it." Naga became uneasy under his father's piercing gaze. "So sorry, shouldn't he be there, Sire?"

"What? Oh no, it doesn't matter. Where's Tsukku-san?"

"In one of the guest houses, Sire."

"Have you told him you want to become Christian next year?"

"Yes, Sire."

"Good. Fetch him."

In moments Toranaga saw the tall, lean priest approach under the flares—his taut face deeply lined, his black tonsured hair without a fleck of gray—and he was reminded suddenly of Yokosé. "Patience is very important, Tsukku-san. *Neh?*"

"Yes, always. But why did you say that, Sire?"

"Oh, I was thinking about Yokosé. How everything was very different then, such a little time ago."

"Ah, yes. God moves in curious ways, yes, Sire. I'm so very pleased you're still within your own borders."

"You wanted to see me?" Toranaga asked, fanning himself, secretly envying the priest his flat stomach and his gift of tongues.

"Only to apologize for what happened."

"What did the Anjin-san say?"

"Many angry words—and accusations that I'd burned his ship."

"Did you?"

"No, Sire."

"Who did?"

"It was an Act of God. The storm came and the ship was burned."

"It wasn't an Act of God. You say you didn't help it, you or any priest, or any Christian?"

"Oh, I helped, Sire. I prayed. We all did. Before God, I believe that ship was an instrument of the Devil—I've said so to you many times. I know it wasn't your opinion and again I ask your forgiveness for opposing you on this. But perhaps this Act of God helped and did not hinder."

"Oh? How?"

"The Father-Visitor's no longer distracted, Sire. Now he can concentrate on Lords Kiyama and Onoshi."

Toranaga said bluntly, "I've heard all this before, Tsukku-san. What practical help can the chief Christian priest give me?"

"Sire, put your trust in—" Alvito caught himself, then said sincerely, "Please excuse me, Sire, but I feel with all my heart that if you put your trust in God, He will help you."

"I do, but more in Toranaga. Meanwhile I hear Ishido, Kiyama, Onoshi, and Zataki have gathered their legions. Ishido will have three or four hundred thousand men in the field against me."

"The Father-Visitor's implementing his agreement with you, Sire. At Yokosé I reported failure, now I think there's hope."

"I can't use hope against swords."

"Yes, but God can win against any odds."

"Yes. If God exists he can win against any odds." Then Toranaga's voice edged even more. "What hope are you referring to?"

"I don't know, actually, Sire. But isn't Ishido coming against *you?* Out of Osaka Castle? Isn't that another Act of God?"

"No. But you understand the importance of that decision?"

"Oh yes, very clearly. I'm sure the Father-Visitor understands that also."

"You say this is his work?"

"Oh, no, Sire. But it is happening."

"Perhaps Ishido will change his mind and make Lord Kiyama commander-in-chief and skulk at Osaka and leave Kiyama and the Heir opposing me?"

"I can't answer that, Sire. But if Ishido leaves Osaka it will be a miracle. *Neh?*"

"Are you seriously claiming this to be another Act of your Christian God?"

"No. But it could be. I believe nothing happens without His knowledge."

"Even after we're dead we still may never know about God." Then Toranaga added abruptly, "I hear the Father-Visitor's left Osaka," and was pleased to see a shadow cross the Tsukku-san's face. The news had come the day they'd left Mishima.

"Yes," the priest was saying, his apprehension increasing. "He's gone to Nagasaki, Sire."

"To conduct a special burial for Toda Mariko-sama?"

"Yes. Ah, Sire, you know so much. We're all clay on the potter's wheel you spin."

"That's not true. And I don't like idle flattery. Have you forgotten?"

"No, Sire, please excuse me. It wasn't meant to be." Alvito became even more on guard, almost wilting. "You're opposed to the service, Sire?"

"It doesn't matter to me. She was a very special person and her example merits honor."

"Yes, Sire. Thank you. The Father-Visitor will be very pleased. But he thinks it matters quite a lot."

"Of course. Because she was *my* vassal and a Christian her example won't go unnoticed—by other Christians. Or by those considering conversion. *Neh?*"

"I would say it will not go unnoticed. Why should it? On the contrary she merits great praise for her self-sacrifice."

"In giving her life that others might live?" Toranaga asked cryptically, not mentioning seppuku or suicide.

"Yes."

Toranaga smiled to himself, noticing that Tsukku-san had never once mentioned the other girl, Kiyama Achiko, her bravery or death or burial, also with great pomp and ceremony. He hardened his voice. "And you know of no one who ordered or assisted in the sabotage of my ship?"

"No, Sire. Other than by prayer."

"I hear your church building in Yedo is going well."

"Yes, Sire. Again thank you."

"Well, Tsukku-san, I hope the labors of the High Priest of the Christians will bear fruit soon. I need more than hope and I've a very long memory. Now, please, I require your services as interpreter." Instantly he sensed the priest's antagonism. "You have nothing to fear."

"Oh, Sire, I'm not afraid of him, please excuse me, I just don't want to be near him."

Toranaga got up. "I require you to respect the Anjin-san. His bravery is unquestioned and he saved the Mariko-sama's life many times. Also he's understandably almost berserk at the moment—the loss of his ship, *neh?*"

"Yes, yes, so sorry."

Toranaga led the way toward the shore, guards with flares lighting their way. "When do I have your High Priest's report on the gun-running incident?"

"As soon as he gets all the information from Macao."

"Please ask him to speed his inquiries."

"Yes, Sire."

"Who were the Christian *daimyos* concerned?"

"I don't know, so sorry, or even if any were involved."

"A pity you don't know, Tsukku-san. That would save me a lot of time. There are more than a few *daimyos* who would be interested to know the truth of that."

Ah, Tsukku-san, Toranaga thought, but you do know and I could press you into a corner now and, while you would twist and thrash around like a cornered snake, at length I'd order you to swear by your Christian God, and then if you did you would have to say: "Kiyama, Onoshi, and probably Harima." But the time's not ready. Yet. Nor ready for you to know I believe you Christians had nothing to do with the sabotage. Nor did Kiyama, or Harima, or even Onoshi. In fact, I'm sure. But it still wasn't an Act of God. It was an Act of Toranaga.

Yes.

But why? you might ask.

Kiyama wisely refused the offer in my letter that Mariko gave him. He had to be given proof of my sincerity. What else could I give but the ship—and the barbarian—that terrified you Christians? I expected to lose both, though I only gave one. Today in Osaka, intermediaries will tell Kiyama and the chief of your priests this is a free gift from me to them, proof of my sincerity: that I am not opposed to the Church, only Ishido. It is proof, *neh?*

Yes, but can you ever trust Kiyama? you will ask quite rightly.

No. But Kiyama is Japanese first and Christian second. You always forget that. Kiyama will understand my sincerity. The gift of the ship was absolute, like Mariko's example and the Anjin-san's bravery.

And how did I sabotage the ship? you might want to know.

What does that matter to you, Tsukku-san? It is enough that I did. And no one the wiser, except me, a few trusted men, and the arsonist. Him? Ishido used *ninja*, why shouldn't I? But I hired one man and succeeded. Ishido failed.

"Stupid to fail," he said aloud.

"Sire?" Alvito asked.

"Stupid to fail to bottle up such an incendiary secret as smuggled muskets," he said gruffly, "and to incite Christian *daimyos* into rebellion against their liege lord, the Taikō. *Neh?*"

"Yes, Sire. If it's true."

"Oh, I'm sure it's true, Tsukku-san." Toranaga let the conversation lapse now that Tsukku-san was clearly agitated and ready to be a perfect interpreter.

They were down by the shore now and Toranaga led, sure-footed in the semidarkness, brushing his weariness aside. As they passed the heads on the shore he saw Tsukku-san cross himself in fear and he thought, how stupid to be so superstitious—and to be afraid of nothing.

The Anjin-san's vassals were already on their feet, bowing, long before he arrived. The Anjin-san was not. The Anjin-san was still sitting staring bleakly out to sea.

"Anjin-san," Toranaga called out gently.

"Yes, Sire?" Blackthorne came out of his reverie and got to his feet. "Sorry, you want talk now?"

"Yes. Please. I bring Tsukku-san because I want talk clearly. Understand? Quick and clear?"

"Yes." Toranaga saw the fixity of the man's eyes in the light of the flares and his utter exhaustion. He glanced at Tsukku-san. "Does he understand what I said?" He watched the priest talk, and listened to the evil-sounding language. The Anjin-san nodded, his accusatory gaze never faltering.

"Yes, Sire," the priest said.

"Now interpret for me, please, Tsukku-san, as before. Everything exact: Listen, Anjin-san, I've brought Tsukku-san so we can talk directly and quickly without missing the meaning of any word. It's so important to me that I ask your patience. I think it's best this way."

"Yes, Sire."

"Tsukku-san, first swear before your Christian God nothing he says will ever pass your lips to another. Like a confessional. *Neh?* As sacred! To me and to him."

"But Sire, this isn't—"

"This you will do. Now. Or I will withdraw all my support, forever, from you and your Church."

"Very well, Sire. I agree. Before God."

"Good. Thank you. Explain to him your agreement." Alvito obeyed, then Toranaga settled himself on the sand dunes and waved his fan against the encroaching night bugs. "Now, please tell me, Anjin-san, what happened at Osaka."

Blackthorne began haltingly, but gradually his mind began to relive it all and soon the words gushed and Father Alvito had difficulty in keeping up. Toranaga listened in silence, never interrupting the flow, just adding cautious encouragement when needed, the perfect listener.

Blackthorne finished at dawn. By then Toranaga knew everything there was to tell—everything the Anjin-san was prepared to tell, he corrected himself. The priest knew it also but Toranaga was sure there was nothing in it the Catholics or Kiyama could use against him or against Mariko or against the Anjin-san, who, by now, hardly noticed the priest.

"You're sure the Captain-General would have put you to the stake, Anjin-san?" he asked again.

"Oh, yes. If it hadn't been for the Jesuit. I'm a heretic in his eyes—fire's supposed to 'cleanse' your soul somehow."

"Why did the Father-Visitor save you?"

"I don't know. It was something to do with Mariko-sama. Without my ship I can't touch them. Oh, they would have thought of that themselves but perhaps she gave them a clue how to do it."

"What clue? What would she know about burning ships?"

"I don't know. *Ninja* got into the castle. Perhaps *ninja* got through the men here. My ship was sabotaged. She saw the Father-Visitor at the castle the day she died. I think she told him how to burn *Erasmus*—in return for my life. But I have no life without my ship, Sire. None."

"You're wrong, Anjin-san. Thank you, Tsukku-san," Toranaga said in dismissal. "Yes, I appreciate your labor. Please get some rest now."

"Yes, Sire. Thank you." Alvito hesitated. "I apologize for the Captain-General. Men are born in sin, most stay in sin though they're Christians."

"Christians are born in sin, we're not. We're a civilized people who understand what sin really is, not illiterate peasants who know no better. Even so, Tsukku-san, if I'd been your Captain-General I would not have let the Anjin-san go while I had him in my grasp. It was a military decision, a good one. I think he'll live to regret he didn't insist—and so will your Father-Visitor."

"Do you want me to translate that, Sire?"

"That was for your ears. Thank you for your help." Toranaga returned the priest's salutation and sent men to accompany him back to his house, then turned to Blackthorne. "Anjin-san. First swim."

"Sire?"

"Swim!" Toranaga stripped and went into the water in the growing light. Blackthorne and the guards followed. Toranaga swam strongly out to sea, then turned and circled the wreck. Blackthorne came after him, refreshed by the chill. Soon Toranaga returned ashore. Servants had towels ready now, fresh kimonos and cha, saké and food.

"Eat, Anjin-san."

"So sorry, not hungry."

"Eat!"

Blackthorne took a few mouthfuls, then retched. "So sorry."

"Stupid. And weak. Weak like a Garlic Eater. Not like hatamoto. *Neh?*"

"Sire?"

Toranaga repeated it. Brutally. Then he pointed at the wreck, knowing that now he had Blackthorne's full attention. "That's nothing. *Shigata ga nai.* Unimportant. Listen: Anjin-san is hatamoto, *neh?* Not Garlic Eater. Understand?"

"Yes, so sorry."

Toranaga beckoned his bodyguard, who handed him the sealed scroll. "Listen, Anjin-san, before Mariko-sama left Yedo, she gave me this. Mariko-sama say if you live after Osaka—if you live, understand—she ask me to give this to you."

Blackthorne took the proffered scroll and, after a moment, broke the seal.

"What message say, Anjin-san?" Toranaga asked.

Mariko had written in Latin: "Thou. I love thee. If this is read by thee then I am dead in Osaka and perhaps, because of me, thy ship is dead too. I may sacrifice this most prized part of thy life because of my Faith, to safeguard my Church, but more to save thy life which is more precious to me than everything —even the interest of my Lord Toranaga. It may come to a choice, my love: *thee or thy ship.* So sorry, but I choose life for thee. This ship is doomed anyway—with or without thee. I will concede thy ship to thine enemy so that thou may live. This ship is nothing. *Build another.* This thou canst do—were you not taught to be a builder of ships as well as a navigator of ships? I believe Lord Toranaga will give thee all the craftsmen, carpenters, and metal craftsmen necessary—*he needs you and your ships*—and from my personal estate I have bequeathed thee all the money necessary. Build another ship and build another life, my love. Take next year's Black Ship, and live forever. Listen, my dear one, my Christian soul prays to see thee again in a Christian heaven—my Japanese *hara* prays that in the next life I will be whatever is necessary to bring thee joy and to be with thee wherever thou art. Forgive me—but thy life is all important. I love thee."

"What message say, Anjin-san?"

"So sorry, Sire. Mariko-sama say this ship not necessary. Say build new ship. Say—"

"Ah! Possible? Possible, Anjin-san?"

Blackthorne saw the *daimyo's* flashing interest. "Yes. If get . . ." He could not remember the word for carpenter.

"If Toranaga-sama give men, ship-making men, *neh?* Yes. I can." In his mind the new ship began to take shape. Smaller, much smaller than *Erasmus*. About ninety to a hundred tons would be all he could manage, for he had never overseen or designed a complete ship by himself before, though Alban Caradoc had certainly trained him as a shipwright as well as pilot. God bless you, Alban, he exulted. Yes, ninety tons to start with. Drake's *Golden Hind* was thereabouts and remember what she endured! I can get twenty cannon aboard and that would be enough to . . . "Christ Jesus, the cannon!"

He whirled and peered at the wreck, then saw Toranaga and all of them staring at him and realized he'd been talking English to them. "Ah, so sorry, Sire. Think too quick. Big guns—there, in sea, *neh?* Must get quick!"

Toranaga spoke to his men, then faced Blackthorne again. "Samurai say everything from ship at camp. Some things fished from sea, shallow, here at low tide, *neh?* Now in camp. Why?"

Blackthorne felt light-headed. "Can make ship. If have big guns can fight enemy. Can Toranaga-sama get gunpowder?"

"Yes. How many carpenters? How much need?"

"Forty carpenters, blacksmiths, oak for timbers, do you have oak here? Then I'll need iron, steel, I'll set up a forge and I'll need a master . . ." Blackthorne realized he was talking in English again. "Sorry. I write on paper. Carefully. And I think carefully. Please, you give men to help?"

"All men, all money. At once. I *need* ship. At once! How fast can you build it?"

"Six months from the day we lay keel."

"Oh, not faster?"

"No, so sorry."

"Later we talk some more, Anjin-san. What else Mariko-sama say?"

"Little more, Sire. Say give money to help ship, her money. Say also sorry if . . . if she help my enemy destroy ship."

"What enemy? What way destroy ship?"

"Not say who—or how, Sire. Nothing clear. Just sorry if. Mariko-sama say *sayonara.* Hope seppuku serves Lord Toranaga."

"Ah yes, serves greatly, *neh?*"

"Yes."

Toranaga smiled at him. "Glad all good now, Anjin-san. Eeeeee, Mariko-sama was right. Don't worry about that!" Toranaga pointed at the hulk. "Build new ship at once. A fighting ship, *neh?* You understand?"

"Understand very much."

"This new ship . . . could this new ship fight the Black Ship?"

"Yes."

"Ah! Next year's Black Ship?"

"Possible."

"What about crew?"

"Please?"

"Seamen—gunners?"

"Ah! By next year can train my vassals as gunners. Not seamen."

"You can have the pick of all the seamen in the Kwanto."

"Then next year possible." Blackthorne grinned. "Is next year possible? War? What about war?"

Toranaga shrugged. "War or no war—still try, *neh?* That's your prey—understand 'prey'? And our secret. Between you and me only, *neh?* The Black Ship."

"Priests will soon break secret."

"Perhaps. But this time no tidal wave or *tai-fun,* my friend. You will watch and I will watch."

"Yes."

"First Black Ship, then go home. Bring me back a navy. Understand?"

"Oh yes."

"If I lose—*karma.* If not, then everything, Anjin-san. Everything as you said. Everything—Black Ship, ambassador, treaty, ships! Understand?"

"Yes. Oh yes! Thank you."

"Thank Mariko-sama. Without her . . ." Toranaga saluted him warmly, for the first time as an equal, and went away with his guards. Blackthorne's vassals bowed, completely impressed with the honor done to their master.

Blackthorne watched Toranaga leave, exulting, then he saw the food. The servants were beginning to pack up the remains. "Wait. Now food, please."

He ate carefully, slowly and with good manners, his own men quarreling for the privilege of serving him, his mind roving over all the vast possibilities that Toranaga had opened up for him. You've won, he told himself, wanting to dance a hornpipe with glee. But he did not. He reread her letter once more. And blessed her again.

"Follow me," he ordered, and led the way toward the camp, his brain already designing the ship and her gunports. Jesus God in heaven, help Toranaga to keep Ishido out of the Kwanto and Izu and please bless Mariko, wherever she is, and let the cannon not be rusted up too much. Mariko was right: *Erasmus* was doomed, with or without me. She's given me back my life. I can build another life and another ship. Ninety tons! My ship'll be a sharp-nosed, floating battle platform, as sleek as a greyhound, better than the *Erasmus* class, her bowsprit jutting arrogantly and a lovely figurehead just below, and her face'll look just like *her,* with her lovely slanting eyes and high cheekbones. My ship'll . . . Jesus God, there's a ton of stuff I can salvage from the wreck! I can use part of the keel, some of the ribs—and there'll be a thousand nails around, and the rest of the keel'll make bindings and braces and everything I need . . . if I've the time.

Yes. My ship'll be like *her,* he promised himself. She'll be trim and miniature and perfect like a Yoshitomo blade, and that's the best in the world, and just as dangerous. Next year she'll take a prize twenty times her own weight, like Mariko did at Osaka, and she'll rip the enemy out of Asia. And then, the following year or the one after, I'll sail her up the Thames to London, her pockets full of gold and the seven seas in her wake. *The Lady* will be her name," he said aloud.

CHAPTER 61

Two dawns later Toranaga was checking the girths of his saddle. Deftly he kneed the horse in the belly, her stomach muscles relaxed, and he tightened the strap another two notches. Rotten animal, he thought, despising horses for their constant trickeries and treacheries and ill-tempered dangerousness. This is me, Yoshi Toranaga-noh-Chikitada-noh-Minowara, not some addle-brained child. He waited a moment and kneed the horse hard again. The horse grunted and rattled her bridle and he tightened the straps completely.

"Good, Sire! Very good," the Hunt Master said with admiration. He was a gnarled old man as strong and weathered as a brine-pickled vat. "Many would've been satisfied the first time."

"Then the rider's saddle would've slipped and the fool would have been thrown and his back maybe broken by noon. *Neh?*"

The samurai laughed. "Yes, and deserving it, Sire!"

Around them in the stable area were guards and falconers carrying their hooded hawks and falcons. Tetsu-ko, the peregrine, was in the place of honor and, dwarfing her, alone unhooded, was Kogo the goshawk, her golden, merciless eyes scrutinizing everything.

Naga led up his horse. "Good morning, Father."

"Good morning, my son. Where's your brother?"

"Lord Sudara's waiting at the camp, Sire."

"Good." Toranaga smiled at the youth. Then because he liked him, he drew him to one side. "Listen, my son, instead of going hunting, write out the battle orders for me to sign when I return this evening."

"Oh, Father," Naga said, bursting with pride at the honor of formally taking up the gauntlet cast down by Ishido in his own handwriting, implementing the decision of yesterday's Council of War to order the armies to the passes. "Thank you, thank you."

"Next: The Musket Regiment is ordered to Hakoné at dawn tomorrow. Next: The baggage train from Yedo will arrive this afternoon. Make sure everything's ready."

"Yes, certainly. How soon do we fight?"

"Very soon. Last night I received news Ishido and the Heir left Osaka to review the armies. So it's committed now."

"Please forgive me that I can't fly to Osaka like Tetsu-ko and kill him, and Kiyama and Onoshi, and settle this whole problem without having to bother you."

"Thank you, my son." Toranaga did not trouble to tell him the monstrous problems that would have to be solved before those killings could become fact. He glanced around. All the falconers were ready. And his guards. He called the Hunt Master to him. "First I'm going to the camp, then we'll take the coast road for four *ri* north."

"But the beaters are already in the hills. . . ." The Hunt Master swallowed the rest of his complaint and tried to recover. "Please excuse my—er—I must have eaten something rotten, Sire."

"That's apparent. Perhaps you should pass over your responsibility to someone

770

else. Perhaps your piles have affected your judgment, so sorry," Toranaga said. If he had not been using the hunt as a cover he would have replaced him. "Eh?"

"Yes, so sorry, Sire," the old samurai said. "May I ask—er—do you wish to hunt the areas you picked last night or would you—er—like to hunt the coast?"

"The coast."

"Certainly, Sire. Please excuse me so I can make the change." The man rushed off. Toranaga kept his eyes on him. It's time for him to be retired, he thought without malice. Then he noticed Omi coming into the stable compound with a young samurai beside him who limped badly, a cruel knife wound still livid across his face from the fight at Osaka.

"Ah, Omi-san!" He returned their salute. "Is this the fellow?"

"Yes, Sire."

Toranaga took the two of them aside and questioned the samurai expertly. He did this out of courtesy to Omi, having already come to the same conclusion when he had talked to the man the first night, just as he had been polite to the Anjin-san, asking what was in Mariko's letter though he had already known what Mariko had written.

"But please put it in your own words, Mariko-san," he had said before she left Yedo for Osaka.

"I am to give his ship to his enemy, Sire?"

"No, Lady," he had said as her eyes filled with tears. "No. I repeat: You are to whisper the secrets you've told me to Tsukku-san at once here at Yedo, then to the High Priest and Kiyama at Osaka, and say to them all that without his ship, the Anjin-san is no threat to them. And you are to write the letter to the Anjin-san as I suggest, now."

"Then they will destroy the ship."

"They will try to. Of course they'll think of the same answer themselves so you're not giving anything away really, *neh?*"

"Can you protect his ship, Sire?"

"It will be guarded by four thousand samurai."

"But if they succeed . . . the Anjin-san's worthless without his ship. I beg for his life."

"You don't have to, Mariko-san. I assure you he's valuable to me, with or without a ship. I promise you. Also in your letter to him say, if his ship's lost, *please build another.*"

"What?"

"You told me he can do that, *neh?* You're sure? If I give him all the carpenters and metalworkers?"

"Oh, yes. Oh, how clever you are! Oh yes, he's said many times that he was a trained shipbuilder. . . ."

"You're quite sure, Mariko-san?"

"Yes, Sire."

"Good."

"Then you think the Christian Fathers will succeed, even against four thousand men?"

"Yes. So sorry, but the Christians will never leave the ship alive, or him alive as long as it's floating and ready for sea. It's too much of a threat to them. This ship is doomed, so there's no harm in conceding it to them. But only you and I know and are to know his only hope is to build another. I'm the only one who can help him do that. Solve Osaka for me and I'll see he builds his ship."

I told her the truth, Toranaga thought, here in the dawn at Yokohama, amid the smell of horses and dung and sweat, his ears hardly listening now to the wounded samurai and Omi, his whole being sad for Mariko. Life is so sad, he told himself, weary of men and Osaka and games that brought so much suffering to the living, however great the stakes.

"Thank you for telling me, Kosami," he said as the samurai finished. "You've done very well. Please come with me. Both of you."

Toranaga walked back to his mare and kneed her a last time. This time she whinnied but he got no more tightness on the girth. "Horses are far worse than men for treachery," he said to no one in particular and swung into the saddle and galloped off, pursued by his guards and Omi and Kosami.

At the camp on the plateau he stopped. Buntaro was there beside Yabu and Hiro-matsu and Sudara, a peregrine on his fist. They saluted him. "Good morning," he said cheerfully, beckoning Omi to be part of their conversation but waving everyone else well away. "Are you ready, my son?"

"Yes, Father," Sudara said. "I've sent some of my men to the mountains to make sure the beaters are perfect for you."

"Thank you, but I've decided to hunt the coast."

At once Sudara called out to one of the guards and sent him riding away to pull back the men from the hills and switch them to the coast. "So sorry, Sire, I should have thought of that and been prepared. Please excuse me."

"Yes. So, Hiro-matsu-san, how's the training?"

Hiro-matsu, his sword inevitably loose in his hands, scowled. "I still think this is all dishonorable and unnecessary. Soon we'll be able to forget it. We'll piss all over Ishido without this sort of treachery."

Yabu said, "Please excuse me, but without these guns and this strategy, Hiro-matsu-san, we'll lose. This is a modern war, this way we've a chance to win." He looked back at Toranaga, who had not yet dismounted. "I heard in the night that Jikkyu's dead."

"You're certain?" Toranaga pretended to be startled. He had got the secret information the day he left Mishima.

"Yes, Sire. It seems he's been sick for some time. My informant reports he died two days ago," Yabu said, gloating openly. "His heir's his son, Hikoju."

"That puppy?" Buntaro said with contempt.

"Yes—I agree he's nothing but a whelp." Yabu seemed to be several inches taller than usual. "Sire, doesn't this open up the southern route? Why not attack along the Tokaidō Road immediately? With the old devil fox dead, Izu's safe now, and Suruga and Totomi are as helpless as beached tuna. *Neh?*"

Toranaga dismounted thoughtfully. "Well?" he asked Hiro-matsu quietly.

The old general replied at once, "If we could grab the road all the way to Utsunoya Pass and all the bridges and get over the Tenryu quickly—with all our communications secure—we'd slice into Ishido's underbelly. We could contain Zataki in the mountains and reinforce the Tokaidō attack and rush on to Osaka. We'd be unbeatable."

Sudara said, "So long as the Heir leads Ishido's armies we're beatable."

"I don't agree," Hiro-matsu said.

"Nor I, so sorry," Yabu said.

"But I agree," Toranaga said, as flat and as grave as Sudara. He had not yet told them about Zataki's possible agreement to betray Ishido when the time was ripe. Why should I tell them? he thought. It's not fact. Yet.

But how do you propose to implement your solemn agreement with your half brother to marry Ochiba to him if he supports you, and at the same time marry Ochiba yourself, if that's her price? That's a fair question, he said to himself. But it's highly unlikely Ochiba would betray Ishido. If she did and that's the price, then the answer's simple: My brother will have to bow to the inevitable.

He saw them all looking at him. "What?"

There was a silence. Then Buntaro said, "What happens, Sire, when we oppose the banner of the Heir?"

None of them had ever asked that question formally, directly, and publicly. "If that happens, I lose," Toranaga said. "I will commit seppuku and those who honor the Taikō's testament and the Heir's undoubted legal inheritance will have to submit themselves humbly at once to his pardon. Those who don't will have no honor. *Neh?*"

They all nodded. Then he turned to Yabu to finish the business at hand, and became genial again. "However, we're not on that battlefield yet, so we continue as planned. Yes, Yabu-sama, the southern route's possible now. What did Jikkyu die of?"

"Sickness, Sire."

"A five-hundred-koku sickness?"

Yabu laughed, but inwardly he was rabid that Toranaga had breached his security net. "Yes," he said. "I would presume so, Sire. My brother told you?" Toranaga nodded and asked him to explain to the others. Yabu complied, not displeased, for it was a clever and devious stratagem, and he told them how Mizuno, his brother, had passed over the money that had been acquired from the Anjin-san to a cook's helper who had been inserted into Jikkyu's personal kitchen.

"Cheap, *neh?*" Yabu said happily. "Five hundred koku for the southern route?"

Hiro-matsu said stiffly to Toranaga, "Please excuse me but I think that's a disgusting story."

Toranaga smiled. "Treachery's a weapon of war, *neh?*"

"Yes. But not of a samurai."

Yabu was indignant. "So sorry, Lord Hiro-matsu, but I presume you mean no insult?"

"He meant no insult. Did you, Hiro-matsu-san?" Toranaga said.

"No, Sire," the old general replied. "Please excuse me."

"Poison, treachery, betrayal, assassination have always been weapons of war, old friend," Toranaga said. "Jikkyu was an enemy and a fool. Five hundred koku for the southern route is nothing! Yabu-sama has served me well. Here and at Osaka. *Neh*, Yabu-san?"

"I always try to serve you loyally, Sire."

"Yes, so please explain why you killed Captain Sumiyori before the *ninja* attack," Toranaga said.

Yabu's face did not change. He was wearing his Yoshitomo sword, his hand as usual loose on the hilt. "Who says that? Who accuses me of that, Sire?"

Toranaga pointed at the pack of Browns forty paces away. "That man! Please come here, Kosami-san." The youthful samurai dismounted, limped forward and bowed.

Yabu glared at him. "Who are you, fellow?"

"Sokura Kosami of the Tenth Legion, attached to the Lady Kiritsubo's bodyguard at Osaka, Sire," the youth said. "You put me on guard outside your quarters—and Sumiyori-san's—the night of the *ninja* attack."

"I don't remember you. You dare to say I killed Sumiyori?"

The youth wavered. Toranaga said, "Tell him!"

Kosami said in a rush, "I just had time before the *ninja* fell on us, Sire, to open the door and shout a warning to Sumiyori-san but he never moved, so sorry, Sire." He turned to Toranaga, quailing under their collective gaze. "He'd—he was a light sleeper, Sire, and it was only an instant after . . . that's all, Sire."

"Did you go into the room? Did you shake him?" Yabu pressed.

"No, Sire, oh no, Sire, the *ninja* came so quickly we retreated at once and counterattacked as soon as we could, it was as I said. . . ."

Yabu looked at Toranaga. "Sumiyori-san had been on duty for two days. He was exhausted—we all were. What does that prove?" he asked all of them.

"Nothing," Toranaga agreed, still cordial. "But later, Kosami-san, you went back to the room. *Neh?*"

"Yes, Sire, Sumiyori-san was still lying in the futons as I'd last seen him and . . . and the room wasn't disturbed, not at all, Sire, and he'd been knifed, Sire, knifed in the back once. I thought it was *ninja* at the time and nothing more about it until Omi-sama questioned me."

"Ah!" Yabu turned his eyes on his nephew, his total *hara* centered on his betrayer, measuring the distance between them. "So you questioned him?"

"Yes, Sire," Omi replied. "Lord Toranaga asked me to recheck all the stories. This was one strangeness I felt should be brought to our Master's attention."

"One strangeness? There's another?"

"Following Lord Toranaga's orders, I questioned the servants who survived the attack, Sire. There were two. So sorry, but they both said you went through their quarters with one samurai and returned shortly afterward alone, shouting '*Ninja!*' Then they—"

"They rushed us and killed the poor fellow with a spear and a sword and almost overran me. I had to retreat to give the alarm." Yabu turned to Toranaga, carefully putting his feet in a better attack position. "I've already told you this, Sire, both personally and in my written report. What have servants to do with me?"

"Well, Omi-san?" Toranaga asked.

"So sorry, Yabu-sama," Omi said, "but both saw you open the bolts of a secret door in the dungeon and heard you say to the *ninja*, 'I am Kasigi Yabu.' This alone gave them time to hide from the massacre."

Yabu's hand moved a fraction. Instantly Sudara leapt in front of Toranaga to protect him and in the same moment Hiro-matsu's sword was flashing at Yabu's neck.

"Hold!" Toranaga ordered.

Hiro-matsu's sword stopped, his control miraculous. Yabu had made no overt motion. He stared at them, then laughed insolently. "Am I a filthy *ronin* who'd attack his liege lord? This is Kasigi Yabu, Lord of Izu, Suruga, and Totomi. *Neh?*" He looked directly at Toranaga. "What am I accused of, Sire? Helping *ninja?* Ridiculous! What have servants' fantasies to do with me? They're liars! Or this fellow—who implies something that can't be proved and I can't defend?"

"There's no proof, Yabu-sama," Toranaga said. "I agree completely. There's no proof at all."

"Yabu-sama, did you do those things?" Hiro-matsu asked.

"Of course not!"

Toranaga said, "But I think you did, so all your lands are forfeit. Please slit your belly today. Before noon."

The sentence was final. This was the supreme moment Yabu had prepared for all his life.

Karma, he was thinking, his brain now working at frantic speed. There's nothing I can do, the order's legal, Toranaga's my liege lord, they can take my head or I can die with dignity. I'm dead either way. Omi betrayed me but that is my *karma*. The servants were all to be put to death as part of the plan but two survived and that is my *karma*. Be dignified, he told himself, groping for courage. Think clearly and be responsible.

"Sire," he began with a show of audacity, "first, I'm guiltless of those crimes, Kosami's mistaken, and the servants liars. Second, I'm the best battle general you have. I beg the honor of leading the charge down the Tokaidō—or the first place in the first battle—so my death will be of direct use."

Toranaga said cordially, "It's a good suggestion, Yabu-san, and I agree whole-heartedly that you're the best general for the Musket Regiment but, so sorry, I don't trust you. Please slit your belly by noon."

Yabu dominated his blinding temper and fulfilled his honor as a samurai and as the leader of his clan with the totality of his self-sacrifice. "I formally absolve my nephew Kasigi Omi-san from any responsibility in my betrayal and formally appoint him my heir."

Toranaga was as surprised as everyone.

"Very well," Toranaga said. "Yes, I think that's very wise. I agree."

"Izu is the hereditary fief of the Kasigi. I will it to him."

"Izu is no longer yours to give. You are my vassal, *neh?* Izu is one of my provinces, to give as I wish, *neh?*"

Yabu shrugged. "I will it to him, even though . . ." He laughed. "It's a lifetime favor. *Neh?*"

"To ask is fair. Your request is refused. And, Yabu-san, all your final orders are subject to my approval. Buntaro-san, you will be the formal witness. Now, Yabu-san, whom do you want as your second?"

"Kasigi Omi-san."

Toranaga glanced at Omi. Omi bowed, his face colorless. "It will be my honor," he said.

"Good. Then everything's arranged."

Hiro-matsu said, "And the attack down the Tokaidō?"

"We're safer behind our mountains." Toranaga breezily returned their salutes, mounted his horse, and trotted off. Sudara nodded politely and followed. Once Toranaga and Sudara were out of range, Buntaro and Hiro-matsu relaxed but Omi did not, and no one took his eyes off Yabu's sword arm.

Buntaro said, "Where do you want to do it, Yabu-sama?"

"Here, there, down by the shore, or on a dung heap—it's all the same to me. I don't need ceremonial robes. But, Omi-san, you will not strike till I've made the two cuts."

"Yes, Sire."

"With your permission, Yabu-san, I will also be a witness," Hiro-matsu said.

"Are your piles up to it?"

The general bristled and said to Buntaro, "Please send for me when he's ready."

Yabu spat. "I'm already ready. Are you?"

Hiro-matsu turned on his heel.

Yabu thought for a moment, then took his scabbarded Yoshitomo sword out of his sash. "Buntaro-san, perhaps you'd do me a favor. Give this to the Anjin-san." He offered him the sword, then frowned. "On second thought, if it's no trouble, will you please send for him, then I can give it to him myself?"

"Certainly."

"And please fetch that stinking priest as well so I can talk directly with the Anjin-san."

"Good. What arrangements do you want made?"

"Just some paper and ink and a brush for my will and death poem, and two tatamis—there's no reason to hurt my knees or to kneel in the dirt like a stinking peasant. *Neh?*" Yabu added with bravado.

Buntaro walked over to the other samurai, who were shifting from one foot to the other with suppressed excitement. Carelessly Yabu sat cross-legged and picked his teeth with a grass stalk. Omi squatted nearby, warily out of sword range.

"Eeeeee," Yabu said. "I was so near success!" Then he stretched out his legs and hammered them against the earth in a sudden flurry of rage. "Eeeeee, so near! Eh, *karma, neh? Karma!*" Then he laughed uproariously and hawked and spat, proud that he still had saliva in his mouth. "*That* on all gods living or dead or yet to be born! But, Omi-san, I die happy. Jikkyu's dead and when I cross the Last River and see him waiting there, gnashing his teeth, I'll be able to spit in his eye forever."

Omi said, meaning it, though watching him like a hawk, "You have done Lord Toranaga a great service, Sire. The coastal route's open now. You're right, Sire, and Iron Fist's wrong and Sudara's wrong. We should attack at once—the guns will get us through."

"That old manure heap! Fool!" Yabu laughed again. "Did you see him go purple when I mentioned his piles? Ha! I thought they were going to burst on him then and there. Samurai? I'm more samurai than he is! I'll show him! You will not strike until I give the order."

"May I thank you humbly for giving me that honor, and also for making me your heir? I formally swear the Kasigi honor is safe in my hands."

"If I didn't think so I wouldn't have suggested it." Yabu lowered his voice. "You were right to betray me to Toranaga. I'd have done the same if I'd been you, though it's all lies. It's Toranaga's excuse. He's always been jealous of my battle prowess, and my understanding the guns and the value of the ship. It's all my idea."

"Yes, Sire, I remember."

"You'll save the family. You're as cunning as a scabby old rat. You'll get back Izu and more—that's all that's important now and you'll hold it for your sons. You understand the guns. And Toranaga. *Neh?*"

"I swear I will try, Sire."

Yabu's eyes dropped to Omi's sword hand, noting his alertly defensive kneeling posture. "You think I'll attack you?"

"So sorry, of course not, Sire."

"I'm glad you're on guard. My father was like you. Yes, you're a lot like him." Without making a sudden movement he put both of his swords on the ground, just out of reach. "There! Now I'm defenseless. A few moments ago I wanted your head—but not now. Now you've no need to fear me."

"There's always a need to fear you, Sire."

Yabu chortled softly and sucked another grass stalk. Then he threw it away. "Listen, Omi-san, these are my last orders as Lord of the Kasigis. You will take my son into your household and use him if he's worth using. Next: Find good husbands for my wife and consort, and thank them deeply for serving me so well. About your father, Mizuno: He's ordered to commit seppuku at once."

"May I request that he be given the alternative of shaving his head and becoming a priest?"

"No. He's too much of a fool, you'll never be able to trust him—how dare he pass on my secrets to Toranaga!—and he'll always be in your way. As to your mother . . ." He bared his teeth. "She's ordered to shave her head and become a nun and join a monastery outside Izu and spend the rest of her life saying prayers for the future of the Kasigis. Buddhist or Shinto—I prefer Shinto. You agree, Shinto?"

"Yes, Sire."

"Good. That way," Yabu added with malicious delight, "she'll stop distracting you from Kasigi matters with her constant whining."

"It will be done."

"Good. You are ordered to avenge the lies against me by Kosami and those treacherous servants. Soon or later, I don't care, so long as you do it before you die."

"I will obey."

"Is there anything I've forgotten?"

Carefully Omi made sure they were not overheard. "What about the Heir?" he asked cautiously. "When the Heir's in the field against us, we lose, *neh?*"

"Take the Musket Regiment and blast a way through and kill him, whatever Toranaga says. Yaemon's your prime target."

"That was my conclusion too. Thank you."

"Good. But better than waiting all that time, put a secret price on his head now, with *ninja* . . . or the Amida Tong."

"How do I find them?" Omi asked, a tremor in his voice.

"The old hag Gyoko, the Mama-san, she's one of those who knows how."

"Her?"

"Yes. But beware of her, and Amidas. Don't use them lightly, Omi-san. Never touch her, always protect her. She knows too many secrets and the pen's a long arm from the other side of death. She was my father's unofficial consort for a year . . . it may even be that her son is my half brother. Eh, beware of her, she knows too many secrets."

"But where do I get the money?"

"That's your problem. But get it. Anywhere, anyhow."

"Yes. Thank you. I will obey."

Yabu leaned closer. At once Omi readied suspiciously, his sword almost out of the scabbard. Yabu was gratified that even defenseless he was still a man to beware of. "Bury that secret very deep. And listen, nephew, remain very good friends with the Anjin-san. Try to get control of the navy he will bring back one day. Toranaga doesn't understand the Anjin-san's real value, but he's right to stay behind the mountains. That gives him time and you time. We've got to get off the land and out to sea—our crews in their ships—with Kasigis in overall command. The Kasigis must go to sea, to command the sea. I order it."

"Yes—oh, yes," Omi said. "Trust me. That *will* happen."

"Good. Lastly, never trust Toranaga."

Omi said with his complete being, "I don't, Sire. I never have. And never will."

"Good. And those filthy liars, don't forget, deal with them. And Kosami." Yabu exhaled, at peace with himself. "Now please excuse me, I must consider my death poem."

Omi got to his feet and backed off and when he was well away he bowed and went another twenty paces. Within the safety of his own guards he sat down once more and began to wait.

Toranaga and his party were trotting along the coast road that circled the vast bay, the sea coming almost up to the road and on his right. Here the land was low-lying and marshy with many mud flats. A few *ri* north this road joined with the main artery of the Tokaidō Road. Northward twenty *ri* more was Yedo.

He had a hundred samurai with him, ten falconers and ten birds on their gloved fists. Sudara had twenty guards and three birds, and rode as advance guard.

"Sudara!" Toranaga called out as though it was a sudden idea. "Stop at the next inn. I want some breakfast!"

Sudara waved acknowledgment and galloped ahead. By the time Toranaga rode up, maids were bowing and smiling, the innkeeper bobbing with all his people. Guards covered north and south, and his banners were planted proudly.

"Good morning, Sire, please what can I get for you to eat?" the innkeeper asked. "Thank you for honoring my poor inn."

"Cha—and some noodles with a little soya, please."

"Yes, Sire."

The food was produced in a fine bowl almost instantly, cooked just the way he liked it, the innkeeper having been forewarned by Sudara. Without ceremony, Toranaga squatted on a veranda and consumed the simple peasant dish with gusto and watched the road ahead. Other guests bowed and went about their own business contentedly, proud that they were staying in the same inn as the great *daimyo*. Sudara toured the outposts, making sure everything was perfect. "Where're the beaters now?" he asked the Master of the Hunt.

"Some are north, some south, and I've got extra men in the hills there." The old samurai pointed back inland toward Yokohama, miserable and sweating. "Please excuse me but have you any idea where our Master'll wish to go?"

"None at all. But don't make any more mistakes today."

"Yes, Sire."

Sudara finished his rounds then reported to Toranaga. "Is everything satisfactory, Sire? Is there anything I can do for you?"

"No, thank you." Toranaga finished the bowl and drank the last of the soup. Then he said in a flat voice, "You were correct to say that about the Heir."

"Please excuse me, I was afraid I might have offended you, without meaning to."

"You were right—so why should I be offended? When the Heir stands against me—what will you do then?"

"I will obey your orders."

"Please send my secretary here and come back with him."

Sudara obeyed. Kawanabi, the secretary—once a samurai and priest—who always traveled with Toranaga, was quickly there with his neat traveling box of papers, inks, seal chops, and brush pens that fitted into his saddled pannier. "Sire?"

"Write this: 'I, Yoshi Toranaga-noh-Minowara, reinstate my son Yoshi Sudara-noh-Minowara as my heir with all his revenues and titles restored.' "

Sudara bowed. "Thank you, Father," he said, his voice firm, but asking himself, *why?*

"Swear formally to abide by all my dictates, testaments—and the Legacy."

Sudara obeyed. Toranaga waited silently until Kawanabi had written the order, then he signed it and made it legal with his chop. This was a small square piece of ivory with his name carved in one end. He pressed the chop against the almost solid scarlet ink, then onto the bottom of the rice paper. The imprint was perfect. "Thank you, Kawanabi-san, date it yesterday. That's all for the moment."

"Please excuse me but you'll need five more copies, Sire, to make your succession inviolate: one for Lord Sudara, one for the Council of Regents, one for the House of Records, one for your personal files, and one for the archives."

"Do them at once. And give me an extra copy."

"Yes, Sire." The secretary left them. Now Toranaga glanced at Sudara and studied the narrow expressionless face. When he had made the deliberately sudden announcement nothing had shown on Sudara, neither on his face nor in his hands. No gladness, thankfulness, pride—not even surprise, and this saddened him. But then, Toranaga thought, why be sad, you have other sons who smile and laugh and make mistakes and shout and rave and pillow and have many women. Normal sons. This son is to follow after you, to lead after you're dead, to hold the Minowaras tight and to pass on the Kwanto and power to other Minowaras. To be ice and calculating, *like you.* No, not like me, he told himself truthfully. I can laugh sometimes and be compassionate sometimes, and I like to fart and pillow and storm and dance and play chess and Nōh, and some people gladden me, like Naga and Kiri and Chano and the Anjin-san, and I enjoy hunting and winning, and winning, and winning. Nothing gladdens you, Sudara, so sorry. Nothing. Except your wife, the Lady Genjiko. The Lady Genjiko's the only weak link in your chain.

"Sire?" Sudara asked.

"I was trying to remember when I last saw you laugh."

"You wish me to laugh, Sire?"

Toranaga shook his head, knowing he had trained Sudara to be the perfect son for what had to be done. "How long would it take you to be sure if Jikkyu is really dead?"

"Before I left camp I sent a top-priority cipher to Mishima in case you didn't already know if it was true or not, Father. I will have a reply within three days."

Toranaga blessed the gods that he had had advance knowledge of the Jikkyu plot from Kasigi Mizuno and a few days' notice of that enemy's death. For a moment he reexamined his plan and could find no flaw in it. Then, faintly nauseated, he made the decision. "Order the Eleventh, Sixteenth, Ninety-fourth, and Ninety-fifth Regiments in Mishima on instant alert. In four days fling them down the Tokaidō."

"Crimson Sky?" Sudara asked, thrown off balance. *"You're attacking?"*

"Yes. I'm not waiting for them to come against me."

"Then Jikkyu's dead?"

"Yes."

"Good," Sudara said. "May I suggest you add the Twentieth and Twenty-third."

"No. Ten thousand men should be enough—with surprise. I've still got to hold all my border in case of failure, or a trap. And there's also Zataki to contain."

"Yes," Sudara said.

"Who should lead the attack?"

"Lord Hiro-matsu. It's a perfect campaign for him."

"Why?"

"It's direct, simple, old-fashioned, and the orders clear, Father. He will be perfect for this campaign."

"But no longer suitable as commander-in-chief?"

"So sorry, Yabu-san was right—guns have changed the world. Iron Fist is out of date now."

"Who then?"

"Only you, Sire. Until after *the* battle I counsel you to have no one between you and *the* battle."

"I'll consider it," Toranaga said. "Now, go to Mishima. You'll prepare everything. Hiro-matsu's assault force will have twenty days to get across the Tenryu River and secure the Tokaidō Road."

"Please excuse me, may I suggest their final objective be a little farther, the crest of the Shiomi Slope. Allow them in all thirty days."

"No. If I make that an order, some men will reach the crest. But the majority will be dead and won't be able to throw back the counterattack, or harass the enemy as our force retreats."

"But surely you'll send reinforcements at once hard on their heels?"

"Our main attack goes through Zataki's mountains. This is a feint." Toranaga was appraising his son very carefully. But Sudara revealed nothing, neither surprise nor approval nor disapproval.

"Ah. So sorry. Please excuse me, Sire."

"With Yabu gone, who's to command the guns?"

"Kasigi Omi."

"Why?"

"He understands them. More than that, he's modern, very brave, very intelligent, very patient—also very dangerous, more dangerous than his uncle. I counsel that if you win, and if he survives, then find some excuse to invite him Onward."

"*If* I win?"

"Crimson Sky has always been a *last* plan. You've said it a hundred times. If we get mauled on the Tokaidō, Zataki will sweep down into the plains. The guns won't help us then. It's a last plan. You've never liked last plans."

"And the Anjin-san? What do you advise about him?"

"I agree with Omi-san and Naga-san. He should be bottled up. The rest of his men are nothing—they're *eta* and they'll cannibalize themselves soon, so they're nothing. I advise that all foreigners should be bottled up or thrown out. They're a plague—to be treated as such."

"Then there's no silk trade. *Neh?*"

"If that was the price then I'd pay it. They're a plague."

"But we must have silk and, to protect ourselves, we must learn about them, learn what they know, *neh?*"

"They should be confined to Nagasaki, under very close guard, and their numbers strictly limited. They could still trade once a year. Isn't money their essential motive? Isn't that what the Anjin-san says?"

"Ah, then he is useful?"

"Yes. Very. He's taught us the wisdom of the Expulsion Edicts. The Anjin-san is very wise, very brave. But he's a toy. He amuses you, Sire, like Tetsu-ko, so he's valuable, though still a toy."

Toranaga said, "Thank you for your opinions. Once the attack is launched you will return to Yedo and wait for further orders." He said it hard and deliberately. Zataki still held the Lady Genjiko, and their son and three daughters hostage at his capital of Takato. At Toranaga's request Zataki had granted Sudara a leave of absence, but only for ten days, and Sudara had solemnly agreed to the bargain and to return within that time. Zataki was famous for his narrow-mindedness about honor. Zataki would and could legally obliterate all the hostages on this point of honor, irrespective of any overt or covert treaty or agreement. Both Toranaga and Sudara knew without any doubt Zataki would do that if Sudara did not return as promised. "You will wait at Yedo for further orders."

"Yes, Sire."

"You will leave for Mishima at once."

"Then it will save time if I go that way." Sudara pointed at the junction ahead.

"Yes. I'll send you a dispatch tomorrow."

Sudara bowed and went to his horse and, with his twenty guards, rode off.

Toranaga picked up the bowl and took a remaining morsel of the now cold noodles. "Oh, Sire, so sorry, do you want some more?" the young maid said breathlessly, running up. She was round-faced and not pretty, but sharp and observant—just as he liked his serving maids, and his women. "No, thank you. What's your name?"

"Yuki, Sire."

"Tell your master he makes good noodles, Yuki."

"Yes, Sire, thank you. Thank you, Sire, for honoring our house. Just raise a knuckle joint for whatever you require and you'll have it instantly."

He winked at her and she laughed, collected his tray, and hurried off. Containing his impatience, he checked the far bend in the road, then examined his surroundings. The inn was in good repair, the tiled surrounds to the well clean and the earth broomed. Out in the courtyard and all around, his men waited patiently but he could detect nervousness in the Hunt Master and decided that today was the man's last day of active duty. If Toranaga had been seriously concerned with the hunt for itself alone, he would have told him to go back to Yedo now, giving him a generous pension, and appointed another in his place.

That's the difference between me and Sudara, he thought without malice. Sudara wouldn't hesitate. Sudara would order the man to commit seppuku now, which would save the pension and all further bother and increase the expertise of the replacement. Yes, my son, I know you very well. You're most important to me.

What about Lady Genjiko and their children, he asked himself, bringing to the fore that vital question. If the Lady Genjiko were not sister to Ochiba—her favorite and cherished sister—I would regretfully allow Zataki to eliminate them all now and so save Sudara an enormous amount of danger in the future, if I die soon, because they are his only weak link. But fortunately Genjiko is Ochiba's sister, and so an important piece in the Great Game, and I don't have to allow that to happen. I should but I won't. This time I have to gamble. So I'll remind myself Genjiko's valuable in other ways—she's as sharp as a shark's spine, makes fine children, and is as fanatically ruthless over her nest as Ochiba, with one enormous difference: Genjiko is loyal to me first, Ochiba to the Heir first.

So that's decided. Before the tenth day Sudara must be back in Zataki's hands. An extension? No, that might make Zataki even more suspicious than he is now, and he's the last man I want suspicious now. Which way will Zataki jump?

You were wise to settle Sudara. If there's a future, the future will be safe in his hands and Genjiko's, providing they follow the Legacy to the letter. And the decision to reinstate him now was correct and will please Ochiba.

He had already written the letter this morning that he would send off to her tonight with a copy of the order. Yes, that will remove one fish bone from her gullet that was making her choke, deliberately set there so long ago for that purpose. It's good to know Genjiko is one of Ochiba's weak links, perhaps her only one. What's Genjiko's weakness? None. At least I haven't found one yet, but if there is one, I'll find it.

He was scrutinizing his falcons. Some were prating, some preening themselves, all in good fettle, all hooded except Kogo, her great yellow eyes darting, watching everything, as interested as he was.

What would you say, my beauty, he asked her silently, what would you say if I told you I must be *impatient* and break out and my main thrust will be along the Tokaidō, and not through Zataki's mountains, as I told Sudara? You'd probably say, why? Then I'd answer, because I don't trust Zataki as far as I can fly. And I can't fly at all. *Neh?*

Then he saw Kogo's eyes snap to the road. He squinted into the distance and smiled as he saw the palanquins and baggage horses approaching around the bend.

"So, Fujiko-san? How are you?"

"Good, thank you, Sire, very good." She bowed again and he noticed she was not in pain from her burn scars. Now her limbs were as supple as ever, and there was a pleasing bloom on her cheeks. "May I ask how the Anjin-san is?" she said. "I heard the journey from Osaka was very bad, Sire."

"He's in good health now, very good."

"Oh, Sire, that's the best news you could have given me."

"Good." He turned to the next palanquin to greet Kiku and she smiled gaily and saluted him with great fondness, saying that she was so pleased to see him and how much she had missed him. "It's been so long, Sire."

"Yes, please excuse me, I'm sorry," he said, heated by her astounding beauty and inner joy in spite of his overwhelming anxieties. "I'm very pleased to see you." Then his eyes went to the last litter. "Ah, Gyoko-san, it's been a long time," he added, dry as tinder.

"Thank you, Lord, yes, and I'm reborn now that these old eyes have had the honor of seeing you again." Gyoko's bow was impeccable and she was carefully resplendent, and he caught the merest flash of a scarlet under kimono of the most expensive silk. "Ah, how strong you are, Sire, a giant among men," she crooned.

"Thank you. You're looking well too."

Kiku clapped her hands at the sally and they all laughed with her. "Listen," he said, happy because of her, "I've made arrangements for you to stay here for a while. Now, Fujiko-san, please come with me."

He took Fujiko aside and after giving her cha and refreshments and chatting about unimportant things he came to the point. "You agreed half a year and I agreed half a year. So sorry, but I must know today if you will change that agreement."

The square little face became unattractive as the joy went out of it. The tip of her tongue touched her sharp teeth for a moment. "How can I change that agreement, Sire?"

"Very easy. It's finished. I order it."

"Please excuse me, Sire," Fujiko said, her voice toneless, "I didn't mean that. I made that agreement freely and solemnly before Buddha with the spirit of my dead husband and my dead son. It cannot be changed."

"I order it changed."

"So sorry, Sire, please excuse me, but then *bushido* releases me from obedience to you. Your contract was equally solemn and binding and any change must be agreed by both parties without duress."

"Does the Anjin-san please you?"

"I am his consort. It is necessary for me to please him."

"Could you continue to live with him if the other agreement did not exist?"

"Life with him is very, very difficult, Sire. All formalities, most politenesses, every kind of custom that makes life safe and worthy and rounded and bearable has to be thrown away, or maneuvered around, so his household is not safe, it has no *wa*—no harmony for me. It's almost impossible to get servants to understand, or for me to understand . . . but, yes, I could continue to do my duty to him."

"I ask you to finish with the agreement."

"My first duty is to you. My second duty is to my husband."

"My thought, Fujiko-san, was that the Anjin-san would marry you. Then you would not be a consort."

"A samurai cannot serve two lords or a wife two husbands. My duty is to my dead husband. Please excuse me, I cannot change."

"With patience everything changes. Soon the Anjin-san will know more of our ways and his household will also have *wa*. He's learned incredibly since he's been—"

"Oh, please, Sire, don't misunderstand me, the Anjin-san's the most extraordinary man I've ever known, certainly the kindest. He's given me great honor and, oh yes, I know his house will be a real house soon, but . . . but please excuse me, I must do my duty. My duty is to my husband, my only husband. . . ." She fought for control. "It must be, *neh?* It must be, Sire, or then all . . . all the shame and the suffering and dishonor are meaningless, *neh?* His death, my child's, his swords broken and buried in the *eta* village. . . . Without duty to him, isn't all our *bushido* an immortal joke?"

"You must answer one question now, Fujiko-san: Doesn't your duty to a request from me, your liege lord, and to an astonishingly brave man who is becoming one of us and is your master, and," he added, believing he recognized the bloom in her face, "your duty to his unborn child, doesn't all that take precedence over a previous duty?"

"I'm . . . I'm not carrying his child, Sire."

"Are you sure?"

"No, not sure."

"Are you late?"

"Yes . . . but only a little and that could be . . ."

Toranaga watched and waited. Patiently. There was much yet to do before he could ride away and cast Tetsu-ko or Kogo aloft and he was avid for that pleasure, but that would be for himself alone and therefore unimportant. Fujiko was important and he had promised himself that at least for today he would pretend that he had won, that he had time and could be patient and arrange matters it was his duty to arrange. "Well?"

"So sorry, Sire, no."

"Then it's no, Fujiko-san. Please excuse me for asking you but it was necessary." Toranaga was neither angry nor pleased. The girl was only doing what was honorable and he had known when he had agreed to the bargain with her that there would never be a change. That's what makes us unique on earth, he thought with satisfaction. A bargain with death is a bargain that is sanctified. He bowed to her formally. "I commend you for your honor and sense of duty to your husband, Usagi Fujiko," he said, mentioning the name that had ceased to be.

"Oh, thank you, Sire," she said at the honor he did to her, her tears streaming from the complete happiness that possessed her, knowing this simple gesture cleansed the stigma from the only husband she would have in this life.

"Listen, Fujiko, twenty days before the *last day* you are to leave for Yedo— whatever happens to me. Your death may take place during the journey and must appear to be accidental. *Neh?*"

"Yes, yes, Sire."

"This will be our secret. Yours and mine only."

"Yes, Sire."

"Until that time you will remain head of his household."

"Yes, Sire."

"Now, please tell Gyoko to come here. I'll send for you again before I go. I have some other things to discuss with you."

"Yes, Sire." Fujiko bowed deeply and said, "I bless you for releasing me from life." She went away.

Curious, Toranaga thought, how women can change like chameleons—one moment ugly, the next attractive, sometimes even beautiful, though in reality they're not.

"You sent for me, Sire?"

"Yes, Gyoko-san. What news have you for me?"

"All sorts of things, Sire," Gyoko said, her well-made-up face unafraid, a glint in her eyes, but her bowels in upheaval. She knew it was no coincidence that this meeting was taking place and her instinct told her Toranaga was more dangerous than usual. "Arrangements for the Guild of Courtesans progress satisfactorily and rules and regulations are being drawn up for your approval. There is a fine area to the north of the city that would—"

"The area I've already chosen is nearer the coast. The Yoshiwara."

She complimented him on his choice, groaning inwardly. The Yoshiwara— Reed Moor—was presently a bog and mosquitoed and would have to be drained and reclaimed before it could be fenced and built on. "Excellent, Sire. Next: Rules and regulations for the *gei-sha* are also being prepared for your perusal."

"Good. Make them short and to the point. What sign are you going to put over the gateway to the Yoshiwara?"

" 'Lust will not keep—something must be done about it.' "

He laughed, and she smiled but did not relax her guard, though she added seriously, "Again may I thank you on behalf of future generations, Sire."

"It's not for you or them I agreed," Toranaga told her, and quoted one of his comments in the Legacy: " Virtuous men throughout history have always decried bawdy houses and Pillow Places, but men aren't virtuous and if a leader outlaws houses and pillowing he's a fool because greater evils will soon erupt like a plague of boils."

"How wise you are."

"And as to putting all the Pillow Places in one area, that means all the unvirtuous may be watched, taxed, and serviced, all at the same time. You're right again, Gyoko-san, 'Lust will not keep.' It soon gets addled. Next?"

"Kiku-san has regained her health, Sire. Perfectly."

"Yes, I saw. How delightful she is! I'm sorry—Yedo's certainly hot and unkind in the summer. You're sure she's fine now?"

"Yes, oh yes, but she has missed you, Sire. We are to accompany you to Mishima?"

"What other rumors have you heard?"

"Only that Ishido's left Osaka Castle. The Regents have formally declared you outlaw—what impertinence, Sire."

"Which way's he planning to attack me?"

"I don't know, Sire," she said cautiously. "But I imagine a two-forked attack, along the Tokaidō with Ikawa Hikoju now that his father, Lord Jikkyu, is dead, and along the Koshu-kaidō, from Shinano, as Lord Zataki has foolishly sided with Lord Ishido against you. But behind your mountains you're safe. Oh, yes, I'm sure you'll live to a ripe old age. With your permission, I'm shifting all my affairs to Yedo."

"Certainly. Meanwhile see if you can find out where the main thrust will be."

"I'll try, oh yes, Sire. These are terrible times, Sire, when brother will go against brother, son against father."

Toranaga's eyes were veiled and he made a note to increase vigilance on Noboru, his eldest son, whose final allegiance was with the Taikō. "Yes," he agreed. "Terrible times. Times of great change. Some bad, some good. You, for example, you're rich now and your son, for example. Isn't he in charge of your saké factory at Odawara?"

"Yes, Sire." Gyoko went gray under her makeup.

"He's been making great profits, *neh?*"

"He's certainly the best manager in Odawara, Sire."

"So I hear. I have a job for him. The Anjin-san's going to build a new ship. I'm providing all craftsmen and materials, so I want the business side handled with *very great care.*"

Gyoko almost collapsed with relief. She had presumed Toranaga was going to obliterate them all before he left for the war, or tax her out of existence, because he'd found out she'd lied to him about the Anjin-san and the Lady Toda, or about

Kiku's unfortunate miscarriage, which was not by chance as she had reported so tearfully a month ago, but by careful inducement, at her insistence with Kiku's dutiful agreement. *"Oh ko,* Sire, when do you want my son in Yokohama? He will ensure it's the cheapest ship ever built."

"I don't want it cheap. I want it the very best—for the most reasonable price. He's to be overseer and responsible under the Anjin-san."

"Sire, you have my guarantee, my future, my future hopes that it will be as you wish."

"If the ship is built perfectly, exactly as the Anjin-san wants, within six months from the first day, then I will make your son samurai."

She bowed low and for a moment was unable to talk. "Please excuse a poor fool, Sire. Thank you, thank you."

"He has to learn everything the Anjin-san knows about building the ship so others can be taught when he leaves. *Neh?*"

"It will be done."

"Next: Kiku-san. Her talents merit a better future than just being alone in a box, one of many women."

Gyoko looked up, again expecting the worst. "You're going to sell her contract?"

"No, she shouldn't be a courtesan again or even one of your *gei-sha.* She should be in a household, one of few ladies, very few."

"But, Sire, seeing you even occasionally, how could she possibly have a better life?"

He allowed her to compliment him and he complimented her back, and Kiku, then said, "Frankly, Gyoko-san, I'm getting too fond of her and I can't afford to be distracted. Frankly she's far too pretty for me—far too perfect. . . . Please excuse me, but this must be another of our secrets."

"I agree, Sire, of course, whatever you say," Gyoko said fervently, dismissing it all as lies, racking her brain for the real reason. "If the person could be someone Kiku could admire, I would die content."

"But only after seeing the Anjin-san's ship under sail within the six months," he said dryly.

"Yes—oh yes." Gyoko moved her fan for the sun was hot now and the air sticky and breathless, trying to fathom why Toranaga was being so generous with both of them, knowing that the price would be heavy, very heavy. "Kiku-san will be distraught to leave your house."

"Yes, of course. I think there should be some compensation for her obedience to me, her liege lord. Leave that with me—and don't mention this to her for the present."

"Yes, Sire. And when do you want my son in Yokohama?"

"I'll let you know that before I leave."

She bowed and tottered away. Toranaga went for a swim. Northward the sky was very dark and he knew it would be raining heavily there. When he saw the small group of horsemen coming from the direction of Yokohama he returned.

Omi dismounted and unwrapped the head. "Lord Kasigi Yabu obeyed, Sire, just before noon." The head had been freshly washed, the hair groomed, and it was stuck on the spike of a small pedestal that was customarily used for the viewing.

Toranaga inspected an enemy as he had done ten thousand times before in his lifetime, wondering as always how his own head would look after death, viewed by his conqueror, and whether terror would show, or agony or anger or horror or all of them or none of them. Or dignity. Yabu's death mask showed only berserk wrath, the lips pulled back into a ferocious challenge. "Did he die well?"

"The best I have ever seen, Sire. Lord Hiro-matsu said the same. The two cuts, then a third in the throat. Without assistance and without a sound." Omi added, "Here is his will."

"You took off the head with one stroke?"

"Yes, Sire. I asked the Anjin-san's permission to use Lord Yabu's sword."

"The Yoshitomo? The one I gave Yabu? He gave it to the Anjin-san?"

"Yes, Sire. He spoke to him through the Tsukku-san. He said, 'Anjin-san, I give you this to commemorate your arrival at Anjiro and as a thank you for the pleasure that little barbarian gave me.' At first the Anjin-san refused to take it, but Yabu begged him to and said, 'None of these manure eaters deserves such a blade.' Eventually he agreed."

Curious, Toranaga thought. I expected Yabu to give the blade to Omi.

"What were his last instructions?" he asked.

Omi told him. Exactly. If they had not all been also written in the will that had been given publicly to the formal witness, Buntaro, he would not have passed all of them on, and indeed, would have invented others. Yabu was right, he thought furiously, reminding himself to remember forever that the pen's a long arm from the grave.

"To honor your uncle's death bravery, I should honor his death wishes. All of them, without change, *neh?*" Toranaga said, testing him.

"Yes, Sire."

"Yuki!"

"Yes, Sire," the maid said.

"Bring cha, please."

She scurried away and Toranaga let his mind weigh Yabu's last wishes. They were all wise. Mizuno was a fool and completely in Omi's way. The mother was an irritating, unctuous old hag, also in Omi's way. "Very well, since you agree, they're confirmed. All of them. And I also wish to approve your father's death wishes before they become final. As a reward for your devotion you are appointed Commander of the Musket Regiment."

"Thank you, Sire, but I don't deserve such an honor," Omi said, exulting.

"Naga will be second-in-command. Next: You're appointed head of the Kasigis and your new fief will be the border lands of Izu, from Atami on the east to Nimazu on the west, including the capital, Mishima, with a yearly income of thirty thousand koku."

"Yes, Sire, thank you. Please . . . I don't know how to thank you. I'm not worthy of such honors."

"Make sure you are, Omi-sama," Toranaga said good-naturedly. "Take possession of the castle at Mishima at once. Leave Yokohama today. Report to Lord Sudara at Mishima. The Musket Regiment will be sent to Hakoné and be there in four days. Next, privately, for your knowledge alone: I'm sending the Anjin-san back to Anjiro. He'll build a new ship there. You'll pass over your present fief to him. At once."

"Yes, Sire. May I give him my house?"

"Yes, you may," Toranaga said, though of course a fief contained everything therein, houses, property, peasants, fishermen, boats. Both men looked off as Kiku's trilling laugh came through the air and they saw her playing the fan-throwing game in the far courtyard with her maid, Suisen, whose contract Toranaga had also bought as a consolation gift to Kiku after the unfortunate miscarriage of his child.

Omi's adoration was clear for all the world to see, much as he tried to hide it, so sudden and unexpected had been her appearance. Then they saw her look toward them. A lovely smile spread over her face and she waved gaily and

Toranaga waved back and she returned to her game.

"She's pretty, *neh?*"

Omi felt his ears burning. "Yes."

Toranaga had originally bought her contract to exclude Omi from her, because she was one of Omi's weaknesses and clearly a prize, to give or withhold, until Omi had declared and proved his real allegiance and had assisted or not assisted in Yabu's removal. And he had assisted, miraculously, and proved himself many times. Investigating the servants had been Omi's suggestion. Many, if not all, of Yabu's fine ideas had come from Omi. Omi had, a month ago, uncovered the details of Yabu's secret plot with some of the Izu officers in the Musket Regiment to assassinate Naga and the other Brown officers during battle.

"There's no mistake, Omi-san?" he had asked when Omi reported to him secretly at Mishima, while he was awaiting the outcome of Mariko's challenge.

"No, Sire. Kiwami Matano of the Third Izu Regiment is outside."

The Izu officer, a jowly, heavyset, middle-aged man, had laid out the whole plot, given the passwords, and explained how the scheme would work. "I couldn't live with the shame of this knowledge anymore, Sire. You are our liege lord. Of course, in fairness I should say the plan was only *if necessary.* I supposed that meant if Yabu-sama decided to change sides suddenly during the battle. So sorry, you were to be the prime target, then Naga-san. Then Lord Sudara."

"When was this plan first ordered and who knows about it?"

"Shortly after the regiment was formed. Fifty-four of us know—I've given all the names in writing to Omi-sama. The plan, code name 'Plum Tree,' was confirmed personally by Kasigi Yabu-sama before he left for Osaka the last time."

"Thank you. I commend your loyalty. You are to keep this secret until I tell you. Then you will be given a fief worth five thousand koku."

"Please excuse me, I deserve nothing, Sire. I beg permission to commit seppuku for having held this shameful secret so long."

"Permission is refused. It will be as I ordered."

"Please excuse me, I do not deserve such reward. At least allow me to remain as I am. This is my duty and merits no reward. Truly I should be punished."

"What's your income now?"

"Four hundred koku, Sire. It's enough."

"I'll consider what you say, Kiwami-san."

After the officer had left he had said, "What did you promise him, Omi-san?"

"Nothing, Sire. He came to me of his own accord yesterday."

"An honest man? You're telling me he's an honest man?"

"I don't know about that, Sire. But he came to me yesterday, and I rushed here to tell you."

"Then he will really be rewarded. Such loyalty's more important than anything, *neh?*"

"Yes, Sire."

"Say nothing of this to anyone."

Omi had left and Toranaga had wondered if Mizuno and Omi had trumped up the plot to discredit Yabu. At once he put his own spies to find out the truth. But the plot had been true, and the burning of the ship had been a perfect excuse to remove the fifty-three traitors, all of whom had been placed among the Izu guards on that night. Kiwami Matano he had sent to the far north with a good, though modest, fief.

"Surely this Kiwami is the most dangerous of all," Sudara had said, the only one admitted to the plot.

"Yes. And he'll be watched all his life and not trusted. But generally there's good in evil people and evil in good people. You must choose the good and get rid of the evil without sacrificing the good. There's *no* waste in my domains to be cast away lightly."

Yes, Toranaga thought with great satisfaction, you certainly deserve a prize, Omi.

"Listen, Omi-san, the battle will begin in a few days. You've served me loyally. On the last battlefield, after my victory, I'll appoint you Overlord of Izu, and make your line of the Kasigi hereditary *daimyos* again."

"So sorry, Sire, please excuse me, but I don't deserve such honor," Omi said.

"You're young but you show great promise, beyond your years. Your grandfather was very like you, very clever, but he had no patience." Again the sound of the ladies' laughter, and Toranaga watched Kiku, trying to decide about her, his original plan now cast aside.

"May I ask what you mean by patience, Sire?" Omi said, instinctively feeling that Toranaga wanted the question to be asked.

Toranaga still looked at the girl, warmed by her. "Patience means restraining yourself. There are seven emotions, *neh?* Joy, anger, anxiety, adoration, grief, fear, and hate. If a man doesn't give way to these, he's patient. I'm not as strong as I might be but I'm patient. Understand?"

"Yes, Sire. Very clearly."

"Patience is very necessary in a leader."

"Yes."

"That lady, for example. She's a distraction to me, too beautiful, too perfect for me. I'm too simple for such a rare creature. So I've decided she belongs elsewhere."

"But, Sire, even as one of your lesser ladies . . ." Omi mouthed the politeness that both men knew a sham, though obligatory, and all the time Omi was praying as he had never prayed before, knowing what was possible, knowing that he could never ask.

"I quite agree," Toranaga said. "But great talent merits sacrifice." He was still watching her throwing her fan, catching her maid's fan in return, her gaiety infectious. Then both the ladies were obscured by the horses. So sorry, Kiku-san, he thought, but I have to pass you on, to settle you out of reach quickly. The truth is, I really am getting too fond of you, though Gyoko would never believe I had told her the truth, nor will Omi, nor even you yourself. "Kiku-san is worthy of a house of her own. With a husband of her own."

"Better a consort of the lowest samurai than wife of a farmer or merchant, however rich."

"I don't agree."

For Omi those words ended the matter. *Karma,* he told himself, his misery overwhelming him. Put your sadness away, fool. Your liege lord has decided, so that is the end of it. Midori is a perfect wife. Your mother is to become a nun, so now your house will have harmony.

So much sadness today. And happiness: *daimyo* of Izu-to-be; Commander of the Regiment; the Anjin-san's to be kept in Anjiro, therefore the first ship is to be built within Izu—*in my fief.* Put aside your sadness. Life is all sadness. Kiku-san has her *karma,* I have mine, Toranaga has his, and my Lord Yabu shows how foolish it is to worry about this or that or anything.

Omi looked up at Toranaga, his mind clear and everything compartmentalized. "Please excuse me, Sire, I beg your forgiveness. I wasn't thinking clearly."

"You may greet her if you wish, before you leave."

"Thank you, Sire." Omi wrapped up Yabu's head. "Do you wish me to bury it—or display it?"

"Put it on a spear, facing the wreck."

"Yes, Sire."

"What was his death poem?"

Omi said:

> " *'What are clouds*
> *But an excuse for the sky?*
> *What is life*
> *But an escape from death?'* "

Toranaga smiled. "Interesting," he said.

Omi bowed and gave the wrapped head to one of his men and went through the horses and samurai to the far courtyard.

"Ah, Lady," he said to her with kind formality. "I'm so pleased to see you well and happy."

"I'm with my Lord, Omi-san, and he's strong and content. How can I be anything but happy."

"*Sayonara,* Lady."

"*Sayonara,* Omi-sama." She bowed, aware of a vast finality now, never quite realizing it before. A tear welled and she brushed it aside and bowed again as he walked away.

She watched his tall, firm stride and would have wept aloud, her heart near breaking, but then, as always, she heard the so-many-times-said words in her memory, kindly spoken, wisely spoken, 'Why do you weep, child? We of the Floating World live only for the moment, giving all our time to the pleasures of cherry blossoms and snow and maple leaves, the calling of a cricket, the beauty of the moon, waning and growing and being reborn, singing our songs and drinking cha and saké, knowing perfumes and the touch of silks, caressing for pleasure, and drifting, always drifting. Listen, child: never sad, always drifting as a lily on the current in the stream of life. How lucky you are, Kiku-chan, you're a Princess of *Ukiyo,* the Floating World, drift, live for the moment. . . .'

Kiku brushed away a second tear, a last tear. Silly girl to weep. Weep no more! she ordered herself. You're so incredibly lucky! You're consort to the greatest *daimyo* himself, even though a very lesser, unofficial one, but what does that matter—*your sons will be born samurai.* Isn't this the most incredible gift in the world? Didn't the soothsayer predict such an incredible good fortune, never to be believed? But now it's true, *neh?* If you must weep there are more important things to weep about. About the growing seed in your loins that the weird-tasting cha took out of you. But why weep about that? It was only an "it" and not a child and who was the father? Truly?

"I don't know, not for certain, Gyoko-san, so sorry, but I think it's my Lord's," she had said finally, wanting his child so much to bind the promise of samurai.

"But say the child's born with blue eyes and a fair skin? It may, *neh?* Count the days."

"I've counted and counted, oh, how I've counted!"

"Then be honest with yourself. So sorry, but both of our futures depend on you now. You've many a birthing year ahead of you. You're just eighteen, child, *neh?* Better to be sure, *neh?*"

Yes, she thought again, how wise you are, Gyoko-san, and how silly I was, bewitched. It was only an "it" and how sensible we Japanese are to know that a child is not a proper child until thirty days after birth when its spirit is firmly fixed in its body and its *karma* inexorable. Oh, how lucky I am, and I want a son and another and another and never a girl child. Poor girl children! Oh gods, bless the soothsayer and thank you thank you thank you for my *karma* that I am favored by the great *daimyo,* that my sons will be samurai and oh, please make me worthy of such marvelousness. . . .

"What is it, Mistress?" little Suisen asked, awed by the joy that seemed to pour out of Kiku.

Kiku sighed contentedly. "I was thinking about the soothsayer and my Lord and my *karma,* just drifting, drifting. . . ."

She went farther out into the courtyard, shading herself with her scarlet umbrella, to seek Toranaga. He was almost hidden by the horses and samurai and falcons in the courtyard, but she could see he was still on the veranda, sipping cha now, Fujiko bowing before him again. Soon it'll be my turn, she thought. Perhaps tonight we can begin a new "it." Oh, please. . . . Then, greatly happy, she turned back to her game.

Outside the gateway Omi was mounting his horse and he galloped off with his guards, faster and ever faster, the speed refreshing him, cleansing him, the pungent sweat-smell of his horse pleasing. He did not look back at her because there was no need. He knew that he had left all his life's passion, and everything that he had adored, at her feet. He was sure he would never know passion again, the spirit-joining ecstasy that ignited man and woman. But this did not displease him. On the contrary, he thought with a newfound icy clarity, I bless Toranaga for releasing me from servitude. Now nothing binds me. Neither father nor mother nor Kiku. Now I can be patient too. I'm twenty-one, I'm almost *daimyo* of Izu, and I've a world to conquer.

"Yes, Sire?" Fujiko was saying.

"You're to go direct from here to Anjiro. I've decided to change the Anjin-san's fief from around Yokohama to Anjiro. Twenty *ri* in every direction from the village, with a yearly income of four thousand koku. You'll take over Omi-san's house."

"May I thank you on his behalf, Sire. So sorry, do I understand that he doesn't know about this yet?"

"No. I'll tell him today. I've ordered him to build another ship, Fujiko-san, to replace the one lost, and Anjiro will be a perfect shipyard, much better than Yokohama. I've arranged with the Gyoko woman for her eldest son to be business overseer for the Anjin-san, and all materials and craftsmen will be paid for out of my treasury. You'll have to help him set up some form of administration."

"*Oh ko,* Sire," she said, immediately concerned. "My time remaining with the Anjin-san will be so short."

"Yes. I'll have to find him another consort—or wife. *Neh?*"

Fujiko looked up, her eyes narrowing. Then she said, "Please, how may I help?"

Toranaga said, "Whom would you suggest? I want the Anjin-san to be content. Contented men work better, *neh?*"

"Yes." Fujiko reached into her mind. Who would compare with Mariko-sama? Then she smiled. "Sire, Omi-san's present wife, Midori-san. His mother hates her, as you know, and wants Omi divorced—so sorry, but she had the astounding bad manners to say it in front of me. Midori-san's such a lovely lady and, oh, so very clever."

"You think Omi wants to be divorced?" Another piece of the puzzle fell in place.

"Oh, no, Sire, I'm sure he doesn't. What man wants really to obey his mother? But that's our law, so he should have divorced her the first time his parents mentioned it, *neh?* Even though his mother's very bad tempered, she surely knows what's best for him, of course. So sorry, I have to be truthful as this is a most important matter. Of course I mean no offense, Sire, but filial duty to one's parents is the corner post of our law."

"I agree," Toranaga said, pondering this fortunate new thought. "The Anjin-san would consider Midori-san a good suggestion?"

"No, Sire, not if you ordered the marriage . . . but, so sorry, there's no need for you to order him."

"Oh?"

"You could perhaps think of a way to make him think of it himself. That would certainly be best. With Omi-san, of course, you just order him."

"Of course. You'd approve of Midori-san?"

"Oh, yes. She's seventeen, her present son's healthy, she's from good samurai stock, so she'd give the Anjin-san fine sons. I suppose Omi's parents will insist Midori give up her son to Omi-san, but if they don't the Anjin-san could adopt him. I know my Master likes her because Mariko-sama told me she teased him about her. She's very good samurai stock, very prudent, very clever. Oh, yes, he'd be very safe with her. Also her parents are both dead now so there'd be no ill feeling from them about her marrying a—marrying the Anjin-san."

Toranaga toyed with the idea. I've certainly got to keep Omi off balance, he told himself. Young Omi can become a thorn in my side too easily. Well, I won't have to do anything to get Midori divorced. Omi's father will absolutely have definite last wishes before he commits seppuku and his wife will certainly insist the most important last thing he does on this earth will be to get their son married correctly. So Midori will be divorced within a few days anyway. Yes, she'd be a very good wife.

"If not her, Fujiko-san, what about Kiku? Kiku-san?"

Fujiko gaped at him. "Oh, so sorry, Sire, you're going to relinquish her?"

"I might. Well?"

"I would have thought Kiku-san would be a perfect unofficial consort, Sire. She's so brilliant and wonderful. Though I can see she would be an enormous distraction for an ordinary man, and, so sorry, it would be years before the Anjin-san would be able to appreciate the rare quality of her singing or dancing or wit. As wife?" she asked, with just enough emphasis to indicate absolute disapproval. "Ladies of the Willow World aren't usually trained the same as . . . as others are, Sire. Their talents lie elsewhere. To be responsible for the finances and the affairs of a samurai house is different from the Floating World."

"Could she learn?"

Fujiko hesitated a long while. "The perfect thing for the Anjin-san would be Midori-san for wife, Kiku-san as consort."

"Could they learn to live with all his—er—*different* attitudes?"

"Midori-san's samurai, Sire. It would be her duty. You would order her. Kiku-san also."

"But not the Anjin-san?"

"You know him better than I, Sire. But in pillow things and . . . it would be better for him to, well, think of it himself."

"Toda Mariko-sama would have made a perfect wife for him. *Neh?*"

"That's an extraordinary idea, Sire," Fujiko replied, without blinking. "Certainly both had an enormous respect for each other."

"Yes," he said dryly. "Well, thank you, Fujiko-san. I'll consider what you said. He'll be at Anjiro in about ten days."

"Thank you, Sire. If I might suggest, the port of Ito and the Yokosé Spa should be included within the Anjin-san's fief."

"Why?"

"Ito just in case Anjiro is not big enough. Perhaps bigger slipways would be necessary for such a big ship. Perhaps they're available there. Yokosé be—"

"Are they?"

"Yes, Sire. An—"

"Have you been there?"

"No, Sire. But the Anjin-san's interested in the sea. So are you. It was my duty to try to learn about ships and shipping, and when we heard the Anjin-san's ship was burned I wondered if it would be possible to build another, and if so, where and how. Izu is a perfect choice, Sire. It will be easy to keep Ishido's armies out."

"And why Yokosé?"

"And Yokosé because a hatamoto should have a place in the mountains where you could be entertained in the style you have a right to expect."

Toranaga was watching her closely. Fujiko appeared so docile and demure but he knew she was as inflexible as he was and not ready to concede either point unless he ordered it. "I agree. And I'll consider what you said about Midori-san and Kiku-san."

"Thank you, Sire," she said humbly, glad that she had done her duty to her master and repaid her debt to Mariko. Ito for its slipways, and Yokosé where Mariko had said their "love" had really begun.

"I'm so lucky, Fujiko-chan," Mariko had told her at Yedo. "Our journey here has brought me more joy than I have the right to expect in twenty lifetimes."

"I beg you to protect him in Osaka, Mariko-san. So sorry, he's not like us, not civilized like us, poor man. His nirvana is life and not death."

That's still true, Fujiko thought again, blessing Mariko's memory. Mariko had saved the Anjin-san, no one else—not the Christian God or any gods, not the Anjin-san himself, not even Toranaga, no one—only Mariko alone. Toda Mariko-noh-Akechi Jinsai had saved him.

Before I die I will put up a shrine at Yokosé and leave a bequest for another at Osaka and another at Yedo. That's going to be one of my death wishes, Toranaga-sama, she promised herself, looking back at him so patiently, warmed by all the other lovely things yet to be done on the Anjin-san's behalf. Midori to wife certainly, *never* Kiku as wife but *only* a consort and not necessarily chief consort, and the fief extended to Shimoda on the very south coast of Izu. "Do you want me to leave at once, Sire?"

"Stay here tonight, then go direct tomorrow. Not via Yokohama."

"Yes. I understand. So sorry, I can take possession of my Master's new fief on his behalf—and all it contains—the moment I arrive?"

"Kawanabi-san will give you the necessary documents before you leave here. Now, please send Kiku-san to me."

Fujiko bowed and left.

Toranaga grunted. Pity that woman's going to end herself. She's almost too valuable to lose, and much too smart. Ito and Yokosé? Ito understandable. Why Yokosé? And what else was in her mind?

He saw Kiku coming across the sun-baked courtyard, her little feet in white tabi, almost dancing, so sweet and elegant with her silks and crimson sunshade, the envy of every man in sight. Ah, Kiku, he thought, I can't afford that envy, so sorry. I can't afford you in this life, so sorry. You should have remained where you were in the Floating World, courtesan of the First Class. Or even better, *gei-sha*. What a fine idea that old hag came up with! Then you'd be safe, the property of many, the adored of many, the central point of tragic suicides and violent quarrels and wonderful assignations, fawned on and feared, showered with money that you'd treat with disdain, a legend—while your beauty lasts. But now? Now I can't keep you, so sorry. Any samurai I give you to as consort takes to his bed a double-edged knife: a complete distraction and the envy of every other man. *Neh?* Few would agree to marry you, so sorry, but that's the truth and this is a day for truths. Fujiko was right. You're not trained to run a samurai household, so sorry. As soon as your beauty goes—oh, your voice will last, child, and your wit, but soon you'll still be cast out on to the dung heap of the world. So sorry, but that's also the truth. Another is that the highest Ladies of the Floating World are best left in their Floating World to run other houses when age is upon them, even the most famous, to weep over lost lovers and lost youth in barrels of saké, watered with your tears. The lesser ones at best to be wife to a farmer or fisherman or merchant, or rice seller or craftsman, from which life you were born—the rare, sudden flower that appears in the wilderness for no reason other than *karma,* to blossom quickly and to vanish quickly.

So sad, so very sad. How do I give you samurai children?

You keep her for the rest of your time, his secret heart told him. She merits it. Don't fool yourself like you fool others. The truth is you could keep her easily, taking her a little, leaving her a lot, just like your favorite Tetsu-ko, or Kogo. Isn't Kiku just a falcon to you? Prized yes, unique yes, but just a falcon that you feed from your fist, to fly at a prey and call back with a lure, to cast adrift after a season or two, to vanish forever? Don't lie to yourself, that's fatal. Why not keep her? She's only just another falcon, though very special, very high-flying, very beautiful to watch, but nothing more, rare certainly, unique certainly, and, oh, so pillowable. . . .

"Why do you laugh? Why are you so happy, Sire?"

"Because you are a joy to see, Lady."

Blackthorne leaned his weight on one of the three hawsers that were attached to the keel plate of the wreck. *"Hipparuuuu!"* he called out. Puuuulll!

There were a hundred samurai naked to their loincloths hauling lustily on each rope. It was afternoon now and low tide, and Blackthorne hoped to be able to shift the wreck and drag her ashore to salvage everything. He had adapted his first plan when he had found to his glee that all the cannon had been fished out of the sea the day after the holocaust and were almost as perfect as the day they had left their foundry near Chatham in his home county of Kent. As well, almost a thousand cannonballs, some grape and chain and many metal things had been recovered. Most were twisted and scored but he had the makings of a ship, better than he had dreamed possible.

"Marvelous, Naga-san! Marvelous!" he had congratulated him when he had discovered the true extent of the salvage.

"Oh, thank you, Anjin-san. Try hard, so sorry."

"Never mind so sorry. All good now!"

Yes, he had rejoiced. Now *The Lady* can be just a mite longer and a mite more abeam, but she'll still have her greyhound look and she'll be a pisscutter to end all pisscutters.

Ah, Rodrigues, he had thought without rancor, I'm glad you're safe and away this year and there'll be another man to sink next year. If Ferriera's Captain-General again, that would be a gift from heaven, but I won't count on it and I'm glad you're safe away. I owe you my life and you were a great pilot.

"Hipparuuuuuuu!" he shouted again and hawsers jerked, the sea dripping off them like sweat, but the wreck did not budge.

Since that dawn on the beach with Toranaga, Mariko's letter in his hands, the cannon discovered so soon afterward, there had not been enough hours in the day. He had drawn beginning plans and made and remade lists and changed plans and very carefully offered up lists of men and materials needed, not wanting any mistakes. And after the day, he worked at the dictionary long into the night to learn the new words he would need to tell the craftsmen what he wanted, to find out what they had already and could do already. Many times, in desperation, he had wanted to ask the priest to help but he knew there was no help there now, that their enmity was inexorably fixed.

Karma, he had told himself without pain, pitying the priest for his misbegotten fanaticism.

"Hipparuuuuuuuu!"

Again the samurai strained against the hold of the sand and the sea, then a chant sprang up and they tugged in unison. The wreck shifted a fraction and they redoubled their efforts, then it jerked loose and they sprawled in the sand. They picked themselves up, laughing, congratulating themselves, and leaned on the ropes again. But now the wreck was stuck firm once more.

Blackthorne showed them how to take the ropes to one side, then to the other, trying to ease the wreck to port or starboard but it was as fixed as though anchored.

"I'll have to buoy it, then the tide'll do the work and lift it," he said aloud in English.

"Dozo?" Naga said, puzzled.

"Ah, gomen nasai, Naga-san." With signs and pictures in the sand he explained, damning his lack of words, how to make a raft and tie it to the spines at low tide; then the next high tide would float the wreck and they could pull it ashore and beach it. At the next low tide it would be easy to manage because they would have laid rollers for it to rest on.

"Ah so desu!" Naga said, impressed. When he explained to the other officers, they also were filled with admiration and Blackthorne's own vassals were puffed with implied importance.

Blackthorne noticed this and he pointed a finger at one. "Where are your manners?"

"What? Oh, so sorry, Sire, please excuse me for offending you."

"Today I will, tomorrow no. Swim out to ship—untie this rope."

The *ronin*-samurai quailed and rolled his eyes. "So sorry, Sire, I can't swim."

Now it was silent on the beach and Blackthorne knew all were waiting to see what would happen. He was furious with himself, for an order was an order and involuntarily he had given a death sentence that was not merited this time. He thought a moment. "Toranaga-sama's orders, all men learn swim. *Neh?* All my vassals swim within thirty days. Better swim in thirty days. You, in water—get first lesson now."

Fearfully the samurai began to walk into the sea, knowing he was a dead man. Blackthorne joined him and when the man's head went under he pulled him up, none too kindly, and made him swim, letting him flounder but never dangerously all the way out to the wreck, the man coughing and retching and holding on. Then he pulled him ashore again and twenty yards from the shallows he shoved him off. "Swim!"

The man made it like a half-drowned cat. Never again would he act self-important in front of his master. His fellows cheered and the men on the beach were rolling in the sand with laughter, those who could swim.

"Very good, Anjin-san," Naga said. "Very wise." He laughed again, then said, "Please, I send men for bamboo. For raft, *neh?* Tomorrow try to get all here."

"Thank you."

"More pull today?"

"No, no thank—" Blackthorne stopped and shaded his eyes. Father Alvito was standing on a dune, watching them.

"No, thank you, Naga-san," Blackthorne said. "All finish here today. Please excuse me a moment." He went to get his clothes and swords but his men brought them to him quickly. Unhurriedly, he dressed and stuck his swords in his sash.

"Good afternoon," Blackthorne said, going over to Alvito. The priest looked drawn but there was friendliness in his face, as there had been before their violent quarrel outside Mishima. Blackthorne's caution increased.

"And to you, Captain-Pilot. I'm leaving this morning. I just wanted to talk a moment. Do you mind?"

"No, not at all."

"What are you going to do, try to float the hulk?"

"Yes."

"It won't help you, I'm afraid."

"Never mind. I'm going to try."

"You really believe you can build another ship?"

"Oh, yes," Blackthorne said patiently, wondering what was in Alvito's mind.

"Are you going to bring the rest of your crew here to help you?"

"No," Blackthorne said, after a moment. "They'd rather be in Yedo. When the ship's near completion . . . there's plenty of time to bring them here."

"They live with *eta,* don't they?"

"Yes."

"Is that the reason you don't want them here?"

"One reason."

"I don't blame you. I heard they're all very quarrelsome now and drunk most of the time. Did you know a week or so ago there was a small riot among them and their house burned down, so the story goes?"

"No. Was anyone hurt?"

"No. But that was only through the Grace of God. Next time . . . It seems one of them has made a still. Terrible what drink does to a man."

"Yes. Pity about their house. They'll build another."

Alvito nodded and looked back at the spines washed by the waves. "I wanted to tell you before I go, I know what the loss of Mariko-san means to you. I was greatly saddened by your story about Osaka, but in a way uplifted. I understand what her sacrifice means . . . Did she tell you about her father, all that other tragedy?"

"Yes. Some of it."

"Ah. Then you understand also. I knew Ju-san Kubo quite well."

"What? You mean Akechi Jinsai?"

"Oh, sorry, yes. That's the name he's known by now. Didn't Mariko-sama tell you?"

"No."

"The Taikō sneeringly dubbed him that: *Ju-san Kubo, Shōgun of the Thirteen Days.* His rebellion—from mustering his men to the great seppuku—lasted only thirteen days. He was a fine man but he hated us, not because we were Christians but because we were foreigners. I often wondered if Mariko became Christian just to learn our ways, to destroy us. He often said I poisoned Goroda against him."

"Did you?"

"No."

"What was he like?"

"A short, bald man, very proud, a fine general and a poet of great note. So sad to end that way, all the Akechis. And now the last of them. Poor Mariko . . . but what she did saved Toranaga, if God wills it." Alvito's fingers touched his rosary. After a moment he said, "Also, Pilot, also before I go I want to apologize for . . . well, I'm glad the Father-Visitor was there to save you."

"You apologize for my ship too?"

"Not for the *Erasmus,* though I had nothing to do with that. I apologize only for those men, Pesaro and the Captain-General. I'm glad your ship's gone."

"*Shigata ga nai,* Father. Soon I'll have another."

"What kind of craft will you try to build?"

"One big enough and strong enough."

"To attack the Black Ship?"

"To sail home to England—and defend myself against anyone."

"It will be a waste, all that labor."

"There'll be another 'Act of God'?"

"Yes. Or sabotage."

"If there is and my new ship fails, I'm going to build another, and if that fails, another. I'm going to build a ship or get a berth and when I get back to England I'm going to beg or borrow or buy or steal a privateer and then I'm coming back."

"Yes. I know. That's why you will never leave. You know too much, Anjin-san. I told you that before and I say it again, but with no malice. Truly. You're a brave man, a fine adversary, one to respect, and I do, and there should be peace between us. We're going to see a lot of each other over the years—if any of us survive the war."

"Are we?"

"Yes. You're too good at Japanese. Soon you'll be Toranaga's personal interpreter. We shouldn't quarrel, you and I. I'm afraid our destinies are interlocked. Did Mariko-san tell you that, too? She told me."

"No. She never said that. What else did she tell you?"

"She begged me to be your friend, to protect you if I could. Anjin-san, I didn't come here to goad you, or to quarrel, but to ask a peace before I go."

"Where are you going?"

"First to Nagasaki, by ship from Mishima. There are trade negotiations to conclude. Then to wherever Toranaga is, wherever the battle will be."

"They'll let you travel freely, in spite of the war?"

"Oh, yes. They need us—whoever wins. Surely we can be reasonable men, and make peace—you and I. I ask it because of Mariko-sama."

Blackthorne said nothing for a moment. "Once we had a truce, because she wanted it. I'll offer you that. A truce, not a peace—providing you agree not to come within fifty miles of where my shipyard is."

"I agree, Pilot, of course I agree—but you've nothing to fear from me. A truce, then, in her memory." Alvito put out his hand. "Thank you."

Blackthorne shook the hand firmly. Then Alvito said, "Soon her funeral will take place at Nagasaki. It's to be in the cathedral. The Father-Visitor will say the service himself, Anjin-san. Part of her ashes are to be entombed there."

"That would please her." Blackthorne watched the wreck for a moment, then looked back at Alvito. "One thing I . . . I didn't mention to Toranaga: Just before she died I gave her a Benediction as a priest would, and the last rites as best I could. There was no one else and she was Catholic. I don't think she heard me, I don't know if she was conscious. And I did it again at her cremation. Would that—would that be the same? Would that be acceptable? I tried to do it before God, not mine or yours, but God."

"No, Anjin-san. We are taught that it would not. But two days before she died she asked for and received absolution from the Father-Visitor and she was sanctified."

"Then . . . then she knew all along she had to die . . . whatever happened, she was a sacrifice."

"Yes, God bless her and cherish her!"

"Thank you for telling me," Blackthorne said. "I've . . . I was always worried my intercession would never work, though I. . . . Thank you for telling me."

"*Sayonara,* Anjin-san," Alvito said, offering his hand again.

"*Sayonara,* Tsukku-san. Please, light a candle for her . . . from me."

"I will."

Blackthorne shook the hand and watched the priest walk away, tall and strong, a worthy adversary. We'll always be enemies, he thought. We both know it, truce or no truce. What would you say if you knew Toranaga's plan and my plan? Nothing more than you've already threatened, *neh?* Good. We understand each other. A truce will do no harm. But we won't be seeing much of each other, Tsukku-san. While my ship's abuilding I'll take your place as interpreter with Toranaga and the Regents and soon you'll be out of trade negotiations, even while Portuguese ships carry the silk. And all that'll change too. My fleet will only be the beginning. In ten years the Lion of England will rule these seas. But first *The Lady,* then all the rest. . . .

Contentedly Blackthorne walked back to Naga and settled plans for tomorrow, then climbed the slope to his temporary house, near Toranaga. There he ate rice and slivered raw fish that one of his cooks had prepared for him and found them delicious. He took a second helping and began to laugh.

"Sire?"

"Nothing." But in his head he was seeing Mariko and hearing her say, 'Oh, Anjin-san, one day perhaps we'll even get you to like raw fish and then you'll be on the road to nirvana—the Place of Perfect Peace.'

Ah, Mariko, he thought, I'm so glad about the real absolution. And I thank thee.

For what, Anjin-san? he could hear her say.

For life, Mariko my darling. Thou. . . .

Many times during the days and the nights he would talk to her in his head, reliving parts of their life together and telling her about today, feeling her presence very close, always so close that once or twice he had looked over his shoulder expecting to see her standing there.

I did that this morning, Mariko, but instead of you it was Buntaro, Tsukku-san beside him, both glaring at me. I had my sword but he had his great bow in his hands. Eeeee, my love, it took all my courage to walk over and greet them formally. Were you watching? You would have been proud of me, so calm and samurai and petrified. He said so stiffly, talking through Tsukku-san, "Lady Kiritsubo and the Lady Sazuko have informed me how you protected my wife's honor and theirs. How you saved her from shame. And them. I thank you, Anjin-san. Please excuse my vile temper of before. I apologize and thank you." Then he bowed to me and went away and I wanted you so much to be there—to know that everything's protected and no one will ever know.

Many times Blackthorne had looked over his shoulder expecting her there, but she was never there and never would be and this did not disturb him. She was with him forever, and he knew he would love her in the good times and in the tragic times, even in the winter of his life. She was always on the edge of his dreams. And now those dreams were good, very good, and intermixed with her were drawings and plans and the carving of the figurehead and sails and how to set the keel and how to build the ship and then, such joy, the final shape of *The Lady* under full sail, bellied by a sharp sou'wester, racing up the Channel, the bit between her teeth, halyards shrieking, spars stretched on a larboard tack and then, 'All sails ho! Tops'ls, mainsails, royals, and top topgallants!' easing out the ropes, giving her every inch, the cannonade of the sails reaching on the other tack and 'Steady as she goes!' every particle of canvas answering his cry, and then at long last, full-bodied, a lady of inestimable beauty turning hard aport near Beachy Head for London . . .

Toranaga came up the rise near the camp, his party grouped around him. Kogo was on his gauntlet and he had hunted the coast and now he was going into the hills above the village. There were still two hours of sun left and he did not want to waste the sun, not knowing when he would ever have the time to hunt again.

Today was for me, he thought. Tomorrow I go to war but today was to put my house in order, pretending that the Kwanto was safe and Izu safe, and my succession—that I will live to see another winter and, in the spring, hunt at leisure. Ah, today has been very good.

He had killed twice with Tetsu-ko and she had flown like a dream, never so perfectly, not even when she'd made the kill with Naga near Anjiro—that beautiful, never-to-be-forgotten stoop to take that wily old cock pigeon. Today she had taken a crane several times her own size and come back to the lure perfectly. A pheasant had been pointed by the dogs and he had cast the falcon to her circling station aloft. Then the pheasant had been flushed and the soaring, climbing, falling had begun, to last forever, the kill beautiful. Again Tetsu-ko had come to the lure and fed from his fist proudly.

Now he was after hare. It had occurred to him that the Anjin-san would enjoy meat. So, instead of finishing for the day, satisfied, Toranaga had decided to go for game for the pot. He quickened his pace, not wanting to fail.

His outriders led the way past the camp and up the winding road to the crest above and he was greatly pleased with his day.

His critical gaze swept over the camp, seeking dangers, and found none. He could see men at weapon training—all regimental training and firing was forbidden while the Tsukku-san was nearby—and that pleased him. To one side, glinting in the sun, were the twenty cannon that had been salvaged with such care and he noticed that Blackthorne was squatting cross-legged on the ground nearby, concentrating over a low table, now like any normal person would sit. Below was the wreck and he noted that it had not yet moved, and he wondered how the Anjin-san would bring it ashore if it could not be pulled ashore.

Because, Anjin-san, you will bring it ashore, Toranaga told himself, quite certain.

Oh, yes. And you will build your ship and I'll destroy her like I destroyed the other one, or give her away, another sop to the Christians who are more important to me than your ships, my friend, so sorry, and the other ships waiting in your home land. Your countrymen will bring those out to me, and the treaty with your Queen. Not you. I need you here.

When the time's right, Anjin-san, I'll tell you why I had to burn your ship, and by then you won't mind because other things will be occupying you, and you'll understand what I told you was still the truth: It was your ship or your life. I chose your life. That was correct, *neh?* Then we'll laugh about the "Act of God," you and I. Oh, it was easy to appoint a special watch of trusted men aboard with secret instructions to spread gunpowder loosely and liberally on the chosen night, having already told Naga—the moment Omi whispered about Yabu's plot—to rearrange the roster so that the following shore and deck watch were only Izu men, particularly the fifty-three traitors. Then a single *ninja* with a flint out of the darkness and your ship was a torch. Of course neither Omi nor Naga was ever party to the sabotage.

So sorry, but so necessary, Anjin-san. I saved your life, which you wanted even above your ship. Fifty times or more I've had to consider giving your life away but so far I've always managed to avoid it. I hope to continue to do that. Why? This is a day for truth, *neh?* The answer is because you make me laugh and I need a friend. I daren't make friends among my own people, or among the Portuguese. Yes, I will whisper it down a well at noon but only when I'm certain I'm alone, that I *need one friend.* And also your knowledge. Mariko-sama was right again. Before you go I want to know everything you know. I told you we both had plenty of time, you and I.

I want to know how to navigate a ship around the earth and understand how a small island nation can defeat a huge empire. Perhaps the answer could apply to us and China, *neh?* Oh yes, the Taikō was right in some things.

The first time I saw you, I said, "There's no excuse for rebellion," and you said, "There's one—if you win!" Ah, Anjin-san, I bound you to me then. I agree. Everything's right if you win.

Stupid to fail. Unforgivable.

You won't fail, and you'll be safe and happy in your large fief at Anjiro, where Mura the fisherman will guard you from Christians and continue to feed them misinformation as I direct. How naïve of Tsukku-san to believe one of my men, even Christian, would steal your rutters and give them secretly to the priests without my knowledge, or my direction. Ah, Mura, you've been faithful for thirty years or more, soon you'll get your reward! What would the priests say if they knew your real name was Akira Tonomoto, samurai—spy at my direction, as well as fisherman, headman, and Christian? They'd fart dust, *neh?*

So don't worry, Anjin-san, I'm worrying about your future. You're in good strong hands and, ah, what a future I've planned for you.

"I'm to be consort to the barbarian, oh oh oh?" Kiku had wailed aloud.

"Yes, within the month. Fujiko-san has formally agreed." He had told Kiku and Gyoko the truth once more, patiently giving the distraught girl face. "And a thousand koku a year after the birth of the Anjin-san's first son."

"Eh, a thou—what did you say?"

He had repeated the promise and added sweetly, "After all, samurai is samurai and two swords are two swords and his sons will be samurai. He's hatamoto, one of my most important vassals, Admiral of all my ships, a close personal adviser—even a friend. *Neh?*"

"So sorry, but Sire—"

"First you'll be his consort."

"So sorry, first, Sire?"

"Perhaps you should be his wife. Fujiko-san told me she didn't wish to marry, ever again, but I think he should be married. Why not you? If you please him enough, and I imagine you could please him enough, and still, dutifully, keep him building his ship . . . *neh?* Yes, I think you should be his wife."

"Oh yes oh yes oh yes!" She had thrown her arms around him and blessed him and apologized for her impulsive bad manners for interrupting and not listening dutifully, and she had left him, walking four paces off the ground where a moment ago she had been ready to throw herself off the nearest cliff.

Ah, ladies, Toranaga thought, bemused and very content. Now she's got everything she wants, so has Gyoko—if the ship's built in time and it will be—so have the priests, so have—

"Sire!" One of the hunters was pointing at a clump of bushes beside the road. He reined in and readied Kogo, loosening the jesses that held her to his fist. "Now," he ordered softly. The dog was sent in.

The hare broke from the brush and raced for cover and at that instant he released Kogo. With immensely powerful thrusts of her wings she hurtled in pursuit, straight as an arrow, overhauling the panicked animal. Ahead, a hundred paces across the rolling land was a brambled copse, and the hare twisted this way and that with frantic speed, making for safety, Kogo closing the gap, cutting corners, knifing ever closer a few feet off the ground. Then she was above her prey and she hacked down and the hare screamed and reared up and darted back, Kogo still in pursuit *ek-ek-ek*ing with rage because she had missed. The hare whirled again in a final dash for sanctuary and shrieked as Kogo struck again and got a firm grip with her talons on its neck and head and bound on fearlessly, closing her wings, oblivious of the animal's frantic contortions and tumblings as, effortlessly, she snapped the neck. A last scream. Kogo let go and leaped into the air for an instant and shook her ruffled feathers into place again with a violent flurry, then settled back onto the warm, twitching body, talons once more in the death grip. Then and only then did she give her shriek of conquest and hiss with pleasure at the kill. Her eyes watched Toranaga.

Toranaga trotted up and dismounted, offering the lure. Obediently the goshawk left her prey and then, as he deftly concealed the lure, she settled on his outstretched gauntlet. His fingers caught her jesses and he could feel her grip through the steel-reinforced leather of the forefinger perch.

"Eeeeee, that was well done, my beauty," he said, rewarding her with a morsel, part of the hare's ear that a beater sliced off for him. "There, gorge on that but not too much—you've still work to do."

Grinning, the beater held up the hare. "Master! It must be three, four times her weight. Best we've seen for weeks, *neh?*"

"Yes. Send it to the camp for the Anjin-san." Toranaga swung into the saddle again and waved the others forward to the hunt once more.

Yes, the kill had been well done, but it had none of the excitement of a peregrine kill. A goshawk's only what it is, a cook's bird, a killer, born to kill anything and everything that moves. Like you, Anjin-san, *neh?*

Yes, you're a short-winged hawk. Ah, but Mariko was peregrine.

He remembered her so clearly and he wished beyond wishing that it had not been necessary for her to go to Osaka and into the Void. But it was necessary, he told himself patiently. The hostages had to be released. Not my kin, but all the others. Now I've another fifty allies committed secretly. Your courage and Lady Etsu's courage and self-sacrifice have bound them and all the Maedas to my side, and through them, the whole western seaboard. Ishido had to be winkled out of his impregnable lair, the Regents split, and Ochiba and Kiyama broken to my fist. You did all this and more: You gave me time. Only time fashions snares and provides lures.

Ah, Mariko-chan, who would have thought a little slip of a woman like you, daughter of Ju-san Kubo, my old rival, the archtraitor Akechi Jinsai, could do so much and wreak so much vengeance so beautifully and with such dignity on the Taikō, your father's enemy and killer. A single awesome stoop, like Tetsu-ko, and you killed all your prey which are my prey.

So sad that you're no more. Such loyalty deserves special favor.

Toranaga was at the crest now and he stopped and called for Tetsu-ko. The falconer took Kogo from him and Toranaga caressed the hooded peregrine on his fist a last time, then he slipped her hood and cast her into the sky. He watched her spiral upward, ever upward, seeking a prey that he would never flush. Tetsu-ko's freedom is my gift to you, Mariko-san, he said to her spirit, watching the falcon circle higher and higher. To honor your loyalty to me and your filial devotion to our most important rule: that a dutiful son, or daughter, may not rest under the same heaven while the murderer of her father still lives.

"Ah, so wise, Sire," the falconer said.

"Eh?"

"To release Tetsu-ko, to free her. I thought the last time you flew her she'd never come back but I wasn't sure. Ah, Sire, you're the greatest falconer in the realm, the best, to *know,* to be so sure when to give her back to the sky."

Toranaga permitted himself a scowl. The falconer blanched, not understanding why, quickly offered Kogo back and retreated hastily.

Yes, Tetsu-ko was due, Toranaga thought testily, but, even so, she was still a symbolic gift to Mariko's spirit and the quality of her revenge.

Yes. But what about all the sons of all the men you've killed?

Ah, that's different, those men all deserved to die, he answered himself. Even so, you're always wary of who comes within arrow range—that's normal prudence. This observation pleased Toranaga and he resolved to add it to the Legacy.

He squinted into the sky once more and watched the falcon, no longer his falcon. She was a creature of immense beauty up there, free, beyond all the tears, soaring effortlessly. Then some force beyond his ken took her and whirled her northward and she vanished.

"Ah, Tetsu-ko, thank you. Bear many daughters," he said, and turned his attention to the earth below.

The village was neat in the lowering sun, the Anjin-san still at his table, samurai training, smoke rising from the cooking fires. Across the bay, twenty *ri* or so, was Yedo. Forty *ri* southeast was Anjiro. Two hundred and ninety *ri* westward was Osaka and north from there, barely thirty *ri,* was Kyoto.

That's where the main battle should be, he thought. Near the capital. Northward, up around Gifu or Ogaki or Hashima, astride the Nakasendō, the Great North Road. Perhaps where the road turns south for the capital, near the little village of Sekigahara in the mountains. Somewhere there. Oh, I'd be safe for years behind my mountains, but this is the chance I've waited for: Ishido's jugular is unprotected.

My main thrust will be along the North Road and not the Tokaidō, the coastal road, though between now and then I'll pretend to change fifty times. My brother will ride with me. Oh yes, I think Zataki will convince himself Ishido has betrayed him to Kiyama. My brother's no fool. And I will keep my solemn oath to seek Ochiba for him. During *the* battle Kiyama will change sides, I think he will change sides, and when he does, if he does, he will fall on his hated rival Onoshi. That will signal the guns to charge, I will roll up the sides of their armies and I will win. Oh yes, I will win—because Ochiba, wisely, will never let the Heir take the field against me. She knows that if she did, I would be forced to kill him, so sorry.

Toranaga began to smile secretly. The moment I have won I will give Kiyama all Onoshi's lands, and invite him to appoint Saruji his heir. The moment I am President of the new Council of Regents we will put Zataki's proposal to the Lady Ochiba, who will be so incensed at his impertinence that, to placate the First Lady of the Land and the Heir, the Regents will regretfully have to invite my brother Onward. Who should take his place as Regent? Kasigi Omi. Kiyama will be Omi's prey . . . yes, that's wise, and so easy because surely by that time Kiyama, Lord of all the Christians, will be flaunting his religion, which is still against our law. The Taikō's Expulsion Edicts are still legal, *neh?* Surely Omi and the others will say, "I vote the Edicts be invoked"? And once Kiyama is gone, never again a Christian Regent, and patiently our grip will tighten on the stupid but dangerous foreign dogma that is a threat to the Land of the Gods, has always threatened our *wa* . . . therefore must be obliterated. We Regents will encourage the Anjin-san's countrymen to take over Portuguese trade. As soon as possible the Regents will order all trade and all foreigners confined to Nagasaki, to a tiny part of

Nagasaki, under very serious guards. And we will close the land to them forever
. . . to them and to their guns and to their poisons.

So many marvelous things to do, once I've won, if I win, when I win. We are
a very predictable people.

It will be a golden age. Ochiba and the Heir will majestically hold Court in
Osaka, and from time to time we will bow before them and continue to rule in
his name, outside of Osaka Castle. Within three years or so, the Son of Heaven
will invite me to dissolve the Council and become Shōgun during the remainder
of my nephew's minority. The Regents will press me to accept and, reluctantly,
I will accept. In a year or two, without ceremony, I will resign in Sudara's favor
and retain power as usual and keep my eyes firmly on Osaka Castle. I will
continue to wait patiently and one day those two usurpers inside will make a
mistake and then they will be gone and somehow Osaka Castle will be gone, just
another dream within a dream, and the real prize of the Great Game that began
as soon as I could think, which became possible the moment the Taikō died, the
real prize will be won: *the Shōgunate.*

That's what I've fought for and planned for all my life. I, alone, am heir to
the realm. I will be Shōgun. And I have started a dynasty.

It's all possible now because of Mariko-san and the barbarian stranger who
came out of the eastern sea.

Mariko-san, it was your *karma* to die gloriously and live forever. Anjin-san,
my friend, it is your *karma* never to leave this land. It is mine to be Shōgun.

Kogo, the goshawk, fluttered on his wrist and settled herself, watching him.
Toranaga smiled at her. I did not choose to be what I am. It is my *karma.*

T HAT YEAR, *at dawn on the twenty-first day of the tenth month, the Month without Gods, the main armies clashed. It was in the mountains near Sekigahara, astride the North Road, the weather foul—fog, then sleet. By late afternoon Toranaga had won the battle and the slaughter began. Forty thousand heads were taken.*

Three days later Ishido was captured alive and Toranaga genially reminded him of the prophecy and sent him in chains to Osaka for public viewing, ordering the eta *to plant the General Lord Ishido's feet firm in the earth, with only his head outside the earth, and to invite passersby to saw at the most famous neck in the realm with a bamboo saw. Ishido lingered three days and died very old.*

JAMES CLAVELL

JAMES CLAVELL is, in his words, "a half-Irish
Englishman with Scots overtones, born in
Australia, a citizen of the U.S.A., residing
in England, California and Canada or
wherever."

CHINA

YELLOW
SEA

KOREA

SEA OF JAPAN

J A P A N

EAST
CHINA
SEA

FORMOSA

O C E A N

P A C I F I C

INSET SCALE (MILES)

0   250   500   750   1,000

K O R E A   S T R A I T

Nagasaki

Kyoto (Miyok...

Osa...

SHIKOKU

KYUSHU

P A C I F I C

SCALE

0   50   100   150 MILES

GUY FLEMING